P9-EKE-306

The Big Book of

FEMALE DETECTIVES

CALGARY PUBLIC LIBRARY

APR   2019

CALGARY PUBLIC LIBRARY

APR 2019

The Big Book of
FEMALE DETECTIVES

Edited and with an Introduction by

Otto Penzler

VINTAGE CRIME/BLACK LIZARD
Vintage Books
A Division of Penguin Random House LLC
New York

A VINTAGE CRIME/BLACK LIZARD ORIGINAL, OCTOBER 2018

Copyright © 2018 by Otto Penzler

All rights reserved. Published in the United States by Vintage Books, a division of Penguin Random House LLC, New York, and distributed in Canada by Random House of Canada, a division of Penguin Random House Canada Limited, Toronto.

Vintage is a registered trademark and Vintage Crime/Black Lizard and colophon are trademarks of Penguin Random House LLC.

This is a work of fiction. Names, characters, places, and incidents either are the product of the authors' imagination or are used fictitiously. Any resemblance to actual persons, living or dead, events, or locales is entirely coincidental.

Due to limitations of space, permission to reprint previously published material can be found on pages 1113–1115.

Library of Congress Cataloging-in-Publication Data
Names: Penzler, Otto, editor.
Title: The big book of female detectives : / edited by Otto Penzler.
Description: New York : Vintage Crime/Black Lizard, 2018.
Identifiers: LCCN 2018026857 (print) | LCCN 2018034802 (ebook) |
ISBN 9780525434757 (ebook) | ISBN 9780525434740 (paperback)
Subjects: LCSH: Detective and mystery stories, American. | Detective and mystery
stories, English. | Women detectives—Fiction. | BISAC: FICTION / Anthologies
(multiple authors). | FICTION / Mystery & Detective / Short Stories. |
FICTION / Mystery & Detective / Women Sleuths.
Classification: LCC PS648.D4 (ebook) | LCC PS648.D4 B49 2018 (print) |
DDC 813/.087208—dc23
LC record available at https://lccn.loc.gov/2018026857

Vintage Crime/Black Lizard Trade Paperback ISBN: 978-0-525-43474-0
eBook ISBN: 978-0-525-43475-7

Book design by Anna B. Knighton

www.blacklizardcrime.com

Printed in the United States of America
10 9 8 7 6 5 4 3 2

To my dear friend and colleague
Luisa Smith,
the best bookseller I've ever known

CONTENTS

Contents

The Golden Age

Mid-Century

The Modern Era

Contents

Bad Girls

INTRODUCTION

MANY ELEMENTS of the detective story as we know it today have appeared in literature through the centuries, beginning with Cain murdering his brother in the Bible to the bloodletting in several of Shakespeare's plays and advancing to the gothic novels of the eighteenth century. Credit for the invention of the classic detective story is generally given to Edgar Allan Poe for his lurid tale "The Murders in the Rue Morgue" in 1841, in which he provided the template for all writers who followed. Brilliant detective? Check. Sidekick who served as the reader's surrogate, asking the questions that we couldn't? Check. Seemingly impossible crime? Check. Baffled police force that relied on an amateur to solve the puzzle? Check.

Perhaps not surprisingly, the history of women detectives in literature accurately mirrored society; how could it not? Much of that history paralleled detective fiction in general, just some years behind the roles of male authors and characters.

A little more than twenty years after the debut of Poe's C. Auguste Dupin, the first female detective character appeared, either Mrs. Paschal in the anonymously published *Revelations of a Lady Detective* (1864) or the eponymous protagonist of Andrew Forrester, Jr.'s *The Female Detective*, published the same year; exact publication dates are disputed.

While the first authors of detective fiction were men, female authors began to be published about a quarter of a century later. Generally credited with being the first woman to tell mystery stories, Anna Katharine Green was actually preceded by Metta Victoria Fuller Victor, who wrote the groundbreaking novel *The Dead Letter*, published in 1867, more than a decade before Green's first novel, *The Leavenworth Case* (1878). Variously regarded as the "mother," "grandmother," or "godmother" of the detective story, Green went on to be a hugely successful author whose career spanned six different decades, her last book, *The Step on the Stair*, finally being published in 1923.

The appearance of both female characters and writers following their male counterpoints was not surprising due to contemporary ideas of femininity in nineteenth-century England and America (apart from some French detective fiction in the nineteenth century, there were virtually no mystery novels published in the rest of the world). Scotland Yard (a metonym for the Metropolitan Police Service) was created in 1829, but the first woman officer wasn't appointed until 1915, a year after the creation of the Women's Police Service. In the United States, the first police force was created in Boston in 1838, but the first woman to be hired as a "policeman" (her official title with the Chicago Police Department) did not occur until 1891.

Credit must be given to the fecund creativity of the author of *Revelations of a Lady Detective*, who invented an imaginary special division of female detectives, preceding the reality of the situation by more than a half century, and to Baroness Orczy, whose Lady Molly was placed in the "Female Department" of Scotland Yard—which didn't exist.

For a woman to take a job as a policewoman or as a private detective was an act of great courage—or desperation. It was regarded as lowly work, almost as damning of a woman's character as if she were an actress. Nonetheless, the Victorian era found quite a few women engaged in the profession in fictional form. Without exception, they were strong, independent women who didn't fret about their reputations as they had a job to do and went about their business with dependable dedication and intelligence. While it is common for these literary figures to rely on their intuition (and occasionally their charm), they display a doggedness and a surprising degree of courage that enables them to solve mysteries.

Charging into the twentieth century, it became more common for female characters, both detectives and criminals, to engage in their respective activities more for sport and entertainment than out of necessity, and nowhere is this more in evidence than in the pulp magazines. America tried to deny alcohol to its people, but it gave women the vote, which changed a wide spectrum of attitudes and practical elements of daily life. Women's hemlines and haircuts became shorter, they wanted to drink and smoke, just as men did, and women took as much freedom and license in the Roaring Twenties as their male counterparts. Sure, a few women in the pages of the popular magazines who were working as private detectives or reporters had positions intended to make them assistants or "girl Fridays," but there they were, in front of the situation, usually smarter than their bosses, frequently bailing them out of difficult situations and, while often proclaiming their fear, equally as feisty and fearless as their sidekicks.

Just as that social revolution of the 1920s changed women's roles in real life as well as in fiction, the upheavals of the 1960s and 1970s, specifically the feminist movement, also had a profound and inevitable effect on women in the world of detective fiction, both as authors and as characters.

Marcia Muller had her first book published by McKay-Washburn, a modest little company that took a chance in 1977 on *Edwin of the Iron Shoes*, which introduced Sharon McCone. It was the first novel that was written by a woman to feature a tough female private eye. That publishing breakthrough opened the gate, and a few others stepped through before a positive crush poured forth. The first and, in many ways, most notable authors to walk in those shoes were Sue Grafton, who brought Kinsey Millhone to readers in 1982 with the first of her worldwide bestselling alphabet series, *"A" Is for Alibi*, and Sara Paretsky, who, in the same year, published the first V. I. Warshawski novel, *Indemnity Only*, the beginning of another series that went on to become an international success.

Paretsky also was the driving force behind the creation of Sisters in Crime, an organization officially formed in 1987 with the intention of attracting more attention to women mystery writers, both in terms of reviews and sales. A look at the mystery section in bookstores and the bestseller lists is undeniable evidence that the organization has achieved its goals.

The stories in this collection span a century and a half and range from the cozy (which is *not* a pejorative, as some of its most popular practitioners have accused it of being) to the hardboiled (which is difficult to define precisely but, like porn, you know it when you read it). They are the distillation of a lifetime of reading (as well as publishing, editing, and retailing) and were selected for a variety of reasons, not the least of which was historical significance. Admittedly, some of the milestones of distaff detection will require a touch more patience than more contemporary female ferrets, but they have their own charm and are worth the reader's attention.

Seeing the evolution of the female detective's style as it gathers strength and credibility through the decades is educational, but that is not the purpose of this book, or not the primary one, anyway. The writers whose work fills these pages are the best of their time, and their stories are among the high points of detective fiction that may be read with no greater agenda than the pure joy that derives from distinguished fiction.

—*Otto Penzler*

THE VICTORIANS AND EDWARDIANS

(BRITISH)

THE MYSTERIOUS COUNTESS

Anonymous

STORIES OF HISTORICAL SIGNIFICANCE are often barely readable. Just because they are the first of some type of story does not always mean they also are among the best examples of that subgenre. This caveat does not apply to the stories in the anonymously published *Revelations of a Lady Detective* (1864), which turn out to be extremely old-fashioned but nonetheless quite charming. They do not have the narrative drive of such of the author's contemporaries as Charles Dickens or Wilkie Collins, and characterization is sparse, not to mention that dialogue is stilted and overly formal, but it is all intrinsically pleasing.

Mrs. Paschal, the heroine of the stories in the book, is not fully developed, but we do know that she works for Scotland Yard in a special division of female detectives. She was widowed early, as she is not yet forty years old when she makes her first appearance, is relatively fearless and creatively adventurous, is an accomplished actress, and has the complete trust of her superior at Scotland Yard.

It is somewhat cavalier to describe Mrs. Paschal as the first female detective, as a convincing argument could be made for the eponymous protagonist of Andrew Forrester, Jr.'s *The Female Detective*. Without getting bogged down in a lengthy discussion of bibliographical points, most of which rely on conjecture, however learned the scholars who debate it, I will leave it with the evidence that the first advertisement for *Revelations of a Lady Detective*, announcing the book as "available" (though no copy has ever been reported), was dated May 15, 1864; the first for *The Female Detective* was dated May 22, 1864. It is a weak argument, and there is more evidence to suggest that Forrester's book appeared first, perhaps as much as six months earlier.

There are many other controversies, notably in the title of the book and the identification of the author. The wonderful scholar Frederic Dannay (half of the Ellery Queen collaboration) attributed authorship to "Anonyma," but the title page of the volume clearly states that the volume is "by the author of '*Anonyma*.'" Additionally, he lists the title as *Experiences of a Detective*, which is no more than a later retitling. He further errs by dating the book 1861, when it was, in fact, published three years later. Much of the mix-up may be attributed to the fact that it is one of the rarest volumes of detective fiction ever published and he wrote his bibliography without ever actually having seen it.

Even today, the authorship has not been conclusively determined. Voices have been heard for Forrester; for Bracebridge Hemyng, who wrote several volumes, perhaps all twelve or thirteen in the "Anonyma" series; and for W. Stephens Hayward, whose byline unambiguously appears on a recent reprint by the British Library but without explanation and should not be trusted.

"Anonyma," incidentally, was the name used by newspapers to pseudonymously refer to the beautiful Catherine Walters, the most famous courtesan of her day, and the fictionalized series of books about her adventures was a sensation.

"The Mysterious Countess" was originally published in *Revelations of a Lady Detective* (London, J. A. Berger—doubtful!—or George Vickers— likely!—, 1864).

The Mysterious Countess

ANONYMOUS

CHAPTER I
The Chief of the Detective Police

I TURNED A FAMILIAR CORNER, and was soon threading the well-known avenues of Whitehall. It was in a small street, the houses in which cover the site of the once splendid palace of the Stuarts, where one king was born and another lost his head, that the head-quarters of the London Detective Police were situated. I stopped at a door of modest pretensions, and knocked three times. I was instantly admitted. The porter bowed when he saw who I was, and at once conducted me into a room of limited dimensions. I had not to wait long. Coming from an inner room, a man of spare build, but with keen searching eyes, like those of a ferret, shook me, in a cold, business-like way, by the hand, and desired me to be seated. His forehead bulged out a little, indicating the talent of which he was the undoubted possessor. All who knew him personally, or by reputation, admired him; he performed the difficult duties of an arduous position with untiring industry and the most praiseworthy skill and perseverance. He left nothing to others, except, of course, the bare execution. This man with the stern demeanour and the penetrating glance was Colonel Warner—at the time of which I am writing, head of the Detective Department of the Metropolitan Police. It was through his instigation that women were first of all employed as detectives. It must be confessed that the idea was not original, but it showed him to be a clever adapter, and not above imitating those whose talent led them to take the initiative in works of progress. Fouché, the great Frenchman, was constantly in the habit of employing women to assist him in discovering the various political intrigues which disturbed the peace of the first empire. His petticoated police were as successful as the most sanguine innovator could wish; and Colonel Warner, having this fact before his eyes, determined to imitate the example of a man who united the courage of a lion with the cunning of a fox, culminating his acquisitions with the sagacity of a dog.

"Sit down, Mrs. Paschal," exclaimed the colonel, handing me a chair.

I did so immediately, with that prompt and passive obedience which always pleased him. I was particularly desirous at all times of conciliating Colonel Warner, because I had not long been employed as a female detective, and now having given up my time and attention to what I may call a new profession, I was anxious to acquit myself as well and favourably as I could, and gain the good-will and approbation of my superior. It is hardly necessary to refer to the circumstances which led me to embark in a career at once strange, exciting, and mysterious, but I may say that my husband died suddenly, leaving me badly off. An offer was made me through a peculiar channel. I accepted it without hesitation, and became one of the much-dreaded, but little-known people called Female Detectives, at the time I was verging upon forty. My brain was vigorous and subtle, and I concentrated all my energies upon the proper fulfilment and execution of those duties which devolved upon me. I met the glance of Colonel Warner and returned it unflinchingly; he liked people to stare back again at him, because it betokened confidence in themselves, and evidenced that they would not shrink in the hour of peril, when danger encompassed them and lurked in front and rear. I was well born and well educated, so that, like an accomplished actress, I could play my part in any drama in which I was instructed to take a part. My dramas, however, were dramas of real life, not the mimetic representations which obtain on the stage. For the parts I had to play, it was necessary to have nerve and strength, cunning and confidence, resources unlimited, confidence, and numerous other qualities of which actors are totally ignorant. They strut, and talk, and give expression to the thoughts of others, but it is such as I who really create the incidents upon which their dialogue is based and grounded.

"I have sent for you," exclaimed the colonel, "to entrust a serious case to your care and judgment. I do not know a woman more fitted for the task than yourself. Your services, if successful, will be handsomely rewarded, and you shall have no reason to complain of my parsimony in the matter of your daily expenses. Let me caution you about hasting—take time—elaborate and mature your plans; for although the hare is swift, the slow and sure tortoise more often wins the race than its fleet opponent. I need hardly talk to you in this way, but advice is never prejudicial to anyone's interests."

"I am very glad, I am sure," I replied, "to hear any suggestions you are good enough to throw out for my guidance."

"Quite so," he said; "I am aware that you possess an unusual amount of common sense, and consequently are not at all likely to take umbrage at what is kindly meant."

"Of what nature is the business?" I asked.

"Of a very delicate one," answered Colonel Warner; "you have heard of the Countess of Vervaine?"

"Frequently; you mean the lady who is dazzling all London at the present moment by the splendour of her equipage and her diamonds, and the magnificent way in which she spends what must be a colossal fortune."

"That's her," said the colonel. "But I have taken great pains to ascertain what her fortune actually consists of. Now, I have been unable to identify any property as belonging to her, nor can I discern that she has a large balance in the hands of any banker. From what source, then, is her income derived?"

I acknowledged that I was at a loss to conjecture.

"Very well," cried Colonel Warner, "the task I propose for you is to discover where, and in what way, Lady Vervaine obtains the funds which enable her to carry on a career, the splendour and the profuseness of which exceed that of a prince of the blood royal during the Augustan age of France, when Louis XIV set an example of extravagance which was pursued to ruination by the dissolute nobility, who surrounded the avenues of his palaces, and thronged the drawing-rooms of his country seats. Will it be an occupation to your mind, do you think? If not, pray decline it at once. It is always bad to undertake a commission when it involves a duty which is repugnant to you."

"Not at all," I replied; "I should like above all things to unravel the secrets of the mysterious countess, and I not only undertake to do so, but promise to bring you the tidings and information you wish for within six weeks."

"Take your own time," said the colonel; "anyone will tell you her ladyship's residence; let me see or hear from you occasionally, for I shall be anxious to know how you are getting on. Once more, do not be precipitate. Take this cheque for your expenses. If you should require more, send to me. And now, good morning, Mrs. Paschal. I hope sincerely that your endeavours may be crowned with the success they are sure to merit."

I took the draft, wished Colonel Warner goodbye, and returned to my own lodgings to ruminate over the task which had just been confided to me.

CHAPTER II
The Black Mask

I imagined that the best and surest way of penetrating the veil of secresy which surrounded the Countess of Vervaine would be to obtain a footing in her household, either as a domestic servant, or in some capacity such as would enable me to play the spy upon her actions, and watch all her movements with the greatest care and closeness. I felt confident that Colonel Warner had some excellent motive for having the countess unmasked; but he was a man who always made you find your own tools, and do your work with as little assistance as possible from him. He told you what he wanted done, and nothing remained but for you to go and do it. The Countess of Vervaine was the young and lovely widow of the old earl of that name. She was on the stage when the notorious and imbecile nobleman made her his wife. His extravagance and unsuccessful speculations in railway shares, in the days when Hudson was king, ruined him, and it was well known that, when he died brokenhearted, his income was very much reduced—so much so, that when his relict began to lead the gay and luxurious life she did, more than one head was gravely shaken, and people wondered how she did it. She thought nothing of giving a thousand pounds for a pair of carriage horses, and all enterprising tradesmen were only too rejoiced when anything rare came in their way, for the Countess of Vervaine was sure to buy it. A rare picture, or a precious stone of great and peculiar value, were things that she would buy without a murmur, and pay the price demanded for them without endeavouring to abate the proprietor's price the value of a penny piece. Personally, she was a rare combination of loveliness and accomplishments. Even the women admitted that she was beautiful, and the men raved about her. She went into the best society, and those of the highest rank and the most exalted social position in London were very glad to be asked to her magnificent and exclusive parties. Fanny, Countess of Vervaine, knew very well that if you wish to become celebrated in the gay and giddy world of fashion, you must be very careful who you admit into your house. It may be convenient, and even necessary, to ask your attorney to dine with you occasionally; but forbear to ask a ducal friend on the same day, because his grace would never forgive you for making so great a blunder. The attorney would go about amongst his friends and tell them all in what company he had been. Your house would acquire the reputation of being an "easy" one, and your acquaintances who were really worth knowing would not any more visit at a house where "anybody" was received with the same cordiality that they had themselves met with. The Countess of Vervaine lived in a large mansion in one of the new, but aristocratic squares in Belgravia. A huge towering erection it was to look at—a corner house with many windows and balconies and verandahs and conservatories. It had belonged to the earl, and he bequeathed it to her with all its wealth of furniture, rare pictures, and valuable books. It was pretty well all he had to leave her, for his lands were all sold, and the amount of ready money standing to his credit at his banker's was lamentably small—so small, indeed, as to be almost insignificant. The earl had been dead a year and a half now. She had mourned six months for him, and at the expiration of that time she cast off her widow's weeds—disdaining the example of royalty to wear them for an indefinite period—and launched into all the gaiety and dissipation that the Babylon of the moderns could supply her with. Very clever and versatile was her ladyship, as well able to talk upon abstruse subjects with a member of a scientific society as to converse with one of her patrician friends upon the merits of the latest fashions which the Parisians had with their usual taste designed.

I dressed myself one morning, after having gained the imformation I have just detailed, and put on the simplest things I could find in my wardrobe, which was as extensive and as full of disguises as that of a costumier's shop. I wished to appear like a servant out of place. My idea was to represent myself as a lady's-maid or under housekeeper. I did not care what situation I took as long as I obtained a footing in the household. When I approached Lady Vervaine's house, I was very much struck by its majestic and imposing appearance. I liked to see the porcelain boxes in the windows filled with the choicest flowers, which a market gardener and floriculturist undertook by contract to change twice a week, so that they should never appear shabby or out of season. I took a delight in gazing at the trailing creepers running in a wild, luxuriant, tropical manner, all over the spacious balconies, and I derived especial pleasure from the contemplation of the orange trees growing in large wooden tubs, loaded with their yellow fruit, the sheen and glimmer of which I could faintly see through the well-cleaned windows of the conservatory, which stood over the porch protecting the entrance to the front door.

I envied this successful actress all the beautiful things she appeared to have in her possession, and wondered why she should be so much more fortunate than myself; but a moment afterwards, I congratulated myself that I was not, like her, an object of suspicion and mistrust to the police, and that a female detective, like Nemesis, was not already upon my track. I vowed that all her splendour should be short-lived, and that in those gilded saloons and lofty halls, where now all was mirth and song and gladness, there should soon be nothing but weeping and gnashing of teeth. I descended the area steps, and even here there was a trace of refinement and good taste, for a small box of mignonette was placed on the sill of each window, and a large Virginia creeper reared its slender limbs against the stuccoed wall.

A request to see the housekeeper brought me into the presence of that worthy. I stated my business to her, and asked her favourable consid-

eration of my case. She shook her head, and said she was afraid that there was no vacancy just at present, but if I would call again, she might perhaps be able to give me a more encouraging reply. I knew perfectly well how to treat a lady of her calibre. Servants in gentlemen's families are generally engaged in making a purse, upon the proceeds of which they are enabled to retire when the domestic harness begins to gall their necks, and they sigh for rest after years of hard work and toil. They either patronize savings' banks, where they get their two and a half per cent., on the principle that every little helps, although they could at the same time obtain six per cent. in foreign guaranteed government stock; but those who work hard, know how to take care of their money, because they understand its value, and they distrust speculative undertakings, as it is the duty of all prudent people to do; or if they distrust the parochial banks, they have a stocking which they keep carefully concealed, the contents of which are to help their possessors to furnish a lodging-house, or take a tavern, when the time arrives at which they think fit to assert their independence and retire from the servitude which they have all along tolerated for a purpose. Armed with a thorough knowledge of the class, I produced a five-pound note, and said that it was part of my savings from my last place, and that I should be happy to make her a present of it, if she would use the influence I was sure she possessed to procure me the situation I was so desirous of obtaining.

This offer produced a relaxation of the housekeeper's sternness. She asked for a reference, which I gave her; we always knew how to arrange those little matters, which were managed without any difficulty; and the result of our interview was, that I was engaged as third lady's-maid at a salary of fifteen pounds a year, and to find myself in tea and sugar. I entered my new place in less than a week, and soon had an opportunity of observing the demeanour of the Countess of Vervaine; at times it was restless and excited. Her manner was frequently pre-occupied, and she was then what is called absent. You might speak to her three or four times before you obtained an answer. She did not appear to hear you. Some weighty matter was occupying her attention, and she was so engrossed by its contemplation that she could not bestow a single thought on external objects. She was very young—scarcely five-and-twenty, and not giving evidence of being so old as that. She was not one of those proud, stern, and haughty aristocrats whom you see in the Park, leaning back in their open carriages as if they were casting their mantle of despisal and scorn to those who are walking. She was not pale, and fagged, and bilious-looking; on the contrary, she was fat and chubby, with just the smallest tinge of rose-colour on her cheek—natural colour, I mean, not the artificial hue which pernicious compounds impart to a pallid cheek.

Now and then there was an air of positive joyousness about her, as if she was enamoured of life and derived the most intense pleasure from existence in this world below, where most of us experience more blows and buffets than we do occurrences of a more gratifying nature. Although not pretending to do so, I studied her with great care, and the result of my observations was that I could have sworn before any court of justice in the world that, to the best of my belief, she had a secret—a secret which weighed her down and crushed her young, elastic spirit, sitting on her chest like a nightmare, and spoiling her rest by hideous visions. In society she showed nothing of this. It was in the company of others that she shone; at home, in her bed-room, with her attendant satellites about her, whom she regarded as nobodies, she gave way to her fits of melancholy, and showed that every shining mirror has its dull side and its leaden reverse. There are some people who are constituted in such a manner by nature, that though they may be standing upon the crater of a volcano given to chronic eruptions, and though they are perfectly cognizant of the perilous position in which they are, will not trouble themselves much about it. It was my private opinion that the ground under the feet of the Countess of Vervaine was mined, and that she knew it, but that she had

adopted that fallacious motto which has for its burden "a short life and a merry one." There was something very mysterious about her, and I made the strongest resolution that I ever made in my life that I would discover the nature of the mystery before many days had passed over my head. The countess had not the remotest idea that I was in any way inimical to her. She regarded me as something for which she paid, and which was useful to her on certain occasions. I believe she looked upon me very much as a lady in the Southern States of America looks upon a slave—a thing to minister to her vanity and obey her commands. Lady Vervaine was one of those fascinating little women who charm you by their simple, winning ways, and you do not dream for a moment that they are not terrestrial angels; did you know them intimately, however, you would discover that they have a will and a temper of their own, such as would render the life of a husband miserable and unhappy if he did not succumb to her slightest wish, and put up with her most frivolous caprice. She was frequently tyrannical with her servants, and would have her most trivial command obeyed to the letter, under pain of her sovereign displeasure. One day she struck me on the knuckles with a hairbrush, because I ran a hair-pin into her head by the merest accident in the world. I said nothing, but I cherished an idea of retaliation nevertheless. We had dressed her on a particular evening for the Opera. She looked very charming; but so graceful was her manner, so pleasant was her bearing, and so unexceptionable her taste, that she could never look anything else.

"Paschal," she said to me.

"Yes, my lady," I replied.

"I shall come home a little before twelve; wait up for me."

"Yes, my lady," I replied again, in the monotonous, parrot-like tone that servants are supposed to make use of when talking to those who have authority over them.

It was a long, dreary evening; there was not much to do, so I took up a book and tried to read; but although I tried to bring my attention upon the printed page, I was unable to succeed in doing so. I was animated with a conviction that I should make some important discovery that night. It is a singular thing, but in my mind coming events always cast their shadows before they actually occurred. I invariably had an intuition that such and such a thing would happen before it actually took place. It was considerably past twelve when the mysterious countess came home; the charms of the opera and the Floral Hall must have detained her until the last moment, unless she had met with some entertaining companion who beguiled the hours by soft speeches and tender phrases, such as lovers alone know how to invent and utter. I began to unrobe her, but after I had divested her of her cloak, she called for her dressing-gown, and told me to go and bring her some coffee. The cook was gone to bed, and I found some difficulty in making the water boil, but at last I succeeded in brewing the desired beverage, and took it upstairs. The countess was, on my return, industriously making calculations, at least so it seemed to me, in a little book bound in morocco leather, and smelling very much like a stationer's shop. She might have been making poetry, or concerting the plot of a drama, but she stopped every now and then, as if to "carry" something, after the manner of mathematicians who do not keep a calculating machine on the premises.

After I had put down the coffee, she exclaimed—

"You can go. Good night."

I replied in suitable terms, and left her, but not to go to my room or to sleep. I hung about the corridor in a stealthy way, for I knew very well that no one else was likely to be about, and I wanted to watch my lady that night, which I felt convinced was going to be prolific of events of a startling nature. The night was a little chilly, but I did not care for that. Sheltering myself as well as I could in the shadow of a doorway, I waited with the amount of resignation and patience that the occasion required. In about half an hour's time the door of the Countess of Vervaine's apartment opened. I listened breathlessly, never

daring to move a muscle, lest my proximity to her should be discovered. What was my surprise and astonishment to see a man issue from the room! He held a light in his hand, and began to descend a flight of stairs by its aid.

I rubbed my eyes to see whether I had not fallen asleep and dreamed a dream; but no, I was wide awake. The man must, I imagined, have been concealed somewhere about the apartment, for I saw no trace of him during the time that I was in the room. He was a person of small size, and dressed in an odd way, as if he was not a gentleman, but a servant out of livery. This puzzled me more than ever, but I had seen a few things in my life which appeared scarcely susceptible of explanation at first, but which, when illuminated by the calm light of reason and dissected by the keen knife of judgment, were in a short time as plain as the sun at noonday. I thought for a brief space, and then I flattered myself that I had penetrated the mystery. I said to myself, *It is a disguise.* The Countess of Vervaine was a little woman. She would consequently make a very small man. The one before me, slowly and with careful tread going down the staircase, was a man of unusually small stature. You would call him decidedly undersized. There was a flabbiness about the clothes he wore which seemed to indicate that they had not been made for him. The coat-sleeves were especially long. This gave strength to the supposition that the countess had assumed male attire for purposes of her own. She could not possibly have had herself measured for a suit of clothes. No tailor in London would have done such a thing. She had probably bought the things somewhere—picking them up at random without being very particular as to their size or fit. I allowed the man to reach the bottom of the staircase before I followed in pursuit. Gliding stealthily along with a care and precision I had often practised in the dead of night at home in order that I might become well versed and experienced in an art so useful to a detective, I went down step by step and caught sight of the man turning an angle which hid him from my view, but as he did so I contrived to glance at his features. I started and felt inclined to shrink. Every lineament of his face was concealed by a hideous black mask. My sensations were not enviable for many a long night afterwards; that dark funereal face-covering was imprinted in an almost indelible manner upon my mind, and once or twice I awoke in bed shivering all over in a cold perspiration, fancying that the black mask was standing over me holding a loaded pistol at my head, and threatening my life if I did not comply with some importunate demand which I felt I could not pay the slightest attention to. Recovering myself, as best I could, I raised my dress, and stepping on my toes, followed the black mask. He descended to the lower regions. He held the light before him, occasionally looking around to see if any one were behind him. I contrived whenever he did this to vanish into some corner or fall in a heap so that the rays of the lamp should not fall upon my erect form. We passed the kitchen, from which the stale cabbage-watery smell arose which always infests those interesting domestic offices after their occupants have retired to rest. I could hear the head cook snoring. He slept in a small room on the basement, and was, I have no doubt, glad to go to bed after the various onerous duties that he had to perform during the day, for the office of cook in a good family is, you know, a sinecure. Aristocratic birth does not prevent the possessor from nourishing a somewhat plebeian appetite which must be satisfied at least four or five times a day. A plain joint is not sufficient, a dozen messes called *entrées* must accompany it, composed of truffles and other evil-smelling abominations, such as are to be met with at the shop of a Parisian epicure. I had not searched the rooms on the basement very closely, but during the cursory investigation I had made, I noticed that there was one which was always kept locked. No one ever entered it. Some said the key was lost, but none of the servants seemed to trouble themselves much about it. It was an empty room, or it was a lumber room. They did not know, neither did they care. This being the state of things existent respecting that room I was astonished to see the man in the black mask produce a key well

oiled so as to make it facile of turning, put it in the lock, turn it, open the door, enter, and disappear, shutting the door after him. It did not take me long to reach the keyhole, to which I applied my eye. The key was not in it, but whether the Black Mask had secured the door inside or not, I could not tell. The time had not then arrived at which it was either necessary or prudent to solve the riddle. I could see inside the room with the greatest ease. The lamp was on the floor, and the Black Mask was on his knees engaged in scrutinizing the flooring. The apartment was utterly destitute of furniture, not even a chair or a common deal table adorned the vacant space, but a few bricks piled on the top of one another lay in one corner. Near them was a little mound of dry mortar, which, from its appearance, had been made and brought there months ago. A trowel such as bricklayers use was not far off. While I was noticing these things the man in the black mask had succeeded in raising a couple of planks from the floor. These he laid in a gentle way on one side. I could perceive that he had revealed a black yawning gulf such as the entrance to a sewer might be. After hesitating a moment to see if his lamp was burning brightly and well, he essayed the chasm and disappeared in its murky depths, as if he had done the same thing before and knew very well where he was going. Perfectly amazed at the discoveries I was making, I looked on in passive wonderment. I was, as may be supposed, much pleased at what I saw, because I felt that I had discovered the way to unravel a tangled skein. Queen Eleanor, when she found out the clue which led her through the maze to the bower of fair Rosamond, was not more delighted than myself, when I saw the strange and mystic proceeding on the part of the Black Mask. When I had allowed what I considered a sufficient time to elapse, I tried the handle of the door—it turned. A slight push and the door began to revolve on its hinges; another one, and that more vigorous, admitted me to the room. All was in darkness. Sinking on my hands and knees, I crawled with the utmost caution in the direction of the hole in the floor. Half a minute's search brought me to it. My hand sank down as I endeavoured to find a resting-place for it. I then made it my business to feel the sides of the pit to discover if there was any ladder, through the instrumentality of whose friendly steps I could follow the Black Mask. There was. Having satisfied myself of this fact, I with as much rapidity as possible took off the small crinoline I wore, for I considered that it would very much impede my movements. When I had divested myself of the obnoxious garment, and thrown it on the floor, I lowered myself into the hole and went down the ladder. Four or five feet, I should think, brought me to the end of the flight of steps. As well as I could judge I was in a stone passage. The air was damp and cold. The sudden chill made me shudder. It was evidently a long way under ground, and the terrestrial warmth was wanting. It had succumbed to the subterraneous vapours which were more searching than pleasant; a faint glimmer of light some distance up the passage showed me that the Black Mask had not so much the best of the chase. My heart palpitated, and I hastened on at the quickest pace I considered consistent with prudence.

CHAPTER III
Bars of Gold and Ingots

I could see that the passage I was traversing had been built for some purpose to connect two houses together. What the object of such a connexion was it was difficult to conceive. But rich people are frequently eccentric, and do things that those poorer and simpler than themselves would never dream of. The Black Mask had discovered the underground communication, and was making use of it for the furtherance of some clandestine operation. The passage was not of great length. The Black Mask stopped and set the light upon the ground. I also halted, lest the noise of my footsteps might alarm the mysterious individual I was pursuing. I had been in many perplexities and exciting situations before, and I had taken a prominent part in more than one

extremely perilous adventure, but I do not think that I was ever, during the whole course of my life, actuated by so strong a curiosity, or animated with so firm a desire to know what the end would be, as I was on the present occasion. In moments such as those which were flitting with the proverbial velocity of time, but which seemed to me very slow and sluggish, the blood flows more quickly through your veins, your heart beats with a more rapid motion, and the tension of the nerves becomes positively painful. I watched the movements of the Black Mask with the greatest care and minuteness. He removed, by some means with which he was acquainted, half a dozen good-sized bricks from the wall, revealing an aperture of sufficient dimensions to permit the passage of a human body. He was not slow in passing through the hole. The light he took with him. I was in darkness. Crawling along like a cat about to commit an act of feline ferocity upon some muscipular abortion, I reached the cavity and raised my eyes to the edge, so as to be able to scrutinize the interior of the apartment into which the Black Mask had gone. It was a small place, and more like a vault than anything else. The light had been placed upon a chest, and its flickering rays fell around, affording a sickly glare very much like that produced on a dark afternoon in a shrine situated in a Roman Catholic Continental church. The sacred edifice is full of darkening shadows, but through the bronzed railings which shut off egress to the shrine, you can see the long wax tapers burning, emitting their fiery tribute to the manes of the dead. The Black Mask had fallen on his knees before a chest of a peculiar shape and make; it was long and narrow. Shooting back some bolts, the lid flew open and disclosed a large glittering pile of gold to my wondering gaze. There was the precious metal, not coined and mixed with alloy, but shining in all the splendour of its native purity. There were bars of gold and ingots, such as Cortez and Pizarro, together with their bold followers, found in Peru, when the last of the Incas was driven from his home, his kingdom, and his friends, after many a sanguinary battle, after many a hard-fought fray. The bars were heavy and valuable, for they were pure and unadulterated. There were many chests, safes, and cases in the vault. Were they all full of gold? If so, what a prize had this audacious robber acquired! He carefully selected five of the largest and heaviest ingots. Each must have been worth at least a thousand pounds. It was virgin gold, such as nuggets are formed of, and, of course, worth a great deal of money. After having made his choice, it was necessary to place the bars in some receptacle. He was evidently a man of resources, for he drew a stout canvas bag from his pocket, and, opening it, placed them inside; but, as he was doing so, the mask fell from his face. Before he could replace the hideous facial covering, I made a discovery, one I was not altogether unprepared for. The black mask—ungainly and repulsive as it was—had hitherto concealed the lovely features of the Countess of Vervaine. With a tiny exclamation of annoyance she replaced the mask and continued her task. I smiled grimly as I saw who the midnight robber was, whose footsteps I had tracked so well, whose movements I had watched so unerringly. It would take but few visits to this treasure vault, I thought to myself, to bring in a magnificent income; and then I marvelled much what the vault might be, and how the vast and almost countless treasure got there. Questions easy to propound, but by no means so facile of reply. At present my attention was concentrated wholly and solely upon the countess. It would be quite time enough next morning to speculate upon the causes which brought about effects of which I was the exultant witness. Having stowed away the ingots in the canvas bag, the mysterious countess rose to her feet, and made a motion indicative of retiring. At this juncture I was somewhat troubled in my mind. Would it be better for me to raise an alarm or to remain quiet? Supposing I were to cry out, who was there to hear my exclamation or respond to my earnest entreaty for help and assistance? Perhaps the countess was armed. So desperate an adventuress as she seemed to be would very probably carry some offensive weapon about her, which it was a fair presumption she would not hesitate to use if

hard pressed, and that lonely passage, the intricacies of which were in all probability known but to herself and me, would forever hide from prying eyes my blanching bones and whitening skeleton. This was not a particularly pleasant reflection, and I saw that it behoved me to be cautious. I fancied that I could regain the lumber room before the countess could overtake me, because it would be necessary for her to shut down and fasten the chest, and when she had done that she would be obliged to replace the bricks she had removed from the wall, which proceeding would take her some little time and occupy her attention while I made my escape. I had gained as much information as I wished, and I was perfectly satisfied with the discovery I had made. The countess was undoubtedly a robber, but it required some skill to succeed in bringing her to justice. In just that species of skill and cunning I flattered myself I was a proficient. Hastily retreating, I walked some distance, but to my surprise did not meet with the ladder. Could I have gone wrong? Was it possible that I had taken the wrong turning? I was totally unacquainted with the ramifications of these subterranean corridors. I trembled violently, for a suspicion arose in my breast that I might be shut in the vault. I stopped a moment to think, and leaned against the damp and slimy wall in a pensive attitude.

CHAPTER IV
In the Vault

Without a light I could not tell me where I was, or in which direction it would be best for me to go. I was in doubt whether it would be better to go steadily on or stay where I was, or retrace my steps. I had a strong inclination to do the latter: whilst I was ruminating a light appeared to the left of me. It was that borne by the Countess of Vervaine. I had then gone wrong. The passage prolonged itself, and I had not taken the right turning. The countess was replacing the bricks, so that it was incumbent upon me to remain perfectly still, which I did. Having accomplished her task, she once more took up her bag, the valuable contents of which were almost as much as she could carry. I was in the most critical position. She would unquestionably replace the planks, and perhaps fasten them in some way so as to prevent my escaping as she had done. My only chance lay in reaching the ladder before her, but how was it possible to do so when she was between myself and the ladder? I should have to make a sudden attack upon her, throw her down, and pass over her prostrate body, all very desirable, but totally impossible. I was defenceless. I believed her to be armed. I should run the risk of having a couple of inches of cold steel plunged into my body or else an ounce of lead would make a passage for itself through the ventricles of my heart, which were not at all desirous of the honour of being pierced by a lady of rank. I sighed for a Colt's revolver, and blamed myself for not having taken the precaution of being armed. Although I wished to capture Lady Vervaine above all things, I was not tired of my life. Once above ground again and in the house I should feel myself more of a free agent than I did in those dreary vaults, where I felt sure I should fall an easy prey to the attacks of an unscrupulous woman. Lady Vervaine pursued her way with a quick step, which showed that she had accomplished her object, and was anxious to get to her own room again, and reach a haven of safety. As for me, I resigned myself to my fate. What could I do? To attack her ladyship would, I thought, be the forerunner of instant death. It would be like running upon a sword, or firing a pistol in one's own mouth. She would turn upon me like a tiger, and in order to save herself from the dreadful consequences of her crime, she would not hesitate a moment to kill me. Serpents without fangs are harmless, but when they have those obnoxious weapons it is just as well to put your iron heel upon their heads and crush them, so as to render them harmless and subservient to your sovereign and conquering will. I followed the Countess of Vervaine slowly, and at a distance, but I dared not approach her. I was usually fertile in expedi-

ents, and I thought I should be able to find my way out of the dilemma in some way. I was not a woman of one idea, and if one dart did not hit the mark I always had another feathered shaft ready for action in my well-stocked quiver. Yet it was not without a sickening feeling of uncertainty and doubt that I saw her ladyship ascend the ladder and vanish through the opening in the flooring. I was alone in the vault, and abandoned to my own resources. I waited in the black darkness in no enviable frame of mind, until I thought the countess had had sufficient time to evacuate the premises, then I groped my way to the ladder and mounted it. I reached the planks and pushed against them with all my might, but the strength I possessed was not sufficient to move them. My efforts were futile. Tired and exhausted, I once more tried the flags which paved the passage, and cast about in my mind for some means of escape from my unpleasant position. If I could find no way of extrication it was clear that I should languish horribly for a time, and ultimately perish of starvation. This was not an alluring prospect, nor did I consider it so. I had satisfied myself that it was impossible to escape through the flooring, as the Countess of Vervaine had in some manner securely fastened the boards. Suddenly an idea shot through my mind with the vivid quickness of a flash of lightning. I could work my way back through the passage, and by feeling every brick as I went, discover those which gave her ladyship admittance into the vault where the massive ingots of solid bullion were kept. I had no doubt whatever that so precious a hoard was visited occasionally by those it belonged to, and I should not only be liberated from my captivity, but I should discover the mystery which was at present perplexing me. Both of these were things I was desirous of accomplishing, so I put my shoulder to the wheel, and once more threaded the circumscribed dimensions of the corridor which led to the place in which such a vast quantity of gold was concealed. I took an immense deal of trouble, for I felt every brick singly, and after passing my fingers over its rough surface gave it a push to see if it yielded. At last, to my inexpressible joy, I reached one which "gave;" another vigorous thrust and it fell through with a harsh crash upon the floor inside. The others I took out more carefully. When I had succeeded in removing them all I entered the bullion vault in the same way in which her ladyship had, and stopped to congratulate myself upon having achieved so much. The falling brick had made a loud noise, which had reverberated through the vault, producing cavernous echoes; but I had not surmised that this would be productive of the consequences that followed it. Whilst I was considering what I should do or how I should dispose myself to sleep for an hour or so—for, in nursery parlance, the miller had been throwing dust in my eyes, and I was weary—I heard a noise in one corner of the vault, where I afterwards found the door was situated. A moment of breathless expectation followed, and then dazzling blinding lights flashed before me and made me close my shrinking eyes involuntarily. Harsh voices rang in my ears, rude hands grasped me tightly, and I was a prisoner. When I recovered my power of vision, I was surrounded by three watchmen, and as many policemen. They manacled me. I protested against such an indignity, but appearances were against me.

"I am willing to come with you," I exclaimed, in a calm voice, because I knew I had nothing to fear in the long run. "But why treat me so badly?"

"Only doing my duty," replied one of the police, who seemed to have the command of the others.

"Why do you take me in custody?" I demanded.

"Why? Come, that's a good joke," he replied.

"Answer my question."

"Well, if you don't know, I'll tell you," he answered, with a grin.

"I have an idea, but I want to be satisfied about the matter."

"We arrest you for *robbing the bank*," he replied, solemnly.

My face brightened. So it was a bank, and the place we were in was the bullion vault of the house. The mystery was now explained. The Countess of Vervaine had by some means discovered her proximity to so rich a place, and had either had the passage built, or had been fortunate enough to find it ready-made to her hand. This was a matter for subsequent explanation.

"I am ready to go with you," I said; "when we arrive at the station-house I shall speak to the inspector on duty."

The man replied in a gruff voice, and I was led from the vault, happy in the reflection that I had escaped from the gloom and darkness of the treasure house.

CHAPTER V
Hunted Down

"Glad to see you, Mrs. Paschal," exclaimed Colonel Warner when I was ushered into his presence. "I must congratulate you upon your tact, discrimination, and perseverance, in running the Countess of Vervaine to earth as cleverly as you did. Rather an unpleasant affair, though, that of the subterranean passage."

"I am accustomed to those little dramatic episodes," I replied: "when I was taken to the station-house by the exultant policeman, the inspector quickly released me on finding who I was. I always carry my credentials in my pocket, and your name is a tower of strength with the executive."

"We must consider now what is to be done," said the colonel; "there is no doubt whatever that the South Belgrave Bank has being plundered to a great extent, and that it is from that source that our mysterious countess has managed to supply her extravagant habits and keep up her transitory magnificence, which she ought to have seen would, from its nature, be evanescent. I am only surprised to think that her depredations were not discovered before; she must have managed everything in a skilful manner, so skilful indeed as to be worthy of the expertest burglar of modern times. I have had the manager of the bank with me this morning, and he is desirous of having the matter hushed up if possible; but I told him frankly that I could consent to nothing of the kind. One of the watchmen or policemen who took you into custody must have gone directly to a newspaper office, and have apprised the editor of the fact, because here is a statement of the circumstance in a daily paper, which seems to have escaped the manager's notice. Newspapers pay a small sum for information, and that must have induced the man to do as he apparently has done. The astute Countess of Vervaine has, I may tell you, taken advantage of this hint, and gone away from London, for I sent to her house this morning, which was shut up. The only reply my messengers could get was that her ladyship had gone out of town, owing to the illness of a near relation, which is, of course, a ruse."

"Clearly," I replied, "she has taken the alarm, and wishes to throw dust in our eyes."

"What do you advise?" asked Colonel Warner, walking up and down the room.

"I should say, leave her alone until her fears die away and she returns to town. It is now the height of the season, and she will not like to be away for any great length of time."

"I don't agree with you, Mrs. Paschal," returned the colonel, testily.

"Indeed, and why not?"

"For many reasons. In the first place, she may escape from the country with the plunder. What is to prevent her from letting her house and furniture in London, and going abroad with the proceeds?"

"There is some truth in that," I said, more than half convinced that the colonel took the correct view of the case.

"Very well, my second reason is that a bird in the hand is worth two in the bush."

Proverbial, but true, I thought to myself.

"Thirdly, I wish to recover as much of the stolen property as I can. A criminal, with full hands, is worth more than one whose digits are empty."

"Do you propose that I shall follow her up?" I demanded.

"Most certainly I do."

"In that case, the sooner I start the better it will be."

"Start at once, if your arrangements will permit you to do so. Servants are not immaculate, and by dint of inquiry at her ladyship's mansion, I have little doubt you will learn something which you will find of use to you."

"In less than a week, colonel," I replied, confidently, "the Countess of Vervaine shall be in the hands of the police."

"In the hands of the police?" What a terrible phrase, full of significance and awful import. Redolent of prison and solitary confinement. Replete with visions of hard-labour, and a long and weary imprisonment, expressive of a life of labour, disgrace, and pain. Perhaps indicative of summary annihilation by the hands of the hangman.

"I rely upon you," said Colonel Warner, shaking my hand. "In seven days from this time I shall expect the fulfilment of your promise."

I assented, and left the office in which affairs of so much importance to the community at large were daily conducted, and in nine cases out of ten brought to a successful issue.

Yet the salary this man received from a grateful nation, or more strictly speaking from its Government, was a bare one thousand a year, while many sinecurists get treble that sum for doing nothing at all. My first care was to return to the Countess of Vervaine's house. It was shut up, but that merely meant that the blinds were down and the shutters closed in the front part. The larger portion of the servants were still there and glad to see me. They imagined that I had been allowed a holiday, or that I had been somewhere on business for her ladyship. I at once sought the housekeeper. "Well, Paschal," she said, "what do you want?"

"I have been to get some money for the countess, who sent me into the City for that purpose, ma'am," I boldly replied, "and she told me I was to come to you, give you ten pounds, and you would give me her address, for she wished you to follow her into the country."

"Oh! indeed. Where is the money?"

I gave the housekeeper ten sovereigns, saying—"You can have five more if you like, I dare say she won't miss it."

"Not she. She has plenty."

The five additional portraits of Her Majesty were eagerly taken possession of by the housekeeper, who blandly told me that the countess would be found at Blinton Abbey, in Yorkshire, whither she had gone to spend a fortnight with some aristocratic acquaintance. I always made a point of being very quiet, civil, and obliging when in the presence of the housekeeper, who looked upon me as remarkably innocent, simple, and hardworking. After obtaining the information I was in search of I remained chatting in an amicable and agreeable manner for a short time, after which I took my leave. When, ho! for the night mail, north. I was accompanied by a superintendent, to whom I invariably intrusted the consummation of arduous enterprises which required masculine strength. He was a sociable man, and we might between us have proved a match for the cleverest thieves in Christendom. In fact we frequently were so, as they discovered to their cost. There is to me always something very exhilarating in the quickly rushing motion of a railway carriage. It is typical of progress, and raises my spirits in proportion to the speed at which we career along, now through meadow and now through woodland, at one time cutting through a defile and afterwards steaming through a dark and sombre tunnel. What can equal such magical travelling? It was night when we reached Blinton. The Abbey was about a mile and a half from the railway station. Neither the superintendent nor myself felt inclined to go to rest, for we had indulged in a nap during the journey from which we awoke very much invigorated. We left our carpet bags in the care of a sleepy railway porter who had only awaited the arrival of the night mail north, and at half-past one o'clock set out to reconnoitre the position of Blinton Abbey. The moon was shining brightly. We pursued a bridle path and found little difficulty in finding the Abbey as we followed the porter's instructions to the letter. All was still as we gazed undisturbed upon the venerable pile which had withstood the blasts of many a winter and reflected the burning rays of innumerable summer suns. I was particularly struck with the chapel, which was grey and sombre before us; the darkened roof, the lofty buttresses, the clustered shafts, all spoke of former grandeur. The scene forcibly recalled Sir Walter Scott's lines,

"If thou would'st view fair Melrose aright,
Go visit it by the pale moonlight;
For the gay beams of lightsome day
Gild but to flout the ruins grey,
When the broken arches are black in night
And each shafted oriel glimmers white;
When the cold light's uncertain shower
Streams on the ruined central tower;
When buttress and buttress alternately
Seem framed of ebon and ivory—
Then go, but go alone the while,
And view St. David's sacred pile."

We halted, inspired with a sort of sacred awe. The chapel, the turreted castle, the pale and silvery moonlight, the still and witching time of night, the deep castellated windows, the embrasures on the roof from which, in days gone by, many a sharp-speaking culverin was pointed against the firm and lawless invader, all conspired to inspire me with sadness and melancholy. I was aroused from my reverie by the hand of the superintendent which sought my arm. Without speaking a word he drew me within the shadow of a recess, and having safely ensconced me together with himself, he whispered the single word, "Look!" in my ear. I did as he directed me, and following the direction indicated by his outstretched finger saw a dark figure stealing out of a side door of Blinton Abbey. Stealthily and with cat-like tread did that sombre figure advance until it reached the base of a spreading cedar tree whose funereal branches afforded a deathlike shade like that of yew trees in a churchyard, when the figure produced a sharp pointed instrument and made a hole as if about to bury something. I could scarcely refrain a hoarse cry of delight for it seemed palpable to me that the Countess of Vervaine was about to dispose of her ill-gotten booty. I blessed the instinct which prompted me to propose a visit to the Abbey in the night-time, although I invariably selected the small hours for making voyages of discovery. I have generally found that criminals shun the light of day and seek the friendly shelter of a too often treacherous night. In a low voice I communicated my suspicions to the superintendent, and he concurred with me. I suggested the instant arrest of the dark figure. The lady was so intently engaged that she did not notice our approach; had she done so she might have escaped into the Abbey. The strong hand of the superintendent was upon her white throat before she could utter a sound. He dragged her remorselessly into the moonlight, and the well-known features of the Countess of Vervaine were revealed indisputably.

"What do you want of me, and why am I attacked in this way?" she demanded in a tremulous voice as soon as the grasp upon her throat was relaxed.

I had meanwhile seized a bag, the same canvas bag which had contained the ingots on the night of the robbery. They were still there. When I heard her ladyship's inquiry, I replied to it. "The directors of the South Belgravia Bank are very anxious to have an interview with your ladyship," I said.

She raised her eyes to mine, and an expression of anguish ran down her beautiful countenance. She knew me, and the act of recognition informed her that she was hunted down. With a rapid motion, so swift, so quick, that it resembled a sleight-of-hand, the Countess of Vervaine raised something to her mouth; in another moment her hand was by her side again, as if nothing had happened. Something glittering in the moonlight attracted my attention. I stooped down and picked it up. It was a gold ring of exquisite workmanship. A spring lid revealing a cavity was open. I raised it to my face. A strong smell of bitter almonds arose. I turned round with a flushed countenance to her ladyship. She was very pale. The superintendent was preparing to place handcuffs around her slender wrists; he held the manacles in his hand and was adjusting them. But she was by her own daring act spared this indignity. A subtle poison was contained in the secret top of her ring, and she had with a boldness peculiar to herself swallowed it before we could anticipate or prevent her rash act. The action of the virulent drug was as quick as it was deadly. She tottered. A smile which seemed to say, the battle is over, and I soon shall be at rest, sat upon her lips. Then she fell heavily to the ground with her features convulsed with a hard spasm, a final pain; her eyes were fixed, her lips parted, and Fanny, the accomplished, lovely, and versatile Countess of Vervaine was no more. I did not regret that so young and fair a creature had escaped the felons' dock, the burglars' doom. The affair created much excitement at the time, and the illustrated papers were full of pictures of Blinton Abbey, but it has long since passed from the public mind, and hundreds of more sensation have cropped up since then. The South Belgravian Bank recovered its ingots, but it was nevertheless a heavy loser through the former depredations of the famous Countess of Vervaine.

THE UNRAVELED MYSTERY

Andrew Forrester, Jr.

ARGUABLY THE FIRST WOMAN IN LITERATURE to take employment as a private detective is Miss Gladden (not her real name, merely, she writes, "the name I assume most frequently while in my business"), often referred to simply as "G." She enters the stage in *The Female Detective* (1864) by Andrew Forrester, Jr., the pseudonym of James Redding Ware (1832–1909). The best evidence of its preeminence indicates that this rare book was first published in May 1864, while the anonymously published *Revelations of a Lady Detective*, long regarded as its predecessor, was published several months later. Both books were preceded by the near-detective volume *Ruth the Betrayer; or, The Female Spy* by Edward Ellis, a "penny dreadful" issued in fifty-two parts in 1862–1863.

Ware's decision to write about a female private investigator was extraordinary, as no such career was open to women in England at the time of his book. As the first-person narrator, "G" is not intent on breaking down barriers, merely attempting to avoid genteel poverty. It is fortunate that she is intuitive, as many elements of her cases rely on intuition and coincidence, though she does occasionally make deductions based on observation.

As Forrester, James Redding Ware also wrote *Revelations of a Private Detective* (1863) and *Secret Service, or Recollections of a City Detective* (1864). A book frequently listed in his bibliography, *The Private Detective*, is simply a later reprint of *Revelations of a Private Detective*. Ware was a prolific playwright and wrote several other books under his own name that did not involve crime (his works covered such topics as dreams, board games, and English slang) until he produced another collection of purportedly true-life experiences, *Before the Bench: Sketches of Police Court Life* (1880).

"The Unraveled Mystery" was originally published in *The Female Detective* (London, Ward & Lock, 1864).

The Unraveled Mystery

ANDREW FORRESTER, JR.

WE, MEANING THEREBY SOCIETY, are frequently in the habit of looking at a successful man, and while surveying him, think how fortunate he has found life, how chances have opened up to him, and how lucky he has been in drawing so many prizes.

We do not, or we will not, see the blanks which he may have also drawn. We look at his success, thinking of our own want of victories, shut our eyes to his failures, and envy his good fortune instead of emulating his industry. For my part I believe that no position or success comes without that personal hard work which is the medium of genius. I never will believe in luck.

When this habit of looking at success and shutting our eyes to failure is exercised in reference, not to a single individual, but to a body, the danger of coming to a wrong conclusion is very much increased.

This argument is very potent in its application to the work of the detective. Because there are many capital cases on record in which the detective has been the mainspring, people generally come to the conclusion that the detective force is made up of individuals of more than the average power of intellect and sagacity.

Just as the successful man in any profession says nothing about his failures, and allows his successes to speak for themselves, so the detective force experiences no desire to publish its failures, while in reference to successes detectives are always ready to supply the reporter with the very latest particulars.

In fact, the public see the right side only of the police embroidery, and have no idea what a complication of mistakes and broken threads there are on the wrong.

Nay, indeed, the public in their admiration of the public successes of the detective force very generously forget their public failures, which in many instances are atrocious.

To what cause this amiability can be attributed it is perhaps impossible to say, but there is a great probability that it arises from the fact that the public have generally looked upon the body as a great public safeguard—an association great at preventing crime.

Be this as it may, it is certain that the detective force is certainly as far from perfect as any ordinary legal organization in England.

But the reader may ask why I commit myself to this statement, damaging as it is to my profession.

My answer is this, that in my recent days such a parliamentary inquiry (of a very brief nature, it must be conceded) has been made into the uses and customs of the detective force, as must have led the public to believe that this power is really a formidable one, as it affects not only the criminal world but society in general.

It had appeared as though the English detectives were in the habit of prying into private life, and as though no citizen were free from a system of spydom, which if it existed would be intolerable, but which has an existence only in imagination.

It is a great pity that the minister who replied to the inquiry should have so faintly shown that the complaint was faint, if not altogether groundless.

I do not suppose the public will believe me with any great amount of faith, and simply because I am an interested party; yet I venture to assert that the detective forces as a body are weak; that they fail in the majority of the cases brought under their supervision; and finally, that frequently their most successful cases have been brought to perfection, not by their own unaided endeavours so much as by the use of facts, frequently stated anonymously, and to which they make no reference in finally giving their evidence. This evidence starts from the statement, "from information I received." Those few words frequently enclose the secret which led to all the after operations which the detective deploys in description, and without which secret his evidence would never have been given at all.

The public, especially that public who have experienced any pressure of the continental system of police, and who shudder at the remembrance of the institution, need have no fear that such a state of things municipal can ever exist in England. It could not be attempted as the force is organized, and it could not meet with success were the constitution of the detective system invigorated, and in its reformed character pressed upon English society, for it would be detected at once as unconstitutional, and resented accordingly.

With these remarks I will to the statement I have to make concerning my part, that of a female detective, in the attempt to elucidate a criminal mystery which has never been cleared up, which from the mode in which it was dealt with, ran little chance of being discovered, and which will now never be explained.

The simple facts of the case, and necessary to be known, are these—

One morning, a Thames boatman found a carpet-bag resting on the abutment of an arch of one of the Thames bridges. This treasure-trove being opened, was found to contain fragments of a human body—no head.

The matter was put into the hands of the police, an inquiry was made, and nothing came of it.

This result was very natural.

There was little or no intellect exercised in relation to the case. Facts were collected, but the deductions that might have been drawn from them were not made, simply because the right men were not set to work to—to sort them, if I may be allowed that expression.

The elucidation, as offered by me at the time, and which was in no way acted upon, was due—I confess it at first starting—not to myself, but to a gentleman who put me in possession of the means of submitting my ultimate theory of the case to the proper authorities.

I was seated one night, studying a simple case enough, but which called for some plotting, when a gentleman applied to see me, with whom I was quite willing to have an interview, though I did not even remotely recognise the name on the card which was sent in to me.

As of course I am not permitted to publish his name, and as a false one would be useless, I will call him Y——.

He told me, in a few clear, curt words, very much like those of a detective high in office, and who has attained his position by his own will, that he knew I was a detective, and wanted to consult with me.

"Oh, very well, if I am a detective, you can consult with me. You have only yourself to please."

He then at once said that he had a theory of the Bridge mystery, as he called it and as I will call it, and that he wanted this theory brought under the consideration of the people at Scotland Yard.

So far I was cautious, asking him to speak.

He did so, and I may say at once that at the end of a minute I threw off the reserve I had maintained and became frank and outspoken with my visitor.

I will not here reproduce his words, because if I did so I should afterwards have to go through them in order to interpolate my own additions, corrections, or excisions.

It is perhaps sufficient to say that his entire theory was based upon grounds relating to his profession as a medical man. Therefore, whenever a statement is made in the following narrative which smacks of the surgery, the reader may fairly lay its origin to Y—— while, on the other hand, the generality of the conclusions drawn from these facts are due to myself.

I shall therefore put the conversations we had at various times in the shape of a perfected history of the whole of them, with the final additions and suggestions in their proper places, though they may have occurred at the very commencement of the argument.

As our statement stood, as it was submitted to the authorities, so now it is laid before the public, official form and unnecessary details alone being excised.

1. The mutilated fragments did not when placed together form anything like an entire body, and the head was wanting.

The first fact which struck the medical man was this, that the dissection had been effected, if not with learning, at least with knowledge. The severances were not jagged, and apparently the joints of the body had not been guessed at. The knife had been used with some knowledge of anatomy.

The inference to be drawn from these facts was this, that whoever the murderer or homicide might be, either he or an accessory, either at or after the fact, was inferentially an educated man, from the simple discovery that there was evidence he knew something of a profession (surgery) which presupposes education.

Now, it is an ordinary rule, in cases of murder where there are two or more criminals, that these are of a class.

That is to say, you rarely find educated men (I am referring here more generally to England) combine with uneducated men in committing crime. It stands evident that criminals in combination presupposes companionship. This assertion accepted, or allowed to stand for the sake of argument, it then has to be considered that all companionship generally maintains the one condition of equality. This generality has gained for itself a proverb, a sure evidence of most widely-extended observation, which runs—"Birds of a feather flock together."

Very well. Now, where do we stand in reference to the Bridge case, while accepting or allowing the above suppositions?

We arrive at this conclusion—

That the state of the mutilated fragments leads to the belief that men of some education were the murderers.

2. The state of the tissue of the flesh of the mutitilated fragments showed that the murder had been committed by the use of the knife.

This conclusion was very easily arrived at.

There is no need to inform the public that the blood circulates through the whole system of veins and arteries in about three minutes, or that nothing will prevent blood from coagulating almost immediately it has left the veins. To talk of streams of blood is to speak absurdly.

If, therefore, an artery is cut, and the heart continues to beat for a couple of minutes after the wound is made, the blood will be almost pumped out of the body, and the flesh, after death, will in appearance bear that relation to ordinary flesh that veal does to ordinary beef—a similar process of bleeding having been gone through with the calf, that of exhausting the body of its blood.

What was the conclusion to be drawn from the fact that the fragments showed by their condition that the murdered man had been destroyed by the use of the knife?

The true conclusion stood thus—that he was murdered by foreigners.

For if we examine a hundred consecutive murders and homicides, committed in England by English people, we shall find that the percentage of deaths from the use of the knife is so small as barely to call for observation. Strangling, beating, poisoning (in a minor degree)—these are the modes of murder adopted in England.

The conclusion, then, may stand that the murder was committed by foreigners.

I am aware that against both the conclusions at which I have arrived it might be urged that educated and uneducated men have been engaged in the same crime; and secondly, that murders by the knife are perpetrated in England.

But in all cases of mystery, if they are to be solved at all, it is by accepting probabilities as certainties, so far as acting upon them is concerned.

3. There was further evidence than supposition to show that the remains were those of a foreigner.

This evidence is divided into a couple of branches. The first depends upon the evidence of the pelves, or hip bones, which formed a portion of the fragments; the second upon the evidence of the skin of the fragments.

First—

It may be remarked by anyone of experience that there is this distinctive difference between foreigners and Englishmen, and one which may be seen in the Soho district any day—that while the hips of foreigners are wider than those of Englishmen, foreign shoulders are not so broad as English; hence it results that while foreigners, by reason of the contrast, look generally wider at the hips than shoulders, Englishmen, for the greater part, look wider at the shoulders than the hips.

This distinction can best be observed in contrasting French and English, or German and English soldiery. Here you find it so extremely evident as not to admit discussion.

Now, was there any evidence in the fragments to which this comparative international argument could apply?

Yes.

The medical gentleman who examined the fragments deposed that they belonged to a slightly-built man. Then followed this remarkable statement, that the hip bones, or pelves, were extremely large.

The second branch of this evidence, relating to the skin, may now be set out.

The report went on to say that the skin was covered with long, strong, straight black hairs.

Now it is very remarkable that the skin should exhibit those appearances which are usually associated with strength, while the report distinctly sets out that the fragments belonged to a slightly-built man.

It strikes the most ordinary thinker at once that his experience tells him that slight, weakly made men are generally distinguishable for weak and thin hair. Most men at once recognise the force of the poetical description of Samson's strength lying in his hair.

There is, then, surely something contradictory in the slight build, and the long, strong black hair, if we judge from our ordinary experience. But if we carry our experience beyond the ordinary, if we go into a French or Italian eating-house in the Soho district, it will be found that scarcely a man is to be found who is destitute of strong hair, for the most part black, upon the face. It need not be added that hair thickly growing on the face is presumptive proof that the entire skin possesses that faculty, the palms of the hands and soles of the feet excepted.[*]

Now follows another intricate piece of evidence. The hairs are stated to be long, black, and strong—that is to say, black, thick, and without any curl in them.

Any man who, by an hospital experience, has seen many English human beings, will agree with me that the body hair here in England is rarely black, rarely long, and generally with a tendency to curl.

Now, go to the French and Italian cafés already referred to, and it will be found that the beards you shall see are black, very strong, and the hairs individually straight.

The third conclusion stands thus:

---

[*] It should be here again pointed out that it is to the doctor that these physiological remarks are to be attributed.

That the bones and skin of the fragments point to their having formed a portion of a foreigner rather than an Englishman.

EVIDENCE OF THE FRAGMENTS. The evidence of the fragments, therefore, goes problematically to prove that the murdered man was an educated foreigner, stabbed to death by one or more educated foreigners.

Now, what evidence can be offered which can support this theory?

Much.

In the first place, the complaints of the French Government to England, and the results of those complaints, very evidently show that London is the resting-place of many determined foreigners. In fact, it is a matter beyond all question, that London has at all times been that sanctuary for refugees from which they could not be torn.

Hence London has always been the centre of foreign exiled disaffection.

Then if it can be shown that foreign exiled disaffection is given to assassination, it stands good that we have here in London foreigners who are ready to assassinate.

Experience shows that this tendency to assassinate on the part of foreign malcontents is a common understanding amongst them. There is no need to refer to the attempts upon the life of the Emperor of the French, upon the life of the father of the late King of Naples—there is no need to point out that in the former cases the would-be assassins have lived in London, and have generally set out from London. All required is, to talk of tyranny with the next twenty foreigners you may meet, good, bad, and indifferent. It will be found that the ordinary theory in reference to a tyrant is, not that he shall be overthrown by the will of the people, but by the act of assassination.

This theory is the natural result, possibly, of that absence of power in the people which we English possess. We take credit to ourselves for abhorring assassination in reference to tyrants; but it should never be forgotten that here we have no need of assassination—the mere will of the people (when it is exerted) being quite enough to carry away all opposition.

Once admit assassination as a valuable aid in destroying tyranny, and you recognise by inference its general value as a medium of justice and relief.

Now apply the argument to the treachery of a member of a secret society, and you will comprehend the suggestion that the murdered man was a member of a secret political society, who was either false, or supposed to be false, to the secret society to which he belonged.

The question now arises—are there foreign secret societies established in London?

Have they an existence abroad? Unquestionably. Even here in open England there are a dozen secret societies of a fellowship-like character—Masons, and Foresters, and Odd Fellows, &c. &c.

And if foreigners have secret societies abroad, in spite of the police, why not here, where they have perfect liberty to form as many secret societies as they like?

Where has the money come from which has rigged out various penniless men, and sent them on the Continent to assassinate this or that potentate?

The inference is good that the money is found by secret societarians. Where else could it come from? Exiles personally are not rich; but if twenty economical professors save two pounds a-piece in six months, there is forty pounds to be applied to a purpose.

Is there any solid evidence beyond that of the fragments to suggest that the murdered man was a foreigner? There is.

In the first place, the state of those fragments showed that death had been recent—say, within two days.

Now, was any man missing during those two days who was in any way suggestively identifiable with the dead man?

If so, no application was made to the police.

Now, if the dead man were an Englishman, and all who knew him were not implicated in his death (a most unlikely supposition), it seems pretty evident that the discovery of the murder following so swiftly on the fact, some clew to the mystery must have been gained.

Granted the supposed Englishman had no relations in London (for it must be accepted as certain that the murder was committed in town, it being hardly within the bounds of possibility to suppose that the remains were brought into London to hide)—granted he had no friends, he must have had either servants, landlady, or employers. If any of these had existed, how certain it is that the publicity of the crime would have been followed by some inquiries by some of these people.

Not one was made.

Not any evidence was offered to the police that could for a moment be looked upon as valuable, although it is not perhaps going too far to say that every soul in London who could comprehend the affair had heard of and talked it over within twenty-four hours of its discovery, thanks to the power and extension of the press.*

But see how thoroughly this absence of all inquiry will fall in with the murdered man having been a foreign refugee resting in this country.

Firstly—these refugees lodge together, and make so free with each other's lodgings, and visit so frequently and so generally, that an English landlady would have some difficulty in telling who was and who was not her lodger. It would be most unlikely that she would miss a foreigner who had been staying with her foreign lodger some weeks. Hence it might readily happen that a man having no locality with which he could be identified, no suspicion would be aroused by his absence from any particular place.

Then see how this supposed poverty of lodging would accord with a refugee who, broken

down by want, might betray his society in order to gain bread, by selling their secrets to his home-police.

Or, on the other hand, he might be an actual police spy, sent by his government to play the refugee and the poverty-stricken wretch, in order the better to penetrate the secrets of conspirators.

Then mark how all chance of recognition is avoided by the absence of the head. In disposing of the fragments, and slinging them over the bridge by means of a rope, it was intended silently to drop the ugly burden into the Thames. The idea of the bag resting on the abutment of the bridge could never have entered into the precautionary measures perfected by the murderers, and yet the necessity of strict secresy was made wonderfully evident in the fact of the head being kept back.

For what purpose? Probably that the chief actors in the murder might be sure of its destruction—perchance that it might be forwarded to the president of a secret society, that the death of the traitor might be proved beyond all dispute.

Another very important line of consideration is the inquiry why such a means of disposing of the remains as that taken was adopted. It will be remarked that the objectionable process of cutting up the body had to be gone through, and that then the dangerous act of carrying or riding with a bag of human remains through the streets to the river had to be effected. And effected *in the night time*, when it must be notorious to all parties the police are particularly alert in inquiring into the nature of the parcels carried past them. It will frequently happen that the police stop and justifiably examine heavy packages which they find being carried in the streets during the night.

The encountering of all these enormous risks, to say nothing of the fear of interruption during the final act of lowering the carpet-bag, all go to presuppose that the murderers were unable to dispose of the body in any less hazardous manner.

---

* I point out as an instance the late case of poisoning a wife and children in a cab. The culprit was discovered within twenty-four hours of the publication of the crime, and by several people in no way connected with the family in which the catastrophe occurred.

What is the mode in which murderers usually seek to hide the more awful traces of their guilt in the shape of the murdered man? They generally adopt the simplest and safest mode—hiding under the ground.

A body buried ten feet in the ground, even though in the close cellar of a house, would give no warning of the hidden secret. A body buried in quicklime, under similar circumstances, would give no warning, though only four or three feet below the surface.

Burial is the most evident and simplest mode of disposing of a dead body. How is it, then, that the murderers in question did not bury, and ran a series of frightful risks, which resulted in the discovery of the remains?

The answer is obvious—they had no means of burial. In other words, the murder being done in a house where there was no command of the ground floor it was impossible to bury the body, and so it had to be disposed of in some other way. The inference therefore, is, that the occupier of the place was a lodger—not a householder.

Now make inquiries in the Soho district and you will find that refugees rarely become householders. Always hoping, perhaps, to return to their countries, never possibly desirous of taking any step which shall appear to themselves like a settling in a foreign land, it will be found that they prefer lodgings, and that the householders in most of the streets frequented by this sort of people are either English people or foreigners who do *not* belong to the refugee class, such as Swiss (chiefly) and the world of waiters, who with their savings have gone into foreign housekeeping.

I am aware that there is one good objection to this part of my scheme, in the remark that the murder might have been committed in a house occupied by the murderer or his friends, but that there might be no yard attached, or a yard too much exposed, or that the ground floor was too publicly in use to admit of time for the removal of the boards, the replacing of the flooring, and the burial of the body.

However, I beg again to urge the doctrine of probabilities. Accepting the theory that it was a murder by foreigners, and not denying the statement that foreign refugees, as a rule, rarely become householders, the probability is greater that the murderers had no ground in which to bury, rather than they had ground at their command, but that circumstances prevented them from using it.

It is true that there is one awkward point in the fact that the bridge selected from which to throw their burden was not so near to the refugee district as the late Suspension Bridge. At first sight it would appear strange that a longer risk should be run by taking the remains to a bridge not the nearest to the scene of the murder. But it must be remembered that the Suspension Bridge had no recesses, while the actual bridge used has many—that the Suspension Bridge was altogether more open and better lit than the other. These suggestions must be taken for what they are worth. I am willing to admit that it still remains extraordinary that the attempt to dispose of the body should have been made at the more distant of the two bridges, and I acknowledge that the apparent advantages of the bridge used over the Suspension do not appear to compensate the extra risk incurred.

Let those who object thoroughly to the whole of this theory, advanced to account for a mystery which has never been cleared up—let them make the most of a weak point.

The probability seems to me that the murdered man was a spy amongst men who, holding to the theory of the justice of assassination, very necessarily recognised its value in relation to a spy in the pay of a tyrant. Nay, to be at once exhaustive in reference to spies, few people will be inclined to deny that the spy, whatever the shape he has taken, has always been dealt with most implacably.

The supposition once accepted that the murderers had no power of burial, the use of the Thames as a hiding place follows almost as a natural consequence. To hide below the water when the earth is not to be opened for the purpose of concealment appears to be a very natural thought. In what other way could the body be so readily disposable?

The Thames offered secrecy, the risk of carriage was surmountable; this means therefore of concealment, though it involved danger to those concerned in the work, was far preferable to leaving the remains in the street—a mode which only a madman would adopt.[*]

Had the bag not lodged on the abutment of the bridge not one hint of the crime, it is evident, would ever have been made public. Or two or more may have been concerned in this crime, but they all kept their counsel well. Whether this silence was the result of brotherhood or fear it is impossible to say—possibly the latter. The very success of this one murder would intimidate any societarian who contemplated betraying his companions.

There has but to be added to the statement already put before the reader, two facts which, however, call for little or no comment.

1. The toll-keeper at one end of the bridge recognised the carpet-bag as a heavy one he had lifted over his toll-bar during the night.

2. He stated that he did this kindness for a woman whom he afterwards thought must have been a man in woman's clothing.

I see no value in this evidence.

1. The identification of the bag was of no value.

2. It does not appear that the man remarked upon any peculiarity of the carrier of the bag till after its discovery on the bridge abutment. And therefore his evidence is not reliable.

All I have now to do is to put in form the result I drew from the above theoretic evidence.

The result in question may be put thus—

DEDUCTION—That a foreign man, of age,

but not aging, was murdered by stabbing by the members of a secret foreign society of educated men which he had betrayed. That this murder was committed by lodgers and most probably on some other floor than the basement, and of a house situated in the Soho district.

A copy of this statement now made to the reader, but somewhat more abridged and technical was forwarded to the authorities—but so far as I have been able to learn it was never accepted as of any value.

The inquiry, as all the world knows, failed.

I do not wonder that it did.

Left in the hands of English police, who set about their work after their ordinary rule, it is evident that if the murder was committed by foreigners, in a foreign colony, there was little chance of discovery.

I believe the chief argument held against me at the time I sent in my report ran as follows: that if my supposition to the effect that the murdered man was a foreign police spy were correct, the publicity given to the discovery of the remains would have led to a communication sooner or later from a foreign prefect of police stating that an officer was missing.

I did not make a reply to the objection, but I could have announced that the French police, for instance, are not at all desirous of advertising their business, and that a French prefect of police would prefer to lose a man, and let the chance of retribution escape, rather than serve justice by admitting that a French political spy had been in London.

The silence of continental police prefects at that time is by no means to be accepted as an evidence that they missed no official who had been sent to England.

The case failed—miserably.

It could not be otherwise.

How would French police succeed, set to work in Bethnal-Green to catch an English murderer?

They would fail—miserably also.

There can be no question about it, to those who have any knowledge of the English police

---

[*] Such a mode was exercised a few months since with several still-born children. Inquiry was set on foot, and the perpetrator of this open mode of disposing of human remains turned out to be a doctor who had suffered so much from delirium tremens that he might be called a madman.

system, and who choose to be candid, that it requires more intellect infused into it. Many of the men are extraordinarily acute and are able to seize facts as they rise to the surface. But they are unable to work out what is below the surface. They work well enough in the light. When once they are in the dark, they walk with their hands open, and stretched out before them.

Had foreign lodging-houses, where frequent numbers of foreigners assemble, been inquired about, had some few perfectly constitutional searches been made, they might have led to the discovery of a fresh blood-stained floor—it being evident that if a spy were fallen upon from behind and stabbed, his blood must have reached the ground and written its tale there.

These blood-stains must still exist if the house in which the murder took place has not been burnt down, but I doubt if ever the police will make an examination of them at this or any other distance of time, owing to the distant date of the crime.

Experience shows that the chances of discovery of a crime are in exact inverse proportion to the time which has elapsed since the murder. Roughly it may be stated that if no clew is obtained within a week from the discovery of a crime, the chances of hunting down the criminal daily become rapidly fewer and fainter.

Let it not be supposed that I am advocating any change in the detective system which would be unconstitutional. Far from it. I am quite sure any unconstitutional remodelment of that force would not be suffered for any length of time to exist—as it was proved by that recent parliamentary protest against an intolerable excess of duty on the part of the police to which I have already referred.

My argument is, that more intellect should be infused into the operation of the police system, that it is impossible routine can always be a match for all shapes of crime, and finally that means should be taken to avoid so much failure as could be openly recorded of the detective police authorities.

Take in point the case I have been mentioning.

What evidence have the public ever read or learnt to show that any other than ordinary measures were taken to clear up any extraordinary crime?

It is clear that while only ordinary measures are in force to detect extraordinary crime, a premium of impunity is offered to the latter description of ill-doing, and one which it is just possible is often pocketed. Be all that as it may, it is certain the Bridge mystery has never been cleared up.

THE REDHILL SISTERHOOD

C. L. Pirkis

THE FIRST OF FOURTEEN NOVELS written by Catherine Louisa Pirkis (1839–1910) was *Disappeared from Her Home* (1877), a mystery novel that lays the foundation of what was to become her best-known work, *The Experiences of Loveday Brooke, Lady Detective* (1894), a short story collection featuring the eponymous character, who is significant in the history of the detective story.

Unlike many of her Victorian sisters in crime, Loveday Brooke is not a breath-taking young beauty with endless energy and resources who becomes involved in solving crimes for the sport of it. She works for a private detective agency out of necessity. As Pirkis writes, "Some five or six years previously, by a jerk of Fortune's wheel, Loveday had been thrown upon the world penniless and all but friendless. Marketable accomplishments she had found she had none, so she had forthwith defied convention, and had chosen for herself a career that had cut her off sharply from her former associates and her position in society."

She is past thirty when her adventures are recorded, and she is as ordinary in appearance as it is possible for someone to be, which proves to be a signifi-cant asset in her profession, and she makes no great effort to be anything else. "Her dress was invariably black," Pirkis writes, "and was almost Quaker-like in its neat primness."

Ebenezer Dyer, the chief of the detective agency, describes her as "the most sensible and practical woman I ever met." Brooke functions very much in the manner of Sherlock Holmes. She makes observations about physical objects and then eliminates all but one possible conclusion. Her skill at ratiocination inevita-bly leads to a solution, and she explains—usually at the conclusion of the case— the observations she's made and the unerring deductions to which they led.

"The Redhill Sisterhood" was originally published in the April 1893 issue of *The Ludgate Monthly*; it was first collected in *The Experiences of Loveday Brooke, Lady Detective* (London, Hutchinson, 1894).

The Redhill Sisterhood

C. L. PIRKIS

"THEY WANT YOU AT REDHILL, NOW," said Mr. Dyer, taking a packet of papers from one of his pigeon-holes. "The idea seems to be gaining ground in manly quarters that in cases of mere suspicion, women detectives are more satisfactory than men, for they are less likely to attract attention. And this Redhill affair, so far as I can make out, is one of suspicion only."

It was a dreary November morning; every gas jet in the Lynch Court office was alight, and a yellow curtain of outside fog draped its narrow windows.

"Nevertheless, I suppose one can't afford to leave it uninvestigated at this season of the year, with country-house robberies beginning in so many quarters," said Miss Brooke.

"No; and the circumstances in this case certainly seem to point in the direction of the country-house burglar. Two days ago a somewhat curious application was made privately, by a man giving the name of John Murray, to Inspector Gunning, of the Reigate police—Redhill, I must tell you, is in the Reigate police district. Murray stated that he had been a greengrocer somewhere in South London, had sold his business there, and had, with the proceeds of the sale, bought two small houses in Redhill, intending to let the one and live in the other. These houses are situated in a blind alley, known as Paved Court, a narrow turning leading off the London and Brighton

coach road. Paved Court has been known to the sanitary authorities for the past ten years as a regular fever nest, and as the houses which Murray bought—numbers 7 and 8—stand at the very end of the blind alley, with no chance of thorough ventilation, I dare say the man got them for next to nothing. He told the Inspector that he had had great difficulty in procuring a tenant for the house he wished to let, number 8, and that consequently when, about three weeks back, a lady, dressed as a nun, made him an offer for it, he immediately closed with her. The lady gave her name simply as 'Sister Monica,' and stated that she was a member of an undenominational Sisterhood that had recently been founded by a wealthy lady, who wished her name kept a secret. Sister Monica gave no references, but, instead, paid a quarter's rent in advance, saying that she wished to take possession of the house immediately, and open it as a home for crippled orphans."

"Gave no references—home for cripples," murmured Loveday, scribbling hard and fast in her note-book.

"Murray made no objection to this," continued Mr. Dyer, "and, accordingly, the next day, Sister Monica, accompanied by three other Sisters and some sickly children, took possession of the house, which they furnished with the barest possible necessaries from cheap shops in the neighbourhood. For a time, Murray said, he thought he had secured most desirable tenants, but during the last ten days suspicions as to their real character have entered his mind, and these suspicions he thought it his duty to communicate to the police. Among their possessions, it seems, these Sisters number an old donkey and a tiny cart, and this they start daily on a sort of begging tour through the adjoining villages, bringing back every evening a perfect hoard of broken victuals and bundles of old garments. Now comes the extraordinary fact on which Murray bases his suspicions. He says, and Gunning verifies his statement, that in whatever direction those Sisters turn the wheels of their donkey-cart, burglaries, or attempts at burglaries, are sure to follow. A week ago they went along towards Horley, where, at an outlying house, they received much kindness from a wealthy gentleman. That very night an attempt was made to break into that gentleman's house—an attempt, however, that was happily frustrated by the barking of the house-dog. And so on in other instances that I need not go into. Murray suggests that it might be as well to have the daily movements of these sisters closely watched, and that extra vigilance should be exercised by the police in the districts that have had the honour of a morning call from them. Gunning coincides with this idea, and so has sent to me to secure your services."

Loveday closed her note-book. "I suppose Gunning will meet me somewhere and tell me where I'm to take up my quarters?" she said.

"Yes; he will get into your carriage at Merstham—the station before Redhill—if you will put your hand out of window, with the morning paper in it. By-the-way, he takes it for granted that you will save the 11.5 train from Victoria. Murray, it seems, has been good enough to place his little house at the disposal of the police, but Gunning does not think espionage could be so well carried on there as from other quarters. The presence of a stranger in an alley of that sort is bound to attract attention. So he has hired a room for you in a draper's shop that immediately faces the head of the court. There is a private door to this shop of which you will have the key, and can let yourself in and out as you please. You are supposed to be a nursery governess on the lookout for a situation, and Gunning will keep you supplied with letters to give colour to the idea. He suggests that you need only occupy the room during the day, at night you will find far more comfortable quarters at Laker's Hotel, just outside the town."

This was about the sum total of the instructions that Mr. Dyer had to give.

The 11.5 train from Victoria that carried Loveday to her work among the Surrey Hills did not get clear of the London fog till well away on the other side of Purley. When the train halted at Merstham, in response to her signal, a tall, soldier-like individual made for her carriage, and, jumping in, took the seat facing her. He introduced himself to her as Inspector Gunning, recalled to her memory a former occasion on which they had met, and then, naturally enough, turned the talk upon the present suspicious circumstances they were bent upon investigating.

"It won't do for you and me to be seen together," he said; "of course I am known for miles round, and anyone seen in my company will be at once set down as my coadjutor, and spied upon accordingly. I walked from Redhill to Merstham on purpose to avoid recognition on the platform at Redhill, and half-way here, to my great annoyance, found that I was being followed by a man in a workman's dress and carrying a basket of tools. I doubled, however, and gave him the slip, taking a short cut down a lane which, if he had been living in the place, he would have known as well as I did. By Jove!" this was added with a sudden start, "there is the fellow, I declare; he has weathered me after all, and has no doubt taken good stock of us both, with the train going at this snail's pace. It was unfortunate that your face should have been turned towards that window, Miss Brooke."

"My veil is something of a disguise, and I will put on another cloak before he has a chance of seeing me again," said Loveday.

All she had seen in the brief glimpse that the train had allowed was a tall, powerfully-built man walking along a siding of the line. His cap was drawn low over his eyes, and in his hand he carried a workman's basket.

Gunning seemed much annoyed at the circumstance. "Instead of landing at Redhill," he said, "we'll go on to Three Bridges and wait there for a Brighton train to bring us back, that will enable you to get to your room somewhere between the lights; I don't want to have you spotted before you've so much as started your work."

Then they went back to their discussion of the Redhill Sisterhood.

"They call themselves 'undenominational,' whatever that means," said Gunning. "They say they are connected with no religious sect whatever, they attend sometimes one place of worship, sometimes another, sometimes none at all. They refuse to give up the name of the founder of their order, and really no one has any right to demand it of them, for, as no doubt you see, up to the present moment the case is one of mere suspicion, and it may be a pure coincidence that attempts at burglary have followed their footsteps in this neighbourhood. By-the-way, I have heard of a man's face being enough to hang him, but until I saw Sister Monica's, I never saw a woman's face that could perform the same kind office for her. Of all the lowest criminal types of faces I have ever seen, I think hers is about the lowest and most repulsive."

After the Sisters, they passed in review the chief families resident in the neighbourhood.

"This," said Gunning, unfolding a paper, "is a map I have specially drawn up for you—it takes in the district for ten miles round Redhill, and every country house of any importance is marked with it in red ink. Here, in addition, is an index to those houses, with special notes of my own to every house."

Loveday studied the map for a minute or so, then turned her attention to the index.

"Those four houses you've marked, I see, are those that have been already attempted. I don't think I'll run them through, but I'll mark them 'doubtful'; you see the gang—for, of course, it is a gang—might follow our reasoning on the matter, and look upon those houses as our weak point.

Here's one I'll run through, 'house empty during winter months,' that means plate and jewellery sent to the bankers. Oh! and this one may as well be crossed off, 'father and four sons all athletes and sportsmen,' that means firearms always handy—I don't think burglars will be likely to trouble them. Ah! now we come to something! Here's a house to be marked 'tempting' in a burglar's list. 'Wootton Hall, lately changed hands and re-built, with complicated passages and corridors. Splendid family plate in daily use and left entirely to the care of the butler.' I wonder, does the master of that house trust to his 'complicated passages' to preserve his plate for him? A dismissed dishonest servant would supply a dozen maps of the place for half-a-sovereign. What do these initials, 'E.L.,' against the next house in the list, North Cape, stand for?"

"Electric lighted. I think you might almost cross that house off also. I consider electric lighting one of the greatest safeguards against burglars that a man can give his house."

"Yes, if he doesn't rely exclusively upon it; it might be a nasty trap under certain circumstances. I see this gentleman also has magnificent presentation and other plate."

"Yes. Mr. Jameson is a wealthy man and very popular in the neighbourhood; his cups and epergnes are worth looking at."

"Is it the only house in the district that is lighted with electricity?"

"Yes; and, begging your pardon, Miss Brooke, I only wish it were not so. If electric lighting were generally in vogue it would save the police a lot of trouble on these dark winter nights."

"The burglars would find some way of meeting such a condition of things, depend upon it; they have reached a very high development in these days. They no longer stalk about as they did fifty years ago with blunderbuss and bludgeon; they plot, plan, contrive, and bring imagination and artistic resource to their aid. By-the-way, it often occurs to me that the popular detective stories, for which there seems too large a demand at the present day, must be, at times, uncommonly useful to the criminal classes."

At Three Bridges they had to wait so long for a return train that it was nearly dark when Loveday got back to Redhill. Mr. Gunning did not accompany her thither, having alighted at a previous station. Loveday had directed her portmanteau to be sent direct to Laker's Hotel, where she had engaged a room by telegram from Victoria Station. So, unburthened by luggage, she slipped quietly out of the Redhill Station and made her way straight for the draper's shop in the London Road. She had no difficulty in finding it, thanks to the minute directions given her by the Inspector.

Street lamps were being lighted in the sleepy little town as she went along, and as she turned into the London Road, shopkeepers were lighting up their windows on both sides of the way. A few yards down this road, a dark patch between the lighted shops showed her where Paved Court led off from the thoroughfare. A side-door of one of the shops that stood at the corner of the court seemed to offer a post of observation whence she could see without being seen, and here Loveday, shrinking into the shadows, ensconced herself in order to take stock of the little alley and its inhabitants. She found it much as it had been described to her—a collection of four-roomed houses of which more than half were unlet. Numbers 7 and 8 at the head of the court presented a slightly less neglected appearance than the other tenements. Number 7 stood in total darkness, but in the upper window of number 8 there showed what seemed to be a night-light burning, so Loveday conjectured that this possibly was the room set apart as a dormitory for the little cripples.

While she stood thus surveying the home of the suspected Sisterhood, the Sisters themselves—two, at least, of them—came into view, with their donkey-cart and their cripples, in the main road. It was an odd little cortège. One Sister, habited in a nun's dress of dark blue serge, led the donkey by the bridle; another Sister, similarly attired, walked alongside the low cart, in which were seated two sickly-looking children. They were evidently returning from one of their long country circuits, and unless they had lost their way and been belated—it certainly seemed a late hour for the sickly little cripples to be abroad.

As they passed under the gas lamp at the corner of the court, Loveday caught a glimpse of the faces of the Sisters. It was easy, with Inspector Gunning's description before her mind, to identify the older and taller woman as Sister Monica, and a more coarse-featured and generally repellant face Loveday admitted to herself she had never before seen. In striking contrast to this forbidding countenance was that of the younger Sister. Loveday could only catch a brief passing view of it, but that one brief view was enough to impress it on her memory as of unusual sadness and beauty. As the donkey stopped at the corner of the court, Loveday heard this sad-looking young woman addressed as "Sister Anna" by one of the cripples, who asked plaintively when they were going to have something to eat.

"Now, at once," said Sister Anna, lifting the little one, as it seemed to Loveday, tenderly out of the cart, and carrying him on her shoulder down the court to the door of number 8, which opened to them at their approach. The other Sister did the same with the other child; then both Sisters returned, unloaded the cart of sundry bundles and baskets, and, this done, led off the old donkey and trap down the road, possibly to a neighbouring costermonger's stables.

A man, coming along on a bicycle, exchanged a word of greeting with the Sisters as they passed, then swung himself off his machine at the corner of the court, and walked it along the paved way to the door of number 7. This he opened with a key, and then, pushing the machine before him, entered the house.

Loveday took it for granted that this man must be the John Murray of whom she had heard. She had closely scrutinized him as he had passed her, and had seen that he was a dark, well-featured man of about fifty years of age.

She congratulated herself on her good fortune in having seen so much in such a brief space of time, and coming forth from her sheltered corner turned her steps in the direction of the draper's shop on the other side of the road.

It was easy to find it. "Golightly" was the singular name that figured above the shop-front, in which were displayed a variety of goods calculated to meet the wants of servants and the poorer classes generally. A tall, powerfully-built man appeared to be looking in at this window. Loveday's foot was on the doorstep of the draper's private entrance, her hand on the door-knocker, when this individual, suddenly turning, convinced her of his identity with the journeyman workman who had so disturbed Mr. Gunning's equanimity. It was true he wore a bowler instead of a journeyman's cap, and he no longer carried a basket of tools, but there was no possibility for anyone, with so good an eye for an outline as Loveday possessed, not to recognize the carriage of the head and shoulders as that of the man she had seen walking along the railway siding. He gave her no time to make minute observation of his appearance, but turned quickly away, and disappeared down a by-street.

Loveday's work seemed to bristle with difficulties now. Here was she, as it were, unearthed in her own ambush; for there could be but little doubt that during the whole time she had stood watching those Sisters, that man, from a safe vantage point, had been watching her.

She found Mrs. Golightly a civil and obliging person. She showed Loveday to her room above the shop, brought her the letters which Inspector Gunning had been careful to have posted to her during the day. Then she supplied her with pen and ink and, in response to Loveday's request, with some strong coffee that she said, with a little attempt at a joke, would "keep a dormouse awake all through the winter without winking."

While the obliging landlady busied herself about the room, Loveday had a few questions to ask about the Sisterhood who lived down the court opposite. On this head, however, Mrs. Golightly could tell her no more than she already knew, beyond the fact that they started

every morning on their rounds at eleven o'clock punctually, and that before that hour they were never to be seen outside their door.

Loveday's watch that night was to be a fruitless one. Although she sat, with her lamp turned out and safely screened from observation, until close upon midnight, with eyes fixed upon numbers 7 and 8 Paved Court, not so much as a door opening or shutting at either house rewarded her vigil. The lights flitted from the lower to the upper floors in both houses, and then disappeared somewhere between nine and ten in the evening; and after that, not a sign of life did either tenement show.

And all through the long hours of that watch, backwards and forwards there seemed to flit before her mind's eye, as if in some sort it were fixed upon its retina, the sweet, sad face of Sister Anna.

Why it was this face should so haunt her, she found it hard to say.

"It has a mournful past and a mournful future written upon it as a hopeless whole," she said to herself. "It is the face of an Andromeda! 'Here am I,' it seems to say, 'tied to my stake, helpless and hopeless.'"

The church clocks were sounding the midnight hour as Loveday made her way through the dark streets to her hotel outside the town. As she passed under the railway arch that ended in the open country road, the echo of not very distant footsteps caught her ear. When she stopped they stopped, when she went on they went on, and she knew that once more she was being followed and watched, although the darkness of the arch prevented her seeing even the shadow of the man who was thus dogging her steps.

The next morning broke keen and frosty. Loveday studied her map and her country-house index over a seven o'clock breakfast, and then set off for a brisk walk along the country road. No doubt in London the streets were walled in and roofed with yellow fog; here, however, bright sunshine played in and out of the bare tree-boughs and leafless hedges on to a thousand frost spangles, turning the prosaic macadamized road into a gangway fit for Queen Titania herself and her fairy train.

Loveday turned her back on the town and set herself to follow the road as it wound away over the hill in the direction of a village called North-field. Early as she was, she was not to have that road to herself. A team of strong horses trudged by on their way to their work in the fuller's-earth pits. A young fellow on a bicycle flashed past at a tremendous pace, considering the upward slant of the road. He looked hard at her as he passed, then slackened pace, dismounted, and awaited her coming on the brow of the hill.

"Good morning, Miss Brooke," he said, lifting his cap as she came alongside of him. "May I have five minutes' talk with you?"

The young man who thus accosted her had not the appearance of a gentleman. He was a handsome, bright-faced young fellow of about two-and-twenty, and was dressed in ordinary cyclists' dress; his cap was pushed back from his brow over thick, curly, fair hair, and Loveday, as she looked at him, could not repress the thought how well he would look at the head of a troop of cavalry, giving the order to charge the enemy.

He led his machine to the side of the foot-path.

"You have the advantage of me," said Love-day; "I haven't the remotest notion who you are."

"No," he said; "although I know you, you cannot possibly know me. I am a north country man, and I was present, about a month ago, at the trial of old Mr. Craven, of Troyte's Hill—in fact, I acted as reporter for one of the local papers. I watched your face so closely as you gave your evidence that I should know it any-where, among a thousand."

"And your name is——?"

"George White, of Grenfell. My father is part proprietor of one of the Newcastle papers. I am a bit of a literary man myself, and sometimes figure as a reporter, sometimes as leader-writer, to that paper." Here he gave a glance towards his side pocket, from which protruded a small vol-ume of Tennyson's poems.

The facts he had stated did not seem to invite comment, and Loveday ejaculated merely:

"Indeed!"

The young man went back to the subject that was evidently filling his thoughts. "I have spe-cial reasons for being glad to have met you this morning, Miss Brooke," he want on, making his footsteps keep pace with hers. "I am in great trouble, and I believe you are the only person in the whole world who can help me out of that trouble."

"I am rather doubtful as to my power of help-ing anyone out of trouble," said Loveday; "so far as my experience goes, our troubles are as much a part of ourselves as our skins are of our bodies."

"Ah, but not such trouble as mine," said White eagerly. He broke off for a moment, then, with a sudden rush of words, told her what that trouble was. For the past year he had been engaged to be married to a young girl, who, until quite recently had been fulfilling the duties of a nursery governess in a large house in the neigh-bourhood of Redhill.

"Will you kindly give me the name of that house?" interrupted Loveday.

"Certainly; Wootton Hall, the place is called, and Annie Lee is my sweetheart's name. I don't care who knows it!" He threw his head back as he said this, as if he would be delighted to announce the fact to the whole world. "Annie's mother," he went on, "died when she was a baby, and we both thought her father was dead also, when suddenly, about a fortnight ago, it came to her knowledge that instead of being dead, he was serving his time at Portland for some offence committed years ago."

"Do you know how this came to Annie's knowledge?"

"Not the least in the world; I only know that I suddenly got a letter from her announc-ing the fact, and at the same time, breaking off her engagement with me. I tore the letter into a thousand pieces, and wrote back saying I would not allow the engagement to be broken off, but would marry her tomorrow if she would have me. To this letter she did not reply; there came instead a few lines from Mrs. Copeland, the lady at Wootton Hall, saying that Annie had thrown up her engagement and joined some Sisterhood, and that she, Mrs. Copeland, had pledged her word to Annie to reveal to no one the name and whereabouts of that Sisterhood."

"And I suppose you imagine I am able to do what Mrs. Copeland is pledged not to do?"

"That's just it, Miss Brooke," cried the young man enthusiastically. "You do such wonderful things; everyone knows you do. It seems as if, when anything is wanted to be found out, you just walk into a place, look round you, and, in a moment, everything becomes clear as noonday."

"I can't quite lay claim to such wonderful powers as that. As it happens, however, in the present instance, no particular skill is needed to find out what you wish to know, for I fancy I have already come upon the traces of Miss Annie Lee."

"Miss Brooke!"

"Of course, I cannot say for certain, but it is a matter you can easily settle for yourself—settle, too, in a way that will confer a great obligation on me."

"I shall be only too delighted to be of any—the slightest service to you," cried White, enthusiastically as before.

"Thank you. I will explain. I came down here specially to watch the movements of a certain Sisterhood who have somehow aroused the suspicions of the police. Well, I find that instead of being able to do this, I am myself so closely watched—possibly by confederates of these Sisters—that unless I can do my work by deputy I may as well go back to town at once."

"Ah! I see—you want me to be that deputy."

"Precisely. I want you to go to the room in Redhill that I have hired, take your place at the window—screened, of course, from observation—at which I ought to be seated—watch as closely as possible the movements of

these Sisters and report them to me at the hotel, where I shall remain shut in from morning till night—it is the only way in which I can throw my persistent spies off the scent. Now, in doing this for me, you will be also doing yourself a good turn, for I have little doubt but what under the blue serge hood of one of the sisters you will discover the pretty face of Miss Annie Lee."

As they had talked they had walked, and now stood on the top of the hill at the head of the one little street that constituted the whole of the village of Northfield.

On their left hand stood the village schools and the master's house; nearly facing these, on the opposite side of the road, beneath a clump of elms, stood the village pound. Beyond this pound, on either side of the way, were two rows of small cottages with tiny squares of garden in front, and in the midst of these small cottages a swinging sign beneath a lamp announced a "Postal and Telegraph Office."

"Now that we have come into the land of habitations again," said Loveday, "it will be best for us to part. It will not do for you and me to be seen together, or my spies will be transferring their attentions from me to you, and I shall have to find another deputy. You had better start on your bicycle for Redhill at once, and I will walk back at leisurely speed. Come to me at my hotel without fail at one o'clock and report proceedings. I do not say anything definite about remuneration, but I assure you, if you carry out my instructions to the letter, your services will be amply rewarded by me and by my employers."

There were yet a few more details to arrange. White had been, he said, only a day and night in the neighbourhood, and special directions as to the locality had to be given to him. Loveday advised him not to attract attention by going to the draper's private door, but to enter the shop as if he were a customer, and then explain matters to Mrs. Golightly, who, no doubt, would be in her place behind the counter; tell her he was the brother of the Miss Smith who had hired her room, and ask permission to go through the shop to that room, as he had been commissioned by his sister to read and answer any letters that might have arrived there for her.

"Show her the key of the side-door—here it is," said Loveday; "it will be your credentials, and tell her you did not like to make use of it without acquainting her with the fact."

The young man took the key, endeavoured to put it in his waistcoat pocket, found the space there occupied and so transferred it to the keeping of a side pocket in his tunic.

All this time Loveday stood watching him.

"You have a capital machine there," she said, as the young man mounted his bicycle once more, "and I hope you will turn it to account in following the movements of these Sisters about the neighbourood. I feel confident you will have something definite to tell me when you bring me your first report at one o'clock."

White once more broke into a profusion of thanks, and then, lifting his cap to the lady, started his machine at a fairly good pace.

Loveday watched him out of sight down the slope of the hill, then, instead of following him as she had said she would "at a leisurely pace," she turned her steps in the opposite direction along the village street.

It was an altogether ideal country village. Neatly-dressed chubby-faced children, now on their way to the schools, dropped quaint little curtsies, or tugged at curly locks as Loveday passed; every cottage looked the picture of cleanliness and trimness, and although so late in the year, the gardens were full of late flowering chrysanthemums and early flowering Christmas roses.

At the end of the village, Loveday came suddenly into view of a large, handsome, red-brick mansion. It presented a wide frontage to the road, from which it lay back amid extensive pleasure grounds. On the right hand, and a little in the rear of the house, stood what seemed to be large and commodious stables, and immediately adjoining these stables was a low-built, red-brick shed, that had evidently been recently erected.

That low-built, red-brick shed excited Loveday's curiosity.

"Is this house called North Cape?" she asked of a man, who chanced at that moment to be passing with a pickaxe and shovel.

The man answered in the affirmative, and Loveday then asked another question: could he tell her what was that small shed so close to the house—it looked like a glorified cowhouse—now what could be its use?

The man's face lighted up as if it were a subject on which he liked to be questioned. He explained that that small shed was the engine-house where the electricity that lighted North Cape was made and stored. Then he dwelt with pride upon the fact, as if he held a personal interest in it, that North Cape was the only house, far or near, that was thus lighted.

"I suppose the wires are carried underground to the house," said Loveday, looking in vain for signs of them anywhere.

The man was delighted to go into details on the matter. He had helped to lay those wires, he said: they were two in number, one for supply and one for return, and were laid three feet below ground, in boxes filled with pitch. These wires were switched on to jars in the engine-house, where the electricity was stored, and, after passing underground, entered the family mansion under its flooring at its western end.

Loveday listened attentively to these details, and then took a minute and leisurely survey of the house and its surroundings. This done, she retraced her steps through the village, pausing, however, at the "Postal and Telegraph Office" to dispatch a telegram to Inspector Gunning.

It was one to send the Inspector to his cipher-book. It ran as follows:

"Rely solely on chemist and coal-merchant throughout the day. —L. B."

After this, she quickened her pace, and in something over three-quarters of an hour was back again at her hotel.

There she found more of life stirring than when she had quitted it in the early morning. There was to be a meeting of the "Surrey Stags," about a couple of miles off, and a good many hunting men were hanging about the entrance to the house, discussing the chances of sport after last night's frost. Loveday made her way through the throng in leisurely fashion, and not a man but what had keen scrutiny from her sharp eyes. No, there was no cause for suspicion there: they were evidently one and all just what they seemed to be—loud-voiced, hard-riding men, bent on a day's sport; but—and here Loveday's eyes traveled beyond the hotel court-yard to the other side of the road—who was that man with a bill-hook hacking at the hedge there—a thin-featured, round-shouldered old fellow, with a bent-about hat? It might be as well not to take it too rashly for granted that her spies had withdrawn, and had left her free to do her work in her own fashion.

She went upstairs to her room. It was situated on the first floor in the front of the house, and consequently commanded a good view of the high road. She stood well back from the window, and at an angle whence she could see and not be seen, took a long, steady survey of the hedger. And the longer she looked the more convinced she was that the man's real work was something other than the bill-hook seemed to imply. He worked, so to speak, with his head over his shoulder, and when Loveday supplemented her eyesight with a strong field-glass, she could see more than one stealthy glance shot from beneath his bent-about hat in the direction of her window.

There could be little doubt about it: her movements were to be as closely watched today as they had been yesterday. Now it was of first importance that she should communicate with Inspector Gunning in the course of the afternoon: the question to solve was how it was to be done?

To all appearance Loveday answered the question in extraordinary fashion. She pulled up her blind, she drew back her curtain, and seated herself, in full view, at a small table in the window recess. Then she took a pocket inkstand from her pocket, a packet or correspondence cards from her letter-case, and with rapid pen, set to work on them.

About an hour and a half afterwards, White, coming in, according to his promise, to report proceedings, found her still seated at the window, not, however, with writing materials before her, but with needle and thread in her hand with which she was mending her gloves.

"I return to town by the first train tomorrow morning," she said as he entered, "and I find these wretched things want no end of stitches. Now for your report."

White appeared to be in an elated frame of mind. "I've seen her!" he cried, "my Annie—they've got her, those confounded Sisters; but they sha'n't keep her—no, not if I have to pull the house down about their ears to get her out."

"Well, now you know where she is, you can take your time about getting her out," said Loveday. "I hope, however, you haven't broken faith with me, and betrayed yourself by trying to speak with her, because, if so, I shall have to look out for another deputy."

"Honour, Miss Brooke!" answered White indignantly. "I stuck to my duty, though it cost me something to see her hanging over those kids and tucking them into the cart, and never say a word to her, never so much as wave my hand."

"Did she go out with the donkey-cart today?"

"No, she only tucked the kids into the cart with a blanket, and then went back to the house. Two old Sisters, ugly as sin, went out with them. I watched them from the window, jolt, jolt, jolt, round the corner, out of sight, and then I whipped down the stairs, and on to my machine, and was after them in a trice and managed to keep them well in sight for over an hour and a half."

"And their destination today was?"

"Wootton Hall."

"Ah, just as I expected."

"Just as you expected?" echoed White.

"I forgot. You do not know the nature of the suspicions that are attached to this Sisterhood, and the reasons I have for thinking that Wootton Hall, at this season of the year, might have an especial attraction for them."

White continued staring at her. "Miss

Brooke," he said presently, in an altered tone, "whatever suspicions may attach to the Sisterhood, I'll stake my life on it, my Annie has had no share in any wickedness of any sort."

"Oh, quite so; it is most likely that your Annie has, in some way, been inveigled into joining these Sisters—has been taken possession of by them, in fact, just as they have taken possession of the little cripples."

"That's it!" he cried excitedly; "that was the idea that occurred to me when you spoke to me on the hill about them, otherwise you may be sure——"

"Did they get relief of any sort at the Hall?" interrupted Loveday.

"Yes; one of the two ugly old women stopped outside the lodge gates with the donkey-cart, and the other beauty went up to the house alone. She stayed there, I should think, about a quarter of an hour, and when she came back, was followed by a servant, carrying a bundle and a basket."

"Ah! I've no doubt they brought away with them something else beside old garments and broken victuals."

White stood in front of her, fixing a hard, steady gaze upon her.

"Miss Brooke," he said presently, in a voice that matched the look on his face, "what do you suppose was the real object of these women in going to Wootton Hall this morning?"

"Mr. White, if I wished to help a gang of thieves break into Wootton Hall tonight, don't you think I should be greatly interested in procuring from them the information that the master of the house was away from home; that two of the men servants, who slept in the house, had recently been dismissed and their places had not yet been filled; also that the dogs were never unchained at night, and that their kennels were at the side of the house at which the butler's pantry is not situated? These are particulars I have gathered in this house without stirring from my chair, and I am satisfied that they are likely to be true. A the same time, if I were a professed burglar, I should not be content with information

that was likely to be true, but would be careful to procure such that was certain to be true, and so would set accomplices to work at the fountain head. Now do you understand?"

White folded his arms and looked down on her.

"What are you going to do?" he asked, in short, brusque tones.

Loveday looked him full in the face. "Communicate with the police immediately," she answered; "and I should feel greatly obliged if you will at once take a note from me to Inspector Gunning at Reigate."

"And what becomes of Annie?"

"I don't think you need have any anxiety on that head. I've no doubt that when the circumstances of her admission to the Sisterhood are investigated, it will be proved that she has been as much deceived and imposed upon as the man, John Murray, who so foolishly let his house to these women. Remember, Annie has Mrs. Copeland's good word to support her integrity."

White stood silent for awhile.

"What sort of a note do you wish me to take to the Inspector?" he presently asked.

"You shall read it as I write it, if you like," answered Loveday. She took a correspondence card from her letter-case, and, with an indelible pencil, wrote as follows—

"Wooton Hall is threatened tonight—concentrate attention there.

"L. B."

White read the words as she wrote them with a curious expression passing over his handsome features.

"Yes," he said, curtly as before. "I'll deliver that, I give you my word, but I'll bring back no answer to you. I'll do no more spying for you—it's a trade that doesn't suit me. There's a straight-forward way of doing straight-forward work, and I'll take that way—no other—to get my Annie out of that den."

He took the note, which she sealed and handed to him, and strode out of the room.

Loveday, from the window, watched him mount his bicycle. Was it her fancy, or did there pass a swift, furtive glance of recognition between him and the hedger on the other side of the way as he rode out of the court-yard?

Loveday seemed determined to make that hedger's work easy for him. The short winter's day was closing in now, and her room must consequently have been growing dim to outside observation. She lighted the gas chandelier which hung from the ceiling and, still with blinds and curtains undrawn, took her old place at the window, spread writing materials before her and commenced a long and elaborate report to her chief at Lynch Court.

About half-an-hour afterwards, as she threw a casual glance across the road, she saw that the hedger had disappeared, but that two ill-looking tramps sat munching bread and cheese under the hedge to which his bill-hook had done so little service. Evidently the intention was, one way or another, not to lose sight of her so long as she remained in Redhill.

Meantime, White had delivered Loveday's note to the Inspector at Reigate, and had disappeared on his bicycle once more.

Gunning read it without a change of expression. Then he crossed the room to the fire-place and held the card as close to the bars as he could without scorching it.

"I had a telegram from her this morning," he explained to his confidential man, "telling me to rely upon chemicals and coals throughout the day, and that, of course, meant that she would write to me in invisible ink. No doubt this message about Wootton Hall means nothing——"

He broke off abruptly, exclaiming: "Eh! what's this!" as, having withdrawn the card from the fire, Loveday's real message stood out in bold, clear characters between the lines of the false one.

Thus it ran:

"North Cape will be attacked tonight—a desperate gang—be prepared for a struggle. Above all, guard the electrical engine-house. On no account attempt

to communicate with me; I am so closely watched that any endeavour to do so may frustrate your chance of trapping the scoundrels. L. B."

That night when the moon went down behind Reigate Hill an exciting scene was enacted at "North Cape." The *Surrey Gazette,* in its issue the following day, gave the subjoined account of it under the heading, "Desperate encounter with burglars."

"Last night, 'North Cape,' the residence of Mr. Jameson, was the scene of an affray between the police and a desperate gang of burglars. 'North Cape' is lighted throughout with electricity, and the burglars, four in number, divided in half—two being told off to enter and rob the house, and two to remain at the engine-shed, where the electricity is stored, so that, at a given signal, should need arise, the wires might be unswitched, the inmates of the house thrown into sudden darkness and confusion, and the escape of the marauders thereby facilitated. Mr. Jameson, however, had received timely warning from the police of the intended attack, and he, with his two sons, all well armed, sat in darkness in the inner hall awaiting the coming of the thieves. The police were stationed, some in the stables, some in out-buildings nearer to the house, and others in more distant parts of the grounds. The burglars effected their entrance by means of a ladder placed to a window of the servants' staircase which leads straight down to the butler's pantry and to the safe where the silver is kept. The fellows, however, had no sooner got into the house than the police issuing from their hiding-place outside, mounted the ladder after them and thus cut off their retreat. Mr. Jameson and his two sons, at the same moment, attacked them in front, and thus overwhelmed by numbers, the scoundrels were easily secured. It was at the engine-house outside that the sharpest struggle took place. The thieves had forced open the door of this engine-shed with their jimmies immediately on their arrival, under the very eyes of the police, who lay in ambush in the stables, and when one of the men, captured in the house, contrived to sound an alarm on his whistle, these outside watchers made a rush for the electrical jars, in order to unswitch the wires. Upon this the police closed upon them, and a hand-to-hand struggle followed, and if it had not been for the timely assistance of Mr. Jameson and his sons, who had fortunately conjectured that their presence here might be useful, it is more than likely that one of the burglars, a powerfully-built man, would have escaped.

"The names of the captured men are John Murray, Arthur and George Lee (father and son), and a man with so many aliases that it is difficult to know which is his real name. The whole thing had been most cunningly and carefully planned. The elder Lee, lately released from penal servitude for a similar offence, appears to have been prime mover in the affair. This man had, it seems, a son and a daughter, who, through the kindness of friends, had been fairly well placed in life: the son at an electrical engineer's in London, the daughter as nursery governess at Wootton Hall. Directly this man was released from Portland, he seems to have found out his children and done his best to ruin them both. He was constantly at Wootton Hall endeavouring to induce his daughter to act as an accomplice to a robbery of the house. This so worried the girl that she threw up her situation and joined a Sisterhood that had recently been established in the neighbourhood. Upon this, Lee's thoughts turned in another direction. He induced his son, who had saved a little money, to throw up his work in London, and join him in his disreputable career. The boy is a handsome young fellow, but appears to have in him the makings of a first-class criminal. In his work as an electrical engineer he had made the acquaintance of the man John Murray, who, it is said, has been rapidly going downhill of late. Murray was the owner of the house rented by the Sisterhood that Miss Lee had joined, and the idea evidently struck the brains of these three scoundrels that this Sisterhood, whose antecedents were a little mysterious, might be utilized to draw off the attention of the police from themselves and from the especial house in the neighbourhood that they had planned to attack. With this end in view, Murray made an application to the police to have the Sisters watched, and still further to give colour to the suspicions he had endeavoured to set afloat concerning them, he and his confederates made feeble attempts at burglary upon the houses at which the Sisters had called, begging for scraps. It is a matter for congratulation that the plot, from beginning to end, has been thus successfully unearthed, and it is felt on all sides that great credit is due to Inspector Gunning and his skilled coadjutors for the vigilance and promptitude they have displayed throughout the affair."

Loveday read aloud this report, with her feet on the fender of the Lynch Court office.

"Accurate, as far as it goes," she said, as she laid down the paper.

"But we want to know a little more," said Mr. Dyer. "In the first place, I would like to know what it was that diverted your suspicions from the unfortunate Sisters?"

"The way in which they handled the children," answered Loveday promptly. "I have seen female criminals of all kinds handling children, and I have noticed that although they may occasionally—even this is rare—treat them with a certain rough sort of kindness, of tenderness they are utterly incapable. Now Sister Monica, I must admit, is not pleasant to look at; at the same time, there was something absolutely beautiful in the way in which she lifted the little cripple out of the cart, put his tiny thin hand round her neck, and carried him into the house. By-the-way I would like to ask some rapid physiognomist how he would account for Sister Monica's repulsiveness of feature as contrasted with young Lee's undoubted good looks—heredity, in this case, throws no light on the matter."

"Another question," said Mr. Dyer, not paying much heed to Loveday's digression: "how was it you transferred your suspicions to John Murray?"

"I did not do so immediately, although at the very first it had struck me as odd that he should be so anxious to do the work of the police for them. The chief thing I noticed concerning Murray, on the first and only occasion on which I saw him, was that he had had an accident with his bicycle, for in the right-hand corner of his lamp-glass there was a tiny star, and the lamp itself had a dent on the same side, had also lost its hook, and was fastened to the machine by a bit of electric fuse. The next morning as I was walking up the hill towards Northfield, I was accosted by a young man mounted on that self-same bicycle—not a doubt of it—star in glass, dent, fuse, all three."

"Ah, that sounded an important keynote, and led you to connect Murray and the younger Lee immediately."

"It did, and, of course, also at once gave the lie to his statement that he was a stranger in the place, and confirmed my opinion that there was nothing of the north-countryman in his accent. Other details in his manner and appearance gave rise to other suspicions. For instance, he called himself a press reporter by profession, and his hands were coarse and grimy as only a mechanic's could be. He said he was a bit of a literary man, but the Tennyson that showed so obtrusively from his pocket was new, and in parts uncut, and totally unlike the well-thumbed volume of the literary student. Finally, when he tried and failed to put my latch-key into his waistcoat pocket, I saw the reason lay in the fact that the pocket was already occupied by a soft coil of electric fuse, the end of which protruded. Now, an electric fuse is what an electrical engineer might almost unconsciously carry about with him, it is so essential a part of his working tools, but it is a thing that a literary man or a press reporter could have no possible use for."

"Exactly, exactly. And it was no doubt, that bit of electric fuse that turned your thoughts to the one house in the neighbourhood lighted by electricity, and suggested to your mind the possibility of electrical engineers turning their talents to account in that direction. Now, will you tell me, what, at that stage of your day's work, induced you to wire to Gunning that you would bring your invisible-ink bottle into use?"

"That was simply a matter of precaution; it did not compel me to the use of invisible ink, if I saw other safe methods of communication. I felt myself being hemmed in on all sides with spies, and I could not tell what emergency might arise. I don't think I have ever had a more difficult game to play. As I walked and talked with the young fellow up the hill, it became clear to me that if I wished to do my work I must lull the suspicions of the gang, and seem to walk into their trap. I saw by the persistent way in which Wootton Hall was forced on my notice that it was wished to fix my suspicions there. I accordingly, to all appearance, did so, and allowed the fellows to think they were making a fool of me."

"Ha! ha! Capital that—the biter bit, with a vengeance! Splendid idea to make that young rascal himself deliver the letter that was to land him and his pals in jail. And he all the time laughing in his sleeve and thinking what a fool he was making of you! Ha, ha, ha!" And Mr. Dyer made the office ring again with his merriment.

"The only person one is at all sorry for in this affair is poor little Sister Anna," said Loveday pityingly; "and yet, perhaps, all things considered, after her sorry experience of life, she may not be so badly placed in a Sisterhood where practical Christianity—not religious hysterics—is the one and only rule of the order."

THE DIAMOND LIZARD

George R. Sims

MOST OF THE BOOKS AND SHORT STORIES of the prolific George Robert Sims (1847–1922) focused on the difficult lives of the poor in London, though he also wrote many detective stories and novels, some of which featured elements of that same social consciousness.

Born in London, he received his education in England and other parts of Europe, receiving a degree from the University of Bonn, then studying in France, where he became intensely interested in gambling. He returned to England to become one of its most popular, prolific, and beloved journalists, writing articles, stories, and poetry, many of them humorous but most frequently devoted to social causes. A bon vivant who enjoyed the fabulous wealth he acquired from his journalism, books, and plays, he died nearly penniless, having lost most of his earnings to gambling and generous support of charities.

Among his mystery novels and short stories, which numbered in the hundreds, most of which were collected in extremely successful books, few are remembered or read today, though he is noted for having created Dorcas Dene, one of the earliest female detectives in literature.

Dene (née Lester) was a beautiful but only modestly successful actress when she left the stage to marry. When her young artist husband goes blind, she takes employment as a private detective to earn money and, combining her beauty and intelligence, quickly becomes one of the most successful detectives in England. Her adventures are recounted in *Dorcas Dene, Detective* (1897) and *Dorcas Dene, Detective: Second Series* (1898). The first volume was selected for *Queen's Quorum*.

As was common for publishers, the collection was disguised as a novel with chapters rather than individual story titles. "The Diamond Lizard" was completed with the section titled "The Price of a Pin," which immediately followed it in the volume.

"The Diamond Lizard" was originally published in *Dorcas Dene, Detective* (London, F. V. White, 1897).

The Diamond Lizard

GEORGE R. SIMS

I HAD RECEIVED a little note from Dorcas Dene, telling me that Paul and her mother had gone to the seaside for a fortnight, and that she was busy on a case which was keeping her from home, so that it would not be of any use my calling at Elm Tree Road at present, as I should find no one there but the servants and whitewashers.

It had been a very hot July, just before the War, but I was unable to leave town myself, having work in hand which compelled me to be on the spot. But I got away from the close, dusty streets during the daytime as frequently as I could, and one hot, broiling afternoon I found myself in a light summer suit on the lawn of the Karsino at Hampton Court, vainly endeavouring to ward off the fierce rays of the afternoon sun with one of those white umbrellas which are common enough on the Continent, but rare enough to attract attention in a land where fashion is one thing and comfort another.

My favourite Karsino waiter, Karl, an amiable and voluble little Swiss, who, during a twenty years' residence in England, had acquired the English waiter's love of betting on horse-races, had personally attended to my wants, and brought me a cup of freshly-made black coffee and a petit verre of specially fine Courvoisier, strongly recommended by the genial and obliging manager. Comforted by the coffee and overpowered by the heat, I was just dropping off into a siesta, when I was attracted by a familiar voice addressing me by name.

I raised my umbrella, and at first imagined that I must have made a mistake. The voice was undoubtedly that of Dorcas Dene, but the lady who stood smiling in front of me was to all outward appearance an American tourist. There was the little courier bag attached to the waist-belt, with which we always associate the pretty American accent during the great American touring season. The lady in front of me was beautifully dressed, and appeared through the veil she was wearing to be young and well-favoured, but her hair was silvery grey and her complexion that of a brunette. Now Dorcas Dene was a blonde with soft brown wavy hair, and so I hesitated for a moment, imagining that I must have fallen into a half doze and have dreamed that I heard Dorcas calling me.

The lady, who evidently noticed my doubt and hesitation, smiled and came close to the garden seat on which I had made myself as comfortable as the temperature would allow me.

"Good afternoon," she said. "I saw you lunching in the restaurant, but I couldn't speak to you then. I'm here on business."

It *was* Dorcas Dene.

"I have half an hour to spare," she said. "My people are at the little table yonder. They've just ordered their coffee, so they won't be going yet."

44

She sat down at the other end of the garden seat, and, following a little inclination of her parasol, I saw that the "people" she alluded to were a young fellow of about three-and-twenty, a handsome woman of about five-and-thirty, rather loudly dressed, and a remarkably pretty girl in a charming tailor-made costume of some soft white material, and a straw hat with a narrow red ribbon round it. The young lady wore a red sailor's-knot tie over a white shirt. The red of the hat-band and the tie showed out against the whiteness of the costume, and were conspicuous objects in the bright sunlight.

"How beautiful the river is from here," said Dorcas, after I had inquired how Paul was, and had learnt that he was at Eastbourne in apartments with Mrs. Lester, and that the change had benefited his health considerably.

As she spoke Dorcas drew a small pair of glasses from her pocket, and appeared very much interested in a little boat with a big white sail, making its way lazily down the river, which glistened like a sheet of silver in the sunlight.

"Yes," I said, "it's a scene that always delights our American visitors, but I suppose you're not here to admire the beauties of the Thames?"

"No," said Dorcas, laughing. "If I had leisure for that I should be at Eastbourne with my poor old Paul. I've a case in hand."

"And the *case* is yonder—the young man, the lady, and the pretty girl with the red tie?"

Dorcas nodded assent. "Yes—she is pretty, isn't she? Take my glasses and include her in the scenery, and then, if you are not too fascinated to spare a glance for anybody else, look at the young gentleman."

I took the hint and the glasses. The young lady was more than pretty; she was as perfect a specimen of handsome English girlhood as I had ever seen. I looked from her to the elder lady, and was struck by the contrast. She was much too bold-looking and showy to be the companion of so modest-looking and bewitching a damsel.

I shifted my glasses from the ladies to the young gentleman.

"A fine, handsome young fellow, is he not?" said Dorcas.

"Yes. Who is he?"

"His name is Claude Charrington. He is the son of Mr. Charrington, the well-known barrister, and I am at the present moment a parlourmaid in his stepmother's service."

I looked at the silver-haired, smart American lady with astonishment.

"A parlour-maid! Like that!" I exclaimed.

"No; I've been home and made up. I have a day out. I should like you to see me as a parlour-maid at the Charringtons—the other servants think I can't have been in very good places; but they are very kind to me, especially Johnson, the footman, and Mrs. Charrington is quite satisfied."

"Does she know you are not really a parlourmaid?"

"Yes. It was she who engaged me to investigate a little mystery which is troubling her very much. I had to be in the house to make my inquiries, and she consented that I should come as a parlour-maid. It is a very curious case, and I am very interested in it."

"Then so am I," I said, "and you must tell me all about it."

"About ten days ago," said Dorcas, "just as I had arranged to have a fortnight at the seaside with Paul, a lady called on me in a state of great agitation.

"She told me that her name was Mrs. Charrington, that she was the second wife of Mr. Charrington, the barrister, and that she was in great distress of mind owing to the loss of a diamond and ruby bracelet, a diamond and ruby pendant, and a small diamond lizard, which had mysteriously disappeared from her jewel case.

"I asked her at once why she had not informed the police instead of coming to me; and she explained that her suspicions pointed to a member of her own family as the thief, and she was terrified to go to the police for fear their investigations should confirm her suspicions, and then the position would be a terrible one.

"I asked her if she had informed her husband of her loss, and if the servants knew of it, and she told me that she had only just discovered it, and had not said a word to any one but her own family solicitor, who had advised her to come to me at once, as the matter was a delicate one. Her husband was away in the country, and she dreaded telling him until she was quite sure the person she suspected was innocent, and she had not yet said anything to the servants, as, of course, if she did they would have a right to insist on the matter being investigated in order that their characters might be cleared. It was a most unpleasant situation, apart from the loss of the valuable jewels, which had been given to her a few days previously as a birthday present. She was in the position of being compelled to conceal her loss for fear of bringing the guilt home to a member of her family."

"And whom does she suspect?" I asked.

"The young gentleman who is paying such marked attention yonder to the pretty girl in the red tie—her stepson, Mr. Claude Charrington," answered Dorcas, picking up her glasses and surveying the "scenery."

"Why does she suspect him?" I asked, following her gaze.

"Mrs. Charrington tells me that her stepson has lately caused his father considerable anxiety owing to his extravagance and recklessness. He has just left Oxford, and is going to the Bar, but he has been very erratic, and lately has evidently been pressed for money. Mrs. Charrington is very fond of him, and he has always appeared to return her affection, and has frequently come to her with his troubles. Mr. Charrington is an irritable man, and inclined to be severe with his son, and the stepmother has frequently acted as peacemaker between them. She has always endeavoured to make Claude look upon her as his own mother.

"A few days before the robbery was discovered Claude laughingly told her that he was 'in a devil of a mess' again, and that in order to get a little ready money to carry on with he had had to pawn his watch and chain for ten pounds. His father had recently given him a sum of money to satisfy some pressing creditors, but had insisted on deducting a certain amount monthly from his allowance until it was paid. Claude showed Mrs. Charrington the ticket for the watch and chain, and jokingly said that if things didn't get better with him he would have to give up all idea of the Bar and go to South Africa and look for a diamond mine. He told her that he hadn't dared tell the Governor how much he owed, and that the assistance had only staved off the more pressing of his creditors.

"Mrs. Charrington urged him to make a clean breast of everything on his father's return. He shook his head, and presently laughed the matter off, saying perhaps something would turn up. He wasn't going to the Governor again if he could possibly help it.

"That was the situation of affairs two days before the robbery was discovered. But two days after he had let his stepmother see the ticket for his watch and chain, Claude Charrington was in funds again. Mrs. Charrington discovered it quite accidentally. Claude took out a pocket-book at the breakfast table to look for a letter, and in taking out an envelope he pulled out a packet of banknotes. Mrs. Charrington remarked on their presence. He said, 'Oh, I've had a stroke of luck,' but he coloured up and looked confused. That evening Mrs. Charrington—who, by the bye, I should tell you was in mourning for her brother, who had just died in India—went to her jewel case, and to her horror discovered that a diamond and ruby bracelet, a diamond and ruby pendant, and a diamond lizard had disappeared. The cases were there, but empty.

"Instantly the idea occurred to her that Claude, knowing she was in mourning, and not likely to wear the jewels for some time, had abstracted them and pawned them—perhaps intending to put them back again as soon as he could get the money.

"She was strengthened in her suspicion by his acquisition of banknotes at a time when, according to his own account, he had pawned his watch to tide over until his allowance became due; his confusion when she noticed the banknotes; and finally by her suddenly remembering that two evenings previously after she had dressed for dinner and was in the drawing-room, she had gone upstairs again to fetch her keys, which she remembered having left on the dressing-table. Outside her room she met Claude with his dog, a fox-terrier, at his heels.

"'I've been hunting all over the place for Jack, Mater,' he said, 'and I heard him in your room. The little beggar was scratching away at the wainscoting like mad. There must be rats there. I had to go in to get him away—I was afraid he'd do some damage.'

"Mrs. Charrington found her keys on the dressing-table, and thought no more of Claude and his explanation until she missed the jewellery. Then it occurred to her that Claude had been in her room and had had an opportunity of using her keys, which not only opened the drawer in which she kept her jewel case, but the case itself."

Dorcas finished her story, and I sat for a moment gazing at the young fellow, who seemed supremely happy. Could it be possible that if he were guilty his crime could trouble him so little?

"The circumstances are very suspicious," I said, presently, "but don't you think Mrs. Charrington ought at once to have taxed her stepson, and given him an opportunity of clearing himself?"

"He would naturally have denied the charge in any circumstances. But presuming him to be innocent, the bare idea that his stepmother could have thought him guilty would have been most painful to him. That is the sort of mistake one can never atone for. No, Mrs. Charrington did the wisest thing she could have done. She decided, if possible, to be sure of his guilt or innocence before letting any one—even her husband—know of her loss."

"And how far do your investigations go in other directions?"

"So far, I am still in the dark. I have had every opportunity of mixing with the servants and studying them, and I don't believe for a moment that they are concerned in the matter. The footman bets, but is worried because he has

not paid back a sovereign he borrowed last week to put on a 'dead cert.,' which didn't come off. The lady's maid is an honourable, high-minded girl, engaged to be married to a most respectable man who has been in a position of trust for some years. I cannot find any suspicious circumstances connected with any of the other servants."

"Then you are inclined to take Mrs. Charrington's view?"

"No, I am not. And yet——. Well, I shall be able to answer more definitely when I have found out a little more about that young lady with the red tie. I have had no opportunity of making inquiries about her. I found out that Claude Charrington was coming here this morning when Johnson came downstairs with a telegram to the manager, 'Reserve window table for two o'clock'; but I had to get home and change to an American lady, and when I got here the little party were already at luncheon."

"But the young lady may have nothing to do with the matter. When a young man pawns some one else's jewellery to provide himself with ready money, surely the last person he would tell would be the young lady he is entertaining at a place like this."

"Quite so," said Dorcas, "but I have seen the young lady rather more closely than you have. I sat at the next table to them in the restaurant. Let us take a little stroll and pass them now."

Dorcas rose, and with her parasol shading her face strolled down on the terrace, and I walked by her side.

As we passed quite close to Claude Charrington and his friends I looked at the young lady. The end of her red necktie was fastened to the shirt *with a diamond lizard*.

"Good heavens!" I said to Dorcas when we were out of hearing, "is that part of the missing jewellery?"

"If it is not, it is at least a curious coincidence. Claude Charrington has access to his stepmother's room and the keys of her jewel case. Jewellery is missing. One of the articles is a diamond lizard. He is here today with a young lady, and that young lady has on jewellery which exactly answers the description of one of the missing articles. Now you know why I am going to find out a little more concerning that young lady and her female companion."

"Do you want an 'assistant'?" I said eagerly.

Dorcas smiled. "Not this time, thank you," she said; "but if I do later I will send you a wire. Now I think I must say good-day, for my 'people' look like making a move, and I mustn't lose them."

"Can't I see you this evening?"

"No, this evening I expect I shall be back at Mrs. Charrington's—you forget I am only a parlour-maid with a day out."

Dorcas nodded pleasantly, and I took the hint and left her.

A few minutes later I saw the Charrington party going back into the hotel, and Dorcas Dene following them at a respectful distance.

I sat down again on my old seat and fell into a reverie, which was interrupted by Karl the waiter, who came ostensibly to know if there was anything he could get me, but really to have a few minutes' chat on his favourite subject—the Turf. Did I know anything good for tomorrow at Sandown?

I told Karl that I did not, and then he told me that he had had a good tip himself—I ought to get on at once. I shifted the conversation from the Turf to general gossip, and then quite innocently I asked him if he knew who the people were who had lunched at the window table and had just left the lawn.

Oh, yes, he knew the young gentleman. That was Mr. Claude Charrington. He was a frequent customer and had often given Karl a good tip. Only a few days ago he had given him a horse at long odds and it had come off.

"And the young lady with the red tie?"

Karl wasn't quite sure—he had seen her only once or twice before. He thought the young lady was an actress at one of the Musical Comedy theatres. The elder lady used to be often there years ago, but she hadn't been for some time until today. He remembered her when she was one of the handsomest women of the day.

I lit a cigarette and said carelessly that I supposed they came with Mr. Charrington.

"No," said Karl; "they were here when he came, and he seemed rather surprised to see the elder lady. I suppose," said Karl, with a grin, "the young gentleman had only invited the younger lady to lunch, and he thought that two was company and three was none, as your English proverb says."

A white napkin waved from the balcony of the restaurant summoned Karl back to his duties, and looking at my watch I found that it was four o'clock, and time for me to make a start for town, where I had an appointment at six.

I thought of nothing but the mystery of the Charrington jewellery in the train, but when I got out at Waterloo I was still unable to find any theory which would satisfactorily reconcile the two opposing difficulties. If Claude Charrington had stolen his stepmother's jewellery to raise money on it he wouldn't have given it away; and if he had given it away it could have nothing to do with his sudden possession of a bundle of banknotes, which his stepmother considered one of the principal proofs of his guilt.

Two days later I received a telegram just before noon:

"Marble Arch, four o'clock.—DORCAS."

I was there punctually to the time, and a few minutes later Dorcas joined me, and we turned into the park.

"Well," I said, "you've found out who the young lady is. You've traced the jewellery—and I suppose there can be no doubt that Claude Charrington is the culprit?"

"I've found out that the young lady is a Miss Dolamore. She is a thoroughly good girl. Her mother, the widow of a naval officer, is in poor circumstances and lives in the country. Miss Dolamore, having a good voice, has gone on the stage. She is in lodgings in Fitzroy Street, Fitzroy Square. The house is kept and let out in apartments by an Italian, one Carlo Rinaldi, married to an Englishwoman—the Englishwoman is the woman who was with Miss Dolamore at Hampton Court."

"Then the elder woman was her landlady?"

"Yes."

"And Claude Charrington is in love with Miss Dolamore!"

"Exactly. They have been about together a great deal. He calls frequently to see her and take her out. It is understood in the house that they are engaged."

"How have you ascertained all this?"

"I visit the house. The first floor was to let and I took it yesterday morning for a friend of mine and paid the rent in advance. I am getting little odds and ends and taking them there for her. There is a delightfully communicative Irish housemaid at the Rinaldi's."

"Then of course it's quite clear that Claude Charrington gave Miss Dolamore that diamond lizard. Have you found out if she has the bracelet and the pendant too? If she hasn't, the lizard may be merely a coincidence. There are plenty of diamond lizards about."

"The bracelet and the pendant are at Attenborough's. They were pawned some days ago by a person giving the name of Claude Charrington and the Charringtons' correct address."

"By Claude Charrington, of course?"

"No; whoever the guilty party is it is not Claude Charrington."

"*Not Claude Charrington!*" I exclaimed, my brain beginning to whirl. "What do you mean? The jewels were in Mrs. Charrington's case—she misses them—one article is in the possession of Claude's sweetheart, a young lady who is on the stage, and the others are pawned in the name of Claude Charrington, and yet you say Claude Charrington had nothing to do with it. Whatever makes you come to such a strange conclusion as that?"

"One fact—and one fact alone. On the very day that we were at Hampton Mr. Charrington, the barrister, returned to town. He arrived in the afternoon, and seemed worried and out of

sorts. His wife had made up her mind to tell him everything, but he was so irritable that she hesitated.

"Yesterday she had an extraordinary story to tell me. When her husband had gone to his chambers in the morning she began to worry about not having told him. She felt that she really ought to do so now he had come back. She went to her jewel case to go over everything once more in order to be quite sure nothing else was missing before she told him her trouble, and there, to her utter amazement, was all the missing property, the bracelet, the pendant, and the diamond lizard."

"Then," I said with a gasp, "Claude Charrington must have redeemed them and put them back!"

"Not at all. The diamond lizard is *still* in Miss Dolamore's possession, and the diamond bracelet and pendant are *still at Attenborough's*."

I stared at Dorcas Dene for a moment in dumb amazement. When at last I could find words to speak my thoughts I exclaimed: "What does this mean? What can it mean? We shall never know, because Mrs. Charrington has her jewels again and your task is ended."

"No—my task is a double one now. Mrs. Charrington engaged me to find out who stole her jewels. When I can tell her that I shall be able to tell her also who endeavoured to conceal the robbery by putting a similar set back in their place. This is no common case of jewel stealing. There is a mystery and a romance behind it—a tangled skein which a Lecoq or a Sherlock Holmes would have been proud to unravel—*and I think I have a clue.*"

PART II
The Prick of a Pin

When Dorcas told me that she had a clue to the mystery of the Charrington jewels, I pressed her to tell me what it was.

"All in good time," she said; "meanwhile you can help me if you will. There is a club in ——

Street, Soho, of which most of the members are foreigners. It is called 'The Camorra.' Carlo Rinaldi, the landlord of the house in which Miss Dolamore is staying, spends his evenings there. It is a gambling club. Visitors are admitted, and the members by no means object to female society. I want you to take me there tomorrow night."

"But, my dear Dorcas—I—I'm not a member."

"No, but you can be a visitor."

"But I don't *know* a member."

"Oh, nonsense," said Dorcas, "you know a dozen. Ask your favourite waiter at any foreign restaurant, and he will be pretty sure to be able to tell you of one of his fellow-employés who can take you."

"Yes," I said, after I had thought for a moment. "If that is so, I think I can arrange it."

"That's a bargain, then," she said. "I will meet you and your friend the member outside Kettner's, in Church Street, tomorrow night at ten o'clock. Till then, good-bye."

"One question more," I said, retaining the hand that was placed in mine. "I assume that your object in going to this club is to watch Miss Dolamore's landlord; but if you have taken his second floor, won't he recognize you and be suspicious?"

Dorcas Dene smiled. "I'll take care there is no danger of his recognizing the lady of the second floor at the Camorra tomorrow night. And now, good afternoon. The Charringtons dine at eight, and I have to wait at table tonight."

Then, with a little nod of adieu, she walked quickly away and left me to think out my plans for capturing a member of the Camorra.

I had very little difficulty in finding a waiter who was a member. He turned up in a very old acquaintance, Guiseppe, of a well-known Strand café and restaurant. Guiseppe easily obtained an evening off, but he demurred when I told him that I wanted him to introduce a lady friend of mine as well as myself to the club. He

was nervous. Was she a lady journalist? I pacified Guiseppe, and the preliminaries were satisfactorily arranged, and at ten o'clock, leaving Guiseppe round the corner, I strolled on to Kettner's, and looked for Dorcas Dene.

There was no trace of her, and I was beginning to think she had been detained, when a stout, rather elderly-looking woman came towards me. She was dressed in a black silk dress, the worse for wear, a shabby black velvet mantle, and a black bonnet, plentifully bedecked with short black ostrich plumes, upon which wind and weather had told their tale. At her throat was a huge cameo brooch. As she came into the light she looked like one of the German landladies of the shilling table d'hôte establishments in the neighbourhood. The woman looked at me searchingly, and then asked me in guttural broken English if I was the gentleman who had an appointment there with a lady.

For a moment I hesitated. It might be a trap.

"Who told you to ask me?"

"Dorcas Dene."

"Indeed," I said, still suspicious, "and who is Dorcas Dene?"

"*I am,*" replied the German frau. "Come, do you think Rinaldi will recognize his second floor?"

"My dear Dorcas," I gasped, as soon as I had recovered from my astonishment, "why *did* you leave the stage?"

"Never mind about the stage," said Dorcas. "Where's the member of the Camorra?"

"He's waiting at the corner."

I had all my work to keep from bursting into a roar of laughter at Guiseppe's face when I introduced him to my lady friend, "Mrs. Goldschmidt." He evidently didn't think much of my choice of a female companion, but he bowed and smiled at the stout, old-fashioned German frau, and led the way to the club. After a few rough-and-ready formalities at the door, Guiseppe signed for two guests in a book which lay on the hall table, and we passed into a large room at the back of the premises, in which were a number of chairs and small tables, a raised platform with a piano, and a bar. A few men and women, mostly foreigners, were sitting about talking or reading the papers, and a sleepy-looking waiter was taking orders and serving drinks.

"Where do they play cards?" I said.

"Upstairs."

"Can I play?"

"Oh, yes, if I introduce you as my friend."

"May ladies play?"

Guiseppe shrugged his shoulders. "If they have money to lose—why not?"

I went to Dorcas. "Is he here?" I whispered.

"No; he's where the playing is, I expect."

"That's where we are going," I said.

Dorcas rose, and she and I and Guiseppe made our way to the upstairs room together.

On the landing we were challenged by a big, square-shouldered Italian. "Only members pass here," he said, gruffly.

Guiseppe answered in Italian, and the man growled out, "All right," and we entered a room which was as crowded as the other was empty.

One glance at the table was sufficient to show me that the game was an illegal one.

Dorcas stood by me among a little knot of onlookers. Presently she nudged my elbow, and I followed her glance. A tall, swarthy Italian, the wreck of what must once have been a remarkably handsome man, sat scowling fiercely as he lost stake after stake. I asked her with my eyebrows if she meant this was Rinaldi, and she nodded her head in assent.

A waiter was in the room taking orders, and bringing the drinks up from the bar below.

"Order two whiskies and seltzers," whispered Dorcas.

Then Dorcas sat down at the end of the room away from the crowd, and I joined her. The waiter brought the whiskies and seltzers and put them down. I paid unchallenged.

A dispute had arisen over at the big table, and the players were shouting one against the other. Dorcas took advantage of the din, and said, close to my ear, "Now you must do as I tell you—I'm going back to the table. Presently Rinaldi will leap up; when he does, seize him by the arms, and hold him—a few seconds will do."

"But——"

"It's all right. Do as I tell you."

She rose, taking her glass, still full of whisky and seltzer, with her. I wondered how on earth she could tell Rinaldi was going to jump up.

The stout old German frau pushed in among the crowd till she was almost leaning over Rinaldi's shoulder. Suddenly she lurched and tilted the entire contents of her glass into the breast pocket of his coat. He sprang up with a fierce oath, the rest of the company yelling with laughter. Instantly I seized him by the arms, as though to prevent him in his rage striking Dorcas. The German woman had her handkerchief out. She begged a thousand pardons, and began to mop up the liquid which was dripping down her victim. Then she thrust her hand into his inner pocket.

"Oh, the pocket-book! Ah, it must be dried!"

Quick as lightning she opened the book, and began to pull out the contents and wipe them with her handkerchief.

Carlo Rinaldi, who had been bellowing like a bull, struggled from me with an effort, and made a grab at the book. Dorcas, pretending to fear he was going to strike her, flung the book to him, and, giving me a quick glance, ran out of the room and down the stairs, and I followed, the fierce oaths of Rinaldi and the laughter of the members of the Camorra still ringing in my ears.

I hailed a taxi and dragged Dorcas into it.

"Phew!" I said, "that was a desperate game to play, Dorcas. What did you want to see in his pocket-book?"

"What I found," said Dorcas quietly. "A pawnticket for a diamond and ruby bracelet and a diamond and ruby pendant, pawned in the name of Claude Charrington. I imagined from the description given me at the pawnbroker's that the man was Rinaldi. Now I know that he pawned them on his own account, because he still has the ticket."

"How did he get them? Did Claude Charrington give them to him or sell them to him, or——"

"No. The person who gave them to Rinaldi is the person who put the new set back in their place."

"Do you know who that is?"

"Yes, now. The fact of Rinaldi having the ticket in his possession supplied the missing link. You remember my telling you how Mrs. Charrington discovered just as she was going to tell her husband of her loss that the jewels were no longer missing?"

"Yes; she found them the day after her husband's return."

"Exactly. Directly she told me, I asked her to let me examine the drawer in which the jewel-case was kept. It lay at the bottom of the left-hand top drawer of a chest near the bed. It was locked, and the keys were carried about by Mrs. Charrington and put on the dressing-table at night after the bedroom door had been bolted.

"As soon as possible I went with Mrs. Charrington to the bedroom. Then I took the keys and opened the drawer. The box she told me was where it was always kept, at the bottom of the drawer underneath layers of pocket-handkerchiefs and several cardboard boxes of odds and ends which she kept there.

"I turned the things over carefully one by one, and on a handkerchief which lay immediately on the top of the jewel-case I saw something which instantly attracted my attention. It was a tiny red spot, which looked like blood. Opening the jewel-case, I carefully examined the jewellery inside, and I found that the pin of the diamond lizard extended slightly beyond the brooch and was very sharp at the point.

"I then examined the keys, and upon the handle of the key of the jewel-box I found a tiny red smear. What had happened was as clear as noonday. Whoever had put the jewels back had pricked his or her finger with the pin of the lizard. The pricked finger had touched the handkerchief and left the little blood-mark. Still

bleeding slightly, the finger had touched the key in turning it in the lock of the jewel-case.

"Saying nothing to Mrs. Charrington, who was in the room with me, I cast my eyes searchingly in every direction. Suddenly I caught sight of a tiny mark on the sheet which was turned over outside the counterpane. It was a very minute little speck, and I knew it to be a bloodstain.

"'Who sleeps on this side near the chest of drawers?' I asked Mrs. Charrington, and she replied that her husband did.

"'Did he hear no noise in the night?'

"'In the night!' she exclaimed with evident astonishment. 'Good gracious! no one could have come into the room last night without our hearing them. Whoever put my jewels back did it in the daytime.'

"I didn't attempt to undeceive her, but I was certain that Mr. Charrington himself had replaced the jewels. He had probably done it in the night when his wife was fast asleep. A night-light burnt all night—she was a heavy sleeper—he had risen cautiously—the matter was a simple one. Only he had pricked his finger with the brooch-pin."

"But what was his motive?" I cried.

"His motive! That was what I wanted to make sure tonight, and I did so when I found the pawnticket in the name of Claude Charrington in the pocket-book of Carlo Rinaldi—Claude Charrington is the father's name as well as the son's."

"Then you think Rinaldi pawned the original jewels for Mr. Charrington? Absurd!"

"It *would* be absurd to think that," said Dorcas, "but my theory is not an absurd one. I have ascertained the history of Carlo Rinaldi from sources at my command. Rinaldi was a valet at the West End. He married a rich man's cast-off mistress. The rich man gave his mistress a sum of money as a marriage portion. He gave her up not only because he had ceased to care for her, but because he had fallen in love and was about to marry again. He was a widower. He lost his first wife when their only child, a son, was a few months old, and he himself quite a young man. The mistress was Madame Rinaldi, the rich man was Claude Charrington."

"Well, where does that lead you?"

"To this. During the time that Mrs. Charrington is sure that the jewels were not in her case I trace them. I find the diamond lizard in the possession of a young lady who lodges in the house of Madame Rinaldi. I find the pendant and bracelet at Attenborough's, and tonight I have seen the pawnticket for them in the possession of Madame Rinaldi's husband. Therefore, there is no doubt in my mind that whoever took the jewels out of Mrs. Charrington's case gave them to the Rinaldis. I have proved by the prick of the finger and the bloodstain that Mr. Charrington put a similar set of jewels to those abstracted back into the empty cases in his wife's jewel-box, therefore he must have been aware that they were missing. Mrs. Charrington has not breathed a word of her loss to any one but myself, therefore he must have been privy to their abstraction, and it is only reasonable to conclude that he abstracted them himself."

"But the lizard in Miss Dolamore's possession must have been given her by Claude, her sweetheart, and he was suddenly flush of money just after the theft—remember that!"

"Yes; I have ascertained how he got that money. Johnson, the footman, told me that the young fellow had given him a tip for the Leger. 'And he gets good information sometimes from a friend of his,' said Johnson. 'Why, only last week he backed a thirty-three to one chance, and won a couple of hundred. But don't say anything to the missis,' said Johnson. 'She might tell the governor, and Mr. Claude isn't in his good books just at present.'"

I agreed with Dorcas that that would account for the young fellow's confusion when his stepmother saw the notes, but I urged there was still the lizard to get over.

"I think that is pretty clear. The Irish housemaid tells me that Madame is very friendly with Miss Dolamore. I shouldn't be surprised if she

went down to Richmond with her that day to show Claude the lizard and get him to buy it for more than it was worth. I know the Rinaldis were pressed at the time for ready money."

I confessed to Dorcas that her theory cleared Claude Charrington of suspicion, but it in no way explained why Mr. Charrington, senior, should send his former mistress his present wife's jewels.

At that moment the cab stopped. We were at Elm Tree Road. Dorcas got out and put out her hand. "I can't tell you why Mr. Charrington stole his wife's jewellery," she said, "because he hasn't told me."

"And isn't likely to," I replied with a laugh.

"You are mistaken," said Dorcas. "I am going to his chambers tomorrow to ask him, and then my task will be done. If you want to know how it ends, come to Eastbourne on Sunday. I am going to spend the day there with Paul."

The sunshine was streaming into the pretty seaside apartments occupied by the Denes, the midday Sunday meal was over, and Paul and Dorcas were sitting by the open window.

I had only arrived at one o'clock, and Dorcas had postponed her story until the meal was over.

"Now," said Dorcas, as she filled Paul's pipe and lighted it for him, "if you want to know the finish of the 'Romance of the Charrington Jewels,' smoke and listen."

"Did you go to Mr. Charrington as you said you would?" I asked as I lit my cigar.

"*Smoke and listen!*" said Dorcas with mock severity in her tone of command. "Of course I went. I sent up my card to Mr. Charrington.

"Ushered into his room he gave me a searching glance and his face changed.

"'This card says "Dorcas Dene, Detective"?' he exclaimed. 'But surely—you—you are very like some one I have seen lately!'

"'I had the pleasure of being your wife's parlour-maid, Mr. Charrington,' I replied quietly.

"'You have dared to come spying in my house!' exclaimed the barrister angrily.

"'I came to your house, Mr. Charrington, at your wife's request. She had missed some jewellery which you presented to her a day or two before you went into the country. Circumstances pointed to your son Claude as the thief, and your wife, anxious to avoid a scandal, called me in instead of the police.'

"The barrister dropped into his chair and rubbed his hands together nervously.

"'Indeed—and she said nothing to me. You are probably aware that you have been investigating a mare's nest—my wife's jewellery is not missing.'

"'No, it is not missing now, because when you returned from the country you put a similar set in its place.'

"'Good heavens, madame!' exclaimed Mr. Charrington, leaping to his feet, 'what do you mean?'

"'Pray be calm, sir. I assure you that I have come here not to make a scandal, but to avoid one. After you gave your wife the jewellery, you for some reason secretly abstracted it. The jewellery you abstracted passed into the possession of Mrs. Rinaldi, whose husband pawned two of the articles at Attenborough's. As your wife is quite aware that for many days her jewellery was missing, I am bound to make an explanation of some kind to her. I have come to you to know what I shall say. You cannot wish her to believe that your son took the jewellery?'

"'Of course Claude must be cleared—but what makes you believe that I put the jewellery back?'

"'On the night you did so you pricked your finger with the pin of the lizard. You left a small bloodstain on the linen that was in the drawer, and when you turned down the sheet to get back into bed again your finger was still bleeding, and left its mark as evidence against you. Come Mr. Charrington, explain the circumstances under which you committed this rob——well, let us say, made this exchange, and I will do my best to find a means of explaining matters to your wife.'

"Mr. Charrington hesitated a moment, and then, having probably made up his mind that it was better to have me on his side than against him, told me his story.

"At the time that he kept up an irregular establishment he made the lady who is now Mrs. Rinaldi many valuable presents of jewellery. Among them were the articles which had resulted in my becoming temporarily a parlour-maid under his roof. When the lady married Rinaldi, he provided for her. But the man turned out a rascal, squandered and gambled away his wife's money, and forced her to pawn her jewellery for him. He then by threats compelled her to forward the tickets to her former protector, and implore him to redeem them for her as she was without ready money to do so herself. The dodge succeeded two or three times, but Mr. Charrington grew tired, and on the last occasion redeemed the jewellery and put it in a drawer in his desk, and replied that he could not return it, as it would only be pawned again. He would keep it until the Rinaldis sent the money to redeem it, and then they could have it.

"Then came his wife's birthday, and he wished to make her a present of some jewellery. He selected a bracelet and a pendant in diamonds and sapphires and a true-lovers'-knot brooch in diamonds, and ordered them to be sent to his chambers.

"He was busy when they came, and put them away for safety in a drawer immediately below the one in which he had some weeks previously placed the jewellery belonging to Mrs. Rinaldi. Mrs. Rinaldi's jewellery, each article in its case, he had wrapped up in brown paper and marked outside 'jewellery,' to distinguish it from other packets which he kept there, and which contained various articles belonging to his late wife.

"On the eve of his wife's birthday he found he would have to leave town for the day without going to his office. He had to appear in a case at Kingston-on-Thames, which had come on much sooner than he had expected. Knowing he would not be back till late at night, he sent a note and his keys to his clerk, telling him to open his desk, take out the jewellery which had recently been forwarded from Streeter's, and send it up to him at his house. He wished his wife many happy returns of the day, apologized for not having his present ready, but said it would be sent up, and she should have it that evening.

"The clerk went to the desk and opened the wrong drawer first. Seeing a neatly tied-up parcel labelled 'jewellery,' he jumped to the conclusion that it was the jewellery wanted. Not caring to trust it to a messenger, he went straight up to the house with it, and handed it to Mrs. Charrington herself, who concluded it was her husband's present. When she opened the parcel she noticed that the cases were not new, and supposed that her husband had bought the things privately. She was delighted with the jewellery—a bracelet and pendant in diamonds and rubies and a diamond lizard.

"When her husband returned to dinner he was horrified to find his wife wearing his former mistress's jewellery. But before he could say a word she kissed him and told him that these things were just what she wanted.

"He hesitated after that to say a mistake had been made, and thought that silence was best. The next day Mrs. Charrington received news of her brother's death, and had to go into deep mourning. The new jewellery was put away, as she would not be able to wear it for many months.

"That afternoon at Mr. Charrington's chambers Rinaldi called upon him. Desperately hard up, he had determined to try and bully Mr. Charrington out of the jewellery. He shouted and swore, and talked of an action at law and exposure, and was delighted to find that his victim was nervous. Mr. Charrington declared that he could not give him the jewellery back. Whereupon Mr. Rinaldi informed him that if by twelve o'clock the next day it was not in his possession he should summon him for detaining it.

"Mr. Charrington rushed off to his jewellers. How long would it take them to find the exact counterpart of certain jewellery if he brought them the things they had to match? And how long would they want the originals? The jewellers said if they had them for an hour and made a

coloured drawing of them they could make up or find a set within ten days.

"That night Charrington abstracted the birthday present he had given his wife from her jewel-box. The next morning at ten o'clock it was in the hands of the jewellers, and at mid-day when Rinaldi called to make his final demand the jewellery was handed over to him.

"Then Mr. Charrington went out of town. On his return the new jewellery was ready and was delivered to him. In the dead of the night, while his wife was asleep, he put it back in the empty cases. And that," said Dorcas, "is—as Dr. Lynn, at the Egyptian Hall, used to say—'how it was done.'"

"And the wife?" asked Paul, turning his blind eyes towards Dorcas; "you did not make her unhappy by telling her the truth?"

"No, dear," said Dorcas. "I arranged the story with Mr. Charrington. He went home and asked his wife for her birthday present. She brought the jewels out nervously, wondering if he had heard or suspected anything. He took the bracelet and the pendant from the cases.

"'Very pretty, indeed, my dear,' he said. 'And so you've never noticed the difference?'

"'Difference?' she exclaimed. 'Why—why—what do you mean?'

"'Why, that I made a dreadful mistake when I bought them and only found it out afterwards. The first that I gave you, my dear, were imitation. I wouldn't confess to you that I had been done, so I took them without your knowing and had real ones made. The real ones I put back the other night while you were fast asleep.'

"'Oh, Claude, Claude,' she cried, 'I am so glad. I did miss them, dear, and I was afraid there was a thief in the house, and I dared not tell you I'd lost them, And now—oh, how happy you've made me!'"

Two months later Dorcas told me that young Claude Charrington was engaged to Miss Dolamore with his father's consent, but he had insisted that she should leave Fitzroy Street at once, and acting on private information which Dorcas had given him, he assured Claude that diamond lizards were unlucky, and as he had seen Miss Dolamore with one on he begged to offer her as his first present to his son's intended a very beautiful diamond true-lovers'-knot in its place. At the same time he induced his wife to let him have her diamond lizard for a much more valuable diamond poodle with ruby eyes.

So those two lizards never met under Mrs. Charrington's roof, and perhaps, all things considered, it was just as well.

THE STIR OUTSIDE THE CAFÉ ROYAL

Clarence Rook

AN ELUSIVE, ENIGMATIC FIGURE, Clarence Rook (1862 or 1863–1915) was born in Faversham, Kent, the son of a bookseller and the town's postmaster. He graduated from Oxford University and became a fairly prolific and successful journalist, writing for the *Globe*, the *Chronicle*, *The Illustrated London News*, *The Idler*, *The Ludgate Monthly*, *The Art Journal*, and various American publications. He was a popular figure in London's literary circle and was strongly praised by George Bernard Shaw.

His best-known work is *Hooligan Nights* (1899), which Rook insisted was a true portrait of life in London's underworld as confided to him by an informant. Doubt has been cast on the verisimilitude of his claim that his book was pure journalism, partially owing to the fact that the same "real-life" character also appears in "The Stakes," an undisguised work of fiction that appeared in 1900 in *Pall Mall Magazine*.

Nora Van Snoop is a determined young woman who knows exactly what to do to bring her quarry to justice. Even though she appears in only this single story, her name has become part of the English language. According to the *Oxford English Dictionary*, the verb "to snoop" is a bastardization of the Dutch word "snoepen," which means "to enjoy stealthily."

"The Stir Outside the Café Royal" was originally published in the September 1898 issue of *The Harmsworth Magazine*.

The Stir Outside the Café Royal

CLARENCE ROOK

COLONEL MATHURIN was one of the aristocrats of crime; at least Mathurin was the name under which he had accomplished a daring bank robbery in Detroit which had involved the violent death of the manager, though it was generally believed by the police that the Rossiter who was at the bottom of some long firm frauds in Melbourne was none other than Mathurin under another name, and that the designer and chief gainer in a sensational murder case in the Midlands was the same mysterious and ubiquitous personage.

But Mathurin had for some years successfully eluded pursuit; indeed, it was generally known that he was the most desperate among criminals, and was determined never to be taken alive. Moreover, as he invariably worked through subordinates who knew nothing of his whereabouts and were scarcely acquainted with his appearance, the police had but a slender clue to his identity.

As a matter of fact, only two people beyond his immediate associates in crime could have sworn to Mathurin if they had met him face to face. One of them was the Detroit bank manager whom he had shot with his own hand before the eyes of his fiancée. It was through the other that Mathurin was arrested, extradited to the States, and finally made to atone for his life of crime. It all happened in a distressingly common-place way, so far as the average spectator was concerned. But the story, which I have pieced together from the details supplied—firstly, by a certain detective sergeant whom I met in a tavern hard by Westminster; and secondly, by a certain young woman named Miss Van Snoop— has an element of romance, if you look below the surface.

It was about half-past one o'clock, on a bright and pleasant day, that a young lady was driving down Regent Street in a hansom which she had picked up outside her boarding-house near Portland Road Station. She had told the cabman to drive slowly, as she was nervous behind a horse; and so she had leisure to scan, with the curiosity of a stranger, the strolling crowd that at nearly all hours of the day throngs Regent Street. It was a sunny morning, and everybody looked cheerful. Ladies were shopping, or looking in at the shop windows. Men about town were collecting an appetite for lunch; flower girls were selling "nice vi'lets, sweet vi'lets, penny a bunch"; and the girl in the cab leaned one arm on the apron and regarded the scene with alert attention. She was not exactly pretty, for the symmetry of her features was discounted by a certain hardness in the set of the mouth. But her hair, so dark as to be almost black, and her eyes of greyish blue set her beyond comparison with the commonplace.

Just outside the Café Royal there was a slight

stir, and a temporary block in the foot traffic. A brougham was setting down, behind it was a victoria, and behind that a hansom; and as the girl glanced round the heads of the pair in the brougham, she saw several men standing on the steps. Leaning back suddenly, she opened the trapdoor in the roof.

"Stop here," she said, "I've changed my mind."

The driver drew up by the kerb, and the girl skipped out.

"You shan't lose by the change," she said, handing him half-a-crown.

There was a tinge of American accent in the voice; and the cabman, pocketing the half-crown with thanks, smiled.

"They may talk about that McKinley tariff," he soliloquised as he crawled along the kerb towards Piccadilly Circus, "but it's better 'n free trade—lumps!"

Meanwhile the girl walked slowly back towards the Café Royal, and, with a quick glance at the men who were standing there, entered. One or two of the men raised their eyebrows; but the girl was quite unconscious, and went on her way to the luncheon-room.

"American, you bet," said one of the loungers. "They'll go anywhere and do anything."

Just in front of her as she entered was a tall, clean-shaven man, faultlessly dressed in glossy silk hat and frock coat, with a flower in his button-hole. He looked around for a moment in search of a convenient table. As he hesitated, the girl hesitated; but when the waiter waved him to a small table laid for two, the girl immediately sat down behind him at the next table.

"Excuse me, madam," said the waiter, "this table is set for four; would you mind——"

"I guess," said the girl, "I'll stay where I am." And the look in her eyes, as well as a certain sensation in the waiter's palm, ensured her against further disturbance.

The restaurant was full of people lunching, singly or in twos, in threes, and even larger parties; and many curious glances were directed to the girl who sat at a table alone and pursued

her way calmly through the menu. But the girl appeared to notice no one. When her eyes were off her plate they were fixed straight ahead—on the back of the man who had entered in front of her. The man, who had drunk a half-bottle of champagne with his lunch, ordered a liqueur to accompany his coffee. The girl, who had drunk an aerated water, leaned back in her chair and wrinkled her brows. They were very straight brows, that seemed to meet over her nose when she wrinkled them in perplexity. Then she called a waiter.

"Bring me a sheet of notepaper, please," she said, "and my bill."

The waiter laid the sheet of paper before her, and the girl proceeded, after a few moments thought, to write a few lines in pencil upon it. When this was done, she folded the sheet carefully, and laid it in her purse. Then, having paid her bill, she returned her purse to her dress pocket, and waited patiently.

In a few minutes the clean-shaven man at the next table settled his bill and made preparations for departure. The girl at the same time drew on her gloves, keeping her eyes immovably upon her neighbour's back. As the man rose to depart, and passed the table at which the girl had been sitting, the girl was looking into the mirror upon the wall, and patting her hair. Then she turned and followed the man out of the restaurant, while a pair at an adjacent table remarked to one another that it was a rather curious coincidence for a man and woman to enter and leave at the same moment when they had no apparent connection.

But what happened outside was even more curious.

The man halted for a moment upon the steps at the entrance. The porter, who was in conversation with a policeman, turned, whistle in hand.

"Hansom, sir?" he asked.

"Yes," said the clean-shaven man.

The porter was raising his whistle to his lips when he noticed the girl behind.

"Do you wish for a cab, madam?" he asked, and blew upon his whistle.

As he turned again for an answer, he plainly

saw the girl, who was standing close behind the clean-shaven man, slip her hand under his coat, and snatch from his hip pocket something which she quickly transferred to her own.

"Well, I'm——" began the clean-shaven man, swinging round and feeling in his pocket.

"Have you missed anything, sir?" said the porter, standing full in front of the girl to bar her exit.

"My cigarette-case is gone," said the man, looking from one side to another.

"What's this?" said the policeman, stepping forward.

"I saw the woman's hand in the gentleman's pocket, plain as a pikestaff," said the porter.

"Oh, that's it, is it?" said the policeman, coming close to the girl. "I thought as much."

"Come now," said the clean-shaven man, "I don't want to make a fuss. Just hand back that cigarette-case, and we'll say no more about it."

"I haven't got it," said the girl. "How dare you? I never touched your pocket."

The man's face darkened.

"Oh, come now!" said the porter.

"Look here, that won't do," said the policeman, "you'll have to come along of me. Better take a four-wheeler, eh, sir?"

For a knot of loafers, seeing something interesting in the wind, had collected round the entrance.

A four-wheeler was called, and the girl entered, closely followed by the policeman and the clean-shaven man.

"I was never so insulted in my life," said the girl.

Nevertheless, she sat back quite calmly in the cab, as though she was perfectly ready to face this or any other situation, while the policeman watched her closely to make sure that she did not dispose in any surreptitious way of the stolen article.

At the police-station hard by, the usual formalities were gone through, and the clean-shaven man was constituted prosecutor. But the girl stoutly denied having been guilty of any offence.

The inspector in charge looked doubtful.

"Better search her," he said.

And the girl was led off to a room for an interview with the female searcher.

The moment the door closed the girl put her hand into her pocket, pulled out the cigarette-case, and laid it upon the table.

"There you are," she said. "That will fix matters so far."

The woman looked rather surprised.

"Now," said the girl, holding out her arms, "feel in this other pocket, and find my purse."

The woman picked out the purse.

"Open it and read the note on the bit of paper inside."

On the sheet of paper which the waiter had given her, the girl had written these words, which the searcher read in a muttered undertone—

"I am going to pick this man's pocket as the best way of getting him into a police-station without violence. He is Colonel Mathurin, alias Rossiter, alias Connell, and he is wanted in Detroit, New York, Melbourne, Colombo, and London. Get four men to pin him unawares, for he is armed and desperate. I am a member of the New York detective force—Nora Van Snoop."

"It's all right," said Miss Van Snoop, quickly, as the searcher looked up at her after reading the note. "Show that to the boss—right away."

The searcher opened the door. After whispered consultation the inspector appeared, holding the note in his hand.

"Now then, be spry," said Miss Van Snoop. "Oh, you needn't worry! I've got my credentials right here," and she dived into another pocket.

"But do you know—can you be sure," said the inspector, "that this is the man who shot the Detroit bank manager?"

"Great heavens! Didn't I see him shoot Will Stevens with my own eyes! And didn't I take service with the police to hunt him out?"

The girl stamped her foot, and the inspector left. For two, three, four minutes, she stood listening intently. Then a muffled shout reached her ears. Two minutes later the inspector returned.

"I think you're right," he said. "We have found enough evidence on him to identify him. But why didn't you give him in charge before to the police?"

"I wanted to arrest him myself," said Miss Van Snoop, "and I have. Oh, Will! Will!"

Miss Van Snoop sank into a cane-bottomed chair, laid her head upon the table, and cried. She had earned the luxury of hysterics. In half an hour she left the station, and, proceeding to a post-office, cabled her resignation to the head of the detective force in New York.

THE MANDARIN

Fergus Hume

A YEAR BEFORE THE PUBLICATION of the first Sherlock Holmes book, Fergusson Wright Hume (1859–1932) had the honor of writing the bestselling mystery novel of the nineteenth century, *The Mystery of a Hansom Cab* (1886). He paid to have it published in Australia, but it quickly had a modest success and he sold all rights to a group of English investors called the Hansom Cab Publishing Company for fifty pounds sterling (not unlike Arthur Conan Doyle, who sold all rights to *A Study in Scarlet* for twenty-five pounds in 1887). It went on to sell more than a half million copies.

Although he had studied to be a barrister, Hume wanted to be a writer and once described how his famous book came to be written. He asked a Melbourne bookseller what sort of book sold best. The bookseller replied that "the detective stories of [Emile] Gaboriau had a large sale; and, as, at this time, I had never even heard of this author, I bought all his works . . . and I determined to write a book of the same class; containing a mystery, a murder, and a description of low life in Melbourne. This was the origin of *Cab*." Hume went on to write an additional 130 novels—all of which have been largely forgotten.

The protagonist in "The Mandarin" is Hagar Stanley, a Gypsy and the niece of a miserly and corrupt owner of a pawnshop in London, where she is employed. Pretty, smart, and honest, she soon learns the trade, becoming an expert in various areas of antiques, and largely takes over the running of the shop. Known for her decency and fearlessness, she is quick to help people in righting wrongs and works as an amateur detective to that end. In the last story, Hagar gets married, and the happy couple become professional traveling booksellers.

"The Mandarin" was originally published in the author's short story collection *Hagar of the Pawn-Shop* (London, Skeffington & Son, 1898).

The Mandarin

FERGUS HUME

THERE WAS SOMETHING VERY QUEER about that lacquer mandarin; and something still queerer about the man who pawned it. The toy itself was simply two balls placed together; the top ball, a small one, was the head, masked with a quaintly-painted face of porcelain, and surmounted by a pagoda-shaped hat jingling with tiny golden bells. The large ball below was the body, gaily tinted to imitate the official dress of a great Chinese lord; and therefrom two little arms terminating in porcelain hands, exquisitely finished even to the long nails, protruded in a most comical fashion. Weighted dexterously within, the mandarin would keel over this side and that, to a perilous angle, but he never went over altogether. When set in motion the big ball would roll, the arms would wag, and the head nod gravely, a little red tongue thrusting itself out at every bow. Then the golden bells would chime melodiously, and rolling, wagging, nodding, the mandarin made all who beheld him laugh, with his innocent antics. He was worthy, in all his painted beauty, to be immortalized by Hans Andersen.

"A very pretty toy?" said Hagar, as the quaint thing tipped itself right and left, front and back. "It comes from China, I suppose?"

She asked this question of the customer, who demanded two pounds on the figure; but in place of answering her, he burst out into a hoarse laugh, and leered unpleasantly at the girl.

"Comes from other side of Nowhere, I reckon, missus!" he said, in a coarse voice; "and a bloomin' rum piece of goods 'tis, anyhow!"

Hagar did not like the man's looks at all, although she was by no means exacting on the score of personal beauty—especially with regard to the male sex. Still, there was something brutal about this fellow which revolted her every sense. He had a bullet-head, with a crop of closely-cut hair; a clean-shaven face of a blue-black dirty hue, where the beard had been removed; a low forehead, a snub nose, a large ugly mouth, and two cunning gray eyes which never looked anyone straight in the face. This attractive gentleman wore a corduroy suit, a red linen handkerchief round his throat, and a fur cap with earflaps on his head. Also he carried a small black pipe between his teeth, and breathed therefrom an atmosphere of the vilest tobacco. Certainly the toy was queer; but the man queerer. Not at all the sort of person likely to be in possession of so delicate a work of Chinese art and fancy.

"Where did you get this?" demanded Hagar, drawing her black brows together and touching with one finger the swaying mandarin.

"It's all on the square, missus!" growled the man in an injured tone. "I didn't prig the blessed thing, if that's yer lay. A pal o' mine as is a sailor brought it from Lord-knows-where an' guv' it me. I wants rhino, I do; so if you kin spring two quid—"

"I'll give you twenty shillings," said Hagar, cutting him short.

"Oh, my bloomin' eyes! if this ain't robbery an' blue murder!" whined the man; "twenty bob! why, the fun you gits out of it's worth more!"

"That's my offer—take it or leave it. I don't believe you came honestly by it, and I'm running a risk in taking it."

"Sling us the blunt, then!" said the customer, sullenly; "it's the likes of you as grinds down the likes of me! Yah! you an' yer preachin'."

"In whose name am I to make out the ticket?" asked Hagar, coldly.

"In the name of Mister William Smith—Larky Bill they calls me; but 'tain't hetiikit to put h'endearin' family names on pawn-tickets. I lives in Sawder Alley, Whitechapel."

"Why didn't you go to a nearer pawn-shop, then?" said Hagar, taking down Mr. Smith's address, without smiling at his would-be wit.

"That's my biz!" retorted Bill, scowling. "'Ere, gimme the tin; an' don't you arsk no questions an' you won't be tol' no lies! D'ye see?"

Hagar stamped her foot. "Here's the money and the ticket. Take yourself and your insolence out of my shop. Quick!"

"I'm gitting!" growled the man, shuffling towards the door. "See 'ere, missus; I comes fur that doll in three months, or it may be four. If it ain't all right an' 'anded up to me proper, I'll break your neck!"

"What's that you say?" Hagar was over the counter, and close at hand by this time. Larky Bill stared open-mouthed at her spirit. "You say another word, my jail-bird," said Hagar, seizing his ear, "and I'll put you into the gutter!"

"Lordy! what a donah!" muttered Bill, rubbing his ear when he found himself outside. "She'll look arter the toy proper. Three months. Tck!" he rapped his thumbnail against his teeth. "I can't get less from the beak; but I've bested Monkey anyhow!"

And with these enigmatic words, Mr. Smith turned on his heel and went to Whitechapel.

There his forebodings were realized, for at the very door of his own house in Sawder Alley, he was taken in charge by a grim policeman, and sent to prison for four months. He had stolen some fruit off a coster's barrow on the day previous to his arrest, and quite expected to be—as he phrased it—nabbed for the theft. Therefore he employed the small remnant of freedom still remaining to him in pawning the mandarin in the most distant pawn-shop he could think of, which happened to be Hagar's. As Mr. Smith left the court to do his four months, a wizen-faced man slouched close to him.

"Bill," he growled, edging against the policeman, "where's that doll?"

"That's all right, Monkey! I've put it where you won't git it!" grunted Smith.

When Black Maria rolled away with Bill inside, the man he had called Monkey stood on the edge of the pavement and cursed freely till a policeman moved him on. He had a particular desire to gain possession of that doll, as he called it; and it was on this account that Larky Bill had taken the trouble to hide it. Monkey never thought of a pawn-shop. It was a case of diamond cut diamond; and one rogue had outwitted the other.

In the meantime, Hagar, quite unaware of the value attached to the Chinese toy, placed it away among other pawned articles upon a high shelf. But it did not always remain there, for Bolker, a child in many ways, notwithstanding his precocious intelligence, found it out, and frequently took it down to play with. Hagar would not have permitted this had she known, as the toy was given into her charge to keep safe, and she would have been afraid of Bolker spoiling the painting or rubbing off the gilding. Bolker knew this, and was clever enough to play with the mandarin only when Hagar was absent. He placed it on the counter, and made it sway in its quaint fashion. The waving arms, the nodding head, and the roseleaf of a tongue slipping in and out, enchanted the lad, and he would amuse himself for hours with it. It was strange that a gilded toy, no doubt made for the amusement of grave

Chinese Emperors, should descend to afford pleasure to an arab of London City. But the mandarin was an exile from the Flowery Land, and rocked as merrily in the dingy pawn-shop as ever he had done in the porcelain palaces of Pekin.

A month or two after the mandarin had been pawned, Bolker announced in the most unexpected manner that he intended to better himself. He had been given, he said, the post of shop-boy in a West-end bookseller's establishment; and as he was fond of literature, he intended to accept it. Hagar rather wondered that anyone should have placed sufficient confidence in this arab to give him a situation; but she kept her wonderment to herself, and permitted him to go. She was sorry to lose the benefit of his acute intelligence, but personally she had no great love for this scampish hunchback; so she saw him depart without displaying much sorrow. Thus Bolker vanished from the pawn-shop and from Carby's Crescent, and ascended into higher spheres.

Nothing new happened after his departure. The mandarin remained untouched on the shelf, and the dust collected over his motionless figure. Hagar quite forgot about the toy and its pawner; and it was only when Larky Bill was released from prison and came to claim his property that she recalled the incident. She took down the figure, dusted it carefully, and set it swaying on the counter before Mr. Smith. Neither Bill nor Hagar noticed that it did not roll as easily and gracefully as usual.

"Here's the quid and interest and ticket," said Bill, tendering all three. "I'm glad to get this 'ere back again. No one's touched it, 'ave they?"

"No. It has been on that shelf ever since you pawned it. Where have you been?"

Larky Bill grinned. "I've been stayin' at a country 'ouse of mine fur my 'ealth's sake," he said, tucking the mandarin under his arm. "Say, missus, a cove called Monkey didn't come smellin' round 'ere fur this h'image?"

"Not that I know of. Nobody asked for the toy."

"Guess it's all right," chuckled Bill, gleefully.

"Lord, to think as how I've done that bloke! Won't he cuss when he knows as I've got 'em!"

What "them" were Mr. Smith did not condescend to explain at that particular moment. He nodded familiarly to Hagar, and went off, still chuckling with the mandarin in charge. Hagar put away the money, and thought that she had seen the last of Bill; but she reckoned wrongly. Two hours afterwards he was back in the shop, mandarin and all, with a pale face, a wild eye, and a mouth full of abuse. At first he swore at large without giving any explanation; so Hagar waited till the bad language was ended, and then asked him quietly what was the matter. For answer Bill plumped down the Chinese toy on the counter, and clutched his fur cap with both hands.

"Matter, cuss you!" he shrieked, furiously— "as if ye didn't know! I've been robbed!"

"Robbed! What nonsense are you talking? And what have I to do with your being robbed?"

Bill gasped, and pointed to the mandarin, who was rolling complacently, with a fat smile on his porcelain visage. "That—that doll!" he spluttered. "I've been robbed!"

"Of the doll?" asked Hagar, impatiently.

"Y' young Jezebel! Of the dimins—dimins!"

"Diamonds!" echoed the girl, starting back in astonishment.

"Yes! Y' know, hang you, y' know! Twenty thousan' poun' of dimins! They was in that doll—inside 'im. They ain't there now! Why not? 'Cause you've robbed me! Thief! Yah!"

"I did not know that there were any jewels concealed in the mandarin," said Hagar, calmly. "Had I known I should have informed the police."

"Blown the gaff, would ye? An' why?"

"Because a man in your position does not possess diamonds, unless he steals them. And now I think of it," added Hagar, quickly, "about the time you pawned this toy Lady Deacey's jewels were stolen. You stole them!"

"P'raps I did, p'raps I didn't!" growled Bill, mentally cursing Hagar for the acuteness of her understanding. "'Tany rate, 'twarn't your biz to prig 'em!"

"I tell you I never touched them! I did not know they were in there!"

"Then who did, cuss you? When I guv you the doll, the dimins were inside; now they ain't. Who took 'em?"

Hagar pondered. It was certainly odd that the diamonds should have been stolen. She had placed the mandarin on the shelf on the day of its pawning, and had not removed it again until she had returned it to its owner. Seeing her silent, Bill turned the toy upside down, and removed a square morsel of the lacquer, which fitted in so perfectly as to seem like one whole piece. Within was the dark hollow of the ball—empty.

"I put them dimins into 'ere with my own 'and," persisted Bill, pointing one grimy finger at the gap; "they were 'ere when I popped it; they ain't 'ere now. Where are they? Who's bin playing with my property?"

"Bolker!" cried Hagar, without thinking. It had just flashed across her mind that one day she had found Bolker amusing himself with the mandarin. At the time she had thought nothing of it, but had replaced the toy on its shelf, and forbidden the lad to meddle with it. But now, recalling the episode, and connecting it with Bolker's sudden departure, she felt convinced that the imp had stolen the concealed jewels. But—as she wondered—how had he become cognizant that twenty thousands pounds' worth of diamonds was hidden in the hollow body of the doll? The thing puzzled her.

"Bolker?" echoed Larky Bill, wrathfully. "And who may that cuss be?"

"He was my shop-boy; but he left three months ago to better himself."

"I dessay! With my dimins, I'll bet. Where is he, that I may cut his bloomin' throat!"

"I shan't tell you," said Hagar, alarmed by the brutal threat of the man, and already regretting that she had been so candid.

"I'll make you! I'll twist your neck!" raged Bill, mad with anger.

He placed his great hands on the counter to vault over; but the next moment he dropped back before the shining tube of a neat little revolver, which leveled itself in Hagar's hands. She had lately purchased it for defense.

"I keep this always by me," said she, calmly, "to protect myself against such rogues as you!"

Bill stared at her blankly, then turned on his heel and left the shop. At the door he paused and shook his fist.

"I'll find that Bolker, and smash the life out of him!" he said, hoarsely; "then, my fine madam, I'll come back to lay you out!" after which he vanished, leaving the mandarin, with its eternal smile, still rocking on the counter.

Hagar put away the pistol, and took up the figure. Now that she knew about the diamonds, and had forced Bill to admit, as he had done indirectly, that they had been stolen from Lady Deacey, she thought it possible that the Chinese toy might belong to the same owner. In spite of her fearlessness, Hagar was not altogether happy in her mind as regards the burglar. If he did not find the diamonds, he was quite capable of returning to murder her. On the whole, Hagar concluded that it would be just as well for society at large, and herself in particular, if Mr. Smith were restored to the prison whence he had lately emerged. After some consideration she resolved to see Vark, the lawyer, and tell him the episode of the mandarin, taking the image with her as evidence. Vark, if anyone, would be able to deal with the intricacies of the affair.

In the meantime, Bill Smith had repaired to the public-house which guarded the narrow entrance to Carby's Crescent, and there was drowning his regrets in strong drink. As he drained his tankard of ale, he fell into conversation with the fat landlord—a brutal-looking prize-fighter, who looked as though he had been in jail—quite a bird of Mr. Smith's feather. These two congenial spirits recognized each other, and became friendly—so friendly, indeed, that Bill thought it a good opportunity to extract information regarding the whereabouts of Bolker. He was too wise to explain his reason for making these inquiries.

"That's a fine gal in the pawn-shop, hay!" said he, with a leer.

"Wot—'Agar? She's a plum, ain't she?—but not for every man's pickin'; oh, no; not she! 'Agar kin look arter herself proper!" said the landlord.

"Does she mind that shorp all alone?"

"Jus' now she does," replied mine host. "She 'ad a boy, a wicked little 'unchback devil; Bolker's 'is name. But he's hoff; gitting a wage in West-end, as I do 'ear."

"Wes'-end?" said Bill, reflectively. "An' where might 'e 'ang out there?"

"Ho, in a swell, slap-up book-shop. Juppins, Son an' Juppins, Les'er Square way. 'Is parients live down 'ere, but Bolker's that set up with 'is good luck as 'e looks down on 'em."

"Do he now!" said Bill, amiably. "I'd twist 'is neck if he wos my kid. No more booze, thankee. I'm orf t' see a pal o' mine."

The result of this conversation was that Mr. Smith repaired to Leicester Square and loafed up and down the pavement before the book-shop. He saw Bolker several times during the day; for, having been told by the landlord that the lad was a hunchback, he had no difficulty recognizing him. Up till the evening he kept a close watch, and when Bolker had put up the shutters and was walking home towards Lambeth, Bill followed him stealthily. All unknowing that he was followed by a black shadow of crime and danger, Bolker paused on Westminster Bridge to admire the red glories of the sunset; then plunged into the network of alleys which make up Lambeth. In a quiet lane by the river he was gripped from behind; a large hand was clapped over his mouth to prevent his crying out, and he was dragged down on to a ruined wharf which ran out through green slime into the turbid waters of the stream.

"Now, then, I've got ye!" said his captor in a savage tone—"an' I've got a knife too, y' bloomin' thief! Jes' y' answer me strife, or I'll cut yer 'ead orf!"

Bolker gasped with alarm; but, not recognizing the threatening face of the man before him, he recovered a little of his native impudence, and began to bluster.

"Here, now, what do you mean by this? What have I done?"

"Done, y' whelp! Opened that doll an' prigged them dimins!"

"Larky Bill!" cried Bolker, at once recognizing his peril. "Here, let me go!"

"Not till y' give up my property—my dimins."

"What property? What diamonds?"

"Oh, y' know what 'm drivin' at, cuss you! Y're the 'unchback as wos in the shorp kep' by that foine gal 'Agar. I popped that doll, with dimins in 'is innards, an' you stole 'm."

"I did nothing of the sort. I—"

"'Ere! drop yer lies, y' imp! Y' know moy naime, y' did, so y' knows more! Jes' look et this knoif! S'elp me but I'll slip it int' ye, ef y' don't tell!"

He threw the terrified boy across his knee, and placed the cold steel at his throat. The rose-red sky spun overhead in the eyes of Bolker, and he thought that his last hour had come. To save himself there was nothing for it but confession.

"What! Wait! I'll tell you!" he gasped. "I did take the diamonds."

"Y' young cuss!" growled Bill, setting the lad on his feet again with a jerk. "An' 'ow did y' know they was inside that himage?"

"Monkey told me."

Bill started to his feet with an oath, but still kept his grip on Bolker's shoulder to prevent him getting away. "Monkey," he said, fiercely. "Wot did 'e tell y'?"

"Why, that Lady Deacey's diamonds were inside the mandarin."

"How did Monkey come to find that doll?"

"He got the office from a girl called Eliza, who saw you pawning the toy."

"Liz sold me," muttered Bill. "I thought as I sawr 'er on that doy. She' mus' ha' twigged that doll under m' arm, and guessed as I popped it. Gord! I'll deal with 'er laiter, I will! Garn, y' dorg and tell me th' rest!" he added, shaking the boy.

"There is no more to tell," whimpered Bolker, his teeth chattering. "Monkey couldn't get the mandarin, 'cause he had not the ticket.

He made friends with me, and asked me to steal it. I wouldn't, until he told me why he wanted it. Then he said that you had stolen twenty thousand pounds' worth of diamonds from Lady Deacey's house in Curzon Street, and had hidden them in the mandarin. He said we'd go whacks if I'd steal them for him. I couldn't get the mandarin, as Hagar's so sharp she would have missed it, and put me in jail for stealing it; so I opened the doll, and took out the diamonds which were in a leather bag."

"Moy bag, moy dimins!" said Bill, savagely. "What did y' do with 'em?"

"I gave them to Monkey, and he cleared out with them. He never gave me a single one; and I don't know where to find him."

"I does," growled Mr. Smith, releasing Bolker, "an' I'll fin' 'im and slit his bloomin' throat. 'Ere! I say, y' come back!" for, taking advantage of his release, Bolker was racing up the wharf.

Bill gave chase, as he wanted to obtain further information from the lad; but Bolker knew the neighborhood better than the burglar, and soon eluded him in the winding alleys.

"It don't matter!" said Bill, giving up the chase and wiping his brow. "Monkey's got the swag. Might ha' guessed as he'd round on me. I'll jest see 'im and Liz, and if I don't make 'm paiy fur this, maiy I——!" Then he clinched his resolve with an oath, which it is unnecessary to repeat here. After relieving his feelings thus, he went in search of his perfidious friend, with murderous thoughts in his heart.

At first he thought that it would be difficult to find Monkey. No doubt the man on obtaining the diamonds had gone off to America, North or South, so as to escape the vengeance of his pal—Bill had always been Monkey's pal—and to live comfortably on the fruits of his villainy. Later on the burglar learnt, rather to his surprise, that Monkey was still in London, and still was haunting the thieves' quarter in Whitechapel. Bill wondered at this choice of a residence when the man had so much money in his possession; but he ascribed this longing to Monkey's love for his old haunts and associates. Neverthe-

less, knowing that Bill was out of prison, it was strange that the man did not look after his skin.

"'E knows wot I am when I'm riz!" said Bill to himself, as he continued his search, "so he ought to get orf while 'is throat ain't cut! Blimme; but I'll 'ave a drop of 'is 'eart's blood fur every one of them bloomin' dimins!"

One evening he found Monkey in the parlor of a low public-house called the Three Kings, and kept by a Jew of ill-fame, who was rather a fence than a landlord.

His traitorous friend, more wizened and shriveled up than ever, was seated in a dark corner, with an unlighted pipe in his mouth, a half-drained tankard of bitter before him, and his hands thrust moodily into his pockets. If Monkey had the diamonds, his appearance belied their possession, for he looked anything but prosperous. There was no appearance of wealth in his looks or manner or choice of abode.

"Wot, Bill, ole pal!" he said, looking up when Mr. Smith hurled himself into the room. "Y've got h'out of quod!"

"Yus! I've got hout to slit yer throat!"

"Lor!" whined Monkey, uncomfortably. "Wot's you accusin' me fur? I ain't done nuffin', s'elp me!"

Bill drew a chair before that of Monkey, and taking out his knife played with it in a significant manner. Monkey shrank back before the glitter of the blade and the ugly look in his pal's eyes, but he did not dare to cry out for assistance, lest the burglar should pounce on him.

"Now, look 'ee 'ere, Monkey," said Bill, with grim deliberation, "I don't want none of yer bloomin' lip, ner his eiather! D' y' see? I've seen that beast of a kid as you put up to steal my dimins, and—"

"Yah! that kid!" cried Monkey, with sudden ferocity. "Wish I'd 'im 'ere; I'd squeeze the 'eart out o' him!"

"Wot fur? Didn't 'e git y' the swag—moy swag—cuss y'?"

"No, 'e didn't; an' ef 'e ses 'e did, 'e's a liar—a bloomin' busted liar, s'elp me! I tell you, Bill, 'e kep' them shiners to 'imself, cuss 'im!"

"Thet's a d——d lie, y' sneakin' dorg!" said Bill, politely.

"M' I die if 'tain't gorspel truth!" yelped Monkey. "Look 'ee 'ere, ole pal——"

"Don't y' call me pal!" interrupted Bill, savagely. "I ain't no pal of yourn, y' terbaccer-faiced son of a bloomin' 'angman! Liz blew the gaff on me poppin' that himage, and y' tried to git m' swag when I was doin' time. An' y' did get it, y'——!"

"I didn't!" snapped Monkey, interrupting in his turn. "The kid stuck to the swag, I tell y'. 'Course I knowed of them dimins!"

"'Course y' did!" growled William, ironically. "Didn't I tell y' 'ow I cracked that crib in Curzon Street, an' prigged th' dimins an' th' himage? Yah! y' cuss!"

"I knows y' did, Bill. An' you tole me 'ow y' stowed the swag inside the doll. My heye! that was sharp of y'; but y' moight 'ev trusted a pal! I didn't know y' popped the doll till Liz told me. She sawr y' goin' in t' that popshorp with the Chiner thing under yer arm; an'——"

"And you'd set 'er arter me!" cried Bill! savagely. "She didn't git int' Lambeth on the chance!"

"Yus," said Monkey, doggedly, "I did put 'er on yer trail. Y' hid the dimins in that image, and cleared out with it. I couldn't foller meself, so I set Liz ont' ye. She tole me as 'ow y'd popped th' thing; so when y' wos doin' time I tried to git it again, tho' that young cuss 'es sold me."

"Blimme! but I've a moind to slit yer throat!" said Bill, furiously. "Wot d' y' mean tryin' to coller my swag?"

"Why, fur yer own sake, Bill, s'elp me. I thort the gal might fin' out. But y' needn't git up, Bill; I didn't git them dimins. The boy hes them."

"That's a lie. I tell y'!"

"'Tain't! When I tole the kid about the dimins he stole 'em sure, an' lef' th' doll so es the pawnshop gal wouldn't fin' out. But I never saw 'im agin, though I watched the shorp like a bloomin' tyke. The boy cleared out with them dimins. I wish I'd 'im 'ere! I'd choke the little d——l!"

Bill reflected, and slipped the knife into his pocket. Without doubt Monkey was speaking the truth; he was too savagely in earnest to be telling a falsehood. Moreover, if he really possessed the diamonds, he would not remain hard up and miserable in the thieves' quarter of dingy Whitechapel. No; Bolker had kept the jewels, and had deceived Monkey; more than that, in the interview on the ruined wharf he had deceived Bill himself. Priding himself on his astuteness, Mr. Smith felt savage at having been sold by a mere boy.

"If I kin on'y git 'im agin!" he thought, when leaving the Three Kings, "I'll take the 'ead orf 'm, and chuck 'is crooked karkuss int' the river mud!"

But he found it difficult to lay hands on Bolker, although for more than a week he haunted the shop in Leicester Square. Warned by his one experience that Bill was a dangerous person to meddle with, Bolker had given notice to his employers, and at present was in hiding. Also, he was arranging a little scheme whereby to rid himself of Larky Bill's inopportunities. Vark was the man who undertook to carry out the details of the scheme; and Hagar was consulted also with regard to its completion. These three people, Vark, Hagar, and Bolker, laid an ingenious trap for unsuspecting Bill, into which he walked without a thought of danger. He had been betrayed by Monkey, by Bolker, by Liz; now he was going to be sold by Vark, the lawyer. Truly, the fates were against Bill at this juncture.

Vark was a thieves' lawyer, and had something in him of a latter-day Fagin; for he not only made use of criminals when he could do so with safety, but also he sold them to justice when they became dangerous. As he saw a chance of making money out of Bill Smith, he resolved to do so, and sent for the man to visit him at once. As Vark had often done business with the burglar, Bill had no idea that it was in the lawyer's mind to betray him, and duly presented himself at the spider's office in Lambeth, like a silly fly. The first thing he saw on entering the room was the mandarin swaying on the table.

"You are astonished to see that," said Vark,

noticing his surprise. "I daresay; but you see, Bill, I know all about your theft of the Deacey diamonds."

"Who tole you?" growled Bill, throwing himself into a chair.

"Hagar of the pawn-shop," replied Vark, slowly and with significance.

Bill's eyes lighted up fiercely, in precisely the way Vark wished. The lawyer had not forgiven Hagar for refusing to marry him, and for curtailing his pickings in the Dix estate. For these reasons he wished her evil; and if he could inoculate the burglar's heart with a spite towards her he was bent on doing so. It appeared from Bill's next speech that he had succeeded.

"Oh, 'twas that gal, wos it?" said Mr. Smith, quietly. "I might ha' guessed it, by seein' that himage. Well, I owe 'er one, I do, and I guess I'll owe 'er another. But that's my biz; 'tain't yourn. Wot d'ye want, y' measly dorg?" he added, looking at the lean form of Vark in a surly manner.

"I want to see you about the Deacey diamonds. Why did you not bring them to me when you stole them?"

"Whoy? 'Cause I didn't b'lieve in ye!" retorted Bill. "I know'd I wos in fur toime when I prigged them apples, an' I wasn't going to trust my swag to y' or Monkey. Y'd ha' sold me."

"Well, Monkey did sell you."

"Yah! 'e didn't get much on th' deal!"

"No; but Bolker did."

"Bolker!" echoed Bill, grinding his teeth: "d' y' know that crooked cuss? Y' do! Well, see 'ere!"—Bill drew his clasp-knife out of his pocket and opened it—"I'm goin' to slip that int' 'im fust toime as I claps eyes on 'is ugly mug!"

"You'd better not, unless you want to be hanged."

"Wot d' I care?" growled Bill, sulkily; "scragged, or time with skilly an' hoakum. It's all th' saime t' me."

"I suppose you wonder where the diamonds are?"

"Yus. I want 'em!"

"That's a pity," said Vark, with irony— "because I am afraid you won't get them."

"Where is them dimins?" asked Bill, laying his open knife on the table.

Vark passed over the question. "I suppose you know that the police are after you for the Deacey robbery?" he said, slipping his hand idly across the table till it was within reach of the knife. "Oh, yes; Lord Deacey offered a reward for the recovery of the jewels. That has been paid, but as you are still at large, the police want you, my friend!"

"Oh, I ain't afraid of y' givin' me up; I'm too useful t' y', I am, and I knows too much about y'. The pealers shawn't put me in quod this toime. Who got the reward?" he asked suddenly.

"Bolker got it."

"D——n him! Bolker!"

"Yes. Monkey made a mistake when he trusted the lad. Bolker thought that he would make more out of honesty than by going shares with Monkey. When he found the jewels, he went off with them to Scotland Yard. Lady Deacey has them now, and Bolker," added Vark, smiling, "has money in the bank."

"Cuss 'im; whoy didn't I cut 'is bloomin' throat down by the river?"

"That is best known to yourself," replied Vark, who was now playing with the knife. "You are in a tight place, my friend, and may get some years for this robbery."

"Yah! No one knows I did it!"

"There is the evidence against you," said Vark, pointing to the mandarin. "You stole that out of Lord Deacey's drawing-room along with the diamonds. You pawned it, and Hagar can swear that you did so. Bolker can swear that the stolen diamonds were inside. With these two witnesses, my poor Bill, I'm afraid you'd get six years or more!"

"Not me!" said Bill, rising. "Y' won't give me up; and I ain't feared of anyone else."

"Why not? There is a reward offered for your apprehension."

"What d' I care? Who'll git it?"

"I will!" replied Vark, coolly, rising.

"You?" Bill recoiled for a moment, and sprang forward. "Cuss you! Y'd sell me, y' shark! Gimme my knife!"

"Not such a fool, Mr. Smith!"

Vark threw the knife into a distant corner of the room, and leveled a revolver at the bullet-head of the advancing burglar. Bill fell back for the moment—fell into the arms of two policemen.

He gave a roar like a wild beast.

"Trapped, by——!" he yelled, and struggled to get free.

The next moment Hagar and Bolker were in the room, and Bill glared at one and the other.

"Y' trapped me, d——n y'!" said he; "wait till I git out!"

"You'll kill me, I suppose?" said Hagar, scornfully.

"No; shawn't kill you, nor yet that little d——l with th' 'unch. There's on'y one cove as I'd swing for—that beastly thief of a lawyer!"

Vark recoiled before the glare in the man's eyes; and as Bill, foaming and cursing, was hurried out of the room, he looked at Hagar with a nervous smile.

"That's bluff," he said, feebly.

"I don't think so," replied Hagar, quietly.

"Good-by, Mr. Vark. I'm afraid you won't live more than seven years; there will be a funeral about the time of Larky Bill's release."

When she went out, Bolker grinned at the lawyer and, with frightful pantomime, he drew a stroke across his neck. Vark looked at the clasp-knife in the corner and shivered. The mandarin on the table rolled and smiled always.

THE OUTSIDE LEDGE: A CABLEGRAM MYSTERY

L. T. Meade & Robert Eustace

THE SUCCESS of Arthur Conan Doyle's Sherlock Holmes stories inspired a sudden dash by a large number of authors to write similar fiction. One of the least likely may have been L. T. Meade, the nom de plume of Elizabeth Thomasina Meade Smith (1844–1914), who was a prolific (approximately two hundred titles) and highly successful author of books for teenage girls.

Unlike the work of many of her contemporaries, Meade's mystery fiction broke significant new ground when it was written and remains highly readable today. Some of her most memorable story collections were written in collaboration with Dr. Clifford Halifax, the pseudonym of Dr. Edgar Beaumont (1860–1921), or with Robert Eustace, the pseudonym of Dr. Eustace Robert Barton (1868–1943). Two of Meade's collections were selected for *Queen's Quorum* as being among the 106 most important short story collections in the history of the genre: *Stories from the Diary of a Doctor* (1894) with Halifax, the first series to feature a physician detective, who happens to be Halifax himself, and *The Brotherhood of the Seven Kings* (1899) with Eustace, the first collection to feature a female criminal.

Stories about Miss Florence Cusack, by Meade and Eustace, appeared in *The Harmsworth Magazine* between April 1899 and March 1901; there were only five stories, and they remained uncollected until 1998. Miss Cusack, like Holmes and his many imitators, had her devoted and admiring "Watson"—Dr. Lonsdale. An unusual element of the stories is that the culprit is known to both the detective and the reader early on, the challenge being to learn how the criminal committed the crime.

"The Outside Ledge: A Cablegram Mystery" was originally published in the October 1900 issue of *The Harmsworth Magazine*; it was first collected in *The Detections of Miss Cusack* (Shelburne, Ontario, The Battered Silicon Dispatch Box Press, 1998).

The Outside Ledge: A Cablegram Mystery

L. T. MEADE & ROBERT EUSTACE

I HAD NOT HEARD from my old friend Miss Cusack for some time, and was beginning to wonder whether anything was the matter with her, when on a certain Tuesday in the November of the year 1892 she called to see me.

"Dr. Lonsdale," she said, "I cannot stand defeat, and I am defeated now."

"Indeed," I replied, "this is interesting. You so seldom are defeated. What is it all about?"

"I have come here to tell you. You have heard, of course, of Oscar Hamilton, the great financier? He is the victim of a series of frauds that have been going on during the last two months and are still being perpetrated. So persistent and so unaccountable are they that the cleverest agents in London have been employed to detect them, but without result. His chief dealings are, as you know, in South African Gold Mines, and his income is, I believe, nearer fifty than thirty thousand a year. From time to time he receives private advices as to the gold crushings, and operates accordingly. You will say, of course, that he gambles, and that such gambling is not very scrupulous, but I assure you the matter is not at all looked at in that light on the Stock Exchange.

"Now, there is a dealer in the same market, a Mr. Gildford, who, by some means absolutely unknown, obtains the same advice in detail, and of course either forestalls Mr. Hamilton, or, on the other hand, discounts the profits he would make, by buying or selling exactly the same shares. The information, I am given to understand, is usually cabled to Oscar Hamilton in cipher by his confidential agent in South Africa, whose *bona fides* is unquestionable, since it is he who profits by Mr. Hamilton's gains.

"This important information arrives as a rule in the early morning about nine o'clock and is put straight into my friend's hands in his office in Lennox Court. The details are discussed by him and his partner Mr. Le Marchant, and he immediately afterwards goes to his broker to do whatever business is decided on. Now, this special broker's name is Edward Gregory, and time after time, not invariably, but very often, Mr. Gregory has gone into the house and found Mr. Gildford doing the identical deals that he was about to do."

"That is strange," I answered.

"It is; but you must listen further. To give you an idea of how every channel possible has been watched, I will tell you what has been done. In the first place it is practically certain that the information found its way from Mr. Hamilton's office to Mr. Gildford's, because no one knows the cipher except Mr. Hamilton and his partner, Mr. Le Marchant."

"Wireless telegraphy," I suggested.

Miss Cusack smiled, but shook her head.

"Listen," she said. "Mr. Gildford, the dealer, is a man who also has an office in Lennox Court, four doors from the office of Mr. Hamilton, also close to the Stock Exchange. He has one small room on the third floor back, and has no clerks. Now Mr. Gregory, Mr. Hamilton's broker, has his office in Draper's Gardens. Yesterday morning an important cable was expected, and extraordinary precautions were adopted. Two detectives were placed in the house of Mr. Gildford, of course unknown to him—one actually took up his position on the landing outside his door, so that no one could enter by the door without being seen. Another was at the telephone exchange to watch if any message went through that way. Thus you will see that telegrams and telephones were equally cut off.

"A detective was also in Mr. Hamilton's office when the cable arrived, the object of his presence being known to the clerks, who were not allowed to use the telephone or to leave the office. The cable was opened in the presence of the younger partner, Mr. Le Marchant, and also in the presence of the detective, by Mr. Hamilton himself. No one left the office, and no communication with the outside world took place. Thus, both at Mr. Gildford's office and at Mr. Hamilton's, had the information passed by any visible channel it must have been detected either leaving the former office or arriving at the latter."

"And what happened?" I inquired, beginning to be much interested in this strange story.

"You will soon know what happened. I call it witchery. In about ten minutes time Mr. Hamilton left his office to visit his broker, Mr. Gregory, at the Stock Exchange, everyone else, including his partner, Mr. Le Marchant, remaining in the office. On his arrival at the Stock Exchange he told Mr. Gregory what he wanted done. The latter went to carry out his wishes, but came back after a few moments to say that the market was spoiled, Mr. Gildford having just arrived and dealt heavily in the very same shares and in the same manner. What do you make of it, Dr. Lonsdale?"

"There is only one conclusion for me to arrive at," I answered; "the information does not pass between the offices, but by some previously arranged channel."

"I should have agreed with you but for one circumstance, which I am now going to confide to you. Do you remember a pretty girl, a certain Evelyn Dudley, whom you once met at my house? She is the only daughter of Colonel Dudley of the Coldstream Guards, and at her father's death will be worth about seven thousand a year."

"Well, and what has she to do with the present state of things?"

"Only this: she is engaged to Mr. Le Marchant, and the wedding will take place next week. They are both going to dine with me tonight. I want you to join the party in order that you may meet them and let me know frankly afterwards what you think of him."

"But what has that to do with the frauds?" I asked.

"Everything, and this is why." She lowered her voice, and said in an emphatic whisper, "I have strong reasons for suspecting Mr. Le Marchant, Mr. Hamilton's young partner, of being in the plot."

"Good heavens!" I cried, "you cannot mean that. The frauds are to his own loss."

"Not at all. He has only at present a small share in the business. Yesterday from a very private source I learned that he was in great financial difficulties, and in the hands of some money-lenders; in short I imagine—mind, I don't accuse him yet—that he is staving off his crash until he can marry Evelyn Dudley, when he hopes to right himself. If the crash came first, Colonel Dudley would not allow marriage. But when it is a *fait accompli* he will be, as it were, forced to do something to prevent his son-in-law going under. Now I think you know about as much of the situation as I do myself. Evelyn is a dear friend of mine, and if I can prevent it I don't want her to marry a scoundrel. We dine at eight—it is now past seven, so if you will dress quickly I can drive you back in my brougham. Evelyn is to spend the night with me, and is already at my house. She will entertain you till I am ready. If nothing happens to prevent it, the wedding is to take place next Monday. You see, therefore, there is no time to lose in clearing up the mystery."

"There certainly is not," I replied, rising. "Well, if you will kindly wait here I will not keep you many minutes."

I went up to my room, dressed quickly, and returned in a very short time. We entered the brougham which was standing at the door, and at once drove off to Miss Cusack's house. She ushered me into the drawing-room, where a tall, dark-eyed girl was standing by the fire.

"Evelyn," said Miss Cusack, "you have often heard me talk of my great friend Dr. Lonsdale. I have just persuaded him to dine with us tonight. Dr. Lonsdale, may I introduce you to Miss Evelyn Dudley?"

I took the hand which Evelyn Dudley stretched out to me. She had an attractive, bright face, and during Miss Cusack's absence we each engaged the other in brisk conversation. I spoke about Miss Cusack, and the girl was warm in her admiration.

"She is my best friend," she said. "I lost my mother two years ago, and at that time I do not know what I should have done but for Florence Cusack. She took me to her house and kept me with her for some time, and taught me what the sin of rebellion meant. I loved my mother so passionately. I did not think when she was taken from me that I should ever know a happy hour again."

"And now, if report tells true, you are going to be very happy," I continued, "for Miss Cusack has confided some of your story to me. You are soon to be married?"

"Yes," she answered, and she looked thoughtful. After a moment she spoke again.

"You are right: I hope to be very happy in the future—happier than I have ever been before. I love Henry Le Marchant better than anyone else on earth."

I felt a certain pity for her as she spoke. After all, Miss Cusack's intuitions were wonderful, and she did not like Henry Le Marchant—nay, more, she suspected him of underhand dealings. Surely she must be wrong. I hoped when I saw this young man that I should be able to divert my friend's suspicions into another channel.

"I hope you will be happy," I said; "you have my best wishes."

"Thank you," she replied. She sat down near the fire as she spoke, and unfurled her fan.

"Ah! there is a ring," she said, the next moment. "He is coming. You know perhaps that he is dining here tonight. I shall be so pleased to introduce you."

At the same instant Miss Cusack entered the room.

"Our guest has arrived," she said, looking from Miss Dudley to me, and she had scarcely uttered the words before Henry Le Marchant was announced.

He was a tall, young-looking man, with a black, short moustache and very dark eyes. His manner was easy and self-possessed, and he looked with frank interest at me when his hostess introduced him.

The next moment dinner was announced. As the meal proceeded and I was considering in what words I could convey to Miss Cusack my impression that she was altogether on a wrong tack, something occurred which I thought very little of at the time, but yet was destined to lead to most important results presently.

The servant had just left the room when a slight whiff of some peculiar and rather disagreeable odour caught my nostrils. I was glancing across the table to see if it was due to any particular fruit, when I noticed that Miss Cusack had also caught the smell.

"What a curious sort of perfume!" she said, frowning slightly. "Evelyn, have you been buying any special new scent today?"

"Certainly not," replied Miss Dudley; "I hate scent, and never use it."

At the same moment Le Marchant, who had taken his handkerchief from his pocket, quickly replaced it, and a wave of blood suffused his swarthy cheeks, leaving them the next instant ashy pale. His embarrassment was so obvious that none of us could help noticing it.

"Surely that is the smell of valerian," I said, as the memory of what it was came to me.

"Yes, it is," he replied, recovering his composure and forcing a smile. "I must apologise to you all. I have been rather nervous lately, and have been ordered a few drops of valerian in water. I cannot think how it got on my handkerchief. My doctor prescribed it for me yesterday."

Miss Cusack made a common-place reply, and the conversation went on as before.

Perhaps my attitude of mind was preternaturally suspicious, but it occurred to me that Le Marchant's explanation was a very lame one. Valerian is not often ordered for a man of his evidently robust health, and I wondered if he were speaking the truth.

Having a case of some importance to attend, I took my departure shortly afterwards.

During the three following days I heard nothing further from Miss Cusack, and made up my mind that her conjectures were all wrong and that the wedding would of course take place.

But on Saturday these hopes were destined to be rudely dispersed. I was awakened at an early hour by my servant, who entered with a note. I saw at once that it was in Miss Cusack's handwriting, and tore it open with some apprehension. The contents were certainly startling. It ran as follows—

"I want your help. Serious developments. Meet me on Royal Exchange steps at nine this morning. Do not fail."

After breakfast I sent for a cab, and drove at once to the city, alighting close to the Bank of England. The streets were thronged with the usual incoming flux of clerks hurrying to their different offices. I made my way across to the Royal Exchange, and the first person I saw was Miss Cusack standing just at the entrance. She turned to me eagerly.

"This is good of you, doctor; I shall not forget this kindness in a hurry. Come quickly, will you?"

We entered the throng, and moved rapidly down Bartholomew Lane into Throgmorton Street; then, turning round sharp to the left, found ourselves in Lennox Court.

I followed my guide with the greatest curiosity, wondering what could be her plans. The next moment we entered a house, and, threading our way up some bare, uncarpeted stairs, reached the top landing. Here Miss Cusack opened a door with a key which she had with her, pushed me into a small room, entered herself, and locked the door behind us both. I glanced around in some alarm.

The little room was quite bare, and here and there round the walls were the marks of where office furniture had once stood. The window looked out on to the back of the house in Lennox Court.

"Now we must act quickly," she said "At 9:30 an important cable will reach Mr. Hamilton's office. This room in which we now find ourselves is next door to Mr. Gildford's office in the next house, and is between that and Mr. Hamilton's office two doors further down. I have rented this room—a quarter's rent for one morning's work. Well, if I am successful, the price will be cheap. It was great luck to get it at all."

"But what are you going to do?" I queried, as she proceeded to open the window and peep cautiously out.

"You will see directly," she answered; "keep back, and don't make a noise."

She leant out and drew the ends of her boa along the little ledge that ran outside just below the window. She then drew it in rapidly.

"Ah, ha! do you remember that, Dr. Lonsdale?" she cried softly, raising the boa to my face.

I started back and regarded her in amazement.

"Valerian!" I exclaimed. "Miss Cusack, what is this strange mystery?"

She raised her hand.

"Hush! not another word yet," she said. Her

eyes sparkled with excitement. She rapidly produced a pair of very thick doeskin gloves, put them on, and stood by the window in an attitude of the utmost alertness. I stood still in the middle of the room, wondering whether I was in a dream, or whether Miss Cusack had taken leave of her senses.

The moments passed by, and still she stood rigid and tense as if expecting something. I watched her in wonderment, not attempting to say a word.

We must have remained in this extraordinary situation fully a quarter of an hour, when I saw her bend forward, her hand shot out of the window, and with an inconceivably rapid thrust she drew it back. She was now grasping by the back of the neck a large tabby cat; its four legs were drawn up with claws extended, and it was wriggling in evident dislike at being captured.

"A cat!" I cried, in the most utter and absolute bewilderment.

"Yes, a cat; a sweet pretty cat, too; aren't you, pussy?" She knelt down and began to stroke the creature, who changed its mind and rubbed itself against her in evident pleasure. The next moment it darted towards her fur boa and began sniffing at it greedily. As it did so Miss Cusack deftly stripped off a leather collar round its neck. A cry of delight broke from her lips as, unfastening a clasp that held an inner flap to the outer leather covering, she drew out a slip of paper.

"In Henry Le Marchant's handwriting," she cried. "What a scoundrel! We have him now."

"Henry Le Marchant's handwriting!" I exclaimed, bending over the slip as she held it in her hand.

"Yes," she answered; "see!"

I read with bated breath the brief communication which the tiny piece of paper contained. It was beyond doubt a replica of the telegram which must have arrived at Hamilton's office a few moments ago.

Miss Cusack also read the words. She flung the piece of paper to the ground. I picked it up.

"We must keep this, it is evidence," I said.

"Yes," she answered, "but this has upset me. I have heard of some curious methods of communication, but never such a one as this before. It was the wildest chance, but thank God it has succeeded. We shall save Evelyn from marrying a man with whom her life would have been intolerable."

"But what could have led you to this extraordinary result?" I said.

"A chain of reasoning starting on the evening when we dined together," she replied. "What puzzled me was this: What had Henry Le Marchant to do with valerian on his handkerchief? It was that fact which set me thinking. His explanation of using it as a nerve sedative was so obviously a lie on the face of it, and his embarrassment was so evident, that I did not trouble myself with this way out of the mystery for a single moment. I went through every conceivable hypothesis with regard to valerian, but it was not till I looked up its properties in a medical book that the first clue came to me. Valerian is, as you of course know, doctor, a plant which has a sort of intoxicating, almost maddening effect on cats, so much so that they will search out and follow the smell to the exclusion of any other desire. They are an independent race of creatures, and not easily trained like a dog. Then the amazing possibility suggested itself to me that the method employed by Mr. Le Marchant to communicate with Mr. Gildford, which has nonplussed every detective in London, was the very simple one employing a cat.

"Come to the window and I will explain. You see that narrow ledge along which our friend pussy strolled so leisurely a moment ago. It runs, as you perceive, straight from Mr. Hamilton's office to that of Mr. Gildford. All Mr. Gildford had to do was to sprinkle some valerian along the ledge close to his own window. The peculiar smell would be detected by a cat quite as far off as the house where Mr. Hamilton's office is. I thought this all out, and, being pretty sure that my surmises were correct, I called yesterday on Henry Le Marchant at the office with the express purpose of seeing if there was a cat there.

"I went with a message from Evelyn. Nestling on his knee as he sat at his table writing in his private room was this very animal. Even then, of course, there was no certainty about my suspicions, but in view of the event which hung upon them—namely his marriage to Evelyn—I was determined to spare no pains or trouble to put them to the test. I have done so, and, thank God, in time. But come, my course now is clear. I have a painful duty before me, and there is not a moment to lose."

As Miss Cusack spoke she took up her fur boa, flicked it slowly backwards and forwards to remove the taint of the valerian, and put it round her neck.

Five minutes later we were both communicating her extraordinary story to the ears of one of the sharpest detectives in London. Before that night Henry Le Marchant and James Gildford were both arrested; and Miss Cusack, excited, worn out, her eyes blazing and her hands trembling, went to poor Evelyn Dudley's home to tell her the result of her day's work. The particulars of that interview she never confided even to me. But the next week she and Evelyn left the country to spend a long winter in the South of France.

Henry Le Marchant and Gildford were convicted of conspiracy to defraud, and were condemned to suffer the severest punishment that the law prescribes in such cases.

But why follow their careers any further? Evelyn's heart very nearly broke, but did not quite, and I am glad to be able to add that she has married a man in every respect worthy of her.

THE FREWIN MINIATURES

Emmuska Orczy

ALTHOUGH BARONESS EMMUSKA ORCZY (1865–1947) was most famous for the creation of the Scarlet Pimpernel, the first hero with a secret identity, she also was notable for producing stories about "the Old Man in the Corner," an arm-chair detective who relied entirely on his cerebral faculties to solve crimes, and about one of the earliest female sleuths, Lady Molly of Scotland Yard.

Lady Molly Robertson-Kirk had an important position in the fictional "Female Department" of Scotland Yard and worked cases almost as a private eye, without assistance until she was ready to have the criminal hauled off. Her exploits, mostly solved by intuition rather than solid police investigation, are narrated by her pretty assistant, Mary, who adores her. Her superiors do not know of Molly's personal agenda, which is to prove her husband innocent of a crime for which he has been convicted and sentenced to twenty years in prison. At the conclusion of the only book of her adventures, she is successful.

Born in Hungary, Baroness Orczy spoke no English until she was fifteen and her family had moved to England, though all her novels, plays, and short stories were written in English. She failed to sell her novel about Sir Percy Blakeney, an effete English gentleman who was secretly a courageous espionage agent during the days of the French Revolution, daringly saving the lives of countless French aristocrats who had been condemned to the guillotine. Orczy and her husband wrote a stage-play version that was produced without success in 1903. After changing the ending, it opened in the West End two years later and became wildly succesful.

The Scarlet Pimpernel was published as a novel in the same year, the first of numerous adventures about the thorn in the side of the bloodthirsty citizens of the Committee of Public Safety and the Committee of General Security and the gendarmerie. His success inspired the following doggerel:

We seek him here . . .
We seek him there . . .
Those Frenchies seek him . . .

79

Everywhere.
Is he in heaven?
Is he in h-ll?
That demned elusive
Pimpernel?

The Scarlet Pimpernel took his name from a wildflower that blossoms and dies in a single night.

"The Frewin Miniatures" was first published in the July 1909 issue of *Cassell's Magazine* and first collected in *Lady Molly of Scotland Yard* (London, Cassell, 1910).

The Frewin Miniatures

EMMUSKA ORCZY

ALTHOUGH, MIND YOU, Lady Molly's methods in connection with the Ninescore mystery were not altogether approved of at the Yard, nevertheless, her shrewdness and ingenuity in the matter were so undoubted that they earned for her a reputation, then and there, which placed her in the foremost rank of the force. And presently, when everyone—public and police alike—were set by the ears over the Frewin miniatures, and a reward of 1,000 guineas was offered for information that would lead to the apprehension of the thief, the chief, of his own accord and without any hesitation, offered the job to her.

I don't know much about so-called works of art myself, but you can't be in the detective force, female or otherwise, without knowing something of the value of most things, and I don't think that Mr. Frewin put an excessive value on his Englehearts when he stated that they were worth £10,000. There were eight of them, all on ivory, about three to four inches high, and they were said to be the most perfect specimens of their kind. Mr. Frewin himself had had an offer for them, less than two years ago, of 200,000 francs from the trustees of the Louvre, which offer, mind you, he had refused. I dare say you know that he was an immensely wealthy man, a great collector himself, as well as dealer, and that several of the most unique and most highly priced works of art found their way into his private collection. Among them, of course, the Engleheart miniatures were the most noteworthy.

For some time before his death Mr. Frewin had been a great invalid, and for over two years he had not been able to go beyond the boundary of his charming property, Blatchley House, near Brighton.

There is a sad story in connection with the serious illness of Mr. Frewin—an illness which, if you remember, has since resulted in the poor old gentleman's death. He had an only son, a young man on whom the old art-dealer had lavished all the education and, subsequently, all the social advantages which money could give. The boy was exceptionally good-looking, and had inherited from his mother a great charm of manner which made him very popular. The Honourable Mrs. Frewin is the daughter of an English peer, more endowed with physical attributes than with worldly goods. Besides that, she is an exceptionally beautiful woman, has a glorious voice, is a fine violinist, and is no mean water-colour artist, having more than once exhibited at the Royal Academy.

Unfortunately, at one time, young Frewin had got into very bad company, made many debts, some of which were quite unavowable, and there were rumours current at the time to the effect that had the police got wind of certain transactions in connection with a brother officer's cheque, a very unpleasant prosecution would have followed. Be that as it may, young Lionel Frewin had to quit his regiment, and presently he went off to Canada, where he is supposed to have gone in for farming. According to the story related by some of the servants at Blatchley House, there were violent scenes between father and son before the former consented to pay some of the young spendthrift's most pressing debts, and then find the further sum of money which was to enable young Frewin to commence a new life in the colonies.

Mrs. Frewin, of course, took the matter very much to heart. She was a dainty, refined, artistic creature, who idolised her only son, but she had evidently no influence whatever over her husband, who, in common with certain English families of Jewish extraction, had an extraordinary hardness of character where the integrity of his own business fame was concerned. He absolutely never forgave his son what he considered a slur cast upon his name by the young spendthrift; he packed him off to Canada, and openly told him that he was to expect nothing further from him. All the Frewin money and the priceless art collection would be left by will to a nephew, James Hyam, whose honour and general conduct had always been beyond reproach.

That Mr. Frewin really took his hitherto idolised son's defalcations very much to heart was shown by the fact that the poor old man's health completely broke down after that. He had an apoplectic fit, and, although he somewhat recovered, he always remained an invalid.

His eyesight and brain power were distinctly enfeebled, and about nine months ago he had a renewed seizure, which resulted in paralysis first, and subsequently in his death. The greatest, if not the only, joy the poor old man had during the two years which he spent pinned to an invalid chair was his art collection. Blatchley House was a perfect art museum, and the invalid would have his chair wheeled up and down the great hall and along the rooms where his pictures and china and, above all, where his priceless minia-

tures were stored. He took an enormous pride in these, and it was, I think, with a view to brightening him up a little that Mrs. Frewin invited Monsieur de Colinville—who had always been a great friend of her husband—to come and stay at Blatchley. Of course, there is no greater connoisseur of art anywhere than that distinguished Frenchman, and it was through him that the celebrated offer of £8,000 was made by the Louvre for the Engleheart miniatures.

Though, of course, the invalid declined the offer, he took a great pleasure and pride in the fact that it had been made, as, in addition to Monsieur de Colinville himself, several members of the committee of art advisers to the Louvre came over from Paris in order to try and persuade Mr. Frewin to sell his unique treasures. However, the invalid was obdurate about that. He was not in want of money, and the celebrated Frewin art collection would go intact to his widow for her life, and then to his heir, Mr. James Hyam, a great connoisseur himself, and art dealer of St. Petersburg and London.

It was really a merciful dispensation of Providence that the old man never knew of the disappearance of his valued miniatures. By the time that extraordinary mystery had come to light he was dead.

On the evening of January the 14th, at half-past eight, Mr. Frewin had a third paralytic seizure, from which he never recovered. His valet, Kennet, and his two nurses were with him at the time, and Mrs. Frewin, quickly apprised of the terrible event, flew to his bedside, whilst the motor was at once despatched for the doctor. About an hour or two later the dying man seemed to rally somewhat, but he appeared very restless and agitated, and his eyes were roaming anxiously about the room.

"I expect it is his precious miniatures he wants," said Nurse Dawson. "He is always quiet when he can play with them."

She reached for the large, leather case which contained the priceless art treasures, and, opening it, placed it on the bed beside the patient. Mr. Frewin, however, was obviously too near death to care even for his favourite toy. He fingered the miniatures with trembling hands for a few moments, and then sank back exhausted on the pillows.

"He is dying," said the doctor quietly, turning to Mrs. Frewin.

"I have something to say to him," she then said. "Can I remain alone with him for a few minutes?"

"Certainly," said the doctor, as he himself discreetly retired; "but I think one of the nurses had better remain within earshot."

Nurse Dawson, it appeared, remained within earshot to some purpose, for she overheard what Mrs. Frewin was saying to her dying husband.

"It is about Lionel—your only son," she said. "Can you understand what I say?"

The sick man nodded.

"You remember that he is in Brighton, staying with Alicia. I can go and fetch him in the motor if you will consent to see him."

Again the dying man nodded. I suppose Mrs. Frewin took this to mean acquiescence, for the next moment she rang for John Chipps, the butler, and gave him instructions to order her motor at once. She then kissed the patient on the forehead and prepared to leave the room; but just before she did so her eyes lighted on the case of miniatures, and she said to Kennet, the valet:

"Give these to Chipps, and tell him to put them in the library."

She then went to put on her furs preparatory to going out. When she was quite ready she met Chipps on the landing, who had just come up to tell her that the motor was at the door. He had in his hand the case of miniatures which Kennet had given him.

"Put the case on the library table, Chipps, when you go down," she said.

"Yes, madam," he replied.

He followed her downstairs, then slipped into the library, put the case on the table as he had been directed, after which he saw his mistress into the motor, and finally closed the front door.

———

About an hour later Mrs. Frewin came back, but without her son. It transpired afterwards that the young man was more vindictive than his father; he refused to go to the latter's bedside in order to be reconciled at the eleventh hour to a man who then had no longer either his wits or his physical senses about him. However, the dying man was spared the knowledge of his son's irreconcilable conduct, for, after a long and wearisome night passed in a state of coma, he died at about 6:00 A.M.

It was quite late the following afternoon when Mrs. Frewin suddenly recollected the case of miniatures, which should have been locked in their accustomed cabinet. She strolled leisurely into the library—she was very fatigued and worn out with the long vigil and the sorrow and anxiety she had just gone through. A quarter of an hour later John Chipps found her in the same room, sitting dazed and almost fainting in an armchair. In response to the old butler's anxious query, she murmured:

"The miniatures—where are they?"

Scared at the abruptness of the query and at his mistress's changed tone of voice, Chipps gazed quickly around him.

"You told me to put them on the table, ma'am," he murmured, "and I did so. They certainly don't seem to be in the room now——" he added, with a sudden feeling of terror.

"Run and ask one of the nurses at once if the case was taken up to Mr. Frewin's room during the night?"

Chipps, needless to say, did not wait to be told twice. He was beginning to feel very anxious. He spoke to Kennet and also to the two nurses, and asked them if, by any chance, the miniatures were in the late master's room. To this Kennet and the nurses replied in the negative. The last they had seen of the miniatures was when Chipps took them from the valet and followed his mistress downstairs with the case in his hands.

The poor old butler was in despair; the cook was in hysterics, and consternation reigned throughout the house. The disappearance of the miniatures caused almost a greater excitement than the death of the master, who had been a dying man so long that he was almost a stranger to the servants at Blatchley.

Mrs. Frewin was the first to recover her presence of mind.

"Send a motor at once to the police station at Brighton," she said very calmly, as soon as she completely realised that the miniatures were nowhere to be found. "It is my duty to see that this matter is thoroughly gone into at once."

Within half an hour of the discovery of the theft Detective Inspector Hankin and Police Constable McLeod had both arrived from Brighton, having availed themselves of Mrs. Frewin's motor. They are shrewd men, both of them, and it did not take them many minutes before they had made up their minds how the robbery had taken place. By whom it was done was quite another matter, and would take some time and some ingenuity to find out.

What Detective Inspector Hankin had gathered was this: While John Chipps saw his mistress into the motor, the front door of the house had, of necessity, been left wide open. The motor then made a start, but after a few paces it stopped, and Mrs. Frewin put her head out of the window and shouted to Chipps some instructions with regard to the nurses' evening collation, which, in view of Mr. Frewin's state, she feared might be forgotten. Chipps, being an elderly man and a little deaf, did not hear her voice distinctly, so he ran up to the motor, and she repeated her instructions to him. In Inspector Hankin's mind there was no doubt that the thief, who must have been hanging about the shrubbery that evening, took that opportunity to sneak into the house, then to hide himself in a convenient spot until he could find an opportunity for the robbery which he had in view.

The butler declared that, when he returned, he saw nothing unusual. He had only been gone a little over a minute; he then fastened and bolted the front door, and, according to his usual custom, he put up all the shutters of the ground-floor windows, including, of course, those in the

library. He had no light with him when he did this accustomed round, for, of course he knew his way well enough in the dark, and the electric chandelier in the hall gave him what light he wanted.

While he was putting up the shutters, Chipps was giving no particular thought to the miniatures, but, strangely enough, he seems to have thought of them about an hour later, when most of the servants had gone to bed and he was waiting up for his mistress. He then, quite casually, and almost absent-mindedly, when crossing the hall, turned the key of the library door, thus locking it from the outside.

Of course, throughout all this we must remember that Blatchley House was not in its normal state that night, since its master was actually dying in a room on the floor above the library. The two nurses and Kennet, the valet, were all awake and with him during the whole of that night. Kennet certainly was in and out of the room several times, having to run down and fetch various things required by the doctor or the nurses. In order to do this he did not use the principal staircase, nor did he have to cross the hall, but, as far as the upper landing and the secondary stairs were concerned, he certainly had not noticed anything unusual or suspicious; whilst when Mrs. Frewin came home she went straight up to the first floor and certainly noticed nothing in any way to arouse her suspicions. But, of course, this meant very little, as she certainly must have been too upset and agitated to see anything.

The servants were not apprised of the death of their master until after their breakfast. In the meanwhile Emily, the housemaid, had been in, as usual, to "do" the library. She distinctly noticed, when she first went in, that none of the shutters were up and that one of the windows was open. She thought at the time that someone must have been in the room before her, and meant to ask Chipps about it, when the news of the master's death drove all thoughts of open windows from her mind. Strangely enough, when Hankin questioned her more closely about it, and she had had time to recollect everything more clearly, she made the extraordinary statement that she certainly had noticed that the door of the library was locked on the outside when she first went into the room, the key being in the lock.

"Then, didn't it strike you as very funny," asked Hankin, "that the door was locked on the outside, and yet that the shutters were unbarred and one of the windows was open?"

"Yes, I did seem to think of that," replied Emily, with that pleasant vagueness peculiar to her class; "but then, the room did not look like burglars—it was quite tidy, just as it had been left last night, and burglars always seem to leave a great mess behind, else I should have noticed," she added, with offended dignity.

"But did you not see that the miniatures were not in their usual place?"

"Oh, they often wasn't in the cabinet, as the master used to ask for them sometimes to be brought to his room."

That was, of course, indisputable. It was clearly evident that the burglar had had plenty of chances to make good his escape. You see, the actual time when the miscreant must have sneaked into the room had now been narrowed down to about an hour and a half, between the time when Mrs. Frewin finally left in her motor to about an hour later, when Chipps turned the key in the door of the library and thus undoubtedly locked the thief in. At what precise time of the night he effected his escape could not anyhow be ascertained. It must have been after Mrs. Frewin came back again, as Hankin held that she or her chauffeur would have noticed that one of the library windows was open. This opinion was not shared by Elliott from the Yard, who helped in the investigation of this mysterious crime, as Mrs. Frewin was certainly very agitated and upset that evening, and her powers of perception would necessarily be blunted. As for the chauffeur: we all know that the strong headlights on a motor are so dazzling that nothing can be seen outside their blinding circle of light.

Be that as it may, it remained doubtful when the thief made good his escape. It was easy enough to effect, and, as there is a square of flagstones in front of the main door and just below the library windows, the thief left not the slightest trace of footprints, whilst the drop from the window is less than eight feet.

What was strange in the whole case, and struck Detective Hankin immediately, was the fact that the burglar, whoever he was, must have known a great deal about the house and its ways. He also must have had a definite purpose in his mind not usually to be found in the brain of a common housebreaker. He must have meant to steal the miniatures and nothing else, since he made his way straight to the library, and, having secured the booty, at once made good his escape without trying to get any other article which could more easily be disposed of than works of art.

You may imagine, therefore, how delicate a task now confronted Inspector Hankin. You see, he had questioned everyone in the house, including Mr. Frewin's valet and nurses, and from them he casually heard of Mrs. Frewin's parting words to her dying husband and of her mention of the scapegrace son, who was evidently in the immediate neighbourhood, and whom she wished to come and see his father. Mrs. Frewin, closely questioned by the detective, admitted that her son was staying in Brighton, and that she saw him that very evening.

"Mr. Lionel Frewin is staying at the Metropole Hotel," she said coldly, "and he was dining with my sister, Lady Steyne, last night. He was in the house at Sussex Square when I arrived in my motor," she added hastily, guessing, perhaps, the unavowed suspicion which had arisen in Hankin's mind, "and he was still there when I left. I drove home very fast, naturally, as my husband's condition was known to me to be quite hopeless, and that he was not expected to live more than perhaps a few hours. We covered the seven miles between this house and that of my sister in less than a quarter of an hour."

This statement of Mrs. Frewin's was, if you remember, fully confirmed both by her sister and her brother-in-law, Lady Steyne and Sir

Michael. There was no doubt that young Lionel Frewin was staying at the Hotel Metropole in Brighton, that he was that evening dining with the Steynes at Sussex Square when his mother arrived in her motor. Mrs. Frewin stayed about an hour, during which time she, presumably, tried to influence her son to go back to Blatchley with her in order to see his dying father. Of course, what exactly happened at that family interview none of the four people present was inclined to reveal. Against that both Sir Michael and Lady Steyne were prepared to swear that Mr. Lionel Frewin was in the house when his mother arrived, and that he did not leave them until long after she had driven away.

There lay the hitch, you see, for already the public jumped to conclusions, and, terribly prejudiced as it is in a case of this sort, it had made up its mind that Mr. Lionel Frewin, once more pressed for money, had stolen his father's precious miniatures in order to sell them in America for a high sum. Everyone's sympathy was dead against the young son who refused to be reconciled to his father, although the latter was dying.

According to one of the footmen in Lady Steyne's employ, who had taken whiskies and sodas in while the interview between Mrs. Frewin and her son was taking place, Mr. Lionel had said, very testily:

"It's all very well, mother, but that is sheer sentimentality. The guv'nor threw me on my beam ends when a little kindness and help would have meant a different future to me; he chose to break my life because of some early peccadilloes—and I am not going to fawn round him and play the hypocrite when he has no intention of altering his will and has cut me off with a shilling. He must be half imbecile by now, and won't know me anyway."

But with all this, and with public opinion so dead against him, it was quite impossible to bring the crime home to the young man. The burglar, whoever he was, must have sneaked into the library some time before Chipps closed the door on the outside, since it was still so found by Emily the following morning. Thereupon the public, determined that Lionel Frewin should in some way be implicated in the theft, made up its mind that the doting mother, hearing of her son's woeful want of money, stole the miniatures herself that night, and gave them to him.

When Lady Molly heard this theory she laughed, and shrugged her pretty shoulders.

"Old Mr. Frewin was dying, was he not, at the time of the burglary?" she said. "Why should his wife, soon to become his widow, take the trouble to go through a laboured and daring comedy of a burglary in order to possess herself of things which would become hers within the next few hours? Even if, after Mr. Frewin's death, she could not actually dispose of the miniatures, the old man left her a large sum of money and a big income by his will, with which she could help her spendthrift son as much as she pleased."

This was, of course, why the mystery in this strange case was so deep. At the Yard they did all that they could. Within forty-eight hours they had notices printed in almost every European language, which contained rough sketches of the stolen miniatures hastily supplied by Mrs. Frewin herself. These were sent to as many of the great museums and art collectors abroad as possible, and, of course, to the principal American cities and to American millionaires. There is no doubt that the thief would find it very difficult to dispose of the miniatures, and until he could sell them his booty would, of course, not benefit him in any way. Works of art cannot be tampered with, or melted down or taken to pieces, like silver or jewellery, and, so far as could be ascertained, the thief did not appear to make the slightest attempt to dispose of the booty, and the mystery became more dark, more impenetrable than ever.

"Will you undertake the job?" said the chief one day to Lady Molly.

"Yes," she replied, "on two distinct conditions."

"What are they?"

"That you will not bother me with useless questions, and that you will send out fresh notices to all the museums and art collectors you can think of, and request them to let you know of any art purchases they may have made within the last two years."

"The last two years!" ejaculated the chief, "why, the miniatures were only stolen three months ago."

"Did I not say that you were not to ask me useless questions?"

This to the chief, mind you; and he only smiled, whilst I nearly fell backwards at her daring. But he did send out the notices, and it was generally understood that Lady Molly now had charge of the case.

It was about seven weeks later when, one morning, I found her at breakfast looking wonderfully bright and excited.

"The Yard has had sheaves of replies, Mary," she said gaily, "and the chief still thinks I am a complete fool."

"Why, what has happened?"

"Only this, that the art museum at Budapest has now in its possession a set of eight miniatures by Engleheart; but the authorities did not think that the first notices from Scotland Yard could possibly refer to these, as they had been purchased from a private source a little over two years ago."

"But two years ago the Frewin miniatures were still at Blatchley House, and Mr. Frewin was fingering them daily," I said, not understanding, and wondering what she was driving at.

"I know that," she said gaily, "so does the chief. That is why he thinks that I am a first-class idiot."

"But what do you wish to do now?"

"Go to Brighton, Mary, take you with me and try to elucidate the mystery of the Frewin miniatures."

"I don't understand," I gasped, bewildered.

"No, and you won't until we get there," she replied, running up to me and kissing me in her pretty, engaging way.

That same afternoon we went to Brighton and took up our abode at the Hotel Metropole. Now you know I always believed from the very first that she was a born lady and all the rest of it, but even I was taken aback at the number of acquaintances and smart friends she had all over the place. It was "Hello, Lady Molly! Whoever would have thought of meeting you here?" and "Upon my word! this is good luck," all the time.

She smiled and chatted gaily with all the folk as if she had known them all her life, but I could easily see that none of these people knew that she had anything to do with the Yard.

Brighton is not such a very big place as one would suppose, and most of the fashionable residents of the gay city find their way sooner or later to the luxurious dining-room of the Hotel Metropole, if only for a quiet little dinner given when the cook is out. Therefore I was not a little surprised when, one evening, about a week after our arrival and just as we were sitting down to the table d'hôte dinner, Lady Molly suddenly placed one of her delicate hands on my arm.

"Look behind you, a little to your left, Mary, but not just this minute. When you do you will see two ladies and two gentlemen sitting at a small table quite close to us. They are Sir Michael and Lady Steyne, the Honourable Mrs. Frewin in deep black, and her son, Mr. Lionel Frewin."

I looked round as soon as I could, and gazed with some interest at the hero and heroine of the Blatchley House drama. We had a quiet little dinner, and Lady Molly having all of a sudden become very silent and self-possessed, altogether different from her gay, excited self of the past few days, I scented that something important was in the air, and tried to look as unconcerned as my lady herself. After dinner we ordered coffee, and as Lady Molly strolled through into the lounge, I noticed that she ordered our tray to be placed at a table which was in very close proximity to one already occupied by Lady Steyne and her party.

Lady Steyne, I noticed, gave Lady Molly a pleasant nod when we first came in, and Sir Michael got up and bowed, saying "How d'ye do?" We sat down and began a desultory conversation together. Soon, as usual, we were joined by various friends and acquaintances who all congregated round our table and set themselves to entertaining us right pleasantly. Presently the conversation drifted to art matters, Sir Anthony Truscott being there, who is, as you know, one of the keepers of the Art Department at South Kensington Museum.

"I am crazy about miniatures just now," said Lady Molly in response to a remark from Sir Anthony.

I tried not to look astonished.

"And Miss Granard and I," continued my lady, quite unblushingly, "have been travelling all over the Continent in order to try and secure some rare specimens."

"Indeed," said Sir Anthony. "Have you found anything very wonderful?"

"We certainly have discovered some rare works of art," replied Lady Molly, "have we not, Mary? Now the two Englehearts we bought at Budapest are undoubtedly quite unique."

"Engleheart—and at Budapest!" remarked Sir Anthony. "I thought I knew the collections at most of the great Continental cities, but I certainly have no recollection of such treasures in the Hungarian capital."

"Oh, they were only purchased two years ago, and have only been shown to the public recently," remarked Lady Molly. "There was originally a set of eight, so the comptroller, Mr. Pulszky, informed me. He bought them from an English collector whose name I have now forgotten, and he is very proud of them, but they cost the country a great deal more money than it could afford, and in order somewhat to recoup himself Mr. Pulszky sold two out of the eight at, I must say, a very stiff price."

While she was talking I could not help noticing the strange glitter in her eyes. Then a curious smothered sound broke upon my ear. I turned and saw Mrs. Frewin looking with glowing and dilated eyes at the charming picture presented by Lady Molly.

"I should like to show you my purchases," said the latter to Sir Anthony. "One or two foreign connoisseurs have seen the two miniatures and declare them to be the finest in existence. Mary," she added, turning to me, "would you be so kind as to run up to my room and get me the small sealed packet which is at the bottom of my dressing-case? Here are the keys."

A little bewildered, yet guessing by her manner that I had a part to play, I took the keys from her and went up to her room. In her dressing-case I certainly found a small, square, flat packet, and with that in my hand I prepared to go downstairs again. I had just locked the bedroom door when I was suddenly confronted by a tall, graceful woman dressed in deep black, whom I at once recognised as the Honourable Mrs. Frewin.

"You are Miss Granard?" she said quickly and excitedly; her voice was tremulous and she seemed a prey to the greatest possible excitement. Without waiting for my reply she continued eagerly:

"Miss Granard, there is no time to be more explicit, but I give you my word, the word of a very wretched, heart-broken woman, that my very life depends upon my catching a glimpse of the contents of the parcel that you now have in your hand."

"But—" I murmured, hopelessly bewildered.

"There is no 'but,'" she replied. "It is a matter of life and death. Here are £200, Miss Granard, if you will let me handle that packet," and with trembling hands she drew a bundle of banknotes from her reticule.

I hesitated, not because I had any notion of acceding to Mrs. Frewin's request, but because I did not quite know how I ought to act at this strange juncture, when a pleasant, mellow voice broke in suddenly:

"You may take the money, Mary, if you wish. You have my permission to hand the packet over to this lady," and Lady Molly, charming, graceful, and elegant in her beautiful directoire gown, stood smiling, with Hankin just visible in the gloom of the corridor.

She advanced towards us, took the small packet from my hands, and held it out towards Mrs. Frewin.

"Will you open it?" she said, "or shall I?"

Mrs. Frewin did not move. She stood as if turned to stone. Then with dexterous fingers my lady broke the seals of the packet and drew from it a few sheets of plain white cardboard and a thin piece of match-boarding.

"There!" said Lady Molly, fingering the bits of cardboard while she kept her fine, large eyes fixed on Mrs. Frewin. "£200 is a big price to pay for a sight of these worthless things."

"Then this was a vulgar trick," said Mrs. Frewin, drawing herself up with an air which did not affect Lady Molly in the least.

"A trick, certainly," she replied with her winning smile. "Vulgar, if you will call it so— pleasant to us all, Mrs. Frewin, since you so readily fell into it."

"Well, and what are you going to do next?"

"Report the matter to my chief," said Lady Molly, quietly. "We have all been very severely blamed for not discovering sooner the truth about the disappearance of the Frewin miniatures."

"You don't know the truth now," retorted Mrs. Frewin.

"Oh, yes I do," replied Lady Molly, still smiling. "I know that two years ago your son, Mr. Lionel Frewin, was in terrible monetary difficulties. There was something unavowable, which he dared not tell his father. You had to set to work to find money somehow. You had no capital at your own disposal, and you wished to save your son from the terrible consequences of his own folly. It was soon after Monsieur de Colinville's visit. Your husband had had his first apoplectic seizure; his mind and eyesight were somewhat impaired. You are a clever artist yourself, and you schemed out a plan whereby you carefully copied the priceless miniatures and then entrusted them to your son for sale to the Art Museum at Budapest, where there was but little likelihood of their being seen by anyone who knew they had belonged to your husband. English people do not stay more than one night there, at the Hotel Hungaria. Your copies were works of art in themselves, and you had no difficulty in deceiving your husband in the state of mind he then was, but when he lay dying you realised that his will would inevitably be proved, wherein he bequeathed the miniatures to Mr. James Hyam, and that these would have to be valued for probate. Frightened now that the substitution would be discovered, you devised the clever comedy of the burglary at Blatchley, which, in the circumstances, could never be brought home to you or your son. I don't know where you subsequently concealed the spurious Engleheart miniatures which you calmly took out of the library and hid away during the night of your husband's death, but no doubt our men will find that out," she added, quietly, "now that they are on the track."

With a frightened shriek Mrs. Frewin turned as if she would fly, but Lady Molly was too quick for her and barred the way. Then, with that wonderful charm of manner and that innate kindliness which always characterized her, she took hold of the unfortunate woman's wrist.

"Let me give you a word of advice," she said, gently. "We at the Yard will be quite content with a confession from you, which will clear us of negligence and satisfy us that the crime has been brought home to its perpetrator. After that, try and enter into an arrangement with your husband's legatee, Mr. James Hyam. Make a clean breast of the whole thing to him and offer him full monetary compensation. For the sake of the family he won't refuse. He would have nothing to gain by bruiting the whole thing abroad, and for his own sake and that of his late uncle, who was so good to him, I don't think you would find him hard to deal with."

Mrs. Frewin paused awhile, undecided and still defiant. Then her attitude softened; she turned and looked full at the beautiful, kind eyes turned eagerly up to hers and, pressing Lady Molly's tiny hand in both her own, she whispered:

"I will take your advice. God bless you."

She was gone, and Lady Molly called Hankin to her side.

"Until we have that confession, Hankin," she said, with the quiet manner she always adopted where matters connected with her work were concerned, "Mum's the word."

"Ay, and after that, too, my lady," replied Hankin, earnestly.

You see, she could do anything she liked with the men and I, of course, was her slave.

Now we have got the confession, Mrs. Frewin is on the best of terms with Mr. James Hyam, who has behaved very well about the whole thing, and the public has forgotten all about the mystery of the Frewin miniatures.

CONSCIENCE

Richard Marsh

RICHARD BERNARD HELDMANN (1857–1915) wrote prolifically under the pseudonym Richard Marsh. When he produced *The Beetle* in 1897, it competed with another supernatural thriller, Bram Stoker's *Dracula*, receiving better reviews and greater sales, and it remains an exciting read to the present day. Heldmann, as Marsh, wrote about eighty volumes of mystery, horror, romance, and humor, beginning his career by writing stories under his own name for boys' magazines. He was caught forging checks, served eighteen months in prison, and, upon his release, began to use the Marsh pseudonym. He wrote relentlessly (eight books were published in a single year), and his publisher had such a backlog that many more were published after his death from a heart attack—possibly due to overwork.

Although his horror fiction provided much of his reputation, he wrote numerous crime and mystery novels and short stories, perhaps most memorably about Judith Lee, whose adventures appeared in twenty-two stories, mostly published in *The Strand Magazine*, the first twelve collected in *Judith Lee: Some Pages from Her Life* (1912), with nine more collected in *The Adventures of Judith Lee* (1916). The last story about her, "The Barnes Mystery," has never been collected.

Judith Lee has the remarkable ability to read lips with ease, and in multiple languages, which makes it possible for her to thwart criminals of all kinds, though she is often reluctant to believe what she "hears." She is highly intelligent, skilled at disguise, and well-versed in martial arts. She is unconnected to the police, encountering a surprisingly large number of forgers, spies, con men, and murderers, turning them over to the authorities as soon as she has sufficient evidence.

"Conscience" was originally published in the October 1911 issue of *The Strand Magazine* under the title "Judith Lee: Some Pages from Her Life: Conscience"; it was first collected in *Judith Lee: Some Pages from Her Life* (London, Methuen, 1912).

Conscience

RICHARD MARSH

I HAD BEEN SPENDING a few days at Brighton, and was sitting one morning on the balcony of the West Pier pavilion, listening to the fine band of the Gordon Highlanders. The weather was beautiful—the kind one sometimes does get at Brighton—blue skies, a warm sun, and just that touch in the soft breeze which serves as a pick-me-up. There were crowds of people. I sat on one end of a bench. In a corner, within a few feet of me, a man was standing, leaning with his back against the railing—an odd-looking man, tall, slender, with something almost Mongolian in his clean-shaven, round face. I had noticed him on that particular spot each time I had been on the pier. He was well tailored, and that morning, for the first time, he wore a flower in his buttonhole. As one sometimes does when one sees an unusual-looking stranger, I wondered hazily what kind of person he might be. I did not like the look of him.

Presently another man came along the balcony and paused close to him. They took no notice of each other; the new-comer looked attentively at the crowd promenading on the deck below, almost ostentatiously disregarding the other's neighbourhood. All the same, the man in the corner whispered something which probably reached his ears alone—and my perception—something which seemed to be a few disconnected words:—

"Mauve dress, big black velvet hat, ostrich plume; four-thirty train."

That was all he said. I do not suppose that anyone there, except the man who had paused and the lazy-looking girl whose eyes had chanced for a moment to wander towards his lips had any notion that he had spoken at all. The new-comer remained for a few moments idly watching the promenaders; then, turning, without vouchsafing the other the slightest sign of recognition, strolled carelessly on.

It struck me as rather an odd little scene. I was constantly being made an unintentional confidante of what were meant to be secrets; but about that brief sentence which the one had whispered to the other there was a piquant something which struck me as amusing—the more especially as I believed I had seen the lady to whom the words referred. As I came on the pier I had been struck by her gorgeous appearance, as being a person who probably had more money than taste.

Some minutes passed. The Mongolian-looking man remained perfectly quiescent in his corner. Then another man came strolling along—big and burly, in a reddish-brown suit, a green felt hat worn slightly on one side of his head. He paused on the same spot on which the first man had brought his stroll to a close, and he paid no attention to the gentleman in the corner, who looked right away from him, even while I could see his lips framing precisely the same sentence:—

"Mauve dress, big black velvet hat, ostrich plume; four-thirty train."

The big man showed by no sign that he had heard a sound. He continued to do as his predecessor had done—stared at the promenaders, then strolled carelessly on.

This second episode struck me as being rather odder than the first. Why were such commonplace words uttered in so mysterious a manner? Would a third man come along? I waited to see—and waited in vain. The band played "God Save the King," the people rose, but no third man had appeared. I left the Mongolian-looking gentleman still in his corner and went to the other side of the balcony to watch the people going down the pier. I saw the gorgeous lady in the mauve dress and big black picture hat with a fine ostrich plume, and I wondered what interest she might have for the round-faced man in the corner, and what she had to do with the four-thirty train. She was with two or three equally gorgeous ladies and one or two wonderfully-attired men; they seemed to be quite a party.

The next day I left Brighton by an early train. In the compartment I was reading the *Sussex Daily News*, when a paragraph caught my eye. "Tragic Occurrence on the Brighton Line." Late the night before the body of a woman had been found lying on the ballast, as if she might have fallen out of a passing train. It described her costume—she was attired in a pale mauve dress and a big black picture hat in which was an ostrich-feather plume. There were other details—plenty of them—but that was enough for me.

When I read that and thought of the man leaning against the railing I rather caught my breath. Two young men who were facing each other at the other end of the compartment began to talk about the paragraph in tones which were audible to all.

"Do you see that about the lady in the

mauve dress who was found on the line? Do you know, I shouldn't wonder a bit if it was Mrs. Farningham—that's her rig-out to a T. And I know she was going up to town yesterday afternoon."

"She did go," replied the other; "and I'm told that when she started she'd had about enough cold tea."

The other grinned—a grin of comprehension.

"If that's so I shouldn't wonder if the poor dear opened the carriage door, thinking it was some other door, and stepped out on to the line. From all I hear, it seems that she was quite capable of doing that sort of thing when she was like that."

"Oh, quite; not a doubt of it. And she was capable of some pretty queer things when she wasn't like that."

I wondered; these young gentlemen might be right; still, the more I thought the more I wondered.

I was very much occupied just then. It was because I had nearly broken down in my work that I had gone for those few days to Brighton. I doubt if I even glanced at a newspaper for some considerable time after that. I cannot say that the episode wholly faded from my memory, but I never heard what was the sequel of the lady who was found on the line, or, indeed, anything more about her.

I accepted an engagement with a deaf and dumb girl who was about to travel with her parents on a long voyage, pretty nearly round the world. I was to meet them in Paris, and then go on with them to Marseilles, where the real journey commenced. The night before I started some friends gave me a sort of send-off dinner at the Embankment Hotel. We were about halfway through the meal when a man came in and sat by himself at a small round table, nearly facing me. I could not think where I had seen him before. I was puzzling my brain when a second man came across the room and strolled slowly by his table. He did not pause, nor did either allow a sign to escape him to show that they were acquaintances, yet I distinctly saw the lips of the man who was seated at the table frame about a dozen words:—

"White dress, star in her hair, pink roses over left breast. Tonight."

The stroller went carelessly on, and for a moment my heart seemed to stand still. It all came back to me—the pier, the band of the Gordon Highlanders, the man with his back against the railings, the words whispered to the two men who had paused beside him. The diner in front of me was the Mongolian-looking man; I should have recognized him at once had not evening dress wrought such a change in him. That whispered sentence made assurance doubly sure. The party with whom I was dining had themselves been struck by the appearance of the lady in the white frock, with the diamond star in her hair and the pink roses arranged so daintily in the corsage of her dress. There had been a laughing discussion about who was the nicest-looking person in the room; more than one opinion had supported the claim of the lady with the diamond star.

In the middle of that dinner I found myself all at once in a quandary, owing to that very inconvenient gift of mine. I recalled the whisper about the lady in the mauve dress, and how the very next day the body of a lady so attired had been found on the Brighton line. Was the whispered allusion to the lady in the white dress to have a similar unpleasant sequel? If there was fear of anything of the kind, what was I to do?

My friends, noticing my abstraction, rallied me on my inattention.

"May I point out to you," observed my neighbour, "that the waiter is offering you asparagus, and has been doing so for about five minutes?"

Looking round, I found that the waiter was standing patiently at my side. I allowed him to help me. I was about to eat what he had given me when I saw someone advancing across the room whom I knew at once, in spite of the alteration which evening dress made in him—it was the big, burly man in the red-brown suit.

The comedy—if it were a comedy—was repeated. The big man, not, apparently, acknowledging the existence of the solitary diner, passed his table, seemingly by the merest chance, in the course of his passage towards another on the other side of the room. With a morsel of food on his fork poised midway between the plate and his mouth, the diner moved his lips to repeat his former words:—

"White dress, star in her hair, pink roses over left breast. Tonight."

The big man had passed, the morsel of food had entered the diner's mouth; nothing seemed to have happened, yet I was on the point of springing to my feet and electrifying the gaily-dressed crowd by crying, "Murder!"

More than once afterwards I wished I had done so. I do not know what would have happened if I had; I have sometimes asked myself if I could say what would *not* have happened. As a matter of fact, I did nothing at all. I do not say it to excuse myself, nor to blame anyone, but it seemed to me, at the moment, that to do anything was impossible, because those with whom I was dining made it so. I was their guest; they took care to make me understand that I owed them something as my hosts. They were in the merriest mood themselves; they seemed to regard it as of the first importance that I should be merry too. To the best of my ability I was outwardly as gay as the rest of them. The lady in the white dress, with her party, left early. I should have liked to give her some hint, some warning—I did neither; I just let her go. As she went across the room one or two members of our party toasted her under their breath. The solitary diner took no heed of her whatever. I had been furtively watching him the whole time, and he never once glanced in her direction. So far as I saw, he was so absorbed in his meal that he scarcely raised his eyes from the table. I knew, unfortunately, that I could not have mistaken the words which I had seen his lips forming. I tried to comfort myself with the reflection that they could not have referred to the vision of feminine loveliness which had just passed from the room.

The following morning I travelled by the

early boat-train to Dover. When the train had left the station I looked at my *Telegraph*. I read a good deal of it; then, at the top of a column on one of the inside pages, I came upon a paragraph headed: "Mysterious Affair at the Embankment Hotel." Not very long after midnight—in time, it seemed, to reach the paper before it went to press—the body of a young woman had been found in the courtyard of the hotel. She was in her night attire. She was recognized as one of the guests who had been staying in the hotel; she had either fallen or been thrown out of her bedroom window.

Something happened to my brain so that I was unconscious of the train, in which I was a passenger, as it sped onwards.

What did that paragraph mean? Could the woman who had been found in her night attire in the courtyard of the Embankment Hotel be the woman who had worn the white dress and a diamond star in her pretty brown hair? There was nothing to show that she was. There was nothing to connect that lightly-clothed body with the whispered words of the solitary diner, with a touch of the Mongol in his face; yet I wondered if it were not my duty to return at once to London and tell my story. But, after all, it was such a silly story; it amounted to nothing; it proved nothing. Those people were waiting for me in Paris; I could not desert them at the last moment, with all our passages booked, for what might turn out to be something even more fantastic than a will-o'-the-wisp.

So I went on to Paris, and, with them, nearly round the world; and I can say, without exaggeration, that more than once that curious-looking gentleman's face seemed to have gone with me. Once, in an English paper which I picked up after we had landed at Hong-Kong, I read about the body of a woman which had been found on the Great Western Railway line near Exeter station—and I wondered. When I went out into the streets and saw on the faces of the people who thronged them something which recalled the solitary diner at the Embankment Hotel—I wondered still more.

More than two years elapsed. In the summer of the third I went to Buxton, as I had gone to Brighton, for a rest. I was seated one morning in the public gardens, with my thoughts on the other side of the world—we had not long returned from the Sandwich Islands—and I was comparing that land of perpetual summer with the crisp freshness of the Buxton air. With my thoughts still far away, my eyes passed idly from face to face of those around me, until presently I became aware that under the shade of a tree on my left a man was sitting alone. When I saw his face my thoughts came back with a rush; it was the man who had been on the pier at Brighton, and at the Embankment Hotel, and who had travelled with me round the world. The consciousness of his near neighbourhood gave me a nasty jar; as at the Embankment Hotel there was an impulsive moment when I felt like jumping on to my feet and denouncing him to the assembled crowd. He was dressed in a cool grey suit; as at Brighton, he had a flower in his buttonhole; he sat upright and impassive, glancing neither to the left nor right, as if nothing was of interest to him.

Then the familiar comedy, which I believe I had rehearsed in my dreams, began again. A man came down the path from behind me, passing before I had seen his face, and under the shady tree paused for an instant to light a cigarette, and I saw the lips of the man on the chair forming words:—

"Grey dress, lace scarf, Panama hat; five-five train:"

His lips framed those nine words only; then the man with the cigarette passed on, and I really do believe that my heart stood still. Comedy? I had an uncomfortable conviction that this was a tragedy which was being played—in the midst of that light-hearted crowd, in that pleasant garden, under those laughing skies. I waited for the action to continue—not very long. In the distance I saw a big, burly person threading his way among the people towards that shady tree, and I knew what was coming. He did not pause even for a single instant, he just went slowly by, within a foot of the chair, and the thin lips shaped themselves into words:—

"Grey dress, lace scarf, Panama hat; five-five train."

The big man sauntered on, leaving me with the most uncomfortable feeling that I had seen sentence of death pronounced on an innocent, helpless fellow-creature. I did not propose to sit still this time and allow those three uncanny beings, undisturbed, to work their evil wills. As at the hotel, the question recurred to me—what was I to do? Was I to go up and denounce this creature to his face? Suppose he chose to regard me as some ill-conducted person, what evidence had I to adduce that any statements I might make were true? I decided, in the first place, to leave him severely alone; I had thought of another plan.

Getting up from my chair I began to walk about the gardens. As had not been the case on the two previous occasions, there was no person in sight who answered to the description—"Grey dress, lace scarf, Panama hat." I was just about to conclude that this time the victim was not in plain view, when I saw a Panama hat in the crowd on the other side of the band. I moved quickly forward; it was certainly on a woman's head. There was a lace scarf spread out upon her shoulders, a frock of a very light shade in grey. Was this the woman whose doom had been pronounced? I went more forward still, and, with an unpleasant sense of shock, recognized the wearer.

I was staying at the Empire Hotel. On the previous afternoon, at tea-time, the lounge had been very full. I saw a tall lady, who seemed to be alone, glancing about as if looking for an empty table. As she seemed to have some difficulty in finding one, and as I had a table all to myself, I suggested, as she came near, that she should have a seat at mine. The manner in which she received my suggestion took me aback. I suppose there are no ruder, more ill-bred creatures in the world than some English women. Whether she thought I wished to force my company upon her and somehow scrape an acquaintance I cannot say. She could not have treated my suggestion

with more contemptuous scorn had I tried to pick her pocket. She just looked down at me, as if wondering what kind of person I could be that I had dared to speak to her at all, and then, without condescending to reply, went on. I almost felt as if she had given me a slap across my face.

After dinner I saw her again in the lounge. She wore some very fine jewellery—she was a very striking woman, beautifully gowned. A diamond brooch was pinned to her bodice. As she approached I saw it was unfastened; it fell within a foot of where I was sitting. I picked it up and offered it to her, with the usual formula.

"I think this is your brooch—you have just dropped it."

How do you think she thanked me? She hesitated a second to take the brooch, as if she thought I might be playing her some trick. Then, when she saw that it was hers, she took it and looked it carefully over—and what do you suppose she said?

"You are very insistent."

That was all, every word—in such ineffable tones! She was apparently under the impression that I had engineered the dropping of that diamond brooch as a further step in my nefarious scheme to force on her the dishonour of my acquaintance.

This was the lady who in the public gardens was wearing a light grey dress, a lace scarf, and a Panama hat. What would she say to me if I told her about the man under the shady tree and his two friends? Yet, if I did not tell her, should I not feel responsible for whatever might ensue? That she went in danger of her life I was as sure as that I was standing there. She might be a very unpleasant, a very foolish woman, yet I could not stand by and allow her quite possibly to be done to death, without at least warning her of the danger which she ran. The sooner the warning was given the better. As she turned into a side path I turned into another, meaning to meet her in the centre of hers and warn her there and then.

The meeting took place, and, as I had more than half expected, I entirely failed to do what I had intended. The glance she fixed on me when she saw me coming and recognized who I was conveyed sufficient information. It said, as plainly as if in so many words, that if I dared to insult her by attempting to address her it would be at my own proper peril. None the less, I did dare. I remembered the woman in the mauve dress, and the woman in the white, and the feeling I had had that by the utterance of a few words I might have saved their lives. I was going to do my best to save hers, even though she tried to freeze me while I was in the act of doing so.

We met. As if scenting my design, as we neared each other she quickened her pace to stride right past. But I was too quick for her; I barred the way. The expression with which, as she recognized my intention, she regarded me! But I was not to be frightened into dumbness.

"There is something I have to say to you which is important—of the very first importance—which it is essential that I should say and you should hear. I have not the least intention of forcing on you my acquaintance, but with your sanction——"

I got as far as that, but I got no farther. As I still continued to bar her path, she turned right round and marched in the other direction. I might have gone after her, I might have stopped her—I did move a step or two; but when I did she spoke to me over her shoulder as she was moving:—

"If you dare to speak to me again I shall claim the protection of the police, so be advised."

I was advised. Whether the woman suffered from some obscure form of mental disease or not I could not say; or with what majesty she supposed herself to be hedged around, which made it the height of presumption for a mere outsider to venture to address her—that also was a mystery to me. As I had no wish to have a scene in the public gardens, and as it appeared that there would be a scene if I did any more to try to help her, I let her go.

I saw her leave the gardens, and when I had seen that I strolled back. There, under the shady tree, still sat the man with the touch of the Mongol in his face.

After luncheon, which I took at the hotel, I had a surprise. There, in the hall, was my gentleman, going through the front door. I spoke to the hall porter.

"Is that gentleman staying in the house?" The porter intimated that he was. "Can you tell me what his name is?" The porter answered promptly, perhaps because it was such an unusual name:—

"Mr. John Tung." Then he added, with a smile, "I used to be in the Navy. When we were on the China station I was always meeting people with names like that—this gentleman is the first I've met since."

An idea occurred to me. I felt responsible for that woman, in spite of her stupidity. If anything happened to her it would lie at my door. For my own sake I did not propose to run the risk. I went to the post-office and I sent a telegram to John Tung, Empire Hotel. The clerk on the other side of the counter seemed rather surprised as he read the words which I wished him to wire.

"I suppose this is all right?" he questioned, as if in doubt.

"Perfectly all right," I replied. "Please send that telegram at once."

I quitted the office, leaving that telegraph clerk scanning my message as if he were still in doubt if it was in order. In the course of the afternoon I had another idea. I wrote what follows on a sheet of paper.

"You threw the woman in the mauve dress on to the Brighton line; you were responsible for the death of the woman in the white dress at the Embankment Hotel; you killed the woman who was found on the Great Western line near Exeter station; but you are going to do no mischief to the woman in the grey dress and the lace scarf and the Panama hat, who is going up to town by the five-five.

"Be sure of that.

"Also you may be sure that the day of reckoning is at hand, when you and your two accomplices will be called to a strict account. In that hour you will be shown no more mercy than you have shown.

"That is as certain as that, at the present moment, you are still alive. But the messengers of justice are drawing near."

There was no beginning and no ending, no date, no address—I just wrote that and left it so. It was wild language, in which I took a good deal for granted that I had no right to take; and it savoured a good deal of melodrama and high-falutin. But then, my whole scheme was a wild-cat scheme; if it succeeded it would be because of that, as it were, very wild-cat property. I put my sheet of paper into an envelope, and I wrote outside it in very large, plain letters, "Mr. John Tung." Then I went into the lounge of the hotel for tea—and I waited.

And I kept on waiting for quite a consider-able time. It was rather early for tea, but as time passed and people began to gather together, and there were still no signs of the persons whose presence I particularly desired, I began to fidget. If none of them appeared I should have to reconsider my plan of campaign. I was just on the point of concluding that the moment had come when I had better think of something else, when I saw Mr. John Tung standing in the door-way and with him his two acquaintances. This was better than I had expected. Their appear-ance together in the public room of the hotel suggested all sorts of possibilities to my mind.

I had that missive prepared. I waited until I had some notion of the quarter of the room in which they proposed to establish themselves, then I rose from my chair and, crossing to the other side of the lounge, left on a table close to that at which they were about to sit—I hoped unnoticed—the envelope on which "Mr. John Tung" was so plainly written. Then I watched for the march of events.

What I had hoped would occur did happen. A waiter, bustling towards the new-comers, saw the envelope lying on a vacant table, picked it up, perceived that it was addressed to Mr. John Tung, and bore it to that gentleman. I could not hear, but I saw what was said. The waiter began:—

"Is this your letter, sir?"

Mr. Tung glanced, as if surprised, at the envelope which the man was holding, then took it from between his fingers and stared at it hard.

"Where did you get this?" he asked.

"It was on that table, sir."

"What table?"

"The one over there, sir."

Mr. Tung looked in the direction in which the man was pointing, as if not quite certain what he meant.

"How came it to be there? Who put it there?"

"Can't say, sir. I saw an envelope lying on the table as I was coming to you, and when I saw your name on it I thought it might be yours. Tea, sir?"

"Tea for three, and bring some buttered toast."

The waiter went. Mr. Tung remained staring at the envelope as if there were something in its appearance which he found a little puzzling. One of his companions spoke to him; but as his back was towards me I could not see what he said—I could guess from the other's answer.

"Some rubbish; a circular, I suppose—the sort of thing one does get in hotels."

Then he opened the envelope, and—I had rather a funny feeling. I was perfectly conscious that from the point of view of a court of law I had not the slightest right to pen a single one of the words which were on the sheet of paper inside that envelope. For all I could prove, Mr. Tung and his friends might be the most inno-cent of men. I might find it pretty hard to prove that the Mongolian-looking gentleman had whispered either of the brief, jerky sentences which I had seen him whisper; and, even if I could get as far as that, there still remained the difficulty of showing that they bore anything like the construction which I had put upon them. If I had misjudged him, if my deductions had been wrong, then Mr. Tung, when he found what was in that envelope, would be more than justified in making a fine to-do. It was quite possible, since I could not have eyes at the back of my head, that someone had seen me leave that envelope on the table, in which case my authorship might be traced, and I should be in a pretty awkward situation. That woman in the grey dress would be shown to have had right on her side when she declined, with such a show of scorn, to allow me even to speak to her. So, while Mr. Tung was tearing open the envelope and taking out the sheet of paper, I had some distinctly uncomfortable moments. Suppose I had wronged him—what was I to do? Own up, make a clean breast of it—or run away?

I had not yet found an answer when I became perfectly certain that none was required. My chance shot had struck him like a bombshell; the change which took place in his countenance when he began to read what was written on that piece of paper was really curious. I should have said he had a visage over whose muscles he exercised great control—Mongols have as a rule. But those words of mine were so wholly unexpected that when he first saw them his expression was, on the instant, one of stunned amazement. He glanced at the opening words, then, dropping his hands to his sides, gazed round the room, as if he were wondering if there were anyone there who could have written them. Then he raised the sheet of paper again and read farther. And, as he read, his breath seemed to come quicker, his eyes dilated, the colour left his cheeks, his jaw dropped open. He presented a unique picture of the surprise which is born of terror.

His companions, looking at him, were affected as he was, without knowing why. The big, burly man leaned towards him; I saw him mutter:—

"You look as if you'd had a stroke. What's the matter? What's that you've got there? Don't look like that. Everyone is staring at you. What's up?"

Mr. Tung did not reply; he looked at the speaker, then at the sheet of paper—that time I am sure he did not see what was on it. Then he crumpled the sheet of paper up in his hand, and without a word strode across the lounge into the hall beyond. His two companions looked after him in bewildered amazement; then they went also, not quite so fast as he had done, but fast enough. And all the people in the lounge looked at each other. The manner of the exit of these three gentlemen had created a small sensation.

My little experiment had succeeded altogether beyond my anticipation. It was plain that I had not misjudged this gentleman. It would be difficult to find a more striking illustration than that presented by Mr. John Tung of the awful accusing conscience which strikes terror into a man's soul. I could not afford to let my acquaintance with these three interesting gentlemen cease at this moment; the woman in the grey dress must still not be left to their tender mercies.

After what seemed to me to be a sufficient interval, I left my tea and went after them into the hall. I was just in time. The three men were in the act of leaving the hotel. As they were moving towards the door a page came up, an official envelope in his hand.

"Mr. John Tung? A telegram for you, sir."

Mr. Tung took it as if it were some dangerous thing, hesitated, glanced at the men beside him, tore it open, read what was on the flimsy sheet of pink paper, and walked so quickly out of the building that his gait almost approached a run. His companions went after him as if they were giving chase. My wire had finished what those few plain words on the sheet of paper had begun.

I was lingering in the hall, rather at a loss as to what was the next step that I had better take, when the woman in the grey dress came out of the lift, which had just descended. A cab was at the door, on which was luggage. Although she must have seen me very clearly, she did not recognize my presence, but passed straight out to the cab. She was going up to London by the five-five train.

I no longer hesitated what to do. I, too, quitted the hotel and got into a cab. It still wanted ten minutes to five when I reached the station. The train was standing by the platform; the grey-frocked lady was superintending the labelling of her luggage—apparently she had no maid. She was escorted by a porter, who had her luggage in charge, to a first-class carriage. On the top of her luggage was the tell-tale thing which has probably done more harm than good—the dressing-bag which is so dear to the hearts of many women, which ostentatiously proclaims the fact that it contains their jewels, probably their money, all that they are travelling with which they value most. One has only to get hold of the average travelling woman's dressing-bag to become possessed of all that she has—from the practical thief's point of view—worth taking—all contained in one portable and convenient package.

At the open door of the compartment next to the one to which the porter ushered her, the big, burly man was standing—rather to my surprise. I thought I had startled him more than that. Presently who should come strolling up but his more slightly built acquaintance. Apparently he did not know him now; he passed into the compartment at whose door he was standing, without a nod or sign of greeting. My glance travelling down the platform, I saw that standing outside a compartment only a few doors off was Mr. John Tung.

This did not suit me at all. I did not propose that those three gentlemen should travel with the grey-frocked lady by the five-five train to town. Rather than that I would have called in the aid of the police, though it would have been a very queer tale that I should have had to tell them. Perhaps fortunately, I hit upon what the old-time cookery books used to call "another way." I had done so well with one unexpected message that I thought I would try another. There were ten minutes before the train started—still time.

I rushed to the ladies' waiting-room. I begged a sheet of paper and an envelope from the attendant in charge. It was a sheet of paper which she gave me—and on it I scribbled:—

"You are watched. Your intentions are known.

"The police are travelling by the five-five train to London in attendance on the lady in the grey dress. If they do not take you on the road they will arrest you when you reach town.

"Then heigh-ho for the gallows!"

I was in doubt whether or not to add that last line. I daresay if I had had a second or two to think I should not have added it; but I had not. I just scrawled it off as fast as I could, folded the sheet of paper, slipped it into the envelope, which I addressed in large, bold letters to Mr. John Tung. The attendant had a little girl with her, of, perhaps, twelve or thirteen years old, who was acting as her assistant. I took her to the waiting-room door, pointed out Mr. Tung, and told her that if she would slip that envelope into the gentleman's hand and come back to me without having told him where she got it from, I would give her a shilling.

Officials were examining tickets, doors were being closed, preparations were being made to start, when that long-legged young person ran off on her errand. She gave Mr. Tung the envelope as he was stepping into the carriage. He had not time even to realize that he had got it before she was off again. I saw him glance with a startled face at the envelope, open it, hurriedly scan what was within, then make a dart into the compartment by which he was standing, emerge with a bag in his hand, and hurry from the station. Conscience had been too much for him again. The big, burly man, seeing him going, went hurrying after him, as the train was in the very act of starting. As it moved along the platform the face of the third man appeared at the window of his compartment, gazing in apparent astonishment after the other two. He might go to London by the five-five if he chose. I did not think it mattered if he went alone. I scanned the newspapers very carefully the next day; as there was no record of anything unusual having happened during the journey or afterwards I concluded that my feeling that nothing was to be feared from that solitary gentleman had been well founded, and that the lady in the grey dress had reached her destination in comfort and safety.

What became of Mr. Tung when he left the station I do not know; I can only say that he did not return to the hotel. That Buxton episode was in August. About a month afterwards, towards the close of September, I was going north. I started from Euston station. I had secured my seat, and, as there were still several minutes before the train went off, I strolled up and down the platform. Outside the open door of one of the compartments, just as he had done at Buxton station, Mr. Tung was standing!

The sight of him inspired me with a feeling of actual rage. That such a dreadful creature as I was convinced he was should go through life like some beast of prey, seeking for helpless victims whom it would be safe to destroy—that he should be standing there, so well dressed, so well fed, so seemingly prosperous, with all the appearance about him of one with whom the world went very well—the sight of him made me positively furious. It might be impossible, for various reasons, to bring his crimes home to him, but I could still be a thorn in his side, and might punish him in a fashion of my own. I had been the occasion to him of one moment in which conscience had mastered him and terror held him by the throat. I might render him a similar service a second time.

I was seized with a sudden desire to give him a shock which would at least destroy his pleasure for the rest of that day. Recalling what I had done at Buxton, I went to the bookstall and purchased for the sum of one penny an envelope and a sheet of paper. I took these to the waiting-room, and on the sheet of paper I wrote three lines—without even a moment's consideration:—

"You are about to be arrested. Justice is going to be done.

"Your time has come.

"Prepare for the end."

I put the sheet of paper containing these words into the envelope, and, waylaying a small boy, who appeared to have been delivering a parcel to someone in the station, I instructed him to hand my gentleman the envelope and then make off. He did his part very well. Tung was standing sideways, looking down the platform, so that he did not see my messenger approaching from behind; the envelope was slipped into his hand almost before he knew it, and the boy was off. He found himself with an envelope in his hand without, I believe, clearly realizing whence it had come—my messenger was lost in the crowd before he had turned; it might have tumbled from the skies for all he could say with certainty.

For him the recurrence of the episode of the mysterious envelope was in itself a shock. I could see that from where I stood. He stared at it, as he had done before, as if it had been a bomb which at any moment might explode. When he saw his own name written on the face of the envelope, and the fashion of the writing, he looked frantically around, as if eagerly seeking for some explanation of this strange thing. I should say, for all his appearance of sleek prosperity, that his nerves were in a state of jumps. His lips twitched; he seemed to be shaking; he looked as if it would need very little to make him run. With fingers which I am sure were trembling he opened the envelope; he took out the sheet of paper—and he read.

When he had read he seemed to be striving to keep himself from playing the cur; he looked across the platform with such an expression on his face and in his eyes! A constable was advancing towards him, with another man by his side. The probability is that, scared half out of his senses, conscience having come into its own, he misinterpreted the intention of the advancing couple. Those three lines, warning him that he was about to be arrested, that his time had come, to prepare for the end, synchronized so perfectly with the appearance of the constable and his companion, who turned out to be a "plain clothes man" engaged in the company's business, that in his suddenly unnerved state he jumped to the conclusion that the warning and its fulfilment had come together—that those two officers of the law were coming to arrest him there and then.

Having arrived at that conclusion, he seems to have passed quickly to another—that he would not be taken alive. He put his hand into his jacket pocket, took out a revolver, which had no doubt been kept there for quite another purpose, put the muzzle to his brow, and while the two men—thinking of him not at all—were still a few yards off, he blew his brains out. He was dead before they reached him—killed by conscience.

They found his luggage in the compartment

in which he had been about to travel. The contents of his various belongings supplied sufficient explanation of his tragic end. He lived in a small flat off the Marylebone Road—alone; the address was contained in his bag. When the police went there they found a miscellaneous collection of articles which had certainly, in the original instance, never belonged to him. There were feminine belongings of all sorts and kinds. Some of them were traced to their former owners, and in each case the owner was found to have died in circumstances which had never been adequately explained. This man seemed to have been carrying on for years, with perfect impunity, a hideous traffic in robbery and murder—and the victim was always a woman. His true name was never ascertained. It was clear, from certain papers which were found in his flat, that he had spent several years of his youth in the East. He seemed to have been a solitary creature—a savage beast alone in its lair. Nothing was found out about his parents or his friends; nor about two acquaintances of whom I might have supplied some particulars. Personally, I never saw nor heard anything of either of them again.

I went on from Euston station by that train to the north. Just as we were about to start, a girl came bundling into my compartment whom I knew very well.

"That was a close shave," she said, as she took her seat. "I thought I should have missed it; my taxi-cab burst a tyre. What's this I heard them saying about someone having committed suicide on the platform? Is it true?"

"I believe there was something of the kind; in fact, I know there was. It has quite upset me."

"Poor dear! You do look out of sorts. A thing like that would upset anyone." She glanced at me with sympathetic eyes. "I was talking about you only yesterday. I was saying that a person with your power of what practically amounts to reading people's thoughts ought to be able to do a great deal of good in the world. Do you think you ever do any good?"

The question was asked half laughingly. We were in a corridor carriage. Two women at the other end of it suddenly got up and went, apparently, in search of another. I had been in no state to notice anything when I had got in; now I realized that one of the women who had risen was the one who had worn the grey dress at Buxton. She had evidently recognized me on the instant. I saw her whisper to her companion in the corridor, before they moved off:—

"I couldn't possibly remain in the same compartment with that half-bred gipsy-looking creature. I've had experience of her before."

I was the half-bred gipsy-looking creature. The experience she had had of me was when I saved her life at Buxton. That I did save her life I am pretty sure. I said to my friend, when they had gone:—

"I hope that sometimes I do do a little good; but even when I do, for the most part it's done by stealth, and not known to fame; and sometimes, even, it's not recognized as good at all."

"Is that so?" replied my friend. "What a very curious world it is."

When I thought of what had happened on the platform which we were leaving so rapidly behind, I agreed with her with all my heart and soul.

THE HIDDEN VIOLIN

M. McDonnell Bodkin

MATTHIAS McDONNELL BODKIN (1850–1933) created two significant characters in the history of the detective story. The first was Paul Beck (named Alfred Juggins when he first appeared in *Pearson's Magazine* in 1897) in *Paul Beck, the Rule of Thumb Detective* (1898). He claims to be not very bright, saying, "I just go by the rule of thumb, and muddle and puzzle out my cases as best I can." He also appears in *The Quests of Paul Beck* (1908), *The Capture of Paul Beck* (1909), *Young Beck, a Chip off the Old Block* (1911, in a minor role), *Pigeon Blood Rubies* (1915), and *Paul Beck, Detective* (1929).

Dora Myrl, Lady Detective (1900) introduces a modern woman who works as a private inquiry agent, a highly unsavory job for a female in the Victorian age. Her arsenal as a crime fighter includes exceptional skill at disguise, the ability to ride a bicycle at high speeds, and a small revolver she carries in her purse. She is young, pretty, smart (she graduates from Cambridge University, is expert at math, and has a medical degree), and witty, and she meets Paul Beck halfway through *The Capture of Paul Beck*. He is twice her age and taken by her beauty, while she admires him as "the greatest detective in the world." They are on opposite sides of the case, but both see that justice is done. They fall in love (Dora having "captured" him) and have a son, who stars in the stories collected as *Young Beck*; Dora makes a cameo appearance, but her career has ended.

Bodkin, whose primary career was as a barrister, was appointed a judge in County Clare, Ireland, served as a Nationalist member of Parliament, and wrote of his courtroom episodes in *Recollections of an Irish Judge* (1914).

"The Hidden Violin" was first collected in *Dora Myrl, Lady Detective* (London, Chatto & Windus, 1900).

The Hidden Violin

M. McDONNELL BODKIN

"I SHOULD LIKE TO, SYLVIA, BUT I CAN'T."

"You must, Dora."

"Must is a strong word, my dear, but it is on my side this time, not yours. There is a tough case there that insists on being finished tomorrow. I can't go."

"But you will, whether you can or not."

She whisked away with a rustling of silk to the other end of Dora Myrl's bright little sitting-room, where the two girls had been sitting in a cosy corner for a cosy cup of afternoon tea. Brightening her eyes and dimpling her cheeks, there was some pleasant surprise which she could hardly hold back.

Dora Myrl's eye followed her keenly.

"They call me a detective, Sylvia, when they want to flatter me. But I don't pretend to guess your conundrum. What is it? You have got a stone up that new-fashioned silk sleeve. Take it out and throw it."

Sylvia stood before her dramatically, her hands close to her sides, her blue eyes dancing with excitement.

"Signor Nicolo Amati is to play there!"

Dora Myrl surrendered at discretion.

"I will go, of course," she said, smilingly.

"Whether you can or not."

"Whether I can or not."

For here was a chance which no girl—and least of all a girl like Dora Myrl, full of vitality to her finger-tips—would miss.

All London—that is to say, literary and artistic London, or the London that thought itself, or wanted other people to think it, literary and artistic—was still brimming over with the story how that famous musical connoisseur, Lord Mellecent, travelling in Northern Italy with his daughter Sylvia, had lit, amid the embowering vines of a little village on the banks of the Po, on a miraculous violin and violinist. He very quickly convinced himself that the violin was the masterpiece of Antonio Stradivarius, and the player a direct descendant of Nicolo Amati, whose name he bore.

For ages this priceless violin had discoursed exquisite music for the simple villagers. Its strings had danced at their weddings and wept at their graves in the hands of generation after generation of the gifted family of the Amati. But young Nicolo was declared, even by the lovers of old times, to be the most wonderful of them all. Beneath his flying fingers this wonderful violin made music more sweet than the song birds in spring-time, more sad than the meaning of the autumn winds.

Lord Mellecent was in a very frenzy of rapture. He loitered about the sunshiny village for a month, till at last he succeeded in carrying violin and violinist away with him to smoky London. It was vaguely hinted that his golden-haired, blue-eyed daughter, Sylvia, aided and abetted in the capture.

Nicolo Amati had known nothing of the science of music. The marvellous melody of which he was master had come to him from—if we may use the phrase—aural tradition alone. His soul was full of sweet sounds which he poured forth from his sympathetic violin as spontaneously as the nightingale. The masterpieces of the great composers were to him the entering on a new region of undreamt delights.

He had come to London in the spring, and London was thrown into a ferment of restless anticipation by the announcement that in the early autumn he would play for the first time in public.

That this public appearance was to be anticipated by a musical "at home" at the house of Lord Mellecent was the exciting news that the Earl's daughter carried to Dora Myrl.

They were at school together, these two, when the three years' difference in their age seemed like an eternity. Dora, the brilliant leader of the school, alike in the playground and in the study, had been kind to the shy, golden-haired girl just arrived, and helped her and petted her into happiness. So a warm friendship had sprung up between the two.

For Sylvia, Dora was still and always "the head girl." The Earl's daughter looked up to the lady detective with a reverence tempered by affection. But of late the wonderful Italian had shared that homage, and they had many talks together about Signor Nicolo Amati. Dora was keenly anxious to see and hear him, on Sylvia's account and on her own, for she was passionately fond of music, and she wished to judge for herself if the new idol was worthy of his incense.

"Of course I know he is incomparable," said Sylvia, wisely, when they had settled down again after the first flurry of the news. "I am one of the three people in London who have heard him. Papa and his old master are the other two. All

the rest are dying of curiosity, just like yourself, Dora. Oh, don't deny it! You suspect my swan is a goose. There are only fifty people invited in all. I have been positively mobbed for cards. I have had to go about disguised for the last fortnight or I would never have escaped with my life."

She was brimming over with delight and babbled incoherently.

"Monsieur Gallasseau is coming, too. You know him, of course. The second best violin player in the world; only he thinks himself the best. Won't it be fun when he finds out! Don't shake your head that way, you solemn old thing; you have not heard our Italian."

"Your Italian, Sylvia?"

"I didn't say mine, and you must not snap up my words like that, or I'll take my card from you. Mind you come in good time. Now I must be off." And before the blush her friend's words had called up had left her fair face, she was out of the room.

There was a subdued excitement amongst the fortunate fifty that were gathered together in the great drawing-room of Mellecent's house in Park Lane, and an impatience even of the dainties that were handed round on silver salvers by soft-footed servants.

Through the low buzz of conversation one name sounded persistently. Broken sentences could be heard here and there.

"I believe he's just wonderful."

"The music of the spheres, my dear."

"His violin is all carved out of one piece of wood, they tell me."

"And he's so young and handsome!"

"They say that Lord Mellecent could never have coaxed him to come but for Sylvia, and that she is just simply——"

"But surely Lord Mellecent would never give his consent. He is too——"

"One can never be sure nowadays. Genius is so much the fashion it can go anywhere and do anything."

Unconscious Sylvia, lovely in pure, soft white, with a bunch of blue ribbon at her throat, sat with Dora Myrl in the front row, close to a dais carpeted in dark red, with a music stand conspicuous in the centre. Her soft cheek was flushed to the wild-rose tint, and her blue eyes alight with eager expectancy.

A sudden hush came upon the people. All the eyes were on the dais. A side door opened, and there appeared the Earl of Mellecent, with a man walking on either side, and half-a-dozen of the most noted musical connoisseurs in London following.

The famous Frenchman, Gallasseau, walked at the Earl's right hand—tall, broad, swarthy, and smiling. But the young Italian on his left caught and held the eyes of the audience. His beauty would have in itself compelled attention apart from the subtle rumours of his genius. He had the figure of a Greek god, black eyes full of light and fire, and a face perfect in curve and colour.

There was a dead silence in the body of the room, and a little buzz of talk upon the dais. The suave Frenchman blandly insisted that his young rival should take precedence, and after a moment's courteous contention Nicolo Amati came forward to the front of the platform.

A wonderful old violin, that glowed a rich, dark, warm red in the taper's light, nestled lovingly at his chin. He held it with a clasp so light it was almost a caress.

In the moment's pause the people fidgeted in their seats in the intensity of expectation. The bow swept the strings and all held their breath to listen.

Never was such music heard since Orpheus drew beasts and trees in his train, and charmed the heart of the grim King of Hades by the magic of his lute. "Sweet, sweet, blinding sweet," it filled all hearts with ecstasy that was almost pain. The melody flowed as life flows, with infinite variety. Love and grief and joy were wakened in their turn. Now the flying bow struck quick, clear notes from the strings like showers of many-coloured sparks; now the magic violin sighed or moaned or sung under the hands of the master. Its pores and fibres

were filled with all the melody it had made and heard, and thrilled with sweet remembrance at his touch.

The music faded away in a long, dying fall that filled all eyes with idle tears. The silence rested for awhile in love with the sweet strains—softly, almost reverently.

Applause broke out at last coming straight from the heart.

As Amati bowed, his dark eyes were lustrous with unshed tears.

"You know the famous Scotch test?" Dora whispered. "'A mon is a player when he can gar himsel' greet wi' his fiddle.'"

Sylvia made no sign, spoke no word, but sat motionless with parted lips and shining eyes like one inspired.

Presently a low murmur arose in which the name of "Gallasseau" was mingled, but there was no heartiness in the sound.

Monsieur Gallasseau was equal to the occasion.

"No, no," he said, shrugging his broad shoulders higher at each "no." "I will not break the charm. The vanquished salutes the victor," he added, bowing smilingly, "but you would not publicly drag me at your chariot wheels, *mon ami*? If the favour might be permitted I would willingly play with you alone and hear you play. But it is too much to ask?"

Before Lord Mellecent could interpose, Amati answered courteously, in good English, softened and made musical by the pure Italian vowels:

"Signor Gallasseau is too modest. But if he will come to my rooms tomorrow at noon my violin and myself are at his service."

The Frenchman bowed his thanks with a smile on his handsome face, in which there was no trace of envy.

Presently the company began to move and melt away softly, as if still under the spell of the music.

Sylvia whispered to Dora, "Don't stir; he will be here for the evening, and will play for us again. I want you to know him well."

"It is not I, signorina," said Amati to Dora

Myrl the same evening, when, almost faint with delight, she murmured her praise of his playing: "it is not I, it is my violin. The music is here always, asleep till the touch of the bow awakens it."

"A wonderful violin!" Lord Mellecent chimed in, settling himself in the saddle for an easy canter on his hobby. "You know the story, of course?" This to Dora. "It is the masterpiece of Stradivarius—we have it under his own hand—and was a gift to his godson, the son of his master, 'Nicolo Amati.' For nearly two hundred years it has made music for the family of Amati, and it is today more lovely than when it came from the master's hand. There is no violin in the world to match it. Look at the scroll; it is chiselled clean, and sharp, and fine. See how perfect is the purfling! Mark the elegant droop of the long corners. Above all, the varnish—the miraculous varnish of which the secret is lost to the world—pure dragon's blood, with a rich inward glow."

He moved the violin softly in the light, and the smooth surface glowed like deep red wine. There was no chip or stain on the gem-like glow; only the under varnish of rich yellow showed through the worn surface of the fainter red where the touch of the players had been through all those years.

Dora, who knew something about violins as she knew something about most things worth knowing, recognised the supreme beauty of the noble instrument in whose heart was hidden such melody.

The music was in her ears and heart all through the night, and all next day its strains kept mingling with the thoughts she strove to concentrate on the details of the "tough case" on which she was engaged.

There was a sudden sound of quick steps on the stairs, and, without knocking, Sylvia burst into the room.

Turning sharply on her office chair, that swung round with the motion of her body, Dora saw the handsome face of Amati appear behind the excited girl with a strange look in his dark eyes.

It was Sylvia who spoke.

"You'll find it, won't you, Dora? I promised him you would. His violin, you know—it's lost, stolen, vanished, but you'll find it!"

"If I can," said Dora quietly. Her lips tightened, and a curious light kindled at the back of her clear grey eyes. "But first I must know all about the loss. Gently, Sylvia; sit down. Sit down, Signor Amati. Now tell me the story."

Amati told it with a running accompaniment of interruptions and exclamations from Sylvia. There was very little to tell. It appeared that Monsieur Gallasseau called at eleven instead of twelve, carrying his violin case with him in the hansom. He was much disappointed that Amati was out. At first he said he would wait for him, but changed his mind in a few moments, and came down, with his violin case still in his hands, and drove away.

On his return before noon Amati heard the story, and missed his violin from its case. He drove straight to the Frenchman's residence, about two miles away.

"When I got there," Amati went on, "I was told that Monsieur's flat was on the fourth floor. There was a porter at the entrance.

"'Can I see Signor Gallasseau?' I asked.

"'He has left strict directions he is not to be disturbed on any account.'

"'Will you kindly take him my card?'

"He went with my card to the lift. There was a moment's delay. I stepped past unobserved and ran swiftly up the shallow stairs."

"Bravo!" said Dora under her breath.

"I opened the door of the sitting-room on the fourth floor. It was not his—it was vacant. But above me I heard the sound of a violin. It was my own. I ran on; louder and sweeter the notes came. He can play—that Signor Gallasseau. I turned the handle of the door; it was locked. I beat upon it with my hands. The music ceased at once. There was a sound of steps in the room and a tinkling of metal. The next moment the door opened and Signor Gallasseau stood before me smiling.

"'Oh, Signor Amati,' he said, 'I am so

charmed to see you. You may go,' this angrily to the porter who came up behind me. 'I have just come from your place; you were not there. Did you mistake the hour or did I? I am so much grieved.'

"I stood for a moment bewildered at his coolness. Then I broke out:

"'I came for the violin you carried away!'

"With a puzzled look on his face he offered me his own violin which lay on the table.

"'But for what,' he said, 'to play upon—is it not? It is at your service. But surely your own is much finer.'

"'My own has been stolen, Signor.'

"'Stolen! It is impossible! You do not know, then, where it is gone?'

"'But I do, Signor,' I answered hotly. 'It is here—here in your room; I heard it played a minute before the door was opened.'

"For a moment he looked angry, then shrugged his shoulders and smiled.

"'Monsieur is droll,' he said. 'But monsieur loves his violin as myself, and it is a fine instrument. Monsieur will be pleased to search my rooms.'

"Then I searched everywhere, looking even in impossible places, and I found nothing!

"'Monsieur is satisfied?' he asked politely.

"'Satisfied that you have hidden it cunningly,' I answered.

"'Monsieur is pleased to be rude, but I can pardon him on account of his loss. Adieu.'

"'Not adieu, Signor. I will come again, believe me.'

"'Monsieur will be welcome.'

"In the street I met Signora Sylvia, and she brought me to you."

Dora listened intently with half-closed eyes and puckered brows.

"Now, I want to ask you a few questions. Don't you say a word, Sylvia. Did Monsieur Gallasseau look you straight in the face?"

"Straight in the face, with a smile on his own. His eyes were never off me while I was in the room."

"Did you notice at his neck—— No, a man would never notice that. But tell me, were there any mirrors in the room?"

"Oh, I had forgotten to mention it; there were four small mirrors with frames of wrought brass hanging by brass chains. But all four had their faces turned to the wall."

"That was strange!"

"Very strange."

"Did you turn them back again, Signor?"

"No, but I looked carefully behind them for an opening in the wall. There was none."

"You are certain the violin was in the room when you knocked?"

"Quite certain; I heard it."

"You could not have mistaken the sound?"

"Can a mother mistake the laugh of her baby, or a lover the voice of his love? No, it is impossible."

"Yet you have not the least notion where the violin was hidden?"

"Not the least."

"But you have, Dora!" broke in Sylvia impetuously.

"That remains to be seen, my dear. Now let us go to business. You say, Signor, there is a vacant set of chambers just under those of Monsieur Gallasseau? Well, I'll take those chambers tomorrow, and I will be glad to see you there as often and as long as you can spare time. That is if you don't object, my dear?"

Sylvia's answer was a pinch and a kiss. The jest cheered her, for she guessed that Dora was not confident without cause.

On the third day, as Amati was visiting Dora in her new quarters, he met Gallasseau on the stairs, and the Frenchman bowed with an amused smile on his handsome face.

That same afternoon, while Dora and Amati sat at tea, the strains of a violin were heard, superlatively sweet.

"Mine! mine!" Amati cried. "Oh, I shall find it!"

He started from his seat excitedly, but Dora's restraining hand was on his arm.

"Softly, softly," she said. "You tried before, remember, and failed. It is my turn now."

"We shall go together."

"If you will, but I doubt if he will admit us both."

They crept softly up the carpeted stairs together. The music sounded clearer and more sweet.

"There is no doubt?" whispered Dora.

"None, none," he answered, with his hand upon the door knob. It was locked, but at the first rattle of the lock the music ceased. They heard four steps across the room, and instantly, as it seemed, the key was turned in the lock, and Monsieur Gallasseau stood in the doorway facing them, smiling.

"Good evening, mademoiselle; good evening, monsieur. Monsieur is come to apologise, is he not?"

"I came to search," Signor Amati answered shortly.

"What, again!" with a contemptuous shrug. "Very good. For this one time. But you observe it is the last. I will be troubled no more."

Dora and Amati made together towards the door. But Gallasseau blocked the entrance, facing them squarely.

"No, no, I will allow one—no more. It is you or mademoiselle. For me, I prefer mademoiselle, of course."

Then Dora asserted herself.

"You must have your wish, monsieur. Signor Amati, if you will do me the favour to wait in my sitting-room, in five minutes I will bring you your violin."

With an amused smile Gallasseau moved backwards from the door, allowing Dora to pass into the room.

"Mademoiselle is so droll!" he said, "but she is welcome, very welcome to my poor rooms to find the violin—if she can."

She gave one quick look round the room, but made no movement to search.

"The mirrors are gone, monsieur?" she said very quietly.

He started for a moment, but answered, still smiling:

"Mademoiselle has heard of my mirrors. Yes, they are gone to be relacquered. If I could have guessed this visit, there would have been mirrors for mademoiselle."

"Oh, I think not, I really think not. You will pardon me for contradicting you, monsieur. Won't you sit down. I hate to keep you standing while I search."

"Mademoiselle will pardon me; I will not sit down in her presence. I prefer to stand and look at mademoiselle, if I may?"

"Why, certainly."

She had moved across the room to a table near the door where the Frenchman's own violin lay. There was a high backed chair close beside.

"Monsieur was seated here playing when he heard the handle turn in the door?"

"It is so, mademoiselle."

"And you opened the door instantly?"

"As mademoiselle observes—instantly."

"The chair is only three yards from the door; there was no time to hide a violin, monsieur."

"No time at all, mademoiselle."

"Unless you hid it quite close of course?"

"Quite close?" repeated the Frenchman vaguely, with a puzzled look on his face.

She changed the subject abruptly.

"Forgive me, monsieur, there is a little band of white ribbon running round your collar; it is drawn quite tight. It must incommode you, I fear. Will you allow me?"

He started back with a frightened look from her outstretched hand.

"Quite right," she went on calmly, "it is really not necessary. You are quick enough to see, monsieur, that the game is up. Turn round."

Monsieur Gallasseau hesitated for a fraction of a second. Then he smiled a very sickly smile.

"Mademoiselle is very clevaire," he said, and turning round showed the violin, like the golden hair of the young lady in the ballad, "hanging down his back."

BEFORE WORLD WAR I
(AMERICAN)

CHRISTABEL'S CRYSTAL

Carolyn Wells

THE PROLIFIC AND BIBLIOPHILIC Carolyn Wells (1862–1942) wrote and edited 170 books, of which 82 are mysteries, many of which had exceptionally ingenious plot ideas, and most of which are achingly dull—reason enough to ignore them. Still, it is difficult to understand that someone so enormously popular and prominent in her lifetime could be so largely forgotten and unread today.

As famous as she was for her mystery novels, sixty-one of which featured the scholarly, book-loving Fleming Stone, Wells was equally noted in her time for such anthologies as *A Nonsense Anthology* (1902), considered a classic of its kind, and her *A Parody Anthology* (1904), which remained in print for more than a half century. Wells also wrote the first instructional manual in the detective fiction genre, *The Technique of the Mystery Story* (1913). Her first mystery novel, *The Clue* (1909), was selected for the Haycraft-Queen Definitive Library of Detective-Crime-Mystery Fiction.

Her affection for satires and parodies led her to write many of them herself, including *Ptomaine Street* (1921), a full-length parody of Sinclair Lewis, and several stories involving Sherlock Holmes, including "The Adventure of the 'Mona Lisa'" (1912) and "The Adventure of the Clothes-Line" (1915).

"Christabel's Crystal" was originally published in the October 15, 1905, issue of the Chicago *Sunday Record-Herald*.

Christabel's Crystal

CAROLYN WELLS

OF ALL THE UNEXPECTED PLEASURES that have come into my life, I think perhaps the greatest was when Christabel Farland asked me to be bridesmaid at her wedding.

I always had liked Christabel at college, and though we hadn't seen much of each other since we were graduated, I still had a strong feeling of friendship for her, and besides that I was glad to be one of the merry house party gathered at Farland Hall for the wedding festivities.

I arrived the afternoon before the wedding-day, and found the family and guests drinking tea in the library. Two other bridesmaids were there, Alice Fordham and Janet White, with both of whom I was slightly acquainted. The men, however, except Christabel's brother Fred, were strangers to me, and were introduced as Mr. Richmond, who was to be an usher; Herbert Gay, a neighbor, who chanced to be calling; and Mr. Wayne, the tutor of Christabel's younger brother Harold. Mrs. Farland was there too, and her welcoming words to me were as sweet and cordial as Christabel's.

The party was in frivolous mood, and as the jests and laughter grew more hilarious, Mrs. Farland declared that she would take the bride-elect away to her room for a quiet rest, lest she should not appear at her best the next day.

"Come with me, Elinor," said Christabel to me, "and I will show you my wedding-gifts."

Together we went to the room set apart for the purpose, and on many white-draped tables I saw displayed the gorgeous profusion of silver, glass, and bric-à-brac that are one of the chief component parts of a wedding of today.

I had gone entirely through my vocabulary of ecstatic adjectives and was beginning over again, when we came to a small table which held only one wedding-gift.

"That is the gem of the whole collection," said Christabel, with a happy smile, "not only because Laurence gave it to me, but because of its intrinsic perfection and rarity."

I looked at the bridegroom's gift in some surprise. Instead of the conventional diamond sunburst or heart-shaped brooch, I saw a crystal ball as large as a fair-sized orange.

I knew of Christabel's fondness for Japanese crystals and that she had a number of small ones of varying qualities; but this magnificent specimen fairly took my breath away. It was poised on the top of one of those wavecrests, which the artisans seem to think appropriately interpreted in wrought-iron. Now, I haven't the same subtle sympathy with crystals that Christabel always has had; but still this great, perfect, limpid sphere affected me strangely. I glanced at it at first with a calm interest; but as I continued to look I became fascinated, and soon found myself obliged (if I may use the expression) to tear my eyes away.

Christabel watched me curiously. "Do you love it too?" she said, and then she turned her eyes to the crystal with a rapt and rapturous gaze that made her appear lovelier than ever. "Wasn't it dear of Laurence?" she said. "He wanted to give me jewels of course; but I told him that I would rather have this big crystal than the Koh-i-nur. I have six others, you know; but the largest of them hasn't one-third the diameter of this."

"It is wonderful," I said, "and I am glad you have it. I must own it frightens me a little."

"That is because of its perfection," said Christabel simply. "Absolute flawless perfection always is awesome. And when it is combined with perfect, faultless beauty, it is the ultimate perfection of a material thing."

"But I thought you liked crystals because of their weird supernatural influence over you," I said.

"That is an effect, not a cause," Christabel replied. "Ultimate perfection is so rare in our experiences that its existence perforce produces consequences so rare as to be dubbed weird and supernatural. But I must not gaze at my crystal longer now, or I shall forget that it is my wedding-day. I'm not going to look at it again until after I return from my wedding-trip; and then, as I tell Laurence, he will have to share my affection with his wedding-gift to me."

Christabel gave the crystal a long parting look, and then ran away to don her wedding-gown. "Elinor," she called over her shoulder, as she neared her own door, "I'll leave my crystal in your special care. See that nothing happens to it while I'm away."

"Trust me!" I called back gaily, and then went in search of my sister bridesmaids.

The morning after the wedding began rather later than most mornings. But at last we all were seated at the breakfast-table and enthusiastically discussing the events of the night before. It seemed strange to be there without Christabel, and Mrs. Farland said that I must stay until the bridal pair returned, for she couldn't get along without a daughter of some sort.

This remark made me look anywhere rather than at Fred Farland, and so I chanced to catch Harold's eye. But the boy gave me such an intelligent, mischievous smile that I actually blushed and was covered with confusion.

Just at that moment Katy the parlor-maid came into the dining-room, and with an anxious expression on her face said: "Mrs. Farland, do you know anything about Miss Christabel's glass ball? It isn't in the present-room."

"No," said Mrs. Farland; "but I suppose Mr. Haley put it in the safe with the silver and jewelry."

"I don't think so, ma'am; for he asked me was he to take any of the cut glass, and I told him you had said only the silver and gold, ma'am."

"But that crystal isn't cut glass, Katy; and it's more valuable than all Miss Christabel's silver gifts put together."

"Oh, my! is it, ma'am? Well, then, won't you please see if it's all right, for I'm worried about it."

I wish I could describe my feelings at this moment. Have you ever been in imminent danger of a fearful catastrophe of any kind, and while with all your heart and soul you hoped it might be averted, yet there was one little, tiny, hidden impulse of your mind that craved the excitement of the disaster? Perhaps it is only an ignoble nature that can have this experience, or there may be a partial excuse for me in the fact that I am afflicted with what sometimes is called the "detective instinct." I say afflicted, for I well know that anyone else who has this particular mental bias will agree with me that it causes far more annoyance than satisfaction.

Why, one morning when I met Mrs. Van Allen in the market, I said: "It's too bad your waitress had to go out of town to attend the funeral of a near relative, when you were expecting company to luncheon." And she was as angry as could be, and called me an impertinent busy-body.

But I just had deduced it all from her glove. You see, she had on one brand-new black-kid glove, and the other, though crumpled up in her hand, I could see never had been on at all. So I knew that she wouldn't start to market early in the morning with such gloves if she had any sort of half-worn black ones at all.

And I knew that she had given away her next-best pair recently—it must have been the night before, or she would have tried them on sooner; and as her cook is an enormous woman, I was sure that she had given them to her waitress. And why would she, unless the maid was going away in great haste? And what would require such a condition of things except a sudden call to a funeral? And it must have been out of town, or she would have waited until morning, and then she could have bought black gloves for herself. And it must have been a near relative to make the case so urgent. And I knew that Mrs. Van Allen expected luncheon guests, because her fingers were stained from paring apples; and why would she pare her own apples so early in the morning except to assist the cook in some hurried preparations? Why, it was all as plain as could be, and every bit true; but Mrs. Van Allen wouldn't believe my explanation, and to this day she thinks I made my discoveries by gossiping with her servants.

Perhaps all this will help you to understand why I felt a sort of nervous exhilaration that had in it an element of secret pleasure, when we learned that Christabel's crystal really was missing.

Mr. Haley, who was a policeman, had remained in the present-room during all of the hours devoted to the wedding celebration, and after the guests had gone he had packed up the silver, gold, and jewels and put them away in the family safe, which stood in a small dressing-room between Mrs. Farland's bedroom and Fred's. He had worn civilian's dress during the evening, and few if any of the guests knew that he was guarding the valuable gifts. The mistake had been in not telling him explicitly to care for the crystal as the most valuable gem of all; but this point had been overlooked, and the ignorant officer had assumed that it was merely a piece of cut glass, of no more value than any of the carafes or decanters. When told that the ball's intrinsic value was many thousands of dollars, and that it

would be next to impossible to duplicate it at any price, his amazement was unbounded, and he appeared extremely grave.

"You ought to have told me," he said. "Sure, it's a case for the chief now!" Haley had been hastily telephoned for to come to Farland Hall and tell his story, and now he telephoned for the chief of police and a detective.

I felt a thrill of delight at this, for I always had longed to see a real detective in the act of detecting.

Of course everybody was greatly excited, and I just gave myself up to the enjoyment of the situation, when suddenly I remembered that Christabel had said that she would leave her crystal in my charge, and that in a way I was responsible for its safety. This changed my whole attitude, and I realized that, instead of being an idly curious observer, I must put all my detective instinct to work immediately and use every endeavor to recover the lost crystal.

First, I flew to my own room and sat down for a few moments to collect my thoughts and lay my plans. Of course, as the windows of the present-room were found in the morning fastened as they were left the night before, the theft must have been committed by someone in the house. Naturally it was not one of the family or the guests of the house. As to the servants, they all were honest and trustworthy—I had Mrs. Farland's word for that. There was no reason to suspect the policeman, and thus my process of elimination brought me to Mr. Wayne, Harold's tutor.

Of course it must have been the tutor. In nine-tenths of all the detective stories I ever have read the criminal proved to be a tutor or secretary or some sort of gentlemanly dependent of the family; and now I had come upon a detective story in real life, and here was the regulation criminal ready to fit right into it. It was the tutor of course; but I should be discreet and not name him until I had collected some undeniable evidence.

Next, I went down to the present-room to search for clues. The detective had not arrived yet, and I was glad to be first on the ground, for I remembered how much importance Sherlock Holmes always attached to the first search. I didn't really expect that the tutor had left shreds of his clothing clinging to the table-legs, or anything absurd like that; but I fully expected to find a clue of some sort. I hoped that it wouldn't be cigar ashes; for though detectives in fiction always can tell the name and price of a cigar from a bit of ash, yet I'm so ignorant about such things that all ashes are alike to me.

I hunted carefully all over the floor; but I couldn't find a thing that seemed the least bit like a clue, except a faded white carnation. Of course that wasn't an unusual thing to find, the day after a wedding; but it surprised me some, because it was the very flower I had given to Fred Farland the night before, and he had worn it in his buttonhole. I recognized it perfectly, for it was wired, and I had twisted it a certain way when I adjusted it for him.

This didn't seem like strong evidence against the tutor; but it was convincing to me, for if Mr. Wayne was villain enough to steal Christabel's crystal, he was wicked enough to manage to get Fred's boutonnière and leave it in the room, hoping thereby to incriminate Fred. So fearful was I that this trick might make trouble for Fred that I said nothing about the carnation; for I knew that it was in Fred's coat when he said good-night, and then we all went directly to our rooms. When the detective came he examined the room, and I know that he didn't find anything in the way of evidence; but he tried to appear as if he had, and he frowned and jotted down notes in a book after the most approved fashion.

Then he called in everybody who had been in the house over night and questioned each one. I could see at once that his questions to the family and guests were purely perfunctory, and that he too had his suspicions of the tutor.

Finally, it was Mr. Wayne's turn. He always was a nervous little man, and now he seemed terribly flustered. The detective was gentle with him, and in order to set him more at ease began to converse generally on crystals. He asked Mr. Wayne if he had traveled much, if he ever had been to Japan, and if he knew much about the making and polishing of crystal balls.

The tutor fidgeted around a good deal and seemed disinclined to look the detective in the eye; but he replied that he never had been to Japan, and that he never had heard of a Japanese rock crystal until he had seen Miss Farland's wedding-gift; and that even then he had no idea of its great value until since its disappearance he had heard its price named.

This sounded well; but his manner was so embarrassed, and he had such an effect of a guilty man, that I felt sure my intuitions were correct and that he himself was the thief.

The detective seemed to think so too, for he said at last: "Mr. Wayne, your words seem to indicate your innocence; but your attitudes do not. Unless you can explain why you are so agitated and apparently afraid, I shall be forced to the conclusion that you know more about this than you have admitted."

Then Mr. Wayne said: "Must I tell all I know about it, sir?"

"Certainly," said the detective.

"Then," said Mr. Wayne, "I shall have to state that when I left my room late last night to get a glass of water from the ice-pitcher, which always stands on the hall-table, I saw Mr. Fred Farland just going into the sitting-room, or present-room, as it has been called for the last few days."

There was a dead silence. This, then, was why Mr. Wayne had acted so embarrassed; this was the explanation of my finding the white carnation there; and I think the detective thought that the sudden turn affairs had taken incriminated Fred Farland.

I didn't think so at all. The idea of Fred's stealing his own sister's wedding-gift was too preposterous to be considered for a moment.

"Were you in the room late at night, Mr. Farland?" asked the detective.

"I was," said Fred.

"Why didn't you tell me this before?"

"You didn't ask me, and as I didn't take the crystal I saw no reason for referring to the fact that I was in the room."

"Why did you go there?"

"I went," said Fred coolly, "with the intention of taking the crystal and hiding it, as a practical joke on Christabel."

"Why did you not do so?"

"Because the ball wasn't there. I didn't think then that it had been stolen, but that it had been put away safely with the other valuables. Since this is not so, and the crystal is missing, we all must get to work and find it somehow before my sister returns."

The tutor seemed like a new man after Fred had spoken. His face cleared, and he appeared intelligent, alert, and entirely at his ease. "Let me help," he said. "Pray command my services in any way you choose."

But the detective didn't seem so reassured by Fred's statements. Indeed, I believe he really thought that Christabel's brother was guilty of theft.

But I believed implicitly every word Fred had uttered and, begging him to come with me, I led the way again to the sitting-room. Mr. Wayne and Janet White came too, and the four of us scrutinized the floor, walls, and furniture of the room over and over again. "There's one thing certain," I said thoughtfully: "The crystal was taken either by someone in the house or someone out of it. We've been confining our suspicions to those inside. Why not a real burglar?"

"But the windows are fastened on the inside," said Janet.

"I know it," I replied. "But if a burglar could slip a catch with a thin-bladed knife—and they often do—then he could slip it back again with the same knife and so divert suspicion."

"Bravo, Miss Frost!" said Mr. Wayne, with an admiring glance at me. "You have the true detective instinct. I'll go outside and see if there are any traces."

A moment later he was on the veranda and excitedly motioning us to raise the window. Fred pushed back the catch and opened the long French window that opened on the front veranda.

"I believe Miss Frost has discovered the mystery," said Mr. Wayne, and he pointed to numerous scratches on the sash-frame. The house had been painted recently, and it was seen easily that the fresh scratches were made by a thin knife-blade pushed between the sashes.

"By Jove!" cried Fred, "that's it, Elinor; and the canny fellow had wit enough to push the catch back in place after he was outside again."

I said nothing, for a moment. My thoughts were adjusting themselves quickly to the new situation from which I must make my deductions. I realized at once that I must give up my theory of the tutor, of course, and anyway I hadn't had a scrap of evidence against him except his fitness for the position. But, given the surety of burglars from outside, I knew just what to do: look for footprints, to be sure.

I glanced around for the light snow that always falls in detective stories just before the crime is committed, and is testified, usually by the village folk, to have stopped just at the crucial moment. But there wasn't a sign of snow or rain or even dew. The veranda showed no footprints, nor could the smooth lawn or flagged walks be expected to. I leaned against the veranda railing in despair, wondering what Sherlock Holmes would do in a provoking absence of footprints, when I saw in the flower-bed beneath several well-defined marks of a man's shoes.

"There you are, Fred!" I cried, and rushed excitedly down the steps.

They all followed, and, sure enough, in the soft earth of the wide flower-bed that surrounded the veranda were strong, clear prints of large masculine footgear.

"That clears us, girls," cried Janet gleefully, as she measured her daintily shod foot against the depressions.

"Don't touch them!" I cried. "Call Mr. Prout the detective."

Mr. Prout appeared, and politely hiding his chagrin at not having discovered these marks before I did, proceeded to examine them closely.

"You see," he said in a pompous and dictatorial way, "there are four prints pointing toward the house, and four pointing toward the street. Those pointing to the street are superimposed upon those leading to the house, hence we deduce that they were made by a burglar who crossed the flower-bed, climbed the veranda, stepped over the rail, and entered at the window. He then returned the same way, leaving these last footprints above the others."

As all this was so palpably evident from the facts of the case, I was not impressed much by the subtlety of his deductions and asked him what he gathered from the shape of the prints.

He looked at the well-defined prints intently. "They are of a medium size," he announced at last, "and I should say that they were made by a man of average height and weight, who had a normal-sized foot."

Well, if that wasn't disappointing! I thought of course that he would tell the man's occupation and social status, even if he didn't say that he was left-handed or that he stuttered, which is the kind of thing detectives in fiction always discover.

So I lost all interest in that Prout man, and began to do a little deducing on my own account. Although I felt sure, as we all did, that the thief was a burglar from outside, yet I couldn't measure the shoes of an absent and unidentified burglar, and somehow I felt an uncontrollable impulse to measure shoes.

Without consulting anybody, I found a tape-measure and carefully measured the footprints. Then I went through the house and measured all the men's shoes I could find, from the stable-boy's up to Fred's.

It's an astonishing fact, but nearly all of them fitted the measurements of the prints on the flower-bed. Men's feet are so nearly universal in size, or rather their shoes are, and too, what with extension soles and queer-shaped lasts, you can't tell anything about the size or style of a man from his footprints.

So I gave up deducing and went to talk to Fred Farland.

"Fred," I said simply, "did you take Christabel's crystal?"

"No," he answered with equal simplicity, and he looked me in the eyes so squarely and honestly that I knew he spoke the truth.

"Who did?" I next inquired.

"It was a professional burglar," said Fred, "and a mighty cute one; but I'm going to track him and get that crystal back before Christabel comes home."

"Let me help!" I cried eagerly. "I've got the true detective instinct, and I know I can do something."

"You?" said Fred incredulously. "No, you can't help; but I don't mind telling you my plan. You see I expect Lord Hammerton down to make me a visit. He's a jolly young English chap that I chummed with in London. Now, he's a first-rate amateur detective, and though I didn't expect him till next month, he's in New York, and I've no doubt that he'd be willing to come right off. No one will know he's doing any detecting; and I'll wager he'll lay his hands on that ball in less than a week."

"Lovely!" I exclaimed. "And I'll be here to see him do it!"

"Yes, the mater says you're to stay a fortnight or more; but mind, this is our secret."

"Trust me," I said earnestly; "but let me help if I can, won't you?"

"You'll help most by not interfering," declared Fred, and though it didn't altogether suit me, I resolved to help that way rather than not at all.

A few days later Lord Hammerton came. He was not in any way an imposing-looking man. Indeed, he was a typical Englishman of the Lord Cholmondeley type, and drawled and used a monocle most effectively. The afternoon he came we told him all about the crystal. The talk turned to detective work and detective instinct. Lord Hammerton opined in his slow languid drawl that the true detective mind was not dependent upon instinct, but was a nicely adjusted mentality that was quick to see the cause back of an effect.

Herbert Gay said that while this doubtless was so, yet it was an even chance whether the cause so skilfully deduced was the true one.

"Quite so," agreed Lord Hammerton amiably, "and that is why the detective in real life fails so often. He deduces properly the logical facts from the evidence before him; but real life and real events are so illogical that his deductions, though true theoretically, are false from mere force of circumstances."

"And that is why," I said, "detectives in story-books always deduce rightly, because the obliging author makes the literal facts coincide with the theoretical ones."

Lord Hammerton put up his monocle and favored me with a truly British stare. "It is unusual," he remarked slowly, "to find such a clear comprehension of this subject in a feminine mind."

They all laughed at this; but I went on: "It is easy enough to make the spectacular detective of fiction show marvelous penetration and logical deduction when the antecedent circumstances are arranged carefully to prove it all; but place even Sherlock Holmes face to face with a total stranger, and I, for one, don't believe that he could tell anything definite about him."

"Oh, come now! I can't agree to that," said Lord Hammerton, more interestedly than he had spoken before. "I believe there is much in the detective instinct besides the exotic and the artificial. There is a substantial basis of divination built on minute observation, and which I have picked up in some measure myself."

"Let us test that statement," cried Herbert Gay. "Here comes Mr. Wayne, Harold's tutor. Lord Hammerton never has seen him, and before Wayne even speaks let Lord Hammerton tell us some detail, which he divines by observation."

All agreed to this, and a few minutes later Mr. Wayne came up. We laughingly explained the situation to him and asked him to have himself deduced.

Lord Hammerton looked at Arthur Wayne for a few minutes, and then said, still in his deliberate drawl: "You have lived in Japan for the past seven years, in Government service in the interior, and only recently have returned."

A sudden silence fell upon us all—not so much because Lord Hammerton made deductions from no apparent evidence, but because we all knew Mr. Wayne had told Detective Prout that he never had been in Japan.

Fred Farland recovered himself first, and said: "Now that you've astonished us with your results, tell us how you attained them."

"It is simple enough," said Lord Hammerton, looking at young Wayne, who had turned deathly white. "It is simple enough, sir. The breast-pocket on the outside of your coat is on the right-hand side. Now it never is put there. Your coat is a good one—Poole, or some London tailor of that class. He never made a coat with an outer breast-pocket on the right side. You have had the coat turned—thus the original left-hand pocket appears now on the right side.

"Looking at you, I see that you have not the constitution which could recover from an acute attack of poverty. If you had it turned from want, you would not have your present effect of comfortable circumstances. Now, you must have had it turned because you were in a country where tailoring is not frequent, but sewing and delicate manipulation easy to find. India? You are not bronzed. China? The same. Japan? Probable; but not treaty ports—there are plenty of tailors there. Hence, the interior of Japan.

"Long residence, to make it incumbent on you to get the coat turned, means Government service, because unattached foreigners are allowed only as tourists. Then the cut of the coat is not so very old, and as contracts run seven or fourteen years with the Japanese, I repeat that you probably resided seven years in the interior of Japan, possibly as an irrigation engineer."

I felt sorry then for poor Mr. Wayne. Lord Hammerton's deductions were absolutely true, and coming upon the young man so suddenly he made no attempt to refute them.

And so as he had been so long in Japan, and must have been familiar with rock crystals for years, Fred questioned him sternly in reference to his false statements.

Then he broke down completely and confessed that he had taken Christabel's crystal because it had fascinated him.

He declared that he had a morbid craving for crystals; that he had crept down to the present-room late that night, merely to look at the wonderful, beautiful ball; that it had so possessed him that he carried it to his room to gaze at for a while, intending to return with it after an hour or so. When he returned he saw Fred Farland, and dared not carry out his plan.

"And the footprints?" I asked eagerly.

"I made them myself," he explained with a dogged shamefacedness. "I did have a moment of temptation to keep the crystal, and so tried to make you think that a burglar had taken it; but the purity and beauty of the ball itself so reproached me that I tried to return it. I didn't do so then, and since—"

"Since?" urged Fred, not unkindly.

"Well, I've been torn between fear and the desire to keep the ball. You will find it in my trunk. Here is the key."

There was a certain dignity about the young man that made him seem unlike a criminal, or even a wrong-doer.

As for me, I entirely appreciated the fact that he was hypnotized by the crystal and in a way was not responsible. I don't believe that man would steal anything else in the world.

Somehow the others agreed with me, and as they had recovered the ball, they took no steps to prosecute Mr. Wayne.

He went away at once, still in that dazed, uncertain condition. We never saw him again; but I hope for his own sake that he never was subjected to such a temptation.

Just before he left, I said to him out of sheer curiosity: "Please explain one point, Mr. Wayne. Since you opened and closed that window purposely to mislead us, since you made those footprints in the flower-bed for the same reason, and since to do it you must have gone out and then come back, why were the outgoing footprints made over the incoming ones?"

"I walked backward on purpose," said Mr. Wayne simply.

THE BULLET FROM NOWHERE

Hugh C. Weir

READERS OF PURE DETECTIVE STORIES have a special fondness for impossible crimes, and Hugh Cosgro Weir (1884–1934), in *Miss Madelyn Mack, Detective* (1914), his only volume of mystery fiction, managed to produce two: "The Bullet from Nowhere" and "The Man with Nine Lives."

Born in Illinois, he became a reporter in Ohio at the age of sixteen before becoming a prolific writer of short stories and magazine articles, with more than three hundred to his credit, as well as a fantastically tireless writer of stories for the screen as well as screenplays, having written at least three hundred, the first of which was for Universal Studios at the age of twenty. All were silent films and are largely unknown today.

Although he wrote mystery stories for such top pulp magazines as *Flynn's Weekly*, Weir is remembered today solely for *Miss Madelyn Mack, Detective*, which he dedicated to Mary Holland: "This is your book. It is you, woman detective of real life, who suggested Madelyn. It was the stories told me from your own note-book of men's knavery that suggested these exploits of Miss Mack."

Miss Mack became a detective while still in college and was immediately successful, her recorded cases narrated in first person by her friend Nora. The young detective denied having any special talents, ascribing her ability to catch criminals to hard work and common sense, though she concludes that imagination is also important, stating that "a woman, I think, always has a more acute imagination than a man!"

Later in life, Weir cofounded with Catherine McNelis an advertising agency and Tower Magazines, of which he was editorial director at the time of his death. Founded in 1929 during the Depression, its magazines (*The New Movie Magazine*, *Detective*, *Home*, and *Love*) became overnight smashes, with total circulation announced at 1.3 million. In 1935, the company abruptly went bankrupt when advertisers claimed they had been defrauded with inflated circulation numbers, and McNelis was found guilty and sentenced to a year and a day in jail.

"The Bullet from Nowhere" was originally published in the October 1914 issue of *MacLean's Magazine*; it was first collected in *Miss Madelyn Mack, Detective* (Boston, The Page Company, 1914).

The Bullet from Nowhere

HUGH C. WEIR

I

LOUDER AND LOUDER, as though the musician had abandoned himself to the wild spirit of his crashing climax, the pealing strains of the "storm scene" from "William Tell" rolled out from the keys of the mahogany piano, through the closed doors of Homer Hendricks's music-room, and down the stairs to the waiting group below.

The slender, white fingers of the musician quivered with feverish energy. Into his thin, pale face, white with the pallor of midnight studies, crept two dull spots of hectic color. His eyes glistened with the gleam of the inspired artist, who behind the printed music sees the soul of the composer.

Save only for his short, pompadoured red hair, bristling above his forehead like a stiff, wiry brush, and his chin, too square and stubborn for a dreamer, Homer Hendricks, who made the law his profession and music his recreation, presented all of the characteristics of the picturesque genius.

The group in the library had crowded close to the hall door, as though fearing to miss a note in the rolling climax from the piano above. Montague Weston, tossing his neglected cigarette aside, was the first to break the spell.

"He's a wonder!" he breathed.

The girl in white at his elbow glanced toward him with swift enthusiasm.

"Doubly so! To think that a man who can make music like that is also rated as the leading corporation lawyer in the State!"

Weston shrugged. "Yes, he calls his piano only his plaything."

The girl lowered her voice. "Is it true—you know this is my first visit here—that he is as eccentric as we read in those sensational newspaper articles?"

A slow smile broke over Weston's face. "That depends on your idea of eccentricity, Miss Morrison. Some persons, for instance, might deem his present performance the height of oddity. Hendricks never plays except when he is alone in his own music-room with the door closed!"

"Really!" The girl's eyes were wide with her amazement.

"And again"—Weston was evidently enjoying the other's naive curiosity—"the fact that Mr. Hendricks has condescended to join our theater party tonight suggests another of his peculiarities. I believe this is the first evening in ten years that he has left his piano before midnight! But then this is a special occasion."

"Hilda Wentworth's birthday?" the girl interjected.

Weston nodded.

"All of the affection of a lonely bachelor without a domestic circle of his own is bound up in Homer Hendricks's love for his niece. And I happen to know, Miss Morrison, how very much alone such a man can be!"

At the wistful note in Weston's voice, the vivacious Miss Morrison glanced away quickly.

"I should not think that would apply to your case!" she said lightly. "If all reports are true, Monty Weston has won almost as great a reputation as a heart-breaker as he has as a trust-breaker!"

"You flatter both my social and my legal ability!" Weston laughed. He glanced at his watch. "By Jove, it's after eight! Where are Hilda and Bob Grayson?"

He turned so suddenly as he put the question that his companion gazed at him in surprise. The second of the two women in the group, Muriel Thornton, smiled shrewdly.

"Hilda went up-stairs a moment ago," she volunteered. "As for Bob," she paused significantly as the shadow deepened on Weston's face. "Where is Bob?" she added artlessly.

The rivalry of Weston and Grayson, the struggling young architect, for the favors of Hilda Wentworth had too long been a matter of gossip for the point of the question to pass unnoticed.

Wilkins, the fourth member of the group, essayed an eager answer in the pause that followed.

"Bob had a business engagement in his rooms, I believe, and left directly after dinner. He was to have been back by eight, though."

Up-stairs, the music still continued. Homer Hendricks had reached the finale of the overture, and Rossini's majestic strains were rolling out with the sweep of a lashing surf.

Weston strolled to the door.

"'William Tell' is nearing the end, I fancy. Listen!"

The speaker was right. It was the end—but not the end that either the musician or his audience were expecting.

Above the crash of the music rang out the sudden, muffled report of a revolver!

From the piano came a long, echoing discord,

as though the player's arm had fallen heavily to the keys.

And then silence—a silence so intense that the low breathing of the group in the library, stricken suddenly motionless, sounded with strange distinctness!

For a moment the quartet stood staring at one another, helpless, dumb, under the spell of an overwhelming bewilderment.

Miss Morrison fell back against the wall, panting like a frightened deer, her eyes staring up the winding stairway as though they would pierce the closed door above and see—what?

Of the two men, Weston was the prompter to act.

Jerking his companion by the elbow as though to arouse him to the necessity of the situation, he sprang out of the doorway, taking the steps to the second floor two at a bound.

John Wilkins, glancing hesitatingly at the women, followed more slowly at his shoulder.

From the end of the upper hall came the sound of running steps as the men reached it. A tall, slight, fair-haired girl, in a green satin evening gown, clutched Weston's arm with a wild, questioning stare.

For the first time Wilkins sensed the spell of tragedy. In the girl's eyes was a gleam of undisguised terror.

"The shot?" she burst out. "It came from——"

Weston nodded shortly, even curtly, as he jerked his head toward the door of the music-room, still closed, and followed the motion with a quick step. Wilkins reached forward and touched the girl's shoulder awkwardly.

"Don't you think I had better escort you below, Miss Wentworth?"

The girl shook off his fingers impatiently.

Weston's hand was on the knob of the music-room door. He turned it abruptly. A puzzled frown swept his face, and he turned it again more violently. The door was locked.

Hilda Wentworth darted to his side, tearing his hand away almost fiercely and beating the panels sharply with her knuckles.

"Uncle! Uncle! It is I, Hilda!"

The silence was unbroken.

The girl redoubled her efforts, tearing at the wood with her fingers and raising her voice almost to a shriek.

Then of a sudden she stepped back, turned with a low, gasping wail, and sank into the arms of a tall, broad-shouldered young man with the build of an athlete, who sprang up the stairs past Wilkins's hesitating figure just in time to catch her.

Weston glanced at the newcomer with a swift hardening of his lips. "Lend a hand here, Grayson!" he jerked out. "We've got to break in this door!"

"In Heaven's name, why?"

"No time for questions, man!" Weston's tones were curt. "Hendricks is in there. We heard a shot. We don't——"

"A shot?"

The words might have been a spur. The speaker lowered the body of the fainting girl to the floor, and sprang to the door with a vigor that made the others stare in spite of the tension of the moment.

Poising himself for an instant, he launched his body toward the oaken panels. There was a sharp splintering of wood.

Weston muttered a low cry of satisfaction and joined him in a second assault. The door shivered on its hinges.

The girl on the floor raised herself on her elbow and watched the two with a white, strained face.

The men drew back with muscles taut and hurled themselves a third time toward the barrier.

II

This time the attack was successful. The door fell inward so abruptly that they were thrown to their knees.

Before they could rise, a satin-clad figure sprang past them from the hall and threw itself with a cry on the body of a man in evening clothes, huddled on the floor.

Just above his left ear showed a gaping bullet-hole, from which a thin stream of blood was already trickling down on to the rug beneath him.

His eyes were fixed in a ghastly stare which permitted no second question as to his condition. Homer Hendricks was dead!

Weston raised the girl to her feet with the commanding gesture of a strong-minded man in a sudden emergency.

"Hilda—Miss Wentworth—you must let us take you down-stairs. This is no place for you."

"Oh, Uncle! Poor Uncle!" sobbed the girl unheeding.

Weston darted a swift glance around the room and toward the stairs. The women below were evidently not yet aware of the situation.

Wilkins from the hall was surveying the scene like a man in a nightmare, with a face from which every vestige of color had fled.

Grayson was still standing by the shattered door, with his hands clenched as though in a quick, nervous spasm.

At Weston's words he approached the girl with an added sentence of entreaty.

She nodded dully, flashed a last, despairing glance at the body on the floor, and suffered him to take her arm without resistance.

There was a certain suggestion of intimacy in the action, which brought a sudden scowl to Weston's features, as he said crisply:

"Of course, Grayson, you will explain to the ladies. As for the rest of it, you had better have them remain until——"

"The police?" Grayson finished inquiringly. "Shall I telephone?"

Weston hesitated, with a glance at Wilkins. The latter was still maintaining his position in the doorway as though fearing to enter.

"The police?" he repeated huskily. His eyes were riveted on the body of Hendricks as though held by a magnet. "I—I suppose so. This is awful, gentlemen!"

The attitude of the three men in the face of the sudden tragedy was curiously suggestive of their characters—Weston, with the crisply directing demeanor of the man accustomed to leadership; Grayson, frankly bewildered, with his attention centered on the girl's distress rather than the harsher features of the situation; Wilkins, passively content to allow another to direct his actions.

Hilda Wentworth gathered up her skirts and gently released herself from Grayson's hand.

In her face was a forced calmness, to a close observer more expressive of inward suffering than even her first outburst of grief.

As Grayson made a move to follow her, she turned with a low sentence. "I would prefer that you stay here, Bob!"

Her, inflection, and the glance which accompanied it, brought another swiftly veiled scowl to Weston's face. He strode to the end of the room and did not turn until Wilkins had led Miss Wentworth to the stairs.

Grayson, in the center of the apartment, had dug his hands into his trousers-pockets and was watching him curiously.

"A beastly bad business, Bob!" Weston spoke nervously, in odd contrast to his former curt tones.

Grayson jerked his head almost imperceptibly toward the motionless body on the carpet.

"What on earth made him do it?"

"*Him* do it?" There was an obvious note of surprise in Weston's voice. "Heavens, Bob, can't you see it's not—not *that*?"

Grayson recoiled as from a blow.

"Not suicide?" His tone raised itself with a shrill suddenness. "Why, man, it must be! You don't mean, you can't mean——"

Weston lifted his eyebrows questioningly. "Do men shoot themselves without a weapon, Bob?"

Grayson sprang abruptly past the other, stooped swiftly over the silent form of Homer Hendricks, and turned his eyes, fiercely across the adjacent stretch of carpet.

Weston watched him somberly.

"Are you convinced?" he queried at length.

Grayson pushed back the only chair in that end of the room, saw that it concealed nothing, and then, seizing an end of the elaborately carved piano, in front of which the body of the dead man rested, tugged until he forced it an inch from the wall.

His eyes swept the crack thus exposed, and he stepped back with a gesture of bewilderment.

"Have you found it?" Weston ventured. There was the barest trace of a sneer in his voice.

Grayson sprang across at him and clutched his shoulder.

"The weapon, man! Where is it? I say it must be here!"

Weston glanced at the other's flushed features calmly.

"I told you, Bob, there was none. Or, perhaps, you think that a dead man can rise to his feet and toss the gun that has ended his life out of the window?"

"The window?" Grayson muttered. Weston's sneer escaped him.

Darting to the three windows of the music-room, he flung back the drawn curtains of each in turn. They were all locked, and neither the glass nor the curtains showed a mark of disturbance.

Weston followed his movements with folded arms.

"There is still the door, Bob. And remember that is the only other possible exit." He hesitated. "If you will take the trouble to raise it from the floor, you will discover a fact which I learned some minutes ago. The key was turned from the *inside* and not from the *outside*!"

Grayson glanced at the other for a long moment in silence; then, stepping across the carpet with the resolution of a man determined to accept only the evidence of his own eyes, he raised the shattered panels until the lock was exposed.

The key, bent by the force of the fall, was still firmly fixed on the inward side of the door!

Grayson rose from his knees like a man groping in a brain-whirling maze.

"Sit down, Bob!" Weston pushed across a chair and forced the other into it. "We've got to face this thing coolly."

"Coolly!" Grayson's voice rose almost to a hysterical laugh. "Good Heavens! Are you a man or a machine? You tell me that Hendricks did not kill himself——"

"Could not!" Weston corrected in a level tone.

"And now," Grayson burst on unheeding, "you show me that he was not——"

"Murdered?" Weston completed calmly. "That is where you are wrong. I have shown you no such inference!"

Grayson passed his hand wearily over his brow.

"We are not dealing with spirits, man! You forget that the windows are fastened, the door locked——"

"I forget nothing!" said Weston coldly.

Grayson kicked back his chair impatiently. "Then, if Hendricks's murderer has not vanished into thin air, how——"

"That, my dear boy," said Weston softly, "is a question which these gentlemen may be able to answer for us!"

As he spoke, he motioned toward the hall.

Wilkins had appeared at the head of the stairs with two newcomers, both of whom were obviously policemen, although only one was in uniform.

Wilkins paused awkwardly at the door, with his hand on the shoulder of the man in civilian clothes.

"Lieutenant Perry, of headquarters," he announced formally, "Mr. Weston and Mr. Grayson!"

Weston extended his hand with a subtle suggestion of deference which brought a gratified flush to the officer's face.

He was a short, stocky, round-headed man with all of the evidences of the stubborn police bulldog, although the suggestion of any pronounced mental ability was lacking.

His eyes swept the body of the dead man and the details of the room with professional stoicism. Motioning to his companion, he knelt over Hendricks's stiffening form.

"Bullet entered at the left ear," he muttered. "Death probably instantaneous!" He straightened with the conventional police frown. "Where's the weapon, gentlemen?"

Grayson was silent, content that Weston should act as spokesman. The latter flung out his hands.

"We thought you could find it for us!" he answered shortly.

"Then you have not found it?" There was a flash of suspicion in the lieutenant's voice.

"We have not!"

The lieutenant jotted down a scrawling line in his note-book.

"Are we to believe this murder, then?" he rasped.

"I should prefer that you draw your own conclusions, Lieutenant!"

For an instant the officer's pencil was poised in the air, then he closed his note-book with a jerk, thrust his pencil into his pocket, and walked quickly to the closed windows, and then to the door. A growing coldness was apparent in every movement.

"Help me here, Burke!" he snapped to his subordinate. "Stand back, gentlemen!" he continued with almost a growl as Weston made a motion as though to assist.

The next moment the broken door was raised slowly back against the wall. The lieutenant's eyes fell on the lock with the twisted key. With a grimness he did not attempt to conceal, he whirled on the two men behind him.

"What kind of a yarn are you trying to give me?" His hand pointed first to the locked door and then to the fastened windows. "Do you think I was born yesterday? Come, gents, out with the truth!"

"The truth?" said Weston curtly.

The lieutenant bristled. "Just so—and the sooner you let me have it the better for all parties concerned! First you tell me there is no weapon, and would have me infer that Mr. Hendricks did not kill himself. Then I find that the room is locked as tight as a drum and there is no possible way for anyone else to have fired the shot—and escape. Do you think I am blind? You are either covering up the fact of suicide, or trying to shield the murderer!"

Lieutenant Perry paused, quite out of breath, with his face very red and his right hand clenched with the violence of his emotions.

The turn of affairs was so abrupt and unexpected that Grayson stood speechless. Weston had made an angry step forward, with his eyes flashing, when a low exclamation from the policeman, Burke, broke the tension.

In his right hand he was holding out a woman's white kid glove, with its thumb stained with a ragged splotch of still fresh blood.

"Found it down by the wall, sir! It was covered up by the door!"

Lieutenant Perry snatched the glove from the other's hand and held it toward the light. On the wrist was a delicately embroidered monogram in white silk.

Grayson with difficulty smothered a sharp cry. Then his eyes sought Weston's face, grown suddenly cold and hard. Both men had recognized the object on the instant. The glove was the property of Hilda Wentworth!

"H. W." The lieutenant deciphered the letters slowly. "And pray, gentlemen," he said mockingly, nodding toward Weston with a grin of exultation, "what person do these interesting initials fit?"

"I think I can answer that question, sir!"

The words came in a clear, cold tone from the doorway, and Hilda Wentworth, pressing her way past Wilkins's resisting arm, stepped into the room.

"The glove is mine, officer!"

She held out her hand, but the lieutenant, with a low laugh that brought the blood flaming to the girl's face, thrust the glove into his pocket.

His eyes flashed from Weston to Grayson significantly.

"I fancy, gentlemen, I have found the explanation of your cock and bull story!" he said slowly.

Grayson sprang forward with a growl.

"You will take those words back or—or——"

Weston caught his shoulder sternly. "Gently, Bob! You are only making a bad matter worse!"

The lieutenant turned to his man, Burke, ignoring Grayson's threatening attitude. "Clear the room and telephone the coroner! As for you, Miss Wentworth, I am sorry, but——"

"What?" asked the girl steadily. Reversing the situation of a few moments before, she seemed the calmest member of the group.

"I am compelled to ask you not to leave the house until I give you permission!" the officer finished brusquely.

A sudden pallor swept Hilda Wentworth's face and for an instant her eyes closed; but she fought back the weakness resolutely. With a curt nod she stepped to the door.

"I am at your service!" she said simply.

Wilkins offered her his arm, and Weston followed the two without a backward glance. Grayson hesitated, still scowling at the lieutenant's stocky figure. The officer was glaring from the face of the dead man to the polished surface of the piano, with his nerves plainly on a feather edge.

Grayson shrugged, and had made a step toward the hall when his gaze was arrested almost mechanically by a glitter of green on the red carpet, near the wall at his right. He had taken a second step when a curious impulse—was it the factor of chance?—caused him to turn swiftly. Lieutenant Perry was bending over the body of Homer Hendricks with his face for the moment averted. Grayson's hand felt hurriedly over the carpet and closed about a small greenish object at his feet. Straightening, he walked rapidly through the doorway.

In the hall, he glanced at the object in his hand. It was a green jade ball, whose diameter was perhaps that of a quarter. Dropping it into his pocket, the young man ran down the stairs.

III

"I have earned a vacation, Nora, and I intend to take it."

Madelyn Mack elevated her arms in a luxurious yawn, as she pushed aside the traveling-bag at her feet. The eight o'clock train had just brought her back from Denver, and six weeks in the tortuous windings of the Ramsen bullion case. I had received her telegram from Buffalo just in time to meet her at the Grand Central station, and we had driven at once to her Fifth Avenue office. As I noted the tired lines under her eyes, and the droop of her shoulders, I could appreciate something of the strain under which she had been laboring. I nodded slowly.

"Yes, you need a vacation," I agreed.

Madelyn impatiently pushed aside a stack of unopened letters. "And I intend to take it!" she repeated almost belligerently. "Business or no business!"

"With a ten-thousand-dollar fee for six weeks' work," I laughed somewhat enviously, "you should worry!"

Madelyn tossed her accumulated correspondence recklessly into a corner of her desk, and drew down its roll-top with a bang.

"I feel like dissipating tonight, Nora. Are you up to a cabaret? A place with noise enough to drown out every echo of work!"

At her elbow the telephone shrilled suddenly. Mechanically Madelyn took down the receiver. Almost with the first sentence over the wire, I could see her features contract.

"Yes, Mr. Grayson, this is Miss Mack talking. What is that?" In a moment she clapped her hand over the transmitter, and turned a wry face to me. "Was I foolish enough to talk about a rest, Nora? Homer Hendricks has just been shot—murder or suicide!"

Her next sentence was directed at the telephone. "Never mind what Lieutenant Perry says, Mr. Grayson! I'll be over at once. Yes, I said *at once*!"

She hung up the receiver, and sprang to her feet.

"Come on, Nora! I'll give you the details on the way!" Her weariness had vanished as though it had never existed.

She slammed the door of the office, leaving her bag where she had tossed it, and jabbed the bell for the elevator. Not until we were in her car that had been waiting at the curb, and speeding up the Avenue, did she speak again.

"You know of Hendricks, the lawyer, of course, and his niece, Hilda Wentworth——"

"You don't mean to say that he has been killed, and the girl is suspected——"

Madelyn shrugged. "The police seem to think so!"

She drew over to her end of the seat, and subsided into an abstracted silence, as we swerved across toward the Drive. I knew that it was hopeless to expect her to volunteer further information, and, indeed, doubted if she possessed it.

When the car whirled up to our destination Madelyn was out on the walk before the last revolution of the wheels had ceased.

We were not more than half-way up the steps of the Hendricks residence when the door flew open, and a young man, who had evidently been stationed in the hall awaiting our arrival, sprang forward to meet us.

Madelyn smiled as she caught his impulsively extended hand.

"Any new developments, Mr. Grayson?"

"None, except that Coroner Smedley is here. He is up-stairs now with the police."

Madelyn led us to the farther end of the veranda.

"Before we go in, it will be just as well if you give me a brief summary of what has happened."

Grayson walked back and forth, his hands clenched at his sides, talking rapidly. Madelyn heard him in silence, the darkness concealing her expression.

"Is that all?" she queried at length. For a moment she stood peering out over the veranda railing. "Miss Wentworth lived with her uncle, I take it?"

"Yes."

"And inherits his property?"

Grayson growled an affirmative.

"Suppose I change my angle, and ask if you are prepared to explain your own whereabouts at the time of the crime?"

"I have done so!"

Madelyn's eyes hardened.

"We won't mince matters, Mr. Grayson. From the police standpoint, Miss Wentworth and yourself, as her probably favored suitor, are the two persons most likely to profit by Mr. Hendricks's death. It may be awkward, perhaps exceedingly awkward, that you were the only two in the house not accounted for at the moment of the shot!"

"I have told you the truth!" Grayson dug his hands into his pockets sullenly.

Madelyn turned abruptly toward the door, and then paused. "Was Mr. Hendricks aware of your sentiments toward his niece?"

Grayson hesitated. "Certainly."

"And was not enthusiastic on the subject?"

"Well, perhaps not—er—enthusiastic." Grayson's stammer was obvious. "To be quite frank, he preferred——"

"Yes?"

"Monty Weston; but, of course——"

"I think that is enough," said Madelyn quietly. "Will you kindly lead the way in?"

Grayson's hand, fumbling in his pockets, was suddenly withdrawn.

"By the way, here is something I almost forgot. I picked it up on the floor of Hendricks's room as we were leaving."

He extended the curious green jade ball he had found in the music-room.

Madelyn's eyes narrowed. Then she said casually, "Quite an interesting little ornament," and dropped it into her bag.

The hall of the Hendricks house was empty. The members of the tragically disrupted theatre party had retreated to the library, and were endeavoring nervously to maintain the semblance of a conversation. The police were still busy upstairs.

"You had better join your friends," said Mad-elyn to Grayson. "We will be down presently." And she ran lightly up the broad stairway, as I followed.

The music-room of Homer Hendricks presented a scene of confusion shattering all the precedents of its peaceful history, and almost sufficient, one was tempted to think, to call back its late master to resent the intrusion on his cherished sanctum.

The body of Mr. Hendricks was still stretched on the carpet where it had fallen. It, and the massive piano, were the only objects in the room that had been left unchanged.

Madelyn gave a shrug of disgust as we paused in the doorway and surveyed the scene of ravage.

"Are you expecting to find gold pieces concealed in the furniture, gentlemen?"

Lieutenant Perry whirled sharply. "May I inquire, Miss Mack, since when have you been in charge of this case?"

The officer essayed a wink toward his companions, who had been increased by two plain-clothes-men and the coroner since Grayson's telephone call.

Madelyn smiled. "Your powers of humor, Lieutenant, are exceeded only by your powers of deduction!"

Her glance wandered over the torn-up room, with its chairs turned upside down, its rugs rolled up from the floor, and even its few objects of bric-a-brac removed from their places, and deposited in a corner. The search for the missing weapon that had done Homer Hendricks to death had been thorough—if nothing else.

Madelyn's eyes rested for a second time on the piano of the dead man. The instrument seemed to exert a peculiar fascination for her. With her glance fixed on the keyboard, which no one had seen fit to close, she bowed to the grinning lieutenant.

"Will I be trespassing if I take a glance around?"

"Oh, help yourself! I reckon we have found about all there is to find!"

"Have you?" said Madelyn lightly.

The police officer righted a chair and sat

down heavily on its cushioned seat, watching Madelyn's lithe figure as she walked across to Hendricks's body. As a matter of fact when she dropped to her knees, and held a pocket magnifying lens close to the white, rigid face of the dead man, she had the unreserved attention of every occupant of the room.

The lieutenant, realizing the fact, shrugged his shoulders. "Miss Sherlock Holmes at work!" he said in a tone loud enough to reach Madelyn's ears.

"I beg your pardon," said Madelyn, without shifting the position of her lens, "have you any information as to when Mr. Hendricks visited this room last, that is, previous to this evening?"

Lieutenant Perry hesitated.

"Why, er——"

"He had not been here for ten days, Miss Mack," spoke up one of his subordinates, and then continuing, before he became aware of the scowl of his superior, "He and his niece were out of town on a visit, and only arrived home today."

"Thank you," said Madelyn, rising, and leaning carelessly against the piano. "May I trouble you with another question, Lieutenant?"

The lieutenant glared silently.

"Did Mr. Hendricks use tobacco?"

"He did not!"

"Thank you!" The suspicion of a smile tinged Madelyn's face.

Lieutenant Perry crossed his left leg carelessly over his knee and thrust his thumbs into the armholes of his waistcoat. The farther plain-clothesman nudged his companion. This attitude of the lieutenant's was a characteristic prelude either to one of his favorite jokes or a verbal fusillade, designed to crush an opponent to the dust.

"If you are quite through with your clue-searching, Miss Mack," he said with mock humbleness, "I would like your expert opinion on a little bit of evidence we have picked up!"

His right hand disengaged itself for a moment and produced the blood-stained glove of Hilda Wentworth. Mr. Perry held it up almost caressingly.

"Would you care to take a squint at this with that high-power lens of yours?"

"Oh, I hardly think so!" said Madelyn indifferently. "That belongs to Miss Wentworth, does it not?"

"Righto!"

"Then, if I might make a suggestion, I would return it to the young lady."

"Oh, you would, would you?" exploded the lieutenant. "What do you think of that, men? That is the richest joke I have heard for a month!"

Madelyn sauntered to the door.

"I may have the pleasure of seeing you below, Lieutenant," she said as she joined me.

The moment she had disappeared from the view of the men in the music-room her assumption of careless indifference vanished. Her lips closed in a tense line, as she paused at the head of the stairs.

"If those imbeciles had only left that room as it was!" Her hands were clenched as though every nerve was a-quiver. "Nora, I have got to have ten minutes alone in there! I must manage it!" She turned abruptly. "Will you kindly give Lieutenant Perry Miss Wentworth's compliments, and tell him she desires an immediate interview with him and the coroner in the library?"

"But," I stammered, "she doesn't!"

Madelyn glared, and then continued as though I had not interrupted her. "They will probably take two of the policemen down-stairs with them. That will leave only one behind. If you can inveigle him outside, Nora, the obligation won't be forgotten!"

"You speak as though I was a siren!" I snapped. "Promise him you will publish his picture in *The Bugle* in the morning," said Madelyn impatiently.

She opened the nearest door, and disappeared behind it, as I returned to the music-room in my role of assumed messenger. I managed to repeat Madelyn's instructions without so much as a quiver at Lieutenant Perry's sudden scowl. With a nod to the coroner, he brushed past me at once.

Madelyn's calculation proved uncannily correct. The two plain-clothes-men followed Coroner Smedley silently down the stairs in the lieutenant's wake. Only a red-faced rounds-man was left twirling his stick disconsolately in the littered room.

"Good evening!" I smiled.

He glanced up with obvious welcome at the prospect of companionship.

I plunged directly to the point. "This is a big case, Mr. Dennis," I began, noting with relief that he was a professional acquaintance of mine. "It ought to mean something to you, eh?"

He grunted non-committally.

"I say, have you a good picture of yourself at home?"

Mr. Dennis looked interested.

"That is, one which would be good enough for publication in *The Bugle*?"

Mr. Dennis looked more interested.

"Because if you have," I continued enticingly, "and will do me a favor, I will see that it is given a good position in tomorrow's story."

"What is the favor?"

"Oh, merely that you let me talk to you for ten minutes in the hall! A friend of mine wants a chance to look over this room without disturbance."

"You mean Miss Mack?" asked Dennis, suspiciously.

I smiled. "That picture of yours would look mighty nice, with a quarter of a column write-up under it. I expect Mrs. Dennis would be so tickled that she would appreciate a present from me of twenty-five copies of the paper to send to her friends!"

Dennis walked abruptly into the hall. "Come on!" he snapped.

As we reached the end of the corridor, I saw Madelyn step quietly into the room we had vacated.

I wondered curiously if Hilda Wentworth would rise to the occasion sufficiently to hold the attention of the suspicious Mr. Perry, and speculated grimly what would be the result

if the lieutenant should return unexpectedly to the upper floor. My fears, however, proved unfounded. Before the ten minutes were over, Madelyn reappeared, beckoned to me pleasantly, and slipped a crumpled bill into Dennis's hand as she passed him.

"I'll look for that picture at the office, Mr. Dennis," I said cordially. And then I turned anxiously to Madelyn. "Did you find anything?"

"Is it fate, or Providence, or just naturally Devil's luck that traps the transgressor?" returned Madelyn irrelevantly. She was tapping a slender blue envelope. "Exhibits A and B in the case of Homer Hendricks," she continued. "A small jade ball, and a spoonful of tobacco ashes. They sound commonplace enough, don't they?" And she thoughtfully descended the stairs.

At the door of the library she faced the group inside with a slight bow. The hum of conversation ceased. From an adjoining alcove, Miss Wentworth, nervously facing a battery of questions from Lieutenant Perry and the coroner, noted our arrival with an expression of hastily concealed relief. It was evident that the task of keeping the gentlemen of the law occupied had taxed the girl's nerves to the utmost.

Grayson had taken a position as near the alcove as he could venture, and was glowering at her inquisitors, apparently not caring whether they saw his scowls or not.

"I will be obliged for a few moments' conversation, gentlemen!" said Madelyn pleasantly. "A very few moments, I assure you. I will talk to Mr. Wilkins first, if I may."

John Wilkins rose from his chair, as I found a vacant seat in the library, and joined Madelyn in the hall. In less than two minutes he returned, with his face wearing an expression of almost laughable bewilderment.

"Evidently the famous Miss Mack does not believe in lengthy cross-examinations," commented Miss Morrison as he resumed his chair.

"She asked me just four questions," said Wilkins dubiously, "and only two of them had to do with the affair up-stairs. She cut me short when I started the account of our finding the body."

Lieutenant Perry, as though to show his disdain, deepened the rasp in his examination of Miss Wentworth as he saw Weston take Wilkins's place in the hall.

Weston glanced at his watch as he returned. "It took me just one minute more than you to pass through the ordeal, old man," he confided to Wilkins, with something like a grin.

Lieutenant Perry stepped out of the alcove with a gesture of finality.

"Have you a version of the case to give to *The Bugle*, Lieutenant?" I asked, as a ring at the doorbell and a shuffling of feet on the veranda announced the belated arrival of other members of the newspaper fraternity.

The lieutenant darted a sullen glance in the direction of Hilda Wentworth. "You may say for me," he said acidly, "that, whether suicide or murder, a certain near relative of the dead man is holding back the truth, and, and——" his eyes traveled slowly around the room, "the police expect to find measures very shortly to make that person speak!"

A low cry broke from Hilda Wentworth. Darting across the room, she caught the lieutenant's arm imploringly.

"Oh, please, sir, don't—don't——"

"I hardly think you need alarm yourself, Miss Wentworth!"

Madelyn was smiling quietly from the doorway. "I trust, Miss Noraker," she continued, addressing me, "that *The Bugle* will do Miss Wentworth the justice, and myself the favor, of announcing that I am prepared to *prove* that no relative of Mr. Hendricks had any connection with his death, or possesses any knowledge of how it was brought about! And furthermore, for Lieutenant Perry's peace of mind, you may add that it is a case not of suicide—but of murder!"

The lieutenant's face went a sudden, pasty yellow. Madelyn slowly drew on her gloves.

"By the way, Lieutenant, if you and the cor-

oner have time to meet me here at ten o'clock tomorrow morning, I will take pleasure in corroborating my statements!"

She bowed to the other occupants of the room. "I will also include in that invitation Miss Wentworth and the gentlemen who were present at the time of the murder."

She stepped back, and, adroitly skirting the group of newly arrived newspaper men, ran lightly across the pavement to her car.

At the steps of the motor I caught her. "Madelyn, just one question, *please*! How in the name of Heaven could the murderer shoot, and then escape through a locked door?"

Madelyn drew down her veil wearily.

"He didn't shoot!" she said shortly.

IV

Hilda Wentworth, haggard-faced after a feverishly tossing night, was toying with her breakfast grapefruit and tea, which the motherly housekeeper had insisted on bringing to her room, when the bell of the telephone tinkled sharply.

Miss Wentworth took down the receiver wearily; but, at the sound of the voice at the other end of the wire, she brightened instantly.

"Good morning! This is Miss Mack. I am not going to ask you if you had a restful night."

"Restful night!" the girl cried hysterically. "Two of those odious policemen have been patrolling the house constantly, and watching my room as though I would steal away with the family spoons if I had a ghost of a chance!"

Miss Mack's exclamation was only partly audible, but the girl smiled wanly.

"I shall be detained perhaps a half an hour longer than I expected this morning, Miss Wentworth. If you will explain this to Lieutenant Perry, and the other gentlemen, I will appreciate it."

Miss Mack hung up the receiver abruptly. It was obvious that she was in a hurry. But there was an inflection in her tones that brought a new color to Hilda Wentworth's face, and she was surprised to find herself return to her breakfast with almost a relish.

For a moment, after she had finished the call, Madelyn sat with a pen poised thoughtfully over a pad of writing paper. Then, tossing the pen aside, she turned to the telephone again.

"Hello! *Bugle* office?" she snapped, as a belated click answered her call. "Oh, is that you, Nora? Can you give me a few moments? Good! I wish you would call at the office of Ambrose Murray, the president of the Third National Bank, and tell him that you were sent by Miss Mack. He may, or may not, have certain information to give you. You will deliver his message to me at the Hendricks home at a quarter after ten. Wait for me outside. Do you understand—outside?"

As the tall, old-fashioned clock in the library of the late Homer Hendricks rang out the stroke of half past ten, it gazed down on a group of six persons, whose attitudes presented an interesting study in contrasting emotions.

In the corner nearest the door stood Lieutenant Perry and Coroner Smedley. The lieutenant had refused the offer of a chair, and the coroner, who worshipped at the Perry shrine for political reasons, essayed to copy the other's majesty of demeanor, his smile of supreme boredom, and even his very attitude.

Grayson had drawn Hilda Wentworth's chair thoughtfully into the shadow of a huge palm, and was bending over her in an effort to buoy her spirits, which was apparently so successful that Weston, seated with Wilkins on the opposite side of the room, scowled savagely.

"Ten thirty!" snapped Mr. Perry, ostentatiously consulting the gold repeater, which the members of the detective department had presented to him on the occasion of his silver wedding anniversary. "I will give Miss Mack just five minutes more. I have work to do!"

"The five minutes will not be necessary, Lieutenant," said a quiet voice from the hall, as Madelyn and I paused in the doorway.

"Quite dramatic!" came from Mr. Perry.

Madelyn's eyes swept the room. Her graceful serenity had disappeared in a sudden tenseness. "You will please follow me up-stairs," she said, moving back.

"Up-stairs?" growled Mr. Perry.

Madelyn turned to the stairway without answer.

Miss Wentworth and Grayson were the first to comply, and the lieutenant, observing that the others were joining them, brought up a sullen rear, with the coroner endeavoring to copy his appearance of contempt.

Madelyn paused at the door of the music-room, and waited silently for us to enter. The shattered door had been temporarily repaired, and placed on a new set of hinges. Madelyn closed it, and stepped to the center of the room. She stood for a moment, staring abstractedly up at a brightly colored Turner landscape. A silence crept through the apartment, so pregnant that even Lieutenant Perry squared his shoulders.

"I am going to tell you the story of a tragedy," began Madelyn, with her eyes still fixed on the landscape as though studying its bold coloring.

"In all of my peculiar experience I have never met with a crime so artistically conceived and so diabolically carried out. From a personal standpoint, I may even say that I owe the author my thanks for one of the most interesting problems which it has been my fortune to confront. In these days of bungled crime, it is a relief to cross wits with one who has really raised murder to a fine art!"

Her left hand mechanically, almost unconsciously, dropped a small round object into the palm of her right hand. It was a green jade ball. From somewhere in the room came a sudden low sound like the hiss of a trampled snake.

Madelyn's eyes dropped to the ball almost caressingly. "I am now about to re-enact the drama of Mr. Homer Hendricks's murder. I hardly think it will be necessary to caution silence until I am quite through!"

She stepped to the piano at the other end of the room, twirled the music stool a moment, and, carefully inspecting its height like a musician critical of trifles, took her seat at the key-board.

Her hands ran lightly over the keys with the touch of the born music-lover. Then, without preamble, she broke into the storm scene from "William Tell."

Miss Wentworth was gazing at Grayson with a sort of dumb wonder. The young man pressed her arm gently.

The expression of superior boredom had entirely left Lieutenant Perry's ruddy features.

Madelyn's fingers seemed fairly to race over the keys. The thundering music of Rossini rolled through the apartment. Madelyn was reaching the climax in that superb musical painting of the war of the elements.

Again that low sibilant sound like a serpent's hiss sounded from somewhere in the taut-nerved audience, to be drowned by the sharp, clear-cut report of a revolver!

Madelyn's fingers wavered, her elbow fell with a sharp discord on the keys, and she staggered back from the stool. In the front of the piano, at a point almost directly opposite her left temple, a small hole, perhaps the diameter of a quarter, had opened in the elaborate carving, and from it curled a thin spiral of blue smoke!

With a jagged splotch of powder extending from her temple to her cheek, Madelyn sprang to her feet. From the rear of the room, a man, crouching forward in his chair, darted toward the door. Lieutenant Perry's hand flashed from his pocket with the instinct of the veteran police-man. At the end of his outflung arm frowned the blue muzzle of a revolver.

"You may arrest Mr. Montague Weston for the murder of Homer Hendricks!" came the quiet voice of Madelyn.

The words, instead of a spur, acted with much the effect of a sledge-hammer on the agi-tated figure of Weston. For an instant he gazed wildly about the room like a man confronted with a ghastly specter. The steady coolness of purpose that had marked his brilliant rise at the bar had shriveled in the heart-stabbing moments

of Madelyn's demonstration. As Lieutenant Perry stretched a hand toward him, he fell in a sobbing heap at the officer's feet.

Madelyn jerked her head significantly from the white, drawn face of Hilda Wentworth to Weston's moaning form. The lieutenant fastened his hand on the man's collar and dragged him to his feet as the coroner flung open the door.

The suddenness of it all had gripped us as by a magnet. The creaking of a chair sounded in the tension with a sharpness that was almost painful. The denouement had occurred with the swift-ness of a film from a moving picture machine—and was blotted out as swiftly as the lieutenant closed the door behind his cowering prisoner.

Grayson breathed a long, deep sigh.

"How, how in thunder, Miss Mack, did——"

Madelyn had resumed her toying with the green jade ball. With a gesture almost like that of a schoolmistress addressing a dense student, she stepped across to the piano, and inserted the ball in the small, round hole in the heavy carv-ing, through which had floated the blue curl of smoke. It exactly matched six other balls of green jade, set into the panels in a fantastic orna-mentation.

"Before this instrument is used again," said Madelyn, as she turned, "I would recommend a thorough overhauling. Just behind the opening which I have filled is the muzzle of a revolver—loaded with a blank cartridge for this morn-ing's purpose, but which has not always been so harmless.

"From its trigger, you will find—as I assured myself last night—a wire spring connecting with one of the treble D flats on the keyboard. When Mr. Hendricks struck it in the overture of 'Wil-liam Tell,' and again when I repeated his action just now, the pressure of the key released the trigger of the weapon, and it was automatically exploded.

"When Weston attached the apparatus—your ten days' absence from the house, Miss Went-worth, giving him ample time—he used a paper substitute for the jade ball he had removed, and probably took occasion, when he entered the room last night, to cover over the exposed opening in the panels.

"Unfortunately for him, the imp of chance was dogging his trail. He dropped the jade ball—and the same perverse imp directed the hand of Nemesis to it.

"The psychological effect of my repetition of the crime, after the shock of the discovery of his apparatus, would have taxed a far stronger set of nerves than those of Mr. Weston!"

She paused, and then added in a musing afterthought, "Perhaps, you can tell me, Mr. Grayson, what cynical philosopher has said that all women are fickle? Mr. Weston happens to be an assiduous devotee of My Lady Nicotine. I fancy that he was so completely under her spell that he sought relief from the task of arranging his murder-spring in his favorite pipe. But she of Nicotine, perhaps in horror at his meditated crime, jilted her slave. As he bent over his work his pipe bowl was tilted ever so slightly—and the ashes, which fell with her favor, again aided the imp of chance to lead me to his trail!"

Madelyn shrugged her shoulders as though she were quite through, and then, with a sudden suggestion, continued, "The motive? What are the two greatest factors that sway men to evil?

"The first, of course, is greed. Weston, himself, will have to supply the details of his betrayal of the trust of Homer Hendricks. It was not until Miss Noraker brought me, just before I entered the house this morning, certain confidential information as to the financial condition of Weston, that I was absolutely certain of this link in my chain of evidence.

"Under an assumed name, he has been engineering certain questionable mining companies, and had even persuaded the man who was his life-long friend to invest a considerable share of his fortune in one of his projects. Faced by the imminence of exposure, and ruin, and unable to conceal longer the truth from Homer Hendricks, Weston's devilish ingenuity suggested the death of the man who had trusted him—and the means of carrying it out."

Madelyn walked slowly to the door, and then turned.

"I have forgotten the second of the two motives that I referred to. Of course, it is the factor of jealousy, or perhaps love. May I mention your name, Miss Wentworth?

"Goaded by the fear of losing you, he pilfered one of your gloves, and dropped it where a schoolboy was bound to see its connection with the crime. I daresay that he would have offered to establish your innocence on your promise to marry him. He could have done it in any one of a dozen ways, of course, without implicating himself."

Madelyn gave a sudden glance toward Wilkins and myself.

"I think that Mr. Grayson wishes to discuss that factor of love somewhat further with Miss Wentworth!"

As we stepped into the hall after her, she softly closed the door of the music-room.

AN INTANGIBLE CLEW

Anna Katharine Green

ANNA KATHARINE GREEN ROHLFS (1846–1935), known variously as the mother, grandmother, and godmother of the American detective story, has popularly and famously been credited with writing the first American detective novel by a woman, *The Leavenworth Case* (1878). The fact that her novel was preceded by *The Dead Letter* in 1867, by Seeley Regester (the nom de plume of Metta Victoria Fuller Victor), is significant mainly to historians and pedants, as *The Dead Letter* sank without notice while *The Leavenworth Case* became one of the bestselling detective novels of the nineteenth century.

That landmark novel introduced Ebenezer Gryce, a stolid, competent, and colorless policeman who bears many of the characteristics of Charles Dickens's Inspector Bucket (from *Bleak House*, 1852–1853) and Wilkie Collins's Sergeant Cuff (from *The Moonstone*, 1868). Gryce, dignified and gentle, inspires confidence even in those he interrogates. The enormous success of *The Leavenworth Case* induced Green to invent many more mysteries for Gryce to solve, including *A Strange Disappearance* (1880) and *Hand and Ring* (1883); the last, *The Mystery of the Hasty Arrow* (1917), was published forty years after the first.

Green also was one of the first authors to produce female detective protagonists, notably Amelia Butterworth, who often worked with Gryce and was of a higher social standing than the policeman, thereby allowing him access to a level of society that otherwise might have presented difficulties, and Violet Strange, a beautiful and wealthy young woman employed by a private detective agency who accepted cases only if they interested her.

"An Intangible Clew" was originally published in *The Golden Slipper and Other Problems for Violet Strange* (New York, G. P. Putnam's Sons, 1915).

An Intangible Clew

ANNA KATHARINE GREEN

"HAVE YOU STUDIED THE CASE?"

"Not I."

"Not studied the case which for the last few days has provided the papers with such conspicuous headlines?"

"I do not read the papers. I have not looked at one in a whole week."

"Miss Strange, your social engagements must be of a very pressing nature just now?"

"They are."

"And your business sense in abeyance?"

"How so?"

"You would not ask if you had read the papers."

To this she made no reply save by a slight toss of her pretty head. If her employer felt nettled by this show of indifference, he did not betray it save by the rapidity of his tones as, without further preamble and possibly without real excuse, he proceeded to lay before her the case in question.

"Last Tuesday night a woman was murdered in this city; an old woman, in a lonely house where she has lived for years. Perhaps you remember this house? It occupies a not inconspicuous site in Seventeenth Street—a house of the olden time?"

"No, I do not remember."

The extreme carelessness of Miss Strange's tone would have been fatal to her socially; but then, she would never have used it socially. This

they both knew, yet he smiled with his customary indulgence.

"Then I will describe it."

She looked around for a chair and sank into it. He did the same.

"It has a fanlight over the front door."

She remained impassive.

"And two old-fashioned strips of particoloured glass on either side."

"And a knocker between its panels which may bring money someday."

"Oh, you do remember! I thought you would, Miss Strange."

"Yes. Fanlights over doors are becoming very rare in New York."

"Very well, then. That house was the scene of Tuesday's tragedy. The woman who has lived there in solitude for years was foully murdered. I have since heard that the people who knew her best have always anticipated some such violent end for her. She never allowed maid or friend to remain with her after five in the afternoon; yet she had money—some think a great deal—always in the house."

"I am interested in the house, not in her."

"Yet, she was a character—as full of whims and crotchets as a nut is of meat. Her death was horrible. She fought—her dress was torn from her body in rags. This happened, you see, before her hour for retiring; some think as early as six in the afternoon. And"—here he made a rapid gesture to catch Violet's wandering attention—"in spite of this struggle; in spite of the fact that she was dragged from room to room—that her person was searched—and everything in the house searched—that drawers were pulled out of bureaus—doors wrenched off of cupboards—china smashed upon the floor—whole shelves denuded and not a spot from cellar to garret left unransacked, no direct clew to the perpetrator has been found—nothing that gives any idea of his personality save his display of strength and great cupidity. The police have even deigned to consult me—an unusual procedure—but I could find nothing, either. Evidences of fiendish purpose abound—of relentless search—but no clew to the man himself. It's uncommon, isn't it, not to have *any* clew?"

"I suppose so." Miss Strange hated murders and it was with difficulty she could be brought to discuss them. But she was not going to be let off; not this time.

"You see," he proceeded insistently, "it's not only mortifying to the police but disappointing to the press, especially as few reporters believe in the No-thoroughfare business. They say, and we cannot but agree with them, that no such struggle could take place and no such repeated goings to and fro through the house without some vestige being left by which to connect this crime with its daring perpetrator."

Still she stared down at her hands—those little hands so white and fluttering, so seemingly helpless under the weight of their many rings, and yet so slyly capable.

"She must have queer neighbours," came at last, from Miss Strange's reluctant lips. "Didn't they hear or see anything of all this?"

"She has no neighbours—that is, after half-past five o'clock. There's a printing establishment on one side of her, a deserted mansion on the other side, and nothing but warehouses back and front. There was no one to notice what took place in her small dwelling after the printing house was closed. She was the most courageous or the most foolish of women to remain there as

she did. But nothing except death could budge her. She was born in the room where she died; was married in the one where she worked; saw husband, father, mother, and five sisters carried out in turn to their graves through the door with the fanlight over the top—and these memories held her."

"You are trying to interest me in the woman. Don't."

"No, I'm not trying to interest you in her, only trying to explain her. There was another reason for her remaining where she did so long after all residents had left the block. She had a business."

"Oh!"

"She embroidered monograms for fine ladies."

"She did? But you needn't look at me like that. She never embroidered any for me."

"No? She did first-class work. I saw some of it. Miss Strange, *if* I could get you into that house for ten minutes—not to see her but to pick up the loose intangible thread which I am sure is floating around in it somewhere—wouldn't you go?"

Violet slowly rose—a movement which he followed to the letter.

"Must I express in words the limit I have set for myself in our affair?" she asked. "When, for reasons I have never thought myself called upon to explain, I consented to help you a little now and then with some matter where a woman's tact and knowledge of the social world might tell without offence to herself or others, I never thought it would be necessary for me to state that temptation must stop with such cases, or that I should not be asked to touch the sordid or the bloody. But it seems I was mistaken, and that I must stoop to be explicit. The woman who was killed on Tuesday might have interested me greatly as an embroiderer, but as a victim, not at all. What do you see in me, or miss in me, that you should drag me into an atmosphere of low-down crime?"

"Nothing, Miss Strange. You are by nature, as well as by breeding, very far removed from everything of the kind. But you will allow me to suggest that no crime is low-down which makes imperative demand upon the intellect and intuitive sense of its investigator. Only the most delicate touch can feel and hold the thread I've just spoken of, and *you* have the most delicate touch I know."

"Do not attempt to flatter me. I have no fancy for handling befouled spider webs. Besides, if I had—if such elusive filaments fascinated me—how could I, well-known in person and name, enter upon such a scene without prejudice to our mutual compact?"

"Miss Strange"—she had reseated herself, but so far he had failed to follow her example (an ignoring of the subtle hint that her interest might yet be caught, which seemed to annoy her a trifle)—"I should not even have suggested such a possibility had I not seen a way of introducing you there without risk to your position or mine. Among the boxes piled upon Mrs. Doolittle's table—boxes of finished work, most of them addressed and ready for delivery—was one on which could be seen the name of—shall I mention it?"

"Not mine? You don't mean mine? That would be too odd—too ridiculously odd. I should not understand a coincidence of that kind; no, I should not, notwithstanding the fact that I have lately sent out such work to be done."

"Yet it was your name, very clearly and precisely written—your whole name, Miss Strange. I saw and read it myself."

"But I gave the order to Madame Pirot on Fifth Avenue. How came my things to be found in the house of this woman of whose horrible death we have been talking?"

"Did you suppose that Madame Pirot did such work with her own hands?—or even had it done in her own establishment? Mrs. Doolittle was universally employed. She worked for a dozen firms. You will find the biggest names on most of her packages. But on this one—I allude to the one addressed to you—there was more to be seen than the name. These words were written on it in another hand. *Send without opening.*

This struck the police as suspicious; sufficiently so, at least, for them to desire your presence at the house as soon as you can make it convenient."

"To open the box?"

"Exactly."

The curl of Miss Strange's disdainful lip was a sight to see.

"You wrote those words yourself," she coolly observed. "While someone's back was turned, you whipped out your pencil and——"

"Resorted to a very pardonable subterfuge highly conducive to the public's good. But never mind that. Will you go?"

Miss Strange became suddenly demure.

"I suppose I must," she grudgingly conceded. "However obtained, a summons from the police cannot be ignored even by Peter Strange's daughter."

Another man might have displayed his triumph by smile or gesture; but this one had learned his rôle too well. He simply said:

"Very good. Shall it be at once? I have a taxi at the door."

But she failed to see the necessity of any such hurry. With sudden dignity she replied:

"That won't do. If I go to this house it must be under suitable conditions. I shall have to ask my brother to accompany me."

"Your brother!"

"Oh, he's safe. He—he knows."

"Your *brother knows*?" Her visitor, with less control than usual, betrayed very openly his uneasiness.

"He does and—*approves*. But that's not what interests us now, only so far as it makes it possible for me to go with propriety to that dreadful house."

A formal bow from the other and the words:

"They may expect you, then. Can you say when?"

"Within the next hour. But it will be a useless concession on my part," she pettishly complained. "A place that has been gone over by a dozen detectives is apt to be brushed clean of its cobwebs, even if such ever existed."

"That's the difficulty," he acknowledged; and did not dare to add another word; she was at that particular moment so very much the great lady, and so little his confidential agent.

He might have been less impressed, however, by this sudden assumption of manner, had he been so fortunate as to have seen how she employed the three quarters of an hour's delay for which she had asked.

She read those neglected newspapers, especially the one containing the following highly coloured narration of this ghastly crime:

"A door ajar—an empty hall—a line of sinister looking blotches marking a guilty step diagonally across the flagging—silence—and an unmistakable odour repugnant to all humanity—such were the indications which met the eyes of Officer O'Leary on his first round last night, and led to the discovery of a murder which will long thrill the city by its mystery and horror.

"Both the house and the victim are well known." Here followed a description of the same and of Mrs. Doolittle's manner of life in her ancient home, which Violet hurriedly passed over to come to the following:

"As far as one can judge from appearances, the crime happened in this wise: Mrs. Doolittle had been in her kitchen, as the tea-kettle found singing on the stove goes to prove, and was coming back through her bedroom, when the wretch, who had stolen in by the front door which, to save steps, she was unfortunately in the habit of leaving on the latch till all possibility of customers for the day was over, sprang upon her from behind and dealt her a swinging blow with the poker he had caught up from the hearthstone.

"Whether the struggle which ensued followed immediately upon this first attack or came later, it will take medical experts to determine. But, whenever it did occur, the fierceness of its character is shown by the grip taken upon her throat and the traces of blood which are to be seen all over the house. If the wretch had lugged her into her workroom and thence to the kitchen, and thence back to the spot of first assault, the evidences could not have been more ghastly. Bits of her clothing torn off by a ruthless hand lay scattered over all these floors. In her bedroom, where she finally breathed her last, there could be seen mingled with these a number of large but worthless glass beads; and close against one of the baseboards, the string which had held them, as shown by the few remaining beads still clinging to it. If in pulling the string from her neck he had hoped to light upon some valuable booty, his fury at his disappointment is evident. You can almost see the frenzy with which he flung the would-be necklace at the wall, and kicked about and stamped upon its rapidly rolling beads.

"Booty! That was what he was after; to find and carry away the poor needlewoman's supposed hoardings. If the scene baffles description—if, as some believe, he dragged her yet living from spot to spot, demanding information as to her places of concealment under threat of repeated blows, and, finally baffled, dealt the finishing stroke and proceeded on the search alone, no greater devastation could have taken place in this poor woman's house or effects. Yet such was his precaution and care for himself that he left no finger-print behind him nor any other token which could lead to personal identification. Even though his footsteps could be traced in much the order I have mentioned, they were of so indeterminate and shapeless a character as to convey little to the intelligence of the investigator.

"That these smears (they could not be called footprints) not only crossed the hall but appeared in more than one place on the staircase proves that he did not confine his search to the lower storey; and perhaps one of the most interesting features of the case lies in the indications given by these marks of the raging course he took through these upper rooms. As the accompanying diagram will show [we omit the diagram] he went first into the large front chamber, thence to the rear where we find two rooms, one unfinished and filled with accumulated stuff most of which he left lying loose upon the floor, and the other plastered, and containing a window opening upon an alleyway at the side, but empty of all furniture and without even a carpet on the bare boards.

"Why he should have entered the latter place, and why, having entered he should have crossed to the window, will be plain to those who have studied the conditions. The front chamber windows were tightly shuttered, the attic ones cumbered with boxes and shielded from approach by old bureaus and discarded chairs. This one only was free and, although darkened by the proximity of the house neighbouring it across the alley, was the only spot on the storey where sufficient light could be had at this late hour for the examination of any object of whose value he was doubtful. That he had come across such an object and had brought it to this window for some such purpose is very satisfactorily demonstrated by the discovery of a worn-out wallet of ancient make lying on the floor directly in front of this window—a proof of his cupidity but also proof of his ill-luck. For this wallet, when lifted and opened, was found to contain two hundred or more dollars in old bills, which, if not the full hoard of their industrious owner, was certainly worth the taking by one who had risked his neck for the sole purpose of theft.

"This wallet, and the flight of the murderer without it, give to this affair, otherwise simply brutal, a dramatic interest which will be appreciated not only by the very able detectives already hot upon the chase, but by all other inquiring minds anxious to solve a mystery of which so estimable a woman has been the unfortunate victim. A problem is presented to the police——"

There Violet stopped.

When, not long after, the superb limousine of Peter Strange stopped before the little house in Seventeenth Street, it caused a veritable sensation, not only in the curiosity-mongers lingering on the sidewalk, but to the two persons within— the officer on guard and a belated reporter.

Though dressed in her plainest suit, Violet Strange looked much too fashionable and far too young and thoughtless to be observed, without emotion, entering a scene of hideous and brutal crime. Even the young man who accompanied her promised to bring a most incongruous element into this atmosphere of guilt and horror, and, as the detective on guard whispered to the man beside him, might much better have been left behind in the car.

But Violet was great for the proprieties and young Arthur followed her in.

Her entrance was a *coup du théâtre*. She had lifted her veil in crossing the sidewalk and her interesting features and general air of timidity were very fetching. As the man holding open the door noted the impression made upon his companion, he muttered with sly facetiousness:

"You think you'll show her nothing; but I'm ready to bet a fiver that she'll want to see it all and that you'll show it to her."

The detective's grin was expressive, notwithstanding the shrug with which he tried to carry it off.

And Violet? The hall into which she now stepped from the most vivid sunlight had never been considered even in its palmiest days as possessing cheer even of the stately kind. The ghastly green light infused through it by the coloured glass on either side of the doorway seemed to promise yet more dismal things beyond.

"Must I go in there?" she asked, pointing, with an admirable simulation of nervous excitement, to a half-shut door at her left. "Is there where it happened? Arthur, do you suppose that there is where it happened?"

"No, no, Miss," the officer made haste to assure her. "If you are Miss Strange" (Violet bowed), "I need hardly say that the woman was struck in her bedroom. The door beside you leads into the parlour, or as she would have called it, her work-room. You needn't be afraid of going in there. You will see nothing but the disorder of her boxes. They were pretty well pulled about. Not all of them though," he added, watching her as closely as the dim light permitted. "There is one which gives no sign of having been tampered with. It was done up in wrapping paper and is addressed to you, which in itself would not have seemed worthy of our attention had not these lines been scribbled on it in a man's handwriting: '*Send without opening.*'"

"How odd!" exclaimed the little minx with widely opened eyes and an air of guileless innocence. "What ever can it mean? Nothing serious I am sure, for the woman did not even know me. She was employed to do this work by Madame Pirot."

"Didn't you know that it was to be done here?"

"No. I thought Madame Pirot's own girls did her embroidery for her."

"So that you were surprised——"

"Wasn't I!"

"To get our message."

"I didn't know what to make of it."

The earnest, half-injured look with which she uttered this disclaimer did its appointed work. The detective accepted her for what she seemed and, oblivious to the reporter's satirical gesture, crossed to the work-room door, which he threw wide open with the remark:

"I should be glad to have you open that box in our presence. It is undoubtedly all right, but we wish to be sure. You know what the box should contain?"

"Oh, yes, indeed; pillow-cases and sheets, with a big S embroidered on them."

"Very well. Shall I undo the string for you?"

"I shall be much obliged," said she, her eye flashing quickly about the room before settling down upon the knot he was deftly loosening.

Her brother, gazing indifferently in from the doorway, hardly noticed this look; but the reporter at his back did, though he failed to detect its penetrating quality.

"Your name is on the other side," observed the detective as he drew away the string and turned the package over.

The smile which just lifted the corner of her lips was not in answer to this remark, but to her recognition of her employer's handwriting in the words under her name: *Send without opening.* She had not misjudged him.

"The cover you may like to take off yourself," suggested the officer, as he lifted the box out of its wrapper.

"Oh, I don't mind. There's nothing to be ashamed of in embroidered linen. Or perhaps that is not what you are looking for?"

No one answered. All were busy watching her whip off the lid and lift out the pile of sheets and pillow-cases with which the box was closely packed.

"Shall I unfold them?" she asked.

The detective nodded.

Taking out the topmost sheet, she shook it open. Then the next and the next till she reached the bottom of the box. Nothing of a criminating nature came to light. The box as well as its contents was without mystery of any kind. This was not an unexpected result of course, but the smile with which she began to refold the pieces and throw them back into the box, revealed one of her dimples which was almost as dangerous to the casual observer as when it revealed both.

"There," she exclaimed, "you see! Household linen exactly as I said. Now may I go home?"

"Certainly, Miss Strange."

The detective stole a sly glance at the reporter. She was not going in for the horrors then after all.

But the reporter abated nothing of his knowing air, for while she spoke of going, she made no move towards doing so, but continued to look about the room till her glances finally settled on a long dark curtain shutting off an adjoining room.

"There's where she lies, I suppose," she feelingly exclaimed. "And not one of you knows who killed her. Somehow, I cannot understand that. Why don't you know when that's what you're hired for?" The innocence with which she uttered this was astonishing. The detective began to look sheepish and the reporter turned aside to hide his smile. Whether in another moment either would have spoken no one can say, for, with a mock consciousness of having said something foolish, she caught up her parasol from the table and made a start for the door.

But of course she looked back.

"I was wondering," she recommenced, with a half wistful, half speculative air, "whether I should ask to have a peep at the place where it all happened."

The reporter chuckled behind the pencil-end he was chewing, but the officer maintained his solemn air, for which act of self-restraint he was undoubtedly grateful when in another minute she gave a quick impulsive shudder not altogether assumed, and vehemently added: "But I couldn't stand the sight; no, I couldn't! I'm an awful coward when it comes to things like that. Nothing in all the world would induce me to look at the woman or her room. But I should like—" here both her dimples came into play though she could not be said exactly to smile— "just one little look upstairs, where he went poking about so long without any fear it seems of being interrupted. Ever since I've read about it I have seen, in my mind, a picture of his wicked figure sneaking from room to room, tearing open drawers and flinging out the contents of closets just to find a little money—a little, little money! I shall not sleep tonight just for wondering how those high-up attic rooms really look."

Who could dream that back of this display of mingled childishness and audacity there lay hidden purpose, intellect, and a keen knowledge of human nature. Not the two men who listened to this seemingly irresponsible chatter. To them she was a child to be humoured and humour her they did. The dainty feet which had already found their way to that gloomy staircase were allowed to ascend, followed it is true by those of the officer who did not dare to smile back at the reporter because of the brother's watchful and none too conciliatory eye.

At the stair head she paused to look back.

"I don't see those horrible marks which the papers describe as running all along the lower hall and up these stairs."

"No, Miss Strange; they have gradually been

rubbed out, but you will find some still showing on these upper floors."

"Oh! oh! where? You frighten me—frighten me horribly! But—but—if you don't mind, I should like to see."

Why should not a man on a tedious job amuse himself? Piloting her over to the small room in the rear, he pointed down at the boards. She gave one look and then stepped gingerly in.

"Just look!" she cried; "a whole string of marks going straight from door to window. They have no shape, have they—just blotches? I wonder why one of them is so much larger than the rest?"

This was no new question. It was one which everybody who went into the room was sure to ask, there was such a difference in the size and appearance of the mark nearest the window. The reason—well, minds were divided about that, and no one had a satisfactory theory. The detective therefore kept discreetly silent.

This did not seem to offend Miss Strange. On the contrary it gave her an opportunity to babble away to her heart's content.

"One, two, three, four, five, six," she counted, with a shudder at every count. "And one of them bigger than the others." She might have added, "It is the trail of one foot, and strangely intermingled at that," but she did not, though we may be quite sure that she noted the fact. "And where, just where did the old wallet fall? Here? or *here*?"

She had moved as she spoke, so that in uttering the last "here," she stood directly before the window. The surprise she received there nearly made her forget the part she was playing. From the character of the light in the room, she had expected, on looking out, to confront a near-by wall, but not a window in that wall. Yet that was what she saw directly facing her from across the old-fashioned alley separating this house from its neighbour; twelve unshuttered and uncurtained panes through which she caught a darkened view of a room almost as forlorn and devoid of furniture as the one in which she then stood.

When quite sure of herself, she let a certain portion of her surprise appear.

"Why, look!" she cried, "if you can't see right in next door! What a lonesome-looking place! From its desolate appearance I should think the house quite empty."

"And it is. That's the old Shaffer homestead. It's been empty for a year."

"Oh, empty!" And she turned away, with the most inconsequent air in the world, crying out as her name rang up the stair, "There's Arthur calling. I suppose he thinks I've been here long enough. I'm sure I'm very much obliged to you, officer. I really shouldn't have slept a wink tonight, if I hadn't been given a peep at these rooms, which I had imagined so different." And with one additional glance over her shoulder, that seemed to penetrate both windows and the desolate space beyond, she ran quickly out and down in response to her brother's reiterated call.

"Drive quickly!—as quickly as the law allows, to Hiram Brown's office in Duane Street."

Arrived at the address named, she went in alone to see Mr. Brown. He was her father's lawyer and a family friend.

Hardly waiting for his affectionate greeting, she cried out quickly. "Tell me how I can learn anything about the old Shaffer house in Seventeenth Street. Now, don't look so surprised. I have very good reasons for my request and—and—I'm in an awful hurry."

"But——"

"I know, I know; there's been a dreadful tragedy next door to it; but it's about the Shaffer house itself I want some information. Has it an agent, a——"

"Of course it has an agent, and here is his name."

Mr. Brown presented her with a card on which he had hastily written both name and address.

She thanked him, dropped him a mocking curtsey full of charm, whispered "Don't tell father," and was gone.

Her manner to the man she next interviewed was very different. As soon as she saw him she subsided into her usual society manner. With just a touch of the conceit of the successful débutante, she announced herself as Miss Strange of Seventy-second Street. Her business with him was in regard to the possible renting of the Shaffer house. She had an old lady friend who was desirous of living downtown.

In passing through Seventeenth Street, she had noticed that the old Shaffer house was standing empty and had been immediately struck with the advantages it possessed for her elderly friend's occupancy. Could it be that the house was for rent? There was no sign on it to that effect, but—etc.

His answer left her nothing to hope for.

"It is going to be torn down," he said.

"Oh, what a pity!" she exclaimed. "Real colonial, isn't it! I wish I could see the rooms inside before it is disturbed. Such doors and such dear old-fashioned mantelpieces as it must have! I just dote on the Colonial. It brings up such pictures of the old days; weddings, you know, and parties;—all so different from ours and so much more interesting."

Is it the chance shot that tells? Sometimes. Violet had no especial intention in what she said save as a prelude to a pending request, but nothing could have served her purpose better than that one word, *wedding*. The agent laughed and giving her his first indulgent look, remarked genially:

"Romance is not confined to those ancient times. If you were to enter that house today you would come across evidences of a wedding as romantic as any which ever took place in all the seventy odd years of its existence. A man and a woman were married there day before yesterday who did their first courting under its roof forty years ago. He has been married twice and she once in the interval; but the old love held firm and now at the age of sixty and over they have come together to finish their days in peace and happiness. Or so we will hope."

"Married! married in that house and on the day that——"

She caught herself up in time. He did not notice the break.

"Yes, in memory of those old days of courtship, I suppose. They came here about five, got the keys, drove off, went through the ceremony in that empty house, returned the keys to me in my own apartment, took the steamer for Naples, and were on the sea before midnight. Do you not call that quick work as well as highly romantic?"

"Very." Miss Strange's cheek had paled. It was apt to when she was greatly excited. "But I don't understand," she added, the moment after. "How could they do this and nobody know about it? I should have thought it would have got into the papers."

"They are quiet people. I don't think they told their best friends. A simple announcement in the next day's journals testified to the fact of their marriage, but that was all. I would not have felt at liberty to mention the circumstances myself, if the parties were not well on their way to Europe."

"Oh, how glad I am that you did tell me! Such a story of constancy and the hold which old associations have upon sensitive minds! But——"

"Why, Miss? What's the matter? You look very much disturbed."

"Don't you remember? Haven't you thought? Something else happened that very day and almost at the same time on that block. Something very dreadful——"

"Mrs. Doolittle's murder?"

"Yes. It was as near as next door, wasn't it? Oh, if this happy couple had known——"

"But fortunately they didn't. Nor are they likely to, till they reach the other side. You needn't fear that their honeymoon will be spoiled that way."

"But they may have heard something or seen something before leaving the street. Did you notice how the gentleman looked when he returned you the keys?"

"I did, and there was no cloud on his satisfaction."

"Oh, how you relieve me!" One—two dimples made their appearance in Miss Strange's fresh, young cheeks. "Well! I wish them joy. Do you mind telling me their names? I cannot think of them as actual persons without knowing their names."

"The gentleman was Constantin Amidon; the lady, Marian Shaffer. You will have to think of them now as Mr. and Mrs. Amidon."

"And I will. Thank you, Mr. Hutton, thank you very much. Next to the pleasure of getting the house for my friend, is that of hearing this charming bit of news in its connection."

She held out her hand and, as he took it, remarked:

"They must have had a clergyman and witnesses."

"Undoubtedly."

"I wish I had been one of the witnesses," she sighed sentimentally.

"They were two old men."

"Oh, no! Don't tell me that."

"Fogies; nothing less."

"But the clergyman? He must have been young. Surely there was some one there capable of appreciating the situation?"

"I can't say about that; I did not see the clergyman."

"Oh, well! it doesn't matter." Miss Strange's manner was as nonchalant as it was charming. "We will think of him as being *very* young."

And with a merry toss of her head she flitted away.

But she sobered very rapidly upon entering her limousine.

"Hello!"

"Ah, is that you?"

"Yes, I want a Marconi sent."

"A Marconi?"

"Yes, to the *Cretic*, which left dock the very night in which we are so deeply interested."

"Good. Whom to? The Captain?"

"No, to a Mrs. Constantin Amidon. But first be sure there is such a passenger."

"*Mrs.!* What idea have you there?"

"Excuse my not stating over the telephone. The message is to be to this effect. Did she at any time immediately before or after her marriage to Mr. Amidon get a glimpse of anyone in the adjoining house? No remarks, please. I use the telephone because I am not ready to explain myself. If she did, let her send a written description to you of that person as soon as she reaches the Azores."

"You surprise me. May I not call or hope for a line from you early tomorrow?"

"I shall be busy till you get your answer."

He hung up the receiver. He recognized the resolute tone.

But the time came when the pending explanation was fully given to him. An answer had been returned from the steamer, favourable to Violet's hopes. Mrs. Amidon had seen such a person and would send a full description of the same at the first opportunity. It was news to fill Violet's heart with pride; the filament of a clew which had led to this great result had been so nearly invisible and had felt so like nothing in her grasp.

To her employer she described it as follows:

"When I hear or read of a case which contains any baffling features, I am apt to feel some hidden chord in my nature thrill to one fact in it and not to any of the others. In this case the single fact which appealed to my imagination was the dropping of the stolen wallet in that upstairs room. Why did the guilty man drop it? and why, having dropped it, did he not pick it up again? But one answer seemed possible. He had heard or seen something at the spot where it fell which not only alarmed him but sent him in flight from the house."

"Very good; and did you settle to your own mind the nature of that sound or that sight?"

"I did." Her manner was strangely businesslike. No show of dimples now. "Satisfied that if any possibility remained of my ever doing this, it would have to be on the exact place of this occurrence or not at all, I embraced your suggestion and visited the house."

"And that room no doubt."

"And that room. Women, somehow, seem to manage such things."

"So I've noticed, Miss Strange. And what was the result of your visit? What did you discover there?"

"This: that one of the blood spots marking the criminal's steps through the room was decidedly more pronounced than the rest; and, what was even more important, that the window out of which I was looking had its counterpart in the house on the opposite side of the alley. In gazing through the one I was gazing through the other; and not only that, but into the darkened area of the room beyond. Instantly I saw how the latter fact might be made to explain the former one. But before I say how, let me ask if it is quite settled among you that the smears on the floor and stairs mark the passage of the criminal's footsteps!"

"Certainly; and very bloody feet they must have been too. His shoes—or rather his one shoe—for the proof is plain that only the right one left its mark—must have become thoroughly saturated to carry its traces so far."

"Do you think that any amount of saturation would have done this? Or, if you are not ready to agree to that, that a shoe so covered with blood could have failed to leave behind it some hint of its shape, some imprint, however faint, of heel or toe? But nowhere did it do this. We see a smear—and that is all."

"You are right, Miss Strange; you are always right. And what do you gather from this?"

She looked to see how much he expected from her, and, meeting an eye not quite as free from all ironic suggestion as his words had led her to expect, faltered a little as she proceeded to say:

"My opinion is a girl's opinion, but such as it is you have the right to have it. From the indications mentioned I could draw but this conclusion: that the blood which accompanied the criminal's footsteps was not carried through the house by his shoes—he wore no shoes; he did not even wear stockings; probably he had none. For reasons which appealed to his judgment, he went about his wicked work barefoot; and it was the blood from his own veins and not from those of his victim which made the trail we have followed with so much interest. Do you forget those broken beads—how he kicked them about and stamped upon them in his fury? One of them pierced the ball of his foot, and that so sharply that it not only spurted blood but kept on bleeding with every step he took. Otherwise, the trail would have been lost after his passage up the stairs."

"Fine!" There was no irony in the bureauchief's eye now. "You are progressing, Miss Strange. Allow me, I pray, to kiss your hand. It is a liberty I have never taken, but one which would greatly relieve my present stress of feeling."

She lifted her hand toward him, but it was in gesture, not in recognition of his homage.

"Thank you," said she, "but I claim no monopoly on deductions so simple as these. I have not the least doubt that not only yourself but every member of the force has made the same. But there is a little matter which may have escaped the police, may even have escaped you. To that I would now call your attention since through it I have been enabled, after a little necessary groping, to reach the open. You remember the one large blotch on the upper floor where the man dropped the wallet? That blotch, more or less commingled with a fainter one, possessed great significance for me from the first moment I saw it. How came his foot to bleed so much more profusely at that one spot than at any other? There could be but one answer: because here a surprise met him—a surprise so startling to him in his present state of mind, that he gave a quick spring backward, with the result that his wounded foot came down suddenly and forcibly instead of easily as in his previous wary tread. And what was the surprise? I made it my business to find out, and now I can tell you that it was the sight of a woman's face staring upon him from the neighbouring house which he had probably been told was empty. The shock disturbed

his judgment. He saw his crime discovered—his guilty secret read, and fled in unreasoning panic. He might better have held on to his wits. It was this display of fear which led me to search after its cause, and consequently to discover that at this especial hour more than one person had been in the Shaffer house; that, in fact, a marriage had been celebrated there under circumstances as romantic as any we read of in books, and that this marriage, privately carried out, had been followed by an immediate voyage of the happy couple on one of the White Star steamers. With the rest you are conversant. I do not need to say anything about what has followed the sending of that Marconi."

"But I am going to say something about your work in this matter, Miss Strange. The big detectives about here will have to look sharp if——"

"Don't, please! Not yet." A smile softened the asperity of this interruption. "The man has yet to be caught and identified. Till that is done I cannot enjoy anyone's congratulations. And you will see that all this may not be so easy. If no one happened to meet the desperate wretch before he had an opportunity to retie his shoelaces, there will be little for you or even for the police to go upon but his wounded foot, his undoubtedly carefully prepared alibi, and later, a woman's confused description of a face seen but for a moment only and that under a personal excitement precluding minute attention. I should not be surprised if the whole thing came to nothing."

But it did not. As soon as the description was received from Mrs. Amidon (a description, by the way, which was unusually clear and precise, owing to the peculiar and contradictory features of the man), the police were able to recognize him among the many suspects always under their eye. Arrested, he pleaded, just as Miss Strange had foretold, an alibi of a seemingly unimpeachable character; but neither it, nor the plausible explanation with which he endeavoured to account for a freshly healed scar amid the callouses of his right foot, could stand before Mrs. Amidon's unequivocal testimony that he was the same man she had seen in Mrs. Doolittle's upper room on the afternoon of her own happiness and of that poor woman's murder.

The moment when, at his trial, the two faces again confronted each other across a space no wider than that which had separated them on the dread occasion in Seventeenth Street, is said to have been one of the most dramatic in the annals of that ancient court room.

PLANTED

James Oppenheim

IF REMEMBERED AT ALL TODAY, the major achievements of James Oppenheim (1882–1932) are in areas unrelated to writing detective fiction specifically and fiction more generally.

He founded the literary magazine *The Seven Arts* and was its primary editor for a year (1916–1917) until he was forced out due to his relentless opposition to American involvement in World War I. Oppenheim's fellow editors were Waldo Frank, George Jean Nathan, Louis Untermeyer, and Paul Rosenfeld, and important contributors to its pages included Sherwood Anderson, Van Wyck Brooks, Robert Frost, D. H. Lawrence, and Amy Lowell.

Oppenheim was a socialist who wrote about labor troubles in his novel *The Nine-Tenths* (1911) and in his famous poem "Bread and Roses" (1911), a title now associated with the 1912 textile workers' strike in Lawrence, Massachusetts. The poem was later set to music in 1976 by Mimi Fariña and again in 1990 by John Denver.

The theme of women's rights appeared in some of his works, but his wife divorced him shortly after he published *Idle Wives* (1914); possible cause and effect are not known.

A popular poet and short story writer in his day, he contributed work to most of the major magazines of the time, including *American Magazine, American Mercury, Century, McClure's, Collier's, Harper's, Hearst's,* and *New Republic.*

In "Planted" (which had the better title of "Mrs. Judas" in the April 1916 issue of England's *The Story-Teller*), Oppenheim created an odd character who in many ways was a throwback to the Victorian era. Ki Polly used her feminine wiles to capture a criminal, letting him fall in love with her, kissing him, but later treating him in a motherly way since she is twelve years older than he is. She appears to be fearless, a necessary element of being a female detective (though it is unclear if she is a private eye or a member of the police force).

"Planted" was originally published in the September 1915 issue of *McClure's Magazine.*

Planted

JAMES OPPENHEIM

AS MRS. POLLY TURNED THE CORNER and came up Manhattan Avenue, she thought she saw a face at one of her windows; and she thought it was the face of Ray Levine. This was very disturbing, especially as it was after midnight, the street was deserted, and she was tired.

Her four-room flat was on the ground floor, and a gas-lamp on the pavement before it brightened the windows. What she saw was a momentary reflection, a gray shadow that assumed the shape of a man's face and then vanished. She may have been mistaken.

Nevertheless she did not dare pause, but walked on to the stoop. Even then, to wait too long would inform the intruder that he had been seen. But if it was Ray Levine! Her heart gave a bound. Seven backward years were bridged, and she and Ray were standing near each other in the court-room, and Ray was full of bitter contempt. Luckily, he was handcuffed to an officer.

"Detective, eh? And catch a man with a kiss? Well, Ki, I hate just one thing, and that's treachery. When I get out—so help me—I'll put a bullet through your heart, Mrs. Judas."

This was not the usual sort of threat; but the young man meant it with all his soul. In spite of her native courage, her heart sickened. In a flash, she saw herself in Ray's big touring car at Niagara Falls, and felt his lips close upon hers. She had indeed betrayed him with a kiss. She had torn out his story—how he had been temporary agent of an express company in a Long Island town, and how he had taken thirty thousand dollars for Flo, that wicked woman of the Tenderloin. She had saved him from Flo, only to land him in prison.

"Perhaps he loved you, Ki," she thought; "perhaps you—you loved him a bit. You sickly fool, is this the end of it, now?"

There was one last hope. She looked eagerly up and down the empty street. But the houses gazed vacantly on the vacant pavements, and in the distance the mist floated smotheringly, closing her in, accentuating her loneliness. Nevertheless, a plain-clothes man might be hidden in some doorway nearby; for on this day of Ray's release he would doubtless be shadowed by Headquarters. Then, too, the Chief may have remembered Ray's threat, in which case the house would be well watched.

She hesitated for a moment. Should she go around the corner to the drug store and telephone to Headquarters? Ray would notice this, and get away; and she had no intention of letting him off. Should she, then, take the risk and go in boldly? To open the door might easily mean the end.

She stood there at the foot of the stoop, a woman alone, tapping one high-heeled shoe on the stone step, swinging the silver mesh bag, which was fat with her "make-up." She had spent the evening working along Broadway, and looked and felt the part. Her clear blue eyes were brilliant with the drinks she had had to take; her cheeks red with rouge; her hat startling with its red feathers; and her stout, tightly-laced body appareled in vivid blue.

After the excitement of the evening, she had the sense of ebb-tide: disgust with herself and her work; that gnawing loneliness she always felt as she returned home to the empty flat; that sense of impending disaster.

She shivered, looked quickly up and down the street again, heard, as it were, the silence of sleep on the city; and then, with heart pounding against her ribs, walked boldly up the stoop, pushed open the outer door, unlocked the inner door, and so entered the dark hall. It smelled of the dirty steam-heated carpet and the accumulated vapors of several suppers. She went to her door, listened, and scolded herself:

"Come, Ki. No worse to go tonight than any other night. But be a good fellow to the end; be a sport, old girl!" With that, she slipped the key into the lock, and with great care pushed the door open a little. Light from the street-lamp outside came in broad shafts through the windows, so that the crowded room was visible. All looked right: the Morris chair beside the center table; the couch in the corner; the photographs on the wall. She heard not the smallest sound.

All at once an anger at her own weakness nerved her. She flung up her head and walked in, leaving the door behind her open. She looked neither to right nor left, but went to the crowded mantel, found a match-box, and struck a match. That was the crucial moment, as she stood there, illuminated, distinct, with the tiny blaze flinging jumping shadows on the wall.

Nothing happened. And a moment later she had reached up, and the lamp on the table blazed. Then she looked about her. She was alone in the room; but the dining-room behind was in darkness, and was effectually screened by the tube-bead curtains that hung in the doorway in dusty silence.

Nevertheless she felt that she was a target; and, humming under her breath to forget her thoughts, she went to the door, shut it tight, the lock clicking, and then with swift steps returned to the mantel and seized the telephone.

"Spring 3100," she said in a low voice. "Send police if they don't answer quick. . . . Yes—yes. . . . Oh, Headquarters? That you, Croly?" She laughed softly. "Yes, this is Mrs. Polly. I'm home. . . . Yes; you're right—it's about Levine. . . . Good enough. Shadowed him, eh? . . . Three men? Good! . . . No, I didn't see the one on the street. . . . Other in the yard? . . . Yes, sure, the roof. So you traced him to this house. Well, he can't get away, then. . . . I'll call you up. Good luck! So long!"

She set the telephone down, and stood a moment, hesitating. Then she had a bright idea. Again she put the transmitter to her lips.

"Murray Hill 7109. . . . Yes."

She waited in silence; and a curious thought came to her—so trivial and absurd, she almost laughed aloud. Two nights before she had heard mice. She was not afraid of mice, but she was of rats; and these little fellows made such a noise that she concluded they were rats. In terror she sat up in her bed, and, not knowing what to do, she began to "meow" like a cat, her voice rising and rising, until suddenly she remembered that others in the house might hear her and think she was possessed of a devil.

"Yes," she thought, with a slight shiver; "I'm so scared I've got to think of funny things."

She felt as if her body were much too large and bullets much too small.

Suddenly she put her lips to the transmitter again.

"7109? . . . Yes. I want to speak to Flo. . . . Oh, that you, Flo? This is Kirah Polly. . . . I'm home, yes. Flo, I want you to jump in your clothes and come here quick. . . . Yes, here. Ray Levine is out. . . . He is. Now, see here, kid; if you don't do this for me, you're done for. Besides, you loved the boy, didn't you, dear? . . . Listen. You know, he threatened to kill me when he got loose. Well, Headquarters has shadowed him: he's close by; and only you can save him. Come quick, now, sweetheart, and catch him before he ruins himself. Take him away. He wrecked himself for you, you know. . . . You will? Bless your heart, Flo! Take a taxi."

The room was steeped in brooding silence. The lamp burned with a slight purr, as of a cat drowsing; sirens were echoes in the far misty night. Mrs. Polly was almost afraid to stir, afraid to hear the rustle of her dress. But she carefully pulled the hat-pins from her hat, laid the hat on the couch, gave her hair a dab or two, and glanced at herself in the mirror.

"My!" she said to herself, "but you look gone, Ki. Rouge on snow." Then slowly she went to the Morris chair, sank into it, and folded her hands in her lap.

She was facing the tube-bead curtains, trying with her sharp eyes to see what lay behind them. She could see nothing. She waited.

She had the strange sensation of sitting in the electric chair and waiting for the annihilating current to be turned on—the killing "juice." Then suddenly the shock went through her, and she sat up. There were two definite steps; a hand parted the curtains; and Levine stepped through.

Their eyes met. Neither really saw the other—they only *felt*. Yet somewhere in the back of her mind Mrs. Polly was telling herself that he looked old and fagged, though his black eyes had lost none of their glitter and his black hair was untouched with gray. He was fairly tall and wiry; and he looked dangerous.

He stood; she sat; neither looked away.

"How did you get in?" she asked under her breath.

Then, to her amazement, she saw that he did not hold a revolver. Somehow, this increased rather than allayed her sense of crisis.

He stepped into the room.

"You left your door unlatched," he said.

He had difficulty in speaking.

"No, I didn't."

"You expected me, anyway."

"I'm never surprised."

"Well," he muttered, staring hard at her, "I heard what you said over the 'phone."

"What of it?" she questioned, returning his gaze.

"Nothing of it. What are you sitting there for?"

"What are you standing there for?"

"Just be careful what you say, Ki."

"And what you do, Ray!"

She met his eyes again; and the power of her clear glance shook him. He looked around the room, muttering.

"Where do you keep your gun?"

"I don't need any gun," she answered very calmly.

He sneered. "A detective without a gun!"

She leaned forward suddenly, and spoke with menacing authority:

"Now you sit down, Ray! Sit down!"

He clenched his fists and took a step toward her.

"Ki," he burst out, "I stand just so much, and then——"

"You sit!" she added sharply.

"Well, I won't sit down."

"Do," she said. "For, when you stand, I can see that you tremble like a child—tremble before a woman."

His dark face grew menacing. He was really handsome; but now there were lines like scars about his mouth.

"Say that again!" he breathed.

"Why!" she exclaimed. "Do you still love me?"

He drew back a little, as if she had struck him.

"Love *you*?"

"You're shaking like a custard. Are you a man?"

"Love—you?" he repeated. Then he sneered. "If I could hate any one worse than I hate you——"

"It's all the same," she said.

"What's the same?"

"Loving—hating. They bind you to the other person. Perhaps you want a drink to steady yourself."

"What do you mean?"

"You can't stand still. Why not sit down?"

"And if I don't?"

"I won't open my mouth again until you do!" She sat back complacently. He stared at her, and then began walking uncertainly about the room. He went to the mantel, and toyed with some of the papers on it. He studied some photographs on the wall. Once or twice he came toward her, and then withdrew.

At last he leaned a fist on the table and looked at her.

"What's your game?" he burst out.

She met his glance without a quiver.

They were silent; the room was desperately still.

"Ki," he began, between his teeth, "I say!" He stopped. She said nothing.

"Huh!" he laughed sneeringly. "All right!"

Slowly she rose, and at once he became alert. She turned from him and went to a corner of the room. He followed swiftly.

"See here." He raised his voice. "What's this? No signaling, Ki!"

She stooped swiftly over a chair, and drew up a doily with a threaded needle sticking through it. She turned toward him, smiling, went back to her chair, sat down, and began to sew.

He stood behind her, amazed.

"Just as you want," he said; and there was a new menace in his voice. She heard him step away, and then draw down the shades of the windows. He came back softly, and leaned over her. She could almost feel his hands closing around her throat; but she embroidered steadily.

"By God!" he burst out.

A moment later he passed her, and sat down on a chair near her.

She leaned toward him, smiling.

"Now we can talk."

"You wicked devil!" he exclaimed.

She smiled at him.

"Am I so wicked, Ray?"

There was something so humanly intimate about this that he started. But he stiffened again.

She went on embroidering, and spoke musingly.

"Flo," she said, "was wicked—with those green eyes of hers, and that heaving bosom, and the hundred devils in her when the lid was lifted. She's the innocence that drives men mad and destroys them. She's as beautiful as ever, and the men—crazy as ever."

"What do you tell me that for, Ki?" he asked gruffly.

"You loved her once."

"I was insane—insane," he muttered angrily.

"And—what are you now?" she asked him slowly.

His nostrils quivered, his breath came quickly.

"Now," he said, "I'm an ex-convict—thanks to you, Ki."

"Thanks to yourself."

"Thanks to you."

"Thanks to Flo."

"To you, I say."

"To the law, I say!"

"Well," he said, in a trembling, childish voice, "I just won't have this any longer—you rotten——"

"Are you crying?" she burst out.

He bit on his lips, screwed up his face, turned from her.

"You damnable woman, I'll have my revenge on you—I will! Ruined my life. Seven years of hell. Can't you see what you did to me?"

He choked down a sob and turned toward her swiftly, slipping his hand in his jacket pocket.

Her heart missed a beat; but she spoke calmly.

"You never knew how I found you in Niagara, did you, Ray?"

"What's that?" he snapped.

"It was fairly clever." She smiled up at him. "You never would have thought of it yourself."

"Thought of what?"

"You see, Ray, all they gave me was your photograph, and the rumor that you were in Niagara. So, when I got off the train, I made for the line-up of chauffeurs. And I said to them that my younger brother had come into a large fortune, and I was afraid he was blowing it on some woman. Had they seen a young man around, answering to description, who was making the coin spin? I went down the line. It was no, until I came to a private car. 'Yes,' says he, 'that must be the man. He bought a car yesterday—a big black shining touring car. He'll be hanging out in Piddy's Inn.' So he took me to you."

He looked at her, puzzled.

"And in cold blood you went ahead?"

"How else should a detective go ahead?"

"Yes! But to make love to me—to take advantage of being a woman!"

"You took advantage of being a temporary agent, and unbonded."

"Yes. But to play with love!"

"How about Flo?"

He sat silent. Her voice lowered:

"You got out this morning, didn't you, son?"

"Son!" he sneered. "That's not what you called me then."

"What did I call you then?"

His face darkened.

"I suppose you don't remember!"

"It's seven years ago."

"So, you didn't even care for me. It was all acting!" He shut his eyes, clenching his fists, breathing between his teeth. He seemed to hate himself. "First one woman ruined me, then another. But I learned one thing in prison."

"What was that?"

He rose slowly, his hand in his pocket, and took a step toward her.

"Revenge."

She met his gaze.

"Sit down, Ray."

"Not for a minute," he answered.

She spoke scornfully:

"Do you think I'm afraid to die?"

"Who's talking about dying?" he mumbled.

"Then take your hand out of your pocket."

"Not till I get ready to."

She bent her head and began to embroider again.

"What's that?" she murmured.

"What's what?"

"Will you please open the hall door," she said, "and see if anyone is outside?"

"Open it yourself," he breathed.

She started to put down her sewing.

"No, you don't!" he cried. "You *are* clever—by heaven, you are. Let him stay in the hall. You sha'n't budge, nor I."

She looked up at him frankly.

"Ray," she said, "do be reasonable with me. You know well enough that you were guilty, and that it was my job to get the evidence and convict you. What, in heaven's name, could I have done? What would you have done in my place?"

"You made love to me," he said.

"Are you a man, Ray?" she asked quickly. "To say a woman made love to you!"

"Women like you and Flo do, Ki."

"Yes, to womanish men."

"Womanish!"

"Yes. I think you are womanish," she answered quietly. "Now, like a woman, you come crying around here, and want revenge because I made love to you."

He began to pace up and down nervously, pausing now and then to look at her.

"But you did ruin me!" he cried. "And in cold blood."

"Not so very cold."

He stopped.

"What do you mean?"

"Sit down and I'll tell you, Ray."

He obeyed her, and sat again in the chair near her.

"Ray," she said softly, "when I went after you seven years ago, my husband had deserted me three years before, at the time my boy died. I was lonesome as a bell-buoy at sea. I was frozen in on myself. But I feel that way now," she murmured, "and that's why it never matters to me whether I die or not. Perhaps you think it easy for a woman to be a detective, and live in the under-world without being part of it, and not be respectable enough to have friends of the real sort. That was the way I felt when I found you. Then you loved me; and it seemed to me as if I had found something."

Color mounted to his cheeks.

"You did care for me, Ki?" he whispered.

"I did, Ray."

He leaned toward her.

"Ki, you honestly cared? Loved?"

"If you call it love," she said weakly.

"But you cared?"

She smiled, her eyes wistful with tears.

"I'm an old fool," she muttered, wiping her eyes with the doily. "You see, when a woman's my age, and nothing to love, she just naturally fastens on every ownerless dog and becomes its mother. And when I found you up there, young and handsome, and blowing your life to bits—well——"

"Well, what?" he asked softly.

"I felt like a mother to you."

He sat up.

"Like a mother! But I loved you, because you were a woman, not a mother to me!"

"Not so fast!" she said. "Remember the day we sat out watching the Falls, up there on the rocks, alone with sky and water?"

"What day?"

"The day you told me everything."

He shivered.

"Well, what of it?"

"Remember what you said to me?"

"What did I say to you?"

"You said I reminded you of your mother, the only woman you had ever really loved——"

He stared at her.

"I said that?"

"Yes."

"But I didn't mean I wanted you to be a mother to me. I loved you."

"What could come of it?" she pleaded. "Ray, I'm more than twelve years older than you."

"What's twelve years?"

She smiled.

"You're the same as ever."

He shuddered.

"The same! Yes, with seven years of hell branded on me."

A vein on his forehead stood out; a dangerous light returned to his eyes.

"You're playing with me again," he muttered. "But I won't take any more of it! I bet you'd make love to me now to get the best of me."

"You think that, Ray?"

"You did it once; you would do it again."

"Ah, no," she sighed. "You see, I didn't play at it then. I did care."

"And now?"

"Now I'm too old; I'm past all that."

"You're not. Your eyes are as bright as ever."

"My husband may still be living."

"What do I care?"

"Can't we be friends, Ray? Really, now, I've often thought of you these past years, and wished it might have been different. Come, let's make the best of it. Perhaps I can put you on your feet again."

"How?" he sneered.

"Well," she said, "you've learned a lot in jail."

"A lot!" he said bitterly. "A lot about crime and vice."

"Just what I meant. You see, I might get you in on the police department—secret service work. I think you could do it."

"With my record!"

"It was a youthful error. They know that."

"I paid pretty heavily for my youthful error!"

"Come," she said, "make the best of it. You look tired out, Ray—pale and worn. And all this strain. And this silly revenge business. Come, let me get you some supper, and we'll celebrate your new life. A new start, tonight!"

He sat musing, and sighed. Then he rose wearily and began to pace around. Suddenly he looked at her suspiciously, and came toward her, leaning against the table. He spoke hoarsely, shaking with a new gust of emotion.

"Ki, what in the name of twenty hells are you trying to do?"

She looked at him.

"What are *you* trying to do?"

"By God, I'm a fool with women. I was fooled twice, and I've paid for it with seven years of being shut in; seven years of being dead; seven years of scheming how I could get revenge on you. You said you cared for me. You cared for me so much that you sent me to prison!"

He leaned nearer; his voice rose.

"Now I've reached the end. I swore, Ki, I would kill you, and I will!"

"I had to send you to prison," she murmured.

"Had to!"

"For your own sake."

"How?"

"To save you from your own folly—yes, and from Flo."

"Yes," he snapped; "from Flo!"

"Now, see here, Ray," she said sharply. "What would have become of you if you had gone on running wild? You, with your crazy nature! And women could twist you around their little fingers! Why, you would have destroyed yourself in dissipation. Isn't that so?"

"Maybe," he growled.

"Think," she said, "of taking thirty thousand dollars for a woman; and then the reckless speed with which you spent it! Perhaps you forget what you said when I turned you over to the police."

"What did I say?"

She smiled.

"You said, 'Thank God, it's over.'"

There was a pause. He sat down again.

"Ah, now, Ray," she said, "come! I did struggle with myself over you. I did care for you. But, if you had been my own son, it might have seemed best for you to pay up—to be shut away until you grew to know better. Why not make the best of it?"

"But you making love to me—" he began again.

"And you loving Flo."

"I never did."

"Not love? What, then? She was like a madness in your blood, even when you were with me. I think you still love her."

He breathed hard, looking down on the floor.

"She was a—a snake!"

"But beautiful."

"Not so beautiful. But that long, twisting neck of hers—and those green eyes—and her laughing at me, and never letting me alone——"

"Never letting you alone?"

"Yes; never taking no for answer, but coming around, dogging me about, making scenes, quarreling, tempting—and then whispering, 'I am nice, Ray, don't you think so?' 'You do care for me, after all, don't you?' And her damned innocence——"

"That fooled you, like the rest!" said Mrs. Polly, smiling.

"How did I know? She going around talking like a saint, and then making love like a hurricane—struggling, fighting— It was like hugging a volcano."

"Often think of her?"

He looked away.

"I hate to think of her."

"You love to think of her. You love that madness in your blood, don't you? You love to feel wild."

"She destroyed me. I was a decent fellow until Flo came."

"Yes; she went around the world, breaking men. A curious business. But she's changed, Ray."

He looked up, interested.

"How, changed?"

"Well, your going to prison for her. It made a different woman of her. It subdued her, scared her. I think she loved you, Ray."

He stared at her.

"Did she?" he asked, like a wistful child.

She smiled.

"I think she really did. So if she comes tonight, while you are here——"

"Yes?"

"Don't be too hard on her. Perhaps you two——"

"We two?"

"Think of it! She's still beautiful. And she and I have been very good friends."

He breathed hard, looking away. Then he turned toward her.

"I've been a fool, Ki," he said.

"Yes," she laughed frankly; "you have, Ray."

"You're really my friend," he said.

"And no silly love business?"

"No. I guess it's Flo."

"Good." She arose. "Now, Ray, I'll get supper. But first——"

"First, what?"

"An evidence of good faith. Give me the gun."

He looked at her quickly, and met her clear, honest eyes. He smiled, put his hand in his pocket, and lifted out the loaded revolver. She took it carefully, and gazed at it.

"So you would have killed me, boy. Well, well!"

She sighed and looked down at him; her lips quivered.

"Listen," she said. "I am going to see how wise you are. You see, I didn't telephone to Flo; just held the 'phone to my lips."

His jaw fell; he stared.

"Why?" he asked.

"Ray," she said solemnly, "Flo is dead."

He trembled all over, and sank back.

"Dead?"

She stepped away from him carefully.

"Yes. Consumption—three years ago."

He leaped to his feet like a maniac.

"Damn you!" he shouted. "You've betrayed me again!"

He started for her, and she raised the revolver.

"Get back," she said quietly.

He paused.

"Ray," she said, "neither did I call up Headquarters. I could have; but you see I wanted to give you a chance to make good. It was all planted."

He stared and stared at her.

"Shall I get supper?" asked Mrs. Polly.

"Oh, Ki!" he broke down.

She gave him one motherly kiss then, and went in to find the coffee pot.

THE PULP ERA

THE WIZARD'S SAFE

Valentine

IN A TYPE OF STORY that is no longer written but that still retains its charm, even in the modern era, a lovely young woman is the brains of an outfit, sometimes a criminal one and sometimes one that battles crime, composed of men who adore her and will quickly make themselves available to do her bidding. Edgar Wallace's Four Square Jane had her group of thieves; L. T. Meade's Madame Koluchy, her gang of killers; David Durham's Fidelity Dove, whose angelic look "made slaves of many men" and belied her thieving ways; and Archibald Thomas Pechey (1876–1961), under the pseudonym Valentine, had Daphne Wrayne who, with the Four Adjusters, righted wrongs that the criminal justice system was unable to.

The early short stories and first book about the group of amateur crime fighters, beginning with *The Adjusters* (1930), was published under the Valentine nom de plume (a name inspired by his mother's maiden name of Valentin) but was continued for forty-five additional novels and short stories using the pseudonym Mark Cross, the first of which was *The Shadow of the Four* (1934).

Books and stories frequently begin with Daphne calling a meeting of her associates, explaining a situation for them, and requesting their help in "adjusting" a miscarriage of justice—a request never denied. The various skills of the members assure a satisfying outcome. The members of the group are Sir Hugh Williamson, a noted African explorer; James Treviller, a handsome young nobleman; Martin Everest, a lawyer; and Alan Sylvester, an actor. They secretly operate outside the law, and the police are suspicious of them. Although they can't positively identify them as the goodhearted vigilantes that they are, the police are confident that Daphne is the head of *some* sort of helpful organization and turn a blind eye to its activities.

"The Wizard's Safe" was originally published in the June 16, 1928, issue of *Detective Fiction Weekly*.

The Wizard's Safe

VALENTINE

THE DUCHESS OF ARLINGTON, stout, comfortable, complacent-looking, sank down with a sigh into the easy chair and smiled affectionately at Daphne Wrayne. All the same she was distinctly puzzled, for it was the first time she had entered that luxurious room.

Daphne herself she had known from babyhood and when she had launched out into that extraordinary enterprise known as the Adjusters she, the duchess, was one of the first to cross-question her upon it. Not that she had learned any more from the girl than the public knew.

The Adjusters had suddenly sprung into being one day in lavishly furnished offices in Conduit Street. Their object, they said, was to handle and solve the cases with which the police were unable to cope—and they charge no fees whatsoever!

But that was a year ago, and today the duchess knew as she gazed at pretty, beautifully dressed Daphne Wrayne smiling at her from her big carved oak chair, that this girl represented the Adjusters as far as the public knew.

She admitted to four mysterious colleagues, but no one had ever seen them. According to her, no one was ever going to see them! But the duchess knew, because the press constantly told her so, that the public, rich and poor alike, brought all sorts of cases to Daphne—and Daphne solved them!

At the moment she was almost the most talked-of young woman in the whole of London, credited with the most amazing powers. Though she herself invariably denied them.

"So this is where you do all your Sherlock Holmes stuff, is it?" said the duchess, gazing round the room. "What an amazin' young woman you are, my dear."

THE BIGGEST BRAINS

"Everybody's talkin' about you—crazy to know who's with you in this show of yours. What on earth you do it for I don't know. The modern young women simply get me beat."

Daphne Wrayne laughed softly.

"Well, it's huge fun."

"Tell that to any one who'll swallow it!" retorted the other with a little sniff. "I haven't known you from babyhood for nothing. You never studied law for those years just for fun—don't tell me!

"Though why on earth you charge no fees in this place, defeats me. D'you know that you've made such a name for yourselves that you could charge some of your clients what you like?"

"I believe we could," calmly, "but as we run the risk almost every week of our lives of being caught, tried and sent to prison—"

"You sit there and tell me that?" amazed.

"I do, and mean it. Oh, mind you, duchess, there'd be no stigma attaching to any one of us. I'm not even sure that any jury would convict us even if we *were* caught. At the same time we've got to work with absolutely clean hands and the moment the public knows we're making money out of this show our hands cease to be absolutely clean. And that's why we never charge any fees.

"Everybody suspected us at first—they were bound to. Philanthropy's rare these days. But gradually they've learned they can trust us. We've solved cases that have baffled the police, and—which is far more important—there's no publicity."

"But how on earth do you do it?"

The girl smiled.

"It's not amazingly difficult, duchess, come to think of it. A capital of a quarter of a million—that's our first asset. Four of the biggest brains in England—that's the second. And those four going everywhere and mixing with everybody and no one with even the vaguest notion of who they are."

"You mean to say I know them?" incredulously.

"Most assuredly," smiling, "though you haven't even an idea that they're my colleagues. And until we trip up, you and the public never will."

EASY ENOUGH

The duchess drew a deep breath.

"It's beyond words!" she said.

"Well, then," went on the girl, "the police are working all the time under a handicap and we're not. If the police, say, have reason to suspect a man of holding stolen property they daren't enter his house and search it unless they're practically sure. If they make a mistake there's big trouble following.

"But that never worries us," with an amused little laugh, "always provided that we don't get caught. There's no one to prosecute us because

no one knows who to prosecute. We can *tell* 'em we're the Adjusters, but that won't help 'em.

"The only one of the Adjusters whom the public has ever seen is Daphne Wrayne. And Daphne Wrayne merely sits in this office like a good little girl. It's her colleagues who pull the chestnuts out of the fire."

The duchess regarded her helplessly. To look at the girl it all seemed so utterly preposterous. Anything less like the popular conception of the tread of a great criminal-hunting organization she found it impossible to imagine.

She studied the rose-leaf skin, the big, serious, brown eyes, the fair, curly hair, and the adorable little mouth. She looked at the slender bare arms, the slim, ringless hands—she looked at the wisp of a black frock that almost shrieked Bond Street in its expensive simplicity. She looked at the amber silk clad legs and the dainty little high-heeled shoes.

"I give it up," she said.

Daphne laughed merrily.

"That's right, my dear," she answered. "Now have a cigarette and tell me what you want to see me about."

THE PROFESSOR'S HOUSE

The duchess took the cigarette offered to her, lit it, and lay back in her chair.

"You saw, of course, that I had my jewels stolen last week?"

"I did."

"I was at the Yard this morning. They haven't got a clew and they told me so. Absolutely baffled. 'I shall go to the Adjusters then,' I said, thinking to annoy them.

"'Can't do better,' said Montarthur, who's in charge of the case. 'If Miss Wrayne can't find 'em, no one can.' Frankly, my dear, I was amazed. How on earth have you managed it?"

"Oh, we've helped the Yard in one or two cases," carelessly. "Sir Arthur Conroy's a darling. So is Montarthur, for that matter. We're huge pals. But let's get back to your case.

"I saw it in the papers, of course, but I didn't read it. I never read the newspaper reports of cases where I'm not consulted."

"I've taken Professor Daventry's house at Ascot for a month," began the duchess, but Daphne stopped her.

"Who's he?"

"A wealthy old recluse—half a dozen letters after his name—written a dozen books on abstruse mathematics, inventive wizard—you'll find him in 'Who's Who'—half a page to his name. Lets his house every year for a month at an exorbitant fee and jogs off to the Riviera."

"Is he there now?"

"He is."

"Right. Go ahead."

The duchess lighted another cigarette.

"Beautiful house called Forest Lodge, sumptuously furnished with every modern convenience imaginable—even down to burglar alarms. Don't wonder at that. He's got some fine pictures and china, too."

"Well?"

"The first night I was there I went to bed and locked all my jewels away in the safe in my bedroom."

"Oh, you've got a safe there?"

"Yes—the latest pattern let into the wall, behind one of the pictures. There are only two keys in existence. I have one and the professor has the other. Mine has never left my possession."

ON MONDAY NIGHT

"And the professor's on the Riviera," smiled Daphne.

"Quite so."

"Who else knows of the existence of this safe?" put in the girl. "Any of the servants in the house?"

"The butler, Daventry's butler, admitted that he did. Incidentally I took over half a dozen of Daventry's servants, but every one of 'em has been with him for years. I took my own maid with me, but I'd trust her with anything."

"I see. Well, go on, duchess."

"As I said I went to bed on Monday night after locking all my jewels up in the safe."

"And the key?"

"Slept with it under my pillow."

"Was it there next morning?"

"It was."

"Your bedroom door locked?"

"It was."

"Windows?"

"Both open at the top, but they're fifty feet from the ground."

"When did you next go to the safe?"

"The following evening before dinner. I took the key out of my vanity bag which had never left my hands all day, opened the safe and—everything gone!"

"What does everything include?"

"Six cases. My diamond necklace, my pearl necklace, my diamond tiara, my diamond pendant, and my two diamond bracelets. And if you put 'em at two hundred thousand pounds, my dear, you're not a long way out."

FOR AN OLD FRIEND

"And the police found nothing?" after a pause.

"All the police found, my dear, were footprints beneath my bedroom window and most of the burglar wires cut."

Daphne's eyebrows went up.

"That's interesting," she said.

For some moments she sat deep in thought frowning at her blotting pad. Then:

"I'll run down and have a chat with Montarthur," she said, "and I think I'll get you to put me up for a day or two, duchess."

"By all means, my dear," with alacrity. "When shall I expect you?"

"Tonight probably," after a little deliberation.

"Got a clew?"

Daphne threw back her head and laughed merrily.

"My dear duchess, I'm a girl, not a magician! You surely don't expect me to have one so soon?"

"Frankly, inspector," said Daphne Wrayne, as she and Montarthur sat together in the latter's private room, "I'm only taking up this case because the Duchess of Arlington is an old friend.

"I don't see the vaguest hope of succeeding where you people have failed, and I tell you so. But I can't very well refuse, and I know you'll understand. Now what can you tell me?"

"Very little, I'm afraid, Miss Wrayne," with a shrug of his shoulders. "We found footprints, very big footprints, in the flower beds immediately below the duchess's window, but there isn't a pair of boots in the house that will fit 'em. We've interviewed all the servants and there isn't one of them we can suspect."

"What about the guests?"

He handed her a list.

"There they are."

Daphne ran her eyes over the paper.

"I know every one of 'em," she remarked laconically. Then: "The duchess tells me that some of the wires were cut?"

"Yes—evidently by a man who knew the wiring. That's the only shadow of a clew we've got. The wires cut were the ones that affected only the duchess's bedroom."

WHAT MIGHT HAVE HAPPENED

"Really? And her windows were open she tells me!"

"They were. But there's not a trace of any sort on the window ledges. Yet she swears her door was locked so that entry could only have been made from the windows."

Daphne shook her head.

"You mustn't forget, inspector, that we don't *know* that the safe was tampered with during the night. She locked up her jewels at twelve on Monday and never opened the safe till six thirty on Tuesday."

"You mean it might have been done during Tuesday, Miss Wrayne?"

"Well, it's possible, isn't it?"

"The duchess swears the key of the safe was never out of her possession."

"My sex swears a lot of things—and believe 'em, too. Find any marks round the safe lock?"

He leaned forward.

"Very tiny traces of wax, Miss Wrayne!" he answered.

Daphne nodded.

"Then that tells us how it was done."

"Yes, but not who did it," ruefully.

She laughed.

"Well, just because two heads are always better than one, inspector, I'm going down there for a night or two. And if by any chance you've missed anything," her brown eyes sparkling deliciously, "Heaven help you!"

She got up from her chair. Then suddenly stopped.

A MOTLEY GANG

"By the way, inspector, you don't happen to know when those alarm wires were installed and why?"

"Yes. I've found that out," he replied. "The professor had them fitted in six months ago. There was an attempted burglary and a successful one there just about a year ago.

"The first was while the professor was in residence himself, but he alarmed the burglars and they got away with nothing. The second was when Lady Castlebrough was in residence. The professor lets his house every summer for Ascot."

"I know. The duchess told me. What went that time?"

"Some of the professor's own silver—not of very great value, though."

"Any points of similarity between that robbery and this one?" queried the girl carelessly.

"None, Miss Wrayne."

"Right! Then I won't bother you any further."

Anyone who had been privileged to peep into a locked room in the Euston the following afternoon, a room whose door bore the commonplace name of James Martin, would have seen five people—four men and a girl—sitting round a fire talking in low tones.

Probably, unless he was an unusually observant person—which few are—he wouldn't have lingered there. For the room was merely a meagerly furnished office such as you may see anywhere.

And the still life was represented by no more than half a dozen deal chairs, a writing table with a few papers and commercial books, and a small safe.

Neither was the animated life, to the casual observer, worthy of more than the merest glance. All the four men were shabbily dressed. One of them, a big bronzed giant of a man with rather nice eyes, wore a muffler round his neck and smoked a brier pipe.

The tall, thin, rather hawklike-looking man who sat next to him had his coat collar turned up and his hands thrust deep into his overcoat pockets as he lounged in his chair.

The elderly, white-haired man with the benevolent face had turned his chair round and was straddling it, his arms resting on the back. The clean-shaven, good-looking, rather boyish man in the shiny blue suit was smoking a cigarette.

THE SHABBY TYPIST

The girl, an amazingly pretty girl, too, was obviously in no better circumstances than those who sat facing her. A city typist perhaps on a few pounds a week judging from her clothes—though even the shabbiness of them couldn't hide the slim beauty of her.

Had you told your casual observer that any one of these five could have written out a check for ten thousand pounds without, as the saying goes, feeling it, he would most probably have dropped down dead from sheer amazement.

Yet there were quite a number of people in Mayfair who would have been prepared to swear that if ever Daphne Wrayne of Conduit Street, Park Street, and Maidenhead had a twin sister, this girl must be she.

Half Debrett would have taken its oath without hesitation that the big bronzed giant was no other than Lord James Trevitter, the best known of all the sporting young English peers.

No less certain would they have been over the hawk-faced man. They would have known him at once as Sir Hugh Williamson, the great explorer.

The theatrical world would have identified the white-haired man in a second as Alan Sylvester, the popular actor manager. Bench and bar wouldn't have hesitated even fractionally over the handsome, clean-shaven, cigarette-smoking man.

They would have been positive that it was Martin Everest, K. C., the biggest criminal barrister of modern times.

DOING THE IMPOSSIBLE

Yet there was scarcely a man in England who wouldn't have given half of all he possessed to know what was only known to these five people. And that was that these men were the Adjusters!

"Jimmy" Trevitter was the first to speak, as he puffed at his brier pipe.

"Let's have it, darling," he began, for he and Daphne Wrayne had been engaged for months past, though no one but those in that room knew of it. "What is it today—blackmail, burglary, arson, or forgery?"

"The Duchess of Arlington's jewels," answered the girl as she drew off her shabby gloves and disclosed daintily manicured hands, strangely at variance with them. "She came to see me this morning."

Martin Everest frowned.

"So the police are at a dead end, Daph?"

"Absolutely—worse luck."

"Like that?"

"Sure," admitted the girl with a little sigh. "I saw Montarthur this morning and told him the duchess had been to me. He was very charming, but I fancy he thought the same as I think—that we've got our work cut out.

"That's the worst of acquiring a reputation like ours. We're expected to do the impossible—"

"We advertised it, my dear, at the start," suggested Williamson with a smile.

"I know, confound it," answered the girl with a little laugh. "And now it's coming home. If only people would come to us at once instead of—here's the case, over ten days old and the duchess expects us to solve it! If she wasn't such a dear old thing I'd have told her to go to Hades."

She opened a packet of cigarettes, took one out, lit it.

"Still we've got to go for it, I suppose. I said I would. I'm off to Ascot tonight. And now I'll tell you all I've got from Montarthur and perhaps you can give me a few suggestions."

It was interesting to watch the four men as she talked, interesting to see how they hung on her words. They were all serious now and you could see in a moment that each one of them realized the quick, alert little brain that lay behind that thoughtful, beautiful young face of the girl who spoke so eagerly to them.

"Incidentally I went in to see Lady Castlebrough this morning," she said, as she came to the end of her story. "I thought it might be as well."

A GOOD DETECTIVE

"Learn anything fresh there?" queried Trevitter.

"I learned something," answered the girl slowly, "though whether it's of any value or not I really don't know.

"You see, the Castlebrough jewels are nearly as valuable as the Arlington jewels, and they're both pretty famous. Is it pure coincidence that the house is let in two consecutive years to two people with wonderful jewels?"

"Are you suspecting the professor, Daph?" asked Everest in the pause that followed.

"A good detective puts *nobody* outside the pale of suspicion at the start, Martin," retorted the girl. "Who knows anything of the professor?"

"I do," said Williamson. "A little, clean-shaven, fussy, didactic sort of a chap. Marvelous mathematical brain and a bit of an expert on criminology. You'll see him at most of the big trials at the Central Criminal Court."

"Quite right. I've seen him," asserted Everest, "though I don't know him to speak to."

"I attend most of 'em myself," smiled the girl, "but I'd hate to have a black mark against me in consequence."

"What's your idea, Daph?" queried Trevitter.

AN INSIDE JOB

"Oh, I haven't got one, Jim. I'm just searching for any suspicious circumstance that will give me a line. And the professor only becomes suspicious because he did exactly the same to Lady Castlebrough as he did to the duchess. He showed both of them over the house, showed *both* of them the safe, and apparently dilated to both of them on its invulnerability!

"Now the duchess locks up her jewels in the safe and they're stolen. But Lady Castlebrough doesn't. She confided to me that she never believes in safes. Says that a burglar always goes for them, first thing.

"In each case there's an attempted burglary the moment after these two people arrive. In the first case some silver of no value is stolen. In the second we find footprints and the jewels gone from the safe. But I'm wondering whether in the *first* case the safe and the jewels weren't the *real* objective?

"Frankly, from what Montarthur tells me, I'm inclined to look on those footprints as a purposeful blind. He's prepared to stake his reputation on the fact that the room was never entered by the window. In which case it was entered by the door.

"And we can assume that it was the work of some one who knew the distribution of the household. Otherwise why did he cut the wires outside the duchess's bedroom?"

"Excellent bit of reasoning, my dear," smiled Everest, "but where are your facts to fit it?"

"Of course, that's the trouble," admitted the girl. "I haven't got any. All the same, Martin, we can at least follow our usual methods."

"You mean *your* unusual methods, my dear," with a chuckle.

"All right. Have it your way," laughing. "But you know as well as I do that because I'm a girl and a young one at that, I help to balance you men."

"That," said Williamson thoughtfully, "is the greatest asset we've got. An impulsive young woman whose extensive legal training can't entirely stop her from remembering that after all she's a woman and therefore must at times follow intuition blindly, lest she be untrue to her sex.

"So, my child, I'll tackle the professor forthwith."

"I want you to," retorted the girl. "He caught the eight fifty-three from Ascot on Saturday morning the sixteenth and was supposed to leave for the Riviera on the eleven o'clock from Victoria."

TELLING IT STRAIGHT

"He had a reservation. Verify that—it shouldn't be difficult. Of course," a little twinkle came into her eyes, "if you'd care to fly over to Cannes to the Megantic Hotel and see if—"

"It's as well money's no object," answered Williamson, with a grin. "You'd break any ordinary firm in a week. Still, there's nothing like doing a job properly.

"I believe half our success is due to the fact that we do so many entirely unnecessary things

that we can't help hitting the necessary one in the process."

Daphne made a little *moue.*

"Well, we get there," she replied. "All the same I can't quite see how we're going to get there this time, and I tell you so straight. It looks seriously to me as if we'd taken on the impossible."

For nearly an hour more they sat there discussing the case from every angle. But that was always Daphne Wrayne's method. She had laid it down emphatically once to a reporter, and her words had been repeated in the next morning's paper to form a controversy that lasted for weeks.

"The police are only out to catch the criminal," she had said. "We're merely after recovering the victim's stolen property. Therefore we're bound to work on different lines for the most part."

HUNTING THE UNUSUAL

"In cases where the police have been called in first and have covered all the ordinary channels without success, we are fairly safe in assuming that we have to look to the *unusual* ones for the solution of the problem. Therefore, if time permits, I call my colleagues together and ask for new ideas.

"No idea that they suggest is too impossible to be dismissed. Each one, however fantastic, has to be labeled and held in readiness in case one single new fact arises to suggest that it has a chance of being the correct solution."

Consequently when Daphne arrived that evening at Forest Lodge, though she was by no means suspecting the professor of any share in the robbery she was holding in her mind the remote possibility that he could have had something to do with it.

"Except for myself and my servants, my dear," said the duchess, "the house is empty. All my guests have gone and I've put off those who were coming—for a couple of days. You're a famous young woman, you know, and I don't want to handicap you in any way."

"The famous young woman," replied the girl airily, "hasn't a notion what to do and doesn't mind admitting it. Still she's trying. Give her some tea, please, and then let her come up and see your room. All pukka detectives do that. No! I'm hanging on to this attaché case. It's highly important."

"What's in it?" asked the duchess interestedly.

"The usual stock in trade," answered Daphne with a little laugh. "An amazingly powerful magnifying glass, a foot-rule, a pair of compasses, a complete apparatus for finger-prints, a very extra-special camera and apparatus, bottles, boxes, *et cetera*. Some detective this child, I assure you!"

She dropped into a chair and producing her case lit a cigarette.

"Any news, duchess?"

"Not a bit. Have you?"

"Nix."

"Any theories?"

"Whole bunches—and no facts to fit 'em."

The duchess regarded her half smiling.

"I wish I could understand you, Daph!" she said. "You look like a schoolgirl on a holiday."

THE MYSTERIOUS ROOM

"Well, that's all I am really—only I'm on an interesting job of work. I don't believe anyone will ever believe in me until I wear horn-rimmed glasses, homemade frocks, and elastic-sided boots. It's a hard world for us women."

She sighed pathetically as she lay back in her chair crossing her slender silken legs. But her eyes were mischievous all the same.

"Then why don't you do it?" retorted the duchess.

"No darned fear! I just love fogging people. Come on!" jumping up. "Let's go and explore the mysterious room."

For nearly an hour the duchess sat in a chair in the corner of her bedroom while Daphne wandered round exploring everything. Scarcely a word passed between them during that hour—but the duchess saw an entirely new Daphne Wrayne.

There was very little of the "schoolgirl on a holiday" now about her. She went over every inch of that room with serious face and wrinkled white forehead. Nothing seemed to escape her notice. Magnifying glass in hand she examined every nook and crevice, safe, doors, floor, ceiling, walls.

Then at last she finished, came slowly over to the fireplace, pulled up a chair, lit another cigarette. She was looking puzzled, almost worried. For some minutes she smoked in silence, her eyes on the fire. Then at last the duchess spoke.

AT A DEAD END

"Well, my dear?" she ventured.

The girl's head came up quickly, and a smile flickered over her face.

"You're rather a sweet person, aren't you?" she queried. "You still persist in believing that I can do what the police have been unable to do. But I'm afraid," a little wistfully, "that I've got to disappoint you.

"Duchess, all I *can* tell you is that I'm absolutely certain the burglar never came in through the window. But then I knew that before I came down here. And yet——" With an impatient gesture she got up from her chair and gazed round the room frowning.

"Those footprints outside were a blind," she said shortly. "They were deliberately done to make you think that the burglar entered by the window. Momentarily, I'm at a dead end. I think I'll go and have a hot tub and dress for dinner."

A look of disappointment crossed the duchess's face, but she merely answered quietly:

"I'll take you and show you your room, my dear."

Dinner was rather a taciturn meal. Daphne in her silver frock, and white shoes and stockings was looking more absurdly schoolgirlish than ever, but she seemed distinctly preoccupied and times without number her eyes kept wandering to the telephone which stood in the corner of the room.

And then suddenly it whirred into one of its calls and she sprang to her feet.

"That may be for me, duchess!" she exclaimed as she ran across the room. Then: "Hello—hello! Yes! It's Daphne Wrayne speaking." A little pause, and very slowly and deliberately: "P. Q. R. 22. Answer, please!"

The duchess looked on open-mouthed, saw the sudden smile that rippled over the girl's face, and heard her go on, relief in her voice:

"Is that you, A 3? Well, have you any news for me?"

The duchess watched her intently. The beautiful face now became grave in a moment, a little frown had developed on the smooth white forehead—Daphne was listening intently, nodding thoughtfully, but still obviously worried.

"Yes, as you say, it's distinctly curious— Oh! Most certainly suspicious! Can't find a single thing to help us—I shall be here all tomorrow in case you find out anything more—Good-by, old man!"

LIKE A FLASH

She hung up the receiver slowly, thoughtfully— came back to her chair and sat down. Absently she picked up her cigarette case.

"Duchess," she said, "if you take my tip you'll never embark on a career like mine. It's just one mass of—"

She stopped suddenly, abruptly. One slim hand had gone up to her mouth. Her whole attitude was that of one who had suddenly been arrested by an amazing idea.

"What's the matter, Daph?"

For the space of seconds the girl sat very still as if carved in stone. Then:

"Duchess! Where's the safe key?"

"In the safe. You left it there."

"Wait here a minute!"

She was out of the room in a flash. In a few minutes she was back again, but now her cheeks were flushed and her eyes were shining.

"Duchess!" her voice was almost quivering. "Come upstairs with me—quickly, please! Oh, don't talk! Just come!"

Up in the bedroom Daphne turned to the amazed woman who was staring helplessly around.

"I want an empty jewel case—quickly!" she said. "Any old one will do."

SOLVING IT

Still regarding her bewilderedly the other went to her chest of drawers, unlocked it.

"Will this do?"

"Fine! Anything in it? No? Good. Come over to the safe!"

Snatching the case from her hands Daphne half pulled her across the room, flung open the safe.

"Now I'm putting it inside—see?"

She thrust the jewel case in, pushed to the safe door, turned the key—waited for the space of seconds. Then once more she turned the key in the lock and pulled open the safe door.

The safe was empty!

In a moment she had seized the duchess by the waist and was whirling her round the room delightedly.

"I've solved it, I've solved it!" she exclaimed. "Your jewels are here, old lady—in this very room! And if I have to pull the darned place to pieces I'll have 'em for you this very night."

"But—but"—stammering—"I don't understand—"

"Lock the door quickly," interrupted the girl, "we don't want anyone in. And don't ask me any questions for a few minutes, for the love of Mike."

She was across the room in a moment and

regardless of her dainty frock was down on her hands and knees tapping on the walls and the floor in the immediate neighborhood of the safe. As for the duchess she could only stand and watch her, speechless.

"I'm afraid we've got to move this chest of drawers!" exclaimed Daphne suddenly, jumping up and pointing to the big mahogany piece that stood immediately under the picture that had hidden the safe. "Can you give me a hand, my dear?"

"Won't we need some help?"

Daphne made an impatient gesture.

"For Heaven's sake, no! There'll be enough scandal as it is presently."

They got it away at last by dint of extensive shoving and pushing. And then Daphne was down on her hands and knees again pulling back the carpet—and suddenly she gave a little cry of triumph.

"Great heavens!" exclaimed the duchess.

No more than that. She simply stood there staring with bulging eyes. At her side, Daphne Wrayne on her knees, rippling delight in every line of her pretty face. And before her a trap door pushed back, a yawning black cavity, and at the bottom of it in a heap—the Duchess of Arlington's jewel cases!

A WONDERFUL SAFE

"Montarthur was positive," said Daphne as she and the duchess sat together over the fire, "that the burglary was *not* done through the window. And the moment I came to examine the window I was equally sure.

"But both of us were led astray by the fact that from twelve o'clock at midnight until six thirty the next evening it was *possible* for anyone to enter this room of yours. All the same Montarthur missed the full significance of two facts which both my colleagues and I spotted.

"The first was that both Lady Castlebrough and yourself possess very famous jewels. The second, that the professor showed you *both* over the house himself, and in each case *dilated on the advantages of the safe*. I'm not saying I suspected the professor from that moment. But I do say that he then became a person who had to be cleared.

"Supposing that the professor had duplicate keys of the house and safe—as he easily could have. What easier than for him to use them? He knows the whole place.

"If by any chance he is discovered in the house, it's his own house, and he can bring up a hundred excuses to cover himself."

She paused a moment to light the inevitable cigarette and then went on:

BEFORE THE CALL

"And the professor came further under my direct notice from the fact that apparently only he knew that you were going to occupy this room. And this was when he made his big mistake.

"He argued that by cutting the wires outside your bedroom only, we should immediately say after seeing the footprints, 'That's how the burglar entered.'

"Instead of which, I said, after examining everything, 'Those footprints were obviously a blind—and what the cut wires tell me is that only a person with a very intimate knowledge of the house could have done this.' Valuable deduction, my dear!"

"I don't wonder the Adjusters are a success," murmured the duchess admiringly. "Daph, you're simply wonderful."

"Frankly," admitted the girl, though the pleasure was showing in her face, "I don't agree. I happen to have a logical mind and that's why I took this game up. You had only been in residence a day, duchess! No one without an intimate knowledge of you and your movements *could* have known in what room you were.

"Montarthur had the records of all the servants from A to Z. It was no use my going over the old ground again. The Adjusters are only called in when the police methods—darned thorough methods, too, let me tell you—have failed.

"The only reason, believe me, why we discover the seemingly impossible is because that's all there is left for us to look for! It isn't such marvelous cleverness, duchess! The mere fact of the police being baffled tells us that only the really fantastic can find the solution to the problem."

"But how did you get to this amazing solution, Daphne?" queried the other. "What gave you the idea of that safe?"

"As you know," answered the girl thoughtfully, "I was up against a dead end, right until the phone bell rang. It was one of my colleagues who called me up and this is what he told."

She leaned forward in her chair checking off the points on her slim fingers.

"The professor canceled his departure on the Saturday morning train—took another reservation on Tuesday morning and went by it. The disappearance of your jewels happened some time after Monday night."

THE PROFESSOR'S TRIP

"The professor, incidentally staying at the Continental, left his hotel on Monday evening at nine o'clock and arrived back about twelve thirty that night. My colleague trots off to Ascot in his car. Makes inquiries.

"The porter remembers the professor traveling up on that particular night—knows him well by sight—and on that particular ten forty train. Quaint, isn't it? Why had he come down? Where had he been? What had he been doing?"

As she paused, smiling at the duchess, the latter drew a deep breath.

"But even then that was an hour and a half before I went to bed!" she said.

"Quite so," replied the girl, "and that proved obviously that the professor didn't go down to *get into his house*. Then why did he go? Obviously to plant those footmarks and make

you think positively that some one had been in the house.

"Then I said to myself: 'Obviously he never entered the house at all, and if he didn't, where are the jewels?' And then in a moment, duchess, the idea came out and hit me between the eyes. If you put something in a box, shut the box, open it again and find that something's gone, then obviously one of two things has happened.

"Either somebody's taken it out, or—it's never been taken out at all! And that's why I left the table in such a hurry to go and test my theory. I took an empty jewel case of my own, shoved it in the safe, locked it, reopened it and—it had gone! The whole thing was clear.

"The professor is an ingenious crook playing for enormous stakes. He tried for the Castlebrough jewels and failed, just because Lady Castlebrough happens to distrust safes. You don't and—well, he nearly got away with it!

"When Montarthur comes to take that safe to pieces, he'll find, I fancy, that it's a masterpiece of ingenuity and shows the amazingly clever mechanical brain of our learned friend. He will find that the turning of the key releases the bottom of the safe, the contents slide through, and the bottom comes up again.

"It's really a masterpiece of construction. I've examined the inside of the safe pretty thoroughly and even now I know I can't detect exactly how it's done!"

She stretched her slender white arms above her head, yawning a little. Then:

"Of course, I've done my part of the job," she said. "You asked me for your jewels and you've got 'em. Naturally I'm now turning the whole business over to Montarthur and he can do what he pleases.

"Though if the professor chooses to swear, as he probably will swear, that he knows nothing whatsoever about this 'peculiarity' of his safe, Montarthur's not going to have a cakewalk to convict him.

"Mind you, I haven't the slightest doubt that

he did it, but it's going to be purely circumstantial. If I were defending him I think I could make out quite a good case for him. Just shows, duchess," with a smile, "what clever people we Adjusters really are!

"All we do is to find the stolen stuff, give it to the rightful owners and get all the kudos. These other poor fish have to get convictions—and that's an appalling business when once you start!"

RED HOT

Frederick Nebel

NOT ONLY WAS LOUIS FREDERICK NEBEL (1903–1967) a prolific writer of pulp fiction, but he achieved that magical gold ring for writers of that era—creating a successful series, meaning that there was always a market for another story or novella. In fact, Nebel, who was at the very top of the B-list authors of the pulp era, wrote several long-running series, mainly for *Black Mask* and its closest rival, *Dime Detective*, in a career that essentially ended after a single decade (1927-1937). His protagonists are tough and frequently violent, but they bring a strong moral code to their jobs, as well as a level of realism achieved by few other pulp writers.

Homicide Captain Steve MacBride, who is as hard-boiled as they come, was a *Black Mask* fixture for nearly a decade, as was his ever-present sidekick, *Free Press* reporter Kennedy, who provides comic relief in most of the thirty-seven stories in which they appear.

Donny "Tough Dick" Donahue of the Interstate agency, with twenty-one adventures, all in *Black Mask*, ran from 1930 to 1935; a half dozen of the best were collected in *Six Deadly Dames* (1950).

The stories featuring Jack Cardigan, an operative for the Cosmos Detective Agency, and Patricia Seaward, who works for him on nearly fifty cases, ran from 1931 to 1937 in the pages of *Dime Detective*; some of the best were published in *The Adventures of Cardigan* (1988). Seaward is as tough as, and a lot smarter than, the big, somewhat thuggish Irish P.I. she assists, and she covers his back on numerous occasions.

Nebel wrote two novels, both of which were filmed: *Sleepers East* (1933), released a year after the novel was published, starring Wynne Gibson, Preston Foster, and Mona Barrie, and *Fifty Roads to Town* (1936), released in 1937, starring Don Ameche, Ann Sothern, Slim Summerville, and Jane Darwell.

"Red Hot" was originally published in the July 1, 1934, issue of *Dime Detective*; it was first collected in *The Complete Casebook of Cardigan, Volume 3: 1934-35* (Boston, Altus, 2012).

Red Hot

FREDERICK NEBEL

CHAPTER I
Hard-Boiled Heir

THE HOTEL CITADEL was small, decent, with a quiet gray front and no doorman. It had a long, narrow lobby hung with pictures of Yosemite, the redwood forests, and Half Moon Bay, and it rose narrowly in a quiet street near the St. Francis and Union Square. The man at the desk was old, neat, with a polished bald head, oval-shaped spectacles, and a sweeping gray mustache, not a hair of which was out of place. The hotel was not stuffy. It was merely quiet, proper, and successful, catering more to the residential trade than to the transient.

Cardigan punched open the single swing-door and came in with a blast of chill, damp wind. His big feet smacked the lozenge-shaped tiles as he headed for the desk singing, "Ta-ra-da-boom-de-ay, ta-ra-da-boom-de-ay," in a low, good-humored voice. He bore down on the desk, a large, bulky man in a battered old fedora; a shaggy ulster with one lapel turned up and the other turned down.

Reaching the desk, he scooped up one of the two house phones and said expansively to the aged clerk: "Good evening, Mr. Birdsong. Think it'll stop raining?"

————

Mr. Birdsong didn't like noisy people; he said fretfully, "It always has stopped, Mr. Cardigan," and petulantly turned a ledger page.

Cardigan laughed, said: "I guess that puts me in my place. Well, sir—" He broke off to say into the transmitter, "Miss Seaward, please." Waiting, he tapped his foot; then, "Pat? . . . This is your favorite detective . . . I want you to come down. . . . Why? A little job on which your sweetness and light are needed, sugar. Right away . . . Of course I'm downstairs."

He hung up, planked down the instrument and rolled off to the corner of the lobby, where he flopped into a large leather chair and shot his legs out straight. He lit a long, black cigar and was just getting into it when Pat came out of the elevator. She carried a small umbrella and looked very smart in black hat, a three-quarter-length, black lapin coat, and black patent-leather pumps. Cardigan rose out of the chair, pushing with his hands.

"I was just about to jump into the tub," Pat said.

"Every time I call up, you're either jumping in a tub or out of one. Don't you ever just sit—and maybe knit?"

"I can't knit."

"You'd be a swell one to live with, either jumping in a tub or jumping out of one. Learn knitting."

"Thank God I only work for you; that's enough."

They were on their way to the door and he said: "There's not much to this job, Patsy I just need you to put on a sob act." He held open the swing-door and followed her out into the street. "Hey, taxi," he yelled.

They climbed in and he gave an address and sat back with his cigar, as the cab headed off through the afternoon drizzle.

"Sob act?" Pat said.

"Sort of. This afternoon a man by the name of Martin Strang walks into the office. He's from Denver and he's worth dough. Well, he's looking for a young fellow by the name of Husted Hull, who happens to be his nephew. Martin Strang's sister married Burton Hull and old Burton Hull died two months ago in Colorado Springs. Hull's wife died four years ago.

"They've been trying for two months to get Husted Hull to come back to Denver for the reading of his old man's will. But the lad won't come back. It seems he's been knocking around the West ever since his mother died. She left him a thousand bucks a month and he had a falling-out with his old man. When the old man died he stipulated that his son Husted must be present at the reading of the will. Well, they wrote and wrote, and Martin Strang wrote, but the only reply they got was a telegram that said, 'Go stand on your head.'

"So Strang came out. He has no idea where Husted Hull lives. The lawyers who send the thousand a month regularly said he's been in San Francisco for three months but the only address is 'General Delivery.' He's lived in Seattle, San Diego, Los Angeles, and so on, but he's always had his mail sent care of General Delivery. Strang said he married about three years ago, about a year after he left home. He said then, I'm told, that he'd never have anything to do with his old man or any other member of the family. Strang came to me and asked me to locate him and make an appointment for them at my office."

"And you located him?"

Cardigan slapped his knee. "I located him.

Did you expect the old master wouldn't? First I called up all the hotels. No luck. Then I tried the telephone company—information. No luck. Then I tried the banks. One bank has a depositor named Husted Hull. I went down and spoke with the manager, laid my cards on the table, and got Hull's address. We're going there now."

"It seems rather futile, doesn't it?"

"Maybe not. This Strang looks to me like a decent old bird. He doesn't care about what he'll get out of it. He's got plenty himself. Soon as he left I called our Denver office on long-distance and they shot back an A-one report on him. He's sore—sore because his nephew's taking this attitude. I guess young Hull was the black sheep, though his mother loved him and left him that thousand a month. If we can get him and Strang together, it may be different. Do you get the setup now?"

The cab drew to the curb and Cardigan, saying, "Guess this is it," climbed out into the cold San Francisco rain. Pat followed and looked up at a four-story building while Cardigan paid the driver. They walked into a glass vestibule, on one wall of which was a series of brass buttons with names beneath. Cardigan pressed one of these and listened. The inner door clicked open and he grabbed Pat's arm and walked her into the hallway. They climbed a narrow stairway to the first landing, which had a door on either side. There were no name plates, but in a moment they heard the click of heels upstairs and they climbed the second staircase. Now they heard laughter, voices, a radio playing. A girl was standing on the second landing.

"Mrs. Hull?" Cardigan asked.

"Yes?" she said politely, with an inquisitive twist of her pretty head.

"Is Mr. Hull in?"

"Yes—yes, of course. Won't you . . . ?" She motioned to the open door.

The apartment foyer was small, with two high-backed chairs standing against the wall. The radio and the voices were beyond.

Cardigan was saying: "This is Miss Seaward, Mrs. Hull. My name's Cardigan. I guess you're busy, but if your husband'd just step out here."

She smiled. "I'll get him."

As she said this, a tall, yellow-haired young man came into the foyer from the inner corridor. A slab of hair lay down over one eyebrow and he held a highball in his hand.

Mrs. Hull took hold of his arm. "Dear, these people—Mr. Cardigan—"

Hull cut in with, "What do you want?" He was looking at Cardigan with pale eyes that suddenly burned with anger, and his hand shook, spilling some of the highball.

"Hughie," his wife said in a plaintive little voice. "Please, Hughie."

"Leggo," he snapped, ripped free of her hand. And again to Cardigan, "Well, what do you want?"

Cardigan stood on wide-planted feet. "Mr. Hull, take it easy."

The anger paused for a moment in Hull's eyes, then receded gradually. He dropped his gaze, jerked it around the small room, shrugged. "I'm sorry," he said.

Cardigan said: "Your uncle's in town."

Hull looked up, scowling. "What does he want?"

Pat stepped forward. "Mr. Hull, he wants you to go back to Denver with him. You must know all the details. He came all the way to San Francisco, just to talk with you, face to face. Why don't you see him? Why don't you?"

Hull looked at her vaguely. "See him?"

"Yes—please."

"No!" Hull snapped, his cheeks reddening. "They've written and written and written and they can all go hang on a limb. I want nothing to do with them. To hell with them. They all panned me when I was a kid. I was the black sheep—to all but my mother; and when she died, I skinned out."

Pat said: "But I understand the will can't be read until you're present. Your father made that stipulation."

"I know, I know!" Hull cried. "He wanted

to leave me ten cents or something. He wanted me to sit there while my cousins and uncle and aunts and whatnot got big money and I got—ten cents. Do you think I'll give them that satisfaction? No!"

Cardigan said, "Suppose you're right," in a blunt, man-to-man voice. "Suppose you're right, Mr. Hull. Suppose you are the black sheep. What of it? I was one myself. But why not show them you've got the guts to go back there and take it on the button?"

Hull was pretty drunk. He laughed. "Nothing doing. I'm getting a thousand a month from my mother's estate. That made them sore. Why, do you know what?" he demanded, his hand shaking, spilling some more of the drink. "Even if that old man of mine left me all he had, I wouldn't take it. Do you call that guts, Mr. Cardigan?"

His wife took hold of his arm again. "Hughie, dear, why don't you go back? It won't take long and then they won't bother you any more?"

He set his thin, pale jaw. "No, Bernice—no!"

"Hughie, please!"

"No, I tell you!" he cried, pulling free. He leveled an arm at Cardigan. "You go back to my uncle and tell him that if he puts his face inside my door I'll punch it off. Tell him that!" He swung around on his heel and plunged out of sight.

Cardigan went after him, saw his heels going in through a doorway, followed him into a large living room noisy with talk and radio music. Two girls and two men were in the room. All were pretty high. A little brunette yelped: "O-o-o-o, look at the great big nice man!"

A fat youth stumbled toward Cardigan with a glass and a bottle. "Have a drink, podner."

"Excuse me—"

"Come on, have a drink t' the last round-up or something."

Cardigan brushed him aside, bent on cornering Hull, who was at the other side of the room mixing another highball. Hull turned as Cardigan came up.

"Listen, Mr. Hull," Cardigan said. "Let's talk sense—"

Hull's eyes seemed to bloat with fresh anger. "I told you, didn't I? Will you please get the hell out of here!"

The little brunette got between them and raised her arms. "Dance with me, big man?" she cooed to Cardigan.

Cardigan picked her up and stood her aside, then took hold of Hull's lapel. "It's only reasonable, Mr. Hull—"

Hull flung his hand away. "You could talk all night and you'd still get the same answer. I'll not give those people the satisfaction of razzing me when the will is read. Now please beat it out of here!"

A big young fellow spun Cardigan around, looked at him and punched him on the jaw. Cardigan wound up on a divan. Bernice Hull ran in and cried: "Stop!"

The big young fellow said: "He insulted Josephine."

The little brunette was crying in a corner.

Cardigan got up and said: "I'd better go, Mrs. Hull."

She seemed to be the only one who was sober. She looked red and embarrassed.

As Cardigan started off, the big young fellow gripped him by the wrist, twisted his arm behind his back. "Say, 'Uncle,'" he said.

"Ralph, stop!" Bernice Hull pleaded.

Cardigan corkscrewed out of the grip, wrenched clear and left the big young fellow standing stupidly alone. "It's all right, Mrs. Hull," he said. "Boys will be boys."

He ducked into the corridor, reached the foyer, and found Pat waiting patiently.

Bernice Hull came running after him, saying: "I'm so sorry, so sorry." Her eyes pleaded with him. "I've begged him to go back, but Husted's so stubborn when he wants to be." Tears were almost in her eyes. "Please forgive us."

Pat said graciously: "Oh, there's nothing to forgive, Mrs. Hull."

Cardigan said: "If your husband changes his mind, I'm at the Cosmos Detective Agency, on Market Street. Or he can call his uncle, Mr. Strang, at the Hotel Farago."

They went downstairs and stood on the sidewalk, looking for a cab. The late afternoon was gray, drab, wet. Fog seemed to smoke sluggishly through the drizzle, and the tops of the taller buildings appeared to be afloat in the thick pall.

Cardigan held Pat's umbrella, a small thing with a short handle, but presently she grabbed it from him, saying: "If you don't mind, I'll hold it myself, because when you hold it, it does neither of us any good. A person would think you were waving a flag. Mrs. Hull's nice, isn't she?"

"She's a pip. But that husband of hers, he looks to me like the wrong end of an accident."

"What are you going to do now?"

"Report to Martin Strang and bail out. I should get into this family dog-fight? Ixnay. I did what I was hired to do. I located Husted Hull and called on him and please keep that damned umbrella out of my ear."

CHAPTER II
The Law Chisels In

When Pat walked in the agency office next morning Cardigan was slipping the telephone receiver slowly back into the hook. A deep furrow lay crookedly across his forehead, his brows were bent, and there was a sharp, compressed look in his eyes. He set the telephone down more quietly than he was accustomed to doing things and stared intently at it.

He said, more to himself than to Pat: "I don't like that."

"What's the matter, chief?" she asked anxiously.

He made a ball of his fist, laid it on the desk. "Maybe nothing. Maybe—" he rose out of his swivel chair—"lots."

"But—"

He cut in: "The manager of the Hotel Farago just called up—Ben Tremaine. When Martin Strang asked him if he knew of a good, reliable detective agency, Tremaine recommended us." He pointed to the telephone. "That was Tremaine just called up. He said Strang's bed hadn't been slept in last night."

"But maybe—"

Cardigan jabbed her with a dark look. "Maybe what?"

"Maybe he—well—didn't feel like sleeping last night."

"There was a standing order for breakfast to be brought up to his room each morning at eight. When the waiter came with it this morning, Strang wasn't there. Under the door there was a bill of fare that is passed around, slipped under the doors, each evening at five thirty."

His lips tightened and he scowled steadily across the room and his fist thumped the desk slowly, rhythmically.

He said: "When we stopped by to see Strang yesterday at four thirty, after that goofy interview with Hull, you remember Strang got sore. Can you blame him? He said he would go around and see Hull himself. I advised him not to. I said Hull would likely take a sock at him. Strang struck me as the kind of guy who wasn't especially afraid of a sock on the jaw. You saw him. He looked like a guy could handle himself, even though he's fifty."

Pat sat down on the edge of a chair, her eyes wide. "Do you think he went?"

Cardigan was terse, clipped. "You hang around here till I get back." He crossed to the clothes-tree, slapped on his misshapen, faded fedora, banged his arms into the sleeves of his shabby, shaggy ulster.

"Wait," said Pat.

She got up and went over and pulled the back of his collar from beneath his coat, plucked off a few stray threads.

He said, "Thanks, Pats," and left the office. He walked down to the dim old lobby, reached the street and stood there for a moment, his forehead still wrinkled, a little knot of muscle at either corner of his mouth. The morning was clear, bright with sunlight, windy. The wind tussled with his hat and overcoat and whipped sheets of discarded newspapers crazily in the air, or skated them wildly along the pavement. He saw a cab idling along and hailed it, climbed in.

Fifteen minutes later he got out in front of the familiar four-storied building. It was a neat street, sharply graded. He paid the driver and rocked into the lobby, pushed the brass button he had pushed the night before, and waited, nibbling on his lip. He pressed the button again, waited another minute, and when there was no answer he pushed the button marked *Janitor*. In a few minutes a small, withered little man opened the door.

Cardigan said: "I can't seem to raise the Hull apartment."

"Maybe they ain't in."

"I think they are. Or I think there's something wrong."

Cardigan showed his identification. "I called on these people last night. Will you come up with me and bring a key?"

"But—"

"Why kill time? If you don't want to let me in, say so, and I'll ring the police."

The man dropped his eyes. "I'll get a key."

He disappeared down the lower hall and when he came back again he was carrying a bunch of keys. Cardigan followed him up two flights of stairs, and the man spent a full minute ringing the apartment bell. Finally, but reluctantly, he inserted a key and opened the door. Cardigan thrust past him, paused in the foyer to listen, heard nothing.

The man stammered, "Whuh—what makes you think—"

"Quiet," Cardigan muttered.

He pushed on into the corridor, looked in the living room. The shades were drawn and a light was burning. He pulled up the shades. He turned and the small man was in his way. Preoccupied, Cardigan brushed him aside, went down the corridor. The small dining room was empty also. The bedroom was empty. Cardigan's scowl deepened and he looked in all the closets, in the bathroom, the kitchenette.

The small man's timid voice said: "What's the matter?"

Cardigan swiveled. "When these people moved in, did they have much baggage?"

"Only suitcases, I think."

"Well, they've scrammed."

"But they just paid a month's rent. Their month ain't up until—"

Cardigan left him and made another tour of the rooms. He emptied several waste baskets, examined their contents, but found nothing of importance. He pulled out the divan cushions and the cushions of two armchairs, replaced them, and stood for a moment with his fists planted on his hips and one side of his mouth sucked inward.

Then he said: "Well, that's that."

"That's—uh—what?" asked the small man.

Cardigan looked through him, said, "Thanks for letting me in," and strode out.

When he blew back into his office, his coat tails flying, Pat turned from the window to say, "Well?"

Cardigan said: "I went there half expecting to find Martin Strang a corpse. Well, I didn't." He scaled his hat across the office and hooked it neatly on a prong of the clothes-tree.

Pat let out a sigh. "Well, thank the Lord for that."

"Don't be in a hurry to thank the Lord, kid. The Hulls have scrammed, bag and baggage. On the way back here I stopped at the Farago Hotel and had a talk with Ben Tremaine. No sign of Martin Strang yet, and no word from him. Tremaine's worried."

"What are you going to do?"

"There's only one thing I can do. Call in the cops. If I let this slide and slide, I'll get in Dutch. Strang's been away from his hotel all night. It's as plain as the nose on your face that something's happened to him. Get me headquarters and ask for McGovern."

"Oh, why McGovern, chief? You know you two always bicker."

"The hell with that. If I got somebody else, Mac'd horn in anyhow."

Pat was reaching for the phone when the outer door opened slowly and Bernice Hull came in. Cardigan put out a hand, said to Pat: "Hold it."

In a louder voice he said: "Good morning, Mrs. Hull."

She looked very small and pretty in a dark cloth coat with a stand-up fur collar. Her smile was wan, a little rueful, as she came into the inner office. Pat stood with her hand still on the telephone and Cardigan, puzzled, said: "I didn't expect to see you, Mrs. Hull."

She dropped her eyes. "I don't suppose I should be here, but I came around anyway. I wanted to see you and I thought—well—I thought perhaps I could see Husted's uncle, too. I forgot what hotel you said he was staying at. But, please," she went on, "don't ever tell Husted about it."

"Why the sudden fade-away from the apartment?"

"Well, you see, Mr. Cardigan, Husted was very worked up last evening. After those people left, he stormed up and down and said he was going to move to a hotel. He said he wouldn't meet his uncle and he said he didn't want to have him coming around. I tried to quiet him and then I walked around the corner to a store and got some things for dinner. But when I came back, Husted was still worked up—and packing. He was determined to move to a hotel, so he wouldn't be bothered. So"—she shrugged—"what could I do?"

"And where are you living now?"

"At the Norman Hotel, in Bush Street."

Cardigan looked at Pat and Pat looked at Cardigan.

Bernice Hull colored a little. "It probably seems foolish, my coming around here, and I know Husted would be angry if he knew it, but—well—I was so embarrassed last night. And I would like to meet his uncle. I do really want Hughie to go back to Denver, but he is stubborn."

———

Cardigan sat on his desk, folded his arms and bent a shrewd stare on the young woman. "I'd like you to meet Martin Strang, too. I think you'd like him and I think he'd like you. But I don't know where he is."

Bernice Hull looked quizzically at him. "But I thought you said yesterday—"

"I said he was stopping at the Hotel Farago. But since last evening he hasn't been stopping there. He's disappeared. His baggage is there, but he isn't."

Her eyes grew very round, her manner was more puzzled than ever. "But where could he have gone?"

"Mrs. Hull, I'd like to know myself."

"Oh, how awful, how terrible!" She looked hopelessly from Cardigan to Pat.

Cardigan's low voice said: "I was just about to phone the police."

Bernice Hull nodded. "But, of course—you'd have to," she cried, in an anxious voice. "He may have been beaten by robbers and left in some vacant lot. Maybe if I told Husted this—then maybe he'd relent and help you find him."

Cardigan smiled. "I don't think his help would do much good. This is a job for the police. I'd supposed maybe Mr. Strang'd gone to your apartment last evening."

"Well, he may have—after we'd gone."

Cardigan said: "Best thing for you to do, Mrs. Hull, is go back to your hotel and say nothing. A cop'll be around before the day's over, just as a matter of routine. If you tell your husband Mr. Strang's gone, he'll want to know where you found it out and when you tell him he may go into another of his Hollywood tempers."

She nodded agreement, then said: "I'll see you later, I hope. I hope I haven't been a nuisance." She smiled sweetly at Cardigan, at Pat; and Cardigan saw her to the door.

When he came back, he said: "What do you think of her now?"

Pat was definite. "I think she's a very fine girl and I feel sorry for her with a husband like Husted Hull."

Cardigan lit a butt, snapped a jet of smoke from one side of his mouth. "Either she's God's most kind and innocent creature or she's a swell actress."

"Oh, nonsense! Are you beginning to doubt her?"

"She just seems too good to be true, but I hope I'm wrong."

"Oh, you give me a pain, chief."

"Hell, you should be a missionary's secretary." He nodded to the telephone. "Get McGovern on the wire."

She was reaching for the instrument when the outer office door banged open and Sergeant McGovern, plain-clothed, with a derby riding cockily over one eyebrow, strode in. Behind him strode Martin Strang, tall, white-faced, in his eyes a cold blue anger. Detective Hunerkopf came last, closing the door, removing his hat, and looking very fat and placid and benign. One of McGovern's hard, keen eyes was narrowed down and there was a tight, sardonic twist to his mouth.

"Fast one, eh?" he chopped off sarcastically.

Cardigan hung his thumbs in his lower vest pockets and said to Pat: "Look, the trapeze act is in again."

Pat eyed him with a look that was half angry, half pleading. She knew that something had gone awfully wrong and she did not want Cardigan to aggravate McGovern's already angry mood.

McGovern came right up to Cardigan and planted an index finger hard against the topmost button of Cardigan's vest. "You," said McGovern, "will have to think up some speedy answers, sonny boy."

Hunerkopf was bowing to Pat and holding his hat off, an inch above his head. "It's always a pleasure kind of to see you, Miss Seaward. I always says to Mac, to Mac I says—"

"Shut up, August!" McGovern growled.

Martin Strang remained in the background, his fists clenched at his sides, his lips locked tightly, though words of wrath ached behind them.

McGovern used his index finger again. "You, Cardigan—"

"Lay off the prologue," Cardigan said; he pushed McGovern out of the way and went across the room to face Strang. "What's the trouble, Mr. Strang?"

Strang muttered passionately, "*You* are asking *me*?"

"Yeah, I'm asking you."

Strang's eyes burned on Cardigan. "I was always chary of detective agencies. I should have known. But I at least thought that the manager of a reputable hotel, when he recommended you—"

Cardigan was blunt without being insolent. "Suppose before you go into that, Mr. Strang, you give me an idea about what I've done."

"Done! You sent me into a trap!"

"I didn't send you anywhere."

"You told me my nephew and his wife lived in Apartment Thirty-two, third floor, at—at that address—Leeward House."

"That's right."

"Well, sir," Martin Strang went on thickly, angrily, "I went there last evening, at about six. I knocked. A small, dapper man opened the door and I asked for Husted Hull. He said to step in. I did. When I stepped in, he closed the door. Then he drew a gun on me, A large, thick-set, oldish man joined him. They took me out, put me in a car, blindfolded me, and drove me somewhere where they held me prisoner all night."

McGovern horned in, "Now the fast answers, Cardigan."

Cardigan said to Strang: "When did they let you go?"

"Let me go! They didn't let me go. I worked free of my bonds in the dark and when, this morning, one of them came in with a flashlight to look at me, I knocked him over and ran out. I went directly to the police, who returned with me to the house, but no one was there by that time."

"Make 'em fast, old sock!" McGovern chuckled.

Cardigan swiveled. "Fat-head, what are you trying to do—say I planted a couple of mugs there to kidnap Mr. Strang?"

"Suppose I said I wouldn't be surprised?"

"I'd say you were actually as thick as you look."

McGovern's bony dark face grew darker. "Watch your tongue, sonny boy!"

"Watch yours!" Cardigan ripped back at him. "You're hired by this city to do police work and not to plagiarize the funny papers."

"Now, now, Mr. Cardigan," Hunerkopf said placidly, "don't let us get all hot and bothered."

"You stay out of this!" McGovern barked.

Hunerkopf sighed and leaned back dolefully in a chair.

"But why," said Pat, "must everyone get angry?"

"And you stay out of it, too," Cardigan told her.

Martin Strang said: "I didn't come here to listen to a lot of bickering. I came to procure results."

Pat laughed ironically. "You certainly had a headstart when you brought Mr. McGovern along."

"Young lady," said McGovern, glaring at her, "I don't have to stand any lip from you!"

She flared: "And you don't have to come in here with your atrociously bad manners, Mr. Know-it-all!"

"Ha, ha, ha," chortled Hunerkopf, wagging his big head.

"August!" McGovern thundered. "You wait for me outside!"

Hunerkopf left the office, sighing, wagging his head.

McGovern's hard, steely gaze swept back to Cardigan and he said in a low, tight voice: "Now, we'll get down to business."

"Business with you meaning that you're going to stand there and steam off, and after it goes on a while I'm going to get sore and take a poke at you."

"Why," demanded McGovern, "did you tell Mr. Strang his nephew was there when he wasn't?"

"I told Mr. Strang his nephew was there because, you dope, he was there."

"Why wasn't he there when Mr. Strang went there?"

"I guess he didn't want to be bothered, so he up and moved."

"Why," McGovern drove on, "did two mugs turn up there and take Mr. Strang and make him a prisoner?"

"Now we're both in virgin territory, Mac. I don't know. I haven't the slightest idea."

Strang said in a loud, accusing voice: "You were the only one in this city who knew I was a wealthy man. You made up that story about finding my nephew. You so worded your report that I would go to that address myself determined to talk with my nephew. You were smart enough not to urge me to go."

"You should write, Mr. Strang. Your imagination's the nuts."

"You will please keep your insolence to yourself."

"Oh, I'm supposed to stand here and take a lot of crap from you and hang my head. Is that it? I didn't ask you for that job. You came to me and I located your nephew and you paid me fifty bucks."

"And you laid that trap!"

Cardigan held out his fist toward Pat. "Hold this, Pats, before it reverts to type."

McGovern jumped in front of him, grabbed his arm. "I can take care of that part of it," he growled darkly.

Cardigan's eyes were beginning to look windy. He gave one vicious wrench of his body, without moving his feet. McGovern stopped against the wall, making a picture of Jack Johnson rattle. McGovern started for his blackjack. Cardigan laid his hand on a rectangular slab of glass, six inches long, two inches thick, which he used for a paperweight.

"Gentlemen, gentlemen," said Martin Strang, not afraid, merely irritated.

Cardigan and McGovern eyed each other stonily for half a minute, and then they relaxed.

Cardigan said to Strang: "I'll get your nephew. If I have to drag him bodily, I'll get him and bring him to you and show you that I did find him, I did talk with him."

"Like hell you will!" McGovern barked.

"But that seems fair enough," Strang said.

McGovern towered. "Mr. Strang, you don't know this potato the way I know him."

"Someday, Mac," Cardigan said, "you're going to make one too many cracks against this agency and just for the fun of it I'm going to sue you. I can prove I saw Husted Hull yesterday afternoon. I'm going to prove it. Now you get the lead out of your pants and scram out of here. You're a carbuncle on the heel of prosperity and besides your face reminds me of calf's liver, which I've always hated."

McGovern looked at Strang. "See! See what I have to take?"

Strang remained neutral, saying: "I'll be at my hotel, the Farago." Then he looked levelly at Cardigan. "You will produce Husted Hull or I'll have a warrant sworn out for your arrest and"—he nodded toward Pat—"the young lady's." He looked at his watch. "I'll give you three hours." He turned and left the office, a fine figure of a man.

McGovern followed, but stopped in the doorway to say, with his tongue in his cheek: "This is one time an ace up your sleeve won't do you any good, sonny boy."

"Roll your hoop, Mac."

"I'm a tough case, hanh?"

"Yeah, a tough case of dandruff."

"Yah!"

Cardigan said to Pat: "I'll bet it wags its ears, too."

Hunerkopf looked in, his hat held an inch above his head. "Good day, Miss Seaward. Good day, Mr. Cardigan. If you're interested, I know where you can buy a whole lug of oranges dirt cheap. Best thing in the world for an acid condition."

"Goom-bye, Augie," Cardigan chuckled.

When the law had gone, Pat said: "Mr. Hunerkopf's a nice old man."

"He's human, anyhow. But don't let that simple manner of his kid you. I often think that behind the scenes it's Hunerkopf that gets the ideas and Mac the promotions. Though Mac's a good cop, too."

"You'd never think you thought that, when you're together."

"Do I ever throw bouquets at anybody? One thing I hate, I hate this back-slapping you see so much. Mac'd jail me in a minute if he thought he could. He'd send me up for a stretch. All in sport, see?"

Pat didn't. She sighed. "You're hopeless."

He took a shot of Bourbon from the neck of a dark amber-colored bottle and smacked a cork back in with the heel of his hand. "Hang around, Pats. The old man is going out to get Exhibit A."

CHAPTER III
Two Guys

Cardigan went along Market to Taylor and up Taylor to Bush. He swung into the severe, modernistic lobby of the Norman Hotel and went directly to one of the writing rooms, where he sat down, thrust a blank sheet of paper into a hotel envelope and addressed the envelope to Husted Hull. He did not want to arouse the hotel's curiosity by asking point-blank for the number of the Hull room. He carried the letter to the desk and said: "Will you please put this in Mr. Hull's box?"

"Certainly," said the young, affable clerk.

Cardigan watched him turn and slip the envelope into one of the pigeon holes. He saw that it was numbered 407 and he was on his way toward the elevator bank by the time the clerk faced front again. Entering a waiting car, he was lifted to the fourth floor. His big feet swung down a wide, airy corridor, and he knocked on the door numbered 407.

Bernice Hull opened it and Cardigan said: "How do you do, Mrs. Hull."

"Oh, Mr. Cardigan," she said brightly, as though she had not seen him a short time before. "Do come in."

Cardigan pushed into a large living room and saw Hull standing with his back to a window. He was holding a highball in his hand and he did not seem pleased.

"Well, so you're back again. How did you find out I'd moved here?"

"Just cruised around the hotels and asked the desk clerks."

Hull made an angry sound in his throat and strode into the bedroom. Bernice went after him and Cardigan heard her urging him to come back to the living room. He did not come and presently Cardigan strolled over and leaned in the bedroom doorway. Hull was sitting on one of the twin beds, taking a long pull at his drink and looking mutinously over the rim of the glass.

"I wish," he said, "you would please stop pestering me. I told you once that I won't see him and that goes. And the more you go on pestering me, the stubborner I'm going to get. Let him go hang his head somewhere. Let them all hang their heads somewhere. This is one time I can get back at them and, boy, I'm going to get back at them."

Cardigan said: "Mr. Hull, give your ears a chance. Personally, I don't give a hoot how you get back at your uncle, but this is different. You see, I'm in a spot now. Your uncle doesn't believe I found you. He doesn't believe I interviewed you. He thinks it was a gag."

Hull stood up. "Swell! Have a drink."

"Uh-uh," Cardigan grunted, shaking his head. "You see, Mr. Hull, after you moved from that apartment last evening, your uncle went there, steamed up, I suppose, to see you."

Hull laughed gleefully. "Swell! I guess I lighted out just in time. Boy, that's a good one! Ha-ha!"

Cardigan was very grave. "No," he said. "The joke is on me."

He explained briefly what had happened.

Hull squinted intently. "You must be crazy!" he said.

"I am not crazy. I have to produce you, to satisfy your uncle and the police. I'm in a spot. If I can't produce you, I'll be arrested."

Bernice gripped her husband's arm. "You'll have to go, Hughie! You must go!"

Hull glared at Cardigan. "It's a trick," he said angrily. "I don't believe he was waylaid. I don't believe it at all. It's just a trick—to get me to see him. He knows that if he gets me in front of him, I'll listen to reason—and I'm not going to do that." He laughed ironically. "You're pretty smart, Mr. Cardigan, but the gag doesn't work." He shook a forefinger violently up and down. "Those people are going to pay for the way they treated me when I was a kid!"

Cardigan folded his arms, looked very grave. "It's no gag, Mr. Hull. I'm in a spot, I tell you. Your uncle believes I tricked him and he's got the cops believing it, too. If it wasn't for that, I'd not be bothering you. But"—he made a gesture—"get your hat and coat."

Hull shook his head. "Don't you believe it. I know a gag when I see it. My mind's made up."

Cardigan smiled coolly. "You're going, Mr. Hull."

Hull scooped up the telephone, said into the mouthpiece: "Send up the house officer—immediately!" He hung up, smiled. "After all, Mr. Cardigan, you've no authority—"

"Why, you dirty rat! For two cents, I'd—"

"Oh, please, please," whimpered Bernice Hull.

Hull said: "Maybe you'd rather go now, instead of being thrown out."

"I'll go now, bright boy. But I'll be back."

Cardigan spun on his heel, strode from the apartment. He stood for a few moments in the lobby, taking quick, irritable puffs at a cigarette. His eyes settled on a pair of large, highly polished black shoes, traveled up a pair of stout legs to a newspaper behind which a man sat. He strolled over and said in a low voice: "Just like an ostrich, Augie."

Hunerkopf lowered the newspaper. "Why, if

it ain't Mr. Cardigan! I always said, it's a small world—"

"You couldn't possibly by any chance have tailed me here, could you?"

"Who, me?" said Hunerkopf, rising and looking very hurt and then saying in an injured tone, "I just like to sit here a lot. I like the atmosphere, kind of. It takes me out of my work."

"There's one thing I like about you, Augie. You're twice the liar I am. Come on outside."

The lumpy detective trailed Cardigan to the sidewalk and they crossed the street and entered a lunch-and-soda fountain.

"Ah," said Hunerkopf, rubbing his hands, "I see they got baked apple on the menu. Good for the system. Join me in a baked apple and we'll—"

"Wait a minute. For once, Augie, keep your mind off your stomach. You'll die of too much health, someday. Listen now—"

"Well, can't I listen while I eat a baked apple? Then we'll be killing two stones with one bird."

Cardigan sighed. "O. K., Augie—O. K."

While Hunerkopf gouged out a tremendous baked apple, Cardigan talked and kept watching the hotel entrance across the street. He wound up by saying: "Will you? You wouldn't want to see me get tossed in jail, would you?"

"Well, no. Trouble with jails, Mr. Cardigan—well, I wrote a long letter to a newspaper once, kind of urging all jails to feed their inmates more fruit—"

"There he comes now. Pay up and—"

"Gosh, I just remembered I ain't got nothing smaller than a twenty."

"You're no dummy," Cardigan said, and paid.

They walked across the street just as Hull and his wife were climbing into a cab. A porter had already stowed their baggage in front. He was about to close the door when Hunerkopf took it away from him, lifted his hat, and said into the cab: "Good day. I'm Hunerkopf from the cops."

He climbed in and Cardigan followed, pull

ing out one of the extra seats. Hunerkopf planted himself between Hull and Bernice. Hull tried to get up, his face white with anger.

"*Sh*, Mr. Hull," Hunerkopf said. And to the driver, "Drive down to Market Street. What's the number, Mr. Cardigan?"

Cardigan gave the address of the agency.

"You can't do this!" Hull cried.

"You wouldn't be nice," Cardigan said, "so this is my come-back."

Hunerkopf tried to make polite conversation with Bernice. "Do you like San Francisco, Mrs. Hull?"

She was troubled, confused. "Y-yes—of course."

"Do you, Mr. Hull?"

"I tell you, I'm not going!"

The cab was speeding.

Hunerkopf patted Hull's knee. "You should take life a little easy, Mr. Hull, like it was a bowl of cherries. Take my partner, Mr. McGovern. He don't. And look at him. Dyspepsia half the time." He drew a package from his pocket. "Have a fig?"

"To hell with your figs!"

"You, Mrs. Hull?"

"N-no, thank you."

Hull yelled: "Stop this cab!"

The driver braked.

Hunerkopf said: "Driver, you stop where I told you to."

It was a short ride and presently the cab pulled up in front of the agency building. They all got out.

Hull was angry and touchy, and when they walked into the office he spun and said: "By God, I'll have you arrested for this! Why don't you spend your time finding criminals instead of picking on honest citizens?"

Hunerkopf held his hat an inch above his head. "We meet again, Miss Seaward."

And Cardigan said: "Pat, phone Mr. Strang and tell him to come right over."

She telephoned.

"Now phone McGovern and tell him, too. I'll show these guys if I'm a bum."

Hull began pacing up and down the inner office. His wife sat troubled in a chair, her anxious eyes following him. Hunerkopf spread himself complacently in a chair and chewed on figs. Cardigan leaned by the window and looked down into Market Street. Ten minutes later he said: "Here comes Mr. Strang now."

Cardigan saw Strang step out of a taxi, pay up, and he saw the taxi start off. Strang started for the building entrance but was accosted by two men. The hair on Cardigan's nape stiffened. He saw Strang turn and move across the street, the two men flanking him.

Cardigan spun, yelled: "Come on, Augie! Pat, stay here with them! Augie, snap on it!"

Cardigan sailed out of the office, plunged down the hallway, down the stairs, out into the street. He caught a glimpse of a sedan whipping away from the opposite curb. He caught a glimpse of Strang in back. Hunerkopf came piling out.

"Hey!" Cardigan yelled. He raised his gun and took a shot at a tire, but the car was already speeding and he missed.

Hunerkopf jumped to the footboard of a parked roadster in which a man sat. "Chase that car," he said.

"Who are you?"

Hunerkopf showed his badge.

The man shook his head. "Not me." He climbed out. "Try it yourself."

"I'll drive," Cardigan snapped, jumping in behind the wheel.

Hunerkopf crashed into the seat beside him. "What?"

"Strang."

"What about him?"

"Two guys."

"Oh."

Cardigan swung the car about in the center of the street and opened it up. It was a fast job. Hunerkopf had his gun out. He pushed up the windshield a bit, but the wind forced it shut again. "They're making a left," he said.

Cardigan screeched the tires on the next left, then made a right turn into Mission Street. "They're heading places," he said.

The sedan was doing about sixty, whipping and roaring through scattered traffic on a busy street. Traffic cops blew whistles. Hunerkopf leaned out to wave at the traffic cops. "Hello, Emil!" he yelled. "Hello, Vincent!"

"Never mind your pals," Cardigan said. "Keep your eyes on that sedan while I watch the traffic. If we ever hit anything, we'll land in San Mateo county. This car can step, but they forgot to put brakes on it."

"Ain't that something?"

"That sedan's no cripple, either."

"They're cutting through Eleventh."

Cardigan followed the sedan through Eleventh, through Division, and out Potrero. "They're heading for the Bayshore highway," he yelled.

In a few minutes they struck the Bayshore road, a fast speedway running south along the tidelands. Cardigan slammed the accelerator pedal against the floorboards. He could do no more. Hunerkopf looked at the speedometer.

"We're doing eighty-two. Did you ever have a blow-out?"

"Why bring that up?"

"I did, once. It's a experience, it is—Look, ain't we sort of gaining, sort of?"

"Inching."

Crash!

The glass windguard on Cardigan's side shattered.

"They like me, Augie—"

Crash!

The one on Hunerkopf's side vanished.

They slid deep into the seats. Another shot drilled the windshield and carried away the rearview mirror.

"I always wanted to buy a little farm and retire," Hunerkopf said.

A fourth bullet shattered the left cowl light. The roadster was gaining.

"In five minutes," Cardigan shouted, "we'll be on 'em."

"Or else, Mr. Cardigan. I'd like to take some pot shots at them tires, but if I blow one that car'll land over on the S.P. tracks and Mr. Strang—"

"There goes the other cowl light. Who the hell got me into this?"

Hunerkopf said: "Here goes."

Left-handed, he fired, emptying his gun. In a moment spots of moisture began to sprinkle the windshield.

"I got it," Hunerkopf said. "I put holes in their gas tank." He reloaded his gun.

Three minutes later the sedan swung from the road onto a large cindered space in front of a gas station. Dust and cinders flew as the wheels were locked. Cardigan braked and slid the roadster into the dust, and cinders peppered the windshield. Two men jumped out of the sedan, knocked over a man standing alongside a touring car, and jumped in.

The roadster's brakes were bad. Cardigan swerved to miss the sedan but the roadster slammed head-on into the rear of the touring car and pushed the touring car up between two gas pumps. The two men leaped out, spun with drawn guns. The roadster's windshield was smashed by the gunfire as Cardigan and Hunerkopf fell out. Hunerkopf fired from a kneeling position. The smaller of the two men fell down, his feet kicking up cinders. The other galloped off, with Cardigan after him. Cardigan fired one shot above his head, another at his feet.

"Dope!" he yelled. "Stop!"

The big man held up his hands, stopped and turned around, his chest rising and falling rapidly, his breath pumping loudly from his open mouth.

"Drop the rod behind you," Cardigan said.

The man dropped it.

Cardigan picked it up, kicked the man in the seat of the pants and said: "Now walk back."

By this time the small man was standing up. Hunerkopf said: "I hardly even hit him."

Mr. Strang was walking toward them, his face gray, grim. "By Judas Priest, Mr. Cardigan," he said, "I was ready to swear you'd got me into another trap!"

"Yeah? Well, let me tell you something, Mr. Strang. For that lousy fifty bucks you gave me, you're sure getting service. Climb in the roadster. We'll lock these bad boys in the rumble and take you back to my office. Your nephew's there and—frankly—I wouldn't mind if you popped him in the snout."

CHAPTER IV
Red Hot

Bernice Hull was crying. She sat in the swivel chair at Cardigan's desk, her arms on the desk, her face buried in her arms. The sobs that wrenched muffled into her arms also made her shoulders convulse. Pat, grave-faced, stood beside her, patting the convulsive shoulders.

She said to McGovern: "Every time you walk in here, something happens. You're like a bull in a China shop."

McGovern rubbed his knuckles. "I take a lot of horsing from that boss of yours, Miss Seaward, but I don't take it from a perfect stranger. If you don't like it, you can lump it."

Hull sat slumped on a chair, a welt on his chin, his head groggy, his eyes a little glazed. McGovern had smacked him.

McGovern looked reproachfully at Pat. "I walk in here. I find you holding a gun on this bird Hull—"

"It was for his own good," she blazed back. "And besides, Cardigan told me to keep him here."

McGovern yelled: "He was insolent!"

"You're just angry," Pat said, "because Cardigan proved what he said he would prove. You're cantankerous—"

"Young woman!" McGovern roared.

The outer door opened and Cardigan swung in, his battered hat crushed low on his forehead, his overcoat buttoned wrong, and his tie over one shoulder.

"Hi, gang," he said.

Hunerkopf came in next, hauling the two manacled men and looking very placid, fat, and self-satisfied. He raised his hat an inch above his head.

"Miss Seaward—"

Cardigan lit a butt. "What's the matter with Hull?"

Pat said: "Oh, Mr. McGovern hit him."

"Where's that Mr. Strang?" McGovern barked darkly.

"Be up in a minute, Mac," Cardigan said. "All the excitement upset his stomach. Then Augie gave him a fig and that made him worse, so he stopped downstairs in the drug store to get a sedative."

"Who are these two guys?"

"We'll probably get around to that later. They snatched Mr. Strang right in front downstairs, as he was getting out of a cab. Augie and I shooed after them. They won't talk, but probably your records at headquarters will."

"Oh, they won't talk!" exploded McGovern. He spun on the smaller of the two men. "Who are you?"

"Who are you?"

"Oh, insolent, eh?"

"Sure."

"Why, you little punk, you—"

"Mac," said Hunerkopf, raising a hand. "Remember, there's ladies present. Besides, you always get indigestion when—"

"Hands up, everybody!" Hull was on his feet, a gun gripped in his hand.

"Oh, I never knew he had a gun!" Pat cried.

"I'm going out," Hull said in a shaky voice. "Get out of my way. Get out of my way!"

"Hughie!" cried Bernice, horrified.

"Drop that, you fool!" Cardigan snarled.

Hull's face was dead white. "Get out of—"

"Hughie!"

Bernice jumped up, her eyes wide and stricken. "Oh, dear God, Hughie, don't—"

He snapped: "Get back, Bernice!"

"But, dear, dear—"

His left hand struck her down.

Strang came walking in saying: "Well, I feel much better—"

"Look out!" Pat cried.

Strang's face froze.

McGovern made a dive for his service gun and at the same time took a lunge toward the window. Hull pivoted. Cardigan fired twice through his pocket and both shots made but one hole in Hull's side. Bernice screamed and Hull crashed to the floor and McGovern yelled: "Sweet work, Cardigan!"

Bernice ran across the office and fell on her husband, screaming again. "Oh, Hughie, Hughie . . . !"

Cardigan pulled his gun out of his pocket, fanned it up and down. Deep wrinkles were on his forehead. He made a face as though a bad taste were in his mouth. He grimaced.

He muttered: "I hated to do that." Then he looked up at Strang. "Well, there's your nephew, Mr. Strang."

Strang pointed. "That man," he said, "is not my nephew."

"What?" McGovern exploded.

"That—man—is—not—Husted Hull."

Bernice looked up, her face anguished, wet with tears. "What are you saying?" she cried passionately.

A tight, breathless silence fell upon the office, and then there came the low groans of Hull. Bernice broke into fresh tears and bent over him, cradling his head in her arms.

"What is this, what is this?" she cried. "What are they saying, saying, *saying*?"

Strang said to Cardigan: "You have been deluded, Mr. Cardigan."

Cardigan's face was dull red, a humid wrath moved far back in his eyes. He spun and took three strides and grabbed the smaller of the two manacled men by the throat.

"Spill it!" he rasped.

"Look out—"

"Spill it! What's the hook-up here?"

"Ugh—look out—"

"Spill it! Where's Husted Hull?"

"D-dead—"

"Where?"

"I—don't—ugh—know—"

"When was he killed?"

"Ouch—over three years ago—somewhere—south—"

Cardigan swung away from him. "Mrs. Hull!"

"Yes?" she said weakly, sitting on the floor now, with her husband resting back against her breast.

His face looked ghostly, his eyes were haggard. He said: "It's no use. I killed him over three years ago. I met him in Caliente and we chummed together, took a little shack up the Coast. I got to know all about him, his family, all the details. I knew he got a thousand a month from his mother's estate. I knew he never saw them and they never saw him. I'm good at forgery. I was able to copy his signature. I—once—back East—did a little time for forgery. So we went out fishing one night and I clipped him and tied an anchor with a steel cable to him and threw him over. The rest was easy. No one knew us around there—it was a lonely spot. I just picked up and left, taking all his things and mine. I sent a wire to the law firm that sent him his money regularly, giving a change of address. I went to Seattle and became Husted Hull and got the monthly checks and no one ever found out. I met and married Bernice—as Husted Hull.

"Last week I met Proctor." He pointed to the smaller of the two men. "I'd known him in prison back East. He wanted to come around to our apartment. I had to tell him I was married and living as Husted Hull. He was broke. I had to give him some money. He saw I was living well and wanted to know my racket. I refused. Then he said I'd have to tell him or else. So I told him. He wanted a cut monthly of five hundred. What could I do?

"Then you came. I was scared stiff at first—

but then I saw you couldn't have known the real Husted Hull. I was desperate. I knew the uncle'd run across me. I called Proctor up while Bernice was out to the store. I said I was moving to a new hotel. I explained what had happened and said that if I stayed at the same address Strang might show up and then I'd lose out and so would he, on the split. He said all right. So Bernice and I moved.

"Proctor must have come to the apartment after we'd left. Let himself in with a master key and waited for Strang. You can see it was a snatch. He knew I couldn't say anything. He knew—he had me—where he—he—he . . ."

His head fell forward.

Strang murmured in a low, passionate voice: "Good . . . Lord!"

Bernice fainted and fell to one side on the floor. Pat ran to her. Now Pat was crying: "Oh, you poor, poor girl—you poor, poor thing."

Cardigan said bitterly: "There's life on the button for you."

Hunerkopf touched one of his eyes. "Yes, me, I always wanted a little farm—Can I do anything to help, Miss Seaward?"

McGovern was on his knees. He said: "Well, he's dead."

"It was either you or him," muttered Cardigan.

McGovern stood up, said in a low voice: "Thanks, kid. You're pretty good."

"Oh, I'm not so good. There I had a red-hot killer under my nose all along and didn't know it."

"Well, yes, you were pretty dumb about that."

Cardigan glared. "Oh, yeah! I suppose you would have known right off the bat!"

"Sure."

"Yes, you would have! Why, everyone knows you won that sergeant's badge at a raffle."

McGovern glared. "Now, look here, Cardigan—"

Pat was standing now and glaring crimson-faced at both of them. "Oh, you idiots!" she cried. "You awful, awful idiots!"

McGovern grimaced bitterly and held a hand against his chest. "My indigestion again," he croaked. "My—"

"See?" said Hunerkopf, pointing a broad index finger. "See?"

Cardigan was lifting up Bernice and saying in a low, muffled voice: "Come on, little girl. It's tough. Cripes, but it's tough."

THE DOMINO LADY COLLECTS

Lars Anderson

ONE OF THE STAPLES of the pulp magazine era was a plethora of costumed characters, largely due to the enormous success of the Shadow, who was soon followed by crime fighters using sobriquets that made them sound more villainous than heroic: Doc Savage, the Spider, the Phantom, the Whisperer, the Ghost, and the Black Bat, among others.

What was unusual was a female masked avenger, but the Domino Lady filled the bill. In her real life she was Ellen Patrick, a gorgeous twenty-two-year-old who swore vengeance on criminals after her policeman father was murdered. She is tall and has curly blond hair, penetrating brown eyes, and a stunning figure.

Her modus operandi generally finds her at a party or social gathering in a thin, low-cut, backless dress that clings to her every curve. When she discovers the item that she came to steal from her adversary, she slips into a bedroom or closet, peels off her dress and dons another one (both dresses so gossamer that they fit in a small handbag), puts on a mask, and returns to the party. Her disguise apparently works, just as Clark Kent removing his glasses appears to make him unrecognizable. When successful, she leaves a card bearing the inscription: "The Domino Lady's Compliments."

There were only six stories about her, five of which appeared in *Saucy Romantic Adventures* and one in *Mystery Adventure Magazine*. They are very much alike, and the prose style is distinguished mainly for its unbridled use of exclamation points!!!

Little is known of the author, whose career appears to have lasted only a few years in the 1930s and all of whose stories were published in the second-level pulps.

"The Domino Lady Collects" was originally published in the May 1936 issue of *Saucy Romantic Adventures*; it was first collected in *Compliments of the Domino Lady* (Bordentown, New Jersey, Bold Venture Press, 2004).

The Domino Lady Collects

LARS ANDERSON

CHAPTER I

GLITTERING SUNSHINE was vainly attempting to bore its way through the closely shuttered Venetian blinds protecting the bedroom windows of an apartment on Wiltshire Boulevard. Across the busy thoroughfare, the fragrant buds of a California spring were shooting into life in the tiny park.

A tousled blonde head, resting in a nest of soft curls sunk deep in a silken pillow, moved slightly, and brown eyes blinked drowsily. A damp, cerise mouth deliciously shaped, opened in a delicate yawn, and, under the coverlet, a shapely leg stirred, languorously.

The Domino Lady, Hollywood's most mysterious female, was awakening!

A fair, pink-skinned arm, prettily rounded, drew aside the coverlet as she squirmed out of bed and glided to the window to pull up the shutters and let the sunshine into the room. Then, taking a cigarette from a silver and black box on her bedside table, she threw herself back on the bed where she lay outside the covers to enjoy the fragrant puffs of smoke that would serve to clear her sleep-drenched and tired brain.

A nightgown of sheerest green silk was but scant concealment for her gorgeous figure. A chastely-rounded body and a slender waist served to accentuate the seductive softness of her hips and the sloping contours of her slim thighs, while

skin like the bloom on a peach glowed rosily in the reflected sunlight.

Abruptly, a musical tinkling broke the stillness of the room. It was the bell of her telephone, which had been specially installed since she objected to the usual jangling one, and, without raising her shining head from the pillow, she picked the instrument up, and answered:

"Yes!" Her soft voice throbbed melodiously with a peculiarly emotional quiver, a little trick of hers. She never knew who might be at the other end of the wire!

"Oh, hello, Eloise!" Her voice resumed its normal tone. "I had intended calling you this morning. Anything new?"

"Not a thing, Ellen!" responded Eloise Schenick, despondently. "This affair has me desperate! If he does as he threatens, and Lew learns of . . ."

"Sh-h-h-h!" cautioned The Domino Lady in a sibilant whisper. "Not over the telephone, dear! You can never tell who might be listening in, you know!"

The sound of a sob came to her over the wire. "I'd forgotten!" murmured her caller, contritely. "I've been so worried that I'm almost crazy! If you can't help me . . ."

The other laughed soothingly.

"Don't take it so hard, kiddo," she advised softly. "You know I'm going to help you. Never fear, that precious husband of yours will not find out a thing. I'll have those letters back before morning, and safe in your hands, or my name isn't Ellen Patrick!"

"Oh, you darling! If you only can . . ."

"All right!" agreed Ellen, quickly, decisively, "I'm taking immediate steps in that direction! And, should they fail, I'll be seeing your friend this evening! So, either way, I promise you results, Eloise! Now, perk up, so Lew Schenick won't smell a mouse . . . 'Bye!"

As she cradled the phone for a moment, a tight little smile played about the corners of her luscious mouth. Then, lifting the instrument once more she spoke briefly:

"This is Miss Ellen Patrick, Apartment 422 . . . Please send a boy up in fifteen minutes."

Sliding from the bed, she peeled the silken nightrobe from her and ran into the ornate bathroom. A needle shower quickly stung her rose body into a state of hot-blooded energy. After a brisk rubdown with a big towel, she slipped into a black velvet negligee which hid her youthful body more completely than the silk nightgown had disclosed it!

Slipping pink-toed feet into black suede slippers, she glided into the living room where she sank into a straight-backed chair before a walnut writing desk. For a long moment she was busy, writing in her usual perfect flowing chirography which was so indicative of her impressive personality. The note she handed the boy a few minutes later was inscribed in white ink on smooth black stationery, and was addressed to "*Mr. Rob Wyatt, The Franklyn Arms.*" It read:

"This is your last chance to come across. If certain letters are not returned to their rightful owner before midnight tonight, I shall be forced to call and pick them up myself."

The distinctive epistle was signed, *The Domino Lady!*

CHAPTER II

Owen Patrick had been one of the most feared politicians in California at one time. An assas-

sin's slug had put a period to his career three years before, and there were those who believed the killer to have been a hired gunman in the employ of the state machine. The big Irishman's dauntless spirit and keen wit had been transplanted in his only child, Ellen.

Before her father's untimely death, the girl had lived a life of comparative ease as befitted the child of Owen Patrick. She had spent four years at Berkeley, a year in the Far East, and then—a cowardly bullet had robbed her of the one who meant more to her than life itself. Small wonder then that she pursued the life of a ruthless, roguish adventuress, at times accepting nigh impossible undertakings simply for the sake of friendship and the love of adventure. At other times, she was coldly involved in hazardous schemes merely to embarrass the authorities, whom she blamed for her father's death, at the same time earning an adequate income wherewith to obtain the luxuries to which she had become accustomed. Of late, she had become well-known and feared as *The Domino Lady!*

Take the present case, for instance. Eloise Schenick, former dancer and wife of Lew Schenick of Trianon Films, Inc., had been a classmate at Berkeley in the old days. Married to a man years her senior, she had been indiscreet, and compromising letters were being held over her head by a well-known Hollywood character. This man, a big game hunter and sometimes character actor, was noted for his triumphs in the wild places, but his hunting was not strictly confined to the carnivore! And his parties were the talk of the town!

Wealthy in his own right, Rob Wyatt's exorbitant demands were but an indication of the inherent cruelty of the man. As a last resort, the tearful Eloise had confided in her old chum, never dreaming that she was addressing the notorious Domino Lady, herself, or that Ellen knew the formidable Wyatt in person. And, as usual, while pitying the victim for her foolishness, the adventure-loving Ellen had unhesitatingly accepted the issue, *gratis!*

Pretty, shapely, talented, the "young avenger,"

as Ellen liked to style herself, was in great demand in society. Many proposals of marriage had fallen to her lot, but she had thus far remained free of marital bonds. At twenty-two, she was known as one of the most beautiful girls in California's Southland. Of medium height and willowy, there was something about her radiant, Nordic beauty that captivated all with whom she came in contact. And, as far as the sex of her was concerned, its appeal had long since been granted!

Lifting the champagne glass to her cerise lips, Ellen Patrick's great brown eyes flitted over the bronzed features of Rob Wyatt, who was leaning toward her in the conservatory of his penthouse atop the sumptuous Franklyn Arms. He was frowning slightly, but she couldn't help admiring his rugged handsomeness, square chin and mouth, the well-knit masculine figure. He was tall, with a finely drawn, rather nervous face, a high-bridged arrogant nose, and lips that were strangely full and impetuous; a man of queer charm and strange moods, admired for his nerve and his attainments in the wild game field, feared for his inherent cruelty of nature, loved hopelessly by many women in his life of whose existence he at times seemed utterly unaware. Ellen had always liked him, though the liking was not unmixed by a strange fear!

"He might be a rounder, a *roué*, even a blackmailer!" thought Ellen, "but there's something darned compelling about him just the same! And there's plenty of ice and iron beneath that velvety exterior, I'll bet me! . . ."

She took a test sip of the wine, breathed: "Heavenly!"

He leaned closer. "The champagne?" he questioned pointedly. "Or the toast?"

She laughed softly as she remembered that he had said: "To you . . . and me . . . and tonight!" just before he had drained the glass.

"What do you think?" she parried pertly, brown eyes narrowing, languorously.

"Why, the toast, of course!" he responded, boldly. "Since it is asking too much that I believe

you to be as coldly indifferent as you would have one think!"

Again, her tinkling laughter sounded. "It *was* a lovely thought!" she admitted; then dropped her eyes before the intensity of his gaze.

During the afternoon, Ellen had worked the magic which had gotten her the invitation to Wyatt's party. But that had been easy. Merely a call on the telephone, since the hunter had been wanting her to come to his penthouse for months without success.

In the sanctity of her luxurious apartment she had prepared herself for the adventure, bathing her gorgeous body and dressing it into a thing altogether lovely to behold. The frock, a smart creation of brown satin, fitted snugly about her white throat after the Russian fashion, but did not prevent the flaunting of her perfect body. Long, brown earrings she had fastened in her tiny pink ears to dangle bewitchingly below her shining coiffure. A bit of exotic perfume, scarlet for her lips, coloring for her smooth cheeks . . . A white silken cape trimmed in white fur . . . why, Rob Wyatt's eyes were but paying her the homage she deserved!

"Why haven't you visited me before?" he was asking.

Ellen recovered quickly: "Perhaps it was only because you didn't impress me as really desiring my company!" she teased, impishly.

"Not a chance, my dear!" he objurgated, firmly. "And I'm sure you've realized the truth after my persistency!"

"But you are reputed to have the pick of Hollywood," she charged, softly, "so you couldn't have missed my presence to any great extent!"

He grinned. Being a very wealthy man, his code was simple. Money could do anything, but anything. It was evident that he enjoyed fencing with this beautiful girl as a prelude to her final abdication to his advances.

"The fact that you've remained aloof disproves your statement!" he murmured. "But if you'd care to prove it, you'll have to include yourself among the most beautiful for my sake, at least!"

Ellen flushed. Wyatt certainly had a way with him. A smooth, impressive, magnetic personality radiating a compelling appeal. The hint of arrogance which showed through the veneer of his suavity added to his charm and desirability in the eyes of most women. Even Ellen felt herself liking him more and more!

Without replying, her eyes wandered to the glittering panorama of the city far below, visible through the open windows that stretched from floor to ceiling on one side of the huge conservatory.

"What a magnificent view!" she remarked.

"Do you like it?" he asked, taking her rounded arm as she rose. "Would you like to walk around the terrace and see the sights?"

Ellen had finished her second glass of champagne, and it had been wonderful. Every sip of her favorite drink seemed to be more tasty than the one preceding it, and a warm glow came into being within her soft body. And her mental reaction turned decidedly to the exhilarating! Rising from her seat, she moved onto the terrace with Wyatt, her slim, pink-tipped hand grasping the crook of his elbow.

Darkness surrounded them there. Chairs and cushioned settees, potted palms and uniquely-boxed plants were everywhere. Ellen quickly found that the sights mentioned by her attentive host included not only the panoramic night view of Hollywood and vicinity, but also several necking parties being indulged in by several others of Rob Wyatt's party guests!

As they strolled along, Ellen caught glimpses of interlocking arms, the paleness of feminine flesh glowing whitely against the somber hue of masculine coats . . . Heard faint murmurs, soft whispers, as caresses were exchanged between the more amorous guests!

The wine had given her a feeling of walking on air as she glided along the terrace, clinging to the arm of Wyatt. As disjointed bits of conversational emotion came to their ears, she laughed, softly.

"Rather a sophisticated party, Mr. Wyatt!"

"Just the usual thing, my dear!" he grinned, placing a big hand over the slender one that was so snugly ensconced in the crook of his arm. "And that's why Hollywood likes Rob Wyatt 'shindigs,' you see!"

"So it would seem!" laughed Ellen.

While strolling, they had come upon an unoccupied settee, and now Wyatt indicated it with a nod of his dark head. "Shall we?"

"So the guests aren't the only ones who get ideas?" she insinuated, softly.

"Could my mind be blank on a night like this?" he retorted in jest, then sobered. "I'm taking a chance on having this crowd around tonight! A chance not many would take, I'm sure . . . but when I knew you were coming here, I couldn't call it off . . ."

She was instantly on guard. "A chance?" she asked, quickly. "Why, what do you mean?"

Laughing couples were everywhere, but Wyatt's sober eyes were only for her. "I've been threatened!" he admitted, softly. "Threatened by the blonde adventuress who has styled herself 'The Domino Lady'! . . ." He broke off, evidently at a loss as to just how to proceed.

Ellen laughed: "Why, that's really absurd!" she exclaimed. "To think of your being molested in your own home while surrounded by friends and servants! Have you called the police?" Her concern was evident in her words and actions, and her host became at once more confiding.

"Why, no, I haven't called the police," he admitted, "because, you see, this little matter does not concern the police! It is strictly private, and something I'd rather not have them meddling with at present. It might cause a scandal, were it to come to light, and I cannot afford any scandal with a lieutenant governorship in the offing!" He whispered the latter sentence with an air of greatest secrecy; and Ellen almost laughed aloud.

"But what are you intending?" she asked, casually. "Surely you do not intend to quietly submit to threats without doing something?"

"I have everything attended to, thanks to the written threat I received," he boasted, patting her bare arm and grinning, knowingly. "You see, there is no entrance to this penthouse excepting through the fire escapes, and steps leading to the lobby. I have men in the fire escapes, and on guard in the lobby. They will come to my aid at the slightest evidence of foul play. And they will be particularly alert during the midnight hour when the little crook is supposed to put in her appearance!"

"Then you're perfectly safe," Ellen assured him with a laugh. She wanted to ask further questions, but refrained. It wouldn't do to arouse Wyatt's suspicions, so she adroitly changed the subject. "Isn't it time for a bit of music?" she asked, glancing at the tiny baguette on her wrist.

"Certainly, if you desire it, beautiful lady!" he grinned, brightening perceptibly. "Since the Wyatt menage is adequately equipped for anything in the way of a good time!"

"Including the perfect host!" she breathed. Ellen thought it a good idea to hand him a compliment, since she had obtained the necessary information from him, and she still had twenty minutes before midnight!

"Never more so than tonight!" he said, softly. "And all because you're numbered among my guests."

He grasped her bare arm, led her into a sumptuous living room. He switched on a powerful radio. The entrancing strains of the dreamy *When I Grow Too Old to Dream* floated out into the room.

"Shall we dance?" he asked.

She nodded, and he was quick to clasp her in his arms. She smiled at his hungry zeal.

"You're a dream! Ellen, beautiful!" he whispered, intensely, as he led her through the steps of the waltz.

Thrills stabbed Ellen. She couldn't help liking the possessive grip of his arm about her slender waist, drawing her close to him. Her lovely curves were flattened to his body, and she experienced an emotion quite unlike any that had before claimed her!

She had danced with many men without responding to their ardor, but, once in a while, she was cognizant of the rising tides within her, indicating that a particular partner was *the* type who could stir her soul to the depths and arouse the latent passions of her affectionate nature. It was so with Rob Wyatt! Willingly, her soft body clung to him in the measured movements of the dance, as light as the proverbial feather in his arms!

Abruptly, Rob Wyatt stood stockstill in the middle of the waltz. He held Ellen close, tilted her shining head upward so that his dark gaze penetrated to the very center of her being, as his hungry mouth closed over her hot, crimson lips. Such a kiss it was, something entirely new to the little adventuress, and it filled her with hungry longings as new and untried desires were given birth in her soft body. For a moment, she returned the kiss, forgetful of all else in the ecstasy of the moment. Then, remembering, she was out of his arms, retreating before him.

"Let's dance again?" breathed Wyatt, hoarsely, holding out his arms to her. Ellen hesitated a moment. Since he was obviously not wishing to press matters, she decided it best to follow suit. She smiled a brilliant smile, her alert mind working at full speed. It was now five minutes of midnight!

"I really should powder my nose first," she replied, pertly.

"It doesn't need it, you know," he demurred.

"And that's a fib," she smiled. "I'll only be a moment!"

As she turned to go, there came an interruption. A servant entered the room, bowed unctuously. "The telephone in the den, sir," he said, "and it is important!"

Wyatt frowned, but went to answer the summons. With a gay little laugh, and a prayer of thanks for the interruption, Ellen disappeared into the ladies' dressing room. It was without occupant at the moment, and Ellen crossed to the bed upon which a pile of hats and wraps were laid out. She had no time to lose, she reflected grimly, as she stooped and grasped the hem of her dress, drew it hurriedly upward over her shapely body. The brown frock was immediately hidden from view beneath the coverlets of the bed. This left the purposeful little intruder's body sheathed in a form-fitting evening dress of black crepe which she had worn beneath the high-collared brown one!

The creation of black, backless and daringly cut in at its décolletage, was the startling costume of the daring Domino Lady!

A moment later, she was creeping from the dressing room, and crossing the conservatory, but now the white silken cape partially covered the black frock, a black domino mask of shining silk masqueraded her eyes, and a small, black automatic sprouted in her determined right fist! *The Domino Lady was on her way to keep her midnight engagement!*

CHAPTER III

Ellen glided softly along a dim-lit corridor until she reached a massive end-door. The cold butt of the automatic steadied her, brought a grim smile to her lips. She reached out, twisted the knob silently, slowly, cautiously. She pushed the door open the barest fraction of an inch and peered in.

A moment later, she was switching on the softly shaded lights of the den which Wyatt had quitted a moment before. The flood of illumination revealed a sumptuous, masculine office with a huge desk set well to the rear of the place.

She wasted no time but hastened across the thick rug to attempt to find what she had come to get. The desk she found cluttered with documents and scribbled notations. To each piece of paper, no matter how small, Ellen gave hurried attention. But success did not come to her, although she wasted precious moments in vain search.

As she worked, a grim smile twitched at her curved lips as she imagined her erstwhile host's reaction when he found the desk tampered with!

Then, the smile was erased as her mind went back to the image when her father's still form had been found in the Keyser Building, riddled with state machine's bullets!

And by his own admission, this man Wyatt was ambitious for a position of power in the state; a creature who was sadistically torturing her friend with indiscreet letters although he did not need the demanded blackmail money! With poignant pain, she recalled that her aid was all that would save her friend, at the same time putting a crimp in the murdering state machine, could she but uncover something incriminating in Wyatt's den.

The penthouse was strangely silent now. Somewhere near, a clock ticked, reminding Ellen of the great need of speed now that midnight was past! There was one remaining drawer to be opened, and she delved into it with a desperate little prayer for aid. One hand encountered a sheath of papers, and she drew them forth, knowing that the precious letters were not numbered among them!

Abruptly, breath caught in her throat. Her brown eyes went wide behind the slits in the domino mask! From beneath the pile, one sheet of paper seemed to leap at her like a coiled serpent! It was heavy and official-appearing, and it was covered with notations and figures of a most incriminating nature! Ellen looked at the small packet, exultant.

This document was a sell-out of state power to Rob Wyatt along with a promised concession to Owens Valley water rights! Its meaning was clear. It was a statement of intention, turning over not only a large political slice of the state to Wyatt henchmen, but a veritable empire in precious irrigation rights!

The full import struck Ellen with the force of a mailed fist, and she was almost surprised by the sudden entrance of Rob Wyatt, now clad in a sleek dressing gown, who closed the massive door behind him!

Under all circumstances, the big game hunter was a cool customer. Serious but entirely calm, he faced Ellen Patrick across the desk, cognizant of the threatening weapon in her hand, but the expression on his face was not that of a man who anticipates the defeat of his plans. A smile played across his enigmatic features, and he seemed quite pleased with himself.

"Well, I must compliment you upon keeping our little engagement, Miss Domino Lady!" Wyatt taunted with a laugh. "As well as upon the charming costume you're wearing! However, I must warn you—no matter how you obtained entrance to this suite—it will require more than that automatic or a melodramatic costume to get you safely out of here! All exits are well-guarded, my dear!"

Ellen paled slightly. She had been in tight corners before, but never one the equal of this! She felt rather than saw the dark eyes caressing her sensuous figure as Wyatt advanced a pace in the face of her gun! She moved but slightly backward, held the gun higher.

"*Hold it!*" The command, softly-spoken, knifed through the room and brought a halt to the calmly, leisurely advancing man. "All your guards can do you no good, once I've let daylight through your heart, Rob Wyatt! And that's exactly what will happen within the next moment unless you obey my orders!"

He took a backward step, thinking fast. He knew that the crackle of the small calibre weapon would not be heard outside the door of the den, or upon the fire-escapes. And this grim, purposeful woman who threatened him might be just another tart with a quick trigger finger and no judgment!

Eyes glowing through the openings in her mask, full lips set in a straight line, a gentle flush on the flower-like cheeks—from the tips of her tiny evening slippers to the very top of her sleek blonde head, she looked like what she was! A determined woman, confident of her own power! She moved forward to face the now-frowning Wyatt.

He tried to regain his composure. "What's your game anyway?"

"Whatever it is, it's not crooked politics!" she rasped, and enjoyed his look of consternation.

"Politics?" He stared at her, hard. "What—what do you know about politics?" he demanded.

She laughed in his face. "Plenty that won't stand a good airing!" she said, softly, teasingly. "And it all concerns your ambitions, and your guarantees of protection, Wyatt! Am I right so far?"

He looked at her as though dazed. He was silent, thinking.

She continued, relentlessly. "I know all the details! And it would delight me to send you to prison where you belong!"

"So what?" he managed, weakly. There was no real force to the words. The terrible threat in her words had burned him to the heart, and his face became a desperate mask pierced by narrowed, dark eyes.

"So what?" she laughed, harshly. "So plenty! I have you right where I want you! I have in my possession all that is necessary to convict you, secure you a nice long stretch in the pen for robbing poor people of their water rights, and conspiring to fix an election!"

He fairly gasped: "You mean . . . ?"

"I mean that unless you hand over those letters I called for right now, I'm giving you the works, and leaving here as I entered, with all the incriminating evidence!"

Wyatt looked at her bleakly. "I should tell you to go . . ."

"But you won't," she interrupted, quickly. "Because you're afraid of me! You're afraid of the evidence I can use against you. Think of it! The big game hunter who was never afraid in his life!"

He broke in harshly: "Don't use that 'big-strong-he-man' stuff on me! It won't get you anywhere! I'm not afraid of anything that I don't have to be. I'm not taking chances, and that's how I've become the biggest shot in town right now! I'm going to give you those letters in return for the documents you've stolen from my desk. Of course," he went on, calmly now, "you won't get far away before I have you back for house-breaking!"

"It suits me," she told him, evenly. "But mark one thing down to be remembered, Wyatt!

You'll never see me again until I call again to secure those documents which will send you where you belong! I'm out to get you from this moment forward, and The Domino Lady never fails to deliver. Don't forget that!"

Wyatt grunted, but his smile was egotistical as he walked to a hidden closet in the corner and returned with a slender packet which he placed upon the desk. Ellen quickly secured it, tossed the Wyatt documents to the waiting man. She smiled as she slipped the packet of letters into a tiny pocket inside the white cape. Then, she moved swiftly, spoke harshly.

"Now, get going!" she rasped, coldly. "Walk to the wall! Face it and place your arms behind you! One false move, and I'll put daylight through you!"

Since there was nothing else to do, Rob Wyatt did as directed with the best grace he could muster under the circumstances. He fumed and swore a terrible vengeance as he nosed the wall and placed his hands behind him. But he was totally unprepared for the next move of his visitor.

Dipping swiftly beneath the cape, Ellen produced a tiny hypodermic syringe which had been previously loaded with a quick-acting drug which, while harmless, would incapacitate the victim for several minutes!

Noiselessly, she went close behind Wyatt, and her soft laugh and a prickling sensation behind the right ear as she used the needle deftly, were his first indication of her intention. Immediately, the room began to blur before his eyes, and a choking darkness crept into his brain!

Swift realization of what had happened swept over him even before the words of his assailant seeped into his darkening brain:

"Just a bit of suspended animation, my dear friend, while The Domino Lady makes her exit!"

If speed were required before, Ellen Patrick outdid herself now. A tiny black card with the inscription *The Domino Lady's Compliments* in white ink was tossed upon the desk as a souvenir of her daring visit. Then, without a glance at the fallen Wyatt, she opened the massive door and exited into the perilous corridor! What if a guard, or a guest had missed the hunter and were lying in wait for her? What if . . . but she had no time for idle speculations. It was a grand test for the nerves of the little adventuress. If she had miscalculated, she could expect trouble in a large dose and with a capital T! If she were lucky—well, that would be a still different story.

Three minutes later, her stilted heels were clicking across the conservatory. She heard a faint shuffling of feet in the direction of the foyer and judged that the guests were leaving. Her lungs expanded and contracted in a deep breath of relief when she found the dressing room vacant, the coats missing, and the place all to herself.

Working with the speed of a burlesque strip-artist, she peeled the incriminating black crepe frock from her lovely, quivering figure. Swiftly, the brown satin dress replaced it. The black gown and the domino were quickly folded and added to the letters which she placed in a large, addressed envelope. This gown of special construction for the purpose, folded neatly about the domino, hypo-needle, and automatic, and the package made no very perceptible bulge beneath the high-necked satin dress. Then, smiling, Ellen Patrick joined the departing guests in the foyer!

"Mr. Wyatt?" a servant was saying as she departed. "Just a wee-nip too much, sir! You know how it is, sir? He will be quite all right in a little while, sir! Thank you, sir!"

And The Domino Lady smiled knowingly to herself as she hesitated in the lobby long enough to drop the large envelope into the mail chute for the morrow's delivery! No taking chances with the incriminating parcel at the last moment, she mused! And her mind was busy with three pleasant subjects as her cab knifed the night traffic of Hollywood Boulevard: Wyatt's discomfiture; Eloise Schenick's thankfulness; and her next encounter with the handsome hunter who never knew any rules.

THE LETTERS AND THE LAW

T. T. Flynn

BLACK MASK is regarded by one and all as the greatest of the mystery pulp magazines, and most experts agree that the Avis of the pulps was *Dime Detective*, which featured some of the greatest names of the era, much as *Black Mask* did: Raymond Chandler, Cornell Woolrich, Erle Stanley Gardner, and George Harmon Coxe. When Harry Steeger, the legendary president of Popular Publications, decided to start a sister publication to his enormously successful *Detective Fiction Weekly*, he called on his regular contributors to write for the new magazine. The first issue (November 1931) included a story by Thomas Theodore Flynn (1902–1979), the prolific author who went on to be a mainstay of both publications.

Eschewing college for a life of adventure, Flynn went to sea at the age of fourteen, working as a common laborer as ship's carpenter, oiler, steersman, fireman, and more. He returned to work on railroads, gathering material for his fiction. After Charles Lindbergh's 1927 solo flight across the Atlantic captivated the nation, Flynn wrote aviation stories, taking flying lessons in the name of accuracy. Sometime after he moved to the West, he began to write westerns, a genre in which he had his greatest success, making a sale to the *Saturday Evening Post*. *The Man from Laramie* appeared as a serial in eight issues from January 2 to February 20, 1954; it was made into a hit movie that starred Jimmy Stewart the following year.

Flynn's most popular crime fiction characters were Mr. Maddox, a racetrack tout and bookie who appeared regularly in *Dime Detective*, and Mike Harris and Trixie Meehan, private eyes who were fixtures in the pages of *Detective Fiction Weekly*. An ongoing storyline is that the very cute Trixie exasperates Harris, first by getting them into trouble and then by being a step ahead of him as they solve a mystery. Unusually for a pulp detective male–female team, there appears to be little sexual chemistry between them.

"The Letters and the Law" was originally published in the June 27, 1936, issue of *Detective Fiction Weekly*.

The Letters and the Law

T. T. FLYNN

CHAPTER I
In the Ring—

MIAMI LOOKED THE SAME—white clouds in the clear blue sky—the February sun bright and hot—when I tipped the Pullman porter and dashed through the station to a taxi.

"Geigler Building on Flagler Street," I panted at the hacker.

"Nice weather we're having," he beamed as he closed the door.

I was mopping perspiration off my face and neck. "Terrific!" I groaned. "What I need is an oversized ice plant."

"Ha-ha—it is a little warm today, isn't it?" he burbled over his shoulder as he drove off. "But think of the weather they're having up north."

"If I think, I'll melt," says I, shoving my heavy overcoat over on the seat and mopping perspiration.

He thought I was kidding him. I don't know what Bradley's office girl thought when I walked in on her, still mopping perspiration.

"Why, it's Mister Harris!" she squealed, hopping out of her chair.

"Hello, Dotty," says I. "Last spring it was Mike, wasn't it?"

"Dotty?" says she, cooling off. "Don't you even remember my *name*?"

"Could I forget it," I remembered just in time. "Prudence, the little lady who couldn't forget her name."

"I thought we agreed to forget all that," she reminded with sweet charity.

"Pay no attention to me," I cracked. "My meter isn't connected yet. Where is Bradley?"

She reached for the phone. "I'll tell him you're here."

"Is he in conference?"

"Why—why, yes and no," says Prudence. "I think he's expecting you; just let me tell him you're here."

"Never mind; I'll tell him myself," I refused, starting toward Bradley's door.

"Really—" Prudence protested weakly.

But I was already opening Bradley's door. . . .

Maybe you've never met me—Mike Harris, of the Blaine Agency. I'm red-headed, five feet and a shadow, and life doesn't seem much more than one case after another. I've got a vacation coming—but I'll give you that later.

Bradley was behind his desk, lighting a fresh cigar.

"I'm here, thanks to you," I snorted, tossing the overcoat on a chair and peeling off my coat and vest.

"So I see. You're a sight for sore eyes, Mike!" says Bradley heartily. He came around the desk and grabbed my hand. "I'm certainly glad to see you, Mike. Yes, sir, I certainly am."

Bradley managed the Miami office. He was gray-haired and immaculate, smooth as a Junior League smile, and hard-boiled as a dowager's determination. Just the man for that stretch of gold coast between Jacksonville and Miami. Bradley could soft-soap a chair full of jittery millions or strong-arm a gold-washed crook with the same finesse.

"Never mind the greeter's lullaby," I handed him sourly. "Where's your ice water? Where's a fan? I'm burning up."

Bradley chuckled. "It isn't *that* hot here, Mike."

"Meet this sun in an overcoat, a winter suit, winter underwear, and socks, and then sing your song," I retorted. "Those ditherwits in the New York office didn't care whether I had on earmuffs or rubbers when they wired me to change trains at the next junction and get down here. Dish me the dirt before I melt on your floor."

"It's a woman," says Bradley, returning to his chair.

"Isn't it always?" I cracked, drawing ice water from the cooler in the corner.

Bradley took the cigar from his mouth and sighed. "But *what* a woman, Mike!"

"So was Eve, and she took the apple."

"In this case," Bradley informed me wryly, "the lady plants the tree, too. Give this Lucille Palmer a brace of free tickets to an opening and she'd leave with the show."

I tossed the paper cup into the waste container and surveyed Bradley. He was deeply affected; more so than I'd ever seen him.

"It must be pretty bad," I said. "Give me the worst. This Lucille Palmer sounds to me like a great discovery."

"In a way she is," Bradley admitted ruefully. "I've met some sharp-witted women in my day, Mike, but I don't believe I've ever seen one who could stay in the money with her. Yes, she's a discovery."

"So was Little America—but what does one do with it? What has the lady done—tampered with your happy home?"

"I," said Bradley severely, "am a very moral man, Mike. But Colonel Wedgewood, the beet-sugar king, unfortunately forgot himself. It would be more truthful to say he lost his reason. Lucille Palmer led him back to the cradle days and made him beg for the bottle."

"So what?"

"So," said Bradley, "it's two hundred grand for the letters—or else."

I gave Bradley a vicious look. "Did you have me sent all the way down here to recover a sap's letters? Tell that peepshow grandpappy to pay off the lady and charge it to education."

"This," said Bradley earnestly, "is no ordinary case, Mike. You know me well enough to know I don't go off half-cocked when a client cries on my shoulder. Colonel Wedgewood has paid off already with jewels, cash, and a long list of expensive odds and ends."

"So now he's left with the odds while the lady keeps the ends? What does he want?"

"Forty-seven torrid letters," Bradley informed me sadly.

I yawned. "Don't you know," I asked wearily, "that if she's asking two hundred grand for those letters, he should tell her to take the squawk to the Supreme Court—or jump off the Hoboken Ferry? No one pays any attention to dirt any more. She couldn't get it into a New York court if she carried a union card. Where is he from?"

"New York and Denver. But a breach of promise suit is not what Colonel Wedgewood fears, Mike. His lawyers can handle that without difficulty. The old man is enough of a fighter not to care much what the newspapers print."

"Then who's crabbing about what?"

Bradley rolled the cigar in his fingers. He looked as sad as a corporation lawyer reviewing a bad case.

"Colonel Wedgewood gave me the complete picture," he sighed. "Relations between the colonel and his wife are strained—very strained. The colonel washed a great deal of the family dirt in those letters. He was in an agitated state of mind at the time; and he felt certain he had found a marvelously understanding girl who was happy to share his troubles and sympathize. So, in the various letters, he wrote it all out, with appropriate comments. If Mrs. Wedgewood's lawyers get hold of those letters, they'll bomb him with some of the things he put down. He'll be forced into a property settlement which will cost him several millions. And that, my boy, is not penny arcade money."

"You make it sound very pitiful," I said sarcastically. "The colonel will have only a couple of million left, I suppose? I could weep at such poverty. Why is he squawking about two hundred thousand if that much will save him several millions? He'll never turn up another deal that will pay him such a percentage."

"On the face of the matter, yes," Bradley admitted. "But Colonel Wedgewood is certain other demands will follow. He has no way of knowing that this Palmer woman won't keep photostatic copies of the letters—which would be quite enough for Mrs. Wedgewood's lawyers. You see, due to the facts the colonel put down in the letters, this Lucille Palmer is quite aware of the situation—and how valuable the letters really are."

"The man certainly went whole hog when he decided to play the fool."

"He couldn't have done worse," Bradley sighed again. "I don't see any way out but to get the letters, and at the same time make certain no photostatic copies exist."

"In other words, you want a miracle—so you send up north for me to do your dirty work?"

"It's an important and delicate case which must be settled quickly and carefully, Mike," Bradley pleaded earnestly. "I couldn't think of two people in the Blaine organization better fitted to do it than you and Trixie Meehan."

That blew me out of the chair yelping: "*What?* Trixie Meehan? Not on your egg-stained vest! I wouldn't work panhandlers' row with that little torpedo! Nix! *Nein!* No! Get it? *NO!* Trixie's raw-hided me for the last time! If you send for her, I take a runout powder and go back to New York. Do I make it plain?"

Bradley's face was red before I finished. He coughed behind his hand, looked distressed.

"Aren't you a little severe on Miss Meehan, Mike? You two have done some great work together. She's tops in her class!"

"So is prussic acid in its class!" I snorted. "I'm not having any of Trixie Meehan this trip—and that's that!"

Bradley coughed again.

"Unfortunately," he sadly informed me, "Miss Meehan is—er—".

"Miss Meehan is right here!" says a voice I know only too well. "And if that sawed-off little eohippus has any more cracks to make about me, I'll add up the check myself!"

CHAPTER II
The Parade

From the next room Trixie swept in—little Trixie, pert as ever—and primed for trouble. And I started back-pedaling fast.

"Am I surprised?" I bleated weakly. "You know—"

"I know," says little Trixie, glaring. "Don't soft-soap *me*, Numbskull!"

Never met Trixie Meehan either? Life has passed you by. Trixie is no bigger than a gadfly. But her blue eyes are so-o-o big, and soft and melting. Trixie's misleading little face has a way of making old men husky and young men weak. Trixie tripping by on the main stem is as soft and helpless as a bit of fluff on an autumn breeze.

But *this* Trixie, who worked Blaine Agency cases with me, was concentrated hell-on-wheels. Her cuddly curves had the strength of an adagio dancer, her fluffy helplessness masked a chilled-steel nerve, her mind clicked eighty to the minute, and Trixie's pink little tongue could take the skin off a chromium gargoyle. *What* a woman—and here she was loaded for bear.

"This *is* a surprise," I got out weakly. "Ha-ha, *what* a surprise. I didn't know you were below the Mason-Dixon line, Trixie."

"I'll bet you didn't," says Trixie.

So I let her have it back twice as nasty. "I took the pledge on you, sister, that last case out West. You're poison to me. You give me nightmares with that razor-edged tongue. I'm not having another helping, if you ask for it on a hot griddle. No more—get me?"

Trixie put her little hands on her little hips and cut me down with a look.

"I get you," she gave me coldly. "But since when were *you* heaven's gift to anyone, Ape?"

"Time!" yelled Bradley. "Call off this cross-country feud until you break this case! I've explained it to you, Miss Meehan. You've got the layout, Mike. The Palmer woman is registered at the Miami-Plaza. She's dealing through a New York law firm. I think they're shysters. One of the partners, a man named Louis Layre, is also at the Miami-Plaza. That's all the help I can give you. Now give me a little help. *I'm* the one that's in hot water here. It's my office that'll get the heat if the Palmer woman puts it over."

Trixie had calmed down. She gave me a nasty look and the lift of her shoulder, and spoke to Bradley. "Are there only two of them?"

"As far as I know."

"Only two," says Trixie demurely. "That shouldn't be hard to handle."

"Now, listen," I said desperately. "I told you—"

"Of course," says Trixie sweetly to me, "if you're a cowardly quitter, Mike. If you're afraid of this Palmer woman—"

"Afraid of her? Me afraid of *any* woman?"

"Hmmmmm," says Trixie, giving me the up-and-up under her long lashes. "Well, we'll see. Mr. Bradley, where is this lovely old sapodillo?"

"Colonel Wedgewood and his wife have opened their Palm Beach villa," Bradley explained hastily. "They're doing the social whirl rather big this winter. This Palmer woman has turned up with her squeeze just when it will be most embarrassing and damaging to the colonel's peace of mind and—er—his wife's good nature. That sent him to us so quickly and—uh—desperately."

"I adore desperate men," Trixie giggled.

I sighed. "I'll take the hook," I said. "But if a certain party gets in my hair I'll run her back to New York so fast her brogues'll smoke. And that's no maybe. Furthermore, *I'll* give the orders."

"Of course, Nitwit," Trixie agreed. "You always try, don't you?"

"Now there you go—"

Bradley waved us down. "The sky's the limit on expenses," says he hurriedly. "Colonel Wedgewood wants results. He's willing to pay through the nose to get them. Could anything be fairer?"

"Or sweeter?" Trixie sighed.

"We'll get results," I promised sourly. "But how he'll pay! Start the swindle sheet with a bottle of good Scotch. I've got to think."

"Dynamite might blast it out quicker," Trixie suggested helpfully.

Bradley stood up with a wild look in his eye. "Go into the next room there and plan it any way you like," he choked. "Only don't bite in the clenches."

Trixie saw my ideas—after an argument which brought Bradley to the door twice. He didn't interrupt because we had the door locked. When we had it settled, I drew a check to the expense account that made Bradley gag, and took the next plane back to New York.

A day's hard work got me luggage, clothes, and a big, lean valet by the name of Bitters. From my room at the Pierre, I wired the Miami-Plaza to reserve a suite for Mr. Michael Harris and manservant.

The next day Bitters and I flew south. Just before dark we hit the crowded Miami-Plaza lobby like good news from home. You could hear the conversation gagging when I breezed in wearing a bright suit that screamed for attention, with Bitters, in ministerial black, towering at my heels, and four bellhops staggering after him with loads of swank luggage.

"Mr. Michael Harris," I gave the pop-eyed clerk. "I reserved a suite by wire."

He fussed with his necktie, opened and

closed his mouth silently, looked at the bellhops ganging behind me, and said, "Uh—yes, sir! Uh—will you register, please?"

I waved my hand languidly up at Bitters.

"I won't," says I. "But my man will. Have me put in my suite quickly, please. And send up the manager."

Near me an over-dressed fat woman made a remark which cut through the sudden quiet.

"How odd!" she said.

I turned, saw her eyeing me through a pair of nose-glasses she held up with a pudgy hand.

"Bitters," says I coldly. "Make a note of anyone who shows interest in me."

"A note?" Bitters gulped, looking around wildly.

"You heard me. A note. A memorandum. I wish to be informed, you idiot, of the presence of any suspicious characters. Do I make myself plain?"

Bitters was breathing heavily through his nose by then. He barely managed to bleat, "Yes, sir. Quite so, sir."

By that time the lady had her glasses down and was breathing hard, too. "Well, I *never*—" she gasped.

"Madame," says I coldly, "you'd better." That got me into the elevator and up to the suite. There I handed each of the bellhops a ten-dollar bill.

"Young men," I told them severely, "I want service. Very good service. I'm willing to pay for what I get. There's more where that came from. Pass the word along. Furthermore, I'll pay twenty dollars for a complete description and report of anyone who tries to pump the staff about me. Do I make myself plain?"

They were pop-eyed by then. The nearest bellhop stuttered, "Are you expecting a sh-shot in the back, Mr. Harris?"

"Son," I told him, "I'm expecting the manager just now. Get him up here."

They did.

The manager was a pudgy, pink-faced man who looked as if he could suavely handle any situation which might arise about the hotel. But he entered the suite warily; and he grew fidgety, and his eyebrows went up when he heard my demands.

"I want four bodyguards while I'm here," I told him coldly. "Big men. Competent men. The uglier their faces, the better. Put two of them outside my door immediately. And have the other two waiting in the lobby every time I come down. Day or night. On second thought, you may need more than four to keep that schedule."

He moistened his lips.

"That, Mr. Harris, will run into quite a sum of money."

"Did I ask you about money? I want the guards."

That sank him. He looked at me askance. His thoughts registered on his face. He was wondering if I was a big-shot dodging trouble up north—and expecting a blow-up down here. Miami, of course, was the happy playground of the big money crooks from all over the north. But usually they buried their differences and lived in harmony while they took the sun and planned future business.

My request for guards was making the manager wonder if I wasn't one of the boys playing foul ball on local hospitality. It flustered him. "I don't understand—I'm afraid I don't understand, Mr. Harris."

"Who asked you to understand? Do I get the bodyguards?"

He bowed, stiffly. "We try to make our guests feel at home, Mr. Harris. Is there any other way we can be of service to you?"

I took out my new bill-fold. It was fat with Colonel Wedgewood's money. Bug-eyed, the manager watched the wad of five-hundred-dollar bills I took out and leafed through.

"Let's see—seventeen thousand. Will you put this in the safe for me? Leave the receipt at the desk."

"Of course, of course—uh—seventeen thousand," he mumbled, counting the bills. "You don't wish to come down and sign for it, Mr. Harris?"

"If I did, I would," I gave him. "But I don't."

He nodded and left in a daze.

The scene had left Bitters breathing heavily through his nose again.

"Unpack!" I snarled at him. "Don't stand there looking as if you're in a psychopathic ward! I didn't hire you to look surprised at what I do."

"Indeed so, sir," Bitters answered hastily. "I understand you perfectly, sir. I mean—er—I'll try to understand you perfectly. Unpack, sir— that was what you wished, wasn't it?" Bitters babbled, looking like his dinner had come to life and snapped at him.

"It is," says I, turning to the bedroom. "Order Scotch and soda."

The manager may have left in a daze, but he gave service. By the time I was dressed for dinner, two big huskies were stationed outside my door. I stepped out, looked them over, and spoke to the one on my right, "What's your name?"

"Joe Jacobs," he rumbled, looking down his nose, past a face that would have made a mother weak. He had a cauliflower ear, a scar on his jaw, and the shoulders and neck of a wrestler.

"And you?" I asked the other man.

He looked down, too, blinked, and said, "Gus Wayland's me name, Boss. What're we supposed to do?" He had a flat nose, long arms, powerful hands, and the trusting brown eyes of a good-natured spaniel.

"All you've got to do, Gus," I explained, "is keep close to me when I tell you to, and not let anyone touch me. You're bodyguards. Get it? Bodyguards."

"*Har*—it's a pipe!" Gus chortled, with a confidential wink.

"Take that smirk off your map!" I ordered. "D'you think you're starring in a two-ring circus?"

Gus straightened his face, snapped to attention—and when I went down to eat a few minutes later both of them trotted at my heels as solemn and formidable as two work elephants behind a fox terrier.

When we disgorged from the elevator into the lobby, two more huskies standing nearby took their cue and closed in also.

"Don't crowd so much or I'll suffocate!" I snarled from inside that towering wall of meat. "Deliver me to the dining room and wait at the door."

The dining room was crowded. My ten-dollar tips had been like a shot of yeast to the hotel staff. The headwaiter led the charge. A "reserved" sign was whisked off a table. Waiters flocked around. The head-waiter himself took my order. Diners turned in their chairs and stared at the show.

I looked around for Trixie Meehan—and spotted her at a table across the room.

Little Trixie was dressed in white. She looked fragile, lovely, and very, very helpless. But she had protection. He was past forty, rather sallow, but well-turned out, jaunty and good-looking in a dinner jacket.

I knew the type. He was a wise boy—New York wise—self-assured, smug. But Trixie had him hooked. He was watching her as if fearful the luscious little tidbit might flit away.

Trixie saw me and ignored me. She was working on her escort as if she had suddenly discovered something devastating.

They left before I did. They were not in sight when I emerged from the dining room. So, with my squad of huskies I paraded the lobby, the patios, and out on the ocean terrace for the benefit of the crowd.

They ate it up. I ignored them, and in half an hour went up to the suite and telephoned Trixie's room.

She was out then, and was still out the next three times I called her. Hours later the telephone beside my bed rang. Trixie cooed over the wire.

"Apsay, do you think you're another Napoleon with that army of flatfeet?"

"Does this look like Moscow?" I snarled back. "Who was that jumble-brain you speared for the dinner check?"

"*And* the evening, Useless," says Trixie. "We're at the Club Monte now. He dances divinely—*and* his taxi technique is devastating. I didn't dream," Trixie sighed, "that the job would turn out as amusing as this."

"Get a load of cold turkey!" I snarled at her. "You aren't here to take up taxi wrestling! Ditch that shined-up Romeo and do something about the Palmer woman's lawyer! I *told* you what to do!"

"So thoughtful of you, too, Mike," Trixie cooed. "I've been with him all evening. As a wealthy young widow, I'm a riot. Louie's weakness is wealth *and* the widow's mite."

"So it's *Louie* already?"

Trixie giggled. "What a man he turned out to be, Mike. *What* a man!"

"Never mind his score card. Will he talk?"

"Louie," says Trixie cheerfully, "is a gentleman—except in the clinches. Besides, he's smart. He asks questions, but he does hate to talk about his business. Give me time."

"You'll be dizzy by then, with a can tied to you. What about La Palmer?"

"Look for the prettiest one," Trixie said sweetly. "She's all of thirty-four—and admits to twenty-five, and gets away with it, if the beauty shop gossip is right. The cats usually are. Her hair is corn-colored and she's about your height, Mike. Tonight she was wearing white and gold—and Louie is in her bad graces because of poor little me. Isn't it thrilling?"

"Bring that powder-rubber home and knock off for the evening."

That got me a giggle. "I'm only starting—and I hope you don't like it," Trixie gave me. "*Au revoir*, Napoleon. Don't fall over your ego." She hung up on me.

That was Trixie—in my hair already. I bawled out Bitters, had a long Scotch and soda, with visions of Trixie cuddling for that shyster, and finally got to sleep.

In the morning when I crawled out of bed, Bitters handed me a note in a hotel envelope. "This was in your box, sir."

It was from Trixie, of course; three words: *She swims early.*

So I swam early, too.

CHAPTER III
Bait

The white beach sand sloped from the hotel terrace to the shallows where mile-long combers broke in creamy smothers. Gay beach umbrellas dotted the sand. An early crowd was out when I hit the ocean with my four husky guards.

We drew a quick gallery. Celebrities were a dime a dozen at the Miami-Plaza, but four ponderous bodyguards were a show. The crowd had nothing to do but look and talk—and they did.

On our second circuit of the beach I spotted the Palmer woman under an umbrella. Bradley was right. What a woman. In her scanty bathing suit she outclassed anything on the beach. She was small, slender, perfect. Her face had a sultry, vivid beauty that was worth money to any smart girl.

And down beside her on one knee, talking vehemently, was Layre, the lawyer. He paid no attention to me as I paraded by. But Lucille Palmer spared one flickering glance of appraisal. Nothing personal. She probably estimated every man.

By the time I turned back along the beach again, Layre was walking away and Lucille Palmer was heading toward the water, adjusting her green rubber cap. I dunked the body also.

The surf was brisk. She swam out and met the breakers shoulder high. I swam out beyond her at an angle, and drifted back in, laying a bearing on her green cap. In the white smother of a breaking wave I rolled in against her.

We both staggered, fighting for footing until the wave washed past. She was annoyed until she recognized me; and then her face changed.

"Excuse me," I gasped. "I'm not a very g-good swimmer!" And I grabbed her hand and balanced myself.

She let me hold on. "You're the man with the bodyguards," she said, studying my face while we both braced for the next wave.

"Yes, ma'am."

The wave hit us, threw us together, and when we were clear she asked, "Why do you need those four big bruisers to guard you? What are you—a—a what they call a big-shot?"

"Oh, dear me, mercy no!" I denied breathlessly. "My lawyers suggested the guards. Isn't this great? Look out—here comes the next wave!"

We went together again. When we came out of the smother, Lucille gave me a sidewise look.

"No," she said dryly, "you couldn't be."

"Couldn't be what, ma'am?"

"A big-shot," she said coldly, wading back to shallower water. And I'll take my hand if you don't mind. Just what are you, Mr. Harris?"

"D-do you know my name?"

Her laugh was throaty. It matched her sultry looks, as she said: "How could I help it? Everyone in the hotel is asking about you."

"Heavens!" I gulped. "I didn't mean to attract attention. I—I think I'd better wire my lawyers—er—Miss—"

That drew me another throaty laugh.

"I'm Lucille Palmer. You *are* a funny man. Tell me why your lawyers insist on those bodyguards?"

I sighed mournfully. "Too much money, I suppose. Kidnapers and all that sort of thing, you know. I've been miserable ever since I inherited the estate."

"Estate?"

"Cousin Jeffry's estate," I sighed. "His health was perfect, too. If the train had been only two minutes later that last time he got drunk—"

"Tch, tch—" Lucille said sympathetically. "So Cousin Jeffry was killed in a train wreck?"

"Not exactly. I don't think the train was wrecked. But if it had been a little late, Jeffry would have gotten over the grade crossing in time. He always was impetuous."

"Impetuous," said Lucille queerly. "It must have been a shock. And you're unsteady now from those waves, aren't you? Here, give me your hand. We'd better sit on the sand and rest a little."

So we sat on the sand—and I told Lucille about the Bon Ton glove counter where I used to work, and the trials of having so much money now.

Lucille patted my hand sympathetically. "You

don't play enough, Michael. And if you wish, you may call me Lucille."

"Lucille," I sighed.

"Lawyers," Lucille murmured dreamily, "have to earn their money by giving advice. But you don't have to be silly enough to take it, Michael."

"Would—would you take a drive with me, Lucille?"

"Of course I would, Michael. And we won't need any bodyguards, will we?"

"Well—"

"No bodyguards," said Lucille firmly. "I'm all the protection you need."

Bitters was at the telephone when I entered the suite. He hung up hastily. I thought he looked guilty. But his voice was as lugubrious as ever.

"Can I mix you a drink, sir?"

"Who were you telephoning?"

"I thought you might need another bottle of Scotch, sir. I took the liberty of ordering it sent up."

"Fair enough," I said. "Go down and get me the papers."

When Bitters was out of the way, I got the switchboard.

"This is 318," I said. "Mr. Harris talking. The telephone was used here a few minutes ago. Who was called?"

"Just a moment, Mr. Harris. Outside, I think— Yes, the Atlantic Hotel. Do you wish the number?"

"Who was being called at the Atlantic Hotel?"

"I can't tell you that, Mr. Harris."

"Never mind the number."

So Bitters had lied. Why? He'd been hired from a New York employment agency. References were in good order. He was the perfect gentleman's gentleman—just what I needed for this act. But now—what about Bitters?

When he returned with the papers, Bitters's long solemn face was slightly disapproving—no different than it had been since we had arrived.

"Will there be anything else, sir?"

"Not now," I said. "I'm going for a drive."

Lucille and I, minus the bodyguards, drove behind a chauffeur in a sixteen-cylinder job I had rented. We came back with a date for dinner.

That afternoon, three bellhops collected their twenty-dollar bills. People had been asking questions about me—a Mrs. Nicolby, the current gossip—Louis Layre, the lawyer—and Lucille Palmer's maid. A business woman was Lucille.

Bradley telephoned: "Colonel Wedgewood is demanding action, Mike. They're crowding him for the money. Any luck?"

"Tell him to stall them. Rome wasn't burned in a day."

"Rome," says Bradley, "never was burned up like Colonel Wedgewood is now over your expense account and the delay. For God's sake, Mike, give me some action for his money!"

"Give him sweet hope," I said. "And you haven't seen an expense account yet." I hung up before Bradley could erupt.

Lucille's black lace frock that evening infuriated every other woman in the dining room. So Lucille felt good. Afterwards we went to the dog races out north of Miami, taking two of my guards, at my insistence.

With palms and pines flanking the grandstand, and the dogs chasing the mechanical rabbit around the brightly lighted arena, while the crowd yelled and rooted, I bet hard and heavy. And lost one—two—three.

"You're reckless with your money," Lucille chided.

Bradley would have groaned at my reply. "It's nothing. I hardly know what to do with the stuff."

I'd told Gus and Joe, my guards, to keep their seats. Lucille and I were edging back to our seats in the grandstand before the fifth race. Lucille's arm, which I held, suddenly went tense. Her eyes, at the moment, were on the seats over to the left. Only one man was looking full at her.

A smooth smile of satisfaction was widening on his face. Smooth, florid, well-barbered, nattily dressed, he had the same wise look as Louis Layre.

The blonde who sat beside him looked like a Broadway chorus girl. And probably had been one.

Lucille Palmer was not smiling. Her makeup emphasized a sudden pallor. I watched her. The fifth race didn't mean anything to her.

I caught her digging fingernails into the palm of her hand. While the pooches were running, she watched that third row ahead, where the blonde and her escort were seated.

Once the man looked around at us. He'd noted where our seats were.

Rasputin, my hound, chased the rabbit in first for a change. The band began to play; the crowd surged from the seats again. Lucille moistened her lips.

"I—I've got to make a telephone call, Michael. Don't bother to come."

"It will be a pleasure," I gave her primly.

I thought she was going to refuse. "Come along, then," she said abruptly.

The closed door of the telephone booth cut off her words. But through the glass she looked nervous, excited. As a matter of fact, she looked frightened.

"Lousy bunch of hounds here tonight."

He'd come down out of the grandstand without his blonde. He was smiling affably. "Cigarette?" he asked, opening a flat case.

I had to think fast to remember the Bon Ton glove counter and Cousin Jeffry. "Why—why, do I know you, sir?"

"Huh—what's that?" He gave a quick, narrow-lidded look. "I get it," he said, half to himself. Then he chuckled. "I know your lady friend, so it's all right, friend. The name is Cushman. Bernard Cushman. What'd you say your name was?"

"Harris, sir. Mr. Michael Harris."

"Well, well—it's a pleasure, Mr. Harris. And here's the little lady herself."

The little lady was edging out of the telephone booth with her hand in her purse. If she didn't have her hand on a gun, I was nobody's business. All color had left her face. The rouge stood out. She was tense, like a cat coming out of a corner ready to fight.

Cushman ignored it with a bland smile. One hand out to shake hands, and the other holding the cigarette case, he said: "You're the last kid I was lookin' for down here. Lots of surprises, eh? Haven't changed your name, have you—gotten married, or anything like that?"

"I'm still Lucille Palmer, Bernie." She had a dangerous note of warning. I wondered what her name had been when they knew each other before.

Cushman chuckled.

"Never mind introducing me, Lucille. I've met Mr. Harris already."

"So I see." Lucille closed her purse with a snap. Her voice had a snap, too. Color was coming back into her cheeks. Her fear was giving away to suppressed fury.

Cushman ignored that, too. He had a bland, smooth manner. "Where you staying?" he questioned.

"Does it matter? I won't be seeing you while I'm here. I'm—busy."

Cushman chuckled again. "First time I've ever seen you too ritzy to pass up old friends. Say—I've got a sweet idea. You an' your friend join us. We're due at a live party in a while."

"No, *thanks!*"

Cushman urged: "You know the fellow—Jack Wetzlaff. He's got a yacht he won in a deal a few months ago. Just brought it down from New York, and he's throwing a party on board tonight."

"Steady, Mike," says I to myself.

I was suddenly all ears. Wetzlaff was in the New York rackets—high up. He'd made plenty; was still making it. The devil only knew what kind of a deal had given him a yacht. Some poor lad had been squeezed hard.

Lucille's anger abruptly vanished. "A yacht?"

"It'll knock your eyes out."

"I didn't know you were running around with Jack Wetzlaff."

"We're like that." Cushman crossed his fingers.

And I horned in. This was a chance to take. Crooks aren't smart. Pour a few drinks into one when he thinks the company is "right," and his tongue usually wags.

"A party on a yacht would be fun," says I, hesitatingly.

"I doubt it," Lucille came back positively. "I think you'd better take me back to the hotel, Michael. I'm getting a headache."

Cushman grinned. "Let's take Lucille back to her hotel, and then you come on to the party with us, Mr. Harris. There'll be an extra girl for you if you want one."

Lucille scorched him with a look. I visibly weakened. She forced a smile.

"If Michael goes, I'll take an aspirin and go, too. Someone might start a poker game. I don't think Michael's poker is good enough."

I felt like a tasty morsel of meat they were bristling over. It didn't matter. Maybe Lucille would talk, too, after a few drinks.

So we went to the party, taking my bodyguards.

CHAPTER IV
A Toast to Treachery

The yacht was tied alongside the causeway, with the fairy-like blaze of lights along the Biscayne Boulevard waterfront gleaming across the water to the west. The fainter lights of Miami Beach showed at the other end of the causeway to the east.

Jack Wetzlaff's yacht had cost someone big money. Windows and portholes were gleaming with light when we went aboard. The party was already high.

I told my men to wait outside—and went in as nervous as a hen with pups. Someone on board might know me. The lid would come off then.

Five minutes later, no one in the mob cared whether I was Dinty Moore or the Emperor of Africa.

There was a good sprinkling of dinner jackets and evening gowns, including Lucille and myself. A smart dick from Centre Street probably could have identified sixty percent of them.

Wetzlaff looked better than his rogue's gallery photograph. He was a short, stocky man, with a blue-black jaw, a pointed nose, ears flat to his head, and patent-leather black hair parted smoothly at the side. A big diamond glinted on his right hand. His face was flushed and he was bawling the words to the song as he hauled a droopy-lidded brunette around in a bad tango.

They'd cleared the saloon floor and were dancing to phonograph music. White-coated stewards were rushing drinks. To give the devil his due, the girls were all lookers. The men were in the money. Your crook is a picker when his bankroll can stand the tariff.

Bernie Cushman's blonde—there was something familiar about Cushman—called herself Verna Shane. She was nice to me. Cushman's orders, I guess.

Wetzlaff spotted us, ditched his girl, came over to greet us. You could tell he and Cushman were thick. Lucille Palmer got the welcome of an old friend. She looked nervous, on edge. She introduced me reluctantly.

"Mr. Wetzlaff—Mr. Harris."

Cushman chuckled and said: "Jack is in Wall Street, Mr. Harris. You might remember him when you're investing money."

Wetzlaff had probably never gotten below Houston Street. He would have been pinched around Broad and Wall. I couldn't resist a crack as I took his moist hand, which, surprisingly, was powerful. I remembered then that Wetzlaff had once been a stevedore.

"I'll remember Mr. Wetzlaff when I need a broker. Everybody's going into Wall Street now, aren't they?" I cracked.

Wetzlaff gave me a quick look. Somebody must have given him the high sign. His face cleared into a welcome smile.

"I'll be on tap for your extra money, Mr. Harris. You won't even have to look me up. I'll get in touch with you."

They seemed to think that was funny—all but Lucille. She said, with a warning edge: "I'll let you know when Michael needs you."

Grinning, Wetzlaff said, "How about a drink?" He looked around, snapped his fingers. A white-coated steward swerved over to us with a tray of glasses—and we were launched in the party in a tide of liquor.

Wetzlaff took Lucille's arm and led her aside. Cushman left his blonde with me. She'd have nothing but a dance.

Maybe it was the liquor—maybe the memory of Trixie and Louis Layre that made me willing enough. But while we danced my mind was working.

Why, I asked myself, had Lucille been so upset when she saw Bernie Cushman? Whom had she telephoned so quickly? Layre, her lawyer? And why had she come out of that telephone booth with her hand in her purse, as if she were expecting a gun? And why, after hearing that Cushman was friends with Jack Wetzlaff, had her guard come down a little?

I couldn't spot a hook-up between all that and Colonel Wedgewood.

Bradley had said Lucille and her lawyer were in Miami Beach alone. They seemed to be putting the screws on Colonel Wedgewood by themselves, with only a two-way split to the money.

But you couldn't tell. Show me a smart woman of the underworld, and usually I'll show you a crook or two behind her. Sometimes more. The molls simply don't work much alone.

Vera was perspiring when we finished the dance. She wanted air. We went out on deck. . . .

My two huskies were standing at the rail, puffing cigarettes. Near them a slim young man in a dinner jacket was staring at the automobile headlights moving along the causeway, between Miami and Miami Beach.

Gus Wayland, the big fellow with the flat nose, the long arms, and the trusting brown eyes of a good-natured spaniel, touched my arm as I passed.

"Can you talk to me a minute, Boss?" he asked hoarsely.

"In just a moment."

The blonde giggled as I parked her at the rail. "Honestly," she said, "that army you drag around paralyzes me, Mr. Harris. What good are they?"

"They're my bodyguard. Suppose someone tried to kidnap me?"

She giggled again. "Get wise, Mike. Do you really think those two gorillas would be any good if some smart boys decided to take you?"

"Why—why, the agency guaranteed them, Miss Shane!"

She eyed me in the moonlight, and shook her head sadly. "I wouldn't believe it if I didn't hear it right here," she stated. "I didn't think there was one left."

"I—I don't understand, Miss Shane."

"You wouldn't." She became scornfully candid for a moment. "Listen, they'd chase those gorillas up the first alley so fast the hams wouldn't know what happened. Somebody sold you a pair of cranberries. Why, that guy there at the rail—" She broke off.

The young man she mentioned was ignoring us.

"Yes?" I prompted.

She shrugged. "Nothing. I'm gettin' gabby like I always do when I hoist a few. Go on and talk with your nursemaid. He's got the fidgets. I guess he's gotta earn his money some way."

Big Gus led me down the deck out of earshot. He ducked his head, so his whisper reached my ear alone. "Listen, Boss!" he husked. "It ain't none of my business. I'm gettin' my dough for taggin' you around an' takin' orders. But I don't like the looks of this gang you muscled into."

"I don't see anything wrong."

"That's what's worryin' Joe an' me. Joe says, 'I'll bet Mr. Harris ain't wise to these eggs. Maybe we better slip it to him straight.'"

"Go on," I said. "Tell me about it."

In the moonlight Gus looked at me doubtfully. "Sometimes," he sighed, "you sound all right, Boss. An' sometimes I ain't so sure. Anyway, if you need bodyguards, this ain't no place for you to be. Joe an' I been lookin' this crowd over. They're mugs."

"What makes you think they're bad for me?"

"Lissen, that guy back there at the rail is watchin' Joe an' me. He's packin' a rod under his arm. Maybe it's all right—but what's he watchin' us for?"

"Thanks," I said. "Keep your mouth buttoned and your eyes open."

My blonde was ready to go in. Lucille Palmer met us inside. "Thanks for giving so much attention to my friend," she said in a voice that would have cut metal.

The blonde smiled sweetly as she left. "Anything for *you*, dearie."

"That girl will make me mad someday," Lucille said ominously.

"She was nice to me," says I timidly.

"She would be," says Lucille through her teeth. "Here, have a drink."

A steward was there with two glasses on his tray. Lucille handed me one, took the other as if she needed it. "Here's to—us," she said, smiling over the rim.

I drank to that. She was all I wanted—as long as she had Colonel Wedgewood's letters. And I wondered if she'd start talking after a few more drinks—

I was still wondering about it when I woke up, coughing and choking.

The biting fumes of ammonia were in my nose and throat. A light was glaring in my eyes. I was lying on a bed with my clothes on. The stocky figure of Jack Wetzlaff was bending over me, holding a handkerchief to my nostrils.

I pushed his hand away and sat up, gasping for breath. Cold, weak, and sick, I saw at once I wasn't aboard the boat. The room was too big. It didn't look like a hotel room either.

"What's the idea?" I gasped, putting my feet over the edge of the bed and rubbing my bleary eyes.

Wetzlaff's smile was not too pleasant. "Got a

head on you, hunh? No wonder, after all those drinks you put down. Your pulse was going ragged, so I thought we'd better wake you up. You can go back to sleep now."

I looked at my wrist watch. It was a quarter to four. "Where am I?" I groaned.

"In my house," Wetzlaff told me. "You're all right. Go on back to sleep."

But I persisted. "What am I doing in your house and where's Miss Palmer?"

"She went home."

"Where's my bodyguards?"

"They went home, too."

"Why didn't I go with them?"

Wetzlaff grinned—and it looked nasty.

"You stayed with the party. Nobody could stop you. I never seen anyone hoist the booze like you did."

I could remember that drink Lucille Palmer had handed me. After that there was some vague talk through the noise and music. I'd sat down, feeling sleepy—

But there'd been no wild drinking. I don't do it. Wetzlaff was lying.

One drink had done it. That meant knockout drops. Had Lucille done that?

Wetzlaff's mention of my weak pulse hinted at part of the truth. I'd been given too strong a dose. My condition had become alarming; he'd worked on me and brought me around.

I wasn't having any more sleep. Sick and weary as I was, and still dopey, I knew this was no place for Mike Harris. If I'd been given knockout drops, there was a reason.

"I think I'll go back to the hotel," I said, standing up giddily.

"It's too late," Wetzlaff said curtly. "Go on back to sleep. You're all right."

I started toward the door. "I'll go back to the hotel," I insisted. "Sorry to have bothered you this way."

I saw it coming—but I couldn't dodge. He hit me on the cheek and knocked me back across the bed.

"All right—you want it, an' you'll get it!" I heard him snarl as I bounced on the mattress.

"An' for much more, I'll take a rod an' put the heat on you myself, you lousy dick!"

CHAPTER V
Moonlight Flight

Wetzlaff's words hit me harder than his fist. I'd fumbled the job. They knew who I was. That explained the doped drink, the watch which had been put on my bodyguards.

I was almost sick enough to lie there and take it. But I was too mad. I'd spent Colonel Wedgewood's money like a drunken sailor. I'd put on an asinine act that had even made Trixie Meehan razz me. And all the while I'd only been making a fool out of myself.

Wetzlaff's lower lip was shoved out in a snarl as he bent over the bed. "Had enough, rat?" he grated. "Or do you have to get the works before you get the idea?"

I was on my side, half doubled up. My left leg was crooked. I kicked him in the stomach as he finished.

He doubled up with a loud grunt, and hurtled back across the room into the wall. When I came off the bed he was bent over, face livid, muscles paralyzed, breath gone for the moment.

I'd have tackled him—but I already knew how strong he was. His right hand was fumbling under his coat. The moment he caught his breath and got the gun, he'd have me.

I got through the doorway just in time. His gun roared behind me. I didn't look around to see where the bullet hit.

I seemed to be in an upstairs hall. Ahead was a flight of stairs going down. Further along the hall, Cushman's blonde was just stepping out of a doorway in a peach silk negligee.

She screamed as the gun went off; screamed again as I dove for the stairs. . . .

The winding flight of steps was only a blur. So was the lighted hall below. Just before I reached the bottom, a man wearing a dinner jacket and holding a liquor glass in his left hand stepped out of a doorway at the right, directly into my path. Vaguely I remembered having seen him on the yacht—

That was all I remembered. He hurled the glass. It splattered the front of my coat—and I was on him an instant later.

His fist hit my shoulder. Then I smashed him on the jaw with my flying weight behind the blow. We crashed to the floor together and brought up with a slam against the front door.

He was out like a bundle of old clothes. My hand felt as if it were broken. In the next room women were crying out, men were shouting, as I staggered up and yanked on the door.

Wetzlaff's yell of warning came down the steps as I left the house. *"Stop him!"* Then I slammed the door behind me so hard the glass shattered.

I dashed over a flagstone terrace onto a smooth lawn. And there was the sea before me— placid and lovely beyond a beach of smooth, white sand.

A low, wooden pier ran out a hundred yards or so into the water. In the dying moonlight, it looked like a dark, spidery tentacle reaching out from shore.

Wetzlaff's yacht probably docked there, I thought, as I dashed across the lawn. Behind me lights went on at the front door. Loud, excited voices clamored on the night. Guns spat after me. . . .

I heard the strident whine of passing bullets. One bullet *plunked* audibly in the sod by my left foot. But the moon was almost down, the light was bad, and I was moving fast toward a fringe of palms and palmetto fringing the lawn and running along the beach.

Unharmed, I reached the black shadows under the first palms and cut along the beach to the right. They didn't seem to be following. It wouldn't have been much use anyway. The undergrowth gave too much cover.

One thing puzzled me. I didn't recognize the beach. It wasn't Miami Beach, or along the shores of Biscayne Bay. The surf had the slow, powerful surge of the open sea.

Wetzlaff's place, obviously, was somewhere along the coast north or south of Miami. There'd be another house somewhere ahead; a telephone, an automobile, perhaps, to get me back to the hotel.

And when I got there Lucille, the wench, was going to get shocked into her age—unless she'd lammed already.

Then I thought of Gus and Joe, my body-guards. If I'd been doped, what of them? Wetzlaff and La Palmer must have known there'd be a kickback from this. They couldn't take chances on those two men talking. By that time I was as cheerful as a flood of tears.

I stopped, listened, heard no sounds of pursuit. So on I went. This stretch of coast was lonely. The dry sand whispered underfoot. The big palm leaves rustled dryly. The undergrowth at my right seemed to grow thicker, wilder.

The moon went down and the night was black. The breaking waves had little ghostly ripples of phosphorescence. Now and then the beach curved gently. No lights appeared.

I was still shaky, weak. My right hand was swollen and sore. The sand made walking hard. I began to tire, but I kept on stubbornly. When daylight came, I wanted to be a long way from Wetzlaff's house. For they'd come after me. They couldn't afford to let me get away. If I rested, went to sleep; if I slowed up and let them get in sight of me after daylight, it would be farewell, sweet farewell for Mike Harris. And I liked him in spite of his dumb mistakes.

So, dopey and half-asleep, I kept going. The palms were black and mysterious on my right, the sea shimmered vaguely on my left, the pale strip of white sand stretched out ahead, and I plodded on—on—on. . . .

Wouldn't there ever be another house? Didn't anyone else live along this stretch of the coast? Then, suddenly, the palms ended—and there was a house with lighted windows, with rest and safety. Sweet safety. Sweet rest.

Mike Harris could still run. I discovered that

as I crossed a lawn and came to the house. Just before I reached the door someone called over at my left: *"Stand still, damn you!"*

And the heartbreaking truth hit me like a blow. The door glass was broken. I had merely made the circuit of an island—and was back at Wetzlaff's house again. They had me, and I was helpless. . . .

CHAPTER VI
Trixie Shows

They came at me from two sides, trapping me there by the door. Three of them. I thought they were going to shoot. Instead, for thirty seconds after they reached me, they hit me with everything but the flagstones underfoot.

Fight back? I tried. What chance did I have? They even kicked me after I went down.

From what they said as I was yanked up again, I gathered they had spotted me returning along the beach, had tumbled to what I had done, and had eased to the house and waited for me.

By that time, the front door was open, the lights were on, and Wetzlaff and his house guests were crowding out.

"Bring him in!" Wetzlaff snarled.

Hired eggs, tough eggs, had jumped me. Two of them held me by the arms and hustled me into a big, brightly-lighted living room. The first thing I saw was my bodyguards, Gus and Joe, sitting gingerly on the edge of straight-backed chairs. Their arms were tied behind, their ankles were loosely tied.

Gus Wayland turned one sorrowful brown eye toward me. The other was black-and-blue and swollen shut.

"Boss," Gus said reproachfully, "I seen it coming."

"But you didn't duck fast enough," Joe Jacobs grumbled sourly. He had the cauliflower ear, the scar on his jaw, and the shoulders of a wrestler. And now, sour and morose, he scowled at me. "These guys say you're a detective," he said.

"Do they?" was all I could think to reply through my swollen lips.

A blue-black stubble covered Wetzlaff's face. He was chewing on the stub of a cigar. The big diamond on his right hand glinted as he took the cigar from his mouth and addressed me with savage sarcasm. "So you thought you'd lam out?"

"I wish I'd kicked you in the jaw before I left," I told him; and reached for a handkerchief to wipe blood from my lip. The mug on my right grabbed my arm. "You've already frisked me!" I snapped. "Don't be so nervous!"

"Shall I crack him, Chief?" he begged Wetzlaff.

"Not now. You've almost ruined him already."

The young man I'd met at the bottom of the steps had a strip of adhesive plaster on his cheek. His look was venomous.

And Bernie Cushman was grinning. Two other men, about his age, were strangers to me. I'd have picked them out as crooks in any crowd. Cushman's blonde was there, dressed again, and four other girls I remembered vaguely as having seen on the yacht. They were molls or they wouldn't be here. Everyone looked sleepy.

Wetzlaff chewed the stump of his cigar again and glowered at me. Then he rolled it over to the corner of his mouth and demanded: "What the hell were you doing with 'Dates' Palmer?"

"That her name?"

"Don't stall with me!"

"I met the lady at the Miami-Plaza. I never saw her before. She told me her name was Lucille Palmer."

"Yeah? What's *your* name?"

"Michael Harris."

"Where you from?"

"Cleveland," says I, with a faint glimmer of hope.

"What were you doing in Miami?"

Wetzlaff was talking as if, after all, he didn't know much about me. Had he been guessing upstairs? I hung on to the original story I'd given Lucille Palmer.

"I came to Miami to enjoy myself," I said.

"And hooked up with 'Dates' Palmer right off?"

"I met her while I was in swimming."

"What was the idea of the flash front and these mugs for bodyguards?"

"I've received kidnaping threats," I gave him with dignity. "My lawyers advised the bodyguards. Will you—you please explain all this?" I asked coldly. "The law, I assure you, will have something to say about it."

Wetzlaff chewed his cigar in silence.

Bernie Cushman shrugged.

"Well," he said, "there he is. What d'you make of him?"

Vera Shane, the blonde, spoke up petulantly. "I told you you were making a mistake, Jack."

Wetzlaff snatched a folded piece of paper from his pocket and shoved it out at me.

"If you're a young squirt on the loose, what the hell are you doing with this letterhead from the Blaine Agency in your billfold? What's this writing on the back?"

He almost caught me off-guard.

"Oh—that?" says I, thinking wildly. "Why— uh—while I was in New York, I hired detectives from the Blaine Agency. Those are some memoranda in my—uh—private shorthand. That top note says to write a letter to my Aunt Louisa, in Omaha, Nebraska. Her oldest son broke his ankle last month, and—'"

"All right, dammit, all right!" Wetzlaff broke in angrily. He glowered at me. "But I don't like the way you went into action upstairs. You didn't act like no damn fool then."

"I—I was frightened, I'll have to admit," says I meekly.

The blonde hummed under her breath: *"What a hell of a mess—what a hell of a mess. When this red-headed lamb gets loose, then what, suckers?"*

Wetzlaff snapped: "Throw him in that attic room! Lock those other two mugs down in the old wine cellar! We've got to get some sleep!"

The attic room was up under the eaves. A rabbit couldn't have crawled through its one small window. The air was hot, stale. An army cot comprised the furniture. The two men who had brought me up locked and bolted the door.

I went to sleep. There wasn't anything else to do.

The sun was glaring through the tiny window when a hand on my shoulder awakened me. One of the men who had brought me in was there by the cot.

"Wetzlaff says to get you washed up and bring you down for grub," he said curtly. "Make it snappy."

By the sun it was about noon. Out of that little hell-hole under the roof, with a quick shower, a shave with a safety razor he handed me, and in my clothes again, I felt better. A radio was playing downstairs. Dishes were clattering, people were talking, when my guard brought me into the dining room.

Wetzlaff set down a glass of beer and pointed to an empty chair on my side of the long table. "Get some groceries," he growled.

The men wore white linens and flannels. The girls were in gay sport clothes. Sleep had helped their dispositions. The guard stood behind my chair and I sat down gaping at Lucille Palmer, seated across from me.

She had blue shadows under her eyes. Overnight she had aged years. And she was in a vile temper.

"So you're here, too?" I queried.

"Oh, for God's sake! Do I have to listen to you gabble and bleat on top of everything else?"

"Dearie," said one of the girls silkily, "you liked it well enough last night."

Lucille snatched up her glass of beer. I thought she was going to hurl it at the speaker. Then she put it down and flared at Wetzlaff: "Tell those floozies to lay off me or I won't be responsible!"

"Let her alone!" Wetzlaff mumbled.

The rest of the meal was more amicable. Wetzlaff harked back to old times. I gathered Lucille had once worked the badger game and Wetzlaff had been one of the gang. He'd come a long way since then.

I gathered further that Lucille had turned a neat trick on Cushman two years before in San Francisco. Cushman had almost taken a rap because of it. He'd threatened to get her then. That explained why she had come out of the telephone booth looking for trouble.

When the meal was over, Wetzlaff spoke bluntly. "All of you scram outside. I'm going to be busy for a little while." Then he directed my guard, "Take him in the living room. I want to talk to him in a few minutes."

In the living room I took a cigarette from a box on a table and smoked moodily. My guard loitered near the hall doorway. He had a gun in a pocket. I knew what to expect if I tried to make another break.

There was a library behind the living room. Wetzlaff was in there with Lucille Palmer. In the quiet which fell I could hear their voices. Wetzlaff's grew louder, threatening. Lucille came back at him angrily. I listened. And what did I hear?

Wetzlaff: "You've got those letters in Miami somewhere! Are you going to cough up?"

La Palmer: "For the tenth time, *no!*"

All ears by then, I heard Wetzlaff angrily say: "I've tried to give you the dope straight! With those letters and the squeeze I can give him, I'll make that two-timing old billy-goat cough up a half million! You've got no business monkeying with a set-up like that!"

Lucille snapped back: "Where do you get off telling me my business? Stick to your racket and I'll stick to mine! You've already spoiled one sweet sucker I was shaping up! There will be hell to pay over him!"

"Yeah?"

"Yeah!" said Lucille, hard and fighting mad.

Silence for a moment. Then Wetzlaff said something in a lower voice. Her reply was shot with sudden panic.

"So *that's* your out? All you guys in the racket are kill-crazy! You—you can't do anything like that!"

Wetzlaff laughed at her, ugly, sneering. After a moment he asked, "Are you going to cough up those letters and take your split?"

"Louis Layre put you onto this, Jack! You're using the same arguments he gave me! The dirty, double-crossing rat!"

"Never mind Layre! Are you going to be reasonable?"

"No!" Lucille fairly screamed at him. "For the last time, *no!*"

Wetzlaff cursed her then. "We'll see about that!" And suddenly I felt sorry for Lucille Palmer.

Something else was on my mind at the same moment, too. A low, droning sound outside the house had swiftly increased in volume. I recognized it now as the motors of an airplane. They were sputtering, missing . . .

The front door opened. One of the men looked into the living room. "Where's Jack?" he asked the guard.

"Next room."

Wetzlaff opened the library door and met him.

"There's an amphibian plane landing here, Jack! Something's wrong with its motors!"

Wetzlaff began to swear again. His face was dark with anger. "We don't want anyone here!"

"Well, it's coming down!"

"I'll see about that!" Wetzlaff spoke over his shoulder to Lucille Palmer. "Wait in here with the boy friend until I get back." And to the guard, "Watch 'em both."

He hurried out with the other man.

I'd moved to the front window by then. Lucille joined me. The corners of her mouth were white, drawn. She was breathing hard from strong emotion.

She ignored me as we stared out the window at the twin-motored amphibian plane which swooped low over the water beyond the pier. It landed amid sheets of spray and taxied with coughing, spitting motors to the beach.

Wetzlaff and his guests hurried down to meet it.

On its landing wheels, the amphibian wallowed slowly up on the smooth, dry sand. The engines stopped. Wetzlaff stepped forward and talked to the pilot.

He broke off as a young woman in a gay sport suit emerged from the plane, ducked under the wing and joined him. The pilot followed her. A few moments later Wetzlaff and the strange young woman started toward the house. She was laughing as they talked. And Wetzlaff was smiling broadly.

A sick feeling suddenly hit the pit of my stomach. That tiny, slender, good-looking little bundle of fluff strolling at Wetzlaff's side was Trixie Meehan!

CHAPTER VII
A Chance to Die

Lucille Palmer recognized Trixie also. I saw her startled expression, saw her bite down on her lower lip. Her eyes flashed to my face. Her expression wasn't pleasant.

Under her breath she said, "So she's here, too!"

Trixie's face was clear as she came to the flagstone terrace with Wetzlaff. Not a line of worry in it. She's never looked more cuddly and helpless, more lovely and happy. Just a lost little girl trustfully meeting the world. The windows were open. I heard her chuckle delightedly.

"Such a *lovely* house, Mr. Gadsden. How nice of you to have it right here where our plane broke down."

Wetzlaff's smirk was almost fatuous. The lug! "For a little lady like you, I'd have a house anywhere I thought she'd drop down. Here, sit under the umbrella at this table. I'll order something cold."

"So thoughtful of you," Trixie cooed.

Wetzlaff called an order in the front door and rejoined her. I heard Trixie telling him how she'd hired the plane for a joy-ride out beyond the Gulf Stream. After they finished the drinks, Wetzlaff stood up and said he'd show her the house.

The guard had closed the door between our room and the hall. Lucille jumped up, walked to the door and called through. "Jack, I want to talk to you a minute!"

Wetzlaff came in alone. Lucille led him to the other end of the room, talked under her breath. I heard Louis Layre's name mentioned. Wetzlaff's face hardened. He nodded and rejoined Trixie in the hall.

Lucille lighted a cigarette and began to hum cheerfully under her breath. I felt like throttling her. She'd knifed Trixie in some way. And if Wetzlaff caught Trixie off-base just once . . .

I was afraid—horribly afraid.

Trixie saw most of the house but the living room. Outside again with Wetzlaff, I saw her staring at the plane. "Someone's helping my pilot," she said.

"One of my men," Wetzlaff said calmly. "He's an expert mechanic; he will find the trouble in no time."

"That's—comforting," Trixie said. Some of her gayety had vanished.

Wetzlaff lighted a cigar, leaned back in his chair and watched the two men working on the plane. He seemed to be waiting for something.

The two men at the plane suddenly started toward the house, one walking ahead of the other. Doubt turned to certainty; then fear swamped me as I made out Trixie's pilot being herded to the house with a gun in his back.

The pilot was pale, flustered, when he reached the terrace. "What's the idea of this gun?" he demanded of Wetzlaff.

The gunner, a long, rangy fellow in dirty white canvas trousers, replied for him. "Chief, he was pullin' a fast one. Nothin' wrong with those motors."

"Yeah?" said Wetzlaff. He was on his feet by then. So was Trixie.

The pilot was a good-looking young fellow. He shrugged. "If they're okay now, we'll take off and call it a day."

"Will you?" said Wetzlaff. "Rough him, Pete."

Callously the gun barrel beat the young pilot to his knees. Blood was trickling out of the poor devil's hair when he reeled to his feet, eyes staring, mouth working.

"*Th-this has gone far enough!*" he gasped. "She—she said it was a joke she was playing when she asked me to find this island and stall the motors and land. But I've had enough!"

At my right shoulder Lucille Palmer laughed nastily. "I knew there was something screwy when that hussy showed up. It's some more of Louis Layre's dirty tricks."

"Get away from me before I forget myself!" I snarled.

Only the guard's drawn automatic kept me from going out that screened window. For Trixie had snapped open her purse and was drawing a gun as she darted back from Wetzlaff's sudden grab.

I groaned as she stumbled over the chair behind her and Wetzlaff caught her arm. Little Trixie didn't have a chance after that. Wetzlaff twisted her arm and forced her to her knees. He tore the gun out of her hand and jerked her to her feet.

"So you're a tough little tart, after all!"

While I clenched my fists and stood taut and trembling, Wetzlaff questioned Trixie, twisting her arm until she moaned. He seemed to have an idea she was hooked up with Louis Layre, the lawyer. He might be doing business with the man, but he obviously didn't trust him.

Trixie gave him no satisfaction. More than a bullying racketeer was needed to break that gallant little kid's spirit.

Wetzlaff finally exploded in rage, "Lock this guy upstairs with that other fellow! This business is spouting enough screwy angles to give a man the d.t.'s!"

So the good-looking young pilot and I landed back up under the eaves. We looked at one another after the door was locked. He was still shaking. He moistened his lips.

"What the hell does this mean?" he groaned.

"What you don't know won't hurt you," I said. "Sit down and stop shaking. You're not dead yet."

"Dead?"

"It's a gag," I said wearily. "What is your name?"

"Jerry Thompson."

"Where are we?"

He stared at me. "Don't you know?"

"Would I ask?"

He sighed. "We're on one of the little islands out beyond the Gulf Stream. About eighty miles from Miami. Last Man Cay it's called. We're off the steam tracks and the air lines to Nassau. Stray conch fishermen are about all that ever drop by. Rich guys have built on some of these isolated cays in the last ten years. Less than an hour from Miami by plane," he said bitterly, "and we might as well be off the edge of the earth."

"We're still hanging on," I said. "Right now there's nothing to do but wait and see what breaks."

I didn't tell him as I tried the door that my heart was almost breaking over what might be happening to Trixie. The door was solid, hopeless. Any attempt to break it down would alarm the house.

The hot afternoon hours dragged by. Suddenly we both rushed to the little window. The amphibian motors had begun to roar.

Through the tiny window we could see the propellers swirling sand off the beach. The amphibian trundled around, took the water, and as the motors died, it floated toward the pier. Two men made the bow fast to the pier with a line and came ashore.

"I wonder what they're going to do," Jerry Thompson said huskily.

"Probably sink it."

He swallowed. "I'm sunk myself then. I've been supporting a wife and two kids with that crate this winter."

An hour later there was activity in the house. Wetzlaff's yacht showed off the end of the pier. A speedboat raced ashore. Wetzlaff and his house guests went down to meet it, carrying suitcases. Lucille Palmer was with them. She didn't seem to be a prisoner.

"Taking her cut and liking it after all," I muttered.

"What's that?" Thompson asked.

"Never mind. But it isn't good news for us."

He groaned. "My wife will be worried. She'll think something's happened to me."

"Too bad," I said. Why tell him his wife was practically a widow already?

Evening came. Darkness fell. No water. No food. I said suddenly, "Are you game to take a chance?"

CHAPTER VIII
Payoff Partners

Thompson looked at me doubtfully. "What kind of a chance?"

"To get out of here. You'll risk a bellyful of lead. But it's probably your only chance to see the family again. Think fast, brother, think fast."

I liked him for his answer. "What do we do?" he asked quietly.

I was already tipping the cot up. As quickly as possible I wrenched a leg off. "Got a knife?" I asked.

Surprisingly, he had. I sharpened the end of the leg. "Grab a sheet and catch," I said.

With the sharpened stick, I attacked the plaster, waist high on the sloping roof, which formed one side of the room. Thompson caught the fragments in the sheet before they rattled on the floor.

It was a screwy idea. But anything was better than waiting for Wetzlaff to get rid of us. Beyond the plaster there were laths, held by light nails. Carefully I pulled them off and got access to the under side of the roof. One strip of board had to be cut through in two places with the knife. Then shingles removed. The cool night air which rushed in was a Godsend to our sweat-covered bodies.

I crawled out first and perched on the slant of the roof. Thompson followed. The moon was up. The ground looked a long way below.

Thompson whispered, "How do we get down?"

"We don't," I said. "We go inside. That girl's in there. And a couple more mugs we've got to take along. And don't tell me it's dangerous and you've had enough or I'll shove you off the roof right here."

"If I do, you can shove," he replied. I loved that Jerry Thompson like a brother from then on.

We crawled over the ticklish slant of the roof until we were above a side-porch roof. Hanging onto Thompson's wrists, I lowered myself. He gasped. He was slipping. I let go and dropped the last two feet. He caught himself, came sliding feet first over the edge a moment later, and I eased him to a footing.

We unscreened a darkened window and slipped into a bedroom.

Gus and Joe were probably still down in the old wine cellar. But where was Trixie? I could hear people shooting craps downstairs. A man swore disgustedly.

"That cleans me!" he exclaimed. "But for ten bucks I'll tow that bunch out in the plane an' sink 'em for you, Buck. I know you've got a weak belly."

A leer was in Buck's reply. "Yeah? And what about the dame?"

Silence down there. I could almost see them looking at one another. Another voice said, "All Wetzlaff said was he didn't want to see her again."

I was sick inside by then, and raging. Those swine mouthing over Trixie's lovely helplessness. To Jerry Thompson I whispered:

"How long will it take you to get out to that plane and start those motors?"

"I ought to do it in ten minutes."

I whispered an idea in his ear.

"Okay," he said under his breath, and slipped back out the window.

And I raised a leg of the bed, removed a castor, and tied it in the end of a pillow case. The result was comforting.

They were still rolling dice downstairs when I tiptoed along the hall and up to the attic floor again. The short hall up there had several more rooms along it. A small electric bulb gave dim light. Without much hope I tapped on the doors. Trixie Meehan's voice said, "Yes?" inside the second door.

"It's Mike."

"Wh-what are you doing out there, Mike?"

"Wait and see."

I unscrewed the light bulb. In the darkness I hammered on her door. Half a minute of that brought steps hurrying up from below. Were they all coming? No; it sounded like one man.

I crouched at the top of the steps and waited. He came tramping up grumbling, "What the hell happened to that light?" Then, louder: "What's the matter up here?"

I swung the pillow case. He pitched forward with a queer, gurgling sound. I broke his fall just enough to avoid jarring the house. When I turned on the light I saw he was the same ill-natured fellow who'd kept a gun on me earlier in the day. He'd left his gun downstairs. But he had the keys I wanted. A moment later Trixie was with me, whispering shakily:

"Mike, you darling! I knew you'd do some-. thing if you could! Where's Wetzlaff? Where's the pilot of my plane?"

"Wetzlaff's gone back to Miami with the Palmer woman. Your pilot's outside. How'd you happen to come here?"

"Your man told me over the telephone this morning that you'd gone to Havana with friends. It didn't make sense. You'd have told me. I met Louis Layre in the lobby. He looked nervous, and said he was in a hurry and would see me in half an hour. I followed him in a taxi. He went on board a yacht moored by the causeway. He wasn't there long. When he left I turned sight-seeing tourist and talked to a sailor guarding the foot of the gangplank.

"He wouldn't let me aboard, but he was willing to kill the time talking. He looked sleepy, and told me the yacht had just come in from an all-night trip. I couldn't get any more out of him. But from a sailor on the yacht tied up just ahead of that one, I found out the boat belonged to a Mr. Wetzlaff, who had a house on Last Man's Cay.

"Wetzlaff's name was all I needed. Louis Layre worried—the Palmer woman not around—you gone—Layre going aboard Wetzlaff's boat which had been out all night—and Wetzlaff owning an island off-shore. I hired that plane and flew out here to see if there were any trace of you."

"Well, you saw."

Trixie shivered in the crook of my arm. "I balled everything up, didn't I, Mike?"

"Sweetness," I said, "you forced Lucille Palmer's hand. Wetzlaff was trying to chisel in on the Wedgewood deal. Louis Layre had sold out to him. Lucille wasn't having any of it. Now she's given in. They're going ashore to crack Wedgewood. The price is now up to half a million. And," says I, "Wedgewood will probably pay if they aren't stopped."

A yell came up from below. "What's keeping you so long up there, Buck? You fooling with that girl?" When Buck didn't reply, we heard them coming up.

I started sweating. Without a gun we were sunk. I thought of going through my room and out on the roof. But there wasn't time.

I'd been listening for the amphibian motors to start. Had something happened to Jerry Thompson? Wouldn't that motor *ever* start?

They were in the second floor hall now, two or three of them, coming fast.

"Get back in your room," I said thickly.

"We're not going to make it, are we?" Trixie said unsteadily.

"Not now, I guess. This is the payoff."

"Then I'll take it with you, Mike."

"Trixie—you're—you're pretty swell!"

"Yes, Mike?" Trixie said with a catch in her voice.

It was almost love—and just then, outside in the night, the amphibian motors racketed out into full-throated thunder. . . .

CHAPTER IX
Bitters

Well, we didn't have love. One of the men below yelled, "It's the plane, boys! Somebody's out there!"

They bolted back downstairs. We had the house to ourselves. I grabbed Trixie's arm and hustled her down so fast her teeth rattled.

When I got her out the back door with directions, I looked for the old wine cellar down in the basement. It wasn't hard to find. One of my keys unlocked the massive door. Dirty, unshaven, haggard, Gus lumbered out croaking:

"What's the score, Boss? Don't tell me they're letting us go!"

"I should tell you anything!" I cracked back. "Just keep coming!"

When we reached the kitchen, I heard a bewildered voice calling in the front hall. "Buck! Pete! Where the hell are you guys?"

My victim had gotten downstairs by himself. We heard him go out the front door, still calling.

I grabbed a newspaper off a chair as we started out the back. Then, on the back porch, I spotted a five-gallon oil can.

"Just what I need to put the frosting on the cake," says I aloud. I took the can back in, unscrewed the cap, slopped some of the contents out, then backed through the doorway and tossed a lighted match.

It was gasoline. The puffing explosion almost blew me out the back porch door.

Gus Wayland gulped: "What the hell you doing, Boss?"

"Disinfecting a rat's nest," I said. "Follow me if you want breakfast in the morning!"

The amphibian motors were roaring just off-shore. The big plane was wallowing parallel to the beach in the opposite direction from which I ran.

The ripping tear of sub-machine gun fire spatted against the sound of the motors. Wetzlaff's men were shooting from the beach as they kept abreast of the slowly moving plane.

Trixie was waiting under the palms where I'd told her to go.

"The plane's going the other way!" she protested as I caught her arm and urged her along.

"Don't argue! Come on!"

"Do you know what you're doing?" Trixie panted indignantly as I half-dragged her along.

"Stop talking, you little nitwit, and run!" I yelled, shaking her arm.

"Nitwit?" Trixie blazed. "Trying to be a caveman again, Ape?"

So we were at it again, fighting as we ran. Where was love now? Bah!

I ran them a quarter of a mile down the beach. By that time the amphibian had circled out from shore and was heading back toward us. I lighted the newspaper, waved the flaming torch. The motors revved up and the plane came racing over the water toward us.

"You knew it was going to pick us up all the time!" Trixie accused.

"If you had any sense you'd have known he was decoying Wetzlaff's men down the other way!" I snapped. I was still jumpy. Suppose Jerry Thompson struck a floating log? Suppose something went wrong at the last minute?

Thompson brought the plane in almost to the beach. We waded out. He helped us aboard. His left arm was wet with blood. "They hit you," I said.

He grinned. "Nipped me in the arm. It's cheap enough for the ticket out of here. Hang on. We're going places."

Windows and walls of the cabin were dotted with bullet holes. That close they'd come to Thompson and the gas tanks. The next moment the up-surge of the plane thrust me down in the seat as Thompson hunted the sky with motors gunned wide open.

Last Man Cay, so formidable, so threatening and menacing, was suddenly only an insignificant patch of land on a limitless, moon-dusted sea. Far below red flames were licking out of a toy-like house.

I had no regrets for that fire. But as we droned through the night sky and the slow minutes dragged, I wondered feverishly whether I had a chance now to keep my promise and break the Wedgewood case in time.

Jerry Thompson was still chipper when he brought us down in a long glide toward the seaplane landing fronting Biscayne Boulevard. He taxied up on the wooden apron and stepped back to us, grinning.

"Now," he said, "for the cops!"

"Great boy, keed!" I said. "But no cops right now. I've got to have a little free time."

"Hey?" says Jerry, squinting at me. "How come?"

"You made a thousand bucks today," I told him. "And repairs on your plane extra."

"Nix. I ain't asking for an extra cut. I got back, didn't I?"

"It's on the expense account," I explained. "The guy who pays will like it or else. But I need time, Jerry. I'm a private dick on a delicate case. You will earn that grand if you help me."

Jerry's face cleared. "Why didn't you say so? I'll get my arm fixed up and report to the missus."

"I'm staying at the Miami-Plaza," I said as I started for the door. "Michael Harris is the name. I'll be seeing you."

We got a taxi on Biscayne Boulevard and drove over the south causeway. Wetzlaff's yacht was not there. That wasn't any help.

People stared at us as we entered the Miami-Plaza. We looked bad. The desk said Lucille Palmer had checked out. My mind was on Bitters as the elevator went up. Would Bitters be here? He was.

I entered so swiftly I caught him coming off my bed with a newspaper in one hand and a glass of my Scotch and soda in the other. His jaw dropped. His eyes bulged. He gasped:

"Why, sir, why—"

"Exactly!" I yelped. "Why, and *why the hell?* Put down that glass, you big tramp!"

His hand was shaking as he obeyed. "You look rather upset, sir," he gulped. "Uh—has anything happened?"

I stood on my toes and slammed an uppercut under his jaw. He went back on the bed. Rubbing my knuckles, I let him have it cold turkey.

"So I went to Havana, did I? Come through with it, you pile of cheese! What do you know about it?"

"I—I don't understand, sir."

"Maybe this'll help you!" I raged, and mashed his nose with the next one.

He was moaning and holding a handkerchief to his bleeding nose when he wallowed up on the bed again. Big Gus Wayland spoke admiringly from the doorway.

"Attaboy, Boss! What a punch! How about lettin' me have him? I gotta crack someone before I feel right again."

"I'll give him to you in a minute if he won't talk."

"This is a case for the police!" Bitters moaned.

"Cops, huh? Well, I'm a copper myself! Who's your friend at the Atlantic Hotel?"

"D-do you know about that?"

"What d'you think?"

"Oh, my soul!" Bitters exclaimed wildly. "What will happen to my references? Let me explain, sir. It's this way, sir. Indeed it is, sir. I didn't know you were a detective. And I happened to mention to a friend I met that you were wealthy. One thing led to another. He asked me questions—"

"What's his name?"

"A Mr. Cushman, sir."

"So that's the nigger in the weeds, eh? You've been fingering wealthy suckers for Bernie Cushman and getting a split afterwards?"

Bitters' silence verified it.

"Where's Cushman now?"

Bitters said nervously: "He—he telephoned about two hours ago and said you wouldn't be back for several days. I—I was to wait here for further word."

I grabbed the telephone and called the Atlantic Hotel. Cushman had checked out. Next I telephoned our branch office. Bradley answered. When he recognized my voice, he yelled:

"So you're finally back? And if you give me a wise-cracking excuse, I won't be responsible! Where have you been? Where is Miss Meehan?"

"Calm down," I suggested.

"Calm down?" Bradley bellowed. "I *am* calm! What have you been doing? Blowing yourself to a good time, I suppose, on that expense money I was fool enough to give you! Do you know what's happened in the meantime?"

"You tell me," I said.

"Colonel Wedgewood," Bradley roared, "called me about two hours ago and fired the Blaine Agency off the case! He says you've bungled everything! He demands an immediate accounting of the expense money! He swore he'd get my job and yours!"

"I can explain—"

"Explain?" Bradley yelled. "Can you explain me back into my job? Can you explain why this case has suddenly gone to pieces in our hands? You know the Blaine Agency policy! Results and no excuses! All you need to explain now is that expense account you blackjacked out of me! And you'd damned well better account for every penny that's been spent!" Bradley warned ominously. He slammed up the receiver.

CHAPTER X
Doubling for Trouble

Sweet welcome home! Bradley's job gone—my job and Trixie Meehan's job probably gone—and an expense account that never could be explained, now that I'd failed. And Colonel Wedgewood due to be nicked for his half million after all. . . .

I called Trixie's room. "Be ready to leave in ten minutes," I told her.

"Who gave you a whip? Simon Legree?"

"This is business and never mind the wise-cracks!" I yelped

"If I minded you," says Trixie, "I'd have been plucking at a straitjacket long ago. What's behind this sudden itch?"

"The sky's just fallen in on our heads! We're going to Palm Beach!"

Trixie, in a pinch, was a trouper. "I'll be ready," she promised instantly.

Joe Jacobs rubbed the livid scar on his jaw. "Palm Beach, hey? We goin' too?"

"You are! Bitters, if we're both not ready in ten minutes, Heaven help you! Joe, tell the desk to get a big car for me to drive to Palm Beach."

I was tying my necktie as I made for the elevator. Bitters hurried between Gus and Joe like a prisoner heading for the guillotine. A minute after we hit the lobby, Trixie joined us.

The car was waiting. Trixie rode beside me, the others in the back. While we raced northward, I told Trixie of my talk with Bradley. She was floored.

"Mike, what can we do now? Colonel Wedgewood may have paid his money by now. They've had time to get to him."

"We'll soon see!" I said savagely, and sent the speedometer crawling higher.

It was after ten-thirty when we rolled across the Lake Worth bridge into Palm Beach. It took me another quarter of an hour to locate and reach the Italian-style villa of Colonel Wedgewood. The house and the high-fenced tropical garden at one side were a riot of light, color, and sound. An Oriental garden party was in progress. They were dancing on a temporary floor out in the scented, swanky garden.

"*This* looks like Wedgewood is worried," I remarked disgustedly.

Trixie said, "You can lay this on his wife. Going in?"

"Come along," says I. "Gus, you and Joe watch that rat."

A doorman in baggy trousers, silk jacket, and turban out of the Arabian Nights answered my ring. He looked down his nose at us. "Only guests in costume are admitted tonight, sir."

"Tell Colonel Wedgewood I want to see him on important business."

"Your name, sir?"

"Never mind my name."

His eyebrows lifted in understanding. "This way, please."

He led us to the right, along a narrow, tiled

hall, and left us in a tiny corner room which was dim and quiet.

"Well," says Trixie. "That was easy."

"Too easy," I said. "I don't like the looks of it."

Some minutes later the door opened and the Sultan Shahriyar himself slipped into the room and closed the door. He was about my size. His gorgeous costume and turban flamed with phony jewels. A black, curly beard covered his face. He carried a package under his arm. And his beard was phony, too.

"Did you bring them?" he demanded in a rasping, querulous voice.

"Bring what?"

"Those letters. Who is this young woman?"

I almost yelled with relief. He thought we represented Wetzlaff or La Palmer.

"Have you got the money in that package?" I asked.

"There is two hundred thousand in bills and a certified check for the rest," he said waspishly. "I had the bank manager go down and certify the check. Where—where are the letters?" He was frantic with anxiety.

I sneered, "No backbone left, eh? We're the detectives who've been working on your case. Hide that money. We'll get your letters back. D'you mean to tell me they've got nerve enough to come here and collect?"

He reacted in a frenzy of rage.

"Yes, you fool! I'm paying to protect myself! I was promised results and all I got was excuses! Tonight I was called to the telephone by a strange man and informed the time was up, and it was going to cost me half a million now for delaying! *Your* useless delays cost me that much extra! Get out of here before I have you thrown out!" He turned to the door to make good the threat.

"It's sink or swim now," says I to Trixie. "Here we go off the end of the dock!"

My arm was around Colonel Wedgewood's neck as I finished. I yanked the spluttering old idiot back on the floor and stopped his mouth by shoving his turban down over his face.

"Hey!" says Trixie. "It's all off now!"

"It's all coming off," I panted. "Look the other way if you're embarrassed."

Five minutes later I was wearing Colonel Wedgewood's costume, including the false beard. The colonel was gagged, tied hand and foot with a light cord and parked behind the sofa.

"I suppose we needed something like this to polish off the day," Trixie said faintly. "Do they hang people here in Florida?"

"Why bring that up?" I said. "It will come soon enough. Keep an eye on that old Romeo and his half million. I'm going hunting."

"For what?"

"That's the hell of it," I confessed. "I don't know. You might try prayer while I'm gone."

The doorman spoke to me deferentially. "Will the gentleman and lady be leaving, sir?"

I shook my head and walked back to the garden party. I felt as insane as this play I was making. What chance did Trixie and I have with the Blaine Agency now?

But this much I knew. Wetzlaff was striking hard and quick for the money. He was sending someone here for it tonight. The doorman evidently had his instructions. Colonel Wedgewood would be notified. That meant me now. They'd bring the letters, of course. And I now had a gun under my left arm.

Meanwhile—what a party!

The tropical garden was hung with colored lanterns. Sultan Shahriyar's court had come to life and was dancing under the moon and stars.

A gay young slave girl in pearls, gauze, and little else but a mask tapped me on the arm and quirked luscious lips.

"Aren't you dancing at all tonight, Colonel Wedgewood?"

They say the flesh is weak. How true!

"Colonel Wedgewood!" my partner reproved with a giggle, after we had made half a round of the floor. "I didn't know you were so—so *impetuous!*"

"*Ah-h-h!*" I sighed, and risked being a little more impetuous.

A moment later she said warningly, *"Oh-h-h—!"*

A hand caught my shoulder. A strong hand. A formidable hand. And a man-sized voice said icily, *"Eustace*, have you lost your mind?"

CHAPTER XI
The Credit and the Cash

It was the Sultana Scheherazade—veiled, jeweled, bangled, and authoritative. No doubt about the authority. She outweighed two of my little slave girl. She was broad in the beam and giving off sparks as she took me off that dance floor like a snowplow going through a drift.

"Eustace, you're a fool! An outrageous, scandalous old fool! Haven't you any respect for me, capering around with that brazen young thing like an old billy-goat! I've a good mind to lock you in your room!"

Through her veil I could see a noticeable mustache over a hard, mean mouth. I forgave that wizened, trussed-up old fossil right there. A woman like this would drive any man to flesh and zip.

The dim light saved my disguise. "Bah!" I growled in my throat and stalked away before she could get set for another wave of abuse.

Not until then did I discover I was sweating again. That had been a close shave. But it was nothing to the shock I got not two minutes later.

An arm slipped through mine out under the palms. A smooth voice said sarcastically, "Has my sweet old daddy got the money ready?"

You're right. It was Lucille Palmer, costumed and veiled also. *"Ah—ah—gggg!"* I gulped in my throat.

She warned me with an edge to her voice, "I haven't got the letters on me, so don't try to pull any fancy tricks!"

"Where are they?" I said, rasping and querulous.

"Give me the money and the certified check and you'll get the letters immediately."

"This way."

"Your voice sounds queer. This isn't too much of a shock to you, is it, Daddy?"

"Grnthh . . ."

"Love," Lucille informed me cheerfully, "comes high. But you had your money's worth, didn't you, Daddy? And you won't need that money much longer anyway."

The nerve of her. I almost forgot I wasn't Colonel Wedgewood and bit back a blistering retort just in time. All the while I was wondering where the devil she had those letters.

"How'd you get in here?" I growled.

She chuckled.

"After I decided to attend your garden party I just had time to get a costume in Miami. I'd have been here sooner but the costumer delayed me."

The doorman had left his post. I stopped her in the hall near the room where Trixie waited, and went in alone. Trixie was gone. Colonel Wedgewood was still behind the couch out of sight. The packet of money was lying on the couch.

I beckoned Lucille in and handed her the package in silence.

She broke the string, opened the paper, looked at the bundles of large-denomination bills and the certified check on top.

"You just couldn't take it, could you, Daddy?" she said sarcastically. "Well, thanks for the sentiment. I'll send flowers when your arteries give way."

"The letters!" I reminded her as she opened the door with that half-million cuddled in her arms.

"They're coming!"

A man in costume, turban, and mask shouldered into the room. A second one stopped me in the doorway.

"You got it?" the first one demanded.

He was Wetzlaff. His companion was Bernie Cushman. Lucille Palmer said sharply, "It's all here. Give the old fool his letters and let's scram out of here."

Wetzlaff laughed unpleasantly.

"Give 'em up until that certified check's been

cashed? Hell, no! He'll get 'em later on—if he toes the line to suit me!"

That was the gag I'd been looking for all along. Why should they give up the letters if they had a chance to hang onto them for a further club? But at least I now knew where they were. Wetzlaff had them.

He was the nearest to me. La Palmer was beyond him. Bernie Cushman was in the doorway. Wetzlaff was sneering as he turned away— and I slugged him right on the button. He went down cold and I grabbed for my gun.

"*It's a plant!*" Lucille squawked. "Lam for the car, Bernie!" She slammed the door as she went out, and Cushman faded with her.

I stayed with Wetzlaff. The letters were more important at the moment. It took me half a minute to locate them and get the packet out from under his costume. And his gun. He wore a business suit underneath, ready for a quick getaway.

"I've got your letters, Grandpop!" I called to the figure behind the sofa. "Now I'll try to get your money!"

But I knew the money was gone. They had a start on me. Their getaway was planned. Bernie Cushman had had time to collect his wits and go for a gun.

The front door was ajar. They'd gone out that way. I followed—and ran smack into a fight out in the street. An automobile was half pulled out from the curb, its motor running. Trixie had Lucille Palmer in the gutter, helpless with a jujutsu armhold. The bundles of bills were around their feet. Gus and Joe were just subduing Bernie Cushman and the driver of the car.

"She almost bumped me as she ran out!" Trixie gasped. "I recognized her and got your men to stop them!"

Gus Wayland knocked Bernie Cushman cold and turned to me uncertainly. "Holy cow, Boss! What happened to you?"

"Never mind!" I panted, grabbing up the bundles of bills and re-wrapping them in the paper. "Hold everything here! I'll be back in a minute!" Chauffeurs from the other cars were gathering around as I started back toward the house. "It's a joke," I called to them. "Don't get excited."

They probably didn't believe me. It didn't matter at the moment. I found Wetzlaff groggily crawling to his feet and feeling for his gun. I held a gun on him while I untied Colonel Wedgewood.

"Here's your letters," I said, cramming them into his hand. "And there's your money. Do you want me to call the cops?"

"Merciful heavens, *no!*" he gasped, staggering to a chair. He was suddenly only a tired, frightened old man. "I heard him refuse to give the letters to you," he said. "You were right. I shouldn't have tried to deal with them. But let them go. You understand I simply can't afford any publicity."

"This kills me!" I groaned. "It's the first time I ever let a crook go when I had him cold. But here goes. Outside, Wetzlaff!"

He went like a shorn lamb.

Gus and Joe threw the lot of them into their car. Bitters had made his escape. "Let's get going," I said. "A fadeout is the quickest way to hush it up."

Not until I was driving across the Lake Worth bridge did Trixie sigh contentedly.

"Mike, are we lucky, or aren't we? Everything fixed up—and both of us here safe and sound?"

"Not bad," says I.

"You said some sweet things on that island, Mike. I've been thinking about them ever since."

"Did I?" says I. "I had to think fast to break this case, didn't I? But I told you if you followed my orders we'd get somewhere."

Trixie moved away from me and blazed, "The next time I stroke a nitwit's ego I hope I'm caught dead! Listen to me, Mike Harris! Of all the conceited—"

Well, I had to drive and listen. It was the same old story. Trixie on my neck with her razor tongue for no reason at all. What a life! What a woman! I ask you.

THE OLD MAIDS DIE

Whitman Chambers

ALTHOUGH ONCE A POPULAR AND PROLIFIC PULP WRITER, Elwyn Whitman Chambers (1896–1968) is most remembered today for the many motion pictures for which he wrote screenplays and for which his novels and stories served as the basis. His pulp fiction fell into the familiar wisecracking hard-boiled school and many of his characters, of whatever name, sounded similar.

One of his many detectives is a little different. Katie Blayne, a police reporter for the *Sun* in an unnamed city, does have snappy dialogue, but it would be a stretch to call her hard-boiled. Among the rivals who work for several newspapers, each trying to get stories before the others, Katie is known as the Duchess, though this is not fully explained. It may have a little to do with her imperious manner, well-earned since she appears to beat the others to the story while helping the police, with whom she has a warm relationship, solve crimes. The Duchess, who could "produce hunches faster than a cigarette machine turns out coffin nails," is Chambers's most enduring character, although he produced twenty novels and scores of short stories.

It is Chambers's screen work that shines more brightly. He wrote the screenplays for such TV series as *Surfside 6* and *77 Sunset Strip*, as well as numerous films, including *Manhandled* (1949), a film noir starring Sterling Hayden, in which lowlife Dan Duryea victimizes Dorothy Lamour, and *Special Agent* (1949), in which William Eythe plays a railroad agent who pursues two brothers who pulled off a huge payroll heist; they are played by Paul Valentine and George Reeves (who later gained fame as television's *Superman*). Films based on his novels include *The Come On* (1956), based on his 1953 novel of the same title, which starred Anne Baxter and Sterling Hayden; *Murder on the Campus* (1933), based on his 1933 novel *The Campanile Murders*, featuring Shirley Grey and Charles Starrett; *Sinner Take All* (1936), based on *Murder for a Wanton* (1934), starring Bruce Cabot and Margaret Lindsay; and *Blonde Ice* (1948), based on *Once Too Often* (1938), with Robert Paige and Leslie Brooks.

"The Old Maids Die" was originally published in the December 26, 1936, issue of *Detective Fiction Weekly*.

The Old Maids Die

WHITMAN CHAMBERS

THE THREE OF US were playing pinochle in the City Hall press room when we got the flash; Jeff Gervin, who covers night police for the *Sun*; Spike Kaylor, who holds down the beat for my paper, the *Bulletin*, and myself. It was a few minutes after midnight.

The radio receiver on top of the battery of phone books blared. "Calling Car 19. Calling Car 19. Go to 748 Myrtle Street. A woman called for help on her telephone and then evidently fainted. Step on it, boys."

Sour-faced Jeff Gervin grunted. "Go on and call for help. See if I care. Deal, will you, Kane?"

I looked at Spike Kaylor, and Spike looked at me. Jeff Gervin glared, one bushy eyebrow higher than the other, his thin lips twisted in a sneer.

"Don't be a pair of saps!" Jeff snorted. "If it's a story, the dicks will bring it in to us. Why borrow trouble? Deal, will you?"

I stood up and Spike Kaylor followed suit.

"Coming, Jeff?" I asked.

"Me? Leave this nice warm press room to go out on a phony call like that? On your way, boobs. Scram."

We scrammed.

Prowl Car 19 was drawn up in front of 748 Myrtle Street and Spike pulled his rattling old flivver in behind it and we tumbled out.

The big two-story house set well back from the street on a lot that took in half a block. Spike pushed through a sagging gate and led the way up a weed-grown gravel path. From the dim glow of a street lamp half a block away I could see that the garden had gone to seed and the house needed paint.

We climbed the creaking, rickety stairs and found the front door ajar. Spike pushed it open and we walked into a long bare hallway.

We heard voices coming from a room at the rear and started down the hall. Spike caught my arm, gasped:

"Good night! Look!"

I swung around, peered through an open door at the right. All at once I felt sweat coming out on my forehead and the pit of my stomach felt empty and sick.

I was looking into a bedroom, an old-fashioned room with furniture of another day. The bed was longer and wider than they make beds now. The covers and the white counterpane were jumbled.

Half covered by them, with one thin bare leg dragging on the floor, lay an old woman with white hair. The upper part of her face and one side of her head was a bloody pulp.

There was blood on the floor, on the ceiling, on the white bedclothes. It seemed hard to believe that one old woman could have had so much blood in her body.

Beside the bed lay a blood-drenched hammer. A window at the far side of the room was open and the old-fashioned lace curtain was fluttering in the breeze.

"Somebody," Spike said in an awed voice, "played that game for keeps. A thorough job, I calls it. Let's see what the bulls have to say."

We went on down the hall, reached the open door of a large sitting room. On a couch at the far side lay another old woman. She looked exactly like the one in the bedroom.

She was lying motionless, staring at the ceiling with dazed and glassy eyes. Now and then she said dully: "A huge Negro. . . . A huge Negro!"

Two coppers stood diffidently watching her and looking like they wished they were somewhere else. One of them saw us, glared, and demanded: "You guys touch anything in that room?"

We didn't pay any attention to him, for from the open door of the small darkened room at one side came a clear cool voice we knew well—too well!

Katie Blayne, better known as the Duchess, was already on the job. Katie covers day police for the *Sun*. She had no more right to be out on this story than—than *I* had!

"Jeff Gervin?" Katie was saying. "No, he's not out here yet. To be charitable, he's hardly had time. I live only two blocks away, you know, and I happened to have my radio tuned to the police band. So I ran over.

"Here's the lay. These twin spinsters, Malvina and Alva Perkins, live in this old house with their nephew, John Perkins. The nephew is a nightwatchman at the Western Chemical Works, and on the job tonight.

"Alva Perkins was a cripple. She slept in a bedroom on the lower floor. Malvina slept upstairs, where she had a bell that her sister could ring if she wanted anything.

"Somewhere around midnight the bell rang frantically. Malvina rushed downstairs to her sister's room. She was just in time to see a big Negro leap out of the open window and disap-

pear. Alva had been beaten to death with a hammer which lay beside the bed.

"Malvina staggered into the hall, yelled help a couple of times into the telephone and then fainted. She was just coming around when the two officers in the prowl car got here, with me on their heels. The cops sent for Captain Wallis and looked things over perfunctorily.

"They found where the window had been jimmied. There weren't any tracks under it because it opens on a gravel path. . . . No, there was no attempt at robbery. The Negro probably heard the other sister coming down the stairs and took a powder. . . .

"Yes, the cops have sent out a general pick-up order. . . . No, they didn't search the neighborhood. The fellow had plenty of time to make a getaway. . . .

"Yes, that's about all now. I'll turn the story over to Jeff when he gets here—if ever."

Katie came out into the sitting room, nodding to Spike and me.

"Sometime," the red-headed, peppery Mr. Kaylor sputtered, "I hope to come out on a story and not find you ahead of me. Don't you ever sleep?"

"Yeah," said an angry voice from the hall doorway, "and don't you ever mind your own business?" It was Jeff Gervin, winded, red-faced, smelling of gin. "It seems to me that a guy by the name of Gervin is covering night police for the *Sun*. If I'm wrong, wise me."

Katie smiled but didn't say anything. One of the coppers asked: "How'd you get here so pronto, Gervin?"

"I came with Captain Wallis. He and McNaught are in the front room with the body."

The old woman on the couch moaned: "A huge Negro!"

Spike started for the telephone in the little room adjoining. Jeff Gervin began to take the Duchess over the coals for butting in on the story. And the two bulls headed for the front bedroom with me on their heels.

We found Captain Wallis and Mike McNaught, his fingerprint expert, looking over the scene of the murder. The coppers told them Miss Perkins's story.

"This," Wallis said slowly, "is bad. There are twenty thousand Negroes living within a radius of a mile from this house. H-m. Any prints on the hammer, Mike?"

"Not a print," Mike McNaught said.

"Try the window he jimmied. Where's this other sister?"

We had started back along the hall when we heard the door bell buzz. One of the cops answered it. A taxi driver said: "Somebody ring for a cab?"

Katie Blayne came running down the hall. "I did," she called.

I fell in behind her and we went out to the street. Katie paused as the driver threw open the cab door.

"Good night, Pinky. It's been nice to have seen you again."

"Where you bound, Duchess?"

"Home, of course."

"You're calling a cab to drive you two blocks? Tell me another, Katie."

"I'll tell you plenty, Pinky Kane," she retorted sharply. "Dust!"

"Suppose I don't choose to dust?"

Katie glared at me. Then she turned, leaped into the cab, and jerked the door shut behind her. I reached for the door handle. The taxi driver said:

"Hold it, pal."

I looked the big gorilla over and decided I wanted none of him.

"Right," I said, and turned toward the house.

II

As the cab rolled off, I ran back to the street and hopped into Spike Kaylor's flivver. Luckily he'd left the ignition key in the lock. I turned it on, revved up the motor and lit out after the cab.

I kept about two blocks behind. The driver, apparently, never knew he was tailed until, half an hour later, we drew up before a large factory

building on the other side of the city. For the first time I realized what Katie had on her mind.

We met on the sidewalk beside the cab. The Duchess said with a sigh: "I might have known it. Don't you ever get tired following me around?"

"Not ever. You see, Duchess, I like you. And I want to see that no harm befalls you in your various wanderings over the city after nightfall."

Katie said something that sounded suspiciously like "Nuts!"

The driver leaned out of his cab. "Lady, I can take this lug like Grant took Richmond. How's about it?"

The Duchess shrugged wearily. "Skip it," she said. "How much do I owe you?"

She paid him off, got a receipt to send in with her weekly swindle sheet, and turned again to me.

"I'd appreciate your letting me handle this interview," she said. "I have an idea about this murder. You needn't ask what it is, because I'm not putting out anything, but I'd like a free hand when we talk to Perkins. O.K.?"

"I won't say a word, Katie. At least not very many. I have an idea or two myself. Let's go."

We rang a bell at the main entrance of the plant and after a long wait the door was opened by a tall thin man of fifty or thereabouts. He eyed us with disapproval as he asked: "What you want?"

"We're from the *Sun* and the *Telegram*, Mr. Perkins," Katie said. "One of your aunts, Miss Alva, was killed tonight. We want to talk to you about it."

He stood there in the doorway blinking at us, an unpleasant-looking fellow with close-set eyes, thin gray hair, and a stoop.

"You can come in, I guess," he said finally.

He led the way along a corridor with offices on either side, down a flight of stairs to the basement, and into a small windowless room which was furnished with three or four uncomfortable chairs, a row of lockers against the wall, and a deal table. On a one-burner gas plate a pot of coffee was boiling. The whole place reeked of acid fumes.

"You can sit down, I guess," John Perkins said heavily. "What happened to Aunt Alva?"

Katie told him. During the brief recital he poured himself a cup of coffee and drank it black and scalding hot. He asked no questions. He seemed hardly interested.

"We were wondering," Katie said finally, "if you knew anything about the killing of your Aunt Alva?"

He didn't bat an eye at the pointed insinuation. "No," he said, "I don't guess I know anything about it. A big Negro you say? No, I don't know any big Negroes."

Katie's eyes glittered. "By the way, Mr. Perkins, have you been the sole support of your two aunts?"

"Me? I should guess not." His voice, now, was bitter. "Them two old women are worth a hundred thousand dollars, more or less." He poured himself another cup of coffee, added heavily: "My father left it to them in trust. When they die, I get it."

"And in the meantime, you're working as a night watchman at fifty or sixty dollars a month?" Katie remarked.

"Forty-five," the drab Mr. Perkins corrected.

"And you're not the least bit resentful?" Katie pursued.

He looked her coldly in the eye; his mouth was grim. "If you think I'm not, you're crazy!" he snapped. And then he chuckled harshly. "I see what you're getting at, I guess. Well, you're wrong. Didn't Aunt Malvina say it was a Negro killed Aunt Alva?"

"That's what she said," Katie admitted. "But she might have made a mistake."

"Aunt Malvina," John Perkins declared, "doesn't make mistakes. Howsomever, I got something here I ought to show you, just in case you and the police get any foolish ideas about me."

We followed him upstairs. He stopped at a time clock near the outer door, took a card from the big rack, handed it to Katie. I peered over her shoulder.

It was Perkins's card. The last stamp on it showed the date and the time: 1:01 A.M. The previous stamp read: 11:59 P.M.

"I have to ring in, you see, every hour," John Perkins explained.

I looked at the clock. I knew the type. I had punched one like it in a warehouse where I worked before I broke into the newspaper racket. Another fellow and I had tried to to set it back when we got to work late one day. We'd discovered it couldn't be rigged.

"You told me," Perkins said, "that Aunt Alva was killed about midnight. I rung in here at one minute to twelve. It takes me a half hour to drive home. You can draw your own conclusions, I guess."

Katie stared at him for a long moment before she asked quietly: "What's the current rate in the Black Belt for a job like that?"

John Perkins grinned. "A hundred dollars, I understand." Then his jaw set and all at once his ice-blue eyes were hard. "I'm not sorry my aunt is dead. She was an old harridan and she got what's been coming to her for a long time. I'm only sorry the fellow didn't kill Aunt Malvina too. Now I guess that's about all I got to say. You people can get the hell out of here."

Which we did.

Just before I left Katie at her home she said abstractedly:

"I talked to Malvina Perkins. She's a mean old woman. And she's a little queer. Perhaps she's even crazy. I wonder—?"

"You wonder if maybe Malvina killed her sister and cooked up the story about the Negro?"

The Duchess merely said "Good night, Pinky. Pleasant dreams."

I drove off laughing to myself. That was Katie. If her first hunch proved to be a dud, she lost no time in giving birth to another. Katie Blayne can produce hunches faster than a cigarette machine turns out coffin nails.

When I got back to the City Hall I found Jeff Gervin and Spike Kaylor having a drink in the press room.

"I'll have one of those," I said.

"Yes, and I'll have the key to my car," Spike shot back. "What was the brilliant idea?"

"I was riding herd on the Duchess. We had a talk with John Perkins. We discovered that those two old maids are plenty wealthy and Perkins is their heir. The dough was left to them by Perkins's father, and Perkins is pretty bitter about it. But—Perkins's time card was punched at one minute to twelve and it's a half hour's run from that factory to his home."

Jeff Gervin grunted. "You and the Duchess get the damnedest ideas. The guy who knocked off the old dame is now cooling in the can. Name of Jim Brown."

I choked on Jeff's bourbon, reached for the water.

"They picked up this Jim Brown just after you ran off with my car," Spike explained. "He was only three blocks away. A big Negro, dead drunk, with a cut on his head and blood all over his hands. He was staggering along the street talking to himself."

"Lyle and Allen spotted him," Jeff took up the story. "They dragged him into their prowl car, took him in to the Perkins dame, and she went into hysterics."

"Identified him on the spot," Spike concluded.

"So that's that," Jeff said. "Nice work, I calls it. Have another drink?"

I had another drink and went home.

The next day about noon I saw Katie Blayne talking to John Forsythe in the anteroom of the Detective Bureau. Forsythe is one of our better criminal lawyers, a fellow who won't look at a case unless important money is involved, but a right guy at that.

A little later, when Forsythe dropped into the press room, I jumped him.

"You're not, by any chance, going to defend this Negro, are you?"

"I am," Forsythe said flatly.

The room at the moment happened to be crowded with a few reporters and more than a few press room habitués: bail bond brokers,

politicians, coppers off duty, and other riff-raff that is constantly getting in our hair. Everybody looked at the tall, immaculate, gray-haired, lean-faced lawyer.

"What's the answer to that one?" fat, moon-faced Willie Blake of the *Sentinel* demanded. "I mean, who's putting up the dough?"

"The *Sun*," Katie Blayne declared, "is putting up the dough."

"How come?" I asked.

"Miss Blayne," said Forsythe, "has convinced her publisher that the boy is innocent. And I am forced to agree."

"Who wouldn't agree," Willie grinned, "for a couple of G's?"

"What makes you think this Jim Brown is innocent?" lanky lantern-jawed Pete Zerker of the *Bulletin* asked reasonably. "How about the identification? How about the blood all over him?"

"The old lady could be mistaken in identifying him," Forsythe pointed out. "And the blood was Jim Brown's own. He had fallen down, you know, and had cut his head."

"Sure," I said. "He fell down when he hopped out that window."

"Furthermore," the attorney went on coolly, "the police found no fingerprints on the lethal weapon. Now do you really believe that a drunken Negro boy, a young fellow who is not very bright anyhow, would have the foresight to wear gloves?"

"The prints were probably smeared," Willie Blake suggested.

"There were no prints," Forsythe stated flatly, "smeared or otherwise."

And that was that—for a while.

III

Jim Brown was arraigned on a charge of first-degree murder the next day and his preliminary hearing was set for a morning three weeks hence.

A little before nine on the morning of the preliminary, Katie Blayne showed up at the press room with a confident smile and a breezy, "Good morning."

"I have here," she announced to Pete Zerker and Willie Blake and me, "a hundred dollars which says that the case against Jim Brown will be dismissed before noon today. You may have all or any part of it."

"You're pretty confident, Duchess," Pete growled.

"You must be nuts," Willie said. "With the old dame identifying him he's a cinch to be bound over to the superior court. If I were you, Duchess, I wouldn't risk my money on a crazy bet like that."

"You let me worry about my money," Katie shot back. "How much would you like, Willie?"

Willie gulped, shrugged, said: "I'll take a fin."

"Pinky?"

"I'll take ten," I said without enthusiasm.

"Pete?"

"I'll take vanilla," Zerker snapped.

At ten o'clock we were all at the press table in the justice court. The D.A. and a couple of his staff came in, looking blustery and important. Then John Forsythe wandered down the aisle, looking very cool and confident, nodding to his friends among the spectators and at the press table.

The judge arrived and finally the bailiff came trailing in with the prisoner, a big, poorly dressed, frightened–looking colored boy who sat down awkwardly beside John Forsythe.

The hearing got under way with the D.A. making a brief statement of the case and calling Miss Malvina Perkins to the stand. The thin, tall old lady bustled over to the witness chair and sat down. Her lips were thin and pressed tightly against her teeth. Her eyes were glittering, too bright. A shrewish, vindictive, bitter old woman, and could you blame her?

After she was sworn, the district attorney rose and with gentle deference began his examination.

"Miss Perkins, please tell the judge what happened in your home on the night of June fourteenth."

"I was in my room on the upper floor," the spinster began in a shrill voice. "It was a few minutes before midnight. I heard my sister ring for me. Frantically. She was an invalid and sleeping on the lower floor. I ran downstairs and into her room. I saw a man, a big Negro, run across the room and leap out the window. My sister was dead, beaten to death."

The D.A. slowly nodded. "Did you see this man's face?" he asked.

"I did."

"Clearly?"

"Clearly."

"Could you identify him if you saw him again?"

"I certainly could."

"Do you see him in this room?"

"Yes!" the old woman hissed.

"Please point him out to the court."

Miss Perkins leveled a skinny finger at the black boy beside John Forsythe.

"That's him!" she screamed. "That's the monster that killed my poor crippled sister."

"Are you absolutely positive, Miss Perkins?" the D.A. persisted gently.

"Certainly I'm positive!" the old lady shot back. "Do you think I could ever forget his horrible face?"

Everybody stared at the prisoner. His face wasn't horrible at all. It was just the face of a bewildered kid.

John Forsythe was whispering to him. The black boy was nodding his head.

Abruptly I felt an electric tension in the room. I forgot to listen to the D.A., to Miss Perkins' testimony.

I watched John Forsythe and the black boy. The kid was grinning now. Forsythe whispered to him again and he wiped the grin away with the back of his hand.

I glanced at Katie. She, too, was watching Forsythe and the prisoner. And there was something in her blue eyes that told me I had lost ten dollars.

She leaned toward me and whispered: "Cover up your ears, Pinky. The dynamite is going off in just a second. See? Mr. Forsythe is lighting the fuse."

I looked around at Forsythe. He was standing now, placidly buttoning the lower button of his neat double-breasted coat.

"If it please, Your Honor," he said.

The district attorney swung around, glaring. "You may have the witness in due time," he snapped. "Until I am finished with her—"

"If the court pleases," Forsythe broke in. "I believe a most regrettable error has been made."

"Error?" The judge glared down over the rims of his spectacles. "What manner of error, Mr. Forsythe?"

"Your bailiff has brought in the wrong prisoner."

"The—the *which*?" the district attorney gasped.

"I'm sure it was all a misunderstanding, Your Honor," Forsythe went on smoothly. "But this young man here is one Ed Higgins, who has just finished serving a sixty-day sentence for assault and battery. On the night Miss Alva Perkins was murdered, Ed Higgins was in jail."

The judge leaned forward, staring at the black boy. "I remember. I sentenced him myself." He swung on the bailiff. "Where is Jim Brown?"

The bailiff winced. "I guess, Your Honor, he's still in the city prison. I—I—"

The judge silenced him with a wave of his hand.

I whispered to Katie: "What did it cost Forsythe to have the wrong prisoner brought in?"

"S-s-s-sh!"

The judge had turned on the white-faced Miss Perkins. "Madame, you are an old woman. And I recall an old song to the effect that all colored people look alike. I could point out that your testimony might have sent an innocent man to the gallows, but I don't think it is necessary. Mr. Forsythe, I don't know how you engineered this coup and I am not going to inquire. The end, certainly, justified the means. Do I hear a motion requesting the case against Jim Brown be dismissed?"

"I make such a motion, Your Honor," Forsythe smiled.

The judge looked over at the D.A. We all looked at the D.A. And saw that that smug gentleman had collapsed in his chair.

"Any objection?" the judge asked.

"No," the district attorney said sadly. "No objection."

The gavel banged. "Case dismissed!"

Back in the press room Katie didn't rub it in—much. She took my ten-spot and Willie's five.

"Thank you kindly, gentlemen," she said. "I'm only sorry it wasn't more."

"If it had been any more," I grumbled, "I wouldn't eat until next pay day. Look here, people. How do you figure that Miss Perkins?"

"Ask me a tough one," Willie Blake said. "That dame deliberately identified the first suspect the cops dragged in. Why? Because she polished off her sister herself. Right, Pete?"

"Wrong, Willie," the *Bulletin*'s reporter came back. "I figure the poor old woman was so overcome with grief and hysteria and a very natural vindictiveness that she really thought Jim Brown was the man she'd seen jumping out the window."

"Well, Duchess?" I asked. "What's your theory?"

"My theory," said Katie, "is not for publication."

"Getting exclusive, huh?" Pete Zerker jeered.

"I have always been exclusive," said the Duchess with a toss of her shapely blond head.

In the days that followed the police went on looking for a big Negro whom Miss Perkins could positively identify, the gang in the press room went on with its routine run of crimes and accidents, and the Duchess went on being mysterious.

And I was worried. I think about as much of Katie Blayne as I do of my right eye, despite the fact that she treats me like she'd treat a nice soft rug—just something pleasant to walk upon.

I was worried because I know Katie, know her every mood. She was getting ready to put something over on us. And when Katie gets that watch-me-pull-a-fast-one look in her big blue eyes, I get ready to drag her out of trouble by the hair of her very lovely head. Of course, there have been occasions when she turned the tables and dragged me out of trouble, but we needn't go into that.

I took Katie out occasionally during these weeks and one night, starting home from a movie in my car, we picked up a two-alarm on the police broadcast.

"Want to go?" I asked, thumbing through my list of stations.

"Did you ever know me to pass up a fire? Where is it?"

"Fourth and Polk."

"Let's get under way."

IV

Fourth and Polk is in the factory district. It took us twenty minutes to get there. We watched a rattan factory go up in smoke and it was about midnight when we ran into Spike Kaylor and Jeff Gervin.

"Hey, you lugs," Jeff called. "How's about a ride back to the Hall?"

I looked at the Duchess. Though now they worked on the same paper, Katie and Jeff, as you may have guessed, were like a couple of strange bulldogs.

"It's all right with me," she shrugged. "Jeff, did you get the name of that fireman who had his hand cut?"

"Did I get—Listen, Duchess! Are you telling me—"

"Skip it. Both of you," I ordered. "Here's the car. Get in, you two."

Jeff and Spike got into the rear seat. As I started off I switched on the radio. It warmed up, the hum died and we heard:

". . . Car 19. Calling Car 19. Go to 748 Myrtle Street. That's the house where Alva Perkins was murdered two months ago. A citizen just phoned he saw a Negro leaving the house. Step on it, boys."

Spike whistled. "Boy, they got the other old maid! Sure as shootin' they—"

"Oh, Pinky, Pinky!" Katie Blayne cried in a voice choked with pain and horror. "Something has gone wrong! Something terrible has happened!"

I shot a quick look at her. Her face was dead white. Her mouth was slack, her lips trembling. There was terror in her eyes.

"That poor old woman!" she groaned, twisting her hands. "That poor old woman!"

"Step on it, mug!" Jeff Gervin snapped. "Get us out there to 748 Myrtle. Open her up, damn it! Won't this crate do better than forty?"

Katie's fingers were suddenly biting into my arm.

"No, no, no!" she cried. "The Western Chemical Works! Quick! Turn around!"

I smelled the whiskey on Jeff's breath as he leaned forward and yelled into my ear.

"To hell with that! Keep going, Kane!"

"Please, Pinky," the Duchess begged. "Please do as I ask you. I know what I'm doing. I know I'm right."

"Take us out to Myrtle Street, I tell you," Jeff ordered angrily.

"I'll take you where I damn well please," I retorted. "If you want out, hop when I swing this corner."

I swung the corner and he didn't hop. We were, then, only half a mile from the Western Chemical plant and I made it in thirty seconds. I drove the car around to the rear of the four-story building, slammed on the brakes and cut the motor.

"Well, we're here, Duchess," I said. "Now what?"

"Come on," she called, and was out of the car.

We trailed her around to the front of the building and she opened the door with a key she pulled out of her handbag. We went in behind her and she closed the door.

"Where'd you get the key?" I asked.

"The plant manager."

She walked straight down the hall to the time

clock. There was a card in the slot. Katie took it out and I saw it was John Perkins' card and was stamped 12:01 A.M.

And then I saw several other things. One was a cheap alarm clock standing on top of the big time clock. The alarm bell had been removed and a spring device attached to the clapper. Hanging from the lever at the side of the time clock, at the end of a two-foot rope, was a window weight.

"He set the alarm clock at midnight," Katie said breathlessly. "When it went off, that spring tripped the window weight."

"And the weight fell about four feet," I said, "and jerked the lever which stamped Perkins' card. Neat."

"All of which," Jeff Gervin grumbled, "adds up to what?"

Jeff was a bit drunk and slow on the pick-up. Nobody answered him.

"Maybe," I suggested half-heartedly, "he just rigged it to get himself a couple of hours sleep. We could look, anyway."

We started down the dim corridor to the stairway.

"This is awful," Katie said, with a catch in her voice. "Someone has made a horrible mistake."

"Hold it, guys!"

It was Spike Kaylor. I checked myself, startled at the tension in Spike's voice. He had dropped to his knees on the stained and rather dirty concrete floor. He rubbed a dark damp spot with his finger, held the finger close to his eyes.

"Blood," he said calmly.

A little chill of apprehension and bewilderment swept down my spine. All at once I didn't like this great dimly lighted chemical plant with its strange and acrid smells.

Spike was crawling along the floor on all fours.

"More of it," he said. "It's smeared. Like something was dragged over it."

"The something," I said, "being a body." I looked sharply at Katie. She was biting her lower lip. There was horror in her fine eyes. "Whose, Duchess," I asked.

"The man who has been tailing Perkins for nearly two months," she said heavily. Then she started forward. "Hurry! He might not be dead yet."

We all ran down the corridor to the stairway which led to the basement. Katie got there first, cried: "Good grief! Look!"

The wide stairway was jammed almost solid with broken crates and boxes, pasteboard cartons, and excelsior.

"One match," Spike remarked, "and this dump would go up like a skyrocket."

Katie hurled aside a smashed crate and started down the stairs. The rest of us turned to and in three or four minutes we cleared enough of a path to worm our way into the basement. There was a light burning in the watchman's little room.

On the floor, sprawled grotesquely just as it had been dumped, lay the body of a man in a blue serge suit. His hat was gone. The top of his bald head was red and pulpy. We knew, by the set and tortured look on his face, by the glassy stare in his eyes, that he was dead.

"You know him, Katie?" I asked.

"Yes. He's a private detective by the name of Jones. My paper hired him." She wrung her hands. "Oh, if only Captain Wallis had listened to me! I knew, I *knew*, that the first murder was planned! And there was only one man who had anything to gain by killing those old maids.

"But Captain Wallis only laughed at me," Katie rushed on hysterically. "Said there was no evidence against Perkins. Said it was just another one of my pipe-dreams. So the *Sun* hired Jones to keep watch on Perkins. And Perkins must have found out he was being watched, and sneaked up on this poor man and—and killed him brutally."

Katie buried her face in her trembling hands.

Spike said: "And then Perkins rushed home and killed his other aunt. He figured to get back here, recover his time card for an alibi and then fire the joint. A neat plan. The dicks picking up that Negro kid right after the first murder was just coincidence. Only—"

"Malvina swore she saw a Negro leap out of her sister's window," I pointed out.

"Of course!" Katie exclaimed. "That was all part of his plan. With the police believing the first old maid was killed by a Negro, they'd naturally suppose that the other had been killed by the same man."

"Yes, but—" I began.

"S-s-s-sh!" Jeff Gervin hissed. "You guys hear that?"

"Hear what?" I whispered. If I heard anything, it was my own knees knocking together.

"Somebody," Jeff rasped, "just shut the front door!"

My heart came up in my throat as I thought of that pile of tinder blocking the stairway.

"Let's go, gang!" I yelled.

I kicked a box out of the way and shoved the Duchess up two steps. Then, for some reason, I looked up.

And peering down at us over the pile of tinder that clogged the stairway was a big black Negro!

No, not a Negro! Just John Perkins, his coat thick with padding, his thin face coated with burnt cork!

John Perkins's head and shoulders disappeared. Then I heard his feet strike the concrete floor three times as he hurled his weight against the pile of broken crates and boxes which filled the stair well.

"Look out!" Spike yelled.

I jerked Katie backward off the steps, lost my balance and fell against Spike and Jeff.

As I scrambled to my feet I saw that the stair well was clogged solidly.

"Look, you lugs!" Jeff Gervin sputtered. "We gotta get out of here!"

"Are you telling me?" Spike snorted. "Where does this corridor lead to?"

V

It led, as we could readily see, to a brick wall at one end and to a steel fire door at the other. It was a cinch the fire door was bolted, but it was our only chance of getting out of the trap we'd blundered into.

I started toward it, heard at that instant the splash of liquid on the pile of tinder in the stair well.

"Gasoline!" Jeff Gervin screamed. "Get back! Get back!"

In an instant the stairway was a crackling, roaring mass of flame. I ran to the steel door at one end of the corridor.

I pounded it, kicked it, hurled my weight against it. It was as solid as Gibraltar.

Catching Katie's hand, I raced her down the hall, past the appalling heat of the stairway and into the watchman's little room. Spike and Jeff came after us.

"Slam that door!" I ordered. "The air in here is O.K. We've got to keep it that way!"

"Yes," Spike said heavily, "and when those big vats of acid out in the main plant let go. What then? I ask you, what then?"

Katie had picked up a newspaper on the table and walked over to the door.

"Help me, Pinky," she said quietly. "You know how the miners do when they're trapped. We'll plug up all the cracks around the door. If we can keep out the monoxide and the acid fumes, the air in here will keep us alive for hours."

"Hours, hell!" Jeff growled bitterly. "The alarm probably isn't even in yet. Another five minutes and the whole inside of this joint will be gutted. I've seen chemical plants go up before."

"Skip it, Jeff!" I snapped, and knelt beside the Duchess and started to plug the cracks around the door.

Katie said in an undertone: "I'm sorry I got you into this, Pinky."

I put my arm around her and drew her close. She put her head against me and I felt a tear drop on my hand.

"Forget it, kid," I said. "You didn't get me into this. We came into it together, just like I wanted to do a lot of things."

She looked up at me. Her face was deathly pale; her eyes were shining.

"Such as?" she asked.

"Such as get married. And go places, and see people, and do things. Together. You and me."

She nodded slowly. "If we'd been married, months ago when you first asked me, I probably wouldn't have been working now. And I wouldn't have blundered into this mess. And you—"

Spike Kaylor abruptly shoved me aside, put his ear to the door. I could hear, very faintly, shouts and a familiar hissing sound as tons of water poured on flames.

"Can you tie it?" Spike yelled jubilantly. "The brave fire laddies are with us. Now how in Sam Hill did they get on the job without us hearing a single siren?"

"Cinch!" Jeff Gervin growled. "The apparatus was coming by here on its way back from the wicker works fire. They just pulled up, hooked on their hoses and—"

Katie had risen to her feet. "And we'll be out of here in a few minutes." She looked at me, smiled a bit sheepishly. "Pinky, do you suppose everybody gets sentimental when they're in a tight spot?"

I groaned. What we'd said hadn't seemed sentimental to me at all.

In ten minutes we were out of it, standing around a body the fireman had carried to the sidewalk.

"Who is he, Kane? What do you make of it?" Battalion Chief Murphy asked me. "We found him in the hallway at the head of the stairs."

"He's the bird who touched it off. He spilled too much gasoline around, I guess, and when it blew it knocked him over. Now I've got to hit for a telephone."

The four of us, Katie and Jeff and Spike and I, climbed into my car. We found telephones in an all-night drug store eight or ten blocks away, and phoned our stories.

Katie and I came out of our booths at the same time. "You had it doped exactly right, Katie," I said. "Perkins had been home and killed his other aunt. How did you do it?"

Katie shrugged. "It wasn't hard. The police didn't find a sign of a fingerprint on the push button beside Miss Perkins's bed. Proving—"

"That the old woman didn't ring for help," I said quickly. "But someone who knew about that button did. Someone who was wearing gloves. John Perkins, of course."

"And Captain Wallis," Katie said bitterly, "laughed at me."

"Don't feel badly, Katie. There was no evidence against Perkins. They couldn't watch him forever, and sooner or later he'd have slipped away and killed Malvina. Let's forget it. Let's forget everything. Everything except what we said while we were down there waiting to go up in smoke. Look! Don't you think it would be a good idea to marry me and get out of this rotten newspaper racket?"

She smiled at me, shook her head, said: "No. No, Pinky."

"Is that final?" I demanded.

"Well—practically final."

"Any time," Jeff Gervin growled. "Any time you two love-birds get through cooing, I'd like to get back to the Hall and kill this pint I just bought. Fires give me a thirst."

Jeff Gervin gives *me* a pain in the neck.

TOO MANY CLIENTS

D. B. McCandless

IT IS NOT A STRETCH to suggest that D. B. McCandless was not a major figure of the pulp writing world. Although he created the series about private investigator Sarah Watson for the highly regarded *Detective Fiction Weekly*, he also wrote for the decidedly down-market *Gangster Stories*.

There is little to keep his name alive other than his creation of Watson, who is a significant presence in the eleven stories in which she was the leading character. Unlike most female pulp detectives, she is not cute, nor does she require a man to help her out of a tough situation. She is, on the contrary, middle-aged, dramatically overweight, and dressed without any attempt to be fashionable or attractive. It is common for her to call her young assistant, Ben Todd, a "whippersnapper" and keep him in the dark as a case progressed.

More than for most pulp fiction, the stories by McCandless require a suspension of disbelief that could test even the least discriminating reader. Rather than focus on reasonable, or even possible, activities, it would be best to appreciate the fast-paced narrative and an original character who may well have inspired Erle Stanley Gardner to create another overbearing female detective and her younger, thinner, long-suffering male partner when he began the Bertha Cool and Donald Lam series he wrote as A. A. Fair.

"Too Many Clients" was originally published in the March 27, 1937, issue of *Detective Fiction Weekly*.

Too Many Clients

D. B. McCANDLESS

THE WOMAN STRIDING DOWN the echoing corridor paused and laid stubby fingers, gloved in black cotton, upon the knob of the door which said: WATSON DETECTIVE AGENCY. In the twilight of the corridor, the woman's craggy face seemed gray, the hard gray of granite, and the nondescript clothes which covered the corseted column of her body seemed gray, too, though strong sunlight would have revealed them as dusty black.

The woman laid one ear to the opaque glass of the door, listened a moment, with craggy chin jutting, to the faint click-clack of typewriter keys, then straightened the antique headgear on her gray hair and swung in the door, shutting it behind her by the simple expedient of kicking it shut with one square-toed shoe.

The long-legged young man pecking at the typewriter looked up. He said: "'Lo, Sarah Watson! How d'yuh spell philatelist?"

"I don't spell it," said Sarah Watson, hoarsely. "What is a philatelist, Ben Todd?"

"A philatelist," said Ben Todd, "is a guy who monkeys with stamps."

"*Monkeys* is right," said Sarah, crossing the dusty floor with resounding tread. "Now, listen, young feller! I know the papers say a damn-fool stamp collector named Barnes has had one of his postage stamps stolen, but if you're writing to Theodore Barnes you can stop writing. I'm boss of this outfit, and I'm not going to get gummed up with any postage stamps."

"Listen," shouted Ben Todd. "The Barnes stamp ain't just a stamp. It's unique. It's the only stamp of its kind in the world. It's hoary with age. It has a history. Men have murdered and died to possess it. . . ."

Ben Todd broke off, staring ahead.

"Murdered and died for it," he murmured, and his wide mouth jerked up in the beginnings of a grin "Oh, well, old girl, you're the boss, as you say. We don't want to be gummed up, of course, with murder and death. . . ."

"Bennie," said Sarah, slamming her purse down on her roll top desk, "Bennie, you're about as subtle as a bull. If you think you can egg me into going after a fool postage stamp by rolling your eyes and talking about danger and death! You throw that letter away, Bennie. . . ."

Ben Todd yawned and ran long fingers through his red hair.

"Sarah," he said, "you're right. It's better to keep our noses out of something we ain't fitted to do. The Barnes stamp is insured, of course, and the insurance company will have their best bloodhounds baying with their noses to the scent. . . ."

"Bennie," said Sarah, firmly, "you're about as wily as a cow. If the insurance company bloodhounds want to bay, let 'em bay. I ain't going to get mixed up with any piddling post-age stamp. . . ."

"Piddling!" shouted Ben Todd. "Piddling!" she says. Listen! The Barnes stamp is worth thirty thousand—"

"Thirty thousand? You mean to say one postage stamp is worth—"

"Sarah, the insurance company is offering three thousand for the return of that stamp."

"Bennie, sit down. Finish that letter. Three thousand! Tell Mr. Theodore Barnes we're starting right now to look for his stamp and when we get our hands on it. . . ."

"When we get our hands on it! Listen, old girl, when we get our hands on that stamp, we'll use special stamp tongs. That stamp is fragile, it's delicate, it's precious."

"I don't give a damn what it is," said Sarah hoarsely. "We're going to find it. You finish that letter, and if you don't know how to spell philatelist—. Take that grin off your face, squirt! I've changed my mind. We ain't going to write that letter, Bennie. Get your hat."

A battered black box on four wheels rattled and chugged and bumped to a stop on Fairview Drive. The woman under the wheel peered to survey the residence set back from the road.

"Bennie," she muttered, "it looks to me like Mr. Barnes should have sold his postage stamp long since and had his lawn shaved."

Ben Todd stared at the imposing pile of white stone and ivy set in the midst of rank grass. He said:

"The old guy has beggared himself for stamps, they say, mortgaged everything to the hilt. They say, too, that—"

"They say, too, that men never gossip," rasped Sarah. "Stop scandal mongering about our future client. Climb out!"

Ben Todd climbed. Sarah joined him at the sagging gates of the Barnes estate.

Ben Todd said: "Right next door stands the house of Sylvester Barnes, old Theodore's brother. They say Sylvester's a philatelist, too—a

rabid one. They say he's been practically foaming at the mouth for years to get the Barnes stamp away from Theodore. They say—"

Sarah turned her back.

"Listen," said Ben Todd, indignantly. "Listen, you old war horse. I got more information."

"Your information's stale," barked Sarah, charging through the gates and up the driveway. "I know all you say they say and a lot more, too. Bennie, there's something going on in that house. Bennie, I heard something. . . ."

The front door of the house flew open. A woman ran out, screaming, stumbling down the wide, white steps.

Sarah put on speed. She seized the screaming woman with competent hands and shook. The woman stopped screaming. She was a middle-aged spinsterish type of woman, with the bright black eyes and jerky movements of a bird. She wore an old-fashioned, black, beaded dress and an old-fashioned, white kitchen apron tied about her waist.

"You Lily Devlin?" said Sarah briskly. "I thought so. Get your chin down on your chest, Lily, way down, and you won't faint. So, you're Theodore Barnes's step-sister? Um! What's going on here? Quick!"

Lily Devlin opened her thin lips. They twisted sidewise as she spoke: "Dead!" she squalled.

"Dead?" repeated Sarah, flatly. "Who's dead?"

"He's dead," moaned Lily Devlin, and slid and fell flat.

Sarah stared down at the crumpled figure a moment, then rounded it and started up the steps.

"Somebody's dead," she said. "Bring her along, Bennie. I'm going to find the corpse."

Sarah strode through the open door. Ben Todd came behind with the woman cradled in his arms.

"Hi!" shouted Sarah. "Hi!"

Sarah's shout penetrated the very cracks of the elaborate ceiling and echoed back. Silence! Sarah wheeled, hands on hips, and stared down at Ben Todd's burden. Lily Devlin opened her eyes. She said: "Theodore couldn't have killed him because Theodore never came downstairs. . . ."

"Good!" said Sarah. "The corpse ain't Theodore, then. That's a relief. Where's Theodore now?"

"Upstairs. I—I went up and called him when the man—the dead man—came. Theodore was lying down. He's sick since the Barnes stamp was stolen. He roused when I knocked and told him a man was here about the stamp—"

"About the stamp?" snapped Sarah. "Go on."

"Theodore must have dozed off again," continued Lily Devlin, "for he never came down and still, the man is dead in there, in the study, with the kitchen knife in his chest!"

Sarah turned toward the stairs with her hands on her broad hips. "Theodore!" she bellowed. "Come down! Theo—"

A figure appeared in the dimness above, a spindle-legged figure in an old-fashioned nightshirt. For a moment, the blob of face on top of the nightshirt bent down over the banister, then the tails of the nightshirt whisked and disappeared.

"Bennie," said Sarah, "go find the corpse."

As Ben Todd started down the hall, Theodore Barnes was coming down the stairs, now wrapped in a dressing gown which hid his lean shanks. His face was no longer a blob. It was visibly a face, a face patterned with the criss-cross lines of age, but topped with a thatch of jet-black hair.

"Madam!" he demanded, his little black eyes stabbing at Sarah. "Who are you? Your entrance here—your unwarranted familiarity—"

"Theodore," announced Sarah firmly, "this is no time for dignity. I came here, in the first place, about that stolen stamp. The stamp will have to wait. There's a dead man somewhere on your premises, Mr. Barnes, with a knife in him. . . ."

"Sarah!" yelled Ben Todd from the rear of the hall "He's here! He's got a knife in him and an empty envelope beside him, the kind of envelope they use for valuable stamps. . . ."

Theodore Barnes brushed by Sarah and sped

toward the voice. Sarah sped after. Lily Devlin collapsed in a hall chair and stayed there, her face buried in thin fingers which curved like bird's claws.

At the end of the hall, a door stood open. Outside the door stood Ben Todd, Theodore Barnes, and Sarah. Inside sat the dead.

The walls of the room were covered with books, except for the single oblong of the French window at the back. The dead man sat behind a desk, leaning far back in a mahogany swivel chair.

The dead man's arms extended rigidly, his clenched fists resting on the desk. Between the fists, lights glinted on a small, transparent envelope, crumpled and empty. The dead eyes stared down blankly at the brown wooden knife handle which protruded from the chest.

Sarah stirred. She rapped Theodore Barnes smartly on his thin shoulder. "Who?" she demanded.

"I—I don't know," quavered Theodore Barnes.

"He came to see you."

"I—I don't know."

"He came to see you about a stamp—*the* stamp . . ."

Theodore Barnes gave a little cry. He charged into the silent room. He said, gasping: "The stamp! Maybe—maybe it's in one of his hands . . ."

Sarah strode forward. She laid strong fingers on Mr. Barnes. She said, firmly: "Mr. Barnes, you go use the phone I saw in the hall. Get the police. The stamp must wait. It would be unthinkable to desecrate the dead. Mr. Barnes, before the police arrive. . . ."

Theodore Barnes's small black eyes squinted into Sarah's clear gray ones. He jerked away and ran out into the hall.

Sarah said, quietly: "Step in, Bennie, and close that door behind you. We've got to see what the corpse has in his fists. . . ."

Two minutes later, Ben Todd softly reopened

the door. He leaned his long length against one side. Sarah leaned against the other. Ben Todd whispered: "Theodore's coming. Sarah, you can't keep . . ."

"Hush!" commanded Sarah and opened her square hand. For a moment, she and Ben Todd stared down at the thing which lay on her extended palm, stared at the length of thin black thread, stared at the five black beads strung upon the thread.

"Evidence," whispered Ben Todd. "Evidence found in a dead man's grip! Sarah, it ain't right to double-cross the cops, and it ain't safe. Sarah, you've got to—"

"Careless," muttered Sarah, staring at the black beads. "Very careless of Lily. I noticed the trimming on her shoulder was snagged."

Running footsteps sounded. Sarah's fist closed, hiding black beads. Theodore Barnes appeared, puffing, his parchment-white face mottled.

"The police—!" he gasped.

"Will be here any minute," finished Sarah. "Good-day, Mr. Barnes. . . ."

"Madam!" protested Theodore Barnes. "The police will want to question you!"

"The police," interrupted Sarah, hoarsely, "can question me at my office. I'm Sarah Watson, private detective. This is my assistant. We came here to offer you our services in connection with the recovery of the Barnes stamp. . . ."

"Ah!" gasped Theodore Barnes, grasping Sarah's arm. "The Barnes stamp! Don't go. We must discuss this. . . ."

"Mr. Barnes," countered Sarah, "there is a dead man here—a dead man who came to discuss the Barnes stamp. . . ."

Sarah broke off, shook Mr. Theodore Barnes's thin fingers from her arm and pointed a stubby finger at the desk.

"There, Mr. Barnes," she said, "is something I should like to discuss—that little piece of white cloth caught on the side of the desk there. Somebody caught a garment there on that splinter recently, Mr. Barnes, while leaning over that

desk. There's a piece like that torn from the hem of your step-sister's apron, Mr. Barnes."

Mr. Barnes bent over the small fragment of white cloth, his face ashen. He said: "Lily! Poor Lily! But, of course, she caught it there when she discovered the body, when she leaned over the desk and looked . . ."

"That," said Sarah grimly, "is what she will tell the police, at least. Drat it! I'd forgot the police. Come on, Ben Todd. We're going."

Sarah stalked out the front door of the ivy-covered Barnes mansion and surveyed the road from beneath grizzled brows.

"No cops yet," she sighed. "You find Lily, Ben Todd. I'm going around back. . . ."

Sarah clattered down the steps with undignified speed and rounded the house. Three minutes later, she came back, breathing rather heavily, to find Ben Todd lounging in the front seat of her car. Ben Todd said: "Lily's disappeared. There's a squad car coming down the road, fast. I'll bet my nonexistent salary that our friend, Sergeant O'Reilly, is in it. If he spots this heap . . ."

Sarah charged into the heap like a battering ram. The heap swept down the right curve of the drive as the police car swept up the left. Ben Todd said: "Well, there goes your last chance to turn over those beads. You never had a case yet, you old harridan, that you didn't double-cross somebody, but when you begin double-crossing the cops, old girl, you're in danger."

"At the present moment," growled Sarah, "we're both in danger. Shut up, Let me think!"

Ben Todd subsided. The old car rattled on, one block, two blocks, making audible speed. Ben Todd sat stiffly, his eyes on Sarah. Sarah's driving technique was growing momentarily more erratic. Sarah's eyes seemed more interested in the reflector above her than the road ahead.

The car hurtled a corner, narrowly missed a curb. "Bennie!" screamed Sarah, above the rattle of speed. "I've made up my mind. The thing to do is take the passenger we got in the back seat straight to the police. . . ."

A figure rose up from the dimness of the car's rear. A knife flashed in that dimness, flashed in a swooping arc toward Sarah's broad back.

Ben Todd twisted, flung himself. Sarah yelled: "Ouch!" Ben Todd's fingers closed over the thin hand holding the knife point between Sarah's shoulder blades.

Sarah said: "Relax, Lily Devlin, and rest yourself. Bennie, don't hurt her. I've changed my mind. We ain't taking her to the cops. Not yet."

Lily Devlin collapsed soundlessly in a corner of the rear seat. Ben Todd remained rigid, half over the back of his seat, staring down at the brown wooden handle of the knife he had taken from Lily Devlin's hand.

Sarah said: "Lily, where did you get that knife?"

"In the kitchen," answered Lily Devlin, and sobbed.

"How many knives like that did you have in your kitchen, Lily?"

"Three. We had four once, all alike, a set, but I gave one to Sylvester's housekeeper. . . ."

"Three?" said Sarah, putting on speed. "One in the dead man. One almost in me. That leaves one—"

"No," Lily Devlin objected. "The third is gone. It was gone when I ran into the kitchen to get one before I hid in your car. I didn't mean to kill you, Mrs. Watson. Mrs. Watson, the police mustn't get me. The police will believe I killed that awful man. They'll believe—Mrs. Watson, I didn't tear that piece out of my apron when I looked at the dead man. I tore it in the kitchen early this morning. But the police will hear all about me and the stamp and the money Theodore owes me for the stamp . . ."

"Lily," said Sarah, grimly, "you're talking too much. You must never talk too much to the driver of a speeding car."

Ten minutes later, Sarah Watson sailed into her office with Ben Todd and Lily Devlin in her wake.

"Lily," said Sarah, pointing, "sit there. Bennie, stand behind her. Now, Lily. This money you say Theodore owes you—how much?"

"Thirty thousand," moaned Lily Devlin, twisting her hands. "Thirty thousand—all I had. He borrowed it years ago, when he bought the stamp they call the Barnes stamp now. Since then, everything has gone so he could keep that stamp. The house is mortgaged. The servants are gone. And no money for me—only worry and work. I threatened to sue Theodore. He wrote out a paper, promising to sell the Barnes stamp and give me the money. I knew it was a trick to stave me off. I refused to accept the paper until he'd signed it before witnesses. I called in his brother, Sylvester, and Sylvester's housekeeper, and Theodore signed and I knew as he signed that he still thought the paper would do me no good. But I took the paper to a lawyer and the lawyer swore it would stand in court and I went back and told Theodore the paper was legal and he'd have to sell the Barnes stamp and—"

"And," interrupted Sarah, "the next day, the Barnes stamp was stolen out of your step-brother's safe?"

"Yes!" gasped Lily Devlin. "How could you know?"

"I know lots," claimed Sarah, emphatically. "And I guess more. Now, when you told Theodore he'd signed away his precious stamp, he raged, of course, and tore his hair. Wait! That reminds me. Tell me, does your step-brother always sleep in his hair?"

"His—?"

"His toupee," insisted Sarah, firmly. "He had it on when he appeared in his nightshirt at the top of the stairs. I wondered if he slept in it?"

Lily Devlin looked up at Ben Todd as though for help. Ben Todd returned the look coldly. He said: "I'd advise you to answer. I'd advise you to answer all questions, Miss Devlin—even embarrassing questions."

"Lily," rasped Sarah, leaning forward and rapping Lily Devlin's whitened knuckles with stubby finger tips, "Lily, we'll forget the toupee.

Just tell me this, Lily—how did the dead man happen to have a hank of black beads off your dress clutched in his dead hand? There, there! Put your head down on your chest, Lily, way down. Bennie, get her some water."

Lily Devlin opened her sharp, black eyes. Sarah wiped trickles of water from Lily's chin. Sarah said: "Lily, you're in a bad fix. You need the services of a first-rate, intelligent, energetic private detective. . . ."

"Sarah," said Ben Todd. "Listen. This dame—"

"Quiet!" barked Sarah. "A client is never a dame."

"Client! By hell, Sarah, you can't take this woman's case! She's guilty!"

"Maybe," said Sarah. "But she means money to us. You hustle her out of here and around to the hotel, young feller, before the cops get any smart ideas about coming here to find her. Move, you long-legged imbecile! Move!"

Sarah Watson sat alone in her dusty office, the roll top desk open before her. The door flew wide. Ben Todd charged in. "Mrs. Watson," he began, belligerently, "I—"

"I know," replied Sarah, grimly. "You quit. We never had a case yet that you didn't quit."

Ben Tod shuffled his feet. He said: "But look, old girl! You've already offered your services to Theodore Barnes. Now, even if this Devlin dame ain't guilty, how in hell can you reconcile working for Theodore and at the same time giving your services to Theodore's step-sister?"

"Giving!" barked Sarah. "I ain't giving my services to anybody. As for offering our services to Theodore—" Sarah picked up the phone and jiggled the hook.

A few moments later, Sarah hung up her receiver and banged down the phone.

"Well," she said, peering under knotted brows at Ben Todd, "That's that. Theodore is willing to pay a thousand for his stamp, over and above what the insurance company will give. Ben Todd, put on your hat. We've got two

clients now, but we could use a third. There's still Sylvester. . . ."

Ben Todd took his head in his hands and groaned.

Sarah said: "Sylvester is mixed up in the Barnes stamp case, somehow, Ben Todd, and I mean to know how. Sylvester Barnes has been hankering after that stamp for years. Sylvester Barnes has one of those brown, wooden-handled knives. We're going to see Sylvester, Bennie, before some insurance company bloodhound gets the same sniff I've got."

Sarah's car rattled once more down elegant Fairview Drive. It chugged past the sagging gates of Theodore Barnes' estate and went on.

"Bennie," explained Sarah, "while you were putting Lily Devlin to bed at the hotel, O'Reilly barged into the office. O'Reilly wanted information. I found out that the corpse in Theodore's study was a gent known in certain circles as Slick Johnny Johns. Slick Johnny was a second-story man out of work. He had a sizable bump on his head, O'Reilly said—a bump the cops are sure knocked him unconscious before he got the knife. O'Reilly also told me that—"

"Wait!" said Ben Todd. "What did you tell O'Reilly?"

"Nothing," snapped Sarah. "Do you think I'm a fool?"

Sarah swept the car into the well-kept grounds of Sylvester Barnes. She drove in under an imposing porte-cochère and slowed and suddenly stepped on the gas and sent the car charging toward the rear, and braked.

The back door opened. A buxom Negress stood framed in light. Sarah jumped out of the car. She stalked slowly toward the door, playing the light of a flash on the ground before her as she went.

"Good evening," she said to the woman in the door, and drew from her capacious purse a shining, wooden-handled knife.

The black woman's eyes rolled down toward the knife. Sarah said:

"I'm representing the Acme Cutlery Company. I understand you have in your kitchen a knife just like this, one of a set of four . . . ?"

"Ain't got it in my kitchen now," said the Negress, backing a little. "Somebody took that knife clean away."

"When?" demanded Sarah. "When did they take it?"

"Dunno," replied the servant. "Missed it tonight."

"Good evening," said Sarah. "And thanks."

Thirty seconds later, Sarah's car shot under the porte-cochère again and braked at the front door of the same house. Sarah mounted the steps and placed an invincible finger upon the bell. The door opened. A massive butler stood in the light.

Sarah said: "Good evening. We represent Mr. Theodore Barnes. We want to see Sylvester Barnes and we want to see him damn' quick."

The butler's eyes goggled at the gun in Sarah's hand. He made a feeble motion with his thick arm.

Sarah said: "Come on in, Bennie. We're invited," and stalked down the wide hall toward an open door from which voices came.

A replica of Mr. Theodore Barnes rose from behind a desk as Sarah entered. The replica was in much better condition than Theodore. The network of wrinkles was absent and the black hair looked real.

"Mr. Sylvester Barnes?" said Sarah "I'm Sarah Watson. This is my assistant, Ben Todd. Your brother, Theodore, has engaged us to find his stamp. We've come to find it. . . ."

Sarah stopped abruptly, her grizzled brows knotted as she peered down at the figure of another man, lounging in a chair in the shadows beyond the desk. As Sarah stared, the figure rose and waved a half-empty glass.

"Madam!" exclaimed the figure, "Madam Watson! A pleasure!"

"Humph!" snorted Sarah. "A bloodhound! You're here on insurance company business, of course, John Rankin? You're here with your nose to the Barnes stamp scent?"

John Rankin waved his glass vaguely, and sat down. He said: "The only scent in my nostrils at

the moment is the scent of good liquor. I've been enjoying said scent for the past two hours. Mr. Sylvester Barnes and I are old cronies."

Sarah grunted. She took a chair uninvited. "John Rankin," she said. "How many times during those two hours has your old crony left you, and how long each time?"

John Rankin looked toward Sylvester Barnes and closed an eye. He said: "Crazy! Crazy as a bat out of hell!".

"Maybe," agreed Sarah ominously, shaking a stubby finger under John Rankin's nose. "Suppose you answer my question, bloodhound, before I get violent."

John Rankin put down his glass. He said: "Mr. Barnes has been in this room with me every minute for the last two hours—well, practically every minute. Say, what is this, anyway, you old amateur dick?"

"This, Mr. Sylvester Barnes," explained Sarah, "needs an alibi. There's a dead man right next door, at Theodore's house, a dead man with a knife in his heart, a dead man who called on Theodore to talk to him about the stolen Barnes stamp. . . ."

John Rankin lunged out of his chair. He charged for the door. Sarah chuckled dryly as the door banged. She swung around and pierced Sylvester Barnes with her gaze.

"Mr. Barnes," she called, grimly, opening her black handbag, "Mr. Barnes, look at this!"

Sylvester Barnes made a strange sound. He put his palms on the desk and hoisted himself up out of his chair. He said: "That—that knife!"

"Exactly," agreed Sarah, drawing the wooden-handled knife out of her bag and holding it up. "Sylvester Barnes," she said, "where is the Barnes stamp?"

Sylvester Barnes sat down, suddenly. He sat down with a thump, and he clenched his hands before him.

"It's preposterous!" he said, in a shaking voice. "My brother knows' better than to try to intimidate me."

"Your brother may know better," said Sarah, "but we don't. Ben Todd, you got your gun covering Sylvester?"

Ben Todd did not answer. Sarah turned in her chair, her hand grasping the knife. Ben Todd was struggling in the grip of the gargantuan butler. Ben Todd's mouth was covered by one of the butler's expansive palms.

Sarah rose, took a step forward. At the same moment, Sylvester Barnes flung himself over the desk, gripped Sarah's right wrist and twisted. The knife clattered to the desk. Sarah wrenched the hurt wrist free and used it to propel a fist at Sylvester Barnes's jaw. Barnes dodged. The force of the blow carried Sarah sprawling half over the desk, hat askew, arms flailing.

Sarah made a wild dive at Sylvester. Sarah's fingers contacted Sylvester's throat, slipped down, scratching, and closed.

Sarah hoisted Sylvester's meager person half over the desk, got back on her own feet and yanked her prey the balance of the way. Still gripping him, she wheeled and surveyed the butler and Ben Todd, and an unholy, totally unfeminine light of glee danced in her gray eyes as she looked.

Ben Todd's mouth was no longer gagged by the butler's broad palm. Ben Todd's mouth was open and grinning the insane grin of battling youth. Ben was battling with a mountain, but even a mountain will collapse if enough dynamite is exploded at strategic points. Ben Todd was intensely and joyously engaged in exploding that dynamite.

As Sarah watched, the last charge of explosive went off against the butler's jaw. The butler fell down. He exhibited no inclination to rise. Sarah sighed gustily. She took a firmer grip on Mr. Sylvester Barnes's throat.

"Good work, Bennie!" she cried. "I'll hold Sylvester. You go out to the black woman in the kitchen. Tell her you represent the Ajax Rope Company. . . ."

Ben Todd was on his way. Sarah turned to Sylvester Barnes and stared into his popping black eyes.

"Sylvester," she said, "I know things. I know that you and Theodore cooked up the theft of the Barnes stamp so that Theodore would have the insurance money to pay off his step-sister and still have the stamp. . . ."

Sylvester Barnes made noises in his throat. The noises were unintelligible but the expression in Sylvester's rather slippery black eyes seemed to satisfy Sarah.

"Yes," she continued, complacently, "I know things. I know about Slick Johnny Johns, the crooked gent your brother hired to come over here and steal back the Barnes stamp after you'd refused to return it. I know about Slick Johnny and I know about the knife in Slick Johnny's chest. I know it's the same knife that you took out of your kitchen before you went after Slick Johnny. . . ."

Sarah released some of the pressure of her fingers from Sylvester Barnes's throat. She waited for him to speak.

"S'help me!" gulped Mr. Barnes. "I never used that knife. I've got it yet. It's in my safe. I hid it there . . . !"

Ben Todd loped into the room with loops of rope over his arm. He said: "Black gal's safe in the kitchen closet. Nobody else in the house."

"Good," said Sarah, complacently, without taking her eyes from Sylvester Barnes. "You tie up the butler, Bennie. Sylvester is going to open his safe for me now," and Sarah cast the wooden-handled knife she had been holding to the desk and placed the business end of her gun against Sylvester's shrinking middle.

Sylvester opened the safe. He pointed a shaking finger at a wooden-handled knife which lay on the shelf. He said: "There! If the man who came here and stole that stamp has a knife in him, I didn't put it there. That's the knife I took with me. . . ."

"Maybe," admitted Sarah, thoughtfully. "On the other hand, that's only the third knife accounted for, Mr. Barnes, and there were four to the set. . . ."

Sarah's voice trailed off. She poked her gun a little deeper into Mr. Barnes and pointed at a large tin box which stood on the top shelf of Mr. Barnes's safe.

"That?" she said. "Is there cash in there?"

Sylvester Barnes gulped. He nodded assent.

"How much?" demanded Sarah.

"Forty thousand. I had it ready to pay Theodore for the stamp. I was willing to pay forty. I never wanted to get involved in this crooked deal. . . ."

"You are involved in it," reminded Sarah. "Deep. Forty thousand, eh? I'll take your case, Mr. Barnes. I'll take your case."

"What?"

"I'll take your case," said Sarah, firmly. "I'll also take the cash, Mr. Barnes—all the cash."

"You can't! This is blackmail! This is robbery! This is a hold-up, a hold-up with weapons. I'll have the police on you! I'll have—"

"You'll carry that tin box to the desk," said Sarah, "and I'll take the cash. After I take the cash, I'll take the stamp, the Barnes stamp, which you took back from Slick Johnny Johns after your brother had hired him to take it away from you. . . ."

Sylvester Barnes cried out in agony, his sliding eyes moving from Sarah's gun to Sarah's implacable face.

"No!" he screamed. "Take the money! Take all of it! But you can't have the stamp. No! You can't have it. I—I haven't got it! I haven't got the Barnes stamp, I tell you. . . ."

"You've got the Barnes stamp," insisted Sarah, "somewhere in that desk. I saw your eyes slide there when I mentioned the stamp. March! I wouldn't like to shoot you dead, Mr. Barnes, but after all, you may go to the chair, anyway, for Slick Johnny Johns's murder, you know."

Sylvester Barnes moved slowly to the desk. He opened the top drawer of the desk. He lifted with trembling fingers a small, transparent envelope. He held the envelope for a moment, gazing down at the grimy blue stamp it covered. . . .

"Thanks," said Sarah, hoarsely, and plucked the Barnes stamp from his hands.

Sarah dropped the glassine-covered stamp into her bag. She said: "Get busy, Ben Todd, and tie up Sylvester. I need my hands free to take the forty thousand dollars out of the box."

Ben Todd got busy. He was breathing heavily and his eyes were grim as they darted from the ropes he was knotting to the soiled bills Sarah was cramming from the tin box into her purse.

Ben Todd knotted the last knot. He dragged Sylvester Barnes, not too gently, toward the spot on the carpet where the butler lay. Sarah Watson clicked shut the maw of her black purse. She said, briskly: "Handle Mr. Sylvester Barnes nice, Bennie. He's a client, you know."

Ben Todd dropped Mr. Barnes with a thud. He strode toward the desk and regarded Sarah with baleful eyes.

"Sarah," he said, through thinned lips. "Put that money back where you got it and put it back quick. I'll stand for assorted murderers for clients but I'll be damned if I'll stand for blackmail and downright theft—"

"You'll stand what I tell you to stand," growled Sarah grimly, "until this case is closed." She put her hand purposefully upon the gun which she had laid on the desk.

Ben Todd stepped back. Sarah took the gun in her left hand and held it there. She used her right hand to lift the French phone from Sylvester Barnes's desk.

"Gotham Hotel?" she barked, a few moments later. "Give me room 301. Lily? Don't be scared. It's me. I want you to meet me at Theodore's house, Lily, in ten minutes. Take a cab and stop at the corner. I'll be waiting for you. . . ."

Sarah hung up. She stared for a moment at the freckles which stood out very clearly on the unwonted pallor of Ben Todd's face. Ben Todd's mouth worked. He said:

"You! You damned old— You're going to round out your double-crossing now by selling Lily Devlin to the cops? You're going to lead her into that house next door—that house you know is full of cops! Listen to me. I didn't want you to take that woman's case, but you took it. You took it and I'm not going to see you double-cross her now. . . ."

"You're not going to see me do anything," said Sarah, placidly. "You're going to stay right here, young feller, and keep an eye on Sylvester, while I give O'Reilly the goods on the murderer of Slick Johnny Johns."

Ten minutes later, Sarah Watson threw open the front door of the Theodore Barnes residence and stalked in, dragging with her a white-faced, shrinking woman as she went.

A cop stopped leaning against the wall and started forward. Sarah said:

"'Lo, Tim! O'Reilly here?"

The cop jerked a fat thumb toward the rear.

Sarah asked: "John Rankin, the insurance dick, with him?"

Tim nodded.

Sarah snapped: "Good!"

Tim said: "Mr. Theodore Barnes is in there, too," and his eyes played speculatively over the woman Sarah was gripping by the arm.

Sarah ordered: "Get O'Reilly out here. Whisper I've got the killer for him and he'll come fast."

The cop sprinted. Lily Devlin sagged against Sarah. Sarah muttered something to her and straightened her hat. O'Reilly appeared, big arms swinging.

Sarah said, curtly: "Good! Stay here, O'Reilly. I'm going in with John Rankin and Theodore Barnes."

O'Reilly gasped. "But—but, by thunder, woman, you've got her!"

Sarah said: "Maybe you'd better send a cop around to the back of the house and have him parked near the study window. He can hide in the ivy vines that cover the house back there. Maybe you'd better be ready yourself, O'Reilly, outside the study door. There were four wooden-handled knives in that set, and I've only accounted for three. . . ."

O'Reilly stepped back, jaw slack, at this cryp-tic utterance. Sarah smiled grimly and swept by him and down the hall to the study door.

Theodore Barnes sat in an easy chair with his back to the desk where the dead man had sat not so long before. Theodore Barnes was smoking a cigarette in a long, amber holder. He took the holder out of his mouth and dropped it as Sarah entered with Lily Devlin in tow.

The other man in the room rose from his seat as she entered, and sat down again, reaching for his half-empty glass as he sat.

Sarah swept past them both. She placed Lily Devlin on a divan near a window. She took her own post behind the divan and focused her piercing gaze on Theodore Barnes.

"Theodore Barnes," she began, "I'm glad the insurance bloodhound is here. He'll make a good witness to the fact that I've recovered the Barnes stamp."

Theodore Barnes sprang from his chair. He slipped on the cigarette-holder which lay in his path and brought up leaning against the desk.

Sarah said complacently: "Yes, Mr. Rankin will make a good witness that I've returned the Barnes stamp to you and that I'm entitled to the insurance company's reward. . . ."

"It's impossible!" shouted Theodore Barnes. "She hasn't got it! She can't have it!"

"I have it," insisted Sarah. "Here it is!"

"Glory!" shouted John Rankin, handing over the stamp Sarah held extended. "Glory! She's done it. The Barnes stamp. She's got it!"

"I've got a good nose, too," said Sarah, com-placently, "and I don't spoil it with the fumes of liquor. Show the stamp to Mr. Theodore Barnes, John Rankin."

"The Barnes stamp!" breathed Theodore Barnes. "It is! Let me have it. It's mine. Give it to me. Give . . . !"

Sarah reached out a firm hand, laid it on Theodore's wrist and extracted from his clutch-ing fingers the Barnes stamp.

"Mr. Barnes," she ordered: "Sit down! There, behind the desk. Don't hesitate, Mr. Barnes. The dead man who sat there is gone. Now, Mr. Barnes!

I have with me thirty thousand dollars cash. When you have made out a receipt for that sum in favor of your brother, Sylvester, in exchange for the Barnes stamp, I'll hand you—"

"You'll hand me my stamp!" screeched Theodore Barnes. "I won't sell my stamp. Give it to me. It's mine. I'll have you ejected for your presumption. I'll have you ejected for your high-handed methods. . . ."

"My high-handed methods recovered the stamp," purred Sarah, calmly.

"I won't sell it!" shouted Theodore Barnes. "It's mine. I never meant to sell it. Give it to me."

"Lily," said Sarah, without taking her eyes from Theodore Barnes, "Lily, hand over to me the paper your step-brother signed, the paper promising to sell the Barnes stamp, the very legal paper, Lily. . . ."

Sarah broke off, snatched the paper which Lily extended and waved it under Theodore's nose.

"You'll be getting off easy," said Sarah. "There might be certain facts I could reveal, Theodore—facts the insurance company would be intensely interested in—facts about certain little plans made by you and your brother?"

Theodore Barnes reached for a pen. Sarah opened her handbag and began to count soiled bills. As she counted, her eyes darted from the bills to Theodore Barnes, hunched over his writing.

Theodore Barnes laid down his pen. Sarah grasped the paper he had written, read it carefully, waved it in the air to dry. She picked up the thick wad of bills she had counted out.

Theodore reached for the bills. Sarah said:

"Come get your money, Lily. I usually charge ten percent for my services, but I've only taken a grand off the thirty thousand in your case, Lily, because I like to see justice done. And now, I'll just step over to Sylvester's and deliver the receipt for the money and the Barnes stamp. . . ."

Theodore Barnes sprang. Something shining flashed in his rising hand. Sarah fell sidewise

against him, her stubby fingers clutching. Lily Devlin uttered a little cry and slid down to the floor. The knife flashed through the spot where Lily had stood a moment before. Sarah's hands reached after the knife.

"Help me, Rankin, you boozy bloodhound," shouted Sarah, and managed to deliver a wallop to the struggling Theodore. "Help!"

The door burst open. The window swung in. Sarah fell back as O'Reilly's big paw wrenched the knife from Theodore's hand and flung it far. Theodore Barnes collapsed, suddenly, in the chair, his face ashen.

"I don't know what possessed me," he muttered, his quick, dark eyes darting from O'Reilly to Sarah to the cop who had come through the window. "Just for a moment, I went wild—seeing the stamp go out of my possession drove me frantic. I didn't mean to hurt anyone. I apologize, humbly. I apologize to you, Mrs. Watson. I apologize to everyone. I'll be myself in a minute. I—"

There was silence for a moment, except for the heavy breathing of O'Reilly. Theodore Barnes lifted his head. He said: "You all understand, I'm sure. The strain of all of this. Ah, Mrs. Watson, of course I must reimburse you for recovering the Barnes stamp. The special thousand dollar reward I offered still holds, of course—"

"Keep it," said Sarah hoarsely. "You'll need it—for lawyers. I don't take fees from murderers. . . ."

O'Reilly yelped. He pounced on the cringing figure behind the desk. Sarah said, thoughtfully: "Of course, I might have taken your thousand, Theodore, if you hadn't been such a damn mean murderer—a murderer that put a knife into a man already unconscious. . . . Yes, Theodore, your brother Sylvester knocked him unconscious when he took the Barnes stamp away. . . ."

"Stop her!" shouted Theodore Barnes. "She doesn't know what she's talking about. She can't prove it. Nobody can prove it. Nobody saw me!"

"I saw you," roared Sarah, "in my mind's eye."

"She's crazy," screamed Theodore Barnes. "John Rankin, say she's crazy! How could I have killed that man? My sister knows I never came down the stairs from my room. My sister knows I was sleeping."

"Theodore," said Sarah, "do you usually sleep with your toupee on straight?"

"Toupee? Madam, what do you mean? You're mad, woman, mad! I couldn't have killed him. I never left my room."

Sarah stooped. Her square-tipped fingers slid into the cuff of Theodore Barnes' dressing gown sleeve. She held up a leaf. She said: "This is the season when the ivy falls, Theodore. You should have remembered that when you climbed down the back of the house."

Theodore Barnes stared at the leaf. He said: "I'm not guilty. The police know I'm not guilty. The police know the corpse had a strand of black beads in its hand, black beads that came from my sister's gown."

"Thank you, Theodore," said Sarah, mildly. "That's what I've been waiting for. The police didn't find the black beads, Theodore, because I found them first. Only two people knew that those black beads were there. Me—and the murderer. Take him, O'Reilly. He has confessed."

———

The Watson antique chugged down elegant Fairview Drive. Sarah said: "Well, Bennie, a good night's work, if I say so myself. Everybody pleased. Sylvester pleased, because he's got the Barnes stamp, and it only cost him the forty grand he was willing to pay, plus a little discomfort. Sylvester's black housekeeper pleased because you let her out of her closet and I slipped her five. Lily Devlin pleased because she's got back her thirty thousand and nobody thinks she did murder to get it. O'Reilly pleased because he's got the murderer and the murderer has confessed. Ben Todd pleased because he's proved again that Sarah Watson is a double-crossing, thieving old—"

"Reprobate," supplied Ben Todd and laughed. "You, Sarah, how about you? You pleased, too, old girl?"

"Um," said Sarah, stepping on the gas. "Let's see. Ten thousand from Sylvester, as commission for negotiating the difficult and delicate transfer of the Barnes stamp. One thousand from Lily for getting her money from Theodore. Three thousand from the insurance company for recovering the stolen stamp. Ten and one and three is fourteen, and fourteen divided by two is seven. Well, yes, Bennie, I am pleased. Moderately pleased!"

RAT RUNAROUND

Roger Torrey

SINCE REPUTATIONS AND LINGERING literary fame usually depend on the publication of novels, not short stories, it is perhaps understandable that Roger Torrey (1901–1946) has been largely forgotten, though he was one of the most prolific, gifted, and popular pulp writers of his era. In a career that lasted only a little more than thirteen years, he produced about 280 stories and novellas, mainly for the best magazines of the time, including *Black Mask*, which published his first story, "Police Business," in its January 1933 issue, and 49 others.

As prodigious as his written output was, his alcoholic intake dwarfed it, becoming legendary even in the hard-drinking world of pulp writers. He met Helen, his second wife, also an alcoholic, in a bar, and she quickly moved into his hotel room, where they established a system of producing fiction that worked for them. He sat at one desk, she at another, with a bottle of booze nearby. The first person to finish the story on which they were working was permitted to drink while the other had to finish the story before being allowed to have a nip. He was only forty-five when he died of alcohol poisoning.

His only novel, *42 Days for Murder*, was published by the un-prestigious house of Hillman-Curl in 1938. Torrey wrote fourteen stories featuring Marge Chalmers and Pat McCarthy, all of which were published in *Black Mask*. McCarthy is an ex-cop who opens his own detective agency, and Chalmers, his sidekick, more often than not keeps him out of trouble while helping to solve the case.

"Rat Runaround" was originally published in the May 1937 issue of *Black Mask*.

Rat Runaround

ROGER TORREY

McCARTHY WAS BEHIND HIS DESK and Marge Chalmers sat at the side. Cantwell stood in front of the desk. He was tall and thin and his long face showed dull pallor. His skin wasn't white but seemed to have no color at all. His hair was a dull mousy brown and it straggled over his eyes, giving him a worried look that his whiny voice upheld.

He said, "Now Mr. McCarthy. It's like I'm telling you. I'm scared. I'm plain scared."

He sounded as though this were the truth. McCarthy leaned comfortably back in his chair and said, "I've heard stories and stories. You got one. One pip. If I ever heard a dirty double-crossing tramp talk, I've heard one now. You get the hell out of this office and be thankful I don't throw you out. Scram, boy, scram."

Marge looked sorrowful and shook her blond head. She said, "Now, Pat! Please!" in a low, sad voice.

Cantwell looked hopeless. "I want to hire a body-guard. You got an agency, ain't you? I've—I can get money. I'm scared, I tell you."

McCarthy winked at Marge. He did it openly, making no attempt at concealing it from the long, lean Cantwell. He yawned, said, "I do all my body-guard work for money." He changed his voice, snapped out:

"Listen, Cantwell. I'll bet you put in five years in the pen and you should have got fifty and done every minute of it. You're out, as far as

I'm concerned. Out cold, like last January. You smell like stir to me and I don't like the smell. Now scram, boy. I'm losing my patience."

Cantwell didn't move from the desk. He twisted a very new, very cheap cap in his hands, said, "Listen! I can get money. Lots of money." He spoke slowly, distinctly, and his eyes pleaded for belief. "I'll be paid for every day I put in stir. I need help but I'll pay for it and pay big."

McCarthy said, "I tell you to get out," and got up from his chair. But he leaned across the desk and said very softly and smoothly:

"What d'ya mean big? What does big mean?"

"Anything you say. You get me by for two weeks and you can name your score."

"All right. Two weeks for two thousand. How's that?"

Cantwell dropped his cap, stooped, and picked it up. His face showed a flush not caused by the bending.

He said, "That's fine. Just fine."

He sounded relieved and his muddy brown eyes cleared slightly. He tried a smile, switched it off and said again, "Just fine."

McCarthy said, "In advance."

"I can get it," Cantwell said hurriedly, "but not for two weeks."

McCarthy shrugged and said to Marge, "He shouldn't have gone to jail. It should have been the goofy house. I should work for conversation."

256

Marge shook her head again. She said, "But Pat! Maybe he's really in danger."

"What of it? He's a no-good double-crossing rat by his own admission and I hope to God he is in danger."

He spoke as if Cantwell weren't in the room, and the tall thin man said desperately, "Oh, hell, Shylock! It's a cut on a hundred and twenty grand. How's that? Worth two weeks' time?"

McCarthy laughed, again spoke to Marge. "You heard his yarn. There were three of them, Cantwell, Plansky, and Thomes. They killed a bank messenger while they were heisting him and they got caught three days later. Cantwell turned State's evidence and got off with a lousy five years. Thomes got hung. Plansky got twenty to life. They only got sixteen hundred on the job. And now he makes talk about a hundred and twenty grand."

He looked at Cantwell then, tapped his forehead with a finger, said, "You're stir screwy, guy. Now get the hell out of here before I heave you out."

A patch of red showed in Cantwell's two cheeks. He lowered his voice and asked, "You ever hear of Herman Wansner?"

"Yeah. He died two years ago."

"I know that. Did you know he was a fence?"

"I heard it."

"Did you know he was robbed the night of the same day we pulled the bank job?"

"And I suppose you robbed him?"

"Plansky, Thomes, and me did. That's the hundred and twenty grand."

McCarthy asked if this was in cash and he sounded skeptical and winked at Marge again. But he sat back down in his chair.

Cantwell said, blurting the words out in haste: "It's as good. It's unregistered bonds and unset stones and it's as good as money in the bank. Wansner never reported the loss because he'd have had to explain where he got the stuff and it was all hotter than a forty-five. We stashed it and I can't get it now."

"Why not?" McCarthy's voice was less skeptical and his light blue eyes were round and hard. His face was long, high cheek-boned and his beard made dark shadow on his jowls. He looked more than a little like an Irish priest and more than a little predatory at the same time.

Cantwell, encouraged by this changed attitude, hurried on with: "The bonds were from a bank job in St. Louis. The stones came from three different jobs in the East. I was in on the stones with Thomes and Plansky in the first place and we shoved 'em with Wansner. But they weren't in the bank job. I pulled that with Frankie Giles. We turned the bonds to Wansner but he never had time to sell them before Plansky and Thomes and I got them and the rocks. You get the idea; we sold them to him and then stole 'em back."

McCarthy said to Marge: "A swell boy, this. I bet his mother never could keep a dime in the house."

Marge was listening intently to Cantwell. She shook her head impatiently at McCarthy, said to Cantwell: "But I don't believe I understand, Mr. Cantwell. Why can't you get these bonds and unset stones now? Didn't you say you hid them?"

Cantwell said patiently, "That's it. Frankie Giles is in town. He knows I know where the stuff is. If I go to my plant, he'd be watching me. He'd take the bonds and the stones both. He knows I robbed Wansner and that I can't go to the police for help."

McCarthy said, "Take him with you and cut him in, if you're afraid of him."

Cantwell took the edge of his right hand and drew it across his throat. "You don't know Frankie Giles. He's bad, and I've lost my guts."

McCarthy laughed harshly and said: "You're in a bad way. Let's figure this out. I can use the dough." He said to Marge, "Hon, you run along and come back in an hour or so and we'll have some lunch. I want to talk this over with pally, here."

Marge looked troubled and shook her head. She said, "It sounds like trouble to me and it sounds like crooked trouble. I don't like it, Pat."

McCarthy walked to the door with her, patting her on the shoulder. He said, "Don't fret, hon," and under his breath, "I'm going to throw a curve on this. It'll work out, hon. You watch."

Marge Chalmers said she intended to do just that. She also said that Pat McCarthy was the kind of fool that needed someone to watch over him and that she seemed to have fallen heir to this job. She sounded a little bitter about this.

An hour later McCarthy said to Cantwell, "Then it's a bet and we'll play it that way."

He looked up, saw Cantwell with his head cocked in a listening position. Cantwell said, in a worried, frightened tone: "Mr. McCarthy, that sounds to me like somebody in the hall."

"What of it? People go back and forth all the time."

"But it sounds like they stopped outside the door."

McCarthy said: "You got the horrors, guy," but went to the outer door. He half turned as he opened it, said:

"I think you're—"

He saw Cantwell's startled face and turned back to the door just as something struck him above the ear. He went to his knees and managed to tip his head in time to see the next blow coming and he tried to dodge this. He knew the attempt was hopeless, even as he did.

Some time later he came out of his daze and saw a strange face bending over him, stayed conscious long enough to feel a needle prick his arm. As he faded back into coma he heard the rattle of excited voices.

An hour later he said, "Sapped!" in a weak voice and, hazily focusing on the room, asked, "Nurse? Hospital?"

He saw a white uniform loom over him, heard a cheerily professional voice say, "Now, Mr. McCarthy. You're not to talk. You've been injured."

"I know that."

"Steady now."

He could again feel his arm bared for the needle, and as the drowsy feeling again overcame him he mumbled, "But how in hell . . ."

"Now, now. You'll hear all about it. You just rest and . . ." The voice died away in the wave of sleep again sweeping over him.

When he next awoke he saw Marge Chalmers by the bed and as his eyes flickered open she asked anxiously, "How goes the battle? Feel better?"

The nurse, standing by the blond girl, said warningly, "Now, Miss Chalmers. He's not to talk very much and he's not to get excited. Concussion's a funny thing and Mr. McCarthy was very close to a fracture."

"Sure. I know."

McCarthy managed to lift his hand to his head and found it bandaged. His voice was both weak and querulous and his eyes were foggy from shock and morphine. He said, "What in hell happened?"

"Don't you remember, Pat?"

"Remember what?"

"Didn't you see them?"

"Who?"

Marge said regretfully, "I was hoping you'd seen them. There were two of them, according to the elevator boy."

"They got away then? That it?"

"Uh-huh! They sapped you and just walked out. I was afraid you had a fractured skull but the X-ray shows it's all right."

McCarthy watched Marge's face and blond head start in slow circles, go around and around, and gradually grow dimmer. He snapped back to consciousness with the odor of ammonia in his nostrils and the nurse, bending over him, said sharply over her shoulder to Marge:

"Now Miss Chalmers! That's enough! He can't stand excitement and talking."

Marge tiptoed toward the door and McCarthy said faintly, "Marge!"

"Yes, Pat!"

"Where's Cantwell?"

"You mustn't talk, Pat."

"Where's Cantwell?"

The nurse interrupted sharply with: "Now Mr. McCarthy. That's enough. You're not allowed to talk. Tomorrow, perhaps."

"Just one question!"

"Well . . ."

"Marge! Where's Cantwell?"

The blond girl said, "Pig-head Irish! I suppose you have to know," in a defensive voice. "I shouldn't tell you, but Cantwell's gone. The two men took him with them after they sapped you. Now you got it."

McCarthy said, "Oh hell!" and closed his eyes. He heard Marge tiptoe from the room, heard the door close, and said, "Oh, nurse!"

She came to the bed. "Now you're to sleep. What is it?"

McCarthy managed a feeble grin, said, "If a man ain't safe in the office of the private cop he's hired to protect him, where in hell *is* he safe?"

"Now you go to sleep. I shouldn't have allowed Miss Chalmers to talk with you."

"You should have tried to keep her from it if she wanted to. That girl's determined." He dropped easily back to sleep, smiling to himself, and the nurse sniffed and looked at the door and muttered:

"Blond hussy! The way she talked to him you'd think she was married to him."

Pat McCarthy patted the rakish bandage that circled his head and covered one eye, and said defensively, "Well, what the hell! Doctor said it was all right if I took it easy." He looked down at his desk, and then up to where Marge stood accusingly in the doorway.

He said, "Come on in and tell me if there's any news. Did you go to the station and tell Shannon and Costello about this screwy set-up?"

Marge said she had and that she thought both Mr. Shannon and Mr. Costello two nice men, even if policemen. And then, "They haven't found a thing yet. I—I just happened to run into something myself." She made this last admission and looked a little frightened and a little proud at the same time. McCarthy stared back at her, then snapped:

"Spit it out. What crack-brained stunt have you done now? Damn it, don't you know this is

no deal for you to play around with? Don't you know this is one of those things?"

"I thought you'd be glad I was helping, Pat." She sounded injured but her eyes didn't back up her voice. She plainly hadn't expected McCarthy to think anything of the kind. She went on with:

"I met a man named Orrie Arnold and he runs around with Frank Giles. He's from St. Louis. That's where those stolen bonds came from."

McCarthy tapped the bandage on his head and said bitterly, "So did I meet somebody that runs around with Frankie Giles. And look what it got me. You'll give that guy a miss from this time on. Get sense; when there's this kind of money involved, people like that are dangerous."

"Oh, this Orrie Arnold isn't dangerous. I've got him sold. He likes me."

"Like hell. Does he know you run around with me?"

She wrinkled her forehead and frowned. "I don't know. He didn't say anything that sounded as though he did."

"It's a cinch he knows it. Whoever sapped me must have followed Cantwell here to the office, so they'd have seen you leave here. After all, we've been running around for some little time. You lay off."

"He might say something. He liked to talk about himself."

McCarthy said seriously, "Now listen, Marge. I mean this. This is no dice. You keep away from this guy right from this minute. You hear me?"

She said, "Yes!" in a sullen voice.

"Now mind. I'm surprised that you'd take a chance with a hood like that."

"He lives at the Carlton Hotel. On Marin Street."

"That's fine. You give him a miss from now on and take in that lower lip before you fall over it. Did Shannon say whether Giles is in town?"

"No, but Orrie Arnold told me he was."

"What does Arnold look like?"

"He's nice looking. Dark. Smooth looking."

McCarthy picked up his hat, winced when

he put it on. He said, "I've got a couple things to do. You go home and I'll call you when I get through."

"Where you going?"

McCarthy looked surprised and answered as though the answer should have been known. "Calling on your boy friend, of course." He patted the bulge a gun made under his left arm. "If I figure him out as one of the guys that smacked me, I'll do my best to make sure you don't see him for some time, hon."

"Pat! You're in no shape to go out looking for trouble."

He grinned at her, said, "I ain't looking for it, hon. It's heading for me and I'm just meeting it half way. You trot on home."

McCarthy pushed Marge out of the office in front of him. On the sidewalk he said, "Home for you, hon," turned, and drove down Marin Street.

The Carlton Hotel was patronized mostly by the sporting class, and looked it. The lobby was slightly overcolored, slightly overdecorated; the bell boys wore uniforms that were just a little too swanky, were just a little too eager to serve. The four boys on the bench snapped to attention as McCarthy walked in, and he picked the first in line and beckoned him to the side and asked:

"Orrie Arnold? What's his room?"

The boy stiffened and made his face blank. He said, "You'll have to ask at the desk, sir."

He then looked down at the corner of the folded bill McCarthy held, said in the same tone:

"It's 417 and he's having a party." He turned sidewise, palmed the bill, and added, "That's right down the hall from the elevator, to your right. You can't miss it."

McCarthy said, "Thank you," and went to the elevator. On the fourth floor he waited until two other passengers for the same floor had gone down the hall and out of sight, and then took the gun from under his arm and put it in the side pocket of his coat. His face got a little whiter and his eyes got a hard glassy sheen to them. He started breathing a little faster.

He went down the hall then, peering at num-

bers as he did, and stopped at 417. He muttered to himself, "Now for it."

He crowded the door and rapped on it with his left hand, keeping the right in his pocket. He heard somebody fumble with the knob and, when the door swung open letting out a blast of sound, he put his left hand against the breast of the man who had opened it and shoved. The man, off balance, staggered back to the center of the room. McCarthy followed him a couple of steps, took the hand with the gun from his pocket, and snapped out:

"Just everybody hold tight and there won't be any trouble. I'm not fooling."

There were four men and three women in the room, and all of them except the man who had opened the door were holding glasses. All were drunk.

The man who had opened the door said, "Whassa idea?"

He was wavering on his feet and his voice was thick. He was very dark, very well dressed, but wore no coat. McCarthy looked past him to the others, said:

"Who's Arnold?"

The dark man took a staggering little step and caught his balance. He said, "Who wanssa know?"

McCarthy said, "I know now. Get your coat."

Arnold's teetering wasn't quite so apparent with this. His voice was a little surer. He focused his eyes on McCarthy with a little effort, said:

"A pinch, huh. It's a bum rap, brother."

Then his eyes showed more intelligence and he said, "Hell! You're no cop! You're—" He stopped with this, took a step back and rested his hand on a table littered with empty glasses and bottles.

McCarthy said, "Yeah, you got it. I'm McCarthy. Put on your coat and come along."

One of the women giggled and said, "Ain't we all invited?"

The man by her said, "Shut up, Babe!" and to McCarthy, "What's the idea in coming in here and putting on an act? You can't come in here and put on an act and—"

McCarthy said, "Shut up, you heel!" and tipped his gun muzzle that way. The man stared at it, grunted, "Ugh—ugh—" and moved slightly behind the woman he'd called Babe. McCarthy made motions with the gun and said:

"Stay in the clear, heel."

The Babe woman had looked at the gun as though she didn't understand what it was. Her eyes suddenly widened and she said, "Why, it's a snatch! It's a kidnap!"

McCarthy snapped, "It's no snatch!" and to Arnold, "Your coat——!"

Arnold said, "You can't get away with this," in a voice that was almost normal, and McCarthy snarled, "Can't I? Watch!"

He brought his right hand back so the gun it held rested against his hip bone, took a step ahead and swung with his left. The blow caught Arnold in the face and Arnold slammed back into the little table holding the glasses and went to the floor. The table and glasses fell on top of him. The Babe woman screamed and McCarthy said:

"Shut up."

He reached down with his left hand and got Arnold by the front of his shirt and hauled him to his feet. He cuffed him then across the face, first with the palm and then with the back of his hand, and Arnold, mind on the gun McCarthy held, took this.

Then McCarthy saw a flash of movement, stepped back, and swung the gun toward a broken-nosed man in the back of the room, and the broken-nosed man let go of the bottle he held by the neck and sullenly held his hands at shoulder height with no word from McCarthy.

McCarthy was breathing hard and noisily. His eyes were hot and glaring and his finger was tight on the trigger of the big gun he held.

He said, "You make a mistake like that again and see what happens. Get your coat, Arnold, or so help me I'll blast you out right here."

Arnold went to the closet and picked a coat. The broken-nosed one said:

"I know where to find you, you——!" to McCarthy. McCarthy said, "Snap it up, Arnold!" and to the broken nose, "And you're a fool if you come looking for me."

The Babe woman said again, "He's snatching Orrie!" in a surprised stupid voice, and the man by her said, "Shut up, kid, for Jees' sake."

McCarthy said, "That's sense. Everybody keep quiet."

He backed to the door, took the key from the lock. He said, "Now listen! I'm walking out of here with Arnold and I'll be watching this door. The first guy that sticks his face out, I'll shoot it off him."

He reached up to the wall telephone, jerked it free, and dropped it on the floor. He opened the door with his left hand, fumbled the key into the outside of the lock, and said:

"O.K., Arnold. Away we go," and to the broken-nosed man, "I *want* you to come out, you heel. I *want* a crack at you."

"You'll get one."

"I hope."

McCarthy took Arnold by the front of the coat and jerked him out after him through the door. He twisted the key in the lock, threw Arnold toward the stairs, and said:

"You're going through the lobby. You're going right. You get it?"

Arnold said he understood. He didn't sound in the least afraid, either. Rather, he sounded a little scornful and more than a little confident. They went through the lobby, McCarthy half a pace behind Arnold; McCarthy's gun, again in his side pocket, jammed against Arnold's side.

In front of the hotel McCarthy said, "Turn right, heel. My car's that way."

Arnold felt himself gun-prodded to McCarthy's battered coupé and McCarthy opened the door. Marge Chalmers, who'd followed Pat, came up and said, "I knew you'd be back, Pat. What are you going to do with him?"

Arnold said, "He's going to turn me loose

right here and now, if he's smart. I can throw my weight around in this town, don't think I can't."

McCarthy stared at Marge, then said, "As long as you're here, you can drive us. I can handle him by myself but why take chances? The beach road will be best. There isn't much traffic and if anybody hears it they'll think it's a back-fire."

He forced Arnold in beside Marge, crowded after him, and Marge kicked the motor into life.

Arnold said to Marge, "You wasn't putting anything over, tramp. I knew you were this lug's. You were so dumb about that act of yours that you were funny."

McCarthy reached across with his gun barrel and swiped it across Arnold's face. He said, in almost a placid voice:

"You ain't got long to talk, brother, but I don't even want to hear you that long. Shut up or papa clout."

They went on for ten minutes in silence. Marge drove, eyes intent on the road, but her cheeks were hot and red and the color didn't come from rouge. McCarthy watched Arnold, a half grin on his face, and the rakish bandage and this constant grin finally got to Arnold. He snapped out:

"You can't get away with this."

"You're here, ain't you? You guys got away with it with Cantwell, didn't you? You're a cinch."

"They saw me go out with you."

"I let you out of the car after I talked to you—that's my story. With the record you got, there isn't going to be any fuss made. I doubt if anybody'll say they saw you go out with me even."

Arnold argued, "The hotel people saw me go out with you," and McCarthy made the grin a little wider and more vindictive and said:

"They saw you and some other guy go out of my office building with Cantwell, too. What's the difference?"

"Cantwell ain't hurt."

McCarthy reached up and tapped the bandage on his head. He said, "I was. Plenty. I'm getting my own back. I'm turning my dog loose."

"It wasn't me that did that."

"Who did?"

"It was Bennie Schultz. The guy that was giving you the argument in the room." Arnold's voice sounded a little eager and hurried. "He's got a broken nose, Schultz has."

McCarthy said in the same indifferent tone, "O.K.! I'll get him next time. You was with him, so it's just the same to me." He watched the road from the corner of his eye, said to Marge:

"Turn on the first cross road, hon. It's O.K. any place off the highway. No houses and no traffic."

Marge twisted the battered coupé off the road and McCarthy stopped her a hundred yards up the dirt road she'd selected. He swung the door open, said to Arnold:

"Come on, guy. Might as well make it easy for me."

Arnold said, "My God! You *mean* it."

McCarthy nodded as though surprised. "It's what Cantwell got. Marge, take the car back to the highway and wait for me. This isn't going to be pretty."

Arnold stared from Marge to McCarthy but he couldn't look long away from the gun McCarthy held. He gripped the car door as though to steady himself, said:

"You *do* mean it. Why, it's murder!"

"Go on, Marge. I'll be there almost as soon as you are. Brace up, Arnold. Take it right."

"What if I tell you where Cantwell is?"

McCarthy let irritation creep into his face. He jerked Arnold away from the car door and Arnold sprawled on the ground. McCarthy snapped at Marge:

"Get going. Damn it, how many times do I have to tell you?"

"Pat, I won't let you do this. It's just cold-blooded murder."

"Get going. So help me, get going or I'll turn loose right here in front of you. Get going, I say."

Marge put the coupé in gear and drove away. McCarthy said to Arnold, and his voice was almost friendly:

"All right, guy. It won't hurt."

Arnold bleated, "So help me, I'll tell you the truth. You can check it. My God, man, don't do this."

McCarthy hesitated just the slightest. His eyes were very watchful. He said, "You was with Frankie Giles when he got the bonds in that St. Louis job, weren't you? This Schultz was along too, wasn't he?"

"I wouldn't lie to you. There was three of us besides Giles. Schultz, Cantwell, and me. We never made a cent out of the job; Cantwell and that gang of his robbed Wansner of the stuff before Wansner paid off. Then he wouldn't pay. That's one reason Frankie's so hot to get the stuff."

McCarthy thought a moment, then said with apparent frankness: "If it wasn't for Cantwell, I'd turn you loose. But he was my client and I'm working for him. I'm going through this mob of yours right in turn."

"I'll tell the truth. He's in a shack on Florence Avenue. I can't tell you the number but I can show it to you. It's the truth." McCarthy hesitated, finally said:

"Will you sign a ticket on that St. Louis job, and show up Giles and Schultz? It's that or staying here." He waved the gun. "That'll give the law something to hang on them."

Arnold saw that McCarthy was weakening. He said promptly, "No. That's at least five years for me, too. No."

McCarthy cocked the gun then. He leaned over Arnold, who promptly fell on his face to the ground, gripping his head with his two arms. McCarthy said, in a persuasive voice:

"O.K. Get it over with."

He held the gun muzzle back of Arnold's ear and Arnold moaned, "I'll sign. I'll sign."

McCarthy said, "Then get the hell off the ground, you crying rat. You can put it out but you can't take it." He had to half carry Arnold to where Marge waited with the car.

Marge drove south on Florence Avenue and Arnold said, "It's in the next block, and at the intersection. It's the third house on our side of the street. Where that cab—" He tensed in his seat and McCarthy said, "Quiet, now!" and to Marge: "Easy does it, hon. Here's that broken-nose guy now, come to check up."

Marge slowed the coupé and the cab pulled away from the curb. The broken-nosed man, Schultz, who had been in Arnold's hotel room, started up the walk to the house. Marge eased ahead to where the cab had been and stopped, and Schultz heard the sound of the motor and turned. He twisted his head in a puzzled way, stared at the coupé and took a couple of steps toward it, then changed his mind and again started for the house. He walked fast and with his head down.

McCarthy opened the door of the car. He said, "You, Arnold! You hold tough!" and then called out: "Hey! Schultz!"

The house had five steps leading up to the porch and Schultz was half way up these. He stopped and turned, but said nothing. McCarthy started to climb from the car, facing Schultz. He had his gun half raised, cocked and ready. And then Arnold shoved him in the back and cried out:

"Bennie!"

McCarthy went to the sidewalk on his hands and knees. Schultz jumped to the top of the steps and turned, light flashing on a gun he held in his hand. He raised it, and as he did, McCarthy, still on knees and one hand, brought his own gun into line and sighted deliberately. He called:

"Schultz! Drop that!"

Schultz fired and McCarthy shot back so closely the two reports lapped. Schultz wavered, then pitched down the steps to the walk.

McCarthy was up and running. Marge was trying to hold Arnold, who'd lost his head. He pulled free, got clear of the car, and started down the sidewalk at a run. By this time, McCarthy was on the porch. He passed the door, brought glass crashing to the porch from a window with the barrel of his gun.

Marge climbed from the car, almost breathless, and saw McCarthy start through the window. She saw him stop, one leg over the sill, heard the racket of his heavy gun as he shot. She sobbed out:

"The fool! The damn fool!" and ran up the walk and toward the house. She got to the porch as another shot roared out inside, and she almost fell through the window and into a bedroom. She heard a heavy fall toward an open door, got to the door and saw McCarthy lying on the floor of a short narrow hall.

She said, *"Pat!"* and somehow managed to scream the word.

McCarthy got to his feet, swearing viciously. He snapped back, "I tried for a guy when I come in here and he ducked back and I missed. Get the hell back in that room and in the clear. I saw that door there slam and was going to try for the guy again, but I fell on this damned rug."

He kicked the rug to one side, roared out, "Did I tell you to get in that room? Move, damn you."

She scuttled back from the hall and into the bedroom and peered out at him. He went down the hall, very cautiously, and into a kitchen, where he saw the back door standing open. He heard the roar of a suddenly accelerated motor and got to this door in time to see a car turn from the alley in back and skid onto Florence Avenue.

Then he went back to the front bedroom and said to Marge: "Let's see if Cantwell's here."

Cantwell was there, his mouth bandaged with tape and with both hands and feet tied with the same material. He was lying on the floor of a small room off the hall and when McCarthy took the tape from his face, it showed battered and discolored. He tried to speak, had trouble doing so, and finally managed to get out:

"Have they gone?"

"Who was here?"

"Frankie Giles, a guy named Schultz, and one named Arnold."

McCarthy grinned and said, "Well, Schultz is here. I was holding on his neck and I bet I didn't miss his Adam's apple an inch either way. I had Arnold but I let him go, in the excitement."

Marge said, in her small determined voice,

"If I'd had a gun, I could have watched him. But I didn't. If you'd killed him that terrible way, Pat McCarthy, I'd have told the law about it. That would have been murder."

"Did you think I was going to? Couldn't you tell I was bluffing? I had to get the straight of this out of him somehow."

Marge said, "I'm not so sure."

With McCarthy helping, Cantwell managed to get out on the porch. A dozen people were already there, staring at the dead man at the bottom of the steps; and a prowl car was just pulling into the curb behind the coupé. Marge and McCarthy shoved Cantwell through the crowd and to their coupé and one of the crowd volunteered:

"A car come out of the alley like a bat out of hell. It picked up a guy that was running down the street."

The prowl car driver worked his way through the crowd, heard this, and said:

"What's this? You did that shooting." He reached out and gripped McCarthy by the shoulder and McCarthy shook the hand off and said:

"Now wait a minute. It's O.K."

He reached for his pocket and the policeman grabbed for his arm again and missed it. McCarthy grinned, brought out identification and said:

"This. We're on the same side, Jack."

The other man from the prowl car came up, waving the crowd back, and McCarthy said, "Let's go into the house."

The prowl car driver looked at the bandage around McCarthy's head, said, "What in hell happened to you?" and McCarthy reached up and felt of the bandage. He said, "Why, I forgot all about that," in a surprised, startled, voice. He said, "Come on in and I'll tell you the score," and took the driver by the arm and started for the house.

Half an hour later, after a carefully vague explanation of the shooting, Cantwell and McCarthy started back toward the center of town. Marge had left some time before with the understanding she'd wait at McCarthy's office for him. They followed the morgue wagon a block down Florence and then McCarthy swung the coupé left and toward his office. Cantwell had surgeon's tape across his nose and one cheek-bone, three stitches in one ear and five more across his forehead. Both eyes were so black and swollen that he could hardly see. He said:

"Thank the Lord you came along," in a voice that sounded as though he meant it. "I couldn't have held out much longer."

"You didn't crack, did you?"

"No. Almost. That Frankie Giles is nuts. He'd do anything. That was him that went out when you came in."

McCarthy said, "Schultz went out, too," and grinned, and Cantwell said, "But so did Arnold. The wrong way."

McCarthy agreed with this and Cantwell continued with: "If it was only Giles that got it instead of Schultz, I'd feel better. Giles is crazy, kill crazy."

McCarthy grinned, said, "His turn next."

They went into McCarthy's office and found it empty and with the door locked. McCarthy prowled around, found a half finished letter in the typewriter that Marge had begun, and said aloud and querulously:

"Now where the hell is she? She always says where she's going, when she's supposed to wait like this."

Cantwell stared at him and said, "Arnold!"

McCarthy grabbed him and shoved him toward the door. He growled out: "Get moving, dope."

He hurried him downstairs and to the coupé, broke speed laws to the Carlton Hotel. The same boy McCarthy had talked with before came to meet them and said to McCarthy:

"If it's Arnold, he's checked out." He looked at the bill McCarthy held and added regretfully:

"I tried to find out where he was going but he didn't leave an address."

"Was there a girl with him?"

"He and some other guy came in with a girl and then went out with that whole party that was in his room upstairs. The girl was blond and pretty."

McCarthy grunted and swung away and Cantwell fell in step with him. Cantwell said, in a worried voice: "I tell you, Mr. McCarthy, this Frankie Giles is crazy. It doesn't look good to me. Not at all."

McCarthy said, "Shut up," and sailed out to his car. The bandage on his head had gotten dirty during the excitement at the Florence Avenue house, and his hat was riding high on this. His face was lined, drawn, and his eyes looked unholy. He was chewing at his lips, staring straight ahead, and on the trip back to his office he had the nervous Cantwell clutching at the seat. He went in, dialed the Central Station, said:

"Shannon, please. Or Costello. Snap it up, man, snap it up."

He listened a moment, said, "You, Shannon? McCarthy. Listen, where can I get hold of Frankie Giles? He's a crook, but I don't think you got anything against him. . . . You've been watching him? . . . Good. Give it to me." He listened a moment, slammed the phone down, and swung on Cantwell. Then he said:

"O.K. Where's the stuff? Where are these hot bonds and stones? Come through, damn you."

Cantwell gulped and shook his head and McCarthy reached over and caught him by the lapel of his coat. He said in a harsh, rough voice that in no way resembled his ordinary tone:

"Where? Damn you, I ain't fooling. If they want to trade in the girl for the stuff I want it ready to give them." He pulled back his fist, asked again, "Where?"

Cantwell didn't look at the fist but he looked at McCarthy's face. He blurted out: "Well— well, it's at the Security Trust. Safe deposit."

"Where's the key?"

"Under the carpet in my room. In a crack. Covered with dirt."

McCarthy gave him a tight-lipped smile, said, "Let's get going." He went outside, hailed a cab and boosted the reluctant Cantwell inside.

They drove to Cantwell's room and Pat held

the gun on him while Cantwell got the key. Then they drove to the bank.

The safe deposit vault of the Security Trust opened directly on the street. There was a small foyer with an armed guard and an attendant at a desk, then a barred door opening into a corridor that led to the vault proper.

McCarthy and Cantwell came through the barred door with McCarthy carrying a small handbag, and McCarthy waved at the attendant and said "Thanks."

They went onto the street with McCarthy slightly in the lead and he saw a Yellow Cab idling in front of them at the curb. Its sign said: Occupied, and he stepped to one side and away from Cantwell and stared impatiently up the street for another. But that instant a gun crashed inside the cab and it lurched away from the curb.

McCarthy, at the report, had jerked his eyes toward Cantwell and saw him start to pitch ahead. McCarthy was carrying the handbag in his right hand and in the instant it took him to drop the bag and get his gun from under his coat the cab was out in traffic, traffic so thick McCarthy couldn't shoot without endangering people on the opposite side of the street. He cursed, picked up the bag with his left hand, and with the gun still in his right, bent over Cantwell.

Cantwell was lying on his face, both arms stretched out straight ahead and with half his body off the sidewalk and in the gutter. Still holding the gun, McCarthy turned him over and saw he was quite dead. McCarthy came to his feet again in time to see the traffic man from the corner bearing down on him, in time to hear the traffic man shout:

"Drop that gun!"

McCarthy dropped the gun but still held the bag in his left hand. As the uniformed man came up he told him: "I was with him. It was somebody in that cab."

The traffic man snorted unbelief but clamoring witnesses, already crowding for their place in the sun, supported this story. The traffic man said:

"Just you wait. There's more to this than that."

McCarthy snorted in turn but waited . . . waited until the Homicide Squad had checked his story with the guard and attendant inside the bank . . . waited while Cantwell's body was photographed and loaded into a morgue bus and taken away . . . waited and expected every minute to be questioned about the bag. He wasn't.

An hour after the shooting McCarthy stamped down the hall to his office, said to the blocky man who lounged outside his door:

"Hello, Shannon! Didn't expect to see you."

Shannon was red-faced, bristly black-haired, and twenty pounds or more overweight. His voice was harsh, bullying, but this was manner alone.

He said, "You might have known I'd come to see you. What's this about Frankie Giles? We ain't got a thing on him but we sure as hell would like to have. We been watching him; damned lucky the department knows where he lives."

McCarthy opened the office, tossed the bag carelessly on his desk. He said, "If I don't hear from my girl by the time it's dark, I'm going to see him. It's at 426 Rosemary Avenue you said, didn't you?"

Shannon said this was correct, and then: "You mean that Miss Chalmers is with that guy?"

"That's it."

Shannon said quietly, "I'm going in with you. I'll take that Giles apart with my own two hands. Let me get Costello on the phone, Irish, he'll want in on the party."

McCarthy said, "Fine. We'll need him."

"How you going to work it?"

"I'm just going in, is all."

Shannon laughed shortly. He said, "Well, five'll get you ten that you're carried out. You want it?"

McCarthy said he'd give the same odds. It was five hours until dark.

Frankie Giles's house was set back from the street about half the length of the lot; the lawn

was green, well kept, and spotted with shrubbery. The shrubbery was trimmed too low to
offer concealment. Close to the corner, a street
light showed the three men in the car every
detail of the yard.

McCarthy grunted, "No chance for anything
but the front door. It was a screwy idea waiting
until dark anyway."

Shannon's harsh voice said, "Maybe and
maybe not." He waved, offered: "It may be
screwy to have about twenty men stashed around
the block to make sure Giles makes no sneak, but
I can't see it."

Costello, Shannon's partner, said, "Shan's
right." He was a mild man, as tall as Shannon
but lacking that man's temper and aggressive-
ness. He was both quieter and smarter.

McCarthy grunted and kept the car rolling
down the street and past the corner. He stopped,
climbed out, and said, "Might as well try it now
as later." Costello said cheerfully, "Right. Let's
go."

McCarthy looked a little embarrassed. He
said, "Now look! I don't know that Giles has got
the girl. I just got that notion. There's no charge
against Giles and there's no reason for you birds
to get into this."

Shannon reached out and pawed at McCarthy's face. He said, awkwardly, "You damn fool!"

Costello said, "If you're right on this we'll
have Giles on a kidnap rap. I hate the guy's
guts, anyway." He gave McCarthy a sudden
direct glance, said, "And if you're right and it's
a snatch, I want that guy to stand trial. None of
this losing your head and shooting wild."

McCarthy didn't answer this but swung up
the walk to the front door. He was slightly in the
lead, Shannon and Costello walking side by side
behind him. He said:

"I don't see any lights inside," and knocked,
and the door swung open instantly and framed a
tall dark girl. She said, "What is it?"

McCarthy put out his hand and swept her to
one side and went through the door, Shannon
and Costello at his heels.

The hall was dark, but only for a moment.

As Shannon and Costello cleared the door the
girl swung it closed. Then lights snapped on
and they saw Arnold at the end of the wide hall,
holding a riot gun. The muzzle of this bore on
them as they stood grouped. McCarthy shot a
glance behind him, saw the girl crouched almost
on the floor, and said, "A plant!"

He raised his hands without waiting for an
order and Costello followed suit, but Shannon
made no move.

Arnold snapped, "Up!" and shoved the gun
ahead.

Shannon said, "Well, I am!" in an injured
tone and raised his hands to shoulder height,
and Arnold grunted, "Wise!" and, to the girl:
"Come along the wall."

He held the gun steady on the three men as
the girl crept along, keeping out of the line of
possible fire, and as she passed him he said:

"Tell Frankie to come here. You keep watch,
Lil."

She said, "Uh-huh!" and passed through the
door at the end of the hall.

Shannon lowered his hands slightly and said,
"What's the idea?"

Arnold said, "Shut up and keep those hands
high."

In another moment Frankie Giles came
through the back door. His coat was off and he
held another riot gun.

He said, "Let's put 'em in the same room
with the gal. If I'd done what I wanted and
traded her for that stuff we'd be out of here right
now."

Arnold said, "So you've said. You help on
this." He ordered the three: "Now come ahead
steady. One at a time. I'll shake 'em down,
Frankie."

Frankie nodded. Arnold set the riot gun
against the wall. He produced a small automatic
from his pocket, motioned to McCarthy, and
said, "Well, come on."

He made McCarthy stand well away from
Shannon and Costello and against the wall, took
the heavy gun from McCarthy's shoulder clip,
and grunted at the weight of it. He said:

"It's a cannon!" and at the same time took a step back and swung the smaller gun he held against McCarthy's face. McCarthy rolled with the blow but went to the floor. Shannon and Costello both stepped ahead but Giles rapped out: "Hold it."

They stopped, Shannon breathing heavily and Costello a little white in the face.

Costello said, "I'll get you guys at the station and so help me God I'll beat you to death. So help me God."

Giles said to Orrie Arnold, "Lay off that stuff, Orrie. That don't do any good." Arnold snarled back, "I'm doing this."

He searched Costello with the same swift efficiency and took a gun, sap, and handcuffs from him. And then waved him back and Shannon ahead. He took the mate to McCarthy's gun from Shannon and slapped at his face with this, but Shannon took a step back and the blow passed in front of him.

Giles said again, "Lay off, Orrie!"

Arnold turned on him and blazed, "I hate cops. Shut your mouth." He returned the automatic to his pocket, put the three guns he'd taken from the prisoners on the floor by his shotgun, and picked this up. Giles said, "First door to the right, boys," and backed into it. Shannon and Costello stood still and when Arnold waved toward the door, Shannon said:

"What about McCarthy?" who was still lying on the floor, out.

Arnold snarled, "Well, pick him up."

With McCarthy between them and with Arnold following, Shannon and Costello turned into the room to the right. With the exception of an iron camp cot and chair it was bare of furniture but it wasn't empty.

Marge Chalmers was sitting on the cot, leaning back against the wall with her hands tied behind her and a gag in her mouth. Her feet, also tied, were resting on the floor.

A very small, very dark Filipino sat in the chair in front of her, holding a nickel-plated revolver pointed at her stomach. He shot one glance at the newcomers and then returned his gaze to the girl. He kept moistening his lips with a small pink tongue, and his eyes weren't nice.

Giles was standing with his shotgun over against the farther wall. He said, "Over here!" and motioned to the floor at one side and to the right of the cot. Costello and Shannon lugged the sagging McCarthy to the spot indicated, let him slump to the floor, and then Giles ordered:

"You two sit on the floor."

They obeyed, watched McCarthy, who was lying on his side with his knees drawn up. His mouth was open and there was a slight trickle of blood leaking down his cheek and temple. The bandage he still wore on his head was awry, and his eyes were closed. Giles looked at him and said reprovingly to Orrie Arnold:

"Why did you smack him so damn hard? Acts like it's a fractured skull to me."

Arnold walked to McCarthy and kicked him in the ribs, though not particularly hard. He said, "The heel! If he'd laid off Cantwell, none of this would have happened. And I'm telling you, Frankie, you made a mistake in not trading this dizzy twist for that stuff. The boy friend would have popped for it and glad to do it."

Giles said, "You better go and see how Lil is making out. I know the place must be staked and she may have seen something."

Arnold looked undecided but finally said, "O.K.!" He went out the door and into the hall and, as he did, Lil cried out in the back of the house. The cry was indistinct but carried a definite note of warning. Giles stared at the hall door a moment, said to the Filipino, "Take this, Tommy, and watch them all."

He handed the Filipino the riot gun and the little dark man put the nickeled revolver on the floor and took the riot gun. He twisted his chair then, so that he could watch the three men on the floor as well as the girl. The move brought his side only a couple of feet away from Marge and she watched him with eyes very bright.

Giles said, "I'll be right back," and followed Arnold from the room.

Costello said, "Ain't this a honey of a thing to run into? I ask you. That twist must have seen some of our cops."

The Filipino tilted his shotgun and said, "You shut up!"

At the same moment Marge lifted her bound feet from the floor, braced herself against the wall, and kicked up and out. She was wearing high-heeled pumps and the heel caught the little dark man under the ear and he went over sidewise, chair and all.

McCarthy half rolled from his position on the floor and went from that position to fall on the Filipino. He bumped the little man's head twice on the floor, drew his fist back and struck him under the ear, then stood up and said to Marge:

"Nice work, kid!"

She gurgled against her gag, rolled her eyes frantically, and he went to her and unfastened the towel that made it. She tried to speak and couldn't. He untied her hands and feet and she tried again to speak and again failed. Then she pointed up to his head and he said:

"Oh, that! I was stalling."

Shannon had the shotgun the Filipino had dropped and Costello had the nickeled revolver. Shannon said, "Then suppose you quit stalling now," to McCarthy and started toward the doorway, but Costello said, "Wait. How many is there, Miss Chalmers?"

She had some difficulty in saying: "Giles and Arnold and a girl." Costello said gloomily, "And me with this pop gun," and stared down at the nickeled gun with distaste.

Shannon said: "You dope! Ours are still in the hall." He started toward the door and McCarthy told Marge:

"If he makes a move, kick him in the face," and followed, after motioning at the Filipino.

Costello and McCarthy were about ten feet behind Shannon as he stopped and peered around the door casing. They saw him step clear of the door and into the hall and out of sight, then heard the shotgun crash. Then he shouted:

"Come on!"

McCarthy went into the hall with a sort of plunging dive that took him past Costello. He saw Shannon raise the shotgun again, saw the girl Lil outlined in the door at the back of the hall. She screamed, ducked back out of sight, and Shannon lowered the shotgun and said:

"I got Arnold." Arnold was lying in the hall, his hands gripped on his belly.

McCarthy passed Shannon, went to where their three guns were still piled on the floor. He said, "That girl is back there with Giles. This is going to take doing."

Shannon dropped the shotgun, said, "Yeah. Him in a dark room and with the girl. He's got it his way."

McCarthy started down the hall toward the door at the end.

Costello said, "I'm with you," and came alongside.

McCarthy gripped him by the shoulder and jerked him back.

With his body at floor level, and well to the side, McCarthy shoved open the door at the back of the hall. As he did so, Costello shot past his ear at a man outlined against a window. The man went to the floor, got up, and made another frantic scramble for the window and succeeded in getting half through it before Costello and McCarthy shot at the same time. He fell outside the house.

Costello pointed with his gun barrel, said, "Arnold's in the hall, and Giles is outside with a couple of slugs in him." He raised his voice, said, "You in there. You twist, Lil. Come out in the light or we start shooting."

Lil came, white-faced and trembling. McCarthy said to Shannon:

"Pfft for your twenty cops. Where are they?"

They heard a hail from outside and Shannon bawled back, "O.K.! All clear. This is Shannon."

And then Marge screamed in a muffled way.

McCarthy turned and raced down the hall. He got to the door of the room, saw Marge braced against the wall back of the couch and holding the Filipino's right hand in the air above his head. He was on his feet and leaning over her, his left hand at her throat and straining to bring down the knife he held in his right.

Marge was twisted on the cot, one hand at the dark man's wrist and the other on his forearm. She was staring up at the knife and McCarthy could see her chest heave as she tried to scream again.

Pat stood in the doorway, sighted deliberately and fired. The knife flew up in the air. The girl followed it with her eyes before she turned them toward the doorway. Both she and the Filipino still held their pose, but the Filipino turned his head as McCarthy reached him, and McCarthy smashed him across the face with his gun barrel as he did.

The little dark man slumped down on top of the girl, and she rolled from under him and said, "I knew you'd come."

McCarthy said, "You bet!" He watched her face whiten as she said:

"I thought he was out. He was just stallin'; just like you were."

McCarthy said, "I got all my fingers yet. This bird ain't."

She stared at him a moment, and then her eyes went blank and she started to slip to the floor. He caught her, said, "It's all over, kid." Still holding her he turned and bellowed:

"Hey, Shannon! Let that big lug of a Costello clean house and you bring me some water."

Shannon's red face looked very good natured. He stood in the doorway and said, "I thought you'd want to know the score. Giles is going to die. Both of you hit him when he was perched on that window-sill." His eyes widened and he stared at the table. "What's that?"

"That's a bunch of unregistered bonds from a St. Louis bank job. I'm going to return them for the reward. This—" McCarthy pointed at a desk tray. He was still taking unset stones out of a little bag from his pocket and putting them on the tray. "This is a bunch of junk that was stolen in three different jobs in the East. There's a guy named Plansky in the big house, that can tell

us where. If he don't, there's enough big stones in the lot to pick the jobs, and they'll be insured and there'll be more reward money for me. All this stuff was fenced with Herman Wansner, who's dead now."

Shannon's grin faded away. He went to the desk, poked the unmounted stones with a stubby finger, and as he did Marge Chalmers said complacently:

"And I get a cut in the reward. Pat's going to be big hearted. Aren't I the lucky girl?"

Shannon said, "You are. Lucky to be alive. That Filipino that was trying to do you in is charged with kidnaping and assault and attempted murder. He'll get plenty years in jail, but he pretty near got you with that knife."

Marge shuddered a little, asked, "What about the girl?" and Shannon shrugged, said, "Maybe a couple years is all. Women get a break, always."

McCarthy said, "I'd say *I* got a break on this. The reward money's going to count up to heavy dough. I think I'll trade the coupé in on a new job, for one thing."

Shannon said, "Good idea," in an absent voice. "That fella Schultz and Arnold are dead. Giles is dying. The Filipino and the gal go to jail. It's a good job."

McCarthy said, "The hell of it is about Cantwell. I was supposed to be guarding him, and Arnold and Giles killed him when I wasn't more than three feet from him." He made a sour face, added, "What a lousy guard *I* am!"

Shannon straightened and the grin came back. He said, "I meant to tell you about that. We would have taken Cantwell if they hadn't killed him. Giles told us a lot of things before he got too sick to talk. Cantwell was really the one that shot the bank messenger in that hold-up. That's the job that Plansky's doing twenty to life on and that they hung Thomes for."

Marge made her eyes wide and horrified. She cried out, "Mr. Shannon! They hung the wrong man!"

Shannon grinned at her. "Well, not quite. Giles did a lot of talking and he knew what he was talking about. It seems Thomes had the hanging coming for another killing he did." His grin widened even more and he ended with, "That makes the whole thing six, two, and even."

McCarthy said to Marge, "That means win, place, and show."

"That's right, Miss Chalmers," Shannon said. "McCarthy and you win the reward, the girl and the Filipino place where they belong—in the big house. The rest of them show. They show in the morgue."

Marge said, "You and Pat think of the cheeriest things to talk about. I never heard of six, two, and even. I never heard of win, place, and show."

Shannon said, "It's a horse-racing term. People that bet on horse races use it."

Marge swung toward McCarthy. She snapped, "That's where the reward money will go. On horse races. We won't have a dime of it in a

month; you watch and see. Betting on horse racing has kept you broke all your life and you know it. I'm telling you, Pat McCarthy, that you're a fool to do it. I'm telling you. . . ."

McCarthy grinned and said to Shannon, "You would have to bring race horses into this. She goes on like this for hours." He looked patient as he turned back to Marge and said, "You were saying, honey . . ."

Shannon scuttled toward the door and said he'd be seeing them. As he went through it he heard Marge say:

"Now don't make a joke of it, Pat, it's no joke. Go ahead. Throw your money to those dirty bookies. But don't come crying to me when you lose it. You'll get no sympathy from me and I'll . . ."

Shannon went down the hall, mumbling, "I guess she don't like horse races."

MURDER WITH MUSIC *AND* COKE FOR CO-EDS

Adolphe Barreaux

THE EARLIEST PULP MAGAZINES tried to appeal to mass readerships, but, as time went by, many tended to aim at a specific taste or demographic, such as readers who wanted mysteries, westerns, fantasy, science fiction, or romance. As the demand for ever more magazines increased, even smaller or more focused subjects were added to newsstand displays, appealing to those who wanted stories devoted to railroads, jungles, airplanes, automobiles, and so on.

One magazine with a wide appeal but a narrow and very specific target audience was *Spicy Detective Stories*, one of the sleaziest of the pulps. Adolphe Barreaux (1899–1985), who had studied at the Yale School of Fine Arts and the Grand Central School of Art, created Sally the Sleuth for *Spicy* in November 1934 with a little two-page strip titled "A Narrow Escape." The material published in this pulp was generally produced by the worst writers of the era, mainly when they failed to sell their work to the better-paying, higher-end magazines. All the stories included illustrations of scantily clad women, frequently in bondage—so racy that the magazines were kept under the counter at most newsstands and sold only to adults. These illustrations were provided by Majestic Studios, a tiny art shop owned by Barreaux from 1936 to 1953; he was also the owner of Trojan Publishing from 1949 to 1955.

Although he worked for a few other pulps from the 1930s to the 1950s, most of Barreaux's work went to *Spicy*, for which he drew the "Sally the Sleuth" strip until 1942, when other artists took it over. Barreaux went on to work for many of the major comic book publishers, including DC, Dell, Ace, and Fox.

Sally works in law enforcement but does not do much actual sleuthing beyond following a suspect, getting caught by him (always the only suspect, by the way), having her clothes torn off, enduring some bondage and torture, and either overpowering the villain herself or being rescued by her boss, the Chief. She is fearless and feisty but not especially intellectual. Sally's exploits were the most popular feature in the magazine and were pioneering as she was the first female central figure in a series of comic strips.

"Murder With Music" was originally published in the September 1937 issue of *Spicy Detective Stories*; "Coke for Co-eds" was originally published in the January 1938 issue of *Spicy Detective Stories*; they were first collected in *The Best of Sally the Sleuth* (Eureka, California, Pulpville Press, 2013).

SALLY THE SLEUTH

Murder With Music
by BARREAUX
YOU VILL SERVE MINE PURPOSE JUST AS THE ODDER GIRL DID. I VILL PLAY MINE MELODIES ON YOU JUST LIKE ON A VIOLIN!
I GO NOW TO MAKE PREPARATIONS. SO I TIE YOU UP FOR A LEETLE WHILE
THERE'S A PILE OF MUSIC. IF I COULD JUST TEAR PIECES OFF THE TITLES AND DROP THEM FROM THE WINDOW.... I'LL TRY IT, ANYWAY
IN LOVE
HELP ME
PRISONER
RELE
-AND STILL THEY'RE COMING DOWN. "HELP ME" -"PRISONER" — SOMEBODY MUST BE IN TROUBLE. I THINK I'D BETTER LOOK INTO THIS
SO THIS IS WHERE THE MONKEY BUSINESS IS GOING ON! PUT UP YOUR HANDS, PROFESSOR SCHMALTZ, I NEVER DID LIKE YOUR LOOKS
ACH!
JUST AS I THOUGHT—HE KEPT THE POOR GIRL'S BODY IN HERE, COVERED WITH WAX TO PREVENT DECOMPOSITION

SALLY THE SLEUTH

Coke for Co-eds

CHILLER-DILLER

Richard Sale

KNOWN TO HIS CONTEMPORARIES as "the Dumas of the pulps" for his prolific output, Richard Bernard Sale (1911–1993) sold his first story while still in college. After a brief stint as a journalist, he wrote stories that started to appear at a prodigious rate in most of the top pulps of the era. During a ten-year period, mainly in the 1930s, he published approximately five hundred stories—about one a week. When he had greater demands, he could write a story in a day.

Sale also started to write novels at this time, beginning with *Not Too Narrow, Not Too Deep* (1936), an allegorical adventure about ten convicts and their escape from a penal colony much like Devil's Island. It was filmed as *Strange Cargo* (1940), starring Clark Gable, Joan Crawford, Peter Lorre, Ian Hunter, and Paul Lukas. Among his outstanding crime novels are *Lazarus No. 7* (1942) and *Passing Strange* (1942).

Hollywood beckoned to Sale as a way to make more money. Among the many films he wrote were *Mr. Belvedere Goes to College* (1949), *When Willie Comes Marching Home* (1950), *Gentlemen Marry Brunettes* (1955), *Abandon Ship* (1957), and the excellent thriller *Suddenly!* (1954), with Frank Sinatra as a would-be presidential assassin. His novel about Hollywood's sleazy side, *The Oscar* (1963), was a huge bestseller and was released in 1966 with a screenplay primarily by Harlan Ellison; it had a large cast of famous actors and other performers, including Stephen Boyd, singer Tony Bennett, comedian Milton Berle, Elke Sommer, Ernest Borgnine, Jill St. John, Eleanor Parker, Joseph Cotten, Edie Adams, Peter Lawford, and Broderick Crawford.

Sale's most popular pulp stories feature "Daffy" Dill, an easygoing, wisecracking reporter who constantly finds himself in hot water, generally due to the machinations of his rival Harry Lyons, only to be saved due to the paper's wise receptionist, Dinah Mason; its editor, known as "the Old Man"; and his Weegee-like pal, the photographer Candid Jones.

"Chiller-Diller" was originally published in the June 24, 1939, issue of *Detective Fiction Weekly*.

Chiller-Diller

RICHARD SALE

CHAPTER I
The Big Story

IT WAS A BIG STORY. The murder was the least important part of it. It was a big story and it wasn't in my department, and I was just as glad. But I got sucked into it anyhow. Yea verily, me, the crime reporter, became I, the cocktail reporter. And all because editors and publishers see eye to eye and a reporter does the bidding.

The beginning of April—it should have been April Fool's Day but it wasn't—I was sitting in the city room of the *Chronicle* with McGuire of the sports department, Sammy Lyons of the waterfront, and Jimmy Verne, who was the best fotog we had on the sheet. It was a Saturday and things were slow and we were chewing the rag and killing time when the door of the Old Man's office burst open and the Old Man stepped out, turbulent, apoplectic, and generally in a stew. I'd never seen the geezer so excited. He was shouting and waving his hands, and he looked like Grumpy out of the seven dwarfs. Not a hair on his pate, the green eyeshade up on his forehead, a white shirt, open vest, and havoc in his face. "Daffy!" he roared. "Verne! Sammy! Kendrick! Where's Kendrick? Get him in here on rewrite! We've got a story and what a story! Hurry up, everyone in here on their toes!"

He took us by surprise so much we all jumped out of our reveries and tore into the doghouse. Kendrick of rewrite brought up the rear. The Old Man plumped into his chair and I yelled, "What is it, chief? What is it? Has the president been assassinated?"

"Cut it out!" snapped the Old Man. "This is no time to kid. Sammy—up to the Hotel St. Clair, Room 414, and see what you can do there. It's loaded with cops and you'll probably get thrown out on your ear but do your best. Scram!"

Sammy left.

"Kendrick. Take these notes I scribbled down and rewrite them into a number one yarn. I'm breaking down page one and reinserting. What a shame today is Saturday instead of Friday! This would be a swell morsel for the week-end. Half the readers will miss it at this point. Scandal, my blades! Scandal and murder, only in this case, the scandal is much more important than the murder!"

"To everybody except the stiff," I said. "I haven't any doubts it was pretty important to the guy who was bumped. Why all the excitement?"

"Ah, Daffy, that Dinah, what a gal, what a newspaperman she turned out to be! She's in the jug."

"The jug?" I roared. "Dinah's in the jug? What is this, Rasputin? What's it all about?"

"Yes, my brainless number one boy, Dinah

Mason is my idea of a newspaperman. I've always said women made bum newspapermen but I'm wrong. She used her head. Not a chance to get the story out, it was all wrapped up in her little brain, the cops grabbed her, they stuck her in the can, and she remembered reading somewhere in a book that a guy is allowed one telephone call. So she asked and they let her make her call. She makes out that she's calling momma to say she won't be home. She spills only four or five sentences before they nab her and kill the connection, and then Halloran calls back and tells me I'll cut my own throat if I run her flash, and I tell him—"

"—you'll cut your own throat. All right," I said. "What's Dinah in for?"

"Nothing, nothing, she found a stiff and they grabbed her as a material witness. We'll spring her, that's your job. But get this. Ever hear of a plug named Al Myers? Flippo Myers?"

I said, "He's crooning up at the Eldomingo Club on Fifty-Third. He's probably the all time con man, gambler, grafter, and whatnot, and I've heard via the grapevine that Al isn't above being a gunman when he gets sore enough. He's got a voice and he sings at the club to get his hand in with the idle rich and then he plays them for a sucker every time. Boy, when it comes to making money dishonestly and not getting nailed for it, Al Myers is the tops. Good-looking cuss too."

The Old Man said, "He and Elsie Whittaker eloped last night."

There was a dead silence. "Elsie Whittaker," I said slowly. "The dizzy little blonde debutramp who's had her pan over every picture magazine and roto section in the country? The only daughter of Fletcher Whittaker, who happens to be worth ten or more millions and traces his ancestry back to the guys who met the pilgrims when they landed? *Wow!*"

"Boy," Jimmy Verne said, "you got something, chief. Is it true?"

"True?" The Old Man spat. Of course it's true. True enough to get somebody killed! Al Myers and Elsie Whittaker were married last night in Harrison, New York, and they're right in the big city at this moment and I've got to nail them. All you guys in the office are going to start calling hotels. I'm going to cover all outgoing trains and all planes—"

"You're in a jam unless this is verified," I said. "I admit it's a very nice thing, the daughter of the original American family marrying a gun-punk out of Hoboken, but you'd better check—"

"You're late," said the Old Man. "I've already called Joe Morris of the Harrison *Sun*, a weekly, and asked him to look up the license and see the minister—no, it was a justice named Gillicuddy, who married them—"

Speak of the devil—the telephone rang and it was Morris from Harrison. "Yeah?" said the Old Man. "Fine. . . . Good. . . . Then you see the guy Gillicuddy now and call back at once. There's fifty bucks in this for you, Joe, and my thanks. Yeah, so long." He hung up. "Well, they got the license all right. Now to check on the marriage."

I was getting tired of the noise and confusion. "But what has Dinah got to do with all this? Where does she come in? How did she get in the jug and how did she fall into this yarn anyhow? She hasn't got enough on the ball to have gone out and dished this up by her lonesome. She was tipped off or she fell into it, and I don't come from Missouri to know that either."

"All right, maybe you're right. I don't know the answer myself. Dinah was picked up at the Hotel St. Clair hovering over the corpse of a friend of yours and mine. You all know her. Jane Willis of the *Dispatch*, that gal who gets in the nicest places and does articles for the society magazines on the side. I guess you'd call her a cocktail reporter. She's dead."

There was a crash. Jimmy Verne had dropped his Speed Graphic and hit his own foot. The look of pallid amazement on his face changed to an "Ouch" as he grabbed his foot and danced. "What's the matter with you?" the Old Man asked.

"The matter with me?" Verne snapped. "Well, I'm only human even if I am a news photographer! I had lunch with that dame at the Press Club this very noon and she borrowed a buck out of my jeans to get uptown! Three hours ago, I was sitting at the Press Club talking to her, and now you come out and say she's dead to this world. What do you expect me to say, 'Here today, gone tomorrow'?"

"The camera's okay," I grinned.

"Holy smoke," Verne said. "You can't believe a thing like that. You eat lunch with someone and three hours later she's cold. You have got a tale, chief. If you can nail Myers—"

The Old Man sat up, smelling something he hadn't known before. "What has Myers got to do with Willis? You think Al Myers and the marriage had anything to do with this girl—"

"What happened to her?" I asked.

"I don't know. She was murdered. Dinah got that much to me. Dinah was looking the scene over and she started to call the paper when the police arrived. They took her right in. I don't know if she's been charged, but I doubt it. Halloran knows Dinah is a reporter for this paper and that she probably had nothing to do with it."

"Where do you get that 'probably' business?" I said. "You know darn well Dinah is too dumb to kill anybody. Is this paper going to stand bail for her? Where is she, the Tombs?"

"Keep your shirt on," the Old Man said. "Be with you in a second. I think Jimmy has an angle."

"Sure I've got an angle," Verne replied. "Maybe I ought to be a reporter instead of a camera toter. Why, didn't any of you guys ever date Jane Willis? She used to be Mrs. Al Myers before she got Renovated in 1936."

The Old Man blinked, then shrieked, "Kendrick! Gimme rewrite! Kendrick! Where the blazes is he?"

You can see what life was like when he smelled a story. All was confusion, but I refused to be strung up again. "Kendrick can wait," I snapped. "Give me the lowdown on how I'm to spring Dinah."

"You get in touch with the *Chronicle*'s lawyer—wait I'll give you written authorization. His name is Watson. Daniel Watson. You'll

like him. You spring her even if it takes bail, but spring her. Take Jimmy with you and get some shots of Dinah in the jug and Dinah coming out. That's a good angle. *Chronicle* reporter suffers for her art." The telephone rang and he grabbed it. "Yeah, yeah, Joe. He did? . . . Thank *you*, Joe. I'll mail the money to you. So long." He hung up. "Well, Gillicuddy says he married the happy couple at two A.M. this morning and that they were both a mite high-ho. McGuire— did you send all those guys out to cover depots, ships, and flying fields?"

"Covered," McGuire said wearily.

"Kenyon is going to realize he is publishing a paper when we break this," said the Old Man. "And if one of you bozos leaks it out before we get through at least two editions, you'll be fired. What a setup. Mr. and Mrs. Fletcher Steele Whittaker, bluebloods in America since the founding of the settlement at Jamestown, Vayginya, announce the marriage of their daughter, Elsie, who's always been a snooty little dickens, to Al Myers, ex-con, gunman pug, and general bait for a cop's bullet. Ah me—"

"Come on, Jimmy," I told Verne. "Let's blow out of here. The place is getting to sound more and more like something out of a Hollywood movie, and I don't want it to get around that I was here when it happened."

"Yah!" the Old Man snorted. "If you had the heart of a real Fourth Estater, you'd see what a swell yarn this is from a human news angle. But you, cluck, all you're worried about is Dinah, a jug, and a corpse."

It was a fact. Not the corpse so much, although I did give Jane Willis more than a mental nod. You can't be a crime reporter and go scooting in the wake of bullets and death without considering ways and means when you hear of a murder. But it was Dinah I was worried about. Murder is a hard rap, and I didn't like Dinah mixed up. Not even if she was clear, because the papers would mention her name, at least, and it's a bum stigma to have tacked onto your moniker.

Downstairs, I got a nickel and telephoned Poppa Hanley. I got through to him, and said, "Poppa, this is Daffy."

Poppa Hanley, for those who came in late, is Lieutenant William Hanley, the homicide bureau's claim to fame and second in command only to Inspector Mike Halloran, who is as tough a walrus as ever came out of Athlone, Eire. "Hello, Daffy," Hanley said cautiously. "Have you heard about Dinah?"

"Sure I've heard about Dinah," I stormed. "What does it all mean, Poppa? I hope your hands are clean or I'm going to be awfully sore at you!"

"Shh," Hanley said. "It's Halloran's case and he's burned. It would have been all right except Dinah was trying to get a news story together instead of calling the cops. He knows she didn't do it, but he's trying to scare the daylights out of her so she won't be a naughty girl again."

"What's the charge?" I said. "Has she been arraigned?"

"No," Hanley said. "And there won't be any charge. He said something about obstructing justice, but he wouldn't dare pull it because the Commish would say he was stalling and for him to get the real killer of the dame. You get a writ of habeas corpus and you'll spring Dinah like a mousetrap."

I went up and saw Watson, the *Chronicle* mouthpiece, and there was a lot of fixing and finagling and we saw a judge named McCall and got the writ okayed and then we trooped over to Centre Street, thus armed with heavy legality, and we burst in upon Inspector Halloran and slapped the writ on his desk, and Watson said, "Charge her up or put up, Inspector. Crime or no crime?"

"Oh, get the dame out of here," Halloran said, growling. "I'm glad to get rid of her. But you tell her to keep her nose out of police business, Daffy, or the next time I'll run her into the ground. Why, that dame was using all the clues and evidence in the room for a cheap news story, spoiling all my leads. I ought to jug her for a year. Get her out of here and tell her to stay out of here."

Hanley was in the hall outside, grinning. "Was Dinah scared?" I said. "I'll bet Halloran really gave her the works."

"Scared?" Poppa said, tugging at a droopy ear lobe, his homely face very much amused. "The old boy told her she was going to fry in the chair and Dinah said, 'I regret that I have but one life to give for my newspaper.' Boy, did he have a slow burn."

So we finally got Dinah out of hock and Verne took a couple of shots. Dinah was very gay. "I wasn't a bit scared," she said. "I knew you had a lot of friends in the police department and that they wouldn't dare electrocute me and take a chance of offending you that way."

Dinah, you see, still believed in Santa Claus.

CHAPTER II
Between the Eyes

You might have thought it was old home week back at the *Chronicle* city room. Dinah Mason sure looked like the most popular girl in the racket. Dinah is the light of my life, the cream in my coffee, and the nail in my shoe. She managed both phases nicely. She wouldn't marry me, and she wouldn't let me marry anyone else either, not that I wanted to.

I can remember back in the days when Dinah first came to the *Chronicle*. She wanted to be George Jean Nathan in those days, fresh out of Alabama U. The Old Man who has the heart of a stone—nay, a cold Siberian stone—promptly put her to receptioning at the telephone of the paper. But Dinah had the stuff, and she worked her way up into the movie department until she now handled not only the cinema reviews, but also interviews and dramatic gossip.

She was sitting on a desk—it was McGuire's—and the rest of us crowded around her in a circle. Even the Old Man. He put his pride in his pocket and came out and he made sure that Kendrick of rewrite was getting everything down in black and white.

"Well," Dinah said, "you could have knocked

me over with a bee's slipstream. Here I was this afternoon, writing a review on a stinker called *Shadows Over Shanghai* when Marian Hans called and said she felt lower than a snake in quicksand, and would I help her out."

Marian Hans was the society editor of the *Chronicle*. The "cocktail" reporter, as we tab those gals and guys who follow the blue-bloods, not-so-blue-bloods, and merely-rich-bloods. I thought to myself that Dinah looked beautiful up there on the desk, her blonde hair looking like a halo under the light, the devil!

"She had a touch of grippe. Well, you know how Marian and Jane Willis went around together and it seems they had a working agreement to split any real stuff which they dug out. That way, they could both devote more time to covering different assignments and then split them."

"I'll see her about that!" the Old Man said. "No reporter of mine splits news with any rival sheet."

"Turn your damper down," I said. "If you cut it out this rag will be running out of news in a week. Society news anyhow. Marian is a truck horse compared to Jane Willis in news garnering. That gal was good. She knew how to dig. I had one date with her, and she was a very nice female, if you like brunettes. I made one pass at her on that date and she jiu-jitsued me into a snowbank. Yeah, Jane Willis was all right."

"Hmm," Dinah said. She studied me coldly before she continued. "So I told Marian I'd cover for her, and she said that Jane Willis was up in the Hotel St. Clair where she had two rooms, and that she had a mild scoop in the society bracket and was splitting the story with Marian. And would I go up and get it for her and write it and give her the by-line. So I did. I went up there. Was I surprised!"

"What happened?" the Old Man said. "Get all this, Kendrick."

"I'm getting it," Kendrick said wearily.

"Well," Dinah went on, "I didn't bother to telephone up from the lobby, Marian had told me the room, so I just went up. And when I got to 414 I knocked on the door and there wasn't any answer. I noticed the door was ajar so I walked right in. Well, you could have—"

"—knocked you over with a crowbar," I finished. "We know all that. Get on to the business."

"Listen," Dinah said evenly, "this is my story and I'll tell it the way I want to tell it or not at all."

"Don't be a woman," snapped the Old Man. "Keep talking."

"Well, she was dead. She was lying right there on the floor. She was on her back, staring straight up. Her eyes were open, and she—just looked—dead. You know that awful yellow color. I felt all dizzy for a minute, and then I saw her typewriter and I saw that she'd been writing a story and I went over and read it. It was just the lead on the Myers-Whittaker marriage, but the lead had the dope. Then the police were there and I was nabbed. If I'd had any brains, I'd have realized that someone had already spotted the corpse and gone for the police. That door was ajar."

"If you'd had any brains," the Old Man sniffed, "you could tell me why Jane Willis was supposed to be murdered. As far as I can see, you walked in and found her dead. She could have dropped dead from shock or surprise."

"Sure," I said. "Maybe a city editor raised her salary."

"Oh, she was murdered all right," Dinah exclaimed. "She was shot."

"Are you getting this, Kendrick?"

"What there is of it."

"She was shot right between the eyes," said Dinah blithely. "Didn't I tell you that? Oh, sure, lads, you could see the bullet hole right there, a little blue hole. I didn't see any blood, only a sort of bubble." She shuddered. "It was no picnic for a gal who gets seasick like I do. And when the police came, they found some splintered glass near her and they said it was a clue but they didn't know what it meant. Just tiny specks of it. They thought the killer had had his cheaters knocked off in the tussle and that maybe the specs had been busted. They were going to check with oculists around town. The four-eyed killer. Hot stuff, chief."

"Good enough," the Old Man admitted. "Anything else?"

"Well, Halloran tried to pin it on me at headquarters but his heart wasn't in it and I could see he was scaring me for trying to pull a fast one and report it to the *Chronicle* before I reported it to the police, so—"

"Telephone, chief," said a copy boy.

The Old Man took it at McGuire's desk. "Eh? . . . That's too bad. . . . Well, it means money but it's worth it. This story will last a week at least. Okay, Hammy, come in, come in wherever you are." He hung up and turned. "Dinah, you need a rest. You need sunlight."

"Sure I do," Dinah said, surprised. "But how come you recognized the fact, Rasputin?" She coughed. "There's a rat in the kindling box somewhere."

"That was Hammy. We can't get an interview out of Fletcher Whittaker and his wife because they're not in New York. There's no point in telephoning them either, just a waste of time and dough. They won't give out by long distance. They're in Miami, Dinah, and you're going down and break through. I want to hear what America's finest family has to say about the heiress marrying the gunman. Nice copy. You get your things together and grab the first plane south this afternoon. I'm calling Kenyon and giving you an expense account but I want the interview first, Dinah, and the suntan second, understand, so snap into it."

"Hey," I said. "You can't do that! How about me?"

"How about you? You're in this burg to stay and you can rot here until you scare up Al Myers and his glamor-girl wife. They're in New York. The police probably want them, I want them, you want them. We want a statement out of them. It looks like Al shot his former wife to keep the news from breaking."

"Hooey," I said. "He would have taken the copy out of the machine. And he doesn't wear glasses. And a newly married guy doesn't take time off from a honeymoon to slip a slug into some one."

"Don't give a hoot. You find Myers and get his story. It ought to be hot. And you find him before the cops get to him or we'll get stale beer instead of champagne."

CHAPTER III
The Upside-Down Smudge

Dinah and Smootsy Dobbins (for a fotog) left on the five o'clock plane for Miami, and I went over with them to see them off. Poppa Hanley came too, which touched Dinah no end. Poppa told the pilot he'd better be careful with the cargo or things would happen. The pilot took one look at Dinah and got the point. You could see he would enjoy the trip. I burned.

Then Poppa and I came back to the big town and we went up to the Hideaway Club and had dinner with Bill Latham. The evening papers were out with the story then, and we had a *Chronicle* sent in. It was a good story but it looked funny to see the by-line *Dinah Mason* under a yarn like that when it should have read *Daffy Dill*.

Well, I thought, Dinah has taken over the cocktail reporter end of it now, and I can settle down to following the killer.

But it wasn't going to be as easy as all that.

Poppa Hanley took one look at the *Chronicle* story and had himself a fine laugh at Dinah's expense. "What's so funny?" I said, annoyed. I was secretly kind of proud of the little woman. "I read it and it seemed like a nice little yarn to me."

"Oh," Poppa said sagaciously, "it's a fine yarn. A very good story indeed. Only it ought to be in a fiction magazine."

"I don't get you," I said.

"Well, it's true that Jane Willis is dead. And it's true that she was murdered. And it's true, we did find glass on the floor, the only clue around the dump. But if Jane Willis was shot between the eyes, Doc Kyne and Inspector Halloran are certainly working on the case in blissful ignorance."

I stared at him. "Poppa, I don't get you!"

"Jane Willis wasn't shot between the eyes, dear. I can see where Dinah got fooled, because it may have looked like that, but it wasn't that."

"Then what was it?"

"I guess when she felt herself going she put a hand to her face. It's an instinctive gesture." He made believe he was passing out and naturally enough, raised a hand to his head to steady it. "Get it?"

"Got it."

"Well, the dame had just finished putting a new typewriter ribbon in her machine. We found the old one in a wastebasket. Her fingers were full of blue-black ink. It so happened she plugged a bullet hole of typewriter ink squarely between her eyes. It *did* look like a slug hole, blue but no blood. Maybe Dinah saw one like that some place before. But Jane Willis wasn't shot."

"What happened to her, you old goat? Cut out the stalling. I've got to call the Old Man and kill this story and rewrite it. He'll have a fit. Boy, Dinah ought to be glad she's on the way to Miami, for even at that distance her ears will burn when he starts calling her four kinds of dope. What happened to Willis? I'm on this case now, you know. It's my assignment."

"It's mine too," Poppa Hanley grunted, looking dour and pulling on one of his droopy ear lobes. "Inspector Halloran handed it to me. I expected I'd get it. . . . Willis? Hmm. Stabbed."

"A chiv, hah?" I said. I shook my head. "Dinah must have been more scared than you looked. Tell me more quickly."

"Stabbed. What more do you want? Someone clipped her through the eardrum with a needle of some sort and plugged her brain. It was a kind of neat thing when you look at it. That's all I know. The weapon wasn't found. We reconstructed it so that Jane Willis was working at the machine on that story when someone drove the needle home."

I said, "But that means the killer was with Jane Willis all the time. Jane knew the guy. Knew him well enough to have him standing there while she wrote a prize yarn. And while she was typing he drove the needle home."

"Sure," said Poppa Hanley. "You're thinking Al Myers. Married to her once. Divorced. Knew her well enough. Well, there's an alarm out for Al, and he'll get picked up sooner or later. A three-state alarm now with descriptions of him and this Elsie Whittaker and her car and his car. But I can take Myers or leave him alone. For one thing, if Myers had done the jabbing with that needle, he wouldn't have left that lead story on his elopement with the Whittaker heiress right in the machine where the cops would grab it. That's no way to keep a marriage secret, and it's a motive for killing the dame. So take it or leave it."

"I'll leave it," I said. "Sit tight."

I telephoned the *Chronicle*. The Old Man had gone home, so I talked with Kendrick and had Dinah's story pulled out and reinserted with the McCoy in news. Then I went back and joined Poppa again and asked him about the needle. "I don't know anything about it," he said. "Doc Kyne is working on the dame now. We can go see her if you'd like."

"I'd like," I said. "But first tell me about the glass you found on the floor. Dinah said glass from a pair of cheaters. You think the killer wore glasses?"

"Naw." Poppa Hanley dismissed the idea with a wave of the hand. "Dinah has an imagination like a dictator."

"Maybe a flash bulb burst. White glass? Burned white from the heat? A fotog?"

I was thinking of Jimmy Verne having had lunch with Jane Willis a couple of hours before she got clipped.

"Nope," said Hanley. "I don't know what but definitely not those. Maybe you and me had better run downtown and I'll show you the stuff, Daffy. Then we can start clean."

We finished dinner and rode Hanley's cruise car down to Centre Street. When we went inside, at the lab, we found Doc Kyne washing his hand and cleaning up. "Well, well," I chirped. "If it isn't the Buzzard. Have you been playing with visceras again?"

"Ha-ha," said Dr. Kyne sourly. "Pardon my ghoulish laughter, Mr. Dill, but I think you are so funny. In a pig's eye."

"Gosh," sighed Hanley, "can't you two guys ever speak civilly to each other?"

"He hasn't any sense of humor," I said.

"My sense of humor is perfectly all right," Dr. Kyne said, "but it's no fun trying to measure the depth of a thrust through an eardrum; Hanley, that was a long needle killed this girl. It went into her a good six inches. Looks like an ice-pick but the wound seems a trifle finer than an ice-pick. Like a hat pin."

"Let's see her," I said.

I will spare you the details because when you have been autopsied by a medical examiner, you don't look like anything much except something that has a crying need for the beautifying touch of an expert mortician. Jane Willis looked pretty bad. Death was hard on her. Her face had always been a trifle on the rough-an'-tough side, and the hue of death, hard and uncompromising, brought out her rugged jaw. The smudge was still apparent on her forehead. I could see how Dinah was fooled.

Even so, there was something funny about the smudge that I couldn't make out just then. It looked sort of silly, not like a print should have at all.

"Wait a second," I said. "I thought you said Jane Willis put her own hand to her head."

"But it's true," said Hanley. "We even found the old typewriter ribbon in the basket where she'd thrown it when she put in the new one."

"That may be," I said. "I'm not saying that Jane Willis didn't put a new typewriter ribbon in her machine. All right, she did. But then she got up and went in and washed her mitts. Why? Because that isn't a typewriter ribbon smudge on her fingertips. Take a look at it. Here, watch."

I took out a piece of paper and raised her cold hand and pressed the fingertips against it. There was no smudge on the paper.

Hanley grunted. "What'd you expect, a print? She's dead. Dead men don't give off prints. The body oils of a healthy living woman would, but she's not secreting body oils any more."

"I'm not talking about a print. I'm talking smudge. That smudge on her fingers doesn't need body oils to come off. Not if it's wet typewriter ribbon ink, as it is supposed to be. But it isn't that. She washed her hands. And she didn't make the smudge on her forehead. What you see on her hands is ink from a fountain pen. It's dry now. That's why it won't smudge off."

Dr. Kyne said, "I think he's right."

I went over to Jane Willis's body and bent down close to her face and looked at the smudge there. "I *thought* there was something screwy about this thing," I said. "It looks like a thumb print. Only it's upside down."

Hanley came over and looked, but the expression in his face said, "So what?"

"When you made that pass at yourself in the Hideaway, making out that you were fainting," I said, "what did you do?"

Hanley did it and his face fell. "Oh-oh," he said. "I get it. That print on her dome is upside down. It's a thumb print upside down. And she couldn't have made it. Not in a normal position. Then how did it get there?"

"Watch," said I. "Consider a hat pin in my right hand. I put my left hand on your head to steady it, maybe while we struggle. My other fingers are in your hair, my thumb on your forehead, upside down. Get it? Then I jab into your eardrum and the deed is did."

Hanley said, "We've got something. Doc, you stay right here and you don't let anyone get near that stiff except Babcock whom I'm gonna send right down." He waved at me. "Come on."

We went upstairs, and Hanley sent Babcock down with the print equipment to take the mold of that print off Jane Willis's face. "And check with Al Myers's when you get it," Hanley called. "And if that don't work, check its type through the files, but *check it!*"

There were reports from the lab on his desk. Report from checking the fingernails: negative. Dust, small particles of wood, no flesh. Report on the glass found: negative, no prints, no trace, apparently cheap frosted glass, used extensively now for junk jewelry which was quite the rage. Junk jewelry probably smashed in scuffle. Junk jewelry is the inexpensive ornamental stuff that is so popular. Did it mean a woman? The hatpin too!

I could see that Poppa was getting bogged down into details so I left him and went home. When I got home, I thought the thing over for quite a while, trying to find a woman in it, but the only woman I could think of was Marian Hans, who had played sick and asked Dinah to pinch-hit for her. It was possible that Marian had pulled a phony, perhaps murdered Jane Willis, then sent Dinah to discover her while she lay in bed with a fairly decent alibi. But why? Marian Hans and Jane Willis had been closer than a pea and its pod. Sharing the news, the dirt, double-dating, pally-wallying. Murder was quite a rap. Even if two gals get in a huff, they don't jab hatpins into each other's ears.

I wired Dinah Mason at the Pancoast in Miami Beach and asked her if she had smelled perfume or powder or seen anything to give a clue as to whether or not the identity of the killer was feminine.

Then I telephoned Marian Hans at her apartment. There was no answer. I didn't give it much chance, just two rings, and then I hung up. I hung up in a hurry because my door was opening. I thought of making a break for the desk where I keep my .31 Colt gravescratcher, but it was too late for that. The door opened and two people came in.

You could have knocked me over with a heavy look.

It was Gentleman Al Myers, and his winsome debutramp bride, Elsie Whittaker.

CHAPTER IV
Finger Girl

Life is full of little surprises. No matter how many times I've written that nothing is ever new, I am constantly eating those words by being surprised out of my very pants.

Myers and Whittaker. There they were. The police of three states were hanging in suspense, waiting for a sight of them. And here they were. Poppa, and Halloran, the city editor of any newsrag in the town, Pop and Mom Whittaker, Dinah Mason: all of them would have given a shirt to be this close to them.

And they picked on me.

"Just tell me one thing," I said slowly. "Is this a bump-off or is it a social visit? I want to say quick prayers for one, or break out the champagne for the other."

The question, needless to say, was prompted by the very ugly automatic pistol in Myers's fist. But even so, the presence of Elsie Whittaker seemed to indicate that the gun was merely to keep my head in line and my hands off a telephone. It didn't look as if the season's glamorous debutante was going in for witnessing murders. On the other hand, men seldom carry guns unless they expect to use them.

"Don't be silly," Myers snapped. "And stay away from that telephone. Keep away from the desk. I'm not going to kill you. Just sit tight a minute."

I relaxed. He wanted help, not homicide. I watched him close the door. He tried to lock it but there wasn't any key. "Never has been a key," I said. "Safest way to keep out burglars is to leave the door unlocked. They get suspicious when they find an open door. I'll bet you thought twice yourself. Now take it easy, Al, and relax. I'm not going to telephone the cops. Why should I? I'm a newshound, not a bull, and you're good for a story just as long as you're not excommunicado in some bullpen."

It was logical, and it happened to be the truth. Myers put the gun away and told Elsie Whittaker to sit down. She looked pale and frightened and I felt sorry for the kid. The blonde hair was askew, the makeup was no longer perfect, and the glamor was gone. She was a young scared matron and she looked it. Myers looked pretty upset himself. He was pallid too, and he lighted a cigarette nervously, so nervously that when the telephone rang, he jumped to the ceiling—well, almost—and back again. Before he could object, I waved him away and picked up the handset and said, "Hello?"

The operator said, "I have your party now, sir."

"What party?" I said, being absentminded.

"The party you just called," she said. "You hung up before the line answered. I have it for you now. Go ahead."

"Hello," I said.

"Who is this?" said Marian Hans.

"Hello, Marian," I said. "This is Daffy. Remember?"

"Well, for pete's sake," said Marian Hans huffily. "You might give me a chance to answer the telephone before you hang up next time."

"How do you feel?"

"Come on, come on," she said, "what's on your mind? You don't give a hoot how I feel. I can't see Daffy Dill getting worried about a cocktail reporter. You once told me that my brand was the onus of the Fourth Estate. . . . Oh well, I feel pretty good. A touch of flu. It hit me like a light and put me down, but the doctor says I'll be okay."

"Still in bed?"

"Yes. But don't ask me where I was when you called. No embarrassing queries please. Washing my hands, let's say. To tell the truth, I feel sort of lousy still, but I'll be okay. Did Dinah see Jane and get that story? Jane called me and said she had a honey. She wouldn't tell me what it was on the phone. Said it might leak and that it was good for page one. I couldn't go myself, so I asked Dinah."

"Dinah got the story," I said. "It was the elopement of Gentleman Al Myers with the society sprout Elsie Whittaker."

Marian groaned. "Did *I* have to miss a natural like that? That was big of Jane to split with us. She could have double-crossed. I think I might have with a yarn like that."

"Look," I said slowly, "you're sick and maybe I shouldn't tell you this. You and Jane were pals. But someone's got to tell you and it's a cinch you don't know yet. I thought you did by now. But you've got to be checked like anyone else."

Her voice changed. "Something happened? To Jane Willis?"

"Yes," I said. "The worst that can happen."

"She's dead?"

"That's got it. Stabbed through the eardrum with a hatpin. You guessed it pretty well."

"Murdered!" she breathed. "She was murdered!"

"She didn't die of old age," I said.

There was a long pause, and I could feel Marian Hans trying to get her bearings. Finally she said, "Daffy—can you come up here right away, Daffy?"

"I think so. Why?"

"I know who killed her," Marian said. "I'm sure I do. You come up here right away."

"I'll arrange it," I said. "Take it easy." I hung up. I turned to face my visitors.

Elsie Whittaker was sitting down opposite me, puffing a cigarette. Al Myers was pacing back and forth. He had put the gun away and he was wearing out the rug. When I finished the phone call, he stopped pacing and stared at me. He looked tigerish. His eyes were shiny and his lantern jaw was set, and he threw an index finger at me and said, "You know I didn't kill that dame. We were divorced. She didn't mean anything to me and she didn't have anything on me to be bumped for. I didn't do it, and you know I didn't do it."

"The police of three states," I pointed out sagely, "are looking for you right now. Looking for *your* car"—I nodded at him—"and looking for her car." I sighed. "Silly silly police. They should be looking for a car belonging to a guy named Vincent Harris."

Myers jerked, startled. "How'd you know that?"

"Simple, my dear Watson. Her car is hot, your car is hot, her families' cars are in the dear old Southland where I yearn to be—Miami, where the sailfish come up like thunder across the Gulf Stream. Vinnie Harris was a pal of yours, still is. Vinnie would lend you his car while the heat was on, and you'd cover him if you got caught."

"I didn't kill Jane," Myers said.

"All right, says you, you didn't. Says I, mayhap you're telling the truth. I don't think you did. Where do I come in? Why bust in here with the spouse and the gat?"

Al Myers sat down and held his head in his hands. Then he looked up at me. "Dill, you've got to help me. The first time in my life, I played a game square, and I'm roped. I'm not kidding. This marriage thing is level. It's got to keep. But it won't keep. Not with cops looking for me, trying to pin the killing of my ex-wife on me. How much of a chance do you think I've got with that?"

"Chance of what?"

"Listen," he said. "Elsie and I are in love. Never mind that dirty smile. We're in love, see? We've been in love for a long time, almost a year now. I'd have married her sooner but I didn't see how it could work out. Her old man is tough as nails on family and breeding and background. He'd eight-ball me from the start. Then, the other night, we thought we'd just go ahead and do it. Elsie said that she could persuade her father to give his approval, but first we'd have to be married. Once married, she was sure she could make him come around. And if he came around, her mother would come around too. So we made the break and did it. And then this happened."

"Well?"

"You only say 'well.' Can't you see? It'll ruin the whole thing. If they don't get the guy who nabbed Jane right away, the whole thing'll be sunk."

"Look," I said. "This isn't a sewing circle. Let's be frank. Fletcher Whittaker has twelve million bucks. I think you married his daughter for a divorce or annulment price. Say no."

Al Myers said, "No. . . . I ought to slug you for that crack."

"Now don't get yourself hurt trying," I said. "There's no point in being an outraged juvenile. Anything I say, you've got coming."

"Listen," Myers said. "I'm in love with this kid. Understand that? I'm in love with her. Ball and chain, for keeps. I've given up the rackets, given the boys the go-by. I've got a job crooning at the Eldomingo, and it's honest and it's all I'm going to do. I'm going to try and get a band behind me of my own. I'm going straight and respectable. You're right. I've got cracks coming because I've been tinhorn all my life. But no more."

"Even by-by to the twelve million bucks?"

"You can look at my books yourself. Or send an accountant to do it if you want. I don't need any more money. Sure, maybe I didn't make it working hard in an office, but I've got dough. Plenty of dough. I've got sixty grand in savings banks, in stocks, in bonds. That's plenty, mister, that's not pennies. And I get a good take-off at the Eldomingo. I don't need her old man's dough. What would I do with it?"

"Black Sheep Turns White," I said. "Headline."

"That's all the truth."

I turned to her. "When did this guy propose to you?"

"He didn't. I did the proposing," she said. "Last November. I told him I was in love with him and asked him to marry me. He took down his hair and told me his past and said no. I've been after him since then. I'm twenty-two, Mr. Dill, old enough to know better. I'm in love, and I think you're hateful."

"*All* right," I said. "Maybe you're both on the level. I could be wrong. But I don't see my hand in this."

"You can whitewash us in your column as much as possible," Myers said. "And maybe I've got some ideas on what happened to Jane."

"Now you're talking," I said. "Give."

"Well," he said, "I don't know so much really. But this much. I tipped off Jane to the elopement."

"Keep talking."

"Five in the afternoon. I went up to the hotel and saw her. We've been friends, I figured I'd do her a favor. I told her about the marriage and I said it was exclusive and told her to hold it until me and the kid got down to Miami to see the folks."

"Well?"

"Well, she knew about it already. She has tipsters in the towns around and about, who look through the license records for her. She knew we'd been married in Harrison before I told her. She said, since she'd found out about it first, she was going to run the story right away. But that's not what I'm getting at. There was someone else there when I was there."

"You were the last to see her alive," I said, "if you saw her that late in the day. If you didn't kill her, it was the guy who was there with her. Who was it?"

"I don't know," Myers said. "Only it wasn't a guy. It was a dame. I didn't see her. I could hear her. She was in the bathroom. I think Jane stuck her in the bathroom when I knocked. But she sneezed once. And I could smell perfume."

"Kind?"

"I wouldn't know. Sweet and sort of heavy. I saw a handkerchief on the table. I snitched it when Jane wasn't looking. I've got it right here."

He handed it to me. There was still a scent on it. Hmm, says I. Then, "Okay, Al. I'll play ball with you. You won't tell me where you're hiding out, so I won't ask you. But right now, I've got some heavy work to do, and I've got to lam. I just had a call from—well, skip it. Anyway, I have someone who thinks she can put the finger on the killer, and I'm on my way."

They had no sooner left than I called the *Chronicle* and got through to Pop Henderson at the morgue. Not the kind of morgue where the stiffs grow like the poppies in Flanders Field. A newspaper morgue, full of clippings from the past. "Pop," I said. "This is Daffy. I'm coming down there later. I want you to get out everything you've got on Gentleman Al Myers."

"All right, Daffy."

Then I left and went downstairs and caught a cab and rode over to the apartment house on 86th Street near Fifth, where Marian Hans lived. I took the elevator up and then knocked on the door. Marian called, "It's open, Daffy. I left it open for you."

I opened the door to go in and I hadn't got it halfway, when I saw the room was black as night. And suddenly there was a flash and a roar, and I felt as though I had been clubbed across the chest. I heard Marian scream once and then I fell forward on my face and passed out cold.

CHAPTER V
The Lowdown

When I came to, I was bouncing around and it hurt a little. I opened my eyes and said, "Where are we going?"

"Hospital," said a familiar voice. "I always told you never to jump a gun. Now you'll know better."

I looked up and the homely, welcome pan of Poppa Hanley loomed down at me. My head was in his lap. I guess I was a sick little boy. We were in an ambulance, I realized next second, for they opened up the siren as they made a turn.

"Am I hit badly?" I asked.

"No," said Hanley. "But you're hit, and hit proper. It's the nicest hole you ever picked up. Does it hurt?"

"Not so much," I said. "But it feels numb and soft."

"You'll be all right."

"Did you see Marian—"

"He's got to keep quiet," the medico in the amb said. "That's not going to help him any."

Poppa Hanley said, "Okay then, Doc. I'll tell him. Marian Hans is dead as the buffalo nickel, Daffy."

"She was alive when I walked in. She called me, said the door was open. I didn't jump a gun, Poppa. I was bushwhacked."

"Then she was killed right after you. She's dead. Drilled clean through the head, almost a contact shot. She didn't have a chance. There was a letter under her pillow for you. I opened it and read it. Sorry, but murder is murder. You know."

"What did it say?"

"I'll read it. It's right here. 'Dear Daffy, I am writing this note, perhaps foolishly, because I know something which the man who killed Jane might kill me for. Taking no chances. Don't expect a sudden end, but I want you to know this just in case. Take the key in my bag which has a tag on it. Number on tag 11098. Go to Mirabeau Bank and open lock-box drawer 11098 in the vaults downstairs. Belonged to Jane. See if there is a gun there. If not, tell cops Al Myers did the job. If so, take that gun to headquarters right away. Marian.'"

I closed my eyes and panted. "You handle that, Poppa. Tell me, did you find a handkerchief on me? A woman's handkerchief? My right coat pocket."

"Didn't look. Wait a second." He stuck his hand in and felt around. "There's nothing in there, kid, but an old beer bottle top."

"Filched," I said. "Wonderful evidence. Gone. Look, Poppa. Three things for you to do. Put out a call for the car belonging to Vinnie Harris, Myers's old sidekick. You'll pick up Myers that way. Then go to my place, take the cigarette box on side table, take it to headquarters and get prints off it. Then take this pill out of me and match it with those in the records of ballistics. It'll match one somewhere. I think—"

Suddenly the world swam, and I knew I was fainting, and as I went, I heard the medico say, "Well, I warned him. Next time he'll keep quiet with a wound like that."

Poppa Hanley grunted, "For two pins, I'd slap your ears down."

And then I was really gone.

———

Next day was Sunday. I was a pretty sick laddie. They tell me the nurse put Garbo to shame. I don't even remember what she looked like. Banks were closed, so Poppa couldn't get into the lock-box drawer. Nothing else happened. Someone sent flowers, forget who. Poppa told me he had the bullet and it was down at ballistics. That's why I was sick. They gave me ether to get the pill out.

Ether makes me sick.

On Monday morning, I felt like a million dollars. Dr. Kerr Kyne, the old Buzzard no less, came in and looked me over and sniffed. "Well, that's hard luck," he said drily. "I'm afraid you're going to live. Entirely a flesh wound, knitting nicely, and you could really leave here tonight, just so you don't use your left arm and tear the wound open again. Your temperature is normal enough. Humpf! Well, I'm on my way to see your cohort's viscera, as you would say. Sorry I can't perform an autopsy on you too."

"Vulture," I said warmly, "I love you!"

He smiled faintly and waved and then left for the post-mortem on Marian Hans. I shivered at the thought. It might very well have been my own post-mortem. I'd never been that close to the line before.

At ten o'clock, Poppa Hanley arrived and we settled down for a session. "In the first place," Hanley said, "I've been down to the lock drawer, and the rod was gone. The drawer was absolutely empty, and the guard told me that someone had been in on Saturday morning before the bank closed."

"Sure! You see? Whoever did it got that gun out before Jane Willis was bumped. If that gun hadn't been recovered, Jane would never have been clipped."

"All right, you button your lip and just listen. You're supposed to be wounded. So the gun is gone. Then Doc Kyne told me this morning that he had finally analyzed the smudge on Willis's forehead this morning, and that it was blue-black mascara, and not a typewriter ribbon. We get along, no?"

"I'm all ears," I said. "Confound and amaze me. Go ahead."

"I picked up the cigarette box in your apartment and took it down to headquarters and got prints off it. But they didn't match Myers's. What are you trying to prove?"

"Have you got Myers yet?"

"Uh-huh. Eight o'clock this morning on Canal Street. You were right. He was in Vinnie Harris's car. But the spouse wasn't with him and he won't talk."

I said, "All right. Now how about the pill you got out of me, and out of Marian Hans?"

Poppa Hanley stuck a cigar in his mouth, and instantly tipped me off that the news was both good and big. Poppa buys the very cheapest cigars on the market because he doesn't smoke them. But whenever Poppa gets excited about a case, a cigar goes in his mouth instead of chewing tobacco, and he chaws it until it's in shreds and utterly disreputable. He started chawing right then and there.

"Well, Daffy," he said, "I don't know what you're aiming at, and I'm not sure that you were in on this, but that pill outa you has done big things."

"I'll guess," I said. "That pill was fired out of the same gun which showed up in another case sometime somewhere. Probably a murder case. The gun wasn't recovered."

Hanley blinked. "Go on. You're not guessing."

"I swear I am. It's the only logical thing."

"I don't believe it. You've hit it on the nose. You couldn't guess a thing like that. You had the *Chronicle* send you up clippings from the morgue on Al Myers."

"True," I said, "but I haven't seen them yet."

As if to substantiate me, the nurse—whose name was Jones and who must have been a beautiful baby—said that a man was here from the *Chronicle* and called himself Rasputin, the Mad Monkey. I said okay and the Old Man breezed in.

In topcoat and hat to cover the bald spot, the Old Man looks fairly respectable. "Hello, my dear boy," he said. "When are you going to quit lousing up this hospital and come back to work? Hanley, we'd better fire the nurse for one thing. She's conducive to illness. Ahem, and me with four children. How do you feel, Target?"

"Good enough," I said, "to know when I'm well off."

"Hmm, a pity," said the Old Man. "Well, I brought up all the trash out of the morgue that you asked for. Think you're well enough to read all this stuff? All kidding aside?"

"I'm well enough to ask for a bonus for being wounded in line of duty for the New York *Chronicle*, the sweatshop which keeps me in velvet."

"You're not well enough to be refused," the Old Man said. "So I'll wait until you come back to the office before I turn the angle down. Look, I've got to get back for the home edition. I didn't tell Dinah that anything had happened to you. She telephoned in this morning, finally got her statement out of the Whittakers. Smart girl, that kid. They wouldn't see her and they wouldn't talk to her. So she sent Smootsy in to fix the phone—the old repair man gag—and Smootsy planted one of those little gadget microphones. That night, they sent the Whittakers a wire saying Myers and Elsie were in Miami and would come home as soon as they were sure they would be welcome. Then Dinah hooked up the dry cells and listened to momma and pater thrash the thing out. It's thumbs down, Daffy. An annulment, a divorce, or goodbye Elsie. There was something about blood will show. And they didn't mean Al Myers either. Another listen, and it develops that Elsie Whittaker was an adopted daughter, and not their own. We checked with the Infant Home, and it's true. Adopted at age of eight months. So Dinah has a story that'll make the other cocktail reporters rip their hair-dos wide open. Take care of him Hanley, I've got to go."

"Listen," I called, "Dinah isn't coming home yet, is she?"

"Told her she could have a week," the Old Man said, and then he was gone.

"Let's see that stuff you've got there," Hanley said.

We looked through it together and we finally reached the story and I shivered at the goodness of my guess. In 1928, Albert Myers had gone on trial in General Sessions for shooting and killing Black Jack Denham in a brawl at a night spot. But when the trial came off, the state's witnesses forgot their stories (intimidation), and the defense attorney had pulled a fast one by demanding that the gun, marked exhibit A, be matched with the bullet taken from Black Jack. Some fun, because someone had switched guns, and the exhibit was a phony and had never fired the murder bullet, and Captain DuBois himself, chief of ballistics, had to admit the fact. Mistrial.

"Well," said Hanley, "that's that. Pretty plain now."

"Sure," I said. "Jane Willis was married to Al Myers in those days and when that killing finished up in a mistrial, Jane figured she had enough of that kind of stuff. Not being chained to a killer for her, so she took the highroad. Now she must have known that Myers had done it, and been afraid she might be killed by him to cover it. So she kept that gun—maybe it was given to her for safekeeping after the switch was made. Anyway, she kept it. As long as she had it—and it was Myers's gun—she was good for life because she told Myers if anything happened to her, that gun would go to the D.A. and Myers's goose would hang high."

"Sure," said Hanley. "Everything is fine except Myers has an alibi for the afternoon Jane Willis was bumped."

"Baloney," I said. "He told me himself he was the last one to see her alive. But Myers didn't kill Willis, Poppa. A woman did."

Hanley just spluttered.

"That's what I said. A dame. A woman. Listen. You run down to headquarters and match that print you got off my cigarette box with the print of the upside down thumb you found on Jane Willis's forehead. You do that, and you've got your killer. You do it, and if they match, you tell me, and I'll give you the dame's name."

"I'll take you at your word," Hanley said. "I'll be back as soon as I check." He shook hands and went out.

CHAPTER VI
No Kidding

He hadn't been gone two minutes—oh, it was less than that—when Miss Jones appeared at the door and said, "Another visitor, Daffy. A lady. Miss Beckwith."

"Never heard of her," I said. "But who am I to turn down a lady? Send her in."

The door opened and Miss Beckwith came in. She wore tortoise-shell glasses and she had buck teeth and black hair and she was dressed like a woman suffrage campaigner of 1918. Nurse Jones closed the door and left and Miss Beckwith came right to my bedside and pulled her hatpin out of the hat on her head and stuck it against my ear before I could move.

"Not an inch," she whispered. "Not an inch, not a sound, or I'll run it home. It's ready to go."

"Son of a gun," I gasped. "You did it!"

I could feel the hatpin pricking the inside of my ear. She had her left hand on my head to steady it, her thumb upside down as it had been upside down on Jane Willis's head. Her right hand held the pin. It was nine inches long if it was anything at all. Black. The end of it was broken. You could see where the glass ornament had been on the end of it, but the edge was jagged where the ornament had broken off. I said, "So that's where the glass came from."

"That's where it came from," she said. "It might interest you to know that Jane Willis broke it when she fell to the floor. She never made a sound. It's an excellent way to kill someone. I read about it in a mystery novel, but it worked better than I ever expected. . . . Quick, what have they done with him?"

"Mrs. Myers, née Elsie Whittaker," I said, "your husband is going to fry in the electric chair. And so are you, because you made a mistake. You left your thumbprint on Jane Willis's head, and you left it on that cigarette box in my apartment. Hanley is matching them both right now. You can bump me off, but it's not going to save you. They'll take you in as a material witness with your husband, sooner or later, and you'll be fingerprinted, and presto, they'll have you."

"Very smart," Elsie Whittaker said. Her voice was very low. Then I thought she was going to cry. "You've spoiled it all!"

That needle was pricking me and I was sweating.

"Well," I said, "it was a long shot, Elsie. You must have loved the guy an awful lot. When he told you his past, he told you about the murder, eh? And the fact that Jane still had the gun?"

"I wasn't going to kill her," she said. "I stole the key to the lock-box and got the gun—"

"Whoa. Whoa, whoa there!" I said. "It wouldn't be as simple as all that. You can't just walk into a bank and get into a lock-box—even though you have the key."

"Naturally!" she snapped. "I'm not a complete dimwit even though I made my début. I've had a lock-box of my own for years."

"Well, how did you get her signature authorizing you to open it?" I wanted to know.

"That was easier than you'd think. I invited her for cocktails, and when she was a little high, I tricked her into putting her signature on a letter of authorization. With that and the key I got into the box and took the gun."

"Smart," I admitted. "And—?"

"And when she found it out, she was furious. She told me to come up there, so I went, alone. Al didn't know anything about it. He still doesn't."

I had a feeling that she was breaking and that her nerve was going and that maybe I was going to get a chance and get the needle out of my ear without dying. I said, "Then why did you kill her, you poor kid?"

Sympathy and women. Yea verily. Always works.

"Al came and then left. I hid in the bathroom. Jane told me that she wanted the gun or she would talk. I'd forgotten she could talk. She said she'd write a newspaper column on the thing that would put Al in the chair. I got in a panic. She went for my bag to get my gun—"

"You should have got rid of it right away," I said, friendly as all get-out. Why not? The needle was still there.

She smiled wryly.

"I know, but I didn't. We wrestled for the gun and she got it and put it in her pocket and told me to go. She sat down and began to type and I walked over and took the hatpin and killed her."

I said, "Leibowitz is a good lawyer for that. He might get you off. No premeditation. But if you kill me, no good."

She smiled, but sort of grimly, and I felt the cold perspiration begin to ooze as she said:

"I left my handkerchief at Jane's. Al picked it up when he was there. That was my handkerchief he gave you. He didn't even know it."

"So you got it back by shooting me and shooting Marian. You're a shooting girl. And using that same gun. A giveaway. Just reopened the whole case against your husband."

"I had to. It was touch and go. Hurry. And the gun was in my bag—"

"You did all that for the love of Al Myers," I said. I was sweating again because I could suddenly sense resentment, and her hand had stopped trembling. I had the buzzer for the nurse in my left hand at the side of the bed and I pressed it. "Have a heart. I've got a girl coming to see me, a girl I'm in love with (how you talk when you're stalling for time!) and you've shot me up enough as it is."

"You spoiled it all for me," Elsie Whittaker said coldly and suddenly. "Why shouldn't I pay you back for it?"

The muscles of her hand tensed, and Miss Jones opened the door. It threw her off a second. I ducked my head. I felt the hatpin against my lower jaw. A snap, and the hatpin broke and the dame ran for the door, pulling the gun from her bag and yelling at Jonesy to get out of the way. Jonesy got out of the way and neatly tripped Whittaker as she went by and Whittaker stumbled out of the door and ran straight into a powerhouse haymaker flung by the one and only William Hanley, of Centre Street. I winced. The sound of that crack hurt me more than the inch of hatpin in my cheek. Then another thud when she hit the floor. Poppa picked up the gun and stared at the celluloid buck teeth, the black wig, and the plain glass cheaters. "Hmm," he said. "An actress, eh? Ham, sister, all ham!"

Jonesy came over and picked the hatpin out of my jaw and washed the wound and said it was all her fault and whatnot.

"Oh, cut it out," I told her. "It was my own fault letting her get that close. Never mind cauterizing. I'm so glad to get stabbed in the jawbone instead of the eardrum I feel like a million bucks! Bring me a bandaid and, Hanley, give me police protection."

Hanley came in looking sheepish. He had the cuffs on the girl and an interne was trying to bring her around. "It seems like I always arrive at the right time, but I didn't mean to. I got downstairs and I figured Babcock could match those prints so I called him at headquarters and told him to do it, and I came right back up again."

My doctor was there then. "I forbid it!" he roared. "We've got to have peace and quiet around this room! No more shenanigans, I don't care who murdered whom, you've got to stay still and rest or I'll not have responsibility—"

The telephone rang.

Nurse Jones whistled. "Daffy, everything happens to you."

"I forbid you to answer it," said the doctor.

But forbidding didn't do any good right at that point.

I picked up the handset. It was long distance. It was Dinah. "Oh, darling," she said, "I just read it in the papers. Are you all right? Are you hurt? It says you're in a hospital! Are you dying? I'm taking the first plane—"

"Dinah, listen!" I snapped. "Chance for a scoop. The killer of Jane Willis and Marian Hans is Elsie Whittaker. You stay down there and beat it over to the Whittaker place with Smootsy and get the lowdown. You get the first statement out of the Whittakers and then scram. Got that?"

"I've got it," Dinah said. "But are you all—"

"How can I help but be all right?" I said. "You ought to see the nurse I've got! One look at her eyes and a dead man would resurrect himself. I'm not kidding."

"Neither am I," Dinah said grimly. "I'll get your darn statement, but then I'm grabbing the first plane north and when I get there, that hussy had better be out of town, or I'll scratch her eyes out and pull her hair off and knit a basket with it. Get me?"

"I get you," I said dreamily. "Stroke my left temple now, Miss Jones. Yes, I get it, Angel-Eyes. Hurry home." And I hung up and smiled at Hanley and told Miss Jones that she had served her purpose and that as a safety precaution, she ought to take a trip to California.

"And he," said Poppa with finality, "ain't kidding."

THE PASSING OF ANNE MARSH

Arthur Leo Zagat

BECOMING FAMOUS as one of "the electric typewriter boys," Arthur Leo Zagat (1896–1949) was one of the most prolific writers of the pulp era, when it was common for writers to produce hundreds of thousands of words a year in order to make a living at a penny a word. Zagat was a master at writing longer stories of twenty thousand words that magazines then featured on their covers as "feature-length novels" or "complete novels."

After serving in World War I, he stayed in Europe to study in Paris, then returned to New York, the city of his birth, and received a law degree from Fordham University but never practiced. Having sold the first story he wrote, he immediately became a full-time writer, becoming one of the most successful authors of horror and supernatural stories that were violent and terrifying, in a genre known as "weird menace."

Producing more than a half million words a year for twenty-five years, Zagat was one of the highest-paid writers of his time, working in various other genres as well as producing his bone-chilling weird tales, and as a regular contributor to such classic pulp magazines as *The Spider*, with a series about the kindly Doc Turner, who was always willing to help those in need, and *Operator #5*, with spy stories featuring the Red Finger.

In the mystery field, he created the much-loved Anne Corbin, née Anne Marsh, who, with her courageous husband, Peter Corbin, wages war on behalf of the oppressed against the tyranny of the criminal combine that has driven her father to suicide.

"The Passing of Anne Marsh" was originally published in the April 1937 issue of *Detective Tales*.

The Passing of Anne Marsh

ARTHUR LEO ZAGAT

"IT'S COMIN' ON TO SNOW, MISS ANNE," a thin querulous voice called. "It's goin' to be a white Christmas."

Faith Parker's work-gnarled fingers were red and ungainly against the gay-hued chintz curtain they held aside from a frost-edged window. Her eyes, peering through the glass, were tiny, birdlike in a countenance yellow and wrinkled as old parchment—sere and sharp-featured. Her flat-breasted, scrawny frame was enveloped by an immaculate white Hoover apron, and there clung to her the spicy redolence of the crisp roast meats, the savory gravies, the toothsome, mouth-melting pastries that made The Tavern on Bolton Turnpike the nightly rendezvous of Laneville's élite.

"It had snowed already the day I came home, just a year ago. There was snow and ice all the way from the college. Lane Hill was all white and the white on the dark boughs of the pines was very beautiful." Anne Marsh spoke as though to herself. She moved with an unconscious lovely grace between dim booths within which holly-decked tables nestled discreetly. Her garb was that of a slim, athletic boy, high-laced leather boots, whipcord breeches, plaid lumberjacket, visored wool cap, but she was utterly feminine. The thick wool of her mackinaw could not hide the tender curves of womanhood. Tight, tawny curls escaped from under the black cap to set off

a wistful small face. Her lips, deeply red and velvet soft, were fashioned for caresses but incongruously were edged with pain. Her long-lashed grey eyes were destined for laughter but mirrored only a lurking, sleepless fear.

"Beautiful," Anne's low, throbbing voice repeated. "The icy air was like wine bubbling in my veins, and I was happy. I was coming home to Dad, Faith, to the man who had been father and mother to me as long as I could remember. For two weeks we were going to tramp together over the hills, and spend long evenings together in our workshop, happily contriving some clever, useless little gadget. I reached home, and . . ."

"Miss Anne! You mustn't . . . !"

"And found Dad dead by his own hand; his name, for years so venerated in the city he loved, a synonym for dishonor." The girl's mouth twitched with a suffering one so young should not have been called on to endure. "He had stolen the charity money entrusted to him to be distributed at Christmas."

"He did not steal it," the older woman denied fiercely. "He did not mean . . ."

"No, he did not mean to take it. Relying on the promises of a half-dozen of Laneville's leaders to replace it before it would have to be paid out, he had borrowed the Community Chest funds to save his Union Light and Power Company, to save the hundreds of small investors and

297

the thousands of laborers who depended upon it for their living from disaster. But his false friends broke the promise they never intended to keep. The company failed, and they bought it in for a song, as they had planned. It was they who were the real thieves, but they stole within the law, safely and cleverly."

"It was that lawyer who told them how to do it Miss Anne. Fulton Zander. He's shrewd. . . ."

"Shrewd and cunning as Satan. He and his clients are called honest men by the same law that says Webster Marsh was a thief. The same law that says I am a thief— It's right, Faith. I *am* a thief, an outlaw. A pariah. . . ."

She checked. Clear and distinct, a cheer came in through the Tavern's walls, the shrill, piping outcry of many merry children.

"Listen," Faith Parker exclaimed. "Listen to them orphans. Would they be cheerin' like that if you hadn't got that home for them by blackmail, or would they be shiverin' in Slum Hollow, blue with cold and hunger?" She turned back to the window. "Look at them, Miss Anne. Come here and look at them."

The girl came alongside of her. Outside, to the left, the wooded height of Lane Hill loomed against the sky's leaden vault; but to the right, across the concrete bridge over Waley's Creek, the highway dipped and she could see over the tall hedge that bordered the road.

Far back from the highway a gabled dwelling of time-darkened ivy-clad brick was stately and dignified as when anciently Joshua Marsh had built it to house his progeny of whom she was the last. Over the pillared portico a newly painted sign said, LANEVILLE CHILDRENS' HOME. On the velvet lawn sloping to the pike, winter had killed the plants and shrubbery, but it was a live and vibrant garden of human flowers. A throng of warmly clad, ruddy-cheeked youngsters darted about, screaming gleefully as the dancing first snowflakes eluded their chubby little hands.

"Oh they *are* happy, Faith." A smile tugged at the corners of Anne's mouth and a little of the bitterness faded from her winsome face. "It was worth the price to give them that."

She grew sober again, remembering the night of dire peril out of which she had wrenched that home for the homeless. She had felt death's hot breath on her neck, that dreadful midnight, and almost the teeth of the law's bulldog had sunk into her soft flesh. If it had not been for Peter . . .

Her glance came away from the gay scene and strained through the sudden thick veil of white crystals that with silent swiftness already obscured the mountain from which Bolton Turnpike curved.

He was somewhere up there, she thought, the youth who so many times had appeared out of his mysterious abode to save her from disaster and so many times had vanished again into that mystery, carrying her heart with him. Peter! She knew of him only that no matter what the odds against him his dark head was jauntily cocked and his blue eyes dauntless, that there was a heart-shaped little scar at the corner of his mouth. . . .

And that his kisses had burned like white flame on her lips.

Her hands tightened, abruptly, on the sill. "Faith," she gasped. "Faith. There's someone . . ." Then she had whirled to the Tavern door, was out in the blinding swirl, was running up the road.

There it was, the form she had glimpsed through a momentary gap in the seething downfall. She had seen the man stagger, fall. Now he was crawling, like some dark beast, on hands and one knee in the highway. Crawling slowly, painfully, while behind him a scarlet stain trailed for a moment, melting the snowy film, and was almost instantly blotted out by a new coating of white.

"Peter," Anne whispered through frozen lips. "Peter. What's the matter? What . . ."

He kept crawling; as if he did not hear her; hitched himself along, slowly, painfully. The leg from which dribbled that gory thread dragged a lifeless, useless thing, behind him.

"Peter." The girl bent to him, got shaking hands on his shoulders. "It's I. It's Anne. Don't you understand, it's Anne Marsh."

He stopped then, twisted his hanging head to look up at her. His lips were whiter than the flakes that settled on them and melted in the feathery vapor of his breath; his cheeks were sunken, quivering; his eyes were dark pits of agony.

"Anne," he groaned. "Get away from me. Go away. They mustn't find you—with me."

"You're hurt, Peter. Your leg's broken."

"Shot," he whispered. "I was almost—free. But a lucky bullet—" He coughed, the spasm seeming to rack every fibre of his lithe, slender body. "They know I came this way. You—leave me. They . . ." He pitched forward, fell inert, a still mound in the snow.

A sudden frigid gust flailed icy particles against Anne's cheek, but it was not the savage onslaught that lined her face with drab despair. Long ago she had surmised Peter to be one of the bandits who skulked in the No Man's Land of Lane Hill and descended from it in swift forays. The police had made many raids into that mountain fastness and had returned empty-handed, but they had routed Peter from his hiding place at last. They must be close on his trail. In minutes, in seconds, perhaps, they would overtake him.

If they found her with him—that's what he had been trying to say—she would be gathered into the net of the law. "Bulldog" Ryan, the plodding, indomitable detective who alone had suspected her own outlawry, would seize the chance to arrest her. Armed with a search warrant he would at least be enabled to probe The Tavern thoroughly, and he would find indubitable proof of her guilt.

"Peter," Anne groaned, going to her knees beside him. "Peter. Wake up. You've got to wake up!"

She shook him with frantic hands. Muted and incoherent through distance a shout reached her from far up the mountain. Another answered. It was nearer. The police! They were still far away, but they were coming fast.

"Peter!" Her palm spatted against his cheek, stingingly. "Wake up."

"Ugh," he grunted. "What?"

"Try and get up, Peter. Try hard." She had an arm under him, was trying to lift him. "If you can hop on your good leg I'll be a crutch for the other. Get up, Peter. Please get up."

He was struggling. He was breathing hard, and his eyes were closed, but he was moving, trying to get his uninjured leg under him, thrusting at ground with his cold-blued hands. Anne threw all her small strength into the effort to aid him. She managed to slide her shoulder under his arm pit, to get his arm over her back. She heaved upward, pain tearing at her chest, tearing at her back, his weight like lead holding her down.

The rising wind howled eerily in the tree-tops she could no longer see. It wasn't the wind. It was the siren of a police car, wailing down the white slope. They dared not go too fast in this white sightlessness but they were coming surely, inexorably.

"That's it, Peter darling." Anne's voice was low, encouraging and very steady. "That's fine." She had one arm around his waist, her other hand clutched the wrist of his arm that was around her neck, and they were erect on their knees. "One more try and we'll make it. When I count three. Do you understand?"

The siren yowled.

The motion of his head was somehow grotesque, as though it were the head of a marionette manipulated by someone unskilled. But it was a nod.

"One . . ." The siren howl was nearer. "Two . . ." The hunters were coming faster than she had thought possible *"Three!"*

Peter's attempt to rise was pathetic in its feebleness, but he did make it. Anne found some unguessed-at reserve of strength in her aching thighs and with that slight aid they miraculously surged to their feet.

It was too late! They were only fifty feet from the tavern's door, but the juggernaut must overtake them before they could possibly reach it!

CHAPTER II
Trapped

"Run, Anne!" Peter muttered, thick-tongued. "You . . . can escape." He had regained a modicum of consciousness, but he was a lax, almost lifeless burden, leaning heavily upon her.

"No!" the girl sobbed. Like a grotesque, three-legged monster in the bleached darkness of the blizzard, the two lurched into the roadside bushes.

Snow-laden withes slapped at them, parted to let them through. Snow poured down, stifling the threshing of the brush, stifling Peter's moan of anguish. Anne, abruptly rigid, put her lips to his ear.

"Quiet, my dear," she whispered. "Be very quiet."

Through the white, almost solid pall the siren's scream was a long, menacing howl borne on the breast of deafening engine thunder that battered against the screening bushes—and roared away.

"They've gone past, Peter," Anne dared a murmur of throbbing triumph. "The snow covered the marks where you fell, as soon as we got off the road, and they didn't see it—"

Voices reached the trembling girl, deep-throated, rumbling. And then another made intelligible words, carrying more clearly through the snow-filled air because it was high-pitched and thin and querulous.

"No, I ain't seen nobody come out of the woods." Faith Parker said. "I been standin' right here too, the past half-hour."

Once more the hoarse rumble. Once more Faith's reply. Was she talking so loudly on purpose, hoping to be overheard?

"You better come inside if you're bound on waiting here. There's a fire an' I can heat up some coffee, an' you can watch the road from here while you're warming up."

The police were at the tavern, then, watching the road, waiting for their prey. They knew that although they had somehow passed him, he must come out of the woods on the highway. The steep ravine through which Waley's Creek ran, on whose lip the restaurant's kitchen door opened, would cut off his escape to the east. West of the road was a treacherous bog, not yet frozen sufficiently to be anything but a death trap for anyone who attempted it in this blinding storm. Death just as sure would overtake the wounded man in the arctic cold of the mountain.

Yes, they could afford to wait there in warmth and comfort while their quarry chose between death or capture.

Anne Marsh's lids were slitted against the driving, icy blasts. She hugged Peter closer to her.

"Try to walk," she said. "Please try to walk."

Perhaps he heard her. Perhaps the movement of his flaccid frame was sheer automatism. At any rate there was some response in him as Anne started off, some little aid to her own painful progress. Otherwise the task she set herself would have been a sheer impossibility.

As it was, every nerve, every cell of her slim young body quivered with exhaustion before she managed to gain the bottom of the creek's ravine and struggle along the narrow shelf of ground that was all that stretched between the ice-scummed water and the side of the gully through which it ran. They were twenty feet away from the tavern.

Anne stumbled to her knees, let her burden slide flaccidly to the ground. For a long minute she remained like that, pulling deep breaths into her lungs.

After awhile she heaved erect again. And then she did a very queer thing. Facing the earthy wall, she tugged at an ice-encrusted root tendril, reached sidewise and pulled at another.

A section of the bank moved out toward her, as if it were a door on hinges. It *was* a door, the earth a mere covering for the boards revealed on its inner side.

With a last fierce effort Anne dragged Peter's motionless form into that space, and the door thudded shut.

Soft footsteps whispered in the dark. A switch clicked. A small windowless room sprang into existence in the yellow light of a single, unshaded bulb, a room that was earth-floored but walled and ceiled by rough, splintered boards. In the center was a time-darkened work bench which had belonged to Webster Marsh.

Every gouge in that old wood was poignant with memory for Anne Marsh, every stain on it spoke of a comradeship few fathers and daughters are ever privileged to know. . . .

But Anne had no time for reminiscence now. Certain strange garments hung from a row of hooks screwed into one wall; disguises that had masked her in her raids on the despoilers of Laneville's poor. She took an armful, bent and deposited them on the floor and heaved the unconscious man onto the rough pallet.

His countenance was no longer blunt-jawed and competent. It was color-drained, and the laxness of fatigue and suffering made it the poignantly pathetic face of a sick boy. His lips moved.

"Anne," they muttered. "I love—" and twisted abruptly, writhing with a pain not physical. "No!" he moaned. "She's his daughter. She's a Marsh. You must hate her. Hate . . ."

"Hush, dear." The girl's cold hand rested on the sweat dewed brow. "Sleep."

He sighed, shrugged more closely into the pile on which he lay, was silent. There were tears in Anne's eyes as she threw off her soaked cap and jacket. What was it that lay between them? The first time she had seen him, up on the hillside where he had rescued her from a kidnap gang he had said something like that when he had discovered who she was.

"If I had known," he had said. "I wouldn't have . . ." But after that he had kissed her, had stopped to kiss her though the police were closing in on him.

Her deft hands unbuckled and tugged off the fur-lined galosh that was wet with something more viscid than thawing ice. Reddened, they rolled up the drenched trouser leg.

Anne shuddered at the scarlet mess the act revealed, but she got to her feet, darted across the room to the closet that contained first aid supplies.

Breath hissed from between her teeth in a gasp of relief as she bathed the blood away. The gash was ugly, but the bullet had only scraped the shin bone, paralyzing but not breaking it.

As she plastered down the end of that white swathing the tramp of heavy feet sounded dully overhead. A door slammed closed. Anne smiled wryly. The police had tired of waiting. They had gone.

She could get hot water now, put up the strengthening broth to heat that Peter would need so badly when he awakened.

She wiped her bloody hands with cotton waste, twisted to the wooden ladder that lifted from the dirt floor and ended against a seemingly solid ceiling. Her hand flashed to the switch as she passed and blackness smashed into the hidden room again.

Anne's feet whispered on the ladder treads. She reached the top of the ladder, fumbled. Her fingers found nailheads in a beam, pressed them in a certain order. Wood scraped on wood and pale luminance slitted the blackness above her. It grew slowly, became an aperture wide enough to let her through.

She went up into the bedroom she had shared with Faith since death and disgrace had taken her home from her and they had pooled their slender resources to build this tavern. She flung across the room to the single, iron-barred window, twisted at those bars. Behind her there was again the sound of scraping wood.

When she turned there was no longer any aperture in the floor. It was a level of wood, solid, unbroken.

This was not the tavern's only secret, not the only hidden thing that Bulldog Ryan would give his pension to unearth. That he suspected their existence Anne knew beyond doubt, but the courts demand more than vague suspicions before they issue a search warrant.

The hot breath of the huge range met her as she opened the door to the kitchen. She stepped out into that grateful warmth, pulled it shut behind her.

"Hello," a toneless voice said. "I see you decided to come back."

Anne twisted to the sound. The doorway framed the speaker; stocky, derby hat crowning his pinched, pointed visage, a mocking sneer twisting at his thin lips.

The police had gone, but Bulldog Ryan had remained behind.

CHAPTER III
Whispers of Doom

"Come back?" Anne Marsh managed to force through the clamping muscles of her throat. "I haven't been anywhere."

"Yeah." Ryan stood stolidly motionless on spread, thick legs, but the girl had an impression that he was advancing on her with that plodding, persistent pace with which he had come after her, always come after her for a fear-filled year. "I been right here the past half-hour an' you ain't gone out. It must be snowin' in your room there an' that's how you got your tootsies an' your pants wet."

The girl said nothing in reply. What was there to say?

"He's in there, huh," the heavy, expressionless voice began again. "Slippery Joe."

"I—I don't know what you're talking about."

"Yeah. I know you're dumb. I know you don't know nothing about Joe, just like you was asleep in there when some guy emptied ten grand outta John Simpson's safe. Somethin' funny about that room. I been wantin' to take a look at it for a long time an' now I'm goin' to."

He *was* moving now. His thick-soled shoes thudding purposefully toward her. "No," Anne whispered, spreading her arms wide. "You can't

go in there." He wouldn't miss the marks her wet boots had made on the floor in there. Not Ryan. They would show him the hidden trapdoor and. . . . "You haven't got a warrant."

"No, I ain't got a warrant. I'm breakin' the law. But there ain't nobody here 'ceptin' you to see me do it, an' there won't nobody ask too many questions when I bring in the guy we been huntin' for a year. *Get outta my way!*"

Spatulate fingers lashed out at Anne, clamped on her shoulder. The kitchen whirled around her and the floor came up to hit her. Anne rose on hands and knees, stayed that way, heart pounding, a soundless scream twisting her lips as Ryan lumbered through the opened door, and vanished within.

It was over. With only one left of those from whom she had set out to exact vengeance and reparation, Ryan had run her down at last. When the tracks had shown him the trapdoor and he'd broken it open he'd go down through it to find not only Peter but also the disguises that would tie her inescapably to certain unsolved crimes.

"Hey!" he snapped. "How the hell did you get in here?"

"That, Mr. Bulldog Ryan, ain't the question."

It was Faith's acidulous voice that sounded in reply. "It's what you mean by breakin' into a lady's bedroom."

Anne didn't know how she regained her feet. But she was erect, and she was where she could see into the room, where she could see Ryan's broad, squat back and the old woman facing him, a kimono fluttering about her bony, angular form, her wrinkled countenance a mask of righteous indignation.

"Get out!"

"Wait." His head moved and the gasping girl knew that no inch of the chamber was escaping his scrutiny. "Wait. Now that I'm in here, I'm goin' to look around."

"Go ahead and look, if you think it's going to do you any good. Maybe it will. Maybe it's the first time you've been in a decent woman's room."

Anne's hand went to her breast. It was coming now. He would see the wet marks on the floor and . . .

There weren't any there! The boards were dry. The old woman had wiped them dry!

Ryan moved around the room with a clumsy diffidence. He came to the window that was latticed by iron bars. He tugged at the black rods, peered out into the white swirl of nothingness without. Then he turned.

"All right," he said heavily. "You two have put it over on me again. Maybe I fell asleep standin' in that kitchen doorway. Maybe the two of you walked in and out of this room and I didn't see you. Yeah. But I've got a hunch there's something queer about this room, and I'm going to find out what it is damn soon."

"What do you mean?" Anne couldn't stop the question, though all she wanted was for Ryan to get out of that room, out of the house.

"I mean that you've got about a week more to stay here. Union Light and Power's bringin' a high tension line in from Bolton along this road and they're goin' to condemn this property for the right of way. Fulton Zander's in court right this mornin', gettin' the papers approved. When their crews start tearin' down I'm goin' to be here, with bells on."

He thudded out into the kitchen and banged the outer door shut.

"Faith," Anne exclaimed. "You slipped out through the front door and around to the creek. I didn't know you knew about the secret entrance."

"I know about that and I know a lot more things. Includin' that we're through here. I'm glad of that. Maybe we'll go away from here now, and live a normal life where you'll be Anne Marsh and not Webster Marsh's daughter. . . ."

"I'm still his daughter, Faith, still the daughter of dishonor. There's Fulton Zander left to deal with."

"You little fool— Here, where are you going?"

"To make some chicken broth. I . . ."

"I'll attend to that. You get some blankets and clean sheets and a pillow and take them down to your Peter. The idea," she sniffed, "of letting that poor hurt boy lay there on them filthy rags."

"You're an angel, Faith. . . ." Anne's arms were around the stringy, dried-up little figure.

The snow laid a blanket of soft white over the roofs of the mansions along East Drive, and edged the windows of the stores on Main Street with unintended beauty. Even Slum Hollow was crisp and white and clean in the sunset glow when the blizzard ended. And in the hovels of the very poor there was a little laughter, for there would be lots of jobs clearing the streets.

The shovellers started along Main Street at dusk and by ten they had reached the bridge over Waley's Creek where Bolton Turnpike came down off Lane Hill. They stopped there— because the state highway plows had opened the road to this point—and leaning on their long shovel handles squinted across the bridge at the windows of The Tavern, bright yellow oblongs in the night. That Marsh girl ran that joint, didn't she? The daughter of that guy Webster Marsh who swiped the Community Chest money last year and made everything so tough?

Yeah. We was pretty sore at him then, even though he bumped himself off, but what was the use keepin' a grudge? After all the charities around town been gettin' money all year in all kinds of funny ways, pretty near as much I guess as they woulda got if old Marsh hadn't done what he did. An' before that the ginks what worked fer his company were treated white, a lot better than this new gang's been doin', cuttin' wages an' not givin' no holidays with pay, an' so on—

Slim, somehow pathetic in the black of the mourning she still wore, Anne Marsh sat at her desk by the door between the dining room and kitchen and covertly read a yellowed clipping that had appeared in the *Laneville Courier* the morning after Christmas—a year ago.

"As long as the naked are unclothed," it ended, "and the hungry unfed, the soul of Webster Marsh shall have no peace."

"Only a little more, Dad," the girl whispered. "There's only one more left who must pay for your rest, and then . . ."

And then, what? The tavern that had grown to mean home to her would be torn down by the first of the New Year. She would be homeless again, her mission accomplished. Where would she and Faith go? What would they do . . . ?

Anne's thoughts abruptly ended. Another voice was whispering from under her desk. A ghostly, disembodied voice it was.

"It's so cosy here, Dickie," the voice said. "So nice to be alone with you here. It's always nice at the tavern but tonight the storm's kept people home, and it's like everything's just for us."

Anne's hand moved under the desktop to the switch that connected the tuned-down loudspeaker there with the one occupied booth. That was another of the secrets of the tavern, the concealed wires by which she had been enabled to listen in on the conversations of her guests, relaxing and guarded by the seeming privacy the little cubicles afforded them. This was how she had learned the plans by which John Lawton had sought to safeguard his payroll money and had been enabled to circumvent them. This was how Dr. Thomas Wayne had betrayed himself. . . .

"Guess we wouldn't be here either if the governor hadn't been called over to Fulton Zander's house so I could grab the car." Anne didn't switch off the talk. She did not make a habit of listening in on lovers' murmurings, but this . . .

"Gee! Won't he be sore?"

"Naw. He seemed all hipped up after that 'phone call. Said something about splitting a melon in cash. . . . Hell! Keep that quiet, Rhoda. I shouldn't have spilled it. He told me to keep mum about it. Reason why he wasn't using the boat was because this here meeting was so all-fired secret."

"Ooh, Dickie, that's positively thrilling. Tell me some more."

"But . . ."

"Oh, you needn't be afraid I'll tell anybody. All the girls tell me their secrets and I never repeat them. Come on, I'll give you an extra kiss if you do."

"Well, to tell you the truth I don't know anything more except that it's the Union Light and Power bunch that's going to be there."

"Oh, it's business." Anne didn't have to glance up into the artfully concealed mirror that would have given her a view of Rhoda's face to know that she was pouting. "I thought it was something interesting."

"Maybe it's more interesting than you think. The governor cracked wise about a stickup making a rich haul if he got a notion to . . ."

The voice clicked off as the kitchen door swung open behind Anne. A neatly dressed waitress came through, swinging supple hips. . . .

"Mary," Anne said, stopping her, "who are the youngsters in booth ten?"

"The girl's some dizzy deb from East Drive."

"And the boy?"

"Him? He's Dickie Lawton."

"I didn't know John Lawton had a son."

"Gosh, where you been, Miss Marsh? Dickie made the winning touchdown for Yale in the Dartmouth game. He's All-American left halfback an' some sugar for the dames."

"Oh yes. I remember now. Look, Mary, tell Hazel Jervis I want her to take the desk. There isn't anything doing tonight and I think I'll go to bed early."

"Sure." The girl swung away with her tray. Anne arose and went through the rear door of the dining room.

The trapdoor scraped shut over Anne's head. She went down into the darkness of the secret room, tiptoed across its floor. Her hands found that which they sought in the blackness.

For a moment there was no sound except

the soft whisper of breathing. Of *two* persons breathing. The girl had not turned on the light because Peter lay here asleep. Peter—her heart sang the name. . . .

And then the song was a dirge as she recalled the muttering of his delirium. "She's his daughter. You must hate her. Hate . . ."

Hate! That was her heritage. But why must *he* hate her?

She stifled a sob. Fabric rustled in the darkness, rubbing against satin-smooth skin. . . . Anne whirled to a sudden footfall, was blinded by yellow light. . . .

Her vision cleared. Peter was crouched against the wall, his hand on the light-switch. His clothing was wrinkled, but dry, his wounded leg straight again. The heart-shaped scar at the corner of his mouth was a white pucker. A small, flat automatic snouted from his fist.

"Up with 'em," he grunted. "Reach."

CHAPTER IV
Conspirators' Cabal

Anne Marsh's hands went over her head. "Peter!" she gasped. "What . . . What's the idea."

Astonishment peered from the youth's blue eyes. "It's—it's you. It's Anne." He pulled the gun dazedly across his forehead. "I heard someone in here, and I thought . . ."

"You'd been found out. But you saw me when the light came on. Why did you still . . . ?" And then she laughed. "Oh, it's because I'm dressed as a boy." Laughed and blushed, remembering that she had made the change with him lying only a yard away, that her dress, her frothy undergarments, still lay at her feet.

His blue eyes laughed with her. "Dressed as a boy but too damned beautiful to be one. You couldn't fool anybody except a sleep-doped dummy like me. Look at your hair. . . ."

"I'll fix that." Anne snatched a checked cap from the hook where the boy's clothing had hung, stuffed her hair into it. She bent, came up with

a handful of black loam from the floor, rubbed it over her face. "How's this?"

She strode toward him, and she was a grimy-faced, shabby street urchin to the last small inch of her. "Watch yer car, mister?" she whined. "Only cost you a nickle."

"You're pretty good, at that." Peter applauded.

"I ought to be. I've had enough practice. But that's enough fooling. Put out the light. I've got to get out of here."

"Out! Where—what . . . ?"

"Put out that light." She stamped her foot. "Please. It's getting late."

The darkness smashed in again. Once more there was the scrape of wood on wood.

Anne climbed to the road. She was a small, lonely figure trotting toward the heart of the city.

Close-drawn window drapes muffled the scrape of the snow shovels that were clearing East Drive. "We're all here," Fulton Zander's acidulous tones remarked, "If everyone is sure he was not followed here we can get down to business."

"What's the idea of all the secrecy?" The question oozed greasily from John Simpson's thick lips. "You'd think we were running a stag, the way you had us sneak in here."

"That's just what my Alice thinks," Donald Reynolds, grey of hair but dissipated of ferret-like countenance twittered.

Zander's fleshless lips scarcely moved. "You'll be able to bribe your Alice with a new diamond for Christmas, Don," he murmured, "and as for you, Simpson, I imagine some of the big depositors in your bank would be interested in knowing you were here tonight; those who hold bonds of the Union Light and Power Company for example—when I move in court tomorrow for a receivership!"

"A receivership!" John Lawton, Laneville's department store owner, spluttered; "I thought we were making money."

"We have been," Zander replied. "*We* have been, but the books show the corporation has been running at a terrific loss. I told you a year ago that there was more to my plan than just getting hold of the outfit. You gave me authority to operate it in accordance with my ideas, and I've done so. I've been . . ."

"Milking the business. Good man!" Tall, completely bald, Dr. Thomas Wayne was too sardonic even to pretend ignorance of Zander's machinations as the others were doing. "Gentlemen!" He lifted a small glass, "I give you Fulton Zander, shrewdest lawyer in seven states."

"I don't like it," the last of the half-dozen seated around the table moaned. "I think we're going too far. I'm sorry I ever threw in with you fellows, I've been sorry ever since—ever since Webster Marsh—killed himself." Fred Harris's neatly manicured hands tugged at his trim van dyke, trembling, and the tiny lights of hysteria jittered in his red-shot eyes. "I keep seeing him in my sleep, pointing a finger at me, accusing. I feel him looking at us now, listening. . . ."

Outside the snow gleamed with an eerie, internal luminance, but along East Drive bomb-like flares waved the orange-red pennants of their flames to illumine the labors of the shovellers. The lurid glare deepened the shadow of a great fir in the Zander grounds so that it was a tar-hued, impenetrable mass lying against the sidewall of the house.

Within that shadow a black shape crouched silent and motionless and somehow feral. A gloved hand held a small round diaphragm against the wood and from this two slender, hollow rubber tubes curved to shell-like ears covered by hair that light would have revealed as tightly curled and tawny.

Fulton Zander's eyes moved to the dapper little man, blue lids folding vulture-like over their pale gaze. "Would you like to refuse your share, Harris, and let me split it up among the rest of us?"

"No. I'll be damned if I will. In for a calf, in for an ox."

"Then I shall proceed." The lawyer's smile was a humorless, vinegary twitch of pallid lips. "I shall not bore you with the manipulations by which it was accomplished, but, as I have already said, while the books of Union Light and Power show it to have run this year at a terrific loss, I have here, in this box, the round sum of fifty thousand dollars in cash. I am reserving ten thousand for myself and distributing eight thousand to each of you. A pretty little Christmas gift from the people of Laneville, gentlemen, I think you will agree."

"Not bad," Simpson rubbed pudgey hands. "Not bad," his buttery accents repeated.

"I take it you are satisfied," Zander murmured. One of his claws moved to his vest pocket, came out with a small key that it fitted into the cash box's lock, clicked over . . .

A dull detonation, the crash of splintering glass, sounded from somewhere outside the room, "What's that," Harris squealed. "What was that?"

The attorney's head jerked up and his beak pointed at the closed door. "An explosion. It sounded like an explosion somewhere at the back of the house."

"Damned right it was," Reynolds shoved himself up out of his seat. "Look. Look at that." His hand pointed to the threshold of the door. Something grey, slender, curled from under it, stretched a lazy tendril into the room. "That's smoke. The house is on fire."

Zander leaped to his feet, a moment behind the others because he took time to relock the money box and shove it under his arm. "Fire," he gasped. "There's no one back there. I gave the servants a night off. We've got to . . ."

He didn't need to finish. Wayne had flung the door open on swirling grey smoke, the others were crowding through it behind him. In that moment darkness smashed down on them, stygian, complete.

Someone shouted incoherently. Someone coughed. Then Fred Harris's cry was a thin squeal in the dark smoke-pall that flickered with a wavering, lurid glow. "The door is wedged."

"Good thing." Zander's voice was cool, collected. "If the bunch of you poured out that way it would be a dead giveaway. Go through the back, the way you came." Feet thudded, obeying.

In the deserted room a window scraped open, scraped closed again, the sound unnoticed.

Snow-glimmer came in through a smashed window, outlining the gleaming kitchen into which the rout burst. The smoke was fading, here, thinner with a strange swiftness.

"What's this?" Dr. Wayne exclaimed, pouncing on a round, black object that lay in the center of the kitchen floor. "Well, I'll be damned. A smoke pot."

He came up with it, and the others crowded around him. Someone struck flame from a cigarette lighter and astonished eyes widened, staring at that which he held.

It was one of the bomb-like road flares that lined East Drive. Its wick was wrapped around with a grease-smeared rag that still smouldered acridly!

"What the hell, Zander?" Lawton grunted. "What kind of trick is this you're pulling on us?"

There was no answer.

"Hey, Zander!" The men peered at one another. There were only five of them. Their host was missing.

"Skipped!" Wayne snarled. "The—that's why he had the front door locked. He got us in here and skipped with the cash."

"You're nuts!" Reynolds, holding the lighter, protested. "Something's happened to him." He turned, shoved through the white-faced knot, went through the kitchen doorway into the narrow passageway from the front of the house. Then he spoke again, his ejaculation a throaty gasp. "Here he is!"

The others, crowding out behind him, saw Zander too. He was a crumpled, grotesquely awkward heap across the threshold of the room in which the interrupted meeting had been held. A blue bruise on his forehead told what it was that had stunned him.

The cash box was nowhere in sight.

CHAPTER V
Caught

Anne Marsh's little heels thudded into the soft ground where she had crouched, listening in on the men who had killed her father as surely as though they had held the poison cup to his lips. She huddled in the ebon shadow that had served her so well, and worked at the boy's jacket she wore, trying to button it over a black metal cash box that held fifty thousand dollars in untraceable cash.

The wide street was a river of eerie light dotted by the mufflered, overcoated forms of laborers. But to her right there was a thick hedge that drowned the radiance, and between her and that shelter there was only ten feet of open ground.

Her muscles tensed, as a sprinter's would, waiting for the starter's gun. Then she was off, a flitting shadow across the white snow blanket.

Strong arms clamped around her, pinning her arms to her side, holding her helpless. "Got you!" a toneless voice exclaimed. "Got you at last! And dead to rights."

Anne moaned, and slumped, knowing it was useless to struggle. Bulldog Ryan's pinched visage glimmered out of the darkness, his thin lips pulling away from his teeth in a grimace of gloating triumph.

"I figured the only way you could get in and out of that damn room of yours was if there was a tunnel through the bank underneath, and I camped out in the bushes across the creek, where I could keep watch. I followed you, and I let you have plenty of rope, and by jingo, you sure have hung yourself with it."

"All right," the girl said, her tones flat, dreary but very steady. "You've got me, and it's all over. Put the handcuffs on me and take me off to jail."

"I'll put the cuffs on you all right," the detective grunted, suiting the action to the word, "but we're not goin' to the station yet. We're goin' back there an' see just what it is you've been up to."

The electric light wires had been clipped outside the house, could not be repaired till a linesman was called, but someone had found candles and the room with the long table was illuminated once more. Fulton Zander was back in his chair, the bruise livid on his forehead.

"Look here, officer." The words slid from his thin, scarcely moving lips. "You've recovered my cash box and that satisfies me. This is the Christmas season and I'm disposed to be charitable. Let the boy go."

A twisted steel chain linked Anne's slender wrist to Ryan's burly one. "Let him go, is it?" The detective's eyes were slitted, dangerous. "*Him—*" His free hand jerked the cap from his prisoner's head and her hair sprang from confinement, a russet nimbus in the wavering candlelight. "*Her*, you mean. You don't know what you're askin'. This is Anne Marsh, gentlemen, the slipperiest crook that ever prowled Laneville. You ought to know it. There ain't one of you here she ain't rooked. I been pluggin' after her for a year an' I got her at last, an' you say let her go. Not if I have to pull you all in for compoundin' a felony."

"You can't do that," Zander snarled. "We'll swear you're lying. A cop's word against six of the most reputable men in Laneville! Which do you think a jury will believe?"

"I've got the cash box and I've got the tracks under the window. That's evidence enough to bear me out, and by God I'll put it over."

"Maybe you will," Simpson wheezed. "But if you try it, we'll break you. There's enough influence in this crowd to break a commissioner, let alone a flatfoot."

Ryan's big hand fisted at his side. "Break and be damned," he growled. "This wench goes behind the bars if I have to turn in my badge the next day."

Anne flung her head back. "You won't have to turn in your badge, Ryan. It's been a clean fight between us, an honest fight. Take me in to prison. I'll sign a confession. And I'll go on the witness stand and tell the world exactly why the directors of Union Light and Power were here, exactly why they're threatening you to keep the fact quiet that they were here."

"And that, gents, is the payoff," Ryan flung at them. "So long. I'll see you in court."

He turned, and there was a curious gentleness in that growl of his. "Come along, Miss Marsh. Come . . ."

"Not so fast!" A lithe, dark-haired figure confronted him in the doorway, a figure whose slender hand thrust the muzzle of a vicious little automatic point-blank at him. "Back up, Ryan. Let go of that chain and grab air. One peep out of any of you, one move, and I'll blast you!"

The detective's thick arms went ceiling-ward. Three voices tangled, each gasping a name.

"Slippery Joe," Ryan whispered.

"Peter!" Anne exclaimed.

And from Fulton Zander, his face livid as the bruise on his brow, gasped: "Peter Corbin!"

It was this last to which the intruder responded. "Yes, Zander. Peter Corbin." His mouth twitched, bitterly. "You didn't know I escaped from the steel-barred hell to which you sent me. You and your boss, Webster Marsh, framing me for sabotage—that you hired done on the Apple Street dynamo to drive the Company stocks down so you could buy it cheap."

"No!" Anne's cry was a low throb, pain torn. "No, Peter. Dad never did anything like that. He couldn't."

"The hell he couldn't." The youth's laugh was icy. "He packed me away in the pen for twenty years, but I crushed out, and I've been skulking in the woods ever since. That's what Webster Marsh did to me. That's why I hate his memory, hate everyone who belongs to him."

"No." the girl moaned, and was across the room in a flash, was leaning over Zander. "Tell him. If there's any good in you at all, tell him Dad didn't do that terrible thing to him."

Her grey eyes held the lawyer's vulpine ones, and there was a breath-bated, tense silence in the room. Silence, utter stillness, the only motion that of the barrel of Peter's automatic flicking from one to another of the group.

"Tell him," Anne's tear-filled voice broke that silence. "You must!"

Zander's fleshless lips moved. "Marsh didn't know anything about it. I rigged the whole thing, and I bought in the stock."

The girl spun to the man she loved. "You heard that, Peter," she cried. "You heard him."

"I heard him." The grim lines of the youth's darkly handsome face broke, and it was boyishly appealing. "I heard him, my darling." And then it was stern again.

"There's a roll of wire in my pocket, Anne, cut into short lengths. Get it out and tie it around their ankles and their wrists. Their handkerchiefs will do for gags."

It was done. Peter and Anne were gone. The six directors who had stolen and milked and wrecked the Union Light and Power Company sat around their leader's long table, unable to move or speak.

In another chair sat Bulldog Ryan, gagged and bound like the rest. Peculiarly enough, there was the faint shadow of a smile on his face, as though he found some secret satisfaction even in defeat.

The scraping of snow shovels were almost inaudible now, as their wielders worked away from the Zander house. A candle guttered, went out. From an infinite distance the howl of the night express came deepthroated and melancholy into the room.

Bulldog Ryan stirred. His shoulders heaved. His wrists came free of the wires that clamped them. It could be seen now that he had used an old trick, swelling them as the girl lashed them, so that they had actually not been bound at all. He bent, unfastened his feet, rose and thumbed the gagging handkerchief from his mouth.

"I got an awful short memory," he grunted, "and I think you birds got the same. Nothin'

happened here tonight. Nothin' at all. Only, I reckon you birds will want to be certain my memory stays bad—so supposin' you ante up about fifty grand for that Christmas Fund."

Starting to work on Fulton Zander's lashings, he sighed. "I'm puttin' in for retirement in the mornin'," he muttered. "I'm gettin' too soft to be on the cops." He paused. "And anyway, there won't be no fun in the job, with only common, ordinary crooks to chase."

Two extracts from the *Laneville Daily Courier* of Dec. 23rd, 1936. The first:

The COURIER'S CHRISTMAS FUND, that had not filled its quota this year, was put far over the top this morning by two anonymous contributions of fifty thousand dollars. One was delivered by Western Union Messenger. No information as to its source could be obtained except that the package in which the currency was wrapped was left at the depot office by two young men who dashed for the midnight express just as the gates were closing. The other fifty thousand was found in the morning mail at the Fund's headquarters. There are absolutely no clues as to its source.

The second:

The popular Tavern on Bolton Turnpike closed its hospitable doors forever today. Miss Faith Parker, one of the co-owners, cashed the condemnation award and immediately left for parts unknown. She refused to confirm or deny the rumor that she was to join Miss Anne Marsh, who, it will be remembered, is the daughter of the late Webster Marsh.

Bulldog Ryan sipped his breakfast coffee as he read the two items with his eyes that held a strange light. The tight-lipped mouth quirked faintly. "Hope the old gal don't have as much trouble findin' her as I did," he muttered.

THE GOLDEN AGE

THE SECRET ADVERSARY

Agatha Christie

ASK ANY READER OF DETECTIVE STORIES to name the author they love most or the author they read when they were young and you will be sure to be given the one name on everybody's list: Agatha Mary Clarissa Miller Christie (1890–1976), the most popular writer of detective fiction who ever lived (her sales in all languages are reported to have surpassed four billion copies).

Christie's remarkably proficient first book, *The Mysterious Affair at Styles* (1920), is generally credited as the volume that initiated what is known as the Golden Age of mystery fiction. This era, bracketed by the two world wars, saw the rise of the fair-play puzzle story and the series detective, whether an official member of the police department (such as Freeman Wills Crofts's Inspector French), a private detective (like Christie's Hercule Poirot, who made his debut in her first novel), or an amateur sleuth (like Dorothy L. Sayers's Lord Peter Wimsey).

But it was Christie who towered above the others, outselling, outproducing, and outliving the rest. The manuscript of her first novel had been rejected by several publishing houses, and John Lane, the eventual publisher, held it for more than a year before offering only £25 for it. Encouraged by the sale, Christie went on to write more than a hundred books and plays, including the longest continuously running play of all time, *The Mousetrap* (since it opened in 1952, there have been more than 27,000 performances—with no closing in sight), as well as one of the best, *Witness for the Prosecution* (1953).

Less famous than Poirot and Miss Marple, Tommy and Tuppence (actually Prudence) were described in the London *Telegraph* as Christie's greatest creation. They meet in this book, Christie's second novel, as longtime friends who fall in love and (not to give away too much) marry. Seeking a life of fun and excitement, they become detectives when they start their own business, The Young Adventurers. Tuppence is the brains of the team while Tommy is the realist. They also appeared in a short story collection, *Partners in Crime* (1929), and four novels, including *Postern of Fate* (1973), the last novel Christie ever wrote, though not the last published, which was *Sleeping Murder* (1976).

The Secret Adversary was originally published in London by The Bodley Head in 1922.

The Secret Adversary

AGATHA CHRISTIE

CONTENTS

PROLOGUE

It was 2 P.M. on the afternoon of May 7, 1915. The *Lusitania* had been struck by two torpedoes in succession and was sinking rapidly, while the boats were being launched with all possible speed. The women and children were being lined up awaiting their turn. Some still clung desperately to husbands and fathers; others clutched their children closely to their breasts. One girl stood alone, slightly apart from the rest. She was quite young, not more than eighteen. She did not seem afraid, and her grave, steadfast eyes looked straight ahead.

"I beg your pardon."

A man's voice beside her made her start and turn. She had noticed the speaker more than once amongst the first-class passengers. There had been a hint of mystery about him which had appealed to her imagination. He spoke to no one. If anyone spoke to him he was quick to rebuff the overture. Also he had a nervous way of looking over his shoulder with a swift, suspicious glance.

She noticed now that he was greatly agitated. There were beads of perspiration on his brow. He was evidently in a state of overmastering fear. And yet he did not strike her as the kind of man who would be afraid to meet death!

"Yes?" Her grave eyes met his inquiringly.

He stood looking at her with a kind of desperate irresolution.

"It must be!" he muttered to himself. "Yes—it is the only way." Then aloud he said abruptly: "You are an American?"

"Yes."

"A patriotic one?"

The girl flushed.

"I guess you've no right to ask such a thing! Of course I am!"

"Don't be offended. You wouldn't be if you knew how much there was at stake. But I've got to trust some one—and it must be a woman."

"Why?"

"Because of 'women and children first.'" He looked round and lowered his voice. "I'm carrying papers—vitally important papers. They may make all the difference to the Allies in the war. You understand? These papers have *got* to be saved! They've more chance with you than with me. Will you take them?"

The girl held out her hand.

"Wait—I must warn you. There may be a risk—if I've been followed. I don't think I have, but one never knows. If so, there will be danger. Have you the nerve to go through with it?"

The girl smiled.

"I'll go through with it all right. And I'm real

proud to be chosen! What am I to do with them afterwards?"

"Watch the newspapers! I'll advertise in the personal column of the *Times*, beginning 'Shipmate.' At the end of three days if there's nothing—well, you'll know I'm down and out. Then take the packet to the American Embassy, and deliver it into the Ambassador's own hands. Is that clear?"

"Quite clear."

"Then be ready—I'm going to say good-bye." He took her hand in his. "Good-bye. Good luck to you," he said in a louder tone.

Her hand closed on the oilskin packet that had lain in his palm.

The *Lusitania* settled with a more decided list to starboard. In answer to a quick command, the girl went forward to take her place in the boat.

CHAPTER I
The Young Adventurers, Ltd.

"Tommy, old thing!"

"Tuppence, old bean!"

The two young people greeted each other affectionately, and momentarily blocked the Dover Street Tube exit in doing so. The adjective "old" was misleading. Their united ages would certainly not have totalled forty-five.

"Not seen you for simply centuries," continued the young man. "Where are you off to? Come and chew a bun with me. We're getting a bit unpopular here—blocking the gangway as it were. Let's get out of it."

The girl assenting, they started walking down Dover Street towards Piccadilly.

"Now then," said Tommy, "where shall we go?"

The very faint anxiety which underlay his tone did not escape the astute ears of Miss Prudence Cowley, known to her intimate friends for some mysterious reason as "Tuppence." She pounced at once.

"Tommy, you're stony!"

"Not a bit of it," declared Tommy unconvincingly. "Rolling in cash."

"You always were a shocking liar," said Tuppence severely, "though you did once persuade Sister Greenbank that the doctor had ordered you beer as a tonic, but forgotten to write it on the chart. Do you remember?"

Tommy chuckled.

"I should think I did! Wasn't the old cat in a rage when she found out? Not that she was a bad sort really, old Mother Greenbank! Good old hospital—demobbed like everything else, I suppose?"

Tuppence sighed.

"Yes. You too?"

Tommy nodded.

"Two months ago."

"Gratuity?" hinted Tuppence.

"Spent."

"Oh, Tommy!"

"No, old thing, not in riotous dissipation. No such luck! The cost of living—ordinary plain, or garden living nowadays is, I assure you, if you do not know——"

"My dear child," interrupted Tuppence, "there is nothing I do *not* know about the cost of living. Here we are at Lyons', and we will each of us pay for our own. That's it!" And Tuppence led the way upstairs.

The place was full, and they wandered about looking for a table, catching odds and ends of conversation as they did so.

"And—do you know, she sat down and *cried* when I told her she couldn't have the flat after all." "It was simply a *bargain*, my dear! Just like the one Mabel Lewis brought from Paris——"

"Funny scraps one does overhear," murmured Tommy. "I passed two Johnnies in the street today talking about some one called Jane Finn. Did you ever hear such a name?"

But at that moment two elderly ladies rose and collected parcels, and Tuppence deftly ensconced herself in one of the vacant seats.

Tommy ordered tea and buns. Tuppence ordered tea and buttered toast.

"And mind the tea comes in separate teapots," she added severely.

Tommy sat down opposite her. His bared head revealed a shock of exquisitely slicked-back red hair. His face was pleasantly ugly—nondescript, yet unmistakably the face of a gentleman and a sportsman. His brown suit was well cut, but perilously near the end of its tether.

They were an essentially modern-looking couple as they sat there. Tuppence had no claim to beauty, but there was character and charm in the elfin lines of her little face, with its determined chin and large, wide-apart grey eyes that looked mistily out from under straight, black brows. She wore a small bright green toque over her black bobbed hair, and her extremely short and rather shabby skirt revealed a pair of uncommonly dainty ankles. Her appearance presented a valiant attempt at smartness.

The tea came at last, and Tuppence, rousing herself from a fit of meditation, poured it out.

"Now then," said Tommy, taking a large bite of bun, "let's get up-to-date. Remember, I haven't seen you since that time in hospital in 1916."

"Very well." Tuppence helped herself liberally to buttered toast. "Abridged biography of Miss Prudence Cowley, fifth daughter of Archdeacon Cowley of Little Missendell, Suffolk. Miss Cowley left the delights (and drudgeries) of her home life early in the war and came up to London, where she entered an officers' hospital. First month: Washed up six hundred and forty-eight plates every day. Second month: Promoted to drying aforesaid plates. Third month: Promoted to peeling potatoes. Fourth month: Promoted to cutting bread and butter. Fifth month: Promoted one floor up to duties of wardmaid with mop and pail. Sixth month: Promoted to waiting at table. Seventh month: Pleasing appearance and nice manners so striking that am promoted to waiting on the Sisters! Eighth month: Slight check in career. Sister Bond ate Sister Westhaven's egg! Grand row! Wardmaid clearly to blame! Inattention in such important matters cannot be too highly censured. Mop and pail again! How are the mighty fallen! Ninth month: Promoted to sweeping out wards, where I found a friend of my childhood in Lieutenant Thomas Beresford (bow, Tommy!), whom I had not seen for five long years. The meeting was affecting! Tenth month: Reproved by matron for visiting the pictures in company with one of the patients, namely: the aforementioned Lieutenant Thomas Beresford. Eleventh and twelfth months: Parlourmaid duties resumed with entire success. At the end of the year left hospital in a blaze of glory. After that, the talented Miss Cowley drove successively a trade delivery van, a motor-lorry, and a general. The last was the pleasantest. He was quite a young general!"

"What blighter was that?" inquired Tommy. "Perfectly sickening the way those brass hats drove from the War Office to the *Savoy*, and from the *Savoy* to the War Office!"

"I've forgotten his name now," confessed Tuppence. "To resume, that was in a way the apex of my career. I next entered a Government office. We had several very enjoyable tea parties. I had intended to become a land girl, a post-woman, and a bus conductress by way of rounding off my career—but the Armistice intervened! I clung to the office with the true limpet touch for many long months, but, alas, I was combed out at last. Since then I've been looking for a job. Now then—your turn."

"There's not so much promotion in mine," said Tommy regretfully, "and a great deal less variety. I went out to France again, as you know. Then they sent me to Mesopotamia, and I got wounded for the second time, and went into hospital out there. Then I got stuck in Egypt till the Armistice happened, kicked my heels there some time longer, and, as I told you, finally got demobbed. And, for ten long, weary months I've been job hunting! There aren't any jobs! And, if there were, they wouldn't give 'em to me. What good am I? What do I know about business? Nothing."

Tuppence nodded gloomily.

"What about the colonies?" she suggested.

Tommy shook his head.

"I shouldn't like the colonies—and I'm perfectly certain they wouldn't like me!"

"Rich relations?"

Again Tommy shook his head.

"Oh, Tommy, not even a great-aunt?"

"I've got an old uncle who's more or less rolling, but he's no good."

"Why not?"

"Wanted to adopt me once. I refused."

"I think I remember hearing about it," said Tuppence slowly. "You refused because of your mother——"

Tommy flushed.

"Yes, it would have been a bit rough on the mater. As you know, I was all she had. Old boy hated her—wanted to get me away from her. Just a bit of spite."

"Your mother's dead, isn't she?" said Tuppence gently.

Tommy nodded.

Tuppence's large grey eyes looked misty.

"You're a good sort, Tommy. I always knew it."

"Rot!" said Tommy hastily. "Well, that's my position. I'm just about desperate."

"So am I! I've hung out as long as I could. I've touted round. I've answered advertisements. I've tried every mortal blessed thing. I've screwed and saved and pinched! But it's no good. I shall have to go home!"

"Don't you want to?"

"Of course I don't want to! What's the good of being sentimental? Father's a dear—I'm awfully fond of him—but you've no idea how I worry him! He has that delightful early Victorian view that short skirts and smoking are immoral. You can imagine what a thorn in the flesh I am to him! He just heaved a sigh of relief when the war took me off. You see, there are seven of us at home. It's awful! All housework and mother's meetings! I have always been the changeling. I don't want to go back, but—oh, Tommy, what else is there to do?"

Tommy shook his head sadly. There was a silence, and then Tuppence burst out:

"Money, money, money! I think about money morning, noon, and night! I dare say it's mercenary of me, but there it is!"

"Same here," agreed Tommy with feeling.

"I've thought over every imaginable way of getting it too," continued Tuppence. "There are only three! To be left it, to marry it, or to make it. First is ruled out. I haven't got any rich elderly relatives. Any relatives I have are in homes for decayed gentlewomen! I always help old ladies over crossings, and pick up parcels for old gentlemen, in case they should turn out to be eccentric millionaires. But not one of them has ever asked me my name—and quite a lot never said 'Thank you.'"

There was a pause.

"Of course," resumed Tuppence, "marriage is my best chance. I made up my mind to marry money when I was quite young. Any thinking girl would! I'm not sentimental, you know." She paused. "Come now, you can't say I'm sentimental," she added sharply.

"Certainly not," agreed Tommy hastily. "No one would ever think of sentiment in connection with you."

"That's not very polite," replied Tuppence. "But I dare say you mean it all right. Well, there it is! I'm ready and willing—but I never meet any rich men! All the boys I know are about as hard up as I am."

"What about the general?" inquired Tommy.

"I fancy he keeps a bicycle shop in time of peace," explained Tuppence. "No, there it is! Now *you* could marry a rich girl."

"I'm like you. I don't know any."

"That doesn't matter. You can always get to know one. Now, if I see a man in a fur coat come out of the *Ritz* I can't rush up to him and say: 'Look here, you're rich. I'd like to know you.'"

"Do you suggest that I should do that to a similarly garbed female?"

"Don't be silly. You tread on her foot, or pick up her handkerchief, or something like that. If she thinks you want to know her she's flattered, and will manage it for you somehow."

"You overrate my manly charms," murmured Tommy.

"On the other hand," proceeded Tuppence, "my millionaire would probably run for his life! No—marriage is fraught with difficulties. Remains—to *make* money!"

"We've tried that, and failed," Tommy reminded her.

"We've tried all the orthodox ways, yes. But suppose we try the unorthodox. Tommy, let's be adventurers!"

"Certainly," replied Tommy cheerfully. "How do we begin?"

"That's the difficulty. If we could make ourselves known, people might hire us to commit crimes for them."

"Delightful," commented Tommy. "Especially coming from a clergyman's daughter!"

"The moral guilt," Tuppence pointed out, "would be theirs—not mine. You must admit that there's a difference between stealing a diamond necklace for yourself and being hired to steal it."

"There wouldn't be the least difference if you were caught!"

"Perhaps not. But I shouldn't be caught. I'm so clever."

"Modesty always was your besetting sin," remarked Tommy.

"Don't rag. Look here, Tommy, shall we really? Shall we form a business partnership?"

"Form a company for the stealing of diamond necklaces?"

"That was only an illustration. Let's have a—what do you call it in book-keeping?"

"Don't know. Never did any."

"I have—but I always got mixed up, and used to put credit entries on the debit side, and vice versa—so they fired me out. Oh, I know—a joint venture! It struck me as such a romantic phrase to come across in the middle of musty old figures. It's got an Elizabethan flavour about it—makes one think of galleons and doubloons. A joint venture!"

"Trading under the name of the Young Adventurers, Ltd.? Is that your idea, Tuppence?"

"It's all very well to laugh, but I feel there might be something in it."

"How do you propose to get in touch with your would-be employers?"

"Advertisement," replied Tuppence promptly. "Have you got a bit of paper and a pencil? Men usually seem to have. Just like we have hairpins and powder-puffs."

Tommy handed over a rather shabby green notebook, and Tuppence began writing busily.

"Shall we begin: 'Young officer, twice wounded in the war——' "

"Certainly not."

"Oh, very well, my dear boy. But I can assure you that that sort of thing might touch the heart of an elderly spinster, and she might adopt you, and then there would be no need for you to be a young adventurer at all."

"I don't want to be adopted."

"I forgot you had a prejudice against it. I was only ragging you! The papers are full up to the brim with that type of thing. Now listen—how's this? 'Two young adventurers for hire. Willing to do anything, go anywhere. Pay must be good.' (We might as well make that clear from the start.) Then we might add: 'No reasonable offer refused'—like flats and furniture."

"I should think any offer we get in answer to that would be a pretty *un*reasonable one!"

"Tommy! You're a genius! That's ever so much more chic. 'No unreasonable offer refused—if pay is good.' How's that?"

"I shouldn't mention pay again. It looks rather eager."

"It couldn't look as eager as I feel! But perhaps you are right. Now I'll read it straight through. 'Two young adventurers for hire. Willing to do anything, go anywhere. Pay must be good. No unreasonable offer refused.' How would that strike you if you read it?"

"It would strike me as either being a hoax, or else written by a lunatic."

"It's not half so insane as a thing I read this morning beginning 'Petunia' and signed 'Best

Boy.' " She tore out the leaf and handed it to Tommy. "There you are. *Times*, I think. Reply to Box so-and-so. I expect it will be about five shillings. Here's half a crown for my share."

Tommy was holding the paper thoughtfully. His face burned a deeper red.

"Shall we really try it?" he said at last. "Shall we, Tuppence? Just for the fun of the thing?"

"Tommy, you're a sport! I knew you would be! Let's drink to success." She poured some cold dregs of tea into the two cups.

"Here's to our joint venture, and may it prosper!"

"The Young Adventurers, Ltd.!" responded Tommy.

They put down the cups and laughed rather uncertainly. Tuppence rose.

"I must return to my palatial suite at the hostel."

"Perhaps it is time I strolled round to the *Ritz*," agreed Tommy with a grin. "Where shall we meet? And when?"

"Twelve o'clock tomorrow. Piccadilly Tube station. Will that suit you?"

"My time is my own," replied Mr. Beresford magnificently.

"So long, then."

"Good-bye, old thing."

The two young people went off in opposite directions. Tuppence's hostel was situated in what was charitably called Southern Belgravia. For reasons of economy she did not take a bus.

She was half-way across St. James's Park, when a man's voice behind her made her start.

"Excuse me," it said. "But may I speak to you for a moment?"

CHAPTER II
Mr. Whittington's Offer

Tuppence turned sharply, but the words hovering on the tip of her tongue remained unspoken, for the man's appearance and manner did not bear out her first and most natural assumption.

She hesitated. As if he read her thoughts, the man said quickly:

"I can assure you I mean no disrespect."

Tuppence believed him. Although she disliked and distrusted him instinctively, she was inclined to acquit him of the particular motive which she had at first attributed to him. She looked him up and down. He was a big man, clean shaven, with a heavy jowl. His eyes were small and cunning, and shifted their glance under her direct gaze.

"Well, what is it?" she asked.

The man smiled.

"I happened to overhear part of your conversation with the young gentleman in Lyons'."

"Well—what of it?"

"Nothing—except that I think I may be of some use to you."

Another inference forced itself into Tuppence's mind:

"You followed me here?"

"I took that liberty."

"And in what way do you think you could be of use to me?"

The man took a card from his pocket and handed it to her with a bow.

Tuppence took it and scrutinized it carefully. It bore the inscription, "Mr. Edward Whittington." Below the name were the words "Esthonia Glassware Co.," and the address of a city office. Mr. Whittington spoke again:

"If you will call upon me tomorrow morning at eleven o'clock, I will lay the details of my proposition before you."

"At eleven o'clock?" said Tuppence doubtfully.

"At eleven o'clock."

Tuppence made up her mind.

"Very well. I'll be there."

"Thank you. Good evening."

He raised his hat with a flourish, and walked away. Tuppence remained for some minutes gazing after him. Then she gave a curious movement of her shoulders, rather as a terrier shakes himself.

"The adventures have begun," she murmured to herself. "What does he want me to do, I wonder? There's something about you, Mr. Whittington, that I don't like at all. But, on the other hand, I'm not the least bit afraid of you. And as I've said before, and shall doubtless say again, little Tuppence can look after herself, thank you!"

And with a short, sharp nod of her head she walked briskly onward. As a result of further meditations, however, she turned aside from the direct route and entered a post office. There she pondered for some moments, a telegraph form in her hand. The thought of a possible five shillings spent unnecessarily spurred her to action, and she decided to risk the waste of ninepence.

Disdaining the spiky pen and thick, black treacle which a beneficent Government had provided, Tuppence drew out Tommy's pencil which she had retained and wrote rapidly: "Don't put in advertisement. Will explain tomorrow." She addressed it to Tommy at his club, from which in one short month he would have to resign, unless a kindly fortune permitted him to renew his subscription.

"It may catch him," she murmured. "Anyway, it's worth trying."

After handing it over the counter she set out briskly for home, stopping at a baker's to buy three-penny-worth of new buns.

Later, in her tiny cubicle at the top of the house she munched buns and reflected on the future. What was the Esthonia Glassware Co., and what earthly need could it have for her services? A pleasurable thrill of excitement made Tuppence tingle. At any rate, the country vicarage had retreated into the background again. The morrow held possibilities.

It was a long time before Tuppence went to sleep that night, and, when at length she did, she dreamed that Mr. Whittington had set her to washing up a pile of Esthonia Glassware, which bore an unaccountable resemblance to hospital plates!

It wanted some five minutes to eleven when Tuppence reached the block of buildings in which the offices of the Esthonia Glassware Co.

were situated. To arrive before the time would look over-eager. So Tuppence decided to walk to the end of the street and back again. She did so. On the stroke of eleven she plunged into the recesses of the building. The Esthonia Glassware Co. was on the top floor. There was a lift, but Tuppence chose to walk up.

Slightly out of breath, she came to a halt outside the ground glass door with the legend painted across it "Esthonia Glassware Co."

Tuppence knocked. In response to a voice from within, she turned the handle and walked into a small rather dirty outer office.

A middle-aged clerk got down from a high stool at a desk near the window and came towards her inquiringly.

"I have an appointment with Mr. Whittington," said Tuppence.

"Will you come this way, please." He crossed to a partition door with "Private" on it, knocked, then opened the door and stood aside to let her pass in.

Mr. Whittington was seated behind a large desk covered with papers. Tuppence felt her previous judgment confirmed. There was something wrong about Mr. Whittington. The combination of his sleek prosperity and his shifty eye was not attractive.

He looked up and nodded.

"So you've turned up all right? That's good. Sit down, will you?"

Tuppence sat down on the chair facing him. She looked particularly small and demure this morning. She sat there meekly with downcast eyes whilst Mr. Whittington sorted and rustled amongst his papers. Finally he pushed them away, and leaned over the desk.

"Now, my dear young lady, let us come to business." His large face broadened into a smile. "You want work? Well, I have work to offer you. What should you say now to £100 down, and all expenses paid?" Mr. Whittington leaned back in his chair, and thrust his thumbs into the armholes of his waistcoat.

Tuppence eyed him warily.

"And the nature of the work?" she demanded.

"Nominal—purely nominal. A pleasant trip, that is all."

"Where to?"

Mr. Whittington smiled again.

"Paris."

"Oh!" said Tuppence thoughtfully. To herself she said: "Of course, if father heard that he would have a fit! But somehow I don't see Mr. Whittington in the rôle of the gay deceiver."

"Yes," continued Whittington. "What could be more delightful? To put the clock back a few years—a very few, I am sure—and re-enter one of those charming *pensionnats de jeunes filles* with which Paris abounds——"

Tuppence interrupted him.

"A *pensionnat*?"

"Exactly. Madame Colombier's in the Avenue de Neuilly."

Tuppence knew the name well. Nothing could have been more select. She had had several American friends there. She was more than ever puzzled.

"You want me to go to Madame Colombier's? For how long?"

"That depends. Possibly three months."

"And that is all? There are no other conditions?"

"None whatever. You would, of course, go in the character of my ward, and you would hold no communication with your friends. I should have to request absolute secrecy for the time being. By the way, you are English, are you not?"

"Yes."

"Yet you speak with a slight American accent?"

"My great pal in hospital was a little American girl. I dare say I picked it up from her. I can soon get out of it again."

"On the contrary, it might be simpler for you to pass as an American. Details about your past life in England might be more difficult to sustain. Yes, I think that would be decidedly better. Then——"

"One moment, Mr. Whittington! You seem to be taking my consent for granted."

Whittington looked surprised.

"Surely you are not thinking of refusing? I can assure you that Madame Colombier's is a most high-class and orthodox establishment. And the terms are most liberal."

"Exactly," said Tuppence. "That's just it. The terms are almost too liberal, Mr. Whittington. I cannot see any way in which I can be worth that amount of money to you."

"No?" said Whittington softly. "Well, I will tell you. I could doubtless obtain some one else for very much less. What I am willing to pay for is a young lady with sufficient intelligence and presence of mind to sustain her part well, and also one who will have sufficient discretion not to ask too many questions."

Tuppence smiled a little. She felt that Whittington had scored.

"There's another thing. So far there has been no mention of Mr. Beresford. Where does he come in?"

"Mr. Beresford?"

"My partner," said Tuppence with dignity. "You saw us together yesterday."

"Ah, yes. But I'm afraid we shan't require his services."

"Then it's off!" Tuppence rose. "It's both or neither. Sorry—but that's how it is. Good morning, Mr. Whittington."

"Wait a minute. Let us see if something can't be managed. Sit down again, Miss——" He paused interrogatively.

Tuppence's conscience gave her a passing twinge as she remembered the archdeacon. She seized hurriedly on the first name that came into her head.

"Jane Finn," she said hastily; and then paused open-mouthed at the effect of those two simple words.

All the geniality had faded out of Whittington's face. It was purple with rage, and the veins stood out on the forehead. And behind it all there lurked a sort of incredulous dismay. He leaned forward and hissed savagely:

"So that's your little game, is it?"

Tuppence, though utterly taken aback, nevertheless kept her head. She had not the faintest comprehension of his meaning, but she was naturally quick-witted, and felt it imperative to "keep her end up" as she phrased it.

Whittington went on:

"Been playing with me, have you, all the time, like a cat and mouse? Knew all the time what I wanted you for, but kept up the comedy. Is that it, eh?" He was cooling down. The red colour was ebbing out of his face. He eyed her keenly. "Who's been blabbing? Rita?"

Tuppence shook her head. She was doubtful as to how long she could sustain this illusion, but she realized the importance of not dragging an unknown Rita into it.

"No," she replied with perfect truth. "Rita knows nothing about me."

His eyes still bored into her like gimlets.

"How much do you know?" he shot out.

"Very little indeed," answered Tuppence, and was pleased to note that Whittington's uneasiness was augmented instead of allayed. To have boasted that she knew a lot might have raised doubts in his mind.

"Anyway," snarled Whittington, "you knew enough to come in here and plump out that name."

"It might be my own name," Tuppence pointed out.

"It's likely, isn't it, that there would be two girls with a name like that?"

"Or I might just have hit upon it by chance," continued Tuppence, intoxicated with the success of truthfulness.

Mr. Whittington brought his fist down upon the desk with a bang.

"Quit fooling! How much do you know? And how much do you want?"

The last five words took Tuppence's fancy mightily, especially after a meagre breakfast and a supper of buns the night before. Her present part was of the adventuress rather than the adventurous order, but she did not deny its possibilities. She sat up and smiled with the air of one who has the situation thoroughly well in hand.

"My dear Mr. Whittington," she said, "let us by all means lay our cards upon the table. And pray do not be so angry. You heard me say yesterday that I proposed to live by my wits. It seems to me that I have now proved I have some wits to live by! I admit I have knowledge of a certain name, but perhaps my knowledge ends there."

"Yes—and perhaps it doesn't," snarled Whittington.

"You insist on misjuding me," said Tuppence, and sighed gently.

"As I said once before," said Whittington angrily, "quit fooling, and come to the point. You can't play the innocent with me. You know a great deal more than you're willing to admit."

Tuppence paused a moment to admire her own ingenuity, and then said softly:

"I shouldn't like to contradict you, Mr. Whittington."

"So we come to the usual question—how much?"

Tuppence was in a dilemma. So far she had fooled Whittington with complete success, but to mention a palpably impossible sum might awaken his suspicions. An idea flashed across her brain.

"Suppose we say a little something down, and a fuller discussion of the matter later?"

Whittington gave her an ugly glance.

"Blackmail, eh?"

Tuppence smiled sweetly.

"Oh no! Shall we say payment of services in advance?"

Whittington grunted.

"You see," explained Tuppence still sweetly, "I'm so very fond of money!"

"You're about the limit, that's what you are," growled Whittington, with a sort of unwilling admiration. "You took me in all right. Thought you were quite a meek little kid with just enough brains for my purpose."

"Life," moralized Tuppence, "is full of surprises."

"All the same," continued Whittington, "some one's been talking. You say it isn't Rita. Was it——? Oh, come in."

The clerk followed his discreet knock into the room, and laid a paper at his master's elbow.

"Telephone message just come for you, sir."

Whittington snatched it up and read it. A frown gathered on his brow.

"That'll do, Brown. You can go."

The clerk withdrew, closing the door behind him. Whittington turned to Tuppence.

"Come tomorrow at the same time. I'm busy now. Here's fifty to go on with."

He rapidly sorted out some notes, and pushed them across the table to Tuppence, then stood up, obviously impatient for her to go.

The girl counted the notes in a business-like manner, secured them in her handbag, and rose.

"Good morning, Mr. Whittington," she said politely. "At least, au revoir, I should say."

"Exactly. Au revoir!" Whittington looked almost genial again, a reversion that aroused in Tuppence a faint misgiving. "Au revoir, my clever and charming young lady."

Tuppence sped lightly down the stairs. A wild elation possessed her. A neighbouring clock showed the time to be five minutes to twelve.

"Let's give Tommy a surprise!" murmured Tuppence, and hailed a taxi.

The cab drew up outside the tube station. Tommy was just within the entrance. His eyes opened to their fullest extent as he hurried forward to assist Tuppence to alight. She smiled at him affectionately, and remarked in a slightly affected voice:

"Pay the thing, will you, old bean? I've got nothing smaller than a five-pound note!"

CHAPTER III
A Set Back

The moment was not quite so triumphant as it ought to have been. To begin with, the resources of Tommy's pockets were somewhat limited. In the end the fare was managed, the lady recollecting a plebeian twopence, and the driver, still holding the varied assortment of coins in his hand, was prevailed upon to move on, which he did after one last hoarse demand as to what the gentleman thought he was giving him?

"I think you've given him too much, Tommy," said Tuppence innocently. "I fancy he wants to give some of it back."

It was possibly this remark which induced the driver to move away.

"Well," said Mr. Beresford, at length able to relieve his feelings, "what the—dickens, did you want to take a taxi for?"

"I was afraid I might be late and keep you waiting," said Tuppence gently.

"Afraid—you—might—be—late! Oh, Lord, I give it up!" said Mr. Beresford.

"And really and truly," continued Tuppence, opening her eyes very wide, "I haven't got anything smaller than a five-pound note."

"You did that part of it very well, old bean, but all the same the fellow wasn't taken in—not for a moment!"

"No," said Tuppence thoughtfully, "he didn't believe it. That's the curious part about speaking the truth. No one does believe it. I found that out this morning. Now let's go to lunch. How about the *Savoy*?"

Tommy grinned.

"How about the *Ritz*?"

"On second thoughts, I prefer the *Piccadilly*. It's nearer. We shan't have to take another taxi. Come along."

"Is this a new brand of humour? Or is your brain really unhinged?" inquired Tommy.

"Your last supposition is the correct one. I have come into money, and the shock has been too much for me! For that particular form of mental trouble an eminent physician recommends unlimited *Hors d'œuvres*, Lobster *à l'américaine*, Chicken Newberg, and Pêche Melba! Let's go and get them!"

"Tuppence, old girl, what has really come over you?"

"Oh, unbelieving one!" Tuppence wrenched open her bag. "Look here, and here, and here!"

"Great Jehosaphat! My dear girl, don't wave Fishers aloft like that!"

"They're not Fishers. They're five times better than Fishers and this one's ten times better!"

Tommy groaned.

"I must have been drinking unawares! Am I dreaming, Tuppence, or do I really behold a large quantity of five-pound notes being waved about in a dangerous fashion?"

"Even so, O King! *Now*, will you come and have lunch?"

"I'll come anywhere. But what have you been doing? Holding up a bank?"

"All in good time. What an awful place Piccadilly Circus is. There's a huge bus bearing down on us. It would be too terrible if they killed the five-pound notes!"

"Grill room?" inquired Tommy, as they reached the opposite pavement in safety.

"The other's more expensive," demurred Tuppence.

"That's mere wicked wanton extravagance. Come on below."

"Are you sure I can get all the things I want there?"

"That extremely unwholesome menu you were outlining just now? Of course you can—or as much as is good for you, anyway."

"And now tell me," said Tommy, unable to restrain his pent-up curiosity any longer, as they sat in state surrounded by the many *hors d'œuvres* of Tuppence's dreams.

Miss Cowley told him.

"And the curious part of it is," she ended, "that I really did invent the name of Jane Finn! I didn't want to give my own because of poor father—in case I should get mixed up in anything shady."

"Perhaps that's so," said Tommy slowly. "But you didn't invent it."

"What?"

"No. *I* told it to you. Don't you remember, I said yesterday I'd overheard two people talking about a female called Jane Finn? That's what brought the name into your mind so pat."

"So you did. I remember now. How extraordinary——" Tuppence tailed off into silence. Suddenly she aroused herself. "Tommy!"

"Yes?"

"What were they like, the two men you passed?"

Tommy frowned in an effort at remembrance.

"One was a big fat sort of chap. Clean shaven, I think—and dark."

"That's him," cried Tuppence, in an ungrammatical squeal. "That's Whittington! What was the other man like?"

"I can't remember. I didn't notice him particularly. It was really the outlandish name that caught my attention."

"And people say that coincidences don't happen!" Tuppence tackled her Pêche Melba happily.

But Tommy had become serious.

"Look here, Tuppence, old girl, what is this going to lead to?"

"More money," replied his companion.

"I know that. You've only got one idea in your head. What I mean is, what about the next step? How are you going to keep the game up?"

"Oh!" Tuppence laid down her spoon. "You're right, Tommy, it is a bit of a poser."

"After all, you know, you can't bluff him forever. You're sure to slip up sooner or later. And, anyway, I'm not at all sure that it isn't actionable—blackmail, you know."

"Nonsense. Blackmail is saying you'll tell unless you are given money. Now, there's nothing I could tell, because I don't really know anything."

"Hm," said Tommy doubtfully. "Well, anyway, what *are* we going to do? Whittington was in a hurry to get rid of you this morning, but next time he'll want to know something more before he parts with his money. He'll want to know how much *you* know, and where you got your information from, and a lot of other things that you can't cope with. What are you going to do about it?"

Tuppence frowned severely.

"We must think. Order some Turkish coffee, Tommy. Stimulating to the brain. Oh, dear, what a lot I have eaten!"

"You have made rather a hog of yourself! So have I for that matter, but I flatter myself that my choice of dishes was more judicious than yours. Two coffees." (This was to the waiter.) "One Turkish, one French."

Tuppence sipped her coffee with a deeply reflective air, and snubbed Tommy when he spoke to her.

"Be quiet. I'm thinking."

"Shades of Pelmanism!" said Tommy, and relapsed into silence.

"There!" said Tuppence at last. "I've got a plan. Obviously what we've got to do is to find out more about it all."

Tommy applauded.

"Don't jeer. We can only find out through Whittington. We must discover where he lives, what he does—sleuth him, in fact! Now I can't do it, because he knows me, but he only saw you for a minute or two in Lyons'. He's not likely to recognize you. After all, one young man is much like another."

"I repudiate that remark utterly. I'm sure my pleasing features and distinguished appearance would single me out from any crowd."

"My plan is this," Tuppence went on calmly, "I'll go alone tomorrow. I'll put him off again like I did today. It doesn't matter if I don't get any more money at once. Fifty pounds ought to last us a few days."

"Or even longer!"

"You'll hang about outside. When I come out I shan't speak to you in case he's watching. But I'll take up my stand somewhere near, and when he comes out of the building I'll drop a handkerchief or something, and off you go!"

"Off I go where?"

"Follow him, of course, silly! What do you think of the idea?"

"Sort of thing one reads about in books. I somehow feel that in real life one will feel a bit of an ass standing in the street for hours with nothing to do. People will wonder what I'm up to."

"Not in the city. Every one's in such a hurry. Probably no one will even notice you at all."

"That's the second time you've made that sort of remark. Never mind, I forgive you. Anyway, it will be rather a lark. What are you doing this afternoon?"

"Well," said Tuppence meditatively. "I *had* thought of hats! Or perhaps silk stockings! Or perhaps——"

"Hold hard," admonished Tommy. "There's a limit to fifty pounds! But let's do dinner and a show tonight at all events."

"Rather."

The day passed pleasantly. The evening even more so. Two of the five-pound notes were now irretrievably dead.

They met by arrangement the following morning and proceeded citywards. Tommy remained on the opposite side of the road while Tuppence plunged into the building.

Tommy strolled slowly down to the end of the street, then back again. Just as he came abreast of the building, Tuppence darted across the road.

"Tommy!"

"Yes. What's up?"

"The place is shut. I can't make anyone hear."

"That's odd."

"Isn't it? Come up with me, and let's try again."

Tommy followed her. As they passed the third floor landing a young clerk came out of an office. He hesitated a moment, then addressed himself to Tuppence.

"Were you wanting the Esthonia Glassware?"

"Yes, please."

"It's closed down. Since yesterday afternoon. Company being wound up, they say. Not that I've ever heard of it myself. But anyway the office is to let."

"Th—thank you," faltered Tuppence. "I suppose you don't know Mr. Whittington's address?"

"Afraid I don't. They left rather suddenly."

"Thank you very much," said Tommy. "Come on, Tuppence."

They descended to the street again where they gazed at one another blankly.

"That's torn it," said Tommy at length.

"And I never suspected it," wailed Tuppence.

"Cheer up, old thing, it can't be helped."

"Can't it, though!" Tuppence's little chin shot out defiantly. "Do you think this is the end? If so, you're wrong. It's just the beginning!"

"The beginning of what?"

"Of our adventure! Tommy, don't you see, if they are scared enough to run away like this, it shows that there must be a lot in this Jane Finn business! Well, we'll get to the bottom of it. We'll run them down! We'll be sleuths in earnest!"

"Yes, but there's no one left to sleuth."

"No, that's why we'll have to start all over again. Lend me that bit of pencil. Thanks. Wait a minute—don't interrupt. There!" Tuppence handed back the pencil, and surveyed the piece of paper on which she had written with a satisfied eye:

"What's that?"

"Advertisement."

"You're not going to put that thing in after all?"

"No, it's a different one." She handed him the slip of paper.

Tommy read the words on it aloud:

"WANTED, any information respecting Jane Finn. Apply Y. A."

CHAPTER IV
Who Is Jane Finn?

The next day passed slowly. It was necessary to curtail expenditure. Carefully husbanded, forty pounds will last a long time. Luckily the weather was fine, and "walking is cheap," dictated Tuppence. An outlying picture house provided them with recreation for the evening.

The day of disillusionment had been a Wednesday. On Thursday the advertisement had duly appeared. On Friday letters might be expected to arrive at Tommy's rooms.

He had been bound by an honourable promise not to open any such letters if they did arrive, but to repair to the National Gallery, where his colleague would meet him at ten o'clock.

Tuppence was first at the rendezvous. She ensconced herself on a red velvet seat, and gazed at the Turners with unseeing eyes until she saw the familiar figure enter the room.

"Well?"

"Well," returned Mr. Beresford provokingly. "Which is your favourite picture?"

"Don't be a wretch. Aren't there *any* answers?"

Tommy shook his head with a deep and somewhat overacted melancholy.

"I didn't want to disappoint you, old thing, by telling you right off. It's too bad. Good money wasted." He sighed. "Still, there it is. The advertisement has appeared, and—there are only two answers!"

"Tommy, you devil!" almost screamed Tuppence. "Give them to me. How could you be so mean!"

"Your language, Tuppence, your language! They're very particular at the National Gallery. Government show, you know. And do remember, as I have pointed out to you before, that as a clergyman's daughter——"

"I ought to be on the stage!" finished Tuppence with a snap.

"That is not what I intended to say. But if you are sure that you have enjoyed to the full the reaction of joy after despair with which I have kindly provided you free of charge, let us get down to our mail, as the saying goes."

Tuppence snatched the two precious envelopes from him unceremoniously, and scrutinized them carefully.

"Thick paper, this one. It looks rich. We'll keep it to the last and open the other first."

"Right you are. One, two, three, go!"

Tuppence's little thumb ripped open the envelope, and she extracted the contents.

"Dear Sir,

"Referring to your advertisement in this morning's paper, I may be able to be of some use to you. Perhaps you could call and see me at the above address at eleven o'clock tomorrow morning.

"Yours truly,
"A. Carter."

"27 Carshalton Gardens," said Tuppence, referring to the address. "That's Gloucester Road way. Plenty of time to get there if we tube."

"The following," said Tommy, "is the plan of campaign. It is my turn to assume the offensive. Ushered into the presence of Mr. Carter, he and I wish each other good morning as is customary. He then says: 'Please take a seat, Mr.—er?' To which I reply promptly and significantly: 'Edward Whittington!' whereupon Mr. Carter turns purple in the face and gasps out: 'How much?' Pocketing the usual fee of fifty pounds, I rejoin you in the road outside, and we proceed to the next address and repeat the performance."

"Don't be absurd, Tommy. Now for the other letter. Oh, this is from the *Ritz*!"

"A hundred pounds instead of fifty!"

"I'll read it:

"Dear Sir,
"Re your advertisement, I should be glad if you would call round somewhere about lunch-time.

"Yours truly,
"Julius P. Hersheimmer."

"Ha!" said Tommy. "Do I smell a Boche? Or only an American millionaire of unfortunate ancestry? At all events we'll call at lunch-time. It's a good time—frequently leads to free food for two."

Tuppence nodded assent.

"Now for Carter. We'll have to hurry."

Carshalton Terrace proved to be an unimpeachable row of what Tuppence called "ladylike looking houses." They rang the bell at No. 27, and a neat maid answered the door. She looked so respectable that Tuppence's heart sank. Upon Tommy's request for Mr. Carter, she showed them into a small study on the ground floor where she left them. Hardly a minute elapsed, however, before the door opened, and a tall man with a lean hawklike face and a tired manner entered the room.

"Mr. Y. A.?" he said, and smiled. His smile was distinctly attractive. "Do sit down, both of you."

They obeyed. He himself took a chair oppo-site to Tuppence and smiled at her encourag-ingly. There was something in the quality of his smile that made the girl's usual readiness desert her.

As he did not seem inclined to open the con-versation, Tuppence was forced to begin.

"We wanted to know—that is, would you be so kind as to tell us anything you know about Jane Finn?"

"Jane Finn? Ah!" Mr. Carter appeared to reflect. "Well, the question is, what do *you* know about her?"

Tuppence drew herself up.

"I don't see that that's got anything to do with it."

"No? But it has, you know, really it has." He smiled again in his tired way, and continued reflectively. "So that brings us down to it again. What do *you* know about Jane Finn?"

"Come now," he continued, as Tuppence remained silent. "You must know *something* to have advertised as you did?" He leaned forward a little, his weary voice held a hint of persuasive-ness. "Suppose you tell me. . . ."

There was something very magnetic about Mr. Carter's personality. Tuppence seemed to shake herself free of it with an effort, as she said:

"We couldn't do that, could we, Tommy?"

But to her surprise, her companion did not back her up. His eyes were fixed on Mr. Carter, and his tone when he spoke held an unusual note of deference.

"I dare say the little we know won't be any good to you, sir. But such as it is, you're welcome to it."

"Tommy!" cried out Tuppence in surprise.

Mr. Carter slewed round in his chair. His eyes asked a question.

Tommy nodded.

"Yes, sir, I recognized you at once. Saw you in France when I was with the Intelligence. As soon as you came into the room, I knew——"

Mr. Carter held up his hand.

"No names, please. I'm known as Mr. Carter here. It's my cousin's house, by the way. She's

willing to lend it to me sometimes when it's a case of working on strictly unofficial lines. Well, now"—he looked from one to the other—"who's going to tell me the story?"

"Fire ahead, Tuppence," directed Tommy. "It's your yarn."

"Yes, little lady, out with it."

And obediently Tuppence did out with it, telling the whole story from the forming of the Young Adventurers, Ltd., downwards.

Mr. Carter listened in silence with a resump-tion of his tired manner. Now and then he passed his hand across his lips as though to hide a smile. When she had finished he nodded gravely.

"Not much. But suggestive. Quite suggestive. If you'll excuse my saying so, you're a curious young couple. I don't know—you might succeed where others have failed. . . . I believe in luck, you know—always have. . . ."

He paused a moment, and then went on.

"Well, how about it? You're out for adven-ture. How would you like to work for me? All quite unofficial, you know. Expenses paid, and a moderate screw?"

Tuppence gazed at him, her lips parted, her eyes growing wider and wider.

"What should we have to do?" she breathed.

Mr. Carter smiled.

"Just go on with what you're doing now. *Find Jane Finn.*"

"Yes, but—who *is* Jane Finn?"

Mr. Carter nodded gravely.

"Yes, you're entitled to know that, I think."

He leaned back in his chair, crossed his legs, brought the tips of his fingers together, and began in a low monotone:

"Secret diplomacy (which, by the way, is nearly always bad policy!) does not concern you. It will be sufficient to say that in the early days of 1915 a certain document came into being. It was the draft of a secret agreement—treaty—call it what you like. It was drawn up ready for sig-nature by the various representatives, and drawn up in America—at that time a neutral country. It was dispatched to England by a special mes-senger selected for that purpose, a young fellow called Danvers. It was hoped that the whole affair had been kept so secret that nothing would have leaked out. That kind of hope is usually disappointed. Somebody always talks!

"Danvers sailed for England on the *Lusitania*. He carried the precious papers in an oilskin packet which he wore next his skin. It was on that particular voyage that the *Lusitania* was torpedoed and sunk. Danvers was among the list of those missing. Eventually his body was washed ashore, and identified beyond any possible doubt. But the oilskin packet was missing!

"The question was, had it been taken from him, or had he himself passed it on into another's keeping? There were a few incidents that strengthened the possibility of the latter theory. After the torpedo struck the ship, in the few moments during the launching of the boats, Danvers was seen speaking to a young American girl. No one actually saw him pass anything to her, but he might have done so. It seems to me quite likely that he entrusted the papers to this girl, believing that she, as a woman, had a greater chance of bringing them safely to shore.

"But if so, where was the girl, and what had she done with the papers? By later advice from America it seemed likely that Danvers had been closely shadowed on the way over. Was this girl in league with his enemies? Or had she, in her turn, been shadowed and either tricked or forced into handing over the precious packet?

"We set to work to trace her out. It proved unexpectedly difficult. Her name was Jane Finn, and it duly appeared among the list of the survivors, but the girl herself seemed to have vanished completely. Inquiries into her antecedents did little to help us. She was an orphan, and had been what we should call over here a pupil teacher in a small school out West. Her passport had been made out for Paris, where she was going to join the staff of a hospital. She had offered her services voluntarily, and after some correspondence they had been accepted. Having seen her name in the list of the saved from the *Lusitania*, the staff of the hospital were naturally very surprised at her not arriving to take up her billet, and at not hearing from her in any way.

"Well, every effort was made to trace the young lady—but all in vain. We tracked her across Ireland, but nothing could be heard of her after she set foot in England. No use was made of the draft treaty—as might very easily have been done—and we therefore came to the conclusion that Danvers had, after all, destroyed it. The war entered on another phase, the diplomatic aspect changed accordingly, and the treaty was never redrafted. Rumours as to its existence were emphatically denied. The disappearance of Jane Finn was forgotten and the whole affair was lost in oblivion."

Mr. Carter paused, and Tuppence broke in impatiently:

"But why has it all cropped up again? The war's over."

A hint of alertness came into Mr. Carter's manner.

"Because it seems that the papers were not destroyed after all, and that they might be resurrected today with a new and deadly significance."

Tuppence stared. Mr. Carter nodded.

"Yes, five years ago, that draft treaty was a weapon in our hands; today it is a weapon against us. It was a gigantic blunder. If its terms were made public, it would mean disaster. . . . It might possibly bring about another war— not with Germany this time! That is an extreme possibility, and I do not believe in its likelihood myself, but that document undoubtedly implicates a number of our statesmen whom we cannot afford to have discredited in any way at the present moment. As a party cry for Labour it would be irresistible, and a Labour Government at this juncture would, in my opinion, be a grave disability for British trade, but that is a mere nothing to the *real* danger."

He paused, and then said quietly:

"You may perhaps have heard or read that there is Bolshevist influence at work behind the present labour unrest?"

Tuppence nodded.

"That is the truth. Bolshevist gold is pouring into this country for the specific purpose of procuring a Revolution. And there is a certain man, a man whose real name is unknown to us, who is working in the dark for his own ends. The Bolshevists are behind the Labour unrest—but this man is *behind the Bolshevists*. Who is he? We do not know. He is always spoken of by the unassuming title of 'Mr. Brown.' But one thing is certain, he is the master criminal of this age. He controls a marvellous organization. Most of the Peace propaganda during the war was originated and financed by him. His spies are everywhere."

"A naturalized German?" asked Tommy.

"On the contrary, I have every reason to believe he is an Englishman. He was pro-German, as he would have been pro-Boer. What he seeks to attain we do not know—probably supreme power for himself, of a kind unique in history. We have no clue as to his real personality. It is reported that even his own followers are ignorant of it. Where we have come across his tracks, he has always played a secondary part. Somebody else assumes the chief rôle. But afterwards we always find that there has been some nonentity, a servant or a clerk, who has remained in the background unnoticed, and that the elusive Mr. Brown has escaped us once more."

"Oh!" Tuppence jumped. "I wonder——"

"Yes?"

"I remember in Mr. Whittington's office. The clerk—he called him Brown. You don't think——"

Carter nodded thoughtfully.

"Very likely. A curious point is that the name is usually mentioned. An idiosyncrasy of genius. Can you describe him at all?"

"I really didn't notice. He was quite ordinary—just like any one else."

Mr. Carter sighed in his tired manner.

"That is the invariable description of Mr. Brown! Brought a telephone message to the man Whittington, did he? Notice a telephone in the outer office?"

Tuppence thought.

"No, I don't think I did."

"Exactly. That 'message' was Mr. Brown's way of giving an order to his subordinate. He overheard the whole conversation of course. Was it after that that Whittington handed you over the money, and told you to come the following day?"

Tuppence nodded.

"Yes, undoubtedly the hand of Mr. Brown!" Mr. Carter paused. "Well, there it is, you see what you are pitting yourselves against? Possibly the finest criminal brain of the age. I don't quite like it, you know. You're such young things, both of you. I shouldn't like anything to happen to you."

"It won't," Tuppence assured him positively.

"I'll look after her, sir," said Tommy.

"And *I*'ll look after *you*," retorted Tuppence, resenting the manly assertion.

"Well, then, look after each other," said Mr. Carter, smiling. "Now let's get back to business. There's something mysterious about this draft treaty that we haven't fathomed yet. We've been threatened with it—in plain and unmistakable terms. The Revolutionary element as good as declare that it's in their hands, and that they intend to produce it at a given moment. On the other hand, they are clearly at fault about many of its provisions. The Government consider it as mere bluff on their part, and, rightly or wrongly, have stuck to the policy of absolute denial. I'm not so sure. There have been hints, indiscreet allusions, that seem to indicate that the menace is a real one. The position is much as though they had got hold of an incriminating document, but couldn't read it because it was in cipher—but we know that the draft treaty wasn't in cipher—couldn't be in the nature of things—so that won't wash. But there's *something*. Of course, Jane Finn may be dead for all we know—but I don't think so. The curious thing is that *they're trying to get information about the girl from us*."

"What?"

"Yes. One or two little things have cropped up. And your story, little lady, confirms my idea. They know we're looking for Jane Finn. Well, they'll produce a Jane Finn of their own—say at a *pensionnat* in Paris." Tuppence gasped, and

Mr. Carter smiled. "No one knows in the least what she looks like, so that's all right. She's primed with a trumped-up tale, and her real business is to get as much information as possible out of us. See the idea?"

"Then you think"—Tuppence paused to grasp the supposition fully—"that it *was* as Jane Finn that they wanted me to go to Paris?"

Mr. Carter smiled more wearily than ever.

"I believe in coincidences, you know," he said.

CHAPTER V
Mr. Julius P. Hersheimmer

"Well," said Tuppence, recovering herself, "it really seems as though it were meant to be."

Carter nodded.

"I know what you mean. I'm superstitious myself. Luck, and all that sort of thing. Fate seems to have chosen you out to be mixed up in this."

Tommy indulged in a chuckle.

"My word! I don't wonder Whittington got the wind up when Tuppence plumped out that name! I should have myself. But look here, sir, we're taking up an awful lot of your time. Have you any tips to give us before we clear out?"

"I think not. My experts, working in stereotyped ways, have failed. You will bring imagination and an open mind to the task. Don't be discouraged if that too does not succeed. For one thing there is a likelihood of the pace being forced."

Tuppence frowned uncomprehendingly.

"When you had that interview with Whittington, they had time before them. I have information that the big *coup* was planned for early in the new year. But the Government is contemplating legislative action which will deal effectually with the strike menace. They'll get wind of it soon, if they haven't already, and it's possible that that may bring things to a head. I hope it will myself. The less time they have to mature their plans the better. I'm just warning you that you haven't much time before you, and that you

needn't be cast down if you fail. It's not an easy proposition anyway. That's all."

Tuppence rose.

"I think we ought to be business-like. What exactly can we count upon you for, Mr. Carter?"

Mr. Carter's lips twitched slightly, but he replied succinctly:

"Funds within reason, detailed information on any point, and *no official recognition*. I mean that if you get yourselves into trouble with the police, I can't officially help you out of it. You're on your own."

Tuppence nodded sagely.

"I quite understand that. I'll write out a list of the things I want to know when I've had time to think. Now—about money——"

"Yes, Miss Tuppence. Do you want to say how much?"

"Not exactly. We've got plenty to go with for the present, but when we want more——"

"It will be waiting for you."

"Yes, but—I'm sure I don't want to be rude about the Government if you've got anything to do with it, but you know one really has the devil of a time getting anything out of it! And if we have to fill up a blue form and send it in, and then, after three months, they send us a green one, and so on—well, that won't be much use, will it?"

Mr. Carter laughed outright.

"Don't worry, Miss Tuppence. You will send a personal demand to me here, and the money, in notes, shall be sent by return of post. As to salary, shall we say at the rate of three hundred a year? And an equal sum for Mr. Beresford, of course."

Tuppence beamed upon him.

"How lovely. You are kind. I do love money! I'll keep beautiful accounts of our expenses— all debit and credit, and the balance on the right side, and a red line drawn sideways with the totals the same at the bottom. I really know how to do it when I think."

"I'm sure you do. Well, good-bye, and good luck to you both."

He shook hands with them, and in another

minute they were descending the steps of 27 Carshalton Terrace with their heads in a whirl.

"Tommy! Tell me at once, who is 'Mr. Carter?'"

Tommy murmured a name in her ear.

"Oh!" said Tuppence, impressed.

"And I can tell you, old bean, he's IT!"

"Oh!" said Tuppence again. Then she added reflectively. "I like him, don't you? He looks so awfully tired and bored, and yet you feel that underneath he's just like steel, all keen and flashing. Oh!" She gave a skip. "Pinch me, Tommy, do pinch me. I can't believe it's real!"

Mr. Beresford obliged.

"Ow! That's enough! Yes, we're not dreaming. We've got a job!"

"And what a job! The joint venture has really begun."

"It's more respectable than I thought it would be," said Tuppence thoughtfully.

"Luckily I haven't got your craving for crime! What time is it? Let's have lunch—oh!"

The same thought sprang to the minds of each. Tommy voiced it first.

"Julius P. Hersheimmer!"

"We never told Mr. Carter about hearing from him."

"Well, there wasn't much to tell—not till we've seen him. Come on, we'd better take a taxi."

"Now who's being extravagant?"

"All expenses paid, remember. Hop in."

"At any rate, we shall make a better effect arriving this way," said Tuppence, leaning back luxuriously. "I'm sure blackmailers never arrive in buses!"

"We've ceased being blackmailers," Tommy pointed out.

"I'm not sure I have," said Tuppence darkly.

On inquiring for Mr. Hersheimmer, they were at once taken up to his suite. An impatient voice cried "Come in" in answer to the pageboy's knock, and the lad stood aside to let them pass in.

Mr. Julius P. Hersheimmer was a great deal younger than either Tommy or Tuppence had pictured him. The girl put him down as thirty-five. He was of middle height, and squarely built to match his jaw. His face was pugnacious but pleasant. No one could have mistaken him for anything but an American, though he spoke with very little accent.

"Get my note? Sit down and tell me right away all you know about my cousin."

"Your cousin?"

"Sure thing. Jane Finn."

"Is she your cousin?"

"My father and her mother were brother and sister," explained Mr. Hersheimmer meticulously.

"Oh!" cried Tuppence. "Then you know where she is?"

"No!" Mr. Hersheimmer brought down his fist with a bang on the table. "I'm darned if I do! Don't you?"

"We advertised to receive information, not to give it," said Tuppence severely.

"I guess I know that. I can read. But I thought maybe it was her back history you were after, and that you'd know where she was now?"

"Well, we wouldn't mind hearing her back history," said Tuppence guardedly.

But Mr. Hersheimmer seemed to grow suddenly suspicious.

"See here," he declared. "This isn't Sicily! No demanding ransom or threatening to crop her ears if I refuse. These are the British Isles, so quit the funny business, or I'll just sing out for that beautiful big British policeman I see out there in Piccadilly."

Tommy hastened to explain.

"We haven't kidnapped your cousin. On the contrary, we're trying to find her. We're employed to do so."

Mr. Hersheimmer leant back in his chair.

"Put me wise," he said succinctly.

Tommy fell in with this demand in so far as he gave him a guarded version of the disappearance of Jane Finn, and of the possibility of her having been mixed up unawares in "some political show." He alluded to Tuppence and himself as "private inquiry agents" commissioned to find her, and added that they would therefore be glad of any details Mr. Hersheimmer could give them.

That gentleman nodded approval.

"I guess that's all right. I was just a mite hasty. But London gets my goat! I only know little old New York. Just trot out your questions and I'll answer."

For the moment this paralysed the Young Adventurers, but Tuppence, recovering herself, plunged boldly into the breach with a reminiscence culled from detective fiction.

"When did you last see the dece—your cousin, I mean?"

"Never seen her," responded Mr. Hersheimmer.

"What?" demanded Tommy, astonished.

Hersheimmer turned to him.

"No, sir. As I said before, my father and her mother were brother and sister, just as you might be"—Tommy did not correct this view of their relationship—"but they didn't always get on together. And when my aunt made up her mind to marry Amos Finn, who was a poor school teacher out West, my father was just mad! Said if he made his pile, as he seemed in a fair way to do, she'd never see a cent of it. Well, the upshot was that Aunt Jane went out West and we never heard from her again.

"The old man *did* pile it up. He went into oil, and he went into steel, and he played a bit with railroads, and I can tell you he made Wall Street sit up!" He paused. "Then he died—last fall—and I got the dollars. Well, would you believe it, my conscience got busy! Kept knocking me up and saying: What about your Aunt Jane, way out West? It worried me some. You see, I figured it out that Amos Finn would never make good. He wasn't the sort. End of it was, I hired a man to hunt her down. Result, she was dead, and Amos Finn was dead, but they'd left a daughter—Jane—who'd been torpedoed in the *Lusitania* on her way to Paris. She was saved all right, but they didn't seem able to hear of her over this side. I guessed they weren't hustling any, so I thought I'd come along over, and speed things

up. I phoned Scotland Yard and the Admiralty first thing. The Admiralty rather choked me off, but Scotland Yard were very civil—said they would make inquiries, even sent a man round this morning to get her photograph. I'm off to Paris tomorrow, just to see what the Prefecture is doing. I guess if I go to and fro hustling them, they ought to get busy!"

The energy of Mr. Hersheimmer was tremendous. They bowed before it.

"But say now," he ended, "you're not after her for anything? Contempt of court, or something British? A proud-spirited young American girl might find your rules and regulations in war time rather irksome, and get up against it. If that's the case, and there's such a thing as graft in this country, I'll buy her off."

Tuppence reassured him.

"That's good. Then we can work together. What about some lunch? Shall we have it up here, or go down to the restaurant?"

Tuppence expressed a preference for the latter, and Julius bowed to her decision.

Oysters had just given place to Sole Colbert when a card was brought to Hersheimmer.

"Inspector Japp, C.I.D. Scotland Yard again. Another man this time. What does he expect I can tell him that I didn't tell the first chap? I hope they haven't lost that photograph. That Western photographer's place was burned down and all his negatives destroyed—this is the only copy in existence. I got it from the principal of the college there."

An unformulated dread swept over Tuppence.

"You—you don't know the name of the man who came this morning?"

"Yes, I do. No, I don't. Half a second. It was on his card. Oh, I know! Inspector Brown. Quiet, unassuming sort of chap."

CHAPTER VI
A Plan of Campaign

A veil might with profit be drawn over the events of the next half-hour. Suffice it to say that no such person as "Inspector Brown" was known to Scotland Yard. The photograph of Jane Finn, which would have been of the utmost value to the police in tracing her, was lost beyond recovery. Once again "Mr. Brown" had triumphed.

The immediate result of this setback was to effect a *rapprochement* between Julius Hersheimmer and the Young Adventurers. All barriers went down with a crash, and Tommy and Tuppence felt they had known the young American all their lives. They abandoned the discreet reticence of "private inquiry agents," and revealed to him the whole history of the joint venture, whereat the young man declared himself "tickled to death."

He turned to Tuppence at the close of the narration.

"I've always had a kind of idea that English girls were just a mite moss-grown. Old-fashioned and sweet, you know, but scared to move round without a footman or a maiden aunt. I guess I'm a bit behind the times!"

The upshot of these confidential relations was that Tommy and Tuppence took up their abode forthwith at the *Ritz*, in order, as Tuppence put it, to keep in touch with Jane Finn's only living relation. "And put like that," she added confidentially to Tommy, "nobody could boggle at the expense!"

Nobody did, which was the great thing.

"And now," said the young lady on the morning after their installation, "to work!"

Mr. Beresford put down the *Daily Mail*, which he was reading, and applauded with somewhat unnecessary vigour. He was politely requested by his colleague not to be an ass.

"Dash it all, Tommy, we've got to *do* something for our money."

Tommy sighed.

"Yes, I fear even the dear old Government will not support us at the *Ritz* in idleness forever."

"Therefore, as I said before, we must *do* something."

"Well," said Tommy, picking up the *Daily Mail* again, "*do* it. I shan't stop you."

"You see," continued Tuppence. "I've been thinking——"

She was interrupted by a fresh bout of applause.

"It's all very well for you to sit there being funny, Tommy. It would do you no harm to do a little brain work too."

"My union, Tuppence, my union! It does not permit me to work before 11 A.M."

"Tommy, do you want something thrown at you? It is absolutely essential that we should without delay map out a plan of campaign."

"Hear, hear!"

"Well, let's do it."

Tommy laid his paper finally aside. "There's something of the simplicity of the truly great mind about you, Tuppence. Fire ahead. I'm listening."

"To begin with," said Tuppence, "what have we to go upon?"

"Absolutely nothing," said Tommy cheerily.

"Wrong!" Tuppence wagged an energetic finger. "We have two distinct clues."

"What are they?"

"First clue, we know one of the gang."

"Whittington?"

"Yes. I'd recognize him anywhere."

"Hum," said Tommy doubtfully, "I don't call that much of a clue. You don't know where to look for him, and it's about a thousand to one against your running against him by accident."

"I'm not so sure about that," replied Tuppence thoughtfully. "I've often noticed that once coincidences start happening they go on happening in the most extraordinary way. I dare say it's some natural law that we haven't found out. Still, as you say, we can't rely on that. But there *are* places in London where simply every one is bound to turn up sooner or later. Piccadilly Circus, for instance. One of my ideas was to take up my stand there every day with a tray of flags."

"What about meals?" inquired the practical Tommy.

"How like a man! What does mere food matter?"

"That's all very well. You've just had a thundering good breakfast. No one's got a better appetite than you have, Tuppence, and by tea-time you'd be eating the flags, pins and all. But, honestly, I don't think much of the idea. Whittington mayn't be in London at all."

"That's true. Anyway, I think clue No. 2 is more promising."

"Let's hear it."

"It's nothing much. Only a Christian name—Rita. Whittington mentioned it that day."

"Are you proposing a third advertisement: Wanted, female crook, answering to the name of Rita?"

"I am not. I propose to reason in a logical manner. That man, Danvers, was shadowed on the way over, wasn't he? And it's more likely to have been a woman than a man——"

"I don't see that at all."

"I am absolutely certain that it would be a woman, and a good-looking one," replied Tuppence calmly.

"On these technical points I bow to your decision," murmured Mr. Beresford.

"Now, obviously this woman, whoever she was, was saved."

"How do you make that out?"

"If she wasn't, how would they have known Jane Finn had got the papers?"

"Correct. Proceed, O Sherlock!"

"Now there's just a chance, I admit it's only a chance, that this woman may have been 'Rita.'"

"And if so?"

"If so, we've got to hunt through the survivors of the *Lusitania* till we find her."

"Then the first thing is to get a list of the survivors."

"I've got it. I wrote a long list of things I wanted to know, and sent it to Mr. Carter. I got his reply this morning, and among other things it encloses the official statement of those saved from the *Lusitania*. How's that for clever little Tuppence?"

"Full marks for industry, zero for modesty. But the great point is, is there a 'Rita' on the list?"

"That's just what I don't know," confessed Tuppence.

"Don't know?"

"Yes. Look here." Together they bent over the list. "You see, very few Christian names are given. They're nearly all Mrs. or Miss."

Tommy nodded.

"That complicates matters," he murmured thoughtfully.

Tuppence gave her characteristic "terrier" shake.

"Well, we've just got to get down to it, that's all. We'll start with the London area. Just note down the addresses of any of the females who live in London or roundabout, while I put on my hat."

Five minutes later the young couple emerged into Piccadilly, and a few seconds later a taxi was bearing them to The Laurels, Glendower Road, N.7, the residence of Mrs. Edgar Keith, whose name figured first in a list of seven reposing in Tommy's pocket-book.

The Laurels was a dilapidated house, standing back from the road with a few grimy bushes to support the fiction of a front garden. Tommy paid off the taxi, and accompanied Tuppence to the front door bell. As she was about to ring it, he arrested her hand.

"What are you going to say?"

"What am I going to say? Why, I shall say—Oh dear, I don't know. It's very awkward."

"I thought as much," said Tommy with satisfaction. "How like a woman! No foresight! Now just stand aside, and see how easily the mere male deals with the situation." He pressed the bell. Tuppence withdrew to a suitable spot.

A slatternly-looking servant, with an extremely dirty face and a pair of eyes that did not match, answered the door.

Tommy had produced a notebook and pencil.

"Good morning," he said briskly and cheerfully. "From the Hampstead Borough Council. The new Voting Register. Mrs. Edgar Keith lives here, does she not?"

"Yaas," said the servant.

"Christian name?" asked Tommy, his pencil poised.

"Missus's? Eleanor Jane."

"Eleanor," spelt Tommy. "Any sons or daughters over twenty-one?"

"Naow."

"Thank you." Tommy closed the notebook with a brisk snap. "Good morning."

The servant volunteered her first remark:

"I thought perhaps as you'd come about the gas," she observed cryptically, and shut the door.

Tommy rejoined his accomplice.

"You see, Tuppence," he observed. "Child's play to the masculine mind."

"I don't mind admitting that for once you've scored handsomely. I should never have thought of that."

"Good wheeze, wasn't it? And we can repeat it *ad lib*."

Lunch-time found the young couple attacking a steak and chips in an obscure hostelry with avidity. They had collected a Gladys Mary and a Marjorie, been baffled by one change of address, and had been forced to listen to a long lecture on universal suffrage from a vivacious American lady whose Christian name had proved to be Sadie.

"Ah!" said Tommy, imbibing a long draught of beer, "I feel better. Where's the next draw?"

The notebook lay on the table between them. Tuppence picked it up.

"Mrs. Vandemeyer," she read, "20 South Audley Mansions. Miss Wheeler, 43 Clapington Road, Battersea. She's a lady's maid, as far as I remember, so probably won't be there, and, anyway, she's not likely."

"Then the Mayfair lady is clearly indicated as the first port of call."

"Tommy, I'm getting discouraged."

"Buck up, old bean. We always knew it was an outside chance. And, anyway, we're only starting. If we draw a blank in London, there's a fine tour of England, Ireland, and Scotland before us."

"True," said Tuppence, her flagging spirits reviving. "And all expenses paid! But, oh, Tommy, I do like things to happen quickly. So far, adventure has succeeded adventure, but this morning has been dull as dull."

"You must stifle this longing for vulgar sensation, Tuppence. Remember that if Mr. Brown is all he is reported to be, it's a wonder that he has not ere now done us to death. That's a good sentence, quite a literary flavour about it."

"You're really more conceited than I am—with less excuse! Ahem! But it certainly is queer that Mr. Brown has not yet wreaked vengeance upon us. (You see, I can do it too.) We pass on our way unscathed."

"Perhaps he doesn't think us worth bothering about," suggested the young man simply.

Tuppence received the remark with great disfavour.

"How horrid you are, Tommy. Just as though we didn't count."

"Sorry, Tuppence. What I meant was that we work like moles in the dark, and that he has no suspicion of our nefarious schemes. Ha ha!"

"Ha ha!" echoed Tuppence approvingly, as she rose.

South Audley Mansions was an imposing looking block of flats just off Park Lane. No. 20 was on the second floor.

Tommy had by this time the glibness born of practice. He rattled off the formula to the elderly woman, looking more like a housekeeper than a servant, who opened the door to him.

"Christian name?"

"Margaret."

Tommy spelt it, but the other interrupted him.

"No, g *u* e."

"Oh, Marguerite; French way, I see." He paused, then plunged boldly. "We had her down as Rita Vandemeyer, but I suppose that's incorrect?"

"She's mostly called that, sir, but Marguerite's her name."

"Thank you. That's all. Good morning."

Hardly able to contain his excitement, Tommy hurried down the stairs. Tuppence was waiting at the angle of the turn.

"You heard?"

"Yes. Oh, *Tommy!*"

Tommy squeezed her arm sympathetically.

"I know, old thing. I feel the same."

"It's—it's so lovely to think of things—and then for them really to happen!" cried Tuppence enthusiastically.

Her hand was still in Tommy's. They had reached the entrance hall. There were footsteps on the stairs above them, and voices.

Suddenly, to Tommy's complete surprise, Tuppence dragged him into the little space by the side of the lift where the shadow was deepest.

"What the——"

"Hush!"

Two men came down the stairs and passed out through the entrance. Tuppence's hand closed tighter on Tommy's arm.

"Quick—follow them. I daren't. He might recognize me. I don't know who the other man is, but the bigger of the two was Whittington."

CHAPTER VII
The House in Soho

Whittington and his companion were walking at a good pace. Tommy started in pursuit at once, and was in time to see them turn the corner of the street. His vigorous strides soon enabled him to gain upon them, and by the time he, in his turn, reached the corner the distance between them was sensibly lessened. The small Mayfair streets were comparatively deserted, and he judged it wise to content himself with keeping them in sight.

The sport was a new one to him. Though familiar with the technicalities from a course of novel reading, he had never before attempted to "follow" anyone, and it appeared to him at once that, in actual practice, the proceeding was fraught with difficulties. Supposing, for instance, that they should suddenly hail a taxi? In books, you simply leapt into another, promised the driver a sovereign—or its modern equivalent—and there you were. In actual fact, Tommy foresaw that it was extremely likely there would be no second taxi. Therefore he would have to run. What happened in actual fact to a young man

who ran incessantly and persistently through the London streets? In a main road he might hope to create the illusion that he was merely running for a bus. But in these obscure aristocratic byways he could not but feel that an officious policeman might stop him to explain matters.

At this juncture in his thoughts a taxi with flag erect turned the corner of the street ahead. Tommy held his breath. Would they hail it?

He drew a sigh of relief as they allowed it to pass unchallenged. Their course was a zigzag one designed to bring them as quickly as possible to Oxford Street. When at length they turned into it, proceeding in an easterly direction, Tommy slightly increased his pace. Little by little he gained upon them. On the crowded pavement there was little chance of his attracting their notice, and he was anxious if possible to catch a word or two of their conversation. In this he was completely foiled; they spoke low and the din of the traffic drowned their voices effectually.

Just before the Bond Street Tube station they crossed the road, Tommy, unperceived, faithfully at their heels, and entered the big Lyons'. There they went up to the first floor, and sat at a small table in the window. It was late, and the place was thinning out. Tommy took a seat at the table next to them, sitting directly behind Whittington in case of recognition. On the other hand, he had a full view of the second man and studied him attentively. He was fair, with a weak, unpleasant face, and Tommy put him down as being either a Russian or a Pole. He was probably about fifty years of age, his shoulders cringed a little as he talked, and his eyes, small and crafty, shifted unceasingly.

Having already lunched heartily, Tommy contented himself with ordering a Welsh rarebit and a cup of coffee. Whittington ordered a substantial lunch for himself and his companion; then, as the waitress withdrew, he moved his chair a little closer to the table and began to talk earnestly in a low voice. The other man joined in. Listen as he would, Tommy could only catch a word here and there; but the gist of it seemed to be some directions or orders which the big man was impressing on his companion, and with which the latter seemed from time to time to disagree. Whittington addressed the other as Boris.

Tommy caught the word "Ireland" several times, also "propaganda," but of Jane Finn there was no mention. Suddenly, in a lull in the clatter of the room, he got one phrase entire. Whittington was speaking. "Ah, but you don't know Flossie. She's a marvel. An archbishop would swear she was his own mother. She gets the voice right every time, and that's really the principal thing."

Tommy did not hear Boris's reply, but in response to it Whittington said something that sounded like: "Of course—only in an emergency . . ."

Then he lost the thread again. But presently the phrases became distinct again whether because the other two had insensibly raised their voices, or because Tommy's ears were getting more attuned, he could not tell. But two words certainly had a most stimulating effect upon the listener. They were uttered by Boris and they were: "Mr. Brown."

Whittington seemed to remonstrate with him, but he merely laughed.

"Why not, my friend? It is a name most respectable—most common. Did he not choose it for that reason? Ah, I should like to meet him—Mr. Brown."

There was a steely ring in Whittington's voice as he replied:

"Who knows? You may have met him already."

"Bah!" retorted the other. "That is children's talk—a fable for the police. Do you know what I say to myself sometimes? That he is a fable invented by the Inner Ring, a bogy to frighten us with. It might be so."

"And it might not."

"I wonder . . . or is it indeed true that he is with us and amongst us, unknown to all but a chosen few? If so, he keeps his secret well. And the idea is a good one, yes. We never know. We look at each other—*one of us is Mr. Brown*—

which? He commands—but also he serves. Among us—in the midst of us. And no one knows which he is. . . ."

With an effort the Russian shook off the vagary of his fancy. He looked at his watch.

"Yes," said Whittington. "We might as well go."

He called the waitress and asked for his bill. Tommy did likewise, and a few moments later was following the two men down the stairs.

Outside, Whittington hailed a taxi, and directed the driver to go to Waterloo.

Taxis were plentiful here, and before Whittington's had driven off another was drawing up to the curb in obedience to Tommy's peremptory hand.

"Follow that other taxi," directed the young man. "Don't lose it."

The elderly chauffeur showed no interest. He merely grunted and jerked down his flag. The drive was uneventful. Tommy's taxi came to rest at the departure platform just after Whittington's. Tommy was behind him at the booking-office. He took a first-class single ticket to Bournemouth, Tommy did the same. As he emerged, Boris remarked, glancing up at the clock: "You are early. You have nearly half an hour."

Boris's words had aroused a new train of thought in Tommy's mind. Clearly Whittington was making the journey alone, while the other remained in London. Therefore he was left with a choice as to which he would follow. Obviously, he could not follow both of them unless——Like Boris, he glanced up at the clock, and then to the announcement board of the trains. The Bournemouth train left at 3:30. It was now ten past. Whittington and Boris were walking up and down by the bookstall. He gave one doubtful look at them, then hurried into an adjacent telephone box. He dared not waste time in trying to get hold of Tuppence. In all probability she was still in the neighbourhood of South Audley Mansions. But there remained another ally. He rang up the *Ritz* and asked for Julius Hersheimmer. There was a click and a buzz. Oh, if only the young American was in his room! There was another click, and then "Hello" in unmistakable accents came over the wire.

"That you, Hersheimmer? Beresford speaking. I'm at Waterloo. I've followed Whittington and another man here. No time to explain. Whittington's off to Bournemouth by the 3:30. Can you get there by then?"

The reply was reassuring.

"Sure. I'll hustle."

The telephone rang off. Tommy put back the receiver with a sigh of relief. His opinion of Julius's power of hustling was high. He felt instinctively that the American would arrive in time.

Whittington and Boris were still where he had left them. If Boris remained to see his friend off, all was well. Then Tommy fingered his pocket thoughtfully. In spite of the carte blanche assured to him, he had not yet acquired the habit of going about with any considerable sum of money on him. The taking of the first-class ticket to Bournemouth had left him with only a few shillings in his pocket. It was to be hoped that Julius would arrive better provided.

In the meantime, the minutes were creeping by: 3:15, 3:20, 3:25, 3:27. Supposing Julius did not get there in time. 3:29. . . . Doors were banging. Tommy felt cold waves of despair pass over him. Then a hand fell on his shoulder.

"Here I am, son. Your British traffic beats description! Put me wise to the crooks right away."

"That's Whittington—there, getting in now, that big dark man. The other is the foreign chap he's talking to."

"I'm on to them. Which of the two is my bird?"

Tommy had thought out this question.

"Got any money with you?"

Julius shook his head, and Tommy's face fell.

"I guess I haven't more than three or four hundred dollars with me at the moment," explained the American.

Tommy gave a faint whoop of relief.

"Oh, Lord, you millionaires! You don't talk the same language! Climb aboard the lugger. Here's your ticket. Whittington's your man."

"Me for Whittington!" said Julius darkly. The train was just starting as he swung himself aboard. "So long, Tommy." The train slid out of the station.

Tommy drew a deep breath. The man Boris was coming along the platform towards him. Tommy allowed him to pass and then took up the chase once more.

From Waterloo Boris took the tube as far as Piccadilly Circus. Then he walked up Shaftesbury Avenue, finally turning off into the maze of mean streets round Soho. Tommy followed him at a judicious distance.

They reached at length a small dilapidated square. The houses there had a sinister air in the midst of their dirt and decay. Boris looked round, and Tommy drew back into the shelter of a friendly porch. The place was almost deserted. It was a cul-de-sac, and consequently no traffic passed that way. The stealthy way the other had looked round stimulated Tommy's imagination. From the shelter of the doorway he watched him go up the steps of a particularly evil-looking house and rap sharply, with a peculiar rhythm, on the door. It was opened promptly, he said a word or two to the doorkeeper, then passed inside. The door was shut to again.

It was at this juncture that Tommy lost his head. What he ought to have done, what any sane man would have done, was to remain patiently where he was and wait for his man to come out again. What he did do was entirely foreign to the sober common sense which was, as a rule, his leading characteristic. Something, as he expressed it, seemed to snap in his brain. Without a moment's pause for reflection he, too, went up the steps, and reproduced as far as he was able the peculiar knock.

The door swung open with the same promptness as before. A villainous-faced man with close-cropped hair stood in the doorway.

"Well?" he grunted.

It was at that moment that the full realization of his folly began to come home to Tommy. But he dared not hesitate. He seized at the first words that came into his mind.

"Mr. Brown?" he said.

To his surprise the man stood aside.

"Upstairs," he said, jerking his thumb over his shoulder, "second door on your left."

CHAPTER VIII
The Adventures of Tommy

Taken aback though he was by the man's words, Tommy did not hesitate. If audacity had successfully carried him so far, it was to be hoped it would carry him yet farther. He quietly passed into the house and mounted the ramshackle staircase. Everything in the house was filthy beyond words. The grimy paper, of a pattern now indistinguishable, hung in loose festoons from the wall. In every angle was a grey mass of cobweb.

Tommy proceeded leisurely. By the time he reached the bend of the staircase, he had heard the man below disappear into a back room. Clearly no suspicion attached to him as yet. To come to the house and ask for "Mr. Brown" appeared indeed to be a reasonable and natural proceeding.

At the top of the stairs Tommy halted to consider his next move. In front of him ran a narrow passage, with doors opening on either side of it. From the one nearest him on the left came a low murmur of voices. It was this room which he had been directed to enter. But what held his glance fascinated was a small recess immediately on his right, half concealed by a torn velvet curtain. It was directly opposite the left-handed door and, owing to its angle, it also commanded a good view of the upper part of the staircase. As a hiding-place for one or, at a pinch, two men, it was ideal, being about two feet deep and three feet wide. It attracted Tommy mightily. He thought things over in his usual slow and steady way, deciding that the mention of "Mr. Brown" was not a request for an individual, but in all probability a password used by the gang. His lucky use of it had gained him admission. So far he had aroused no suspicion. But he must decide quickly on his next step.

Suppose he were boldly to enter the room on the left of the passage. Would the mere fact of his having been admitted to the house be sufficient? Perhaps a further password would be required, or, at any rate, some proof of identity. The doorkeeper clearly did not know all the members of the gang by sight, but it might be different upstairs. On the whole it seemed to him that luck had served him very well so far, but that there was such a thing as trusting it too far. To enter that room was a colossal risk. He could not hope to sustain his part indefinitely; sooner or later he was almost bound to betray himself, and then he would have thrown away a vital chance in mere foolhardiness.

A repetition of the signal knock sounded on the door below, and Tommy, his mind made up, slipped quickly into the recess, and cautiously drew the curtain farther across so that it shielded him completely from sight. There were several rents and slits in the ancient material which afforded him a good view. He would watch events, and any time he chose could, after all, join the assembly, modelling his behaviour on that of the new arrival.

The man who came up the staircase with a furtive, soft-footed tread was quite unknown to Tommy. He was obviously of the very dregs of society. The low beetling brows, and the criminal jaw, the bestiality of the whole countenance were new to the young man, though he was a type that Scotland Yard would have recognized at a glance.

The man passed the recess, breathing heavily as he went. He stopped at the door opposite, and gave a repetition of the signal knock. A voice inside called out something, and the man opened the door and passed in, affording Tommy a momentary glimpse of the room inside. He thought there must be about four or five people seated round a long table that took up most of the space, but his attention was caught and held by a tall man with close-cropped hair and a short, pointed, naval-looking beard, who sat at the head of the table with papers in front of him. As the new-comer entered he glanced up, and with a correct, but curiously precise enunciation, which attracted Tommy's notice, he asked:

"Your number, comrade?"

"Fourteen, guv'nor," replied the other hoarsely.

"Correct."

The door shut again.

"If that isn't a Hun, I'm a Dutchman!" said Tommy to himself. "And running the show darned systematically too—as they always do. Lucky I didn't roll in. I'd have given the wrong number, and there would have been the deuce to pay. No, this is the place for me. Hullo, here's another knock."

This visitor proved to be of an entirely different type to the last. Tommy recognized in him an Irish Sinn Feiner. Certainly Mr. Brown's organization was a far-reaching concern. The common criminal, the well-bred Irish gentleman, the pale Russian, and the efficient German master of the ceremonies! Truly a strange and sinister gathering! Who was this man who held in his finger these curiously variegated links of an unknown chain?

In this case, the procedure was exactly the same. The signal knock, the demand for a number, and the reply "Correct."

Two knocks followed in quick succession on the door below. The first man was quite unknown to Tommy, who put him down as a city clerk. A quiet, intelligent-looking man, rather shabbily dressed. The second was of the working classes, and his face was vaguely familiar to the young man.

Three minutes later came another, a man of commanding appearance, exquisitely dressed, and evidently well born. His face, again, was not unknown to the watcher, though he could not for the moment put a name to it.

After his arrival there was a long wait. In fact Tommy concluded that the gathering was now complete, and was just cautiously creeping out from his hiding-place, when another knock sent him scuttling back to cover.

This last-comer came up the stairs so quietly that he was almost abreast of Tommy before the young man had realized his presence.

He was a small man, very pale, with a gentle almost womanish air. The angle of the cheek-bones hinted at his Slavonic ancestry, otherwise there was nothing to indicate his nationality. As he passed the recess, he turned his head slowly. The strange light eyes seemed to burn through the curtain; Tommy could hardly believe that the man did not know he was there and in spite of himself he shivered. He was no more fanciful than the majority of young Englishmen, but he could not rid himself of the impression that some unusually potent force emanated from the man. The creature reminded him of a venomous snake.

A moment later his impression was proved correct. The new-comer knocked on the door as all had done, but his reception was very different. The bearded man rose to his feet, and all the others followed suit. The German came forward and shook hands. His heels clicked together.

"We are honoured," he said. "We are greatly honoured. I much feared that it would be impossible."

The other answered in a low voice that had a kind of hiss in it:

"There were difficulties. It will not be possible again, I fear. But one meeting is essential—to define my policy. I can do nothing without—Mr. Brown. He is here?"

The change in the German's voice was audible as he replied with slight hesitation:

"We have received a message. It is impossible for him to be present in person." He stopped, giving a curious impression of having left the sentence unfinished.

A very slow smile overspread the face of the other. He looked round at a circle of uneasy faces.

"Ah! I understand. I have read of his methods. He works in the dark and trusts no one. But, all the same, it is possible that he is among us now. . . ." He looked round him again, and again that expression of fear swept over the group. Each man seemed to be eyeing his neighbour doubtfully.

The Russian tapped his cheek.

"So be it. Let us proceed."

The German seemed to pull himself together. He indicated the place he had been occupying at the head of the table. The Russian demurred, but the other insisted.

"It is the only possible place," he said, "for— Number One. Perhaps Number Fourteen will shut the door?"

In another moment Tommy was once more confronting bare wooden panels, and the voices within had sunk once more to a mere undistinguishable murmur. Tommy became restive. The conversation he had overheard had stimulated his curiosity. He felt that, by hook or by crook, he must hear more.

There was no sound from below, and it did not seem likely that the doorkeeper would come upstairs. After listening intently for a minute or two, he put his head round the curtain. The passage was deserted. Tommy bent down and removed his shoes, then, leaving them behind the curtain, he walked gingerly out on his stockinged feet, and kneeling down by the closed door he laid his ear cautiously to the crack. To his intense annoyance he could distinguish little more; just a chance word here and there if a voice was raised, which merely served to whet his curiosity still farther.

He eyed the handle of the door tentatively. Could he turn it by degrees so gently and imperceptibly that those in the room would notice nothing? He decided that with great care it could be done. Very slowly, a fraction of an inch at a time, he moved it round, holding his breath in his excessive care. A little more—a little more still—would it never be finished? Ah! at last it would turn no farther.

He stayed so for a minute or two, then drew a deep breath, and pressed it ever so slightly inward. The door did not budge. Tommy was annoyed. If he had to use too much force, it would almost certainly creak. He waited until the voices rose a little, then he tried again. Still nothing happened. He increased the pressure. Had the beastly thing stuck? Finally, in desperation, he pushed with all his might. But the door remained firm, and at last the truth dawned upon him. It was locked or bolted on the inside.

For a moment or two Tommy's indignation got the better of him.

"Well, I'm damned!" he said. "What a dirty trick!"

As his indignation cooled, he prepared to face the situation. Clearly the first thing to be done was to restore the handle to its original position. If he let it go suddenly, the men inside would be almost certain to notice it, so, with the same infinite pains, he reversed his former tactics. All went well, and with a sigh of relief the young man rose to his feet. There was a certain bulldog tenacity about Tommy that made him slow to admit defeat. Checkmated for the moment, he was far from abandoning the conflict. He still intended to hear what was going on in the locked room. As one plan had failed, he must hunt about for another.

He looked round him. A little farther along the passage on the left was a second door. He slipped silently along to it. He listened for a moment or two, then tried the handle. It yielded, and he slipped inside.

The room, which was untenanted, was furnished as a bedroom. Like everything else in the house, the furniture was falling to pieces, and the dirt was, if anything, more abundant.

But what interested Tommy was the thing he had hoped to find, a communicating door between the two rooms, up on the left by the window. Carefully closing the door into the passage behind him, he stepped across to the other and examined it closely. The bolt was shot across it. It was very rusty, and had clearly not been used for some time. By gently wriggling it to and fro, Tommy managed to draw it back without making too much noise. Then he repeated his former manœuvres with the handle—this time with complete success. The door swung open—a crack, a mere fraction, but enough for Tommy to hear what went on. There was a velvet *portière* on the inside of this door which prevented him from seeing, but he was able to recognize the voices with a reasonable amount of accuracy.

The Sinn Feiner was speaking. His rich Irish voice was unmistakable:

"That's all very well. But more money is essential. No money—no results!"

Another voice which Tommy rather thought was that of Boris replied:

"Will you guarantee that there *are* results?"

"In a month from now—sooner or later as you wish—I will guarantee you such a reign of terror in Ireland as shall shake the British Empire to its foundations."

There was a pause, and then came the soft, sibilant accents of Number One:

"Good! You shall have the money. Boris, you will see to that."

Boris asked a question:

"Via the Irish Americans, and Mr. Potter as usual?"

"I guess that'll be all right!" said a new voice, with a transatlantic intonation, "though I'd like to point out, here and now, that things are getting a mite difficult. There's not the sympathy there was, and a growing disposition to let the Irish settle their own affairs without interference from America."

Tommy felt that Boris had shrugged his shoulders as he answered:

"Does that matter, since the money only nominally comes from the States?"

"The chief difficulty is the landing of the ammunition," said the Sinn Feiner. "The money is conveyed in easily enough—thanks to our colleague here."

Another voice, which Tommy fancied was that of the tall, commanding-looking man whose face had seemed familiar to him, said:

"Think of the feelings of Belfast if they could hear you!"

"That is settled, then," said the sibilant tones. "Now, in the matter of the loan to an English newspaper, you have arranged the details satisfactorily, Boris?"

"I think so."

"That is good. An official denial from Moscow will be forthcoming if necessary."

There was a pause, and then the clear voice of the German broke the silence:

"I am directed by—Mr. Brown, to place the summaries of the reports from the different unions before you. That of the miners is most satisfactory. We must hold back the railways. There may be trouble with the A.S.E."

For a long time there was a silence, broken only by the rustle of papers and an occasional word of explanation from the German. Then Tommy heard the light tap-tap of fingers, drumming on the table.

"And—the date, my friend?" said Number One.

"The 29th."

The Russian seemed to consider:

"That is rather soon."

"I know. But it was settled by the principal Labour leaders, and we cannot seem to interfere too much. They must believe it to be entirely their own show."

The Russian laughed softly, as though amused.

"Yes, yes," he said. "That is true. They must have no inkling that we are using them for our own ends. They are honest men—and that is their value to us. It is curious—but you cannot make a revolution without honest men. The instinct of the populace is infallible." He paused, and then repeated, as though the phrase pleased him: "Every revolution has had its honest men. They are soon disposed of afterwards."

There was a sinister note in his voice.

The German resumed:

"Clymes must go. He is too far-seeing. Number Fourteen will see to that."

There was a hoarse murmur.

"That's all right, guv'nor." And then after a moment or two: "Suppose I'm nabbed."

"You will have the best legal talent to defend you," replied the German quietly. "But in any case you will wear gloves fitted with the fingerprints of a notorious housebreaker. You have little to fear."

"Oh, I ain't afraid, guv'nor. All for the good of the cause. The streets is going to run with blood, so they say." He spoke with a grim relish. "Dreams of it, sometimes, I does. And diamonds and pearls rolling about in the gutter for anyone to pick up!"

Tommy heard a chair shifted. Then Number One spoke:

"Then all is arranged. We are assured of success?"

"I—think so." But the German spoke with less than his usual confidence.

Number One's voice held suddenly a dangerous quality:

"What has gone wrong?"

"Nothing; but——".

"But what?"

"The Labour leaders. Without them, as you say, we can do nothing. If they do not declare a general strike on the 29th——"

"Why should they not?"

"As you've said, they're honest. And, in spite of everything we've done to discredit the Government in their eyes, I'm not sure that they haven't got a sneaking faith and belief in it."

"But——"

"I know. They abuse it unceasingly. But, on the whole, public opinion swings to the side of the Government. They will not go against it."

Again the Russian's fingers drummed on the table.

"To the point, my friend. I was given to understand that there was a certain document in existence which assured success."

"That is so. If that document were placed before the leaders, the result would be immediate. They would publish it broadcast throughout England, and declare for the revolution without a moment's hesitation. The Government would be broken finally and completely."

"Then what more do you want?"

"The document itself," said the German bluntly.

"Ah! It is not in your possession? But you know where it is?"

"No."

"Does anyone know where it is?"

"One person—perhaps. And we are not sure of that even."

"Who is this person?"

"A girl."

Tommy held his breath.

"A girl?" The Russian's voice rose contemptuously. "And you have not made her speak? In Russia we have ways of making a girl talk."

"This case is different," said the German sullenly.

"How—different?" He paused a moment, then went on: "Where is the girl now?"

"The girl?"

"Yes."

"She is——"

But Tommy heard no more. A crashing blow descended on his head, and all was darkness.

CHAPTER IX
Tuppence Enters Domestic Service

When Tommy set forth on the trail of the two men, it took all Tuppence's self-command to refrain from accompanying him. However, she contained herself as best she might, consoled by the reflection that her reasoning had been justified by events. The two men had undoubtedly come from the second floor flat, and that one slender thread of the name "Rita" had set the Young Adventurers once more upon the track of the abductors of Jane Finn.

The question was what to do next? Tuppence hated letting the grass grow under her feet. Tommy was amply employed, and debarred from joining him in the chase, the girl felt at a loose end. She retraced her steps to the entrance hall of the mansions. It was now tenanted by a small lift-boy, who was polishing brass fittings, and whistling the latest air with a good deal of vigour and a reasonable amount of accuracy.

He glanced round at Tuppence's entry. There

was a certain amount of the gamin element in the girl, at all events she invariably got on well with small boys. A sympathetic bond seemed instantly to be formed. She reflected that an ally in the enemy's camp, so to speak, was not to be despised.

"Well, William," she remarked cheerfully, in the best approved hospital-early-morning style, "getting a good shine up?"

The boy grinned responsively.

"Albert, miss," he corrected.

"Albert be it," said Tuppence. She glanced mysteriously round the hall. The effect was purposely a broad one in case Albert should miss it. She leaned towards the boy and dropped her voice: "I want a word with you, Albert."

Albert ceased operations on the fittings and opened his mouth slightly.

"Look! Do you know what this is?" With a dramatic gesture she flung back the left side of her coat and exposed a small enamelled badge. It was extremely unlikely that Albert would have any knowledge of it—indeed, it would have been fatal for Tuppence's plans, since the badge in question was the device of a local training corps originated by the archdeacon in the early days of the war. Its presence in Tuppence's coat was due to the fact that she had used it for pinning in some flowers a day or two before. But Tuppence had sharp eyes, and had noted the corner of a three-penny detective novel protruding from Albert's pocket, and the immediate enlargement of his eyes told her that her tactics were good, and that the fish would rise to the bait.

"American Detective Force!" she hissed.

Albert fell for it.

"Lord!" he murmured ecstatically.

Tuppence nodded at him with the air of one who has established a thorough understanding.

"Know who I'm after?" she inquired genially.

Albert, still round-eyed, demanded breathlessly:

"One of the flats?"

Tuppence nodded and jerked a thumb up the stairs.

"No. 20. Calls herself Vandemeyer. Vandemeyer! Ha! ha!"

Albert's hand stole to his pocket.

"A crook?" he queried eagerly.

"A crook? I should say so. Ready Rita they call her in the States."

"Ready Rita," repeated Albert deliriously. "Oh, ain't it just like the pictures!"

It was. Tuppence was a great frequenter of the kinema.

"Annie always said as how she was a bad lot," continued the boy.

"Who's Annie?" inquired Tuppence idly.

"'Ouse-parlourmaid. She's leaving today. Many's the time Annie's said to me: 'Mark my words, Albert, I wouldn't wonder if the police was to come after her one of these days.' Just like that. But she's a stunner to look at, ain't she?"

"She's some peach," allowed Tuppence carelessly. "Finds it useful in her lay-out, you bet. Has she been wearing any of the emeralds, by the way?"

"Emeralds? Them's the green stones, isn't they?"

Tuppence nodded.

"That's what we're after her for. You know old man Rysdale?"

Albert shook his head.

"Peter B. Rysdale, the oil king?"

"It seems sort of familiar to me."

"The sparklers belonged to him. Finest collection of emeralds in the world. Worth a million dollars!"

"Lumme!" came ecstatically from Albert. "It sounds more like the pictures every minute."

Tuppence smiled, gratified at the success of her efforts.

"We haven't exactly proved it yet. But we're after her. And"—she produced a long-drawn-out wink—"I guess she won't get away with the goods this time."

Albert uttered another ejaculation indicative of delight.

"Mind you, sonny, not a word of this," said Tuppence suddenly. "I guess I oughtn't to have put you wise, but in the States we know a real smart lad when we see one."

"I'll not breathe a word," protested Albert

eagerly. "Ain't there anything I could do? A bit of shadowing, maybe, or such like?"

Tuppence affected to consider, then shook her head.

"Not at the moment, but I'll bear you in mind, son. What's this about the girl you say is leaving?"

"Annie? Regular turn up, they 'ad. As Annie said, servants is some one nowadays, and to be treated accordingly, and, what with her passing the word round, she won't find it so easy to get another."

"Won't she?" said Tuppence thoughtfully. "I wonder——"

An idea was dawning in her brain. She thought a minute or two, then tapped Albert on the shoulder.

"See here, son, my brain's got busy. How would it be if you mentioned that you'd got a young cousin, or a friend of yours had, that might suit the place. You get me?"

"I'm there," said Albert instantly. "You leave it to me, miss, and I'll fix the whole thing up in two ticks."

"Some lad!" commented Tuppence, with a nod of approval. "You might say that the young woman could come in right away. You let me know, and if it's O.K. I'll be round tomorrow at eleven o'clock."

"Where am I to let you know to?"

"*Ritz*," replied Tuppence laconically. "Name of Cowley."

Albert eyed her enviously.

"It must be a good job, this tec business."

"It sure is," drawled Tuppence, "especially when old man Rysdale backs the bill. But don't fret, son. If this goes well, you shall come in on the ground floor."

With which promise she took leave of her new ally, and walked briskly away from South Audley Mansions, well pleased with her morning's work.

But there was no time to be lost. She went straight back to the *Ritz* and wrote a few brief words to Mr. Carter. Having dispatched this, and Tommy not having yet returned—which did

not surprise her—she started off on a shopping expedition which, with an interval for tea and assorted creamy cakes, occupied her until well after six o'clock, and she returned to the hotel jaded, but satisfied with her purchases. Starting with a cheap clothing store, and passing through one or two second-hand establishments, she had finished the day at a well-known hairdresser's. Now, in the seclusion of her bedroom, she unwrapped that final purchase. Five minutes later she smiled contentedly at her reflection in the glass. With an actress's pencil she had slightly altered the line of her eyebrows, and that, taken in conjunction with the new luxuriant growth of fair hair above, so changed her appearance that she felt confident that even if she came face to face with Whittington he would not recognize her. She would wear elevators in her shoes, and the cap and apron would be an even more valuable disguise. From hospital experience she knew only too well that a nurse out of uniform is frequently unrecognized by her patients.

"Yes," said Tuppence aloud, nodding at the pert reflection in the glass, "you'll do." She then resumed her normal appearance.

Dinner was a solitary meal. Tuppence was rather surprised at Tommy's non-return. Julius, too, was absent—but that to the girl's mind was more easily explained. His "hustling" activities were not confined to London, and his abrupt appearances and disappearances were fully accepted by the Young Adventurers as part of the day's work. It was quite on the cards that Julius P. Hersheimmer had left for Constantinople at a moment's notice if he fancied that a clue to his cousin's disappearance was to be found there. The energetic young man had succeeded in making the lives of several Scotland Yard men unbearable to them, and the telephone girls at the Admiralty had learned to know and dread the familiar "Hullo!" He had spent three hours in Paris hustling the Prefecture, and had returned from there imbued with the idea, possibly inspired by a weary French official, that the true clue to the mystery was to be found in Ireland.

"I dare say he's dashed off there now," thought Tuppence. "All very well, but this is very dull for *me*! Here I am bursting with news, and absolutely no one to tell it to! Tommy might have wired, or something. I wonder where he is. Anyway, he can't have 'lost the trail' as they say. That reminds me——" And Miss Cowley broke off in her meditations, and summoned a small boy.

Ten minutes later the lady was ensconced comfortably on her bed, smoking cigarettes and deep in the perusal of *Garnaby Williams, the Boy Detective*, which, with other three-penny works of lurid fiction, she had sent out to purchase. She felt, and rightly, that before the strain of attempting further intercourse with Albert, it would be as well to fortify herself with a good supply of local colour.

The morning brought a note from Mr. Carter:

"Dear Miss Tuppence,

"You have made a splendid start, and I congratulate you. I feel, though, that I should like to point out to you once more the risks you are running, especially if you pursue the course you indicate. Those people are absolutely desperate and incapable of either mercy or pity. I feel that you probably underestimate the danger, and therefore warn you again that I can promise you no protection. You have given us valuable information, and if you choose to withdraw now no one could blame you. At any rate, think the matter over well before you decide.

"If, in spite of my warnings, you make up your mind to go through with it, you will find everything arranged. You have lived for two years with Miss Dufferin, The Parsonage, Llanelly, and Mrs. Vandemeyer can apply to her for a reference.

"May I be permitted a word or two of advice? Stick as near to the truth as possible—it minimizes the danger of 'slips.' I suggest that you should represent yourself to be what you are, a former V.A.D., who has chosen domestic service as a profes-

sion. There are many such at the present time. That explains away any incongruities of voice or manner which otherwise might awaken suspicion.

"Whichever way you decide, good luck to you.

"Your sincere friend,
"Mr. Carter."

Tuppence's spirits rose mercurially. Mr. Carter's warnings passed unheeded. The young lady had far too much confidence in herself to pay any heed to them.

With some reluctance she abandoned the interesting part she had sketched out for herself. Although she had no doubts of her own powers to sustain a rôle indefinitely, she had too much common sense not to recognize the force of Mr. Carter's arguments.

There was still no word or message from Tommy, but the morning post brought a somewhat dirty postcard with the words: "It's O.K." scrawled upon it.

At ten-thirty Tuppence surveyed with pride a slightly battered tin trunk containing her new possessions. It was artistically corded. It was with a slight blush that she rang the bell and ordered it to be placed in a taxi. She drove to Paddington, and left the box in the cloak room. She then repaired with a handbag to the fastnesses of the ladies' waiting-room. Ten minutes later a metamorphosed Tuppence walked demurely out of the station and entered a bus.

It was a few minutes past eleven when Tuppence again entered the hall of South Audley Mansions. Albert was on the look-out, attending to his duties in a somewhat desultory fashion. He did not immediately recognize Tuppence. When he did, his admiration was unbounded.

"Blest if I'd have known you! That rig-out's top-hole."

"Glad you like it, Albert," replied Tuppence modestly. "By the way, am I your cousin, or am I not?"

"Your voice too," cried the delighted boy. "It's as English as anything! No, I said as a friend of mine knew a young gal. Annie wasn't best pleased. She's stopped on till today—to oblige, *she* said, but really it's so as to put you against the place."

"Nice girl," said Tuppence.

Albert suspected no irony.

"She's style about her, and keeps her silver a treat—but, my word, ain't she got a temper. Are you going up now, miss? Step inside the lift. No. 20 did you say?" And he winked.

Tuppence quelled him with a stern glance, and stepped inside.

As she rang the bell of No. 20 she was conscious of Albert's eyes slowly descending beneath the level of the floor.

A smart young woman opened the door.

"I've come about the place," said Tuppence.

"It's a rotten place," said the young woman without hesitation. "Regular old cat—always interfering. Accused me of tampering with her letters. Me! The flap was half undone anyway. There's never anything in the waste-paper basket—she burns everything. She's a wrong 'un, that's what she is. Swell clothes, but no class. Cook knows something about her—but she won't tell—scared to death of her. And suspicious! She's on to you in a minute if you as much as speak to a fellow. I can tell you——"

But what more Annie could tell, Tuppence was never destined to learn, for at that moment a clear voice with a peculiarly steely ring to it called:

"Annie!"

The smart young woman jumped as if she had been shot.

"Yes, ma'am."

"Who are you talking to?"

"It's a young woman about the situation, ma'am."

"Show her in then. At once."

"Yes, ma'am."

Tuppence was ushered into a room on the right of the long passage. A woman was standing by the fireplace. She was no longer in her first youth, and the beauty she undeniably possessed was hardened and coarsened. In her youth she must have been dazzling. Her pale gold hair, owing a slight assistance to art, was coiled low on her neck, her eyes, of a piercing electric blue, seemed to possess a faculty of boring into the very soul of the person she was looking at. Her exquisite figure was enhanced by a wonderful gown of indigo charmeuse. And yet, despite her swaying grace, and the almost ethereal beauty of her face, you felt instinctively the presence of something hard and menacing, a kind of metallic strength that found expression in the tones of her voice and in that gimlet-like quality of her eyes.

For the first time Tuppence felt afraid. She had not feared Whittington, but this woman was different. As if fascinated, she watched the long cruel line of the red curving mouth, and again she felt that sensation of panic pass over her. Her usual self-confidence deserted her. Vaguely she felt that deceiving this woman would be very different to deceiving Whittington. Mr. Carter's warning recurred to her mind. Here, indeed, she might expect no mercy.

Fighting down that instinct of panic which urged her to turn tail and run without further delay, Tuppence returned the lady's gaze firmly and respectfully.

As though that first scrutiny had been satisfactory, Mrs. Vandemeyer motioned to a chair.

"You can sit down. How did you hear I wanted a house-parlourmaid?"

"Through a friend who knows the lift-boy here. He thought the place might suit me."

Again that basilisk glance seemed to pierce her through.

"You speak like an educated girl?"

Glibly enough, Tuppence ran through her imaginary career on the lines suggested by Mr. Carter. It seemed to her, as she did so, that the tension of Mrs. Vandemeyer's attitude relaxed.

"I see," she remarked at length. "Is there anyone I can write to for a reference?"

"I lived last with a Miss Dufferin, The Parsonage, Llanelly. I was with her two years."

"And then you thought you would get more money by coming to London, I suppose?

Well, it doesn't matter to me. I will give you £50—£60—whatever you want. You can come in at once?"

"Yes, ma'am. Today, if you like. My box is at Paddington."

"Go and fetch it in a taxi, then. It's an easy place. I am out a good deal. By the way, what's your name?"

"Prudence Cooper, ma'am."

"Very well, Prudence. Go away and fetch your box. I shall be out to lunch. The cook will show you where everything is."

"Thank you, ma'am."

Tuppence withdrew. The smart Annie was not in evidence. In the hall below a magnificent hall porter had relegated Albert to the background. Tuppence did not even glance at him as she passed meekly out.

The adventure had begun, but she felt less elated than she had done earlier in the morning. It crossed her mind that if the unknown Jane Finn had fallen into the hands of Mrs. Vandemeyer, it was likely to have gone hard with her.

CHAPTER X
Enter Sir James Peel Edgerton

Tuppence betrayed no awkwardness in her new duties. The daughters of the archdeacon were well grounded in household tasks. They were also experts in training a "raw girl," the inevitable result being that the raw girl, once trained, departed elsewhere where her newly-acquired knowledge commanded a more substantial remuneration than the archdeacon's meagre purse allowed.

Tuppence had therefore very little fear of proving inefficient. Mrs. Vandemeyer's cook puzzled her. She evidently went in deadly terror of her mistress. The girl thought it probable that the other woman had some hold over her. For the rest, she cooked like a *chef*, as Tuppence had an opportunity of judging that evening. Mrs. Vandemeyer was expecting a guest to dinner, and Tuppence accordingly laid the beautifully

polished table for two. She was a little exercised in her own mind as to this visitor. It was highly possible that it might prove to be Whittington. Although she felt fairly confident that he would not recognize her, yet she would have been better pleased had the guest proved to be a total stranger. However, there was nothing for it but to hope for the best.

At a few minutes past eight the front door bell rang, and Tuppence went to answer it with some inward trepidation. She was relieved to see that the visitor was the second of the two men whom Tommy had taken upon himself to follow.

He gave his name as Count Stepanov. Tuppence announced him, and Mrs. Vandemeyer rose from her seat on a low divan with a quick murmur of pleasure.

"It is delightful to see you, Boris Ivanovitch," she said.

"And you, madame!" He bowed low over her hand.

Tuppence returned to the kitchen.

"Count Stepanov, or some such," she remarked, and affecting a frank and unvarnished curiosity: "Who's he?"

"A Russian gentleman, I believe."

"Come here much?"

"Once in a while. What d'you want to know for?"

"Fancied he might be sweet on the missus, that's all," explained the girl, adding with an appearance of sulkiness: "How you do take one up!"

"I'm not quite easy in my mind about the *soufflé*," explained the other.

"You know something," thought Tuppence to herself, but aloud she only said: "Going to dish up now? Right-o."

Whilst waiting at table, Tuppence listened closely to all that was said. She remembered that this was one of the men Tommy was shadowing when she had last seen him. Already, although she would hardly admit it, she was becoming uneasy about her partner. Where was he? Why had no word of any kind come from him? She had arranged before leaving the *Ritz* to have all letters or messages sent on at once by special messenger to a small stationer's shop near at hand where Albert was to call in frequently. True, it was only yesterday morning that she had parted from Tommy, and she told herself that any anxiety on his behalf would be absurd. Still, it was strange that he had sent no word of any kind.

But, listen as she might, the conversation presented no clue. Boris and Mrs. Vandemeyer talked on purely indifferent subjects: plays they had seen, new dances, and the latest society gossip. After dinner they repaired to the small boudoir where Mrs. Vandemeyer, stretched on the divan, looked more wickedly beautiful than ever. Tuppence brought in the coffee and liqueurs and unwillingly retired. As she did so, she heard Boris say:

"New, isn't she?"

"She came in today. The other was a fiend. This girl seems all right. She waits well."

Tuppence lingered a moment longer by the door which she had carefully neglected to close, and heard him say:

"Quite safe, I suppose?"

"Really, Boris, you are absurdly suspicious. I believe she's the cousin of the hall porter, or something of the kind. And nobody even dreams that I have any connection with our—mutual friend, Mr. Brown."

"For heaven's sake, be careful, Rita. That door isn't shut."

"Well, shut it then," laughed the woman.

Tuppence removed herself speedily.

She dared not absent herself longer from the back premises, but she cleared away and washed up with a breathless speed acquired in hospital. Then she slipped quietly back to the boudoir door. The cook, more leisurely, was still busy in the kitchen and, if she missed the other, would only suppose her to be turning down the beds.

Alas! The conversation inside was being carried on in too low a tone to permit of her hearing anything of it. She dared not reopen the door, however gently. Mrs. Vandemeyer was sitting almost facing it, and Tuppence respected her mistress's lynx-eyed powers of observation.

Nevertheless, she felt she would give a good deal to overhear what was going on. Possibly, if anything unforeseen had happened, she might get news of Tommy. For some moments she reflected desperately, then her face brightened. She went quickly along the passage to Mrs. Vandemeyer's bedroom, which had long French windows leading on to a balcony that ran the length of the flat. Slipping quickly through the window, Tuppence crept noiselessly along till she reached the boudoir window. As she had thought it stood a little ajar, and the voices within were plainly audible.

Tuppence listened attentively, but there was no mention of anything that could be twisted to apply to Tommy. Mrs. Vandemeyer and the Russian seemed to be at variance over some matter, and finally the latter exclaimed bitterly:

"With your persistent recklessness, you will end by ruining us!"

"Bah!" laughed the woman. "Notoriety of the right kind is the best way of disarming suspicion. You will realize that one of these days—perhaps sooner than you think!"

"In the meantime, you are going about everywhere with Peel Edgerton. Not only is he, perhaps, the most celebrated K.C. in England, but his special hobby is criminology! It is madness!"

"I know that his eloquence has saved untold men from the gallows," said Mrs. Vandemeyer calmly. "What of it? I may need his assistance in that line myself someday. If so, how fortunate to have such a friend at court—or perhaps it would be more to the point to say *in* court."

Boris got up and began striding up and down. He was very excited.

"You are a clever woman, Rita; but you are also a fool! Be guided by me, and give up Peel Edgerton."

Mrs. Vandemeyer shook her head gently.

"I think not."

"You refuse?" There was an ugly ring in the Russian's voice.

"I do."

"Then, by Heaven," snarled the Russian, "we will see——"

But Mrs. Vandemeyer also rose to her feet, her eyes flashing.

"You forget, Boris," she said. "I am accountable to no one. I take my orders only from—Mr. Brown."

The other threw up his hands in despair.

"You are impossible," he muttered. "Impossible! Already it may be too late. They say Peel Edgerton can *smell* a criminal! How do we know what is at the bottom of his sudden interest in you? Perhaps even now his suspicions are aroused. He guesses——"

Mrs. Vandemeyer eyed him scornfully.

"Reassure yourself, my dear Boris. He suspects nothing. With less than your usual chivalry, you seem to forget that I am commonly accounted a beautiful woman. I assure you that is all that interests Peel Edgerton."

Boris shook his head doubtfully.

"He has studied crime as no other man in this kingdom has studied it. Do you fancy that you can deceive him?"

Mrs. Vandemeyer's eyes narrowed.

"If he is all that you say—it would amuse me to try!"

"Good heavens, Rita——"

"Besides," added Mrs. Vandemeyer, "he is extremely rich. I am not one who despises money. The 'sinews of war,' you know, Boris!"

"Money—money! That is always the danger with you, Rita. I believe you would sell your soul for money. I believe——" He paused, then in a low, sinister voice he said slowly: "Sometimes I believe that you would sell—*us*!"

Mrs. Vandemeyer smiled and shrugged her shoulders.

"The price, at any rate, would have to be enormous," she said lightly. "It would be beyond the power of anyone but a millionaire to pay."

"Ah!" snarled the Russian. "You see, I was right!"

"My dear Boris, can you not take a joke?"

"Was it a joke?"

"Of course."

"Then all I can say is that your ideas of humour are peculiar, my dear Rita."

Mrs. Vandemeyer smiled.

"Let us not quarrel, Boris. Touch the bell. We will have some drinks."

Tuppence beat a hasty retreat. She paused a moment to survey herself in Mrs. Vandemeyer's long glass, and be sure that nothing was amiss with her appearance. Then she answered the bell demurely.

The conversation that she had overheard, although interesting in that it proved beyond doubt the complicity of both Rita and Boris, threw very little light on the present preoccupations. The name of Jane Finn had not even been mentioned.

The following morning a few brief words with Albert informed her that nothing was waiting for her at the stationer's. It seemed incredible that Tommy, if all was well with him, should not send any word to her. A cold hand seemed to close round her heart. . . . Supposing . . . She choked her fears down bravely. It was no good worrying. But she leapt at a chance offered her by Mrs. Vandemeyer.

"What day do you usually go out, Prudence?"

"Friday's my usual day, ma'am."

Mrs. Vandemeyer lifted her eyebrows.

"And today is Friday! But I suppose you hardly wish to go out today, as you only came yesterday."

"I was thinking of asking you if I might, ma'am."

Mrs. Vandemeyer looked at her a minute longer, and then smiled.

"I wish Count Stepanov could hear you. He made a suggestion about you last night." Her smile broadened, cat-like. "Your request is very—typical. I am satisfied. You do not understand all this—but you can go out today. It makes no difference to me, as I shall not be dining at home."

"Thank you, ma'am."

Tuppence felt a sensation of relief once she was out of the other's presence. Once again she admitted to herself that she was afraid, horribly afraid, of the beautiful woman with the cruel eyes.

In the midst of a final desultory polishing of her silver, Tuppence was disturbed by the ringing of the front door bell, and went to answer it. This time the visitor was neither Whittington nor Boris, but a man of striking appearance.

Just a shade over average height, he nevertheless conveyed the impression of a big man. His face, clean-shaven and exquisitely mobile, was stamped with an expression of power and force far beyond the ordinary. Magnetism seemed to radiate from him.

Tuppence was undecided for the moment whether to put him down as an actor or a lawyer, but her doubts were soon solved as he gave her his name: Sir James Peel Edgerton.

She looked at him with renewed interest. This, then, was the famous K.C. whose name was familiar all over England. She had heard it said that he might one day be Prime Minister. He was known to have refused office in the interests of his profession, preferring to remain a simple Member for a Scotch constituency.

Tuppence went back to her pantry thoughtfully. The great man had impressed her. She understood Boris's agitation. Peel Edgerton would not be an easy man to deceive.

In about a quarter of an hour the bell rang, and Tuppence repaired to the hall to show the visitor out. He had given her a piercing glance before. Now, as she handed him his hat and stick, she was conscious of his eyes raking her through. As she opened the door and stood aside to let him pass out, he stopped in the doorway.

"Not been doing this long, eh?"

Tuppence raised her eyes, astonished. She read in his glance kindliness, and something else more difficult to fathom.

He nodded as though she had answered.

"V.A.D. and hard up, I suppose?"

"Did Mrs. Vandemeyer tell you that?" asked Tuppence suspiciously.

"No, child. The look of you told me. Good place here?"

"Very good, thank you, sir."

"Ah, but there are plenty of good places nowadays. And a change does no harm sometimes."

"Do you mean——?" began Tuppence.

But Sir James was already on the topmost stair. He looked back with his kindly, shrewd glance.

"Just a hint," he said. "That's all."

Tuppence went back to the pantry more thoughtful than ever.

CHAPTER XI
Julius Tells a Story

Dressed appropriately, Tuppence duly sallied forth for her "afternoon out." Albert was in temporary abeyance, but Tuppence went herself to the stationer's to make quite sure that nothing had come for her. Satisfied on this point, she made her way to the *Ritz*. On inquiry she learnt that Tommy had not yet returned. It was the answer she had expected, but it was another nail in the coffin of her hopes. She resolved to appeal to Mr. Carter, telling him when and where Tommy had started on his quest, and asking him to do something to trace him. The prospect of his aid revived her mercurial spirits, and she next inquired for Julius Hersheimmer. The reply she got was to the effect that he had returned about half an hour ago, but had gone out immediately.

Tuppence's spirits revived still more. It would be something to see Julius. Perhaps he could devise some plan for finding out what had become of Tommy. She wrote her note to Mr. Carter in Julius's sitting-room, and was just addressing the envelope when the door burst open.

"What the hell——" began Julius, but checked himself abruptly. "I beg your pardon, Miss Tuppence. Those fools down at the office would have it that Beresford wasn't here any longer—hadn't been here since Wednesday. Is that so?"

Tuppence nodded.

"You don't know where he is?" she asked faintly.

"I? How should I know? I haven't had one

darned word from him, though I wired him yesterday morning."

"I expect your wire's at the office unopened."

"But where is he?"

"I don't know. I hoped you might."

"I tell you I haven't had one darned word from him since we parted at the depot on Wednesday."

"What depot?"

"Waterloo. Your London and South Western road."

"Waterloo?" frowned Tuppence.

"Why, yes. Didn't he tell you?"

"I haven't seen him either," replied Tuppence impatiently. "Go on about Waterloo. What were you doing there?"

"He gave me a call. Over the phone. Told me to get a move on, and hustle. Said he was trailing two crooks."

"Oh!" said Tuppence, her eyes opening. "I see. Go on."

"I hurried along right away. Beresford was there. He pointed out the crooks. The big one was mine, the guy you bluffed. Tommy shoved a ticket into my hand and told me to get aboard the cars. He was going to sleuth the other crook." Julius paused. "I thought for sure you'd know all this."

"Julius," said Tuppence firmly, "stop walking up and down. It makes me giddy. Sit down in that armchair, and tell me the whole story with as few fancy turns of speech as possible."

Mr. Hersheimmer obeyed.

"Sure," he said. "Where shall I begin?"

"Where you left off. At Waterloo."

"Well," began Julius, "I got into one of your dear old-fashioned first-class British compartments. The train was just off. First thing I knew a guard came along and informed me mighty politely that I wasn't in a smoking-carriage. I handed him out half a dollar, and that settled that. I did a bit of prospecting along the corridor to the next coach. Whittington was there right enough. When I saw the skunk, with his big sleek fat face, and thought of poor little Jane in his clutches, I felt real mad that I hadn't got a gun with me. I'd have tickled him up some.

"We got to Bournemouth all right. Whittington took a cab and gave the name of an hotel. I did likewise, and we drove up within three minutes of each other. He hired a room, and I hired one too. So far it was all plain sailing. He hadn't the remotest notion that any one was on to him. Well, he just sat around in the hotel lounge, reading the papers and so on, till it was time for dinner. He didn't hurry any over that either.

"I began to think that there was nothing doing, that he'd just come on the trip for his health, but I remembered that he hadn't changed for dinner, though it was by way of being a slap-up hotel, so it seemed likely enough that he'd be going out on his real business afterwards.

"Sure enough, about nine o'clock, so he did. Took a car across the town—mighty pretty place by the way, I guess I'll take Jane there for a spell when I find her—and then paid it off and struck out along those pine-woods on the top of the cliff. I was there too, you understand. We walked, maybe, for half an hour. There's a lot of villas all the way along, but by degrees they seemed to get more and more thinned out, and in the end we got to one that seemed the last of the bunch. Big house it was, with a lot of piny grounds around it.

"It was a pretty black night, and the carriage drive up to the house was dark as pitch. I could hear him ahead, though I couldn't see him. I had to walk carefully in case he might get on to it that he was being followed. I turned a curve and I was just in time to see him ring the bell and get admitted to the house. I just stopped where I was. It was beginning to rain, and I was soon pretty near soaked through. Also, it was almighty cold.

"Whittington didn't come out again, and by and by I got kind of restive, and began to mouch around. All the ground floor windows were shuttered tight, but upstairs, on the first floor (it was a two-storied house) I noticed a window with a light burning and the curtains not drawn.

"Now, just opposite to that window, there was a tree growing. It was about thirty foot away from the house, maybe, and I sort of got it into my head that, if I climbed up that tree,

I'd very likely be able to see into that room. Of course, I knew there was no reason why Whittington should be in that room rather than in any other—less reason, in fact, for the betting would be on his being in one of the reception-rooms downstairs. But I guess I'd got the hump from standing so long in the rain, and anything seemed better than going on doing nothing. So I started up.

"It wasn't so easy, by a long chalk! The rain had made the boughs mighty slippery, and it was all I could do to keep a foothold, but bit by bit I managed it, until at last there I was level with the window.

"But then I was disappointed. I was too far to the left. I could only see sideways into the room. A bit of curtain, and a yard of wallpaper was all I could command. Well, that wasn't any manner of good to me, but just as I was going to give it up, and climb down ignominiously, some one inside moved and threw his shadow on my little bit of wall—and, by gum, it was Whittington!

"After that, my blood was up. I'd just *got* to get a look into that room. It was up to me to figure out how. I noticed that there was a long branch running out from the tree in the right direction. If I could only swarm about half-way along it, the proposition would be solved. But it was mighty uncertain whether it would bear my weight. I decided I'd just got to risk that, and I started. Very cautiously, inch by inch, I crawled along. The bough creaked and swayed in a nasty fashion, and it didn't do to think of the drop below, but at last I got safely to where I wanted to be.

"The room was medium-sized, furnished in a kind of bare hygienic way. There was a table with a lamp on it in the middle of the room, and sitting at that table, facing towards me, was Whittington right enough. He was talking to a woman dressed as a hospital nurse. She was sitting with her back to me, so I couldn't see her face. Although the blinds were up, the window itself was shut, so I couldn't catch a word of what they said. Whittington seemed to be doing all the talking, and the nurse just listened. Now and then she nodded, and sometimes she'd shake her head, as though she were answering questions. He seemed very emphatic—once or twice he beat with his fist on the table. The rain had stopped now, and the sky was clearing in that sudden way it does.

"Presently, he seemed to get to the end of what he was saying. He got up, and so did she. He looked towards the window and asked something—I guess it was whether it was raining. Anyway, she came right across and looked out. Just then the moon came out from behind the clouds. I was scared the woman would catch sight of me, for I was full in the moonlight. I tried to move back a bit. The jerk I gave was too much for that rotten old branch. With an almighty crash, down it came, and Julius P. Hersheimmer with it!"

"Oh, Julius," breathed Tuppence, "how exciting! Go on."

"Well, luckily for me, I pitched down into a good soft bed of earth—but it put me out of action for the time, sure enough. The next thing I knew, I was lying in bed with a hospital nurse (not Whittington's one) on one side of me, and a little black-bearded man with gold glasses, and medical man written all over him, on the other. He rubbed his hands together, and raised his eyebrows as I stared at him. 'Ah!' he said. 'So our young friend is coming round again. Capital. Capital.'

"I did the usual stunt. Said: 'What's happened?' And 'Where am I?' But I knew the answer to the last well enough. There's no moss growing on my brain. 'I think that'll do for the present, sister,' said the little man, and the nurse left the room in a sort of brisk well-trained way. But I caught her handing me out a look of deep curiosity as she passed through the door.

"That look of hers gave me an idea. 'Now then, doc,' I said, and tried to sit up in bed, but my right foot gave me a nasty twinge as I did so. 'A slight sprain,' explained the doctor. 'Nothing serious. You'll be about again in a couple of days.'"

"I noticed you walked lame," interpolated Tuppence.

Julius nodded, and continued:

"'How did it happen?' I asked again. He replied dryly. 'You fell, with a considerable portion of one of my trees, into one of my newly-planted flower-beds.'

"I liked the man. He seemed to have a sense of humour. I felt sure that he, at least, was plumb straight. 'Sure, doc,' I said, 'I'm sorry about the tree, and I guess the new bulbs will be on me. But perhaps you'd like to know what I was doing in your garden?' 'I think the facts do call for an explanation,' he replied. 'Well, to begin with, I wasn't after the spoons.'

"He smiled. 'My first theory. But I soon altered my mind. By the way, you are an American, are you not?' I told him my name. 'And you?' 'I am Dr. Hall, and this, as you doubtless know, is my private nursing home.'

"I didn't know, but I wasn't going to put him wise. I was just thankful for the information. I liked the man, and I felt he was straight, but I wasn't going to give him the whole story. For one thing he probably wouldn't have believed it.

"I made up my mind in a flash. 'Why, doctor,' I said, 'I guess I feel an almighty fool, but I owe it to you to let you know that it wasn't the Bill Sikes business I was up to.' Then I went on and mumbled out something about a girl. I trotted out the stern guardian business, and a nervous breakdown, and finally explained that I had fancied I recognized her among the patients at the home, hence my nocturnal adventures.

"I guess it was just the kind of story he was expecting. 'Quite a romance,' he said genially, when I'd finished. 'Now, doc,' I went on, 'will you be frank with me? Have you here now, or have you had here at any time, a young girl called Jane Finn?' He repeated the name thoughtfully. 'Jane Finn?' he said. 'No.'

"I was chagrined, and I guess I showed it. 'You are sure?' 'Quite sure, Mr. Hersheimmer. It is an uncommon name, and I should not have been likely to forget it.'

"Well, that was flat. It laid me out for a space. I'd kind of hoped my search was at an end. 'That's that,' I said at last. 'Now, there's another matter. When I was hugging that darned branch I thought I recognized an old friend of mine talking to one of your nurses.' I purposely didn't mention any name because, of course, Whittington might be calling himself something quite different down here, but the doctor answered at once. 'Mr. Whittington, perhaps?' 'That's the fellow,' I replied. 'What's he doing down here? Don't tell me *his* nerves are out of order?'

"Dr. Hall laughed. 'No. He came down to see one of my nurses, Nurse Edith, who is a niece of his.' 'Why, fancy that!' I exclaimed. 'Is he still here?' 'No, he went back to town almost immediately.' 'What a pity!' I ejaculated. 'But perhaps I could speak to his niece—Nurse Edith, did you say her name was?'

"But the doctor shook his head. 'I'm afraid that, too, is impossible. Nurse Edith left with a patient tonight also.' 'I seem to be real unlucky,' I remarked. 'Have you Mr. Whittington's address in town? I guess I'd like to look him up when I get back.' 'I don't know his address. I can write to Nurse Edith for it if you like.' I thanked him. 'Don't say who it is wants it. I'd like to give him a little surprise.'

"That was about all I could do for the moment. Of course, if the girl was really Whittington's niece, she might be too cute to fall into the trap, but it was worth trying. Next thing I did was to write out a wire to Beresford saying where I was, and that I was laid up with a sprained foot, and telling him to come down if he wasn't busy. I had to be guarded in what I said. However, I didn't hear from him, and my foot soon got all right. It was only ricked, not really sprained, so today I said good-bye to the little doctor chap, asked him to send me word if he heard from Nurse Edith, and came right away back to town. Say, Miss Tuppence, you're looking mighty pale!"

"It's Tommy," said Tuppence. "What can have happened to him?"

"Buck up, I guess he's all right really. Why shouldn't he be? See here, it was a foreign-looking guy he went off after. Maybe they've gone abroad—to Poland, or something like that?"

Tuppence shook her head.

"He couldn't without passports and things. Besides I've seen that man, Boris Something, since. He dined with Mrs. Vandemeyer last night."

"Mrs. Who?"

"I forgot. Of course you don't know all that."

"I'm listening," said Julius, and gave vent to his favourite expression. "Put me wise."

Tuppence thereupon related the events of the last two days. Julius's astonishment and admiration were unbounded.

"Bully for you! Fancy you a menial. It just tickles me to death!" Then he added seriously: "But say now, I don't like it, Miss Tuppence, I sure don't. You're just as plucky as they make 'em, but I wish you'd keep right out of this. These crooks we're up against would as soon croak a girl as a man any day."

"Do you think I'm afraid?" said Tuppence indignantly, valiantly repressing memories of the steely glitter in Mrs. Vandemeyer's eyes.

"I said before you were darned plucky. But that doesn't alter facts."

"Oh, bother *me*!" said Tuppence impatiently. "Let's think about what can have happened to Tommy. I've written to Mr. Carter about it," she added, and told him the gist of her letter.

Julius nodded gravely.

"I guess that's good as far as it goes. But it's for us to get busy and do something."

"What can we do?" asked Tuppence, her spirits rising.

"I guess we'd better get on the track of Boris. You say he's been to your place. Is he likely to come again?"

"He might. I really don't know."

"I see. Well, I guess I'd better buy a car, a slap-up one, dress as a chauffeur, and hang about outside. Then if Boris comes, you could make some kind of signal, and I'd trail him. How's that?"

"Splendid, but he mightn't come for weeks."

"We'll have to chance that. I'm glad you like the plan." He rose.

"Where are you going?"

"To buy the car, of course," replied Julius, surprised. "What make do you like? I guess you'll do some riding in it before we've finished."

"Oh," said Tuppence faintly, "I *like* Rolls-Royces, but——"

"Sure," agreed Julius. "What you say goes. I'll get one."

"But you can't at once," cried Tuppence. "People wait ages sometimes."

"Little Julius doesn't," affirmed Mr. Hersheimmer. "Don't you worry any. I'll be round in the car in half an hour."

Tuppence got up.

"You're awfully good, Julius. But I can't help feeling that it's rather a forlorn hope. I'm really pinning my faith to Mr. Carter."

"Then I shouldn't."

"Why?"

"Just an idea of mine."

"Oh; but he must do something. There's no one else. By the way, I forgot to tell you of a queer thing that happened this morning."

And she narrated her encounter with Sir James Peel Edgerton. Julius was interested.

"What did the guy mean, do you think?" he asked.

"I don't quite know," said Tuppence meditatively. "But I think that, in an ambiguous, legal, without prejudishish lawyer's way, he was trying to warn me."

"Why should he?"

"I don't know," confessed Tuppence. "But he looked kind, and simply awfully clever. I wouldn't mind going to him and telling him everything."

Somewhat to her surprise, Julius negatived the idea sharply.

"See here," he said, "we don't want any lawyers mixed up in this. That guy couldn't help us any."

"Well, I believe he could," reiterated Tuppence obstinately.

"Don't you think it. So long. I'll be back in half an hour."

Thirty-five minutes had elapsed when Julius

returned. He took Tuppence by the arm, and walked her to the window.

"There she is."

"Oh!" said Tuppence with a note of reverence in her voice, as she gazed down at the enormous car.

"She's some pace-maker, I can tell you," said Julius complacently.

"How did you get it?" gasped Tuppence.

"She was just being sent home to some bigwig."

"Well?"

"I went round to his house," said Julius. "I said that I reckoned a car like that was worth every penny of twenty thousand dollars. Then I told him that it was worth just about fifty thousand dollars to me if he'd get out."

"Well?" said Tuppence, intoxicated.

"Well," returned Julius, "he got out, that's all."

CHAPTER XII
A Friend in Need

Friday and Saturday passed uneventfully. Tuppence had received a brief answer to her appeal from Mr. Carter. In it he pointed out that the Young Adventurers had undertaken the work at their own risk, and had been fully warned of the dangers. If anything had happened to Tommy he regretted it deeply, but he could do nothing.

This was cold comfort. Somehow, without Tommy, all the savour went out of the adventure, and, for the first time, Tuppence felt doubtful of success. While they had been together she had never questioned it for a minute. Although she was accustomed to take the lead, and to pride herself on her quick-wittedness, in reality she had relied upon Tommy more than she realized at the time. There was something so eminently sober and clear-headed about him, his common sense and soundness of vision were so unvarying, that without him Tuppence felt much like a rudderless ship. It was curious that Julius, who was undoubtedly much cleverer than Tommy, did not give her the same feeling of support. She had accused Tommy of being a pessimist, and it is certain that he always saw the disadvantages and difficulties which she herself was optimistically given to overlooking, but nevertheless she had really relied a good deal on his judgment. He might be slow, but he was very sure.

It seemed to the girl that, for the first time, she realized the sinister character of the mission they had undertaken so light-heartedly. It had begun like a page of romance. Now, shorn of its glamour, it seemed to be turning to grim reality. Tommy—that was all that mattered. Many times in the day Tuppence blinked the tears out of her eyes resolutely. "Little fool," she would apostrophize herself, "don't snivel. Of course you're fond of him. You've known him all your life. But there's no need to be sentimental about it."

In the meantime, nothing more was seen of Boris. He did not come to the flat, and Julius and the car waited in vain. Tuppence gave herself over to new meditations. Whilst admitting the truth of Julius's objections, she had nevertheless not entirely relinquished the idea of appealing to Sir James Peel Edgerton. Indeed, she had gone so far as to look up his address in the *Red Book*. Had he meant to warn her that day? If so, why? Surely she was at least entitled to demand an explanation. He had looked at her so kindly. Perhaps he might tell them something concerning Mrs. Vandemeyer which might lead to a clue to Tommy's whereabouts.

Anyway, Tuppence decided, with her usual shake of the shoulders, it was worth trying, and try it she would. Sunday was her afternoon out. She would meet Julius, persuade him to her point of view, and they would beard the lion in his den.

When the day arrived Julius needed a considerable amount of persuading, but Tuppence held firm. "It can do no harm," was what she always came back to. In the end Julius gave in, and they proceeded in the car to Carlton House Terrace.

The door was opened by an irreproachable butler. Tuppence felt a little nervous. After all, perhaps it *was* colossal cheek on her part. She had decided not to ask if Sir James was "at home," but to adopt a more personal attitude.

"Will you ask Sir James if I can see him for a few minutes? I have an important message for him."

The butler retired, returning a moment or two later.

"Sir James will see you. Will you step this way?"

He ushered them into a room at the back of the house, furnished as a library. The collection of books was a magnificent one, and Tuppence noticed that all one wall was devoted to works on crime and criminology. There were several deep-padded leather arm-chairs, and an old-fashioned open hearth. In the window was a big roll-top desk strewn with papers at which the master of the house was sitting.

He rose as they entered.

"You have a message for me? Ah"—he recognized Tuppence with a smile—"it's you, is it? Brought a message from Mrs. Vandemeyer, I suppose?"

"Not exactly," said Tuppence. "In fact, I'm afraid I only said that to be quite sure of getting in. Oh, by the way, this is Mr. Hersheimmer, Sir James Peel Edgerton."

"Pleased to meet you," said the American, shooting out a hand.

"Won't you both sit down?" asked Sir James. He drew forward two chairs.

"Sir James," said Tuppence, plunging boldly, "I dare say you will think it is most awful cheek of me coming here like this. Because, of course, it's nothing whatever to do with you, and then you're a very important person, and of course Tommy and I are very unimportant." She paused for breath.

"Tommy?" queried Sir James, looking across at the American.

"No, that's Julius," explained Tuppence. "I'm rather nervous, and that makes me tell it badly. What I really want to know is what you meant by what you said to me the other day? Did you mean to warn me against Mrs. Vandemeyer? You did, didn't you?"

"My dear young lady, as far as I recollect I only mentioned that there were equally good situations to be obtained elsewhere."

"Yes, I know. But it was a hint, wasn't it?"

"Well, perhaps it was," admitted Sir James gravely.

"Well, I want to know more. I want to know just *why* you gave me a hint."

Sir James smiled at her earnestness.

"Suppose the lady brings a libel action against me for defamation of character?"

"Of course," said Tuppence. "I know lawyers are always dreadfully careful. But can't we say 'without prejudice' first, and then say just what we want to."

"Well," said Sir James, still smiling, "without prejudice, then, if I had a young sister forced to earn her living, I should not like to see her in Mrs. Vandemeyer's service. I felt it incumbent on me just to give you a hint. It is no place for a young and inexperienced girl. That is all I can tell you."

"I see," said Tuppence thoughtfully. "Thank you very much. But I'm not *really* inexperienced, you know. I knew perfectly that she was a bad lot when I went there—as a matter of fact that's *why* I went——" She broke off, seeing some bewilderment on the lawyer's face, and went on: "I think perhaps I'd better tell you the whole story, Sir James. I've a sort of feeling that you'd know in a minute if I didn't tell the truth, and so you might as well know all about it from the beginning. What do you think, Julius?"

"As you're bent on it, I'd go right ahead with the facts," replied the American, who had so far sat in silence.

"Yes, tell me all about it," said Sir James. "I want to know who Tommy is."

Thus encouraged Tuppence plunged into her tale, and the lawyer listened with close attention.

"Very interesting," he said, when she finished. "A great deal of what you tell me, child, is already known to me. I've had certain theories of my own about this Jane Finn. You've done extraordinarily well so far, but it's rather too bad of—what do you know him as?—Mr. Carter to pitchfork you two young things into an affair of this kind. By the way, where did Mr. Hersheimmer come in originally? You didn't make that clear?"

Julius answered for himself.

"I'm Jane's first cousin," he explained, returning the lawyer's keen gaze.

"Ah!"

"Oh, Sir James," broke out Tuppence, "what do you think has become of Tommy?"

"H'm." The lawyer rose, and paced slowly up and down. "When you arrived, young lady, I was just packing up my traps. Going to Scotland by the night train for a few days' fishing. But there are different kinds of fishing. I've a good mind to stay, and see if we can't get on the track of that young chap."

"Oh!" Tuppence clasped her hands ecstatically.

"All the same, as I said before, it's too bad of—of Carter to set you two babies on a job like this. Now, don't get offended, Miss —er——"

"Cowley. Prudence Cowley. But my friends call me Tuppence."

"Well, Miss Tuppence, then, as I'm certainly going to be a friend. Don't be offended because I think you're young. Youth is a failing only too easily outgrown. Now, about this young Tommy of yours——"

"Yes." Tuppence clasped her hands.

"Frankly, things look bad for him. He's been butting in somewhere where he wasn't wanted. Not a doubt of it. But don't give up hope."

"And you really will help us? There, Julius! He didn't want me to come," she added by way of explanation.

"H'm," said the lawyer, favouring Julius with another keen glance. "And why was that?"

"I reckoned it would be no good worrying you with a petty little business like this."

"I see." He paused a moment. "This petty little business, as you call it, bears directly on

a very big business, bigger perhaps than either you or Miss Tuppence know. If this boy is alive, he may have very valuable information to give us. Therefore, we must find him."

"Yes, but how?" cried Tuppence. "I've tried to think of everything."

Sir James smiled.

"And yet there's one person quite near at hand who in all probability knows where he is, or at all events where he is likely to be."

"Who is that?" asked Tuppence, puzzled.

"Mrs. Vandemeyer."

"Yes, but she'd never tell us."

"Ah, that is where I come in. I think it quite likely that I shall be able to make Mrs. Vandemeyer tell me what I want to know."

"How?" demanded Tuppence, opening her eyes very wide.

"Oh, just by asking her questions," replied Sir James easily. "That's the way we do it, you know."

He tapped with his finger on the table, and Tuppence felt again the intense power that radiated from the man.

"And if she won't tell?" asked Julius suddenly.

"I think she will. I have one or two powerful levers. Still, in that unlikely event, there is always the possibility of bribery."

"Sure. And that's where I come in!" cried Julius, bringing his fist down on the table with a bang. "You can count on me, if necessary, for one million dollars. Yes, sir, one million dollars!"

Sir James sat down and subjected Julius to a long scrutiny.

"Mr. Hersheimmer," he said at last, "that is a very large sum."

"I guess it'll have to be. These aren't the kind of folk to offer sixpence to."

"At the present rate of exchange it amounts to considerably over two hundred and fifty thousand pounds."

"That's so. Maybe you think I'm talking through my hat, but I can deliver the goods all right, with enough over to spare for your fee."

Sir James flushed slightly.

"There is no question of a fee, Mr. Hersheimmer. I am not a private detective."

"Sorry. I guess I was just a mite hasty, but I've been feeling bad about this money question. I wanted to offer a big reward for news of Jane some days ago, but your crusted institution of Scotland Yard advised me against it. Said it was undesirable."

"They were probably right," said Sir James dryly.

"But it's all O.K. about Julius," put in Tuppence. "He's not pulling your leg. He's got simply pots of money."

"The old man piled it up in style," explained Julius. "Now, let's get down to it. What's your idea?"

Sir James considered for a moment or two.

"There is no time to be lost. The sooner we strike the better." He turned to Tuppence. "Is Mrs. Vandemeyer dining out tonight, do you know?"

"Yes, I think so, but she will not be out late. Otherwise, she would have taken the latchkey."

"Good. I will call upon her about ten o'clock. What time are you supposed to return?"

"About nine-thirty or ten, but I could go back earlier."

"You must not do that on any account. It might arouse suspicion if you did not stay out till the usual time. Be back by nine-thirty. I will arrive at ten. Mr. Hersheimmer will wait below in a taxi, perhaps."

"He's got a new Rolls-Royce car," said Tuppence with vicarious pride.

"Even better. If I succeed in obtaining the address from her, we can go there at once, taking Mrs. Vandemeyer with us if necessary. You understand?"

"Yes." Tuppence rose to her feet with a skip of delight. "Oh, I feel so much better!"

"Don't build on it too much, Miss Tuppence. Go easy."

Julius turned to the lawyer.

"Say, then. I'll call for you in the car round about nine-thirty. Is that right?"

"Perhaps that will be the best plan. It would

be unnecessary to have two cars waiting about. Now, Miss Tuppence, my advice to you is to go and have a good dinner, a *really* good one, mind. And don't think ahead more than you can help."

He shook hands with them both, and a moment later they were outside.

"Isn't he a duck?" inquired Tuppence ecstatically, as she skipped down the steps. "Oh, Julius, isn't he just a duck?"

"Well, I allow he seems to be the goods all right. And I was wrong about its being useless to go to him. Say, shall we go right away back to the *Ritz*?"

"I must walk a bit, I think. I feel so excited. Drop me in the park, will you? Unless you'd like to come too?"

"I want to get some petrol," he explained. "And send off a cable or two."

"All right. I'll meet you at the *Ritz* at seven. We'll have to dine upstairs. I can't show myself in these glad rags."

"Sure. I'll get Felix to help me choose the menu. He's some head waiter, that. So long."

Tuppence walked briskly along towards the Serpentine, first glancing at her watch. It was nearly six o'clock. She remembered that she had had no tea, but felt too excited to be conscious of hunger. She walked as far as Kensington Gardens and then slowly retraced her steps, feeling infinitely better for the fresh air and exercise. It was not so easy to follow Sir James's advice, and put the possible events of the evening out of her head. As she drew nearer and nearer to Hyde Park corner, the temptation to return to South Audley Mansions was almost irresistible.

At any rate, she decided, it would do no harm just to go and *look* at the building. Perhaps, then, she could resign herself to waiting patiently for ten o'clock.

South Audley Mansions looked exactly the same as usual. What Tuppence had expected she hardly knew, but the sight of its red-brick stolidity slightly assuaged the growing and entirely unreasonable uneasiness that possessed her. She was just turning away when she heard a piercing whistle, and the faithful Albert came running from the building to join her.

Tuppence frowned. It was no part of the programme to have attention called to her presence in the neighbourhood, but Albert was purple with suppressed excitement.

"I say, miss, she's a going!"

"Who's going?" demanded Tuppence sharply.

"The crook. Ready Rita. Mrs. Vandemeyer. She's a-packing up, and she's just sent down word for me to get her a taxi."

"What?" Tuppence clutched his arm.

"It's the truth, miss. I thought maybe as you didn't know about it."

"Albert," cried Tuppence, "you're a brick. If it hadn't been for you we'd have lost her."

Albert flushed with pleasure at this tribute.

"There's no time to lose," said Tuppence, crossing the road. "I've got to stop her. At all costs I must keep her here until——" She broke off. "Albert, there's a telephone here, isn't there?"

The boy shook his head.

"The flats mostly have their own, miss. But there's a box just round the corner."

"Go to it then, at once, and ring up the *Ritz Hotel*. Ask for Mr. Hersheimmer, and when you get him tell him to get Sir James and come on at once, as Mrs. Vandemeyer is trying to hook it. If you can't get him, ring up Sir James Peel Edgerton, you'll find his number in the book, and tell him what's happening. You won't forget the names, will you?"

Albert repeated them glibly. "You trust to me, miss, it'll be all right. But what about you? Aren't you afraid to trust yourself with her?"

"No, no, that's all right. *But go and telephone. Be quick.*"

Drawing a long breath, Tuppence entered the Mansions and ran up to the door of No. 20. How she was to detain Mrs. Vandemeyer until the two men arrived, she did not know, but somehow or other it had to be done, and she must accomplish the task single-handed. What had occasioned this precipitate departure? Did Mrs. Vandemeyer suspect her?

Speculations were idle. Tuppence pressed the bell firmly. She might learn something from the cook.

Nothing happened and, after waiting some minutes, Tuppence pressed the bell again, keeping her finger on the button for some little while. At last she heard footsteps inside, and a moment later Mrs. Vandemeyer herself opened the door. She lifted her eyebrows at the sight of the girl.

"You?"

"I had a touch of toothache, ma'am," said Tuppence glibly. "So thought it better to come home and have a quiet evening."

Mrs. Vandemeyer said nothing, but she drew back and let Tuppence pass into the hall.

"How unfortunate for you," she said coldly. "You had better go to bed."

"Oh, I shall be all right in the kitchen, ma'am. Cook will——"

"Cook is out," said Mrs. Vandemeyer, in a rather disagreeable tone. "I sent her out. So you see you had better go to bed."

Suddenly Tuppence felt afraid. There was a ring in Mrs. Vandemeyer's voice that she did not like at all. Also, the other woman was slowly edging her up the passage. Tuppence turned at bay.

"I don't want——"

Then, in a flash, a rim of cold steel touched her temple, and Mrs. Vandemeyer's voice rose cold and menacing:

"You damned little fool! Do you think I don't know? No, don't answer. If you struggle or cry out, I'll shoot you like a dog."

The rim of steel pressed a little harder against the girl's temple.

"Now then, march," went on Mrs. Vandemeyer. "This way—into my room. In a minute, when I've done with you, you'll go to bed as I told you to. And you'll sleep—oh yes, my little spy, you'll sleep all right!"

There was a sort of hideous geniality in the last words which Tuppence did not at all like. For the moment there was nothing to be done, and she walked obediently into Mrs. Vandemeyer's bedroom. The pistol never left her forehead. The room was in a state of wild disorder, clothes were flung about right and left, a suit-case and a hat box, half-packed, stood in the middle of the floor.

Tuppence pulled herself together with an effort. Her voice shook a little, but she spoke out bravely.

"Come now," she said. "This is nonsense. You can't shoot me. Why, every one in the building would hear the report."

"I'd risk that," said Mrs. Vandemeyer cheerfully. "But, as long as you don't sing out for help, you're all right—and I don't think you will. You're a clever girl. You deceived *me* all right. I hadn't a suspicion of you! So I've no doubt that you understand perfectly well that this is where I'm on top and you're underneath. Now then— sit on the bed. Put your hands above your head, and if you value your life don't move them."

Tuppence obeyed passively. Her good sense told her that there was nothing else to do but accept the situation. If she shrieked for help there was very little chance of any one hearing her, whereas there was probably quite a good chance of Mrs. Vandemeyer's shooting her. In the meantime, every minute of delay gained was valuable.

Mrs. Vandemeyer laid down the revolver on the edge of the washstand within reach of her hand, and, still eyeing Tuppence like a lynx in case the girl should attempt to move, she took a little stoppered bottle from its place on the marble and poured some of its contents into a glass which she filled up with water.

"What's that?" asked Tuppence sharply.

"Something to make you sleep soundly."

Tuppence paled a little.

"Are you going to poison me?" she asked in a whisper.

"Perhaps," said Mrs. Vandemeyer, smiling agreeably.

"Then I shan't drink it," said Tuppence firmly. "I'd much rather be shot. At any rate that would make a row, and some one might hear it. But I won't be killed off quietly like a lamb."

Mrs. Vandemeyer stamped her foot.

"Don't be a little fool! Do you really think I want a hue and cry for murder out after me? If you've any sense at all, you'll realize that poisoning you wouldn't suit my book at all. It's a sleeping draught, that's all. You'll wake up tomorrow morning none the worse. I simply don't want the bother of tying you up and gagging you. That's the alternative—and you won't like it, I can tell you! I can be very rough if I choose. So drink this down like a good girl, and you'll be none the worse for it."

In her heart of hearts Tuppence believed her. The arguments she had adduced rang true. It was a simple and effective method of getting her out of the way for the time being. Nevertheless, the girl did not take kindly to the idea of being tamely put to sleep without as much as one bid for freedom. She felt that once Mrs. Vandemeyer gave them the slip, the last hope of finding Tommy would be gone.

Tuppence was quick in her mental processes. All these reflections passed through her mind in a flash, and she saw where a chance, a very problematical chance, lay, and she determined to risk all in one supreme effort.

Accordingly, she lurched suddenly off the bed and fell on her knees before Mrs. Vandemeyer, clutching her skirts frantically.

"I don't believe it," she moaned. "It's poison—I know it's poison. Oh, don't make me drink it"—her voice rose to a shriek—"don't make me drink it!"

Mrs. Vandemeyer, glass in hand, looked down with a curling lip at this sudden collapse.

"Get up, you little idiot! Don't go on drivelling there. How you ever had the nerve to play your part as you did I can't think." She stamped her foot. "Get up, I say."

But Tuppence continued to cling and sob, interjecting her sobs with incoherent appeals for mercy. Every minute gained was to the good. Moreover, as she grovelled, she moved imperceptibly nearer to her objective.

Mrs. Vandemeyer gave a sharp impatient exclamation, and jerked the girl to her knees.

"Drink it at once!" Imperiously she pressed the glass to the girl's lips.

Tuppence gave one last despairing moan.

"You swear it won't hurt me?" she temporized.

"Of course it won't hurt you. Don't be a fool."

"Will you swear it?"

"Yes, yes," said the other impatiently. "I swear it."

Tuppence raised a trembling left hand to the glass.

"Very well." Her mouth opened meekly.

Mrs. Vandemeyer gave a sigh of relief, off her guard for the moment. Then, quick as a flash, Tuppence jerked the glass upward as hard as she could. The fluid in it splashed into Mrs. Vandemeyer's face, and during her momentary gasp, Tuppence's right hand shot out and grasped the revolver where it lay on the edge of the washstand. The next moment she had sprung back a pace, and the revolver pointed straight at Mrs. Vandemeyer's heart, with no unsteadiness in the hand that held it.

In the moment of victory, Tuppence betrayed a somewhat unsportsman-like triumph.

"Now who's on top and who's underneath?" she crowed.

The other's face was convulsed with rage. For a minute Tuppence thought she was going to spring upon her, which would have placed the girl in an unpleasant dilemma, since she meant to draw the line at actually letting off the revolver. However, with an effort Mrs. Vandemeyer controlled herself, and at last a slow evil smile crept over her face.

"Not a fool, then, after all! You did that well, girl. But you shall pay for it—oh, yes, you shall pay for it! I have a long memory!"

"I'm surprised you should have been gulled so easily," said Tuppence scornfully. "Did you really think I was the kind of girl to roll about on the floor and whine for mercy?"

"You may do—someday!" said the other significantly.

The cold malignity of her manner sent an unpleasant chill down Tuppence's spine, but she was not going to give in to it.

"Supposing we sit down," she said pleasantly.

"Our present attitude is a little melodramatic. No—not on the bed. Draw a chair up to the table, that's right. Now I'll sit opposite you with the revolver in front of me—just in case of accidents. Splendid. Now, let's talk."

"What about?" said Mrs. Vandemeyer sullenly.

Tuppence eyed her thoughtfully for a minute. She was remembering several things. Boris's words, "I believe you would sell— *us*!" and her answer, "The price would have to be enormous," given lightly, it was true, yet might not there be a substratum of truth in it? Long ago, had not Whittington asked: "Who's been blabbing? Rita?" Would Rita Vandemeyer prove to be the weak spot in the armour of Mr. Brown?

Keeping her eyes fixed steadily on the other's face, Tuppence replied quietly:

"Money——"

Mrs. Vandemeyer started. Clearly, the reply was unexpected.

"What do you mean?"

"I'll tell you. You said just now that you had a long memory. A long memory isn't half as useful as a long purse! I dare say it relieves your feelings a good deal to plan out all sorts of dreadful things to do to me, but is that *practical*? Revenge is very unsatisfactory. Every one always says so. But money"—Tuppence warmed to her pet creed—"well, there's nothing unsatisfactory about money, is there?"

"Do you think," said Mrs. Vandemeyer scornfully, "that I am the kind of woman to sell my friends?"

"Yes," said Tuppence promptly. "If the price was big enough."

"A paltry hundred pounds or so!"

"No," said Tuppence. "I should suggest—a hundred thousand!"

Her economical spirit did not permit her to mention the whole million dollars suggested by Julius.

A flush crept over Mrs. Vandemeyer's face.

"What did you say?" she asked, her fingers playing nervously with a brooch on her breast. In that moment Tuppence knew that the fish was hooked, and for the first time she felt a horror of her own money-loving spirit. It gave her a dreadful sense of kinship to the woman fronting her.

"A hundred thousand pounds," repeated Tuppence.

The light died out of Mrs. Vandemeyer's eyes. She leaned back in her chair.

"Bah!" she said. "You haven't got it."

"No," admitted Tuppence, "I haven't—but I know some one who has."

"Who?"

"A friend of mine."

"Must be a millionaire," remarked Mrs. Vandemeyer unbelievingly.

"As a matter of fact he is. He's an American. He'll pay you that without a murmur. You can take it from me that it's a perfectly genuine proposition."

Mrs. Vandemeyer sat up again.

"I'm inclined to believe you," she said slowly.

There was silence between them for some time, then Mrs. Vandemeyer looked up.

"What does he want to know, this friend of yours?"

Tuppence went through a momentary struggle, but it was Julius's money, and his interests must come first.

"He wants to know where Jane Finn is," she said boldly.

Mrs. Vandemeyer showed no surprise.

"I'm not sure where she is at the present moment," she replied.

"But you could find out?"

"Oh, yes," returned Mrs. Vandemeyer carelessly. "There would be no difficulty about that."

"Then"—Tuppence's voice shook a little— "there's a boy, a friend of mine. I'm afraid something's happened to him, through your pal Boris."

"What's his name?"

"Tommy Beresford."

"Never heard of him. But I'll ask Boris. He'll tell me anything he knows."

"Thank you." Tuppence felt a terrific rise in her spirits. It impelled her to more audacious efforts. "There's one thing more."

"Well?"

Tuppence leaned forward and lowered her voice.

"Who is Mr. Brown?"

Her quick eyes saw the sudden paling of the beautiful face. With an effort Mrs. Vandemeyer pulled herself together and tried to resume her former manner. But the attempt was a mere parody.

She shrugged her shoulders.

"You can't have learnt much about us if you don't know that *nobody knows who Mr. Brown is. . . .*"

"You do," said Tuppence quietly.

Again the colour deserted the other's face.

"What makes you think that?"

"I don't know," said the girl truthfully. "But I'm sure."

Mrs. Vandemeyer stared in front of her for a long time.

"Yes," she said hoarsely, at last, "*I* know. I was beautiful, you see—very beautiful——"

"You are still," said Tuppence with admiration.

Mrs. Vandemeyer shook her head. There was a strange gleam in her electric-blue eyes.

"Not beautiful enough," she said in a soft dangerous voice. "Not—beautiful—enough! And sometimes, lately, I've been afraid. . . . It's dangerous to know too much!" She leaned forward across the table. "Swear that my name shan't be brought into it—that no one shall ever know."

"I swear it. And, once's he's caught, you'll be out of danger."

A terrified look swept across Mrs. Vandemeyer's face.

"Shall I? Shall I ever be?" She clutched Tuppence's arm. "You're sure about the money?"

"Quite sure."

"When shall I have it? There must be no delay."

"This friend of mine will be here presently. He may have to send cables, or something like that. But there won't be any delay—he's a terrific hustler."

A resolute look settled on Mrs. Vandemeyer's face.

"I'll do it. It's a great sum of money, and besides"—she gave a curious smile—"it is not—wise to throw over a woman like me!"

For a moment or two, she remained smiling, and lightly tapping her fingers on the table. Suddenly she started, and her face blanched.

"What was that?"

"I heard nothing."

Mrs. Vandemeyer gazed round her fearfully.

"If there should be some one listening——"

"Nonsense. Who could there be?"

"Even the walls might have ears," whispered the other. "I tell you I'm frightened. You don't know him!"

"Think of the hundred thousand pounds," said Tuppence soothingly.

Mrs. Vandemeyer passed her tongue over her dried lips.

"You don't know him," she reiterated hoarsely. "He's—ah!"

With a shriek of terror she sprang to her feet. Her outstretched hand pointed over Tuppence's head. Then she swayed to the ground in a dead faint.

Tuppence looked round to see what had startled her.

In the doorway were Sir James Peel Edgerton and Julius Hersheimmer.

CHAPTER XIII
The Vigil

Sir James brushed past Julius and hurriedly bent over the fallen woman.

"Heart," he said sharply. "Seeing us so suddenly must have given her a shock. Brandy—and quickly, or she'll slip through our fingers."

Julius hurried to the washstand.

"Not there," said Tuppence over her shoulder. "In the tantalus in the dining-room. Second door down the passage."

Between them Sir James and Tuppence lifted Mrs. Vandemeyer and carried her to the bed.

There they dashed water on her face, but with no result. The lawyer fingered her pulse.

"Touch and go," he muttered. "I wish that young fellow would hurry up with the brandy."

At that moment Julius re-entered the room, carrying a glass half full of the spirit which he handed to Sir James. While Tuppence lifted her head the lawyer tried to force a little of the spirit between her closed lips. Finally the woman opened her eyes feebly. Tuppence held the glass to her lips.

"Drink this."

Mrs. Vandemeyer complied. The brandy brought the colour back to her white cheeks, and revived her in a marvellous fashion. She tried to sit up—then fell back with a groan, her hand to her side.

"It's my heart," she whispered. "I mustn't talk."

She lay back with closed eyes.

Sir James kept his finger on her wrist a minute longer, then withdrew it with a nod.

"She'll do now."

All three moved away, and stood together talking in low voices. One and all were conscious of a certain feeling of anticlimax. Clearly any scheme for cross-questioning the lady was out of the question for the moment. For the time being they were baffled, and could do nothing.

Tuppence related how Mrs. Vandemeyer had declared herself willing to disclose the identity of Mr. Brown, and how she had consented to discover and reveal to them the whereabouts of Jane Finn. Julius was congratulatory.

"That's all right, Miss Tuppence. Splendid! I guess that hundred thousand pounds will look just as good in the morning to the lady as it did over night. There's nothing to worry over. She won't speak without the cash anyway, you bet!"

There was certainly a good deal of common sense in this, and Tuppence felt a little comforted.

"What you say is true," said Sir James meditatively. "I must confess, however, that I cannot help wishing we had not interrupted at the minute we did. Still, it cannot be helped, it is only a matter of waiting until the morning."

He looked across at the inert figure on the bed. Mrs. Vandemeyer lay perfectly passive with closed eyes. He shook his head.

"Well," said Tuppence, with an attempt at cheerfulness, "we must wait until the morning, that's all. But I don't think we ought to leave the flat."

"What about leaving that bright boy of yours on guard?"

"Albert? And suppose she came round again and hooked it. Albert couldn't stop her."

"I guess she won't want to make tracks away from the dollars."

"She might. She seemed very frightened of 'Mr. Brown.'"

"What? Real plumb scared of him?"

"Yes. She looked round and said even walls had ears."

"Maybe she meant a dictaphone," said Julius with interest.

"Miss Tuppence is right," said Sir James quietly. "We must not leave the flat—if only for Mrs. Vandemeyer's sake."

Julius stared at him.

"You think he'd get after her? Between now and tomorrow morning. How could he know, even?"

"You forget your own suggestion of a dictaphone," said Sir James dryly. "We have a very formidable adversary. I believe, if we exercise all due care, that there is a very good chance of his being delivered into our hands. But we must neglect no precaution. We have an important witness, but she must be safeguarded. I would suggest that Miss Tuppence should go to bed, and that you and I, Mr. Hersheimmer, should share the vigil."

Tuppence was about to protest, but happening to glance at the bed she saw Mrs. Vandemeyer, her eyes half-open, with such an expression of mingled fear and malevolence on her face that it quite froze the words on her lips.

For a moment she wondered whether the faint and the heart attack had been a gigantic sham, but remembering the deadly pallor she could hardly credit the supposition. As she looked the expression disappeared as by magic, and Mrs. Vandemeyer lay inert and motionless as before. For a moment the girl fancied she must have dreamt it. But she determined nevertheless to be on the alert.

"Well," said Julius, "I guess we'd better make a move out of here any way."

The others fell in with his suggestion. Sir James again felt Mrs. Vandemeyer's pulse.

"Perfectly satisfactory," he said in a low voice to Tuppence. "She'll be absolutely all right after a night's rest."

The girl hesitated a moment by the bed. The intensity of the expression she had surprised had impressed her powerfully. Mrs. Vandemeyer lifted her lids. She seemed to be struggling to speak. Tuppence bent over her.

"Don't—leave——" she seemed unable to proceed, murmuring something that sounded like "sleepy." Then she tried again.

Tuppence bent lower still. It was only a breath.

"Mr.—Brown——" The voice stopped.

But the half-closed eyes seemed still to send an agonized message.

Moved by a sudden impulse, the girl said quickly:

"I shan't leave the flat. I shall sit up all night."

A flash of relief showed before the lids descended once more. Apparently Mrs. Vandemeyer slept. But her words had awakened a new uneasiness in Tuppence. What had she meant by that low murmur: "Mr. Brown"? Tuppence caught herself nervously looking over her shoulder. The big wardrobe loomed up in a sinister fashion before her eyes. Plenty of room for a man to hide in that. . . . Half-ashamed of herself, Tuppence pulled it open and looked inside. No one—of course! She stooped down and looked under the bed. There was no other possible hiding-place.

Tuppence gave her familiar shake of the shoulders. It was absurd, this giving way to nerves! Slowly she went out of the room. Julius and

Sir James were talking in a low voice. Sir James turned to her.

"Lock the door on the outside, please, Miss Tuppence, and take out the key. There must be no chance of anyone entering that room."

The gravity of his manner impressed them, and Tuppence felt less ashamed of her attack of "nerves."

"Say," remarked Julius suddenly, "there's Tuppence's bright boy. I guess I'd better go down and ease his young mind. That's some lad, Tuppence."

"How did you get in, by the way?" asked Tuppence suddenly. "I forgot to ask."

"Well, Albert got me on the phone all right. I ran round for Sir James here, and we came right on. The boy was on the look-out for us, and was just a mite worried about what might have happened to you. He'd been listening outside the door of the flat, but couldn't hear anything. Anyhow he suggested sending us up in the coal lift instead of ringing the bell. And sure enough we landed in the scullery and came right along to find you. Albert's still below, and must be just hopping mad by this time." With which Julius departed abruptly.

"Now then, Miss Tuppence," said Sir James, "you know this place better than I do. Where do you suggest we should take up our quarters?"

Tuppence considered for a moment or two.

"I think Mrs. Vandemeyer's boudoir would be the most comfortable," she said at last, and led the way there.

Sir James looked round approvingly.

"This will do very well, and now, my dear young lady, do go to bed and get some sleep."

Tuppence shook her head resolutely.

"I couldn't, thank you, Sir James. I should dream of Mr. Brown all night!"

"But you'll be so tired, child."

"No, I shan't. I'd rather stay up—really."

The lawyer gave in.

Julius reappeared some minutes later, having reassured Albert and rewarded him lavishly for his services. Having in his turn failed to persuade Tuppence to go to bed, he said decisively:

"At any rate, you've got to have something to eat right away. Where's the larder?"

Tuppence directed him, and he returned in a few minutes with a cold pie and three plates.

After a hearty meal, the girl felt inclined to pooh-pooh her fancies of half an hour before. The power of the money bribe could not fail.

"And now, Miss Tuppence," said Sir James, "we want to hear your adventures."

"That's so," agreed Julius.

Tuppence narrated her adventures with some complacence. Julius occasionally interjected an admiring "Bully." Sir James said nothing until she had finished, when his quiet "well done, Miss Tuppence," made her flush with pleasure.

"There's one thing I don't get clearly," said Julius. "What put her up to clearing out?"

"I don't know," confessed Tuppence.

Sir James stroked his chin thoughtfully.

"The room was in great disorder. That looks as though her flight was unpremeditated. Almost as though she got a sudden warning to go from some one."

"Mr. Brown, I suppose," said Julius scoffingly.

The lawyer looked at him deliberately for a minute or two.

"Why not?" he said. "Remember, you yourself have once been worsted by him."

Julius flushed with vexation.

"I feel just mad when I think of how I handed out Jane's photograph to him like a lamb. Gee, if I ever lay hands on it again, I'll freeze on to it like—like hell!"

"That contingency is likely to be a remote one," said the other dryly.

"I guess you're right," said Julius frankly. "And, in any case, it's the original I'm out after. Where do you think she can be, Sir James?"

The lawyer shook his head.

"Impossible to say. But I've a very good idea where she *has* been."

"You have? Where?"

Sir James smiled.

"At the scene of your nocturnal adventures, the Bournemouth nursing home."

"There? Impossible. I asked."

"No, my dear sir, you asked if anyone of the name of Jane Finn had been there. Now, if the girl had been placed there it would almost certainly be under an assumed name."

"Bully for you," cried Julius. "I never thought of that!"

"It was fairly obvious," said the other.

"Perhaps the doctor's in it too," suggested Tuppence.

Julius shook his head.

"I don't think so. I took to him at once. No, I'm pretty sure Dr. Hall's all right."

"Hall, did you say?" asked Sir James. "That is curious—really very curious."

"Why?" demanded Tuppence.

"Because I happened to meet him this morning. I've known him slightly on and off for some years, and this morning I ran across him in the street. Staying at the *Métropole*, he told me." He turned to Julius. "Didn't he tell you he was coming up to town?"

Julius shook his head.

"Curious," mused Sir James. "You did not mention his name this afternoon, or I would have suggested your going to him for further information with my card as introduction."

"I guess I'm a mutt," said Julius with unusual humility. "I ought to have thought of the false name stunt."

"How could you think of anything after falling out of that tree?" cried Tuppence. "I'm sure anyone else would have been killed right off."

"Well, I guess it doesn't matter now, anyway," said Julius. "We've got Mrs. Vandemeyer on a string, and that's all we need."

"Yes," said Tuppence, but there was a lack of assurance in her voice.

A silence settled down over the party. Little by little the magic of the night began to gain a hold on them. There were sudden creaks in the furniture, imperceptible rustlings in the curtains. Suddenly Tuppence sprang up with a cry.

"I can't help it. I know Mr. Brown's somewhere in the flat! I can *feel* him."

"Sure, Tuppence, how could he be? This door's open into the hall. No one could have come in by the front door without our seeing and hearing him."

"I can't help it. I *feel* he's here!"

She looked appealingly at Sir James, who replied gravely:

"With due deference to your feelings, Miss Tuppence (and mine as well for that matter), I do not see how it is humanly possible for anyone to be in the flat without our knowledge."

The girl was a little comforted by his words.

"Sitting up at night is always rather jumpy," she confessed.

"Yes," said Sir James. "We are in the condition of people holding a séance. Perhaps if a medium were present we might get some marvellous results."

"Do you believe in spiritualism?" asked Tuppence, opening her eyes wide.

The lawyer shrugged his shoulders.

"There is some truth in it, without a doubt. But most of the testimony would not pass muster in the witness-box."

The hours drew on. With the first faint glimmerings of dawn, Sir James drew aside the curtains. They beheld, what few Londoners see, the slow rising of the sun over the sleeping city. Somehow, with the coming of the light, the dreads and fancies of the past night seemed absurd. Tuppence's spirits revived to the normal.

"Hooray!" she said. "It's going to be a gorgeous day. And we shall find Tommy. And Jane Finn. And everything will be lovely. I shall ask Mr. Carter if I can't be made a Dame!"

At seven o'clock Tuppence volunteered to go and make some tea. She returned with a tray, containing the teapot and four cups.

"Who's the other cup for?" inquired Julius.

"The prisoner, of course. I suppose we might call her that?"

"Taking her tea seems a kind of anti-climax to last night," said Julius thoughtfully.

"Yes, it does," admitted Tuppence. "But, anyway, here goes. Perhaps you'd both come, too, in case she springs on me, or anything. You see, we don't know what mood she'll wake up in."

Sir James and Julius accompanied her to the door.

"Where's the key? Oh, of course, I've got it myself."

She put it in the lock, and turned it, then paused.

"Supposing, after all, she's escaped?" she murmured in a whisper.

"Plumb impossible," replied Julius reassuringly.

But Sir James said nothing.

Tuppence drew a long breath and entered. She heaved a sigh of relief as she saw that Mrs. Vandemeyer was lying on the bed.

"Good morning," she remarked cheerfully. "I've brought you some tea."

Mrs. Vandemeyer did not reply. Tuppence put down the cup on the table by the bed and went across to draw up the blinds. When she turned, Mrs. Vandemeyer still lay without a movement. With a sudden fear clutching at her heart, Tuppence ran to the bed. The hand she lifted was cold as ice. . . . Mrs. Vandemeyer would never speak now. . . .

Her cry brought the others. A very few minutes sufficed. Mrs. Vandemeyer was dead—must have been dead some hours. She had evidently died in her sleep.

"If that isn't the cruellest luck," cried Julius in despair.

The lawyer was calmer, but there was a curious gleam in his eyes.

"If it is luck," he replied.

"You don't think—but, say, that's plumb impossible—no one could have got in."

"No," admitted the lawyer. "I don't see how they could. And yet—she is on the point of betraying Mr. Brown, and—she dies. Is it only chance?"

"But how——"

"Yes, *how*! That is what we must find out." He stood there silently, gently stroking his

chin. "We must find out," he said quietly, and Tuppence felt that if she was Mr. Brown she would not like the tone of those simple words.

Julius's glance went to the window.

"The window's open," he remarked. "Do you think——"

Tuppence shook her head.

"The balcony only goes along as far as the boudoir. We were there."

"He might have slipped out——" suggested Julius.

But Sir James interrupted him.

"Mr. Brown's methods are not so crude. In the meantime we must send for a doctor, but before we do so, is there anything in this room that might be of value to us?"

Hastily, the three searched. A charred mass in the grate indicated that Mrs. Vandemeyer had been burning papers on the eve of her flight. Nothing of importance remained, though they searched the other rooms as well.

"There's that," said Tuppence suddenly, pointing to a small, old-fashioned safe let into the wall. "It's for jewellery, I believe, but there might be something else in it."

The key was in the lock, and Julius swung open the door, and searched inside. He was some time over the task.

"Well," said Tuppence impatiently.

There was a pause before Julius answered, then he withdrew his head and shut to the door.

"Nothing," he said.

In five minutes a brisk young doctor arrived, hastily summoned. He was deferential to Sir James, whom he recognized.

"Heart failure, or possibly an overdose of some sleeping-draught." He sniffed. "Rather an odour of chloral in the air."

Tuppence remembered the glass she had upset. A new thought drove her to the washstand. She found the little bottle from which Mrs. Vandemeyer had poured a few drops.

It had been three parts full. Now—*it was empty*.

CHAPTER XIV
A Consultation

Nothing was more surprising and bewildering to Tuppence than the ease and simplicity with which everything was arranged, owing to Sir James's skilful handling. The doctor accepted quite readily the theory that Mrs. Vandemeyer had accidentally taken an overdose of chloral. He doubted whether an inquest would be necessary. If so, he would let Sir James know. He understood that Mrs. Vandemeyer was on the eve of departure for abroad, and that the servants had already left? Sir James and his young friends had been paying a call upon her, when she was suddenly stricken down and they had spent the night in the flat, not liking to leave her alone. Did they know of any relatives? They did not, but Sir James referred him to Mrs. Vandemeyer's solicitor.

Shortly afterwards a nurse arrived to take charge, and the other left the ill-omened building.

"And what now?" asked Julius, with a gesture of despair. "I guess we're down and out for good."

Sir James stroked his chin thoughtfully.

"No," he said quietly. "There is still the chance that Dr. Hall may be able to tell us something."

"Gee! I'd forgotten him."

"The chance is slight, but it must not be neglected. I think I told you that he is staying at the *Métropole*. I should suggest that we call upon him there as soon as possible. Shall we say after a bath and breakfast?"

It was arranged that Tuppence and Julius should return to the *Ritz*, and call for Sir James in the car. This programme was faithfully carried out, and a little after eleven they drew up before the *Métropole*. They asked for Dr. Hall, and a page-boy went in search of him. In a few minutes the little doctor came hurrying towards them.

"Can you spare us a few minutes, Dr. Hall?" said Sir James pleasantly. "Let me introduce you

to Miss Cowley. Mr. Hersheimmer, I think, you already know."

A quizzical gleam came into the doctor's eye as he shook hands with Julius.

"Ah, yes, my young friend of the tree episode! Ankle all right, eh?"

"I guess it's cured owing to your skilful treatment, doc."

"And the heart trouble? Ha ha!"

"Still searching," said Julius briefly.

"To come to the point, can we have a word with you in private?" asked Sir James.

"Certainly. I think there is a room here where we shall be quite undisturbed."

He led the way, and the others followed him. They sat down, and the doctor looked inquiringly at Sir James.

"Dr. Hall, I am very anxious to find a certain young lady for the purpose of obtaining a statement from her. I have reason to believe that she has been at one time or another in your establishment at Bournemouth. I hope I am transgressing no professional etiquette in questioning you on the subject?"

"I suppose it is a matter of testimony?"

Sir James hesitated a moment, then he replied:

"Yes."

"I shall be pleased to give you any information in my power. What is the young lady's name? Mr. Hersheimmer asked me, I remember——" He half turned to Julius.

"The name," said Sir James bluntly, "is really immaterial. She would be almost certainly sent to you under an assumed one. But I should like to know if you are acquainted with a Mrs. Vandemeyer?"

"Mrs. Vandemeyer, of 20 South Audley Mansions? I know her slightly."

"You are not aware of what has happened?"

"What do you mean?"

"You do not know that Mrs. Vandemeyer is dead?"

"Dear, dear, I had no idea of it! When did it happen?"

"She took an overdose of chloral last night."

"Purposely?"

"Accidentally, it is believed. I should not like to say myself. Anyway, she was found dead this morning."

"Very sad. A singularly handsome woman. I presume she was a friend of yours, since you are acquainted with all these details."

"I am acquainted with the details because—well, it was I who found her dead."

"Indeed," said the doctor, starting.

"Yes," said Sir James, and stroked his chin reflectively.

"This is very sad news, but you will excuse me if I say that I do not see how it bears on the subject of your inquiry?"

"It bears on it in this way, is it not a fact that Mrs. Vandemeyer committed a young relative of hers to your charge?"

Julius leaned forward eagerly.

"That is the case," said the doctor quietly.

"Under the name of——?"

"Janet Vandemeyer. I understood her to be a niece of Mrs. Vandemeyer's."

"And she came to you?"

"As far as I can remember in June or July of 1915."

"Was she a mental case?"

"She is perfectly sane, if that is what you mean. I understood from Mrs. Vandemeyer that the girl had been with her on the *Lusitania* when that ill-fated ship was sunk, and had suffered a severe shock in consequence."

"We're on the right track, I think?" Sir James looked round.

"As I said before, I'm a mutt!" returned Julius.

The doctor looked at them all curiously.

"You spoke of wanting a statement from her," he said. "Supposing she is not able to give one?"

"What? You have just said that she is perfectly sane."

"So she is. Nevertheless, if you want a statement from her concerning any events prior to May 7, 1915, she will not be able to give it to you."

They looked at the little man, stupefied. He nodded cheerfully.

"It's a pity," he said. "A great pity, especially as I gather, Sir James, that the matter is important. But there it is, she can tell you nothing."

"But why, man? Darn it all, why?"

The little man shifted his benevolent glance to the excited young American.

"Because Janet Vandemeyer is suffering from a complete loss of memory."

"What?"

"Quite so. An interesting case, a *very* interesting case. Not so uncommon, really, as you would think. There are several very well known parallels. It's the first case of the kind that I've had under my own personal observation, and I must admit that I've found it of absorbing interest." There was something rather ghoulish in the little man's satisfaction.

"And she remembers nothing," said Sir James slowly.

"Nothing prior to May 7, 1915. After that date her memory is as good as yours or mine."

"Then the first thing she remembers?"

"Is landing with the survivors. Everything before that is a blank. She did not know her own name, or where she had come from, or where she was. She couldn't even speak her own tongue."

"But surely all this is most unusual?" put in Julius.

"No, my dear sir. Quite normal under the circumstances. Severe shock to the nervous system. Loss of memory proceeds nearly always on the same lines. I suggested a specialist, of course. There's a very good man in Paris—makes a study of these cases—but Mrs. Vandemeyer opposed the idea of publicity that might result from such a course."

"I can imagine she would," said Sir James grimly.

"I fell in with her views. There *is* a certain notoriety given to these cases. And the girl was very young—nineteen, I believe. It seemed a pity that her infirmity should be talked about—might damage her prospects. Besides, there is no special treatment to pursue in such cases. It is really a matter of waiting."

"Waiting?"

"Yes, sooner or later, the memory will return—as suddenly as it went. But in all probability the girl will have entirely forgotten the intervening period, and will take up life where she left off—at the sinking of the *Lusitania*."

"And when do you expect this to happen?"

The doctor shrugged his shoulders.

"Ah, that I cannot say. Sometimes it is a matter of months, sometimes it has been known to be as long as twenty years! Sometimes another shock does the trick. One restores what the other took away."

"Another shock, eh?" said Julius thoughtfully.

"Exactly. There was a case in Colorado——" The little man's voice trailed on, voluble, mildly enthusiastic.

Julius did not seem to be listening. He had relapsed into his own thoughts and was frowning. Suddenly he came out of his brown study, and hit the table such a resounding bang with his fist that every one jumped, the doctor most of all.

"I've got it! I guess, doc, I'd like your medical opinion on the plan I'm about to outline. Say Jane was to cross the herring pond again, and the same thing was to happen. The submarine, the sinking ship, every one to take to the boats—and so on. Wouldn't that do the trick? Wouldn't it give a mighty big bump to her subconscious self, or whatever the jargon is, and start it functioning again right away?"

"A very interesting speculation, Mr. Hersheimmer. In my own opinion, it would be successful. It is unfortunate that there is no chance of the conditions repeating themselves as you suggest."

"Not by nature, perhaps, doc. But I'm talking about art."

"Art?"

"Why, yes. What's the difficulty? Hire a liner——"

"A liner!" murmured Dr. Hall faintly.

"Hire some passengers, hire a submarine—that's the only difficulty, I guess. Governments are apt to be a bit hide-bound over their engines of war. They won't sell to the first-comer. Still,

I guess that can be got over. Ever heard of the word 'graft,' sir? Well, graft gets there every time! I reckon that we shan't really need to fire a torpedo. If every one hustles round and screams loud enough that the ship is sinking, it ought to be enough for an innocent young girl like Jane. By the time she's got a life-belt on her, and is being hustled into into a boat, with a well-drilled lot of artistes doing the hysterical stunt on deck, why—she ought to be right back where she was in May, 1915. How's that for the bare outline?"

Dr. Hall looked at Julius. Everything that he was for the moment incapable of saying was eloquent in that look.

"No," said Julius, in answer to it, "I'm not crazy. The thing's perfectly possible. It's done every day in the States for the movies. Haven't you seen trains in collision on the screen? What's the difference between buying up a train and buying up a liner? Get the properties and you can go right ahead!"

Dr. Hall found his voice.

"But the expense, my dear sir." His voice rose. "The expense! It will be *colossal*!"

"Money doesn't worry me any," explained Julius simply.

Dr. Hall turned an appealing face to Sir James, who smiled slightly.

"Mr. Hersheimmer is very well off—very well off indeed."

The doctor's glance came back to Julius with a new and subtle quality in it. This was no longer an eccentric young fellow with a habit of falling off trees. The doctor's eyes held the deference accorded to a really rich man.

"Very remarkable plan. Very remarkable," he murmured. "The movies—of course! Your American word for the kinema. Very interesting. I fear we are perhaps a little behind the times over here in our methods. And you really mean to carry out this remarkable plan of yours."

"You bet your bottom dollar I do."

The doctor believed him—which was a tribute to his nationality. If an Englishman had suggested such a thing, he would have had grave doubts as to his sanity.

"I cannot guarantee a cure," he pointed out. "Perhaps I ought to make that quite clear."

"Sure, that's all right," said Julius. "You just trot out Jane, and leave the rest to me."

"Jane?"

"Miss Janet Vandemeyer, then. Can we get on the long distance to your place right away, and ask them to send her up; or shall I run down and fetch her in my car?"

The doctor stared.

"I beg your pardon, Mr. Hersheimmer. I thought you understood."

"Understood what?"

"That Miss Vandemeyer is no longer under my care."

CHAPTER XV
Tuppence Receives a Proposal

Julius sprang up.

"What?"

"I thought you were aware of that."

"When did she leave?"

"Let me see. Today is Monday, is it not? It must have been last Wednesday—why, surely— yes, it was the same evening that you—er—fell out of my tree."

"That evening? Before, or after?"

"Let me see—oh yes, afterwards. A very urgent message arrived from Mrs. Vandemeyer. The young lady and the nurse who was in charge of her left by the night train."

Julius sank back again into his chair.

"Nurse Edith—left with a patient—I remember," he muttered. "My God, to have been so near!"

Dr. Hall looked bewildered.

"I don't understand. Is the young lady not with her aunt, after all?"

Tuppence shook her head. She was about to speak when a warning glance from Sir James made her hold her tongue. The lawyer rose.

"I'm much obliged to you, Hall. We're very grateful for all you've told us. I'm afraid we're now in the position of having to track Miss

Vandemeyer anew. What about the nurse who accompanied her; I suppose you don't know where she is?"

The doctor shook his head.

"We've not heard from her, as it happens. I understood she was to remain with Miss Vandemeyer for a while. But what can have happened? Surely the girl has not been kidnapped."

"That remains to be seen," said Sir James gravely.

The other hesitated.

"You do not think I ought to go to the police?"

"No, no. In all probability the young lady is with other relations."

The doctor was not completely satisfied, but he saw that Sir James was determined to say no more, and realized that to try and extract more information from the famous K.C. would be mere waste of labour. Accordingly, he wished them good-bye, and they left the hotel. For a few minutes they stood by the car talking.

"How maddening," cried Tuppence. "To think that Julius must have been actually under the same roof with her for a few hours."

"I was a darned idiot," muttered Julius gloomily.

"You couldn't know," Tuppence consoled him. "Could he?" She appealed to Sir James.

"I should advise you not to worry," said the latter kindly. "No use crying over spilt milk, you know."

"The great thing is what to do next," added Tuppence the practical.

Sir James shrugged his shoulders.

"You might advertise for the nurse who accompanied the girl. That is the only course I can suggest, and I must confess I do not hope for much result. Otherwise there is nothing to be done."

"Nothing?" said Tuppence blankly. "And— Tommy?"

"We must hope for the best," said Sir James. "Oh yes, we must go on hoping."

But over her downcast head his eyes met Julius's, and almost imperceptibly he shook his head. Julius understood. The lawyer considered the case hopeless. The young American's face grew grave. Sir James took Tuppence's hand.

"You must let me know if anything further comes to light. Letters will always be forwarded."

Tuppence stared at him blankly.

"You are going away?"

"I told you. Don't you remember? To Scotland."

"Yes, but I thought——" The girl hesitated.

Sir James shrugged his shoulders.

"My dear young lady, I can do nothing more, I fear. Our clues have all ended in thin air. You can take my word for it that there is nothing more to be done. If anything should arise, I shall be glad to advise you in any way I can."

His words gave Tuppence an extraordinarily desolate feeling.

"I suppose you're right," she said. "Anyway, thank you very much for trying to help us. Good-bye."

Julius was bending over the car. A momentary pity came into Sir James's keen eyes, as he gazed into the girl's downcast face.

"Don't be too disconsolate, Miss Tuppence," he said in a low voice. "Remember, holiday-time isn't always all play-time. One sometimes manages to put in some work as well."

Something in his tone made Tuppence glance up sharply. He shook his head with a smile.

"No, I shan't say any more. Great mistake to say too much. Remember that. Never tell all you know—not even to the person you know best. Understand? Good-bye."

He strode away. Tuppence stared after him. She was beginning to understand Sir James's methods. Once before he had thrown her a hint in the same careless fashion. Was this a hint? What exactly lay behind those last brief words? Did he mean that, after all, he had not abandoned the case; that, secretly, he would be working on it still while——

Her meditations were interrupted by Julius, who adjured her to "get right in."

"You're looking kind of thoughtful," he remarked as they started off. "Did the old guy say anything more?"

Tuppence opened her mouth impulsively, and then shut it again. Sir James's words sounded in her ears: "Never tell all you know—not even to the person you know best." And like a flash there came into her mind another memory. Julius before the safe in the flat, her own question, and the pause before his reply, "Nothing." Was there really nothing? Or had he found something he wished to keep to himself? If he could make a reservation, so could she.

"Nothing particular," she replied.

She felt rather than saw Julius throw a sideways glance at her.

"Say, shall we go for a spin in the park?"

"If you like."

For a while they ran on under the trees in silence. It was a beautiful day. The keen rush through the air brought a new exhilaration to Tuppence.

"Say, Miss Tuppence, do you think I'm ever going to find Jane?"

Julius spoke in a discouraged voice. The mood was so alien to him that Tuppence turned and stared at him in surprise. He nodded.

"That's so. I'm getting down and out over the business. Sir James today hadn't got any hope at all, I could see that. I don't like him—we don't gee together somehow—but he's pretty cute, and I guess he wouldn't quit if there was any chance of success—now, would he?"

Tuppence felt rather uncomfortable, but clinging to her belief that Julius also had withheld something from her, she remained firm.

"He suggested advertising for the nurse," she reminded him.

"Yes, with a 'forlorn hope' flavour to his voice! No—I'm about fed up. I've half a mind to go back to the States right away."

"Oh no!" cried Tuppence. "We've got to find Tommy."

"I sure forgot Beresford," said Julius contritely. "That's so. We must find him. But after—well, I've been day-dreaming ever since I started on this trip—and these dreams are rotten poor business. I'm quit of them. Say, Miss Tuppence, there's something I'd like to ask you."

"Yes?"

"You and Beresford. What about it?"

"I don't understand you," replied Tuppence with dignity, adding rather inconsequently: "And, anyway, you're wrong!"

"Not got a sort of kindly feeling for one another?"

"Certainly not," said Tuppence with warmth. "Tommy and I are friends—nothing more."

"I guess every pair of lovers has said that sometime or another," observed Julius.

"Nonsense!" snapped Tuppence. "Do I look the sort of girl that's always falling in love with every man she meets?"

"You do not. You look the sort of girl that's mighty often getting fallen in love with!"

"Oh!" said Tuppence, rather taken aback. "That's a compliment, I suppose?"

"Sure. Now let's get down to this. Supposing we never find Beresford and—and——"

"All right—say it! I can face facts. Supposing he's—dead! Well?"

"And all this business fiddles out. What are you going to do?"

"I don't know," said Tuppence forlornly.

"You'll be darned lonesome, you poor kid."

"I shall be all right," snapped Tuppence with her usual resentment of any kind of pity.

"What about marriage?" inquired Julius. "Got any views on the subject?"

"I intend to marry, of course," replied Tuppence. "That is, if"—she paused, knew a momentary longing to draw back, and then stuck to her guns bravely—"I can find some one rich enough to make it worth my while. That's frank, isn't it? I dare say you despise me for it."

"I never despise business instinct," said Julius. "What particular figure have you in mind?"

"Figure?" asked Tuppence, puzzled. "Do you mean tall or short?"

"No. Sum—income."

"Oh, I—I haven't quite worked that out."

"What about me?"

"*You?*"

"Sure thing."

"Oh, I couldn't!"

"Why not?"

"I tell you I couldn't."

"Again, why not?"

"It would seem so unfair."

"I don't see anything unfair about it. I call your bluff, that's all. I admire you immensely, Miss Tuppence, more than any girl I've ever met. You're so darned plucky. I'd just love to give you a real, rattling good time. Say the word, and we'll run round right away to some high-class jeweller, and fix up the ring business."

"I can't," gasped Tuppence.

"Because of Beresford?"

"No, no, *no!*"

"Well then?"

Tuppence merely continued to shake her head violently.

"You can't reasonably expect more dollars than I've got."

"Oh, it isn't that," gasped Tuppence with an almost hysterical laugh. "But thanking you very much, and all that, I think I'd better say no."

"I'd be obliged if you'd do me the favour to think it over until to-morrow."

"It's no use."

"Still, I guess we'll leave it like that."

"Very well," said Tuppence meekly.

Neither of them spoke again until they reached the *Ritz*.

Tuppence went upstairs to her room. She felt morally battered to the ground after her conflict with Julius's vigorous personality. Sitting down in front of the glass, she stared at her own reflection for some minutes.

"Fool," murmured Tuppence at length, making a grimace. "Little fool. Everything you want—everything you've ever hoped for, and you go and bleat out 'no' like an idiotic little sheep. It's your one chance. Why don't you take it? Grab it? Snatch at it? What more do you want?"

As if in answer to her own question, her eyes fell on a small snapshot of Tommy that stood on her dressing-table in a shabby frame. For a moment she struggled for self-control, and then abandoning all pretence, she held it to her lips and burst into a fit of sobbing.

"Oh, Tommy, Tommy," she cried, "I do love you so—and I may never see you again. . . ."

At the end of five minutes Tuppence sat up, blew her nose, and pushed back her hair.

"That's that," she observed sternly. "Let's look facts in the face. I seem to have fallen in love—with an idiot of a boy who probably doesn't care two straws about me." Here she paused. "Anyway," she resumed, as though arguing with an unseen opponent, "I don't *know* that he does. He'd never have dared to say so. I've always jumped on sentiment—and here I am being more sentimental than anybody. What idiots girls are! I've always thought so. I suppose I shall sleep with his photograph under my pillow, and dream about him all night. It's dreadful to feel you've been false to your principles."

Tuppence shook her head sadly, as she reviewed her back-sliding.

"I don't know what to say to Julius, I'm sure. Oh, what a fool I feel! I'll have to say *something*—he's so American and thorough, he'll insist upon having a reason. I wonder if he did find anything in that safe——"

Tuppence's meditations went off on another tack. She reviewed the events of last night carefully and persistently. Somehow, they seemed bound up with Sir James's enigmatical words. . . .

Suddenly she gave a great start—the colour faded out of her face. Her eyes, fascinated, gazed in front of her, the pupils dilated.

"Impossible," she murmured. "Impossible! I must be going mad even to think of such a thing. . . ."

Monstrous—yet it explained everything. . . .

After a moment's reflection she sat down and wrote a note, weighing each word as she did so. Finally she nodded her head as though satisfied, and slipped it into an envelope which she addressed to Julius. She went down the passage to his sitting-room and knocked at the door. As she had expected, the room was empty. She left the note on the table.

A small page-boy was waiting outside her own door when she returned to it.

"Telegram for you, miss."

Tuppence took it from the salver, and tore it open carelessly. Then she gave a cry. The telegram was from Tommy!

CHAPTER XVI
Further Adventures of Tommy

From a darkness punctuated with throbbing stabs of fire, Tommy dragged his senses slowly back to life. When he at last opened his eyes, he was conscious of nothing but an excruciating pain through his temples. He was vaguely aware of unfamiliar surroundings. Where was he? What had happened? He blinked feebly. This was not his bedroom at the *Ritz*. And what the devil was the matter with his head?

"Damn!" said Tommy, and tried to sit up. He had remembered. He was in that sinister house in Soho. He uttered a groan and fell back. Through his almost-closed lids he reconnoitred carefully.

"He is coming to," remarked a voice very near Tommy's ear. He recognized it at once for that of the bearded and efficient German, and lay artistically inert. He felt that it would be a pity to come round too soon; and until the pain in his head became a little less acute, he felt quite incapable of collecting his wits. Painfully he tried to puzzle out what had happened. Obviously somebody must have crept up behind him as he listened and struck him down with a blow on the head. They knew him now for a spy, and would in all probability give him short shrift. Undoubtedly he was in a tight place. Nobody knew where he was, therefore he need expect no outside assistance, and must depend solely on his own wits.

"Well, here goes," murmured Tommy to himself, and repeated his former remark.

"Damn!" he observed, and this time succeeded in sitting up.

In a minute the German stepped forward and

placed a glass to his lips, with the brief command "Drink." Tommy obeyed. The potency of the draught made him choke, but it cleared his brain in a marvellous manner.

He was lying on a couch in the room in which the meeting had been held. On one side of him was the German, on the other the villainous-faced doorkeeper who had let him in. The others were grouped together at a little distance away. But Tommy missed one face. The man known as Number One was no longer of the company.

"Feel better?" asked the German, as he removed the empty glass.

"Yes, thanks," returned Tommy cheerfully.

"Ah, my young friend, it is lucky for you your skull is so thick. The good Conrad struck hard." He indicated the evil-faced doorkeeper by a nod. The man grinned.

Tommy twisted his head round with an effort.

"Oh," he said, "so you're Conrad, are you? It strikes me the thickness of my skull was lucky for you too. When I look at you I feel it's almost a pity I've enabled you to cheat the hangman."

The man snarled, and the bearded man said quietly:

"He would have run no risk of that."

"Just as you like," replied Tommy. "I know it's the fashion to run down the police. I rather believe in them myself."

His manner was nonchalant to the last degree. Tommy Beresford was one of those young Englishmen not distinguished by any special intellectual ability, but who are emphatically at their best in what is known as a "tight place." Their natural diffidence and caution fall from them then like a glove. Tommy realized perfectly that in his own wits lay the only chance of escape, and behind his casual manner he was racking his brains furiously.

The cold accents of the German took up the conversation:

"Have you anything to say before you are put to death as a spy?"

"Simply lots of things," replied Tommy with the same urbanity as before.

"Do you deny that you were listening at that door?"

"I do not. I must really apologize—but your conversation was so interesting that it overcame my scruples."

"How did you get in?"

"Dear old Conrad here." Tommy smiled deprecatingly at him. "I hesitate to suggest pensioning off a faithful servant, but you really ought to have a better watchdog."

Conrad snarled impotently, and said sullenly, as the man with the beard swung round upon him:

"He gave the word. How was I to know?"

"Yes," Tommy chimed in. "How was he to know? Don't blame the poor fellow. His hasty action has given me the pleasure of seeing you all face to face."

He fancied that his words caused some discomposure among the group, but the watchful German stilled it with a wave of his hand.

"Dead men tell no tales," he said evenly.

"Ah," said Tommy, "but I'm not dead yet!"

"You soon will be, my young friend," said the German.

An assenting murmur came from the others.

Tommy's heart beat faster, but his casual pleasantness did not waver.

"I think not," he said firmly. "I should have a great objection to dying."

He had got them puzzled, he saw that by the look on his captor's face.

"Can you give us any reason why we should not put you to death?" asked the German.

"Several," replied Tommy. "Look here, you've been asking me a lot of questions. Let me ask you one for a change. Why didn't you kill me off at once before I regained consciousness?"

The German hesitated, and Tommy seized his advantage.

"Because you didn't know how much I knew—and where I obtained that knowledge. If you kill me now, you never will know."

But here the emotions of Boris became too much for him. He stepped forward waving his arms.

"You hell-hound of a spy," he screamed. "We will give you short shrift. Kill him! Kill him!"

There was a roar of applause.

"You hear?" said the German, his eyes on Tommy. "What have you to say to that?"

"Say?" Tommy shrugged his shoulders. "Pack of fools. Let them ask themselves a few questions. How did I get into this place? Remember what dear old Conrad said—*with your own password*, wasn't it? How did I get hold of that? You don't suppose I came up those steps haphazard and said the first thing that came into my head?"

Tommy was pleased with the concluding words of this speech. His only regret was that Tuppence was not present to appreciate its full flavour.

"That is true," said the working man suddenly. "Comrades, we have been betrayed!"

An ugly murmur arose. Tommy smiled at them encouragingly.

"That's better. How can you hope to make a success of any job if you don't use your brains?"

"You will tell us who has betrayed us," said the German. "But that shall not save you—oh, no! You shall tell us all that you know. Boris, here, knows pretty ways of making people speak!"

"Bah!" said Tommy scornfully, fighting down a singularly unpleasant feeling in the pit of his stomach. "You will neither torture me nor kill me."

"And why not?" asked Boris.

"Because you'd kill the goose that lays the golden eggs," replied Tommy quietly.

There was a momentary pause. It seemed as though Tommy's persistent assurance was at last conquering. They were no longer completely sure of themselves. The man in the shabby clothes stared at Tommy searchingly.

"He's bluffing you, Boris," he said quietly.

Tommy hated him. Had the man seen through him?

The German, with an effort, turned roughly to Tommy.

"What do you mean?"

"What do you think I mean?" parried Tommy, searching desperately in his own mind.

Suddenly Boris stepped forward, and shook his fist in Tommy's face.

"Speak, you swine of an Englishman—speak!"

"Don't get so excited, my good fellow," said Tommy calmly. "That's the worst of you foreigners. You can't keep calm. Now, I ask you, do I look as though I thought there were the least chance of your killing me?"

He looked confidently round, and was glad they could not hear the persistent beating of his heart which gave the lie to his words.

"No," admitted Boris at last sullenly, "you do not."

"Thank God, he's not a mind reader," thought Tommy. Aloud he pursued his advantage:

"And why am I so confident? Because I know something that puts me in a position to propose a bargain."

"A bargain?" The bearded man took him up sharply.

"Yes—a bargain. My life and liberty against——" He paused.

"Against what?"

The group pressed forward. You could have heard a pin drop.

Slowly Tommy spoke.

"The papers that Danvers brought over from America in the *Lusitania*."

The effect of his words was electrical. Every one was on his feet. The German waved them back. He leaned over Tommy, his face purple with excitement.

"*Himmel!* You have got them, then?"

With magnificent calm Tommy shook his head.

"You know where they are?" persisted the German.

Again Tommy shook his head. "Not in the least."

"Then—then——" angry and baffled, the words failed him.

Tommy looked round. He saw anger and bewilderment on every face, but his calm assurance had done its work—no one doubted but that something lay behind his words.

"I don't know where the papers are—but I believe that I can find them. I have a theory——"

"Pah!"

Tommy raised his hand, and silenced the clamours of disgust.

"I call it a theory—but I'm pretty sure of my facts—facts that are known to no one but myself. In any case what do you lose? If I can produce the papers—you give me my life and liberty in exchange. Is it a bargain?"

"And if we refuse?" said the German quietly.

Tommy lay back on the couch.

"The 29th," he said thoughtfully, "is less than a fortnight ahead——"

For a moment the German hesitated. Then he made a sign to Conrad.

"Take him into the other room."

For five minutes, Tommy sat on the bed in the dingy room next door. His heart was beating violently. He had risked all on this throw. How would they decide? And all the while that this agonized questioning went on within him, he talked flippantly to Conrad, enraging the cross-grained doorkeeper to the point of homicidal mania.

At last the door opened, and the German called imperiously to Conrad to return.

"Let's hope the judge hasn't put his black cap on," remarked Tommy frivolously. "That's right, Conrad, march me in. The prisoner is at the bar, gentlemen."

The German was seated once more behind the table. He motioned to Tommy to sit down opposite to him.

"We accept," he said harshly, "on terms. The papers must be delivered to us before you go free."

"Idiot!" said Tommy amiably. "How do you think I can look for them if you keep me tied by the leg here?"

"What do you expect, then?"

"I must have liberty to go about the business in my own way."

The German laughed.

"Do you think we are little children to let you walk out of here leaving us a pretty story full of promises?"

"No," said Tommy thoughtfully. "Though infinitely simpler for me, I did not really think you would agree to that plan. Very well, we must arrange a compromise. How would it be if you attached little Conrad here to my person. He's a faithful fellow, and very ready with the fist."

"We prefer," said the German coldly, "that you should remain here. One of our number will carry out your instructions minutely. If the operations are complicated, he will return to you with a report and you can instruct him further."

"You're tying my hands," complained Tommy. "It's a very delicate affair, and the other fellow will muff it up as likely as not, and then where shall I be? I don't believe one of you has got an ounce of tact."

The German rapped the table.

"Those are our terms. Otherwise, death!"

Tommy leaned back wearily.

"I like your style. Curt, but attractive. So be it, then. But one thing is essential, I must see the girl."

"What girl?"

"Jane Finn, of course."

The other looked at him curiously for some minutes, then he said slowly, and as though choosing his words with care:

"Do you not know that she can tell you nothing?"

Tommy's heart beat a little faster. Would he succeed in coming face to face with the girl he was seeking?

"I shall not ask her to tell me anything," he said quietly. "Not in so many words, that is."

"Then why see her?"

Tommy paused.

"To watch her face when I ask her one question," he replied at last.

Again there was a look in the German's eyes that Tommy did not quite understand.

"She will not be able to answer your question."

"That does not matter. I shall have seen her face when I ask it."

"And you think that will tell you anything?" He gave a short disagreeable laugh. More than ever, Tommy felt that there was a factor somewhere that he did not understand. The German looked at him searchingly. "I wonder whether, after all, you know as much as we think?" he said softly.

Tommy felt his ascendancy less sure than a moment before. His hold had slipped a little. But he was puzzled. What had he said wrong? He spoke out on the impulse of the moment.

"There may be things that you know which I do not. I have not pretended to be aware of all the details of your show. But equally I've got something up my sleeve that *you* don't know about. And that's where I mean to score. Danvers was a damned clever fellow——" He broke off as if he had said too much.

But the German's face had lightened a little.

"Danvers," he murmured. "I see——" He paused a minute, then waved to Conrad. "Take him away. Upstairs—you know."

"Wait a minute," said Tommy. "What about the girl?"

"That may perhaps be arranged."

"It must be."

"We will see about it. Only one person can decide that."

"Who?" asked Tommy. But he knew the answer.

"Mr. Brown——"

"Shall I see him?"

"Perhaps."

"Come," said Conrad harshly.

Tommy rose obediently. Outside the door his gaoler motioned to him to mount the stairs. He himself followed close behind. On the floor above Conrad opened a door and Tommy passed into a small room. Conrad lit a hissing gas burner and went out. Tommy heard the sound of the key being turned in the lock.

He set to work to examine his prison. It was a smaller room than the one downstairs, and there was something peculiarly airless

about the atmosphere of it. Then he realized that there was no window. He walked round it. The walls were filthily dirty, as everywhere else. Four pictures hung crookedly on the wall representing scenes from "Faust." Marguerite with her box of jewels, the church scene, Siebel and his flowers, and Faust and Mephistopheles. The latter brought Tommy's mind back to Mr. Brown again. In this sealed and closed chamber, with its close-fitting heavy door, he felt cut off from the world, and the sinister power of the arch-criminal seemed more real. Shout as he would, no one could ever hear him. The place was a living tomb. . . .

With an effort Tommy pulled himself together. He sank on to the bed and gave himself up to reflection. His head ached badly; also, he was hungry. The silence of the place was dispiriting.

"Anyway," said Tommy, trying to cheer himself, "I shall see the chief—the mysterious Mr. Brown and with a bit of luck in bluffing I shall see the mysterious Jane Finn also. After that——"

After that Tommy was forced to admit the prospect looked dreary.

CHAPTER XVII
Annette

The troubles of the future, however, soon faded before the troubles of the present. And of these, the most immediate and pressing was that of hunger. Tommy had a healthy and vigorous appetite. The steak and chips partaken of for lunch seemed now to belong to another decade. He regretfully recognized the fact that he would not make a success of a hunger strike.

He prowled aimlessly about his prison. Once or twice he discarded dignity, and pounded on the door. But nobody answered the summons.

"Hang it all!" said Tommy indignantly. "They can't mean to starve me to death." A new-born fear passed through his mind that this might, perhaps, be one of those "pretty ways" of making a prisoner speak, which had been attributed to Boris. But on reflection he dismissed the idea.

"It's that sour faced brute Conrad," he decided. "That's a fellow I shall enjoy getting even with one of these days. This is just a bit of spite on his part. I'm certain of it."

Further meditations induced in him the feeling that it would be extremely pleasant to bring something down with a whack on Conrad's egg-shaped head. Tommy stroked his own head tenderly, and gave himself up to the pleasures of imagination. Finally a bright idea flashed across his brain. Why not convert imagination into reality? Conrad was undoubtedly the tenant of the house. The others, with the possible exception of the bearded German, merely used it as a rendezvous. Therefore, why not wait in ambush for Conrad behind the door, and when he entered bring down a chair, or one of the decrepit pictures, smartly on to his head. One would, of course, be careful not to hit too hard. And then—and then, simply walk out! If he met anyone on the way down, well—— Tommy brightened at the thought of an encounter with his fists. Such an affair was infinitely more in his line than the verbal encounter of this afternoon. Intoxicated by his plan, Tommy gently unhooked the picture of the Devil and Faust, and settled himself in position. His hopes were high. The plan seemed to him simple but excellent.

Time went on, but Conrad did not appear. Night and day were the same in this prison room, but Tommy's wrist-watch, which enjoyed a certain degree of accuracy, informed him that it was nine o'clock in the evening. Tommy reflected gloomily that if supper did not arrive soon it would be a question of waiting for breakfast. At ten o'clock hope deserted him, and he flung himself on the bed to seek consolation in sleep. In five minutes his woes were forgotten.

The sound of the key turning in the lock awoke him from his slumbers. Not belonging to the type of hero who is famous for awaking in full possession of his faculties, Tommy merely blinked at the ceiling and wondered vaguely where he was. Then he remembered, and looked at his watch. It was eight o'clock.

"It's either early morning tea or breakfast," deduced the young man, "and pray God it's the latter!"

The door swung open. Too late, Tommy remembered his scheme of obliterating the unprepossessing Conrad. A moment later he was glad that he had, for it was not Conrad who entered, but a girl. She carried a tray which she set down on the table.

In the feeble light of the gas burner Tommy blinked at her. He decided at once that she was one of the most beautiful girls he had ever seen. Her hair was a full rich brown, with sudden glints of gold in it as though there were imprisoned sunbeams struggling in its depths. There was a wild-rose quality about her face. Her eyes, set wide apart, were hazel, a golden hazel that again recalled a memory of sunbeams.

A delirious thought shot through Tommy's mind.

"Are you Jane Finn?" he asked breathlessly.

The girl shook her head wonderingly.

"My name is Annette, monsieur."

She spoke in a soft, broken English.

"Oh!" said Tommy, rather taken aback. *"Française?"* he hazarded.

"Oui, monsieur. Monsieur parle français?"

"Not for any length of time," said Tommy. "What's that? Breakfast?"

The girl nodded. Tommy dropped off the bed and came and inspected the contents of the tray. It consisted of a loaf, some margarine, and a jug of coffee.

"The living is not equal to the *Ritz*," he observed with a sigh. "But for what we are at last about to receive the Lord has made me truly thankful. Amen."

He drew up a chair, and the girl turned away to the door.

"Wait a sec," cried Tommy. "There are lots of things I want to ask you, Annette. What are you doing in this house? Don't tell me you're Conrad's niece, or daughter, or anything, because I can't believe it."

"I do the *service*, monsieur. I am not related to anybody."

"I see," said Tommy. "You know what I asked you just now. Have you ever heard that name?"

"I have heard people speak of Jane Finn, I think."

"You don't know where she is?"

Annette shook her head.

"She's not in this house, for instance?"

"Oh no, monsieur. I must go now—they will be waiting for me."

She hurried out. The key turned in the lock.

"I wonder who 'they' are," mused Tommy, as he continued to make inroads on the loaf. "With a bit of luck, that girl might help me to get out of here. She doesn't look like one of the gang."

At one o'clock Annette reappeared with another tray, but this time Conrad accompanied her.

"Good morning," said Tommy amiably. "You have *not* used Pear's soap, I see."

Conrad growled threateningly.

"No light repartee, have you, old bean? There, there, we can't always have brains as well as beauty. What have we for lunch? Stew? How did I know? Elementary, my dear Watson—the smell of onions is unmistakable."

"Talk away," grunted the man. "It's little enough time you'll have to talk in, maybe."

The remark was unpleasant in its suggestion, but Tommy ignored it. He sat down at the table.

"Retire, varlet," he said, with a wave of his hand. "Prate not to thy betters."

That evening Tommy sat on the bed, and cogitated deeply. Would Conrad again accompany the girl? If he did not, should he risk trying to make an ally of her? He decided that he must leave no stone unturned. His position was desperate.

At eight o'clock the familiar sound of the key turning made him spring to his feet. The girl was alone.

"Shut the door," he commanded. "I want to speak to you."

She obeyed.

"Look here, Annette, I want you to help me get out of this."

She shook her head.

"Impossible. There are three of them on the floor below."

"Oh!" Tommy was secretly grateful for the information. "But you would help me if you could?"

"No, monsieur."

"Why not?"

The girl hesitated.

"I think—they are my own people. You have spied upon them. They are quite right to keep you here."

"They're a bad lot, Annette. If you'll help me, I'll take you away from the lot of them. And you'd probably get a good whack of money."

But the girl merely shook her head.

"I dare not, monsieur; I am afraid of them."

She turned away.

"Wouldn't you do anything to help another girl?" cried Tommy. "She's about your age too. Won't you save her from their clutches?"

"You mean Jane Finn?"

"Yes."

"It is her you came here to look for? Yes?"

"That's it."

The girl looked at him, then passed her hand across her forehead.

"Jane Finn. Always I hear that name. It is familiar."

Tommy came forward eagerly.

"You must know *something* about her?"

But the girl turned away abruptly.

"I know nothing—only the name." She walked towards the door. Suddenly she uttered a cry. Tommy stared. She had caught sight of the picture he had laid against the wall the night before. For a moment he caught a look of terror in her eyes. As inexplicably it changed to relief. Then abruptly she went out of the room. Tommy could make nothing of it. Did she fancy that he had meant to attack her with it? Surely not. He rehung the picture on the wall thoughtfully.

Three more days went by in dreary inaction. Tommy felt the strain telling on his nerves. He saw no one but Conrad and Annette, and the girl had become dumb. She spoke only in monosyllables. A kind of dark suspicion smouldered in her eyes. Tommy felt that if this solitary confinement went on much longer he would go mad. He gathered from Conrad that they were waiting for orders from "Mr. Brown." Perhaps, thought Tommy, he was abroad or away, and they were obliged to wait for his return.

But the evening of the third day brought a rude awakening.

It was barely seven o'clock when he heard the tramp of footsteps outside in the passage. In another minute the door was flung open. Conrad entered. With him was the evil-looking Number 14. Tommy's heart sank at the sight of them.

"Evenin', guv'nor," said the man with a leer. "Got those ropes, mate?"

The silent Conrad produced a length of fine cord. The next minute Number 14's hands, horribly dexterous, were winding the cord round his limbs, while Conrad held him down.

"What the devil——?" began Tommy.

But the slow, speechless grin of the silent Conrad froze the words on his lips.

Number 14 proceeded deftly with his task. In another minute Tommy was a mere helpless bundle. Then at last Conrad spoke:

"Thought you'd bluffed us, did you? With what you knew, and what you didn't know. Bargained with us! And all the time it was bluff! Bluff! You know less than a kitten. But your number's up now all right, you b—— swine."

Tommy lay silent. There was nothing to say. He had failed. Somehow or other the omnipotent Mr. Brown had seen through his pretensions. Suddenly a thought occurred to him.

"A very good speech, Conrad," he said approvingly. "But wherefore the bonds and fetters? Why not let this kind gentleman here cut my throat without delay?"

"Garn," said Number 14 unexpectedly. "Think we're as green as to do you in here, and have the police nosing round? Not 'alf! We've ordered the carriage for your lordship tomorrow mornin', but in the meantime we're not taking any chances, see!"

"Nothing," said Tommy, "could be plainer than your words—unless it was your face."

"Stow it," said Number 14.

"With pleasure," replied Tommy. "You're making a sad mistake—but yours will be the loss."

"You don't kid us that way again," said Number 14. "Talking as though you were still at the blooming *Ritz*, aren't you?"

Tommy made no reply. He was engaged in wondering how Mr. Brown had discovered his identity. He decided that Tuppence, in the throes of anxiety, had gone to the police, and that his disappearance having been made public the gang had not been slow to put two and two together.

The two men departed and the door slammed. Tommy was left to his meditations. They were not pleasant ones. Already his limbs felt cramped and stiff. He was utterly helpless, and he could see no hope anywhere.

About an hour had passed when he heard the key softly turned, and the door opened. It was Annette. Tommy's heart beat a little faster. He had forgotten the girl. Was it possible that she had come to his help?

Suddenly he heard Conrad's voice:

"Come out of it, Annette. He doesn't want any supper tonight."

"Oui, oui, je sais bien. But I must take the other tray. We need the things on it."

"Well, hurry up," growled Conrad.

Without looking at Tommy the girl went over to the table, and picked up the tray. She raised a hand and turned out the light.

"Curse you"—Conrad had come to the door—"why did you do that?"

"I always turn it out. You should have told me. Shall I relight it, Monsieur Conrad?"

"No, come on out of it."

"Le beau petit monsieur," cried Annette, pausing by the bed in the darkness. "You have tied him up well, *hein*? He is like a trussed chicken!" The frank amusement in her tone jarred on the boy; but at that moment, to his amazement, he felt her hand running lightly over his bonds, and something small and cold was pressed into the palm of his hand.

"Come on, Annette."

"Mais me voilà."

The door shut. Tommy heard Conrad say:

"Lock it and give me the key."

The footsteps died away. Tommy lay petrified with amazement. The object Annette had thrust into his hand was a small penknife, the blade open. From the way she had studiously avoided looking at him, and her action with the light, he came to the conclusion that the room was overlooked. There must be a peephole somewhere in the walls. Remembering how guarded she had always been in her manner, he saw that he had probably been under observation all the time. Had he said anything to give himself away? Hardly. He had revealed a wish to escape and a desire to find Jane Finn, but nothing that could have given a clue to his own identity. True, his question to Annette had proved that he was personally unacquainted with Jane Finn, but he had never pretended otherwise. The question now was, did Annette really know more? Were her denials intended primarily for the listeners? On that point he could come to no conclusion.

But there was a more vital question that drove out all others. Could he, bound as he was, manage to cut his bonds? He essayed cautiously to rub the open blade up and down on the cord that bound his two wrists together. It was an awkward business, and drew a smothered "Ow" of pain from him as the knife cut into his wrist. But slowly and doggedly he went on sawing to and fro. He cut the flesh badly, but at last he felt the cord slacken. With his hands free, the rest was easy. Five minutes later he stood upright with some difficulty, owing to the cramp in his limbs. His first care was to bind up his bleeding wrist. Then he sat on the edge of the bed to think. Conrad had taken the key of the door, so he could expect little more assistance from Annette. The only outlet from the room was the door, consequently he would perforce have to wait until the two men returned to fetch him. But when they did . . . Tommy smiled! Moving with infinite caution in the dark room, he found and unhooked the famous picture. He felt an economical pleasure that his first plan would not be wasted. There was now nothing to do but to wait. He waited.

The night passed slowly. Tommy lived through an eternity of hours, but at last he heard footsteps. He stood upright, drew a deep breath, and clutched the picture firmly.

The door opened. A faint light streamed in from outside. Conrad went straight towards the gas to light it. Tommy deeply regretted that it was he who had entered first. It would have been pleasant to get even with Conrad. Number 14 followed. As he stepped across the threshold, Tommy brought the picture down with terrific force on his head. Number 14 went down amidst a stupendous crash of broken glass. In a minute Tommy had slipped out and pulled to the door. The key was in the lock. He turned it and withdrew it just as Conrad hurled himself against the door from the inside with a volley of curses.

For a moment Tommy hesitated. There was the sound of some one stirring on the floor below. Then the German's voice came up the stairs.

"Gott im Himmel! Conrad, what is it?"

Tommy felt a small hand thrust into his. Beside him stood Annette. She pointed up a rickety ladder that apparently led to some attics.

"Quick—up here!" She dragged him after her up the ladder. In another moment they were standing in a dusty garret littered with lumber. Tommy looked round.

"This won't do. It's a regular trap. There's no way out."

"Hush! Wait." The girl put her finger to her lips. She crept to the top of the ladder and listened.

The banging and beating on the door was terrific. The German and another were trying to force the door in. Annette explained in a whisper:

"They will think you are still inside. They cannot hear what Conrad says. The door is too thick."

"I thought you could hear what went on in the room?"

"There is a peep-hole into the next room. It was clever of you to guess. But they will not think of that—they are only anxious to get in."

"Yes—but look here——"

"Leave it to me." She bent down. To his amazement, Tommy saw that she was fastening the end of a long piece of string to the handle of a big cracked jug. She arranged it carefully, then turned to Tommy.

"Have you the key of the door?"

"Yes."

"Give it to me."

He handed it to her.

"I am going down. Do you think you can go halfway, and then swing yourself down *behind* the ladder, so that they will not see you?"

Tommy nodded.

"There's a big cupboard in the shadow of the landing. Stand behind it. Take the end of this string in your hand. When I've let the others out—*pull!*"

Before he had time to ask her anything more, she had flitted lightly down the ladder and was in the midst of the group with a loud cry:

"Mon Dieu! Mon Dieu! Qu'est-ce qu'il y a?"

The German turned on her with an oath.

"Get out of this. Go to your room!"

Very cautiously Tommy swung himself down the back of the ladder. So long as they did not turn round . . . all was well. He crouched behind the cupboard. They were still between him and the stairs.

"Ah!" Annette appeared to stumble over something. She stooped. "Mon Dieu, voilà la clef!"

The German snatched it from her. He unlocked the door. Conrad stumbled out, swearing.

"Where is he? Have you got him?"

"We have seen no one," said the German sharply. His face paled. "Who do you mean?"

Conrad gave vent to another oath.

"He's got away."

"Impossible. He would have passed us."

At that moment, with an ecstatic smile Tommy pulled the string. A crash of crockery came from the attic above. In a trice the men were pushing each other up the rickety ladder and had disappeared into the darkness above.

Quick as a flash Tommy leapt from his hiding-place and dashed down the stairs, pulling the girl with him. There was no one in the hall. He fumbled over the bolts and chain. At last they yielded, the door swung open. He turned. Annette had disappeared.

Tommy stood spell-bound. Had she run upstairs again? What madness possessed her! He fumed with impatience, but he stood his ground. He would not go without her.

And suddenly there was an outcry overhead, an exclamation from the German, and then Annette's voice, clear and high:

"Ma foi, he has escaped! And quickly! Who would have thought it?"

Tommy still stood rooted to the ground. Was that a command to him to go? He fancied it was.

And then, louder still, the words floated down to him:

"This is a terrible house. I want to go back to Marguerite. To Marguerite. *To Marguerite!*"

Tommy had run back to the stairs. She wanted him to go and leave her. But why? At all costs he must try and get her away with him. Then his heart sank. Conrad was leaping down the stairs, uttering a savage cry at the sight of him. After him came the others.

Tommy stopped Conrad's rush with a straight blow with his fist. It caught the other on the point of the jaw and he fell like a log. The second man tripped over his body and fell. From higher up the staircase there was a flash, and a bullet grazed Tommy's ear. He realized that it would be good for his health to get out of this house as soon as possible. As regards Annette he could do nothing. He had got even with Conrad, which was one satisfaction. The blow had been a good one.

He leapt for the door, slamming it behind him. The square was deserted. In front of the house was a baker's van. Evidently he was to have been taken out of London in that, and his body found many miles from the house in Soho. The driver jumped to the pavement and tried to bar Tommy's way. Again Tommy's fist shot out, and the driver sprawled on the pavement.

Tommy took to his heels and ran—none too soon. The front door opened and a hail of bullets followed him. Fortunately none of them hit him. He turned the corner of the square.

"There's one thing," he thought to himself, "they can't go on shooting. They'll have the police after them if they do. I wonder they dared to there."

He heard the footsteps of his pursuers behind him, and redoubled his own pace. Once he got out of these by-ways he would be safe. There would be a policeman about somewhere—not that he really wanted to invoke the aid of the police if he could possibly do without it. It meant explanations, and general awkwardness. In another moment he had reason to bless his luck. He stumbled over a prostrate figure, which started up with a yell of alarm and dashed off down the street. Tommy drew back into a doorway. In a minute he had the pleasure of seeing his two pursuers, of whom the German was one, industriously tracking down the red herring!

Tommy sat down quietly on the doorstep and allowed a few moments to elapse while he recovered his breath. Then he strolled gently in the opposite direction. He glanced at his watch. It was a little after half-past five. It was rapidly growing light. At the next corner he passed a policeman. The policeman cast a suspicious eye on him. Tommy felt slightly offended. Then, passing his hand over his face, he laughed. He had not shaved or washed for three days! What a guy he must look.

He betook himself without more ado to a Turkish Bath establishment which he knew to be open all night. He emerged into the busy daylight feeling himself once more, and able to make plans.

First of all, he must have a square meal. He had eaten nothing since midday yesterday. He turned into an A.B.C. shop and ordered eggs and bacon and coffee. Whilst he ate, he read a morning paper propped up in front of him. Suddenly he stiffened. There was a long article

on Kramenin, who was described as the "man behind Bolshevism" in Russia, and who had just arrived in London—some thought as an unofficial envoy. His career was sketched lightly, and it was firmly asserted that he, and not the figurehead leaders, had been the author of the Russian Revolution.

In the centre of the page was his portrait.

"So that's who Number 1 is," said Tommy with his mouth full of eggs and bacon. "Not a doubt about it, I must push on."

He paid for his breakfast, and betook himself to Whitehall. There he sent up his name, and the message that it was urgent. A few minutes later he was in the presence of the man who did not here go by the name of "Mr. Carter." There was a frown on his face.

"Look here, you've no business to come asking for me in this way. I thought that was distinctly understood?"

"It was, sir. But I judged it important to lose no time."

And as briefly and succinctly as possible he detailed the experiences of the last few days.

Half-way through, Mr. Carter interrupted him to give a few cryptic orders through the telephone. All traces of displeasure had now left his face. He nodded energetically when Tommy had finished.

"Quite right. Every moment's of value. Fear we shall be too late anyway. They wouldn't wait. Would clear out at once. Still, they may have left something behind them that will be a clue. You say you've recognized Number 1 to be Kramenin? That's important. We want something against him badly to prevent the Cabinet falling on his neck too freely. What about the others? You say two faces were familiar to you? One's a Labour man, you think? Just look through these photos, and see if you can spot him."

A minute later, Tommy held one up. Mr. Carter exhibited some surprise.

"Ah, Westway! Shouldn't have thought it. Poses as being moderate. As for the other fellow, I think I can give a good guess." He handed another photograph to Tommy, and smiled at the other's exclamation. "I'm right, then. Who is he? Irishman. Prominent Unionist M.P. All a blind, of course. We've suspected it—but couldn't get any proof. Yes, you've done very well, young man. The 29th, you say, is the date. That gives us very little time—very little time indeed."

"But——" Tommy hesitated.

Mr. Carter read his thoughts.

"We can deal with the General Strike menace, I think. It's a toss-up—but we've got a sporting chance! But if that draft treaty turns up—we're done. England will be plunged in anarchy. Ah, what's that? The car? Come on, Beresford, we'll go and have a look at this house of yours."

Two constables were on duty in front of the house in Soho. An inspector reported to Mr. Carter in a low voice. The latter turned to Tommy.

"The birds have flown—as we thought. We might as well go over it."

Going over the deserted house seemed to Tommy to partake of the character of a dream. Everything was just as it had been. The prison room with the crooked pictures, the broken jug in the attic, the meeting room with its long table. But nowhere was there a trace of papers. Everything of that kind had either been destroyed or taken away. And there was no sign of Annette.

"What you tell me about the girl puzzled me," said Mr. Carter. "You believe that she deliberately went back?"

"It would seem so, sir. She ran upstairs while I was getting the door open."

"H'm, she must belong to the gang, then; but, being a woman, didn't feel like standing by to see a personable young man killed. But evidently she's in with them, or she wouldn't have gone back."

"I can't believe she's really one of them, sir. She—seemed so different——"

"Good-looking, I suppose?" said Mr. Carter with a smile that made Tommy flush to the roots of his hair. He admitted Annette's beauty rather shamefacedly.

"By the way," observed Mr. Carter, "have you shown yourself to Miss Tuppence yet? She's been bombarding me with letters about you."

"Tuppence? I was afraid she might get a bit rattled. Did she go to the police?"

Mr. Carter shook his head.

"Then I wonder how they twigged me."

Mr. Carter looked inquiringly at him, and Tommy explained. The other nodded thoughtfully.

"True, that's rather a curious point. Unless the mention of the *Ritz* was an accidental remark?"

"It might have been, sir. But they must have found out about me suddenly in some way."

"Well," said Mr. Carter, looking round him, "there's nothing more to be done here. What about some lunch with me?"

"Thanks awfully, sir. But I think I'd better get back and rout out Tuppence."

"Of course. Give her my kind regards and tell her not to believe you're killed too readily next time."

Tommy grinned.

"I take a lot of killing, sir."

"So I perceive," said Mr. Carter dryly. "Well, good-bye. Remember you're a marked man now, and take reasonable care of yourself."

"Thank you, sir."

Hailing a taxi briskly Tommy stepped in, and was swiftly borne to the *Ritz*, dwelling the while on the pleasurable anticipation of startling Tuppence.

"Wonder what she's been up to. Dogging 'Rita' most likely. By the way, I suppose that's who Annette meant by Marguerite. I didn't get it at the time." The thought saddened him a little, for it seemed to prove that Mrs. Vandemeyer and the girl were on intimate terms.

The taxi drew up at the *Ritz*. Tommy burst into its sacred portals eagerly, but his enthusiasm received a check. He was informed that Miss Cowley had gone out a quarter of an hour ago.

CHAPTER XVIII
The Telegram

Baffled for the moment, Tommy strolled into the restaurant, and ordered a meal of surpassing excellence. His four days' imprisonment had taught him anew to value good food.

He was in the middle of conveying a particularly choice morsel of Sole à la Jeanette to his mouth, when he caught sight of Julius entering the room. Tommy waved a menu cheerfully, and succeeded in attracting the other's attention. At the sight of Tommy, Julius's eyes seemed as though they would pop out of his head. He strode across, and pump-handled Tommy's hand with what seemed to the latter quite unnecessary vigour.

"Holy snakes!" he ejaculated. "Is it really you?"

"Of course it is. Why shouldn't it be?"

"Why shouldn't it be? Say, man, don't you know you've been given up for dead? I guess we'd have had a solemn requiem for you in another few days."

"Who thought I was dead?" demanded Tommy.

"Tuppence."

"She remembered the proverb about the good dying young, I suppose. There must be a certain amount of original sin in me to have survived. Where is Tuppence, by the way?"

"Isn't she here?"

"No, the fellows at the office said she'd just gone out."

"Gone shopping, I guess. I dropped her here in the car about an hour ago. But, say, can't you shed that British calm of yours, and get down to it? What on God's earth have you been doing all this time?"

"If you're feeding here," replied Tommy, "order now. It's going to be a long story."

Julius drew up a chair to the opposite side of the table, summoned a hovering waiter, and dictated his wishes. Then he turned to Tommy.

"Fire ahead. I guess you've had some few adventures."

"One or two," replied Tommy modestly, and plunged into his recital.

Julius listened spell-bound. Half the dishes that were placed before him he forgot to eat. At the end he heaved a long sigh.

"Bully for you. Reads like a dime novel!"

"And now for the home front," said Tommy, stretching out his hand for a peach.

"We-el," drawled Julius, "I don't mind admitting we've had some adventures too."

He, in his turn, assumed the rôle of narrator. Beginning with his unsuccessful reconnoitring at Bournemouth, he passed on to his return to London, the buying of the car, the growing anxieties of Tuppence, the call upon Sir James, and the sensational occurrences of the previous night.

"But who killed her?" asked Tommy. "I don't quite understand."

"The doctor kidded himself she took it herself," replied Julius dryly.

"And Sir James? What did he think?"

"Being a legal luminary, he is likewise a human oyster," replied Julius. "I should say he 'reserved judgment.'" He went on to detail the events of the morning.

"Lost her memory, eh?" said Tommy with interest. "By Jove, that explains why they looked at me so queerly when I spoke of questioning her. Bit of a slip on my part, that! But it wasn't the sort of thing a fellow would be likely to guess."

"They didn't give you any sort of hint as to where Jane was?"

Tommy shook his head regretfully.

"Not a word. I'm a bit of an ass, as you know. I ought to have got more out of them somehow."

"I guess you're lucky to be here at all. That bluff of yours was the goods all right. How you ever came to think of it all so pat beats me to a frazzle!"

"I was in such a funk I had to think of something," said Tommy simply.

There was a moment's pause, and then Tommy reverted to Mrs. Vandemeyer's death.

"There's no doubt it was chloral?"

"I believe not. At least they call it heart failure induced by an overdose, or some such claptrap. It's all right. We don't want to be worried with an inquest. But I guess Tuppence and I and even the highbrow Sir James have all got the same idea."

"Mr. Brown?" hazarded Tommy.

"Sure thing."

Tommy nodded.

"All the same," he said thoughtfully, "Mr. Brown hasn't got wings. I don't see how he got in and out."

"How about some high-class thought transference stunt? Some magnetic influence that irresistibly impelled Mrs. Vandemeyer to commit suicide?"

Tommy looked at him with respect.

"Good, Julius. Distinctly good. Especially the phraseology. But it leaves me cold. I yearn for a real Mr. Brown of flesh and blood. I think the gifted young detectives must get to work, study the entrances and exits, and tap the bumps on their foreheads until the solution of the mystery dawns on them. Let's go round to the scene of the crime. I wish we could get hold of Tuppence. The *Ritz* would enjoy the spectacle of the glad reunion."

Inquiry at the office revealed the fact that Tuppence had not yet returned.

"All the same, I guess I'll have a look round upstairs," said Julius. "She might be in my sitting-room." He disappeared.

Suddenly a diminutive boy spoke at Tommy's elbow:

"The young lady—she's gone away by train, I think, sir," he murmured shyly.

"What?" Tommy wheeled round upon him.

The small boy became pinker than before.

"The taxi, sir. I heard her tell the driver Charing Cross and to look sharp."

Tommy stared at him, his eyes opening wide in surprise. Emboldened, the small boy proceeded. "So I thought, having asked for an A.B.C. and a Bradshaw."

Tommy interrupted him:

"When did she ask for an A.B.C. and a Bradshaw?"

"When I took her the telegram, sir."

"A telegram?"

"Yes, sir."

"When was that?"

"About half-past twelve, sir."

"Tell me exactly what happened."

The small boy drew a long breath.

"I took up a telegram to No. 891—the lady was there. She opened it and gave a gasp, and then she said, very jolly like: 'Bring me up a Bradshaw, and an A.B.C., and look sharp, Henry.' My name isn't Henry, but——"

"Never mind your name," said Tommy impatiently. "Go on."

"Yes, sir. I brought them, and she told me to wait, and looked up something. And then she looks up at the clock, and 'Hurry up,' she says. 'Tell them to get me a taxi,' and she begins a-shoving on of her hat in front of the glass, and she was down in two ticks, almost as quick as I was, and I seed her going down the steps and into the taxi, and I heard her call out what I told you."

The small boy stopped and replenished his lungs. Tommy continued to stare at him. At that moment Julius rejoined him. He held an open letter in his hand.

"I say, Hersheimmer"—Tommy turned to him—"Tuppence has gone off sleuthing on her own."

"Shucks!"

"Yes, she has. She went off in a taxi to Charing Cross in the deuce of a hurry after getting a telegram." His eye fell on the letter in Julius's hand. "Oh; she left a note for you. That's all right. Where's she off to?"

Almost unconsciously, he held out his hand for the letter, but Julius folded it up and placed it in his pocket. He seemed a trifle embarrassed.

"I guess this is nothing to do with it. It's about something else—something I asked her that she was to let me know about."

"Oh!" Tommy looked puzzled, and seemed waiting for more.

"See here," said Julius suddenly, "I'd better put you wise. I asked Miss Tuppence to marry me this morning."

"Oh!" said Tommy mechanically. He felt dazed. Julius's words were totally unexpected. For the moment they benumbed his brain.

"I'd like to tell you," continued Julius, "that

before I suggested anything of the kind to Miss Tuppence, I made it clear that I didn't want to butt in in any way between her and you——"

Tommy roused himself.

"That's all right," he said quickly. "Tuppence and I have been pals for years. Nothing more." He lit a cigarette with a hand that shook ever so little. "That's quite all right. Tuppence always said that she was looking out for——"

He stopped abruptly, his face crimsoning, but Julius was in no way discomposed.

"Oh, I guess it'll be the dollars that'll do the trick. Miss Tuppence put me wise to that right away. There's no humbug about her. We ought to gee along together very well."

Tommy looked at him curiously for a minute, as though he were about to speak, then changed his mind and said nothing. Tuppence and Julius! Well, why not? Had she not lamented the fact that she knew no rich men? Had she not openly avowed her intention of marrying for money if she ever had the chance? Her meeting with the young American millionaire had given her the chance—and it was unlikely she would be slow to avail herself of it. She was out for money. She had always said so. Why blame her because she had been true to her creed?

Nevertheless, Tommy did blame her. He was filled with a passionate and utterly illogical resentment. It was all very well to *say* things like that—but a *real* girl would never marry for money. Tuppence was utterly cold-blooded and selfish, and he would be delighted if he never saw her again! And it was a rotten world!

Julius's voice broke in on these meditations.

"Yes, we ought to get along together very well. I've heard that a girl always refuses you once—a sort of convention."

Tommy caught his arm.

"Refuses? Did you say *refuses*?"

"Sure thing. Didn't I tell you that? She just rapped out a 'no' without any kind of reason to it. The eternal feminine, the Huns call it, I've heard. But she'll come round right enough. Likely enough, I hustled her some——"

But Tommy interrupted regardless of decorum.

"What did she say in that note?" he demanded fiercely.

The obliging Julius handed it to him.

"There's no earthly clue in it as to where she's gone," he assured Tommy. "But you might as well see for yourself if you don't believe me."

The note, in Tuppence's well-known schoolboy writing, ran as follows:

"Dear Julius,
"It's always better to have things in black and white. I don't feel I can be bothered to think of marriage until Tommy is found. Let's leave it till then.
                    "Yours affectionately,
                              "Tuppence."

Tommy handed it back, his eyes shining. His feelings had undergone a sharp reaction. He now felt that Tuppence was all that was noble and disinterested. Had she not refused Julius without hesitation? True, the note betokened signs of weakening, but he could excuse that. It read almost like a bribe to Julius to spur him on in his efforts to find Tommy, but he supposed she had not really meant it that way. Darling Tuppence, there was not a girl in the world to touch her! When he saw her—— His thoughts were brought up with a sudden jerk.

"As you say," he remarked, pulling himself together, "there's not a hint here as to what she's up to. Hi—Henry!"

The small boy came obediently. Tommy produced five shillings.

"One thing more. Do you remember what the young lady did with the telegram?"

Henry gasped and spoke.

"She crumpled it up into a ball and threw it into the grate, and made a sort of noise like 'Whoop!' sir."

"Very graphic, Henry," said Tommy. "Here's your five shillings. Come on, Julius. We must find that telegram."

They hurried upstairs. Tuppence had left the key in her door. The room was as she had left it. In the fireplace was a crumpled ball of orange and white. Tommy disentangled it and smoothed out the telegram.

"Come at once, Moat House, Ebury, Yorkshire, great developments—TOMMY."

They looked at each other in stupefaction. Julius spoke first:

"*You* didn't send it?"

"Of course not. What does it mean?"

"I guess it means the worst," said Julius quietly. "They've got her."

"*What?*"

"Sure thing! They signed your name, and she fell into the trap like a lamb."

"My God! What shall we do?"

"Get busy, and go after her! Right now! There's no time to waste. It's almighty luck that she didn't take the wire with her. If she had we'd probably never have traced her. But we've got to hustle. Where's that Bradshaw?"

The energy of Julius was infectious. Left to himself, Tommy would probably have sat down to think things out for a good half-hour before he decided on a plan of action. But with Julius Hersheimmer about, hustling was inevitable.

After a few muttered imprecations he handed the Bradshaw to Tommy as being more conversant with its mysteries. Tommy abandoned it in favour of an A.B.C.

"Here we are. Ebury, Yorks. From King's Cross. Or St. Pancras. (Boy must have made a mistake. It was King's Cross, not *Charing* Cross) 12:50, that's the train she went by. 2:10, that's gone. 3:20 is the next—and a damned slow train too."

"What about the car?"

Tommy shook his head.

"Send it up if you like, but we'd better stick to the train. The great thing is to keep calm."

Julius groaned.

"That's so. But it gets my goat to think of that innocent young girl in danger!"

Tommy nodded abstractedly. He was thinking. In a moment or two, he said:

"I say, Julius, what do they want her for, anyway?"

"Eh? I don't get you?"

"What I mean is that I don't think it's their game to do her any harm," explained Tommy, puckering his brow with the strain of his mental processes. "She's a hostage, that's what she is. She's in no immediate danger, because if we tumble on to anything, she'd be damned useful to them. As long as they've got her, they've got the whip hand of us. See?"

"Sure thing," said Julius thoughtfully. "That's so."

"Besides," added Tommy, as an afterthought, "I've great faith in Tuppence."

The journey was wearisome, with many stops, and crowded carriages. They had to change twice, once at Doncaster, once at a small junction. Ebury was a deserted station with a solitary porter, to whom Tommy addressed himself:

"Can you tell me the way to the Moat House?"

"The Moat House? It's a tidy step from here. The big house near the sea, you mean?"

Tommy assented brazenly. After listening to the porter's meticulous but perplexing directions, they prepared to leave the station. It was beginning to rain, and they turned up the collars of their coats as they trudged through the slush of the road. Suddenly Tommy halted.

"Wait a moment." He ran back to the station and tackled the porter anew.

"Look here, do you remember a young lady who arrived by an earlier train, the 12:50 from London? She'd probably ask you the way to the Moat House."

He described Tuppence as well as he could, but the porter shook his head. Several people had arrived by the train in question. He could not call to mind one young lady in particular. But he was quite certain that no one had asked him the way to the Moat House.

Tommy rejoined Julius, and explained. Depression was settling down on him like a leaden weight. He felt convinced that their quest was going to be unsuccessful. The enemy had over three hours' start. Three hours was more than enough for Mr. Brown. He would not ignore the possibility of the telegram having been found.

The way seemed endless. Once they took the wrong turning and went nearly half a mile out of their direction. It was past seven o'clock when a small boy told them that "t' Moat House" was just past the next corner.

A rusty iron gate swinging dismally on its hinges! An overgrown drive thick with leaves. There was something about the place that struck a chill to both their hearts. They went up the deserted drive. The leaves deadened their footsteps. The daylight was almost gone. It was like walking in a world of ghosts. Overhead the branches flapped and creaked with a mournful note. Occasionally a sodden leaf drifted silently down, startling them with its cold touch on their cheek.

A turn of the drive brought them in sight of the house. That, too, seemed empty and deserted. The shutters were closed, the steps up to the door overgrown with moss. Was it indeed to this desolate spot that Tuppence had been decoyed? It seemed hard to believe that a human footstep had passed this way for months.

Julius jerked the rusty bell handle. A jangling peal rang discordantly, echoing through the emptiness within. No one came. They rang again and again—but there was no sign of life. Then they walked completely round the house. Everywhere silence, and shuttered windows. If they could believe the evidence of their eyes the place was empty.

"Nothing doing," said Julius.

They retraced their steps slowly to the gate.

"There must be a village handy," continued the young American. "We'd better make inquiries there. They'll know something about the place, and whether there's been any one there lately."

"Yes, that's not a bad idea."

Proceeding up the road, they soon came to a little hamlet. On the outskirts of it, they met a workman swinging his bag of tools, and Tommy stopped him with a question.

"The Moat House? It's empty. Been empty for years. Mrs. Sweeney's got the key if you want to go over it—next to the post office."

Tommy thanked him. They soon found the post office, which was also a sweet and general fancy shop, and knocked at the door of the cottage next to it. A clean, wholesome-looking woman opened it. She readily produced the key of the Moat House.

"Though I doubt if it's the kind of place to suit you, sir. In a terrible state of repair. Ceilings leaking and all. 'Twould need a lot of money spent on it."

"Thanks," said Tommy cheerily. "I dare say it'll be a washout, but houses are scarce nowadays."

"That they are," declared the woman heartily. "My daughter and son-in-law have been looking for a decent cottage for I don't know how long. It's all the war. Upset things terribly, it has. But excuse me, sir, it'll be too dark for you to see much of the house. Hadn't you better wait until tomorrow?"

"That's all right. We'll have a look around this evening, anyway. We'd have been here before only we lost our way. What's the best place to stay at for the night round here?"

Mrs. Sweeny looked doubtful.

"There's the *Yorkshire Arms*, but it's not much of a place for gentlemen like you."

"Oh, it will do very well. Thanks. By the way, you've not had a young lady here asking for this key today?"

The woman shook her head.

"No one's been over the place for a long time."

"Thanks very much."

They retraced their steps to the Moat House. As the front door swung back on its hinges, protesting loudly, Julius struck a match and examined the floor carefully. Then he shook his head.

"I'd swear no one's passed this way. Look at the dust. Thick. Not a sign of a footmark."

They wandered round the deserted house.

Everywhere the same tale. Thick layers of dust apparently undisturbed.

"This gets me," said Julius. "I don't believe Tuppence was ever in this house."

"She must have been."

Julius shook his head without replying.

"We'll go over it again tomorrow," said Tommy. "Perhaps we'll see more in the daylight."

On the morrow they took up the search once more, and were reluctantly forced to the conclusion that the house had not been invaded for some considerable time. They might have left the village altogether but for a fortunate discovery of Tommy's. As they were retracing their steps to the gate, he gave a sudden cry, and stooping, picked something up from among the leaves, and held it out to Julius. It was a small gold brooch.

"That's Tuppence's!"

"Are you sure?"

"Absolutely. I've often seen her wear it."

Julius drew a deep breath.

"I guess that settles it. She came as far as here, anyway. We'll make that pub our headquarters, and raise hell round here until we find her. Somebody *must* have seen her."

Forthwith the campaign began. Tommy and Julius worked separately and together, but the result was the same. Nobody answering to Tuppence's description had been seen in the vicinity. They were baffled—but not discouraged. Finally they altered their tactics. Tuppence had certainly not remained long in the neighbourhood of the Moat House. That pointed to her having been overcome and carried away in a car. They renewed inquiries. Had any one seen a car standing somewhere near the Moat House that day? Again they met with no success.

Julius wired to town for his own car, and they scoured the neighbourhood daily with unflagging zeal. A grey limousine on which they had set high hopes was traced to Harrogate, and turned out to be the property of a highly respectable maiden lady!

Each day saw them set out on a new quest. Julius was like a hound on the leash. He followed up the slenderest clue. Every car that had passed through the village on the fateful day was tracked down. He forced his way into country properties and submitted the owners of the motors to a searching cross-examination. His apologies were as thorough as his methods, and seldom failed in disarming the indignation of his victims; but, as day succeeded day, they were no nearer to discovering Tuppence's whereabouts. So well had the abduction been planned that the girl seemed literally to have vanished into thin air.

And another preoccupation was weighing on Tommy's mind.

"Do you know how long we've been here?" he asked one morning as they sat facing each other at breakfast. "A week! We're no nearer to finding Tuppence, *and next Sunday is the 29th!*"

"Shucks!" said Julius thoughtfully. "I'd almost forgotten about the 29th. I've been thinking of nothing but Tuppence."

"So have I. At least, I hadn't forgotten about the 29th, but it didn't seem to matter a damn in comparison to finding Tuppence. But today's the 23rd, and time's getting short. If we're ever going to get hold of her at all, we must do it before the 29th—her life won't be worth an hour's purchase afterwards. The hostage game will be played out by then. I'm beginning to feel that we've made a big mistake in the way we've set about this. We've wasted time and we're no forrader."

"I'm with you there. We've been a couple of mutts, who've bitten off a bigger bit than they can chew. I'm going to quit fooling right away!"

"What do you mean?"

"I'll tell you. I'm going to do what we ought to have done a week ago. I'm going right back to London to put the case in the hands of your British police. We fancied ourselves as sleuths. Sleuths! It was a piece of damn-fool foolishness! I'm through! I've had enough of it. Scotland Yard for me!"

"You're right," said Tommy slowly. "I wish to God we'd gone there right away."

"Better late than never. We've been like a couple of babes playing 'Here we go round the

Mulberry Bush.' Now I'm going right along to Scotland Yard to ask them to take me by the hand and show me the way I should go. I guess the professional always scores over the amateur in the end. Are you coming along with me?"

Tommy shook his head.

"What's the good? One of us is enough. I might as well stay here and nose round a bit longer. Something *might* turn up. One never knows."

"Sure thing. Well, so long. I'll be back in a couple of shakes with a few inspectors along. I shall tell them to pick out their brightest and best."

But the course of events was not to follow the plan Julius had laid down. Later in the day Tommy received a wire:

"Join me Manchester Midland Hotel. Important news—JULIUS."

At 7:30 that night Tommy alighted from a slow cross-country train. Julius was on the platform.

"Thought you'd come by this train if you weren't out when my wire arrived."

Tommy grasped him by the arm.

"What is it? Is Tuppence found?"

Julius shook his head.

"No. But I found this waiting in London. Just arrived."

He handed the telegraph form to the other. Tommy's eyes opened as he read:

"Jane Finn found. Come Manchester Midland Hotel immediately—PEEL EDGERTON."

Julius took the form back and folded it up.

"Queer," he said thoughtfully. "I thought that lawyer chap had quit!"

CHAPTER XIX
Jane Finn

"My train got in half an hour ago," explained Julius, as he led the way out of the station. "I reckoned you'd come by this before I left London, and wired accordingly to Sir James. He's booked rooms for us, and will be round to dine at eight."

"What made you think he'd ceased to take any interest in the case?" asked Tommy curiously.

"What he said," replied Julius dryly. "The old bird's as close as an oyster! Like all the darned lot of them, he wasn't going to commit himself till he was sure he could deliver the goods."

"I wonder," said Tommy thoughtfully.

Julius turned on him.

"You wonder what?"

"Whether that was his real reason."

"Sure. You bet your life it was."

Tommy shook his head unconvinced.

Sir James arrived punctually at eight o'clock, and Julius introduced Tommy. Sir James shook hands with him warmly.

"I am delighted to make your acquaintance, Mr. Beresford. I have heard so much about you from Miss Tuppence"—he smiled involuntarily—"that it really seems as though I already know you quite well."

"Thank you, sir," said Tommy with his cheerful grin. He scanned the great lawyer eagerly. Like Tuppence, he felt the magnetism of the other's personality. He was reminded of Mr. Carter. The two men, totally unlike so far as physical resemblance went, produced a similar effect. Beneath the weary manner of the one and the professional reserve of the other, lay the same quality of mind, keen-edged like a rapier.

In the meantime he was conscious of Sir James's close scrutiny. When the lawyer dropped his eyes the young man had the feeling that the other had read him through and through like an open book. He could not but wonder what the final judgment was, but there was little chance of learning that. Sir James took in everything, but gave out only what he chose. A proof of that occurred almost at once.

Immediately the first greetings were over Julius broke out into a flood of eager questions. How had Sir James managed to track the girl? Why had he not let them know that he was still working on the case? And so on.

Sir James stroked his chin and smiled. At last he said:

"Just so, just so. Well, she's found. And that's

the great thing, isn't it? Eh! Come now, that's the great thing?"

"Sure it is. But just how did you strike her trail? Miss Tuppence and I thought you'd quit for good and all."

"Ah!" The lawyer shot a lightning glance at him, then resumed operations on his chin. "You thought that, did you? Did you really? H'm, dear me."

"But I guess I can take it we were wrong," pursued Julius.

"Well, I don't know that I should go so far as to say that. But it's certainly fortunate for all parties that we've managed to find the young lady."

"But where is she?" demanded Julius, his thoughts flying off on another tack. "I thought you'd be sure to bring her along?"

"That would hardly be possible," said Sir James gravely.

"Why?"

"Because the young lady was knocked down in a street accident, and has sustained slight injuries to the head. She was taken to the infirmary, and on recovering consciousness gave her name as Jane Finn. When—ah!—I heard that, I arranged for her to be removed to the house of a doctor—a friend of mine, and wired at once for you. She relapsed into unconsciousness and has not spoken since."

"She's not seriously hurt?"

"Oh, a bruise and a cut or two; really, from a medical point of view, absurdly slight injuries to have produced such a condition. Her state is probably to be attributed to the mental shock consequent on recovering her memory."

"It's come back?" cried Julius excitedly.

Sir James tapped the table rather impatiently.

"Undoubtedly, Mr. Hersheimmer, since she was able to give her real name. I thought you had appreciated that point."

"And you just happened to be on the spot," said Tommy. "Seems quite like a fairy tale."

But Sir James was far too wary to be drawn.

"Coincidences are curious things," he said dryly.

Nevertheless Tommy was now certain of what he had before only suspected. Sir James's presence in Manchester was not accidental. Far from abandoning the case, as Julius supposed, he had by some means of his own successfully run the missing girl to earth. The only thing that puzzled Tommy was the reason for all this secrecy. He concluded that it was a foible of the legal mind.

Julius was speaking.

"After dinner," he announced, "I shall go right away and see Jane."

"That will be impossible, I fear," said Sir James. "It is very unlikely they would allow her to see visitors at this time of night. I should suggest tomorrow morning about ten o'clock."

Julius flushed. There was something in Sir James which always stirred him to antagonism. It was a conflict of two masterful personalities.

"All the same, I reckon I'll go round there tonight and see if I can't ginger them up to break through their silly rules."

"It will be quite useless, Mr. Hersheimmer."

The words came out like the crack of a pistol, and Tommy looked up with a start. Julius was nervous and excited. The hand with which he raised his glass to his lips shook slightly, but his eyes held Sir James's defiantly. For a moment the hostility between the two seemed likely to burst into flame, but in the end Julius lowered his eyes, defeated.

"For the moment, I reckon you're the boss."

"Thank you," said the other. "We will say ten o'clock then?" With consummate ease of manner he turned to Tommy. "I must confess, Mr. Beresford, that it was something of a surprise to me to see you here this evening. The last I heard of you was that your friends were in grave anxiety on your behalf. Nothing had been heard of you for some days, and Miss Tuppence was inclined to think you had got into difficulties."

"I had, sir!" Tommy grinned reminiscently. "I was never in a tighter place in my life."

Helped out by questions from Sir James, he gave an abbreviated account of his adventures.

The lawyer looked at him with renewed interest as he brought the tale to a close.

"You got yourself out of a tight place very well," he said gravely. "I congratulate you. You displayed a great deal of ingenuity and carried your part through well."

Tommy blushed, his face assuming a prawn-like hue at the praise.

"I couldn't have got away but for the girl, sir."

"No." Sir James smiled a little. "It was lucky for you she happened to—er—take a fancy to you." Tommy appeared about to protest, but Sir James went on. "There's no doubt about her being one of the gang, I suppose?"

"I'm afraid not, sir. I thought perhaps they were keeping her there by force, but the way she acted didn't fit in with that. You see, she went back to them when she could have got away."

Sir James nodded thoughtfully.

"What did she say? Something about wanting to be taken to Marguerite?"

"Yes, sir. I suppose she meant Mrs. Vandemeyer."

"She always signed herself Rita Vandemeyer. All her friends spoke of her as Rita. Still, I suppose the girl must have been in the habit of calling her by her full name. And, at the moment she was crying out to her, Mrs. Vandemeyer was either dead or dying! Curious! There are one or two points that strike me as being obscure—their sudden change of attitude towards yourself, for instance. By the way, the house was raided, of course?"

"Yes, sir, but they'd all cleared out."

"Naturally," said Sir James dryly.

"And not a clue left behind."

"I wonder——" The lawyer tapped the table thoughtfully.

Something in his voice made Tommy look up. Would this man's eyes have seen something where theirs had been blind? He spoke impulsively:

"I wish you'd been there, sir, to go over the house!"

"I wish I had," said Sir James quietly. He sat for a moment in silence. Then he looked up. "And since then? What have you been doing?"

For a moment, Tommy stared at him. Then it dawned on him that of course the lawyer did not know.

"I forgot that you didn't know about Tuppence," he said slowly. The sickening anxiety, forgotten for a while in the excitement of knowing Jane Finn was found at last, swept over him again.

The lawyer laid down his knife and fork sharply.

"Has anything happened to Miss Tuppence?" His voice was keen-edged.

"She's disappeared," said Julius.

"When?"

"A week ago."

"How?"

Sir James's questions fairly shot out. Between them Tommy and Julius gave the history of the last week and their futile search.

Sir James went at once to the root of the matter.

"A wire signed with your name? They knew enough of you both for that. They weren't sure of how much you had learnt in that house. Their kidnapping of Miss Tuppence is the counter-move to your escape. If necessary they could seal your lips with a threat of what might happen to her."

Tommy nodded.

"That's just what I thought, sir."

Sir James looked at him keenly. "*You* had worked that out, had you? Not bad—not at all bad. The curious thing is that they certainly did not know anything about you when they first held you prisoner. You are sure that you did not in any way disclose your identity?"

Tommy shook his head.

"That's so," said Julius with a nod. "Therefore I reckon some one put them wise—and not earlier than Sunday afternoon."

"Yes, but who?"

"That almighty omniscient Mr. Brown, of course!"

There was a faint note of derision in the American's voice which made Sir James look up sharply.

"You don't believe in Mr. Brown, Mr. Hersheimmer?"

"No, sir, I do not," returned the young American with emphasis. "Not as such, that is to say. I reckon it out that he's a figurehead—just a bogy name to frighten the children with. The real head of this business is that Russian chap Kramenin. I guess he's quite capable of running revolutions in three countries at once if he chose! The man Whittington is probably the head of the English branch."

"I disagree with you," said Sir James shortly. "Mr. Brown exists." He turned to Tommy. "Did you happen to notice where that wire was handed in?"

"No, sir, I'm afraid I didn't."

"H'm. Got it with you?"

"It's upstairs, sir, in my kit."

"I'd like to have a look at it sometime. No hurry. You've wasted a week"—Tommy hung his head—"a day or so more is immaterial. We'll deal with Miss Jane Finn first. Afterwards, we'll set to work to rescue Miss Tuppence from bondage. I don't think she's in any immediate danger. That is, so long as they don't know that we've got Jane Finn, and that her memory has returned. We must keep that dark at all costs. You understand?"

The other two assented, and, after making arrangements for meeting on the morrow, the great lawyer took his leave.

At ten o'clock, the two young men were at the appointed spot. Sir James had joined them on the doorstep. He alone appeared unexcited. He introduced them to the doctor.

"Mr. Hersheimmer—Mr. Beresford—Dr. Roylance. How's the patient?"

"Going on well. Evidently no idea of the flight of time. Asked this morning how many had been saved from the *Lusitania*. Was it in the papers yet? That, of course, was only what was to be expected. She seems to have something on her mind, though."

"I think we can relieve her anxiety. May we go up?"

"Certainly."

Tommy's heart beat sensibly faster as they followed the doctor upstairs. Jane Finn at last! The long-sought, the mysterious, the elusive Jane Finn! How wildly improbable success had seemed! And here in this house, her memory almost miraculously restored, lay the girl who held the future of England in her hands. A half groan broke from Tommy's lips. If only Tuppence could have been at his side to share in the triumphant conclusion of their joint venture! Then he put the thought of Tuppence resolutely aside. His confidence in Sir James was growing. There was a man who would unerringly ferret out Tuppence's whereabouts. In the meantime Jane Finn! And suddenly a dread clutched at his heart. It seemed too easy. . . . Suppose they should find her dead . . . stricken down by the hand of Mr. Brown?

In another minute he was laughing at these melodramatic fancies. The doctor held open the door of a room and they passed in. On the white bed, bandages round her head, lay the girl. Somehow the whole scene seemed unreal. It was so exactly what one expected that it gave the effect of being beautifully staged.

The girl looked from one to the other of them with large wondering eyes. Sir James spoke first.

"Miss Finn," he said, "this is your cousin, Mr. Julius P. Hersheimmer."

A faint flush flitted over the girl's face, as Julius stepped forward and took her hand.

"How do, Cousin Jane?" he said lightly.

But Tommy caught the tremor in his voice.

"Are you really Uncle Hiram's son?" she asked wonderingly.

Her voice, with the slight warmth of the Western accent, had an almost thrilling quality. It seemed vaguely familiar to Tommy, but he thrust the impression aside as impossible.

"Sure thing."

"We used to read about Uncle Hiram in the papers," continued the girl, in her low soft tones. "But I never thought I'd meet you one day. Mother figured it out that Uncle Hiram would never get over being mad with her."

"The old man was like that," admitted Julius. "But I guess the new generation's sort of different. Got no use for the family feud business. First thing I thought about, soon as the war was over, was to come along and hunt you up."

A shadow passed over the girl's face.

"They've been telling me things—dreadful things—that my memory went, and that there are years I shall never know about—years lost out of my life."

"You didn't realize that yourself?"

The girl's eyes opened wide.

"Why, no. It seems to me as though it were no time since we were being hustled into those boats. I can see it all now." She closed her eyes with a shudder.

Julius looked across at Sir James, who nodded.

"Don't worry any. It isn't worth it. Now, see here, Jane, there's something we want to know about. There was a man aboard that boat with some mighty important papers on him, and the big guns in this country have got a notion that he passed on the goods to you. Is that so?"

The girl hesitated, her glance shifting to the other two. Julius understood.

"Mr. Beresford is commissioned by the British Government to get those papers back. Sir James Peel Edgerton is an English Member of Parliament, and might be a big gun in the Cabinet if he liked. It's owing to him that we've ferreted you out at last. So you can go right ahead and tell us the whole story. Did Danvers give you the papers?"

"Yes. He said they'd have a better chance with me, because they would save the women and children first."

"Just as we thought," said Sir James.

"He said they were very important—that they might make all the difference to the Allies. But, if it's all so long ago, and the war's over, what does it matter now?"

"I guess history repeats itself, Jane. First there was a great hue and cry over those papers, then it all died down, and now the whole caboodle's started all over again—for rather different reasons. Then you can hand them over to us right away?"

"But I can't."

"What?"

"I haven't got them."

"You—haven't—got them?" Julius punctuated the words with little pauses.

"No—I hid them."

"You *hid* them?"

"Yes. I got uneasy. People seemed to be watching me. It scared me—badly." She put her hand to her head. "It's almost the last thing I remember before waking up in the hospital. . . ."

"Go on," said Sir James, in his quiet penetrating tones. "What do you remember?"

She turned to him obediently.

"It was at Holyhead. I came that way—I don't remember why. . . ."

"That doesn't matter. Go on."

"In the confusion on the quay I slipped away. Nobody saw me. I took a car. Told the man to drive me out of the town. I watched when we got on the open road. No other car was following us. I saw a path at the side of the road. I told the man to wait."

She paused, then went on. "The path led to the cliff, and down to the sea between big yellow gorse bushes—they were like golden flames. I looked round. There wasn't a soul in sight. But just level with my head there was a hole in the rock. It was quite small—I could only just get my hand in, but it went a long way back. I took the oilskin packet from round my neck and shoved it right in as far as I could. Then I tore off a bit of gorse—My! but it did prick—and plugged the hole with it so that you'd never guess there was a crevice of any kind there. Then I marked the place carefully in my own mind, so that I'd find it again. There was a queer boulder in the path just there—for all the world like a dog sitting up begging. Then I went back to the road. The car was waiting, and I drove back. I just caught the train. I was a bit ashamed of myself for fancying things maybe, but, by and by, I saw the man opposite me wink at a woman who was sitting next to me, and I felt scared again, and was glad the papers were safe. I went out in the corridor to get a little air. I thought I'd slip into another carriage. But the woman called me back, said

I'd dropped something, and when I stooped to look, something seemed to hit me—here." She placed her hand to the back of her head. "I don't remember anything more until I woke up in the hospital."

There was a pause.

"Thank you, Miss Finn." It was Sir James who spoke. "I hope we have not tired you?"

"Oh, that's all right. My head aches a little, but otherwise I feel fine."

Julius stepped forward and took her hand again.

"So long, Cousin Jane. I'm going to get busy after those papers, but I'll be back in two shakes of a dog's tail, and I'll tote you up to London and give you the time of your young life before we go back to the States! I mean it—so hurry up and get well."

CHAPTER XX
Too Late

In the street they held an informal council of war. Sir James had drawn a watch from his pocket. "The boat train to Holyhead stops at Chester at 12:14. If you start at once I think you can catch the connection."

Tommy looked up, puzzled.

"Is there any need to hurry, sir? Today is only the 24th."

"I guess it's always well to get up early in the morning," said Julius, before the lawyer had time to reply. "We'll make tracks for the depot right away."

A little frown had settled on Sir James's brow.

"I wish I could come with you. I am due to speak at a meeting at two o'clock. It is unfortunate."

The reluctance in his tone was very evident. It was clear, on the other hand, that Julius was easily disposed to put up with the loss of the other's company.

"I guess there's nothing complicated about this deal," he remarked. "Just a game of hide-and-seek, that's all."

"I hope so," said Sir James.

"Sure thing. What else could it be?"

"You are still young, Mr. Hersheimmer. At my age you will probably have learnt one lesson. 'Never underestimate your adversary.'"

The gravity of his tone impressed Tommy, but had little effect upon Julius.

"You think Mr. Brown might come along and take a hand? If he does, I'm ready for him." He slapped his pocket. "I carry a gun. Little Willie here travels round with me everywhere." He produced a murderous-looking automatic, and tapped it affectionately before returning it to its home. "But he won't be needed this trip. There's nobody to put Mr. Brown wise."

The lawyer shrugged his shoulders.

"There was nobody to put Mr. Brown wise to the fact that Mrs. Vandemeyer meant to betray him. Nevertheless, *Mrs. Vandemeyer died without speaking.*"

Julius was silenced for once, and Sir James added on a lighter note:

"I only want to put you on your guard. Good-bye, and good luck. Take no unnecessary risks once the papers are in your hands. If there is any reason to believe that you have been shadowed, destroy them at once. Good luck to you. The game is in your hands now." He shook hands with them both.

Ten minutes later the two young men were seated in a first-class carriage *en route* for Chester.

For a long time neither of them spoke. When at length Julius broke the silence, it was with a totally unexpected remark.

"Say," he observed thoughtfully, "did you ever make a darned fool of yourself over a girl's face?"

Tommy, after a moment's astonishment, searched his mind.

"Can't say I have," he replied at last. "Not that I can recollect, anyhow. Why?"

"Because for the last two months I've been making a sentimental idiot of myself over Jane! First moment I clapped eyes on her photograph my heart did all the usual stunts you read about in novels. I guess I'm ashamed to admit it, but I came over here determined to find her and fix it all up, and take her back as Mrs. Julius P. Hersheimmer!"

"Oh!" said Tommy, amazed.

Julius uncrossed his legs brusquely and continued:

"Just shows what an almighty fool a man can make of himself! One look at the girl in the flesh, and I was cured!"

Feeling more tongue-tied than ever, Tommy ejaculated "Oh!" again.

"No disparagement to Jane, mind you," continued the other. "She's a real nice girl, and some fellow will fall in love with her right away."

"I thought her a very good-looking girl," said Tommy, finding his tongue.

"Sure she is. But she's not like her photo one bit. At least I suppose she is in a way—must be—because I recognized her right off. If I'd seen her in a crowd I'd have said 'There's a girl whose face I know' right away without any hesitation. But there was something about that photo"—Julius shook his head, and heaved a sigh—"I guess romance is a mighty queer thing!"

"It must be," said Tommy coldly, "if you can come over here in love with one girl, and propose to another within a fortnight."

Julius had the grace to look discomposed.

"Well, you see, I'd got a sort of tired feeling that I'd never find Jane—and that it was all plumb foolishness anyway. And then—oh, well, the French, for instance, are much more sensible in the way they look at things. They keep romance and marriage apart——"

Tommy flushed.

"Well, I'm damned! If that's——"

Julius hastened to interrupt.

"Say now, don't be hasty. I don't mean what you mean. I take it Americans have a higher opinion of morality than you have even. What I meant was that the French set about marriage in a business-like way—find two people who are suited to one another, look after the money affairs, and see the whole thing practically, and in a business-like spirit."

"If you ask me," said Tommy, "we're all too damned business-like nowadays. We're always saying, 'Will it pay?' The men are bad enough, and the girls are worse!"

"Cool down, son. Don't get so heated."

"I feel heated," said Tommy.

Julius looked at him and judged it wise to say no more.

However, Tommy had plenty of time to cool down before they reached Holyhead, and the cheerful grin had returned to his countenance as they alighted at their destination.

After consultation, and with the aid of a road map, they were fairly well agreed as to direction, so were able to hire a taxi without more ado and drive out on the road leading to Treaddur Bay. They instructed the man to go slowly, and watched narrowly so as not to miss the path. They came to it not long after leaving the town, and Tommy stopped the car promptly, asked in a casual tone whether the path led down to the sea, and hearing it did paid off the man in handsome style.

A moment later the taxi was slowly chugging back to Holyhead. Tommy and Julius watched it out of sight, and then turned to the narrow path.

"It's the right one, I suppose?" asked Tommy doubtfully. "There must be simply heaps along here."

"Sure it is. Look at the gorse. Remember what Jane said?"

Tommy looked at the swelling hedges of golden blossom which bordered the path on either side, and was convinced.

They went down in single file, Julius leading. Twice Tommy turned his head uneasily. Julius looked back.

"What is it?"

"I don't know. I've got the wind up somehow. Keep fancying there's some one following us."

"Can't be," said Julius positively. "We'd see him."

Tommy had to admit that this was true. Nevertheless, his sense of uneasiness deepened. In spite of himself he believed in the omniscience of the enemy.

"I rather wish that fellow would come along," said Julius. He patted his pocket. "Little William here is just aching for exercise!"

"Do you always carry it—him—with you?" inquired Tommy with burning curiosity.

"Most always. I guess you never know what might turn up."

Tommy kept a respectful silence. He was impressed by little William. It seemed to remove the menace of Mr. Brown farther away.

The path was now running along the side of the cliff, parallel to the sea. Suddenly Julius came to such an abrupt halt that Tommy cannoned into him.

"What's up?" he inquired.

"Look there. If that doesn't beat the band!"

Tommy looked. Standing out half obstructing the path was a huge boulder which certainly bore a fanciful resemblance to a "begging" terrier.

"Well," said Tommy, refusing to share Julius's emotion, "it's what we expected to see, isn't it?"

Julius looked at him sadly and shook his head.

"British phlegm! Sure we expected it—but it kind of rattles me, all the same, to see it sitting there just where we expected to find it!"

Tommy, whose calm was, perhaps, more assumed than natural, moved his feet impatiently.

"Push on. What about the hole?"

They scanned the cliff-side narrowly. Tommy heard himself saying idiotically:

"The gorse won't be there after all these years."

And Julius replied solemnly:

"I guess you're right."

Tommy suddenly pointed with a shaking hand.

"What about that crevice there?"

Julius replied in an awestricken voice:

"That's it—for sure."

They looked at each other.

"When I was in France," said Tommy reminiscently, "whenever my batman failed to call me, he always said that he had come over queer. I never believed it. But whether he felt it or not, there *is* such a sensation. I've got it now! Badly!"

He looked at the rock with a kind of agonized passion.

"Damn it!" he cried. "It's impossible! Five years! Think of it! Bird's-nesting boys, picnic parties, thousands of people passing! It can't be there! It's a hundred to one against its being there! It's against all reason!"

Indeed, he felt it to be impossible—more, perhaps, because he could not believe in his own success where so many others had failed. The thing was too easy, therefore it could not be. The hole would be empty.

Julius looked at him with a widening smile.

"I guess you're rattled now all right," he drawled with some enjoyment. "Well, here goes!" He thrust his hand into the crevice, and made a slight grimace. "It's a tight fit. Jane's hand must be a few sizes smaller than mine. I don't feel anything—no—say, what's this? Gee whiz!" And with a flourish he waved aloft a small discoloured packet. "It's the goods all right. Sewn up in oilskin. Hold it while I get my penknife."

The unbelievable had happened. Tommy held the precious packet tenderly between his hands. They had succeeded!

"It's queer," he murmured idly, "you'd think the stitches would have rotted. They look just as good as new."

They cut them carefully and ripped away the oilsilk. Inside was a small folded sheet of paper. With trembling fingers they unfolded it. The sheet was blank! They stared at each other, puzzled.

"A dummy?" hazarded Julius. "Was Danvers just a decoy?"

Tommy shook his head. That solution did not satisfy him. Suddenly his face cleared.

"I've got it! *Sympathetic ink!*"

"You think so?"

"Worth trying anyhow. Heat usually does the trick. Get some sticks. We'll make a fire."

In a few minutes the little fire of twigs and leaves was blazing merrily. Tommy held the sheet of paper near the glow. The paper curled a little with the heat. Nothing more.

Suddenly Julius grasped his arm, and pointed to where characters were appearing in a faint brown colour.

"Gee whiz! You've got it! Say, that idea of yours was great. It never occurred to me."

Tommy held the paper in position some minutes longer until he judged the heat had done its work. Then he withdrew it. A moment later he uttered a cry.

Across the sheet in neat brown printing ran the words:

WITH THE COMPLIMENTS OF MR. BROWN.

CHAPTER XXI
Tommy Makes a Discovery

For a moment or two they stood staring at each other stupidly, dazed with the shock. Somehow, inexplicably, Mr. Brown had forestalled them. Tommy accepted defeat quietly. Not so Julius.

"How in tarnation did he get ahead of us? That's what beats me!" he ended up.

Tommy shook his head, and said dully:

"It accounts for the stitches being new. We might have guessed. . . ."

"Never mind the darned stitches. How did he get ahead of us? We hustled all we knew. It's downright impossible for anyone to get here quicker than we did. And, anyway, how did he know? Do you reckon there was a dictaphone in Jane's room? I guess there must have been."

But Tommy's common sense pointed out objections.

"No one could have known beforehand that she was going to be in that house—much less that particular room."

"That's so," admitted Julius. "Then one of the nurses was a crook and listened at the door. How's that?"

"I don't see that it matters anyway," said Tommy wearily. "He may have found out some months ago, and removed the papers, then—— No, by Jove, that won't wash! They'd have been published at once."

"Sure thing they would! No, some one's got ahead of us today by an hour or so. But how they did it gets my goat."

"I wish that chap Peel Edgerton had been with us," said Tommy thoughtfully.

"Why?" Julius stared. "The mischief was done when we came."

"Yes——" Tommy hesitated. He could not explain his own feeling—the illogical idea that the K.C.'s presence would somehow have averted the catastrophe. He reverted to his former point of view. "It's no good arguing about how it was done. The game's up. We've failed. There's only one thing for me to do."

"What's that?"

"Get back to London as soon as possible. Mr. Carter must be warned. It's only a matter of hours now before the blow falls. But, at any rate, he ought to know the worst."

The duty was an unpleasant one, but Tommy had no intention of shirking it. He must report his failure to Mr. Carter. After that his work was done. He took the midnight mail to London. Julius elected to stay the night at Holyhead.

Half an hour after arrival, haggard and pale, Tommy stood before his chief.

"I've come to report, sir. I've failed—failed badly."

Mr. Carter eyed him sharply.

"You mean that the treaty——"

"Is in the hands of Mr. Brown, sir."

"Ah!" said Mr. Carter quietly. The expression on his face did not change, but Tommy caught the flicker of despair in his eyes. It convinced him as nothing else had done that the outlook was hopeless.

"Well," said Mr. Carter after a minute or two, "we mustn't sag at the knees, I suppose. I'm glad to know definitely. We must do what we can."

Through Tommy's mind flashed the assurance: "It's hopeless, and he knows it's hopeless!"

The other looked up at him.

"Don't take it to heart, lad," he said kindly. "You did your best. You were up against one of the biggest brains of the century. And you came very near success. Remember that."

"Thank you, sir. It's awfully decent of you."

"I blame myself. I have been blaming myself ever since I heard this other news."

Something in his tone attracted Tommy's attention. A new fear gripped at his heart.

"Is there—something more, sir?"

"I'm afraid so," said Mr. Carter gravely. He stretched out his hand to a sheet on the table.

"Tuppence——?" faltered Tommy.

"Read for yourself."

The typewritten words danced before his eyes. The description of a green toque, a coat with a handkerchief in the pocket marked P.L.C. He looked an agonized question at Mr. Carter. The latter replied to it:

"Washed up on the Yorkshire coast—near Ebury. I'm afraid—it looks very much like foul play."

"My God!" gasped Tommy. "*Tuppence!* Those devils—I'll never rest till I've got even with them! I'll hunt them down! I'll——"

The pity on Mr. Carter's face stopped him.

"I know what you feel like, my poor boy. But it's no good. You'll waste your strength uselessly. It may sound harsh, but my advice to you is: Cut your losses. Time's merciful. You'll forget."

"Forget Tuppence? Never!"

Mr. Carter shook his head.

"So you think now. Well, it won't bear thinking of—that brave little girl! I'm sorry about the whole business—confoundedly sorry."

Tommy came to himself with a start.

"I'm taking up your time, sir," he said with an effort. "There's no need for you to blame yourself. I dare say we were a couple of young fools to take on such a job. You warned us all right. But I wish to God *I*'d been the one to get it in the neck. Good-bye, sir."

Back at the *Ritz*, Tommy packed up his few belongings mechanically, his thoughts far away. He was still bewildered by the introduction of tragedy into his cheerful commonplace existence. What fun they had had together, he and Tuppence! And now—oh, he couldn't believe it—it couldn't be true! *Tuppence—dead!* Little Tuppence, brimming over with life! It was a dream, a horrible dream. Nothing more.

They brought him a note, a few kind words of sympathy from Peel Edgerton, who had read the news in the paper. (There had been a large headline: EX-V.A.D. FEARED DROWNED.) The letter ended with the offer of a post on a ranch in the Argentine, where Sir James had considerable interests.

"Kind old beggar," muttered Tommy, as he flung it aside.

The door opened, and Julius burst in with his usual violence. He held an open newspaper in his hand.

"Say, what's all this? They seem to have got some fool idea about Tuppence."

"It's true," said Tommy quietly.

"You mean they've done her in?"

Tommy nodded.

"I suppose when they got the treaty she—wasn't any good to them any longer, and they were afraid to let her go."

"Well, I'm darned!" said Julius. "Little Tuppence. She sure was the pluckiest little girl——"

But suddenly something seemed to crack in Tommy's brain. He rose to his feet.

"Oh, get out! You don't really care, damn you! You asked her to marry you in your rotten cold-blooded way, but I *loved* her. I'd have given the soul out of my body to save her from harm. I'd have stood by without a word and let her marry you, because you could have given her the sort of time she ought to have had, and I was only a poor devil without a penny to bless himself with. But it wouldn't have been because I didn't care!"

"See here," began Julius temperately.

"Oh, go to the devil! I can't stand your coming here and talking about 'little Tuppence.' Go and look after your cousin. Tuppence is my girl! I've always loved her, from the time we played together as kids. We grew up and it was just the same. I shall never forget when I was in hospital, and she came in in that ridiculous cap and apron! It was like a miracle to see the girl I loved turn up in a nurse's kit——"

But Julius interrupted him.

"A nurse's kit! Gee whiz! I must be going to Colney Hatch! I could swear I've seen Jane in a nurse's cap too. And that's plumb impossible! No, by gum, I've got it! It was her I saw talking to Whittington at that nursing home in Bournemouth. She wasn't a patient there! She was a nurse!"

"I dare say," said Tommy angrily, "she's probably been in with them from the start. I shouldn't wonder if she stole those papers from Danvers to begin with."

"I'm darned if she did!" shouted Julius. "She's my cousin, and as patriotic a girl as ever stepped."

"I don't care a damn what she is, but get out of here!" retorted Tommy also at the top of his voice.

The young men were on the point of coming to blows. But suddenly, with an almost magical abruptness, Julius's anger abated.

"All right, son," he said quietly, "I'm going. I don't blame you any for what you've been saying. It's mighty lucky you did say it. I've been the most almighty blithering darned idiot that it's possible to imagine. Calm down"—Tommy had made an impatient gesture—"I'm going right away now—going to the London and North Western Railway depot, if you want to know."

"I don't care a damn where you're going," growled Tommy.

As the door closed behind Julius, he returned to his suit-case.

"That's the lot," he murmured, and rang the bell.

"Take my luggage down."

"Yes, sir. Going away, sir?"

"I'm going to the devil," said Tommy, regardless of the menial's feelings.

That functionary, however, merely replied respectfully:

"Yes, sir. Shall I call a taxi?"

Tommy nodded.

Where was he going? He hadn't the faintest idea. Beyond a fixed determination to get even with Mr. Brown he had no plans. He re-read Sir James's letter, and shook his head. Tuppence must be avenged. Still, it was kind of the old fellow.

"Better answer it, I suppose." He went across to the writing-table. With the usual perversity of bedroom stationery, there were innumerable envelopes and no paper. He rang. No one came. Tommy fumed at the delay. Then he remembered that there was a good supply in Julius's sitting-room. The American had announced his immediate departure, there would be no fear of running up against him. Besides, he wouldn't mind if he did. He was beginning to be rather ashamed of the things he had said. Old Julius had taken them jolly well. He'd apologize if he found him there.

But the room was deserted. Tommy walked across to the writing-table, and opened the middle drawer. A photograph, carelessly thrust in face upwards, caught his eye. For a moment he stood rooted to the ground. Then he took it out, shut the drawer, walked slowly over to an arm-chair, and sat down still staring at the photograph in his hand.

What on earth was a photograph of the French girl Annette doing in Julius Hersheimmer's writing-table?

CHAPTER XXII
In Downing Street

The Prime Minister tapped the desk in front of him with nervous fingers. His face was worn and harassed. He took up his conversation with Mr. Carter at the point it had broken off.

"I don't understand," he said. "Do you really mean that things are not so desperate after all?"

"So this lad seems to think."

"Let's have a look at his letter again."

Mr. Carter handed it over. It was written in a sprawling boyish hand.

"Dear Mr. Carter,
"Something's turned up that has given me a jar. Of course I may be simply making

an awful ass of myself, but I don't think so. If my conclusions are right, that girl at Manchester was just a plant. The whole thing was prearranged, sham packet and all, with the object of making us think the game was up—therefore I fancy that we must have been pretty hot on the scent.

"I think I know who the real Jane Finn is, and I've even got an idea where the papers are. That last's only a guess, of course, but I've a sort of feeling it'll turn out right. Anyhow, I enclose it in a sealed envelope for what it's worth. I'm going to ask you not to open it until the very last moment, midnight on the 28th, in fact. You'll understand why in a minute. You see, I've figured it out that those things of Tuppence's are a plant too, and she's no more drowned than I am. The way I reason is this: as a last chance they'll let Jane Finn escape in the hope that she's been shamming this memory stunt, and that once she thinks she's free she'll go right away to the cache. Of course it's an awful risk for them to take, because she knows all about them—but they're pretty desperate to get hold of that treaty. *But if they know that the papers have been recovered by us,* neither of those two girls' lives will be worth an hour's purchase. I must try and get hold of Tuppence before Jane escapes.

"I want a repeat of that telegram that was sent to Tuppence at the *Ritz*. Sir James Peel Edgerton said you would be able to manage that for me. He's frightfully clever.

"One last thing—please have that house in Soho watched day and night.

> "Yours, etc.,
> "Thomas Beresford."

The Prime Minister looked up.

"The enclosure?"

Mr. Carter smiled dryly.

"In the vaults of the Bank. I am taking no chances."

"You don't think"—the Prime Minister hesitated a minute—"that it would be better to open it now? Surely we ought to secure the document, that is, provided the young man's guess turns out to be correct, at once. We can keep the fact of having done so quite secret."

"Can we? I'm not so sure. There are spies all round us. Once it's known I wouldn't give that"—he snapped his fingers—"for the life of those two girls. No, the boy trusted me, and I shan't let him down."

"Well, well, we must leave it at that, then. What's he like, this lad?"

"Outwardly, he's an ordinary clean-limbed, rather block-headed young Englishman. Slow in his mental processes. On the other hand, it's quite impossible to lead him astray through his imagination. He hasn't got any—so he's difficult to deceive. He worries things out slowly, and once he's got hold of anything he doesn't let go. The little lady's quite different. More intuition and less common sense. They make a pretty pair working together. Pace and stamina."

"He seems confident," mused the Prime Minister.

"Yes, and that's what gives me hope. He's the kind of diffident youth who would have to be *very* sure before he ventured an opinion at all."

A half smile came to the other's lips.

"And it is this—boy who will defeat the master criminal of our time?"

"This—boy, as you say! But I sometimes fancy I see a shadow behind."

"You mean?"

"Peel Edgerton."

"Peel Edgerton?" said the Prime Minister in astonishment.

"Yes. I see his hand in *this*." He struck the open letter. "He's there—working in the dark, silently, unobtrusively. I've always felt that if anyone was to run Mr. Brown to earth, Peel Edgerton would be the man. I tell you he's on the case now, but doesn't want it known. By the way, I got rather an odd request from him the other day."

"Yes?"

"He sent me a cutting from some American

paper. It referred to a man's body found near the docks in New York about three weeks ago. He asked me to collect any information on the subject I could."

"Well?"

Carter shrugged his shoulders.

"I couldn't get much. Young fellow about thirty-five—poorly dressed—face very badly disfigured. He was never identified."

"And you fancy that the two matters are connected in some way?"

"Somehow I do. I may be wrong, of course."

There was a pause, then Mr. Carter continued:

"I asked him to come round here. Not that we'll get anything out of him he doesn't want to tell. His legal instincts are too strong. But there's no doubt he can throw light on one or two obscure points in young Beresford's letter. Ah, here he is!"

The two men rose to greet the new-comer. A half whimsical thought flashed across the Premier's mind. "My successor, perhaps!"

"We've had a letter from young Beresford," said Mr. Carter, coming to the point at once. "You've seen him, I suppose?"

"You suppose wrong," said the lawyer.

"Oh!" Mr. Carter was a little nonplussed.

Sir James smiled, and stroked his chin.

"He rang me up," he volunteered.

"Would you have any objection to telling us exactly what passed between you?"

"Not at all. He thanked me for a certain letter which I had written to him—as a matter of fact, I had offered him a job. Then he reminded me of something I had said to him at Manchester respecting that bogus telegram which lured Miss Cowley away. I asked him if anything untoward had occurred. He said it had—that in a drawer in Mr. Hersheimmer's room he had discovered a photograph." The lawyer paused, then continued: "I asked him if the photograph bore the name and address of a Californian photographer. He replied: 'You're on to it, sir. It had.' Then he went on to tell me something I *didn't* know. The original of that photograph was the French girl, Annette, who saved his life."

"What?"

"Exactly. I asked the young man with some curiosity what he had done with the photograph. He replied that he had put it back where he found it." The lawyer paused again. "That was good, you know—distinctly good. He can use his brains, that young fellow. I congratulated him. The discovery was a providential one. Of course, from the moment that the girl in Manchester was proved to be a plant everything was altered. Young Beresford saw that for himself without my having to tell it him. But he felt he couldn't trust his judgment on the subject of Miss Cowley. Did I think she was alive? I told him, duly weighing the evidence, that there was a very decided chance in favour of it. That brought us back to the telegram."

"Yes?"

"I advised him to apply to you for a copy of the original wire. It had occurred to me as probable that, after Miss Cowley flung it on the floor, certain words might have been erased and altered with the express intention of setting searchers on a false trail."

Carter nodded. He took a sheet from his pocket, and read aloud:

"Come at once, Astley Priors, Gatehouse, Kent. Great developments—TOMMY."

"Very simple," said Sir James, "and very ingenious. Just a few words to alter, and the thing was done. And the one important clue they overlooked."

"What was that?"

"The page-boy's statement that Miss Cowley drove to Charing Cross. They were so sure of themselves that they took it for granted he had made a mistake."

"Then young Beresford is now?"

"At Gatehouse, Kent, unless I am much mistaken."

Mr. Carter looked at him curiously.

"I rather wonder you're not there too, Peel Edgerton?"

"Ah, I'm busy on a case."

"I thought you were on your holiday?"

"Oh, I've not been briefed. Perhaps it would be more correct to say I'm preparing a case. Any more facts about that American chap for me?"

"I'm afraid not. Is it important to find out who he was?"

"Oh, I know who he was," said Sir James easily. "I can't prove it yet—but I know."

The other two asked no questions. They had an instinct that it would be mere waste of breath.

"But what I don't understand," said the Prime Minister suddenly, "is how that photograph came to be in Mr. Hersheimmer's drawer?"

"Perhaps it never left it," suggested the lawyer gently.

"But the bogus inspector? Inspector Brown?"

"Ah!" said Sir James thoughtfully. He rose to his feet. "I mustn't keep you. Go on with the affairs of the nation. I must get back to—my case."

Two days later Julius Hersheimmer returned from Manchester. A note from Tommy lay on his table:

"Dear Hersheimmer,
"Sorry I lost my temper. In case I don't see you again, good-bye. I've been offered a job in the Argentine, and might as well take it.

"Yours,
"Tommy Beresford."

A peculiar smile lingered for a moment on Julius's face. He threw the letter into the waste-paper basket.

"The darned fool!" he murmured.

CHAPTER XXIII
A Race Against Time

After ringing up Sir James, Tommy's next procedure was to make a call at South Audley Mansions. He found Albert discharging his professional duties, and introduced himself without more ado as a friend of Tuppence's. Albert unbent immediately.

"Things has been very quiet here lately," he said wistfully. "Hope the young lady's keeping well, sir?"

"That's just the point, Albert. She's disappeared."

"You don't mean as the crooks have got her?"

"They have."

"In the Underworld?"

"No, dash it all, in this world!"

"It's a h'expression, sir," explained Albert. "At the pictures the crooks always have a restoorant in the Underworld. But do you think as they've done her in, sir?"

"I hope not. By the way, have you by any chance an aunt, a cousin, a grandmother, or any other suitable female relation who might be represented as being likely to kick the bucket?"

A delighted grin spread slowly over Albert's countenance.

"I'm on, sir. My poor aunt what lives in the country has been mortal bad for a long time, and she's asking for me with her dying breath."

Tommy nodded approval.

"Can you report this in the proper quarter and meet me at Charing Cross in an hour's time?"

"I'll be there, sir. You can count on me."

As Tommy had judged, the faithful Albert proved an invaluable ally. The two took up their quarters at the inn in Gatehouse. To Albert fell the task of collecting information. There was no difficulty about it.

Astley Priors was the property of a Dr. Adams. The doctor no longer practised, had retired, the landlord believed, but he took a few private patients—here the good fellow tapped his forehead knowingly—"balmy ones! You understand!" The doctor was a popular figure in the village, subscribed freely to all the local sports—"a very pleasant, affable gentleman." Been there long? Oh, a matter of ten years or so—might be longer. Scientific gentleman, he was. Professors and people often came down from town to see him. Anyway, it was a gay house, always visitors.

In the face of all this volubility, Tommy felt doubts. Was it possible that this genial, well-known figure could be in reality a dangerous criminal? His life seemed so open and above-board. No hint of sinister doings. Suppose it was all a gigantic mistake? Tommy felt a cold chill at the thought.

Then he remembered the private patients— "balmy ones." He inquired carefully if there was a young lady amongst them, describing Tuppence. But nothing much seemed to be known about the patients—they were seldom seen outside the grounds. A guarded description of Annette also failed to provoke recognition.

Astley Priors was a pleasant red-brick edifice, surrounded by well-wooded grounds which effectually shielded the house from observation from the road.

On the first evening Tommy, accompanied by Albert, explored the grounds. Owing to Albert's insistence they dragged themselves along painfully on their stomachs, thereby producing a great deal more noise than if they had stood upright. In any case, these precautions were totally unnecessary. The grounds, like those of any other private house after nightfall, seemed untenanted. Tommy had imagined a possible fierce watchdog. Albert's fancy ran to a puma, or a tame cobra. But they reached a shrubbery near the house quite unmolested.

The blinds of the dining-room window were up. There was a large company assembled round the table. The port was passing from hand to hand. It seemed a normal, pleasant company. Through the open window scraps of conversation floated out disjointedly on the night air. It was a heated discussion on county cricket!

Again Tommy felt that cold chill of uncertainty. It seemed impossible to believe that these people were other than they seemed. Had he been fooled once more? The fair-bearded, spectacled gentleman who sat at the head of the table looked singularly honest and normal.

Tommy slept badly that night. The following morning the indefatigable Albert, having cemented an alliance with the greengrocer's boy, took the latter's place and ingratiated himself with the cook at Malthouse. He returned with the information that she was undoubtedly "one of the crooks," but Tommy mistrusted the vividness of his imagination. Questioned, he could adduce nothing in support of his statement except his own opinion that she wasn't the usual kind. You could see that at a glance.

The substitution being repeated (much to the pecuniary advantage of the real greengrocer's boy) on the following day, Albert brought back the first piece of hopeful news. There *was* a French young lady staying in the house. Tommy put his doubts aside. Here was confirmation of his theory. But time pressed. Today was the 27th. The 29th was the much-talked-of "Labour Day," about which all sorts of rumours were running riot. Newspapers were getting agitated. Sensational hints of a Labour *coup d'état* were freely reported. The Government said nothing. It knew and was prepared. There were rumours of dissension among the Labour leaders. They were not of one mind. The more far-seeing among them realized that what they proposed might well be a death-blow to the England that at heart they loved. They shrank from the starvation and misery a general strike would entail, and were willing to meet the Government half-way. But behind them were subtle, insistent forces at work, urging the memories of old wrongs, deprecating the weakness of half-and-half measures, fomenting misunderstandings.

Tommy felt that, thanks to Mr. Carter, he understood the position fairly accurately. With the fatal document in the hands of Mr. Brown, public opinion would swing to the side of the Labour extremists and revolutionists. Failing that, the battle was an even chance. The Government with a loyal army and police force behind them might win—but at a cost of great suffering. But Tommy nourished another and a preposterous dream. With Mr. Brown unmasked and captured he believed, rightly or wrongly, that the whole organization would crumble ignominiously and instantaneously. The strange permeating influence of the unseen chief held it together. Without him, Tommy believed an instant panic would set in; and, the honest men left to themselves, an eleventh-hour reconciliation would be possible.

"This is a one-man show," said Tommy to himself. "The thing to do is to get hold of the man."

It was partly in furtherance of this ambitious design that he had requested Mr. Carter not to open the sealed envelope. The draft treaty was Tommy's bait. Every now and then he was aghast at his own presumption. How dared he think that he had discovered what so many wiser and clever men had overlooked? Nevertheless, he stuck tenaciously to his idea.

That evening he and Albert once more penetrated the grounds of Astley Priors. Tommy's ambition was somehow or other to gain admission to the house itself. As they approached cautiously, Tommy gave a sudden gasp.

On the second floor window some one standing between the window and the light in the room threw a silhouette on the blind. It was one Tommy would have recognized anywhere! Tuppence was in that house!

He clutched Albert by the shoulder.

"Stay here! When I begin to sing, watch that window."

He retreated hastily to a position on the main drive, and began in a deep roar, coupled with an unsteady gait, the following ditty:

I am a Soldier
A jolly British Soldier;
You can see that I'm a Soldier by my feet . . .

It had been a favourite on the gramophone in Tuppence's hospital days. He did not doubt but that she would recognize it and draw her own conclusions. Tommy had not a note of music in his voice, but his lungs were excellent. The noise he produced was terrific.

Presently an unimpeachable butler, accompanied by an equally unimpeachable footman, issued from the front door. The butler remonstrated with him. Tommy continued to sing, addressing the butler affectionately as "dear old whiskers." The footman took him by one arm, the butler by the other. They ran him down the drive, and neatly out of the gate. The butler threatened him with the police if he intruded again. It was beautifully done—soberly and with perfect decorum. Anyone would have sworn that the butler was a real butler, the footman a real footman—only, as it happened, the butler was Whittington!

Tommy retired to the inn and waited for Albert's return. At last that worthy made his appearance.

"Well?" cried Tommy eagerly.

"It's all right. While they was a-running of you out the window opened, and something was chucked out." He handed a scrap of paper to Tommy. "It was wrapped round a letter-weight."

On the paper were scrawled three words: "Tomorrow—same time."

"Good egg!" cried Tommy. "We're getting going."

"I wrote a message on a piece of paper, wrapped it round a stone, and chucked it through the window," continued Albert breathlessly.

Tommy groaned.

"Your zeal will be the undoing of us, Albert. What did you say?"

"Said we was a-staying at the inn. If she could get away, to come there and croak like a frog."

"She'll know that's you," said Tommy with a sigh of relief. "Your imagination runs away with you, you know, Albert. Why, you wouldn't recognize a frog croaking if you heard it."

Albert looked rather crest-fallen.

"Cheer up," said Tommy. "No harm done. That butler's an old friend of mine—I bet he knew who I was, though he didn't let on. It's not their game to show suspicion. That's why we've found it fairly plain sailing. They don't want to discourage me altogether. On the other hand, they don't want to make it too easy. I'm a pawn in their game, Albert, that's what I am. You see, if the spider lets the fly walk out too easily, the fly might suspect it was a put-up job. Hence the usefulness of that promising youth, Mr. T. Beresford, who's blundered in just at the right moment for them. But later, Mr. T. Beresford had better look out!"

Tommy retired for the night in a state of some elation. He had elaborated a careful plan for the following evening. He felt sure that the inhabitants of Astley Priors would not interfere with him up to a certain point. It was after that that Tommy proposed to give them a surprise.

About twelve o'clock, however, his calm was rudely shaken. He was told that some one was demanding him in the bar. The applicant proved to be a rude-looking carter well coated with mud.

"Well, my good fellow, what is it?" asked Tommy.

"Might this be for you, sir?" The carter held out a very dirty folded note, on the outside of which was written: "Take this to the gentleman at the inn near Astley Priors. He will give you ten shillings."

The handwriting was Tuppence's. Tommy appreciated her quick-wittedness in realizing that he might be staying at the inn under an assumed name. He snatched at it.

"That's all right."

The man withheld it.

"What about my ten shillings?"

Tommy hastily produced a ten-shilling note, and the man relinquished his find. Tommy unfastened it.

"Dear Tommy,

"I knew it was you last night. Don't go this evening. They'll be lying in wait for you. They're taking us away this morning. I heard something about Wales—Holyhead, I think. I'll drop this on the road if I get a chance. Annette told me how you'd escaped. Buck up.

"Yours,
"Twopence."

Tommy raised a shout for Albert before he had even finished perusing this characteristic epistle.

"Pack my bag! We're off!"

"Yes, sir." The boots of Albert could be heard racing upstairs.

Holyhead? Did that mean that, after all—— Tommy was puzzled. He read on slowly.

The boots of Albert continued to be active on the floor above.

Suddenly a second shout came from below.

"Albert! I'm a damned fool! Unpack that bag!"

"Yes, sir."

Tommy smoothed out the note thoughtfully.

"Yes, a damned fool," he said softly. "But so's some one else! And at last I know who it is!"

CHAPTER XXIV
Julius Takes a Hand

In his suite at Claridge's, Kramenin reclined on a couch and dictated to his secretary in sibilant Russian.

Presently the telephone at the secretary's elbow purred, and he took up the receiver, spoke for a minute or two, then turned to his employer.

"Some one below is asking for you."

"Who is it?"

"He gives the name of Mr. Julius P. Hersheimmer."

"Hersheimmer," repeated Kramenin thoughtfully. "I have heard that name before."

"His father was one of the steel kings of America," explained the secretary, whose business it was to know everything. "This young man must be a millionaire several times over."

The other's eyes narrowed appreciatively.

"You had better go down and see him, Ivan. Find out what he wants."

The secretary obeyed, closing the door noiselessly behind him. In a few minutes he returned.

"He declines to state his business—says it is entirely private and personal, and that he must see you."

"A millionaire several times over," murmured Kramenin. "Bring him up, my dear Ivan."

The secretary left the room once more, and returned escorting Julius.

"Monsieur Kramenin?" said the latter abruptly.

The Russian, studying him attentively with his pale venomous eyes, bowed.

"Pleased to meet you," said the American. "I've got some very important business I'd like to talk over with you, if I can see you alone." He looked pointedly at the other.

"My secretary, Monsieur Grieber, from whom I have no secrets."

"That may be so—but I have," said Julius dryly. "So I'd be obliged if you'd tell him to scoot."

"Ivan," said the Russian softly, "perhaps you would not mind retiring into the next room——"

"The next room won't do," interrupted Julius. "I know these ducal suites—and I want this one plumb empty except for you and me. Send him round to a store to buy a penn'orth of peanuts."

Though not particularly enjoying the American's free and easy manner of speech, Kramenin was devoured by curiosity. "Will your business take long to state?"

"Might be an all-night job if you caught on."

"Very good, Ivan. I shall not require you again this evening. Go to the theatre—take a night off."

"Thank you, your excellency."

The secretary bowed and departed.

Julius stood at the door watching his retreat. Finally, with a satisfied sigh, he closed it, and came back to his position in the centre of the room.

"Now, Mr. Hersheimmer, perhaps you will be so kind as to come to the point?"

"I guess that won't take a minute," drawled Julius. Then, with an abrupt change of manner: "Hands up—or I shoot!"

For a moment Kramenin stared blindly into the big automatic, then, with almost comical haste, he flung up his hands above his head. In that instant Julius had taken his measure. The man he had to deal with was an abject physical coward—the rest would be easy.

"This is an outrage," cried the Russian in a high hysterical voice. "An outrage! Do you mean to kill me?"

"Not if you keep your voice down. Don't go edging sideways towards that bell. That's better."

"What do you want? Do nothing rashly. Remember my life is of the utmost value to my country. I may have been maligned——"

"I reckon," said Julius, "that the man who let daylight into you would be doing humanity a good turn. But you needn't worry any. I'm not proposing to kill you this trip—that is, if you're reasonable."

The Russian quailed before the stern menace in the other's eyes. He passed his tongue over his dry lips.

"What do you want? Money?"

"No. I want Jane Finn."

"Jane Finn? I—never heard of her!"

"You're a darned liar! You know perfectly who I mean."

"I tell you I've never heard of the girl."

"And I tell you," retorted Julius, "that Little Willie here is just hopping mad to go off!"

The Russian wilted visibly.

"You wouldn't dare——"

"Oh, yes, I would, son!"

Kramenin must have recognized something in the voice that carried conviction, for he said sullenly:

"Well? Granted I do know who you mean—what of it?"

"You will tell me now—right here—where she is to be found."

Kramenin shook his head.

"I daren't."

"Why not?"

"I daren't. You ask an impossibility."

"Afraid, eh? Of whom? Mr. Brown? Ah, that tickles you up! There is such a person, then? I doubted it. And the mere mention of him scares you stiff!"

"I have seen him," said the Russian slowly. "Spoken to him face to face. I did not know it until afterwards. He was one of a crowd. I should not know him again. Who is he really? I do not know. But I know this—he is a man to fear."

"He'll never know," said Julius.

"He knows everything—and his vengeance is swift. Even I—Kramenin!—would not be exempt!"

"Then you won't do as I ask you?"

"You ask an impossibility."

"Sure that's a pity for you," said Julius cheerfully. "But the world in general will benefit." He raised the revolver.

"Stop," shrieked the Russian. "You cannot mean to shoot me?"

"Of course I do. I've always heard you Revolutionists held life cheap, but it seems there's a difference when it's your own life in question. I gave you just one chance of saving your dirty skin, and that you wouldn't take!"

"They would kill me!"

"Well," said Julius pleasantly, "it's up to you. But I'll just say this. Little Willie here is a dead cert, and if I was you I'd take a sporting chance with Mr. Brown!"

"You will hang if you shoot me," muttered the Russian irresolutely.

"No, stranger, that's where you're wrong. You forget the dollars. A big crowd of solicitors will get busy, and they'll get some high-brow doctors on the job, and the end of it all will be that they'll say my brain was unhinged. I shall spend a few months in a quiet sanatorium, my mental health will improve, the doctors will declare me sane again, and all will end happily for little Julius. I guess I can bear a few months' retirement in order to rid the world of you, but don't you kid yourself I'll hang for it!"

The Russian believed him. Corrupt himself, he believed implicitly in the power of money. He had read of American murder trials running much on the lines indicated by Julius. He had bought and sold justice himself. This virile young American, with the significant drawling voice, had the whip hand of him.

"I'm going to count five," continued Julius, "and I guess, if you let me get past four, you needn't worry any about Mr. Brown. Maybe he'll send some flowers to the funeral, but *you* won't

smell them! Are you ready? I'll begin. One—two—three—four——"

The Russian interrupted with a shriek:

"Do not shoot. I will do all you wish."

Julius lowered the revolver.

"I thought you'd hear sense. Where is the girl?"

"At Gatehouse, in Kent. Astley Priors, the place is called."

"Is she a prisoner there?"

"She's not allowed to leave the house—though it's safe enough really. The little fool has lost her memory, curse her!"

"That's been annoying for you and your friends, I reckon. What about the other girl, the one you decoyed away over a week ago?"

"She's there too," said the Russian sullenly.

"That's good," said Julius. "Isn't it all panning out beautifully? And a lovely night for the run!"

"What run?" demanded Kramenin, with a stare.

"Down to Gatehouse, sure. I hope you're fond of motoring?"

"What do you mean? I refuse to go."

"Now don't get mad. You must see I'm not such a kid as to leave you here. You'd ring up your friends on that telephone first thing! Ah!" He observed the fall on the other's face. "You see, you'd got it all fixed. No, sir, you're coming along with me. This your bedroom next door here? Walk right in. Little Willie and I will come behind. Put on a thick coat, that's right. Fur lined? And you a Socialist! Now we're ready. We walk downstairs and out through the hall to where my car's waiting. And don't you forget I've got you covered every inch of the way. I can shoot just as well through my coat pocket. One word, or a glance even, at one of those liveried menials, and there'll sure be a strange face in the Sulphur and Brimstone Works!"

Together they descended the stairs, and passed out to the waiting car. The Russian was shaking with rage. The hotel servants surrounded them. A cry hovered on his lips, but at the last minute his nerve failed him. The American was a man of his word.

When they reached the car, Julius breathed a sigh of relief. The danger-zone was passed. Fear had successfully hypnotized the man by his side.

"Get in," he ordered. Then as he caught the other's sidelong glance, "No, the chauffeur won't help you any. Naval man. Was on a submarine in Russia when the Revolution broke out. A brother of his was murdered by your people. George!"

"Yes, sir?" The chauffeur turned his head.

"This gentleman is a Russian Bolshevik. We don't want to shoot him, but it may be necessary. You understand?"

"Perfectly, sir."

"I want to go to Gatehouse in Kent. Know the road at all?"

"Yes, sir, it will be about an hour and a half's run."

"Make it an hour. I'm in a hurry."

"I'll do my best, sir." The car shot forward through the traffic.

Julius ensconced himself comfortably by the side of his victim. He kept his hand in the pocket of his coat, but his manner was urbane to the last degree.

"There was a man I shot once in Arizona——" he began cheerfully.

At the end of the hour's run the unfortunate Kramenin was more dead than alive. In succession to the anecdote of the Arizona man, there had been a tough from 'Frisco, and an episode in the Rockies. Julius's narrative style, if not strictly accurate, was picturesque!

Slowing down, the chauffeur called over his shoulder that they were just coming into Gatehouse. Julius bade the Russian direct them. His plan was to drive straight up to the house. There Kramenin was to ask for the two girls. Julius explained to him that Little Willie would not be tolerant of failure. Kramenin, by this time, was as putty in the other's hands. The terrific pace they had come had still further unmanned him. He had given himself up for dead at every corner.

The car swept up the drive, and stopped before the porch. The chauffeur looked round for orders.

"Turn the car first, George. Then ring the bell, and get back to your place. Keep the engine going, and be ready to scoot like hell when I give the word."

"Very good, sir."

The front door was opened by the butler. Kramenin felt the muzzle of the revolver pressed against his ribs.

"Now," hissed Julius. "And be careful."

The Russian beckoned. His lips were white, and his voice was not very steady:

"It is I—Kramenin! Bring down the girl at once! There is no time to lose!"

Whittington had come down the steps. He uttered an exclamation of astonishment at seeing the other.

"You! What's up? Surely you know the plan——"

Kramenin interrupted him, using the words that have created many unnecessary panics:

"We have been betrayed! Plans must be abandoned. We must save our own skins. The girl! And at once! It's our only chance."

Whittington hesitated, but for hardly a moment.

"You have orders—from *him*?"

"Naturally! Should I be here otherwise? Hurry! There is no time to be lost. The other little fool had better come too."

Whittington turned and ran back into the house. The agonizing minutes went by. Then— two figures hastily huddled in cloaks appeared on the steps and were hustled into the car. The smaller of the two was inclined to resist and Whittington shoved her in unceremoniously. Julius leaned forward, and in doing so the light from the open door lit up his face. Another man on the steps behind Whittington gave a startled exclamation. Concealment was at an end.

"Get a move on, George," shouted Julius.

The chauffeur slipped in his clutch, and with a bound the car started.

The man on the steps uttered an oath. His hand went to his pocket. There was a flash and a report. The bullet just missed the taller girl by an inch.

"Get down, Jane," cried Julius. "Flat on the bottom of the car." He thrust her sharply forward, then standing up, he took careful aim and fired.

"Have you hit him?" cried Tuppence eagerly.

"Sure," replied Julius. "He isn't killed, though. Skunks like that take a lot of killing. Are you all right, Tuppence?"

"Of course I am. Where's Tommy? And who's this?" She indicated the shivering Kramenin.

"Tommy's making tracks for the Argentine. I guess he thought you'd turned up your toes. Steady through the gate, George! That's right. It'll take 'em at least five minutes to get busy after us. They'll use the telephone, I guess, so look out for snares ahead—and don't take the direct route. Who's this, did you say, Tuppence? Let me present Monsieur Kramenin. I persuaded him to come on the trip for his health."

The Russian remained mute, still livid with terror.

"But what made them let us go?" demanded Tuppence suspiciously.

"I reckon Monsieur Kramenin here asked them so prettily they just couldn't refuse!"

This was too much for the Russian. He burst out vehemently:

"Curse you—curse you! They know now that I betrayed them. My life won't be safe for an hour in this country."

"That's so," assented Julius. "I'd advise you to make tracks for Russia right away."

"Let me go, then," cried the other. "I have done what you asked. Why do you still keep me with you?"

"Not for the pleasure of your company. I guess you can get right off now if you want to. I thought you'd rather I tooled you back to London."

"You may never reach London," snarled the other. "Let me go here and now."

"Sure thing. Pull up, George. The gentleman's not making the return trip. If I ever come to Russia, Monsieur Kramenin, I shall expect a rousing welcome, and——"

But before Julius had finished his speech, and before the car had finally halted, the Russian had swung himself out and disappeared into the night.

"Just a mite impatient to leave us," commented Julius, as the car gathered way again. "And no idea of saying good-bye politely to the ladies. Say, Jane, you can get up on the seat now."

For the first time the girl spoke.

"How did you 'persuade' him?" she asked.

Julius tapped his revolver.

"Little Willie here takes the credit!"

"Splendid!" cried the girl. The colour surged into her face, her eyes looked admiringly at Julius.

"Annette and I didn't know what was going to happen to us," said Tuppence. "Old Whittington hurried us off. *We* thought it was lambs to the slaughter."

"Annette," said Julius. "Is that what you call her?"

His mind seemed to be trying to adjust itself to a new idea.

"It's her name," said Tuppence, opening her eyes very wide.

"Shucks!" retorted Julius. "She may think it's her name, because her memory's gone, poor kid. But it's the one real and original Jane Finn we've got here."

"What——?" cried Tuppence.

But she was interrupted. With an angry spurt, a bullet embedded itself in the upholstery of the car just behind her head.

"Down with you," cried Julius. "It's an ambush. These guys have got busy pretty quickly. Push her a bit, George."

The car fairly leapt forward. Three more shots rang out, but went happily wide. Julius, upright, leant over the back of the car.

"Nothing to shoot at," he announced gloomily. "But I guess there'll be another little picnic soon. Ah!"

He raised his hand to his cheek.

"You are hurt?" said Annette quickly.

"Only a scratch."

The girl sprang to her feet.

"Let me out! Let me out, I say! Stop the car. It is me they're after. I'm the one they want. You shall not lose your lives because of me. Let me go." She was fumbling with the fastenings of the door.

Julius took her by both arms, and looked at her. She had spoken with no trace of foreign accent.

"Sit down, kid," he said gently. "I guess there's nothing wrong with your memory. Been fooling them all the time, eh?"

The girl looked at him, nodded, and then suddenly burst into tears. Julius patted her on the shoulder.

"There, there—just you sit tight. We're not going to let you quit."

Through her sobs the girl said indistinctly:

"You're from home. I can tell by your voice. It makes me home-sick."

"Sure I'm from home. I'm your cousin—Julius Hersheimmer. I came over to Europe on purpose to find you—and a pretty dance you've led me."

The car slackened speed. George spoke over his shoulder:

"Cross-roads here, sir. I'm not sure of the way."

The car slowed down till it hardly moved. As it did so a figure climbed suddenly over the back, and plunged head first into the midst of them.

"Sorry," said Tommy, extricating himself.

A mass of confused exclamations greeted him. He replied to them severally:

"Was in the bushes by the drive. Hung on behind. Couldn't let you know before at the pace you were going. It was all I could do to hang on. Now then, you girls, get out!"

"Get out?"

"Yes. There's a station just up that road. Train due in three minutes. You'll catch it if you hurry."

"What the devil are you driving at?" demanded Julius. "Do you think you can fool them by leaving the car?"

"You and I aren't going to leave the car. Only the girls."

"You're crazed, Beresford. Stark staring mad! You can't let those girls go off alone. It'll be the end of it if you do."

Tommy turned to Tuppence.

"Get out at once, Tuppence. Take her with you, and do just as I say. No one will do you any harm. You're safe. Take the train to London. Go straight to Sir James Peel Edgerton. Mr. Carter lives out of town, but you'll be safe with him."

"Darn you!" cried Julius. "You're mad. Jane, you stay where you are."

With a sudden swift movement, Tommy snatched the revolver from Julius's hand, and levelled it at him.

"Now will you believe I'm in earnest? Get out, both of you, and do as I say—or I'll shoot!"

Tuppence sprang out, dragging the unwilling Jane after her.

"Come on, it's all right. If Tommy's sure—he's sure. Be quick. We'll miss the train."

They started running.

Julius's pent-up rage burst forth.

"What the hell——"

Tommy interrupted him.

"Dry up! I want a few words with you, Mr. Julius Hersheimmer."

CHAPTER XXV
Jane's Story

Her arm through Jane's, dragging her along, Tuppence reached the station. Her quick ears caught the sound of the approaching train.

"Hurry up," she panted, "or we'll miss it."

They arrived on the platform just as the train came to a standstill. Tuppence opened the door of an empty first-class compartment, and the two girls sank down breathless on the padded seats.

A man looked in, then passed on to the next carriage. Jane started nervously. Her eyes dilated with terror. She looked questioningly at Tuppence.

"Is he one of them, do you think?" she breathed.

Tuppence shook her head.

"No, no. It's all right." She took Jane's hand in hers. "Tommy wouldn't have told us to do this unless he was sure we'd be all right."

"But he doesn't know them as I do!" The girl shivered. "You can't understand. Five years! Five long years! Sometimes I thought I should go mad."

"Never mind. It's all over."

"Is it?"

The train was moving now, speeding through the night at a gradually increasing rate. Suddenly Jane Finn started up.

"What was that? I thought I saw a face—looking in through the window."

"No, there's nothing. See." Tuppence went to the window, and lifting the strap let the pane down.

"You're sure?"

"Quite sure."

The other seemed to feel some excuse was necessary:

"I guess I'm acting like a frightened rabbit, but I can't help it. If they caught me now they'd——" Her eyes opened wide and staring.

"*Don't!*" implored Tuppence. "Lie back, and *don't think*. You can be quite sure that Tommy wouldn't have said it was safe if it wasn't."

"My cousin didn't think so. He didn't want us to do this."

"No," said Tuppence, rather embarrassed.

"What are you thinking of?" said Jane sharply.

"Why?"

"Your voice was so—queer!"

"I *was* thinking of something," confessed Tuppence. "But I don't want to tell you—not now. I may be wrong, but I don't think so. It's just an idea that came into my head a long time ago. Tommy's got it too—I'm almost sure he has. But don't *you* worry—there'll be time enough for that later. And it mayn't be so at all! Do what I tell you—lie back and don't think of anything."

"I'll try." The long lashes drooped over the hazel eyes.

Tuppence, for her part, sat bolt upright—much in the attitude of a watchful terrier on guard. In spite of herself she was nervous. Her eyes flashed continually from one window to the other. She noted the exact position of the communication cord. What it was that she feared, she would have been hard put to it to say. But in her own mind she was far from feeling the confidence displayed in her words. Not that she disbelieved in Tommy, but occasionally she was shaken with doubts as to whether anyone so simple and honest as he was could ever be a match for the fiendish subtlety of the arch-criminal.

If they once reached Sir James Peel Edgerton in safety, all would be well. But would they reach him? Would not the silent forces of Mr. Brown already be assembling against them? Even that last picture of Tommy, revolver in hand, failed to comfort her. By now he might be overpowered, borne down by sheer force of numbers. . . . Tuppence mapped out her plan of campaign.

As the train at length drew slowly into Charing Cross, Jane Finn sat up with a start.

"Have we arrived? I never thought we should!"

"Oh, I thought we'd get to London all right. If there's going to be any fun, now is when it will begin. Quick, get out. We'll nip into a taxi."

In another minute they were passing the barrier, had paid the necessary fares, and were stepping into a taxi.

"King's Cross," directed Tuppence. Then she gave a jump. A man looked in at the window, just as they started. She was almost certain it was the same man who had got into the carriage next to them. She had a horrible feeling of being slowly hemmed in on every side.

"You see," she explained to Jane, "if they think we're going to Sir James, this will put them off the scent. Now they'll imagine we're going to Mr. Carter. His country place is north of London somewhere."

Crossing Holborn there was a block, and the taxi was held up. This was what Tuppence had been waiting for.

"Quick," she whispered. "Open the right-hand door!"

The two girls stepped out into the traffic. Two minutes later they were seated in another taxi and were retracing their steps, this time direct to Carlton House Terrace.

"There," said Tuppence, with great satisfaction, "this ought to do them. I can't help thinking that I'm really rather clever! How that other taxi man will swear! But I took his number, and I'll send him a postal order tomorrow, so that he won't lose by it if he happens to be genuine. What's this thing swerving—— Oh!"

There was a grinding noise and a bump. Another taxi had collided with them.

In a flash Tuppence was out on the pavement. A policeman was approaching. Before he arrived Tuppence had handed the driver five shillings, and she and Jane had merged themselves in the crowd.

"It's only a step or two now," said Tuppence breathlessly. The accident had taken place in Trafalgar Square.

"Do you think the collision was an accident, or done deliberately?"

"I don't know. It might have been either."

Hand-in-hand, the two girls hurried along.

"It may be my fancy," said Tuppence suddenly, "but I feel as though there was some one behind us."

"Hurry!" murmured the other. "Oh, hurry!"

They were now at the corner of Carlton House Terrace, and their spirits lightened. Suddenly a large and apparently intoxicated man barred their way.

"Good evening, ladies," he hiccupped. "Whither away so fast?"

"Let us pass, please," said Tuppence imperiously.

"Just a word with your pretty friend here." He stretched out an unsteady hand, and clutched Jane by the shoulder. Tuppence heard other footsteps behind. She did not pause to ascertain whether they were friends or foes. Lowering her head, she repeated a manœuvre of childish days, and butted their aggressor full in the capacious middle. The success of these unsportsman-like tactics was immediate. The man sat down abruptly on the pavement. Tuppence and Jane took to their heels. The house they sought was some way down. Other footsteps echoed behind them. Their breath was coming in choking gasps as they reached Sir James's door. Tuppence seized the bell and Jane the knocker.

The man who had stopped them reached the foot of the steps. For a moment he hesitated, and as he did so the door opened. They fell into the hall together. Sir James came forward from the library door.

"Hullo! What's this?"

He stepped forward, and put his arm round Jane as she swayed uncertainly. He half carried her into the library, and laid her on the leather couch. From a tantalus on the table he poured out a few drops of brandy, and forced her to drink them. With a sigh she sat up, her eyes still wild and frightened.

"It's all right. Don't be afraid, my child. You're quite safe."

Her breath came more normally, and the colour was returning to her cheeks. Sir James looked at Tuppence quizzically.

"So you're not dead, Miss Tuppence, any more than that Tommy boy of yours was!"

"The Young Adventurers take a lot of killing," boasted Tuppence.

"So it seems," said Sir James dryly. "Am I right in thinking that the joint venture has ended in success, and that this"—he turned to the girl on the couch—"is Miss Jane Finn?"

Jane sat up.

"Yes," she said quietly, "I am Jane Finn. I have a lot to tell you."

"When you are stronger——"

"No—now!" Her voice rose a little. "I shall feel safer when I have told everything."

"As you please," said the lawyer.

He sat down in one of the big arm-chairs facing the couch. In a low voice Jane began her story.

"I came over on the *Lusitania* to take up a post in Paris. I was fearfully keen about the war, and just dying to help somehow or other. I had been studying French, and my teacher said they were wanting help in a hospital in Paris, so I wrote and offered my services, and they were accepted. I hadn't got any folk of my own, so it made it easy to arrange things.

"When the *Lusitania* was torpedoed, a man came up to me. I'd noticed him more than once—and I'd figured it out in my own mind that he was afraid of somebody or something. He asked me if I was a patriotic American, and told me he was carrying papers which were just life or death to the Allies. He asked me to take charge of them. I was to watch for an advertisement in the *Times*. If it didn't appear, I was to take them to the American Ambassador.

"Most of what followed seems like a nightmare still. I see it in my dreams sometimes. . . . I'll hurry over that part. Mr. Danvers had told me to watch out. He might have been shadowed from New York, but he didn't think so. At first I had no suspicions, but on the boat to Holyhead I began to get uneasy. There was one woman who had been very keen to look after me, and chum up with me generally—a Mrs. Vandemeyer. At first I'd been only grateful to her for being so kind to me; but all the time I felt there was something about her I didn't like, and on the Irish boat I saw her talking to some queer-looking men, and from the way they looked I saw that they were talking about me. I remembered that she'd been quite near me on the *Lusitania* when Mr. Danvers gave me the packet, and before that she'd tried to talk to him once or twice. I began to get scared, but I didn't quite see what to do.

"I had a wild idea of stopping at Holyhead, and not going on to London that day, but I soon saw that that would be plumb foolishness. The only thing was to act as though I'd noticed nothing, and hope for the best. I couldn't see how they could get me if I was on my guard. One thing I'd done already as a precaution—ripped open the oilskin packet and substituted blank paper, and then sewn it up again. So, if anyone did manage to rob me of it, it wouldn't matter.

"What to do with the real thing worried me no end. Finally I opened it out flat—there were only two sheets—and laid it between two of the advertisement pages of a magazine. I stuck the two pages together round the edge with some gum off an envelope. I carried the magazine carelessly stuffed into the pocket of my ulster.

"At Holyhead I tried to get into a carriage with people that looked all right, but in a queer way there seemed always to be a crowd round me shoving and pushing me just the way I didn't want to go. There was something uncanny and frightening about it. In the end I found myself in a carriage with Mrs. Vandemeyer after all. I went out into the corridor, but all the other carriages were full, so I had to go back and sit down. I consoled myself with the thought that there were other people in the carriage—there was quite a nice-looking man and his wife sitting just opposite. So I felt almost happy about it until just outside London. I had leaned back and closed my eyes. I guess they thought I was asleep, but my eyes weren't quite shut, and suddenly I saw the nice-looking man get something out of his bag and hand it to Mrs. Vandemeyer, and as he did so he *winked*. . . .

"I can't tell you how that wink sort of froze me through and through. My only thought was to get out in the corridor as quick as ever I could. I got up, trying to look natural and easy. Perhaps they saw something—I don't know—but suddenly Mrs. Vandemeyer said 'Now,' and flung something over my nose and mouth as I tried to scream. At the same moment I felt a terrific blow on the back of my head. . . ."

She shuddered. Sir James murmured something sympathetically. In a minute she resumed:

"I don't know how long it was before I came back to consciousness. I felt very ill and sick. I was lying on a dirty bed. There was a screen round it, but I could hear two people talking in the room. Mrs. Vandemeyer was one of them. I tried to listen, but at first I couldn't take much in. When at last I did begin to grasp what was going on—I was just terrified! I wonder I didn't scream right out there and then.

"They hadn't found the papers. They'd got

the oilskin packet with the blanks, and they were just mad! They didn't know whether *I*'d changed the papers, or whether Danvers had been carrying a dummy message, while the real one was sent another way. They spoke of"—she closed her eyes—"torturing me to find out!

"I'd never known what fear—really sickening fear—was before! Once they came to look at me. I shut my eyes and pretended to be still unconscious, but I was afraid they'd hear the beating of my heart. However, they went away again. I began thinking madly. What could I do? I knew I wouldn't be able to stand up against torture very long.

"Suddenly something put the thought of loss of memory into my head. The subject had always interested me, and I'd read an awful lot about it. I had the whole thing at my finger-tips. If only I could succeed in carrying the bluff through, it might save me. I said a prayer, and drew a long breath. Then I opened my eyes and started babbling in *French!*

"Mrs. Vandemeyer came round the screen at once. Her face was so wicked I nearly died, but I smiled up at her doubtfully, and asked her in French where I was.

"It puzzled her, I could see. She called the man she had been talking to. He stood by the screen with his face in shadow. He spoke to me in French. His voice was very ordinary and quiet, but somehow, I don't know why, he scared me worse than the woman. I felt he'd seen right through me, but I went on playing my part. I asked again where I was, and then went on that there was something I *must* remember—*must* remember—only for the moment it was all gone. I worked myself up to be more and more distressed. He asked me my name. I said I didn't know—that I couldn't remember anything at all.

"Suddenly he caught my wrist, and began twisting it. The pain was awful. I screamed. He went on. I screamed and screamed, but I managed to shriek out things in French. I don't know how long I could have gone on, but luckily I fainted. The last thing I heard was his voice saying: 'That's not bluff! Anyway, a kid of her age wouldn't know enough.' I guess he forgot American girls are older for their age than English ones, and take more interest in scientific subjects.

"When I came to, Mrs. Vandemeyer was sweet as honey to me. She'd had her orders, I guess. She spoke to me in French—told me I'd had a shock and been very ill. I should be better soon. I pretended to be rather dazed—murmured something about the 'doctor' having hurt my wrist. She looked relieved when I said that.

"By and by she went out of the room altogether. I was suspicious still, and lay quite quiet for some time. In the end, however, I got up and walked round the room, examining it. I thought that even if anyone *was* watching me from somewhere, it would seem natural enough under the circumstances. It was a squalid, dirty place. There were no windows, which seemed queer. I guessed the door would be locked, but I didn't try it. There were some battered old pictures on the walls, representing scenes from *Faust*."

Jane's two listeners gave a simultaneous "Ah!" The girl nodded.

"Yes—it was the place in Soho where Mr. Beresford was imprisoned. Of course, at the time I didn't even know if I was in London. One thing was worrying me dreadfully, but my heart gave a great throb of relief when I saw my ulster lying carelessly over the back of a chair. *And the magazine was still rolled up in the pocket!*

"If only I could be certain that I was not being overlooked! I looked carefully round the walls. There didn't seem to be a peep-hole of any kind—nevertheless I felt kind of sure there must be. All of a sudden I sat down on the edge of the table, and put my face in my hands, sobbing out a 'Mon Dieu! Mon Dieu!' I've got very sharp ears. I distinctly heard the rustle of a dress, and slight creak. That was enough for me. I was being watched!

"I lay down on the bed again, and by and by Mrs. Vandemeyer brought me some supper. She was still sweet as they make them. I guess she'd been told to win my confidence. Presently she produced the oilskin packet, and asked me if I recognized it, watching me like a lynx all the time.

"I took it and turned it over in a puzzled sort of way. Then I shook my head. I said that I felt I *ought* to remember something about it, that it was just as though it was all coming back, and then, before I could get hold of it, it went again. Then she told me that I was her niece, and that I was to call her 'Aunt Rita.' I did obediently, and she told me not to worry—my memory would soon come back.

"That was an awful night. I'd made my plan whilst I was waiting for her. The papers were safe so far, but I couldn't take the risk of leaving them there any longer. They might throw that magazine away any minute. I lay awake waiting until I judged it must be about two o'clock in the morning. Then I got up as softly as I could, and felt in the dark along the left-hand wall. Very gently, I unhooked one of the pictures from its nail—Marguerite with her casket of jewels. I crept over to my coat and took out the magazine, and an odd envelope or two that I had shoved in. Then I went to the washstand, and damped the brown paper at the back of the picture all round. Presently I was able to pull it away. I had already torn out the two stuck-together pages from the magazine, and now I slipped them with their precious enclosure between the picture and its brown paper backing. A little gum from the envelopes helped me to stick the latter up again. No one would dream the picture had ever been tampered with. I rehung it on the wall, put the magazine back in my coat pocket, and crept back to bed. I was pleased with my hiding-place. They'd never think of pulling to pieces one of their own pictures. I hoped that they'd come to the conclusion that Danvers had been carrying a dummy all along, and that, in the end, they'd let me go.

"As a matter of fact, I guess that's what they did think at first and, in a way, it was dangerous for me. I learnt afterwards that they nearly did away with me then and there—there was never much chance of their 'letting me go'—but the first man, who was the boss, preferred to keep me alive on the chance of my having hidden them, and being able to tell where if I recovered my memory. They watched me constantly for weeks. Sometimes they'd ask me questions by the hour—I guess there was nothing they didn't know about the third degree!—but somehow I managed to hold my own. The strain of it was awful, though . . .

"They took me back to Ireland, and over every step of the journey again, in case I'd hidden it somewhere *en route*. Mrs. Vandemeyer and another woman never left me for a moment. They spoke of me as a young relative of Mrs. Vandemeyer's whose mind was affected by the shock of the *Lusitania*. There was no one I could appeal to for help without giving myself away to *them*, and if I risked it and failed—and Mrs. Vandemeyer looked so rich, and so beautifully dressed, that I felt convinced they'd take her word against mine, and think it was part of my mental trouble to think myself 'persecuted'—I felt that the horrors in store for me would be too awful once they knew I'd been only shamming."

Sir James nodded comprehendingly.

"Mrs. Vandemeyer was a woman of great personality. With that and her social position she would have had little difficulty in imposing her point of view in preference to yours. Your sensational accusations against her would not easily have found credence."

"That's what I thought. It ended in my being sent to a sanatorium at Bournemouth. I couldn't make up my mind at first whether it was a sham affair or genuine. A hospital nurse had charge of me. I was a special patient. She seemed so nice and normal that at last I determined to confide in her. A merciful providence just saved me in time from falling into the trap. My door happened to be ajar, and I heard her talking to some one in the passage. *She was one of them!* They still fancied it might be a bluff on my part, and she was put in charge of me to make sure! After that, my nerve went completely. I dared trust nobody.

"I think I almost hypnotized myself. After a while, I almost forgot that I was really Jane Finn.

I was so bent on playing the part of Janet Vandemeyer that my nerves began to play me tricks. I became really ill—for months I sank into a sort of stupor. I felt sure I should die soon, and that nothing really mattered. A sane person shut up in a lunatic asylum often ends by becoming insane, they say. I guess I was like that. Playing my part had become second nature to me. I wasn't even unhappy in the end—just apathetic. Nothing seemed to matter. And the years went on.

"And then suddenly things seemed to change. Mrs. Vandemeyer came down from London. She and the doctor asked me questions, experimented with various treatments. There was some talk of sending me to a specialist in Paris. In the end, they did not dare risk it. I overheard something that seemed to show that other people—friends—were looking for me. I learnt later that the nurse who had looked after me went to Paris, and consulted a specialist, representing herself to be me. He put her through some searching tests, and exposed her loss of memory to be fraudulent; but she had taken a note of his methods and reproduced them on me. I dare say I couldn't have deceived the specialist for a minute—a man who has made a lifelong study of a thing is unique—but I managed once again to hold my own with them. The fact that I'd not thought of myself as Jane Finn for so long made it easier.

"One night I was whisked off to London at a moment's notice. They took me back to the house in Soho. Once I got away from the sanatorium I felt different—as though something in me that had been buried for a long time was waking up again.

"They sent me in to wait on Mr. Beresford. (Of course I didn't know his name then.) I was suspicious—I thought it was another trap. But he looked so honest, I could hardly believe it. However, I was careful in all I said, for I knew we could be overheard. There's a small hole, high up in the wall.

"But on the Sunday afternoon a message was brought to the house. They were all very disturbed. Without their knowing, I listened. Word had come that he was to be killed. I needn't tell the next part, because you know it. I thought I'd have time to rush up and get the papers from their hiding-place, but I was caught. So I screamed out that he was escaping, and I said I wanted to go back to Marguerite. I shouted the name three times very loud. I knew the others would think I meant Mrs. Vandemeyer, but I hoped it might make Mr. Beresford think of the picture. He'd unhooked one the first day—that's what made me hesitate to trust him."

She paused.

"Then the papers," said Sir James slowly, "are still at the back of the picture in that room."

"Yes." The girl had sunk back on the sofa exhausted with the strain of the long story.

Sir James rose to his feet. He looked at his watch.

"Come," he said, "we must go at once."

"Tonight?" queried Tuppence, surprised.

"Tomorrow may be too late," said Sir James gravely. "Besides, by going tonight we have the chance of capturing that great man and supercriminal—Mr. Brown!"

There was dead silence, and Sir James continued:

"You have been followed here—not a doubt of it. When we leave the house we shall be followed again, but not molested, *for it is Mr. Brown's plan that we are to lead him.* But the Soho house is under police supervision night and day. There are several men watching it. When we enter that house, Mr. Brown will not draw back—he will risk all, on the chance of obtaining the spark to fire his mine. And he fancies the risk not great—since he will enter in the guise of a friend!"

Tuppence flushed, then opened her mouth impulsively.

"But there's something you don't know—that we haven't told you." Her eyes dwelt on Jane in perplexity.

"What is that?" asked the other sharply. "No hesitations, Miss Tuppence. We need to be sure of our going."

But Tuppence, for once, seemed tongue-tied.

"It's so difficult—you see, if I'm wrong—oh, it would be dreadful." She made a grimace at the unconscious Jane. "Never forgive me," she observed cryptically.

"You want me to help you out, eh?"

"Yes, please. *You* know who Mr. Brown is, don't you?"

"Yes," said Sir James gravely. "At last I do."

"At last?" queried Tuppence doubtfully. "Oh, but I thought——" She paused.

"You thought correctly, Miss Tuppence. I have been morally certain of his identity for some time—ever since the night of Mrs. Vandemeyer's mysterious death."

"Ah!" breathed Tuppence.

"For there we are up against the logic of facts. There are only two solutions. Either the chloral was administered by her own hand, which theory I reject utterly, or else——"

"Yes?"

"Or else it was administered in the brandy you gave her. Only three people touched that brandy—you, Miss Tuppence, I myself, and one other—Mr. Julius Hersheimmer!"

Jane Finn stirred and sat up, regarding the speaker with wide astonished eyes.

"At first, the thing seemed utterly impossible. Mr. Hersheimmer, as the son of a prominent millionaire, was a well-known figure in America. It seemed utterly impossible that he and Mr. Brown could be one and the same. But you cannot escape from the logic of facts. Since the thing was so—it must be accepted. Remember Mrs. Vandemeyer's sudden and inexplicable agitation. Another proof, if proof was needed.

"I took an early opportunity of giving you a hint. From some words of Mr. Hersheimmer's at Manchester, I gathered that you had understood and acted on that hint. Then I set to work to prove the impossible possible. Mr. Beresford rang me up and told me, what I had already suspected, that the photograph of Miss Jane Finn had never really been out of Mr. Hersheimmer's possession——"

But the girl interrupted. Springing to her feet, she cried out angrily:

"What do you mean? What are you trying to suggest? That Mr. Brown is *Julius*? Julius—my own cousin!"

"No, Miss Finn," said Sir James unexpectedly. "Not your cousin. The man who calls himself Julius Hersheimmer is no relation to you whatsoever."

CHAPTER XXVI
Mr. Brown

Sir James's words came like a bomb-shell. Both girls looked equally puzzled. The lawyer went across to his desk, and returned with a small newspaper cutting, which he handed to Jane. Tuppence read it over her shoulder. Mr. Carter would have recognized it. It referred to the mysterious man found dead in New York.

"As I was saying to Miss Tuppence," resumed the lawyer, "I set to work to prove the impossible possible. The great stumbling-block was the undeniable fact that Julius Hersheimmer was not an assumed name. When I came across this paragraph my problem was solved. Julius Hersheimmer set out to discover what had become of his cousin. He went out West, where he obtained news of her and her photograph to aid him in his search. On the eve of his departure from New York he was set upon and murdered. His body was dressed in shabby clothes, and the face disfigured to prevent identification. Mr. Brown took his place. He sailed immediately for England. None of the real Hersheimmer's friends or intimates saw him before he sailed—though indeed it would hardly have mattered if they had, the impersonation was so perfect. Since then he had been hand and glove with those sworn to hunt him down. Every secret of theirs has been known to him. Only once did he come near disaster. Mrs. Vandemeyer knew his secret. It was no part of his plan that that huge bribe should ever be offered to her. But for Miss Tuppence's fortunate change of plan, she would have been far away from the flat when we arrived there. Exposure stared him in the face. He took a desperate step, trusting in his assumed character to avert suspicion. He nearly succeeded—but not quite."

"I can't believe it," murmured Jane. "He seemed so splendid."

"The real Julius Hersheimmer *was* a splendid fellow! And Mr. Brown is a consummate actor. But ask Miss Tuppence if she also has not had her suspicions."

Jane turned mutely to Tuppence. The latter nodded.

"I didn't want to say it, Jane—I knew it would hurt you. And, after all, I couldn't be sure. I still don't understand why, if he's Mr. Brown, he rescued us."

"Was it Julius Hersheimmer who helped you to escape?"

Tuppence recounted to Sir James the exciting events of the evening, ending up: "But I can't see *why*!"

"Can't you? I can. So can young Beresford, by his actions. As a last hope Jane Finn was to be allowed to escape—and the escape must be managed so that she harbours no suspicions of its being a put-up job. They're not averse to young Beresford's being in the neighbourhood, and, if necessary, communicating with you. They'll take care to get him out of the way at the right minute. Then Julius Hersheimmer dashes up and rescues you in true melodramatic style. Bullets fly—but don't hit anybody. What would have happened next? You would have driven straight to the house in Soho and secured the document which Miss Finn would probably have entrusted to her cousin's keeping. Or, if he conducted the search, he would have pretended to find the hiding-place already rifled. He would have had a dozen ways of dealing with the situation, but the result would have been the same. And I rather fancy some accident would have happened to both of you. You see, you know rather an inconvenient amount. That's a rough outline. I admit I was caught napping; but somebody else wasn't."

"Tommy," said Tuppence softly.

"Yes. Evidently when the right moment came

to get rid of him—he was too sharp for them. All the same, I'm not too easy in my mind about him."

"Why?"

"Because Julius Hersheimmer is Mr. Brown," said Sir James dryly. "And it takes more than one man and a revolver to hold up Mr. Brown. . . ."

Tuppence paled a little.

"What can we do?"

"Nothing until we've been to the house in Soho. If Beresford has still got the upper hand, there's nothing to fear. If otherwise, our enemy will come to find us, and he will not find us unprepared!" From a drawer in the desk, he took a service revolver, and placed it in his coat pocket.

"Now we're ready. I know better than even to suggest going without you, Miss Tuppence——"

"I should think so indeed!"

"But I do suggest that Miss Finn should remain here. She will be perfectly safe, and I am afraid she is absolutely worn out with all she has been through."

But to Tuppence's surprise Jane shook her head.

"No. I guess I'm going too. Those papers were my trust. I must go through with this business to the end. I'm heaps better now anyway."

Sir James's car was ordered round. During the short drive Tuppence's heart beat tumultuously. In spite of momentary qualms of uneasiness respecting Tommy, she could not but feel exultation. They were going to win!

The car drew up at the corner of the square and they got out. Sir James went up to a plain-clothes man who was on duty with several others, and spoke to him. Then he rejoined the girls.

"No one has gone into the house so far. It is being watched at the back as well, so they are quite sure of that. Anyone who attempts to enter after we have done so will be arrested immediately. Shall we go in?"

A policeman produced a key. They all knew Sir James well. They had also had orders respecting Tuppence. Only the third member of the party was unknown to them. The three entered the house, pulling the door to behind them. Slowly they mounted the rickety stairs. At the top was the ragged curtain hiding the recess where Tommy had hidden that day. Tuppence had heard the story from Jane in her character of "Annette." She looked at the tattered velvet with interest. Even now she could almost swear it moved—as though *some one* was behind it. So strong was the illusion that she almost fancied she could make out the outline of a form. . . . Supposing Mr. Brown—Julius—was there waiting. . . .

Impossible of course! Yet she almost went back to put the curtain aside and make sure. . . .

Now they were entering the prison room. No place for any one to hide here, thought Tuppence, with a sigh of relief, then chided herself indignantly. She must not give way to this foolish fancying—this curious insistent feeling that *Mr. Brown was in the house*. . . . Hark! what was that? A stealthy footstep on the stairs? There *was* some one in the house! Absurd! She was becoming hysterical.

Jane had gone straight to the picture of Marguerite. She unhooked it with a steady hand. The dust lay thick upon it, and festoons of cobwebs lay between it and the wall. Sir James handed her a pocket-knife, and she ripped away the brown paper from the back. . . . The advertisement page of a magazine fell out. Jane picked it up. Holding apart the frayed inner edges she extracted two thin sheets covered with writing!

No dummy this time! The real thing!

"We've got it," said Tuppence. "At last. . . ."

The moment was almost breathless in its emotion. Forgotten the faint creakings, the imagined noises of a minute ago. None of them had eyes for anything but what Jane held in her hand.

Sir James took it, and scrutinized it attentively.

"Yes," he said quietly, "this is the ill-fated draft treaty!"

"We've succeeded," said Tuppence. There was awe and an almost wondering unbelief in her voice.

Sir James echoed her words as he folded the paper carefully and put it away in his pocketbook, then he looked curiously round the dingy room.

"It was here that our young friend was confined for so long, was it not?" he said. "A truly sinister room. You notice the absence of windows, and the thickness of the close-fitting door. Whatever took place here would never be heard by the outside world."

Tuppence shivered. His words woke a vague alarm in her. What if there *was* some one concealed in the house? Some one who might bar that door on them, and leave them to die like rats in a trap? Then she realized the absurdity of her thought. The house was surrounded by police who, if they failed to reappear, would not hesitate to break in and make a thorough search. She smiled at her own foolishness—then looked up with a start to find Sir James watching her. He gave her an emphatic little nod.

"Quite right, Miss Tuppence. You scent danger. So do I. So does Miss Finn."

"Yes," admitted Jane. "It's absurd—but I can't help it."

Sir James nodded again.

"You feel—as we all feel—*the presence of Mr. Brown.* Yes"—as Tuppence made a movement—"not a doubt of it—*Mr. Brown is here*. . . ."

"In this house?"

"In this room. . . . You don't understand? *I am Mr. Brown*. . . ."

Stupefied, unbelieving, they stared at him. The very lines of his face had changed. It was a different man who stood before them. He smiled a slow cruel smile.

"Neither of you will leave this room alive! You said just now we had succeeded. *I* have succeeded! The draft treaty is mine." His smile grew wider as he looked at Tuppence. "Shall I tell you how it will be? Sooner or later the police will break in, and they will find three victims of Mr. Brown—three, not two, you understand, but fortunately the third will not be dead, only wounded, and will be able to describe the attack with a wealth of detail! The treaty? It is in the hands of Mr. Brown. So no one will think of searching the pockets of Sir James Peel Edgerton!"

He turned to Jane.

"You outwitted me. I make my acknowledgments. But you will not do it again."

There was a faint sound behind him, but, intoxicated with success, he did not turn his head.

He slipped his hand into his pocket.

"Checkmate to the Young Adventurers," he said, and slowly raised the big automatic.

But, even as he did so, he felt himself seized from behind in a grip of iron. The revolver was wrenched from his hand, and the voice of Julius Hersheimmer said drawlingly:

"I guess you're caught redhanded with the goods upon you."

The blood rushed to the K.C.'s face, but his self-control was marvellous, as he looked from one to the other of his two captors. He looked longest at Tommy.

"You," he said beneath his breath. "*You!* I might have known."

Seeing that he was disposed to offer no resistance, their grip slackened. Quick as a flash his left hand, the hand which bore the big signet ring, was raised to his lips. . . .

"'*Ave, Cæsar! te morituri salutant,*' " he said, still looking at Tommy.

Then his face changed, and with a long convulsive shudder he fell forward in a crumpled heap, whilst an odour of bitter almonds filled the air.

CHAPTER XXVII
A Supper Party at the *Savoy*

The supper party given by Mr. Julius Hersheimmer to a few friends on the evening of the 30th will long be remembered in catering circles. It took place in a private room, and Mr. Hersheimmer's orders were brief and forcible. He gave carte blanche—and when a millionaire gives carte blanche he usually gets it!

Every delicacy out of season was duly provided. Waiters carried bottles of ancient and royal vintage with loving care. The floral decorations defied the seasons, and fruits of the earth as far apart as May and November found themselves miraculously side by side. The list of guests was small and select. The American Ambassador, Mr. Carter, who had taken the liberty, he said, of bringing an old friend, Sir William Beresford, with him, Archdeacon Cowley, Dr. Hall, those two youthful adventurers, Miss Prudence Cowley and Mr. Thomas Beresford, and last, but not least, as guest of honour, Miss Jane Finn.

Julius had spared no pains to make Jane's appearance a success. A mysterious knock had brought Tuppence to the door of the apartment she was sharing with the American girl. It was Julius. In his hand he held a cheque.

"Say, Tuppence," he began, "will you do me a good turn? Take this, and get Jane regularly togged up for this evening. You're all coming to supper with me at the *Savoy*. See? Spare no expense. You get me?"

"Sure thing," mimicked Tuppence. "We shall enjoy ourselves. It will be a pleasure dressing Jane. She's the loveliest thing I've ever seen."

"That's so," agreed Mr. Hersheimmer fervently.

His fervour brought a momentary twinkle to Tuppence's eye.

"By the way, Julius," she remarked demurely, "I—haven't given you my answer yet."

"Answer?" said Julius. His face paled.

"You know—when you asked me to—marry you," faltered Tuppence, her eyes downcast in the true manner of the early Victorian heroine, "and wouldn't take no for an answer. I've thought it well over——"

"Yes?" said Julius. The perspiration stood on his forehead.

Tuppence relented suddenly.

"You great idiot!" she said. "What on earth induced you to do it? I could see at the time you didn't care a twopenny dip for me!"

"Not at all. I had—and still have—the highest sentiments of esteem and respect—and admiration for you——"

"H'm!" said Tuppence. "Those are the kind of sentiments that very soon go to the wall when the other sentiment comes along! Don't they, old thing?"

"I don't know what you mean," said Julius stiffly, but a large and burning blush overspread his countenance.

"Shucks!" retorted Tuppence. She laughed, and closed the door, reopening it to add with dignity: "Morally, I shall always consider I have been jilted!"

"What was it?" asked Jane as Tuppence rejoined her.

"Julius."

"What did he want?"

"Really, I think, he wanted to see you, but I wasn't going to let him. Not until tonight, when you're going to burst upon every one like King Solomon in his glory! Come on! *We're going to shop!*"

To most people the 29th, the much-heralded "Labour Day," had passed much as any other day. Speeches were made in the Park and Trafalgar Square. Straggling processions, singing the *Red Flag*, wandered through the streets in a more or less aimless manner. Newspapers which had hinted at a general strike, and the inauguration of a reign of terror, were forced to hide their diminished heads. The bolder and more astute among them sought to prove that peace had been effected by following their counsels. In the Sunday papers a brief notice of the sudden death of Sir James Peel Edgerton, the famous K.C., had appeared. Monday's paper dealt appreciatively with the dead man's career. The exact manner of his sudden death was never made public.

Tommy had been right in his forecast of the situation. It had been a one-man show. Deprived of their chief, the organization fell to pieces. Kramenin had made a precipitate return to Russia, leaving England early on Sunday morning. The gang had fled from Astley Priors in a panic, leaving behind, in their haste, various damaging documents which compromised them hope-

lessly. With these proofs of conspiracy in their hands, aided further by a small brown diary taken from the pocket of the dead man which had contained a full and damning résumé of the whole plot, the Government had called an eleventh-hour conference. The Labour leaders were forced to recognize that they had been used as a cat's paw. Certain concessions were made by the Government, and were eagerly accepted. It was to be Peace, not War!

But the Cabinet knew by how narrow a margin they had escaped utter disaster. And burnt in on Mr. Carter's brain was the strange scene which had taken place in the house in Soho the night before.

He had entered the squalid room to find that great man, the friend of a lifetime, dead—betrayed out of his own mouth. From the dead man's pocket-book he had retrieved the ill-omened draft treaty, and then and there, in the presence of the other three, it had been reduced to ashes. . . . England was saved!

And now, on the evening of the 30th, in a private room at the *Savoy*, Mr. Julius P. Hersheimmer was receiving his guests.

Mr. Carter was the first to arrive. With him was a choleric-looking old gentleman, at sight of whom Tommy flushed up to the roots of his hair. He came forward.

"Ha!" said the old gentleman, surveying him apoplectically. "So you're my nephew, are you? Not much to look at—but you've done good work, it seems. Your mother must have brought you up well after all. Shall we let bygones be bygones, eh? You're my heir, you know; and in future I propose to make you an allowance—and you can look upon Chalmers Park as your home."

"Thank you, sir, it's awfully decent of you."

"Where's this young lady I've been hearing such a lot about?"

Tommy introduced Tuppence.

"Ha!" said Sir William, eyeing her. "Girls aren't what they used to be in my young days."

"Yes, they are," said Tuppence. "Their clothes are different, perhaps, but they themselves are just the same."

"Well, perhaps you're right. Minxes then—minxes now!"

"That's it," said Tuppence. "I'm a frightful minx myself."

"I believe you," said the old gentleman, chuckling, and pinched her ear in high good-humour. Most young women were terrified of the "old bear," as they termed him. Tuppence's pertness delighted the old misogynist.

Then came the timid archdeacon, a little bewildered by the company in which he found himself, glad that his daughter was considered to have distinguished herself, but unable to help glancing at her from time to time with nervous apprehension. But Tuppence behaved admirably. She forbore to cross her legs, set a guard upon her tongue, and steadfastly refused to smoke.

Dr. Hall came next, and he was followed by the American Ambassador.

"We might as well sit down," said Julius, when he had introduced all his guests to each other. "Tuppence, will you——"

He indicated the place of honour with a wave of his hand.

But Tuppence shook her head.

"No—that's Jane's place! When one thinks of how she's held out all these years, she ought to be made the queen of the feast tonight."

Julius flung her a grateful glance, and Jane came forward shyly to the allotted seat. Beautiful as she had seemed before, it was as nothing to the loveliness that now went fully adorned. Tuppence had performed her part faithfully. The model gown supplied by a famous dressmaker had been entitled "A tiger lily." It was all golds and reds and browns, and out of it rose the pure column of the girl's white throat, and the bronze masses of hair that crowned her lovely head. There was admiration in every eye, as she took her seat.

Soon the supper party was in full swing, and with one accord Tommy was called upon for a full and complete explanation.

"You've been too darned close about the whole business," Julius accused him. "You let on to me that you were off to the Argentine—

though I guess you had your reasons for that. The idea of both you and Tuppence casting me for the part of Mr. Brown just tickles me to death!"

"The idea was not original to them," said Mr. Carter gravely. "It was suggested, and the poison very carefully instilled, by a past-master in the art. The paragraph in the New York paper suggested the plan to him, and by means of it he wove a web that nearly enmeshed you fatally."

"I never liked him," said Julius. "I felt from the first that there was something wrong about him, and I always suspected that it was he who silenced Mrs. Vandemeyer so appositely. But it wasn't till I heard that the order for Tommy's execution came right on the heels of our interview with him that Sunday that I began to tumble to the fact that he was the big bug himself."

"I never suspected it at all," lamented Tuppence. "I've always thought I was so much cleverer than Tommy—but he's undoubtedly scored over me handsomely."

Julius agreed.

"Tommy's been the goods this trip! And, instead of sitting there as dumb as a fish, let him banish his blushes, and tell us all about it."

"Hear! hear!"

"There's nothing to tell," said Tommy, acutely uncomfortable. "I was an awful mug—right up to the time I found that photograph of Annette, and realized that she was Jane Finn. Then I remembered how persistently she had shouted out that word 'Marguerite'—and I thought of the pictures, and—well, that's that. Then of course I went over the whole thing to see where I'd made an ass of myself."

"Go on," said Mr. Carter, as Tommy showed signs of taking refuge in silence once more.

"That business about Mrs. Vandemeyer had worried me when Julius told me about it. On the face of it, it seemed that he or Sir James must have done the trick. But I didn't know which. Finding that photograph in the drawer, after that story of how it had been got from him by Inspector Brown, made me suspect Julius. Then I remembered that it was Sir James who had discovered the false Jane Finn. In the end, I couldn't make up my mind—and just decided to take no chances either way. I left a note for Julius, in case he was Mr. Brown, saying I was off to the Argentine, and I dropped Sir James's letter with the offer of the job by the desk so that he would see it was a genuine stunt. Then I wrote my letter to Mr. Carter and rang up Sir James. Taking him into my confidence would be the best thing either way, so I told him everything except where I believed the papers to be hidden. The way he helped me to get on the track of Tuppence and Annette almost disarmed me, but not quite. I kept my mind open between the two of them. And then I got a bogus note from Tuppence—and I knew!"

"But how?"

Tommy took the note in question from his pocket and passed it round the table.

"It's her handwriting all right, but I knew it wasn't from her because of the signature. She'd never spell her name 'Twopence,' but anyone who'd never seen it written might quite easily do so. Julius *had* seen it—he showed me a note of hers to him once—but *Sir James hadn't!* After that everything was plain sailing. I sent off Albert post-haste to Mr. Carter. I pretended to go away, but doubled back again. When Julius came bursting up in his car, I felt it wasn't part of Mr. Brown's plan—and that there would probably be trouble. Unless Sir James was actually caught in the act, so to speak, I knew Mr. Carter would never believe it of him on my bare word——"

"I didn't," interposed Mr. Carter ruefully.

"That's why I sent the girls off to Sir James. I was sure they'd fetch up at the house in Soho sooner or later. I threatened Julius with the revolver, because I wanted Tuppence to repeat that to Sir James, so that he wouldn't worry about us. The moment the girls were out of sight I told Julius to drive like hell for London, and as we went along I told him the whole story. We got to the Soho house in plenty of time and met Mr. Carter outside. After arranging things with him we went in and hid behind the curtain in the recess. The policemen had orders to say, if they were asked, that no one had gone into the house. That's all."

And Tommy came to an abrupt halt.

There was silence for a moment.

"By the way," said Julius suddenly, "you're all wrong about that photograph of Jane. It *was* taken from me, but I found it again."

"Where?" cried Tuppence.

"In that little safe on the wall in Mrs. Vandemeyer's bedroom."

"I knew you found something," said Tuppence reproachfully. "To tell you the truth, that's what started me off suspecting you. Why didn't you say?"

"I guess I was a mite suspicious too. It had been got away from me once, and I determined I wouldn't let on I'd got it until a photographer had made a dozen copies of it!"

"We all kept back something or other," said Tuppence thoughtfully. "I suppose secret service work makes you like that!"

In the pause that ensued, Mr. Carter took from his pocket a small shabby brown book.

"Beresford has just said that I would not have believed Sir James Peel Edgerton to be guilty unless, so to speak, he was caught in the act. That is so. Indeed, not until I read the entries in this little book could I bring myself fully to credit the amazing truth. This book will pass into the possession of Scotland Yard, but it will never be publicly exhibited. Sir James's long association with the law would make it undesirable. But to you, who know the truth, I propose to read certain passages which will throw some light on the extraordinary mentality of this great man."

He opened the book, and turned the thin pages.

". . . It is madness to keep this book. I know that. It is documentary evidence against me. But I have never shrunk from taking risks. And I feel an urgent need for self-expression. . . . The book will only be taken from my dead body. . . .

". . . From an early age I realized that I had

exceptional abilities. Only a fool underestimates his capabilities. My brain power was greatly above the average. I know that I was born to succeed. My appearance was the only thing against me. I was quiet and insignificant—utterly nondescript. . . .

". . . When I was a boy I heard a famous murder trial. I was deeply impressed by the power and eloquence of the counsel for the defence. For the first time I entertained the idea of taking my talents to that particular market. . . . Then I studied the criminal in the dock. . . . The man was a fool—he had been incredibly, unbelievably stupid. Even the eloquence of his counsel was hardly likely to save him. I felt an immeasurable contempt for him. . . . Then it occurred to me that the criminal standard was a low one. It was the wastrels, the failures, the general riff-raff of civilization who drifted into crime. . . . Strange that men of brains had never realized its extraordinary opportunities. . . . I played with the idea. . . . What a magnificent field—what unlimited possibilities! It made my brain reel. . . .

". . . I read standard works on crime and criminals. They all confirmed my opinion. Degeneracy, disease—never the deliberate embracing of a career by a far-seeing man. Then I considered. Supposing my utmost ambitions were realized—that I was called to the bar, and rose to the height of my profession? That I entered politics—say, even, that I became Prime Minister of England? What then? Was that power? Hampered at every turn by my colleagues, fettered by the democratic system of which I should be the mere figurehead! No—the power I dreamed of was absolute! An autocrat! A dictator! And such power could only be obtained by working outside the law. To play on the weaknesses of human nature, then on the weaknesses of nations—to get together and control a vast organization, and finally to overthrow the existing order, and rule! The thought intoxicated me. . . .

". . . I saw that I must lead two lives. A man like myself is bound to attract notice. I must have a successful career which would mask my true activities. . . . Also I must cultivate a personality. I modelled myself upon famous K.C.'s. I reproduced their mannerisms, their magnetism. If I had chosen to be an actor, I should have been the greatest actor living! No disguises—no grease paint—no false beards! Personality! I put it on like a glove! When I shed it, I was myself, quiet, unobtrusive, a man like every other man. I called myself Mr. Brown. There are hundreds of men called Brown—there are hundreds of men looking just like me. . . .

". . . I succeeded in my false career. I was bound to succeed. I shall succeed in the other. A man like me cannot fail. . . .

". . . I have been reading a life of Napoleon. He and I have much in common. . . .

". . . I make a practice of defending criminals. A man should look after his own people. . . .

". . . Once or twice I have felt afraid. The first time was in Italy. There was a dinner given. Professor D——, the great alienist, was present. The talk fell on insanity. He said, 'A great many men are mad, and no one knows it. They do not know it themselves.' I do not understand why he looked at me when he said that. His glance was strange. . . . I did not like it. . . .

". . . The war has disturbed me. . . . I thought it would further my plans. The Germans are so efficient. Their spy system, too, was excellent. The streets are full of these boys in khaki. All empty-headed young fools. . . . Yet I do not know. . . . They won the war. . . . It disturbs me. . . .

". . . My plans are going well. . . . A girl butted in—I do not think she really knew anything. . . . But we must give up the Esthonia. . . . No risks now. . . .

". . . All goes well. The loss of memory is vexing. It cannot be a fake. No girl could deceive ME! . . .

". . . The 29th. . . . That is very soon. . . ." Mr. Carter paused.

"I will not read the details of the *coup* that was planned. But there are just two small entries that refer to the three of you. In the light of what happened they are interesting.

". . . By inducing the girl to come to me of her own accord, I have succeeded in disarming her. But she has intuitive flashes that might be dangerous. . . . She must be got out of the way. . . . I can do nothing with the American. He suspects and dislikes me. But he cannot know. I fancy my armour is impregnable. . . . Sometimes I fear I have underestimated the other boy. He is not clever, but it is hard to blind his eyes to facts. . . ."

Mr. Carter shut the book.

"A great man," he said, "Genius, or insanity, who can say?"

There was silence.

Then Mr. Carter rose to his feet.

"I will give you a toast. The Joint Venture which has so amply justified itself by success!"

It was drunk with acclamation.

"There's something more we want to hear," continued Mr. Carter. He looked at the American Ambassador. "I speak for you also, I know. We'll ask Miss Jane Finn to tell us the story that only Miss Tuppence has heard so far—but before we do so we'll drink her health. The health of one of the bravest of America's daughters, to whom is due the thanks and gratitude of two great countries!"

CHAPTER XXVIII
And After

"That was a mighty good toast, Jane," said Mr. Hersheimmer, as he and his cousin were being driven back in the Rolls-Royce to the *Ritz*.

"The one to the joint venture?"

"No—the one to you. There isn't another girl in the world who could have carried it through as you did. You were just wonderful!"

Jane shook her head.

"I don't feel wonderful. At heart I'm just tired and lonesome—and longing for my own country."

"That brings me to something I wanted to say. I heard the Ambassador telling you his wife hoped you would come to them at the Embassy right away. That's good enough, but I've got another plan. Jane—I want you to marry me! Don't get scared and say no at once. You can't love me right away, of course, that's impossible. But I've loved you from the very moment I set eyes on your photo—and now I've seen you I'm simply crazy about you! If you'll only marry me, I won't worry you any—you shall take your own time. Maybe you'll never come to love me, and if that's the case I'll manage to set you free. But I want the right to look after you, and take care of you."

"That's what I want," said the girl wistfully. "Some one who'll be good to me. Oh, you don't know how lonesome I feel!"

"Sure thing I do. Then I guess that's all fixed up, and I'll see the archbishop about a special license tomorrow morning."

"Oh, Julius!"

"Well, I don't want to hustle you any, Jane, but there's no sense in waiting about. Don't be scared—I shan't expect you to love me all at once."

But a small hand was slipped into his.

"I love you now, Julius," said Jane Finn. "I loved you that first moment in the car when the bullet grazed your cheek. . . ."

Five minutes later Jane murmured softly:

"I don't know London very well, Julius, but is it such a very long way from the *Savoy* to the *Ritz*?"

"It depends how you go," explained Julius unblushingly. "We're going by way of Regent's Park!"

"Oh, Julius—what will the chauffeur think?"

"At the wages I pay him, he knows better than to do any independent thinking. Why, Jane, the only reason I had the supper at the *Savoy* was so that I could drive you home. I didn't see how I was ever going to get hold of you alone. You and Tuppence have been sticking together like Siamese twins. I guess another day of it would have driven me and Beresford stark staring mad!"

"Oh. Is he——?"

"Of course he is. Head over ears."

"I thought so," said Jane thoughtfully.

"Why?"

"From all the things Tuppence didn't say!"

"There you have me beat," said Mr. Hersheimmer. But Jane only laughed.

In the meantime, the Young Adventurers were sitting bolt upright, very stiff and ill at ease, in a taxi which, with a singular lack of originality, was also returning to the *Ritz* via Regent's Park.

A terrible constraint seemed to have settled down between them. Without quite knowing what had happened, everything seemed changed. They were tongue-tied—paralysed. All the old *camaraderie* was gone.

Tuppence could think of nothing to say.

Tommy was equally afflicted.

They sat very straight and forbore to look at each other.

At last Tuppence made a desperate effort.

"Rather fun, wasn't it?"

"Rather."

Another silence.

"I like Julius," essayed Tuppence again.

Tommy was suddenly galvanized into life.

"You're not going to marry him, do you hear?" he said dictatorially. "I forbid it."

"Oh!" said Tuppence meekly.

"Absolutely, you understand."

"He doesn't want to marry me—he really only asked me out of kindness."

"That's not very likely," scoffed Tommy.

"It's quite true. He's head over ears in love with Jane. I expect he's proposing to her now."

"She'll do for him very nicely," said Tommy condescendingly.

"Don't you think she's the most lovely creature you've ever seen?"

"Oh, I dare say."

"But I suppose you prefer sterling worth," said Tuppence demurely.

"I—oh, dash it all, Tuppence, you know!"

"I like your uncle, Tommy," said Tuppence, hastily creating a diversion. "By the way, what are you going to do, accept Mr. Carter's offer of a Government job, or accept Julius's invitation and take a richly remunerated post in America on his ranch?"

"I shall stick to the old ship, I think, though it's awfully good of Hersheimmer. But I feel you'd be more at home in London."

"I don't see where I come in."

"I do," said Tommy positively.

Tuppence stole a glance at him sideways.

"There's the money, too," she observed thoughtfully.

"What money?"

"We're going to get a cheque each. Mr. Carter told me so."

"Did you ask how much?" inquired Tommy sarcastically.

"Yes," said Tuppence triumphantly. "But I shan't tell you."

"Tuppence, you are the limit!"

"It has been fun, hasn't it, Tommy? I do hope we shall have lots more adventures."

"You're insatiable, Tuppence. I've had quite enough adventures for the present."

"Well, shopping is almost as good," said Tuppence dreamily. "Think of buying old furniture, and bright carpets, and futurist silk curtains, and a polished dining-table, and a divan with lots of cushions——"

"Hold hard," said Tommy. "What's all this for?"

"Possibly a house—but I think a flat."

"Whose flat?"

"You think I mind saying it, but I don't in the least! *Ours*, so there!"

"You darling!" cried Tommy, his arms tightly round her. "I was determined to make you say it. I owe you something for the relentless way you've squashed me whenever I've tried to be sentimental."

Tuppence raised her face to his. The taxi proceeded on its course round the north side of Regent's Park.

"You haven't really proposed now," pointed out Tuppence. "Not what our grandmothers would call a proposal. But after listening to a rotten one like Julius's, I'm inclined to let you off."

"You won't be able to get out of marrying me, so don't you think it."

"What fun it will be," responded Tuppence. "Marriage is called all sorts of things, a haven, and a refuge, and a crowning glory, and a state of bondage, and lots more. But do you know what I think it is?"

"What?"

"A sport!"

"And a damned good sport too," said Tommy.

DIAMOND CUT DIAMOND

Frederic Arnold Kummer

THE PROLIFIC FREDERIC ARNOLD KUMMER (1873–1943), the son of German immigrants, began his career as an engineer and soon became a successful businessman before turning to writing, which quickly became his full-time occupation.

He wrote for the various popular fiction magazines (*All-Story Weekly*, *Blue Book*, *The Cavalier*, among others) where his old-fashioned, complex crime stories were serialized. He learned to change with the times in order to sell his work, replacing the genteel manners, quaint dialogue, and relatively civilized criminal characters of the early twentieth century with the volatile actions and emotions; harsh, crisp speech; and violent murders that characterize the tougher crime novels that were in vogue in the 1930s.

Noted for his mystery novels, both under his own name and the pseudonym Arnold Fredericks, Kummer also wrote fantasy, children's books, and, most notably, plays—both dramatic and musical, collaborating with Sigmund Romberg, who wrote the music for *The Magic Melody* (1919); Victor Herbert, who wrote the music for *My Golden Girl* (1920); and Gustav Strube, who wrote the score for the grand opera *The Captive* (1938).

More than two dozen of his novels, plays, and stories served as the basis for silent films, including *The Green God* (1911; film 1918), *The Brute* (1912; film 1914), *A Song of Sixpence* (1913; film 1917), and *The Painted Woman* (1917; filmed as *The Slave Market*, 1917). The heavy doses of romance in Kummer's plays, musicals, motion pictures, novels, and stories spilled over into his detective stories.

In "Diamond Cut Diamond," Elinor Vance is a woman of independent means who uses her wealth, intelligence, and charms to help those in trouble, defining herself as "a female Robin Hood," though she doesn't steal. She merely sets up elaborate schemes to catch criminals or to foil their nefarious plans.

"Diamond Cut Diamond" was originally published in the December 13, 1924, issue of *Liberty Magazine*.

Diamond Cut Diamond

FREDERIC ARNOLD KUMMER

"DO YOU MEAN TO SAY," Elinor asked slowly, two scarlet spots showing against the dull white of her cheeks, "that you think this girl a thief?"

Donald McRae gave an uneasy glance about the big studio room.

"I mean to say all the evidence points that way," he replied lamely.

"As a student of criminal psychology, Don, you should be a better judge of human nature. And as a friend of the district attorney—"

"Elinor, for heaven's sake be sensible. Just because you spend your time digging up these unfortunate women, sympathizing with them, is no reason why I should ask the district attorney or anybody else to do the impossible. With all your money I should think you'd go in for something more sensible—worth while. Travel, for instance. Or art."

"Don't be a fool, Don. I've been everywhere, from Tokio to Kalamazoo. You know that. As for art, it's too often merely an excuse for rotten studio parties, nowadays. I'm trying to give a little help to some people who can't help themselves. Can you think of any better way to spend one's time and money?"

"All right. Suit yourself. But I don't see how I can do anything for this girl. As a lawyer—"

"As a lawyer, perhaps not." Elinor's voice was soft as an April shower. "But as a friend—a man who claims to care for me—"

Donald sprang to his feet, thrusting the red-brown hair from his forehead with a characteristic gesture.

"I do," he exclaimed, "and you know it."

"Then why won't you try to help me?"

"Elinor, sit down." He waved to a chair, resumed his own. "Let us go over this girl's case in detail. Then if you can point out to me anything I can do, why—I promise you I'll do it."

"Fair enough." Elinor threw herself on the couch. "I told you, didn't I, that she'd been employed for over a year as secretary by a Mr. Jacob Krantz, of Krantz & Co., jewelers, in Maiden Lane?"

"Yes."

"Well—last month—on the seventeenth, to be exact—young Mr. Krantz, who travels for the firm, came in from a business trip and placed on his father's desk a leather case containing unset diamonds to the value of thirty-four thousand dollars. They were of various sizes, wrapped in seven small packets of white tissue paper. Mr. Krantz states he opened the packets, examined and counted their contents in his son's presence, as was his invariable custom, and found everything to be correct."

"To whom did he make this statement? The police?"

"No. To me. I went to see him. But I'll come to that later. Mr. Krantz, it seems, after taking the packets from his son's case, placed them on a small wooden tray on the desk. Then he called his secretary—Pennington's her name—Jane Pennington—and told her to take the stones to the office of his partner, Mr. Stern, at the other end of the suite. It was Mr. Stern's business to verify Mr. Krantz's count and then lock the diamonds in the safe."

"I see. How did Krantz summon his secretary?"

"By calling to her through the door leading to the outer office. He had to turn his head, but did *not* have to leave his desk. His son was standing alongside of him."

"You think, then," Donald said quickly, detecting a certain significance in Elinor's words, "that while his father's head was turned young Krantz might have—"

"It is at least possible," remarked Elinor.

"But highly improbable. A member of the firm. Entrusted with the task of carrying thousands of dollars' worth of stones about the country on business trips. One would hardly think he would wait to commit a theft directly under his father's nose. What happened then?"

"Miss Pennington took the tray and carried it down the corridor to the office of Mr. Stern. The corridor is some twenty feet long, narrow, and rather dark, in spite of the ground-glass partitions along either side of it. She was alone while passing through it, of course. As soon as she had placed the tray on Mr. Stern's desk she hurried to the front office, took her hat and coat from a rack, and went to lunch.

"Five minutes later Mr. Stern dashed into his partner's office with the news that one of the packets, containing diamonds to the value of eight thousand dollars, was missing. His stenographer, Miss Grasty, who was with him at the time, verified his statement.

"Mr. Krantz thought it significant that Miss Pennington had gone out over fifteen minutes ahead of her regular time. He at once sent for a private detective. When Miss Pennington came back from lunch he accused her. Both he and his son swore that there were seven packets of stones on the tray when it was turned over to her.

"She denied everything, said she had not counted the packets herself, explained her leaving the office so early by saying she had a headache and wanted to go to the drugstore to get something for it.

"She was searched, of course, but nothing was found on her. Mr. Krantz said he didn't expect to find anything—that her purpose in leaving the office so quickly had been to turn the stones over to a confederate, or hide them somewhere, to be recovered later."

"Did she meet anyone while she was out?"

"Yes. In a drugstore two blocks away."

"Who?"

"A young man named Ashton—James Ashton—with whom, it seems, she is in love. He's an electrician, I believe, employed by the New Jersey Chemical Company."

"H-m!" Donald gave Elinor a curious look. "Everything you've told me," he said, "seems to point inexorably to the girl's guilt. Isn't there anything to be said in her favor?"

"Nothing, except that I believe her," Elinor said quietly.

"Did Krantz turn her over to the police?"

"No. It wasn't her arrest he wanted, so much as the diamonds. He let her go. Under the watchful eye of the detective, of course. Gave her twenty-four hours in which to produce the jewels or make the loss good. He thought she might weaken, I suppose, and come across with the missing stones."

"Fair enough. Most men would have let the police give her the third degree."

"I don't know. He still had that in reserve. It was young Krantz who suggested the arrangement. An oily little rat. I forgot to tell you that Miss Pennington said he had been making advances to her for some time. Tried to kiss her once when she stayed after office hours. She slapped his face."

"H-m. Well, that often happens with good-looking girls who work in offices. Doesn't prove anything. What happened then?"

"Well, not having any relatives or friends ready to put up eight thousand dollars for her, she went home, to the house where she boards. She might have told young Ashton about her trouble, but she was—well, ashamed. And afraid, too, that he'd get after Krantz and beat him up, I guess.

"Along about half-past eight young Krantz came to see her. Offered to make the loss good if she'd move over to his flat. The usual proposition. Being a decent girl, she ordered him out. They had some words.

"Miss Whiteley, my secretary, who lives in the same house, overheard the row, and, according to instructions, reported the matter to me.

"Well, to make a long story short, I had Miss Pennington brought here and heard her story. The next day I went down to the office with her and paid Krantz the eight thousand. So that's that."

"H-m. Rather a quixotic thing to do, it seems to me. How do you know she wasn't lying?"

"I know women," Elinor said quietly.

"Maybe. You certainly have a generous heart, and are therefore easily imposed upon. I sometimes think, Elinor, that you rather fancy yourself in this role of a female Robin Hood, always ready to take up the cudgels on behalf of the under dog. It's a charming idea, but if you don't look out you'll find yourself in a nasty mess, someday. Well, I've heard the story. What did you expect me to do?"

"I don't believe, Donald," Elinor remarked, a trace of irony in her voice, "that I really expected you to do anything. But I thought there might be just a chance you could get your friend, Inspector Doyle, to have young Krantz watched, arrested, perhaps, when he tries to dispose of those stones. He took them. I'm convinced of that."

"You'd have to produce more evidence than you have now to make headquarters think so. As for disposing of the stones—provided he's got them—I don't doubt, being in the business, he'll have his own ways of doing that. Unset diamonds of moderate size are pretty much alike. You're asking the impossible."

Elinor sat with her chin cupped in one hand, gazing moodily at the Chinese rug. There was sullen anger in her wide, dark eyes; the set of her slender shoulders bespoke a fixed determination.

"All right," she said. "Then I'll have to go it alone."

"Look here, Elinor!" Donald exclaimed. "Be careful. Don't try anything dangerous. Is it worth it? Eight thousand dollars?"

"It's the principle of the thing. Krantz and his son practically have made this girl admit herself a thief. And she isn't one. I'd stake my last dollar on it.

"Think what it means to her self-respect—to the man she loves. How is she going to explain the loss of her position? The story's bound to get around. She's crushed, wiped out, done. Afraid to look the world in the face, because she feels she's been branded as a crook.

"I want to give her back her courage, her hope, her faith, her love. And if there's any way it can be done, short of murder, I'm going to do it. I trust I make myself quite clear, Mr. McRae," she finished.

After Don had gone, Elinor lay flat on her back on the couch for over an hour, staring up at the ceiling. When she finally rose to her feet it was in response to a message from her secretary, Miss Whiteley.

"Mr. Ashton's here," the secretary said. "Are you ready to see him?"

"What sort of a looking fellow is he, Helen?" Elinor asked, smiling.

"Well—not the kind of a man I'd care to start an argument with, if that's what you mean."

"Good!" Elinor's eyes snapped. "Show him in."

Miss Sadie Pollock, the young woman who had taken Jane Pennington's place as private secretary to Mr. Krantz, glanced at the caller who had just entered the office with a look of cool disdain. He was a tall, eager-faced young man, neatly but by no means smartly dressed. A workman, Miss Pollock thought.

"Well?" she asked.

"I want to see Mr. Krantz. Mr. Jacob Krantz. Personally. About buying some stones," the young man announced.

Miss Pollock retired to the inner office, trying to conceal her surprise. A man like that buying diamonds! It seemed incredible. Presently she returned.

"Mr. Krantz will see you at once," she said.

The diamond dealer rose from his chair with outstretched hand as his caller came into the room.

"Sit down." He waved toward a chair. "I understand you wish to buy some stones."

"No," the man replied, taking a seat. "I don't want to buy any."

"Then why did you tell my secretary so?" Mr. Krantz growled, his good nature vanishing like a puff of smoke. "My time is valuable. If you are an agent or canvasser of any sort—" He glanced significantly toward the door.

The young man did not at once reply. Instead he felt in his pocket and, drawing out a small, round object, rolled it across the glass top of Mr. Krantz's desk.

"I told your secretary I wanted to see you about buying some stones," he said. "You, however, were to do the buying. Here is a diamond I would like to sell."

Mr. Krantz's hard little eyes gleamed with cupidity as he gazed at the jewel before him. An uncut stone, in shape a rough octahedron, it was about the size of a small cherry.

"We don't buy from strangers," he said, making a shrewd guess as to the stone's value. "At least, not as a rule. Where did you get it?"

"What's that to you?" The man shrugged his shoulders. "Maybe I've just got back from South Africa. Or Brazil." He gave the diamond dealer a brazen wink. "You can have it for two thousand."

Mr. Krantz spoke softly through the telephone for a moment. Almost at once his partner, Mr. Stern, came into the office, fat, bland, smiling.

"How much can we offer for this, Sam?" Mr. Krantz said, handing him the diamond.

Mr. Stern sat down at a little table equipped with a pair of delicate, glass-covered scales, magnifying glasses, and other devices incident to the jewel trade. He was busy for several moments weighing the stone, testing its colors, its refraction. Presently he rose and placed the diamond on his partner's desk.

"About fifteen hundred," he announced, with elaborate carelessness. "It ain't worth more, considering the risk of cutting."

Mr. Krantz grunted assent. Both he and Mr. Stern were quite well aware that the stone would have been cheap at two thousand, but their caller looked like a person in need of money.

"All right." The man shrugged his shoulders. "Cash." Mr. Krantz frowned.

"Cash? There ain't no comeback, is there?"

"No. The stone is mine, all right. But for certain reasons I'd rather not take a check."

Mr. Krantz unlocked the safe behind him, drew out some packages of bills. He, too, saw advantages in a cash transaction.

Whereupon Mr. Krantz paid over the money. The young man rose.

"I may bring you in another one, before long," he said, and, with a curious smile, left the office.

"What do you think, Sam?" Mr. Krantz asked when the door had closed behind him.

"Smuggled, of course. It's a South African stone. Fine water. Ought to cut fine, too." He took the bit of crystal and balanced it in his hand. "Good for a thousand profit. I wonder if he knew its value. He seemed mighty anxious to sell. I hope he comes back again."

"If he does," Mr. Krantz grunted, "we'll offer less. There's something fishy about it."

The young man *did* come back a few days later, bringing with him an even larger and finer stone than the one he had brought before. He asked three thousand dollars for it. Mr. Krantz refused to pay a cent more than two, and Mr. Stern backed him up.

"We're taking a big chance," Mr. Krantz grumbled, as he began to count out the purchase price. "How do we know where you got these stones? We don't want to do anything crooked."

"They weren't smuggled," the man said, "and they weren't stolen. You can bank on it."

"Then all I can say is, young fellow," remarked Mr. Krantz, "you must have a private diamond mine right here in America."

"Nothing like that, either." The man rose. "I—I really can't explain." Smiling apologetically, he hurried from the office.

The instant he had gone Mr. Krantz turned to his son, who had been sitting at a desk in a far corner of the room.

"Jump, Morris! Follow him," he said. "Don't lose sight of him. We got to find out where he's getting them stones."

With a quick nod young Mr. Krantz put on his hat and went out.

Mr. Morris Krantz was slim, dark, quick, and noiseless in his movements, and therefore well-equipped for the task which lay ahead of him. Without looking directly at his quarry, he strolled toward the elevator.

The man paid no attention to him. When the car reached the ground floor he hurried to the sidewalk and began to walk rapidly in the direction of the Hudson Terminal. Mr. Krantz followed, not too closely, and when his quarry got into a subway train managed to enter the same car at its other end without being observed and rode to the terminus of the underground line in Jersey City. He was immediately behind his man, however, at the railroad ticket office in Jersey City, and when the former asked for a ticket to Hillsdale Mr. Krantz bought one to the same place.

At the station the man jumped into a taxicab and drove off. Mr. Krantz did the same.

"Just follow that car," he told the chauffeur. "Not too close, though. I don't want them to know they're being followed."

The first car, after proceeding for about a mile through the straggling suburban town, turned into a side street on the outskirts and presently stopped before a small, unimportant-looking frame house. Noting its location, Mr. Krantz told his driver to go on to the next corner and

turn. Here he got out, paid his fare, and walked back to the house at which the man had stopped.

The house stood in a wide, shaded lot, and behind it was a small brick building, in appearance a garage. As Mr. Krantz passed the front of the place he saw the man he had been following leave the house by a rear door and proceed down a gravel walk to the garage. A light presently flashed inside. Mr. Krantz hurried around to the back of the lot and along a narrow lane to the brick building with windows on both sides. Cautiously he peered in.

His first glance told him the place was not a garage. Instead, it seemed to be some sort of a laboratory. In its center was a square concrete pedestal, on which stood an oblong box, made apparently of firebrick. Heavy cables, leading to brass attachments at either end, made Mr. Krantz conclude that the apparatus was electrical in its nature. The man busied himself for a moment with the binding screws at one end of the box, glanced at his wrist watch, then snapped off the lights and went out. Mr. Krantz watched him as he returned to the house; the activity in the illuminated rear kitchen caused him to conclude that his man had gone in for dinner.

But Mr. Krantz was far too excited himself to think about food. An idea of tremendous importance had come to him, one which even yet he could not completely grasp. Had the man locked the door? He thought not, and a quick investigation told him that he was right. Like a shadow he slipped into the room.

The place was in semidarkness, and he did not dare to switch on the lights for fear they would be observed from the house. One thing, however, was visible: the box on the concrete pedestal shone in the darkness with a fierce white glow, giving off an odor suggestive of intense heat.

At the far end of the room he discerned a flight of steps leading to the floor above. In a moment he had ascended and found himself in a low loft, filled with trunks, old furniture, and books. There were cracks in the rough pine floor; he took out his pocket knife and widened one of them until he could see through quite clearly.

An hour passed, and he was beginning to wonder whether the man was coming back, when he suddenly heard footsteps, the opening and closing of a door. Immediately the room beneath him was flooded with brilliant light.

There were two persons in the place now, one the young man he had been following, the other a dark and slender girl, wearing an apron of brown linen. The former was busy for a time, adjusting some apparatus at one side of the room. The girl, meanwhile, went to the oblong box at the center of the room, and, after turning a switch, took up a pair of tongs and plunged them into the glowing mass with which it was filled.

A blinding glare met Mr. Krantz's eyes, then he saw that the girl held in her tongs a white-hot object about the size of an orange, which she at once dropped into a tub of water on the floor at her side.

There was a prodigious hissing, accompanied by clouds of steam. For several moments the girl waited, glancing at an open book which lay on a small table. Then she took up her tongs, and fishing about in the water of the tub, brought up a round, black mass.

Her companion now joined her, and with a hammer proceeded to break open the object as one might crack a nut; thereupon they gazed eagerly at something contained within it, showing, meanwhile, the greatest delight. Then, with a few words which Mr. Krantz could not hear, the man switched off the lights and, with his companion, went out.

The turning of a key in the lock of the door was distinctly audible, and also the closing of the heavy window shutters. The building had evidently been closed for the night.

With sweat streaming down his back, Mr. Krantz descended to the floor below. If the things he had seen meant what he thought they did, it was well that he had come.

One thing was certain—he would have to find out before he left the place, provided he could leave it at all, now that the door was locked. That, he argued, was to prevent anyone from entering from without; a quick inspection of the windows with the aid of a lighted match told him he would have no difficulty in making his escape from within. And the fact that the shutters were closed made it possible for him to turn on the lights without danger of detection from the house.

It took him several moments to locate the switch; but, this done, the room was at once illuminated with a very brilliant greenish-white light.

The dark object which the man had broken open with the hammer still lay on the table. It consisted of a rough, granular shell of what looked like cast iron.

As Mr. Krantz examined it an expression of amazement crossed his face.

Inside, occupying a small cavity, was a grayish crystal about the size of a large pea. He glanced at it eagerly for a moment, then thrust it into his waistcoat pocket.

The book lying open on the table next attracted his attention. It was a work on industrial chemistry. One of the paragraphs was marked. Mr. Krantz stared at it with bulging eyes as he read:

Ever since the successful experiments by Henri Moissan, scientists have known that the manufacture of crystallized carbon, or diamonds, is well within the possibilities of the modern electric furnace. Moissan made actual diamonds, but they were very small. Only the proper development of his process is needed to make them of any size desired.

But the problem is of no interest to the scientist, because, unlike synthetic rubber, or indigo, carbon crystals have no value in the industrial world. Nor would their production on a large scale attract the manufacturer, since his investment would become so much junk the moment his product was put on the market.

The mere knowledge that quantity production was at hand would at once reduce the value of all the diamonds in the world, even the Kohinoor, to the price of so much glass. Hence the manufacture of diamonds is not likely to be attempted, unless by some individual operating in the strictest secrecy, and marketing his product with the utmost care.

With a groan Mr. Krantz turned from the book. All the diamonds in the world worth no more than so much glass! And Krantz & Co. had over a quarter of a million dollars' worth of stones in their vaults!

Scarcely able to think, he raised one of the windows, unfastened the shutters, and, having switched off the lights, dropped noiselessly to the ground outside.

Was the thing real? He could scarcely believe it. And yet how else explain the uncut diamonds the young man had brought to the office, had sold at far below their real market value?

He had one in his waistcoat pocket now. As he waited for the New York train he drew the diamond across the pane of the station window. It cut a deep, white mark.

In the private office of Mr. Jacob Krantz three very white-faced men sat about the senior partner's desk the next day. Mr. Krantz himself was so filled with dismay that his features had shriveled up to the semblance of a dried apple. Mr. Stern was as gray as a death mask. Young Morris Krantz, his sleek hair on end, his eyes wide and fearful, had just finished an account of his adventures.

"Sam," Mr. Krantz remarked slowly, "what do you think we should do?"

"Do?" Mr. Stern picked up the uncut stone and gazed at it helplessly. "We can't do nothing. If diamonds can be made in a lab'ratory, like Morris here says, we might just as well now go out of business. Why, if the story got in the newspapers we couldn't sell our stock at five cents on the dollar!"

"For why should it get in the newspapers, Sam?" Mr. Krantz asked. "These people is cleaning up a thousand or two a week selling us some stones. Ain't it the last thing in the world

they'd want to do—have their secret made public? I ain't afraid they'll tell anybody. I got a better idea, Sam. Let's have a talk with this fellow. Tell him we're on to his secret and are ready to market his product for him fifty-fifty. Make him sign an agreement not to sell through anybody but us. Point out to him that if he ain't careful he'll lose the whole works."

Mr. Stern nodded slowly in agreement.

"You're right, Jake," he said. "We better get out to Jersey at once and have a talk with him. Tell him where he gets off."

A knock at the door followed his words. Miss Pollock came in bearing a letter. Mr. Krantz tore it open, read aloud the contents:

Dear Mr. Krantz:
Please be at the above address tonight at eight o'clock. Bring your son and your partner, Mr. Stern, with you. Ask for Miss Vance, on the sixth floor. We want to talk to you about diamonds.

"That's that," said Mr. Krantz, dropping the note on his desk. "Sam, I ain't feeling well. Think I'll get a cup of coffee."

Elinor came into the living room wearing a gown of green and silver which made Donald McRae catch his breath. He could combat the girl's intelligence, her gay insolence, but her beauty always left him helpless.

"It's good of you to come here, Donald," she said sinking into a chair. "You remember what I told you about Miss Pennington. Well, I've taken action in her case, and—"

"You haven't been doing anything you shouldn't, I hope," he said, noting the seriousness of her smile. "Of course, if you're in any trouble—"

"Thanks, old dear. I'm not—yet. But I may need your help before the evening's over. You have authority to make arrests, haven't you?"

"Yes." Donald lit a cigarette, regarding Elinor with a puzzled frown. What deviltry was she up to now? An amazing woman, who would stop at nothing to gain her ends. She enjoyed the risks to which she was forever subjecting herself as other women might enjoy a hand of bridge. Even now she was gazing at him like some mischievous elf.

"What's the game?" he asked suddenly.

"Don't look so downhearted, old dear," she laughed. "The worst I'm capable of tonight is a little blackmail."

"Blackmail?" Donald gasped.

"Well, you might call it that." She went to the door and called to someone in the next room. A tall, eager-faced young man came in, accompanied by a slender and very charming girl of twenty. Elinor took the latter's hand.

"Miss Pennington," she said, smiling, "this is my friend, Mr. McRae, and Mr. Ashton, Mr. McRae." She nodded to the young man with the eager face. "Mr. Ashton is an electrician—a chemist. He and I have been making some very interesting experiments at his private laboratory over in New Jersey, looking to establishing Miss Pennington's innocence of the crime of which she has been accused. We hope we have succeeded."

Mr. Ashton slipped his arm about his companion's waist.

"If we haven't," he said grimly, "somebody's due for an awful beating up before the evening's over."

"Remember, please," Elinor said, placing her hand on his arm, "you promised not to start anything—"

"Well—" he turned away grimly—"I guess that goes. Till the evening's over, anyway. Glad to have met you—" He nodded to McRae. "Come along, Jane." With his arm still about the slender girl, Ashton returned to the adjoining room.

"She won't marry him," Elinor whispered, "until her innocence has been proved. Her pride, you know. She's afraid he might still think—" A timid knock at the door stopped her, then she opened it.

Mr. Krantz, Mr. Stern, and young Morris filed in solemnly. Even in their perturbed state

of mind they did not fail to note the costly fittings of the room. "A thousand a week, easy," Mr. Krantz muttered to himself, glancing at Mr. McRae.

"My lawyer," Elinor said, introducing him.

"If I'd known it was a case of lawyers," Mr. Krantz remarked, staring uneasily at Donald, "I could've brought my own."

"I don't think you'll need one," Elinor remarked gaily. "Would you gentlemen mind stepping into the dining room?"

"Dining room! If you should ask me now, miss, to eat anything—"

"It isn't that. There's something I want to show you." She swept aside the curtains at the end of the room. "Just go in and take a seat. Don't fall over the chairs."

Her caution was needed. The room was in almost total darkness. Guided by the light which came through the parted curtains, the four men slowly filed into the room, Donald bringing up the rear. A semicircle of chairs confronted them, two of which were already occupied, but the women who sat in them were not recognizable in the dim light.

"Find chairs, everybody," Elinor cried. "We're ready to begin."

In a state of complete bewilderment, Mr. Krantz and his companions sat down.

A faint whirring sound came from the rear of the room where Mr. Ashton stood.

Then a moving picture suddenly appeared on a screen suspended against the opposite wall. Mr. Krantz gave a groan. The picture showed a small room, fitted up as a laboratory, and near the center of it, beside a table, stood Elinor herself, a pair of tongs in her hand. Presently, using the tongs, she lifted a small white-hot object from a box on the table and dropped it into a tub of water at her feet. A short delay ensued, then the little audience saw her take the object from the tub, saw the young man who had now joined her break it open on the top of the table, whereupon they both proceeded to examine its contents with the utmost care.

Suddenly the scene blacked out, to be at once

resumed with young Mr. Krantz as its central figure. For a few moments only was he visible, but during this time he moved swiftly and distinctly as he picked up the two halves of the dark object on the table, gazed at them for an instant, removed something from one of them, and thrust it into his waistcoat pocket. Almost immediately thereafter this picture, too, faded out and the dining room was suddenly flooded with light.

Mr. Krantz and his companions looked about, blinked.

Young Morris, recognizing Jane Pennington as one of the two women who sat near him, rose to his feet snarling like a trapped fox.

James Ashton stepped toward him, his fists clenched. Elinor swept into the half circle made by the chairs.

"Just a moment, please, everybody!" she exclaimed, raising her hand. "What you have just seen is a picture of a small private laboratory at Hillsdale, New Jersey, belonging to my friend, Mr. James Ashton. The picture was taken last night, by means of an automatic camera and the specially installed vacuum lamps with which the place is equipped.

"Mr. Krantz, Jr., forced his way into the place and, as you have seen, stole a diamond belonging to me worth two thousand dollars. Mr. Ashton and myself watched him do it through an opening in the door. There is a gentleman here who has authority to make an arrest."

"But—" Mr. Krantz, Sr., rose unsteadily to his feet—"that ain't the point, miss. Here's your diamond." He took the stone from his pocket and handed it to Elinor. "That ain't what we want to talk to you about. It—it's the diamond business.

"I don't like to say too much before witnesses," he continued, glancing pointedly at McRae and the two women, "but Morris ain't no thief. He only took that stone as evidence. We know what you're up to, and we want to make a deal with you. Can't we talk this thing over in private? If anybody should be arrested, y'understand, and the story gets in the newspapers, we'd all be sunk! Ruined!"

Elinor regarded him with a frosty smile.

"Mr. Krantz," she said, "before I talk to you about the diamond business, there's another matter I want settled.

"You accused this young lady—" she indicated Jane Pennington—"of stealing eight thousand dollars' worth of diamonds from you. I lent her the money to make the loss good. Miss Pennington didn't steal the stones. I think your son did. If he is ready to confess and return them to you, well and good. If not, he'll be under arrest for burglary inside of two minutes. Is that clear?"

With a look of fury Mr. Krantz turned on young Morris.

"What you got to say for yourself, you?" he demanded, pointing a shaky forefinger.

"Better say it quick, too," Mr. Ashton added grimly. "If you know what's good for you." His clenched hands moved restlessly; he seemed to have difficulty in controlling them.

For a moment young Krantz hesitated, his face green with fear. Then he slowly drew a leather wallet from his pocket and took from it a little package.

"Here," he muttered, thrusting the package into his father's hand. "I—I found them on the floor."

"That clears Miss Pennington," Elinor remarked pleasantly, turning to the elder Mr. Krantz, "and leaves you owing me eight thousand dollars."

"I'll make out a check!" Mr. Krantz shouted, drawing a fountain pen from his pocket.

"Fair enough," Elinor told him. "And while you're about it you might add a couple of thousand more to cover my loss on those diamonds I sold you, and another ten, say for laceration of Miss Pennington's feelings. We'll call it a wedding present. Yes—twenty in all. And don't try to stop payment on the check tomorrow, either. If you do, your son goes to jail as sure as he's a foot high."

Completely bewildered, Mr. Krantz made out the check, handed it over. Never in all his career had he been so much at sea. Still, he reflected, the eight thousand dollars was justly owing, since he now had the diamonds back, and what difference did a few additional thousands make, compared with the prospect of manufacturing diamonds by the million.

"Now, miss," he whispered eagerly, "let's you and me talk a little business about them diamonds you made."

"Diamonds I made?" Elinor said, laughing. "I don't admit making any diamonds."

"Of course you don't, miss. I understand that. You couldn't admit it. If you did, you'd never be able to sell another one. But between you and me—" he glanced pointedly at the stone Elinor still held in her hand—"you made that one all right, for Morris saw you do it."

"You're mistaken, Mr. Krantz. This stone, as well as the other two I sold you, I bought from an importer down in Maiden Lane. I'm afraid your son didn't understand what he saw at that laboratory last night. Mr. Ashton and I were making some experiments in criminal psychology. I never told you I could make diamonds. Must you really go?"

Mr. Krantz essayed to speak, but at the sight of Elinor's cool face, of Mr. Ashton's grim one, his voice failed him. Supported by his son, by Mr. Stern, he sagged slowly across the living room and out into the hall. When the door had closed behind them Donald turned to Elinor with a queer smile.

"Sometimes, Elinor," he exclaimed, "I think you're the devil."

"If I am," she grinned, "I hope I'm a good little devil."

"I think she's an angel," Miss Pennington whispered, taking Elinor's hand.

"I know darned well she is," said Ashton, and sweeping Jane into his arms, he kissed her quite shamelessly before them all.

LOCKED DOORS

Mary Roberts Rinehart

AS THE CREATOR of what is generally known as the "Had-I-But-Known" school, Mary Roberts Rinehart (1876–1958) regularly had her plucky heroines put themselves in situations from which they needed to be rescued. That school of detective story has often been parodied and maligned, but it was so well handled by Rinehart that she was, for decades, one of the most successful and beloved mystery writers in America, producing the first mystery novel ever to appear on the bestseller list, *The Man in Lower Ten* (1909). She had written it as a serial published in *The All-Story Magazine* (January–April 1906), which then published *The Circular Staircase* (November, December 1907, January–March 1908), which was then published in book form, a year before her first book, *The Man in Lower Ten*.

Probably her most successful work, *The Circular Staircase* was adapted by Rinehart and Avery Hopwood for the stage as *The Bat* in 1920, by which time she had become the highest-paid writer in America. The book had already served as the basis for a silent film, *The Circular Staircase* (1915); the play, which had some differences from the novel, inspired more than one film, including the silent *The Bat* (1926) and a sound version titled *The Bat Whispers* (1930).

Rinehart's most famous character is Hilda Adams, whose propensity for getting involved in crimes and mysteries garners her the nickname "Miss Pinkerton" after Allan Pinkerton, the famous real-life detective. She is encouraged in her sleuthing endeavors by George Patton, a small-time country detective who goes on to become a police inspector. He is a recurring presence in the series and appears to be interested in deepening his relationship with the dedicated nurse; she calls it "nonsense," though there are numerous hints that she welcomes the attention and returns some of the attraction. She overhears private conversations, listens to people who are sick or wounded and therefore not at their peak strength, and provides information to Patton. It is her stated conviction that she is betraying no trust and, since criminals act against society, society must use every means at its disposal to bring them to justice.

"Locked Doors" was originally published in her short story collection *Mary Roberts Rinehart Crime Book* (New York, Farrar & Rinehart, 1925).

Locked Doors

MARY ROBERTS RINEHART

CHAPTER I: DANGEROUS ASSIGNMENT

"YOU PROMISED," I reminded Mr. Patton, "to play with cards on the table."

"My dear young lady," he replied, "I have no cards! I suspect a game, that's all."

"Then—do you need me?"

The detective bent forward, his arms on his desk, and looked me over carefully.

"What sort of shape are you in? Tired?"

"No."

"Nervous?"

"Not enough to hurt."

"I want you to take another case, following a nurse who has gone to pieces," he said, selecting his words carefully. "I don't want to tell you a lot—I want you to go in with a fresh mind. It promises to be an extraordinary case."

"How long was the other nurse there?"

"Four days."

"She went to pieces in four days!"

"Well, she's pretty much unstrung. The worst is, she hasn't any real reason. A family chooses to live in an unusual manner, because they like it, or perhaps they're afraid of something. The girl was, that's sure. I had never seen her until this morning, a big, healthy-looking young woman; but she came in looking back over her shoulder as if she expected a knife in her back. She said she was a nurse from St. Luke's

and that she'd been on a case for four days. She'd left that morning after about three hours' sleep in that time, being locked in a room most of the time, and having little but crackers and milk for food. She thought it was a case for the police."

"Who is ill in the house? Who was her patient?"

"There is no illness, I believe. The French governess had gone, and they wished the children competently cared for until they replaced her. That was the reason given her when she went. Afterward she—well, she was puzzled."

"How are you going to get me there?"

He gathered acquiescence from my question and smiled approval.

"Good girl!" he said. "Never mind how I'll get you there. You are the most dependable woman I know."

"The most curious, perhaps?" I retorted. "Four days on the case, three hours' sleep, locked in and yelling 'Police!' Is it out of town?"

"No, in the heart of the city, on Beauregard Square. Can you get some St. Luke's uniforms? They want another St. Luke's nurse."

I said I could get the uniforms, and he wrote the address on a card.

"Better arrive about five," he said.

"But—if they are not expecting me?"

"They will be expecting you," he replied enigmatically.

"The doctor, if he's a St. Luke's man—"

"There is no doctor."

It was six months since I had solved, or helped to solve, the mystery of the buckled bag for Mr. Patton. I had had other cases for him in the interval, cases where the police could not get close enough. As I said when I began this record of my crusade against crime and the criminal, a trained nurse gets under the very skin of the soul. She finds a mind surrendered, all the crooked little motives that have fired the guns of life revealed in their pitifulness.

Gradually I had come to see that Mr. Patton's point of view was right; that if the criminal uses every means against society, why not society against the criminal? At first I had used this as a flag of truce to my nurse's ethical training; now I flaunted it, a mental and moral banner. The criminal against society, and I against the criminal! And, more than that, against misery, healing pain by augmenting it sometimes, but working like a surgeon, for good.

I had had six cases in six months. Only in one had I failed to land my criminal, and that without any suspicion of my white uniform and rubber-soled shoes. Although I played a double game no patient of mine had suffered. I was a nurse first and a police agent second. If it was a question between turpentine compresses—stupes, professionally—and seeing what letters came in or went out of the house, the compress went on first, and cracking hot too. I am not boasting. That is my method, the only way I can work, and it speaks well for it that, as I say, only one man escaped arrest—an arson case where the factory owner hanged himself in the bathroom needle shower in the house he had bought with the insurance money, while I was fixing his breakfast tray. And even he might have been saved for justice had the cook not burned the toast and been obliged to make it fresh.

I was no longer staying at a nurses' home. I had taken a bachelor suite of three rooms and bath, comfortably downtown. I cooked my own breakfasts when I was off duty and I dined at a restaurant near. Luncheon I did not bother much about. Now and then Mr. Patton telephoned me and we lunched together in remote places where we would not be known. He would tell me of his cases and sometimes he asked my advice.

I bought my uniforms that day and took them home in a taxicab. The dresses were blue, and over them for the street the St. Luke's girls wear long cloaks, English fashion, of navy blue serge, and a blue bonnet with a white ruching and white lawn ties. I felt curious in it, but it was becoming and convenient. Certainly I looked professional.

At three o'clock that afternoon a messenger brought a small box, registered. It contained a St. Luke's badge of gold and blue enamel.

At four o'clock my telephone rang. I was packing my suitcase according to the list I keep pasted in the lid. Under the list, which was of uniforms, aprons, thermometer, instruments, a nurse's simple set of probe, forceps, and bandage scissors, was the word "box." This always went in first—a wooden box with a lock, the key of which was round my neck. It contained skeleton keys, a small black revolver of which I was in deadly fear, a pair of handcuffs, a pocket flashlight, and my badge from the chief of police. I was examining the revolver nervously when the telephone rang, and I came within an ace of sending a bullet into the flat below.

Did you ever notice how much you get out of a telephone voice? We can dissemble with our faces, but under stress the vocal cords seem to draw up tight and the voice comes thin and colorless. There's a little woman in the flat beneath—the one I nearly bombarded—who sings like a bird at her piano half the day, scaling vocal heights that make me dizzy. Now and then she has a visitor, a nice young man, and she disgraces herself, flats F, fogs E even, finally takes cowardly refuge in a wretched mezzo-soprano and cries herself to sleep, doubtless, later on.

The man who called me had the thin-drawn voice of extreme strain—a youngish voice.

"Miss Adams," he said, "this is Francis Reed speaking. I have called St. Luke's and they referred me to you. Are you free to take a case this afternoon?"

I fenced. I was trying to read the voice. "This afternoon?"

"Well, before night anyhow; as—as early this evening as possible."

The voice was strained and tired, desperately tired. It was not peevish. It was even rather pleasant.

"What is the case, Mr. Reed?"

He hesitated. "It is not illness. It is merely— the governess has gone and there are two small children. We want someone to give her undivided attention to the children."

"I see."

"Are you a heavy sleeper, Miss Adams?"

"A very light one." I fancied he breathed freer.

"I hope you are not tired from a previous case?" I was beginning to like the voice.

"I'm quite fresh," I replied almost gaily. "Even if I were not, I like children, especially well ones. I shan't find looking after them very wearying, I'm sure."

Again the odd little pause. Then he gave me the address on Beauregard Square, and asked me to be sure not to be late. "I must warn you," he added, "we are living in a sort of casual way. Our servants left us without warning. Mrs. Reed has been getting along as best she could. Most of our meals are being sent in."

I was thinking fast. No servants! A good many people think a trained nurse is a sort of upper servant. I've been in houses where they were amazed to discover that I was a college woman and, finding the two things irreconcilable, have openly accused me of having been driven to such a desperate course as a hospital training by an unfortunate love affair.

"Of course you understand that I will look after the children to the best of my ability, but that I will not replace the servants."

I fancied he smiled grimly.

"That of course. Will you ring twice when you come?"

"Ring twice?"

"The doorbell," he replied impatiently.

I said I would ring the doorbell twice.

The young woman below was caroling gaily, ignorant of the six-barreled menace over her head. I knelt again by my suitcase, but packed little and thought a great deal. I was to arrive before dusk at a house where there were no servants and to ring the doorbell twice. I was to be a light sleeper, although I was to look after two healthy children. It was not much in itself, but, taken in connection with the previous nurse's appeal to the police, it took on new possibilities.

At six I started out to dinner. It was early spring and cold, but quite light. At the first corner I saw Mr. Patton waiting for a streetcar, and at his quick nod I saw I was to get in also. He did not pay my fare or speak to me. It was a part of the game that we were never seen together except at the remote restaurant I mentioned before. The car thinned out and I could watch him easily. Far downtown he alighted and so did I. The restaurant was near. I went in alone and sat down at a table in a recess, and very soon he joined me. We were in the main dining-room but not of it, a sop at once to the conventions and to the necessity, where he was so well known, for caution.

"I got a little information—on—the affair we were talking of," he said as he sat down. "I'm not so sure I want you to take the case after all."

"Certainly I shall take it," I retorted with some sharpness. "I've promised to go."

"Tut! I'm not going to send you into danger unnecessarily."

"I am not afraid."

"Exactly. A lot of generals were lost in the Civil War because they were not afraid and wanted to lead their troops instead of saving themselves and their expensive West Point training by sitting back in a safe spot and directing the fight. Any fool can run into danger. It takes intellect to keep out."

I felt my color rising indignantly. "Then you brought me here to tell me I am not to go?"

"Will you let me read you two reports?"

"You could have told me that at the corner!"

"Will you let me read you two reports?"

"If you don't mind I'll first order something to eat. I'm to be there before dark."

"Will you let me——"

"I'm going, and you know I'm going. If you don't want me to represent you I'll go on my own. They want a nurse, and they're in trouble."

I think he was really angry. I know I was. If there is anything that takes the very soul out of a woman, it is to be kept from doing a thing she has set her heart on, because some man thinks it dangerous. If she has any spirit, that rouses it.

Mr. Patton quietly replaced the reports in his wallet and his wallet in the inside pocket of his coat, and fell to a judicial survey of the menu. But although he did not even glance at me he must have felt the determination in my face, for he ordered things that were quickly prepared and told the waiter to hurry.

"I have wondered lately," he said slowly, "whether the mildness of your manner at the hospital was acting, or the chastening effect of three years under an order book."

"A man always likes a woman to be a sheep."

"Not at all. But it is rather disconcerting to have a pet lamb turn round and take a bite out of one."

"Will you read the reports now?"

"I think," he said quietly, "they would better wait until we have eaten. We will probably both feel calmer. Suppose we arrange that nothing said before the oysters counts?"

I agreed, rather sulkily, and the meal went off well enough. I was anxious enough to hurry but he ate deliberately, drank his demitasse, paid the waiter, and at last met my impatient eyes and smiled.

"After all," he said, "since you are determined to go anyhow, what's the use of reading the reports? Inside of an hour you'll know all you need to know." But he saw that I did not take his teasing well, and drew out his pocketbook.

They were two typewritten papers clamped together.

They are on my desk before me now. The first one is endorsed:

Statement by Laura J. Bosworth, nurse, of St. Luke's Home for Graduate Nurses.

Miss Bosworth says:

I do not know just why I came here. But I know I'm frightened. That's the fact. I think there is something terribly wrong in the house of Francis M. Reed, 71 Beauregard Square. I think a crime of some sort has been committed. There are four people in the family, Mr. and Mrs. Reed and two children. I was to look after the children.

I was there four days and the children were never allowed out of the room. At night we were locked in. I kept wondering what I would do if there was a fire. The telephone wires are cut so no one can call the house, and I believe the doorbell is disconnected too. But that's fixed now. Mrs. Reed went round all the time with a face like chalk and her eyes staring. At all hours of the night she'd unlock the bedroom door and come in and look at the children.

Almost all the doors through the house were locked. If I wanted to get to the kitchen to boil eggs for the children's breakfast— for there were no servants, and Mrs. Reed was young and didn't know anything about cooking—Mr. Reed had to unlock about four doors for me.

If Mrs. Reed looked bad, he was dreadful—sunken eyed and white and wouldn't eat. I think he has killed somebody and is making away with the body.

Last night I said I had to have air, and they let me go out. I called up a friend from a pay-station, another nurse. This morning she sent me a special-delivery letter that I was needed on another case, and I got away. That's all; it sounds foolish, but try it and see if it doesn't get on your nerves.

Mr. Patton looked up at me as he finished reading.

"Now you see what I mean," he said. "That woman was there four days, and she is as temperamental as a cow, but in those four days her nervous system went to smash."

"Doors locked!" I reflected. "Servants gone; state of fear—it looks like a siege!"

"But why a trained nurse? Why not a policeman, if there is danger? Why anyone at all, if there is something that the police are not to know?"

"That is what I intend to find out," I replied. He shrugged his shoulders and read the other paper:

Report of Detective Bennett on Francis M. Reed, April 5, 1913:

Francis M. Reed is thirty-six years of age, married, a chemist at the Olympic Paint Works. He has two children, both boys. Has a small independent income and owns the house on Beauregard Square, which was built by his grandfather, General F. R. Reed. Is supposed to be living beyond his means. House is usually full of servants, and grocer in the neighborhood has had to wait for money several times.

On March twenty-ninth he dismissed all servants without warning. No reason given, but a week's wages instead of notice.

On March thirtieth he applied to the owners of the paint factory for two weeks' vacation. Gave as his reason nervousness and insomnia. He said he was "going to lay off and get some sleep." Has not been back at the works since. House under surveillance this afternoon. No visitors.

Mr. Reed telephoned for a nurse at four o'clock from a store on Eleventh Street. Explained that his telephone was out of order.

Mr. Patton folded up the papers and thrust them back into his pocket. Evidently he saw I was determined, for he only said:

"Have you got your revolver?"

"Yes."

"Do you know anything about telephones? Could you repair that one in an emergency?"

"In an emergency," I retorted, "there is no time to repair a telephone. But I've got a voice and there are windows. If I really put my mind to it you will hear me yell at headquarters."

He smiled grimly.

CHAPTER II: HOUSE OF MYSTERY

The Reed house is on Beauregard Square. It is a small, exclusive community, the Beauregard neighborhood; a dozen or more solid citizens built their homes there in the early 70's, occupying large lots, the houses flush with the streets and with gardens behind. Six on one street, six on another, back to back with the gardens in the center, they occupied the whole block. And the gardens were not fenced off, but made a sort of small park unsuspected from the streets. Here and there bits of flowering shrubbery sketchily outlined a property, but the general impression was of lawn and trees, free of access to all the owners. Thus with the square in front and the gardens in the rear, the Reed house faced in two directions on the early spring green.

In the gardens the old tar walks were still there, and a fountain which no longer played, but on whose stone coping I believe the young Beauregard Squarites made their first climbing ventures.

The gardens were always alive with birds, and later on from my windows I learned the reason. It seems to have been a custom sanctified by years, that the crumbs from the twelve tables should be thrown into the dry basin of the fountain for the birds. It was a common sight to see stately butlers and chic little waitresses in black and white coming out after luncheon or dinner with silver trays of crumbs. Many a scrap of gossip, as well as scrap of food, has been passed along at the old stone fountain, I believe. I know that it was there that I heard of the "basement ghost" of Beauregard Square—a whisper at first, a panic later.

I arrived at eight o'clock and rang the doorbell twice. The door was opened at once by Mr. Reed, a tall, blond young man carefully dressed. He threw away his cigarette when he saw me and shook hands. The hall was brightly lighted and most cheerful; in fact the whole house was ablaze with light. Certainly nothing could be less mysterious than the house, or than the debonair young man who motioned me into the library.

"I told Mrs. Reed I would talk to you before you go upstairs," he said. "Will you sit down?"

I sat down. The library was even brighter than the hall, and now I saw that although he smiled as cheerfully as ever his face was almost colorless, and his eyes, which looked frankly enough into mine for a moment, went wandering off round the room. I had the impression somehow that Mr. Patton had had of the nurse at headquarters that morning—that he looked as if he expected a knife in his back. It seemed to me that he wanted to look over his shoulder and by sheer will power did not.

"You know the rule, Miss Adams," he said: "When there's an emergency get a trained nurse. I told you our emergency—no servants and two small children."

"This should be a good time to secure servants," I said briskly. "City houses are being deserted for country places, and a percentage of servants won't leave town."

He hesitated. "We've been doing very nicely, although of course it's hardly more than just living. Our meals are sent in from a hotel, and— well, we thought, since we are going away so soon, that perhaps we could manage."

The impulse was too strong for him at that moment. He wheeled and looked behind him, not a hasty glance, but a deliberate inspection that took in every part of that end of the room. It was so unexpected that it left me gasping.

The next moment he was himself again.

"When I say that there is no illness," he said, "I am hardly exact. There is no illness, but there has been an epidemic of children's diseases among the Beauregard Square children and we are keeping the youngsters indoors."

"Don't you think they could be safeguarded without being shut up in the house?"

He responded eagerly. "If I only thought—" he checked himself. "No," he said decidedly; "for a time at least I believe it is not wise."

I did not argue with him. There was nothing to be gained by antagonizing him. And as Mrs. Reed came in just then, the subject was dropped.

She was hardly more than a girl, almost as blond as her husband, very pretty, and with the weariest eyes I have ever seen, unless perhaps the eyes of a man who has waited a long time for deathly tuberculosis.

I liked her at once. She did not attempt to smile. She rather clung to my hand when I held it out.

"I am glad St. Luke's still trusts us," she said. "I was afraid the other nurse— Frank, will you take Miss Adams's suitcase upstairs?"

She held out a key. He took it, but he turned at the door.

"I wish you wouldn't wear those things, Anne. You gave me your promise yesterday, you remember."

"I can't work round the children in anything else," she protested.

"Those things" were charming. She wore a rose silk negligee trimmed with soft bands of lace and blue satin flowers, a petticoat to match that garment, and a lace cap.

He hesitated in the doorway and looked at her—a curious glance, I thought, full of tenderness, reproof—apprehension perhaps.

"I'll take it off, dear," she replied to the glance. "I wanted Miss Adams to know that, even if we haven't a servant in the house, we are at least civilized. I—I haven't taken cold." This last was clearly an afterthought.

He went out then and left us together. She came over to me swiftly.

"What did the other nurse say?" she demanded.

"I do not know her at all. I have not seen her."

"Didn't she report at the hospital that we were—queer?"

I smiled. "That's hardly likely, is it?"

Unexpectedly she went to the door opening into the hall and closed it, coming back swiftly.

"Mr. Reed thinks it is not necessary, but— there are some things that will puzzle you. Perhaps I should have spoken to the other nurse. If—if anything strikes you as unusual, Miss Adams, just please don't see it! It is all right, everything is all right. But something has occurred—not very much, but disturbing—and we are all of us doing the very best we can."

She was quivering with nervousness.

I was not the police agent then, I'm afraid.

"Nurses are accustomed to disturbing things. Perhaps I can help."

"You can, by watching the children. That's the only thing that matters to me—the children. I don't want them left alone. If you have to leave them call me."

"Don't you think I will be able to watch them more intelligently if I know just what the danger is?"

I think she very nearly told me. She was so tired, evidently so anxious to shift her burden to fresh shoulders.

"Mr. Reed said," I prompted her, "that there was an epidemic of children's diseases. But from what you say—"

But I was not to learn, after all, for her husband opened the hall door.

"Yes, children's diseases," she said vaguely. "So many children are down. Shall we go up, Frank?"

The extraordinary bareness of the house had been dawning on me for some time. It was well lighted and well furnished. But the floors were innocent of rugs, the handsome furniture was without arrangement and, in the library at least, stood huddled in the center of the room. The hall and stairs were also uncarpeted, but there were marks where carpets had recently lain and had been jerked up.

The progress up the staircase was not calculated to soothe my nerves. The thought of my little revolver, locked in my suitcase, was poor comfort. For with every four steps or so Mr. Reed, who led the way, turned automatically and peered into the hallway below; he was listening, too, his head bent slightly forward. And each time that he turned, his wife behind me turned also. Cold terror suddenly got me by the spine, and yet the hall was bright with light.

(Note: Surely fear is a contagion. Could one isolate the germ of it and find an antitoxin? Or is it merely a form of nervous activity run amuck, like a runaway locomotive, colliding with other nervous activities and causing catastrophe? Take this up with Mr. Patton. But would he know? He, I am almost sure, has never been really afraid.)

I had a vision of my oxlike predecessor making this head-over-shoulder journey up the staircase, and in spite of my nervousness I smiled. But at that moment Mrs. Reed behind me put a hand on my arm, and I screamed. I remember yet the way she dropped back against the wall and turned white.

Mr. Reed whirled on me instantly. "What did you see?" he demanded.

"Nothing at all." I was horribly ashamed. "Your wife touched my arm unexpectedly. I dare say I am nervous."

"It's all right, Anne," he reassured her. And to me, almost irritably:

"I thought you nurses had no nerves."

"Under ordinary circumstances I have none."

It was all ridiculous. We were still on the staircase.

"Just what do you mean by that?"

"If you will stop looking down into that hall I'll be calm enough. You make me jumpy."

He muttered something about being sorry and went on quickly. But at the top he went through an inward struggle, evidently succumbed, and took a final furtive survey of the hallway below. I was so wrought up that had a door slammed anywhere just then I think I should have dropped where I stood.

The absolute silence of the house added to the strangeness of the situation. Beauregard Square is not close to a trolley line, and quiet is the neighborhood tradition. The first rubber-tired vehicles in the city drew up before Beauregard Square houses. Beauregard Square children speak in low voices and never bang their spoons on their plates. Beauregard Square servants wear felt-soled shoes. And such outside noises as venture to intrude themselves must filter through double brick walls and doors built when lumber was selling by the thousand acres instead of the square foot.

Through this silence our feet echoed along the bare floor of the upper hall, as well lighted as belowstairs and as dismantled, to the door of the day nursery. The door was locked—double locked, in fact. For the key had been turned in the old-fashioned lock, and in addition an ordinary bolt had been newly fastened on the outside of the door. On the outside! Was that to keep me in? It was certainly not to keep anyone or anything out. The feeblest touch moved the bolt.

We were all three outside the door. We seemed to keep our compactness by common consent. No one of us left the group willingly; or, leaving it, we slid back again quickly. That was my impression, at least. But the bolt rather alarmed me.

"This is your room," Mrs. Reed said. "It is generally the day nursery, but we have put a bed and some other things in it. I hope you will be comfortable."

I touched the bolt with my finger and smiled into Mr. Reed's eyes.

"I hope I am not to be fastened in!" I said.

He looked back squarely enough, but somehow I knew he lied.

"Certainly not," he replied, and opened the door.

If there had been mystery outside, and bareness, the nursery was charming—a corner room with many windows, hung with the simplest of nursery papers and full of glass-doored closets filled with orderly rows of toys. In one corner a small single bed had been added without spoiling the room. The window sills were full of flowering plants. There was a bowl of goldfish on a stand, and a tiny dwarf parrot in a cage was covered against the night air by a bright afghan. A white-tiled bathroom connected with this room and also with the night nursery beyond.

Mr. Reed did not come in. I had an uneasy feeling, however, that he was just beyond the door. The children were not asleep. Mrs. Reed left me to let me put on my uniform. When she came back her face was troubled.

"They are not sleeping well," she complained. "I suppose it comes from having no exercise. They are always excited."

"I'll take their temperatures," I said. "Sometimes a tepid bath and a cup of hot milk will make them sleep."

The two little boys were wide awake. They sat up to look at me and both spoke at once.

"Can you tell fairy tales out of your head?"

"Did you see Chang?"

They were small, sleek-headed, fair-skinned youngsters, adorably clean and rumpled.

"Chang is their dog, a Pekinese," explained the mother. "He has been lost for several days."

"But he isn't lost, Mother. I can hear him crying every now and then. You'll look again, Mother, won't you?"

"We heard him through the furnace pipe," shrilled the smaller of the two. "You said you would look."

"I did look, darlings. He isn't there. And you promised not to cry about him, Freddie."

Freddie, thus put on his honor, protested he was not crying for the dog. "I want to go out and take a walk, that's why I'm crying," he wailed. "And I want Mademoiselle, and my buttons are all off. And my ear aches when I lie on it."

The room was close. I threw up the windows, and turned to find Mrs. Reed at my elbows. She was glancing out apprehensively.

"I suppose the air is necessary," she said, "and these windows are all right. But—I have a reason for asking it—please do not open the others."

She went very soon, and I listened as she went out. I had promised to lock the door behind her, and I did so. The bolt outside was not shot.

After I had quieted the children with my mildest fairy story I made a quiet inventory of my new quarters. The rough diagram of the second floor is the one I gave Mr. Patton later. That night, of course, I investigated only the two nurseries. But, so strangely had the fear that hung over the house infected me, I confess that I made my little tour of bathroom and clothes-closet with my revolver in my hand!

I found nothing, of course. The disorder

of the house had not extended itself here. The bathroom was spotless with white tile, the large clothes-closet which opened off the passage between the two rooms was full of neatly folded clothing for the children. The closet was to play its part later, a darkish little room faintly lighted by a ground-glass transom opening into the center hall, but dependent mostly on electric light.

Outside the windows Mrs. Reed had asked me not to open was a porte-cochere roof almost level with the sills. Then was it an outside intruder she feared? And in that case, why the bolts on the outside of the two nursery doors? For the night nursery, I found, must have one also. I turned the key, but the door would not open.

I decided not to try to sleep that night, but to keep on watch. So powerfully had the mother's anxiety about her children and their mysterious danger impressed me that I made frequent excursions into the back room. Up to midnight there was nothing whatever to alarm me. I darkened both rooms and sat, waiting for I know not what; for some sound to show that the house stirred, perhaps. At a few minutes after twelve faint noises penetrated to my room from the hall, Mr. Reed's nervous voice and a piece of furniture scraping over the floor. Then silence again for half an hour or so.

Then—I was quite certain that the bolt on my door had been shot. I did not hear it, I think. Perhaps I felt it. Perhaps I only feared it. I unlocked the door; it was fastened outside.

There is a hideous feeling of helplessness about being locked in. I pretended to myself at first that I was only interested and curious. But I was frightened; I know that now. I sat there in the dark and wondered what I would do if the house took fire, or if some hideous tragedy enacted itself outside that locked door and I were helpless.

By two o'clock I had worked myself into a panic. The house was no longer silent. Someone was moving about downstairs, and not stealthily. The sounds came up through the heavy joists and flooring of the old house.

I determined to make at least a struggle to free myself. There was no way to get at the bolts, of course. The porte-cochere roof remained and the transom in the clothes-closet. True, I might have raised an alarm and been freed at once, but naturally I rejected this method. The roof of the porte-cochere proved impracticable. The tin bent and cracked under my first step. The transom then.

I carried a chair into the closet and found the transom easy to lower. But it threatened to creak. I put liquid soap on the hinges—it was all I had, and it worked very well—and lowered the transom inch by inch. Even then I could not see over it. I had worked so far without a sound, but in climbing to a shelf my foot slipped and I thought I heard a sharp movement outside. It was five minutes before I stirred. I hung there, every muscle cramped, listening and waiting. Then I lifted myself by sheer force of muscle and looked out. The upper landing of the staircase, brilliantly lighted, was to my right. Across the head of the stairs had been pushed a cotbed, made up for the night, but it was unoccupied.

Mrs. Reed, in a long, dark ulster, was standing beside it, staring with fixed and glassy eyes at something in the lower hall.

CHAPTER III: DEADLY FEAR

Some time after four o'clock my door was unlocked from without; the bolt slipped as noiselessly as it had been shot. I got a little sleep until seven, when the boys trotted into my room in their bathrobes and slippers and perched on my bed.

"It's a nice day," observed Harry, the elder. "Is that bump your feet?"

I wriggled my toes and assured him he had surmised correctly.

"You're pretty long, aren't you? Do you think we can play in the fountain today?"

"We'll make a try for it, son. It will do us all good to get out into the sunshine."

"We always took Chang for a walk every day, Mademoiselle and Chang and Freddie and I."

Freddie had found my cap on the dressing-table and had put it on his yellow head. But now, on hearing the beloved name of his pet, he burst into loud grief-stricken howls.

"Want Mam'selle," he cried. "Want Chang too. Poor Freddie!"

The children were adorable. I bathed and dressed them and, mindful of my predecessor's story of crackers and milk, prepared for an excursion kitchenward. The nights might be full of mystery, murder might romp from room to room, but I intended to see that the youngsters breakfasted. But before I was ready to go down breakfast arrived.

Perhaps the other nurse had told the Reeds a few plain truths before she left; perhaps, and this I think was the case, the cloud had lifted just a little. Whatever it may have been, two rather flushed and blistered young people tapped at the door that morning and were admitted, Mr. Reed first, with a tray, Mrs. Reed following with a coffeepot and cream.

The little nursery table was small for five, but we made room somehow. What if the eggs were underdone and the toast dry? The children munched blissfully. What if Mr. Reed's face was still drawn and haggard and his wife a limp little huddle on the floor? She sat with her head against his knee and her eyes on the little boys, and drank her pale coffee slowly. She was very tired, poor thing. She dropped asleep sitting there, and he sat for a long time, not liking to disturb her.

It made me feel homesick for the home I didn't have. I've had the same feeling before, of being a rank outsider, a sort of defrauded feeling. I've had it when I've seen the look in a man's eyes when his wife comes to after an operation. And I've had it, for that matter, when I've put a new baby in its mother's arms for the first time. I had it for sure that morning, while she slept there and he stroked her pretty hair.

I put in my plea for the children then.

"It's bright and sunny," I argued. "And if you are nervous I'll keep them away from other children. But if you want to keep them well you must give them exercise."

It was the argument about keeping them well that influenced him, I think. He sat silent for a long time. His wife was still asleep, her lips parted.

"Very well," he said finally, "from two to three, Miss Adams. But not in the garden back of the house. Take them on the street."

I agreed to that. "I shall want a short walk every evening myself," I added. "That is a rule of mine. I am a more useful person and a more agreeable one if I have it."

I think he would have demurred if he dared. But one does not easily deny so sane a request. He yielded grudgingly.

That first day was calm and quiet enough. Had it not been for the strange condition of the house and the necessity for keeping the children locked in I would have smiled at my terror of the night. Luncheon was sent in; so was dinner. The children and I lunched and supped alone. As far as I could see, Mrs. Reed made no attempt at housework; but the cot at the head of the stairs disappeared in the early morning and the dog did not howl again.

I took the boys out for an hour in the early afternoon. Two incidents occurred, both of them significant. I bought myself a screw driver—that was one. The other was our meeting with a slender young woman in black who knew the boys and stopped them. She proved to be one of the dismissed servants—the waitress, she said.

"Why, Freddie!" she cried. "And Harry too! Aren't you going to speak to Nora?"

After a moment or two she turned to me, and I felt she wanted to say something, but hardly dared.

"How is Mrs. Reed?" she asked. "Not sick, I hope?" She glanced at my St. Luke's cloak and bonnet.

"No, she is quite well."

"And Mr. Reed?"

"Quite well also."

"Is Mademoiselle still there?"

"No, there is no one there but the family. There are no maids in the house."

She stared at me curiously. "Mademoiselle

has gone? Are you cer— Excuse me, miss. But I thought she would never go. The children were like her own."

"She is not there, Nora."

She stood for a moment debating, I thought. Then she burst out, "Mr. Reed made a mistake, miss. You can't take a houseful of first-class servants and dismiss them the way he did, without half an hour to get out bag and baggage, without making talk. And there's talk enough all through the neighborhood."

"What sort of talk?"

"Different people say different things. They say Mademoiselle is still there, locked in her room on the third floor. There's a light there sometimes, but nobody sees her. And other folks say Mr. Reed is crazy. And there is worse being said than that."

But she refused to tell me any more— evidently concluded she had said too much and got away as quickly as she could, looking rather worried.

I was a trifle over my hour getting back, but nothing was said. To leave the clean and tidy street for the disordered house was not pleasant. But once in the children's suite, with the goldfish in the aquarium darting like tongues of flame in the sunlight, with the tulips and hyacinths of the window-boxes glowing and the orderly toys on their white shelves, I felt comforted. After all, disorder and dust did not imply crime.

But one thing I did that afternoon—did it with firmness and no attempt at secrecy, and after asking permission of no one. I took the new screw driver and unfastened the bolt from the outside of my door.

I was prepared, if necessary, to make a stand on that issue. But although it was noticed, I knew, no mention was made to me.

Mrs. Reed pleaded a headache that evening, and I believe her husband ate alone in the dismantled dining-room. For every room on the lower floor, I had discovered, was in the same curious disorder.

At seven Mr. Reed relieved me to go out. The children were in bed. He did not go into the day

nursery, but placed a straight chair outside the door of the back room and sat there, bent over, elbows on knees, chin cupped in his palm, staring at the staircase. He roused enough to ask me to bring an evening paper when I returned.

When I am on a department case I always take my off-duty in the evening by arrangement and walk round the block. Some time in my walk I am sure to see Mr. Patton himself if the case is big enough, or one of his agents if he cannot come. If I have nothing to communicate it resolves itself into a bow and nothing more.

I was nervous on this particular jaunt. For one thing my St. Luke's cloak and bonnet marked me at once, made me conspicuous; for another, I was afraid Mr. Patton would think the Reed house no place for a woman and order me home.

It was a quarter to eight and quite dark before he fell into step beside me.

"Well," I replied rather shakily; "I'm still alive, as you see."

"Then it is pretty bad?"

"It's exceedingly queer," I admitted, and told my story. I had meant to conceal the bolt on the outside of my door, and one or two other things, but I blurted them all out right then and there, and felt immeasurably better at once.

He listened intently.

"It's fear of the deadliest sort," I finished.

"Fear of the police?"

"I—I think not. It is fear of something in the house. They are always listening and watching at the top of the front stairs. They have lifted all the carpets, so that every footstep echoes through the whole house. Mrs. Reed goes down to the first door, but never alone. Today I found that the back staircase is locked off at top and bottom. There are doors."

I gave him my rough diagram of the house. It was too dark to see it.

"It is only tentative," I explained. "So much of the house is locked up, and every movement of mine is under surveillance. Without baths there are about twelve large rooms, counting the third floor. I've not been able to get there, but I thought that tonight I'd try to look about."

"You had no sleep last night?"

"Three hours—from four to seven this morning."

We had crossed into the public square and were walking slowly under the trees. Now he stopped and faced me.

"I don't like the look of it, Miss Adams," he said. "Ordinary panic goes and hides. But here's a fear that knows what it's afraid of and takes methodical steps for protection. I didn't want you to take the case, you know that; but now I'm not going to insult you by asking you to give it up. But I'm going to see that you are protected. There will be someone across the street every night as long as you are in the house."

"Have you any theory?" I asked him. He is not strong for theories generally. He is very practical. "That is, do you think the other nurse was right and there is some sort of crime being concealed?"

"Well, think about it," he prompted me. "If a murder has been committed, what are they afraid of? The police? Then why a trained nurse and all this caution about the children? A ghost? Would they lift the carpets so they could hear the specter tramping about the house?"

"If there is no crime, but something—a lunatic perhaps?" I asked.

"Possibly. But then why this secrecy and keeping out the police? It is, of course, possible that your respected employers have both gone off mentally, and the whole thing is a nightmare delusion. On my word it sounds like it. But it's too much for credulity to believe they've both gone crazy with the same form of delusion."

"Perhaps I'm the lunatic," I said despairingly. "When you reduce it like that to an absurdity I wonder if I didn't imagine it all, the lights burning everywhere and the carpets up, and Mrs. Reed staring down the staircase, and I locked in a room and hanging on by my nails to peer out through a closet transom."

"Perhaps. But how about the deadly sane young woman who preceded you? She had no imagination. Now about Reed and his wife—how do they strike you? They get along all right and that sort of thing, I suppose?"

"They are nice people," I said emphatically. "He's a gentleman and they're devoted. He just looks like a big boy who's got into an awful mess and doesn't know how to get out. And she's backing him up. She's a dear."

"Humph!" said Mr. Patton. "Don't suppress any evidence because she's a dear and he's a handsome big boy, Miss Adams!"

"I didn't say he was handsome," I snapped.

"Did you ever see a ghost or think you saw one?" he inquired suddenly.

"No, but one of my aunts has. Hers always carry their heads. She asked one a question once and the head nodded."

"Then you believe in things of that sort?"

"Not a particle—but I'm afraid of them."

He smiled, and shortly after that I went back to the house. I think he was sorry about the ghost question, for he explained that he had been trying me out, and that I looked well in my cloak and bonnet. "I'm afraid of your chin generally," he said; "but the white lawn ties have a softening effect. In view of the ties I have almost the courage—"

"Yes?"

"I think not, after all," he decided. "The chin is there, ties or no ties. Good night, and—for heaven's sake don't run any unnecessary risks."

The change from his facetious tone to earnestness was so unexpected that I was still standing there on the pavement when he plunged into the darkness of the square and disappeared.

CHAPTER IV: TERROR ABOVE

At ten minutes after eight I was back in the house. Mr. Reed admitted me, going through the tedious process of unlocking outer and inner vestibule doors and fastening them again behind me. He inquired politely if I had had a pleasant walk, and without waiting for my reply fell to reading the evening paper. He seemed to have forgotten me absolutely. First he scanned the headlines; then he turned feverishly to something farther on and ran his fingers down along a column. His lips were twitching, but evidently he did not find what he expected—or feared—for he threw the paper away and did not glance at it again. I watched him from the angle of the stairs.

Even for that short interval Mrs. Reed had taken his place at the children's door. She wore a black dress, long sleeved and high at the throat, instead of the silk negligee of the previous evening, and she held a book. But she was not reading. She smiled rather wistfully when she saw me.

"How fresh you always look!" she said. "And so self-reliant. I wish I had your courage."

"I am perfectly well. I dare say that explains a lot. Kiddies asleep?"

"Freddie isn't. He has been crying for Chang. I hate night, Miss Adams. I'm like Freddie. All my troubles come up about this time. I'm horribly depressed." Her blue eyes filled with tears.

"I haven't been sleeping well," she confessed. I should think not!

Without taking off my things I went down to Mr. Reed in the lower hall.

"I'm going to insist on something," I said. "Mrs. Reed is highly nervous. She says she has not been sleeping. I think if I gave her an opiate and she gets an entire night's sleep it may save her a breakdown."

I looked straight in his eyes, and for once he did not evade me.

"I'm afraid I've been very selfish," he said. "Of course she must have sleep. I'll give you a powder, unless you have something you prefer to use."

I remembered then that he was a chemist, and said I would gladly use whatever he gave me.

"There is another thing I wanted to speak about, Mr. Reed," I said. "The children are mourning their dog. Don't you think he may have been accidentally shut up somewhere in the house in one of the upper floors?"

"Why do you say that?" he demanded sharply.

"They say they have heard him howling."

He hesitated for barely a moment. Then: "Possibly," he said. "But they will not hear him again. The little chap has been sick, and he—died today. Of course the boys are not to know."

No one watched the staircase that night. I gave Mrs. Reed the opiate and saw her comfortably into bed. When I went back fifteen minutes later she was resting, but not asleep. Opiates sometimes make people garrulous for a little while—sheer comfort, perhaps, and relaxed tension. I've had stockbrokers and bankers in the hospital give me tips, after a hypodermic of morphia, that would have made me wealthy had I not been limited to my training allowance of twelve dollars a month.

"I was just wondering," she said as I tucked her up, "where a woman owes the most allegiance—to her husband or to her children?"

"Why not split it up," I said cheerfully, "and try doing what seems best for both?"

"But that's only a compromise!" she complained, and was asleep almost immediately. I lowered the light and closed the door, and shortly after I heard Mr. Reed locking it from the outside.

With the bolt off my door and Mrs. Reed asleep my plan for the night was easily carried out. I went to bed for a couple of hours and slept calmly. I awakened once with the feeling that someone was looking at me from the passage into the night nursery, but there was no one there. However, so strong had been the feeling that I got up and went into the back room. The children were asleep, and all doors opening into the hall were locked. But the window on to the porte-cochere roof was open and the curtain blowing. There was no one on the roof.

It was not twelve o'clock and I still had an hour. I went back to bed.

At one I prepared to make a thorough search of the house. Looking from one of my windows I thought I saw the shadowy figure of a man across the street, and I was comforted. Help was always close, I felt. And yet, as I stood inside my door in my rubber-soled shoes, with my ulster over my uniform and a revolver and my skeleton keys in my pockets, my heart was going very fast. The stupid story of the ghost came back and made me shudder, and the next instant I was remembering Mrs. Reed the night before, staring down into the lower hall with fixed glassy eyes.

My plan was to begin at the top of the house and work down. The thing was the more hazardous, of course, because Mr. Reed was most certainly somewhere about. I had no excuse for being on the third floor. Down below I could say I wanted tea, or hot water—anything. But I did not expect to find Mr. Reed up above. The terror, whatever it was, seemed to lie below.

Access to the third floor was not easy. The main staircase did not go up. To get there I was obliged to unlock the door at the rear of the hall with my own keys. I was working in bright light, trying my keys one after another, and watching over my shoulder as I did so. When the door finally gave it was a relief to slip into the darkness beyond, ghosts or no ghosts.

I am always a silent worker. Caution about closing doors and squeaking hinges is second nature to me. One learns to be cautious when one's only chance of sleep is not to rouse a peevish patient and have to give a body-massage, as like as not, or listen to domestic troubles—"I said" and "he said"—until one is almost crazy.

So I made no noise. I closed the door behind me and stood blinking in the darkness. I listened. There was no sound above or below. Now houses at night have no terror for me. Every nurse is obliged to do more or less going about in the dark. But I was not easy. Suppose Mr. Reed should call me? True, I had locked my door and had the key in my pocket. But a dozen emergencies flew through my mind as I felt for the stair rail.

There was a curious odor through all the back staircase, a pungent, aromatic scent that, with all my familiarity with drugs, was strange to me. As I slowly climbed the stairs it grew more powerful. The air was heavy with it, as though no windows had been opened in that part of the house. There was no door at the top of this staircase, as there was on the second floor. It opened into an upper hall, and across from the head of the stairs was a door leading into a room. This door was closed. On this staircase, as on all the others, the carpet had been newly lifted. My electric flash

showed the white boards and painted borders, the carpet tacks, many of them still in place. One, lying loose, penetrated my rubber sole and went into my foot.

I sat down in the dark and took off the shoe. As I did so my flash, on the step beside me, rolled over and down with a crash. I caught it on the next step, but the noise had been like a pistol shot.

Almost immediately a voice spoke above me sharply. At first I thought it was out in the upper hall. Then I realized that the closed door was between it and me.

"Ees that you, Meester Reed?"

Mademoiselle!

"Meester Reed!"—plaintively. "Eet comes up again, Meester Reed! I die! Tomorrow I die!"

She listened. On no reply coming she began to groan rhythmically, to a curious accompaniment of creaking. When I had gathered up my nerves again I realized that she must be sitting in a rocking-chair. The groans were really little plaintive grunts.

By the time I had got my shoe on she was up again, and I could hear her pacing the room, the heavy step of a woman well fleshed and not young. Now and then she stopped inside the door and listened; once she shook the knob and mumbled querulously to herself.

I recovered the flash, and with infinite caution worked my way to the top of the stairs. Mademoiselle was locked in, doubly bolted in. Two strong bolts, above and below, supplemented the door lock.

Her ears must have been very quick, or else she felt my softly padding feet on the boards outside, for suddenly she flung herself against the door and begged for a priest, begged piteously, in jumbled French and English. She wanted food; she was dying of hunger. She wanted a priest.

And all the while I stood outside the door and wondered what I should do. Should I release the woman? Should I go down to the lower floor and get the detective across the street to come in and force the door? Was this the terror that held the house in thrall—this babbling old Frenchwoman calling for food and a priest in one breath?

Surely not. This was a part of the mystery, not all. The real terror lay below. It was not Mademoiselle, locked in her room on the upper floor, that the Reeds waited for at the top of the stairs. But why was Mademoiselle locked in her room? Why were the children locked in? What was this thing that had turned a home into a jail, a barracks, that had sent away the servants, imprisoned and probably killed the dog, sapped the joy of life from two young people? What was it that Mademoiselle cried "comes up again"?

I looked toward the staircase. Was it coming up the staircase?

I am not afraid of the thing I can see, but it seemed to me, all at once, that if anything was going to come up the staircase I might as well get down first. A staircase is no place to meet anything, especially if one doesn't know what it is.

I listened again. Mademoiselle was quiet. I flashed my light down the narrow stairs. They were quite empty. I shut off the flash and went down. I tried to go slowly, to retreat with dignity, and by the time I had reached the landing below I was heartily ashamed of myself. Was this shivering girl the young woman Mr. Patton called his right hand?

I dare say I should have stopped there, for that night at least. My nerves were frayed. But I forced myself on. The mystery lay below. Well, then, I was going down. It could not be so terrible. At least it was nothing supernatural. There must be a natural explanation. And then that silly story about the headless things must pop into my head and start me down trembling.

The lower rear staircase was black dark, like the upper, but just at the foot a light came in through a barred window. I could see it plainly and the shadows of the iron grating on the bare floor. I stood there listening. There was not a sound.

It was not easy to tell exactly what followed. I stood there with my hand on the rail. I'd been very silent; my rubber shoes attended to that. And one moment the staircase was clear, with a patch of light at the bottom. The next, something was there, halfway down—a head, it seemed to me, with a pointed hood like a monk's

cowl. There was no body. It seemed to lie at my feet. But it was living. It moved. I could tell the moment when the eyes lifted and saw my feet, the slow back-tilting of the head as they followed up my body. All the air was squeezed out of my lungs; a heavy hand seemed to press on my chest. I remember raising a shaking hand and flinging my flashlight at the head. The flash clattered on the stair tread, harmless. Then the head was gone and something living slid over my foot.

I stumbled back to my room and locked the door. It was two hours before I had strength enough to get my aromatic ammonia bottle.

CHAPTER V: A GHOST WALKS

It seemed to me that I had hardly dropped asleep before the children were in the room, clamoring.

"The goldfish are dead!" Harry said, standing soberly by the bed. "They are all dead with their stummicks turned up."

I sat up. My head ached violently.

"They can't be dead, old chap." I was feeling about for my kimono, but I remembered that when I had found my way back to the nursery after my fright on the back stairs I had lain down in my uniform. I crawled out, hardly able to stand. "We gave them fresh water yesterday, and—"

I had got to the aquarium. Harry was right. The little darting flames of pink and gold were still. They floated about, rolling gently as Freddie prodded them with a forefinger, dull eyed, pale bellies upturned. In his cage above the little parrot watched out of a crooked eye.

I ran to the medicine closet in the bathroom. Freddie had a weakness for administering medicine. I had only just rescued the parrot from the result of his curiosity and a headache tablet the day before.

"What did you give them?" I demanded.

"Bread," said Freddie stoutly.

"Only bread?"

"Dirty bread," Harry put in. "I told him it was dirty."

"Where did you get it?"

"On the roof of the porte-cochère!"

Shade of Montessori! The rascals had been out on that sloping tin roof. It turned me rather sick to think of it.

Accused, they admitted it frankly.

"I unlocked the window," Harry said, "and Freddie got the bread. It was out in the gutter. He slipped once."

"Almost went over and made a squash on the pavement," added Freddie. "We gave the little fishes the bread for breakfast, and now they're gone to God."

The bread had contained poison, of course. Even the two little snails that crawled over the sand in the aquarium were motionless. I sniffed the water. It had a slightly foreign odor. I did not recognize it.

Panic seized me then. I wanted to get away and take the children with me. The situation was too hideous. But it was still early. I could only wait until the family roused. In the meantime, however, I made a nerve-racking excursion out onto the tin roof and down to the gutter. There was no more of the bread there. The porte-cochère was at the side of the house. As I stood balancing myself perilously on the edge, summoning my courage to climb back to the window above, I suddenly remembered the guard Mr. Patton had promised and glanced toward the square.

The guard was still there. More than that, he was running across the street toward me. It was Mr. Patton himself. He brought up between the two houses with absolute fury in his face.

"Go back!" he waved. "What are you doing out there, anyhow? That roof's as slippery as the devil!"

I turned meekly and crawled back with as much dignity as I could. I did not say anything. There was nothing I could bawl from the roof. I could only close and lock the window and hope that the people in the next house still slept. Mr. Patton must have gone shortly after, for I did not see him again.

I wondered if he had relieved the night watch, or if he could possibly have been on guard himself all that chilly April night.

Mr. Reed did not breakfast with us. I made a point of being cheerful before the children, and their mother was rested and brighter than I had seen her. But more than once I found her staring at me in a puzzled way. She asked me if I had slept.

"I wakened only once," she said. "I thought I heard a crash of some sort. Did you hear it?"

"What sort of a crash?" I evaded.

The children had forgotten the goldfish for a time. Now they remembered and clamored their news to her.

"Dead?" she said, and looked at me.

"Poisoned," I explained. "I shall nail the windows over the porte-cochère shut, Mrs. Reed. The boys got out there early this morning and picked up something—bread, I believe. They fed it to the fish and—they are dead."

All the light went out of her face. She looked tired and harassed as she got up.

"I wanted to nail the window," she said vaguely, "but Mr. Reed— Suppose they had eaten that bread, Miss Adams, instead of giving it to the fish!"

The same thought had chilled me with horror. We gazed at each other over the unconscious heads of the children and my heart ached for her. I made a sudden resolution.

"When I first came," I said to her, "I told you I wanted to help. That's what I'm here for. But how am I to help either you or the children when I do not know what danger it is that threatens? It isn't fair to you, or to them, or even to me."

She was much shaken by the poison incident. I thought she wavered.

"Are you afraid the children will be stolen?"

"Oh, no."

"Or hurt in any way?" I was thinking of the bread on the roof.

"No."

"But you are afraid of something?"

Harry looked up suddenly. "Mother's never afraid," he said stoutly.

I sent them both in to see if the fish were still dead.

"There is something in the house downstairs that you are afraid of?" I persisted.

She took a step forward and caught my arm. "I had no idea it would be like this, Miss Adams. I'm dying of fear!"

I had a quick vision of the swathed head on the back staircase, and some of my night's terror came back to me. I believe we stared at each other with dilated pupils for a moment. Then I asked:

"Is it a real thing?—surely you can tell me this. Are you afraid of a reality, or—is it something supernatural?" I was ashamed of the question. It sounded so absurd in the broad light of that April morning.

"It is a real danger," she replied. Then I think she decided that she had gone as far as she dared, and I went through the ceremony of letting her out and of locking the door behind her.

The day was warm. I threw up some of the windows and the boys and I played ball, using a rolled handkerchief. My part, being to sit on the floor with a newspaper folded into a bat and to bang at the handkerchief as it flew past me, became automatic after a time.

As I look back I see a pair of disordered young rascals in Russian blouses and bare round knees doing a great deal of yelling and some very crooked throwing; a nurse sitting tailor fashion on the floor, alternately ducking to save her cap and making vigorous but ineffectual passes at the ball with her newspaper bat. And I see sunshine in the room and the dwarf parrot eating sugar out of his claw. And below, the fish in the aquarium floating belly-up with dull eyes.

Mr. Reed brought up our luncheon tray. He looked tired and depressed, and avoided my eyes. I watched him while I spread the bread and butter for the children. He nailed shut the windows that opened on to the porte-cochere roof and when he thought I was not looking he examined the registers in the wall to see if the gratings were closed. The boys put the dead fish in a box and made him promise a decent interment in the garden. They called on me for an epitaph, and I scrawled on top of the box:

These fish are dead
Because a boy called Fred
Went out on a porch roof when he should
Have been in bed.

I was much pleased with it. It seemed to me that an epitaph, which can do no good to the departed, should at least convey a moral. But to my horror Freddie broke into loud wails and would not be comforted.

It was three o'clock, therefore, before they were both settled for their afternoon naps and I was free. I had determined to do one thing, and to do it in daylight—to examine the back staircase inch by inch. I knew I would be courting discovery, but the thing had to be done, and no power on earth would have made me essay such an investigation after dark.

It was all well enough for me to say to myself that there was a natural explanation; but this had been a human head, of a certainty; that something living and not spectral had slid over my foot in the darkness. I would not have gone back there again at night for youth, love, or money. But I did not investigate the staircase that day, after all.

I made a curious discovery after the boys had settled down in their small white beds. A venturesome fly had sailed in through an open window, and I was immediately in pursuit of him with my paper bat. Driven from the cornice to the chandelier, harried here, swatted there, finally he took refuge inside the furnace register.

Perhaps it is my training—I used to know how many million germs a fly packed about with it, and the generous benevolence with which it distributed them; I've forgotten—but the sight of a single fly maddens me. I said that to Mr. Patton once, and he asked what the sight of a married one would do. So I sat down by the register and waited. It was then that I made the curious discovery that the furnace belowstairs was burning, and burning hard. A fierce heat assailed me as I opened the grating. I drove the fly out of cover, but I had no time for him. The furnace going full on a warm spring day! It was strange.

Perhaps I was stupid. Perhaps the whole thing should have been clear to me. But it was not. I sat there bewildered and tried to figure it out. I went over it point by point:

The carpets up all over the house, lights going full all night and doors locked.

The cot at the top of the stairs and Mrs. Reed staring down.

The bolt outside my door to lock me in.

The death of Chang.

Mademoiselle locked in her room upstairs and begging for a priest.

The poison on the porch roof.

The head without a body on the staircase and the thing that slid over my foot.

The furnace going, and the thing I recognized as I sat there beside the register—the unmistakable odor of burning cloth.

Should I have known? I wonder. It looks so clear to me now.

I did not investigate the staircase for the simple reason that my skeleton key, which unfastened the lock of the door at the rear of the second-floor hall, did not open the door. I did not understand at once and stood stupidly working with the lock. The door was bolted on the other side. I wandered as aimlessly as I could down the main staircase and tried the corresponding door on the lower floor. It, too, was locked. Here was an impasse for sure. As far as I could discover the only other entrance to the back staircase was through the window with the iron grating.

As I turned to go back I saw my electric flash, badly broken, lying on a table in the hall. I did not claim it.

The lower floor seemed entirely deserted. The drawing-room and library were in their usual disorder, undusted and bare of floor. The air everywhere was close and heavy; there was not a window open. I sauntered through the various rooms, picked up a book in the library as an excuse and tried the door of the room behind. It was locked. I thought at first that something moved behind it, but if anything lived there it did not stir again. And yet I had a vivid impression that just on the other side of the door ears as keen as mine were listening. It was broad day, but I backed away from the door and out into the wide hall. My nerves were still raw, no doubt, from the night before.

I was to meet Mr. Patton at half after seven that night, and when Mrs. Reed relieved me at seven I had half an hour to myself. I spent it in Beauregard Gardens, with the dry fountain in the center. The place itself was charming, the trees still black but lightly fringed with new green, early spring flowers in the borders, neat paths and, bordering it all, the solid, dignified backs of the Beauregard houses. I sat down on the coping of the fountain and surveyed the Reed house. Those windows above were Mademoiselle's. The shades were drawn, but no light came through or round them. The prisoner— for prisoner she was by every rule of bolt and lock—must be sitting in the dark. Was she still begging for her priest? Had she had any food? Was she still listening inside her door for whatever it was that was "coming up"?

In all the other houses windows were open; curtains waved gently in the spring air; the cheerful signs of the dinner hour were evident nearby—moving servants, a gleam of stately shirt bosom as a butler mixed a salad, a warm radiance of candlelight from dining-room tables and the reflected glow of flowers. Only the Reed house stood gloomy, unlighted, almost sinister.

Beauregard Place dined early. It was one of the traditions, I believe. It liked to get to the theater or the opera early, and it believed in allowing the servants a little time in the evenings. So, although it was only something after seven, the evening rite of the table crumbs began to be observed. Came a colored butler, bowed to me with a word of apology, and dumped the contents of a silver tray into the basin; came a pretty mulatto, flung her crumbs gracefully and smiled with a flash of teeth at the butler.

Then for five minutes I was alone.

It was Nora, the girl we had met on the street, who came next. She saw me and came round to me with a little air of triumph.

"Well, I'm back in the square again, after all, miss," she said. "And a better place than the Reeds'. I don't have the doilies to do."

"I'm very glad you are settled again, Nora."

She lowered her voice. "I'm just trying it out," she observed. "The girl that left said I wouldn't stay. She was scared off. There have been some queer doings—not that I believe in ghosts or anything like that. But my mother in the old country had the second-sight, and if there's anything going on I'll be right sure to see it."

It took encouragement to get her story, and it was secondhand at that, of course. But it appeared that a state of panic had seized the Beauregard servants. The alarm was all below-stairs and had been started by a cook who, coming in late and going to the basement to prepare herself a cup of tea, had found her kitchen door locked and a light going beyond. Suspecting another maid of violating the tea canister she had gone soft-footed to the outside of the house and had distinctly seen a gray figure crouching in a corner of the room. She had called the butler, and they had made an examination of the entire basement without result. Nothing was missing from the house.

"And that figure has been seen again and again, miss," Nora finished. "McKenna's butler Joseph saw it in this very spot, walking without a sound and the street light beyond there shining straight through it. Over in the Smythe house the laundress, coming in late and going down to the basement to soak her clothes for the morning, met the thing on the basement staircase and fainted dead away."

I had listened intently. "What do they think it is?" I asked.

She shrugged her shoulders and picked up her tray.

"I'm not trying to say and I guess nobody is. But if there's been a murder it's pretty well known that the ghost walks about until the burial service is read and it's properly buried."

She glanced at the Reed house.

"For instance," she demanded, "where is Mademoiselle?"

"She is alive," I said rather sharply. "And even if what you say were true, what in the world would make her wander about the basements? It seems so silly, Nora, a ghost haunting damp cellars and laundries with stationary tubs and all that."

"Well," she contended, "it seems silly for them to sit on cold tombstones—and yet that's where they generally sit, isn't it?"

Mr. Patton listened gravely to my story that night.

"I don't like it," he said when I had finished. "Of course the head on the staircase is nonsense. Your nerves were ragged and our eyes play tricks on all of us. But as for the Frenchwoman—"

"If you accept her you must accept the head," I snapped. "It was there—it was a head without a body and it looked up at me."

We were walking through a quiet street, and he bent over and caught my wrist.

"Pulse racing," he commented. "I'm going to take you away, that's certain. I can't afford to lose my best assistant. You're too close, Miss Adams; you've lost your perspective."

"I've lost my temper!" I retorted. "I shall not leave until I know what this thing is, unless you choose to ring the doorbell and tell them I'm a spy."

He gave in when he saw that I was firm, but not without a final protest. "I'm directly responsible for you to your friends," he said. "There's probably a young man somewhere who will come gunning for me if anything happens to you. And I don't care to be gunned for. I get enough of that in my regular line."

"There is no young man," I said shortly.

"Have you been able to see the cellars?"

"No, everything is locked off."

"Do you think the rear staircase goes all the way down?"

"I haven't the slightest idea."

"You are in the house. Have you any suggestions as to the best method of getting into the house? Is Reed on guard all night?"

"I think he is."

"It may interest you to know," he said finally, "that I sent a reliable to break in there last night quietly, and that he—couldn't do it. He got a leg through a cellar window, and came near not getting it out again. Reed was just inside in the dark." He laughed a little, but I guessed that the thing galled him.

"I do not believe that he would have found anything if he had succeeded in getting in. There has been no crime, Mr. Patton, I am sure of that. But there is a menace of some sort in the house."

"Then why does Mrs. Reed stay and keep the children if there is danger?"

"I believe she is afraid to leave him. There are times when I think that he is desperate."

"Does he ever leave the house?"

"I think not, unless—"

"Yes?"

"Unless he is the basement ghost of the other houses."

He stopped in his slow walk and considered it.

"It's possible. In that case I could have him waylaid tonight in the gardens and left there, tied. It would be a holdup, you understand. The police have no excuse for coming in yet. Or, if we found him breaking into one of the other houses we could get him there. He'd be released, of course, but it would give us time. I want to clean the thing up. I'm not easy while you are in that house."

We agreed that I was to wait inside one of my windows that night, and that on a given signal I should go down and open the front door. The whole thing, of course, was contingent on Mr. Reed leaving the house some time that night. It was only a chance.

"The house is barred like a fortress," Mr. Patton said as he left me. "The window with the grating is hopeless. We tried it last night."

CHAPTER VI: TERROR BELOW

I find that my notes of that last night in the house on Beauregard Square are rather confused, some written at the time, some just before. For instance, on the edge of a newspaper clipping I find this:

Evidently this is the item. R—— went pale on reading it. Did not allow wife to see paper.

The clipping is an account of the sudden death of an elderly gentleman named Smythe, one of the Beauregard families.

The next clipping is less hasty and is on a yellow symptom record. It has been much folded—I believed I tucked it in my apron belt:

If the rear staircase is bolted everywhere from the inside, how did the person who locked it, either Mr. or Mrs. Reed, get back into the body of the house again? Or did Mademoiselle do it? In that case she is no longer a prisoner and the bolts outside her room are not fastened.

At eleven o'clock tonight Harry wakened with earache. I went to the kitchen to heat some mullein oil and laudanum. Mrs. Reed was with the boy and Mr. Reed was not in sight. I slipped into the library and used my skeleton keys on the locked door to the rear room. It was empty even of furniture, but there is a huge box there, with a lid that fastens down with steel hooks. The lid is full of small airholes. I had no time to examine further.

It is one o'clock. Harry is asleep and his mother is dozing across the foot of his bed. I have found the way to get to the rear staircase. There are outside steps from the basement to the garden. The staircase goes down all the way to the cellar evidently. Then the lower door in the cellar must be only locked, not bolted from the inside. I shall try to get in the cellar.

The next is a scrawl:

Cannot get to the outside basement steps. Mr. Reed is wandering round lower floor.

I reported Harry's condition and came up again. I must get to the back staircase.

I wonder if I have been able to convey, even faintly, the situation in that highly respectable old house that night: The fear that hung over it, a fear so great that even I, an outsider and stout of nerve, felt it and grew cold; the unnatural brilliancy of light that bespoke dread of the dark; the hushed voices, the locked doors and staring, peering eyes; the babbling Frenchwoman on an upper floor, the dead fish, the dead dog. And, always in my mind, that vision of dread on the back staircase and the thing that slid over my foot.

At two o'clock I saw Mr. Patton, or whoever was on guard in the park across the street, walk quickly toward the house and disappear round the corner toward the gardens in the rear. There had been no signal, but I felt sure that Mr. Reed had left the house. His wife was still asleep across Harry's bed. As I went out I locked the door behind me, and I took also the key to the night nursery. I thought that something disagreeable, to say the least, was inevitable, and why let her in for it?

The lower hall was lighted as usual and empty. I listened, but there were no restless footsteps. I did not like the lower hall. Only a thin wooden door stood between me and the rear staircase, and anyone who thinks about the matter will realize that a door is no barrier to a head that can move about without a body. I am afraid I looked over my shoulder while I unlocked the front door, and I know I breathed better when I was out in the air.

I wore my dark ulster over my uniform and I had my revolver and keys. My flash, of course, was useless. I missed it horribly. But to get to the staircase was an obsession by that time, in spite of my fear of it, to find what it guarded, to solve its mystery. I worked round the house, keeping close to the wall, until I reached the garden. The night was the city night, never absolutely dark. As I hesitated at the top of the basement steps it seemed to me that figures were moving about among the trees.

The basement door was unlocked and open. I was not prepared for that, and it made me, if anything, more uneasy. I had a box of matches with me, and I wanted light as a starving man wants food. But I dared not light them. I could only keep a tight grip on my courage and go on. A small passage first, with whitewashed stone walls, cold and scaly under my hand; then a large room, and still darkness. Worse than darkness, something crawling and scratching round the floor.

I struck my match, then, and it seemed to me that something white flashed into a corner and disappeared. My hands were shaking, but I managed to light a gas jet and to see that I was in the laundry. The staircase came down here, narrower than above, and closed off with a door.

The door was closed and there was a heavy bolt on it but no lock.

And now, with the staircase accessible and a gaslight to keep up my courage, I grew brave, almost reckless. I would tell Mr. Patton all about this cellar, which his best men had not been able to enter. I would make a sketch for him— coal-bins, laundry tubs, everything. Foolish, of course, but hold the gas jet responsible—the reckless bravery of light after hideous darkness.

So I went on, forward. The glow from the laundry followed me. I struck matches, found potatoes and cases of mineral water, bruised my knees on a discarded bicycle, stumbled over a box of soap. Twice out of the corner of my eye and never there when I looked I caught the white flash that had frightened me before. Then at last I brought up before a door and stopped. It was a curiously barricaded door, nailed against disturbance by a plank fastened across, and, as if to make intrusion without discovery impossible, pasted round every crack and over the keyhole with strips of strong yellow paper. It was an ominous door. I wanted to run away from it, and I wanted also desperately to stand and look at it and imagine what might lie beyond. Here again was the strange, spicy odor that I had noticed in the back staircase.

I think it is indicative of my state of mind that

I backed away from the door. I did not turn and run. Nothing in the world would have made me turn my back to it.

Somehow or other I got back into the laundry and jerked myself together. It was ten minutes after two. I had been just ten minutes in the basement!

The staircase daunted me in my shaken condition. I made excuses for delaying my venture, looked for another box of matches, listened at the end of the passage, finally slid the bolts and opened the door. The silence was impressive. In the laundry there were small, familiar sounds—the dripping of water from a faucet, the muffled measure of a gas meter, the ticking of a clock on the shelf. To leave it all, to climb into that silence—

Lying on the lower step was a curious instrument. It was a sort of tongs made of steel, about two feet long, and fastened together like a pair of scissors, the joint about five inches from the flattened ends. I carried it to the light and examined it. One end was smeared with blood and short, brownish hairs. It made me shudder, but—from that time on I think I knew. Not the whole story, of course, but somewhere in the back of my head, as I climbed in that hideous quiet, the explanation was developing itself. I did not think it out. It worked itself out as, step after step, match after match, I climbed the staircase.

Up to the first floor there was nothing. The landing was bare of carpet. I was on the first floor now. On each side, doors, carefully bolted, led into the house. I opened the one into the hall and listened. I had been gone from the children fifteen minutes and they were on my mind. But everything was quiet.

The sight of the lights and the familiar hall gave me courage. After all, if I was right, what could the head on the staircase have been but an optical delusion? And I was right. The evidence—the tongs—was in my hand. I closed and bolted the door and felt my way back to the stairs. I lighted no matches this time. I had only a few, and on this landing there was a little light from the grated window, although the staircase above was in black shadow.

I had one foot on the lowest stair, when suddenly overhead came the thudding of hands on a closed door. It broke the silence like an explosion. It sent chills up and down my spine. I could not move for a moment. It was the Frenchwoman!

I believe I thought of fire. The idea had obsessed me in that house of locked doors. I remember a strangling weight of fright on my chest and of trying to breathe. Then I started up the staircase, running as fast as I could lift my weighted feet, I remember that, and getting up perhaps a third of the way. Then there came a plunging forward into space, my hands out, a shriek frozen on my lips, and—quiet.

I do not think I fainted. I know I was conscious of my arm doubled under me, a pain and darkness. I could hear myself moaning, but almost as if it were someone else. There were other sounds, but they did not concern me much. I was not even curious about my location. I seemed to be a very small consciousness surrounded by a great deal of pain.

Several centuries later a light came and leaned over me from somewhere above. Then the light said, "Here she is!"

"Alive?" I knew that voice, but I could not think whose it was.

"I'm not— Yes, she's moaning."

They got me out somewhere and I believe I still clung to the tongs. I had fallen on them and had a cut on my chin. I could stand, I found, although I swayed. There was plenty of light now in the back hallway, and a man I had never seen was investigating the staircase.

"Four steps off," he said. "Risers and treads gone and the supports sawed away. It's a trap of some sort."

Mr. Patton was examining my broken arm and paid no attention. The man let himself down into the pit under the staircase. When he straightened, only his head rose above the steps. Although I was white with pain to the very lips I laughed hysterically.

"The head!" I cried. Mr. Patton swore under his breath.

They half led, half carried me into the library. Mr. Reed was there, with a detective on guard over him. He was sitting in his old position, bent forward, chin in palms. In the blaze of light he was a pitiable figure, smeared with dust, disheveled from what had evidently been a struggle. Mr. Patton put me in a chair and dispatched one of the two men for the nearest doctor.

"This young lady," he said curtly to Mr. Reed, "fell into that damnable trap you made in the rear staircase."

"I locked off the staircase—but I am sorry she is hurt. My—my wife will be shocked. Only I wish you'd tell me what all this is about. You can't arrest me for going into a friend's house."

"If I send for some member of the Smythe family will they acquit you?"

"Certainly they will," he said. "I—I've been raised with the Smythes. You can send for anyone you like." But his tone lacked conviction.

Mr. Patton made me as comfortable as possible, and then, sending the remaining detective out into the hall, he turned to his prisoner.

"Now, Mr. Reed," he said. "I want you to be sensible. For some days a figure has been seen in the basements of the various Beauregard houses. Your friends, the Smythes, reported it. Tonight we are on watch, and we see you breaking into the basement of the Smythe house. We already know some curious things about you, such as dismissing all the servants on half an hour's notice and the disappearance of the French governess."

"Mademoiselle! Why, she—" He checked himself.

"When we bring you here tonight, and you ask to be allowed to go upstairs and prepare your wife, she is locked in. The nurse is missing. We find her at last, also locked away and badly hurt, lying in a staircase trap, where someone, probably yourself, has removed the steps. I do not want to arrest you, but, now I've started, I'm going to get to the bottom of all this."

Mr. Reed was ghastly, but he straightened in his chair.

"The Smythes reported this thing, did they?" he asked. "Well, tell me one thing. What killed the old gentleman—old Smythe?"

"I don't know."

"Well, go a little further." His cunning was boyish, pitiful. "How did he die? Or don't you know that either?"

Up to this point I had been rather a detached part of the scene, but now my eyes fell on the tongs beside me.

"Mr. Reed," I said, "isn't this thing too big for you to handle by yourself?"

"What thing?"

"You know what I mean. You've protected yourself well enough, but even if the—the thing you know of did not kill old Mr. Smythe you cannot tell what will happen next."

"I've got almost all of them," he muttered sullenly. "Another night or two and I'd have had the lot."

"But even then the mischief may go on. It means a crusade; it means rousing the city. Isn't it the square thing now to spread the alarm?"

Mr. Patton could stand the suspense no longer.

"Perhaps, Miss Adams," he said, "you will be good enough to let me know what you are talking about."

Mr. Reed looked up at him with heavy eyes.

"Rats," he said. "They got away, twenty of them, loaded with bubonic plague."

I went to the hospital the next morning. Mr. Patton thought it best. There was no one in my little flat to look after me, and although the pain in my arm subsided after the fracture was set I was still shaken.

He came the next afternoon to see me. I was propped up in bed, with my hair braided down in two pigtails and great hollows under my eyes.

"I'm comfortable enough," I said, in response to his inquiry; "but I'm feeling all of my years. This is my birthday. I am thirty today."

"I wonder," he said reflectively, "if I ever reach the mature age of one hundred, if I will carry in my head as many odds and ends of information as you have at thirty!"

"I?"

"You. How in the world did you know, for instance, about those tongs?"

"It was quite simple. I'd seen something like them in the laboratory here. Of course I didn't know what animals he'd used, but the grayish brown hair looked like rats. The laboratory must be the cellar room. I knew it had been fumigated—it was sealed with paper, even over the keyhole."

So, sitting there beside me, Mr. Patton told me the story as he had got it from Mr. Reed—a tale of the offer in an English scientific journal of a large reward from some plague-ridden country of the East for an anti-plague serum. Mr. Reed had been working along bacteriological lines in his basement laboratory, mostly with guinea pigs and tuberculosis. He was in debt; the offer loomed large.

"He seems to think he was on the right track," Mr. Patton said. "He had twenty of the creatures in deep zinc cans with perforated lids. He says the disease is spread by fleas that infest the rats. So he had muslin as well over the lids. One can had infected rats, six of them. Then one day the Frenchwoman tried to give the dog a bath in a laundry tub and the dog bolted. The laboratory door was open in some way and he ran between the cans, upsetting them. Every rat was out in an instant. The Frenchwoman was frantic. She shut the door and tried to drive the things back. One bit her on the foot. The dog was not bitten, but there was the question of fleas.

"Well, the rats got away, and Mademoiselle retired to her room to die of plague. She was a loyal old soul; she wouldn't let them call a doctor. It would mean exposure, and after all what could the doctors do? Reed used his serum and she's alive.

"Reed was frantic. His wife would not leave. There was the Frenchwoman to look after, and I think she was afraid he would do something desperate. They did the best they could, under the circumstances, for the children. They burned most of the carpets for fear of fleas, and put poison everywhere. Of course he had traps too.

"He had brass tags on the necks of the rats, and he got back a few—the uninfected ones. The other ones were probably dead. But he couldn't stop at that. He had to be sure that the trouble had not spread. And to add to their horror the sewer along the street was being relaid, and they had an influx of rats into the house. They found them everywhere in the lower floor. They even climbed the stairs. He says that the night you came he caught a big fellow on the front staircase. There was always the danger that the fleas that carry the trouble had deserted the dead creatures for new fields. They took up all the rest of the carpets and burned them. To add to the general misery the dog Chang developed unmistakable symptoms and had to be killed."

"But the broken staircase?" I asked. "And what was it that Mademoiselle said was coming up?"

"The steps were up for two reasons: The rats could not climb up, and beneath the steps Reed says he caught in a trap two of the tagged ones. As for Mademoiselle the thing that was coming up was her temperature—pure fright. The head you saw was poor Reed himself, wrapped in gauze against trouble and baiting his traps. He caught a lot in the neighbors' cellars and some in the garden."

"But why," I demanded, "why didn't he make it all known?"

Mr. Patton laughed while he shrugged his shoulders.

"A man hardly cares to announce that he has menaced the health of a city."

"But that night when I fell—was it only last night?—someone was pounding above. I thought there was a fire."

"The Frenchwoman had seen us waylay Reed from her window. She was crazy."

"And the trouble is over now?"

"Not at all," he replied cheerfully. "The trouble may be only beginning. We're keeping Reed's name out, but the Board of Health has issued a general warning. Personally I think his six pets died without passing anything along."

"But there was a big box with a lid—"

"Ferrets," he assured me. "Nice white ferrets with pink eyes and a taste for rats." He held out a thumb, carefully bandaged. "Reed had a couple under his coat when we took him in the garden. Probably one ran over your foot that night when you surprised him on the back staircase."

I went pale. "But if they are infected!" I cried; "and you are bitten—".

"The first thing a nurse should learn," he bent forward smiling, "is not to alarm her patient."

"But you don't understand the danger," I said despairingly. "Oh, if only men had a little bit of sense!"

"I must do something desperate then? Have the thumb cut off, perhaps?"

I did not answer. I lay back on my pillows with my eyes shut. I had given him the plague, had seen him die and be buried, before he spoke again.

"The chin," he said, "is not so firm as I had thought. The outlines are savage, but the dimple— You poor little thing; are you really frightened?"

"I don't like you," I said furiously. "But I'd hate to see anyone with—with that trouble."

"Then I'll confess. I was trying to take your mind off your troubles. The bite is there, but harmless. Those were new ferrets; had never been out."

I did not speak to him again. I was seething with indignation. He stood for a time looking down at me; then, unexpectedly, he bent over and touched his lips to my bandaged arm.

"Poor arm!" he said. "Poor, brave little arm!" Then he tiptoed out of the room. His very back was sheepish.

THE TEA-LEAF

Edgar Jepson & Robert Eustace

BORN IN ENGLAND, Edgar Alfred Jepson (1863–1938) graduated from Balliol College, Oxford, then spent five years in Barbados before returning to take a job as an editor at *Vanity Fair*, where he worked with Richard Middleton and the libidinous Frank Harris. He became involved, albeit tangentially, with such members of the Decadent Movement as Ernest Dowson, John Gawsworth (with whom he collaborated on several short stories), and Arthur Machen.

The first novel Jepson wrote under his own name, *Sibyl Falcon* (1895), features a female adventurer; he followed with such fantasy novels and thrillers as *The Mystery of the Myrtles* (1909), which involves human sacrifice, and *The Moon Gods* (1930), a lost-race novel. He may be more widely read as a translator than as a novelist, however, having brought many works by Maurice Leblanc to English-language readers. His son, Selwyn Jepson, was a prolific mystery writer, and his granddaughter is the noted British novelist Fay Weldon.

Dr. Eustace Robert Barton (1868–1943), using the pseudonym Robert Eustace, is known mainly for his collaborations with other writers, including several additional stories with Edgar Jepson; a novel, *The Stolen Pearl: A Romance of London* (1903), with the once-popular mystery writer Gertrude Warden; several books with L.T. Meade; and, most famously, a novel, *The Documents in the Case* (1930), with Dorothy L. Sayers.

Much like Craig Kennedy and Dr. Thorndyke, Ruth Kelstern, although an amateur detective in this story, brought scientific methods to her work, undoubtedly a skill learned in her father's laboratory, where she assisted him in a high-paying job.

"The Tea-Leaf" was originally published in the October 1925 issue of *The Strand Magazine*; it was first published in book form in *Great Short Stories of Detection, Mystery and Horror*, edited by Dorothy L. Sayers (London, Gollancz, 1928).

The Tea-Leaf

EDGAR JEPSON & ROBERT EUSTACE

ARTHUR KELSTERN and Hugh Willoughton met in the Turkish bath in Duke Street, St. James's, and rather more than a year later in that Turkish bath they parted. Both of them were bad-tempered men, Kelstern cantankerous and Willoughton violent. It was indeed difficult to decide which was the worse-tempered; and when I found that they had suddenly become friends, I gave that friendship three months. It lasted nearly a year.

When they did quarrel they quarrelled about Kelstern's daughter Ruth. Willoughton fell in love with her and she with him and they became engaged to be married. Six months later, in spite of the fact that they were plainly very much in love with one another, the engagement was broken off. Neither of them gave any reason for breaking it off. My belief was that Willoughton had given Ruth a taste of his infernal temper and got as good as he gave.

Not that Ruth was at all a Kelstern to look at. Like the members of most of the old Lincoln-shire families, descendants of the Vikings and the followers of Canute, one Kelstern is very like another Kelstern, fair-haired, clear-skinned, with light-blue eyes and a good bridge to the nose. But Ruth had taken after her mother: she was dark with a straight nose, dark-brown eyes of the kind often described as liquid, dark-brown hair, and as kissable lips as ever I saw. She

was a proud, rather self-sufficing, high-spirited girl, with a temper of her own. She needed it to live with that cantankerous old brute Kelstern. Oddly enough in spite of the fact that he always would try to bully her, she was fond of him; and I will say for him that he was very fond of her. Probably she was the only creature in the world of whom he was really fond. He was an expert in the application of scientific discoveries to indus-try; and she worked with him in his laboratory. He paid her five hundred a year, so that she must have been uncommonly good.

He took the breaking off of the engagement very hard indeed. He would have it that Wil-loughton had jilted her. Ruth took it hard too: her warm colouring lost some of its warmth; her lips grew less kissable and set in a thinner line. Willoughton's temper grew worse than ever; he was like a bear with a perpetually sore head. I tried to feel my way with both him and Ruth with a view to help to bring about a reconciliation. To put it mildly, I was rebuffed. Willoughton swore at me; Ruth flared up and told me not to meddle in matters that didn't concern me. Nevertheless my strong impression was that they were miss-ing one another badly and would have been glad enough to come together again if their stupid vanity could have let them.

Kelstern did his best to keep Ruth furious with Willoughton. One night I told him—it was no business of mine; but I never did give a tinker's curse for his temper—that he was a fool to meddle and had much better leave them alone. It made him furious, of course; he would have it that Willoughton was a dirty hound and a low blackguard—at least those were about the mildest things he said of him. It struck me of a sudden that there must be something much more serious in the breaking off of the engagement than I had guessed.

That suspicion was strengthened by the immense trouble Kelstern took to injure Willoughton. At his clubs, the Athenæum, the Devonshire, and the Savile, he would display an astonishing ingenuity in bringing the conversation round to Willoughton; then he would declare that he was a scoundrel and a blackguard of the meanest type. Of course it did Willoughton harm, though not nearly as much harm as Kelstern desired, for Willoughton knew his job as few engineers knew it; and it is very hard indeed to do much harm to a man who really knows his job. People have to have him. But of course it did him some harm; and Willoughton knew that Kelstern was doing it. I came across two men who told me that they had given him a friendly hint. That did not improve Willoughton's temper.

An expert in the construction of those ferroconcrete buildings which are rising up all over London, he was as distinguished in his sphere as Kelstern in his. They were alike not only in the matters of brains and bad temper but I think that their minds worked in very much the same way. At any rate both of them seemed determined not to change their ordinary course of life because of the breaking off of that engagement.

It had been the habit of both of them to have a Turkish bath, at the baths in Duke Street, at four in the afternoon on the second and last Tuesday in every month. To that habit they stuck. The fact that they must meet on those Tuesdays did not cause either of them to change his hour of taking his Turkish bath by the twenty minutes which would have given them no more than a passing glimpse of one another. They continued to take them, as they always had, simultaneously. Thick-skinned? They were thick-skinned. Neither of them pretended that he did not see the other; he scowled at him; and he scowled at him most of the time. I know this, for sometimes I had a Turkish bath myself at that hour.

It was about three months after the breaking off of the engagement that they met for the last time at that Turkish bath, and there parted for good.

Kelstern had been looking ill for about six weeks: there was a greyness and a drawn look to his face; and he was losing weight. On the second Tuesday in October he arrived at the bath punctually at four, bringing with him, as was his habit, a thermos flask full of a very delicate China tea. If he thought that he was not perspiring freely enough he would drink it in the hottest room; if he did perspire freely enough, he would drink it after his bath. Willoughton arrived about two minutes later. Kelstern finished undressing and went into the bath a couple of minutes before Willoughton. They stayed in the hot room about the same time; Kelstern went into the hottest room about a minute after Willoughton. Before he went into it he sent for his thermos flask which he had left in the dressing room and took it into the hottest room with him.

As it happened, they were the only two people in the hottest room; and they had not been in it two minutes before the four men in the hot room heard them quarrelling. They heard Kelstern call Willoughton a dirty hound and a low blackguard, among other things, and declare he would do him in yet. Willoughton told him to go to the devil twice. Kelstern went on abusing him and presently Willoughton fairly shouted: "Oh, shut up, you old fool! Or I'll make you!"

Kelstern did not shut up. About two minutes later Willoughton came out of the hottest room, scowling, walked through the hot room into the shampooing room and put himself into the hands of one of the shampooers. Two or three minutes after that a man of the name of Helston went into the hottest room and fairly yelled.

Kelstern was lying back on a blood-drenched couch, with the blood still flowing from a wound over his heart.

There was a devil of a hullabaloo. The police were called in; Willoughton was arrested. Of course he lost his temper and, protesting furiously that he had had nothing whatever to do with the crime, abused the police. That did not incline them to believe him.

After examining the room and the dead body the detective-inspector in charge of the case came to the conclusion that Kelstern had been stabbed as he was drinking his tea. The thermos flask lay on the floor in front of him and some of the tea had evidently been spilt, for some tea leaves—the tea in the flask must have been carelessly strained off the leaves by the maid who filled it—lay on the floor about the mouth of the empty flask. It looked as if the murderer had taken advantage of Kelstern's drinking his tea to stab him while the flask rather blocked his vision and prevented him from seeing what he would be at.

The case would have been quite plain sailing but for the fact that they could not find the weapon. It had been easy enough for Willoughton to take it into the bath in the towel in which he was draped. But how had he got rid of it? Where had he hidden it? A Turkish bath is no place to hide anything in. It is as bare as an empty barn—if anything, barer; and Willoughton had been in the barest part of it. The police searched every part of it—not that there was much point in doing that, for Willoughton had come out of the hottest room, and gone through the hot room into the shampooers' room. When Helston started shouting murder, Willoughton had rushed back with the shampooers to the hottest room and there he had stayed. Since it was obvious that he had committed the murder the shampooers and the bathers had kept their eyes on him. They were all of them certain that he had not left them to go to the dressing rooms; they would not have allowed him to do so.

It was obvious that he must have carried the weapon into the bath, hidden in the folds of the towel in which he was draped, and brought it away in the folds of that towel. He had laid the towel down beside the couch on which he was being shampooed; and there it still lay when they came to look for it, untouched, with no weapon in it, with no traces of blood on it. There was not much in the fact that it was not stained with blood, since Willoughton could have wiped the knife, or dagger, or whatever weapon he used, on the couch on which Kelstern lay. There were no marks of any such wiping on the couch; but the blood, flowing from the wound, might have covered them up.

There was no finding the weapon; and its disappearance puzzled the police and later puzzled the public.

Then the doctors who made the autopsy came to the conclusion that the wound had been inflicted by a circular, pointed weapon nearly three-quarters of an inch in diameter. It had penetrated rather more than three inches and supposing that its handle was only four inches long it must have been a sizeable weapon, quite impossible to overlook. The doctors also discovered a further proof of the theory that Kelstern had been drinking his tea when he was stabbed. Half-way down the wound they found two halves of a tea leaf which had evidently fallen on to Kelstern's body, been driven into the wound and cut in half by the weapon. Also they discovered that Kelstern was suffering from cancer. This fact was not published in the papers; I heard it at the Devonshire.

Willoughton was brought before the magistrates and to most people's surprise did not reserve his defence. He went into the witness box and swore that he had never touched Kelstern, that he had never had anything to touch him with, that he had never taken any weapon into the Turkish bath and so had had no weapon to hide, that he had never even seen any such weapon as the doctors described. He was committed for trial.

The papers were full of the crime; everyone was discussing it; and the question which occupied everyone's mind was: where had Willoughton hidden the weapon? People wrote to the papers to suggest that he had ingeniously put it in some place under everybody's eyes and that it had been overlooked because it was so obvious. Others suggested that, circular and pointed, it must be very like a thick lead pencil, that it was a thick lead pencil; and that was why the police had overlooked it in their search. The police had not overlooked any thick lead pencil; there had been no thick lead pencil to overlook. They hunted England through—Willoughton did a lot of motoring—to discover the man who had sold him this curious and uncommon weapon. They did not find the man who had sold it to him; they did not find a man who sold such weapons at all. They came to the conclusion that Kelstern had been murdered with a piece of a steel, or iron, rod filed to a point like a pencil.

In spite of the fact that only Willoughton *could* have murdered Kelstern, I could not believe that he had done it. The fact that Kelstern was doing his best to injure him professionally and socially was by no means a strong enough motive. Willoughton was far too intelligent a man not to be very well aware that people do not take much notice of statements to the discredit of a man whom they need to do a job for them; and for the social injury he would care very little. Besides, he might very well injure, or even kill, a man in one of his tantrums; but his was not the kind of bad temper that plans a cold-blooded murder; and if ever a murder had been deliberately planned, Kelstern's had.

I was as close a friend as Willoughton had, and I went to visit him in prison. He seemed rather touched by my doing so, and grateful. I learnt that I was the only person who had done so. He was subdued and seemed much gentler. It might last. He discussed the murder readily enough and naturally with an harassed air. He said quite frankly that he did not expect me, in the circumstances, to believe that he had not committed it; but he had not, and he could not for the life of him conceive who had. I did believe that he had not committed it; there was something in his way of discussing it that wholly

convinced me. I told him that I was quite sure that he had not killed Kelstern; and he looked at me as if he did not believe the assurance. But again he looked grateful.

Ruth was grieving for her father; but Willoughton's very dangerous plight to some degree distracted her mind from her loss. A woman can quarrel with a man bitterly without desiring to see him hanged; and Willoughton's chance of escaping hanging was not at all a good one. But she would not believe for a moment that he had murdered her father.

"No; there's nothing in it—nothing whatever," she said firmly. "If Dad had murdered Hugh I could have understood it. He had reasons—or at any rate he had persuaded himself that he had. But whatever reason had Hugh for murdering Dad? It's all nonsense to suppose that he'd mind Dad's trying all he knew to injure him, as much as that. All kinds of people are going about trying to injure other people in that way, but they don't really injure them very much; and Hugh knows that quite well."

"Of course they don't; and Hugh wouldn't really believe that your father was injuring him much," I said. "But you're forgetting his infernal temper."

"No: I'm not," she protested. "He might kill a man in one of his rages on the spur of the moment. But this wasn't the spur of the moment. Whoever did it had worked the whole thing out and came along with the weapon ready."

I had to admit that that was reasonable enough. But who had done it? I pointed out to her that the police had made careful enquiries about everyone in the bath at the time, the shampooers and the people taking their baths, but they had found no evidence whatever that any one of them had at any time had any relations, except that of shampooer, with her father.

"Either it was one of them, or somebody else who just did it and got right away, or there's a catch somewhere," she said, frowning thoughtfully.

"I can't see how there can possibly have been anyone in the bath except the people who are known to have been there," said I. "In fact, there can't have been."

Then the Crown subpœnaed her as a witness for the prosecution. It seemed rather unnecessary and even a bit queer, for it could have found plenty of evidence of bad blood between the two men without dragging her into it. Plainly it was bent on doing all it knew to prove motive enough. Ruth seemed more upset by the prospect of going into the witness box than I should have expected her to be. But then she had been having a very trying time.

On the morning of the trial I called for her after breakfast to drive her down to the New Bailey. She was pale and looked as if she had had a poor night's rest, and, naturally enough, she seemed to be suffering from an excitement she had to control. It was not like her to show any excitement she might be feeling.

We had of course been in close touch with Willoughton's solicitor, Hamley; and he had kept seats for us just behind him. He wished to have Ruth at hand to consult should some point turn up on which she could throw light, since she knew more than anyone about the relations between Willoughton and her father. I had timed our arrival very well; the jury had just been sworn in. Of course the Court was full of women, the wives of Peers and bookmakers and politicians, most of them overdressed and overscented.

Then the judge came in; and with his coming the atmosphere of the Court became charged with that sense of anxious strain peculiar to trials for murder. It was rather like the atmosphere of a sick room in a case of fatal illness, but worse.

It was unfortunate for Willoughton that the judge was Garbould. A hard-faced, common-looking fellow, and coarse in the grain, he has a well-founded reputation as a hanging judge and the habit of acting as an extra counsel for the prosecution.

Willoughton came into the box, looking under the weather and very much subdued. But he certainly looked dignified and he said that he was not guilty in a steady enough voice.

Greatorex, the leading Counsel for the Crown, opened the case for the prosecution. There was no suggestion in his speech that the police had discovered any new fact.

Then Helston gave evidence of finding the body of the dead man and he and the other three men who had been with him in the hot room gave evidence of the quarrel they had overheard between Willoughton and the dead man, and that Willoughton came out of the hottest room, scowling and obviously furious. One of them, a fussy old gentleman of the name of Underwood, declared that it was the bitterest quarrel he had ever heard. None of the four of them could throw any light on the matter of whether Willoughton was carrying the missing weapon in the folds of the towel in which he was draped; all of them were sure that he had nothing in his hands.

The medical evidence came next. In cross-examining the doctors who had made the autopsy, Hazeldean, Willoughton's counsel, established the fact quite definitely that the missing weapon was of a fair size; that its rounded blade must have been over half an inch in diameter and between three and four inches long. They were of the opinion that to drive a blade of that thickness into the heart, a handle of at least four inches in length would be necessary to give a firm enough grip. It might have been a piece of a steel, or iron, rod sharpened like a pencil. At any rate it was certainly a sizeable weapon, not one to be hidden quickly, or to disappear wholly in a Turkish bath. Hazeldean could not shake their evidence about the tea leaf; they were confident that it had been driven into the wound and cut in half by the blade of the missing weapon, and that that went to show that the wound had been inflicted while Kelstern was drinking his tea.

Detective-Inspector Brackett, who was in charge of the case, was cross-examined at great length about his search for the missing weapon. He made it quite clear that it was nowhere in that Turkish bath, neither in the hot rooms, nor the shampooing room, nor the dressing rooms, nor the vestibule, nor the office. He had had the plunge bath emptied; he had searched the roofs, though it was practically certain that the skylight above the hot room, not the hottest, had been shut at the time of the crime. In re-examination he scouted the idea of Willoughton's having had an accomplice who had carried away the weapon for him. He had gone into that matter most carefully.

The shampooer stated that Willoughton came to him scowling so savagely that he wondered what had put him into such a bad temper. In cross-examining him Arbuthnot, Hazeldean's junior, made it clearer than ever that, unless Willoughton had already hidden the weapon in the bare hottest room, it was hidden in the towel. Then he drew from the shampooer the definite statement that Willoughton had set down the towel beside the couch on which he was shampooed, that he had hurried back to the hot rooms in front of the shampooer; that the shampooer had come back from the hot rooms, leaving Willoughton still in them discussing the crime, to find the towel lying just as Willoughton had set it down, with no weapon in it and no trace of blood on it.

Since the Inspector had disposed of the possibility that an accomplice had slipped in, taken the weapon from the towel, and slipped out of the bath with it, this evidence really made it clear that the weapon had never left the hottest room.

Then the prosecution called evidence of the bad terms on which Kelstern and Willoughton had been. Three well-known and influential men told the jury about Kelstern's efforts to prejudice Willoughton in their eyes and the damaging statements he had made about him. One of them had felt it to be his duty to tell Willoughton about this; and Willoughton had been very angry. Arbuthnot, in cross-examining, elicited the fact that any damaging statement that Kelstern made about anyone was considerably discounted by the fact that everyone knew him to be in the highest degree cantankerous.

I noticed that during the end of the cross-examination of the shampooer, and during this evidence, Ruth had been fidgeting and turning to look impatiently at the entrance to the Court, as if she were expecting someone. Then, just as she was summoned to the witness box, there came in a tall, stooping, grey-headed, grey-bearded man of about sixty, carrying a brown-paper parcel. His face was familiar to me; but I could not place him. He caught her eye and nodded to her. She breathed a sharp sigh of relief and bent over and handed a letter she had in her hand to Willoughton's solicitor and pointed out the grey-bearded man to him. Then she went quietly to the witness box.

Hamley read the letter and at once bent over and handed it to Hazeldean and spoke to him. I caught a note of excitement in his hushed voice. Hazeldean read the letter and appeared to grow excited too. Hamley slipped out of his seat and went to the grey-bearded man who was still standing just inside the door of the Court and began to talk to him earnestly.

Greatorex began to examine Ruth; and naturally I turned my attention to her. His examination was directed also to show on what bad terms Kelstern and Willoughton had been. Ruth was called on to tell the jury some of Kelstern's actual threats. Then—it is astonishing how few things the police fail to ferret out in a really important case—the examination took a curious turn. Greatorex began to question Ruth about her own relations with Willoughton and the plain trend of his questions was to bring out the fact that they had not merely been engaged to be married but had also been lovers.

I saw at once what the prosecution was aiming at. It was trying to make use of the tendency of a British jury and a British judge, in a natural effort to champion morality, to hang a man or a woman, who is on trial for murder, for behaving immorally in relations with the other sex. There was no better way of prejudicing Willoughton than by proving that he had seduced Ruth under the promise of marriage.

Of course Hazeldean was on his feet at once protesting that this evidence was irrelevant and inadmissible; and of course Garbould was against him—he does not enjoy the nickname by which he is known to the junior bar for nothing. Hazeldean was magnificent. He had one of the worst rows with Garbould he had ever had; and he has had many. Garbould is a fool to let him have these rows. Hazeldean always gets the better of him, or seems to; and it does him good with the jury. But then Garbould was raised to the bench not for intelligence but for political merit. He ruled that the questions were admissible and put one or two to Ruth himself.

Then Willoughton lost his temper and protested that this had nothing to do with the case and that it was an outrage. Willoughton has a ringing voice of considerable volume. He is not at all an easy man to hush when he does not wish to hush; and they were some time hushing him. By the time they succeeded Garbould was purplish-red with fury. Anything that he could do to hang Willoughton would certainly be done. But, observing the jury, my impression was that Willoughton's outburst had done him good with it and that Hazeldean's protests had shaken its confidence in Garbould. When I looked at the faces, just a trifle sickly, of the counsel for the prosecution, I felt sure that the Crown had bungled this business rather badly.

Greatorex, assisted by Garbould, went on with his questions; and Ruth, defiant rather than abashed, and looking in her flushed animation a more charming creature than ever, admitted that she and Willoughton had been lovers; that more than once when he had brought her home from a dance or a theatre he had not left her till the early morning. One of the maids had spied on them; and the Crown had the facts.

I was afraid, in spite of Hazeldean's protests, that the fact that Willoughton had seduced her under the promise of marriage, as Greatorex put it, would do him great harm with the jury—very likely it would hang him.

Then Ruth, still flushed, but not greatly discomposed, said: "That would be a reason for my father's murdering Mr. Willoughton, not for Mr. Willoughton's murdering my father."

That brought Garbould down upon her like a ton of bricks. She was there to answer questions, not to make idle remarks and so forth and so on.

Then Greatorex came to the breaking off of the engagement and put it to her that Willoughton had broken it off, had in fact jilted her after compromising her. That she would not have for a moment. She declared that they had had a quarrel and she had broken it off. To that she stuck and there was no shaking her, though Garbould himself took a hearty hand in trying to shake her.

In the middle of it Willoughton, who was looking quite himself again, now that the atmosphere of the Court might be said to be charged almost with violence, said in a very unpleasant, jeering voice: "What she says is perfectly true—what's the good of bothering her?"

Again Garbould was to the fore, and angrily reprimanded him for speaking, bade him keep silent, and said that he would not have his Court turned into a beargarden.

"With the bear on the bench," said Hazeldean to Arbuthnot in a whisper that carried well.

Two or three people laughed. One of them was a juryman. By the time Garbould had finished with him I did not think that that juryman would have convicted Willoughton, if he had actually seen him stab Kelstern.

Willoughton was writing a note which was passed to Hazeldean.

Hazeldean rose to cross-examine Ruth with a wholly confident air. He drew from her the facts that her father had been on excellent terms with Willoughton until the breaking off of the engagement; that in that matter he had taken her part warmly; and that when the maid who had spied upon them had informed him of her relations with Willoughton he had been very little more enraged than he was already.

Then Hazeldean asked: "Is it a fact that since the breaking off of your engagement the prisoner has more than once begged you to forgive him and renew it?"

"Four times," said Ruth.

"And you refused?"

"Yes," said Ruth. She looked at Willoughton queerly and added: "He wanted a lesson."

"Did he then beg you at least to go through

the form of marriage with him, and promise to leave you at the church door?"

"Yes."

"And you refused?"

"Yes," said Ruth.

Garbould bent forward and said in his most unpleasant tone: "And why did you reject the opportunity of repairing your shameful behaviour?"

"It wasn't shameful," Ruth almost snapped; and she scowled at him frankly. Then she added naïvely: "I refused because there was no hurry. He would always marry me if I changed my mind and wanted to."

There was a pause. To me it seemed clearer than ever that the Crown had bungled badly in raising the question of the relations between her and Willoughton since he had evidently been more than ready to save her from any harm that might come of their indiscretion. But then, with a jury, you can never tell. Then Hazeldean started on a fresh line.

In sympathetic accents he asked: "Is it a fact that your father was suffering from cancer in a painful form?"

"It was beginning to grow very painful," said Ruth sadly.

"Did he make a will and put all his affairs in order a few days before he died?"

"Three days," said Ruth.

"Did he ever express an intention of committing suicide?"

"He said that he would stick it out for a little while and then end it all," said Ruth. She paused and added: *"And that is what he did do."*

One might almost say that the Court started. I think that everyone in it moved a little, so that there was a kind of rustling murmur. Garbould threw himself back in his seat with a snort of incredulity and glowered at Ruth.

"Will you tell the Court your reasons for that statement?" said Hazeldean.

Ruth seemed to pull herself together; the flush had faded from her face and she was looking very tired; then she began in a quiet, even voice: "I never believed for a moment that Mr.

Willoughton murdered my father. If my father had murdered Mr. Willoughton it would have been a different matter."

Garbould leaned forward and snarled that it was not her beliefs or fancies that were wanted, but facts.

I did not think that she heard him; she was concentrating on giving her reasons exactly; she went on in the same quiet tone: "Of course, like everybody else I puzzled over the weapon: what it was and where it had got to. I did not believe that it was a pointed piece of a half-inch steel rod. If anybody had come to the Turkish bath meaning to murder my father and hide the weapon, they wouldn't have used one so big and so difficult to hide, when a hat-pin would have done just as well and could be hidden much more easily. But what puzzled me most was the tea leaf in the wound. All the other tea leaves that came out of the flask were lying on the floor. Inspector Brackett told me they were. And I couldn't believe that one tea leaf had fallen on to my father at the very place above his heart at which the point of the weapon had penetrated the skin and got driven in by it. It was too much of a coincidence for me to swallow. But I got no nearer understanding it than anyone else."

Garbould broke in in a tone of some exasperation and told her to come to the facts. Hazeldean rose and protested that the witness should not be interrupted; that she had solved a mystery which had puzzled some of the best brains in England, and she should be allowed to tell her story in her own way.

Again Ruth did not appear to listen to them, and when they stopped she went on in the same quiet voice: "Of course I remembered that Dad had talked of putting an end to it; but no one with a wound like that could get up and hide the weapon. Then, the night before last I dreamt that I went into the laboratory and saw a piece of steel rod, pointed, lying on the table at which my father used to work."

"Dreams now!" murmured Garbould contemptuously; and he leaned back and folded his hands over his stomach.

"I didn't think much of the dream, of course," Ruth went on. "I had been puzzling about it all so hard for so long that it was only natural to dream about it. But after breakfast I had a sudden feeling that the secret was in the laboratory if I could only find it. I did not attach any importance to the feeling; but it went on growing stronger; and after lunch I went to the laboratory and began to hunt.

"I looked through all the drawers and could find nothing. Then I went round the room looking at everything and into everything, instruments and retorts and tubes and so on. Then I went into the middle of the floor and looked slowly round the room pretty hard. Against the wall, near the door, lying ready to be taken away, was a gas cylinder. I rolled it over to see what gas had been in it and found no label on it."

She paused to look round the Court as if claiming its best attention; then she went on: "Now that was very queer because every gas cylinder must have a label on it—so many gases are dangerous. I turned on the cylinder and nothing came out of it. It was quite empty. Then I went to the book in which all the things which come in are entered, and found that ten days before Dad died he had had in a cylinder of CO_2 and seven pounds of ice. Also he had had seven pounds of ice every day till the day of his death. It was the ice and the CO_2 together that gave me the idea. CO_2, carbon dioxide, has a very low freezing point—eighty degrees centigrade—and as it comes out of the cylinder and mixes with the air it turns into very fine snow; and that snow, if you compress it, makes the hardest and toughest ice possible. It flashed on me that Dad could have collected this snow and forced it into a mould and made a weapon that would not only inflict that wound but would *disappear instantly*!"

She paused again to look round the Court at about as rapt a lot of faces as any narrator could desire. Then she went on: "I knew that that was what he had done. I knew it for certain. Carbon dioxide ice would make a hard, tough dagger, and it would melt quickly in the hottest room of a Turkish bath and leave no smell because it is scentless. So there wouldn't be any weapon. And it explained the tea leaf too. Dad had made a carbon dioxide dagger perhaps a week before he used it, perhaps only a day. And he had put it into the thermos flask as soon as he had made it. The thermos flask keeps out the heat as well as the cold, you know. But to make sure that it couldn't melt at all he kept the flask in ice till he was ready to use the dagger. It's the only way you can explain that tea leaf. It came out of the flask sticking to the point of the dagger and was driven into the wound!"

She paused again and one might almost say that the Court heaved a deep sigh of relief.

Then Garbould asked in an unpleasant and incredulous voice: "Why didn't you take this fantastic theory straight to the police?"

"But that wouldn't have been any good," she protested quickly. "It was no use my knowing it myself; I had to make other people believe it; I had to find evidence. I began to hunt for it. I felt in my bones that there was some. What I wanted was the mould. I found it!"

She uttered the words in a tone of triumph and smiled at Willoughton; then she went on: "At least I found bits of it. In the box into which we used to throw odds and ends, scraps of material, damaged instruments, and broken test tubes, I found some pieces of vulcanite; and I saw at once that they were bits of a vulcanite container. I took some wax and rolled it into a rod about the right size and then I pieced the container together on the outside of it—at least most of it—there are some small pieces missing. It took me nearly all night. But I found the most important bit—*the pointed end*!"

She dipped her hand into her handbag and drew out a black object about nine inches long and three quarters of an inch thick and held it up for everyone to see.

Someone, without thinking, began to clap; and there came a storm of applause that drowned the voice of the Clerk calling for order and the bellowing of Garbould.

When the applause died down, Hazeldean, who never misses the right moment, said: "I have no more questions to ask the witness, my lord," and sat down.

That action seemed to clinch it in my eyes and, I have no doubt, it clinched it in the eyes of the jury.

The purple Garbould leant forward and almost bellowed at Ruth: "Do you expect the jury to believe that a well-known man like your father died in the act of deliberately setting a dastardly trap to hang the prisoner?"

Ruth looked at him, shrugged her shoulders, and said with a calm acceptance of the facts of human nature one would expect to find only in a much older woman: "Oh, well, Daddy was like that. And he certainly believed he had very good reasons for killing Mr. Willoughton."

There was that in her tone and manner which made it absolutely certain that Kelstern was not only like that but that he had acted according to his nature.

Greatorex did not re-examine Ruth; he conferred with Hazeldean. Then Hazeldean rose to open the case for the defence. He said that he would not waste the time of the Court, and that in view of the fact that Miss Kelstern had solved the problem of her father's death, he would only call one witness, Professor Mozley.

The grey-headed, grey-bearded, stooping man, who had come to the Court so late, went into the witness box. Of course his face had been familiar to me; I had seen his portrait in the newspapers a dozen times. He still carried the brown-paper parcel.

In answer to Hazeldean's questions he stated that it was possible, not even difficult, to make a weapon of carbon dioxide hard enough and tough enough and sharp enough to inflict such a wound as that which had caused Kelstern's death. The method of making it was to fold a piece of chamois leather into a bag, hold that bag with the left hand, protected by a glove, over the nozzle of a cylinder containing liquid carbon dioxide, and open the valve with the right hand. Carbon dioxide evaporates so quickly that its freezing point, 80° centigrade, is soon reached; and it solidifies in the chamois leather

bag as a deposit of carbon dioxide snow. Then turn off the gas, spoon that snow into a vulcanite container of the required thickness, and ram it down with a vulcanite plunger into a rod of the required hardness. He added that it was advisable to pack the container in ice while filling it and ramming down the snow, then put the rod into a thermos flask; and keep it till it is needed.

"And you have made such a rod?" said Hazeldean.

"Yes," said the Professor, cutting the string of the brown-paper parcel. "When Miss Kelstern hauled me out of bed at half past seven this morning to tell me her discoveries, I perceived at once that she had found the solution of the problem of her father's death, which had puzzled me considerably. I had breakfast quickly and got to work to make such a weapon myself for the satisfaction of the Court. Here it is."

He drew a thermos flask from the brown paper, unscrewed the top of it, and inverted it. There dropped into his gloved hand a white rod about eight inches long. He held it out for the jury to see.

"This carbon dioxide ice is the hardest and toughest ice we know of; and I have no doubt that Mr. Kelstern killed himself with a similar rod. The difference between the rod he used and this is that his rod was pointed. I had no pointed vulcanite container; but the container that Miss Kelstern pieced together is pointed. Doubtless Mr. Kelstern had it specially made, probably by Messrs. Hawkins & Spender."

He dropped the rod back into the thermos flask and screwed on the top.

Hazeldean sat down. The juryman who had been reprimanded by Garbould leaned forward and spoke earnestly to the foreman. Greatorex rose.

"With regard to the point of the rod, Professor Mozley: would it remain sharp long enough to pierce the skin in that heat?" he asked.

"In my opinion it would," said the Professor. "I have been considering that point and bearing in mind the facts that Mr. Kelstern would from his avocation be very deft with his hands, and being a scientific man, would know exactly what to do, he would have the rod out of the flask and the point in position in very little more than a second—perhaps less. He would, I think, hold it in his left hand and drive it home by striking the butt of it hard with his right. The whole thing would not take him two seconds. Besides, if the point of the weapon had melted the tea leaf would have fallen off it."

"Thank you," said Greatorex, and turned and conferred with the Crown solicitors.

Then he said: "We do not propose to proceed with the case, my lord."

The foreman of the jury rose quickly and said: "And the jury doesn't want to hear anything more, my lord. We're quite satisfied that the prisoner isn't guilty."

Garbould hesitated. For two pins he would have directed the case to proceed. Then his eye fell on Hazeldean, who was watching him; I fancied that he decided not to give him a chance of saying more disagreeable things.

Looking black enough, he put the question formally to the jury, who returned a verdict of "Not guilty," and then he discharged Willoughton.

I came out of the Court with Ruth, and we waited for Willoughton.

Presently he came out of the door and stopped and shook himself. Then he saw Ruth and came to her. They did not greet one another. She just slipped her hand through his arm; and they walked out of the New Bailey together.

We made a good deal of noise, cheering them.

THE ALMOST PERFECT MURDER

Hulbert Footner

AS A FRIEND of the great bibliophile Christopher Morley, William Hulbert Footner (1879–1944) decided to use him as a major character in *The Mystery of the
Folded Paper* (1930), his first book about Amos Lee Mappin, an author and amateur criminologist who appeared in ten novels and resembles Charles Dickens's
Mr. Pickwick.

Footner was born in Hamilton, Ontario, and after he went to school in New
York City and began his journalism career there, moved back to Canada to
take a newspaper job in Alberta. He had brief careers as an actor, playwright,
and screenwriter. His early fiction reflects that northern locale as he set his
mystery-adventure novels in northwest Canada. He returned to the United
States and wrote detective stories and novels about Mappin and the breathtak-
ingly gorgeous Madame Rosika Storey, who describes herself as "a practical
psychologist—specializing in the feminine." She is intuitive and highly intelligent, as well as being fearless, hunting down killers and going undercover to
break up criminal gangs. She made her debut in *The Under Dogs* (1925) and
appeared in eight additional books, mostly short collections such as *Madame
Storey* (1926), *The Velvet Hand: New Madame Storey Mysteries* (1928), and *The
Almost Perfect Murder: More Madame Storey Mysteries* (1933).

"The Almost Perfect Murder" was originally published in *The Almost Perfect
Murder* (London, Collins, 1933).

The Almost Perfect Murder

HULBERT FOOTNER

I

FAY BRUNTON was one of those stars who suddenly shine out on Broadway in full effulgence, and are almost as quickly darkened. Most people will remember her name, but I doubt if many could name the parts in which she appeared. But to those of us who knew her, she remains a vivid and lovely memory; she was so beautiful! And that was not all of it; beauty is not uncommon on Broadway: it was her great sweetness of nature that endeared her to us; her girlishness; her simplicity. She was not a great actress; her smile was her passport to popular favour.

My employer, Madame Storey, who knows everybody in the great world, had become acquainted with Fay, and through her I had met the girl. By degrees, I can hardly say how, Fay and I had become intimate friends. She brought colour and incident into my life. To a plain Jane like me, she was marvellous. I was the recipient of all her charming confidences—or nearly all; and as well as I could, I steered her with my advice amongst the pitfalls that beset a popular favourite. For one in the limelight she was incredibly ignorant of evil. And you could not bear to show her the ugly side of life.

How bitterly I regretted that I had not warned her against Darius Whittall in the begin-

ning. But I had thought that her natural goodness would protect her. Goodness, however, is apt to be blind. Whittall's name had been connected with Fay's for several months, but he was only one of many. I had hoped that one of the young men would win out; particularly one who was called Frank Esher, a fine fellow. I banked on the fact that Fay had been shy about mentioning his name in her confidences. As for Whittall, he was a notorious evil-liver. His wife had committed suicide some weeks before. To me he was no better than a murderer.

How well I remember the morning that Fay came to our offices to tell us. It must have been November, for the trees in Gramercy Park had shed their leaves, though the grass was still green. This was during Fay's second season when she was appearing with huge success in *Wild Hyacinth*. She came in beaming, and I marked the gleam of a new pearl necklace under her partly-opened sables. What a vision of youthful loveliness she made, sparkling with a childlike excitement!

She had Mrs. Brunton with her. This lady was not her real mother, but an ageing actress whom Fay had rescued from a cheap boarding-house, and set up as her official chaperone. Such an arrangement is not unusual on the stage. Mrs. Brunton was a typical stage mamma; overdressed, over-talkative; a foolish woman, but devoted to Fay, and people put up with her on that account.

When Fay came to call, business was dropped for the time being. I took her in to my mistress. What a complement they made to each other! the one so dark and tall and wise; the other simple, fair, and girlish. Alongside my mistress, the girl looked the least bit colourless, but that was inevitable. There is only one Madame Storey. Fay was not aware that she suffered by comparison with the other, and if she had known, I doubt if she would have minded.

Mrs. Brunton was in a great flutter. "Oh, I hope we're not interrupting anything important! Fay couldn't wait a minute! What I have been through since last night you wouldn't believe! I didn't sleep a wink! And then to be hauled out of my bed at eight o'clock! *Eight o'clock!* And dragged here half-dressed. Is there a mirror anywhere? I know I'm a sight . . . !"

And so on; and so on. The exasperating thing about that woman was that her talk never meant anything. She surrounded herself with a cloud of words. Nobody ever paid any attention to what she said. Talk with her was a sort of nervous habit, like biting the fingernails.

Meanwhile Mme. Storey was gazing into Fay's face with searching kindness. Nervously pulling off one of her gloves, the girl mutely exhibited the third finger of her left hand. I caught a glimpse of an emerald that took my breath away.

"Who is it?" asked Mme. Storey.

"Darius Whittall," she murmured.

It was a horrible shock to me. Fortunately none of them was looking at me at the moment. The thought of seeing my friend in all her youth and loveliness handed over to that *murderer*—for such he was in all essentials—was more than I could bear. The bottom seemed to drop out of everything.

Mme. Storey's face showed no change upon hearing the announcement, though she must have known Darius Whittall better than I did.

She enfolded the girl in her arms, and murmured her good wishes.

Meanwhile Mrs. Brunton in the background was talking away like steam puffing out of a boiling kettle. I perceived a certain glint of anxiety in the old lady's eye; she knew that Darius Whittall was no paragon for a husband. But he was so rich! so rich! who could blame a mother? She was relieved when Mme. Storey appeared to make no difficulties about the match.

"Well, I never thought he'd be the one!" said Mme. Storey with an appearance of great cheerfulness.

"Neither did I," said Fay, laughing.

"Are you dreadfully in love with him?"

"I suppose so . . . I don't know . . . Don't ask me to examine my feelings!"

"Look at her!" cried Mrs. Brunton. "Isn't that enough? Radiantly happy!"

"But if you're going to marry the man," said Mme. Storey, laughing, "surely you must know the state of your feelings!"

"I want to marry him," said Fay quickly. "Very much. I suppose it's because he needs me so."

Mme. Storey's expression said: Hum! But she did not utter it. She asked when it was going to be.

"Soon," said Fay. "There's no reason for delay. It will be very quiet, of course."

"Of course," said Mme. Storey.

Fay seemed to feel that some further explanation was required. "It's true his wife has only been dead two months," she said. "But as Darius pointed out, she had not been a real wife to him for years before that."

"Poor woman!" said Madame Storey.

We all echoed that. "Poor woman!"

By this time I was aware that my mistress was not any better pleased with Fay's announcement than I had been; but she was too wise to burst out with objections as I might have done.

"Why do you suppose she killed herself?" she said thoughtfully.

"Oh, don't you know?" said Fay. "She was in love with somebody else. Darius talks about her so nicely. He offered to let her divorce him, but she wouldn't because of her religion. A Catholic, you know. I suppose she could see no way but to end it all. Darius honours her for it."

"Oh, don't talk about it!" cried Mrs. Brunton. "Don't let that cloud darken this happy day! How that poor man has suffered! And such a gentleman with it all. Such delicacy! I could tell you things about him! But never mind!"

What has he given *her*? I thought.

Fay and Mme. Storey ignored her interruption. "But *I* think," the former went on with gentle censure, "that she ought to have considered what a dreadful blow it would be to her husband."

"Still," said Mme. Storey dryly, "if she had not done it, you would not be marrying him now."

"No-o," said Fay innocently. "I suppose not. . . . Of course Darius is going to sell the house at Riverdale," she continued with an involuntary shiver. "I shouldn't care to live there where it happened."

Mme. Storey struck out on a new line. "Well! Well!" she said, "what a poor guesser I am! Frank Esher was the one I backed."

I saw a spark of animosity leap out of the old woman's eye. I suppose it occurred to her, too, that my seemingly candid mistress was trying to gum her game.

"Oh, Frank Esher!" said Fay pettishly. "Don't speak of him!"

"He was so good-looking!" said Mme. Storey dreamily.

"Good-looking, yes," said Fay with some heat. "But impossible. You don't know! Oh, impossible!"

"I liked him," said Mme. Storey, "because there seemed to be a genuine fire in him. Most young fellows are so tame! I should have thought he would make a wonderful lover."

Fay, silenced, looked at her with rather a stricken expression in the candid blue eyes.

Mrs. Brunton rushed in to fill the breach. "Fire!" she snorted. "Preserve us from that kind of fire. That's all *I* have to say. I don't speak of his rudeness to me. I am nobody. He treated Fay as if she was just an ordinary girl. No sense of the difference in their positions. A dreadful young man! He spoiled everything. So different from Mr. Whittall. He is such a gentleman. You never catch him making a vulgar display of his feelings!"

Fay had recovered her speech. "That incident is closed," she said. "Frank was simply a thorn in my side."

But Mme. Storey would not let Frank drop. "By the way, what has become of him?" she asked. "I haven't seen him for ages."

"We quarrelled," said Fay with an impatient shrug. "He was always quarrelling with me. He said that would be the last time, and he went away somewhere. Peru or China or somewhere. Nobody knows where he's gone. Now I have a little peace."

But the look in her eyes belied her words.

There was a lot more talk. Like every young girl when she first gets herself engaged, Fay could hardly speak a sentence without bringing in the name of her lover. One would have thought Darius was the Oracle. Considering the manner of man he was, it was absurd and it was piteous.

Darius had no objection to her finishing out the run of *Wild Hyacinth*. But after this season, of course, she would retire. Darius had bought a town house. No, not a big place on the Avenue; Darius hated show. A dear little house in the East Seventies; Darius had said that was the smartest thing now. Very plain outside, and a perfect bower within. Like a French maisonette. Darius had such original ideas. And so on.

When they got up to go, Fay said to me wistfully: "You haven't congratulated me, Bella."

What was I to say? The tears sprang to my eyes. Fortunately she considered that the emotion was suitable to the circumstances. "Oh, I want you to be happy! I want you to be happy!" I stammered.

The words did not please her. She withdrew herself from my arms somewhat coldly.

II

When the door closed behind them I broke down. Mme. Storey looked at me sympathetically. "Ah, Bella, you are very fond of her, aren't you?" she murmured. "This is damnable!"

In my eagerness I involuntarily clasped my hands. "Ah, but you won't . . . you won't let it go on!" I implored her.

"I?" she said in great surprise. "How on earth could I stop it, my dear?"

"Oh, but you could! you could!" I wailed. "You can do anything!"

She shook her head. "As an outsider I have no business to interfere. And, anyhow, my better sense tells me it would be worse than useless. If I said a word to her against her Darius, she'd rush off and marry him the same day. You saw how she looked at you just now. . . . No! it's a tragedy, but it's beyond our mending. If I have learned anything it is that we cannot play Providence in the lives of others. We can only look on and pity her . . ."

"That's what your head says," I murmured. "What about your heart?"

She rose, and began to pace the long room. "Ah, don't drag in heart," she said, almost crossly one would have thought; "I can't set out to save every foolish girl who is determined to make a mess of her life!"

"I can't bear it!" I said.

She continued to walk up and down the long room. That room had been expressly chosen for its length, so that she could pace it while she was thinking. How well it suited her! the bare and beautiful apartment, with its rare old Italian furnishings and pictures. She herself was wearing a Fortuny gown adapted from the same period; and when you turned your back to the windows which looked out on matter-of-fact New York, you were transported right back to sixteenth-century Florence.

I felt that anything more I might say would only damage my suit, so I remained silent. But I couldn't stop the tears from running down.

Mme. Storey looked at me uneasily every time she turned.

"We must get to work," she said crossly. I obediently took up my note-book. "Oh, well," she said in a different tone. "For your sake, Bella . . ." She returned to her desk, and took the telephone receiver off its hook. "We'll see if we cannot dig up something in the circumstances surrounding Mrs. Whittall's death that will give this foolish girl cause to stop and think what she is doing."

She called up Police Headquarters. "Rumsey," she said, "do you remember the case of Mrs. Darius Whittall who killed herself about two months ago? . . . Well, I suppose there was an inquest or investigation of some sort, and that the findings are on file somewhere. Come and see me this afternoon, will you? and bring the papers with you. I want to go over them with you. . . . I'll tell you when I see you . . . Thanks, at four then. Good-bye."

Our worthy friend arrived promptly to his hour. Inspector Rumsey was not a distinguished-looking man, but he was true-blue. He owed part of his reputation, perhaps, to his friendship for my mistress, who often helps him with the more subtle points of his cases. He in return, I need hardly say, is able to render us invaluable assistance.

The papers he laid before my mistress told a simple and straightforward tale. On the night of Sunday, September 11th, Mrs. Whittall had dined alone at their place in Riverdale. Her husband was dining with friends in the city. After dinner, that is to say about nine-thirty, she had complained of the heat, and had asked her maid, Mary Thole, for a light wrap, saying that she would walk in the grounds for a few minutes. Almost immediately after she left the house, the sound of a shot was heard. Everybody in the house heard it, since the windows were all open.

The butler and the second man rushed out to the spot whence it came, a little pavilion or summer-house placed on a slight knoll overlooking the river, about two hundred yards from the house. They found the body of their mistress lying at full length on the gravel outside the entrance to the pavilion. She had evidently fallen with considerable force, for her hair was partly down, the hairpins lying about. An ornamental comb which she wore was found about four feet from her body. One of her slippers was off. So it was judged that she had shot herself within the pavilion, and had fallen backwards down the steps. There were three steps. There was a bullet hole in her right temple, and so far as the servants could judge she was already dead. The revolver was still lying in her partly opened hand. Upon a microscopic examination of the gun later, the prints upon it were found to be those of Mrs. Whittall's fingers.

The body was immediately carried into the house and laid upon the bed. The family physician was telephoned for. The powder marks around the wound could be seen by all. In his confusion and excitement, the butler felt that he ought to notify his master of what had happened before sending for the police. Nobody in the house knew where Mr. Whittall was dining that night, and the butler started telephoning around to his clubs, and to the houses of his most intimate friends in the endeavour to find him. He could not get any word of him. He was still at the telephone when Mr. Whittall returned home. This would be about eleven. Mr. Whittall's first act was to telephone to the local police station. He upbraided the butler for not having done so at once. A few minutes later the police were in the house.

Mrs. Whittall's own maid had identified the revolver as one belonging to her mistress. She had testified that she had seen nothing strange in the behaviour of her mistress before she left the house. So far as she could tell, there was nothing special on her mind. She was a very quiet lady, and saw little company. She had left no letter in explanation of her act. Not more than a minute or so could have elapsed between the time she left the house and the sound of the shot, so she must have proceeded direct to the pavilion and done the deed. Indeed, it happened so quickly it seemed as if she must have run there.

The doctor testified that Mrs. Whittall was dead when he saw her. Death must have been instantaneous. The bullet had passed through her brain and was lodged against the skull on the other side from the point of entrance. Questioned as to her possible reasons for the deed, he said he knew of none. The dead woman was in normal health, and though he had known her for many years, and was a friend, she did not often have occasion to send for him in a professional capacity. She seemed normal in mind. He admitted though, that she might have been seriously disturbed without his knowing anything of it, since she was a very reticent woman, who spoke little about her own affairs.

Mr. Whittall testified that the revolver found in the dead woman's hand was one which he had given her some three months previously. It was a Matson, 32 calibre, an automatic of the latest pattern. She had not asked for a gun. He had given it to her of his own motion, believing that every woman ought to have the means of defending herself at hand. He did not know for sure if she had ever practised shooting it, but he believed not. Only one shot had been fired from it. He understood that she had kept it in the top drawer of the chiffonier in her room, but he had never seen it there. He had not noticed anything unwonted in her behaviour on that day, or he would never have left her alone. It was true, though, that she had suffered from periods of deep depression. She brooded on the fact that she had no children, and looked forward with dread to a childless old age.

Such, in effect, were the contents of the papers which Inspector Rumsey spread before us. Tea and cigarettes followed. Mme. Storey looked disappointed at the outcome.

"Merely a perfunctory investigation, of course," said Inspector Rumsey. "Nobody suspected there might be something peculiar in the case. Nobody wished to turn up anything peculiar."

"I had hoped that there would be enough in these papers to accomplish my purpose," said Mme. Storey gravely. "By showing them to a certain person, I mean. But there is not. So we must dig further into this business. It is not a job that I look forward to!"

"What can you expect to do now, after two months?" said the Inspector.

"Oh, there are plenty of leads. Firstly: if Mr. Whittall was dining in New York that night, it is strange that he should have arrived home in Riverdale as early as eleven."

"Right!"

"Secondly: if it was such a hot night, why should Mrs. Whittall have called for a wrap? When one steps outside to cool off, one doesn't wrap up. It is indicated that she meant to stay out awhile."

"Right!"

"Thirdly: Whittall's explanation of his wife's alleged depression is mere nonsense. It is a simple matter for a rich woman to adopt a child if she is lonely."

The Inspector nodded.

"Fourthly: when a person shoots himself dead one of two things happens. Occasionally the grip on the gun is spasmodic, and remains fixed in death. More often in the act of death all the muscles relax. In that case when she fell from the steps the gun would have been knocked from her hand, just as the comb was knocked from her head. As a matter of fact, they say the gun was found lying in her *open hand*. I am forced to the conclusion that it was placed there afterwards."

I looked at her, struck with horror.

"In that case she must have been decoyed to the pavilion," said the Inspector.

"That is for us to find out."

"The double identification of the gun as hers is an awkward point to get over," he suggested.

"Matson 32's are sold by the hundreds," said Mme. Storey. "There is no evidence that this one bore any distinguishing marks. Why not another of the same design?"

"In that case Mrs. Whittall's gun would have been found."

"Maybe it was."

The Inspector slowly nodded. "A case begins to shape itself," he said. "What do you want me to do?"

"It is not yet a matter of public interest," said Mme. Storey. "As soon as we have sufficient evidence that it is, we will put it in your hands. In the meantime I wish you'd trace where and when Whittall bought the gun that he gave his wife, and the number of it. You have better facilities for doing that than I have."

He nodded.

III

A pleasant-faced young woman, very neatly and plainly dressed, came into my office somewhat shyly, and mutely offered me a printed slip which had been filled in. I read at a glance that the bearer was Mary Thole, who had been sent by Mrs. ——'s Employment Agency as an applicant for the position of maid. One of our operatives had brought about this visit without the girl's suspecting what we wanted of her. I looked at her with a strong interest. Through my association with Mme. Storey I have learned to read character to some degree, and I said to myself that the lady who secured this girl would be lucky. Good servants are rare.

I took her in to Madame Storey.

"Do you know who I am?" asked my mistress.

"Yes, Madame, I read in the papers . . ."

"Good! then you know something of my business. I may as well tell you at once that I do not need a maid. That was merely a pretext."

The girl looked at her, greatly startled.

"Oh, you have nothing to fear," Mme. Storey went on. "I merely wished to satisfy myself that you were an honest and a faithful girl. I am satisfied of it. I mean to be frank with you. Mr. Whittall has engaged himself to marry a friend of mine, a beautiful young girl. I think that is a great shame."

"Oh, yes, Madame!" she said earnestly. "He . . . he is not a good man!"

"So I think myself," said Mme. Storey dryly. "I want you to tell me all the circumstances surrounding Mrs. Whittall's death."

The girl's eyes widened in horror, and she pressed one hand to her cheek. "Oh, Madame, do you think . . . do you think . . . that *he* . . . !"

"Hush!" said Mme. Storey. "Answer my questions carefully, and we'll see."

The girl went on in a daze, more to herself than to us: "Of course, I always knew it was due to him . . . in a way . . . he made it impossible for her to live . . . but I never thought that he might actually . . ."

"Don't jump to conclusions," warned Mme. Storey. She reseated herself at her desk.

"May I ask you something?" said Mary humbly.

"Certainly."

"Is it . . . is it the beautiful young actress, Miss Brunton?"

"Yes. What put that into your head?"

"Well, it came to my mistress's ears that her name was being connected with Mr. Whittall's, and she heard she was a nice girl, so it seemed a great shame to her on the girl's account. So she asked Miss Brunton and her mother to come to Oakhurst—that was the name of the house—to lunch and spend the afternoon. She wanted to stop any scandal that was going about, that might hurt the girl. That was the sort of woman she was; thinking of everybody before herself."

"Hm!" said my mistress, "and did they come?"

"Yes, Madame, and my mistress told me the girl was a dear—that was her own word, and she hoped she could really make friends with her."

"Was Mr. Whittall present at this luncheon?"

"No, Madame. My mistress had fixed a day when she knew he would be out of town."

"When was this?"

"I cannot say to a day. Late in August some time. Two weeks, maybe three, before my mistress died."

"What can you tell me about that visit?"

"Not much, Madame. I was busy about my work, of course. When the car drove up to carry them away, I peeped out of the window, and I had a glimpse of the young lady, as she turned around to say good-bye. Such a beautiful young lady! She was happy and smiling, so I supposed everything had gone well."

"You cannot tell me anything they did?"

"Nothing, except I heard they had tea sent out to the pavilion."

"Who served it?"

"The butler would be at the tea-wagon, Madame, and the second man serving."

"What were the relations, generally, between Mr. and Mrs. Whittall?" asked Mme. Storey.

Mary looked uncomfortable. She said in a low voice: "They were living apart, Madame—though under the same roof, since before I came. They never quarrelled before the servants, of course. They were cold to each other. It was the gossip among the servants that Mr. Whittall was always trying to persuade her to get a divorce, and she wouldn't because it was against the laws of her church."

"So is self-destruction," remarked Mme. Storey gravely.

Mary looked up quickly. Evidently this was a new thought to her.

"You considered that Mrs. Whittall was an unhappy woman?" asked Mme. Storey.

The girl nodded. "But I never heard her complain," she added quickly.

"Had she ever spoken of adopting a child?"

"Not seriously, Madame. Once I heard her say that a child was entitled to a father as well as a mother."

"Now let us come to the day of the tragedy," said Mme. Storey. "I want you to tell me everything that happened that day, beginning with the morning."

"I can't tell you much," said Mary. "What happened at night seems to have driven it all out of my head. . . . It was Sunday. I suppose Madame went to early mass as usual. She would not let me get up on Sunday mornings to dress her, nor would she have the car. She walked to church. Then came breakfast. I tidied up her room then. I don't remember anything about the morning; I suppose she was writing letters. After lunch she slept; I dressed her when she got up. I scarcely saw her during the day. She wanted us to rest on Sundays. Dinner was always earlier; half-past six. I had heard downstairs that the master was dining out. Mrs. Whittall didn't dress for dinner on Sundays. She came up from the table in less than half an hour. I was in her room then. . . ."

"How did she look?"

"Quite as usual, Madame. Calm and pale."

"What happened then?"

"A few minutes later a special delivery letter was brought to the door."

"Ha!" said Mme. Storey. "Why was this never mentioned before?"

"Nobody asked me about it, Madame." For the first time an evasive note sounded in the girl's honest voice.

"Was not such a thing very unusual?"

"No, Madame. Mrs. Whittall's mail was very large, she was interested in so many charities and committees. So many people wrote to her asking for one thing or another. There were often special delivery letters; telegrams too."

"Did you have this letter in your hands?"

"Yes, Madame. I carried it from the door to my mistress."

"Describe it."

"Just an ordinary white envelope with the address written on it. No printing."

"Did you recognise the handwriting?"

"No, Madame."

"Was it a man's handwriting?"

"I don't know. I just gave it a careless glance." Again the evasive note. However, Mme. Storey chose to ignore it.

"Then what happened?"

"Mrs. Whittall said she wouldn't want me any more, and I went away."

"Then?"

"After a while, an hour maybe, she sent for me back again."

"You found her changed then?"

Mary looked at Mme. Storey in a startled way. "Y-yes, Madame," she faltered. "Her cheeks were red. She was nervous. She tried to hide it."

"Where was the letter then?"

"It wasn't anywhere about. It was never seen again."

"Was there a fireplace in the room?"

Mary looked frightened again. "Y-yes, Madame."

"Did you not look there afterwards—next day perhaps?"

The girl hung her head. "Y-yes, Madame."

"And found some scraps of burned paper?"

"Yes, Madame," This very low. "I swept them up."

Once more, to my surprise, Mme. Storey dropped this line of questioning for the moment. "What did Mrs. Whittall say to you?" she asked.

"She said her afternoon dress was too hot, Madame, and she wanted to change. So I started to get a négligée from the wardrobes, but she said no, she had a fancy to put on her blue net evening dress that she had never worn. She wanted her hair done in a different way, too. I was a long time dressing her. It was the first time I had ever found her hard to suit. At the end she asked for her blue velvet evening cloak, as she wanted to walk in the grounds for the cool."

"Had she ever done that before?"

"Not as far as I know, Madame."

"Describe the blue dress."

"A simple little frock, Madame. Just a plain, tight bodice of charmeuse, and a full skirt of net in points over underskirts of malines. A scarf of blue malines went with it. She had never worn it because she said it was too young for her."

"How old was Mrs. Whittall?"

"Thirty-seven, Madame. . . . She wasn't old at all!" the girl went on warmly. "She was beautiful! She was beautiful all over!"

"Where did she keep her revolver?" asked Mme. Storey.

"In the top drawer of the chiffonier in the bedroom. I could feel it lying at the bottom of the drawer when I put things away."

"Were you in the bedroom when you were dressing her that Sunday night?"

"No, Madame; in the dressing-room, which adjoined."

"Did she leave the room at any time while you were dressing her?"

"No, Madame."

"Did you leave the room?"

"No, Madame. The wardrobes were right there along the wall."

"When she was dressed, who left the room first?"

"She did, Madame. I remained to tidy things up. I was still in the dressing-room when I heard . . . when I heard . . ."

"I know," said Mme. Storey gently. "Please attend well to what I am going to ask you. When Mrs. Whittall left the room where did she go?"

"Out through the door into the hall, Madame, and down the stairs. I heard her heels on the stairs. She was in a hurry."

"She did not go into the bedroom first?"

"No, Madame."

"Did she have anything in her hands when she went out of the dressing-room?"

"No, Madame."

"Did the blue cloak have a pocket in it?"

"Only a tiny pocket inside for a handkerchief." Mary held up thumb and finger, indicating a space of an inch and a half.

"Would it have been possible for her to conceal the revolver inside that tight bodice?"

"No, Madame."

"Then I ask you, was it possible that she could have carried her revolver out of the house with her?"

The girl stared at her with wide eyes of horror. "No, Madame! No! No! . . . I never thought it out before. . . . Oh, my poor mistress!"

She broke down completely. Mme. Storey lit a cigarette, to give her time to recover herself.

"Well, after that we know pretty well what happened," my mistress said soothingly. "Just a few more questions. . . . Did it occur to you at any time before your master came home, to look

in the chiffonier drawer to see if Mrs. Whittall's gun was there?"

"No, Madame. I never thought. I scarcely knew what I was doing."

"When did you first see Mr. Whittall?"

"He came running up the stairs to the bedroom where the . . . where the body was lying. He ordered us all out of the room. 'I must be alone with my dead!' he said. Those were his words. Very dramatic."

"Hm!" said Mme. Storey with a hard smile. "And then?"

"In just a minute he called me back into the room by myself, and started to question me, very excited."

"What sort of questions?"

"I can't remember exactly. . . . Like the questions you were asking me. What she was doing all day? What made her go out, and so on."

"Did you tell him about the letter which came?"

"Yes, Madame, because he asked if any message had come."

"What did he say when you told him about the letter?"

"He didn't say anything, then. Later, when we were waiting to be questioned by the police, he sort of said to me and Mr. Frost, the butler, and Mr. Wilkins, the second man—we were the only ones who knew about the letter; he said maybe it would be better if nothing was said about it, and we agreed, of course, not wishing to raise any scandal about the mistress."

"What can you tell me about his subsequent actions?"

"Well, Madame, whenever he got a chance, I saw him looking, looking about the sitting-room and the bedroom . . ."

"For the letter?"

"So I supposed."

"Did you know then that it had been burned?"

"Yes, Madame; I had looked before he came home."

"Why didn't you tell him it had been burned?"

"I didn't want to give him that satisfaction."

"What else?"

"Well, as long as the police were in the house, Mr. Whittall was right there with them. After they had gone he went out. He took a flashlight with him, because I could see it flashing down the path to the pavilion. Then I lost him. He was out of the house about ten minutes. When he came back he wanted me to go to bed. But I asked to stay up . . . by her. He went to bed."

"Can you tell me what became of the pistol that was found in Mrs. Whittall's hand?"

"The police captain took it away with him that night. Later I heard that Mr. Whittall had given it to him."

"Now to go back," said Mme. Storey. "When your mistress sent for you to dress her, you said you found her excited. Do you mean pleasurably so?"

"Yes . . . no . . . I can hardly say, Madame. When I thought over it afterwards, I supposed she had made up her mind then to end it all, and was just sort of wrought up."

"That was reasonable. But you know now that you were wrong."

Mary nodded. "I don't know what to think now," she said unhappily.

"That letter," said Mme. Storey—and Mary instantly began to look nervous, "what do you think was in it, Mary?"

"How should I know?" she said. "A girl like me, just a lady's maid."

"But you thought it had something to do with the tragedy."

"Not direct."

"Well, indirectly, then."

"Whatever I may have thought is proved wrong now."

"Tell me what you thought."

"I don't think I ought," was the stubborn reply. "I told you the truth when I said I didn't know the handwriting. It was only a guess."

Mme. Storey tried another tack. "Mary," she said, "Mr. Whittall has told his fiancée that his wife killed herself because she was in love with another man."

"That's a lie!" she said excitedly. "At least,

the way he means it. My mistress was a good woman!"

"I am sure of it!" said Mme. Storey gravely. "But I can also understand how a woman, married to a man like Whittall, might conceive an honourable love for another man, and still remain true to her marriage vows."

The girl broke into a helpless weeping. Still she stubbornly held her tongue.

At length Mme. Storey said: "Mary, your mistress was foully murdered. Don't you want to see justice done?"

"Yes! . . . Yes!" she sobbed. "But I don't see how *he* could have done it. I don't know what to think! I don't see any use in raking up a scandal!"

"The whole story must be opened to the light now," said Mme. Storey gravely. "If that is done, no possible blame can attach to your mistress's name. Wouldn't you rather tell me here than be forced to tell in open court?"

Mary nodded.

"Then, Mary, from whom did you think that letter had come?"

"Mr. Barry Govett," she whispered.

I exclaimed inwardly. Barry Govett!

"You mustn't lay too much on that!" Mary went on, as well as she could for sobbing. "I am ready to swear there was nothing wrong between them. I don't believe they ever saw each other alone but once. That was at our house in the summer. Mr. Govett called unexpected. He didn't stay but an hour. I happened to go into my mistress's sitting-room where they were, and I saw them. I saw by the way they looked at each other how . . . how it was with them both. How it would always be. I had never seen anything like that. . . ." She was unable to go on.

IV

Barry Govett was the most prominent bachelor in New York society. I had been reading about him in the papers for years. His name regularly headed the list of men present at every fashionable entertainment, and one was continually being informed of his visiting this great person or that in Newport, Saratoga, Lenox, Tuxedo, and Palm Beach. Prominent as he was at this time, he must have been still more prominent a few years ago when the cotillion was still a feature of every ball. I have always wondered what a cotillion was. Barry Govett was the cotillion leader *par excellence*. They said then that one had to engage him months ahead.

All this I had gathered from the gossip weeklies, which, like every other stenographer whose social life was limited to a boarding-house, I used to read with avidity. Barry Govett was their *pièce de resistance*. Before all this happened, he was once pointed out to me in court costume at a great fancy dress ball; and I thought then that he had the most beautifully turned leg I had ever seen on a man. He must have been over forty then, but still conveyed the effect of a young man; very handsome in his style. But too much the cotillion leader for me. When I thought over this I wondered what a woman like Mrs. Whittall could have seen in him. One never knows!

The moment he entered the outer office I was aware of a personality. Of course, no man could occupy so lofty a position for years, even if it was only at the head of a frivolous society, without acquiring great aplomb. Close at hand in the daylight, I saw that there was little of the youth remaining about him, though his figure was still slim, but I liked him better than I had expected. He had a long, oval face, almost ascetic looking, with nice blue eyes, though they were always pleasantly watchful, and betrayed little. He was wonderfully turned out, of course, but nothing spectacular. It was the perfection of art that conceals art. I was immediately sensible of his charm too, though I had discounted it in advance. The smile and the bow conveyed no intimation that he saw in me merely the humble secretary.

I took him in to Mme. Storey. She was playing the great lady that afternoon, and the black ape Giannino in green cap and jacket with golden bells was seated in the crook of her left arm. Mr. Govett hastened forward, and gracefully kissed her hand. I wondered if Giannino would snatch at his none-too-well-covered poll. We were always amused to see how the ape would receive a new person. He is an individual of very strong likes and dislikes. However, he only made a face at Mr. Govett, and hissed amicably. Indeed, Mr. Govett held out his elbow, and Giannino hopped upon it, and stroked his face. This was a great victory.

"Dear lady!" said Mr. Govett, "this is an undeserved privilege. To be invited to tea with you, and" (looking around the room) "alone!"

"Just me and Giannino and my friend Miss Brickley," said Mme. Storey.

He whirled around and bowed to me again, murmuring: "Charmed!" My hand was horribly self-conscious in the expectation that he might offer to kiss it. I wondered if it was quite clean. Which way would I look! I could see too that Mme. Storey was wickedly hoping that he might. Fortunately he did not.

"Miss Brickley has been dying to meet you," she said slyly.

"Ah! you do me too much honour!" he said.

I was rather fussed, and therefore I was bound not to show it. "Well, you're such a famous man," I said.

"Now you're spoofing me," he said. "It's not much to be a hero of the society notes, is it?"

Tea was waiting, and we attacked it forthwith. Mr. Govett, stroking Giannino's pompadour, and feeding him sugar, supplied most of the conversation. His gossip was extremely amusing, without being malicious—well not *very* malicious. No doubt he suited his talk to his company.

Had we heard that Bessie Van Brocklin was going to give a zoological dinner? It was in honour of her new cheetah. He didn't know quite what a cheetah was; the name sounded ominous. The Princess Yevrienev had promised to bring her lion cubs, and the Goldsby-Snows would be on hand with their falcons. Somebody else had a wolf, and he had heard a rumour that there was an anaconda being kept in the dark. Oh, and of course, there were plenty of monkeys in society, zoological and otherwise. It ought to be a brilliant affair.

Had we heard the latest about Freddy Vesey? Freddy had been dining with the Stickneys, who were the last householders on Madison Square. Carried away by his boyhood recollections of old New York, Freddy had leaped into the fountain, causing great excitement among the park-benchers. An Irish policeman was convinced that it was an attempted suicide. Freddy had argued with him at length from the middle of the fountain. Freddy had refused to come out until the policeman promised to let him off. No, Freddy had not undressed before jumping in, he was happy to say, and thereby the world was saved a shocking disclosure of the means by which he preserved his ever youthful figure.

All the while this was going on, I could see that Mr. Govett was wondering why he had been asked to tea with us. He knew, of course, that we had something more to do than gossip in that place. But he betrayed no particular anxiety.

Finally they lighted their cigarettes. Giannino, who adores cigarettes, though they invariably make him sick, coolly stole Mr. Govett's from between his lips, and fled up to the top of a picture frame, where he sat and mocked at us. I dislodged him with a stick which I keep for the purpose, and depriving him of his booty, carried him to his little house in the middle room.

When I came back Mme. Storey was saying: "Have you heard that Darius Whittall is going to marry Fay Brunton?"

"That was a foregone conclusion, wasn't it?" said Mr. Govett with a shrug.

"Not to me!"

"Ah, yes, of course, the adorable Brunton is a friend of yours." I could see by his eyes that he was thinking: Is *this* what I was brought here for?

"Is Whittall a friend of yours?" asked Mme. Storey.

"No!" he said shortly.

"Barry, you and I have known each other for a good many years," said Mme. Storey, "and I

have confidence in your discretion, though you always make-believe not to have any . . ."

"Thanks, dear lady."

"What do you think of me?"

"I think you're an angel!"

"Oh, not that tosh!"

"I think you're the greatest woman in New York!"

"That's not what I want either. In all these affairs that I have been engaged in, are you satisfied that I have always taken the side of decency?"

"Oh, yes!" he said quite simply. "What a question!"

"Good! Then I ask for your confidence in this affair. I am investigating the circumstances surrounding the death of Mrs. Whittall."

He gave a start, which he instantly controlled. One could not have said that he showed more than anybody might have shown upon hearing such an announcement. "Good Heavens!" he murmured, "do you think there was anything more than . . ."

"She was murdered, Barry."

"Oh, my God!" he whispered. His face turned greyish; his hands shook. I thought the man was going to faint; but even while I looked at him, he steadied himself. I never saw such an exhibition of self-control. He drew a long breath.

"How can I help?" he asked quietly.

"By being quite frank with me."

He looked at me in a meaning way.

"Miss Brickley is familiar with all the circumstances," said Mme. Storey, "and she possesses my entire confidence. Nothing that transpires in this room is ever heard outside of it, unless I choose that it shall be."

"Of course," he murmured. "Still, I don't see how I . . ."

"Mrs. Whittall was lured out to the pavilion by a letter which we have reason to suppose she thought you had written."

He jumped up involuntarily, staring at her like one insane; then dropped limply into his chair again. It was some moments before he could speak. "But I never wrote to her in my life!"

"Then how could she have known your handwriting?" asked Mme. Storey.

"Well, I mean nothing but social notes; answers to invitations and so on." He saw that he had made a slip, and added hastily: "How do you know that she *did* recognise my handwriting?"

"We mustn't waste the afternoon fencing with each other," said Mme. Storey mildly. "You are aware of something that would help me very much in this matter."

"What makes you think so?" he asked with an innocent air.

"You betrayed it just now. It leaped out of your eyes."

"I'm sure I don't know what you mean."

"Barry, nothing can be altogether hidden. Your secret is known to a few people."

"I have so many secrets!" he said with a silly-sounding laugh.

"You were in love with her."

"If you imply by that . . ." he began excitedly.

"I imply nothing. From all accounts Mrs. Whittall must have been a saint."

"She was," he said. "And of course I loved her. Everybody who knew her loved her. In our world she moved like a creature apart. She was really good."

"Of course," said Mme. Storey. "But that is not what I mean."

He remained obstinately silent.

"Why did you call on her unexpectedly one afternoon last summer?" Mme. Storey asked bluntly.

He stared at her in confusion. "Why . . . why for no special reason," he stammered.

"On that afternoon," pursued my mistress relentlessly, "you told her that you loved her, and she confessed that it was returned."

He suddenly gave up. "Rosika, you are super-human!" he said simply. "I am in your hands . . . we all are!" He relaxed in his chair, and his chin sank on his breast. The guard had fallen from his eyes, and he looked old and heart-broken. Mme. Storey gave him his own time to speak.

"You understand," he said at last, "my only object in trying to put you off was to protect her memory—not that it needed protection, but only from misrepresentation."

"I understood that from the beginning," said my mistress.

"It is true that I was in love with her," he went on. "Since many years ago. Almost from the time that Whittall first brought her home. We called her St. Cecilia. I watched her once cutting roses in her garden, when she didn't know anybody was near. At first it didn't hurt much. I had no aspirations. She was like a beautiful dream in my life, which redeemed it from triviality. I fed my dream with what glimpses of her came my way.

"Later, all that was changed. It hurt then! Because I knew that she must be unhappy, and I longed to make her happy. I wanted her so! Up to the afternoon that you spoke of we had scarcely ever been alone together, and we had never exchanged any intimate speech. But before that, even in a crowd, I had been aware that she had a sympathy for me. In short, she loved me. You may well wonder at that—a man like me! But you see . . . she saw beneath the grinning mask I wear. She brought out the best in me, that I have hidden for so many years. Even then I had no thought of . . . I knew her too well!

"And then on the day you speak of, a note was brought to me by special delivery from her. I had stored away scraps of her handwriting; invitations and so on, and I never doubted but that it was from her. Just four words: 'Come to me quickly!' I flew. When I entered her sitting-room, she seemed surprised, but I thought that was just a woman's defence. I took her in my arms. She surrendered for a moment, just a little moment; then she thrust me away.

"She denied having written to me. For a moment I did not believe her—I had already burned the note, so I could not show it to her; however, she made it abundantly clear she had not written it. Then we realised somebody must be trying to entrap us, and we were alarmed. But she said nobody could hurt us if we kept our heads up and walked straight. She sent me away. Yes, it was for good! for good! There was never any doubt about that. We were never to attempt to see each other alone; we were not to write—except in case of desperate need. It was I who exacted that. If the need was desperate, either of us might write to the other.

"When I heard of her death—by her own hand as I thought . . . I felt betrayed; I felt if things had come to *that* pass she might have sent for me first. . . . Oh, well, you are not interested in my state of mind! How gladly I would have put a pistol to my own head! I did not do so because I could not bear to sully her name by having it connected with mine. And so I kept on with the same old round, showing the same old grin! I dared not stop for fear of people saying: 'Oh, old Barry Govett is broken-hearted because of, well, you know!' . . . A pretty world, isn't it?" He finished with a harsh laugh.

Nobody said anything for a while.

Finally he raised his head. "But you have given me a renewed interest in life," he said grimly. "The same hand that forged that letter to me afterwards forged the letter that lured her out to the pavilion."

"There can be no doubt of that," said Mme. Storey.

"By God!" said Govett quietly. "If the law doesn't get him, *I will!*"

"Slowly!" said Mme. Storey. "There is no proof yet."

V

I see upon referring to my notes that this took place upon a Friday afternoon. Mr. Govett had not much more than left our place when Fay Brunton dropped in. She looked sweet enough to eat. To our relief she had left the inevitable mother behind on this occasion. Fay did not take tea, but dined at six in order to have a short rest before going to the theatre. She had just fifteen minutes before dinner, she said, and had rushed around to tell us—her news, after what we had just heard, was like a bombshell. I could scarcely repress a cry of dismay.

"Darius and I have decided to get married on Sunday morning."

My mistress never changed a muscle of her smile.

"What!" she said with mock reproach, "must you abandon us so soon?"

"I am not abandoning you!" said Fay, giving her a kiss. "It's the most wonderful plan!" she went on happily. "You know little Larrimore, my understudy, who is dying to have a chance at the part? Well, she is to have it. For a whole week! It's all been fixed up. It will be given out that I am indisposed. The fact of our marriage will be allowed to leak out later. And if Larrimore makes good she can keep the part. It's only that I don't want anybody to lose any money through me.

"We are to be married on Sunday morning in the hotel. Strictly private, of course. And immediately afterwards we'll hop on a train for Pinehurst. Think of Pinehurst after weather like this! And what do you think? Darius has secured the loan of a private car from the president of the railway! I've never been in a private car; have you? And then a whole wonderful week in the woods!"

"Wonderful!" cried Mme. Storey, and there was not a tinge of anything but sympathy in her voice. "But am I not to see you again? Tomorrow is Saturday, and you have two performances."

"How about tonight after the show?" suggested Fay.

Mme. Storey shook her head. "I have an engagement." (This was not true.) "How about tomorrow night after the show?" she went on. "I must have a chance to give you a little party before you step off into the gulf. Come here. My flat is too far uptown."

Fay looked dubious. "I should love it," she said, "but Darius, you know. He hates parties."

The expression in my mistress's eyes said: Damn Darius! But she laughed good-humouredly. "Oh, I don't mean a *party*, my dear. Just you and Darius and Mrs. Brunton; Bella and I."

"I should love it," said Fay. "If Darius doesn't mind."

"Why should Darius mind?" demanded my mistress. "Doesn't he like me?"

"Oh, yes!" said Fay quickly. "He admires you ever so much!"

"Then why should he mind?"

The girl could not withstand the point-blank question. "Well, you see," she faltered, "he thinks . . . that you do not like him very much . . . that you disapprove of him."

"Fay," challenged my mistress, "have I ever by word or look given you any reason to suppose such a thing?"

"Oh, no, Rosika! And so I have told him. Over and over. . . . But he still thinks so."

"Now, look here," said Mme. Storey. "I am never the one to interfere between a married pair—or a soon-to-be-married pair, but you must make a stand somewhere, my child, or you'll soon find yourself a loving little slave. I mean when you are in the right. Now this particular notion of Darius's is a silly notion, isn't it?"

"Y-yes," said Fay.

"Then you should not give in to it. . . . But look here, I'll make it easier for you. Let's pretend that it's your party. You tell Darius that you have asked Bella and me to your hotel for supper after the show on your last night, and he could not possibly object, could he?"

Fay's face lighted up. "Oh, no!" she cried. "That will be splendid!"

"All right!" said Mme. Storey. "Expect us about quarter to twelve. You'll have it in your own rooms, of course, where we may be quite free."

"Now I must run!" said Fay.

"Oh, wait a minute!" pleaded Mme. Storey, slipping her arm through the girl's. "This is the last moment I shall see you alone! There are so many things I want to talk to you about! . . . And now you have driven them all out of my head. . . . Is the little nest ready in the East Seventies?"

"It will be when we get back from Pinehurst." Fay launched into an enthusiastic description.

"And what happens to Oakhurst?" asked Mme. Storey.

"Oh, didn't I tell you? Darius has put it into the hands of Merryman. It's to be sold, lock, stock, and barrel."

"And quite right, too. . . . By the way, do you know what Darius's movements will be tomorrow? I must see him if I can, in order to remove this ridiculous wrong impression he has got of me."

"You're so kind, Rosika! All I know is, he's going to sleep at his rooms in the Vandermeer tonight, in order to be on hand early for all the things he has to see to tomorrow."

"Well, I'll call him up at the Vandermeer."

Arm in arm, they had been moving slowly out through my office with me at their heels. They had now reached the door. Mme. Storey kissed the girl fondly. My mistress was playing an elaborate game, but at least there was nothing insincere about *that* gesture.

"One last thing," she said. "I want to make you a little gift of some sort . . ."

Fay made a gesture of dissent.

"When the news comes out you will be showered with all sorts of useless things. I should like to give you something that you *want*. What shall it be?"

"Oh, I'd much rather leave it to you, dear."

"Well, I must think of something original." She feigned to be considering deeply. "I have it!" she said. "I will give you a beautifully mounted gun with your name chased on the handle. Every woman ought to have a gun."

"Oh, thank you!" said Fay. "But I have one! Darius says too that every woman ought to have a gun. He gave me one months ago."

"Oh, yes, I remember," said Mme. Storey. "What sort of gun?"

"A Matson 32, automatic."

I shivered inwardly. Did the man buy them wholesale?

"Do you carry it about with you?" asked Mme. Storey, laughing.

"Oh, no," said Fay simply. "I keep it in my bottom drawer."

"Ah, well, I'll have to think of something else then," said Mme. Storey.

They embraced, and Fay went.

The instant the door closed after her, Mme. Storey said to me: "Quick, Bella! Your hat!" She went to the window to wave her hand to Fay when she issued below. While standing there, she continued to speak rapidly to me. "Pick up a taxi, and go to Merryman's. That's the big real estate office on Madison Avenue near Forty-Fourth Street. If it's closed, you'll have to look up the address of one of the partners in the telephone book, and go to his house. Apologise for disturbing him and say that your employer (who wishes to remain unknown for the moment) has just learned that the Whittall property in Riverdale has come into the market. Ask for an order to view the place tomorrow. Explain that, owing to your employer's leaving for the West, tomorrow is the only day he will have for the purpose. . . . Wait a minute! Fay is just getting into her car. . . . Now she's off. Run along!"

VI

Next morning we drove up to Riverdale in Mme. Storey's own limousine, but instead of her regular chauffeur, we had Crider at the wheel, an admirable fellow, quiet and keen; the chief of all our operatives. I pointed out to Mme. Storey that if anybody at the house was curious about us, it would be an easy matter to find out who we were by tracing the number of our licence.

"It doesn't matter," she said. "By tonight it will all be decided one way or the other."

Riverdale, as everybody knows, is not a "dale" at all, but a bold hill on the mainland, just to the North of Manhattan Island. On the one side it overlooks the Hudson River; on the other the flat expanse of the Bronx with Van Cortlandt Park. The original village may have started down by the river, but now the whole rocky height is thickly covered with handsome new villas standing in their limited plots. It is an exceedingly well-to-do community, but not fashionable. Fashion has fled farther from town. "Oakhurst," however, is a survival. It was built and laid out by the first Darius Whittall in the days when "a mansion on the Hudson" was synonymous with everything that was opulent and eminent.

The grounds were of considerable extent. We drove in through beautiful wrought-iron gates and past a lodge in the English style. The house was invisible from the road. We wound through a wood of evergreens and oaks before coming to it in the midst of its lawns. It was a long, irregular structure built of native stone. It had no particular architectural pretensions, but the years had mellowed it. It looked dignified and comfortable. This was the back of the house really; the principal rooms faced the glorious prospect over the Hudson with the Palisades beyond.

We drove up under a *porte cochère*, and upon alighting, were received by an irreproachable butler. This must have been Frost. I showed him our order to view the place, and Mme. Storey expressed a wish to be shown the grounds first. Whereupon he handed us over to the second man, a sort of embryo butler; younger, fresh-faced; not yet able to subdue his curiosity and interest at the sight of a woman so beautiful as Madame Storey. He conducted us around the side of the house to the head gardener, who was directing the operations of several men engaged in setting out shrubs.

So we began our perambulations. There was only one thing about the grounds that really interested us; i.e., the pavilion; but of course we said nothing about it, waiting until we should arrive there in proper order. In front of the house the ground fell away gradually in beautiful flower-beds and terraces, to the edge of a steep declivity which dropped to the river. The steep part was wooded in order to mask the railway tracks below. At this season it was all rather sere and leafless, except the grass, which was clipped and rolled to the semblance of green velvet. Stables, garage, and other offices were all concealed behind shrubbery to the north of the house.

We could see the pavilion off to the left as we faced the river; that is to say the southerly side. On this side the hill ran out in a little point ending in a knoll, and on the knoll was the pavilion, in the form of a little Greek temple with a flattened dome and a circle of Doric columns. The winding path which led to it was bordered with rhododendrons, backed with arbour vitæ. As we approached, I pictured the beautiful woman running down that path thinking she was going to the man she loved, and I seemed to hear the shot that ended everything for her. At the foot of the three steps one instinctively looked for bloodstains in the grey gravel; but, of course, all such marks had been erased long since.

Mme. Storey said to the gardener: "I should like to sit down here for five minutes to look at the view. Will you come back?"

The man bowed and hurried away to look after his subordinates.

As we mounted the three steps Mme. Storey laid her hand against the first pillar to the right. "Here," she murmured, "the murderer waited concealed, gun in hand."

I shivered.

Inside, there was a circle of flat-topped marble benches. The view from that spot is world famous. One could see both up and down the glorious river for miles. Only within the last few years the foreground had been defaced by the cutting of new streets and the building of showy houses.

"Our first job is to decide how the murderer got here," said Mme. Storey. "He must have familiarised himself with the spot beforehand."

"But, of course, he knew the spot!" I said, in surprise.

"Mustn't jump to conclusions, my Bella!" she said with a smile. "To go upon the assumption that we already know everything would only be to warp the judgment. All that we can say so far is, some person unknown to us stood behind that pillar and shot Mrs. Whittall."

I thought she was over-scrupulous.

As soon as we looked down to the left, the means of access was clear. The present boundary of the Whittall property was only about a hundred feet away on this side. It was marked by a rough stone wall, not very high; any determined person could have scrambled over it. On the other side of the wall a new street had been laid off down to the river. There were several new houses looking over the wall, and a boating club house down at the end. Once over the wall it was an easy climb through the dead leaves and thin undergrowth up to the pavilion.

"If one followed that street back over the hill and down into the valley on the other side," said Mme. Storey, "it would bring one out somewhere in the vicinity of the subway terminal at Van Cortlandt Park. That is the way he came. You cannot trace anybody on the subway."

She went on: "Now, what did Whittall do with his wife's revolver?"

"A search?" I asked anxiously, thinking what a little time we had.

"Oh, sit down," she said, suiting the action to the word. "And appear to be enjoying the view like me." She produced a cigarette, and lighted it. "Let us search in our heads first. Let us put it through a process of elimination. We have something to go on in this instance because we know our man."

She presently went on: "During that minute when he was left alone with the body, he took the revolver out of the drawer and dropped it in his pocket. All during the time when the police were in the house it lay there in his pocket, burning him! As soon as he could, he left the house with his little flashlight as Mary has told us, and came this way. He was looking for the letter then. He was afraid that his wife might have carried it out in her hand, and dropped it when she fell. Not finding any letter he had to dispose of the gun. Well, there he was. He dared not stay out more than a few minutes. Put yourself in his place, Bella. What would he do with it?"

I shook my head helplessly.

"I think his first impulse would be to toss it from him as far as he could," Mme. Storey resumed. "But it was night, you see, and the risk would be too great that the morning light would reveal it. There are too many men working on this place! For the same reason he wouldn't dare hide it in the shrubbery. He would next think of burying it, but I don't suppose Whittall had ever dug a hole in his life. Besides, he would have to get a tool, which would take time, and anyway, where in this carefully manicured place *could* he have buried it without leaving tell-tale marks? Then there's the river, that's the ideal hiding-place. But it's too far away. It would take him twenty minutes to go and come, not counting the time he spent looking for the letter, and we have Mary's word for it that he was not out of the house more than ten. . . . I think he would have risked the trip to the river, Bella, had he not known of water nearer to. For a guilty person with a heavy object to hide instinctively thinks of water!"

We saw the gardener returning along the path.

Mme. Storey smiled on him. "I have a horror of mosquitoes," she said to him as he came up, "and I want to ask you if there is any standing water on the place, or nearby. Any pond or pool or basin."

"No, Madame," was the reply. "Nothing of that sort anywhere in the neighbourhood."

"But are you *sure*?" she persisted sweetly. "They say that even a pan of water is enough if it's allowed to stand."

"Well, there's an old well down at the foot of the front lawn," he said good-humouredly. "But I hardly think the insects could breed there, because it's twenty feet down to the water."

"Still I'd like to look at it," said Mme. Storey. "If you wouldn't mind."

"Certainly, Madame."

He pointed out a path which led down to the right. As he led the way, he gave us the history of the old well. "The original house on this property stood on the edge of the steep bank, and this was the well belonging to it. When Mr. Whittall's grandfather pulled the old house down, he did not fill up the well, but built an ornamental well-house over it. But the late Mrs. Whittall thought it was incongruous, as it was, and she had it removed. Her idea was to bring over an

antique well-curb from Italy, but for some reason this was never done, and so at present it just has a temporary cover over it."

In a hundred yards or so we came to the spot. It was on the lowest level of the gardens and terraces in front of the house. One could picture the old-fashioned farmhouse which had once stood there. The magnificent elm which had shaded it had been allowed to remain. The brickwork of the well projected a few inches above the ground, and over it had been laid a heavy wooden cover with a trap in the middle, having a ring.

"Will that open?" asked Mme. Storey, pointing.

He got down on his knees to pull it up, looking bored at these vagaries of my mistress, but still respectful.

"I want to look in it," she said.

He made place for her, and she in turn got down on her knees to peer into the black hole.

Suddenly she clasped her breast. "Oh, my pin!" she cried. "It fell in!" And got up with a face of tragedy.

The old gardener scratched his head. I think he was a Scotsman. He looked utterly disgusted. Oh, the folly of these gentlefolk! his expression said.

"It must be recovered!" my mistress said agitatedly. What an admirable actress she was! "It must be recovered! I value it above price!"

"Well, ma'am, I suppose it can be got," the man said slowly. "There's not above three feet of water in the bottom. I have a block and tackle in the toolhouse. I will send one of the men down."

"My chauffeur shall go down," said Mme. Storey.

"No need of that, ma'am."

"No, I insist! My chauffeur shall go down. If the others will help him I shall see that all are well rewarded for their trouble. And you, too!"

"As you wish, Madame." He went off to summon help.

With a slight smile, Mme. Storey pressed an emerald bar-pin that she had unfastened from somewhere or other into my hand, and sent me for Crider. I found him still sitting like a wooden image at the wheel of the car. I gave him the emerald, which he pinned inside his clothes, and whispered his instructions. His eyes gleamed. We returned to the old well.

The under-gardeners had gathered to help, and the old man was dragging block and tackle towards the spot.

"This will take some time, I suppose," said Mme. Storey when he came up. "We had better be looking over the house while we wait."

So we went back up the slope.

We had no particular interest in the interior of the house, but we went over everything dutifully under the guidance of the butler. It was one of the most attractive houses I ever was in. If I had never heard anything else about the mistress of it I would have known by the inside of her house that she was a superior woman. It had nothing of the awful perfection usual to the houses of the very rich; nothing of the museum look. It was full of character. There were no "period" rooms.

In order to give Crider plenty of time we made our tour last as long as possible, but we had returned to the main floor before any word came from him. There was a central hall which was furnished with comfortable chairs. Mme. Storey said to the butler:

"If we may, we will wait here a little while. It is so cold outside."

"Certainly, Madame," he said, and withdrew. We had a feeling, though, that he was lingering somewhere close by. Well, after all, we were strangers in the house.

In a few minutes we heard a car approach swiftly through the crunching gravel, and come to a stop with a grinding of brakes. Mme. Storey and I looked at each other significantly. She shrugged. We heard the car door slam outside, feet came running up the steps, and the front door was flung open. There stood the master of the house. The light was behind him, and I could not read his expression.

The thought instantly flew into my head that the butler, recognising Mme. Storey, or per-

haps suspecting us on general principles, had telephoned to him. He had had just about time enough to drive up from town.

VII

"What! Mme. Storey!" Whittall cried very affably. "What a surprise! I had no idea that you were interested in my property. Why didn't you let me know?"

She ignored the question. "It is beautiful!" she said blandly, "but I am afraid it is too expensive for me."

They shook hands. I could see his face now. He had it under pretty good control, but his eyes were narrow and sharp with curiosity. He was a handsome man in his way, with dark, bright eyes in which there was something both defiant and shifty. It was the look of a schoolboy who knows he has a bad name, and is determined to brazen it out. Why had not Fay Brunton's instincts taken alarm? I wondered. But perhaps Whittall only had that look when he faced my mistress.

"Oh, it's too expensive for anybody to own as a residence now," he said with a laugh. "I supposed it would be bought by a real estate operator, and subdivided. . . . Have you seen everything?"

"Yes, thank you," said Mme. Storey. "We were just waiting for a few minutes. I had the misfortune to lose a piece of jewellery in the grounds, and they are looking for it."

"Ah, I am so sorry!" While he smiled in polite sympathy, his sharp eyes sought to bore into her, but my mistress's face presented a surface as smooth as tinted china.

"We might as well go and see what they are about," she said, moving towards the door.

"Don't hurry away!" he begged. "I don't often have the chance of entertaining you."

However, at this moment the butler appeared, to announce that Madame's pin had been found, and we all moved out to the front steps. Crider was there, and the head gardener. Crider passed over the emerald, and with a meaning look gave his mistress to understand that he had been successful in his other quest. A great relief filled me. Whittall had not come home in time to frustrate us. Mme. Storey was loud in her protestations of thankfulness. She opened her purse to reward the gardener and his men.

"Where was it found?" asked Whittall.

The gardener spoke up. "At the bottom of the old well, sir."

It must have given Whittall a hideous shock. I scarcely had the heart to look at him. He uttered no sound; his eyes were divested of all sense. His florid face went greyish, leaving a network of tiny, purplish veins outlined against the greyness. Several times he essayed to speak before any sound came out.

"Come inside a minute," he gabbled. "Come inside . . . come inside!"

Mme. Storey looked at Crider, and he followed us inside. My mistress had no notion of trusting herself alone with that madman. Whittall led the way across the hall, walking with such quick short steps as to give almost a comic effect. He opened the door of the library for us to pass in. He was for shutting it in Crider's face, but Mme. Storey stopped him with a steady look. So Crider entered and waited with his back against the door. It was a beautiful, quiet room upholstered in maroon, with three tall windows reaching to the floor.

Whittall was in a pitiably unnerved state. Consider the height that he had fallen from. On the eve of his marriage, too. He drew a bottle from a cabinet, and poured himself a drink with shaking hands. Gulped it down at a draught. He went to the windows and jerked at the curtain cords senselessly, though they were already opened to their widest. Again, one was reminded of something comic in his attempt to make out that there was nothing the matter. Finally he asked in a thick voice:

"Am I to have any explanation of this extraordinary visit?"

"I would not insist on it, Whittall," said my mistress, almost regretfully, one would have said.

"I do insist on it," he said quickly.

"Very well. It was not an emerald pin, of course, that I was looking for at the bottom of the well."

"What was it then?"

She turned to the door. "What did you find there, Crider?"

"A Matson 32 automatic, Madame. The magazine is full."

"Hand it over!" said Whittall.

Crider, naturally, made no move to obey.

"This is mere folly," said my mistress calmly; "it is to be handed over to an authority higher than yours."

"Of what do you accuse me?" he cried wildly.

"Of nothing yet, except throwing this gun down the well."

"It's a lie! It's a lie! I never saw it before!"

"Then why all this excitement?"

He turned away biting his fingers.

"This is worse than useless," said Mme. Storey. "Open the door, Crider."

Whittall instantly became abject and cringing. "Wait a minute!" he implored. "Give me a chance to explain. Oh, my God! this frightful unexpected accusation has driven me out of my senses. Give me a chance to recover myself. Don't you see what you are doing? You are ruining me beyond hope. And all for nothing! All for nothing! I am as innocent as a child!"

I am afraid we all smiled grimly at this last cry of his. However, Mme. Storey waited.

"Give me a little time!" he muttered. He took another drink. He then said in a stronger voice: "Send those people out of the room, and I'll tell you all."

"These two are my trusted employees," said Mme. Storey. "We three are as one. You may explain or not, just as it suits you."

After a moment's hesitation he said: "I will explain on one condition, that, if my explanation is a reasonable one, you promise you will not proceed against me immediately. But if you are determined to proceed against me anyhow, what's the use of my telling *you* anything. You can go ahead and be damned to you."

This was too much for Crider. "I'll trouble you to be civil to Madame Storey," he said, flushing.

My mistress silenced him with a gesture. To Whittall she said coolly: "I am not prepared to proceed against you yet. As to the future I make no promises. Are you willing on your part to give me your word of honour that you will not marry until this matter is cleared up?"

"Certainly!" he said quickly. "Word of honor. . . . But, don't tell Fay yet. It would break her heart."

"I have no intention of doing so, yet," said Mme. Storey dryly.

There was a considerable silence.

"We are waiting for the explanation," said Mme. Storey at length.

Whittall turned around. He had evidently decided on his course. "It is true that that is my wife's gun," he said without hesitation, "and that I threw it down the well. But I swear as God is in His Heaven that I did not shoot her. The reason I acted as I did was to prevent a scandal. I immediately suspected that she had been murdered. Well, a dirty scandal would not have given her back to me; it would only have besmirched her reputation still further."

"I know all about the 'other man,'" said Mme. Storey coolly. "I have talked with him. If you are suggesting that he shot her, I answer that it is impossible that he could have done so."

Whittall's face was a study while she was saying this. Finally he shrugged. "In that case," he said sullenly, "I know no more than the next man who did it."

"What gave you reason to suspect that it was murder?" asked Mme. Storey.

"Oh, the general circumstances."

"Nobody else suspected such a thing."

He shrugged indifferently.

Nothing more seemed to be forthcoming, and presently Mme. Storey said: "Your explanation so far is no explanation."

He turned away, visibly in a state of indecision. Then he flung around again. "Oh, hell! I suppose it's all got to come out now!" he cried. "I was warned of her murder!"

"Beforehand?" Mme. Storey asked sternly.

"No. What do you think I am? . . . Shortly after it was committed. That is why I came home so early . . . I was dining with a friend. I was called to the telephone. A voice, unknown to me, said without any preliminary explanation: 'Your wife has just been shot. If you want to avoid a nasty scandal, you had better hurry home and dispose of her revolver, so that it will look like a suicide.'"

I could not help smiling at this tale. It sounded so preposterous. Mme. Storey, however, was grave enough.

"A man's voice or a woman's voice?" she asked.

"A man's."

"Can you offer corroboration of this?"

"Certainly."

"Where were you dining, and with whom?"

"What right have *you* to cross-examine me?" he said, scowling.

"Oh, if you'd rather tell the district attorney . . ." said Mme. Storey calmly.

"I was with Max Kreuger, the manager of Miss Brunton's company," he said sullenly. "We were at the Norfolk. It is not a hotel that I frequent, but we had some private business to discuss, and I didn't want to be recognised."

"Yet the person who called you up knew where to find you?"

He flung out his hands violently. "You'll have to figure that out as best you can! It beats me!"

Mme. Storey took a thoughtful turn up and down.

Whittall went on: "It has been established by a dozen witnesses that the fatal shot was fired at nine-thirty. Kreuger will testify that at that hour I was dining with him in the Norfolk—ten miles away from here. So your case against me collapses. Kreuger will tell you further that about ten minutes past ten I was called to the 'phone. Naturally I did not tell him the nature of the message I received. But he'll tell you that I left immediately. Before eleven I was back here. I suppose the taxicab driver who brought me here can be found too, if he is looked for . . . Kreuger is in his office now. Come with me and question him, and let this ridiculous charge be laid once and for all."

Mme. Storey agreed to the proposal. Again she pointed out to Whittall that she had not yet made any charge.

There was a brief discussion as to how we should dispose ourselves for the drive to town. Naturally we did not intend to let Whittall out of our sight. I thought we all ought to go in Mme. Storey's car, but she ruled otherwise. She and I and Whittall would ride in his car, she said, and Crider could bring her car along after.

While Whittall waited for us in his car, biting his fingers with impatience, Mme. Storey gave Crider his private instructions: "Do not follow us, but drive to your own place as quickly as possible, and change. Telephone Younger to come and get the car. You had also better get in touch with Stephens. Get back to the Adelphi theatre as soon as you can. Whittall will be there in Max Kreuger's office. You and Stephens between you are to keep Whittall under observation until further notice, reporting to me at my office by 'phone as often as you are able."

That was hardly a cheerful drive. Mme. Storey and Whittall sat side by side on the back seat without exchanging a single word the whole way. Whittall crouched in his corner, scowling and biting his fingers. If Fay could have watched him then, that in itself ought to have given her pause. Whittall had a skilful chauffeur, of course. He had a special instinct to warn him of a traffic policeman. When the road was clear he opened his throttle to its widest, and we sped like a bullet. Then at certain moments he abruptly slowed down, and sure enough, presently the brass buttons would appear. We made Times Square in twenty-five minutes.

The Adelphi was one of the newer theatres in that neighbourhood. Its name has been changed now. At this time Whittall was reputed to be the owner, but I do not know if this was so. It was perfectly clear though that Max Kreuger was Whittall's creature. *Wild Hyacinth*, I should say, was not showing at the Adelphi, but at the Yorktown, farther down Broadway, which had a greater seating capacity.

A deceitful air of activity pervaded the offices. Apart from rehearsals, theatrical business seems to consist of lengthy conversations which end exactly where they begin. There were a number of depressed-looking actors of both sexes sitting around the outer office waiting for an interview with the manager. Yet Kreuger as we presently discovered was alone in his office, with his heels cocked up on his desk. Whittall marched straight into the private office with us at his heels. Snatching the cigar from his lips, Kreuger leaped to his feet. He was a rosy, plump little man of the type that I have heard described as a fore-and-aft Jew; a blond. He looked astonished, as well he might, at the combination which faced him.

Without the slightest preamble, Whittall cried out with a wave of his hand: "There he is. Ask him what you want." And went to the window where he turned his back to us.

Kreuger, greatly flustered, began to pull chairs out, and to mumble courtesies.

"Never mind, thanks," said Mme. Storey. "We won't sit down. Just answer a few questions, please. It is by Mr. Whittall's wish that we have come."

"Anything, Madame Storey, anything within my power!" the little man murmured fulsomely.

"What were you doing on the evening of Sunday, September 11th?"

Kreuger was horridly taken aback. He stared at us in a witless fashion and pulled at his slack lower lip. His distracted eyes sought his master for guidance, but received none, Whittall's back being turned.

"Well, speak up, can't you?" barked Whittall, without turning around.

"Yes . . . yes . . . of course," stammered Kreuger, sparring for time. "Let me see . . . September 11th . . . I can't seem to remember offhand. I shall have to look it up."

"That was the night of Mrs. Whittall's death," Mme. Storey reminded him.

"Oh, to be sure! that dreadful night!" said Kreuger in suitable tones of horror. "That was the night of the private showing of the super-film 'Ashes of Roses.' I looked in at that."

This was certainly not the answer that Whittall looked for. He whirled around with a face of terror. I rejoiced that we had caught the villains napping, as it seemed. Something had gone wrong with their concerted story.

"Tell the truth!" gasped Whittall.

"Eh? . . . What?" stammered Kreuger, blinking.

"Tell the truth, I said!" cried Whittall in a fury, banging the desk.

"Oh, to be sure! To be sure!" stuttered the demoralised Kreuger. "Mr. Whittall and I had dinner together that night. At the Hotel Norfolk."

I smiled to myself. This came a little late, I thought. It sounded as if it had been got by heart.

"Why did you not say so at once?" asked Mme. Storey.

"Well, it was a private meeting, Madame. We had business to discuss. I didn't think that Mr. Whittall wanted it known."

"At what time did you meet?"

"Half-past seven."

"Describe what happened."

"Well, we had our dinner. Afterwards we went out to the smoking lounge. Shortly after ten, a boy came through paging Mr. Darius Whittall. Mr. Whittall was surprised, because he had not thought that anybody knew where he was. Everybody in the room looked up, hearing *that* name. At first Mr. Whittall wasn't going to identify himself. Just some trifler, he said, or a newspaper reporter. But he was curious to find out who had got hold of his name. So after the boy had gone on, he went out to the office. In a minute or two he came back. He looked very agitated. All he said was: 'Something wrong at home.' He got his hat and coat, and jumped in a taxicab."

"Now are you satisfied that I didn't do it?" cried Whittall.

"Quite!" said Mme. Storey.

I was surprised at this answer. Still I supposed she had her own reasons for making it.

She asked them both a number of further questions, which they answered readily. Whittall rapidly quieted down. It had the effect of a genuine cross-examination, but knowing my mistress so well, I could see that she was only stalling for time. She did not want Whittall to get away from there until Crider was waiting outside to pick him up. Nothing of moment to the case was brought out by their answers.

Finally we went. The street outside was crowded, and I could not pick out Crider anywhere, but I had no doubt he was safely at his post. Just the same I felt that we were doing wrong to go away and leave Whittall like that, free to work his own nefarious schemes. And as we drove away in a taxicab I voiced something to that effect.

"But we have no reason to order him detained," said Mme. Storey calmly. "He didn't shoot his wife."

"What!" I cried, astonished. "You still doubt that!"

"No," said Mme. Storey, smiling at the heat I betrayed. "I'm sure he didn't."

"But obviously that man Kreuger was ready to swear to anything that would please him!"

"Obviously!" she agreed.

"And the story about the telephone call—fancy anybody calling him up and saying: 'Your wife has been shot.' Just like that. Why, it's preposterous!"

"Quite!" said Mme. Storey. "Whittall is far too clever a man to have offered me so preposterous a story if it were not true. There is nothing so preposterous as the truth sometimes."

"Well, if he didn't do it himself he certainly *had* it done," I said excitedly. "And that telephone message was from his hireling telling him that the job was accomplished."

But Mme. Storey still shook her head.

"What makes you so sure Whittall wasn't responsible?" I asked helplessly.

"It's so simple," she said. "If Whittall had

plotted to shoot his wife, he would have shot her with her own gun, wouldn't he? And then we never would have known."

I looked at her in silence. Why, of course! My theory went down like a house of cards.

"No," she went on gravely, "here's the best part of the day gone, and we're almost where we were yesterday evening. . . . Well, not quite. Because Whittall told one little lie, which will appear later."

"Then are we up against a blank wall?" I asked, discouraged.

"Oh, no," was her surprising answer. "I know who did it."

I looked my breathless question.

But she only shook her head. "No evidence," she said, frowning. "Not a shred! It's almost the perfect crime, my Bella!"

VIII

Mme. Storey and I returned to the office. We found her car waiting out in front for orders. The chauffeur, Younger, handed over the gun fished from the well at Oakhurst, which Crider had given him for safe keeping. Mme. Storey, in my presence, marked the gun for subsequent identification. We found a number of matters awaiting our attention, which we got out of the way as quickly as possible. Meanwhile, we ordered in a light lunch of sandwiches and milk.

While she munched her sandwiches, Mme. Storey paced slowly up and down the long room, considering deeply. With the last bite she evidently finished mapping out her course of action. Her first move was to call up Fay Brunton in her dressing-room at the theatre. They had an aimless friendly talk, which was, however, not so aimless on my mistress's part as might have been supposed, for she found out: (a) that Fay had not seen nor heard from Darius Whittall since we had left him: (b) that she was still looking forward to the supper party in her rooms that night. I also marked this bit:

"I saw the new film 'Ashes of Roses' last night," said Mme. Storey. (I knew this was not true.) "Have you seen it?" Fay's answer ran to some length. It was evidently in the negative, for Mme. Storey said: "Well, you ought to. It's really quite tremendous." The talk then passed to other matters.

Mme. Storey then called up Inspector Rumsey at Headquarters. She asked him if he had succeeded in tracing Whittall's purchase of the guns. He replied that he had full information. She then got him to tell her what his movements would be that afternoon and night, so that we could get in touch with him any time we might need him.

Crider called us up to report that Darius Whittall had called upon the President of the —— Railroad. Crider was not able to say, of course, what was the occasion of the visit. Upon hearing this Mme. Storey instructed Crider to send Stephens to the —— Terminal to find out as best he could what order had been received respecting the President's private car.

I must try to set down in order all that we did that afternoon. The significance of much of it did not become clear to me until night. First; an operative was despatched to the garage run in connection with the Hotel Madagascar (where Fay lived) with instructions to learn what he could about the movements of Miss Brunton's cars on the night of September 11th. Fay kept two cars; a brougham which was driven by a chauffeur and a smart little convertible that she drove herself. It appeared that in this very up-to-date garage a complete record was kept of the movements of all the cars stored there. Every time they went out their mileage was taken, and again when they came in. This was to prevent their use for unauthorised purposes.

Second; an operative (this one a woman) was sent to interview Miss Beatrice Dufaye, the well-known cinema star, in the guise of a representative of some mythical magazine. Miss Dufaye was the star of "Ashes of Roses," a picture which was the sensation of the moment, and at present she was resting at her country place at Glen Cove before starting work on her next picture. Among other things, this operative was instructed to ask certain questions relative to the private showing of "Ashes of Roses" on September 11th. This had been made a great social occasion in theatrical circles.

A third operative was instructed to learn the present whereabouts of Mr. Frank Esher. Esher, you will remember, was the young man who was deeply in love with Fay Brunton, and for whom we suspected she had a tenderness in return. After a quarrel or a series of quarrels, he had flown off to parts unknown. This operative was furnished with the address of his last employers, his club, and his last home address.

Finally I received my assignment. "Bella," said my mistress, "I want you to go to Tiffany's with me, to help choose Fay's wedding present."

It struck me as very strange that we should spend our time this way when matters were at such a critical juncture; and especially as we were determined to prevent this wedding if we could. However, I said nothing. We used up a good hour choosing the most beautiful amongst all the tiny platinum and jewelled watches they showed us.

"Take it to the hotel," said Mme. Storey, "and give it to her maid to keep until Fay returns from the theatre. You may let the maid have a peep at it as a great favour. This ought to put you on an intimate footing at once. You will no doubt find her packing her mistress's things for the journey tomorrow. It will seem quite natural for you to show curiosity in Fay's pretty things. Take plenty of time. Fay cannot get home until nearly six if she comes at all. Ordinarily, on matinée days, she has dinner in her dressing-room. I want you to find out what Fay was doing on the night of September 11th."

"What Fay was doing?" I echoed, greatly disquieted.

Mme. Storey looked at me in a way which did not allay my uneasiness. "Have patience, Bella. I cannot yet foresee how all this is going to turn out."

She drove off up to Riverdale again with the object of recovering the gun which Whittall had presented to the Captain of the precinct. It was from this gun that the fatal shot had been fired.

I proceeded to the Madagascar, that towering palace of luxury. Fay, like most women in her position, had two maids, one of whom waited upon her in the hotel, and one at the theatre. I was already slightly acquainted with Katy Meadows, her hotel maid, and of course the nature of my errand immediately broke the ice between us. Katy was a pretty, vivacious Irish girl with naturally rosy cheeks. Fay spoiled her. Katy looked on me as a sort of superior servant like herself, and was quite free with me. She went into raptures over the watch.

Just as Mme. Storey had said, I found her packing. Fay's things were spread over the whole suite. I did not have to express any curiosity, for Katy insisted on showing me everything; hats, wraps, dresses, lingerie, shoes in endless profusion. It was immoral that one woman should possess so much, but oh! what a fascinating display! Unfortunately, I had something else on my mind, and was unable to give myself up to the contemplation of it. The suite consisted of three rooms; a corner sitting-room with Fay's bedroom on one side and Mrs. Brunton's on the other.

After we had finished rhapsodising over the watch I lingered on. Katy was bustling from room to room bearing armfuls of Fay's things that had to be packed. She was in a great state of fluster.

"Four o'clock!" she cried. "Mercy! I must get a move on me! They're going to have a supper party here after the show, and everything must be out of here before that, and the place tidied up.... But don't you go, Miss Brickley. Sit down and talk to me. It keeps me going. . . ."

In the end it was not at all difficult to get what I wanted. I led up to the matter as I had heard Mme. Storey do over the 'phone.

"I went to see 'Ashes of Roses' last night. It's a dandy picture. Have you seen it?"

"No," said Katy. "I must wait until it shows in the cheaper houses."

"That was a great party they had the night of the private showing last September," I went on. "I suppose your folks went. They say all the famous people on Broadway were there."

"Mrs. Brunton went," said Katy unsuspiciously, "but at the last moment Miss Fay wouldn't go. Said she didn't feel good."

"I thought she was never sick," I ventured.

"Oh, not sick," said Katy. "Just wanted to stay quiet and read. I left her in bed reading. I remember that's the night I saw A. J. Burchell, in 'Well-Dressed Wives.' Don't you love him?"

So much for that.

While I was in the suite, things were still arriving from the shops. I remember I was looking at a marvellous négligée when the telephone rang. From Katy's responses I understood that it was Fay calling from the theatre. Fay was evidently issuing somewhat complicated instructions, to which Katy returned breathless affirmatives.

Katy finally hung up, and turned around with wide eyes. "What do you think!" she cried. "They've changed all their plans. They're going away this evening instead of tomorrow morning!"

I thought that was the end of everything. Mme. Storey had gone up to Riverdale, and I didn't know when she'd get back. Luckily Katy was too much excited herself to notice the effect that her announcement had on me.

"For the Lord's sake," she cried. "You never know what they're going to do next! . . . I'm to pack the dressing-case and the small wardrobe trunk, and leave everything else to Maud. I'm to take the things to the —— Terminal—my own things too, and meet them in the Grand Concourse at six-thirty!"

There was only one thing for me to do, and that was to get out as quick as I could. Which I did. What was I to do? I felt desperate. If I tried to go after Mme. Storey, likely I would only pass her somewhere coming back. I didn't dare call up the police station at Riverdale, because I didn't know if she would give her right name there, and if I mentioned it, I might upset all her plans. There was nothing for it but to return to the office and wait for her. At the worst, I was prepared to go myself to the Terminal, and denounce Whittall in public, though I died for it.

To my great relief that was not required of me. At the end of an hour, Mme. Storey came into the office bringing a very pretty young lady whom I had not seen before. She introduced her as Miss Larrimore. I was too excited at the moment to remember that this was the name of Fay's understudy.

"Miss Larrimore wanted to see our offices," Mme. Storey explained amiably.

Perceiving from my face that something had happened, Mme. Storey allowed the girl to pass on into the long room, while she lingered in my office. I hurriedly made my communication. Mme. Storey was not in the least disturbed. Indeed, she laughed merrily.

"I fancied that some such move might be made," she said. "So I kidnapped Fay's understudy. I expect they're looking for her now."

"But . . . but where did you find her?" I asked, amazed.

"Oh, I knew that after reporting at the theatre for every performance, she was free to go home if Fay had turned up in good health. So I went to her boarding-house, and asked her to go for a drive. We'll take her back directly. It will be fun!"

From her handbag Mme. Storey took an automatic pistol, and put a mark on it in my presence, before dropping it in the drawer of my desk. This weapon was identical with the one which had been recovered from the well at Oakhurst that morning.

My mistress did not hurry herself at all. After showing Miss Larrimore her artistic treasures she announced that she would drive her uptown. "I'm going to drop in on Fay at the theatre," said Mme. Storey. "You come along too."

It was not the first time that Mme. Storey and I had applied at the stage door of the Yorktown theatre, and we were admitted without question. The star of the company was allotted two rooms on the level of the stage; the outer was used to receive her friends in, while the inner was devoted to the mysteries of make-up and dress. When the outer door was opened we heard the voices of several people within. Mme. Storey slyly bade Miss Larrimore to enter first, while she hung back with a smile. Cries of relief greeted the understudy.

"Oh, here you are!"

Then Mme. Storey entered with me at her heels. They were all there; Whittall, Kreuger, Mrs. Brunton, and Fay. My mistress's appearance created a startling effect. Whittall was arrested in full flight, so to speak. The man froze where he stood. His face turned livid. Kreuger was frankly terrified; while Mrs. Brunton was herself, for once. She snarled. She could not have known what had taken place that day, but she saw clearly enough that her darling scheme was endangered. Fay swam towards us, perfectly candid in her gladness. Whittall made an involuntary move to stop her—then he saw it was useless.

"Rosika and Bella!" cried Fay. "What a lucky chance! I was just about to write you. Darius said it would sound too casual to telephone. I am afraid our little party for tonight must be off, my dears. But Darius says we shall have a big one as soon as we get back. Our plans are all changed. It turns out that the private car is required in New York on Tuesday, and we have to use it tonight or not at all. I suppose I am silly, but my heart was set on that private car. So we're off at seven o'clock. Miss Larrimore will play my part tonight. We'll be married in Pinehurst tomorrow."

Mme. Storey looked at Whittall with a cold smile. He visibly writhed under it. He had given her his word of honour, you remember. The tension of that moment was almost unbearable. Everybody in the room was aware of it except the two girls who were laughingly whispering about the night's performance. There was something inexpressibly touching in the sight of their happy ignorance.

Finally Mme. Storey spoke. "I'm afraid I've got the thankless job of throwing a monkey-wrench into the works," she said.

"What do you mean?" asked Fay, laughing.

"I can't let Mr. Whittall go away tonight."

One can imagine what a hell of rage and frustration Whittall was undergoing during those moments. I don't suppose that the arrogant millionaire's will had ever been crossed before.

"What!" said Fay, opening her eyes wide.

"Some time ago," said Mme. Storey coolly, "Mr. Whittall promised to back me in a scheme I was getting up to open a studio building for poor artists. My plans are ripe now, and I have called a meeting for tomorrow. I am counting on him."

"Oh, but surely," said Fay, more and more surprised, "under the circumstances, can't somebody appear for him? can't it be put off for a few days?"

"No," said Mme. Storey with cold firmness.

From astonishment Fay graduated to indignation. Suspecting enmity in my mistress, she turned from her. "Darius!" she said.

What a bitter moment for him! He hesitated. His eyes glittered in the direction of my mistress with an expression of reckless rage. But upon meeting her cold glance they fell again. He knew that the word "murder" had only to be whispered to destroy his chances forever. "I gave her my word," he mumbled, grinding his teeth. "I've got to stick to it."

Fay's gentle eyes flashed. She could see now that there was much more in this than appeared on the surface. But pride would not allow her to ask any more questions. She was much angrier at her renegade lover than she was at Mme. Storey.

"Oh, well, of course it doesn't make any difference," she said, tossing her head. She slipped her hand under Miss Larrimore's arm. "I'm only sorry on your account, my dear." She drew the other girl into the inner room.

IX

The events which succeeded this scene were simply baffling to me. Katy was ordered back from the station to the hotel, and told to unpack all her mistress's things and put them away. The private car was cancelled. At this, Mrs. Brunton could no longer contain her feelings. She burst out at Mme. Storey wildly.

"How dare you come here interfering in our private affairs! What does your silly meeting mean to us when Darius and Fay are going to be married! I never heard of such a thing. . . ."

The outburst was quite natural. Mrs. Brunton had had a hard life, and Whittall's twenty millions blinded her to all other considerations. There is no doubt but she loved Fay as if she had been her own child.

Now Whittall, when he heard this, executed a rapid *volte-face*. A moment before he had seemed absolutely suffocated with rage against Mme. Storey; now he turned against Mrs. Brunton, and roughly silenced her. "Mme. Storey is our friend," he said. "You have no reason to speak to her in that manner. This is important. She knows what she is doing."

Mrs. Brunton didn't know what to make of it, and no more did I. To my further astonishment, Mme. Storey allowed a reconciliation to be patched up, and when I left she and Whittall were chatting together as amicably as you please. Since Fay was to go on as usual, her supper had been ordered in. I can't tell you what happened after that, because I had been sent to the office with private instructions to receive the reports of the various operatives who had been detailed on the case, and forward them to Mme. Storey at the theatre. I supposed that she and Whittall remained at the theatre throughout the performance, exchanging compliments—and watching each other.

During the evening Mme. Storey called me up to say that the little party would take place in Fay's rooms after the performance as at first arranged, and that I was to be there. She instructed me to get in touch with Inspector Rumsey, and to ask him to be waiting in the lobby of the Madagascar at quarter to twelve. I possessed no key to Mme. Storey's plans, and this latter message caused a feeling of dread to weigh on my breast.

In due course I went home to change my dress, and then proceeded to the hotel. I saw the Inspector waiting in the lobby, and nodded to him as I passed. When I was shown up to Fay's suite I found that I was the first to arrive. Katy pounced on me to learn the inner reasons for her mistress's second extraordinary change of plans, but I had no heart to gossip with the maid.

There was a table ready set for six persons. It looked lovely with its snowy cloth set off with glass and silver and flowers. All around the white panelled walls relieved with an old messotint or two there were pink-shaded lights bracketed in threes, and casting down a pleasant glow on the comfortable furniture covered with crisp cretonnes. Only the most expensive places dare to be as simple as that. There were flowers everywhere in the room. To me there was a horrible irony in the sight of all this dainty preparation for such a scene.

Fay, Mrs. Brunton, Darius Whittall, and Kreuger came in together. Their faces gave nothing away.

"Where is Mme. Storey?" I asked involuntarily.

"She'll be up directly," said Fay. "She met a friend in the lobby."

I supposed this was Rumsey.

Fay and Mrs. Brunton disappeared within their respective bedrooms to remove their wraps. When Fay left the room something of the inferno of passion that was consuming Whittall broke through the mask he wore. He looked at me as much as to say: What the hell are you doing here? I paid no attention. Mme. Storey entered, and he smiled at her obsequiously. Mme. Storey lit a cigarette, and lingered in the sitting-room exchanging some trivial remarks with Whittall until Fay returned. She then said something about tidying herself, and entered Fay's room alone.

When she came back we sat down at the table, and the waiters entered. Mme. Storey, alone of the women, was not in evening dress, nevertheless by her mere presence she dominated the scene. Everybody else was trying to be funny. There was a ghastly hollowness about it. Whittall was the loudest of all. Fay seemed pleasant towards him, but I suspected that her pleasant manner concealed a certain reserve. Mrs. Brunton seemed to be satisfied that everything was going well, as long as there was plenty of noise.

Fay occupied the place of honour at the head

of the table, with Mme. Storey on one hand, and me on the other. Kreuger sat next to Mme. Storey, and Mrs. Brunton next to me. Whittall faced Fay across the table. Fay, I remember, was wearing a pale pink gown embroidered with self-coloured beads in a quaint design. It lent her beauty an exquisite fragility. When he thought nobody was looking at him, I would catch Whittall gazing at her like a lost soul.

The meal, I suppose, left nothing to be desired. I cannot remember what we ate or drank. Someday I hope I may be invited to such a perfect little supper when my mind is at peace. This one was wasted on all of us. It was soon over, and the cigarettes lighted. Mrs. Brunton chattered on.

"There was twenty-one hundred dollars in the house tonight. That's a hundred and fifty more than capacity."

"How do you do that sum?" asked Whittall facetiously.

"Standees," said Mrs. Brunton. ". . . And *what* a house! So warm and responsive. I could have hugged them to my breast!"

"Rather an armful," put in Whittall.

"And when she finished her waltz song, didn't they rise to her! Oh, it was wonderful! Never have I heard such applause! And didn't she look sweet when she came out to acknowledge it? I declare her pretty eyes were full of real tears!"

"Well, I thought maybe it was the last time," said Fay.

"I thought they would *never* let her go!" Mrs. Brunton rhapsodised. "She took fourteen calls!"

"Oh, mamma!" protested Fay, laughing. "Draw it mild!"

"Fourteen!" said Mrs. Brunton firmly. "I said it, and I stick to it! Fourteen!"

She appealed to Whittall and to Kreuger, and they made haste to agree in order to shut her up.

"One doesn't have to exaggerate the successes of a girl like Fay," she went on complacently. "I saw Mildred Mortimer and her mother hidden away at the back of the house. I can imagine what *their* feelings were!"

Such was Mrs. Brunton's style. She turned it on like a tap. She had been something of a

beauty in her day, and she looked quite handsome tonight in her black evening gown, with her hair freshened up with henna, and prettily dressed.

Whittall, I remember, made an effort to break up the party. "Fay, you look tired," he said. "I think we'd better beat it."

Fay protested. Kreuger, always eager to take a hint from his master, pushed his chair back. No one else moved. I saw Mme. Storey, for whom this suggestion was really intended, glance at her wrist watch. Then she helped herself to a cigarette, and gave the conversation a fresh start.

The crisis was precipitated by an innocent question of Fay's. "Why are you so quiet, Rosika?"

"I am thinking of that poor lady who is dead," said Mme. Storey gravely.

It was like an icy hand laid on each heart there. A deathly silence fell on us. It seemed to last forever. I felt paralysed. Mrs. Brunton was the first to recover herself. She was afraid of Mme. Storey, and dared not be openly rude, but her anger was evident enough in her voice.

"Oh, I say! What a thing to bring up at such a time and place! I'm surprised at you, Mme. Storey!"

"We are all thinking of her," said Mme. Storey. "It would be better to clear our minds of the subject."

"*I* wasn't thinking of her, I assure you!"

Even the gentle Fay was resentful. "It's not fair to Darius," she murmured.

"Darius is a man and must face things!"

I glanced at Whittall. He had the look of one braced to receive a fatal stroke.

"I am so sorry for her!" murmured Fay distressfully. "I often think about her and wonder . . . But, Rosika, is it *my* fault that I am happy? that I have everything, while she is dead?"

Mme. Storey made no reply to this.

"She solved her problems in her own way!" cried Mrs. Brunton excitedly. "Who shall blame her? Can't you leave her in peace?"

"She did not kill herself," said Mme. Storey slowly. "She was murdered."

Again that awful silence. Horror crushed us.

Whittall lost his grip on himself. "You promised me . . . you promised me . . . !" he cried shakily, "that you would not tell her . . ."

"We had better not talk about promises," said Mme. Storey with a steady look at him.

"Darius! . . . you already knew this!" gasped Fay.

He could make no answer.

Fay turned to Mme. Storey. "Rosika . . . how do you know? . . . how do you know?" she faltered.

"She received a letter that evening which drew her out to the pavilion. She was unarmed when she left the house."

"Then it's quite clear," said Fay, laughing hysterically. "The letter must have been from her lover. He pleaded with her for the last time, and when she was obdurate he shot her in a fit of desperation."

"She was shot within three minutes of leaving the house," said Mme. Storey relentlessly. "Not much time for pleading. No! Somebody was waiting for her in the pavilion with the gun ready."

"But it *must* have been her lover!" wailed Fay.

Mme. Storey sat looking straight ahead of her, pale and immovable as Nemesis. "It was somebody who is amongst us here," she said.

You could hear the tight breasts around the table labouring for breath. Each of us glanced with furtive dread at our companions. Whittall broke again.

"Well, who? . . . who? . . . who?" he cried wildly. "Out with it!"

"Somebody amongst us here?" quavered Mrs. Brunton in a high falsetto. "I never heard of such a thing!"

The ageing woman with her touched-up cheeks and dyed hair looked like a caricature of herself. Everybody around the table looked stricken, clownish, scattered in the wits. I'm sure I was no exception. Only my beautiful mistress was as composed as Death.

"Fay," she asked, "what were you doing on the evening of September eleventh?"

I turned absolutely sick at heart. Mrs. Brunton and Whittall loudly and angrily protested. The exquisite girl shrank away from Mme. Storey, and went as pale as paper. Apart from the noisy voices of the others I heard her dismayed whisper.

"Rosika! . . . I? . . . I? . . . Oh, Rosika, surely you can't think that I . . ."

"This is too much!" cried Mrs. Brunton, jumping up. "Must we submit to be insulted here in our own rooms? Mr. Whittall, are you going to permit this to go any further?"

"No!" cried Whittall, banging the table. "This woman is taking too much on herself! She has no right to catechise us!"

Mme. Storey looked at me. "Bella," she said, "admit the gentleman who is waiting outside."

As well as my legs would serve me I got to the door. Inspector Rumsey was in the corridor. He came in.

With a wave of the hand, Mme. Storey introduced him to the gaping company. "Inspector Rumsey and I are acting in concert in this matter," she said. "I suppose you will allow that he has a right to ask questions."

Rumsey quietly sat down in a chair away from the table.

"Now, Fay," said Mme. Storey.

The girl raised her gentle eyes in an imploring and reproachful glance upon her friend. "Oh, Rosika, how can you?" she murmured.

Mme. Storey's face was like a mask. "I must do my duty as I see it. Answer my question, please."

Fay put a hand over her eyes. "That was the night of the first showing of 'Ashes of Roses'," she murmured. "I did not go. I was not well. I went to bed when Mamma went out."

"But you got up again," said Mme. Storey remorselessly. "I have a report from the garage where you keep your cars, stating that you telephoned for the convertible at 8:10 that night, and that it was handed over to you at the door of your hotel five minutes later. It was returned to the garage at half-past ten."

"Oh, yes," murmured Fay feebly. "I forgot."

Mrs. Brunton and Whittall looked dumfounded. As for me, I simply could not believe my ears.

"Where did you go?" asked Mme. Storey.

"I . . . I was just driving around for the air. I don't remember exactly."

"According to the custom of the garage," Mme. Storey continued, "a reading of the speedometer was taken when the car went out, and again when it was returned. The elapsed mileage was twenty miles. That is just the distance to Riverdale and back."

Fay sat up suddenly. "I never went to Riverdale!" she cried sharply.

"Then where did you go?" persisted Mme. Storey.

A deep blush overspread Fay's face and neck. "Well, if you must know," she said a little defiantly, "I picked up Frank Esher in front of his house and took him for a drive."

Again Mrs. Brunton and Whittall looked at her open-mouthed.

The Inspector spoke up cheerfully. Like everybody else, he wished to be on Fay's side. "That will be easy to verify," he said, taking out his note-book.

"Unfortunately," said Mme. Storey coldly, "Mr. Esher has disappeared."

"Well, anyhow," cried Whittall, "you can't convict her of a crime simply because she chanced to take a drive that night. It's ridiculous!"

"Ridiculous!" echoed Mrs. Brunton.

"I have not yet done," said Mme. Storey. "Inspector, will you please state what you learned respecting the purchase of the guns."

Rumsey consulted the note-book. "On May 24th Mr. Darius Whittall purchased two Matson 32 calibre automatics from Lorber and Staley's. He has an account there. Those were the only pistols of that design he ever purchased from them. One was numbered 13417, the other 13418."

Mme. Storey turned to Whittall. "Are you willing to concede that you gave one of these pistols to your wife, and one to Fay?" she asked.

"I refuse to answer without advice of counsel," he muttered.

"It doesn't matter," said Mme. Storey, undisturbed; "for we already know from other sources that you gave one to your wife and one to Fay, making the same remark to each. . . . Fay, where is yours?"

"In the bottom drawer of my bureau," came the prompt reply.

"Will you fetch it, please?"

Fay called for Katy. The girl immediately appeared in the doorway, looking white and scared. Evidently she had overheard at least part of what had occurred.

"Bring me the gun from the bottom drawer of my bureau."

The strangeness of this request completed the demoralisation of the maid. She stood there like one incapable of motion. Fay herself sprang up and ran into the next room. From there we heard her cry:

"It's gone!"

Then her excited questioning of the maid. Katy swore that she had neither touched nor even seen the gun. She had not yet reached that drawer when her packing was interrupted, she said. The girl got the idea, somehow, that her own honesty was in question. She had no idea that her words were convicting her mistress. Fay finally came back to her seat with a wandering and vacant air. She kept repeating: "I can't imagine . . . ! I can't imagine . . . !" The Inspector looked very grave.

Mme. Storey remorselessly resumed: "I recovered Mrs. Whittall's pistol this morning. It is in my possession, properly marked for identification. The number of it is 13417. The pistol found in Mrs. Whittall's hand, that is to say the one from which the fatal shot was fired, was subsequently given by Mr. Whittall to the Captain of the precinct. I obtained it from the Captain this afternoon. The number is 13418. Here it is."

She produced the weapon from a little bag that she carried on her arm. She handed the sinister black object to Rumsey, who read off the number, 13418, and handed it back to her.

At first I couldn't take it in. Neither could Fay. Her wandering eyes, like a child's, searched from one face to another for the explanation. Mrs. Brunton and Whittall were sitting there, literally frozen with horror. Rumsey had got up. It was from his grave and compassionate gaze at Fay that I realised she stood convicted in his eyes. What a dreadful moment!

Fay burst into tears, and dropped her head between her outstretched arms on the table. "Oh, how can you! . . . How can you!" she sobbed.

At that something seemed to break inside of me. I forgot everything; my duty to my mistress; everything. I was only conscious of the weeping girl whom I loved. I got to my feet. "It's a shame! It's a shame!" I heard myself crying. "She didn't do it! She *couldn't* have done it! Look at her! What does your evidence amount to beside that!"

Fay reached for me like a frightened child, and I took her in my arms.

Mme. Storey never looked at me. No muscle of her face changed. "The rest lies with you, Inspector," she said quietly.

Rumsey's distress comes back to me now. Then I was oblivious to everything. "It will be all right. . . . It will be all right," he kept saying. "I'm sure that a further investigation will clear everything up. But I'm sorry . . . I would not be justified . . . I must ask the young lady . . ."

Mrs. Brunton jumped up with a shriek. "Is he going to *arrest* her!"

"Don't call it an arrest, ma'am; a brief detention. . . ."

"Oh, no! no! no!" Mrs. Brunton flung herself down beside the girl, and wrapped her arms around Fay's knees. "It's all lies!" she cried. "All lies! . . . It was *I* who shot Mrs. Whittall!"

I have scarcely the heart to describe the painful scene that followed. Fay was broken-hearted, of course, but the shock to her proved to be less than Mme. Storey had feared. It turned out that for weeks past, Fay had divined that her companion was carrying a load of guilt on her breast, though, of course, the girl had no idea of its nature. She was already secretly estranged from the woman who passed as her mother.

Nevertheless she loyally wished to accompany her to Police Headquarters, but the rest of us dissuaded her from it. Kreuger went with Mrs. Brunton, but Darius Whittall remained with us. He had to learn his fate. Before Mme. Storey and I, he said with a despairing hangdog air:

"It was not my fault, Fay."

She looked at him with gravely accusing eyes. There was nothing childish about her then. "No," she said quietly, "but you were not sorry when it happened." Unfastening the pearls from about her neck, and drawing off the ring, she handed them over.

He knew it was final. He went away, a broken man.

When we three were alone together, Fay wept again. Mme. Storey looked as uncomfortable as a boy in the presence of emotion. From the little bag she took the gun she had produced at the table.

"Here is your gun, Fay," she said. "I took it out of your drawer when I went into your room to change my hat."

We opened our eyes at that. Nothing so simple had ever occurred to us.

"I hope you can forgive me for those terrible moments I gave you," Mme. Storey went on. "I couldn't help myself. That woman covered her tracks so well, there was nothing for it but to force a confession."

Fay forgave her freely.

"I owe Bella an apology, too," Mme. Storey said with a rueful glance in my direction. "For keeping her in the dark. You see, I needed that outburst from Bella to give the scene verisimilitude."

This made me feel rather foolish, but of course I was not troubling about a little thing like that then.

"I am alone now," sobbed Fay.

Mme. Storey murmured the name of Frank Esher. "I suggest that that woman may have fomented the trouble between you and him because he was poor," she said.

"She was always against him," Fay agreed.

"Why don't you write to him now?"

"I don't know where he is!" mourned Fay.

"In care of the British-American Development Company, Georgetown, British Guiana," said Mme. Storey dryly.

"Oh, Rosika!" This with her face hidden on my shoulder.

"In fact, why not cable?" said Mme. Storey.

"Oh, Rosika. You do it for me."

"Well, as a matter of fact, I have cabled already," said Mme. Storey.

I cannot do better than conclude by appending Mrs. Brunton's subsequent confession to the police—her real name was Elinor Tinsley. All that was so baffling in the case therein becomes clear.

"I am aware that anything I say may be used against me. I want to tell the truth now. I'm glad it's out. It was too great a load to bear. I did it for her; for the one whom I called my daughter. I loved her as much as I could my own child. In spite of all I said, I knew that she had not sufficient talent to maintain her as a star. So many new faces coming to the front each year. I wanted to secure her future. I wanted her to have the best.

"When Mr. Whittall began to pay her attention I saw our chance in him. But his wife was in the way. He was anxious for a divorce, but she wouldn't. I couldn't forget about it. I brooded and brooded on it. I felt I had to act quickly, because Mr. Whittall had a reputation for fickleness. I was afraid he'd take a fancy to somebody else. Once he told me the name of a man he thought his wife was secretly in love with—I won't mention it here; and that gave me my first idea.

"I got a sample of Mrs. Whittall's handwriting by writing her a begging letter under an assumed name, and I practised and practised until I was able to imitate it. Then I sent a letter as coming from her to this man I told you about, hoping that it would result in throwing them into each other's arms, and that there would have to be a divorce then. But weeks passed and nothing happened. I was no further forward than before.

"Then one day Mrs. Whittall asked my daughter and me to have lunch and tea with her at her place. And when we were having tea out in the pavilion, the whole thing seemed to unroll itself before me. I thought of the first showing of 'Ashes of Roses' that was coming soon, and what a good chance that would give me, and I made up my mind I would try again that night. I knew I wouldn't have any trouble with Fay, because she doesn't care for pictures, and I could easily persuade her not to go.

"I got a sample of that man's handwriting on another pretext, and I practised until I was able to write a letter that looked like his. I bought the gun at —— (a big department store) for cash, so the sale couldn't be traced. I knew the kind of gun Mr. Whittall had bought for his wife, and I got the same. I wanted to make it look like suicide. Then I wrote a letter to Mrs. Whittall in this man's name, asking her to come to me, for God's sake, in the little pavilion at nine-thirty that night. Of course, she ought to have known, after the other letter, but I figured if she was in love she wouldn't stop to think. If she hadn't come, I'd just have tried something else. I sent the letter the same afternoon with a special delivery stamp on it. Through a messenger it could have been traced.

"My daughter and I had special invitations to see the private showing of 'Ashes of Roses' that night. Without seeming to, I persuaded Fay to stay at home. I took a taxicab to the theatre, arriving there about eight-fifteen. I had the gun in my reticule. I greeted many friends in the lobby, so I could prove an alibi if anything went wrong. I took a seat on the side aisle, beside one of the exits, and when the lights were put out, it was easy for me to slip out through that exit without anybody seeing.

"I took the West Side subway to the end of the line, and walked up the hill to Riverdale, and on down the other side towards the river. I had fixed in my mind the road that ran alongside the wall of the Whittall property. I climbed the wall, and went up the hill to the pavilion. I was in plenty of time. I took the gun in my hand

and waited, hidden behind a pillar. I kept my gloves on so I wouldn't leave any finger-print on the gun. When Mrs. Whittall came running in, I pressed the gun to her temple and pulled the trigger. She fell back outside. She never made a sound. I closed her hand over the gun as well as I could, and went back the way I came.

"I had found out from Mr. Kreuger that he and Mr. Whittall would be dining at the Hotel Norfolk that night. I wanted to warn Mr. Whittall to secure his wife's gun. I knew he'd be glad enough to hush up any scandal. But I was afraid to stop at Van Cortlandt for fear somebody might remember seeing me in a telephone booth. So I rode on the subway down to 145th Street, and telephoned from a pay station there. Then I rode on the subway down to Times Square, and took a taxi to the hotel. That is all I have to say."

THE LOVER OF ST. LYS

F. Tennyson Jesse

BORN IN ENGLAND as the great-grandniece of the poet Alfred, Lord Tennyson, Fryniwyd Tennyson Jesse (1888–1958) studied art but turned to journalism when she was twenty, working for the London *Times* and *The Daily Mail*. In 1914, she moved to New York, became a war correspondent, and worked for the National Relief Commission, then headed by J. Edgar Hoover. She married when the war ended, and she and her husband lived in many places all around the world.

Avowing that her special interest was in murder, Jesse wrote several articles for the highly respected *Notable British Trials* series. Her *Murder and Its Motives* (1924) is a pioneering work that explores the subject in a general sense and continues with illustrative case studies. She wrote *A Pin to See the Peepshow* (1934), a long novel based on a famous British murder case in which the author chose to ascribe a husband's death to "accidental murder," which may have been a kindness to his wife.

Jesse's best-known work is *The Solange Stories* (1931), a collection of stories about a young Frenchwoman, Solange Fontaine, who is "gifted by nature with an extra-spiritual sense that warn[s] her of evil." The volume was selected by Ellery Queen for *Queen's Quorum* as one of the 106 greatest short story collections in the history of detective fiction. Several additional Solange Fontaine stories were discovered and collected long after Jesse's death in *The Adventures of Solange Fontaine* (1995).

"The Lover of St. Lys" was originally published in 1918 in *The Premier Magazine*; it was first collected in *The Adventures of Solange Fontaine* (London, Thomas Carnacki, 1995).

The Lover of St. Lys

F. TENNYSON JESSE

IT WAS IN A LITTLE GREY TOWN set high in the mountainous country behind the Riviera that Solange and her father decided to spend their summer holiday. St. Lys, seen once on a motor-tour, had enraptured them both—a town of mellow, fluted tiles, of grey walls, of steep streets that were shadowed ways of coolness even at noonday, and ramparts that circled round the mountain crest as though hacked out of the living rock, so sheer and straight they were. It was a restful place, the very townspeople, with their clear, dark eyes and rough-hewn faces, strong of jaw and cheekbone, tender with pure skins and creamy colours, seemed redolent of peace. Here was a town for tired workers, especially for workers in such dark and dragging ways as those which the Fontaines explored—the ways of crime, not taken as detectives or allies of the law, but studied as scientists, with the end always in view of throwing light on causes rather than on actual deeds. The next generation—it was to save this by greater knowledge that Dr. Fontaine laboured, assisted by Solange, and here at least they could hope to continue their new book on the detection of poisons undisturbed by those sudden irruptions of the actual, such as the affair of the negro girl at Marseilles, which so violently tore the tissues of their ordered life.

"Besides," as Solange said, "Terence and Raymond will be able to come up from Nice and see us, and that will be ever so much nicer than always being alone."

Her father glanced at her sharply, to see whether there were any change of her quiet, clear pallor, but eye and cheek were as calm as ever. Terence Corkery—the Consul from Nice—he was an old friend, and as such Solange was wont to treat him, in that affectionate yet aloof way of hers, but young Raymond Ker, with the alertness of a newer civilisation in his confident jaw and bright eyes—he was a comparatively new acquaintance, and though it was true he had been with Solange through much—the tragic affair of the "Green Parrakeet," and the more grotesque happening at the draper's shop in Marseilles— yet it was unlike Solange to admit any man to quite that degree of intimacy so swiftly. Therefore, Dr. Fontaine had wondered, but the clear oval of his daughter's face gave him no clue. He resigned himself to the fact that he could read the countenance of a homicidal maniac with greater ease and accuracy than the familiar features of his daughter.

Corkery was unable to leave Nice while the Fontaines were at St. Lys that year, but, true to his promise, Raymond, protesting that he was merely on the look-out for "copy," arrived at the grey town in the mountains one heavenly evening in June. Solange objected.

"How can you expect copy here, Raymond? This is the abode of innocence and peace. Nothing ever happens, except births and deaths, and the few there are of the latter are invariably from old age!"

"You forget you are a stormy petrel, Solange," replied Raymond, only half-jesting. "I always have hopes of something happening where you are."

But as Solange looked annoyed, and he remembered her distaste for crime encountered in individuals, he changed the conversation. And just at first it looked as though Raymond were out in his theory, and as though peace must always be absolute at St. Lys. Never was there a place that seemed so as though the *bon Dieu* kept it in His pocket, as the Fontaines' old servant, Marie, expressed it. There were not many people to know, socially speaking, and the only family with whom the Fontaines visited on at all a society footing— though both Solange and her father cared little for that sort of thing and made friends with every butcher and baker—was that of the De Tourvilles. M. De Tourville was the lord of the manor, a moth-eaten old castle, beautiful from sheer age and fitness for its surroundings, picturesque enough to set all Raymond's American enthusiasms alight, but shabby to an extent that made Madame De Tourville's conversation one perpetual wail. She was a thin, feverish-looking woman, not without a burnt-out air of handsomeness in her straight features and large eyes, but looking older than her husband, though she was a year or so the younger. He was a very picturesque figure, as he went about the windy town in the long blue cloak he affected, his head, where the dark hair was only beginning to be faintly silvered, bare, and his thin, hawk-like face held high. A queer man, perhaps, said the townspeople, with his sudden tempers, his deep angers, his impulsive kindnesses, but a man of whom they were all proud. They felt the beauty of his presence in the town, though they could not have expressed it. Madame they liked less; she came from the hard Norman country, and was reported to be more than a little miserly, more so than was necessary

even on the meagre income of the De Tourville family.

It was for his sake that everyone had been glad, and not a little curious, when a very rich lady, a young lady, who was a cousin and ward of the De Tourvilles, had come to live with them at the castle. That money should come into the old place, even if only temporarily, was felt to be right, and deep in the minds of the women was the unspoken wonder as to how thin, feverish madame would fare with a young girl in the household. For though he was forty-five, M. De Tourville had the romantic air which, to some young girls, is more attractive than youth.

So much detail about the De Tourvilles was common gossip, and had filtered from the notary's wife, viâ the hotel-keeper's wife, to Marie, and thence to Solange. She herself had visited the château several times, for mutual friends in Paris had supplied letters of introduction, and she knew enough of the De Tourville household to have interested Raymond in them before she and her father took him to call at the château.

Raymond was of opinion that Solange had not exaggerated in depicting the household as interesting. There was something about the bleak château, with its faded tapestries and ill-kept terraces, which would have stirred romance in the dullest, but when added to it was a family that to nerves at all sensitive gave a curious impression of under-currents, then interest was bound to follow. Several times during that call Raymond wondered whether Solange had got her "feeling" about this household, whether that was what interested her, or whether for once he were being more sensitive, perhaps unduly so. For Solange talked gaily, seemed her usual self.

The De Tourville couple were as she had pictured them. The chief interest lay in the personality of Mademoiselle Monique Levasseur, the young ward. She was not, strictly speaking, pretty, but she had a force born of her intense vitality, her evident joy in life. Her dark eyes, large and soft, with none of the beadiness of most brown eyes, glowed in the healthy pallor of her face, her rather large, mobile mouth was deeply red, and her whole girlish form—too thin, with that exquisite appealing meagreness which means extreme youth—seemed vibrant with life. Yet she had her softnesses too—for her cousin, Edmund De Tourville. Her schoolgirl worship was evident in the direction of her limpid gaze, her childish eagerness to wait on him, which he was too much *galant homme* to allow. How much of it all did the wife see, wondered Raymond? He watched the quiet, repressed woman as she dispensed tea, and could gather little from her impassivity. Once he caught a gleam, not between man and girl, but between man and wife—a gleam that surely spoke of the intimacy that needs no words—and felt oddly reassured. The couple understood each other, probably smiled, not heartlessly, tenderly even, with the benignant pity of knowledge, at the schoolgirl enthusiasm. Doubtless that was the under-current that he had felt in the relations between the three. Yet, only a few minutes later, he doubted whether that impression were the true one. For, as they were about to leave, M. De Tourville spoke a few words low to the girl, and she got up and left the room, to reappear a moment later with a little tray, on which was a medicine-bottle and a glass. Everyone looked as they felt, a little surprised, and Edmund De Tourville, measuring out a dose of the medicine carefully, said, smiling:

"You must pardon these domesticities, but the wife has not been well for some time, and the doctor lays great stress on the importance of her taking her drops regularly. Is it not so, Thérèse?"

And Madame De Tourville, obediently draining the little glass, replied that it was. Nothing much in that little incident, but as the girl bore the tray away again her guardian opened the door for her, and slipped out after her; and Raymond, who was by the door, was made the unwilling, but inevitably curious, spectator of an odd little scene. The door did not quite close, and swung a little way open again after De Tourville had pulled it after him, and Raymond saw the girl put the tray down on the buffet which stood in the passage, saw De Tourville catch her

as she turned to come back, and saw the hurried kiss that he pressed on her upturned brow. It was not at all a passionate kiss, though. But the girl glowed beneath it like the rose, and Raymond, with a sudden compunction, moved across the room, so that he was away from the door when his host came in. He was not surprised that Monique Levasseur did not return.

That evening Raymond said to Solange, as they were smoking their after-dinner cigarettes in the hotel garden, which hung on the mountain side, the one word:

"Well?"

And Solange, looking up at him, laughed.

"Well? You mean about this afternoon? You're getting very elliptic, my friend."

"One can, with you."

"And—'well' meant do I think there is anything—anything odd?"

He nodded.

"Yes," said Solange, "I do. But I can't for the life of me say what."

"The girl is obviously in love with him."

"Oh, that—yes. That doesn't matter. She is of the age. But a schoolgirl's rave on a man much older than herself wouldn't make me feel there was anything odd, not if he were married ten deep. No, it was something—something more sinister than that."

"What do you make of the girl?" asked Raymond.

"A personality, evidently. But of the passive kind."

"Passive?" ejaculated Raymond, in surprise; "she struck me as being most amazingly vital, and vital people aren't passive."

"Vital women can be. For the height of femininity is an acutely enhanced passivity. The women who made history, the Helens and Cleopatras, didn't go out and do things, they just lay about and things happened. In the annals of crime, also, you will find frequently that women who are as wax have not only inspired crimes, but helped to commit them, or even committed them alone, acting under the orders of their lovers, as Jeanne Weiss did when she tried to poison her husband. It is a definite type. There are, of course, women who are the dominating force, such as Lady Macbeth; but the other kind is quite as forceful in its effects."

"You are not suggesting, I suppose, that little Monique Levasseur—"

"No, indeed. I got nothing but what was sweet and rather pathetic and feminine with her. But the fact remains that passionate passivity may turn to anything."

And Solange drifted off to discussion of actual cases, such as those of the two sinister Gabrielles—she who was wife of Fenayrou, and she who was accomplice of Eyraud, and from them to that most pathetic of all the examples of feminine docility, Mary Blandy, who poisoned her father for the sake of her lover. And after that, secret poisoning, that abominable and most enthralling of all forms of murder, held them talking about its manifestations till Dr. Fontaine came out to smoke a last pipe.

A month flew past in that enchanted city of towers, and though the Fontaines met the family from the château now and then, no greater degree of intimacy was arrived at between them; indeed, since the arrival of Raymond, the De Tourvilles seemed to withdraw themselves and Monique much more than they had before. Then one day, M. De Tourville arrived at the hotel, only a day before the Fontaines were leaving it, with a request that only intimacy or a great necessity justified. He soon proved that he had the latter to urge him. He told them that his wife, who had been ailing for a long time, as they were aware, had been ordered away, and had left the day before for Switzerland, for a sanatorium, and he asked them whether they would be so good as to take charge of Mademoiselle Levasseur, and escort her to Paris to the house of her former *gouvernante*, at whose school she had been before coming to St. Lys? He could not as a man alone—despite his grey hairs, he added with a smile—continue to look after Monique. But if Monsieur and Mademoiselle Fontaine would accord him this favour, he could himself come to Paris later, and make sure that all was

well with his ward. What he said was very reasonable, and Solange and her father agreed willingly.

But Raymond saw the long look that the girl turned on her guardian from the window of the train as they were starting, saw the meaning glance with which he replied, and somehow that little scene in the passage flashed up against his memory, clear and vivid. Solange said nothing much, but she was kindness itself to the girl, who was plainly depressed at leaving the god of her adoration, and not till the Fontaines had themselves arrived in Switzerland, whither they were bound—a fact she had not thought needful to mention to M. De Tourville—did Solange say anything to her father. And then it was only to express a little wonder that at the place where M. De Tourville, when she had asked him, had said his wife was staying, there was no trace of any lady of that name to be found.

Raymond had gone over to New York by then, and this little discovery, which would so have interested him, he was not destined to know till the following spring. For in February of the next year—which is when spring begins in the gracious country of southern France, Solange somehow made her father feel that another little stay in St. Lys—which, as a matter of fact, had rather bored him—was just what he wanted, and there Raymond, once again on his travels, joined them for a fleeting week. It was less than a year since they had first met the De Tourvilles at St. Lys, yet in that time two things had happened which vitally altered life at the château. Madame De Tourville had died in Switzerland, without ever having returned to her home, and M. De Tourville was married to the ward who had so plainly adored him in the days gone by.

Solange had enjoyed those months which had elapsed between the two visits to St. Lys. Her work had been purely theoretical during the whole of that time; any problems which the continued presence of Raymond might have evoked had been in abeyance owing to his protracted absence on business for his paper, and her father's book had been a success in the only way that appealed to him and his daughter—a success among the *savants* of their particular line of work. Yet, when she heard of the new marriage of De Tourville, she went back to St. Lys, though she knew it meant for her work of the kind she liked least.

When Raymond heard of the changes at the château his mouth and eyes fell open, and he stared at Solange, marvelling that she could tell him so tranquilly. True, she had not seen what he had, that furtive kiss, but yet, where was her gift, what had happened to her famous power of feeling evil, of being aware of dangers to society in her fellow-men, dangers even only contemplated? She had told him calmly, in answer to his questions, that the death of Madame De Tourville seemed certainly mysterious. She had never returned to the home from which she had been so secretively hurried away, no one but her husband, who had joined her in Switzerland, had seen her die—that is to say, no one who knew her in the little world of St. Lys, and as for anyone else, they had only her husband's word to take. She had simply ceased to be, as quietly and unobtrusively as she had lived, and the graceful, passionate young girl, who, however unconsciously, had been her rival, had taken her place.

Yet, or so thought Raymond, when first he met him on this second visit, De Tourville did not look a happy man. There was a haunted expression in his deep-set eyes, a queer watchfulness about his manner, a brooding there had never been before about his eagle face. Perhaps, as Solange suggested, this was because his young bride—as adoring and far more charming than before, as the new-opened rose surpasses the tightly folded bud—was ailing in health. The air of the mountains seemed too keen for her, or the fates envied her her transparent happiness—no cloud upon that! If she, too, were involved in that which Raymond could hardly bear even in his thoughts to bring against the man, then was she the most perfect example of the man-

moulded woman of whom Solange had spoken, who had ever existed.

There were days on which she seemed almost her old self, though her husband always watched to see she did not tire herself, but again there were other days, increasing in number, when it seemed that she lost strength with every breath she drew, and then nothing but her husband's ministrations would satisfy her, no hand but his was allowed so much as to alter her cushions or give her a glass of water. And, watching the man as he waited on her, and detecting that haunted something in his face, Raymond thought what a bitter irony it was, if indeed he had unlawfully hurried his wife out of this world, that now this more dearly loved woman for whom he had sinned should also be drawing nearer to the brink, and, most poignant irony of all, if his hand had indeed given, in the much-paraded medicine, poison to the first wife, how every time the second refused to accept anything save at that same hand it must seem to him, in his conscience-ridden mind, as though nothing which his hand poured out could bring anything but death.

Yet all that was sheer trickery of the mind, and a man strong enough to carry through a crime would perhaps be beyond such promptings of the nerves? But De Tourville did not seem so immune, Raymond thought, and Solange was forced to agree with him. She, too, was beginning to look worried, to his practised eyes, and he could not but feel a shade of triumph. What if it were he, after all, who had detected what those acute senses of hers had passed over? Yet when he examined himself, Raymond was not sure what he wanted. If De Tourville had indeed hurried his wife away—as he had undeniably hurried with indecent haste into his second marriage—did he still want him to be found out and tried for the crime? What then of the fragile Monique, with her big eyes where happiness fought with physical discomfort, and won every time they rested on her husband? A murderer was a dreadful thing, a secret poisoner the basest of murderers, yet what had the first Madame De Tourville to recommend her, to put it with brutal frankness? Nothing compared with this ardent, gracious girl. And, as though the gods themselves were of Raymond's mind, Monique De Tourville's health began to mend, and with that mending the shadow seemed to pass from the face of her husband. He seemed as a man who has taken a new lease of life, as though in his veins also the blood flowed more strongly, and in his heart resurgent life beat higher. On one thing he was determined—to remove his young wife from the place that had seemed to agree with her so ill. Never again, so he declared, should her life be risked in the château, even though it had been in his family for a thousand years, and, to the horror of the town, the historical old place was put up for sale, and bought by an American millionaire. Raymond's good offices were called in over the deal; indeed it was he, triumphing over scruples, who had first led the wealthy personage down to St. Lys to see the castle. The sale had been concluded, all was ready for the departure of Monique and her husband for South America—a climate M. De Tourville had persuaded himself was just what she needed—when the most terrible yet most thrilling day St. Lys had ever known was upon it.

Solange had announced that she was going up to the château to see if she could help the still delicate Monique with her final arrangements—the De Tourvilles were leaving in an automobile to catch the Paris express at midday. Solange had seemed to Raymond's observant eyes oddly watchful of late; he marked well-known symptoms in her, but could not fathom their cause.

Did she, like himself, suspect the picturesque Edmund De Tourville, and even if so, had she, after her individualistic fashion, which often made her take the law into her own hands when she judged fit, decided that Monique's happiness was the important thing, and that Edmund must be allowed to go free for the sake of the girl who hung upon him? It would not be unlike Solange. If, according to her classification of criminals into the congenital and the occasional, De Tourville merely came into the latter, and had only committed the one crime that almost any of us may, if hard enough pressed, and would be safe never to commit another, then it was more than possible she would think he should be allowed to work out his own salvation. If, on the other hand, she had cause to consider him one of those born killers to whom their own desires are sufficient warrant to prey upon society, then, he knew, she would not sacrifice the community to one girl—even apart from the fact that the girl herself might be the next victim. Human tigers, such as are the born killers, are creatures who tire quickly, and who have violent reactions.

Or was he, Raymond, perhaps conjuring up out of a few unfortunately suspicious circumstances a crime that had never been committed, and had the death of Thérèse De Tourville, after all, been merely a convenient but purely natural happening? But against that hope was his knowledge that Solange was aware of something odd in the *affaire* De Tourville, though she had never admitted so much to him.

He walked by her side up to the château on this May morning with a strange quickening of the heart. There seemed a hush as of expectation in the crisp, still air; on the quiet lips of Solange; above all, in the watchful look of De Tourville, whose eyes bore the look of one who is calculating time as though every minute were precious.

Monique alone was radiant, stronger than she had been for some time past, fired with excitement at the thought of the new life in the new world. Raymond had long persuaded himself that, whatever sinister meaning lay behind the drama of the château, she had had no hand in it. Wax as she was in her husband's hands, Raymond told himself her glance was too frank and clear for a guilt to lie behind those eyes.

The big *salon* at the château was dismantled, the pictures were gone from the walls, and packing-cases, already labelled, stood about the bare floor. Edmund had had to sell his family place, but he was taking the most loved of his possessions with him.

"*Chérie*, how sweet of you to come!" cried Monique, springing up from the crate on which she was sitting, already attired in her little close-fitting motor-bonnet that framed her face like a nun's coif, the soft, white chiffon veil streaming behind her, only her full, passionate lips giving the lie to the conventual aspect of her. She kissed Solange, then held out both hands eagerly to Raymond.

"Oh, I'm so excited! And I believe Edmund is, too, though he pretends he isn't. I think he is afraid of something happening to prevent us going!"

"What should happen?" asked Edmund, more harshly than was his wont in addressing her.

"Exactly! That's what I say. What should or could? But I do feel you're anxious all the same, Edmund."

And Monique nodded with an air of womanly wisdom that was new to her.

At that moment a knocking was heard at the great door—an old wooden structure with a heavy iron knocker. The rapping was insistent, even violent, and to each person there came the sudden feeling that something beyond the usual stood there and made that urgent summons. Of all the people there none seemed so disturbed as Edmund De Tourville. His dark face became very pale, but he did not move.

They heard old Henri, the butler, shuffle to the door, and the next moment came the sound of confused protests, asseverations, then over all rose a voice they knew, but which seemed to two of the people in the *salon* to be a voice out of a dream.

Quick, sharp footsteps came near, the door was flung wide open, and Thérèse De Tourville stood upon the threshold, her head flung back, her eyes blazing in her white face, surveying them all as they stared at her. Then Solange moved swiftly forward to Monique's side, as though to protect her. The girl had fallen back and was staring at this ghost from the dead year, and Raymond's face was like hers. Only De Tourville and Solange did not look amazed; for his part he seemed as a man stricken by a blow he has long dreaded.

"Thérèse—Thérèse," the unfortunate man stammered, "have you no pity?"

"Pity!" said Madame De Tourville—the only Madame De Tourville—in a harsh voice. "No, I do not pity. I leave that to you, who cannot even carry out what you begin, who weaken in everything. Pity!"

Raymond interposed. He never knew—did not dare ask himself—whether his first feeling had not been regret that Thérèse De Tourville still lived, that her husband had not, as she taunted him, finished what he had begun; but he did know that the immediate thing was to try and shield Monique from greater pain than she must inevitably be made to feel.

"There can be no need for Madame De—for Monique to be here," he said. "Solange, take her away."

"Yes," said De Tourville, with a groan, "take her away quickly!"

"Not till she has heard!" cried Thérèse; and planted her tall, thin form against the door.

Behind her the frightened faces of the servants could be seen peering.

Then De Tourville broke down.

"Thérèse, I beg of you—anything but that! I will give you anything you like—the money, all of it; we both will! But do not say anything, I implore you! Thérèse—"

Then Monique astonished them all. She gently shook off Solange's detaining hand and went and stood by Edmund, looking at the other woman fiercely.

"Go on!" she said. "What have you to say that can hurt me? You are here, and I am not his wife! What can anything else matter?"

"You don't understand," said Raymond urgently. "Come away."

"What don't I understand?"

"Your Edmund," began Madame De Tourville, "is not only a bigamist! He is a murderer, an assassin, or would be if he had had the heart to finish what he began! What do you say to that, you white-faced bit of sentiment?"

"Edmund, it isn't true?" stammered Monique, her eyes fixed on him.

He could only bow his head in reply; all the fight seemed to have gone out of him.

Again Monique surprised them. She flung her arms round Edmund and held him fiercely.

"Edmund—and you were willing to do that for me?"

Wonder, sorrow, and—yes—triumph rang in her voice. In that moment Raymond Ker learnt more about women than in the whole of his thirty years previously.

"Take her away quickly, before she learns the truth!" said Solange urgently to Edmund above the girl's head.

His eyes met hers with desperation in their haggard depths. He swung Monique's frail figure up in his arms and made to carry her from the room, but Thérèse only laughed and still barred the way.

"For you!" she said. "For you! You little fool! Did you think he had tried to poison *me*? It was all arranged between us! I was to disappear and be given out for dead, and he was to marry you and kill you for the money! It is you he has been poisoning, not me!"

And she laughed again.

"It isn't possible!" cried Raymond. "De Tourville, why don't you say something? Don't you see it's killing Monique?"

"Tell her—I can't!" muttered De Tourville to Solange.

Monique had dropped her hands from him and had taken a step back; in her white, stricken face her eyes looked suddenly dim, like those of a dying bird. Solange took her gently by the arm.

"Monique, it's true," she said. "I'm afraid you've got to know it's true. But he repented, Monique; he hadn't the heart to go on with it. He grew to love you too dearly. Monique—"

"What does all that matter!" said Monique. "He tried to kill me—to kill me! Oh, it's a joke! You're making it up, all of you! Say it's a joke, say it isn't true! Say it—say it!"

No one stirred; and her voice, which had sharpened to the wild scream of a child, fell into monotony again.

"So it's true? All that time I was ill—that I was so thirsty, that my throat hurt so, and I was so sick—you were doing it, Edmund? When no one but you looked after me, you were doing it all the time?"

"Not all the time. He could not go on with it," said Solange. "You remember when you began to get better? That was when he found he cared for you too much."

"It doesn't matter," repeated Monique.

"Well, it's brought me back, anyway," said Madame De Tourville coarsely. "I wasn't going to be cheated because a weak fool had succumbed to your pretty face and soft ways. Where did I come in, I should like to know? At first when I wrote and said what a long time it was taking, he always replied that he had to go cautiously, that Dr. Fontaine and this so-clever *demoiselle* were here, and would suspect if anything happened too soon. And I went on believing him. Then I got suspicious. I kept on picturing them together—my husband and this girl he ought to have killed long ago—and I knew if he wasn't killing her he must be kissing her. So I made inquiries, and found out they were going to do a flit, with the money that should have been mine by now, mine and his. And here I am."

She finished her extraordinary speech, with its astounding egotism, its brutal claims on what could not conceivably be considered hers, and folded her strong arms across her meagre chest, shooting out her hard jaw contemptuously. There could be little doubt which was the stronger willed of the two—she or her husband.

"The question is," remarked Solange, in what she purposely made a very matter-of-fact tone, "what is going to be done about it all now? I suppose everyone in the town saw you come here, madame?"

"Certainly. I am sick of hiding myself."

"You do not mind going to prison with your husband, then?"

"I care for nothing except to get him from that girl. The money is lost, of course. Well and good, but at least he sha'n't have the girl, either."

Solange turned to Monique.

"Monique, it rests with you," she said gently. "Are you going to prosecute? To give information against these people? They trapped you into a marriage that was a sham, because it was their only way of making sure of the money, and then they tried to kill you. Are you going to let them go free?"

Monique had followed the speech carefully, her lips sometimes moving soundlessly as though she were repeating the words that Solange used to herself the better to impress them upon her dazed brain. Slowly she turned her eyes, as with a strong effort of will, from the face of Solange to that of Edmund De Tourville. He had not spoken since his outburst to Solange, but he had not taken his eyes from Monique. Now he made no appeal, he only moistened his lips with his tongue and waited.

"I won't hurt you," said Monique slowly.

"Oh, the hussy, the wretch!" cried Madame De Tourville. "She is not going to prosecute because she still wants him. She couldn't be with him if he went to prison, and she still wants him. Shameful hussy, that's what I call you!"

And the odd thing was that Madame De Tourville was perfectly genuine in her indignation.

"Monique, I can't thank you," said De Tourville slowly. "Thanks from me to you would be an insult. I can only tell you—"

"Ah, la la, they will pay each other compliments in a minute!" broke in Madame De Tourville. "It's as well I made up my mind to what I did before I came here."

"What do you mean?" asked Monique quickly.

"I mean that I called in on monsieur the magistrate on my way, and he and his gendarmes are waiting at the door now for me and my husband. Oh, I wasn't going to run the risk of your forgiving him!"

And Thérèse turned, walked across the hall, where the pale-faced servants fell back from her in fear, and opened the door to the police.

"Well," said Raymond to Solange late that evening—"well, what do you know about that? They'll get twenty years with hard labour if they get a day, and that woman gave the whole thing

away deliberately when she could have got off scot free. Monique would never have brought the charge. It's jolly hard on her, the whole story'll have to come out now."

"Exactly," said Solange, "that's why Thérèse has done it. That woman has two passions—money and her husband. She thought the former was the stronger when she planned to let him marry the girl as a preliminary to poisoning her, and so it might have been if De Tourville had not played her false. Then she could keep quiet no longer, and she thinks a lifetime in prison cheap so long as she is avenged on him. It is all a question of values. After all, murder is the action behind which lies more distortion of value than behind any other in the world, so you must not be surprised that, when you have found someone who can think it worth while to murder, they are abnormal in their other values also."

"Perhaps not—but it isn't only Madame De Tourville who needs explaining. What of him? A weak man who repented, who couldn't be true even to an infamous contract?"

"More or less, though in a man of his type there would always be a thousand complications and subtleties that make any sweeping statement rather crude. He is a potential criminal, but in happier circumstances no one—including himself—would have ever found it out. If he could have made his getaway, I don't believe he would ever have done a criminal act again. In time he would doubtless have persuaded himself that the whole thing was a nightmare, and had never taken place; have believed that he had always been devoted to Monique, and that his only sin was a bigamous marriage, which his great love almost excused. If Thérèse had never turned up to trouble them, he would probably have forgotten even that."

"And Monique?"

"Ah, she is a true type of the *femme aux hommes*. She only lives and breathes in the loved man. You see, even as a young girl fresh from school she started an affair with Edmund, the wife did not exist for her in the strength of her passion, and it was that passion, so innocently undisguised, that first put the whole foul scheme into their heads. For you turned up, a young, eligible man, and they got panicky as they realised that she had only to marry for them to lose her money. If it were not you, it was only a question of time before it was someone else."

"Solange, when did you guess? Did you not at one time think as I did, that De Tourville had got rid of his wife by foul means so as to marry Monique?"

"I certainly should have thought so if I had gone on the facts alone, but I went on two other things as well—my knowledge of types and my 'feeling.'"

"I got my 'feeling' about that household. I couldn't hide it from you, who knew me, and the person I got it with most was Thérèse. That he was of the type to fit in with her I knew— she is of the race of strong women, of the Mrs. Mannings and the Brinvilliers of the criminal world; he is one of the Macbeths. But the odd thing is this—if it had been he who was of the dominating criminal type instead of his wife, then he and Monique would have in all probability done as you suspected. She is no criminal as things are, but she is so completely the type of waxen woman that it would only have rested with the man to make her another Marie Vitalis or Jeanne Weiss. At first I thought as you did, and when I did not find Madame De Tourville in Switzerland, I thought it all the more, though I still couldn't fit it in with their characters as I thought they were. Then I heard of the marriage with Monique, and I came back here determined to find out what was wrong. Monique's failing health struck me as very suspicious, and gradually from one little thing and another I put the crime together."

"What would you have done if Monique had gone on being ill? Given him away, or gone to him privately?" asked Raymond.

"The former, I think, always depending on what Monique wished. For if he could have gone on with it, it would have meant he was impossible to save. But I had hardly got all my facts,

hardly tabulated her symptoms and watched them together, when his heart began to fail him, or to prompt him, whichever way you like to put it. I shall always be glad that it was so before I told him that I knew."

"Then you did?"

"Yes, I should have told him earlier, of course, if I had seen no signs of relenting on his part, but I held out to the last minute, even at the cost of a little more physical suffering for poor little Monique, so as to give him the chance of saving his own soul alive. I knew that if ever it did come out, the knowledge that he had done so would be the only thing to save them both from madness."

"And in his new intention—taking her away— you would have helped—you did help—knowing she was not his wife?"

"My dear, who was hurt by it?" said Solange. "When you have seen as many people hurt as I have, that will be your chief consideration, too. I have told you Monique is a *grande amoureuse*. Her life is bound up in him, and that was what I was out to save, not merely from his poison, but from the poison of his wife's tongue. They would have lived very happily in South America, both have been virtuous, and the chief criminal—his wife—would have had the severest punishment possible in the loss of husband and money. As it is, Monique may die of her hurt."

"Actually die of a broken heart? And in the twentieth century?"

"She may indeed, for she is not a twentieth-century type—she is eternal. At present she is very ill of it with papa and a hospital nurse in attendance, as you know. There is only one hope for her which may materialise, as she has at least the balm of knowing that Edmund relented of his own free will."

"And what's that?"

"That her need of love is greater than her need of any one particular lover. That sometimes happens, you know."

"She'll never love again," asserted Raymond with conviction.

"I shall be more surprised if she can live without," said Solange.

And the conversation wandered away from Monique Levasseur, and plunged—always in theoretic fashion—into the ways of love. Here Raymond refused to follow Solange, as he did in the psychology of matters criminal, and they parted company after an hour of arguing over the route.

Raymond was certain he was far more nearly right than Solange; she was only sure she was right for herself, though very probably wrong for the rest of the world. Yet a few months later it was proved that she had been right in her hope for Monique. A romantic Englishman, who attended the trial of the De Tourvilles, and "wrote up" Monique as the heroine, was one of the many men who proposed to her on that occasion, and he succeeded in persuading her into what was to be a very happy love-marriage.

MISOGYNY AT MOUGINS

Gilbert Frankau

A CRITICISM ONCE LEVELED at the books that Gilbert Frankau (1884–1952) wrote about Peter Jackson is that he may have been too fond of his central character, and the central character was Frankau himself.

Although he wrote a few novels of crime, suspense, and espionage, including *The Lonely Man* (1932) and *Winter of Discontent* (1941; US title: *Air Ministry, Room 28*, 1942), as well as several short story collections that include mystery tales, including *Concerning Peter Jackson and Others* (1931), *Wine, Women, and Waiters* (1932), *Secret Services* (1934), and *Experiments in Crime* (1937), Frankau was famous mainly for his poetry, notably the volumes devoted to the experiences of World War I, and his once-popular novels set against the backgrounds of both the First and Second World Wars. He had been commissioned an officer in the British Army in 1914 and fought in some of the war's bloodiest battles—Loos, Ypres, and Somme—but suffered from shell shock and was moved to a desk job in 1916 writing propaganda. He was married three times and, by his own admission, was involved with many other women. One of his children is the noted novelist Pamela Frankau.

The detective in "Misogyny at Mougins," the beautiful Romanian Kyra Sokratesco, a friend of the Chief of the Secret Police of the Sûreté, appears in several short stories—the only series character created by Frankau (apart from Peter Jackson).

"Misogyny at Mougins" was originally published in *Concerning Peter Jackson and Others* (London, Hutchinson, 1931).

Misogyny at Mougins

GILBERT FRANKAU

I

MY WIFE WAS AWAY—and the limousine with her. The scenario of my new novel seemed to have struck a sex-rock. My Russian butler had developed his seasonal influenza. While, to cap all, it had been raining continually for three liquid January days.

"I have the *cafard*," I told Kyra over the telephone. "The black cockchafer of despair gnaws at my vitals. Suicide beckons to me. But come over if you must."

So she came over, on foot in a mackintosh; and I lit a wood fire for her; and the housemaid, deputizing for the butler, gave us an imitation of tea.

"Me, too," she said, toasting her little wet feet at the wood fire; "suicide beckons. But I shall not commit it in your study. The 'Hotel Tivoli' at Nice will be the place of my *hara-kiri*. A female has to be in the fashion, you see. And there was another yesterday!"

"Surely not another!" My *cafard* left me.

"Yes, my friend. Another. That makes five since Christmas. And all women; all rich; all at dawn, and from the same balcony into the same street."

"An epidemic," I suggested, smiling a little at Kyra's melodramatics.

"Of falling over balconies? Impossible. Either the devil is in that hotel——"

"A plausible theory——"

"Or else a maniac. A homicidal maniac——"

"Disguised as a page-boy——"

"Disguised somehow. And anyhow it is my duty——"

"Say, rather, your pleasure, Kyra——"

"Only if you come with me, Gilbert——"

"And risk a scandal——"

"Pah! What is a little scandal? From Toulon to San Raphael, the gossips think the worst of us. Does it matter, therefore, if we carry the banner of our supposed passion a few kilometres farther, out of the Var into the Alpes Maritimes, into the pleasant city of Nice?"

The argument, with my wife, who approves of Kyra, at home, would have been unanswerable. With my wife away, however, I hesitated—until after breakfast next day, which was a fine one, as only a Beauvallon day can be a fine one after three of rain.

"Perhaps," said Kyra, when I drove my little open run-about to her gateway, "it would be wiser to put a rug over the suitcases."

"Wisdom," said I, "is only another name for cowardice. Let gossip observe the suitcases."

"So you have telegraphed to your wife," she said.

As a matter of fact I had telegraphed to my wife, "Going Nice with Kyra, address 'Tivoli.'" But the deduction annoyed me; and I drove in silence, by the sea-road, for the best part of ten kilometres.

"We have a liver this morning," decided Kyra at the eleventh.

"We are a grass widower," I retorted.

"Let us discuss our suicides," retorted she.

So we discussed our suicides—all five of them. The Baroness Rosendahl, of Vienna. Mrs. Winser, of Cincinnati, Lady Frensham, of Hertford Street, Mayfair, W. Madame Lantresac, of Paris. And the last of the victims, Frau Direktorin Müller, of Berlin.

"A series of coincidences," I suggested, as we chugged up the Esterels.

"Too remarkable for a series of coincidences," opined Kyra. "However, let us suspend imagination till we arrive."

We arrived, through Cannes, at midday; and the receptionist of that large and lavish hotel, the "Tivoli," smiled upon us—with the porters cuddling our suitcases—when he heard our requirements. "A little apartment for the lady—and for me, *une chambre*."

"Next door to Madame's apartment, no doubt," smiled the receptionist; and his mouth fell wide open at my answer: "But no. I would prefer it some distance away."

"*Tu vois*," I said to Kyra, as the lift bore us upwards. "We shall be worse than a scandal. We shall be conspicuous, eccentric!"

"What is more important," retorted Kyra, "is that we shall be on the sixth floor."

II

We all have our especial weaknesses; and because one of mine happens to be vertigo, I felt distinctly queasy by the end of the next half-hour. Six floors facing the Mediterranean Sea may not compare with a recessed skyscraper facing Park Avenue; but the "association of ideas" between the stone balustrade over which Kyra would keep leaning and the cemented courtyard below us made me very pleased with terra firma and lunch.

"They just overbalanced," I said, while we were lunching. "And I don't blame them. That balcony is a death-trap. The architect who built this hotel ought to be shot."

"Mrs. Winser, of Cincinnati," replied Kyra, "at any rate according to her photographs, was almost a dwarf. Five foot high at the utmost. The balustrade over which you disliked my leaning is three foot nine and a half."

After lunch, despite protests, Kyra returned to the sixth-floor balcony, and studied it intently for a good half-hour. Then she borrowed a hundred francs from me; rang for the floor waiter, and asked the "open sesame" of all waiters: "You are an Italian, of course. From what part of Italy do you come?"

"*Da Genova*," replied our man, who was square-headed and stocky, and almost light of hair.

"A pleasant city," said Kyra. "Of the most intelligent inhabitants. I have many friends in Genoa." And in three minutes she had her Italian talking, as only a pretty woman can.

It was a tragedy, he said. Worse—it was bad for the *albergo*. And everyone of the *belle signore* on his floor, too. The English lady had had number six hundred and seven; and the American lady this very apartment. He remembered the American lady particularly. Yes, it was true. This Signora Vinser had been a very short lady. Yes. That was right. She could not have fallen over the balustrade. She must have climbed on to it. And the German lady, she was short and fat, too.

"Indeed," went on our waiter, "they were of a type, all five of them. What type? How shall I describe it? There are so many such here in Nizza. You see them everywhere, and every season. We call them 'the comfortable ones.' They dance; but they do not gamble. They read the papers, and go for a little walk on the Promenade des Anglais, and after lunch they sleep for an hour or two, and in the evenings they play the bridge."

His hundred francs he pocketed with a *"tante grazie,"* but no servility; adding, just before he left us: "But yes. The newspapers reported rightly. All five were quite alone when *it* happened. Because in each case it happened almost at the same moment. Just as the sun was rising, between five and six o'clock."

Alone with me, Kyra fell Kyraish; and smoked three of her Rumanian cigarettes without a word.

"I am at a disadvantage," she confessed after the third one. "Were we in the Var, the police would tell me everything. Here, in the Alpes Maritimes, there is nobody. I am a poor lone damsel. And I am baffled. I think I shall make you take me home."

"Without sending for the manager of the hotel, Kyra? Surely you will do *that*? In all the best detective stories——"

Whereupon, furious, she told me first to *tache* my *lingura*; and then to ring for the chambermaid, who came smirking, and was presented with another of my hundred-franc notes.

The chambermaid proved less sympathetic than the floor waiter. "What would you?" she said. "All rich women go a little crazy in their fifties. It is just the bad luck that we should have had five of them on this sacred sixth floor."

"You think they were all crazy, then?" said Kyra.

"The German lady was. Undoubtedly. She told me that she believed in spirits. And the American lady, too, she believed in them. Especially in her husband's. He was killed in France, she told me. So his spirit could not get back to America. 'I have come to find him,' she said once. 'He needs me. Of that I am very sure.'"

"And the others?" asked Kyra.

"Of them I know nothing. I was not here when they suicided themselves. But the night porter, who is my cousin, he told me that the lady from England used to talk to herself. He heard her doing it—the night before *it* happened, when he was taking her up in the lift."

The chambermaid, my hundred-franc note tucked in her apron pocket, went out still smirking. "There remain for cross-examination," said I, "her cousin, the night porter; and, if my hundred-franc notes last us, the *valet-de-chambre*." But just as I said this, the telephone rang to say that a gentleman who would give no name particularly wanted to see Miss Sokratesco; and a minute or two later, who should come in on us but our friend the Chef de la Sûreté, imagined in Toulon.

"If I intrude on pleasure," said our friend, "pray forgive me. But this hotel is being watched; and when your arrival was reported, I naturally concluded——"

"Your conclusion is an accurate one, Chief," admitted Kyra; and she added, laughing: "If it is necessary to save any reputations, the telegraph office at Sainte Maxime——"

"That also," interrupted the Chief, "has been reported." And he permitted himself a guffaw.

"But this is no time for guffawing," he went on. "Affairs are serious. And international. I break no confidences when I tell you that the Frau Direktorin Müller was a personage in Germany; and that Paris is perturbed, more than perturbed, about this succession of apparent suicides. Paris thinks we have a murderer, and a very cunning one, to deal with. The whole of the Sûreté has been mobilized."

"As far as one can gather," I broke in, "without results."

The Chief, whose temper is of the best, did not resent the interruption. Neither, to my surprise, did he deny its truth.

"We are in black darkness," he admitted. "All five crimes, if crimes they are, seem motiveless. Neither jewels nor money are missing. We can trace no love-affairs. With the exception of the Baroness Rosendahl, who divorced the Baron nearly twenty years ago, all the victims are widows. They appear to have no children. In no case do their fortunes pass to one particular individual. Three lived on annuities. Madame Winser's money will be divided among no fewer than twenty-seven relatives; Frau Müller's goes mainly to charity. And after the most careful, indeed the most exhaustive inquiries, we are positive that no human being could have been anywhere near them when their deaths occurred.

"And what is more," added the Chief, "we can trace no common contact, except——"

"Except," put in Kyra, "the floor waiter——"

"Who only comes on duty at seven in the morning; and a young man who gives dancing lessons here, by name Auguste Roux."

Auguste Roux, of whom the Chief then produced a perfect brigade of photographs, appeared to be the usual type of French dancing boy. He had the mouth of a rabbit; and his forehead indicated a similar brain power. The police had examined him that morning. All five of the dead ladies, he admitted, had been his clients. All five had taken their lessons privately. They had paid his usual fee, and been *tres gentilles* with their *pourboires*. He himself always left the hotel after the dancing. He could therefore throw no light on the mysterious deaths.

"He, too," said the Chief, grinning at me, "is under observation. But so far it has been equally fruitless. As I said before, we are in black darkness. Yet a woman—one little, rich, and not too youthful woman—might assist."

"How?" Kyra spoke.

"She might take dancing lessons, Mademoiselle."

"Then you suspect this *gigolo*?"

"Not of murder. But of knowing more than he will tell us. He is frightened, I think. And when a rabbit is frightened——"

"One strokes it," suggested Kyra, looking very intently at her own exquisite hands.

III

To the average mind, of which I hope I am the possessor, there is something inordinately comic about disguises. Also, I feel that it counts for many Platonic points in my favour that the Kyra whom I escorted in to dinner that evening stirred only one desire in me—and that, to laugh.

Had I been, however, as the gossips proclaim me, her lover, I think that I should have cried to see so much loveliness disappear. All Kyra's loveliness—or nearly all of it—had disappeared. Before me sat a middle-aged woman—over-rouged and over-powdered, and with slightly discoloured teeth. A blonde wig—so obviously a wig!—covered her sleek, dark head; a high frock, the young bosom and the smooth throat. What she wore under that frock I know not. But her boyish figure had acquired a gruesome plumpness. And most of that plumpness was decked, as a velvet cushion in a jeweller's window, with gems.

"And the young lady?" asked the waiter who had served our luncheon. "Does she not dine with you?"

"Alas!" I answered. "Mademoiselle had the bad news. She left this afternoon—hurriedly." Which last—Kyra having departed with the same ostentation that "her friend, Madame Gardiano," had arrived to occupy her vacant apartment—was more or less true.

We dined well, though conversation, even in Rumanian, proved a little difficult. And some while after dinner, with the band playing a fox-trot, our rabbit appeared.

"Madame would like to dance?" he suggested.

"But I dance so badly," said Kyra.

Auguste Roux, however, would brook no denial.

I was well into my second cigar when "Madame Gardiano" took the floor with him; but soon, in sheer pity, I let the weed out. It seemed heartless, you see, to enjoy fine tobacco while a fellow-creature was being tortured. And torture is the only word applicable to Auguste Roux's ordeal.

On the whole he bore the ordeal manfully. But when he brought "Madame Gardiano" back to me, his mouth was twitching; and in sheer pity I offered him drink.

"*Une fine*," he gasped; and Kyra smiled on him, fatly, as it is possible that the Frau Direktorin may have smiled on him, saying:

"A little later, if you are not too busy, we might have another one. A tango, perhaps. In Rumania we dance much tango; but little fox-trot."

"Madame Gardiano's" tango, however, proved even more devastating than her fox-trot; and little as I admire *gigolos*, I would not have grudged Auguste a mention in despatches for his courage in suggesting: "A little course of lessons, Madame. Just to acquire the French manner. The *nuances*, if you understand."

"Private lessons?" smirked "Madame Gardiano."

"Of course, Madame. All my lessons are given in private." And on parting—inspired by yet another brandy and another of my hundred-franc notes, which he clutched from me under the table—he kissed her hand.

"The poor little rabbit," said Kyra, alone with me some hour and a half later. "I begin to feel sorry for him. And he is all of a dancer. Once or twice it was almost impossible for me not to let myself go with him. He has sympathy, too. What I told him about my dear husband——"

"Your what, Kyra?"

"My dear husband. General Gardiano of the Imperial Cavalry. It was he, you remember, who led the first charge against von Mackensen. An ardent soul, Gilbert. One of those who, doubtless, survive after they pass over. Indeed, only six weeks ago, when I was dining with our dear Queen in Bucaresti, he appeared to me, in his white uniform with his silver helmet, and wearing all his medals——"

"Kyra," began I severely.

But Kyra only laughed till the blonde wig toppled sideways; and continued laughterful, whenever we were alone together, which was not often, for three whole days. But on the fourth day, when she came upstairs from her dancing lesson, there was no laughter in her—and it seemed to me that, for the first time in our acquaintance, she must be afraid.

"You are ill?" I said, going to her.

"I am not ill."

"You have discovered something?"

"No. No."

"You have. Tell me!"

"No. Not——" her hands shook—"not till I'm certain. I—I shall need your car tonight. And a pistol. And—and I must see the Chief. Be a dear, and telephone for him. Now. At once."

IV

It was six o'clock before I could get the Chief on the telephone; but he came in ten minutes; and Kyra, who seemed to have recovered from the worst of her fright, received him with her wig off, and a cigarette between "Madame Gardiano's" over-rouged lips.

"Eh bien!" said the Chief. "You have found out the truth? You have news for us?"

"I have no news—yet," answered Kyra. "And the truth seems impossible. There is no motive, either. No human motive, anyway. But the murderer—if murder it be—lives in Mougins, at number thirteen, Rue de la République. And there I visit him, by appointment, at ten o'clock tonight."

"Who made this appointment?" asked the Chief.

"Our *gigolo*. But he is only an innocent go-between. All he gets is his little *bénéfice*——"

"Yet the home of our *gigolo*'s mother"—the Chief referred to his notebook—"is also in Mougins. At the same number in the same Rue de la République. His mother——"

"She is innocent, too, my friend. Nobody could suspect——"

"But what do you suspect, Mademoiselle?"

"Something that is beyond even the powers of the French Sûreté to deal with," said Kyra; and for the second time in our acquaintance it seemed to me that she was afraid.

She kept her own counsel, however; though the Chief did his best to probe her suspicions. All she asked of him was his spare pistol, one of those deadly Brownings which a woman can conceal in her handbag; and that he should watch the house.

"If you hear a shot," she said, "break your way in."

"Rely on me," answered the Chief; and at about seven o'clock he left us—me in a panic, Kyra again calm.

We dined in her apartment, lightly. I took a couple of brandies with little soda. She drank only Evian water. At a quarter to nine I fetched my run-about from the garage. Ten minutes later we were sweeping down the Promenade des Anglais, lights blazing from the big hotels to the right of us; on our left the sea.

"Are they following?" I asked.

"At about fifty metres." Kyra, shrouded to the eyes in a cloak that could only have belonged to "Madame Gardiano," had glanced over her shoulder. "Hurry a little. I must be on time."

I put my foot down; and our pace quickened. Soon the sea lay behind us, and the racecourse, and the Octroi Station on the National Road. We swung into Cagnes at a fair seventy-five kilometres; were blocked there, and again at Antibes. But nine-forty to the second found us in Cannes.

Through Cannes the police-car still followed. But once across the railway-bridge, it hooted; and I drew to the right for it, catching a glimpse of the Chief's face. There were three men with the Chief; but none in uniform.

"Good," said Kyra. "I shall feel safer—if I know they have surrounded the house."

So I slackened speed; and when we came into Mougins the police-car was not to be seen. Nothing was to be seen, in that up-and-down street of shuttered houses, except a man drawing water from a pavement-tap, and a lone pussy scaling a garden wall.

Just beyond that wall, acting on Kyra's orders, I braked the run-about; and, dismounting, knocked on a barred door, to which a woman in servant's dress came quickly, asking: "Is it Madame Gardiano? If so, will she be pleased to enter?" And because that woman's mouth was narrow, with the projecting teeth of the bunny-rabbit, my heart misgave me as I helped "Madame Gardiano" to the pavement and she passed within.

I knew nothing, beyond what I have related here, of Kyra's motives for this nocturnal visit. But I smelt a trap, with the *gigolo* to bait it. And smelling that trap, I felt glad only of two circumstances—of the bulge in my own hip-pocket and the lowness of the garden wall. It is open to doubt, however—for I am by nature a disciplined animal—whether anything would have made me scale that wall, or remove the bulge from my hip-pocket, except the Chief's careful whistle, his signalling hand.

"It is all watched," whispered the Chief, once I stood in the shrubbery beside him, "except that window. Take it—while I go round." Then he disappeared, a shadow among shadows; while I crept to the shutters of the long French window he had indicated, and crouched there, waiting for the bark of Kyra's pistol, fingering my own.

I must have been crouching, I imagine, a good five minutes—and all that time (let it be imputed to me for virtue!) telling myself to thank my stars for not being in love with Kyra Sokratesco—before I heard the unmistakable click of an electric-light switch, the unmistakable opening and closing of a badly-fitted door. And even then—so that it really is quite obvious I am not in love with her—I had no sensation of Kyra's presence within two feet of me, till I heard a man's voice say in tolerable French, "Please to sit there, Madame Gardiano. Yes. Just there, with your back to the long window. And please do not think of *me*. Think only of your dear one. Yes. Of your dear one: of the General who has passed over so gallantly, fighting for his country and his king."

And after that, for the window-frames of the house fitted as badly as the door-frames, I heard the chair creak as Kyra sat on it. But because the shutters were of the cheap Provençal type, plain board and not slatted, I could see nothing. And neither could the Chief.

The Chief came back before the man spoke again: and I managed to indicate to him that Kyra was just inside. He, too, had his pistol out. And I had the impression, as we crouched together, that he was in a state of the intensest excitement. Twice the held breath made a little whistle through his nostrils. Once he muttered to himself; and though the mutter was almost inaudible, it sounded to me like the echo of what I myself was thinking: "It is too much. *C'est trop.*" Then all thought left me; as it will do when all a man's senses concentrate in his ears.

For the man beyond the shutters had turned off the light; and was speaking again, very slowly, and with a peculiar enunciation that brought back memories of certain experiments of which I, then an insomniac, had once been the subject, though to no good end.

"All is prepared," said the voice. "Let your eyes close. You are sleepy. You are very, very sleepy. When you sleep, you are well. Do you wish to be well? Answer me?"

"Yes," answered Kyra, "I wish to be well."

"And happy?"

"And happy."

"Then sleep. While my eyes watch for you. Sleep. Sleep. Sleep."

Silence followed; and in my imagination I could see the man's hands making their hypnotic passes, while Kyra feigned sleep. And presently it seemed to me that her feigning must have accomplished its purpose; for the man's voice went on again: "You sleep. But I bid your eyes to open. I bid your ears to hear."

Kyra did not answer; but a faint moan came from her. And in that moment I had the impulse, almost uncontrollable, to break in. I looked at the Chief; and saw, even in the semi-darkness, that his eyes had hardened. His free hand was feeling cautiously at the shutter. Then the man spoke and Kyra moaned again; and I knew suddenly that the hypnotic slumber was not feigned, but real.

"Your eyes are open," went on the voice. "And your ears hear me. Listen, you—you useless one. You, who are middle-aged, and wealthy, and—and without a husband. The earth is full of

women such as you are. But women such as you cumber it. You serve no purpose here. Do you hear me? You serve no purpose."

"I serve no purpose," answered Kyra—and her voice was strange.

Her voice terrified me. But for a long while I heard no more of it, only the voice of the hypnotist, working on the defenceless soul. And into that soul he poured a horror of itself, and a poison; as one pours poison into a well. On earth— he said—that soul could have no abiding-place. Because earth, and the people thereof, hated it. Yes. Even the humble people——

"Those who bring you food! Those who bring you drink! The boy who dances with you! Why do they do these things for you? For love? Surely not? Only for money. And even taking your money, they despise you. You are loathsome to them. When they see you at your high balcony, they wonder why you do not throw yourself from it. Yet to one, you were never loathsome. And that One is waiting. Waiting for the moment when you—even as he—shall be no longer earth-bound; when you shall come to him at sunrise, not in the vile flesh, but in the free spirit. And always he is very close to you, that Waiting One. Yet closest when you stand on that high balcony of yours at sunrise. For look! I—even I, whose eyes are your eyes—will lift the curtain which is between you. Look! For the sun is rising. Look down on your beloved, earth-bound one. Look down on him. And see!"

And on that there began that work which was first done in Endor, and which still goes on today.

How it was done, we—beyond the window— knew not. Because, though sounds reached us, the sounds were no longer human; being more beast-like—the pant of hot breathing, the scratch of claws on woodwork, the beat of wings. And when those sounds ceased, no sound reached us—until the man's voice commanded, very loudly: "Awake! Awake! It is finished. Madame Gardiano, I order you: awake!"

And then—then the pistol-shot. Within two

feet of us! And the Chief's whistle. And the two of us tearing—tearing at the shutter-boards with crazy hands.

V

The Chief and I had those shutter-boards away in thirty seconds. But there was no need to smash the windows, for Kyra herself opened them; and even through the rouge of Madame Gardiano I saw that her face was gray.

"A—a monster," she stammered. "Somebody had to. So I did. Don't—don't step on him, Chief. He may not be dead yet. The—the light's by the door."

Then she staggered past us, into the garden; and I saw the rest through a haze which was some of it her own dark hair, and some of it the blonde wig she had worn, and some of it the smoke which still curled, as pistol-smoke will curl, like wisps from pipe tobacco about the room.

A body lay in that room; and a great ball of glass, overturned from a black velvet stand, beside the body. Over these knelt the Chef de la Sûreté. While beyond, a door was opening, to show a rabbit-mouthed woman, already handcuffed, and the face of one of the Chief's men. But the Chief signalled to shut the door; and instantly the rabbit-mouthed woman vanished; and in a moment or so he ran out to us in the garden, saying: "My pistol, Mademoiselle. My pistol." And once he had got the pistol he ran back again, very quickly into the room.

Nor could I, despite all the emotions of the past hours, and all the emotions of that bundle of queer femininity which kept muttering, half in and half out of arms, "He put me under. He put me under—though I fought against him," restrain my admiration as I watched the man whose business is to reveal truth arrange that which the *Eclaireur de Nice* reported two days later as "A Fortune-Teller's Suicide," with confirmatory details from "the deceased's servant *la nommée Constance Roux*," and an *agent de la Sûreté* who "happened to be passing when the shot was fired."

And again I admired the Chief when, some hours later—after telling us the whole story from Auguste Roux's first tentative: "If Madame is interested in spiritism, I know of a real medium," to that final moment of horror which had seemed "like—like drowning among jelly-fish"—a rejuvenated Kyra walked out on to her balcony, and stood staring at the sunrise and the sea.

For it was his quick brain which grasped the situation; he and not I who sprang after her; who pulled her backwards—even while her left foot was feeling blindly upwards for a niche in that three-foot-nine balustrade.

INTRODUCING SUSAN DARE

Mignon G. Eberhart

ONCE ONE OF AMERICA'S most successful and beloved mystery writers, Mignon Good Eberhart (1899–1996) enjoyed a career that spanned six decades and produced sixty books, beginning with *The Patient in Room 18* (1929) and concluding with *Three Days for Emeralds* (1988). Her first five books featured Sarah Keate, a middle-aged spinster, nurse, and amateur detective who works closely with Lance O'Leary, a promising young police detective in an unnamed midwestern city. This unlikely duo functions effectively, despite Keate's penchant for stumbling into dangerous situations from which she must be rescued. She is inquisitive and supplies O'Leary with valuable information.

Equally unlikely is the fact that six films featuring Nurse Keate and O'Leary were filmed over a three-year period in the 1930s. *While the Patient Slept* (1935) featured Aline MacMahon as Nurse Keate and Guy Kibbee as O'Leary. *The Murder of Dr. Harrigan* (1936) starred Kay Linaker in the lead role, renamed Nurse Sally Keating and now much younger. *Murder by an Aristocrat* (1936) has Marguerite Churchill as Keating, and *The Great Hospital Mystery* (1937) features a much older Jane Darwell, before Warner Brothers–First National decided to go younger again with a lovely Ann Sheridan starring in both *The Patient in Room 18* (1938) and *Mystery House* (1938).

Eberhart's other series detective is Susan Dare, who, like her creator, is a mystery writer. Young, attractive, charming, romantic, and gushily emotional, she has a habit of stumbling into real-life murders.

"Introducing Susan Dare" was originally published in the April 1934 issue of *Delineator*; it was first collected in *The Cases of Susan Dare* (Garden City, New York, Doubleday, Doran, 1934).

Introducing Susan Dare

MIGNON G. EBERHART

SUSAN DARE watched a thin stream of blue smoke ascend without haste from the long throat of a tiger lily. Michela, then, had escaped also. She was not, however, on the long veranda, for the clear, broadening light of the rising moon revealed it wide and empty, and nothing moved against the silvered lawn which sloped gently toward the pine woods.

Susan listened a moment for the tap of Michela's heels, did not hear it or any other intrusive sound, and then pushed aside the bowl of lilies on the low window seat, let the velvet curtains fall behind her, and seated herself in the little niche thus formed. It was restful and soothing to be thus shut away from the house with its subtly warring elements and to make herself part of the silent night beyond the open windows.

A pity, thought Susan, to leave. But after tonight she could not stay. After all, a guest, any guest, ought to have sense enough to leave when a situation develops in the family of her hostess. The thin trail of smoke from the lily caught Susan's glance again and she wished Michela wouldn't amuse herself by putting cigarette ends in flowers.

A faint drift of voices came from somewhere, and Susan shrank farther into herself and into the tranquil night. It had been an unpleasant dinner, and there would be still an hour or so before she could gracefully extract herself and escape again. Nice of Christabel to give her the guest house—the small green cottage across the terrace at the other side of the house, and through the hedge and up the winding green path. Christabel Frame was a perfect hostess, and Susan had had a week of utter rest and content.

But then Randy Frame, Christabel's young brother, had returned.

And immediately Joe Bromfel and his wife Michela, guests also, had arrived, and with them something that had destroyed all content. The old house of the Frames, with its gracious pillars and long windows and generous dim spaces, was exactly the same—the lazy Southern air and the misty blue hills and the quiet pine woods and the boxed paths through the flowers—none of it had actually changed. But it was, all the same, a different place.

A voice beyond the green velvet curtains called impatiently: "Michela—Michela——"

It was Randy Frame. Susan did not move, and she was sure that the sweeping velvet curtains hid even her silver toes. He was probably at the door of the library, and she could see, without looking, his red hair and lithe young body and impatient, thin face. Impatient for Michela. Idiot, oh, idiot, thought Susan. Can't you see what you are doing to Christabel?

His feet made quick sounds upon the parquet floor of the hall and were gone, and Susan herself made a sharply impatient movement. Because the Frame men had been red-haired, gallant, quick-tempered, reckless, and (added Susan to the saga) abysmally stupid and selfish, Randy had accepted the mold without question. A few words from the dinner conversation floated back into Susan's memory. They'd been talking of fox hunting—a safe enough topic, one would have thought, in the Carolina hills. But talk had veered—through Michela, was it?—to a stableman who had been shot by one of the Frames and killed. It had happened a long time ago, had been all but forgotten, and had nothing at all to do with the present generation of Frames. But Christabel said hurriedly it had been an accident; dreadful. She had looked white. And Randy had laughed and said the Frames shot first and inquired afterward and that there was always a revolver in the top buffet drawer.

"Here she is," said a voice. The curtains were pulled suddenly backward, and Randy, a little flushed, stood there. His face fell as he discovered Susan's fair, smooth hair and thin lace gown. "Oh," he said. "I thought you were Michela."

Others were trailing in from the hall, and a polite hour or so must be faced. Queer how suddenly and inexplicably things had become tight and strained and unpleasant!

Randy had turned away and vanished without more words, and Tryon Welles, strolling across the room with Christabel, was looking at Susan and smiling affably.

"Susan Dare," he said. "Watching the moonlight, quietly planning murder." He shook his head and turned to Christabel. "I simply don't believe you, Christabel. If this young woman writes anything, which I doubt, it's gentle little poems about roses and moonlight."

Christabel smiled faintly and sat down. Mars, his black face shining, was bringing in the coffee tray. In the doorway Joe Bromfel, dark and bulky and hot-looking in his dinner coat, lingered a moment to glance along the hall and then came into the room.

"If Susan writes poems," said Christabel lightly, "it is her secret. You are quite wrong, Tryon. She writes——" Christabel's silver voice hesitated. Her slender hands were searching, hovering rather blindly over the tray, the large amethyst on one white finger full of trembling purple lights. It was a barely perceptible second before she took a fragile old cup and began to pour from the tall silver coffeepot. "She writes murders," said Christabel steadily. "Lovely, grisly ones, with sensible solutions. Sugar, Tryon? I've forgotten."

"One. But isn't that for Miss Susan?"

Tryon Welles was still smiling. He, the latest arrival, was a neat gray man with tight eyes, pink cheeks, and an affable manner. The only obvious thing about him was a rather finical regard for color, for he wore gray tweed with exactly the right shades of green—green tie, green shirt, a cautious green stripe in gray socks. He had reached the house on the heels of his telephoned message from town, saying he had to talk business with Christabel, and he had not had time to dress before dinner.

"Coffee, Joe?" asked Christabel. She was very deft with the delicate china. Very deft and very graceful, and Susan could not imagine how she knew that Christabel's hands were shaking.

Joe Bromfel stirred, turned his heavy dark face toward the hall again, saw no one, and took coffee from Christabel's lovely hand. Christabel avoided looking directly into his face, as, Susan had noticed, she frequently did.

"A sensible solution," Tryon Welles was saying thoughtfully. "Do murders have sensible solutions?"

His question hung in the air. Christabel did not reply, and Joe Bromfel did not appear to hear it. Susan said:

"They must have. After all, people don't murder just—well, just to murder."

"Just for the fun of it, you mean?" said Tryon Welles, tasting his coffee. "No, I suppose not. Well, at any rate," he went on, "it's nice to know your interest in murder is not a practical one."

He probably thought he was making light and pleasant conversation, reflected Susan. Strange that he did not know that every time he said the word "murder" it fell like a heavy stone in that silent room. She was about to wrench the conversation to another channel when Michela and Randy entered from the hall; Randy was laughing and Michela smiling.

At the sound of Randy's laugh, Joe Bromfel twisted bulkily around to watch their approach, and, except for Randy's laugh, it was entirely silent in the long book-lined room. Susan watched too. Randy was holding Michela's hand, swinging it as if to suggest a kind of frank camaraderie. Probably, thought Susan, he's been kissing her out in the darkness of the garden. Holding her very tight.

Michela's eyelids were white and heavy over unexpectedly shallow dark eyes. Her straight black hair was parted in the middle and pulled severely backward to a knot on her rather fat white neck. Her mouth was deeply crimson. She had been born, Susan knew, in rural New England, christened Michela by a romantic mother, and had striven to live up to the name ever since. Or down, thought Susan tersely, and wished she could take young Randy by his large and outstanding ears and shake him.

Michela had turned toward a chair, and her bare back presented itself to Susan, and she saw the thin red line with an angle that a man's cuff, pressing into the creamy flesh, had made. It was unmistakable. Joe Bromfel had seen it, too. He couldn't have helped seeing it. Susan looked into her coffee cup and wished fervently that Joe Bromfel hadn't seen the imprint of Randy's cuff, and then wondered why she wished it so fervently.

"Coffee, Michela?" said Christabel, and something in her voice was more, all at once, than Susan could endure. She rose and said rather breathlessly:

"Christabel darling, do you mind—I have some writing to do——"

"Of course." Christabel hesitated. "But wait—I'll go along with you to the cottage."

"Don't let us keep you, Christabel," said Michela lazily.

Christabel turned to Tryon Welles and neatly forestalled a motion on his part to accompany her and Susan.

"I won't be long, Tryon," she said definitely. "When I come back—we'll talk."

A clear little picture etched itself on Susan's mind: the long, lovely room, the mellow little areas of light under lamps here and there, one falling directly upon the chair she had just left, the pools of shadows surrounding them; Michela's yellow satin, and Randy's red head and slim black shoulders; Joe, a heavy, silent figure, watching them broodingly; Tryon Welles, neat and gray and affable, and Christabel with her gleaming red head held high on her slender neck, walking lightly and gracefully amid soft mauve chiffons. Halfway across the room she paused to accept a cigarette from Tryon and to bend to the small flare of a lighter he held for her, and the amethyst on her finger caught the flickering light of it and shone.

Then Susan and Christabel had crossed the empty flagstone veranda and turned toward the terrace.

Their slippered feet made no sound upon the velvet grass. Above the lily pool the flower fragrances were sweet and heavy on the night air.

"Did you hear the bullfrog last night?" asked Christabel. "He seems to have taken up a permanent residence in the pool. I don't know what to do about him. Randy says he'll shoot him, but I don't want that. He *is* a nuisance of course, bellowing away half the night. But after all—even bullfrogs—have a right to live."

"Christabel," said Susan, trying not to be abrupt, "I must go soon. I have—work to do——"

Christabel stopped and turned to face her. They were at the gap in the laurel hedge where a path began and wound upward to the cottage.

"Don't make excuses, Susan honey," she said gently. "Is it the Bromfels?"

A sound checked Susan's reply—an unexpectedly eerie sound that was like a wail. It rose and swelled amid the moonlit hills, and Susan gasped and Christabel said quickly, though with a catch in her voice: "It's only the dogs howling at the moon."

"They are not," Susan said, "exactly cheerful. It emphasizes——" She checked herself abruptly on the verge of saying that it emphasized their isolation.

Christabel had turned in at the path. It was darker there, and her cigarette made a tiny red glow. "If Michela drops another cigarette into a flower I'll kill her," said Christabel quietly.

"What——"

"I said I'd kill her," said Christabel. "I won't, of course. But she—oh, you've seen how things are, Susan. You can't have failed to see. She took Joe—years ago. Now she's taking Randy."

Susan was thankful that she couldn't see Christabel's face. She said something about infatuation and Randy's youth.

"He is twenty-one," said Christabel. "He's no younger than I was when Joe—when Joe and I were to be married. That was why Michela was here—to be a guest at the wedding and all the parties." They walked on for a few quiet steps before Christabel added: "It was the day before the wedding that they left together."

Susan said: "Has Joe changed?"

"In looks, you mean," said Christabel, understanding. "I don't know. Perhaps. He must have changed inside. But I don't want to know that."

"Can't you send them away?"

"Randy would follow."

"Tryon Welles," suggested Susan desperately. "Maybe he could help. I don't know how, though. Talk to Randy, maybe."

Christabel shook her head.

"Randy wouldn't listen. Opposition makes him stubborn. Besides, he doesn't like Tryon. He's had to borrow too much money from him."

It wasn't like Christabel to be bitter. One of the dogs howled again and was joined by others. Susan shivered.

"You are cold," said Christabel. "Run along inside, and thanks for listening. And—I think you'd better go, honey. I meant to keep you for comfort. But——"

"No, no, I'll stay—I didn't know——"

"Don't be nervous about being alone. The dogs would know it if a stranger put a foot on the place. Good-night," said Christabel firmly, and was gone.

The guest cottage was snug and warm and tranquil, but Susan was obliged finally to read herself to sleep and derived only a small and fleeting satisfaction from the fact that it was over a rival author's book that she finally grew drowsy. She didn't sleep well even then, and was glad suddenly that she'd asked for the guest cottage and was alone and safe in that tiny retreat.

Morning was misty and chill.

It was perhaps nine-thirty when Susan opened the cottage door, saw that mist lay thick and white, and went back to get her rubbers. Tryon Welles, she thought momentarily, catching a glimpse of herself in the mirror, would have nothing at all that was florid and complimentary to say this morning. And indeed, in her brown knitted suit, with her fair hair tight and smooth and her spectacles on, she looked not unlike a chill and aloof little owl.

The path was wet, and the laurel leaves shining with moisture, and the hills were looming gray shapes. The house lay white and quiet, and she saw no one about.

It was just then that it came. A heavy concussion of sound, blanketed by mist.

Susan's first thought was that Randy had shot the bullfrog.

But the pool was just below her, and no one was there.

Besides, the sound came from the house. Her feet were heavy and slow in the drenched grass—the steps were slippery and the flagstones wet. Then she was inside.

The wide hall ran straight through the house, and away down at its end Susan saw Mars. He was running away from her, his black hands outflung, and she was vaguely conscious that he was shouting something. He vanished, and instinct drew Susan to the door at the left which led to the library.

She stopped, frozen, in the doorway.

Across the room, sagging bulkily over the

arm of the green damask chair in which she'd sat the previous night, was a man. It was Joe Bromfel, and he'd been shot, and there was no doubt that he was dead.

A newspaper lay at his feet as if it had slipped there. The velvet curtains were pulled together across the window behind him.

Susan smoothed back her hair. She couldn't think at all, and she must have slipped down to the footstool near the door for she was there when Mars, his face drawn, and Randy, white as his pajamas, came running into the room. They were talking excitedly and were examining a revolver which Randy had picked up from the floor. Then Tryon Welles came from somewhere, stopped beside her, uttered an incredulous exclamation, and ran across the room too. Then Christabel came and stopped, too, on the threshold, and became under Susan's very eyes a different woman—a strange woman, shrunken and gray, who said in a dreadful voice:

"Joe—Joe——"

Only Susan heard or saw her. It was Michela, hurrying from the hall, who first voiced the question.

"I heard something—what was it? What——" She brushed past Christabel.

"Don't look, Michela!"

But Michela looked—steadily and long. Then her flat dark eyes went all around the room and she said: "Who shot him?"

For a moment there was utter shocked stillness.

Then Mars cleared his throat and spoke to Randy.

"I don' know who shot him, Mista Randy. But I saw him killed. An' I saw the han' that killed him——"

"Hand!" screamed Michela.

"Hush, Michela." Tryon Welles was speaking. "What do you mean, Mars?"

"They ain't nothin' to tell except that, Mista Tryon. I was just comin' to dust the library and was right there at the door when I heard the shot, and there was just a han' stickin' out of them velvet curtains. And I saw the han' and I saw the

revolver and I—I do' know what I did then." Mars wiped his forehead. "I guess I ran for help, Mista Tryon."

There was another silence.

"Whose hand was it, Mars?" said Tryon Welles gently.

Mars blinked and looked very old.

"Mista Tryon, God's truth is, I do' know. I do' know."

Randy thrust himself forward.

"Was it a man's hand?"

"I reckon it was maybe," said the old Negro slowly, looking at the floor. "But I do' know for sure, Mista Randy. All I saw was—was the red ring on it."

"A red *ring?*" cried Michela. "What do you mean——"

Mars turned a bleak dark face toward Michela; a face that rejected her and all she had done to his house. "A red ring, Miz Bromfel," he said with a kind of dignity. "It sort of flashed. And it was red."

After a moment Randy uttered a curious laugh.

"But there's not a red ring in the house. None of us runs to rubies—" He stopped abruptly. "I say, Tryon, hadn't we better—well, carry him to the divan. It isn't decent to—just leave him—like that."

"I suppose so—" Tryon Welles moved toward the body. "Help me, Randy——"

The boy shivered, and Susan quite suddenly found her voice.

"Oh, but you can't do that. You can't——" She stopped. The two men were looking at her in astonishment. Michela, too, had turned toward her, although Christabel did not move. "But you can't do that," repeated Susan. "Not when it's—murder."

This time the word, falling into the long room, was weighted with its own significance. Tryon Welles's gray shoulders moved.

"She's perfectly right," he said. "I'd forgotten—if I ever knew. But that's the way of it. We'll have to send for people—doctor, sheriff, coroner, I suppose."

Afterward, Susan realized that but for Tryon Welles the confusion would have become mad. He took a quiet command of the situation, sending Randy, white and sick-looking, to dress, telephoning into town, seeing that the body was decently covered, and even telling Mars to bring them hot coffee. He was here, there, everywhere: upstairs, downstairs, seeing to them all, and finally outside to meet the sheriff . . . brisk, alert, efficient. In the interval Susan sat numbly beside Christabel on the love seat in the hall, with Michela restlessly prowling up and down the hall before their eyes, listening to the telephone calls, drinking hot coffee, watching everything with her sullen, flat black eyes. Her red-and-white sports suit, with its scarlet bracelets and earrings, looked garish and out of place in that house of violent death.

And Christabel. Still a frozen image of a woman who drank coffee automatically, she sat erect and still and did not speak. The glowing amethyst on her finger caught the light and was the only living thing about her.

Gradually the sense of numb shock and confusion was leaving Susan. Fright was still there and horror and a queer aching pity, but she saw Randy come running down the wide stairway again, his red hair smooth now above a sweater, and she realized clearly that he was no longer white and sick and frightened; he was instead alert and defiantly ready for what might come. And it would be, thought Susan, in all probability, plenty.

And it was.

Questions—questions. The doctor, who was kind, the coroner, who was not; the sheriff, who was merely observant—all of them questioning without end. No time to think. No time to comprehend. Time only to reply as best one might.

But gradually out of it all certain salient facts began to emerge. They were few, however, and brief.

The revolver was Randy's, and it had been taken from the top buffet drawer—when no one knew or, at least, would tell. "Everybody knew it was there," said Randy sulkily. The fingerprints on it would probably prove to be Randy's and Mars's, since they picked it up.

No one knew anything of the murder, and no one had an alibi, except Liz (the Negro second girl) and Minnie (the cook), who were together in the kitchen.

Christabel had been writing letters in her own room: she'd heard the shot, but thought it was only Randy shooting a bullfrog in the pool. But then she'd heard Randy and Mars running down the front stairway, so she'd come down too. Just to be sure that that was what it was.

"What else did you think it could be?" asked the sheriff. But Christabel said stiffly that she didn't know.

Randy had been asleep when Mars had awakened him. He had not heard the sound of the shot at all. He and Mars had hurried down to the library. (Mars, it developed, had gone upstairs by means of the small back stairway off the kitchen.)

Tryon Welles had walked down the hill in front of the house to the mail box and was returning when he heard the shot. But it was muffled, and he did not know what had happened until he reached the library. He created a mild sensation at that point by taking off a ring, holding it so they could all see it, and demanding of Mars if that was the ring he had seen on the murderer's hand. However, the sensation was only momentary, for the large clear stone was as green as his neat green tie.

"No, suh, Mista Tryon," said Mars. "The ring on the han' I saw was red. I could see it plain, an' it was red."

"This," said Tryon Welles, "is a flawed emerald. I asked because I seem to be about the only person here wearing a ring. But I suppose that, in justice to us, all our belongings should be searched."

Upon which the sheriff's gaze slid to the purple pool on Christabel's white hand. He said, however, gently, that that was being done, and would Mrs. Michela Bromfel tell what she knew of the murder.

But Mrs. Michela Bromfel somewhat spiritedly knew nothing of it. She'd been walking in the pine woods, she said defiantly, glancing obliquely at Randy, who suddenly flushed all over his thin face. She'd heard the shot but hadn't realized it was a gunshot. However, she was curious and came back to the house.

"The window behind the body opens toward the pine woods," said the sheriff. "Did you see anyone, Mrs. Bromfel?"

"No one at all," said Michela definitely.

Well, then, had she heard the dogs barking? The sheriff seemed to know that the kennels were just back of the pine woods.

But Michela had not heard the dogs.

Someone stirred restively at that, and the sheriff coughed and said unnecessarily that there was no tramp about, then, and the questioning continued. Continued wearily on and on and on, and still no one knew how Joe Bromfel had met his death. And as the sheriff was at last dismissing them and talking to the coroner of an inquest, one of his men came to report on the search. No one was in the house who didn't belong there; they could tell nothing of footprints; the French windows back of the body had been ajar, and there was no red ring anywhere in the house.

"Not, that is, that we can find," said the man.

"All right," said the sheriff. "That'll be all now, folks. But I'd take it kindly if you was to stay around here today."

All her life Susan was to remember that still, long day with a kind of sharp reality. It was, after those first moments when she'd felt so ill and shocked, weirdly natural, as if, one event having occurred, another was bound to follow, and then upon that one's heels another, and all of them quite in the logical order of things. Even the incident of the afternoon, so trivial in itself but later so significant, was as natural, as unsurprising as anything could be. And that was her meeting with Jim Byrne.

It happened at the end of the afternoon, long and painful, which Susan spent with Christabel, knowing somehow that, under her frozen surface, Christabel was grateful for Susan's presence. But there were nameless things in the air between them which could be neither spoken of nor ignored, and Susan was relieved when Christabel at last took a sedative and, eventually, fell into a sleep that was no more still than Christabel waking had been.

There was no one to be seen when Susan tiptoed out of Christabel's room and down the stairway, although she heard voices from the closed door of the library.

Out the wide door at last and walking along the terrace above the lily pool, Susan took a long breath of the mist-laden air.

So this was murder. This was murder, and it happened to people one knew, and it did indescribable and horrible things to them. Frightened them first, perhaps. Fear of murder itself came first—simple, primitive fear of the unleashing of the beast. And then on its heels came more civilized fear, and that was fear of the law, and a scramble for safety.

She turned at the hedge and glanced backward. The house lay white and stately amid its gardens as it had lain for generations. But it was no longer tranquil—it was charged now with violence. With murder. And it remained dignified and stately and would cling, as Christabel would cling and had clung all those years, to its protective ritual.

Christabel. Had she killed him? Was that why she was so stricken and gray? Or was it because she knew that Randy had killed him? Or was it something else?

Susan did not see the man till she was almost upon him, and then she cried out involuntarily, though she as a rule was not at all nervous. He was sitting on the small porch of the cottage, hunched up with his hat over his eyes and his coat collar turned up, furiously scribbling on a pad of paper. He jumped up as he heard her breathless little cry and whirled to face her and took off his hat all in one motion.

"May I use your typewriter?" he said.

His eyes were extremely clear and blue and lively. His face was agreeably irregular in feature, with a mouth that laughed a great deal, a chin that took insolence from no man, and generous width of forehead. His hair was thinning but not yet showing gray and his hands were unexpectedly fine and beautiful. "Hard on the surface," thought Susan. "Terribly sensitive, really. Irish. What's he doing here?"

Aloud she said: "Yes."

"Good. Can't write fast enough and want to get this story off tonight. I've been waiting for you, you know. They told me you wrote things. My name's Byrne. James Byrne. I'm a reporter. Cover special stories. I'm taking a busman's holiday. I'm actually on a Chicago paper and down here for a vacation. I didn't expect a murder story to break."

Susan opened the door upon the small living room.

"The typewriter's there. Do you need paper? There's a stack beside it."

He fell upon the typewriter absorbedly, like a dog upon a bone. She watched him for a while, amazed at his speed and fluency and utter lack of hesitancy.

Presently she lighted the fire already laid in the tiny fireplace and sat there quietly, letting herself be soothed by the glow of the flames and the steady rhythm of the typewriter keys. And for the first time that day its experiences, noted and stored away in whatever place observations are stored, began to arouse and assort and arrange themselves and march in some sort of order through her conscious thoughts. But it was a dark and macabre procession, and it frightened Susan. She was relieved when Jim Byrne spoke.

"I say," he said suddenly, over the clicking keys, "I've got your name Louise Dare. Is that right?"

"Susan."

He looked at her. The clicking stopped.

"Susan. Susan Dare," he repeated thoughtfully. "I say, you can't be the Susan Dare that writes murder stories!"

"Yes," said Susan guardedly, "I can be that Susan Dare."

There was an expression of definite incredulity in his face. "But you——"

"If you say," observed Susan tensely, "that I

don't look as if I wrote murder stories, you can't use my typewriter for your story."

"I suppose you are all tangled up in this mess," he said speculatively.

"Yes," said Susan, sober again. "And no," she added, looking at the fire.

"Don't commit yourself," said Jim Byrne dryly. "Don't say anything reckless."

"But I mean just that," said Susan. "I'm a guest here. A friend of Christabel Frame's. I didn't murder Joe Bromfel. And I don't care at all about the rest of the people here except that I wish I'd never seen them."

"But you do," said the reporter gently, "care a lot about Christabel Frame?"

"Yes," said Susan gravely.

"I've got all the dope, you know," said the reporter softly. "It wasn't hard to get. Everybody around here knows about the Frames. The thing I can't understand is why she shot Joe. It ought to have been Michela."

"What——" Susan's fingers were digging into the wicker arms of her chair, and her eyes strove frantically to plumb the clear blue eyes above the typewriter.

"I say, it ought to have been Michela. She's the girl who's making the trouble."

"But it wasn't—it couldn't—Christabel wouldn't——"

"Oh, yes, she could," said the reporter rather wearily. "All sorts of people could do the strangest things. Christabel could murder. But I can't see why she'd murder Joe and let Michela go scot-free."

"Michela," said Susan in a low voice, "would have a motive."

"Yes, she's got a motive. Get rid of a husband. But so had Randy Frame. Same one. And he's what the people around here call a Red Frame—impulsive, reckless, bred to a tradition of—violence."

"But Randy was asleep—upstairs——"

He interrupted her.

"Oh, yes, I know all that. And you were approaching the house from the terrace, and Tryon

Welles had gone down after the mail, and Miss Christabel was writing letters upstairs, and Michela was walking in the pine woods. Not a damn alibi among you. The way the house and grounds are laid out, neither you nor Tryon Welles nor Michela would be visible to each other. And anyone could have escaped readily from the window and turned up innocently a moment later from the hall. I know all that. Who was behind the curtains?"

"A tramp——" attempted Susan in a small voice. "A burglar——"

"Burglar nothing," said Jim Byrne with scorn. "The dogs would have had hysterics. It was one of you. *Who?*"

"I don't know," said Susan. *"I don't know!"* Her voice was uneven, and she knew it and tried to steady it and clutched the chair arms tighter. Jim Byrne knew it, too, and was suddenly alarmed.

"Oh, look here, now," he cried. "Don't look like that. Don't cry. Don't——"

"I am not crying," said Susan. "But it wasn't Christabel."

"You mean," said the reporter kindly, "that you don't want it to be Christabel. Well——" He glanced at his watch, said, "Golly," and flung his papers together and rose. "There's something I'll do. Not for you exactly—just for—oh, because. I'll let part of my story wait until tomorrow if you want the chance to try to prove your Christabel didn't murder him."

Susan was frowning perplexedly.

"You don't understand me," said the reporter cheerfully. "It's this. You write murder mysteries, and I've read one or two of them. They are not bad," he interpolated hastily, watching Susan. "Now, here's your chance to try a real murder mystery."

"But I don't want——" began Susan.

He checked her imperatively.

"You do want to," he said. "In fact, you've got to. You see—your Christabel is in a spot. You know that ring she wears——"

"When did you see it?"

"Oh, does it matter?" he cried impatiently.

"Reporters see everything. The point is the ring."

"But it's an amethyst," said Susan defensively.

"Yes," he agreed grimly. "It's an amethyst. And Mars saw a red stone. He saw it, it has developed, on the right hand. And the hand holding the revolver. And Christabel wears her ring on her right hand."

"But," repeated Susan, "it *is* an amethyst."

"M-m," said the reporter. "It's an amethyst. And a little while ago I said to Mars: 'What's the name of that flowering vine over there?' And he said: 'That red flower, suh? That's wisteria.'"

He paused. Susan felt exactly as if something had clutched her heart and squeezed it.

"The flowers were purple, of course," said the reporter softly. "The color of a dark amethyst."

"But he would have recognized Christabel's ring," said Susan after a moment.

"Maybe," said the reporter. "And maybe he wishes he'd never said a word about the red ring. He was scared when he first mentioned it, probably; hadn't had a chance to think it over."

"But Mars—Mars would confess to murdering rather than——"

"No," said Jim Byrne soberly. "He wouldn't. That theory sounds all right. But it doesn't happen that way. People don't murder or confess to having murdered for somebody else. When it is a deliberate, planned murder and not a crazy drunken brawl, when anything can happen, there's a motive. And it's a strong and urgent and deeply personal and selfish motive and don't you forget it. I've got to hurry. Now then, shall I send in my story about the wisteria——"

"Don't," said Susan choking. "Oh, don't. Not yet."

He picked up his hat. "Thanks for the typewriter. Get your wits together and go to work. After all, you ought to know something of murders. I'll be seeing you."

The door closed, and the flames crackled. After a long time Susan moved to the writing table and drew a sheet of yellow manuscript paper toward her, and a pencil, and wrote: Characters; possible motives; clues; queries.

It was strange, she thought, not how different real life was to its written imitation, but how like. How terribly like!

She was still bent over the yellow paper when a peremptory knock at the door sent her pencil jabbing furiously on the paper and her heart into her throat. It proved to be, however, only Michela Bromfel, and she wanted help.

"It's my knees," said Michela irritably. "Christabel's asleep or something, and the three servants are all scared of their shadows." She paused to dig savagely at first one knee and then the other. "Have you got anything to put on my legs? I'm nearly going crazy. It's not mosquito bites. I don't know what it is. Look!"

She sat down, pulled back her white skirt and rolled down her thin stockings, disclosing just above each knee a scarlet blotchy rim around her fat white legs.

Susan looked and had to resist a wild desire to giggle. "It's n-nothing," she said, quivering. "That is, it's only jiggers—here, I'll get you something. Alcohol."

"Jiggers," said Michela blankly. "What's that?"

Susan went into the bathroom. "Little bugs," she called. Where was the alcohol? "They are thick in the pine woods. It'll be all right by morning." Here it was. She took the bottle in her hand and turned again through the bedroom into the tiny living room.

At the door she stopped abruptly. Michela was standing at the writing table. She looked up, saw Susan, and her flat dark eyes flickered.

"Oh," said Michela. "Writing a story?"

"No," said Susan. "It's not a story. Here's the alcohol."

Under Susan's straight look Michela had the grace to depart rather hastily, yanking up her stockings and twisting them hurriedly, and clutching at the bottle of alcohol. Her red bracelets clanked, and her scarlet fingernails looked as if they'd been dipped in blood. Of the few people who might have killed Joe Bromfel, Susan reflected coolly, she would prefer it to be Michela.

It was just then that a curious vagrant memory began to tease Susan. Rather it was not so much a memory as a memory *of* a memory—something that sometime she had known and now could not remember. It was tantalizing. It was maddeningly elusive. It floated teasingly on the very edge of her consciousness.

Deliberately, at last, Susan pushed it away and went back to work. Christabel and the amethyst. Christabel and the wisteria. Christabel.

It was dark and still drizzly when Susan took her way down toward the big house.

At the laurel hedge she met Tryon Welles.

"Oh, hello," he said. "Where've you been?"

"At the cottage," said Susan. "There was nothing I could do. How's Christabel?"

"Liz says she is still asleep—thank heaven for that. God, what a day! You oughtn't to be prowling around alone at this time of night. I'll walk to the house with you."

"Have the sheriff and other men gone?"

"For the time being. They'll be back, I suppose."

"Do they know any more about—who killed him?"

"I don't know. You can't tell much. I don't know of any evidence they have unearthed. They asked me to stay on." He took a quick puff or two of his cigarette and then said irritably: "It puts me in a bad place. It's a business deal where time matters. I'm a broker—I ought to be going back to New York tonight——" He broke off abruptly and said: "Oh, Randy—" as young Randy's pale, thin face above a shining mackintosh emerged from the dusk—"let's just escort Miss Susan to the steps."

"Is she afraid of the famous tramp?" asked Randy and laughed unpleasantly. He'd been drinking, thought Susan, with a flicker of anxiety. Sober, Randy was incalculable enough; drinking, he might be dangerous. Could she do anything with him? No, better leave it to Tryon Welles. "The tramp," Randy was repeating loudly. "Don't be afraid of a tramp. It wasn't any tramp killed Joe. And everybody knows it. You're safe enough, Susan, unless you've got some evidence. Have you got any evidence, Susan?"

He took her elbow and joggled it urgently.

"She's the quiet kind, Tryon, that sees everything and says nothing. Bet she's got evidence enough to hang us all. Evidence. That's what we need. Evidence."

"Randy, you're drunk," said Susan crisply. She shook off his clutch upon her arm and then, looking at his thin face, which was so white and tight-drawn in the dusk, was suddenly sorry for him. "Go on and take your walk," she said more kindly. "Things will be all right."

"Things will never be the same again," said Randy. "Never the same—do you know why, Susan?" He's very drunk, thought Susan; worse than I thought. "It's because Michela shot him. Yes, sir."

"Randy, shut up!"

"Don't bother me, Tryon, I know what I'm saying. And Michela," asserted Randy with simplicity, "makes me sick."

"Come on, Randy." This time Tryon Welles took Randy's arm. "I'll take care of him, Miss Susan."

The house was deserted and seemed cold. Christabel was still asleep, Michela nowhere to be seen, and Susan finally told Mars to send her dinner on a tray to the cottage and returned quietly like a small brown wraith through the moist twilight.

But she was an oddly frightened wraith.

She was alone on the silent terrace, she was alone on the dark path—strange that she felt as if someone else were there, too. Was the bare fact of murder like a presence hovering, beating dark wings, waiting to sweep downward again?

"Nonsense," said Susan aloud. "Nonsense——" and ran the rest of the way.

She was not, however, to be alone in the cottage, for Michela sat there, composedly awaiting her.

"Do you mind," said Michela, "if I spend the night here? There's two beds in there. You

see—" she hesitated, her flat dark eyes were furtive—"I'm—afraid."

"Of what?" said Susan, after a moment. "Of whom?"

"I don't know who," said Michela, "or what."

After a long, singularly still moment Susan forced herself to say evenly:

"Stay if you are nervous. It's safe here." Was it? Susan continued hurriedly: "Mars will send up dinner."

Michela's thick white hand made an impatient movement.

"Call it nerves—although I've not a nerve in my body. But when Mars comes with dinner—just be sure it *is* Mars before you open the door, will you? Although as to that—*I* don't know. But I brought my revolver—loaded." She reached into her pocket, and Susan sat upright, abruptly. Susan, whose knowledge of revolvers had such a wide and peculiar range that any policeman, learning of it, would arrest her on suspicion alone, was nevertheless somewhat uneasy in their immediate vicinity.

"Afraid?" said Michela.

"Not at all," said Susan. "But I don't think a revolver will be necessary."

"I hope not, I'm sure," said Michela somberly and stared at the fire.

After that, as Susan later reflected, there was not much to be said. The only interruption during the whole queer evening was the arrival of Mars and dinner.

Later in the evening Michela spoke again, abruptly. "I didn't kill Joe," she said. And after another long silence she said unexpectedly: "Did Christabel ask you how to kill him and get by with it?"

"No!"

"Oh." Michela looked at her queerly. "I thought maybe she'd got you to plan it for her. You—knowing so much about murders and all."

"She didn't," said Susan forcefully. "And I don't plan murders for my friends, I assure you. I'm going to bed."

Michela, following her, put the revolver on the small table between the two beds.

If the night before had been heavy with apprehension, this night was an active nightmare. Susan tossed and turned and was uneasily conscious that Michela was awake and restless, too.

Susan must have slept at last, though, for she waked up with a start and sat upright, instantly aware of some movement in the room. Then she saw a figure dimly outlined against the window. It was Michela.

Susan joined her. "What are you doing?"

"Hush," whispered Michela. Her face was pressed against the glass. Susan looked, too, but could see only blackness.

"There's someone out there," whispered Michela. "And if he moves again I'm going to shoot."

Susan was suddenly aware that the ice-cold thing against her arm was the revolver.

"You are not," said Susan and wrenched the thing out of Michela's hand. Michela gasped and whirled, and Susan said grimly: "Go back to bed. Nobody's out there."

"How do you know?" said Michela, her voice sulky.

"I don't," said Susan, very much astonished at herself, but clutching the revolver firmly. "But I do know that you aren't going to start shooting. If there's any shooting to be done," said Susan with aplomb, "I'll do it myself. Go to bed."

But long after Michela was quiet Susan still sat bolt upright, clutching the revolver and listening.

Along toward dawn, out of the *mêlée* of confused, unhappy thoughts, the vagrant little recollection of a recollection came back to tantalize her. Something she'd known and now did not know. This time she returned as completely as she could over the track her thoughts had taken in the hope of capturing it by association. She'd been thinking of the murder and of the possible suspects; that if Michela had not murdered Joe, then there were left Randy and Christabel and Tryon Welles. And she didn't want it to be Christabel; it must not be Christabel. And that left Randy and Tryon Welles. Randy had a motive, but Tryon Welles had not. Tryon Welles wore a ring habitually, and Randy did not. But the ring was an emerald. And Christabel's ring was what Mars called red. Red—then what would he have called Michela's scarlet bracelet? Pink? But that was a bracelet. She wrenched herself back to dig at the troublesome phantom of a memory. It was something trivial—but something she could not project into her conscious memory. And it was something that somehow she needed. Needed now.

She awoke and was horrified to discover her cheek pillowed cosily upon the revolver. She thrust it away. And realized with a sinking of her heart that day had come and, with it, urgent problems. Christabel, first.

Michela was still silent and sulky. Crossing the terrace, Susan looked at the wisteria winding upward over its trellis. It was heavy with purple blossoms—purple like dark amethysts.

Christabel was in her own room, holding a breakfast tray on her lap and looking out the window with a blank, unseeing gaze. She was years older; shrunken somehow inside. She was pathetically willing to answer the few questions that Susan asked, but added nothing to Susan's small store of knowledge. She left her finally, feeling that Christabel wanted only solitude. But she went away reluctantly. It would not be long before Jim Byrne returned, and she had nothing to tell him—nothing, that is, except surmise.

Randy was not at breakfast, and it was a dark and uncomfortable meal. Dark because Tryon Welles said something about a headache and turned out the electric light, and uncomfortable because it could not be otherwise. Michela had changed to a thin suit—red again. The teasing ghost of a memory drifted over Susan's mind and away again before she could grasp it.

As the meal ended Susan was called to the telephone. It was Jim Byrne saying that he would be there in an hour.

On the terrace Tryon Welles overtook her again and said: "How's Christabel?"

"I don't know," said Susan slowly. "She looks—stunned."

"I wish I could make it easier for her," he said. "But—I'm caught, too. There's nothing I can do, really. I mean about the house, of course. Didn't she tell you?"

"No."

He looked at her, considered, and went on slowly.

"She wouldn't mind your knowing. You see— oh, it's tragically simple. But I can't help myself. It's like this: Randy borrowed money of me— kept on borrowing it, spent it like water. Without Christabel knowing it, he put up the house and grounds as collateral. She knows now, of course. Now I'm in a pinch in business and have got to take the house over legally in order to borrow enough money on it myself to keep things going for a few months. Do you see?"

Susan nodded. Was it this knowledge, then, that had so stricken Christabel?

"I hate it," said Tryon Welles. "But what can I do? And now Joe's—death—on top of it—" He paused, reached absently for a cigarette case, extracted a cigarette, and the small flame from his lighter flared suddenly clear and bright. "It's—hell," he said, puffing, "for her. But what can I do? I've got my own business to save."

"I see," said Susan slowly.

And quite suddenly, looking at the lighter, she did see. It was as simple, as miraculously simple as that. She said, her voice to her own ears marvelously unshaken and calm: "May I have a cigarette?"

He was embarrassed at not having offered it to her: he fumbled for his cigarette case and then held the flame of the lighter for her. Susan was very deliberate about getting her cigarette lighted. Finally she did so, said, "Thank you," and added, quite as if she had the whole thing planned: "Will you wake Randy, Mr. Welles, and send him to me? Now?"

"Why, of course," he said. "You'll be in the cottage?"

"Yes," said Susan and fled.

She was bent over the yellow paper when Jim Byrne arrived.

He was fresh and alert and, Susan could see,

prepared to be kind. He expected her, then, to fail.

"Well," he said gently, "have you discovered the murderer?"

"Yes," said Susan Dare.

Jim Byrne sat down quite suddenly.

"I know who killed him," she said simply, "but I don't know why."

Jim Byrne reached into his pocket for a handkerchief and dabbed it lightly to his forehead. "Suppose," he suggested in a hushed way, "you tell all."

"Randy will be here in a moment," said Susan. "But it's all very simple. You see, the final clue was only the proof. I knew Christabel couldn't have killed him, for two reasons: one is, she's inherently incapable of killing anything; the other is— she loved him still. And I knew it wasn't Michela, because she is, actually, cowardly; and then, too, Michela had an alibi."

"Alibi?"

"She really *was* in the pine woods for a long time that morning. Waiting, I think, for Randy, who slept late. I know she was there, because she was simply chewed by jiggers, and they are only in the pine woods."

"Maybe she was there the day before."

Susan shook her head decidedly.

"No, I know jiggers. If it had been during the previous day they'd have stopped itching by the time she came to me. And it wasn't during the afternoon, for no one went in the pine woods then except the sheriff's men."

"That would leave, then, Randy and Tryon Welles."

"Yes," said Susan. Now that it had come to doing it, she felt ill and weak; would it be her evidence, her words, that would send a fellow creature over that long and ignominious road that ends so tragically?

Jim Byrne knew what she was thinking.

"Remember Christabel," he said quietly.

"Oh, I know," said Susan sadly. She locked her fingers together, and there were quick footsteps on the porch.

"You want me, Susan?" said Randy.

"Yes, Randy," said Susan. "I want you to tell me if you owed Joe Bromfel anything. Money— or—or anything."

"How did you know?" said Randy.

"Did you give him a note—anything?"

"Yes."

"What was your collateral?"

"The house—it's all mine——"

"When was it dated? Answer me, Randy."

He flung up his head.

"I suppose you've been talking to Tryon," he said defiantly. "Well, it was dated before Tryon got his note. I couldn't help it. I'd got some stocks on margin. I had to have——"

"So the house actually belonged to Joe Bromfel?" Susan was curiously cold. Christabel's house. Christabel's brother.

"Well, yes—if you want to put it like that."

Jim Byrne had risen quietly.

"And after Joe Bromfel, to Michela, if she knows of this and claims it?" pressed Susan.

"I don't know," said Randy. "I never thought of that."

Jim Byrne started to speak, but Susan silenced him.

"No, he really didn't think of it," she said wearily. "And I knew it wasn't Randy who killed him because he didn't, really, care enough for Michela to do that. It was—Tryon Welles who killed Joe Bromfel. He had to. For he had to silence Joe and then secure the note and, probably, destroy it, in order to have a clear title to the house, himself. Randy—did Joe have the note here with him?"

"Yes."

"It was not found upon his body?"

It was Jim Byrne who answered: "Nothing of the kind was found anywhere."

"Then," said Susan, "after the murder was discovered and before the sheriff arrived and the search began, only you and Tryon Welles were upstairs and had the opportunity to search Joe's room and find the note and destroy it. Was it you who did that, Randy?"

"*No—no!*" The color rose in his face.

"Then it must have been then that Tryon Welles found and destroyed it." She frowned.

"Somehow, he must have known it was there. I don't know how—perhaps he had had words with Joe about it before he shot him and Joe inadvertently told him where it was. There was no time for him to search the body. But he knew——"

"Maybe," said Randy reluctantly, "I told him. You see—I knew Joe had it in his letter case. He—he told me. But I never thought of taking it."

"It was not on record?" asked Jim Byrne.

"No," said Randy, flushing. "I—asked him to keep it quiet."

"I wonder," said Susan, looking away from Randy's miserable young face, "just how Tryon Welles expected to silence you."

"Well," said Randy dully, after a moment, "it was not exactly to my credit. But you needn't rub it in. I never thought of this—I was thinking of—Michela. That she did it. I've had my lesson. And if he destroyed the note, how are you going to prove all this?"

"By your testimony," said Susan. "And besides—there's the ring."

"Ring," said Randy. Jim Byrne leaned forward intently.

"Yes," said Susan. "I'd forgotten. But I remembered that Joe had been reading the newspaper when he was killed. The curtains were pulled together back of him, so, in order to see the paper, he must have had the light turned on above his chair. It wasn't burning when I entered the library, or I should have noted it. So the murderer had pulled the cord of the lamp before he escaped. And ever since then he has been very careful to avoid any artificial light."

"What are you talking about?" cried Randy.

"Yet he had to keep on wearing the ring," said Susan. "Fortunately for him he didn't have it on the first night—I suppose the color at night would have been wrong with his green tie. But this morning he lit a cigarette and I saw."

"Saw what, in God's name," said Randy burstingly.

"That the stone isn't an emerald at all," replied Susan. "It's an Alexandrite. It changed color under the flare of the lighter."

"Alexandrite!" cried Randy impatiently. "What's that?"

"It's a stone that's a kind of red-purple under artificial light and green in daylight," said Jim Byrne shortly. "I had forgotten there was such a thing—I don't think I've ever happened to see one. They are rare—and costly. Costly," repeated Jim Byrne slowly. "This one has cost a life——"

Randy interrupted: "But if Michela knows about the note, why, Tryon may kill her——" He stopped abruptly, thought for a second or two, then got out a cigarette. "Let him," he said airily.

It had been Tryon Welles, then, prowling about during the night—if it had been anyone.

He had been uncertain, perhaps, of the extent of Michela's knowledge—but certain of his ability to deal with her and with Randy, who was so heavily in his debt.

"Michela doesn't know now," said Susan slowly. "And when you tell her, Randy—she might settle for a cash consideration. And, Randy Frame, somehow you've got to recover this house for Christabel and do it honestly."

"But right now," said Jim Byrne cheerily, "for the sheriff. And my story."

At the doorway he paused to look at Susan. "May I come back later," he said, "and use your typewriter?"

"Yes," said Susan Dare.

THE BLOODY CRESCENDO

Vincent Starrett

ONE OF AMERICA'S GREATEST BOOKMEN, Charles Vincent Emerson Starrett (1886–1974) produced innumerable essays, biographical works, critical studies, and bibliographical pieces on a wide range of authors and subjects, all while managing the "Books Alive" column for the *Chicago Tribune* for many years. His autobiography, *Born in a Bookshop* (1965), should be required reading for bibliophiles of all ages.

Few would argue that Starrett's most outstanding achievements were his writings about Sherlock Holmes, most notably *The Private Life of Sherlock Holmes* (1933), a comprehensive biography of the great detective, and "The Unique 'Hamlet,'" lauded by Sherlockians for decades as the best pastiche ever written.

He described himself as a Dofob—Eugene Field's useful word—which is a "damned old fool over books," and, when a friend called at his home, Starrett's daughter answered the door and told the visitor that her father was "upstairs, playing with his books." Upon Starrett's death, she offered the best tombstone inscription that a bibliophile could hope for: "The Last Bookman."

Among his many fictional works were numerous mystery short stories and several detective novels, including *Murder on "B" Deck* (1929), *Dead Man Inside* (1931), and *The End of Mr. Garment* (1932). His 1934 short story, "Recipe for Murder," was expanded to the full-length novel *The Great Hotel Murder* (1935), which was the basis for the film of the same title and released the same year; it starred Edmund Lowe and Victor McLaglen.

"The Bloody Crescendo," often reprinted as "Murder at the Opera," was originally published in the October 1934 issue of *Real Detectives*; it was first collected in *The Eleventh Juror and Other Crime Classics* (Shelburne, Ontario, The Battered Silicon Dispatch Press, 1995).

The Bloody Crescendo

VINCENT STARRETT

TWO CIRCUMSTANCES marked the *première* of the new opera as notable, even in anticipation. First, and perhaps foremost, it was by all accounts a sensational musical event; something that was going to be talked about in the press and from the pulpit. Second, in spite of her recent scandalous divorce from Palestrina, Edna Colchis was going to sing—and Palestrina was going to direct her.

The murder of Mrs. Emmanuel B. Letts during the sulphurous first act was, of course, unpredictable.

From her seat in the Diamond Circle— specifically, the Hassard box (Mondays and Fridays)—Sally Cardiff watched the surge and flow of opulent Chicago, with the little smile of one for whom such spectacles were providentially ordained. When, occasionally, she replied to the remarks of young Arnold Castle, at her side, she did so pleasantly but without removing her eyes from the scene of colorful congestion.

Young Mr. Castle was cynical. "Fifty per cent of them are here to see what happens between those two," he observed. "This Colchis now," he continued irritably, "what do they expect her to do? Blow up in the middle of the performance?"

His cigar lighter, which he clicked exasperatingly as he talked, was a magnificent affair. It was of gold, by Lemaire, and contained everything but running hot and cold water.

"If she felt that way," said Miss Cardiff, "she would not appear at all. But nothing will go wrong. They are both artists—and egotists."

"As for the opera," persisted Castle, "I suspect it has been greatly overrated. They say there isn't a *tune* in the whole show. Just discord!"

She laughed lightly. "Why do you come?" Then she blushed: "Never mind!" Her smiling gaze swung to the nearer boxes and her voice fell. "Mrs. Letts is wearing her fabulous necklace tonight. You see, it isn't a myth, after all."

"It's vulgar," said young Mr. Castle. "She's a lighthouse. Besides, it's dangerous. In times like these she should keep her jewels in a vault. I wouldn't feel safe with that thing in a church. Who's the fat bounder behind her?"

Miss Cardiff said *"Sh!"* The fat bounder had turned his head in their direction. Mrs. Hassard answered the question. "That's Higginson," she said briefly.

"Get out!" cried Castle, enlightened. Everybody knew who Higginson was. He was Mrs. Letts's secret-service department, an ex-prizefighter employed by Mrs. Letts as private detective and, if occasion should arise, slugger. The job was a sinecure, for the police also kept a friendly eye on the exits and entrances of the wealthy Mrs. Letts. It was easier to prevent an attempt upon her middle-aged person than to imagine what might happen to the heads of the department if any such attempt were made.

"He looks uncomfortable," added young Mr. Castle.

Hassard grinned satirically. "He doesn't like dressing up. He'd be more at home at the back of the house, talking to the fireman."

"Do you think so?" murmured Miss Cardiff. "I was thinking that he rather liked his part."

"He's too fat," observed the critical Castle. "Out of training. Soft living and locking up nights agrees with him. A child could stop him. I think I might even take him on myself," he added appraisingly.

Miss Cardiff again said *"Sh!"* and continued immediately: "Please don't! I never shall forget the time you tried to thrash a taxi driver."

"I won't touch him tonight," grinned Castle. "I suppose he's here to keep an eye on the necklace. Anyway, there are plenty of dicks in the house—eh, Hassard?"

Hassard thought it likely there were a number of detectives scattered through the house—all as uncomfortable in evening dress as Higginson.

Sally Cardiff continued to be fascinated by the audience. From time to time she put her glasses to her eyes, the better to observe some specimen of interest. She saw everything. Everything pleased her. The human values represented were, she knew, in large part spurious; but the circumstance had no power to spoil her appreciation of the cosmic whole. Life was like that. And life was exhilarating—quietly exhilarating.

Mrs. Letts, meanwhile, sat calmly in her chair, nodded occasionally to an arriving acquaintance, but for the most part placid and phlegmatic. She had once been beautiful, and she was still an attractive woman. She had oodles of money—more money than any of the peacocks around her—but she was not a snob. She was simply elderly and a bit tired. She had greeted the Hassards and their party as they came in, and then had forgotten about them. After a time she appeared to nod, and was not shaken from her lethargy until a rapturous burst of applause noted the coming of the famous maestro.

Palestrina paused in his impressive march and bowed profoundly. The applause redoubled. He raised his baton, and it subsided almost abruptly.

"He's got the hair, all right," commented young Mr. Castle.

"Sh!" said Miss Cardiff, for the third time.

The baton descended and there stole through the house the opening notes of the overture to "The Robber Kitten"—a small, wailing cry from the violins, quickly abetted by the bull fiddles. The audience shivered deliciously. The cry mounted eerily on little cat feet until it was a strident shriek; then it dropped to the first whispering wail. The crescendo was repeated. It was heard a third time. Then all the violins and fiddles went crazy together and filled the auditorium with harsh, discordant sound. This continued for some time. Somewhere in the background of it all a wild, high melody persisted—a tortured, uncomfortable strain—and the brasses joined the uproar, at intervals, with savage gusts of laughter.

The critics, in retrospect, decided that the whole had been "a succession of unpleasant sense impressions telling a brutal story with dramatic emphasis."

Whatever the critics may have thought, the house was stunned; then thunders of applause swept the auditorium. Palestrina turned and bowed in several directions. . . .

But the questing eyes of Sally Cardiff, at that moment, caught a familiar face in the glow of an orchestra light; and she put up her glasses for a better view. *Interesting!* The man playing one of the first violins was almost the double of Palestrina, the conductor. They might even have changed places without suspicion—as far as personal appearance went.

Again the baton was upraised, and again the kitten's wail crept through the place, to end abruptly with the shriek of the adult felines. And as the wild cry failed the figure of a man stole from the wings, costumed to represent an enormous cat. He was in full evening dress below the jaw, but a furred headpiece set with pointed ears created the impression of feline masculinity; his tremendous mustachios stood out like bristling antennæ. Orlando Diaz, the famous tenor. As Grimalkin, the Robber Kitten.

He began to sing.

Nobody, of course, paid the slightest attention to Mrs. Emmanuel B. Letts. Yet it might have been observed that at the beginning of the performance she had leaned forward in her chair—to use her glasses—and that a little later she had leaned back again. In point of fact, she did this several times. Her interest in cats, however, was notorious. She was the patron saint of a cat hospital.

The performance went on. More cat-eared, whiskered singers stole on and off the stage. The row was terrific. Colchis appeared and sang divinely—if the word may be applied to the singing of an almost diabolic role—and no mishap occurred to mar the flagrant felicity of the situation.

At the conclusion of the first act the applause was boisterous. Colchis popped in and out of the wings like an animated jack-in-the-box, receiving flowers, while Diaz was even more modest than usual. He was, indeed, the last to appear, to take his bow, and he contrived to lend to the simple act a suggestion of protest. In every gesture he seemed to say that the triumph belonged to Colchis.

"Smart man," commented Sally Cardiff, on whom no nuance of behavior was lost. "He minimizes the Colchis triumph by appearing to abet it."

But at last the ovations were at an end, and the audience dispersed to the lobbies and lounges to smoke and wrangle over the performance. Many sat on in their seats, among them Mrs. Emmanuel B. Letts, to whom—after a respectful moment—Higginson bent forward and addressed a superficial word. What he said, it developed later, was merely: "Well, modom, what did you think of it?"

But Mrs. Letts was already quite dead. She was never to know how the story ended. Rather, she was to furnish—for days to come—a news

sensation more fascinating than any the city had known in years.

"Murder!" shrieked the newsboys in the snowy streets, even before the first performance of "The Robber Kitten" was at an end. And then they shrieked: "Murder-wurder! All about the turrible-urrible murder-wurder in the opery-wopery!" Or words to that effect. Emerging from the great casino into the worst blizzard the city had experienced since '69, the jackdaws and peacocks of the social set were assaulted by the ferocious clamor of the gamins.

Only a few had the faintest inkling of what had occurred almost under their noses.

And Mrs. Emmanuel B. Letts sat on in her gilded box, her fabulous necklace still gleaming on her mottled throat, while silent men stood by and waited the emptying of the great barn that had become her tomb.

Robbery, it seemed apparent, could not have been the motive. There was the famous necklace to prove that. Unless the murderer had somehow failed at the last moment. Was it possible that he had—with consummate cleverness—committed his crime, then been forced to escape without his plunder?

The idea occurred to Dallas, chief of the Detective Bureau, but he put it out of his mind for the time. It seemed unlikely. Jealousy, thought Dallas—or hatred—would be a more likely motive. These wealthy society women! He knew them. They purred and cooed and "deared" one another, but each loathed the ground on which the other walked. For that a woman had turned the trick, Dallas had no doubt at all. It looked, he said, like a woman's job. Academically, a detective has no right to a strong opinion until he has a fact or two upon which to base it; but in actuality all detectives are prejudiced from the beginning.

Only two opera parties had been asked to remain—those occupying the boxes immediately adjoining that of Mrs. Letts. It was obviously impracticable to hold the entire audience.

But the theater staff was on hand in a phalanx—all the ushers, and the box-office bandits, and the hat-check robbers, and the numerous management. Not to mention a terrified young man and young woman from the audience, who were regarded by Dallas with the deepest possible suspicion. The two had occupied main-floor seats on stolen tickets, which they averred they had purchased from a scalper.

Around the scene of the crime a magnificent activity was apparent. Detectives from the Bureau and from the coroner's office dashed in and out of the lethal box. Reporters jostled and quarreled around the door. Flashlights exploded, and the acrid powder smoke drifted out across the vacant auditorium like an aftermath of battle. In the mezzanine lobby beyond the tier of boxes, the presumptive witnesses huddled on long sofas or paced nervously in the deep pile of the carpet.

Dallas and the coroner sat perilously on the extreme outward ledge of the box, facing the corpse, with Higginson at one side. The background was occupied by two burly detectives from the Bureau.

"Well, Higginson," the detective chief began abruptly, "it looks as if the first explanation ought to come from you."

There could be little doubt of it, since presumably the man had sat behind the murdered woman throughout the whole first act. There was, however, this in his favor: he had himself reported the demise at the conclusion of that first installment. Thereafter, for two long and ghastly further installments, with Dallas as his shadowy companion, he had continued to sit behind the stiffening body. Somebody had to sit there, to keep Mrs. Letts from toppling from her chair.

This had been Dallas's idea. It had occurred to him that nothing was to be gained by stopping the performance and dismissing the audience. And removal of the body would only have created a sensation that he had no wish to father. There was always the possibility, too, that the murderess—if unsuspicious—might return to the scene of her crime. She would hardly dare to leave the building, argued Dallas, thus invit-ing an individual attention. It was the detective's whim to ascertain which of the friends of Mrs. Emmanuel B. Letts—female—would first attempt to greet her after the performance. He held a high opinion of the nerve and subtlety of women.

As it happened, nobody made the attempt.

Higginson, although subdued, was faintly peevish. He knew Dallas very well indeed. "Honest to God, Chief," he answered, speaking his own tongue for the first time in weeks, "I told you all I know about it."

"Tell me again," said Dallas. "I want Marlowe and Duffield to hear the whole story. And the coroner," he added.

Messrs. Marlowe and Duffield, of the Bureau, bent their united gaze on the unhappy man.

Higginson's wild eye avoided contact with the body in the gilded chair. The incredible scene was now lighted by a blaze of electricity, in which the fabulous necklace glinted and sparkled like a proscenium arch.

"I got a telephone call, boys," said Higginson, in a low voice. "That's the way it was. During the first act. An usher came to the box. He just put his hand in and touched my arm. I was sitting back a bit—just over there. I slipped outside, and he said I was wanted on the telephone. It was a message for Mrs. Letts, he said."

"Did you tell her you were leaving the box?" asked Duffield swiftly.

"No, I didn't, Duffy." Higginson also knew Messrs. Marlowe and Duffield. "There didn't seem to be any use. It was probably some nuisance, I figured, and I could take care of it as well as her. If I'd told her, she'd just have sent *me*, anyway."

Duffield nodded.

"So I just slipped out and went to the phone myself. It was downstairs in the lobby—the public telephone near the east door. Oh, I know what you're all thinking! I ought to have known better. Who would call her on that telephone, eh? Who would know the number? I know! Good God, do you suppose I'd have gone if I'd known what was going to happen?"

"What happened at the telephone, Hig?" The question came from Marlowe. There was a certain sympathy in his voice that Higginson was quick to sense and appreciate.

"Not a damn thing, Joe! Just a voice I didn't know, saying, 'Is that you, Higginson?' And I said, 'Yes—who's this?' And he said, 'Hold the wire a minute. There's an important message coming for Mrs. Letts.'"

"And you held the wire," finished Duffield dryly. "Meanwhile, this bird—or somebody else—was beating it around to the box you'd left and knifing Mrs. Letts!"

Higginson nodded slowly. "Yes," he agreed. "I guess that's what happened, Duffy."

"It was a man on the telephone, though. You're sure of that?" The detective's voice was strident. Outside, the witnesses pricked up their ears.

"Oh, it was a man on the *telephone*, all right," cut in Dallas, with a faint sneer. "But it wasn't necessarily a man that did this job."

"Why so, Chief?" There was disagreement in Duffield's query.

"Motive," answered the chief laconically. His voice sank. "You can't imagine a *man* caring enough, one way or another, to kill this old woman, can you?"

"One way or another about what?" asked Duffield.

"Anything," said Dallas vaguely. He added: "If it was a man, Duff, it'd be a case of robbery—and the necklace would be gone. Look at it!"

"*Mmmm,*" admitted the other. "It's a whooperdoo, all right."

"It's a lallapaloosa," said Dallas.

"Ever any attempts on her before, Hig?" asked Marlowe.

"Not in my time."

"Is that her glove?" The detective indicated a long and crumpled white object on the floor of the box.

"It's hers," answered Higginson gloomily.

The left hand and arm of the murdered Mrs. Letts were bare to the shoulder. The right hand and arm were gloved to a point above the elbow.

They all studied the impassive woman for a moment, while Mrs. Letts's eyes continued to stare blankly across the empty pit. She seemed to be accepting, with her usual placidity, this new experience of death and dissolution.

Her opera glasses lay on the floor a little distance from the body. Duffield picked them up. "Looks as if somebody had stepped on these," he observed. "This scratch is pretty fresh."

Higginson shrugged. "Afraid *I* did that, Duffy," he confessed. "Last week. She lent 'em to me—at 'The Love of Three Oranges,' I dropped 'em and kicked 'em around a bit."

"At the *what*?" demanded Duffield, incredulously.

"'The Love of Three Oranges,'" said Higginson. "It's another opera."

"My God!" said Duffield.

"Forget that," snapped Dallas, impatiently. "It's obvious what happened. Hig got his call—I *suppose* he did—and left the box. While he was gone, the dame who did the job slid inside, crawled up behind the victim, and pushed a knife into her back. A very neat job too! Not a sound, apparently—although there might have been a little squeal, with perfect safety. I understand there was noise enough on the stage to cover almost anything. There was during the last two acts, anyway, while I was here. Then she slipped back to her own box and waited for the show to go on. All we've got to do," he concluded sardonically, "is find the woman."

The coroner was thoughtful. "It took nerve," he remarked, at last. "You think one of these dames . . . outside . . . ?"

"Sure, it took nerve," said Dallas. "No, I don't think one of these we've got did it—not necessarily. But they were nearest to this compartment. Maybe one of them saw something—or heard something. Anyway, if there was any society row on, they'll be sure to have heard of it. We've got to start somewhere. Let's have 'em in and get it over with."

"All right," said the coroner. "When did Higginson discover Mrs. Letts was dead?"

"At the end of the first act. He didn't notice

anything wrong when he came back. It was dark in the box. He was tired of waiting at the telephone, and he sort of sneaked in and took his seat quietly. That right, Higginson?"

"That's about it," agreed Higginson.

"When he did discover it, he called *me*," concluded Dallas, "and I called *you*. And here we are," he added cheerfully.

"How about the usher that called Higginson away?"

"Left with Higginson and didn't come back. Knows nothing about it—he *says*."

"Call them in," said the coroner.

There entered first, as it happened, Miss Sally Cardiff. The summoner—Detective Sergeant Duffield—for obscure reasons of his own (reasons having to do with her eyes and hair)—had singled her out as the first victim of the inquisition.

She stopped short inside the curtains. Her eyes were very wide. They were even eager.

"Then it's true!" said Sally Cardiff.

Slightly taken aback, Dallas answered. "What's true?" he asked.

"That Mrs. Letts has been murdered!"

"Where did you hear that?" asked Dallas.

"I can *see* it—now! But I knew it before. It could only be that. Why else should the place be running over with policemen and reporters? What else could all the whispering mean? Why detain the box holders nearest to Mrs. Letts and send the rest of the audience away? And, by the way, I think *that* was a mistake, Mr. Detective."

Her eyes sparkled with animation. "Why," she said, "I knew there was something up when I saw Higginson bolt out of the box. And when *you* returned—"

"The deuce you did," said the chief of detectives. He recovered a bit from his astonishment. "When would that be, Miss Cardiff? I mean, when you saw Higginson bolt out of the box?"

"At the end of the first act. I saw him lean over and say something to Mrs. Letts. Perhaps I didn't actually *see* it—but I sensed his movement—you know? And a minute later I saw him get up and leave. I supposed Mrs. Letts had been taken ill."

"Do you know Higginson?"

"I do not. But I have seen him before—with Mrs. Letts."

"It is Mrs. Letts that you know?"

"Only casually—to speak to—in such places as this. She nodded to us all when she came in, but there was no conversation."

"Not in the same set, perhaps?" inquired the detective, with pensive malice.

But there was no sting in the question for Sally Cardiff. "Exactly," she smiled. Then the words burst from her quickly: "Who killed her?"

Dallas laughed shortly and silently. "That's what we are trying to find out. You appear to be a young woman with ideas. Have you any that might help us to answer your own question?"

Miss Cardiff was suddenly apologetic. "I'm sorry," she murmured. "I just can't help being curious. I'm a—a nuisance that way! I haven't a suspicion in the world."

But her eyes still glanced avidly in all directions—seeing everything, appraising everything. She was burning to ask a dozen questions, and a little ashamed of her curiosity. After all, what was it to her? She was probably under suspicion herself! Oddly, she felt no sense of crawling flesh in the presence of the murdered woman. Only a desire to look—to question—even to touch. To go down on her hands and knees and hunt upon the floor for clues. Good heavens! Was *this* the result of all her philosophy and reading? To make of her an amateur detective—stirred to a morbid *Who-lust* by the smell of blood?

For an instant she felt a little silly. Dallas was watching her.

"So you think it was a mistake for me to send away the audience?" he continued. "Just why, Miss Cardiff, if you don't mind?"

She hesitated. "I hardly know," she answered. "It was an impulsive remark—perhaps intuitive. I know, of course, that nobody from our own box went near this place; but I suppose I *can't* answer for the persons in the box beyond. I think your action struck me as being rather the obvious thing, Mr. . . . ."

"My name is Dallas," said Dallas, politely.

"Mr. Dallas. So obvious, in fact, as in all likelihood to be wrong. You see? That is, the man who did this would hardly—unless, of course, he were very clever indeed, and realized that the obvious thing might be overlooked—"

She was speaking, ultimately, to herself, and frowning very prettily over it, it occurred to Duffield.

Dallas studied her with profound interest. "Why do you say the *man*?" he asked suddenly.

"But wasn't it?" she cried. She stooped swiftly to the floor of the box. "Mrs. Letts's glove! See how it has been torn back from the elbow. No woman ever removed a glove that way. Why, it's almost inside out. And he's snapped a button off. Did you find the button, Mr. Dallas?"

Dallas laughed harshly. "We hadn't quite got around to that glove yet, Miss Cardiff," he answered, and swung sharply on his underlings. "Find that button, quick!"

Miss Cardiff studied the distance between the chair occupied by the corpse and the low railing of the box. "It might have jumped over the rail," she observed, "if the glove was removed in haste. And probably it was."

"Hustle downstairs and see if that button's under the balcony, Marlowe," snapped the chief of detectives. "You, too, Duffield!" Then he cleared his throat with some violence. "You are a remarkable young woman, Miss Cardiff," he continued mildly. "What else does the glove tell you?"

He waited almost respectfully for her reply.

"You see," she answered, holding out the glove for his inspection, "in a long glove of this sort there is a gusset, or opening, in the center of the palm; it extends to a point some inches upward on the wrist. This is buttoned at the top by three buttons, and it's easier to open the buttons and work the hand out through the opening than it is to take off the glove. That's the way Mrs. Letts would have done it, herself, if—for instance—she just wanted to cool her fingers."

"I see," said Dallas. "And a man wouldn't do it that way?"

"He might, I suppose; but it's unlikely. His first thought would be to turn the glove back at the top and rip it downward."

"And a woman *wouldn't*? I see!"

Miss Cardiff turned the glove back into its proper shape. "Now here," she continued calmly, "is a point that is perhaps in favor of *your* theory. Notice how the finger tips are stained. They are—"

But Dallas fairly snatched the glove from her hand.

"It's blood!" he crowed. "By George, Miss Cardiff, it's blood!" By his gleeful shout he tacitly accepted her, for the moment, as his fellow worker in the vineyard of detection—a tremendous compliment.

Miss Cardiff retrieved the glove and sniffed it. "No," she said, "it's rouge. I thought it was; that's why I said what I did."

For an instant Dallas was petrified. Then, "Of course!" he bellowed. "Of course it's rouge!" He smiled. "Then it *was* a woman, after all."

"It *may* have been," admitted Miss Cardiff, and then they both looked accusingly, for a moment, at the dead lips of Mrs. Emmanuel B. Letts. It was plainly to be seen that no rouge had been upon those lips for a long time. Certainly no scarlet rouge.

The chief of detectives thrust his head over the railing and called down to his searchers below.

"Just got it, Chief," floated upward the voice of Duffield. "By golly, she was right! It popped over like a blooming poker chip."

"Come up here again," said Dallas jovially, "and take some lessons from a detective that knows her business. . . . By George, Miss Cardiff," he continued with enthusiasm, "you are a howling wonder! There's one thing, though, that you won't discover for a time—and neither will I."

Miss Cardiff looked anxious. "What is that?" she asked.

"*Why* the murderess found it necessary to remove that glove. It's certain that Mrs. Letts didn't take it off, herself; so the other woman must have. You've made that clear, at least."

Miss Cardiff's brow cleared.

"Oh," she said, "I thought you knew why the glove had been removed. Surely the impression of the ring is quite plain on the poor woman's third finger. And from the little bulge in the corresponding finger of the glove, the stone must have been a heavy one. Obviously, a valuable ring has been stolen."

Dallas sat stunned. For a long moment he stared his complete amazement. When he spoke it was in a husky whisper.

"A ring," he echoed. "A valuable ring?" Then his eyes swung to the gleaming, glittering toy on the dead woman's throat. His bewilderment at last found other words. "She took a ring—and left that necklace?"

"Of course," smiled Sally Cardiff cheerily. "The necklace is an imitation."

Could a woman have committed the crime? Sally Cardiff doubted it. Dallas, of course, was simply prejudiced. Intuition was a funny thing. It whispered to Dallas—a man—that a woman had done this deed. To Sally Cardiff—a woman—it whispered that a man had done it. Perhaps she, also, was prejudiced.

The blow, of course, delivered from behind—and by a person stretched along the floor, and therefore *upward*—had been, no doubt, a vigorous one. But there are powerful women in the world. And perhaps the murderer had *not* stretched himself on the floor to deliver his blow. Mrs. Letts had sat well back in the box—it was dark—he could have been in the shadow of the curtains. It was all really much simpler than it appeared. But the glove button *was* an evidence of masculinity, Dallas to the contrary notwithstanding.

And yet—what of the rouge on the finger tips? Women, at times, shook hands with one another. And not heartily, as men did. They purred softly and touched finger tips! It was possible that Mrs. Letts had greeted some such creature before entering the box—and that the creature, an instant before, had dabbed at her lips.

If only the weapon could be found! Mrs. Letts had been wearing an evening dress of silver metal cloth. It had been cut high, since her back was none too lovely. The knife had penetrated the cloth to reach the flesh. Miss Cardiff hummed softly to herself. There were possibilities in the situation. But the knife was with the murderer—or the murderess. Have it your own way, Mr. Dallas! Probably it had been cleaned, anyway, and restored to its original innocence.

"And yet . . ." murmured Miss Cardiff, puckering her forehead.

It was quite late. Indeed, it was quite early. It was, in point of fact, 3 A.M. Mrs. Letts had been dead about six hours, roughly speaking. Maybe five-and-a-half. Let Dallas figure it. What difference did it make? But it *did* make a difference—didn't it? It was a legitimate supposition that the murderer—who was not a fool—had selected his time. Roughly. He couldn't be sure of Higginson, of course. Higginson *might* have left the telephone without waiting for the "important message for Mrs. Letts"; in which case . . . Anyway, the murderer had worked rapidly.

He had telephoned from somewhere *inside* the opera house. Even Dallas must be sure of that. However, there were a number of telephones in the building; they were scattered about the several lobbies and lounges, in convenient corners. For that matter, there were telephones in the *office*! At the ticket window! In every room occupied by a member of the management!

It was a shocking thought.

"*Tut!*" said Miss Cardiff.

A minute later it was less shocking. Even a member of the official staff would not have been fool enough to telephone through the switchboard. He would have gone to a public telephone. His call would then be received by an *outside* operator and would re-enter the opera house by way of another public telephone. The number of the second public telephone would be known, of course, to the murderer. Very simple. Very clever.

Miss Cardiff drew her robe more comfortably about her shoulders. The room was cooling off.

It seemed that weeks had passed since her interview with Dallas. She had been at home for more than an hour. On the way home there had been much conversation. The others had been able to tell Dallas nothing at all. Young Mr. Castle had been all for arresting Higginson at once. The Hassards had seen nothing—heard nothing—but the opera. Had the occupants of the other box? They were all closer to Mrs. Letts than the Hassard group. Closer socially. They knew more about her.

But what was there to know?

There was Emmanuel B. Letts, of course. He was still living—somewhere in the East. The divorce had occurred at least ten years before the *première* of "The Robber Kitten." It had been quiet enough: whatever scandal attached— and there was nothing sensational that one remembered—had attached to the banker Letts. As far as the murder was concerned, he seemed a bit out of the picture.

Miss Cardiff reviewed the episodes of the opera. Mrs. Letts had died during the first act. At what point? Was the uproar, at the moment, particularly furious? The overture, after all, had been the noisiest part of the performance; and Mrs. Letts was placidly alive when the overture had concluded. She recalled a trifling incident to prove it. The overture had ended, the applause of the audience had subsided, and the lines of the opera had begun. Mrs. Letts had put up her glasses and leaned forward in her chair. After a time she had leaned back again. That was all. But it proved conclusively that Mrs. Letts was not murdered during the overture.

But did it prove . . .

"Oh dear!" murmured Sally Cardiff.

Was it conceivable that Mrs. Letts had been murdered in that instant of leaning forward and leaning back again? The moment would have been admirably propitious for a murderer intent on avoiding the chair back. And the racket, at the time, surely had been sufficient. Diaz was singing an aria describing his exploits as the Robber Kitten, and doing a good job of it. The house was intent on the stage. Immediately thereafter there had been a duet between Diaz and Colchis, which could hardly have been described as a lullaby. It was a bit screechy. The orchestra, in the instrumental intervals, had been consistently boisterous. A tiny little scream in Mrs. Letts's box might well have gone unnoted.

Miss Cardiff continued to recall the incidents of the evening. Something had struck her as odd. What was it?

After a moment it occurred to her. The man in the orchestra pit who had looked like Palestrina!

She bit her lips on the fantastic thought that flashed through her mind. Mrs. Letts was a noted patron of the opera. She knew everybody. Without her guarantee it was doubtful if the opera could survive. Undoubtedly she knew Palestrina.

But did musicians use rouge?

Absurd!

Did conductors? Did Palestrina?

What wild and ridiculous nonsense! Palestrina, in point of sober fact, was actively conducting his orchestra at the moment Mrs. Letts lay back in her chair and died. Wasn't he? Of course he was. A houseful of people could testify to that. He had been right there from the beginning.

Very well! But for the sake of the argument— what if Palestrina had *not* been there, behind the conductor's stand, all the time? At *any* time! Was the likeness between himself and the violin player in the orchestra so great that one could pass as the other? Was it possible that a violin player could, without the genius of Palestrina, conduct an orchestra with Palestrina's genius?

Would it have been possible for a violin player to escape from the orchestra pit—at the conclusion of the overture, say—and go about another business?

"Oh dear!" murmured Miss Cardiff again. She sat up straight in her chair. "I'm getting quite, quite mad. But I do wish I had looked for that man in the orchestra again. *Did* he go away? And, if he did, *did* he come back?"

Then another thought occurred to her, more paralyzing than the first. . . .

The newspapers, in the morning, called attention to the statement of the coroner's physician with reference to the violence of the blow given Mrs. Letts by her assailant. It had been, it appeared, very powerful. The flesh about the wound was bruised and discolored. The inference was that only a man could have delivered such a stroke. The newspapers were inspired to this utterance by Dallas, himself, who was anxious that his private theory concerning a woman should remain in obscurity. No use warning one's suspects in advance of the big pinch. His woman obsession was one he was loath to give up, although Sally Cardiff had shaken it.

Duffield, meanwhile, had turned up a sensation. It completely revolutionized Dallas's notions when he heard about it. The word came to him over the telephone, and the chief of detectives banged his fist on the desk and swore with savage triumph.

"Good work, Duff," he said. "Wait there till I join you. I'm coming right away."

Duffield, a bit of a genius himself, had been visited by an inspiration. . . . A pilot had crashed the night before—a commercial pilot—while eastbound for New York, and now lay cursing in a small hospital in Northern Indiana. The newspaper account had been brief. Duffield had read it in an early edition. The pilot, it appeared, was concerned about the fate of his passenger; but as there had been no passenger found in the wreckage, the Indiana authorities had assumed the man to be delirious.

Duffield, without orders, had hurried to the Indiana hospital—by fast plane—and was at the pilot's bedside when he telephoned his superior. Dallas joined him at top speed, by early train. Top speed was what the company called it; but in actuality the Middle West was all but snowbound.

"Listen, Chief," said the subordinate, when he had taken his superior aside, "he said it again, right after I telephoned you!"

"The deuce he did!" said Dallas.

"Yep. There was a doctor with us, and he heard it too. He thought the fellow was trying to say 'Let's go!' which is a common phrase, it seems, among fliers. I didn't try to tell him anything different."

Dallas grinned happily. He inhaled the aseptic odors of the hospital corridor with appreciation. "It looks good to me, Duff," he said.

"It's the goods," said Duffield. "What the pilot was saying was 'Letts,' as sure as you're a foot high. His passenger was Emmanuel B. Letts—and Emmanuel B. Letts is missing! They must have left Chicago sometime last night. They got caught in the blizzard, tried to go over it—or around it—or something—and finally they crashed."

"Is this fellow going to die?"

"No—he's going to pull through."

"I suppose," said Dallas reflectively, "it couldn't have been that—"

"Not a chance," interrupted Duffield. "I thought of that. I thought maybe this fellow had done the job, himself, and was making a sneak. But why? He ain't a gunman or a gangster. He's a professional pilot. It only makes it harder, that way, Chief! There's no sense looking for a hard answer. This fellow couldn't have had anything against Mrs. Letts. The other way it's easy. A woman's husband—"

"All right," said Dallas. "It just occurred to me. Well, we've got to find Letts. Where was the crash?"

"About five miles from here—out in the country."

"Who found the pilot?"

"A farmer. He lives near where it happened. He telephoned the police here, when he heard the crash, and they went out and got him. Got the pilot."

"No suspicions, of course," said Dallas, "so they wouldn't look around. I'll bet they've trampled the snow like a flock of elephants."

Duffield shrugged. "Well," he said, "the snow's been falling pretty steady ever since. There wouldn't have been any footprints, anyway."

"He couldn't go far," mused Dallas. Then he

brightened and spoke more cheerfully. "Maybe he was hurt! He'd almost *have* to be. Maybe the farmer's got him. Anyway, he's hiding somewhere."

"They ain't always hurt," said Duffield, morosely. "First thing he'd think of 'd be a train. He'd have to get that *here*."

"Would he?" questioned Dallas. "Well, that's something. You've looked up the morning trains, I suppose?"

"The storm has shot schedules all to hell," said Duffield. "The train you came on should have left Chicago last night. There's plenty of time as far as trains are concerned."

"This fellow have anything in his pockets?"

"Nothing we want."

"*Hmph*," grumbled Dallas. "Well, you're a good dick, Duffy! Let's get going."

They assured themselves that there was no chance of the pilot's miraculous recovery and disappearance during their absence, then plunged into the snow-clad streets. Their first visit was to the railroad station. No stranger had been inquiring for trains East, however, and they pushed on to police headquarters, where their advent created a sensation. Dallas was a very famous detective.

"I'll go with you, myself," said the chief of police, with flattering emphasis. "My driver knows every road in the county."

"He'll need a snow plow," observed Duffield grimly. "I wish criminals would stop operating in the winter."

The drive to the scene of the accident was cold and difficult; but at last they stood beside the twisted framework of the plane—a gaunt and melancholy spectacle with its insulation of gleaming snow. A glance was sufficient to tell the experienced Chicagoan detectives that a hunt for clues would be useless. They stood in snow to their knees and looked gloomily at the tragic tangle of wood and metal. They kicked their aching feet against the dead motors, and swore thoughtfully.

"Any roadhouses near here?" asked Dallas, at length. "Hotels? Any place he could have gone?"

"There's Braxton's," said the police chief. "It's five miles the other way."

"Letts wouldn't necessarily know his directions," said Dallas. "All right. Let's go to Braxton's."

They drove toilsomely to Braxton's—a two-story shack whose creaking signboard, festooned with snow bunting, announced its *raison d'être* in a single laconic word: TOURISTS. The slattern in charge was unimpressed by their descent. No guests had come to her the night before, nor during the morning hours either. She brightened when they ordered coffee, which they drank standing.

Then again the snow-piled highway took them. They were heading back, now, toward the town. On all sides stretched desolate miles of glistening white. Trees were hung with it. Fences drooped with its weight.

Not far from the wrecked plane the land fell away into a hollow, from out of which now rose a lazy question mark of smoke.

"What's that?" asked Dallas.

"Neilson's," answered the police chief briefly. "The fellow that found the pilot," he explained. "He don't know anything about it."

"Oh?" said Dallas. "Let's have a look at him, anyway. There seems to be a bit of a path there."

They swung inward and upward for a piece; then their wheels spun uselessly in unbroken drifts of snow and ice. Duffield climbed out of the car.

"Get back to the road, if you can," he said. "I'll go up to the house."

He plunged forward on foot, wading in snow to his waist, and at length breasted the hillock. Behind him the stalled car fumed and chugged, endeavoring to back.

Duffield's eyes fell first on the low dwelling of the farmer Neilson, all but snowbound in the hollow. Then he saw something else. From an upper window a man was watching him who, after an instant, began frantically to wave his arms. He seemed to be summoning Duffield to the house. Neilson, no doubt—but what the devil did the fellow want? Had he seen the car?

He strode onward with large steps and at length burst a path to the farmhouse door. The man at the window had disappeared. In the doorway, suddenly, were two men. The second man was obviously Neilson; he could be no one else. But the first man was a man of substance and position if ever Duffield had seen one. He was tall and powerful, running a bit to flesh, and his garments were expensive and of the latest cut. Obviously, too, they had been exposed to the elements.

The big man was excited. "I heard your car from the window," he said, "and I thought I had a glimpse of it. Are you going up to town?"

There was no doubt in Duffield's mind. He had never seen Emmanuel B. Letts or his portrait; but he knew that this was Emmanuel B. Letts.

"Why, yes," he drawled. "Wanta come along?"

"You bet," said the stranger. "I had a breakdown, last night, and had to put in for repairs. I'll tell you about it as we go along."

"Reckon I heard about that," smiled Duffield. "Your pilot's in the hospital, ain't he?"

"Pilot?" echoed the other. "No, no—I heard about that, myself. Poor chap! No, I was driving. Wait till I get my traps." He hurried away upstairs, leaving Neilson staring at Duffield with deep suspicion.

"You don't belong in these parts," said the farmer, after a moment. "What was it you was wanting, when you came along?"

"Your house guest," answered Duffield promptly. He swung his heavy overcoat aside, then swung back the jacket underneath. Before the menace of his little badge the farmer fell away. "Not a word out of you," continued the detective. In a swift whisper he asked: "What did he give you?"

Neilson's eyes fell, then lifted. "A hundred dollars," he said defiantly.

"Keep it," said Duffield. "What'd he tell you?"

"He was with the pilot that was wrecked; but he didn't want it known. It was a secret trip, he said, and would hurt business if it was spread around."

"Keep your mouth shut till you're told to open it," said Duffield, "and I'll keep still about the hundred."

Letts was lumbering down the crooked stairs, clutching his satchel. He was now attired in a significant leather jacket.

"I'll be glad to get away," said the big man happily. "Not but what your hospitality has been fine, Mr. Neilson; but I've got things to do, after all." He turned on Duffield with belated suspicion. "You live around here, I suppose? Just breaking a path to town, eh?"

"Right you are," said Duffield jovially. "And glad to have you with me, Mr. . . . ?" He hesitated before the name.

"I'll make it worth your while," nodded Letts. "My name is Rogers. Maybe you can tell me about the trains out of town. I'm a stranger in the neighborhood, myself."

They fought their way through the drifts, stepping where possible in the holes made by Duffield in his advance upon the house. As they crested the rise, the detective noted that his companions had worked the car back into the road. Two of them—Dallas and the local chief—were performing a slow dance in the snow, pausing occasionally to kick their aching feet against the framework of the car. The chauffeur sat stolidly behind his wheel.

"Friends of mine," said Duffield, in answer to the other's inquiring glance. "All going up to town, the same as we are."

They finished their plunge to the roadway and stopped beside the car. Dallas and the police chief were trying not to stare.

"In you go, boys," cried Duffield. "This gentleman is going along as far as the railway station."

The police chief climbed in beside his chauffeur. Dallas slipped into the rear seat and made room for the newcomer beside him. The last to enter the car was Duffield. The car started with a jerk.

"This is Mr. Rogers, Chief," said Duffield, chattily. "He wants to catch the first train East."

Dallas smiled blandly on their sudden prisoner. He had looked at a portrait of Emmanuel B. Letts before leaving Chicago. He softly rubbed his knuckles.

"I sympathize with Mr. Rogers," he murmured; and laid his heavy hand on the other's shoulder.

Young Mr. Castle was annoyed. He had no objections to playing chauffeur to Sally Cardiff—it was his ambition to land a permanent job in that and other servile capacities—but her detectival activities set his back up. The excitement of Mrs. Letts's murder had gone to her head, apparently. He was forced to admit, however, that Miss Cardiff was not unduly excited. She was eager, but calm enough, all things considered. She was even dispassionate. Her theories of the murder were fantastic, they were the utmost nonsense; but she argued them plausibly. Somewhere, he felt certain, there was a flaw in her reasoning; but he was never able—while she was talking—to put his finger on it.

"And the publicity of it," he had stormed at her. "Suppose you were right! Can't you just see the newspapers? My dear girl, there would be nothing left for you to do but open a private inquiry agency."

"My curiosity is impersonal," she explained. "It's just—just curiosity! I really don't care two straws whether the murderer gets justice or doesn't. It's the chase—you know. My wits against his—and both of us against the police. I don't think I'm morbid, Arnold. As for Dallas—can't you see him taking all the credit? Why, I'll *hand* it to him. I'll toss it to him as I would to a—a fish!"

"Good old sea lion," grinned Castle.

That had been their latest discussion of the subject. It all flickered, cinema-like, through his mind as he sat behind the wheel of his gray roadster and looked up at the gloomy windows of the big warehouse beside which, at the moment, he was parked. Sally Cardiff was inside.

In time she emerged. On the instant all his dissatisfaction fell away. Her face was beaming.

Her step was brisk and triumphant. With what decision her tall heels clicked on the stone flags! And what a glorious small person, in all aspects, was this Sally Cardiff!

"Don't get out," she said, climbing in beside him. She sank back with a long sigh of relief. "It's over," she said.

"You've failed?" he asked quickly—hopefully.

"I've won!"

He drove the roadster furiously through a narrow crack between two taxicabs, beat a changing traffic light by an eyelash, and turned a corner in haste.

"Where to?" he asked, after a time.

"I'm wondering," said Miss Cardiff. "To the Detective Bureau, I suppose. Not that I fancy myself, now, in the role of tale teller; but there's the chance that I'll be able to keep Dallas from making a fool of himself."

"You're quite sure you're not making—*er*—committing an error, yourself?"

"Oh, quite!"

He sighed. "What did you find in the warehouse?" There had been a package under her arm when she emerged. Now it lay across her knee. He eyed it with suspicion.

But she did not lift the parcel. Instead, she opened her small purse, with infinite care, and extracted a tiny envelope.

"Slow down," she ordered, "and look inside."

He almost expected to see a human eyeball staring up at him from the inside of the envelope.

What he saw was exactly nothing. Or did she mean that thread of dust that had settled in a corner of the envelope? As he looked, she shifted the container in her hands; and the thread of dust turned over on its side and glinted.

He looked quickly away. "What is it?"

"Mrs. Letts, you will recall, wore a metal-cloth evening dress. It was cut high. The knife passed through it. This is a shred of the material."

"Get out!" he scoffed. But he was astounded.

"Actually. It can't be anything else. It adhered to the point of the knife."

Castle was stunned. "Oh, come off, Sally!" he cried at last. "It couldn't!"

"It did. Ordinarily, it wouldn't. I mean, it wouldn't adhere to an ordinary knife. This knife was not ordinary. It was rather a blunt knife, with a damaged tip. You remember what the coroner's physician said about the wound? An unusually violent blow was required. That was why. The blade didn't have a point."

He was still incredulous. "And you found it—still clinging to the knife?"

"Oh, no! It was on the jacket of the other man. Almost under the arm. I'm glad it was a rough jacket. The knife, of course, was cleaned—but this little shred—just a twisted thread or two—remained in the broken tip. It was dislodged by the murderer's second thrust—*later*—and remained among the hairs of the jacket."

"Well, I'll be hanged!"

"Somebody will be," smiled Miss Cardiff.

"And the knife proves this, too?"

"Yes—the point is damaged, as I explained. I've got it here, with the jacket."

"How on earth did you get away with them?"

"I simply dared them to stop me."

"Great Scott!" said young Mr. Castle, feebly inadequate. After a moment he asked: "Won't they tell?"

"I don't know. I warned them not to—but I suppose they know, by now, what I was really after. I don't care much. The rest of it is up to Dallas. After all, I'm not a policeman."

Castle smiled a mirthless smile. "No?" he interrogated; and answered himself with grave irony: "No—I suppose not!"

They were incongruous figures on the steps of the Detective Bureau—that sinister gray building with its dingy corridors.

A staring desk sergeant directed them to Dallas's office. In the outer chamber a hard but smirking secretary stopped them. Dallas, it appeared, was in conference.

"My God," said Castle, "do they have them here, too?"

Miss Cardiff smiled attractively. "If you could just slip my name in to him," she whispered, "I think he might consent to see us. In fact, I'm sure of it." She proffered her visiting card.

The secretary smirked and frowned and smirked again. "I ain't saying I haven't heard of you, Miss Cardiff," he observed. "Well, just wait a minute, and maybe—"

He disappeared through a swinging door, into a room across which they saw another door. They heard the second door close behind him.

They waited exactly two minutes.

Then Dallas came hurriedly into the anteroom. He was very courteous.

"I'm glad to see you, Miss Cardiff," he said, ignoring Castle. "But I *am* busy—there's no use denying it. If it's important . . . ?"

"It *is* rather important, I think," answered Miss Cardiff. "I've come to tell you who killed Mrs. Letts."

The chief of detectives stared, speechless. After a moment, "Oh!" he murmured. After another moment he grinned. "To tell you the truth, Miss Cardiff, we've got the fellow, ourselves. Brought him up from Indiana, last night. I was questioning him when you arrived. You were certainly right about his being a man."

"He was running away, then?" cried Sally Cardiff.

"Just as fast as he could go," agreed Dallas.

"And he has confessed?"

"He *will* confess, before I get through with him," said Dallas grimly. "At the moment, between ourselves, he's holding out."

"What does he say? Of course, he hasn't a leg to stand on!"

"I agree with you, but he hasn't been able to see that—yet. Look here, have you got proof?"

"Positively."

"Good enough! It isn't customary to discuss these matters, but with *you* I will." Dallas was at once flattering and unctuous. He needed proof—it was all he did need.

"He admits he attended the opera—privately—but swears he knows nothing of the murder. Gave a very good imitation of a man being shocked, when we told him. Says his presence in Chicago was entirely due to business matters—very important! So important that he came here from the East secretly. Something to do with a bank merger which, if it got out, would upset business to beat the—to beat the band. Affect the stock market, and so on. Very plausible. He had his story all ready, obviously. So secret that, after the opera—and incidentally after the murder—he took a fast plane to get back to New York. Unfortunately, he crashed in Indiana. We were on the job—and we got him."

Miss Cardiff had listened to this explanation with growing wonder. "Who under the sun are you talking about?" she asked, at length.

"Emmanuel B. Letts," said Dallas. "Former husband of Mrs. Emmanuel B. Letts, deceased. Who are *you* talking about?"

"Oh, my goodness!" cried Sally Cardiff. "You've got the wrong man!"

For an instant they stared at each other in silence. It was Dallas who spoke first. "Oh, I think not," he said. But his eyes were worried.

"But you *have*," she insisted. "I *know* it!"

The smirking secretary put his head in at the door for an instant. He made signs to Dallas.

"Get out of here!" roared Dallas in a fury. Then with an effort he controlled himself. "You were saying, Miss Cardiff?"

"I think," said Sally Cardiff, "I'd better tell you my story from the beginning, Mr. Dallas. I'm sure you must have forgotten the most important clue of all—the rouge on Mrs. Letts's glove."

"That rouge!" said Dallas scornfully. "It had nothing to do with it."

"It had everything to do with it. Does Mr. Letts use rouge?"

"Of course not. At least, I'm certain he doesn't."

"So am I. If you'd said he did, I'd have been bothered. Listen, Mr. Dallas. Mrs. Letts wasn't killed by anybody in the audience. She was killed by someone on the stage."

Into the harassed eyes of the detective chieftain crept a look of relieved understanding. He understood it all now. This attractive girl had simply gone cuckoo. She had been thinking too hard about the murder. It often happened that way.

He smiled tolerantly. "I hardly think that can be the case, Miss Cardiff," he said. "After all, the people on the stage had their own business to attend to. They were singing—and dancing—and carrying on—and Mrs. Letts, you will remember, was killed during the first act."

"You think I'm crazy?" Sally Cardiff laughed delightedly. "I give you my word, Mr. Dallas, if you arrest Mr. Letts for this crime, you will have a very nasty time on your hands—afterwards!"

The worried look again crept into Dallas's eyes.

"Well, well," he cried jovially, "let's hear your story, Miss Cardiff. I'm sure it will be an interesting one—and very clever."

For the second time she opened her tiny purse and extracted her envelope. She laid it in his hand. Then she fumbled with her parcel. There emerged a shaggy jacket of theatrical aspect and a gaudy dagger somewhat battered at the tip—but all the more formidable by reason of the damage. A toy that had become an ugly weapon.

"The envelope," continued Sally Cardiff crisply, "contains a few threads of Mrs. Letts's dress. These other things came out of a theatrical warehouse, this afternoon—the warehouse where 'The Robber Kitten' is in storage till its next performance. This is the knife that murdered Mrs. Letts. The threads clung to this battered tip, you see, and later were transferred to the jacket of an actor who was murdered in the play. Not really murdered, you understand. In the opera! It took nerve to pretend to murder a man on the stage after *really* murdering a woman in the audience!"

She paused impressively; but Dallas had no words to utter.

"There is a rehearsal on at the opera house, right now, Mr. Dallas. It will last until five o'clock. Our man will be there. Will you come with me?"

For a long minute Dallas met the challenge of her eyes. Then he wilted.

"And Letts?" he questioned.

"Why not bring him along?"

There was another silence. Then Dallas spoke with epoch-marking decision.

"I'll do it," he said. "Wait till I get my hat."

The orchestra was hard at work and, miraculously, playing something tuneful. But there was little time for listening, and after a few moments of unconscious lagging Castle hastened after his companions. No questions were asked of them. Here and there in the darkened house were other groups, standing or sitting: officials, critics, members of the company not engaged on the stage.

They crowded through a small door, concealed by curtains, climbed a flight of steps, and suddenly found themselves backstage. Only Letts and Dallas—and on different errands—had been in such a place before. A number of performers were standing around; but small attention was paid the newcomers. The light behind the scenes was gratifyingly dim.

"Now, Mr. Dallas, we must work quickly—before we are suspected. I almost wish you had worn a disguise."

"Good Lord!" gulped Dallas. "I never wore one in my life."

"We've simply got to find the telephone he used," said Sally Cardiff. "The one he *must* have used. Remember, it was a public telephone. He would never have operated through the switchboard. Now where would the dressing rooms be, Mr. Letts?"

The mountainous Letts indicated.

"I see. Very well, then—he would go first to his dressing room, remove his mustache and his furry ears, pick up his dagger, then return to this section. Without his costume—it was only a headdress, after all—he would appear to be just a man in evening garments. The house was in darkness—the play was going on. Everybody was intent on the story. His make-up would not be noted. If he left by the door by which we entered, he would be out among the audience in a jiffy—just a quiet man walking up the aisle."

"There are no telephones in the audito-rium proper, Miss Cardiff," said Emmanuel B. Letts positively. "They're all in the lobbies and lounges."

"Yes—and so he did *not* go out into the audience. The nearest exit light is over there." She walked swiftly to the door she had indicated and opened it. "Exactly! This is an entrance to the mezzanine lobby—an exit, if you like." She put her head outside and cocked it at an angle of interrogation. "And at the far end of this corridor there's a telephone booth! Quite perfect, you see. He knew beforehand exactly what he would do. He knew the number of the other telephone he was to call. From the first booth he called the second booth; and when a boy answered, he asked that Higginson be summoned from Mrs. Letts's box. Higginson came—and was asked to hold the wire. Then the other man quietly stood his receiver on the shelf and hurried to the front."

She stepped into the corridor, and the others followed.

"Why did nobody see him?" asked Castle suddenly. "The lobbies and lounges are studded with pages and ushers."

For a moment Sally Cardiff was stunned. It was a question she had never asked herself. Was it possible, after all, that there had been more than one person in the plot? *Had* somebody seen the murderer and kept silence?

"For that matter," said Dallas, a shrewd eye suddenly on Emmanuel B. Letts, "why did nobody but the boy who summoned him see Higginson go to the telephone and return? We questioned the whole staff about that."

But Emmanuel B. Letts knew the answer. "I think I can answer both questions, Miss Cardiff," he said gallantly. "The opera was being presented for the first time. The ushers, once their charges were safely seated, slipped off to their own points of vantage—wherever they may be—and watched the opera. They always do it, unless it is something familiar and boring to them. Most of them, in fact, are students of music—that's why they have these jobs."

"Why, yes," smiled Sally Cardiff, "I think

that must have been it. At any rate," she continued, briskly, "he met nobody—nobody, at any rate, who later connected him with the crime. He knew Mrs. Letts's box, and he slipped in quickly. Then I think he dropped softly to his knees. Mrs. Letts's back was to him. She must have been very close to his hand.

"He knelt," she continued, "at a moment when the orchestra was playing its loudest, or when the orchestra and chorus were in full swing together. Obviously he had no immediate business, himself, on the stage. Everything was planned with the utmost care."

"And the rouge?" asked Dallas.

"He had it on his face. It was part of his make-up. Some of it he rubbed off, no doubt, before leaving his dressing room. But it worried him. He knew it would be noticed if *he* was noticed. I think as he hurried along the corridors, before reaching the lounge and entering the box, his nervousness kept him dabbing at his cheeks— possibly he thought that way to conceal his features. The rouge would adhere to his finger tips, and then—after the murder—when he tried to remove the glove—you see?"

Dallas nodded unwillingly. "The rouge was on the finger tips of the glove," he reminded her. "It was once your opinion—"

"No, yours—*yours* always! I said it *might* have been a woman *or* a man; but I always believed the murderer to have been a man. First he attempted, as I pointed out, to tear the glove off by turning it inside out—a wholly masculine idea. It wouldn't work that way—so, he tugged at the fingers."

"Why did he want the ring?"

"I don't know—but I think, now, that robbery was not his motive. I doubt that he knew the necklace wasn't genuine. To him it would seem real enough. It was only when I saw it at close quarters that I realized it was false."

"Why did he kill her?"

"I don't know, Mr. Dallas—I only know he did."

"What was she to him?" persisted the chief of detectives.

"I can only guess."

Emmanuel B. Letts was registering embarrassment. He coughed deprecatingly. "One hears gossip," he said. Then he stopped and tried again. "I don't pretend that this has hit me very hard, Dallas. There's been nothing between Mrs. Letts and myself for a long time. Still, I'm shocked; and I'd like to see justice done. As I say, one hears gossip—whether or not one wishes to. People persist in believing that I must still be interested in her actions." He shrugged and his face twisted.

"Well, she met him in Italy, when she was there. She helped him, as she had helped others. I suppose, ultimately, she thought she had fallen in love with him. She was not—" he hesitated— "wholly admirable. I'm sorry to say that. For him, of course, it was—to be brutal—just duck soup! An elderly woman with tons of money; and all she asked in return was a little—shall we say?—attention."

Sally Cardiff looked at him with horror and compassion. And over and above and back-grounding his unhappy disillusionment rose now from the theater the triumphant strains of a great love chorus.

"Then that," said Sally Cardiff, in a low voice, "explains a great deal, Mr. Letts. When she discovered that—"

"Exactly."

"Exactly what?" demanded Dallas, annoyed.

"He was the co-respondent in the Colchis-Palestrina divorce," said Sally Cardiff. "Obviously, he was through with *her*—with Mrs. Letts. She had helped him to rise, and then when he no longer needed her—"

Dallas digested this information. "That would give *her* a reason for hating *him*," he agreed. "If *she* had killed *him*, I could understand it. But—"

Miss Cardiff nodded. "It's still puzzling," she admitted.

"It's crazy," said Dallas.

"Unless she were going to break him, in some way," contributed young Mr. Castle, with sudden inspiration.

Miss Cardiff looked startled, as so did Dallas. Emmanuel B. Letts, wiser in the ways of the world even than the policeman, only nodded his head.

A glorious tenor voice was now ringing through the auditorium—soaring on wings of song. When its last note had died away there came from the stage and from the interior of the house a burst of spontaneous applause that reached the group that stood and plotted in the lobby.

Then voices were heard—closer at hand.

"They're coming," gasped Sally Cardiff, in sudden panic. "Mr. Dallas—shall you—shall I—"

For the first time she was nervous. But it was not fear—if anything it was stage fright.

"Leave it to Dallas," counseled young Mr. Castle; and he attempted to draw her away. But she slipped from his grasp and stepped quickly through the lobby door into the wings.

A tall young man, obviously Italian, was striding toward the dressing rooms. His face was still flushed with pleasure at the recognition of his peers. He paused and looked with benevolent curiosity at the group that suddenly confronted him—prepared, if it was their wish, to be amiable for a moment or two. Perhaps an autograph . . .

"Mr. Diaz," said Sally Cardiff casually, "there is only one thing that still bothers me. Well, two! But first of all—what was your *reason* for murdering Mrs. Letts?"

Orlando Diaz did not collapse. For an instant, though, he wavered, and Dallas stepped forward. Then a long sigh passed the tenor's lips and he drew himself upright. He bowed profoundly to the small person who stood before him.

"It was because, dear lady, she had threatened to end my operatic career—and because I knew she could do it."

"And the ring?" she continued. "The ring you took from her finger?"

"It was my own, dear lady—one that I had

given her. It was foolish to take it. It would have been foolish to leave it. Either way, it would have pointed to me."

She nodded her understanding, and, turning, took the arm of Arnold Castle. Even as they moved to leave they saw Dallas again step forward.

But at the door she stopped him. "I can't go yet," she said. "I simply can't, Arnold. Run back, like an angel, and find Palestrina. I've simply *got* to know. Ask him if he has a brother in the orchestra."

Mr. Castle ran back. After a time he returned. "He *has*," he reported. "A *twin* brother."

"I was sure it must be something like that."

After a long silence, during which the car sped nowhere in particular, his secret admiration burst its seals. "Sally," he said, "you're simply *great*! Do you mind if—like good old Watson—I ask one final question?"

"Of course not, silly!"

"What under the canopy was the first thing that led you to suspect Diaz? Someone on the stage, rather than someone in the audience!"

"It was that belated curtain call. You remember it? They clapped and clapped and clapped—and still he didn't come. At last he *did* come. It was most unlike him—unlike *any* opera star. I wondered where he had been, and what he had been doing. And after a while I knew something had kept him. He just got back in time—and I think it was a very narrow squeak for Diaz."

"It was," agreed Arnold Castle, with conviction. "All the good it did him in the end! Do you know, Sally, I think I'm a little afraid of you! It's rather alarming to contemplate—er—having a detective in the family—er—"

Miss Cardiff blushed a little.

"Don't be silly," she said. "There'll be times when I'll be grateful for a good old Watson."

BURGLARS MUST DINE

E. Phillips Oppenheim

KNOWN BY READERS and especially his publishers as "The Prince of Story-tellers," Edward Phillips Oppenheim (1866–1946) was a prolific author who gave his readers exactly what they hoped for: thrilling, fast-paced stories that afforded them a glimpse of the lives of the rich and famous. He was the right man for the job, as his bestselling books made him both fabulously rich and happy to enjoy every shilling of that wealth.

In addition to his 115 novels (including five under the pseudonym Anthony Partridge), Oppenheim produced hundreds of short stories that were published in top magazines for top dollar, all of them being collected in forty-four volumes. His staggering output was achieved by dictating to a secretary (whom he then allowed to edit his work and send it off, commonly not bothering to review it)—but not past the cocktail hour, which frequently meant a party for a hundred or more people aboard the yacht on which he lived.

Leaving school at an early age to work in his father's leather business, he worked all day and then wrote until late at night. He had thirty books published by the time he turned forty and sold the leather business to devote himself full time to writing novels of international intrigue, mystery, and crime. The plot-driven stories feature beautiful, glamorous, mainly vacuous young women, while the men are often heroic, though there is little to distinguish them from one another.

Oppenheim's most important book is *The Great Impersonation* (1920), a Haycraft-Queen cornerstone title in which a disgraced English aristocrat overcomes his alcoholism when England needs him to outwit the Germans as the First World War looms. It was filmed three times, all with the same title as the book: in 1921, as a silent starring James Kirkwood; in 1935, starring Edmund Lowe and Valerie Hobson; and in 1942, updating the story line to focus on events leading to World War II, starring Ralph Bellamy and Evelyn Ankers.

Lucy Mott meets "Violet Joe," the male protagonist in the series, in a story titled "Ask Miss Mott," originally published in the February 9, 1935, issue of *Collier's Magazine.* It was substantially revised and given a new title, "Burglars Must Dine," when it was collected in book form in *Ask Miss Mott* (London, Hodder & Stoughton, 1936); the story published here is taken from the book.

Burglars Must Dine

E. PHILLIPS OPPENHEIM

MISS LUCY MOTT'S first client in the secondary profession which she had so recently adopted made his appearance in sufficiently unusual and alarming fashion.

There was a crash of glass behind her chair, the swinging up of a sash, and a stooping figure sprang lightly into the room. Not only was this unceremonious entrance in itself terrifying—all the more so as Miss Mott's little office was situated on the sixth floor of a block of apartments—but the intruder entered wearing a narrow, black mask over the upper part of his face.

Miss Mott swung round in her chair and gasped in amazement. It was, however, an astonishing but undeniable fact. A burglar, who would appear to have descended from the clouds, had pushed open her window, entered her office and was now crossing the room towards her in haste. Her hand shot out for the telephone.

"Don't touch that, please," the newcomer said.

Miss Mott, new to such adventures, made the fatal mistake of hesitating to parley.

"Why not?" she demanded. "How dare you! What do you want?"

She realized then that she had already lost valuable time. She turned once more towards the telephone, but she was too late. There was a grip upon her arm, not exactly painful but exceedingly firm. She was conscious at that moment of only two things. The first was the compelling power of those flashing eyes through the slits of the mask, the second a fragrant perfume of violets.

"A moment, if you please," the newcomer said. "I owe you an explanation. You shall have it. Please leave the telephone alone. You will only cause trouble if you use it."

Miss Mott remained silent, a condition of mental inactivity for which the ease and confidence of the man's tone were alike responsible.

"There's nothing to be alarmed at, I can assure you," he went on. "I am in the same profession as you, only at the other end. Honor among thieves, you know. What a horrid draft! Will you promise me not to use the telephone if I go back and close the window?"

"What do you mean by saying that I am in the same profession as you?" she demanded.

"You're Miss Mott, aren't you?" he said. "Niece of my old friend Superintendent Wragge of Scotland Yard. You have conducted for some years a correspondence column in a woman's magazine entitled 'Home Talks,' and you have been so successful that you have started a little Information Bureau of your own. You see, I know all about you! May I close the window?"

"I shall catch my death of cold if you don't," Miss Mott said.

"Will you promise not to use the telephone?"

"I suppose so," she said grudgingly.

He recrossed the room, looked regretfully at the broken pane and drew the curtain over it. When he returned he was binding a handkerchief around his finger.

"You had better explain what you are doing here," she said. "Honest people don't wear masks during business hours or break through windows. And perhaps you will tell me while you are about it where on earth you came from?"

"May I sit down?" he asked.

She indicated the clients' chair drawn up to the side of her desk. He took it at once, moving it, she noticed, a trifle nearer to the table so that he was within reach of the telephone. He removed his black Homburg hat with a word of apology and placed it on the floor by his side.

"Well," he said, "I came up by the fire escape, if you want to know."

"By the fire escape," she repeated wonderingly.

"And if you want to know more still I have not come far. I have come from the floor below."

"The bridge club?"

He nodded. "Yes, the Hyacinth Bridge Club."

"Have you been stealing things from there?" she asked.

He drew a package which was protruding from his pocket—an oblong parcel securely wrapped up in brown paper.

"Quite right," he said. "I committed a theft. It was not such an easy affair as I had hoped either."

Lucy Mott shrunk a little away from the parcel. Somehow or other it had a sinister appearance. "What is it?" she asked. "I don't like the looks of it."

He patted it with his hand and sighed. "You are quite right," he said. "It is a messy affair, more vicious than any atomic bomb that was ever made. Harmless enough to look at, but a very incriminating weapon to use or to have found in one's possession."

"Then why did you steal it?"

He smiled. "Well, that's another matter. The thing is—I want to get rid of it for a few hours. May I leave it in your charge?"

"Certainly not," Lucy replied coldly. "I am not a receiver of stolen property."

"But this," he pleaded, "is an unusual affair. I can assure you, Miss Mott, that notwithstanding my appearance and actions I am not a criminal. I dabble in irregularities but I also have leanings towards philanthropy. On the present occasion I have stolen this compromising and, I have to admit, dangerous package to save the reputation, perhaps the life, of a very charming and popular lady whose disappearance would be regretted by all of her friends."

Miss Mott looked at him severely. The curious part of the whole affair was that she felt herself inclined to believe him.

"I am still, however," he went on slowly, "only half-way through the job. I need your help to conclude the affair. I do not know whether you have as yet formulated your scale of charges, but if you are not prohibitive I should like, for a suitable fee, to engage you for the rest of the evening."

"What would be the nature of the services you require from me?" Lucy asked gently.

"I should like to ask your permission to leave your office and descend to the elevator as though I had been an ordinary caller," he said. "Furthermore, I should like you to relieve me of this package for the time being, place it in that brief case," he added, pointing across the room, "take it home with you while you change your clothes, and bring it back to a rendezvous, which we have yet to fix upon, where you will dine with me tonight."

Curiosity grew in Lucy Mott and amazement shone out of her eyes. "I suppose you are real?" she said. "This is not some sort of a dream?" she added hastily.

"I am an actual human being," he assured her, stretching out his hand. "Would you like to feel my fingers to be sure of it?"

"Certainly not," she said. "I have felt them round my arm and I expect I shall have a bruise there tomorrow. You climb through my window wearing a mask, you smash a perfectly good pane of glass to get at the fastening, you confess to have committed a burglary, and you have the impertinence to ask me to take care of the proceeds and dine with you—a perfect stranger—tonight. By the way, what is your name?"

"Ah," he said. "That is a problem."

"Well, you must have one, you know," she said. "You seem to be taking it for granted that I am as eccentric a person as you are. But you can't expect a young woman to dine with a man whose name she doesn't even know."

"My name is Joseph," he said.

"Joseph who?" she asked.

"Joseph of Arimathea, if you like," he answered carelessly.

"So when I arrive at the restaurant where you propose to entertain me tonight," she said, "I am to ask for Mr. Arimathea!"

"You won't need to ask for anyone," he said. "I shall be sitting there waiting for you."

"Wearing that atrocious thing?" she asked, pointing to the mask.

"Not likely," he said. "You will see me as I present myself sometimes. Later, when we are better acquainted, you may discover that my appearance often varies according to my health—and the circumstances."

Lucy sat upright in her chair. "Listen, Mr. Joseph," she said, "we are wasting time. Supposing you tell me what is in that package."

"Something with which you would not like to be found," he said.

"The usual stuff, I suppose? Letters?"

"Nothing of the sort. I cannot at present divulge to anyone the contents of this package. I only want you to keep it for me until this evening. If I could find any way of destroying it here I would do so. There isn't any means, however. I have to rely on you."

"Why not take it away yourself?"

"Because," he explained, "if I have been rightly informed, the elevator does not mount as high as this, and on my way out, therefore, I shall have to pass the door of the Hyacinth Club. If my escapade of this evening has been discovered they might be waiting for me."

"The police?"

"Possibly the police," he admitted, "although sometimes these affairs are not fought out with the police."

"Where exactly did you steal the package from?" she insisted.

"Have you ever been inside the Hyacinth Club?" he enquired.

"Never."

"There is a small room, very much like what we call in golf clubs a locker room, with steel cupboards where members can keep their parcels or some of them even a change of clothes. It is rather a convenience for members living a little way out-of-town. Through influential friends in a different branch of the profession I obtained a master key and stole this packet from one of those lockers."

"How interesting!" Miss Mott exclaimed. "And afterwards?"

"Afterwards I crawled out of the window, risked a short drop on to a small balcony and from there by the fire escape I ascended to your apartment."

"And why was I chosen for this honor?"

"To tell you the truth," he explained, "I had managed to enter the club without being seen by taking the tradesmen's elevator, but I knew that my luck would not hold. Besides, the hall porter is on duty now."

"And did you wear that mask all the time that you were in the club?"

"I put it on when I began to climb the fire escape," he said. "I should be ashamed of it if I were really working professionally. It is old-fashioned. The new cut has long flaps!"

"You seem to me to be very talkative," she said.

"So far," he said, "I seem to have talked too much without having made much progress. What I want you to promise, if you will be so kind, is that in your capacity as a helper of men and women you will slip into an evening gown at eight o'clock—black would suit you very well, I think, with your perfect hair and your perfect complexion—and with the package which I propose to leave with you in a brief case, meet me at some not too well-known restaurant, say Mario's, at half-past eight."

"Thank you," she said. "I never dine out."

"My dear Miss Mott," he said, "is it not true that you have embarked upon a career of adventure, that you have committed yourself professionally to become the helper of anyone in difficulties?"

"I suppose it is more or less true."

"You are the Miss Mott, the *one* Miss Mott, who advises her clients in all cases of difficulty and who teaches people how to live their lives to the best advantage. It is your ambition to penetrate into every nook and cranny of the world of human beings. I have heard all about you, you see! How can you lead the life adventurous if you refuse to dine with a humble and, you must believe me, not vicious criminal?

"There is much that you still have to learn concerning my profession. I will be your instructor. I will show you how to circumvent the efforts of the more dangerous members of my craft. Besides, I shall probably, by dinner-time, be in a position to satisfy your curiosity regarding the contents of the package."

"You are really going to leave it with me—to trust me with it?" she asked.

"I should trust you with most things in life," he said.

"I think," she said, "that you are mad!"

"And I," he said, "think that you are terribly attractive. That little dash of color—anger, I'm afraid—becomes you, and I wish I could believe that I were the first to tell you that your eyes are marvellous. At half-past eight, then, I shall be waiting for you in the hall of Mario's. Don't be surprised if at first you fail to recognize me. I have many personalities.

"I promise you one thing, however. I will not present myself in the guise of a bespectacled clergyman from somewhere in the northern counties. Nothing so amateurish as that. At half-past eight then!"

He rose to his feet, picked up his hat and moved towards the door.

"I will not be there," she declared positively.

"I shall hope for the best," he said, as, with his back towards her, he removed his mask and disappeared.

About an hour after the departure of her strange visitor, Lucy Mott, carrying a small brief case in which she had cautiously placed the fateful package, descended the two flights of stairs and arrived at the elevator terminus. Her heart gave a little jump as she glanced towards the entrance to the Hyacinth Club.

A police sergeant and a constable were standing on either side of the door and from inside came the sound of voices. The constable as soon as he saw her descend the stairs carrying the brief case, stepped forward. The sergeant, however, touched him on the arm, whispered a word in his ear and saluted Miss Mott.

She paused at the entrance to the elevator. "Is there anything wrong here, Sergeant?" she asked.

"A little trouble, Miss Mott," he said. "We shall know the exact nature of it later on."

He was obviously disinclined to say more. The elevator boy took her case and Miss Lucy Mott was transported to the ground floor. She stepped into a taxicab and was driven home. The thrill of her afternoon adventure had passed, leaving behind it a dull sort of depression which she could not shake off.

More than once she was inclined to return to her apartment, and hand over her brief case to the sergeant with a full explanation of how she obtained possession of its contents. She had lost her confidence in that debonnair malefactor, and her cheeks burned when she reflected how easily she had fallen victim to his wiles. Nevertheless, she told herself with a certain grim satisfaction, the end was not yet.

Lucy Mott's visitor kept his word to the letter. Even before the swing doors of the restaurant could be opened to receive her he was moving across the little reception lounge with the welcoming smile of a host upon his lips.

She accepted his hand dolefully. "I only came," she said, "because I was curious."

"And you will remain," he said, as they descended the stairs towards the bar, "because you are going to have a delightful dinner."

"What have you been doing to yourself?" she asked, as they took their places at a small table in the bar.

"I just went through the usual routine," he said. "Bath, a light evening shave, and a change into decent clothes."

"Don't be stupid," she said. "You look about fifteen years older than I expected to find you, and although you have been frightfully clever about it I don't believe that those lines in your face are natural. Those gray streaks in your hair too make me suspicious."

He laughed softly. Whatever her ideas about her companion might have been Miss Mott was at least obliged to confess that he was a very attractive and distinguished-looking person.

"We semi-criminals," he said, "get into the way of this sort of thing. We are quite accustomed to being blonds one evening and brunets the next. You may yet see me as Santa Claus. How thankful you should be that you are entirely on the right side of the fence. You will never need to disguise yourself.

"On the whole I am glad that you did not wear black, although I am afraid it was a matter of obstinacy on your part. Gray with your complexion is a perfect color. You are very distracting, Miss Mott."

"I did not come here to listen to nonsense," she said.

"Of course not," he assured her. "We will talk sensibly before long. This has been a strenuous day. We are going to have another cocktail each, and then I will take you to the little corner table upstairs which I have engaged. You shall read the menu of the dinner I have ordered and, after that, when I am quite sure that nothing would induce you to get up and leave me until after it has been served, I shall tell you just as much as I can of what you are dying to hear."

Lucy looked at him reflectively. After all, he did not exaggerate. Hers were very beautiful blue eyes, very beautifully set.

They mounted the stairs a few minutes afterwards and were ushered to their table by bowing waiters, the wine steward, a maitre d'hotel, and the manager.

Miss Mott accepted a cushion for her back, read the menu and gave a sigh of content. She had a weakness for exquisite food.

"You were quite right," she said. "Nothing would induce me to leave until after the strawberries, and as to what you have to tell me about the Hyacinth Club I have perhaps later information even than you."

He looked at her swiftly. "Yes?"

The monosyllable was crisp, interrogative. She continued after a moment's pause. "The whole place was upset when I came downstairs. There were policemen there. Either there had been a robbery which had been discovered or some other tragedy had happened."

"What time did you leave?"

"Seven o'clock."

"How do you know that there were police there?" he asked. "You didn't go inside the club?"

"There was a sergeant and a constable outside. They nearly stopped me when they saw I was carrying a brief case, but fortunately the sergeant happened to know who I was. He interceded and they let me go."

Her companion gave vent to a little exclamation. "Good grief! That was a narrow shave."

"I suppose I am to take it for granted," she said stiffly, "that you left me in the position of being subject to arrest as a receiver of stolen goods?"

"It was one of those situations," he said, "in which someone *had* to take a risk."

"But why should I be forced to take it?" she said indignantly. "Why should I be forced to run the gauntlet of a police inspection for your sake? You—a perfect stranger."

"Bad luck," he said. "Things turn out that way sometimes. By the by, you brought my property back with you, I suppose?"

"I did not," she said firmly. "Now perhaps you're going to take my dinner away from me.

I'm not going to run any further risks by carting about the results of a robbery. I left it at home in my room until you can explain the situation. In case I do not get another course, may I have a piece more toast to finish my caviar with?"

The waiter sprang attentively to the table. Miss Mott was promptly served. Her companion leaned forward and spoke to the maitre d'hotel.

"Send out for the latest edition of the *Evening News* for me, will you?" he said.

The man hurried off with an acquiescent bow.

"What do you want an evening paper for?" asked Miss Mott.

"I thought I should like to see the nature of the trouble at the Hyacinth Club," he said. "It would interest me to know what exactly they believe is stolen and if they have any description of the so-called thief."

"I shall be able to describe him all right," Lucy said.

Her companion sighed. "So you would give me away, would you?"

A cigarette girl appeared with the evening paper. Lucy Mott's companion turned inquiringly towards her.

"Will you excuse me if I glance at the 'Stop Press' news?" he asked.

"Certainly," she said. "I am rather interested in it myself."

He shook the paper open and glanced at the back page. For a moment or two he remained rigid. Looking at him curiously, Lucy found herself unable to decide whether his steady gaze indicated indifference or whether he had really found disturbing news. With calm fingers he folded up the paper.

"Well," she asked, "did you find what you wanted?"

"Rather more than I wanted," he said. "Take my advice—finish that delicious sole otero—they do it so well here—and don't worry about what happened at the Hyacinth Club."

"I may be allowed a certain amount of curiosity, I suppose?"

He sampled the champagne, nodded approval,

raised the foaming glass to his lips and set it down empty. "The news," he said, "might spoil your dinner."

"It certainly will not," she assured him. "I am not your partner in crime. The worst thing that could happen to me would be the annoyance of having to hand over that package to the police and explain how I came by it."

"You would not try to shield me, then?"

"I do not know the exact gravity of your crime," Lucy replied. "Has anything happened at the Hyacinth Club besides the robbery?"

"There seems to have been some sort of an accident," he said gloomily.

"For which you were responsible, no doubt."

"It was one of the issues which I was trying to prevent."

"Tell me about it at once," Lucy said.

He pushed the paper towards her, his little finger pointing to the few hastily printed lines under a heading in thick black type.

Colonel Warsley, honorary secretary of the Hyacinth Bridge Club in Booker's Buildings, was found shot to death in his private office this evening.

An exclamation of horror broke from Lucy's lips. She looked searchingly into her companion's face as she pushed back the paper.

"You knew this all the time?"

He shook his head. "No, Miss Mott. I did not."

There was a brief silence. The pleasant half-jesting atmosphere seemed to have been dispelled. Their next course was served. Lucy Mott began to eat with mechanical appetite. She felt her heart beating quickly. It was possible that she was dining with a murderer.

"Don't let this unfortunate incident spoil your dinner, Miss Mott," he said. "I am not sure that it is not the best thing that could have happened."

"How can you say that when the poor man is dead? How can you be so callous?"

He shrugged his shoulders. "Did you know Warsley?" he asked.

"We've exchanged greetings on the stairs."

"Well, that should have been enough. You are a person of observation. Were you inclined to like him?"

"That has nothing to do with it," Lucy said.

"On the contrary, it has a great deal to do with it," he insisted. "Everyone who knew Warsley—except his wife—knew that he was a wrong 'un. Unofficially you represent the law. You know that wrong 'uns ought to be punished."

"Let's talk about something else," she said.

"It is rather grim, isn't it?" he admitted. "I'll tell you what—let's dance."

Lucy shook her head. "I couldn't—with you," she said bluntly. "You act like a man who takes nothing in life seriously."

"I can assure you I do," he said. "I find this change of your attitude towards me very serious indeed. You probably think that I made away with Warsley."

"Well, it would not be such a ridiculous suspicion, would it?" she said, turning upon him with flashing eyes. "You appear to treat the matter lightly enough. But I should think that when my evidence is given to the police you might find yourself in quite a serious position."

"So you are going to give evidence against me?" he said.

"I shall tell the truth," Lucy said.

"Very well," he agreed. "I will take what's coming to me. At the present moment, though, what is coming to us both is that wonderful dish of asparagus and after that strawberries! Do you think I could dwell on such trifles if I had just qualified for the gallows?"

Despite herself Lucy smiled.

"I don't know what to think about you," she said. "You puzzle me completely."

"Embrace my motto then for the rest of the meal," he said. "'Let us eat, drink, and be merry, for tomorrow we die.' Too often quoted, perhaps, but the soundest piece of philosophy in the world—especially as I believe that the strawberries are really ripe."

To a certain extent there ensued a faint revival of their former light-heartedness. They even danced twice, and for those few minutes, during which Lucy Mott discovered that her companion was the best dance partner she had ever had, she forgot everything.

It was nearly half-past twelve when, with the gradual emptying of the room, the little party came to an end.

"You will allow me to drive you back to your apartment?" he said, as she came out from the cloakroom. "It would give me a great deal of pleasure."

She shook her head. "I shall take a taxi, thanks. Whatever may happen, I have had a wonderful evening and I thank you very much for it."

"I'm afraid that there is one question which I must ask you," he said, looking down at her. "What do you propose doing with my property?"

Lucy looked around. There was no one in their immediate vicinity. "I am going to take it to Scotland Yard tomorrow morning," she said, "and tell them how I came by it. I am very sorry, but I have no alternative."

"You're going to tell them the whole story?"

"Everything."

The enigma of his faint smile, which she was to understand later on, temporarily defeated her. It seemed half quizzical, half plaintive.

"Anyway, I get the night in peace," he murmured.

"If your conscience will permit it," she said, as he escorted her across the pavement.

Lucy Mott found herself in a curiously hysterical mood during that drive home. She was inclined to laugh and to cry and at the bottom of her heart she regretted her solitude. When she had mounted to her rooms and taken off her evening wrap she dragged out the brief case from under the bed where she had left it, placed it upon a chair and opened it.

Then for a moment all the disturbances of the evening seemed as nothing. She felt the color receding from her cheeks, felt an actual pain at the back of her eyes from their dilated stare. The case was empty!

Superintendent Wragge was an official highly thought of at New Scotland Yard. He was careful, shrewd, and he had the reputation of seldom, if ever, making a mistake. A trifle overcautious, he was esteemed by the younger school. He listened to his niece's story on the following afternoon with the deepest interest. When she had finished he asked her a few questions.

"This young man who broke into your office and with whom you dined afterwards—did he never tell you his name?"

"Joseph," she said. "That was as much as I could get out of him."

Superintendent Wragge's lips were pursed. He whistled softly. "Violet Joe!"

"Is there actually someone with that nickname?" Lucy asked. "My burglar used a perfume of violets, I'm sure. He wore violets last night in his buttonhole and," she added with a faint blush, "he had the impertinence to send me an enormous bunch this morning from a florist's in Bond Street."

Her uncle chuckled. "You seem to have made quite an impression upon him," he said.

"It makes me furious even now," she said, "when I remember how he talked and behaved. Tell me, is there some well-known criminal or anyone on the Yard's books who has the nickname of Violet Joe?"

Superintendent Wragge became more thoughtful. "There is a gang about which we know scarcely anything doing very serious work in London at the present moment," he said. "They are supposed to be directed by one or two men of very important social position. The nickname of one of them is Violet Joe."

Lucy Mott asked her next question with a certain amount of hesitation. "Is there anything definite—anything very serious against him?"

Her uncle shook his head. "Nothing at present. All the same we should like to establish his identity. By the way, do you know where I was

all the morning when you called and found me out?"

"They wouldn't tell me," she said.

"I was at the inquest on Colonel Warsley, the late secretary of the Hyacinth Club."

Lucy's face was alight with interest. "Tell me about it. What was the verdict?"

"Suicide when temporarily insane," Wragge said. "The usual thing."

She drew a long breath of relief. "Well, I'm glad about that at any rate," she said. "Was there anything in the evidence about valuable property being missed from the locker room of the club?"

Superintendent Wragge stroked his chin thoughtfully. "Not exactly. Yet in a way you have solved the mystery. I think I can explain now the whole episode of last night."

Lucy leaned forward eagerly. "For heaven's sake, go on."

"It seems that this Colonel Warsley and his wife were accustomed to play competitive bridge matches with any two players who fancied themselves, and there is no doubt but that they were extraordinarily successful. Warsley himself, it appears, was always looked upon with a certain amount of suspicion, but he was tolerated on account of his wife, who is exceedingly well connected, very popular, and apparently a delightful personality.

"Notwithstanding this, however, there were rumors in the club that on the occasion of these matches Colonel Warsley and Lady Emily Warsley, his wife, played with marked cards. There was a secret committee meeting, and it was arranged yesterday that at six o'clock, when everyone was busy in the card rooms, the secretary's safe and all the private lockers were to be opened and searched. This scheme was duly carried out."

"Did they find anything?" Lucy asked breathlessly.

"Not a thing," the superintendent replied. "Colonel Warsley's locker, which was known to have contained several unopened packs of cards the day before, was empty."

There was a brief silence. The superintendent was looking at his niece. With a little flush upon her cheeks she was working out the significance of her uncle's narration.

"I see," she murmured. "My burglar knew somehow or other what was going to happen, raided the lockers first, found the marked cards and escaped with them. Naturally he did not wish to be seen leaving the club. He confessed to me that he had entered secretly.

"I suppose he had arranged matters too so that when I left my club last night without any parcel or bag my rooms would be searched and they would be taken away. Otherwise, he knew that I would keep my word and bring them to Scotland Yard this morning. Tell me, was the scandal mentioned at all at the inquest?"

"Only in a very vague and sympathetic manner," Superintendent Wragge said. "When the question of motive was raised one member of the jury asked if it was true that there had been any scandal in the club which might have affected the secretary. The attorney who was watching the case on behalf of Lady Emily Warsley got up at once and admitted that, as was common in many card clubs where the stakes ran high, there had been certain rumors concerning the existence of marked cards.

"He thought it should be publicly known that the club premises had been thoroughly searched, including the private rooms of Colonel Warsley, and that nothing in the least incriminating had been found. He branded the accusation as a libel and the chairman of the committee of the club who was present got up and said that he was convinced that the rumors which had been referred to were entirely false.

"The coroner, in his few words, declared that no suspicion of any sort attached itself to the dead man, who was known to have been in poor health and a very unhappy disposition."

"I think," Lucy Mott said, with a severity which she was very far from feeling, "that he might have trusted me."

Her uncle shook his head. "If your burglar friend, my dear Lucy, was really acting for Lady Emily Warsley, as seems likely, he would remember that he had the living to think of as well as the dead.

"You know, it is perfectly possible at such a game as bridge for marked cards to be used and for only one person to know about them. On the other hand, if the truth came out it would be very hard indeed not to implicate both partners. I think your friend's discretion under the circumstances was perfectly justified."

Lucy Mott sighed a little petulantly. "I cannot help feeling that I was rather made use of."

Her uncle smiled. "You must remember, my dear," he pointed out, "that your friend took risks. If ever the time should come when you are able definitely to identify Violet Joe it might be a serious matter for him."

Lucy Mott took her leave with a faint and rather vague smile upon her lips. Somehow or other she fancied that that time would never come.

THE MISSING CHARACTER

Phyllis Bentley

KNOWN MAINLY AS A REGIONAL WRITER, Phyllis Eleanor Bentley (1894–1977) made few contributions to mystery fiction beyond her short stories featuring Miss Marian Phipps, a detective novelist who helps her friend Detective-Sergeant Tarrant, who is a young policeman when she meets him but is later promoted to Inspector-Sergeant.

Bentley is largely known for her bestselling novel *Inheritance* (1932), which made her a celebrity. Set in the West Riding region of Yorkshire, its sympatheticic portrayal of textile workers and mill owners spanning more than a century earned her enormous critical praise. She continued to write significant works about the region, including two more novels in what became known as the *Inheritance* trilogy, and two short story collections, *Tales of the West Riding* (1965) and *More Tales of the West Riding* (1974). *Inheritance* was filmed for British television in 1967 with Michael Goodliffe, John Thaw (later famous as Inspector Morse), and James Bolam.

Her literary fame earned Bentley numerous honors, notably her being given the Order of the British Empire in 1970. Prior to that, she had the rare distinction for an author of being pictured on a cigarette card, an honor usually reserved for athletes and film stars.

The few forays into crime fiction that Bentley made were mainly the twenty-four stories featuring Miss Phipps (although her West Riding collections featured several crime stories). "The Missing Character" (frequently reprinted as "Author in Search of a Character") was the first, published in 1937 in *Woman's Home Companion*; every other story in the series was first published in *Ellery Queen's Mystery Magazine*.

The Miss Phipps stories are cozy detective tales in the tradition of Agatha Christie, in which good triumphs over evil, the crimes solved by a no-longer-young lady novelist, told with gentle humor.

"The Missing Character" was originally published in the July 1937 issue of *Woman's Home Companion*; it was first collected in *Chain of Witnesses: The Cases of Miss Phipps* (Norfolk, Virginia, Crippen & Landru, 2014).

The Missing Character

PHYLLIS BENTLEY

IT WAS HALF-PAST TWO on a warm afternoon in autumn; the passengers in the northbound Pullman had lunched, wisely perhaps but certainly well, and were all ungracefully asleep in their corners, their open mouths and crimson faces cocked roofward at odd angles, like a bed of red dahlias turning to the sun. All, that is, except two persons who faced each other across a table at the far end of the coach. They were awake and indeed their eyes were particularly wide open, for each was staring glassily at a point just above the other's head. The table between them was strewn with writing materials, which, however, neither seemed inclined to use. That they were engaged in some mental travail seemed probable; with each mile the train rushed northward the woman's bushy white hair seemed to grow wilder, the young man's agreeable, plain face more haggard, the eyes of both more distraught.

Miss Marian Phipps, the novelist, was busy with a problem of characterization which had held up her work for the past three weeks. It concerned the heroine of her new novel, who was just about to emerge from her brain onto the written page. The girl had stuck on the threshold so long because Miss Phipps was utterly unable to decide her appearance. It was necessary for the plot that the hero should feel for her, at first sight, a love equally tenacious, respectful, and adoring; now Miss Phipps could not decide what kind of girl, if any, nowadays could command from a contemporary such a passion. She would probably be dark, Miss Phipps had decided; but was she richly rosy, full of life, with flashing eyes, or pale, mysterious, slender? As fast as Miss Phipps pronounced for one type, she revoked the decision in favor of another.

On this, the twenty-second day of the struggle, she had as a last hope booked a seat in the Edinburgh express. She did not in the least wish to go to Edinburgh, but found long train journeys stimulating to the creative faculties. But already a considerable number of miles had gone by, and she was no nearer her solution; she felt hot, tired, cross, and in urgent need of an excuse for ceasing work.

The train took a sudden curve without slowing; Miss Phipps and the large young man found their feet and their papers mixed in consequence. With mutual loathing in their hearts they murmured apologies and disentangled their property. For the first time Miss Phipps observed the young man's notebook; always avid for human detail, she tried to read it upside down. "S-u-l-l-e-n," she spelled; "aged 35, sullen and vehement." At once her large mouth widened to a smile; her eyes beamed behind her old-fashioned pince-nez.

"You are a novelist too?" she exclaimed joyfully.

The young man gave her an unresponsive glare. He did not want to talk to Miss Phipps. He did not admire Miss Phipps. As an object of vision he found her definitely unpleasing. The round pink face, the untidy white hair, the too-glowing smile, the bright blue jumper, the lop-sided pince-nez moored by a chain to a kind of bollard on her substantial bosom—these clashed with his notions of female beauty; that she was a "lady novelist" as well was just, he thought, what might have been expected. "Only needs a Peke to be complete," he decided disgustedly.

"You are a novelist too?" repeated Miss Phipps, beaming.

"Certainly not," snapped the large young man.

"I beg your pardon," said Miss Phipps in an icy tone. "From a phrase in your notebook, which I confess I took a childish pleasure in deciphering from this angle, I surmised I might be addressing a fellow-craftsman."

The young man was rather startled. "More in the old girl than meets the eye," he thought. Coloring, he stammered apologies. "I was thinking of something else," he explained. "I'm a good deal worried just now by a serious problem."

Miss Phipps forgave him. "It's no crime not to be a novelist," she said. "Rather the reverse, perhaps, nowadays. And whoever we are, we all have our problems."

There was a hint of question in her last sentence and the young man was caught by it. "I'm a detective," he blurted. "Detective-Sergeant Tarrant, of the Southshire police headquarters."

"Really!" cried Miss Phipps, impressed. "A detective! On a murder case, perhaps? Do tell me all about it. My name is Marian Phipps."

The young man gave a heavy sigh. "I'm afraid I haven't read any of your novels," he said gloomily.

Miss Phipps had a stock rejoinder for this remark; she always replied: "No? You prefer the lighter fiction?" and found it not ineffective. But this time, hot on a murder trail, she would forgo her mild revenge. With one plump little hand she waved her novels out of court. "Do tell me about your problem," she urged. "It will clear your thoughts to put them into words. Besides, I might be able to help. Psychology, you know. Characterization. Do tell me. I'm not a very discreet person, I'm afraid; but I don't live anywhere near Southshire."

Detective-Sergeant Tarrant rumpled his hair and sighed again, but more hopefully.

"Will you promise not to write up the story if I tell you?" he inquired.

Miss Phipps considered. "I will promise," she said, "that I will not use the story for five years, and that when I do, it will be unrecognizable."

Tarrant laughed. "Now that's the sort of promise you can believe," he said heartily. "Well, I'll tell you. I'd be glad enough of any help; I don't mind admitting I'm stuck with it myself."

He sat up, flicked the pages of his notebook, and began in a brisk official tone:

"On Wednesday last, September thirteenth, I was summoned at one-thirty A.M. by the local police to a house on the front in the seaside resort of Brittlesea; house called Lorel Manor, property of a financier named Ambrose Stacey. Large new house, standing in large grounds; newest architecture, modern pool in rose garden. The call was received at the station at one-twenty A.M. from the butler, who stated that he had been awake in bed, reading, when he heard loud screams from Mrs. Stacey at approximately one-fifteen A.M. He went down to investigate, found her in hysterics on the landing, and called the police."

"But who was dead?" demanded Miss Phipps impatiently.

"I went to Lorel Manor and found the whole household assembled on the upper landing," continued the detective with a repressive glance. "In their midst was lying Mr. Ambrose Stacey, dead. His neck was broken. It was plain that he had fallen down the short flight of stairs leading from his bedroom, a large octagonal apartment almost entirely surrounded by windows, to the main landing below."

"An accident!" exclaimed Miss Phipps, disappointed.

"On the contrary," said Tarrant grimly. "A piece of strong string was found dangling from the rail of the chromium balustrade at the very top of the stairs. The end was broken; a similar piece of string with a broken end was found attached to the opposite balustrade; on measuring—"

"You needn't labor the point," said Miss Phipps. "The string was put there to be fallen over and he fell over it. Go on."

"Mr. and Mrs. Stacey had entered the house by means of Mr. Stacey's latchkey," continued the detective, consulting his notebook, "shortly after one o'clock. They had been dining—with a business friend of Mr. Stacey's. The butler heard them come in and go straight upstairs to their room. About one-ten Mr. Stacey, desiring a whisky and soda, found that the siphon was not in its usual place on the tray in his room; he went downstairs to find it, with fatal results."

"Ah," said Miss Phipps, "the siphon was not in its usual place."

"The problem is," said the detective, "who tied that string?"

"Who was in the house at the time?" demanded the novelist.

"Mrs. Eleanor Stacey, the second wife of the deceased; Rachel, his daughter by his first wife; Rachel's nursery governess, the butler, the cook, the housemaid, the parlormaid. Not, however, Mr. Stacey's secretary, Jack Thornhill."

"From your tone, Mr. Thornhill's absence seems to have a special significance?" queried Miss Phipps.

"His absence was perhaps rather fortunate for Mr. Thornhill," said the detective. "He has an alibi for the whole night, in Leeds; I'm going now to investigate it. It's only fair to say, however, that it has been investigated three times already. He was speaking at a birthday dinner in Leeds at half-past nine; I don't see what you can do against that. It's more than two hundred miles from Leeds to Brittlesea."

"Mr. Thornhill is young and handsome. I take it?" said Miss Phipps, her voice warm with interest.

The detective nodded. "If you like that varnished type," he said.

"And Mrs. Stacey is also young and handsome?"

The detective nodded again, emphatically.

"And Ambrose Stacey was neither young nor handsome?"

"He was fifty-nine," replied Tarrant consideringly, "but really I'm not so sure about the handsome. A very big powerful fellow, with penetrating blue eyes and thick graying hair which stands up from his head, if you know what I mean."

"*En brosse,*" suggested Miss Phipps.

"Very likely," said the detective. "Mrs. Stacey is prostrate with grief; you'd certainly think she was devoted to him. She is really very beautiful, you know; young and fair and gentle. Early twenties."

"Poor before she married?" inquired Miss Phipps.

"Yes. Poor and county. Expensive tastes, I daresay. And she gets a pretty fair amount of cash by the will," said Tarrant. "*And* young Thornhill dotes on her. From appearances you'd judge she loved her husband. But plainly she's the first to be suspected." He sighed.

Miss Phipps gave him a shrewd look. "Was the deceased financier what for the sake of brevity we call a gentleman?" she asked.

"Lord, no!" replied the detective more cheerfully. "No more a gentleman than I am."

Miss Phipps surveyed him with approval. "Tell me more," she said.

"Stacey was a thorough rascal, but a dashed interesting chap," went on Tarrant. "Ambrose Stacey wasn't his real name."

"I thought it sounded a little pseudo," said the novelist.

"Oh, you did?" said the detective, glancing at her respectfully. "Well, he had one of those obscure middle-European names, you know, which may mean anything. He'd been everywhere and done everything, and collected a lot of cash in rather odd ways, and I expect also made a lot of enemies. It may be one of them who's bumped him off; that's the trouble, from my point of view. He married his first wife when he was poor, in the middle-European days, and she never quite fitted into his new setting. He was apt to find consolation elsewhere for that, if you understand me; but at any rate he must have been a decent father, for his daughter, Rachel, simply adores him. The first Mrs. Stacey died seven years ago, and he remained faithful to her memory, outwardly at least, till he married Eleanor. That was just the early spring of this year."

"And Rachel?" said Miss Phipps thoughtfully. "The daughter?"

"Well, of course I thought of her at once," said the detective. "She's twelve years old and the door of her room is just at the foot of the fatal stairs; and string tied to banisters—it sounds like a child's practical joke."

"A curious set of circumstances, if so," commented Miss Phipps. "A child chances to seize the only possible five minutes when the joke could bring disaster. For in the morning Mr. and Mrs. Stacey would presumably be called by a maid with tea, going *up* the stairs."

"Don't let that worry you," said the detective grimly, "for it wasn't a practical joke. The small landing outside the Staceys' room is lighted by a wall lamp which turns on by a switch at the bedroom door. The bulb had been removed from it."

"Tchk!" exclaimed Miss Phipps. "How shocking!"

"The bulb was lying at the foot of the lamp, intact; therefore it had not fallen but been placed there. Nobody admits removing it," concluded the detective.

"Worse and worse," said Miss Phipps distressfully. "And the child? Rachel?"

"She's a pretty little thing, but delicate; thin and pale and as nervy as you make 'em," replied Tarrant. "Of course, I've only seen her in trouble, you may say; she was in despair about her father. But everyone tells me what a nervy delicate child she is; why, Mrs. Stacey had moved her to her present bedroom from a more distant one, so as to be able to hear her if she woke and cried in the night. At twelve years old, you know. Yes, poor kid; she's clever but nervy."

"Oh, dear!" sighed Miss Phipps, twitching her bushy eyebrows mournfully. "I'm unhappy about this case, very."

"Why?" said the detective.

"Aren't you?" demanded Miss Phipps, looking at him shrewdly.

"Yes. But I don't see how she could have done it," said Tarrant. "Five past one, light there, no string; ten past one, string there, no light. How could she suddenly leave the bedroom and begin to fidget on her hands and knees just outside the door? What could she say if her husband looked out to see what she was doing? Why didn't she remove the string and replace the light before screaming to the butler?"

"Oh," said Miss Phipps slowly, "you're thinking of Mrs. Stacey."

"Of course. Aren't you?"

"Never mind. Go on," said Miss Phipps firmly. "What steps did you take to solve the mystery?"

"I looked," said Tarrant, "first for the bulb and then for the siphon."

"Very proper," said Miss Phipps nodding. "A good point. You looked for the siphon. And where did you find it?"

"In young Thornhill's room," said Tarrant. "That's why I'm investigating his alibi for the third time. He says, however, that Stacey came into his room that morning as he was packing his case for his journey to Leeds, to have a last word with him; Stacey wanted a drink, pulled out his flask, and sent Thornhill for the nearest siphon, which of course was the one in his bedroom. A silly story, but in view of Stacey's habits it may be true. Thornhill says that as he returned, siphon in hand, he met Rachel going to her bedroom, and Rachel corroborates this, time and place."

"Oh, I'm delighted to hear it!" cried Miss Phipps with joy. "It's a very great relief to me indeed; I'm simply delighted to hear it."

"But why?" demanded Tarrant in some exasperation. "That doesn't clear young Thornhill of removing the siphon on his own, for a murderous motive."

"I never thought it did," said Miss Phipps. "But he has an alibi. Oh, I am so delighted to hear it, so delighted!"

"What do you see in this case that I don't, I wonder?" said the detective thoughtfully.

"My dear boy," said Miss Phipps firmly, "you said yourself that the method sounded childish. Rachel had the best opportunity of placing the string—better than anyone else in the house; her door is just at the foot of the stairs; you said so."

"But it wasn't a practical joke, because of the light," objected Tarrant.

"Exactly. The fall was quite premeditated," said Miss Phipps, "quite intended. But might it not," said Miss Phipps sadly, "might it not have been premeditated by Rachel?"

"You mean she meant to murder her father?" cried Tarrant. He paused to consider. "Good God!" He struck the table with his hand. "She knew about the siphon!"

"To my mind," observed Miss Phipps calmly, "that's just what clears her of the suspicion of murder and that's why I was so delighted to hear of it."

"Miss Marian Phipps," said the detective, "you're a very exasperating woman."

"My dear boy," observed Miss Phipps very earnestly, "I beg you not to take my criticism unkindly. But, if you will allow me to say so, you're making a great mistake. You're paying too much attention to the mechanics of your plot—bulbs and strings and siphons—and neglecting your human element, your characterization. Why should Rachel murder her father?"

"She had no reason on earth," said the detective. "She adored him."

"Exactly," said Miss Phipps. "Then dismiss that idea altogether from your mind and consider the facts you have laid before me. Don't you see what they all point to? The origin of the tragedy remains as yet obscure to me, because your sketch of the characters is so lamentably imperfect. But one fact emerges clearly. Don't you see that *the wrong person tripped over that string?*"

"What?" shouted Tarrant; his voice was so loud that several of the dahlias stirred and nodded. "How do you reach such a preposterous conclusion?"

"But you told me yourself," objected Miss Phipps mildly, "Mrs. Stacey moved Rachel's bedroom so that she could hear the child if she cried in the night. What do you do when you hear a child cry in the night? You hurry to soothe her. Who, then, often ran down those stairs in the night? Eleanor Stacey. Who knew that fact? Everyone in the household, including Rachel. So much is established fact. I then went one step further and said: What do highly-strung children often feel toward their stepmothers?"

"You mean Rachel meant to murder Mrs. Stacey out of jealousy? Good God! And she's such a nice little kid; I was so sorry for her. How horrible!"

"That's what I thought," said Miss Phipps sweetly. "But don't you see, the siphon clears her. She adored her father. She knew that he might come down to fetch the missing siphon. Would she, then, place the string there just that night? No; for to do so was to risk her father's life, and there were many other nights. Therefore Rachel did not place the string that night. But the string was placed that night. Therefore we must look elsewhere for the murderer—and how gladly," said Miss Phipps, beaming, "we do so."

"Rachel's only a child; she mightn't have worked all that out about the siphon; she might have forgotten all about the siphon," said Tarrant in a tone of gloom.

"In that case the siphon has no significance at all," snapped Miss Phipps. "For I refuse to believe that either young Thornhill or Eleanor would risk a method of killing Ambrose so dangerous to Eleanor; while if Eleanor was to be killed, the siphon had no part to play. We are just where we were before."

At this moment the train burst through a series of bridges with a lamentable clatter; the passengers, startled awake, tossed up and down as they took down hats and picked up handbags; evidently the train was approaching some station.

"We're much worse than we were before," shouted Tarrant above the din. "I had one clue, and at least the identity of the victim was clear, but now you've thrown away the siphon and confused even the object of the crime. If Eleanor Stacey was the intended victim, an entirely fresh set of motives must be found. I wish—"

"You wish I'd never spoken to you," said Miss Phipps regretfully. "That I can well understand. I really don't know," she added with a sigh, "how I came to commit such an impropriety—"

The detective colored and protested.

"—as to interrupt someone else's cerebration," concluded Miss Phipps firmly. "It was unpardonable and I offer you my sincerest apologies. How did I come to do such a thing? Good gracious!" she exclaimed. "I remember now! Mr. Tarrant! You've been deceiving me! You have omitted from your account of this tragedy one of the characters."

"I don't think so," said the detective, hesitating. "The servants had only been there since the marriage this spring. I don't think so."

"But I'm sure," insisted Miss Phipps. "Positive! Listen. Ambrose Stacey, aged fifty-nine. Eleanor his wife, fair and gentle, in her twenties. Rachel, child, aged twelve. Jack Thornhill, in his twenties. Then who was sullen and vehement and in the thirties?"

The detective stared.

"I read it in your notebook," cried Miss Phipps, pointing impatiently. "Who was aged thirty-five, sullen and vehement?"

Tarrant, startled, flipped the pages. "That was Rosa Dorlan, Rachel's nursery governess," he discovered.

"How long had she been with the Staceys?" cried Miss Phipps eagerly.

"Seven years," said Tarrant.

The station, an animated scene with porters, passengers, newsboys, and buffet attendants darting hither and thither like gnats above a flower bed, burst upon them.

"Then there you are!" cried Miss Phipps hastily in triumph. "Don't you see? Don't you see her? Rosa. Handsome. Dark. Ripe. Flushed cheeks. Vehement. Sullen. Involved with Stacey. Hopes to be his wife. The new wife comes. Finds child neurotic and unhappy. Dissatisfied with Rosa. Keeps child near her night and day. Often comes down in night to see her. Nurse knows this. String. Wife trips. End of wife. Nurse not lose job. Indispensable again to Stacey. Perhaps his wife. Siphon a chance, an accident. Wrong person killed. Great distress of Rosa. So great, she forgot to replace bulb and remove string. How's that?"

"So good," said Detective-Sergeant Tarrant, standing up and reaching for his hat, "that I shall get out at this station and go straight back to Brittlesea. It will make so much difference to—er, to all concerned, to have their innocence clearly established." He pulled out an official card and offered it to her respectfully. "If you have any ideas on any future murder problems, Miss Phipps," he said, "I wish you would drop me a line about them. Meanwhile, if there is anything I can do—"

"You've done it," sighed Miss Phipps happily, snatching her pencil and writing: "Fair, young, gentle."

MURDER IN THE MOVIES

Karl Detzer

LIKE SO MANY WRITERS, Karl Detzer (1891–1987) had several careers first, many experiences of which served as colorful backgrounds or story ideas for future work. At sixteen, he took a job at his hometown newspaper, the Fort Wayne *Journal Gazette*, as a reporter and photographer, and remained a reporter for several papers in the area until he joined the army in 1916. Sent to Mexico to fight Pancho Villa's insurgents, he then went to France and took command of the newly formed Department of Criminal Investigation to battle the wave of criminals trying to take advantage of a chaotic government after years of war. He returned to the United States in 1920 to face a court-martial for having tortured and cruelly treated prisoners, with more than a hundred witnesses against him, but he was acquitted and resigned from the army.

He soon decided that he could earn a living as a writer and gained prominence for his series of articles about the "Fire House Gang" for *The Saturday Evening Post*, based on incidents he observed while riding with firemen. He replicated the idea and tone for a series based on his riding along with the Michigan State Police, also for the *Post*, which served as the basis for a movie, *Car 99* (1935), starring Fred MacMurray and Ann Sheridan.

Detzer went on to write more than a thousand stories and articles, as well as several books, most notably *True Tales of the D.C.I.* (1925), which contained, in fact, fictionalized accounts of some of his exploits.

"Murder in the Movies" was originally published in the May 1937 issue of *The American Legion Monthly*.

Murder in the Movies

KARL DETZER

JACK HARTER WAS MURDERED; no argument there. He died of a .32-caliber bullet through his heart. That's in the record. The murder took place on sound stage Number 21 on the Titanic studio lot in Hollywood, the night of April 13th. The time was somewhere between eleven o'clock and eleven-five, which is close enough.

This much is history and nobody denies it. So why do I bring it up? Because this month the Hollywood fan magazines began picking the case to pieces again, saying the whole story hasn't been told; ran pictures of Jack Harter, and Marie Fleming, and Sam Masterford, and Joe Gatski, and Joan Nelson, and Rose Graham, with question marks all around them. One of the magazines even used my picture. It said, "Has property man told all?" Think of that!

The writers of a Hollywood fan magazine have to have something to write about, I suppose. But there isn't any mystery in the Jack Harter case, and never was, except between eleven o'clock that night and four in the morning. By the time the city police got there (and I admit we were a bit slow in calling them) all the cops needed to do was write the answer down in the book.

I'm telling it now, just the way it happened, so that there needn't be any more pictures surrounded by question marks.

To begin with, there were thirteen of us on Stage 21 at the instant the murder occurred, on the night of the thirteenth, and maybe that had something to do with it, and maybe not. Thirteen on the stage, and one man guarding the door.

It had been a tough day on Joe Gatski's unit. Gatski was the supervisor, what's called an associate producer on some lots. He was the big shot on this particular production, understand, responsible to the front office for bringing it in under schedule and holding down costs and making it good box office. He picked the story, and the writers, and the director, and the star, and the extras, and the camera and sound crews, everybody. It was his baby.

This was a fourteen-day job, according to the production charts, which means that from the time the camera first turned over on it till the last retake was in the cutting room, would be two weeks. And not ten minutes over. What's more, it looked as if we'd beat the schedule, too.

We started grinding the morning of the first, and here it was the thirteenth at eleven o'clock at night, and only one shot to finish before midnight, and we'd wrap it up in thirteen days. Thirteenth of the month, thirteen days of shooting, and thirteen people on the sound stage, and up pops a murder. Quite a combination of cause and effect, if you believe some people.

That morning the call board had us booked

for a location shot out in Cahuenga Pass at eight o'clock. We had that shot in the can before eleven, and were at the studio and through with lunch and all set up to go on the back lot at one o'clock. This was a trucking shot in the Paris street, a retake of one we'd done the week before. Joe Gatski had picked it to pieces in the rushes, and ordered Sam Masterford to shoot it over.

Then we went back to the sound stage and worked in a couple of added comedy gags that Gatski had figured out which couldn't have got by the Hays office, but we shot them anyhow. Everything going fine, you see, until three o'clock, and then Gatski came out on the stage and began to cause trouble. He didn't think we were putting our heart into his gags, so he turned on the old temperament. That was easy for Gatski.

You'd think from the way he hollered and swooned and swore that this was a million-dollar opus we were shooting. But it wasn't. It was a little item called "Back of the Boulevard." Maybe you remember it, that mystery piece laid in Paris where an American detective saves the life of the Park Avenue girl. If it cost a nickel over a hundred grand to produce, well, the business manager must have been cheating again. Just an ordinary Class B flicker, for double runs in the nabe houses—that's all it was intended for.

Marie Fleming was the star and Jack Harter played opposite her. Funny coincidence, too, because Jack used to be her husband, and not so long ago, either. She married him in 1931, when they both were just a couple of contract players. By the next year her name was in the lights on the marquee, a full-time star. And in 1931 she met Clem Batting, and she divorced Jack and married Clem before you could say Joseph B. Mankiewitz.

Jack never was a star and never would be. But everybody figured he was good for male leads for ten more years and for good character parts the rest of his life. He was a good actor, you see, but not one of these pretty boys.

I say it was a coincidence, Marie and Jack playing opposite each other. But nothing more than that. They didn't get hostile to each other the way a lot of people do after the divorce. It was always "Hi, Jack!" when she met him, and he'd answer "'Lo, Marie!" and they'd act glad to see each other. Why, one night the newspapers got pictures of them dancing together at the Troc.

You'd think that it would be easy to handle them in a love scene, then, wouldn't you? Well, it wasn't. Sam Masterford, the director of this opus, had plenty of trouble whenever they got together. And in this fade-out shot, it was a real headache.

Oh, they went through all the motions of falling into each other's arms; they followed the book on dialogue; and he planted the kiss on her lips for a good long ten count. But somehow, it didn't jell. It was phony, if you get what I mean. The customers wouldn't believe it in a thousand years.

So here we were, on the night of April 13th, making the fade-out again. It was a simple dolly shot, of the two of them going into the clinch, while the camera trucked forward on them. Do it right once, and the picture'd be finished.

It's always a tough proposition, in the last hours of any production, whether it's a colossal super-super or just a plain quickie. Like an orchestra winding up faster and faster for the final big um-pah. Nerves are ready to snap, and the emotions come right up to the skin where it's worn thin. It takes only one small drink to get a man drunk on the cleanup night. You get mad easy, and you find yourself laughing like hell at something that really isn't funny. And you're just as like as not to fall in love with anybody that happens to be around.

I can't explain it exactly. But ask anybody that's ever worked in a studio. Grover Jones should have written a piece about it.

To make things worse this night, here was Joe Gatski being a general nuisance and giving bad advice and getting in everybody's way. Sam Masterford, the director, was trying to hold things together. He was sweating and pale. It was like trying to drive a four-horse chariot with Joe Gatski scaring the horses. We started shooting the fade-out at eight o'clock, and had made two takes on it, neither of which satisfied Masterford, and were in the middle of the third when Gatski hollered, "Cut!"

"What's wrong with that?" Jack Harter asked.

"Everything," Gatski answered. He could have an insulting voice when he wanted to, and this night he sure did want to. "There's two ways of doing that scene, Harter," he said, "Clark Gable's way and your way. And strange as it may seem, the people like Gable's way best. You better try it."

Sam Masterford said, "I thought they were going through it pretty well that time, Joe."

Joe didn't even look at him. He just said, "*You* thought, did you? You better tell it to Louella, so she can put in her newspaper colyum. 'Sam Masterford has a thought.'"

Sam started to answer, then he put his hands in the pockets of his slacks and walked slowly out into the lights. Sweat was running off his long, thin nose and his lips were moving in and out, but he wasn't saying anything.

"What about it, Sam?" Marie asked.

"We'll rest a few minutes," the director answered. "Then we'll do it again."

The gaffer—he's the chief electrician—hollered "Save 'em!" and the light operators up on the scaffolds threw their switches and the big floods and stone lights went out, and the spots and baby spots on the floor dimmed. Marie was still in Jack's arms all this time. He sort of pushed her away now and crossed to his dressing table and sat down and began to pat his forehead with a piece of cotton, very carefully, to take off the perspiration without smearing the make-up. And Joan Nelson, the hairdresser, came up behind Marie and started to fix her back hair where it had got mussed up in Jack's arms.

Marie's stand-in was over by the bulletin board, and Marie called to her: "You run along home, honey. I'll not need you again tonight."

Her voice seemed to startle Joe Gatski, for he got up quickly and walked out to the middle of the set.

"Listen, you two!" he yelled. "You, Fleming, and you, Harter. I'm sick of this. Me, spending all this money to get a fade-out right, and you double-crossing me! Now, when you put on that scene, put it on hot! What I mean, hot!"

Gatski was a little man, about forty years old, with a bay window like a basketball and a voice like a baseball umpire's. He began tramping up and down now, and his heels, hitting the floor, made echoes up against the roof, in spite of the acoustic lining. And as soon as he was through with Marie and Jack, he turned on Masterford.

"You call yourself a director?" he hollered. "A director! Why, you couldn't direct a dog and pony act! You know this is costing me money? You know what money is? Or don't you know anything?"

Masterford didn't answer, just kept on sweating, all over his pale, high, narrow forehead, and blinking his gray eyes behind his thick glasses. A good director, Sam Masterford, even if he did get his start in horse operas. He looked at his watch after a while and called, "Ready, Marie? How about you, Jack? Okay, then. All ready, everybody. This is going to be the one we print."

He always said that when things weren't breaking right, and he had to shoot a scene over and over. Sort of pep talk. All directors use it. It's their idea of psychology.

Well, we all were hoping he was right this time. Rose Graham, the script girl, held her script book up so no one could see her yawn, and went back to the little folding chair in front of the camera and sat down.

The three men on the scaffolds got set, and when Otto Schmidt, the gaffer, yelled "Lights!" they threw on the heat. The set wasn't much, just a plain interior with a window and a sunlight arc shining through it, and a table with some books on it down left, and this door. In the previous scene Jack had come in the door and halted, and then the camera panned around to show Marie looking at him. She lifted her arms to him slowly while the camera trucked forward, and then the script called for a cut to this dolly shot of the two of them.

We started in on it again, the fourth take since supper. Some directors would have been boiling, but Sam stayed cool, on the surface at least. The cameras were grinding, and everybody was hoping this would be the last one when Gatski began to yell again.

"If I wanted Ann Harding in this production, I'd hire her," he said to Marie. "Who ever gave you the idea that the fade-out was supposed to cool off the audience? The idea is to send 'em out heated up!"

Marie answered, in a voice everybody could hear, "You're a worm, Joe."

"After how I build you up!" he screamed. "Talking to me like that! Why, you little—" But he choked up trying to find a word.

"Hold everything, Mr. Gatski!" Jack Harter hollered. "Don't say it to her!"

"Oh," Joe answered, surprised, because featured players aren't in the habit of speaking up to supervisors. "So you don't want us to pick up your option, eh?"

"I don't give a damn," Jack told him, and you could see he meant it. "I'm through with pictures."

"You said it," Joe snapped.

"And with you potbellied leeches that—"
Sam Masterford broke in.

"Come on, everybody. Our nerves are shaky. Let's rest again. Get out and take a breath of air." He hesitated and added quickly, "But no liquor, understand that!"

"Give us fifteen minutes, Sam," Marie begged.

"Sure," he answered, and the gaffer yelled to save 'em and the lights went out again, and Joe Gatski groaned, remembering he was paying the grips and the camera crew and the sound men overtime.

"I'll go over to Charley's and get a cup of coffee," Marie explained. "Come on, Jack."

We watched them leave the set, Marie and her ex-husband, arm in arm, and I couldn't help thinking what a screwy business the movies turned out to be. How anybody can keep his senses!

When they had gone, Joe Gatski said to himself, "A worm, eh? After all I done for her! And that louse thinking he could get away with taking her part!"

He started to walk again, back beyond another set, at the other side of the sound stage, and his heels hit the floor, bang, bang, bang. Marie and Jack were gone about fifteen minutes, maybe twenty. It was five minutes to eleven when they got back, according to Murphy's watch. Murphy was the studio policeman at the stage door who checked every last person in and out.

The way we knew they were back was that we heard Marie laugh. It was a genuine laugh. Not one of those things they turn on for the sound track. I remember thinking, "Well, it did her good to get that crack at Gatski off her chest."

When they came in, Lanny Hoard, the writer, was with them. This "Back of the Boulevard" was his. Lanny had a soft spot in his heart for Marie . . . everybody who read the gossip colyums knew that. She wasn't his big moment, or anything like that, but he liked to write pictures for her. And didn't often get the chance.

Marie played triangle stories usually, because she'd got typed that way, and Lanny wrote mysteries. And nothing else. There's a gag around the studio that he had a special key on his typewriter with "Gunfire!" on it. You know the sort of stuff. Melodrama.

He was a young fellow, around thirty-one or two, and not bad-looking for a writer.

Marie and Jack were in the middle of the set by now, after looking in their mirrors, and Sam Masterford yelled, "Burn 'em!" The gaffer lifted his hand and the lights all went on in a blaze, and Lanny ducked back into the shadows.

At that moment, according to Archie Murphy, the cop at the door, there were twenty-two people on the set. No one could get in or out without passing him, and he had a reputation for keeping an accurate list.

Well, Masterford looked around and saw that everybody was ready, and then he asked Rose Graham, "Okay?"

You see, the script girl is responsible for any

holes in the picture. It's up to her to make sure that one scene hooks up to the rest without any change in costume, or the way the players have their hair combed, or in the length of the ashes on their cigars. Detail, you understand. Script girl has to see everything, and remember it.

Now, when Masterford asked her if this scene was okay, she studied Jack carefully, then Marie, and finally she nodded sort of uncertainly. Masterford followed her eyes. He was a good director, remember, and I guess he saw the same thing she did. I know that I noticed it right away.

It wasn't anything you could put your finger on. But there *was* a change. Not in Jack, but in Marie. She was prettier, if anything, and it wasn't make-up, either, and it wasn't the lights. She was just naturally prettier.

Of course, there isn't anything you can do in a case like that, except pray that it will hold out till you get the shot made. But Masterford didn't seem to be in any hurry.

"Well, are you going to shoot the scene?" Gatski wanted to know.

"Sure," Masterford said, and looked around again.

The gaffer called, "Lights okay."

"Sound okay," came out of the loud-speaker in the sound booth.

Assistant Director Bill Cook hollered, "Everybody quiet!"

"Look here a minute, Marie," Sam interrupted. He sounded troubled, all of a sudden. Marie looked at him, and now she wasn't pretty. I don't know why, but when she took her eyes off Jack, she just wasn't.

"Okay," Sam agreed after a minute, so she smiled at Jack again, and Jack smiled, making the prettiest two-shot you could imagine.

"Turn 'em," Sam said in a peculiar tone, like a sound track that's picked up an echo.

The camera chief pressed the button and answered, "She's turning."

"Camera," Sam called. "Action."

So there were Marie and Jack, under the lights, slipping closer and closer together, with the sound mike swinging over them to pick up their words.

"Jack!" Marie whispered. That was her final line, okay. You see, Jack Harter was playing a character named Jack. The script had him answer, "You, Judy! You, forever!" as they clinched.

But Jack didn't say, "You, Judy!" He said nothing. He just took Marie and held her close while his lips met hers. The camera chief was counting, wagging his finger like a referee for this ten-count fade-out. Only it went more than ten. It went about fifteen before Sam Masterford yelled, "Cut!"

Lanny Hoard whistled and called, "Atta boy!" He was a little fellow, not much taller than Joe Gatski, and he had a shrill voice.

"We do it over," Sam said. "You blew your line, Jack."

Lanny yelled, "What the hell if he did! It's a natural the way he did it! Leave the line out! I wrote it, and I admit it doesn't belong. His way, it's a natural!"

"A natural," Sam repeated. "Oh, yes."

"It's okay," Gatski called. "Wrap it up and go home!"

Sam stood a minute, rubbing the side of his nose, and I looked back at the stage, just to see what he was looking at, I guess, and there Marie and Jack were, still in each other's arms, as if they hadn't heard a word. I tell you, it made even me laugh, it was so comical. I wondered, "Why did she ever quit him for a lug like Clem Batting?"

Of course she wasn't married to Batting, now, either. That had lasted only a year, when Clem walked out on her, so, I thought, maybe Jack's on the inside track again.

I ran to my lockers, along the rear wall, where I keep my properties. You don't dare turn your back to properties without putting locks on them. The mixer opened the door of his sound booth and came down the steps, lighting his pipe. Lanny Hoard called, "Marie, can I speak to you?"

But she still wasn't listening. I was standing where I could see everything, Marie and Jack still on the set, the chief pushing his camera aside, and the script girl still sitting. The stage was dim.

Jack Harter wasn't talking now. Neither was Marie. They were just looking at each other. Hungrily.

Sam Masterford had walked off the set, looking back and sort of shrugging, and I saw him head toward the hooks on the east wall, where we hung our wraps. In the dark he bumped into Joe Gatski, but I was only twenty feet from them, and didn't hear Gatski say a word. Sam told the police afterward that Gatski mumbled, "Excuse me," which doesn't sound like Gatski.

Joan Nelson, the hairdresser, snapped shut her curler and eyelash box, and started toward the exit without saying good night to anybody. Lanny Hoard saw her go and walked quickly after her, as if he had an idea. The second camera man and one of the grips, a stage hand who'd been pushing the camera truck on the trucking shot, were at the door in plain sight of Murphy, the cop, when the shot sounded, so they were out, as far as suspects went. But where the gaffer went, nobody knew. And when the time came, he wouldn't tell.

I still was facing Jack Harter when it happened. It just went *plop*, not very loud. I couldn't even tell which direction the report came from, whether from the floor or the scaffolds overhead.

For ten seconds nothing happened. Neither Marie nor Jack moved an inch. Then Jack started to bend forward. Doc Herring, the studio night surgeon, said Jack died instantly. But he didn't fall instantly. I guess he was looking too hard at Marie for that. He bent a little, then straightened, and slid to the floor. His head bumped the table, and he lay quiet on his back.

Still nobody hollered. Marie dropped to her knees, whispering, "Jack! Oh, Jack! Speak to me!"

I didn't move. Couldn't. Just looked. So did Rose Graham. Only she listened, too. And saw and heard more than the rest of us. Being a script girl, that was second nature to her.

Lanny Hoard came out of the shadows with a strained, peculiar expression on his face, both mad and surprised. He was holding up his right hand, and I saw he had a coin in his fingers. It turned out to be a nickel.

"What happened?" he asked. I heard Joe Gatski's heels slapping the floor behind Lanny, and of course Joe took charge. He's good at that. Maybe that's how he held his job so long.

He asked, "Why did the damn fool shoot himself?"

Marie looked at him, and if I ever saw hate, it was in her eyes. But she didn't answer; not with words. Just picked up Jack's head and put it gently in her lap and kissed his forehead, and the tears made zigzag lines down her yellow make-up.

By this time Gatski was hollering. "Don't leave nobody get out! Where's Sam Masterford?"

"Coming," the director yelled, running forward, trying to get his arms into his topcoat sleeves, and looking astonished and scared.

Gatski hollered, "Call Infirmary! Doctor! Police! No, no! Studio police! Come quick! Tell 'em Joe Gatski says so. Lights! Watch your dress, Marie—that blood will spoil it! It's charged to this production."

Nobody else said a word. But we were all there, thirteen of us. Twelve living, and Jack dead. Murphy the cop didn't leave the door, just blew five blasts of his whistle, over and over, calling help.

The gaffer threw some switches, and about a dozen lights flashed on, all seeming to point at Jack Harter's face. There was plenty of excitement.

Cap Wright, the night police chief, came at Doc Herring's heels, with a brace of studio cops behind him. Doc didn't even take out his stethoscope, just opened Jack's eyes and looked at them, then dusted off his hands and pulled Marie to her feet.

"Chair," he said quietly, and when I brought it, "Sit down, Miss Fleming. He's dead, of course. Who—" The doc didn't finish.

Cap Wright did that for him, though, right away.

"Who knocked him off?" he asked. He was a big man, ugly, with bug eyes. Honest, everybody said, but not exactly jolly. He'd fought off too many gate crashers, trying to meet the stars, to have a nice personality.

Joe Gatski answered him, and what he said shocked most of us. "Who knocked him off?" he repeated. "Why, Marie did it."

Cap Wright grunted, "Hell to pay! Why'd she do it?"

Then I spoke up. I said, "She didn't."

"Oh," Cap Wright answered, sort of relieved.

Joe Gatski got mad and hollered at me, "What the hell do you know?"

Cap shushed him and asked, "Where's the gun?"

That hadn't occurred to us. We all looked around the floor, but no gun. Gatski told Cap to find it quick, but Cap didn't bother to answer. He lined us up, all except Marie. She still sat there, pinching her fingers and not looking pretty any more. Joe Gatski started to walk away, but Cap hollered, and he turned, sort of surprised, and came back.

Cap asked Rose Graham, "Just where were you, miss?"

"Sitting in that chair, right here," she pointed with her foot.

"That's right," the camera chief agreed. "All the time she set there."

Cap turned on him and asked, "Where was you, Dutch?"

"Pushing my camera, here, like this," the chief answered.

I said, "That's right. I could see them both."

"Could they both see you?" Cap asked suspiciously.

Rose spoke up. "I could," she said.

"Did he have anything in his hands?" Cap wanted to know.

She nodded. "A whisk broom. He was brushing his coat."

Cap laughed, it striking him funny I had a brush when he was thinking of a gun. He asked Rose, "Did Miss Fleming have anything in her hands?"

"No," she answered. "Miss Fleming didn't

shoot him. Neither did the prop man nor Dutch. And I didn't. The shot came from back there." She pointed toward the corner of the stage, past an unfinished set of a library interior, with a statue of some kind on a bookshelf.

"How'd you know?" Joe Gatski asked.

"The sound came from there," she answered.

Doc Herring asked her to repeat that, and she pointed again.

"Where was Harter standing?" he inquired, and when I showed him, Doc said, "She's correct. The course of the slug is from left to right. Whoever shot him stood over there—" he pointed, too—"some little distance."

We all looked toward the corner, which was light enough now, but had been plenty dark when Jack was shot. The two cops came back from prowling around and said nobody was hiding on the stage, and they could find no gun.

Cap Wright said, "Well, one of you did it. For the moment we'll count Miss Fleming out. And you, miss—" he nodded to Rose—"and Dutch and this prop man—" he pointed at me. "That leaves eight." He began to count them off. "Mr. Gatski, Mr. Masterford, the gaffer, this detective writer, this fellow." He pointed to the grip.

Murphy, the cop, interrupted: "He's okay, sir. Him and the second camera man were right inside the door when it happened. It wasn't them."

"Um," Cap answered. "There's still six to pick from. Guess I'll have to question all of you."

"Of course," Sam Masterford answered sensibly. "That's only right. Start on me."

But Cap didn't. He started by looking at the gaffer. I looked, too, and what I saw surprised me. For the gaffer was drunk. Extremely. Liquor was sticking out his ears, you might say. He hadn't been drunk when we wrapped up the picture fifteen minutes ago. We'd have known it, for he was a guy you had to watch; he'd even been warned that he'd lose his job if he brought another bottle on the lot.

Cap said, "What's wrong, Otto?"

"Hell with you," the gaffer answered, and Cap had his men search him, and while they searched, Cap asked, "Where were you, Otto, when the shot was fired?"

But the gaffer just said, "I don't like studio cops."

They found no gun on him, but something else. In his bill fold was a thing you'd not expect to find on a studio technician. A picture from some fan magazine. A picture of Marie Fleming.

Cap asked Marie politely, "He a friend of yours?" and pointed to the gaffer. She shook her head. But it set Cap to wondering about the rest of us, and when his eyes came to Lanny Hoard, he frowned and remembered what the gossip colyums were saying about Lanny being that way about Marie.

"Where were you, Hoard?" he asked Lanny suddenly.

Lanny answered sarcastically, "Mr. Pinkerton grills suspect. Well, I was about to phone."

"No dirty cracks necessary," Cap told him. "You're so good at figuring things out, figure this one! Who saw you phoning?"

Lanny looked startled, and said, "Why—no one." He turned to Joan Nelson, and I remembered—he had followed the hairdresser off the set.

"He was talking to me," Joan backed him up. "Then he walked toward the phone and I started for the door."

"What did he talk to you about?" Cap asked.

Hoard answered, and you could see him getting red: "I borrowed a nickel of her. Hadn't a cent in my pants and wanted to phone for my car."

"That's right," Joan admitted, and Lanny held up the coin.

"I'd just got studio operator," he said, "and she told me to deposit five cents, and I heard the shot. I didn't put through the call."

Cap grunted, and went and whispered to his two cops, and they left the set, one going outdoors and the other starting to hunt inside again.

Gatski was getting nervous. He said impatiently, "Well, do something!"

"All right. What were you doing?" Cap asked him, but Gatski had no time to answer. Marie, who hadn't spoken yet, answered for him.

"He was pulling the trigger," she said in a flat voice.

Sam Masterford went right over to her and began to talk soothingly, and Gatski tramped up and down and swore, and asked Cap Wright to search him, and called Marie names. So Cap got the story, prying it out of us, about the argument between Gatski and Marie and Jack.

"Well, where were you, Mr. Gatski?" Cap asked again.

"He should ask a supervisor where he was!" Gatski answered sort of jerkily. "I was by the water cooler. Taking a stomach tablet. I had the heartburn."

"Alone?"

Gatski yelled, "Of course alone! Do I ask for the spotlight when I take a stomach tablet?"

Cap said to himself, "Mr. Gatski alone at the cooler, this writer alone at the telephone, the gaffer nobody knows where, but drunk."

Masterford broke in quietly, "I was alone, too. I'd gone for my coat and hat and stopped to put on my rubbers. They went on hard. I was still working on them when I heard it."

Cap went and looked at the hooks where the wraps hung, and then asked Sam, "Did you pass anybody, going toward that corner?"

"Just Mr. Gatski," Sam said, and he told about bumping into Joe, and Joe's "Excuse me."

Cap said, "Uh-huh," and looked at the sound mixer. He was the only one that hadn't confessed to being alone in the dark somewhere. Cap asked, "What's your name?"

"Battinger," the mixer answered.

Cap repeated, "Battinger?" He thought it over, still was thinking when Lanny Hoard spoke.

"Wasn't Clem Batting's real name Battinger?" he asked.

Then I remembered. When Marie divorced

Jack to marry Clem, the newspaper colyumists had dug up Clem's real name.

"Clem's my brother," the mixer said.

Marie looked at him quickly, with a scared expression, as if that were a secret she hadn't meant to tell. But Joan, the hairdresser, spoke up again at once. "Mr. Battinger was ahead of me on the way to the door when the shot was fired. I could see him. I'd just left Lanny."

While Cap was thinking this over, the cop he'd sent off stage came back and whispered to him, and he nodded and looked at Lanny, then back at the mixer.

"So Clem's your brother," he said. "But the girl claims she saw you heading toward the door when the shot was fired. If you didn't do it, it's a good thing you've got an alibi."

He didn't seem satisfied, however. When the cop came back still without the gun, Cap searched us all, regardless. He got the three women to help him search each other, even, but there wasn't any gun. All this took time. It was three o'clock and we were getting nowhere fast, when suddenly Rose spoke up.

"You're running in a circle," she accused, and Cap said:

"Yeh? You could do better?"

Rose blushed easy, but she stuck to it. And everybody listened. Everybody around a studio knows about script girls and what kind of eyes and ears they've got.

"You know already it's one of us," she said, "and you yourself limit it to one out of six."

"That's right," Cap agreed.

"Of those six, let's start with Otto, then," Rose said. "He's got a picture of Miss Fleming in his pocket. But regardless of that, he's just plain drunk."

"Not drunk," the gaffer denied.

"He'll not tell us what he was doing at the minute," she admitted, "but that's explainable. He was drinking on the set and didn't want to lose his job."

Cap argues, "We can't find any bottle."

"I saw Otto hide a bottle once before," Rose said. She walked back along the wall, where a battery of lights stood ready to work on the rose trellis set in the morning. She looked into the barrel of each light and finally called Cap. "He spilled it, you see," she pointed out as Cap lifted an empty bottle from the light. "Didn't put the cork back in. There's the liquor, running down inside the light."

"My bottle," Otto grunted, and Cap asked:

"What does it prove?"

"Why, that he was drinking when the shot occurred," Rose said. "The sound scared him, and he dropped the stopper. There it is, on the floor. It was too dark to find it, so he did the next best thing. Put the bottle away open."

Cap admitted, "It's possible. That would put the gaffer at the opposite corner of the stage from the murderer, in spite of the picture in his pocket."

"That leaves five," Rose said. "As for Battinger, he has Joan's alibi." She looked at the sound mixer, and he tried to smile. "That's enough, isn't it? In spite of his being the brother of Marie's former husband?"

Cap didn't like to count the mixer out, but at last he said, "For the time being, okay. That leaves—"

"Joan herself," Rose said, "which is ridiculous. And Mr. Gatski, and Sam Masterford, and Lanny Hoard."

Lanny cried, "You're crazy, Rose. You've got to show a motive."

"Yes, when writing a melodrama," she answered, without looking at him. "But this isn't a script. It's facts. The sort of things I'm used to, day in and day out."

Lanny started to storm, and Cap told him to shut up.

"Lanny either talked himself into a hole or out of it a bit ago," Rose said. "He claimed he had the receiver off the hook, with the operator listening for the sound of a nickel hitting the bell, when the shot was fired."

Cap smiled. "Smart girl," he said. "I thought of that, too. Hoard told the truth. My man checked with the operator. She heard the shot, and Hoard saying, 'What the hell!'"

"That leaves two," Rose went on, holding up two fingers, "Mr. Gatski and Sam Masterford."

Joe Gatski began to holler all over again and nothing could stop him this time. He said he'd get the girl's job, and he talked about his lawyers, and walked up and down, banging his heels on the floor. At last Cap got him quiet, telling him what this girl said wasn't important. But Joe went on giving her filthy looks just the same.

She said, "Sam was putting on his rubbers, over by that wall. The murderer—" she hesitated, as if she didn't like the taste of the word on her tongue, then in spite of herself she repeated it—"the murderer was standing somewhere near the end of that unfinished library set there, and Sam was in behind it. And Mr. Gatski was back near the rose trellis set you see over there."

"Why, that's right," Gatski yelled. "I couldn't shoot around corners!"

"How do you know where Gatski was?" Cap asked.

"My ears told me," Rose said. "Haven't you heard him walk? He runs the same way, hitting the floor first with his heels. I think he'll drive me crazy sometimes on a set. To get to the place from which the shot was fired, and back again, in that short time, he'd have had to run. But he didn't run. I was listening."

Sam Masterford looked sort of astonished.

"So you put me behind the eight ball in your calculations?" he asked.

Rose answered, "No. Behind the pistol. You shot Jack."

Sam didn't say a word. Not a word. Just blinked his gray eyes behind his glasses and looked at Marie. She got up to her feet, slowly, and if a woman ever had suffering in her face, she did at that moment.

"So it was you, Sam," she whispered. "Sam, I understand now. All this talk about you loving me!"

Gatski grumbled, "It's screwy, perfectly screwy! Sam Masterford wouldn't shoot a—"

"Mr. Masterford saw the same thing I did," Rose went on, speaking to Lanny Hoard. "The reason Jack blew up on his last line was that there wasn't any line. They were just falling in love all over again." Marie sobbed out loud, but Rose couldn't stop. "It wasn't acting at all," she explained. "Someone called the scene a natural. It was. Sam recognized it. He tried to change it. Didn't like it, and didn't even want to shoot it. He put it off as long as he could. But Marie kept right on looking at Jack the same way."

Still Sam didn't say a word.

"He has his rubbers on," Rose added. "Remember, he called attention to them, said he had a hard time getting them on. You can't hear a man run in rubbers."

Lanny broke in, half-defending Sam. "You didn't find any gun on him!"

"That's right," Cap agreed, "we haven't found any gun."

Rose looked toward the library set, with its bookshelves half-full. She said, "Did you look back of the books?"

The two cops began to tear down the books. There the gun was, on the top shelf.

Rose said, "Sam and I worked on a quickie together, six or eight years back. One of the first sound-effect jobs. He ran in a scene then of a fellow hiding a gun in the bookshelves of a library. I've always remembered it."

"Oh," Sam said, and sweat began running again off his long, thin nose. "I see. That's where the idea came from," and then he asked the only question in his own defense. "Why didn't Gatski put it there? Or Hoard?"

"They weren't near enough," Rose answered, "and besides, they couldn't reach that high shelf, Sam."

"They could throw it up," he sort of argued.

"Not without me hearing it," she reminded him.

Cap turned to her. "Thanks, miss," he started to say, but Joe Gatski had pulled out his watch by this time, and he interrupted:

"Four o'clock!" he exclaimed. "And we

haven't called the city police!" He started for the phone, but turned around quickly. "Remember, holding you here was none of my doing. I'm paying no overtime after eleven o'clock. Charge it up to Masterford."

Sam just shrugged, and didn't say anything. He never was much of a hand to talk. He didn't even take the stand at the trial. Claimed he

didn't remember anything about it. He didn't of course, but the public couldn't believe that. Never will. Somebody's hiding something, they think, but the reason for that is, they've never been on a set on a cleanup night. Anything can happen to anybody the last hours of any production. Like I said before, somebody ought to write a piece about it.

THE GILDED PUPIL

Ethel Lina White

ALTHOUGH SHE BEGAN WRITING stories, essays, and poems as a child, the Welsh-born Ethel Lina White (1876–1944) did not publish her first novel, *The Wish-Bone* (1927), until she was past her fiftieth birthday. Her first three books were general fiction, after which she wrote more than a dozen mystery novels, beginning with *Put Out the Light* (1931).

Though White was one of England's most popular mystery writers during the 1930s and early 1940s, her books are seldom read today, her reputation resting mainly on the motion pictures, inspired by her extremely suspenseful novels, that are in constant rerun on classic movie channels.

The Spiral Staircase, directed by Robert Siodmak and starring Dorothy McGuire and Ethel Barrymore, was released in 1946; it was based on White's 1933 novel *Some Must Watch*. It was remade in 1975 with Jacqueline Bisset and Christopher Plummer, and again as a made-for-television movie in 2000 with Nicollette Sheridan and Judd Nelson.

Even more successful was *The Lady Vanishes*, directed by Alfred Hitchcock and starring Margaret Lockwood, Michael Redgrave, and Paul Lukas. Released in 1938, it was inspired by White's 1936 novel *The Wheel Spins*. It, too, has been remade twice, once in 1979, starring Elliott Gould, Cybill Shepherd, and Angela Lansbury, and again as a made-for-television movie in 2013 with Tuppence Middleton, Keeley Hawes, and Julian Rhind-Tutt. *Her Heart in Her Throat* (1942; the British title was *Midnight House*) was filmed as *The Unseen* (1945), starring Joel McCrea, Gail Russell, and Herbert Marshall.

"The Gilded Pupil" was first published in *Detective Stories of To-day*, edited by Raymond Postgate (London, Faber & Faber, 1940).

The Gilded Pupil

ETHEL LINA WHITE

THE ESSENTIAL PART of this tale is that Ann Shelley was an Oxford M.A.

Unfortunately, so many other young women had the same idea of going to College and getting a Degree, that she found it difficult to harness her qualifications with a job. Therefore she considered herself lucky when she was engaged as resident governess to Stella Williams, aged fifteen—the only child of a millionaire manufacturer.

It was not until her final interview with Stella's mother, in a sunroom which was a smother of luxury, that she understood the exact nature of her duties. Lady Williams—a beautiful porcelain person, with the brains of a butterfly—looked at her with appealing violet eyes.

"It's so difficult to explain, Miss Shelley. Of course, my husband considers education comes first, but what *I* want is someone to exercise a moral influence on Stella. She—she's not normal."

"Thymus gland?" hinted Ann.

"Oh, far worse. She won't wash."

Ann thought of the times she had been sent upstairs to remove a water-mark, because she had overslept, or wanted to finish a thriller; and she began to laugh.

"That's normal, at her age," she explained. "Schoolgirls often scamp washing."

Lady Williams looked sceptical, but relieved.

"The trouble began," she said, "when she was too old for a nurse. Nannie used to wash and dress her, like a baby. But she refuses to let her maid do anything but impersonal things, like clothes. It's her idea of independence. She's terribly clever and Socialistic. She'll try to catch you out."

"That sounds stimulating," smiled Ann.

All the same, she was not impressed pleasantly by her new pupil. Stella was unattractive, aggressive, and superior. Her sole recommendation to Ann's favour was her intelligence, which was far above the average.

On her first Saturday half-holiday, Ann walked out to the grounds of Arlington Manor—the residence of the Earl of Blankshire—to visit her old governess, Miss West. It was a May day of exciting weather, with concealed lighting bursting through a white windy sky. She thrilled with a sense of liberation, when she turned to the road through the woods, where the opening beeches were an emerald filigree against the blue shadows of the undergrowth.

Miss West's cottage suggested a fairy-tale, with its thatched roof and diamond-paned windows. It stood in a clearing, and was surrounded by a small garden, then purple with clumps of irises.

Ann's knock was answered by the maid, Maggie—a strapping country girl. She showed the visitor into the bed-sitting-room, where her mistress, who was crippled with rheumatism, was sitting up in bed.

Miss West was an old woman, for she had also been governess to Ann's mother. Her mouth and chin had assumed the nutcracker of age, so that she looked rather like an old witch, with her black blazing eyes and snowy hair.

Her dominant quality was her vitality. Ann could still feel it playing on her, like a battery, as they exchanged greetings.

"I love your little house," she remarked later, when Maggie had brought in tea. "But it's very lonely. Are you ever nervous?"

"Nervous of what?" asked Miss West. "There's nothing here to steal, and no money. Everyone knows that the Earl is my banker."

This was her way of explaining that she was a penniless pensioner of the Earl, whom she had taught, in his nursery days.

"Every morning, someone comes down from the Manor, with the day's supplies," she said. "At night, a responsible person visits me for my orders and complaints. . . . Oh, you needn't look down your nose. The Earl is in *my* debt. He is prolonging my life at a trifling expense to himself; but I saved his life, when he was a child, at the risk of my own."

Her deep voice throbbed as she added, "I still feel there is nothing so precious as Life."

Later, in that small bewitched room, Ann was to remember her words.

"Life's big things appeal most to me," she confessed. "Oxford was wonderful—every minute of it. And I'm just living for my marriage with Kenneth. I told you I was engaged. He's a doctor on a ship, and we'll have to wait. In between, I'm just marking time."

"You have the important job of moulding character," Miss West reminded her. "How does your gilded pupil progress?"

"She's a gilded pill." Ann grimaced. "A gilded pupill."

"Is Oxford responsible for your idea of humour?" asked Miss West, who had a grudge against a University education.

"No, it's the result of living in a millionaire's family. Please, may I come to see you, every Saturday afternoon? You make me feel re-charged."

Although Miss West had acted like a mental tonic, Ann was conscious of a period of stagnation, when she walked back through the wood. She taught, in order to live, and went to see an old woman, as recreation. Life was dull.

It might not have appeared so flat, had she known that she was marked down already for a leading part in a sinister drama, and that she had been followed all the way to the cottage.

For the next few weeks life continued to be monotonous for Ann, but it grew exciting for Stella, as, gradually, she felt the pull of her governess's attraction. Ann had a charming appearance and definite personality. She made no attempt to rouse her pupil's personal pride by shock-tactics, but relied on the contrast between her own manicured hands and the girl's neglected nails.

Presently she was able to report progress to the young ship's doctor.

"My three years at Oxford have not been wasted," she wrote. "The Gilded Pupill has begun to wash."

In her turn she became fonder of Stella, especially when she discovered that the girl's aggressive manner was a screen for an inferiority-complex.

"I always feel people hate me," she confided to her governess one day. "I'm ashamed of having a millionaire father. *He* didn't make his money. Others make it for him. He ought to pay them a real spending-income, and, automatically, increase the demand, and create fresh employment."

Ann found these Socialistic debates rather a trial of tact, but she enjoyed the hours of study. Stella was a genuine student, and always read up her subject beforehand, so that lessons took somewhat the form of discussions and explanations. Ann was spared the drudgery of correcting French exercises and problems in Algebra.

But her gain was someone else's loss. She had no idea how seriously she was restricting the activities of another character in the Plot.

Doris—the schoolroom maid—searched daily amid the fragments in the wastepaper-basket for something which she had been ordered to procure. And she searched in vain.

When Stella's devotion to the bathroom was deepening to passion, she began to grow jealous of her governess's private hours.

"Do you go to the Pictures on Saturday?" she asked.

"No. I visit an old witch in a cottage in the wood."

"Take me with you."

"You'd be bored. It's my old governess."

"*Your* governess? I'd love to see her. *Please.*"

Ann had to promise a vague "someday." Although she was sorry to disappoint Stella, she could not allow her to encroach on her precious liberty.

By this time, however, her time-table was an established fact to the brains of the Plot. Therefore, the next Saturday she visited Miss West she was followed by a new trailer.

She noticed him when she came out of the great gates of the millionaire's mansion, because he aroused a momentary sense of repugnance. He was fair and rather womanish in appearance, but his good looks were marred by a cruel red triangular mouth.

He kept pace with her on the opposite side of the street, when she was going through the town, but she shook him off later on. Therefore it gave her quite a shock when she turned into the beech-avenue—now a green tunnel—to hear his footsteps a little distance in the rear.

Although she was furious with herself, she hurried to reach the cottage, which was quite close. The door was opened before she could knock, because her arrival was the signal for Maggie's release. It was Ann herself who had suggested the extra leisure for the maid while she kept the old lady company.

Miss West, whose bed faced the window, greeted her with a question.

"When did you lose your admirer?"

"Who?" asked Anne, in surprise.

"I refer to the weedy boy who always slouches past the minute after your knock."

"I've never noticed him. . . . But I thought I was followed here today by a specially unpleasant-looking man."

"Hum. We'd better assume that you were. . . . How much money have you in your bag?"

"More than I care to lose."

"Then leave all the notes with me. I'll get the Manor folk to return them to you by registered post. . . . And remember, if the man attacks you on your way home, don't resist. Give him your bag—and run."

"You're arranging a cheerful programme for me," laughed Ann.

She might not have felt so amused had she known that the whole time she was inside the cottage the man was not far away, crouched behind a belt of rhododendrons. Inside a deep pocket of his full belted coat was coiled something like a gigantic black slug.

It was a stocking stuffed with sand.

When nine struck, Miss West told her to go.

"Maggie is due now, any minute," she told her, "and so is the housekeeper from the Manor. Good-bye—and don't forget it means 'God be with you.'"

Ann was not nervous, but when she walked down the garden path she could not help contrasting the dark green twilight of the woods with the sun-splashed beech avenue of the afternoon. Clumps of fox-gloves glimmered whitely through the gloom, and in the distance an owl hooted to his mate.

She passed close by the bushes where the man was hiding. He could have touched her had he put out his hand. She was his quarry, whom he had followed to the cottage, so he looked at her intently.

Her expensive bag promised a rich haul. Yet

he let her go by, and waited, instead, for some-one who was of only incidental interest to the Plot.

A few minutes later Maggie charged down the avenue like a young elephant, for she was late. She had not a nerve in her body, and only threepence in her purse. As she passed the rho-dodendron thicket, a shadow slipped out of it like an adder—a black object whirled round in the air—and Maggie fell down on the ground like a log.

The mystery attack was a nine-days' wonder, for bag-snatching was unknown in the district. But while Maggie was recovering from slight concussion in hospital, Ann had the unpleasant task of mentally bludgeoning her pupil out of a "rave." After the weekly visit of the hairdresser, Stella appeared in the school-room with her hair cut and waved in the same fashion as Ann's.

"Like it?" she asked self-consciously.

"It's charming." Ann had to be tender with the inferiority-complex. "But I liked your old style better. That was *you*. Don't copy me, Stella. I should never forgive myself if I robbed you of your individuality."

Stella wilted like a pimpernel in wet weather.

"I'm not going to have a crush on you," she declared. "Too definitely feeble. But we're friends, aren't we? Let's have a sort of Friend's Charter, with a secret signature, when we write to each other. Like this." She scrawled a five-fingered star on a piece of paper and explained it eagerly. "My name."

Ann was aware that Doris, the school-room maid, was listening with a half-grin, and she decided to nip the nonsense in the bud.

"You'll want a Secret Society next, you baby," she said, as she crumpled up the paper. "Now, suppose we call it a day and go to the Pictures."

Stella especially enjoyed that afternoon's entertainment, because the film was about a kid-napped girl, and she was excited by the personal implication.

"If a kidnapper ever got me, I'd say 'Good luck' to him. He'd deserve it," she boasted as they drove home. "They wouldn't decoy me into a taxi with a fake message."

Ann's private feeling was that Stella's intelli-gence was not likely to be tested, since she ran no possible risk. Lady Williams was nervous on the score of her valuable jewellery, so the house was burglar-proof, with flood-lit grounds and every kind of electric alarm.

Besides this, Stella either went out in the car, driven by a trusted chauffeur, or took her walks with a positive pack of large dogs.

So it was rather a shock to Ann when the girl lowered her voice.

"I'll tell you a secret. They've had a shot for me. They sent one of our own cars to the danc-ing class; but I noticed Hereford wasn't driving, so I wouldn't get in. I wouldn't tell them at home because of Mother. She's beautiful and sweet, but she'd go to a Queen's Hall Concert expect-ing a Walt Disney Silly Symphony."

Ann, who was still under the influence of the Picture, was horrified.

"Stella," she cried, "I want you to promise me something. If ever you get a note, signed by me, *take no notice of it*."

"I promise. But if you signed it with our star, I'd *know* it was genuine. And if you were in dan-ger, nothing and no one would stop me from coming to your rescue."

"Single-handed, like the screen heroines, who blunder into every trap?"

"Not me. I'll bring the police with me. . . . Isn't that our school-room maid coming down the drive? Isn't she gorgeous?"

Doris, transformed by a Marina cap and gen-erous lip-stick, minced past the car. She had to be smart, because she was meeting a fashionable gentleman with a cruel red mouth.

When she saw him in the distance, she antici-pated his question by shaking her head.

"No good swearing at me," she told him. "I can't get what isn't there. But I've brought you something else."

She gave him a sheet of crumpled paper on which was the rough drawing of a star.

The next time Ann went to the cottage in the wood the door was opened by the new maid—an ice-cold competent brunette in immaculate livery. There was no doubt she was a domestic treasure and a great improvement on Maggie; but Ann was repelled by the expression of her thin-lipped mouth.

"I don't like your new maid's face," she said to her old governess when Coles had carried out the tea-table.

"Neither do I," remarked Miss West calmly. "She's far too good for my situation—yet she's no fool. My opinion is she's wanted by the police and has come here to hide. It's an ideal spot."

"But you won't keep her?"

"Why not? She's an excellent maid. There's no reason why I should not benefit by the special circumstances, if any. After all it's only my suspicion."

"What about her references?"

"Superlative. Probably forged. The housekeeper hadn't time to enquire too closely. The place isn't popular after the attack on Maggie."

"But I don't like to think of you alone at her mercy."

"Don't worry about me. She's been to the cupboard and found out it's bare. I've nothing to lose."

Ann realized the sense of Miss West's argument, especially as she was in constant touch with the Manor. Not long afterwards she wondered whether she had misjudged the woman, for she received a letter by the next morning's post which indicated that she was not altogether callous.

Its address was the cottage in the wood.

"Dear Madam," it ran. "Pardon the liberty of my writing to you, but I feel responsible for Miss West in case anything happens sudden to her and there's an Inquest. I would be obliged if you would tell me is her heart bad and what to do in case of a sudden attack. I don't like to trouble her ladyship as I am a stranger to her and Miss West bites my head off if I ask her. I could not ask you today because she is suspicious of whispering. Will you kindly drop me a line in return and oblige, Yours respectfully, Marion Coles."

Ann hastily wrote the maid a brief note saying that Miss West had good health—apart from the crippling rheumatism—but recommending a bottle of brandy in case of emergency. She posted it, and forgot the matter.

Meanwhile, Miss West was finding Coles's competency a pleasant change after Maggie's slipshod methods. On the following Saturday, when she carried in her mistress's lunch, Miss West looked, with approval, at her spotless apron and muslin collar.

After she had finished her well-cooked cutlet and custard, she lay back and closed her eyes in order to be fresh for Ann's visit. The cottage was very peaceful with a flicker of green shade outside the window; there was none of the noisy clatter from the kitchen which used to advertise the fact when Maggie washed up—only the ticking of the grandfather's clock and the cooing of wood-pigeons.

She had begun to doze when she heard the opening of the front door. Her visitor was before her usual time.

"Ann," she called.

Instead of her old pupil, a strange woman entered the bedroom. Her fashionably thin figure was defined by a tight black suit, and a halo hat revealed a sharp rouged face.

As Miss West stared at her, she gave a cry of recognition.

"*Coles.*"

The woman sneered at her like a camel.

"Here's two gentlemen come to see you," she announced.

As she spoke, two men, dressed with flashy smartness, sauntered into the room. One was blond and handsome except for a red triangular mouth; the other had the small cunning eyes and low-set ears of an elementary criminal type.

"Go out of my room," ordered Miss West. "Coles, you are discharged."

The men only laughed as they advanced to the bed.

"We're only going to make you safer, old lady," said the fair man. "You might fall out of bed and hurt yourself. See?"

Miss West did not condescend to struggle while her feet and hands were secured with cords. Her wits told her that she would need to conserve every ounce of strength.

"Aren't you taking an unnecessary precaution with a bedridden woman?" she asked scornfully.

"Nothing too good for you, sweetheart," the fair man told her.

"Why have you come here? My former maid has told you that there is nothing of value in my cottage."

"Nothing but you, Beautiful."

"How dare you be insolent to me? Take off your hats in a lady's presence."

The men only laughed. They sat and smoked cigarettes in silence until a knock on the front door made them spring to their feet.

"Let her in," ordered the ringleader.

Miss West strained at her cords as Coles went out of the room. Her black eyes glared with helpless fury when Ann entered and stood—horror-stricken—in the doorway.

"Don't *dare* touch her," she cried.

The men merely laughed again as they seized the struggling girl, forced her down on a bedroom chair, and began to bind her ankles.

"Ann," commanded the old governess. "Keep still. They're three to one. An elementary knowledge of arithmetic should tell you resistance is useless. But I forgot. You were finished at Oxford."

The pedantic old voice steadied Ann's nerves.

"Are *you* all right, Miss West?" she asked coolly.

"Quite comfortable, thanks."

"Good." Ann turned to the men. "What do you want?"

They did not answer, but nodded to Coles, who placed a small table before Ann. With the deft movements of a well-trained maid, she arranged stationery—stamped with Miss West's address—and writing materials.

Then the fair man explained the situation.

"The Williams kid wot you teach is always pestering you to come here and see the old lady. Now, you're going to write her a nice little note inviting her to tea this afternoon."

Ann's heart hammered as she realized that she had walked into a trap. The very simplicity of the scheme was its safeguard. She was the decoy-bird. The kidnappers had only to instal a spy in the Williams household to study the habits of the governess.

Unfortunately she had led them to an ideal rendezvous—the cottage in the wood.

"*No,*" she said.

The next second she shivered as something cold was pressed to her temple.

"We'll give you five minutes to make up your mind," said the fair man, glancing at the grandfather's clock. "Then, we shoot."

Ann gritted her teeth. In that moment her reason told her that she was probably acting from false sentiment and a confused set of values. But logic was of no avail. Like the intellectual youth of the Nation, who went over the top while probably cursing the insanity of War, she knew she had to sacrifice herself for an Ideal.

She could not betray her trust.

"No," she said again.

The second man crossed to the bed and pressed his revolver to Miss West's head.

"Her too," he said.

Ann looked at her old governess, in an agony, imploring her forgiveness.

"She's only fifteen," she said piteously, as though in excuse.

"And I'm an old woman," grunted Miss West. "Your reasoning is sound. But you forget someone younger than your pupil. Your unborn son."

Ann's face quivered, but she shook her head.

Then the old governess spoke with the rasp of authority in her voice.

"Ann, I'm ashamed of you. What is money compared with two valuable lives, not to mention those still to come? I understand these— gentlemen—do not wish to injure your pupil. They only want to collect a ransom."

"That's right, lady," agreed the fair man. "We won't do her no harm. This will tell the old man all he'll want to know."

He laid down a typewritten demand note on the table and added a direction to Ann.

"When we've gone off with the kid, nip off to the old man as fast as you can and give him this."

"With her legs tied to a chair?" asked the deep sarcastic voice of the old woman.

"She's got her hands free, ain't she? Them knots will take some undoing, but it's up to her, ain't it?"

"True. No doubt she will manage to free herself. . . . But suppose she writes this note and the young lady does not accept the invitation? What then?"

The fair man winked at his companion.

"Then you'll both be unlucky," he replied.

Ann listened in dull misery. She could not understand the drift of Miss West's questions. They only prolonged the agony. Both of them knew they could place no reliance on the promises of the kidnappers. The men looked a pair of merciless beasts.

If she wrote that note, she would lure her poor little gilded pupil to her death.

She started as her governess spoke sharply to her.

"*Ann*, you've heard what these gentlemen have said." She added in bitter mockery of their speech, "*Gentlemen* what keeps their hats on in the presence of ladies, wouldn't never break their word. *Write that note.*"

Ann could not believe her ears. Yet she could feel the whole force of her vitality playing on her like an electric battery. It reminded her of a former experience when she was a child. Her uncle, who paid for her education, was an Oxford don,

and he raised an objection against Miss West because she was unqualified.

In the end he consented to give his niece a viva-voce examination, on the result of which depended the governess's fate.

Ann passed the test triumphantly, but she always felt, privately, that Miss West supplied the right answers as she sat staring at her pupil with hypnotic black eyes.

Now she knew that the old magic was at work again. Miss West was trying to tell her something without the aid of words.

Suddenly the knowledge came. Her old governess was playing for time. Probably she was expecting some male visitors from the Manor, as the Earl and his sons often came to the cottage. What she, herself, had to do was to stave off the five-minute sentence of death by writing a note to Stella which was hallmarked as a forgery, so that the girl would not come.

As she hesitated she remembered that she had extracted a promise from her pupil to disregard any message. The question was, whether it would be obeyed, for she knew the strength of her fatal attraction and that Stella was eager to visit the cottage.

Hoping for the best, she began to write, disguising her handwriting by a backward slant.

"Dear Stella"—

With an oath the man snatched up the paper and threw it on the floor in a crumpled ball.

"None of them monkey tricks," he snarled. "We know your proper writing. And sign it with *this.*"

Ann's hope died as the man produced the letter which she had written to Coles about Miss West's health, and also Stella's rough drawing of a star. She was defeated by the evidence—a specimen of her handwriting—for which Doris the school-room maid had searched in vain— and the secret signature.

"I—can't," she said, feebly pushing away the paper.

Again the pistol was pressed to her head.

"Don't waste no time," growled the fair man.

"Don't waste no time," echoed Miss West. "Ann, *write*."

There was a spark in the old woman's eyes and the flash of Wireless. Impelled to take up the pen, Ann wrote quickly in a firm hand, and signed her note with a faithful copy of the star.

The men hung over her, watching every stroke, and comparing the writing with Coles's letter.

"Don't put no dots," snarled the fair man, who plainly suspected a cypher when Ann inserted a period.

He read the note again when it was finished, and then passed it to his companion, who pointed to a word suspiciously. The old woman and the girl looked at each other in an agony of suspense as they waited for the blow to fall.

Then the fair man turned sharply to Miss West.

"Spell 'genwin,'" he commanded.

As she reeled off the correct spelling, he glanced doubtfully at his companion, who nodded.

"O.K.," he said.

Miss West's grim face did not relax, and Ann guessed the reason. She was nerving herself for the second ordeal of Coles's inspection.

Fortunately, however, the men did not want their female confederate's opinion. The job was done and they wanted to rush it forward to its next stage. The fair man sealed the note and whistled on his fingers.

Instantly the weedy youth who had followed Ann to the cottage appeared from behind a clump of laurels in the drive, wheeling a bicycle. He snatched the letter from Coles and scorched away round the bend of the road.

Ann slumped back in her chair, feeling unstrung in every fibre. Nothing remained but to wait—wait—and pray Stella would not come.

The time seemed to pass very slowly inside the room. The men smoked in silence until the carpet was littered with cigarette stubs and the air veined with smoke. Miss West watched the clock as though she would galvanize the crawling minute-hand.

"Don't come," agonized Ann. "Stella, *don't come*."

But absent treatment proved a failure, for Coles, who was hiding behind a curtain, gave a sudden hoot of triumph.

"The car's come."

"Push the girl to the front," commanded the fair man.

He helped to lift Ann's chair to the window, so that she saw the Williams' Lanchester waiting in front of the cottage. Stella stood on the drive, and the chauffeur, Hereford, was in the act of shutting the door. He sprang back to his seat, backed, saluted, and drove swiftly away.

Ann watched the car disappear with despairing eyes. She could not scream, because fingers were gripping her windpipe, nearly choking her. But Stella could distinguish the pale-blue blur of her frock behind the diamond-paned window, and she waved her hand as she ran eagerly up the garden path.

Had Ann been normal, she might have guessed the truth from Stella's reaction to the scene when she burst into the room. Instead of appearing surprised, she dashed to Ann and threw her arms around her.

"They didn't fool *me*," she whispered.

Then she began to fight like a boxing-kangaroo in order to create the necessary distraction, while the police-car came round the bend of the drive.

The prelude to a successful raid was the millionaire's call for prompt action when his daughter brought him Ann's note.

"It's her writing and our private star," she told him. "But—read it." He glanced at the few lines and laughed.

"An impudent forgery," he said.

"No, it's an S.O.S. It looks like a second try for me."

After she had told her father about the first unsuccessful attempt to kidnap her, he realized the importance of nipping the gang's activities in the bud.

This seems the place to print the note which was the alleged composition of an Oxford M.A.

"Dear Stella, Miss West will be pleased if you will come to tea this afternoon. Don't waste no time, and don't run no risks. Let Hereford drive you in the car. To prove this is genuine, I'm signing it with our star, same as you done, one day in the school-room.

Yours, Ann Shelley, M.A."

THE CASE OF THE HUNDRED CATS

Gladys Mitchell

AS ONE OF THE FIRST MEMBERS of London's prestigious Detection Club in the 1930s, and with nearly eighty books to her credit, Gladys Maude Winifred Mitchell (1901–1983) should be as familiar as her contemporaries, Agatha Christie and Dorothy L. Sayers, with whom she was once ranked as "one of the Big Three women mystery writers" of the Golden Age, but that hasn't been the case for many years.

One of the biggest problems for the lack of popularity may be that Mitchell's series character, Dame Beatrice Bradley, who appeared in sixty-six novels and several short stories, is so reptilian in tone and appearance that people are surprised that she doesn't have a forked tongue. Mitchell often denigrates conventions of the genre, notably when she parodies Christie's novel *The Mysterious Affair at Styles* (1920) with *The Mystery of a Butcher's Shop* (1929). Additionally, many of Bradley's cases are heavily laden with Freudian psychology, and it is suggested in the books that she is descended from a long line of witches, so it is no surprise that the supernatural often plays a role in her adventures—not a particularly welcome element for many readers of detective stories.

Mitchell worked as a teacher for more than twenty-five years, first out of economic necessity, then during World War II because of England's shortage of teachers. She had tremendous enthusiasm for the teachings of Freud, so made Dame Beatrice a psychiatrist with her own practice as well as a psychiatric consultant to the Home Office. Enviably, Bradley remains the same age in the last novel about her, *The Crozier Pharaohs* (1984), as she was in the first, *Speedy Death* (1929).

"The Case of the Hundred Cats" was originally published in *Fifty Famous Detectives of Fiction*, edited anonymously (London, Odhams Press, 1938); it was first collected in *Sleuth's Alchemy: Cases of Mrs. Bradley and Others*, edited by Nicholas Fuller (Norfolk, Virginia, Crippen & Landru, 2005).

The Case of the Hundred Cats

GLADYS MITCHELL

FROM THE VERY FIRST I myself suspected the aunt. We had been asked to see a patient who suffered from periodic loss of memory, but Mrs. Bradley—who was carrying out a delicate Home Office job at the time—was not prepared to undertake the case, so I thought I would ring up John.

"Is that the house where they keep all those cats?" he asked.

"I don't know, John."

"Well, it is. That woman takes drugs."

"You won't accept the case, then?"

"No, I won't. They called me in last month, and I told them then what I thought. Mrs. What's it is trying to get the other one's money. She'll get her certified if she possibly can."

I wrote to Mrs. Dudley, the woman who had sent me the letter, and told her to bring the patient to see me.

The two of them came next day, a woman of fifty or so, in very sombre clothes, with a heavy face purple with powder and too much eye shadow on, and a frail, anæmic-looking younger woman who seemed too timid even to give her name.

Ethel let them in to the consulting room, and I sat behind the largest of the three desks, fountain pen in hand, and horn-rimmed goggles on nose, and tried not to look like the prettiest secretary in London.

"Mrs. and Miss Dudley?" I asked, making rapid hieroglyphics on a pad.

"Mrs. and Miss Dudley. Yes, that's right," the elder lady said.

"Then, may I see Miss Dudley alone?"

"No, no!" said the girl, in a whining voice. "I had really rather you didn't!"

"You see, I'm afraid you're not quite clear——" said the aunt.

I looked from one to the other.

"It is customary for the patients themselves to describe to me their symptoms. In this way I can tell whether the case is of sufficient importance for Mrs. Bradley to handle," I said with exceptional rudeness. I disliked Mrs. Dudley at sight, and as for the niece, I never saw anyone who made me feel more irritable. "Then do I understand—oh, then you are not Mrs. Bradley?" the elder lady said.

"I'm the secretary. It is my duty to keep Mrs. Bradley's engagement book up to date. If I think there is no case of sufficient importance for her I send the patients elsewhere—to Sir John MacGovern, for example. But, of course, I can't tell anything about the case until I have questioned the patient alone," I added, turning to the younger woman again.

I saw them look at each other—just a flash, but unmistakable when you're looking out for such a response. The elder woman cleared her throat a little. People often dislike me—I am too pretty and too efficient, I suppose. The first antagonises women, the second men. It is unfortunate for me, in a way.

The elder woman rose.

"Very well. I suppose you mean you want to question us separately. Where shall I wait?"

I rang for Ethel to show her into the lounge. It was eleven o'clock. Ethel, I knew, would settle her down in the lounge and bring her sweet biscuits and coffee, and perhaps a Turkish cigarette, thus producing, as exactly as possible, the psychological effects of the lounge of one of the big London stores, where women of this type seem to spend their time. Besides, these would keep her occupied whilst I questioned the patient, and, even if she wondered all the time what was being asked and answered, experience had informed us that her wondering would be of a comparatively charitable kind.

As soon as she had gone I settled down to it.

"Do you want to come to Mrs. Bradley for some treatment?" I enquired. The patient looked at me with her large, weak, silly, blue eyes, and nodded.

"Is that the truth? Or did your aunt bring you here against your will?" I said. It was a pretty direct suggestion, but she ignored it.

"I wanted to come. I am very ill. I think I am going to die," the poor foolish creature observed, in the same thin, wailing voice as she had used when her aunt was in the room.

"You take drugs, don't you?" I said, remembering what John had told me over the telephone.

"Sometimes. When the cats get very bad."

"The cats?"

"I do love them. They are dears. But they scratch me sometimes. Look!" She glanced fearfully round at the door, then showed me her neck and shoulder, pulling the blouse away with such nervous fingers that one of the buttons flew off.

"I must sew that on before auntie sees it," she said.

We both went down on our knees in search of

it, and when it was found she stuffed it into the pocket of her suit, beneath a handkerchief.

"I'm scratched all over," she said.

"But all these scratches are dangerous! How many cats have you got?"

"A hundred, and I love them all," she said. The bending about had brought colour into her cheeks, and she looked a good deal prettier.

"A hundred?" I said. "And when you lose your memory, do you forget the cats?"

"No, never. I always remember the cats. At least, the cats are the last things I think about when I lose my memory, and the first things I think about when it comes back to me."

"Do you wander away from your home?"

"Oh, yes. They find me usually at the Zoo."

"At the Zoo? What makes you go there?"

"I haven't the slightest idea. I'm always looking at birds when I go to the Zoo. I believe I think I'm a cat."

She was gaining much more confidence. She was leaning forward a little, absorbed in what she was saying. "You see," she added, "I really live two lives."

"Most people live more than two lives. They live six or seven," I assured her.

At Adelheim, where I was trained, they always insisted that we must adopt a brisk and businesslike cheerfulness with the patients.

But this patient, who had begun to creep out of her shell, instantly drew back again, and, for a bit, would not answer my questions at all, except with a nervous laugh.

"What do you want Mrs. Bradley to do? Do you know?" I demanded.

"I only want her to write a certificate, and send a copy of it to my banker, to say I am perfectly sane," the poor girl replied, with a sudden return to composure which took my breath away.

"But who on earth thinks you are anything else?" I said, as though in great surprise. As a matter of fact, most of these underdeveloped, hysterical subjects *do* think that some one believes them to be insane.

She shrugged. Then she got up abruptly.

"You'll ask her to see me, won't you? Before

I lose my memory again? Mrs. Bradley, I mean. You'll get her to see me, won't you? When auntie isn't there. Like this. Like this."

"I'll ask her," I answered. (Whether she'll come is another matter, I thought.) "Yes, I'll certainly ask her. Do you know—have you any idea—what brings on these lapses of memory? Does your aunt—do you quarrel at all?"

"Quarrel? One doesn't—quarrel with grown-up people."

I was annoyed.

"How old are you then, Miss Dudley?"

"Miss Dudley! How funny that sounds? They always call me Lily. That's what you'll put on the certificate for me, won't you? Lily Dudley is sane."

She went out, looking at me over her shoulder with those great, pale, silly, blue eyes.

I telephoned Mrs. Bradley, and she told me to call at her Kensington house and have tea. She was fairly late getting in, so we made it dinner, instead, and I wore my new pansy-black. Mrs. Bradley eyed it approvingly.

"And what supreme idiocy have you committed this time, child?" said she.

I told her about the case. She grinned, looking just like an alligator.

"I must attend another sitting of this Lunacy Laws Commission thing tomorrow, but on Thursday I could see these Dudleys," she said. "Make the appointment for three in the afternoon, at their private house. I like to know the environment of these loss of memory cases. And I want to see the letter. You have it, haven't you, child?"

I took it out of my handbag, and passed it across the table.

"Aha!" said Mrs. Bradley. In her sea-green dinner gown and with her yellow skin, she looked like a smiling snake. I watched her, fascinated, as she took the letter in her skinny claw and with horrible cackles read it.

"Treasure it, child," she said. "You had better come with me on Thursday. Now go and ring up our friend, Inspector Toogarde, and tell him to keep a watch on the house. If he can find any manner or means of excuse, he's to see that

the young woman is arrested. The sooner that's done, the better."

"The *young* woman? Oh—to keep her safe from the aunt!" We had never before employed protective arrest in a case, but I had heard of it.

"To keep her safe from the aunt," said Mrs. Bradley. She cackled wildly. She took me to the theatre after dinner and we picked up John in the vestibule.

"What's this about these cats?" asked Mrs. Bradley.

"Cats?" said John. "Oh, did Nancy tell you? Cats. Oh, yes." He stampeded us into our stalls and then studied the programme. Mrs. Bradley gave him a dig in the ribs.

"And you'd better write to Mrs. Dudley, and tell her my fee is payable in advance," she said to me.

"Very well, if you wish it," I said.

"I'm listening," John remarked, caressing his lower ribs.

"Tell me about the cats, child. The curtain goes up, or should do, in ten minutes' time."

"Well, just that they keep cats, you know. The whole place swarms with cats. And the stink! Phew! Awful! And yet, a funny thing." He paused; a habit he has.

"Go on!" we said together.

"Mixed with this awful catty stench, which pervades the whole of the house, there was a faint odour of sanctity, so to speak, which seemed just vaguely familiar," said John, caressing his chin.

"Proceed," said Mrs. Bradley.

"Oh, I don't know. I could have placed it but for the all-pervasive stench of those beastly cats. I connect it with that American show we visited last year. You know the place I mean."

Mrs. Bradley's eyes were snapping.

"Go on, child, do," she said.

"I can't. Don't know any more. I knew the woman was taking drugs. I said so. Gave her to understand I'd put the police on her track."

"And what stuff do you think it was? Cocaine?" I demanded, abruptly. We had never had a dope-fiend on our books.

John laughed.

"It wasn't cocaine."

"What do you know about poisons, John?" asked Mrs. Bradley, suddenly.

"Nothing, beyond what all alienists learn in a routine way for rapid diagnosis or morbid symptoms, of course."

"Interesting," said Mrs. Bradley absently. "I wish I could cut that conference tomorrow. But I can't. I'm down to speak. Let me beg of you, child," she said to me, "on no account to go round to that house alone."

I promised, and the curtain went up just then. During the intervals Mrs. Bradley would not discuss the case, but bought us pink gins and made weird hieroglyphics all over her programme while we stood in the bar and drank them.

"Keep me in touch with any developments, child," she said that night, before we parted. John took me out to supper. It was an extension night. We danced a good deal, and I was so tired that Ethel had to wake me in the morning.

"I brought your early tea, miss, nearly an hour ago, but you was off that sound!" she said. "So now I've brought your breakfast, and here's the letters, miss."

So I breakfasted in bed, and read Mrs. Dudley's second letter. They were going away to Broadstairs, it announced, and if I would write the certificate which had been asked for—they understood from the medical directory that I was entirely qualified to do this—they need not trouble us further. The letter bore the postmark of ten P.M., and was headed, "Nine forty-five."

I rang up Mrs. Bradley at her house. The conference began at eleven, so I knew she would still be at home.

"Telephone Inspector Toogarde and tell him to watch the house. I *wish* he'd arrest the niece, tell him," said Mrs. Bradley.

Next day I called for her and we both went round to what Americans would call the Dudley residence. It was an old house with a basement.

"Well, any developments, Albert?" asked Mrs. Bradley, for the inspector had put a man outside the door.

"No, ma'am." He saluted.

"Not even a light in the basement?" asked Mrs. Bradley. The constable looked puzzled.

"Yes. There *was* a light in the basement. I never thought anything of it. There wasn't no noise," he observed.

"Oh, wasn't there?" said Mrs. Bradley briskly. "When your officer comes along, you'd better tell him to go down and dig for the body."

She went up to the door and knocked. There was silence. Then there came the sound of footsteps, and, at the same time, a kind of rushing noise. Mrs. Bradley pulled me aside so that both of us were pressed against the coping at the top of the short flight of steps.

"Lean back as far as you can. Here come the cats," she said. As soon as the door was opened, out they came—Siamese, Persian, tabby, Manx, males and females—one animal, I am certain, was a lynx, and I'm sure I saw a Scottish wildcat, but they all shot past so quickly that it was impossible almost to see them. Then a whining voice said sadly:

"Oh, dear! That's all auntie's cats."

"*Your* cats, you mean," said Mrs. Bradley sharply. She put out a yellow claw, seized the woman by the wrist and stared down at the writhing fingers.

"Albert, child, do you want your promotion?" she called. The prisoner bent her head towards Mrs. Bradley's wrist.

"Not 'arf ma'am, please," said the policeman grinning. He swung up the steps and grabbed Mrs. Bradley's captive, who was fighting and clawing, more like a cat herself than a human being.

"Quiet, will you?" demanded the constable. The prisoner began to cry. "And what shall I charge her with, ma'am?—assault and battery, or is it an R.S.P.C.A. case with all them cats?"

"Charge her with murder, and see how she likes it," said Mrs. Bradley brutally. And sure enough, it was not much later that she and John were watching Inspector Toogarde taking the body up from under the basement floor. Mrs. Bradley sighed when she saw me again.

"It's a pity I had that conference yesterday. Still, Toogarde has got his prisoner, and I expect that's all he'll care."

"But did that spineless creature *really* murder her aunt?" I could not believe it possible.

Mrs. Bradley looked at her yellow wrist where teeth-marks were plainly visible. She did not answer the question. There was no need.

"There were one or two interesting points about the story you told me," she said, "although I don't think you noticed. The first thing that struck me was that evidently you had taken it for granted that the older woman must be the married woman. This was not necessarily true. Then came the extraordinary contrast between the way the younger woman spoke when something important was on hand, and her remarks when the matter under discussion was not germane to her purpose."

"Oh? Do you mean the lucid way she told me her aunt was going to get her certified, and wanted me to testify she was sane?" I began to see the point of that interview now.

"It was when you told me she wanted you to send a copy of the certificate to her banker, that I became so extremely suspicious," said Mrs. Bradley. "It so happens that one of the most unpleasant experiences of my life was when I helped to certify a perfectly sane man on the evidence of relatives who wanted to administer his estate. Luckily, we put that right in time, but since then, as soon as I hear lunacy and bankers mentioned together, all my suspicions are aroused. In this particular case, for instance, if Miss Dudley were the older woman and Mrs. Dudley the younger, why didn't the younger one undeceive you?"

"Well, why didn't the older one? It was equally apparent to her."

"I fancy, if you refer to your notes of the conversation, that she did attempt to put you right on the point, but that you yourself interrupted her, and then you sent her away. Well, the whole thing sounded, to my possibly morbid mind, just sufficiently extraordinary to warrant my interference. But I think the affair was well on its way by the time they came to you here. Of course, it was the *aunt* who took drugs, I knew that from your description of her face. It was the niece who procured enough of the valerian for murder."

"Valerian?"

"Cats," said Mrs. Bradley succinctly. "It was when John mentioned the cats and their smell and then the other smell which he almost thought he could recognise, that I began to smell, not a rat, but a murder. You see, in that American hospital he mentioned, they gave the patients small doses of valerian as a sedative. They stain the stuff pink there, and slightly flavour it with essence of clove. It was the clove, I dare say, that he smelt."

"But I still don't understand about the certificate."

"*Miss* Dudley, the older lady, the aunt by marriage, had made a will in niece *Mrs.* Dudley's favour. The latter wanted *Miss* Dudley— *Lily* Dudley—certified sane, so that, *whatever* happened later, the will remained valid and no other relatives could plead unsound mind in the testatrix, because of our medical and psychanalytical evidence."

"But how do you *know* that the young one was Mrs. Dudley? The thing seems to turn upon that."

"When I grasped her hand at the door, I looked for the mark of the wedding ring, child. It was there."

MID-CENTURY

MURDER WITH FLOWERS

Q. Patrick

HUGH CALLINGHAM WHEELER (1912–1987) and Richard Wilson Webb (1901–c.1970) collaborated on the series featuring Peter and Iris Duluth, but both authors were part of a coterie of writers that mixed and matched on many other books published as by Q. Patrick, Patrick Quentin, and Jonathan Stagge. It was when Wheeler and Webb moved to the United States in the 1930s that they created the Duluth series, which changed their books from a recognizably British style to American in speech and tone.

Wheeler and Webb created the Patrick Quentin byline with *A Puzzle for Fools* (1936), which introduced Peter Duluth, a theatrical producer who stumbles into detective work by accident, and Iris Pattison, an actress suffering from melancholia whom he meets at a sanitarium where he has gone to treat his alcoholism. He eventually marries her. Iris is irresistibly curious about mysteries and draws her husband into helping her solve them. The highly successful Duluth series of nine novels inspired two motion pictures, *Homicide for Three* (1948), starring Warren Douglas as Peter and Audrey Long as his wife, Iris, and *Black Widow* (1954), with Van Heflin (Peter), Gene Tierney (Iris), Ginger Rogers, George Raft, and Peggy Ann Garner. Webb dropped out of the collaboration in the early 1950s and Wheeler continued using the Quentin name but abandoned the Duluth series to produce stand-alone novels until 1965.

Oddly, all the Duluth novels were published using the Patrick Quentin nom de plume but the short stories were originally published as by Q. Patrick—until they, as well as non-series stories, were collected in *The Ordeal of Mrs. Snow and Other Stories* (1961), which was selected for *Queen's Quorum*.

"Murder with Flowers" was originally published in the December 1941 issue of *The American Magazine*; it was first collected in *The Puzzles of Peter Duluth* by Patrick Quentin (Norfolk, Virginia, Crippen & Landru, 2016).

Murder with Flowers

Q. PATRICK

IRIS AND I WERE DANCING at the Opal Room. A rumba orchestra was doing wicked things. We were very groomed and expensive and chic that night. Very gay, too, because it was our first wedding anniversary and we were pleased about it.

Other people were dancing there, too, I suppose. I didn't notice them, except maybe to feel sorry for them for not having Iris, wonderful and dangerous in a gown that didn't cover much territory above the hips.

"Darling," she said, "we do a mean rumba, don't we?"

"Yes, darling," I said. "We do."

"Mr. and Mrs. Peter Duluth!" she said. "Twelve months later, and it still sounds— voluptuous!"

It was then that we saw the Black Beard.

He was sitting alone at a table close to the dance floor. A massive, imperial gentleman, immaculately black and white, with a white carnation in his lapel. His beard sprouted magnificently— jet-black and godlike.

There was an empty champagne bottle at his side. It didn't look as if it was the first empty champagne bottle that had been there that evening. He was gazing at it and weaving slightly in his chair.

We were only a couple of feet away when he looked up and saw us. At least, it was Iris he saw. Naturally. Somewhere, above the beard, his eyes

lit up, and the beard waggled in a roguish, satyr smile. One heavy lid lowered at Iris in a ponderous wink.

Then suddenly, as he really focused on her, his face went blank, and another expression came—a kind of shocked amazement that was almost horror. "You!" he said.

He tried to get up, sank back, and then did get up. He leaned across the table toward us. Very slowly, he said, "I warned you. On page eighty-four I warned you. You must be mad dining out tonight—of all nights—when your picture is all over *The Onlooker?*"

That was an odd thing for a complete stranger to say. But I didn't rumba Iris away. Something kept us there. I think it was the Ancient Mariner quality of the black beard and the steady, unwavering stare.

He swayed slightly. The black beard bobbed in a refined little hiccup.

"The white rose!" he said, "And the red rose!" And then, emphatically: "They mean blood."

He stopped. I pushed Iris backward and then sideways. Fantastically, I was a little scared. I don't think Iris was. I think she was just curious.

She smiled suddenly and said, "Go on. The white rose and the red rose . . . What about them?"

"The white rose—and the red rose. They're out. You know they're out."

He raised one of the large hands. The gesture practically toppled him forward into the champagne bottle. Pointing a weighty, ambassadorial finger, he said, "It's life or death for you, young lady. You must realize that." He paused. "The elephant hasn't forgotten."

The music was throbbing, and all around us sleek, expensive people were dancing sleekly and expensively. He was only an old drunk with a black beard. There was nothing to be alarmed about.

And yet . . .

"Life or death," he said. "You mustn't die, young lady. You are too beautiful to die."

No one around seemed to have noticed anything. The music was seething. I started pushing Iris away from the man.

We were on the opposite side of the floor when I said, "Is that Beard a part of your past, darling?"

"I—I never even saw him before." There was a shaken look in her eyes. "Life or death! Why should the white rose and the red rose mean blood—for me?"

"Just drunken nonsense," I said.

"He said my picture was in *The Onlooker*. It isn't in *The Onlooker*, Peter. Or is it?"

"I don't know," I said.

We neither of us read *The Onlooker*. But millions of other people do. It tells you all about everything so snappily. We pretended we had lost interest then. We went on acting like two elegant people being gay on their wedding anniversary. But it was all rather synthetic.

Suddenly Iris said, "After all, Peter, you're a famous play producer and I'm a sort of actress. Maybe I am in *The Onlooker*."

"Maybe."

"Let's—let's buy a copy."

"Yes. Let's."

We scuttled off the dance floor. That showed just how skin-deep our indifference was.

The Opal Room is part of the ultra-swank St. Anton Hotel. We hurried through the tables with the music *tom-tomming* behind us. We were out in corridors with inch-thick carpets and enormous mirrors. We reached a sort of central lounge which housed a magazine stand.

We went to the stand. Everyone turned and stared at Iris. They always do—especially after midnight. One man stared in particular. He was thin and sharp-nosed and youngish in a gay trench coat with a light gray hat. I noticed him vaguely because he was biting his nails. Biting them savagely and looking at Iris, with something nasty about his mouth.

At the stand I said, "*The Onlooker*, please," to a depressed blonde.

She gave it to me. Iris snatched it and started leafing through the pages. I stood at her side.

Two women with exotic perfumes swished by, patting their necks. The man in the gray trench coat stood there nibbling at his nails and watching Iris sidelong behind a cigarette.

"*Farming*," read Iris. "*Sports* . . . female discus-throwing champion . . . that's not me . . . *Theater* . . . Circus opens at Lawrence Stadium tomorrow . . . No . . . *Art* . . . Oh, look, Peter!"

I was looking, all right. It was uncanny. There under the heading *Art* was a photograph. It was a photograph of a very beautiful woman, a woman whom anyone except a husband could easily have taken for Iris. Dark, with those same amazing eyes, that devastating bone structure.

Under the photograph it said: *Eulalia Crawford*. And under that: *She does everything except stick pins in them*.

"Eulalia Crawford!" said Iris.

"She's a dead ringer for you."

"Nonsense." Iris looked ominous. "She's at least ten years older."

"Not to a drunken Beard in a dim light," I said, trying to wriggle out of that. "It's obvious he mistook you for her."

We read what it said about Eulalia Crawford. It didn't help much. It told us that Eulalia Crawford was a "pulchritudinous, amazingly talented" doll-maker. She had a studio downtown. She made the smartest portrait dolls for the smartest people. In fact, after a modest beginning designing carnival figures, she had lifted the doll business into the realms of art. "I do everything with dolls," she had told the reporter laughingly, "except stick pins in them."

"Eulalia Crawford, the doll-maker!" said Iris. "Peter, I've—I've heard of her. She—she's a sort of a relative."

"A relative?"

"Yes." Iris looked excited. "A fifth cousin, or something like that."

"It explains why you look alike," I said. "But that's all it explains."

"But she's in danger—terrible danger," said Iris slowly. "I could tell he meant it, Peter. The Beard, I mean. I could tell from his face. He really knows there's danger for her. The red rose, and the white rose, he said life or death."

We stood there in that elegant lounge. From somewhere far off the rumba sidled through to us, a torrid echo of the South. I looked up. I caught the eye of the man in the gray trench coat. He glanced away.

"If there's danger for Eulalia," said Iris suddenly, "we must warn her."

"Warn her?"

"Yes." Iris looked beautiful and purposeful. "After all, she's blood of my blood and—"

"But just because a crazy, drunken Beard—"

"He wasn't a crazy Beard. He was very sane."

"Then, if you think so, go back and get the truth out of him."

She shook her head. "He'd be suspicious once he knew I wasn't Eulalia. And if I was Eulalia he'd know I wouldn't have to ask him the truth. I must telephone Eulalia."

"But what will you say?" I asked.

"Tell her about the Beard and the red rose and the white rose and page eighty-four and the elephant." Iris looked calm.

She started toward a lighted sign saying *Telephones*. I sighed and followed. As I did so, I happened to glance over my shoulder, and I noticed that the man in the gray trench coat was strolling very casually after us.

Iris reached the Manhattan phone book ahead of me. Efficiently, she started turning pages, murmuring, "Crawford, Eulalia . . . Crawford, Eulalia . . . Here she is."

She disappeared into a phone booth. The man in the trench coat loitered aimlessly. Soon Iris came out again, and said: "Cousin Eulalia—I liked that 'Cousin!'—wasn't there, Peter. But she's expected any minute. A man answered, a man with a stammer."

"A stammer?"

"Yes. A stammer. He said it would be fine for us to go down right away."

I stared. "You mean we're going to Eulalia *now*?"

"We certainly are." She looked dreamy and thrilled to the bone. "We've wined and dined and danced, Peter. Now we plunge into a romantic adventure, and that, darling, is exactly my idea of how to celebrate our first anniversary."

I had a strong feeling that I didn't agree.

The man with the gray trench coat seemed to have lost interest. I saw him ahead of us, moving away down the lounge toward the main door of the hotel.

I went back to the Opal Room and paid my check. I peered through the dancers, looking for the wretched Beard who had started the trouble. I couldn't see him.

When I got back to Iris, she had unchecked her silver fox cape and had it over her shoulders. She looked exactly the way a girl in a silver fox cape should look—slender and beautiful and distinguished. We started toward the swinging doors leading to the street.

Iris said, "You noticed that man in the gray trench coat, Peter? I—I didn't like him." Her expression was rather odd. "The way he looked at me. Almost as if he knew me and . . ."

"And what?"

But she didn't say any more about it, because at that moment we got tangled up with a large, liveried doorman who started calling us a taxi. We got into it and I gave Eulalia Crawford's address.

II

It was raining—a slight drizzle spattering the windows of the taxi. Iris seemed remote, her thoughts like a thin layer of cellophane between us. Once she turned to look out of the rear window. She didn't say anything. Then, later, as we swung off Fifth Avenue somewhere in the 'teen streets, she turned around again.

Softly she said, "I may be crazy, Peter. But I think we're being followed. Look."

I scrambled around and stared out through the rear window. I could see the bright headlights of a private automobile. It was just swinging off Fifth Avenue behind us.

"It's been there ever since we left the St. Anton," said Iris.

I protested strenuously. "Do we have to go through with this screwball idea?"

"It's such a heavenly screwball idea," said Iris. "And if someone *is* following us . . ."

"What?"

"Then it probably means the whole thing is serious. All the more reason to warn Eulalia."

The taxi was crawling now in a dimly lit, deserted side street. The driver was peering out of his window at the house numbers. The other car was still behind us.

"Two-thirty-five," said the driver. "Here we are."

He had stopped in front of a house. There were lighted windows in it, and the door, white-painted, showed a brightly illuminated hallway. I paid the fare and we stepped out. The taxi drove off.

And then it all happened, like something in one of those artificially speeded-up movies.

The car which had been dawdling behind us suddenly accelerated and came roaring forward. We swung around. We stood there by the curb, hypnotized for a moment, watching the car zoom through the dead, dark street toward us.

And as we watched it, something hurtled out of it—something large and red, soaring through the air and splashing on the damp sidewalk at our feet. We both stared down at it. I felt a kind of amazement, teetering over into horror. Because the thing was a bouquet of roses—deep scarlet roses.

I was still staring stupidly at the roses when

Iris gave a little cry, grabbed at my arm, and said, "Duck, Peter!"

I followed her lead, half collapsing to the sidewalk, and only just in time.

A split second later the sharp report of a gun snarled, once and then again. I heard bullets, whistling close to my ear.

"The door!" shouted Iris. "Get to the door!"

Quicker than seemed humanly possible, we both half ran, half scrambled to the outer, glass-paneled door of two-thirty-five. I tugged the door open and pushed Iris in. I dashed in behind her, slamming the door.

The second inner door was locked. We were trapped there in the little hallway. Outside in the street I could hear the car engine roaring at a standstill. What was to prevent the gunman getting out of the car and coming here?

I looked around wildly at the buzzers. I saw Eulalia Crawford's name coupled with another woman's name. I made a stab at the buzzer. I hit the wrong one.

I stared dazedly. The car engine was still roaring outside. Then an answering buzz sounded in the inner door. Like a flash Iris pushed the door inward. I didn't know what was going on in the street any more. I think I heard the car drive away. But I didn't care. I slammed the door behind us.

"Eulalia's studio," panted Iris. "The man on the phone said it was on the top floor."

We started tumbling up the stairs. What sort of a wedding anniversary was this turning out to be?

Iris said breathlessly, "Did you see the man who shot at us?"

I hadn't. I said so. "But *you* did?"

She nodded. "I saw him. Peter, he was wearing a gray trench coat and a gray hat. He was the man who bit his nails. The man who was in the vestibule of the St. Anton."

That was a shock, and yet suddenly it gave a sort of sense to the fantastic thing that had happened.

"The man from the St. Anton," repeated Iris. "And the bouquet of red roses! The red rose—and the white rose."

We had reached the top floor but one, and were hurrying down a dimly lit hallway when a door opened and a woman in a pink wrapper peered out. In an uneasy moment I realized she was the woman whose buzzer I had pressed by mistake.

I muttered, "Sorry. A mistake. We want Miss Crawford."

She slammed her door shut.

I joined Iris on the top landing. There was only one apartment up there. Its door had the elegantly painted legend: *Eulalia Crawford, Dolls, Inc.* Outside the door, propped against the wall, was a dainty red cellophane umbrella. There was a small puddle of water on the linoleum beneath it.

"See! Her umbrella's still dripping, Peter. That means she hasn't been in long."

Iris looked radiant now. Her finger went forward to press the little buzzer in the doorframe. Shaken as I was, seeing her do that made me sensible again.

"Stop!" I said. "Don't press the buzzer."

Her hand remained poised. "Why ever not, Peter?"

"You've got to be sensible. The man at the St. Anton, he—he mistook you for Eulalia Crawford, the way the Beard did. He saw you reading *The Onlooker*. He followed us to this house. He was sure then, so he shot at you. He tried to kill you because he thought you were Eulalia."

"Bright boy," said Iris. "Go to the head of the class." Her hand moved slowly toward the buzzer.

"Don't, Iris. I'm not going to let you get into this any deeper."

"Nonsense." Iris looked determined. "Eulalia's the only one who can explain. And if you think I'm going through life never knowing why I was shot at, you're crazy."

She rang the buzzer then, imperiously. We waited, but there was no reply.

"That's funny."

She rang again. After the drone of the buzzer stopped, a deep silence enveloped the top floor of two-thirty-five.

Iris stooped down then, so that she could see under the door. "The lights are on inside, Peter. And the umbrella's dripping. She *must* be in."

Her hand slipped to the doorknob. She turned it and, surprisingly, the door opened.

Iris stepped into the little hall. This was mad, crazy . . . I followed her, closing the door behind us.

It was an ordinary little hall. But I didn't like the silence. I don't quite know why. Possibly because, if Eulalia was there, she had no right to be so quiet. Ahead of us was the main room, the studio.

We could see only part of it, through the archway leading from the hall. But it was rather a weird sight—because of the dolls. There were dozens of them, sprawled over everything—life-size dolls, middling-size dolls, small dolls, dolls of women in evening gowns, and men in tuxedoes, dolls of different nationalities, dolls of clowns, ballet dancers, trapeze artists in tights—every sort of doll. And somehow they were sinister.

Iris was almost on the threshold of the studio. Softly she called, "Miss Crawford."

I tautened. Nothing happened.

Iris stepped into the studio. She made a sound—a sharp, choking sound.

"Iris! What is it? What—?"

I ran to join her. The swarm of dolls stared from their dozens of baleful, sightless eyes. All through those awful moments, I was conscious of them as a sort of horror background. But they were only a background. Because I saw at once what Iris had seen. Part of the studio had not been visible from the hall. It was visible now, all right.

There was a desk—a large, modernistic desk. It was, inevitably, strewn with dolls, little dolls. But it wasn't the dolls. In a chair in front of the desk was a woman. She was wearing a lemon-yellow evening gown. I couldn't see her face, because she was slumped forward, the little dolls clustering around her. But I could see her back. And I could see the knife plunged deep into the flesh between the shoulder blades.

"Peter—is—is she dead?" Iris ran toward the woman, her hand going out.

"Don't touch her, Iris!"

I was at her side. I was looking down at the woman's face. It was in profile, resting on her hands, gazing pointlessly at a little over-turned doll of a blonde woman in spangled tights. That was really the worst moment.

"Eulalia!" breathed Iris.

But I could only think—*Iris*. In those awful seconds the resemblance was like a blow on the mouth. Eulalia Crawford was older, yes. But she was terrifyingly like Iris—the hair, the lovely, serene profile, the way the cheekbones curved.

My thoughts were reeling. Just a few moments before, Iris had been shot at. Why? Because she was mistaken for Eulalia Crawford. That's what I had thought. But . . . what about this? Hadn't Eulalia been dead—even then when the bouquet of red roses was hurled at us from the car?

Iris's voice came dimly: "Peter, the—the man who answered the phone. The man with the stammer. He must have murdered her. He urged me to come. He left the door open so we could get in. Because he wanted us to get in. He wanted people to think that we—" She had moved around the desk. Sharply she called, "Look, Peter! Oh, look!"

I joined her, numbly. She was pointing.

There behind the desk, strewn haphazardly across the carpet in a sort of nightmare canopy, were dozens of roses. But this time the roses were not red. They were white.

Iris's hand went down to the desk, supporting her. There was a blue book lying there with gold lettering. She touched it, and it moved, revealing something beneath it—a piece of paper with writing on it.

Iris picked it up and stared at it. "Peter, she—she must have been writing this when it happened."

Quaveringly, she started to read.

Dear Lina:
I have to write to you to warn you. Because there's danger—mortal danger. The white rose—and the red rose—

Iris handed the letter to me. "There's more. But I—I can't read it." She paused. "Lina! Eulalia—and now Lina, too." She was very pale. Suddenly she said, "Peter, what are we going to do?"

What, indeed? Call the police? That was the normal thing to do when you discovered a body. But could we call the police? What could we say? We had broken into a strange woman's apartment. Why? Because of the red rose and the white rose.

What were the red rose and the white rose? We didn't know. Who had told us about them? A drunken black-beard. Who was the drunken black-beard? We didn't know. Where could we find him to check our story? We didn't know. Why hadn't we, a reputable play producer and his reputable wife, called the police in the first place if we thought something criminal was afoot? We didn't know. At least, we did know. It was our wedding anniversary, and we thought we'd have some fun. Fun!

The whole madhouse tale scuttled through my thoughts. Who on earth would believe that? Certainly not the hardheaded police.

I glanced at the front door. The sight of it decided me. It seemed to decide Iris too. Almost simultaneously we said, "Come on. Let's get out of here."

Together we ran to the front door. Iris's hand went forward for the knob.

It was then that we heard the scratch of a key in the lock outside.

Wildly I thought, *That other name by the buzzer—Eulalia's roommate!*

The door was pushed open inward. And a woman stood there. I shall never have more than the vaguest impression of that woman. A youngish woman with very blonde hair and very red lips.

She was just as startled as we. She came toward us, staring. Every possible sign of guilt must have been scrawled across our faces. Eulalia's roommate went on staring.

"Who—who are you?" she asked.

Who were we? We stood there, stiff and lifeless as the dolls.

"What are you doing here?"

Then her eyes left us. She gazed into the room beyond. I saw the horror coming into her face. And then she screamed. "Eulalia!" And, with a rising hysterical crescendo, "You killed her! You murdered her!"

After that she wasn't saying any actual words. It was just a long, animal scream.

We were beyond any reasonable process of thought then. The woman's blind terror infected us, too. With amazing teamwork born of panic, Iris and I dashed toward the woman, pushing her aside, and bolted along the landing outside to the stairs. In a split second we were stumbling downward.

III

We were out on the dark street, out in the drizzle—running. And, miraculously, there was a taxi. I hailed it. By a supreme effort we managed to change ourselves into a languid couple in evening dress who nonchalantly needed a taxi.

"Where to?" said the driver.

"Where to?" echoed Iris. "Oh—uptown. Somewhere gay and expensive. The Continental, I think. Yes, the Continental."

That was smart of her. I would have given our home address. Now that we were fugitives from justice that might well have been fatal.

After the horror of two-thirty-five, the impeachably upper-crust atmosphere of the Continental was soothing. We were taken to a table. The lights were dim and the orchestra was playing a dreamy waltz. Everyone was dancing. Dancing seemed a very sensible thing to do. We danced.

I loved it—having Iris close in my arms. For a few misguided moments I really started thinking this was a nice wedding anniversary after all. Then, inevitably, Iris brought us back to reality.

"Running out like that!" she said softly. "We were crazy, Peter. We lost our nerve."

She was soft and warm in my arms. "Yes," I said. "We did."

"That girl who broke in on us, that roommate of Eulalia's," said Iris. "Of course, she thinks we killed Eulalia."

"Yes," I said dreamily. Iris waltzes divinely.

"And when the police come, she'll be able to give them a perfect description of us. So will the woman whose buzzer we rang. And the two taxi drivers—the one who took us there and the one who brought us here. It oughtn't to be hard for the police to catch up with us."

"True," I agreed, worried.

Suddenly I didn't want to dance any more. I wanted a drink. We had the waiter bring highballs to our table. Mine didn't help my mood any. Iris's romantic adventure!

Iris was clasping her drink in both hands, looking ethereal. Slowly she said, "You know, Peter, we've done everything but confess to that murder."

"Exactly."

"Probably the police are after us even now. And it's not only that. The man with the gray trench coat shot at us once. Maybe he wants to shoot at us again."

"Goody," I said dourly.

"And I don't see how we can possibly exonerate ourselves unless—"

"Unless—what?"

"Unless we find out the truth. I mean the truth about the red roses and the white roses. Then we could go to the police and make a clean breast of it."

"And how could we find out the truth?"

"I don't know," Iris confessed helplessly, and then opened her pocketbook. "Maybe this! This letter Eulalia had started to write."

She pulled it out and handed it to me.

I groaned. "So you stole valuable evidence, too! That's another ten years on our sentence."

"I'm sorry, darling," Iris looked rueful. "I just forgot to put it down."

I stared with a jaundiced eye at the brief, cryptic scrawl.

Dear Lina:
I have to write to you to warn you—

Iris leaned over and looked too. "We know that—about warning Lina of the red rose and the white rose. But that other line I couldn't read. Can you make it out?"

I stared at the sprawling, indecipherable script. "'The white rose and the red rose are out,'" I read. "'And the—something . . . The—the crocus is opening.'"

The note broke off there. We stared at each other. "The crocus!" exclaimed Iris. "The red rose—the white rose—the opening crocus."

"The whole damn' botanical garden."

"Lina would know," said Iris. "There's danger for her—just the way there was danger for Eulalia. Lina would be able to tell us everything."

"Lina—U. S. A.," I said. "She's going to be a cinch to locate."

Iris wasn't listening. Suddenly her eyes lit up. "The Beard!" she exclaimed.

"To hell with the Beard," I said.

"But, Peter, the Beard knows everything. *He* could prove our story was really on the level. If we took the Beard to the police, everything might be all right."

"I might remind you that we don't know the Beard's name. We don't know where he lives or what—"

"That doesn't matter." Iris was her old, enthusiastic self again. "There aren't so many black beards in New York." She rose, wrapping her silver fox around her. "Come on. We're going to find the Beard."

Five minutes later we were in a taxi driving back to the St. Anton. I was sure the Beard wouldn't be there any more. But Iris was bubbling over with hope again.

He wasn't at the Opal Room, of course. We weaved through the tables, fine-combing the guests. Then we divided forces and started excavating the lounges. I had no success. I was returning empty-handed to the main vestibule when Iris came running radiantly toward me.

"The doorman!" she exclaimed. "He's a lovely doorman. He got the Beard a taxi about an hour ago. And he heard him tell the driver to go to the Gray Goose."

The Gray Goose was a half-way fashionable night club in the Fifties. We bundled ourselves into yet another taxi and dashed to the Gray Goose.

We didn't check our coats. We went straight into the ballroom. Two pianos were playing boogie-woogie. A few couples were dancing; but most of them were snuggled up in booths. We started pushing into booth after booth, systematically, peering. And in the last booth we found him.

He was more majestic even than my memory of him. Words could not do justice to the splendors of his beard.

"Hello," said Iris.

Slowly, little by little, he moved his head. Slowly his eyes lit up in a wicked, goatish leer. "Buriful girl," he said.

Iris slipped into the booth, sitting down across from him. I squeezed in after her. She leaned forward, saying urgently, "You remember me, don't you? The Opal Room. You mistook me for Eulalia Crawford."

"Y're not Eulalia Cr'wford." His great hand unfolded from the stem of his champagne glass, groped forward, and fell—flop—on Iris's. "Y're much more buriful th'n Eulalia. Younger. My mistake!"

Such superb drunkenness seemed to nonplus even Iris. "You *must* remember me," she pleaded earnestly. "You told me about the white rose and the red rose."

The Beard's hand left Iris's. He giggled. Then, suddenly, he brandished his arm at a hovering waiter. "Drink!" he said. "Drink for the buriful girl. Champagne."

As the waiter slipped away, the Beard's aimless gaze settled for the first time on me. "Who'sh tha'?" he demanded.

"He's just with me," said Iris. "He's—he's not important."

That was startling, to say the least. Iris was looking rather wild-eyed now. She said desperately, "You've *got* to understand. Please. This is terribly important for us. It's—it's life or death. The elephant never forgets. You mustn't forget. Page eighty-four. You've got to help us."

"Nasty man! Buriful girl." The Beard sank back into his red leather corner. "Tell that man—go away. Won't have him here."

Iris gave a rather sickly smile. Then she leaned toward me and breathed, "It's no good, darling. He just doesn't like you. But he likes me. Maybe, if you go away, *I* can get something out of him."

"But I don't want to leave you with that drunken—"

"Go to the bar, darling," she whispered. "Wait for me there. I'll try to get him to talk."

I went to the bar and, perching myself on a high stool, ordered a highball. I was on my second drink when Iris appeared from the inner room. She was looking a little dazed, but rather triumphant, too.

"What a man!" she said. And then, "But I've got Lina."

"You've got Lina? You mean—you know who she is?"

"No. But I know her name, where she lives. He's terribly canny, Peter, the Beard. He's not telling a thing. But I tricked that out of him. Because he thought it was funny. 'Listen,' he said, 'isn't this funny?' And he chanted it."

"Chanted what?"

"A name. Lina Oliver Wendell *Holmes* Brown. Sixteen-seventeen, Smith Street, Brooklyn."

Iris chanted it, too. Personally, I thought the Beard was right. It was a riotously funny name.

Iris was looking pale. "I've been thinking, Peter. And—and there's only one thing to do. The Beard is hopeless until he sobers up. Now, Lina . . ."

"Lina?"

"Lina knows the whole story. This thing that happened to Eulalia—I think it's going to happen to Lina."

"Of course it is," I said savagely. "She's got the red rose and the white rose and the crocus after her. And, so far as I care, they can all catch up with her and—"

"No, darling. They mustn't catch up with her. Don't you see?. Time's everything. Maybe we can still warn Lina in time. And, if we warn her, then she'll have to tell us the truth. That's the only way we can get out of this—this jam."

I was beginning to see. "You want us to go to Lina now?" I glanced at my watch. "Now—at two-forty-five A.M."

"Oh, I know it's crazy. Everything's crazy." Iris's lips were trembling. "But, darling—please go to Lina now."

"Me! You mean I have to go alone?"

"Darling, I can't let the Beard get away now. I simply can't. We need him. I've got to cling to him through thick and thin. But you don't."

I finished my drink in one gulp. I didn't want to go to Brooklyn.

"Peter, I know it's late. But here—" She fumbled in her pocketbook and brought out Eulalia's letter. "If you show her this, she'll know you're on the level. You—you will go, won't you?"

I took the letter. I kissed her. "I'll go."

"Darling!" she smiled. "And, as soon as you're through, go straight back to the apartment. I'll try and get there as soon as possible—with the Beard."

"With the Beard? Do we have to adopt the Beard, too?"

"Of course. Tomorrow morning he'll be sober. Tomorrow morning he'll be worth his weight in roses." Iris was adamant. "Remember, darling. Lina Oliver Wendell *Holmes* Brown."

I nodded. "Sixteen-seventeen. Smith Street. Brooklyn."

"Oh, darling," she whispered.

I kissed her again. She was utterly beautiful and magnificent and exciting. And I left her to the tender mercies of the amorous Beard. I've never hated doing anything so much in my life.

IV

Sixteen-seventeen Smith Street was a squat, dirty house in a row of uniformly squat and dirty houses. The Browns, I discovered, lived in the basement, and judging from the lighted window, someone was awake—either Mr. or Mrs. Oliver Wendell Holmes Brown. I located the buzzer and pressed it.

The door was pulled open almost before I'd stopped ringing. The speed of it all startled me. In the obscure light from the hall I could see the woman who stood there on the threshold only dimly—a dark, fluttering little thing with big, big eyes.

"Oliv—!" She broke off with a birdlike, swooping gesture of her hand. "Oh, I—I thought it was my husband." And then, before I had time to open my mouth, she was explaining nervously, "My husband works late at the restaurant. He—he forgot his key. I was waiting up for him."

We stood there in the dark area, watching each other.

"Are you Lina Oliver Wendell Holmes Brown?" I asked.

"Yes, yes."

Thank heavens, Lina was alive, anyway!

"What do you want?" She started a little chirping laugh and then, as if the unconventional hour of my visit suddenly frightened her, she added jerkily, "What do you want—so late at night?"

"I've come for Eulalia Crawford," I said.

"Eulalia!" The words came in a thin little Phoebe-bird peep, and Lina's small hands took wing again. Impulsively one hand alighted on my sleeve. She was pulling me into the hall. She closed the door behind us. She was almost running ahead. Her face was ashen.

I followed into the living-room. There was too much old-fashioned furniture in it, but it was kind of pathetically neat. There were two framed photographs on the mantel—a photograph of a muscular blonde in tights with a toothy smile, and another photograph of a dark little slip of a thing gleaming with tawdry spangles. That second picture was Lina herself. I could tell. She was older now, though.

She was hovering in front of me, staring.

"What is it? Why did Eulalia send you?"

I thought of Eulalia's letter. That was as good an opening gambit as any.

I pulled the crumpled piece of paper from my pocket. Watching her, I held it out. "Eulalia wrote this to you," I said.

She stared at the fantastic note. "The white rose—and the red rose!" She looked up. Her lips were as pale as her cheeks. "The roses . . ."

I didn't say anything.

Her tongue came out, wetting her lips. I've never seen such real terror in any human eyes. "The letter isn't finished. It isn't in an envelope. It isn't finished. You—you brought it—" She broke off. "What's happened to Eulalia?" And then, in a small, tortured sob, "She's dead! They killed her!"

How had she guessed that? What was I to say? "Mrs. Brown—" I began, and found it difficult to go on.

She stepped back. "They killed Eulalia. And you brought this letter to me. *You* brought it!" She was still backing away. "You're one of them. You've come to get me, too. The roses . . ."

It was then that the sound of the front door buzzer echoed sharply in the hall. Lina swirled around. "Oliver!"

She dashed away from me, calling her husband's name despairingly. I could hear her little footsteps pattering in the hall. "Oliver!"

I heard the basement front door open.

"Oliver—"

Lina's voice stopped in a little choking gasp. There was a moment of entire silence. Then another voice sounded, a man's voice—a voice that stammered hesitatingly. It said, "H-hello, Lina, d-darling. I'm sure you're g-glad to s-see me."

The sound of that stammering voice toppled me off whatever solid ground there was left. The stammering voice which had answered Iris over Eulalia's phone, the voice of the man who had murdered Eulalia!

I glanced wildly around the stuffy Victorian room. I took a pointless step toward the hall.

And then, ripping through the silence, two revolver shots sounded in brutal, rapid succession. One . . . two . . . just like that.

The nearness of those shrill explosions was appalling. The quiet that came after was appalling, too. And then, sprouting out of that quietness like a thin, weak tendril, twined a small wailing sound that shriveled into a hissing sigh. A sigh—then the small, subdued noise of a little body crumpling to the floor.

All that came in a second. I hadn't time even to move a finger before it was over, and I heard the clatter of footsteps running away from the door.

I dashed forward out of the living-room into the hall. I knew what I was going to see, of course.

Lina was there, tumbled in a little limp heap by the open front door. There was blood. But it wasn't the blood that was the worst. Thrown over the little prostrate body, like a bizarre funeral canopy, were roses—dozens of pure white roses.

Some of the petals weren't white any more. They were a vivid scarlet where the blood had splashed them. I dropped to my knees, bending dazedly over Lina. The red rose and the white rose—they mean blood!

Vaguely, as I knelt there by the night's second corpse, I realized I could still hear the running footsteps of the murderer growing fainter on the dark street outside. Blindly obedient to impulse, I jumped up and ran out. I clambered up the iron stairs to the street and stood there at their head.

I could just see the man. He was running to a parked car. I could make him out, a thin, tall figure. I had been thinking, instinctively in terms of the man with the gray trench coat, who bit his nails. But, as he reached the car, I caught a glimpse of his profile in the light from a street lamp. It was gaunt and angular, but it wasn't the same profile. He wasn't wearing a trench coat, either. And the most arresting thing about that fleeing figure was his hair. For it was a vivid, gleaming white.

So there were two men with guns abroad that night!

Long before I could have done anything to stop it, the murder car sprang forward and roared away out of sight. I stood there at the head of the iron stairs, trembling under the delayed impact of shock.

The gunfire had not shaken Brooklyn out of its small-hours' sleep. Probably the cavernous pit of the basement had muffled the reports. In any case, the alarm had not as yet been sounded. But soon Oliver Wendell Holmes Brown himself would return from the restaurant. Soon the cry of "Murder" would echo through the night, shattering the stillness, spreading like ripples across a black lake.

That brought me back to thinking violently about myself. Here I was hopelessly committed to this second corpse—I, Peter Duluth, the man who, almost certainly, was under suspicion of one murder already.

There was only one possible thing to do next. Poor Lina was dead, her secret still undisclosed. There was nothing I could do for her. So long as I stayed there I was jeopardizing my entire future and Iris's.

Get away, Peter Duluth. Get away—now. Scram!

I made my second major retreat that night. I walked out on Oliver Wendell Holmes Brown, the waiter or whatever he was. I left him to face his tragic homecoming—alone.

V

When I let myself into our apartment, it was in total darkness. Iris wasn't there. I turned on all the lights, hating Iris's not being there. It was half past four. Surely all the night clubs were closed by now.

I mixed myself a drink and gulped at it while I paced up and down the room. I was full of forebodings. Iris had already been shot at that night. And the Beard—we knew nothing about him. Why had we assumed so readily that he was a friend? For all we knew, he was one of the gang.

Why had I left Iris to cope with him alone?

I worked myself up into a frenzy of nerves. I'd never felt so helpless. And then, about half an hour later, I heard the incalculably sweet sound of her key scratching the front door lock. I ran out into the hall just as the door opened. And she was there. Iris was there.

She stepped into the apartment and then turned back to the corridor, crooning, "Come on, Pussy. This way, Pussy."

I started toward her, saying, "Iris . . ." Then I stopped dead in my tracks.

Slowly progressing into the room was a large, ponderous figure in black, a figure with the massive dignity of a Supreme Court Justice. But, defying all laws of probability, he was moving on all fours. One large hand padded forward and then another, the substantial rump proceeding soberly behind. The solemn face with its majestic black beard looked unutterably out of place when it stared up at me from six inches above the floor.

The Beard navigated the threshold. Iris closed the door behind him. She turned to me. She looked beautiful but frayed.

"Hello, Peter," she said. "He's been like this ever since we came out of the elevator. He thinks he's a pussy cat."

She was trying hard to smile.

I was still suffering from my gnawing anxiety at her absence. "Where—where have you been?"

"Driving up and down Fifth Avenue," said Iris, "looking for Easter Bunnies."

"You can't see Easter Bunnies in September," I said sensibly.

"*He* can." Iris shot a withering glance at the sportive Beard. "He could see Niagara Falls in Times Square at this point." And then, despairingly: "Peter, *what* shall we do with him?"

"You haven't got anything out of him?"

"Nothing!" Iris wrung her hands. "It's hopeless. I don't even know his name. He—he just says to call him Pussy."

"Pussy!" said the Beard gravely.

And started a laborious attempt to sit up on his haunches. Fantastically, although I've never seen a drunker man, he had not lost one particle of his dignity.

I looked at Iris over his head. She looked back

at me. "At least I managed to bring him home," she said wearily. And then, thinking about me, "But—but Lina. Did you see her? Did you get anything?"

"Lina," I said, "is dead."

"Dead! Iris's lips went pale. "You mean you found her dead like—like Eulalia?"

"She was alive when I got there. She was murdered right under my nose."

Iris's eyes were bleak. Very softly she breathed, "And the roses?"

"Of course the roses. White roses. Her body was strewn with them."

"Peter!"

The Beard, who had been squatting there imperviously, suddenly sat down on the carpet. Iris and I exchanged a harassed glance.

"We'd better get him on a couch in the living-room," said Iris. "I can't bear this—this weaving around."

Somehow we managed together to propel the Beard to a couch. He seemed to like it. He nestled back and closed his eyes.

"Now," said Iris to me, "tell me everything."

I did. I told her that whole miserable Brooklyn saga. When I had finished, we both turned and stared at the Beard.

"He's our only hope now," breathed Iris. Ponderous lids still hid his eyes. Impulsively Iris bent over him, took his large shoulders and shook him. His eyes popped open. "You've got to listen," said Iris passionately. "Lina's dead. Eulalia's dead. The white rose and the red rose—they've murdered Eulalia Crawford and Lina Oliver Wendell Holmes Brown."

"Eulalia," repeated the Beard slowly. "Lina."

"Yes, yes. You've got to help us. Eulalia and Lina are dead—*murdered*!"

The Beard lifted a large hand and started beating solemn, unrhythmical time in the air. "Eulalia, Lina . . . Zelide, Edwina," he said. "Eulalia, Lina . . . Zelida, Edwina."

Iris glanced at me triumphantly. "Tell us," she said sharply. "Tell us. Who is Zelide? Who—is—Zelide?"

The Beard stared. "A bird," he said.

"A bird!" Iris shrugged hopelessly. "Edwina, then. Who is Edwina?"

"'N elephant," said the Beard promptly. Then his eyes shut once more. He started to snore. The drunken oracle had obviously said his last say.

"It's no good, darling," I said.

"But—but it's got to be." Iris swirled round. "I've been with him for hours. That was the only time he answered me. Peter we've got to wake him up. We've got to get him sober."

I looked hopelessly at that vast monument asleep on the couch. I said, "We might try black coffee."

"Coffee—yes." Iris became excited. "We'll make some. Right now."

She hurried into the kitchen. I followed. Cans and percolators and things clattered around, and a few minutes later the coffee was done.

We went into the living-room together, Iris carrying the coffee on the tray as if it were butter on a lordly dish.

"I—" she began.

Then she stopped. Because the couch where the Beard had been so epically asleep was empty.

Iris put down the coffee. We both started a feverish and unsuccessful search of the apartment, under the piano and everywhere. We went out into the hall. The front door was open, telling its own story.

"He's gone," wailed Iris.

That was self-evident. The Beard had been far craftier than we had anticipated. He must have pretended to be asleep. And, during the minutes we had spent in the kitchen, he had made his getaway. The priceless bird had flown.

A mean gray stain of dawn was tinging the sky as we went to bed.

The first thing that swam into my consciousness when I awoke again at some indeterminate daylight hour was the rustle of paper. I opened heavy eyelids. Iris was standing by my bed, fully dressed, and indomitably beautiful. But I didn't like the way she looked. It made me suddenly awake. She looked pale and ominous. In her hand she was clutching a morning paper.

"Hello, darling," she said brightly.

"The paper," I said. "Does it say anything about us?"

She didn't speak. She sat down by me and spread the paper out in front of me. It was the front page. At the bottom left corner, I saw the headline screaming about the two mysterious murders. I scanned the column below. There was all the stuff you would expect. Two women killed in different parts of the city . . . white roses strewn over both. Then there was a paragraph. It read:

Miss Doris Lomas, Eulalia Crawford's roommate, surprised two suspicious characters red-handed in the apartment when she returned from a dance. Miss Lomas told the police how she opened the front door of the apartment and saw a man and a woman actually bending over the body of Miss Crawford. They fled when they saw her. But she was able to give a detailed description of both of them . . .

Detailed description was right! Miss Lomas had a very keen eye. There followed a description of Iris and me, exact to the last zipper.

As I read on, distraught, I reached this:

Mrs. Clarence Stark, who lives in the apartment below, also saw the murder suspects, and her description fits closely with that of Miss Lomas. Already the taxi driver who drove them to Miss Crawford's apartment from the luxurious St. Anton Hotel has been traced. A second taxi is believed to have driven them from the scene of the crime to the Continental. There the trail ends. But the police are sanguine that soon . . .

I stopped. I couldn't read any more. Iris's hand slipped into mine.

"The hunt," said Iris, "is up. The bloodhounds are in full, baying pursuit."

———

It was so indeed. Our worst fears had been justified. Now we were officially stamped as probable murderers pursued by the Law.

"We've only got a little time," said Iris. "A very little time. And we've got to do a lot of thinking."

"We needn't bother thinking," I said gloomily. "We can save that for the long evenings in the penitentiary."

Iris looked at me and decided I wasn't being co-operative. She went out, and came back soon with a tray of breakfast. Balancing the tray with one hand, she pushed the paper off my lap onto the floor. Then she put the tray down in front of me.

"Zelide," she mused. "The Beard called her a bird. Why a bird? We've got the facts if only we could put them together. The white rose, the red rose, the crocus and—Edwina, the elephant."

She broke off with a sudden little cry. Her body had gone tense. She was staring down at something on the carpet.

"Peter," she breathed, "The elephant!" Then she plunged onto her knees by the bedside. I heard her fingers rustling the newspaper wildly. "Peter! I think I've got it."

I pushed the breakfast tray aside. I rolled out of bed onto the floor beside her. "I saw the advertisement. I never realized."

She grabbed my arm and pointed triumphantly at the newspaper. I stared. Staring back at me from a large ad in the paper were three prancing elephants.

"See, Peter? Eulalia's letter to Lina. We read it wrong. Eulalia's writing was so bad. We thought she said, 'The *crocus* is opening.' She didn't. She said, 'The *circus* is opening!'"

Above the elephants, in bold, black letters, were the words: THE CIRCUS IS IN TOWN. GALA OPENING TODAY AT THE LAWRENCE STADIUM.

"That's the clue," breathed Iris. "The circus! Why didn't we guess? Edwina, the elephant. And—and Eulalia had those dolls—those clowns, trapeze artists, and things."

"There was a photograph of Lina in Brooklyn," I cut in, remembering. "A photograph of her all dressed in spangles. She must have been with the circus one time!"

"So must Eulalia. Carnival dolls! Don't you remember how *The Onlooker* said she'd started her career making carnival dolls? That's the tie-up between them. Now the others. Zelide. That sounds like a circus name, Zelide—the bird. Zelide . . . Oh, look, Peter."

Once again Iris was crouched over the paper. She was pointing at the bottom of the advertisement. There, listed with the other attractions, was the announcement: *Madame Zelide, World-Famous Aerialist, with her Amazing Bird Ballet.*

"Zelide—the bird!" exclaimed Iris.

We stayed there crouched together on the floor, staring at each other.

"See how it all makes sense now?" cried Iris. "Eulalia and Lina and Zelide—they must all have been together in the circus."

"And Edwina the elephant?"

That didn't faze her. "Eulalia, Lina, Zelide, and this elephant, Edwina, they all ganged up together and did something connected with roses—something that harmed the man who bites his nails and the man who stutters. That happened in the past. And now the two men are having their revenge." She tossed back her lovely dark hair and looked radiant. "We'll be okay now, darling. Zelide will be able to straighten everything out."

I clambered back into bed and started eating my breakfast. But I wasn't given any peace. Iris clambered onto the bed, too, reached over my coffee for the telephone book and started leafing through it madly.

"What you doing?" I said.

"Lawrence Stadium," she muttered. "Lawrence Stadium . . . Here we are."

She dialed a number. Then she began chattering excitedly into the phone to several different stadium extensions, asking for Madame Zelide. Her face, which had been alight with hope, went grave. Then she turned to me, whispering, "Zelide's not there."

I dunked toast in my coffee. "Then ask to speak to Edwina, the elephant," I said.

Iris withered me and said into the phone, "Do you know where I could reach Madame Zelide, please? . . . Okay . . . Thanks."

She slammed down the receiver. "Zelide," she said, "is staying at the St. Anton. See how it all ties up?"

"At the St. Anton?"

"That explains what happened to us last night. The two gunmen must have divided up the job. The one who stutters was detailed to get Eulalia and Lina. The one who bites his nails was detailed to get Zelide at the St. Anton. While he was there he saw me, mistook me for Eulalia, and figured his buddy had slipped up on the job. So he tried to kill me. That makes sense, doesn't it?"

Iris picked up the telephone again. She dialed. After a brief talk with someone at the St. Anton she hung up disconsolately. "It's no good, Peter. Zelide went out last night and she hasn't come back yet—or called."

"I thought as much," I said darkly. "Farewell, Zelide—corpse number three."

She laid her head against my shoulder. It was nice, even though it did get in the way of my breakfast. She seemed to be thinking. Finally she looked at her watch. "The circus begins at two."

"So what?" I demanded.

"So—we go to the circus." Iris pushed herself around so that she was staring vehemently into my face. "That's the only place we can hope to find out anything." She paused. "You never know. Maybe we'll even stumble into the Beard there. Don't they have bearded men in circuses?"

"Bearded ladies, darling," I said. "Maybe that's it. Maybe the Beard is a lady."

Iris patted her hair and looked far away.

"The Beard is *not* a lady," she said. "You can take that from me."

VI

It was about one-thirty when we left the apartment. Iris was elaborately glamorous in an outfit which culminated in an exotic Dietrich veil. I, very Palm Beach and groomed, sported a pair of heavy sunglasses. The veil and the sunglasses were a forlorn attempt at disguise. The aggressive chic was intended to disconcert policemen, too; because Iris had the bizarre theory that the more over-privileged you seemed the less criminal you looked.

We made the circus, unmolested. And the moment after I'd bought ringside tickets and we'd joined the festive throng scrambling into the great stadium I felt more secure.

Iris looked at her watch and said, "It's going to start any minute, Peter."

"So—what do we do?"

"Zelide, of course." She looked tense through the veil. "We've got to see if she's come. We've got to warn her before the performance begins."

We both looked around through the crowd. Iris said, "Downstairs to the side shows. That's the way to get backstage."

We started wriggling and pushing through children. We were running down broad stone stairs, and finally, with a kind of breathless rush, we reached the broad, long basement where the side shows were.

We stopped then, and stared.

Animals were everywhere, in cages with lurid, jungle backdrops. Macaws, flaming scarlet, were screeching and the tallest man in the world was sharing a sandwich with a tattooed lady. Strolling toward us, hand in hand, were the fat woman and a little golden-haired midget.

We hurried to the fat woman and the midget. Iris asked urgently, "Where can we find Madame Zelide, please?"

The midget jerked with a tiny thumb over her shoulder. "Dressing-rooms back there, lady. They'll tell you."

We left them and hurried on through the animal cages toward the rear of the basement. There, at the end of the long room, we found ourselves in an insane outcrop of elephants. Elephants were everywhere.

Iris gave a little exclamation, pointed, and breathed, "Peter, look! Edwina!"

I looked, and she was right. The legendary Edwina was quite definitely there. She was in an open stall of her own in regal solitude, a vast brown elephant with tree-trunk legs, vague kindly eyes, and an immense pink ribbon around her neck. A message hung on the stall said in large letters: EDWINA, THE OLDEST ELEPHANT IN CAPTIVITY.

"Edwina," said Iris in an awed whisper, and fluttered with her hand. "If the Beard's right, Peter, she knows the whole truth about the roses."

Edwina lifted her trunk into a sort of esse-bend, flicked her ears above the pink ribbon, and whistled. And then, from the distant arena, a crash of cymbals blared.

The circus had begun.

I said urgently, "We'd better get to Zelide."

There was an archway ahead. We hurried to it and found ourselves at the mouth of one of the vast entrances to the arena itself. Here there was wild activity as the opening parade started swaying out into the ring.

Iris grabbed a clown. "Zelide?" she said, "Where's Zelide's room?"

The clown pointed backward. "Down the corridor, first to the left, first to the right—the third room."

We scurried on to Zelide's room.

Iris knocked on the closed door. Nothing happened. She knocked again.

"She's not there, Peter. She—" Impulsively Iris pushed the door inward. I stepped in after her. The room was empty. I closed the door behind us.

The room was tawdry. It smelled of stale make-up. A curtained closet bulged with theatrical costumes. There was a cluttered dressing table. And a mirror above it, encircled with pinned-up photographs.

I went to the dressing table and looked at the photographs. Iris was with me. All the pictures were of the same woman—a blonde with a dazzling smile. They were all signed scrawlingly: *Zelide*. The face was dimly familiar. Then I remembered the photograph at Lina's home.

"We're on the track," I said. "Lina had a photograph of Zelide, at her house."

"And the doll at Eulalia's," breathed Iris. "Do you remember the little blonde doll in tights that was on the desk by Eulalia's head? That must have been Zelide, too."

We looked at each other.

"What are we going to do, Peter? She isn't here. It's no use staying." Then, desperately, "She can't be dead, too."

She broke off. She was looking down at the dressing table. Balanced precariously between jars of cold cream was a brown-paper package. It had Zelide's name on it and a plastering of stamps. It was marked: URGENT, RUSH, SPECIAL DELIVERY.

Iris and I had the same idea simultaneously. Both our hands went out for that package. I got it first. *Rush, urgent . . .* It might be something. It just might.

"Unwrap it!" Iris cried.

I started tearing off the wrappings. "It's—it's only a book," I said.

But I went on unwrapping it. And suddenly we saw the book. It came out with the back of the dust cover on top. It consisted of a single, large photograph of a majestic gentleman with a magnificent, sprouting black beard.

"Peter!" exclaimed Iris. "It's the Beard!"

I turned the book over. I looked dazedly at the title. It said: CRIMES OF OUR TIMES. And, underneath, the author's name: EMMANUEL CATT, AMERICA'S MOST DISTINGUISHED CRIMINOLOGIST.

"The Beard!" said Iris again. "The Beard wrote it. And last night he called himself Pussy, because his name's Catt," she added. "Peter, look. There's a note clipped inside. Open it, Peter."

My hand was rather wobbly as I moved to open the book. I pushed the back dust cover off, and it flopped limply. And then I gave a grunt of surprise. The binding under the paper cover was blue—blue with gold lettering. That conjured up sharp memories.

"This book!" I said. "There was a blue book

with gold lettering on Eulalia's desk. He must have sent each of them a book."

There was a note clipped to the flyleaf. It said, in neat, meticulous handwriting: *See page 84.* Just that. *See page 84.* Period.

"Page eighty-four!" exclaimed Iris. "That's what the Beard said to me. 'I warned you on page eighty-four.'"

I leafed shakily through the book, glancing at the chapter headings as the pages flicked by. One chapter would be called: The Mystery of Something or Other; the next, the Mystery of Something Else. Suddenly I stopped.

On page 84 began Chapter Eleven. And it was called: *The Mystery of the White Rose and the Red Rose.* Penciled into the top corner were the words: *The Red Rose and the White Rose are out. You must realize your danger, Madame Zelide. E. C.*

"Here!" said Iris, awed. "The solution was here all the time in the book."

"Lina can't have gotten her book," I said, "because she had not been warned when I got there."

Tensely we both stared down, scanning the first paragraph of Chapter Eleven. It read:

Perhaps the most fascinating of all modern crimes is the strange case of Tito Forelli, the trapeze artist, who hurtled to his death, at the gala opening of the circus in New York on September 18, 1931. To me, the enduring interest of the case lies in two facts: Firstly, that three women, all telling the same story brought a murder conviction where there was no particle of concrete evidence; secondly that the protagonists of the drama bore the fragrant, fairy-tale names of "White Rose," and "Red Rose." Forelli's partners in the trapeze act, the two Rosa Brothers, inevitably earned their colorful names, since one had bright red hair, while the other was prematurely white. They . . .

Suddenly Iris breathed, "Peter! Listen. Someone's coming."

I started. We both stood there motionless.

And, with a queer kind of menacing distinctness, footsteps sounded on the bare cement of the corridor outside. The ominous human *tap-tap*, coming closer and closer, made Zelide's dressing-room a trap.

We had broken in unauthorized. If we were discovered there might be a scene which would make us conspicuous. And, with the police after us, that was the one thing we couldn't afford.

The footsteps were up to the door now. They stopped dead outside. I saw the curtained clothes closet. I grabbed Iris's arm. Dropping the book back on the table, I pulled her with me behind the curtain, clattering it along the iron rail to conceal us.

We were only just in time. As we pressed back against Madame Zelide's downy feather capes, I heard the door of the dressing-room open. Through a little crack in the curtains, I could see the table with the book lying on its crumpled wrapping paper. Then the person who had come into the room walked into my range of vision.

I caught my breath. He was the man from the St. Anton; the man with the gray trench coat; the man who had shot at Iris; the gunman who bit his nails!

Just seeing him was a shock. But there was something else. He was hatless, and for the first time I saw his hair. It was red.

For an excruciatingly prolonged moment he stood there by the table, gnawing at his nail. Then he picked up the Beard's book and opened it.

I saw his fingers turning the leaves rapidly. Then he gave a sharp little grunt. Furtively he slipped the book under his arm. Then, as quickly as he had come, he left.

Iris and I scrambled out of the closet together. Iris said hoarsely, "Peter, did you see his hair? The man who killed Lina and Eulalia had pure white hair, didn't he? You told me. White hair—red hair. *They* are the roses. The two gunmen were the Roses all along. And the roses they threw were a sort of trade-mark."

It had been as simple as that! "The protagonists bore *the fragrant, fairy-tale names of White Rose and Red Rose.*" The two trapeze artists who had murdered their partner, Tito Forelli, ten years ago, had been convicted on the evidence of the three women *"all telling the same story."* The two Rosa Brothers now seemed to be taking a terrible revenge on the women whose evidence had convicted them—Eulalia, Lina, Zelide.

I remembered the Beard's sinister remark: *"The white rose and the red rose are out."* Not out in the garden. No. Out of *prison!*

Iris and I stared at each other. She said, "The Red Rose came here to steal the book because he didn't want Zelide warned. That means Zelide is still alive. That means they're still after her."

Her reasoning was a little higgledy-piggledy, but she'd most likely got the right idea. Emmanuel Catt must have read of the release of the two Rosa Brothers. He must have realized the great danger for the three women which that release would precipitate and he had sent each of them a copy of his book, to warn them. His warning had failed miserably with Eulalia and Lina. And now the book for Zelide had been stolen.

Zelide might be here any minute. Heaven alone knew where the drunken Beard could be found. Iris and I were the only ones now who could warn her of the terrifying vendetta which had singled her out for its third victim. Zelide's life was in our hands now.

VII

We hurried out of the dressing-room into the corridor with no conscious plan. From far away I could hear the brassy blare of the circus band.

The passage was empty. The Red Rose had betaken himself off as neatly as he had come.

We stood there a moment ineffectually. The band had thumped into *Yankee Doodle.* Somehow that rollicking music in the distance made the immediate silence far deeper.

Suddenly the silence and the loneliness were shattered. From around the far end of the corridor debouched a wild, riotous assembly. In that motley swarm of people I made out the fat woman, the tallest man in the world, a couple of flaxen-haired midgets, youths in green tumbler uniforms, a plump, important ringmaster and a bevy of young, blonde aerialists in feather capes.

They were all in a state of high jubilation. Some were brandishing wine bottles, others were humming snatches of the *Mendelssohn Wedding March.* A fringe of clowns pranced around the edges like excited poodles.

There were two people in the center of the group around whom the gala pandemonium was focused. One of them was a swarthy, Greek-looking man, broad and beaming. The other was a woman whose arm was looped through his—a blonde with a mauve toque perched on stiffly waved hair.

That muscular blonde, that patently just-married blonde on the arm of her happy groom, was to me the sheerest dream of delight. There was no mistaking that flashing, toothy smile which had grinned at me from so many photographs. Zelide at last!

The procession came closer and closer. The voice of the top-hatted ringmaster rose importantly: "Ah, Madame Zelide, you scare us. You are not at your hotel. You do not come for the performance. No one knows where you are. Something terrible has happened to Madame, we say. And now it is this—this happy event—a bride. Madame Zelide no longer." He kissed his own plump forefinger. "From now on, Madame Annapopaulos."

"Madame Annapopaulos!" chorused the crowd in happy unison.

"Ah," said Madame Zelide Annapopaulos coyly, beaming at her groom, "but the circus she still come first. I say to Dmitri, my career she always comes first. I say to Dmitri, whatever happens, I must take the performance. So I come. I am here."

"Madame Zelide is here for the performance," chanted the blonde aerialists in well-trained reverence.

I had never seen so much innocent joy. And the irony of it surged over me. Last night Zelide had been saved by Cupid. While gunmen, out for her life's blood, prowled the elegant lobbies of the St. Anton, she had been amorously, respectably, and securely lodged in the arms of Mr. Annapopaulos.

The procession had swarmed right up to us now and was already pouring past us through the door into Zelide's dressing-room. The happy bride and groom were swept straight past us into the room out of sight.

"Twenty minutes, Madame," said a voice inside the room. "In twenty minutes our ballet goes on. You must be quick. *Quick*."

They had all vanished from sight into the room now, all except two clowns who stood in the doorway.

Iris said, "Come on, Peter. We've got to warn her before she goes on for her act."

We both started forward toward the dressing-room door. The clowns were still there, standing with their motley, rainbow backs toward us.

Iris prodded at one and said, "Let us by, please. We've got to see Madame Zelide."

Inside the room we could hear loud, raucous laughs and the clinking of glasses. Slowly the two clowns turned around—a blue clown and a white clown. They stood there, blocking the doorway, staring at us.

"Please let us in," said Iris again. "We have to see Madame Zelide at once."

The eyes of the white clown flickered unpleasantly. Suddenly he swung around and shut the door of the dressing-room, so that we were barricaded from the people inside. There were only the clowns, then, and us—no one else in that deserted corridor.

"Let us by—" began Iris.

And then she stopped, with a little piping gasp. Because, very slowly, the white clown lifted a cupped hand to his mouth and gnawed at his thumbnail. The hand stayed there for a split second, then it swooped down to the broad pocket of his costume. Long before we could do anything, he had whipped out a revolver. He was aiming it directly at Iris.

"One peep out of either of you," he said, "and I'll shoot the dame in the belly."

With the gun still pointed straight at Iris, the Red Rose talked to the blue clown out of the corner of his mouth. "This is the guy and the dame I told you about—the dame I thought was Eulalia last night."

The blue clown shifted sparse shoulders and stammered, "I—I th-thought s-so."

Iris was very pale. Probably I was, too. I thought of Eulalia dead and Lina dead. I looked into those bright, fanatical eyes. The Rosa Brothers had been trapeze artists. Of course, it would have been simple for them to get themselves hired, incognito, at the circus.

I knew just how far to trust that revolver.

"Get moving," said the Red Rose. He jerked his painted head. "Down the passage. Get moving."

We had to, of course. I took Iris's hand. We started down the empty passage in the direction the Red Rose indicated. The two clowns fell in behind. The Red Rose's revolver was pressed against Iris's back.

"Left, here," said the Red Rose. "Down that passage to the left."

We turned into it, Iris and I, hand in hand. It was a narrower passage with no doors in it, a lonely, gray passage.

"If we see anyone," said the Red Rose, "and if you bat an eyelid, I shoot." After a pause, explaining, he added. "I don't know what you know or what your game is. But we got important work to do. We ain't having you or no one else butting in, see?"

We came to the end of the corridor. There was a door, a tall, steel door. Hanging from a hook on the wall was a key. White Rose took the key. He opened the door outward. Inside there were stairs going down into blackness.

"Turn around," said the Red Rose.

We turned around. We stared straight into his clown's face, straight at the revolver.

"Back down those stairs," he said.

We moved slowly backward, down, down into darkness. The Red Rose loomed above. Was he going to shoot now?

The revolver shifted slightly in his hand. He said, "You're lucky you're still alive. Just keep thinking about that."

Then suddenly we didn't see him any more. There was nothing but utter darkness and the vague, musty smells of a cellar. The door above us had been slammed shut.

I heard the rattle of a key in the lock. Then there was no noise but our own quick breathing. I was relieved because as the Red Rose had said, we were alive.

We stood there, precariously, halfway down the dark stairs that led to—what?

Iris said huskily, "We must find the lights."

Lights—in that darkness!

She started up the stairs again, gropingly. I felt in my pocket for matches. I brought out a box and made a little flickering light.

"The switch must be by the door."

We reached the steel, impregnable door. There was a switch right by it. Before the match sputtered out, I twisted the switch.

Nothing happened.

I flicked it around and around. No light came. It was broken.

Iris said, "We must go down into the cellar. Maybe there's another way out."

We started down the stairs, lighting match after match, penuriously, because there were not very many. We were down in the bowels of the cellar, tripping over old gym horses, slats, broken poles, all the odd, useless junk that ends up in a sports stadium cellar.

Then suddenly, after a match had burnt out, Iris gave a little cry, stumbled, and clutched me. "Peter, light a match. Quick. I think there are steps here."

I lit the last match but one. As its cone of flame sprouted, I saw that Iris was right. We were in a corner by the wall, and concrete stairs led up. We scrambled up them. The match went out. Falteringly I lit the last match. I held it above us. The steps seemed to lead straight to the ceiling.

"They must lead somewhere."

Iris was scrambling ahead. She reached the top. "Keep the match alight," she said; and, instantaneously, the match flickered out. There were queer, shuffling sounds in the darkness. Then Iris said, "The ceiling's wood. I think it's loose."

She gave a cry of jubilation. Because suddenly there was light, a square of light. And I saw Iris against it in silhouette. Iris, glamorous, chic, elegant, and disheveled, standing at the top of the steps, her hands above her head supporting a square trap door. There was straw everywhere.

She wriggled herself up. I went after her, squeezing through.

Straw was all around us on the floor. Vaguely I began to realize we were in a stall, an animal stall. With a tingle of excitement I recognized it. It was empty now. But we had been here before. This was where Edwina and her train had been.

"Quick," I said, gripping Iris's arm. "We've got to get to Zelide's dressing-room. What's the time?"

Iris glanced at her little wrist watch. "Two forty-five. Maybe it's too late. Maybe she's already in the arena."

Together, we ran out of the open stall, through the great archway and headlong into the entrance to the arena itself. The music was playing, loudly, throbbingly. People were everywhere, stagehands, hangers-on, whatever they were, all crowded around the entrance to the ring.

We pushed into the crowd. Iris was ahead. Then she swung round, clutching my hand. "Look, Peter."

In front of us, almost near enough to touch and yet infinitely unget-at-able, I saw a serried row of hippy, feathered blondes marching smartly away over the red, white, and blue sawdust toward the distant center of the ring. Marching grandiosely at their head was a single, even more majestically feathered blonde.

Madame Zelide herself!

We were at the very brink of the ring. We started running forward.

Iris called, "Madame Zelide!"

Then she stopped, because someone had gripped her from behind. I was gripped, too.

A voice said, "Are you nuts? You can't go on there. The performance is on."

We swung around desperately and stared at a lot of nondescript men.

"We've got to get to Zelide," I said. "It's a matter of life or death."

One of the men spat. Another man, an old, gnarled man with spectacles, had a newspaper. He was staring at us through the spectacles with a queer, intent sort of stare. He looked down at the front page. "Murder of Eulalia Crawford," he read. "Wanted by the police, a man and a woman answering . . ."

The other men were crowding around excitedly, looking at the paper, too. We stood there, circled by them. For a moment I felt like a trapped animal.

Really before either of us knew it, Iris and I were pushing through the circle, scrambling away and running—running like mad.

"The audience," Iris panted. "We've got our tickets, Peter. That's the best place to lose ourselves—in the audience."

Vaguely I was conscious of confusion, shouts behind us, but we rushed on through the deserted sideshows, past the bored cage animals, upstairs to the actual entrance to the auditorium. I had the tickets ready in my hand. We swung through doors and automatically became anonymous, just two molecules in a vast body of people.

VIII

Our seats were ringside seats, I knew—a box. No attendants were around at the moment. Iris and I started down through the tiers toward the front of the great oval house.

In the arena, the feathered, bespangled blondes were splaying out to the rhythm of the band, each of them moving to her own indi-

vidual hanging trapeze. I could see the stately figure of Madame Zelide herself, bowing in the center of the ring. Very magnificent she looked.

We were down at the front row now. Ahead of us I could see two empty boxes. I didn't know whether one was ours or not. I didn't care. I navigated Iris ahead into one. I followed.

The sound of footsteps and voices came from behind us. Guiltily we spun around. Iris gave a little gasp. I stared, like a fool.

Coming down the steps between the packed rows of seats were a man and four impeccably *Social Register* dowagers. And the man, infinitely respectable in discreet, ambassadorial serge, wore a beard—a black beard, a magnificent, godlike beard. His eyes, perhaps, were ever so slightly rheumy and morning-afterish, but he proceeded down the steps with all the sober dignity in the world.

Emmanuel Catt, America's Most Distinguished Criminologist, had come to the circus. For one paralyzed second, Iris and I stared at him. Then, as one, we pounced.

Iris said, "You! At last we've found you."

The Beard drew himself up. He fixed us both with a cold eye and said, "I haven't the pleasure of knowing you, and there is straw in your hair. Please let me pass."

So he didn't know us! So the Beard, sober among his dowagers, was a respectable Dr. Jekyll who disowned the evil, alcoholic, midnight acquaintances of his drunken Mr. Hyde other self.

"But you must remember us." Iris stared at him. "How could you forget—after last night? Pussy!"

The dowagers gave one glacial, co-operative sniff and swept into the next box. A faint flush tinged the Beard's cheeks. "Ah—last night, I—ah—was not myself."

"But the Rosa Brothers," said Iris wildly. "They've murdered Eulalia and Lina! It was in all the papers! And now it's Zelide!"

"I haven't seen a paper," the Beard said mechanically. Then he realized what Iris had said. "Murdered Eulalia and Lina?" he gasped.

"Yes, yes. And now they're here at the circus disguised as clowns. They're after Zelide. She's right here—out in the ring."

The Beard was utterly shaken. "But she must be mad. I warned her."

Suddenly there came the ominous rolling of drum taps. As one, Iris and I and the astounded Beard swung around to face the ring.

The moment for the great Bird Ballet had come. Like clockwork, with the first roll on the drums, the blonde "birds" lifted their arms and gripped their trapezes. Rather ponderously, they began to swing onto the trapezes and then levitate as the ropes carried them upward. The drums rolled on.

And Zelide still stood there in the center of the ring. A huge trapeze was lowering above her head. The blonde "birds," in mass ascension, soared higher and higher. Vaguely I saw men up there, men in fancy costumes, hanging high up on the ropes, maneuvering them. Zelide gave a final bow.

The trapeze, lowered from above, came closer and closer. She lifted a hand for it.

And then, as the thunderous drum-roll reached its climax, something incalculably unexpected happened. Suddenly, as if materializing from nowhere, there were roses—a shower of roses tumbling down, down, splashing to the sawdust and around Zelide's feet.

Red roses . . . and white roses . . . red roses . . . and white roses . . .

The audience buzzed its approval. A pretty gesture, the final touch of showmanship. But, to us, the appalling, sinister implication of those roses was almost more than we could endure.

And, as we stood there, taut as steel, helpless, Zelide reached for the trapeze. She was easing herself up onto the bar.

It was then that Iris screamed, "Look! 'Way up there in the ropes!"

She stared up. I stared up. The Beard stared up. And we saw them—saw them up there almost at the peak of the giant arched roof. Two clowns, swinging expertly on ropes, close to the cables that supported Madame Zelide's trapeze.

Two clowns—a blue clown and a white clown. Clowns who, to the vast audience, were just another prop in the pageant; just part of the act.

The Red Rose and the White Rose.

And, as we stared up, I caught the sudden flash of something in the shaft of light from a baby spot. Something in the hand of the Red Rose—something gleaming and steely.

A knife!

Of course! That was the crazy plan—to cut halfway through one of Madame Zelide's trapeze ropes, to wait until she started to swing, and let her hurtle herself to her doom.

"Look!" I clutched at the Beard's arm. "The two clowns up there—they're the Roses."

"*They* dropped the roses," said Iris.

"And the Red Rose has a knife. I saw it gleaming. He was cutting through one of the trapeze ropes. Don't you see? When Zelide gets high enough, when she starts to swing . . ."

For one teetering second the three of us—Iris, the Beard, and I—stood petrified in the box.

Then the two clowns started swarming down their ropes. All the other men were swarming down, too, past the ascending blonde aerialists. No one else but us would have singled out the Roses. No one but Iris and I, who were supposed to be safely locked in the cellar, could possibly have guessed what they had done—guessed that, right there in front of an audience of thousands, they have prepared their fantastically brazen and cunning plot to murder Zelide.

The Roses were halfway to earth. Madame Zelide was rocking on the trapeze, ready to make her triumphant aerial ascent.

Overcome with a common, desperate urgency, the Beard and Iris and I started scrambling over the front of the box and dropped down into the ring. Somewhere behind us the Beard's dowagers screamed. It was a fuse setting off a splutter of shouts and calls behind us. But, indifferent to them, we started running over the bright red, white, and blue sawdust toward Madame Zelide and the trapeze.

The drum-roll went on. Slowly, portentously, Madame Zelide and her trapeze started to rise upward, slowly upward. Attendants were running after us now, agitated, angry, with thumping footsteps and hoarse, high voices.

The Beard was ahead, his role of respectable escort to dowagers abandoned. A bearded Jupiter running with the fleetness of Mercury. We stumbled on through the sawdust. The Roses on their ropes were slipping nearer and nearer to earth. They were of vital importance. But first there was Zelide. Zelide had to be stopped in her regal ascent.

We reached the trapeze. The Beard was still ahead. It was a mad, March-hare moment. Zelide was dangling above our heads, getting higher and higher. I saw her tightsheathed legs swinging. I saw the Beard running ahead of me, immensely dignified and portentous.

Suddenly the legs and the Beard made contact. I saw Emmanuel Catt, America's Most Distinguished Criminologist, leap with extraordinary dexterity into the air. I saw his large hands fold over Zelide's ankles and tug her from the ascending trapeze.

Then, in a wild, farcical heap, the bearded dignitary and the world-famous, would-be-loved aerialist were tumbling together on the sawdust in an inextricable confusion of blonde hair, black beard, and roses—red and white roses.

The ringmaster was shouting and swishing with his whip. The attendants were closing in all around us. The whole vast auditorium was in an uproar.

The whole picture had become a kind of idiot's blur to me. Only one thing was vivid—the realization that the blue clown and the white clown had clambered down their ropes to earth. The two of them stood there for a second, staring at our swirling little group. Then they started running, swiftly for the far exit from the arena.

Vaguely I heard Madame Zelide's voice, high, shrill with furious indignation. Vaguely I heard the Beard's voice, answering gravely. But this was no time for explanations. I rushed to the Beard. I grabbed his arm.

"The White Rose and the Red Rose are escaping," I pointed. "There! We've got to get them."

I had a brief glimpse of Zelide's face, saw it grow pale with horror beneath the sawdust-sprinkled blonde hair. "The White Rose and the Red Rose!" she gasped. "They're *here*?"

That was all, because the Beard and Iris and I were on the run again. The three of us, buoyed up by the wild exhilaration of the chase, started dashing across the huge arena after the fast-vanishing figures of the two clowns.

"Hurry, darling!" Iris cried.

It was surely the maddest race in history. Behind us, stumbling, shouting, panting, came tumblers, attendants, aerialists, everyone and anyone who happened to be around. At first, I think, they were chasing us. Then with a majestic spurt of speed, Madame Zelide, herself, caught up with us. Her tights were twisted, her blonde hair was wild, but she was splendid and formidable, and she was shouting, "Get them! Murderers!"

The gigantic audience had gone crazy. I didn't blame them. They had come to see a circus. Now they had a lunatic track-race on their hands. The roar of them surged over us like a titanic wave.

"The Roses," panted Zelide. "So they try to kill me like they kill poor Forelli. They—"

"I warned you," put in Emmanuel Catt, lumbering at her side. "I sent you a copy of my book with a note. I marked page eighty-four. I never dreamed that you would not read it."

"Nothing I get, no book, no note."

"The Red Rose stole it," put in Iris.

"I should have guessed they were here," panted Zelide, her blonde hair streaming. "Just as I go on, Edwina, she break the line in her act. She charge at two clowns. I should have guessed."

Ahead, we could see the White Rose and the Red Rose. They had almost reached the exit. People were lounging around it, staring blankly. We shouted out to them to stop the clowns. But they didn't get the idea at all. The two Roses slipped into the little group of watchers—and disappeared.

"After them!" I shouted.

IX

We padded on at the head of our motley band. We reached the exit to the accompaniment of a final roar from the circus audience. We plunged into the little tangled group that was clustered there.

I saw a large, swarthy, prosperous man in a cutaway with a pink carnation. Zelide's husband, Mr. Annapopaulos himself!

He pushed to his wife's side. "Zelide, what have we? What then goes on?"

"The Roses," stammered Zelide. "They are out of prison. They try to take their revenge, to murder me."

Everyone seethed some more.

"The clowns!" I exclaimed. "The two clowns who just ran in here. They're the murderers!"

I stopped because another voice broke in harshly: "That's the guy. That guy and that lady—them's the ones wanted in the papers for the Crawford murder."

I spun round, to see the gnarled old man with the spectacles, who had almost captured Iris and me before we got to Zelide. He was pointing at us. And suddenly, from nowhere, three policemen appeared.

I never thought I'd be glad to see policemen. We rushed to them and we all started talking at once. Emmanuel Catt won. The beard gave him added weight in official eyes. Maybe they even knew him by reputation. ". . . tried to cut through Madame Zelide's trapeze rope and kill her . . . attempted murder . . . two other murders . . . desperate criminals . . . disguised as clowns . . . just went through here . . ."

Everyone started chattering then. The gnarled old murderer-catcher, in particular. He pointed down a corridor and shouted, "They went that way. Two clowns."

They started running then, the three of them, down the corridor which the old man had indicated. The Beard and Iris and Madame Zelide and Mr. Annapopaulos and I followed, with the others scrambling after us.

"At least one of them has a revolver," shouted Iris. "They're dangerous."

We sped on, tumbling down one corridor, then another. There was always someone who had seen them, someone pointing ahead and shouting, "That way! That way!"

We passed Zelide's dressing-room—and on. Suddenly, as the corridor wound to the left, I realized what was happening. Obviously the Roses had not planned this escape beforehand. If their cunning project had worked, they would merely have slipped down their ropes, mixed with the throng of other clowns, and actually watched the murder "accident" take place.

Iris and I, by our escape from the cellar, had thrown a monkey wrench into their schedule.

From now on they would have to improvise. But, circus performers from 'way back, they certainly knew all the ropes at the stadium, and they had the key to the cellar into which they had locked us. Almost definitely they would try to escape that way. Down into the cellar, locking the steel door behind them, under the ring, and then up into the animal stalls, far away from the hue and cry.

I pushed through the crowd until I could grab one of the policemen. "Let the others go on," I said. "You come with me. I think I know how we can head them off."

The policeman looked blank but came. In a second we were hurrying back against the crowd, shoving our way forcibly. Iris noticed us first, then Zelide and Mr. Annapopaulos, then the Beard. They too started pushing their way after us.

I caught Iris's eye and nodded.

Soon the crowd, hot on the chase, had swirled on toward the cellar door, abandoning us.

"Quick," I exclaimed. "Get to the animal stalls."

They obeyed me—just because they were too dazed to do anything else. We ran on, down corridor after corridor until we reached the side entrance to the arena. We passed it, hurried under the tall archway, and then, suddenly, we were in the animal stalls. No one was there. No one at all.

Right in front of us, ranged along the walls on either side, were the elephant stalls. And the elephants themselves, their act over, lumbered around in them.

I said, "There's a trap door from the cellar. It comes up in one of the elephant stalls. I'm almost sure they'll be sneaking up that way."

"Which stall?" said the policeman sharply.

I didn't know. I looked at Iris. She was uncertain, too.

"I—I think it was over there." She pointed to a stall to the right.

We hurried toward it, a taut, keyed-up group—the Beard and the policeman, Mr. Annapopaulos with his prosperous arm around his bride's waist, Iris in the Dietrich veil, and me in what was left of my Palm Beach suit.

The elephants shuffled and watched us.

"Yes," Iris said. "I'm almost sure it's here."

She stopped, with a little scream. We all stood petrified in our steps. Because, from behind us, an all too familiar voice had sounded, steely, and very, very low:

"Hands up. Every one of you. Turn around. Stick your hands up."

Slowly, in unison, like some weird sort of circus act, the six of us wheeled around, our hands groping up into the air above our heads. We stood there, staring, the six of us: the policeman, the criminologist, the bridegroom, the aerialist, and Iris and me, the two suckers.

Standing there in front of the other row of elephants and squarely behind two pointed revolvers, were the clowns, the white clown and the blue clown—those nightmare clowns who, once again, had turned the tables.

And it was all so tragically simple. Iris had picked the wrong stall. The Rosa Brothers had come up from the trap door behind us. They had us beautifully under control—but beautifully. Even the policeman was without a plan.

And the Roses were very much on the job. In the grotesquely painted faces the two pairs of eyes were cruelly bright and steady. The Red Rose's pink tongue slid out over his scarlet lips. He was staring straight at Zelide.

"Step forward, Zelide," he said. "Out here, away from the others."

Zelide gave a little moan. Mr. Annapopaulos kept his large arm stubbornly around her waist. Neither of them moved.

"We got you at last, Zelide. Just like we got Eulalia and Lina. Ten years we had to wait—ten years sweltering behind bars where you put us. You—" The eyes were fanatical now, half crazy. "Get forward."

The elephants weaved with their trunks all around us, shuffled their straw, flicked their ears, and looked bored. Somewhere along the line one of them trumpeted and started an uproarious clatter.

Zelide looked grimly at Mr. Annapopaulos. "It is no use, Dmitri. You too must not suffer. I go."

"No, no . . ."

"Yes."

I admired her then. Zelide was a really brave woman.

"Come out, Zelide." The White Rose had the rest of us covered. The Red Rose kept his revolver pointed on Zelide. She took a step forward, very erect.

"This way." The Red Rose jerked along the stalls with his revolver. "Down here."

Zelide moved forward. The Red Rose stepped in behind her. They started up the aisle between the elephant stalls. It was horrible. A sort of mock execution, a terrible, half-mad mockery of an execution.

Zelide moved along. The elephant down the line trumpeted again. Zelide walked more quickly. She reached a stall. The Red Rose was close behind her. Then, like lightning, Zelide dived into the open stall. There was a scuffling and the wild trumpeting again.

Then Zelide's voice screaming, "Edwina! Get him, Edwina! The Red Rose! Get him!"

It was sheer lunacy from then on. The Red Rose stiffened. I saw him jerk the revolver around. I saw his finger on the trigger. A shot was fired. The trumpeting teetered over into a wild, animal scream of fury. Then an elephant was charging—a vast mammoth of an elephant charging, breaking out of the stall, head raised, trunk bristling, a huge, inexorable elephant with an immense pink ribbon around its neck. Edwina!

I saw the Red Rose hesitate, stare in horror at that terrifying sight. Then he started to run, and Edwina was lumbering after him.

"Get him, Edwina. Get him!"

The White Rose still had us covered. At least, up till then, he had. But, as Zelide's voice rang out again, he faltered and glanced over his shoulder. Instantly, all with the same idea, Mr. Annapopaulos, the policeman, the Beard, and I leaped forward, knocked the revolver out of his hand, and tumbled him to the floor.

I scrambled up, leaving the White Rose to the tender mercies of the others. I wheeled around to Edwina. I was just in time to see her head trundle down. Then there was a scream—a human scream. I saw the immense pink ribbon flapping. Then I saw other colors. I saw the white of the clown, waving helplessly in the air, encircled by the viselike trunk.

Zelide ran out of the stall. Iris and I ran forward, too.

For a moment the Red Rose was, madly, up in the air there, screaming. Then he was hurled to the ground.

Zelide rushed forward. "Edwina!" she shouted. "Leave him alone now. Don't kill him. Leave him, Edwina!"

Even in its fury, the elephant seemed to hear and obey. She backed, trumpeting, shaking her trunk.

Zelide and Iris and I rushed forward. The Red Rose was there, twisting and turning in the straw. I pounced on him. He had no strength left. I saw Zelide's eyes gleaming with triumph.

"Edwina—she save me. I know if I can get him to her stall, she save me. The Roses—they remember and hate for ten years. But Edwina remembers forever. Edwina, the elephant, she never forgets."

The others were hurrying to us now, lugging the White Rose with them. I pulled the dazed Red Rose to his feet. We all crowded around.

"Edwina, she is shot. But a little revolver shot—to Edwina it is a mere flea-bite, yes?" Zelide was coping enthusiastically with Edwina.

Edwina seemed to love it. She was puffing a little, but she was perfectly calm again. And her trunk stopped weaving. Ever so delicately, she curled its tip around Zelide's waist.

"Edwina!" we shouted. "Edwina! Bravo, Edwina!"

And, she smirked. I swear she did.

X

There was high festivity and merry-making in the dressing-room of Madame Zelide, world-famous, world-beloved aerialist. The Red Rose and the White Rose had been taken away by the police. Soon we, too, would have to follow to the police station. But at the moment our joy was unconfined.

Sweet red wine was pouring with abandon. Madame Zelide and Mr. Annapopaulos, giving vent to their warm Southern temperaments, were kissing everyone at random.

They kissed me, both of them; they kissed Iris. They even dared to kiss the Beard, who, dowagers forgotten, was beaming broadly, perched on a stool. Everything was confusion.

No one seemed to realize that Iris and I were still at sea. We'd been through hellfire. We'd run the gamut of every kind of emotion. We'd got straw in our hair—actually and figuratively. But we still had only the mistiest idea of what it was all about.

That didn't seem to matter.

At the peak of the toasts, the door burst open, and the ringmaster, resplendent in top hat and tails, surged in on a wave of enthusiastic blonde aerialists. He rushed to Madame Zelide and kissed her. Then he swept the Beard and Iris and me into a mass embrace.

"You save the circus!" he said. "When it happens, when you tug Madame from the trapeze, I say—the end. The most terrible thing! But now we find the trapeze rope—she was half cut through. Those fiends, those madmen! Certainly Madame would have plunged to her death. You save us from the most terrible of tragedies." His enthusiasm mounted: "Free tickets. For every performance I give you free tickets. The best—boxes."

I managed to disentangle myself.

"But if only someone would tell us something, anything. For example: Why did Edwina hate the Roses?"

Madame Zelide gulped red wine and stared. "But they were so cruel to her—always. Edwina, she love Tito Forelli. The Roses hate him. Once they attack him, the two of them together, and Edwina went to his rescue. After that they hate her, too. Always they think out mean, cruel tricks to plague her. Edwina does not forget. No."

"But why," added Iris, in an attempt to get someone to stick to the point, "why did the Roses hate Tito Forelli?"

Emmanuel Catt rose majestically. We were obviously now entering his domain. "That," he began, "is one of the most fascinating cases in criminal history. I have—ah—made a study of it in my book, *Crimes of Our Times*. I shall give you a copy. The murder of Tito Forelli shows the psychopathic jealousy motive coupled with the perfect crime and the relentless Nemesis as supremely as any . . ."

"But it is so easy to say," broke in Zelide, who seemed in no mood to hand over the spotlight to a mere criminologist. "Ten years ago Forelli is the partner of the Roses in a trapeze act. He is the star, by far the best. And the Roses were madly jealous."

"Professional jealousy at its—" began the Beard.

"And there was Eulalia Crawford, too," Zelide dived in. "The girl who then makes the carnival figures for us. She is beautiful, attractive. And she loves Forelli. That makes the Roses even more madly jealous, because the Red Rose, too, loves Eulalia. The White Rose, he was never so bright in the head, just the—how do you say?—shadow of his brother, ready to do anything for the Red Rose, die for him, kill for him."

"A typical moronic assistant, a gangster's bodyguard."

"And so, the Red Rose, his jealousy gets stronger and stronger and his hate. And, together with his brother, he thinks out a plan to kill Forelli so that the Red Rose can have Eulalia. The plan, it is perfect, they think. During the trapeze act they will drop Forelli, they will send him hurtling to his death. All the world will think it is an accident, yes—a simple accident. It happens often with aerialists. No one will suspect."

Zelide paused for breath. The Beard charged in: "The perfect theoretical murder, no evidence, no clues."

"Dmitri, more wine for Mr. Catt," broke in Zelide torridly. "You see, Mr. Duluth, it worked, their plan—yes. And they were proud—proud as clever murderers who would never be discovered. In the papers, everything, it said—accident. Tito Forelli die by accident. Partners absolved. Eulalia then was to be for the Red Rose. But they were fools, stupid fools. For Eulalia hated Red Rose and suspected them.

"She was cunning, Eulalia. She know they are vain, boastful. She praises them, how clever they are, feeds their vanity. There is little Lina, she was with our ballet then, and she was Eulalia's greatest friend. There was I, too. I then was only an unknown little aerialist, and I, too, am a friend of Eulalia's. She comes to ask, makes us hide in a room, and she brings the Roses in. She praises them, so cunningly: '*You are so clever and so smart, so much more clever than Forelli.*'

"And they fall in the trap. When Lina and I are there as witnesses, we hear the Red Rose laugh and say boastfully to Eulalia, '*Sure, we more clever than that Forelli. We fixed him. We got his number okay.*'"

"So Eulalia," broke in the Beard gravely, "tricked them through their vanity into a murder confession in front of witnesses. Although there was no shred of evidence, the three women went to the police. The police believed them. And, afterward, the jury believed them, too. The Rosa Brothers were sent to prison as murderers for ten years."

"And they never forgive us," said Zelide. "Oh, in time we forget. Until this afternoon everything was from my mind. But the Roses never forgot."

So that was it! Sketchily, vaguely as it had been told in competitive duet, the story emerged plain as glass. Two mean, revengeful, small-time crooks who had planned what they thought was the perfect murder, only to be outwitted by three girls.

Two small-time crooks, brooding in prison, harping on their wounded pride and their hatred for the woman one of them had loved and her friends. Two crooks, distorted by their hate, living only for one thing—release and revenge, a second chance to prove themselves smarter than the women who had defeated them.

And the revenge of the Rosas had reaped terrible havoc—for themselves, for two of the women, for all of us. But it was over now, thanks to Edwina, whose slow, stubborn impulse to revenge had been even stronger than theirs.

Everyone, the ringmaster, the fluttering blonde "birds," Mr. Annapopaulos, they had all been listening to that strange tale in rapt astonishment.

But the Beard was now the central figure. He stood in Jove-like splendor, twisting the glass of cheap red wine rather shudderingly. I could imagine how he felt about it after last night's champagne.

"All along," he said, "since my study of the case, I felt there would be great danger when the Rosa Brothers were released. I know their type—the little Caesars, the little men with the big egos and a vast capacity for hate and revenge. Yesterday I tried to warn the three women. I should have done much more. But last night I—was unfortunately not quite myself."

He paused there and looked at Iris. The black beard twitched. Slowly, almost infinitesimally, an eyelid lowered in a wink. It was clear that Emmanuel Catt's lamentable exuberance of the night before was to be our own particular little secret.

"I admit I was a failure, a tragic failure," he said. "But now I drink to the two people who, knowing nothing at all about the issues at stake, managed, by their ingenuity and their courage, at least to save—Madame Zelide. I propose a toast. I toast the two most resourceful people I have ever encountered. I toast Mr. and Mrs. Duluth!"

Everyone grabbed glasses, even the respectful blonde aerialists. There were shouts, applause, confusion. Glasses were waved on high. Feather capes fluttered.

I turned to look at Iris. How did she manage to be so utterly beautiful after all we'd been through? I lifted my glass to her. She lifted hers to me. She smiled—that quick, dazzling smile which always catches the breath right out of me.

"Mr. and Mrs. Duluth," she breathed. "Twelve months later, darling—and it still sounds voluptuous."

I leaned forward and kissed her. Her lips were so soft and warm, so very, very right.

"Mr. and Mrs. Duluth!" shouted the blonde "birds" with an abandon which almost certainly stemmed from the red wine. "Bravo, Mr. and Mrs. Duluth! Bravo!"

I hated taking my lips away from Iris's. I could have done without the ecstatic aerialists, too, and Madame Zelide, and Mr. Annapopaulos, and the ringmaster, and the Beard.

But I didn't really care. Because, suddenly, I was sure of one thing. Against all odds, it had turned out to be a good wedding anniversary, after all. It certainly had.

An honest-to-goodness, super-colossal wedding anniversary!

VACANCY WITH CORPSE

H. H. Holmes

IT IS A LITTLE ODD to call H. H. Holmes a pseudonym of Anthony Boucher, since that itself is the pseudonym of William Anthony Parker White (1911–1968), who took the nom de plume when he realized there were seventy-five other authors named William White.

Born in Oakland, California, White received a B.A. from the University of Southern California and an M.A. in German from the University of California, Berkeley. He later became sufficiently proficient in French, Spanish, and Portuguese to translate mystery stories into English, becoming the first to translate Jorge Luis Borges into English.

As Anthony Boucher, he wrote five well-regarded fair-play detective novels, beginning with *The Case of the Seven of Calvary* (1937). His novel *Nine Times Nine* (1940) was voted the ninth best locked-room mystery of all time in a poll of fellow writers and critics; it was written under the pseudonym H. H. Holmes, taken from an infamous nineteenth-century serial killer.

Boucher wrote prolifically in the 1940s, producing at least three scripts a week for such popular radio programs as *Sherlock Holmes*, *The Adventures of Ellery Queen*, and *The Casebook of Gregory Hood*. He served as the longtime mystery reviewer of *The New York Times* (1951–1968) and *Ellery Queen's Mystery Magazine* (1957–1968). He was one of the founders of the Mystery Writers of America in 1946. The annual World Mystery Convention is familiarly known as the Bouchercon in his honor, and the Anthony Awards are also named for him.

Sister Ursula, who appeared in only two novels and a handful of short stories, is a member of the (fictional) Order of Martha of Bethany, which engages in hospital work, teaching, and even cleaning. She is noted for her kindliness. As the daughter of a police captain, she had decided to become a policewoman until her health sabotaged her plans. It comes as no surprise, then, when she declares, "I am going to find the murderer . . . you see, I am not inexperienced in detection."

"Vacancy with Corpse" was originally published in the February 1946 issue of *Mystery Book Magazine*.

Vacancy with Corpse

H. H. HOLMES

FELICITY CAIN'S HAIR had started out to be red. It had stayed red until halfway through her high school days. This was why she had come to be known as "Liz." You can't call a freckle-faced carrot-top Felicity. That suggests lace and dimity and demureness, and there was nothing demure about Liz, not even after her hair turned the brownish blond you've seen in her publicity pictures.

The freckles had vanished when the red hair changed color, but her eyes still had a greenish glint, and her spirit was still flamboyantly flame-crowned. Yet, here in the quiet, civilized atmosphere of the fashionable cocktail lounge, atop San Francisco's most impressive skyscraper, with the clink of ice and glass to soothe the ear, she was more strikingly lovely than Ben Latimer ever remembered. It was a beauty that fascinated him, left him oddly breathless.

Out of the broad plate glass windows there was a noble view of the bay, bright with the afternoon sun. But he had no eyes for the view—not when Felicity was around. She had her arm in a sling, the result of an airplane accident—she was America's most noted aviatrix—but the injury made no difference to Latimer. She still looked good to him.

He grinned as he set down his glass. "You're like the bay, Liz," he said. "Wonderful."

She smiled back. "You really mean I'm an institution, like the Barbary Coast, the cable cars—and the Cains! See any guide book."

Ben Latimer winced. "No. You're wrong." He waved his arm. "See that view. At first glance it's perfect beauty. But look again and you notice a carrier and a couple of destroyers. There's toughness under that beauty."

"La, sir!" Liz said. "And likewise fie. Is that any way to speak of the woman you love? Don't you know I'm all sweet femininity? At least as long as this damned arm keeps me grounded."

Ben laughed. "It's funny, Liz. When I think about you, it's always with red hair. Even when I look at you I can't get over being surprised."

"And when I think of you I still see you back on campus in a letterman's sweater. I just can't get used to the idea that you're now a policeman."

"Detective-lieutenant, Liz, please," he corrected her. "Can you imagine the society pages of the papers writing up the marriage of a Cain to a mere policeman?"

"I know." Her green eyes sparkled with glee. "At our wedding, do we line up your squad, or whatever you call them, and march out of the church under an arch of crossed rubber hoses."

Ben shook his head. "No rubber hoses in war time," he said solemnly. "In fact, we haven't had a single voluntary confession since the rubber shortage started."

Liz fished in her glass, and said, "I like onions better than olives any time."

"What's the matter?"

"Why? What should be?"

"Whenever you begin making irrelevant remarks like an Odets character, I know you're shying away from something that bothers you. What is it?"

Liz hesitated. "I don't know how to converse with a policeman."

"That's never bothered you before."

"I've never done it before. I mean I've always just talked to Ben—my Ben!" A smile softened her face, a smile such as you never saw in any of the press photos. "Now I want to consult with Detective-lieutenant Latimer."

Ben Latimer frowned. "What on earth kind of official business can you have on your mind? Remember I'm on Homicide."

Liz vigorously nodded her brownish blond head. "Uh-huh."

It wasn't a gag. Her face was serious. She kept it averted as she carefully drew geometric patterns with the cocktail's tooth-pick.

"All right," Ben said. "I'll try to look official even though I'm in plainclothes. What's the trouble? Anybody I know? No, that doesn't sound official. What, madam, is your complaint?"

"It isn't mine. It's Graffer's."

"Your grandfather? You mean there's something sinister about his illness?"

"Of course not!" Liz smiled. "Graffer's illness, God bless him, is just age and heart and things. You don't think Dr. Frayne could be fooled, do you? This is something else. It's—it's funny. Ben, if you hated a man and he was going to—to die, wouldn't you just say to yourself, 'Goody, goody,' and that'd be that?"

"No," Ben said reflectively. "That's not the way some minds work. You might say, 'Damn it, he can't die all of himself and do me out of the pleasure of killing him.' Is that what you mean?"

"Uh-huh. Graffer's been getting notes. Crazy notes. *The Black Angel cannot claim you who belong to us.* Strange things like that."

Ben frowned. "It happens to every judge, I guess, if he's been on the bench as long as your grandfather was. Half the time they're from neurotic cranks. Are they signed, these notes?"

"With a rubber stamp of a pointing hand. You know, what printers call a fist. I don't know what it means."

"The Fist." Ben nodded. "It's an imitation Black Hand racket which sprang up in the Italian colony here. And your grandfather did send Almoneri and de Santis to the gallows."

"But it's so silly," Liz insisted. "That was twenty years ago. And now, when maybe he's dying, why should they suddenly write him threatening notes? Perhaps I shouldn't take them seriously. It must be some screwy kind of a gag. But Graffer wanted me to tell you about it."

Ben shook his head. "I don't know if it's silly, at that. You remember Vitelli wasn't hanged? He got paroled a few weeks ago. He managed to disappear somehow and he hasn't been reporting either to parole or alien authorities. Does your grandfather want a police guard?"

"Uh-huh. Only quiet-like. You know Mother. You know what a policeman in the house would do to her. Especially at a time like this with my cousin, Sherry, coming and the servants changing all the time. Also, Graffer didn't tell anybody but me. Not even Graffer's secretary, Roger Garvey, knows. So could you arrange it somehow?"

"I'll fix things." Ben spoke in reassuring tones. "If it's to be secret, I can't do more than put a couple of men to watch the entrances to the house." He groped in his pocket. "Here—give your grandfather this whistle. It may set his mind at ease."

"Thanks, Ben. It seems so funny, talking to you official-like. You never did mention your work around me. Not even when you were on that suitcase murder and all the papers were full of it. Then, again, maybe I'd better not know too much. Just keep you for my Ben and not think of you that way."

A bespectacled, studious looking young man at the next table rose, started out of the room, but detoured to halt beside them.

"Felicity!" The man was Roger Garvey, "Graffer's" secretary. He grinned. "Headed home? Oh, hello, Latimer."

"Hi, Garvey," Ben grunted.

Liz smiled at the difference between the two men. They were equally tall, equally well-built, but made from different molds. Ben's suit looked rather sloppy beside the sleek perfection of Roger Garvey's well-tailored gray. Then, again, the detective's broken nose—which had healed remarkably well from a wound inflicted by a three-time murderer—served to emphasize the pleasing profile of her grandfather's handsome secretary. Even Ben's easy casualness seemed rather crude when contrasted with Roger's graceful suavity.

"Roger's right, Ben," she said. "I should be headed home. Mother's got so much to do."

"I'll squire you on the cable car, Felicity," Roger Garvey suggested. "Ridiculous nuisance, this having to leave one's car home. And I've no doubt the street-car will be full of filthy workmen in oil-stained overalls. Oh, well! The Japanese war'll be over soon. Until then, I suppose we have to put up with these things."

Ben's face turned brick red. He opened his mouth to make an angry retort, but Liz gave him a warning glance so he only said, "Take good care of her, Garvey."

"That's something I like to do, Latimer. I'll never forgive you for getting the inside track. I suppose we'll be seeing you at the great family dinner tonight?"

"Sorry. I'm on duty."

The secretary looked wise. "Oh, you remember that Sherry's to be there?"

Ben didn't answer for a minute. There was no sound but the clinking of glasses and the babble of voices.

"Yes, I remember," Ben said at last. "Tell her I'll try and get around tomorrow."

"I'm sure that even in her present state she'll be anxious to see you, Latimer. Don't you think so, Felicity?"

Liz said, "Come on. You can't tempt Ben when he's on duty. The only way we could invei-gle him to the house tonight would be to stage a murder for him."

After they had left Detective-lieutenant Ben Latimer sat alone at the table for some minutes. He frowned, and his finger outlined a pointing fist on the damp surface. Then his frown deepened and he murmured, "Sherry!"

He was unreasonably annoyed when the waiter brought him a glass of light brown wine.

CHAPTER II

Mrs. Vicky Cain's hair was red, too, and people used to think that Liz had inherited hers from her mother. If so, it would have been a striking example of the transmission of acquired characteristics, and worthy of note in learned journals.

Usually Mrs. Cain's face was as skilfully made up as her hennaed hair, and she never looked old enough to have a famous aviatrix for a daughter. But now, as she greeted Liz, her face was hot and dripping, and her charmingly decorative apron had failed to protect her best tea-gown from unidentifiable stains.

As for the house, it was old-fashioned but wonderfully kept up. There were deep-piled rugs, waxed hardwood floors, paneled walls and tapestries, Chippendale cabinets, urns and Oriental vases, and over-stuffed furniture, all blending into the color scheme with excellent taste. At one side of the great front hall was the massive staircase, with its heavy newel-post and bronze figures, leading up to the second floor.

"Mother!" Liz gasped. "What *have* you been doing?"

Mrs. Cain sighed. "It isn't what I've been doing, it's what other people have been doing. It's all because Mary wanted to bend wires."

"To bend wires?"

Roger Garvey apparently foresaw trouble. He said, "Good evening, Mrs. Cain," and vanished upstairs unobtrusively, to his secretarial duties.

"Yes, she took a course in night school, and now she's gone into your Uncle Brian's factory." Mrs. Cain sighed deeply. "What's the good of my hiring good cooks if your Uncle Brian keeps stealing them away?"

Liz smiled and nodded. "Oh. The way you spoke it sounded as if she'd gone into an institution to cut out paper dolls. Well, airplanes are important to the progress of our country. Remember that."

"But why did your Uncle Brian need Mary to build airplanes?" Mrs. Vicky Cain persisted. "She's better off in the kitchen."

Liz patted her arm. "Don't worry, Mother. The agency will find us another cook. They always do."

"But that isn't the worst of it," went on Mrs. Cain, smoothing her stained apron. "Today your grandfather decided to move into the west bedroom because he says he wants to be facing the sea when he dies. Which isn't very cheerful, you'll admit. As if we didn't have trouble enough being without servants. How the nurse, Miss Kramer, and I ever got him moved there, I'm sure I don't know!"

"When did the cook leave?" Liz asked.

"This morning. I had to go out and do the marketing myself and the butcher was short of meat, and there are so many guests coming, I guess we'll have to eat out of cans. When there was enough food, they wouldn't let us buy it because that was hoarding, and now there isn't any left. And if there was, we couldn't get it anyway. So I don't know where we are. Do you? It's completely beyond me."

Liz laughed. "I certainly can't answer that one. Now I'm going upstairs, darling, and change into slacks, and be useful. Mother, haven't you anything but gold lamé to wear in the kitchen?"

Mrs. Cain gave a hasty glance downward and a look of surprise spread over her face.

"Certainly, Liz. But I forgot. You know, I'm used to wearing something nice in the afternoon."

Liz shook her head reproachfully and began to climb the broad staircase. This had been San Francisco's showplace once, she reflected—the Cain Mansion. Now all its grand old neighbor-ing houses, on top of the hill, had been converted into three- or four-flat dwellings, housing families whom the Cains did not know. The onetime "mansion" had become just a funny old building. Her mother's ideas were like that, too—all very well for a life of privilege, but hopeless in these changed times. Nothing that might happen in the way of new ideas, new modes of living could ever have demolished her mother's concept of the world and her place in it.

Liz paused in front of the room to which her grandfather had been moved. She was about to knock when Roger Garvey came out.

"Miss Kramer says he's asleep," the secretary told her.

"All right," Liz said. "He needs all the sleep he can get, poor man." She smiled at Roger. "Miss Kramer knows her business. I believe she's the most efficient nurse Graffer has had."

The natty secretary lingered. "Had you anything important you wanted to say to your grandfather? I might be able to help you."

Liz shook her head. "No. I just wanted to find out how he was."

Garvey betrayed curiosity. "I thought perhaps you had some message for him?"

"No, nothing. I've got to go change now, Roger."

But he stood blocking her way in the hall. "Felicity, won't you listen?" he pleaded. Behind his gold-rimmed glasses his eyes had begun to glow.

"I'm sorry, Roger. Let's not go all over that again."

"Tell me, Felicity. What do you suppose your detective-lieutenant thinks of your cousin Sherry now?"

"I'm damned if I know," Liz said truthfully, and pushed her way past him to her room.

Sleek Roger! It was like him to remind her. If she could only forget that she'd caught Ben Latimer on the rebound from Sherry, forget it as completely as she was sure that Ben himself had forgotten it by now. But with Sherry coming here today to see her dying grandfather, Liz's mind was upset, anyway. And Roger's question hadn't helped her.

She changed as rapidly as one can with a bad arm. The doorbell rang as she started downstairs, and she finished the flight at top speed. She was careful to use the banister, however, as she was taking no chances on being grounded for a longer time. Notwithstanding her worry about Sherry and Ben, she still retained all her childhood friendship for her pretty cousin. It would be good to see Sherry again, in spite of the fact that Ben had once cared for her so much.

But it was Uncle Brian Cain who was at the front door. And it was Mrs. Cain who let him in. When Liz arrived he was removing his gloves in the front hall, with a puzzled expression upon his face.

"Liz," he called to his niece as soon as he saw her, "come here and translate. I am trying to persuade your mother that I never stole anybody's cook in my life."

At that moment, the doorbell rang again. Liz smiled at her young and distinguished looking uncle and dashed past him to the door. But it was only Dr. Frayne, their family physician, complete with the bag and the beard that always reminded Liz of a doctor from some period motion picture.

"Hi, Frayne!" Uncle Brian called out. "How's the last bearded medico outside of a museum?"

Dr. Frayne grunted. "Sir, I retired happily ten years ago, and settled down to cultivating my roses and my beard," he said. "Just because this war called me back into practise, I don't intend to relinquish everything. How's your father?"

Uncle Brian shrugged. "I haven't seen him yet."

"Miss Kramer says Graffer's asleep," Liz added.

"I'll run up and have a look at him," the doctor said. "Has the prodigal Sherry returned yet, Vicky?"

Mrs. Cain shook her head.

"Curious to see her, after this great transfor-

mation." Dr. Frayne winked at Liz. "Think I'll invite myself to dinner. Thanks."

Mrs. Cain stared after him as he mounted the stairs, leaving his black bag on the table near the newel-post.

"Don't say it, Mother," Liz cautioned her. "Don't say anything. One more won't make it any worse. Oh, Uncle Brian, did you see the *News* this evening?"

Uncle Brian Cain was lighting a cigar. "No. Why?"

"Your new plane got plenty of space on the front page as a result of that last flight to China," Liz said. "Isn't that what's known as knocking them into the aisles?"

Cain chuckled. "Now, Liz, you know I'm not interested in the publicity. The main thing is we're doing a job—a good job, if I do say it myself. Until the cut-backs come, we'll manage to keep up production and turn out the latest quirks in aircraft."

The doorbell rang again. Liz flung the door open, and threw both arms around her cousin Sherry's neck, without any thought of the bad arm.

It wasn't the twinge of pain that made her draw back. It was the feel of the heavy white wool and the scent of starchy cleanness. But the young woman she had embraced wasn't Sherry. It was a stranger—a nun in a hood, stiff linen and robes, with a rosary at her waist. Sherry was the girl standing beside her.

Liz gasped, drew back, and remained very still while her mother and her uncle uttered loud greetings. It is a strange thing to look at your closest girlhood friend and see her in the convent garb of a novice.

"Sister Ursula, I want you to meet my cousin, Felicity Cain," Sherry was saying. Her voice was still low and rich and warm. "This is Sister Ursula who came up with me."

"Oh, there are two of you!" Mrs. Cain exclaimed in surprise. "I should have known nuns always travel in pairs, but I just can't get used to thinking of you as a nun, Sherry. I fixed up the north room for you. Luckily we have another spare bedroom, so we can manage to take care of you both splendidly."

The doorbell rang again. Mrs. Cain gave a start and turned.

"Now who can that be?"

The latest ringer of the front doorbell was a small, middle-aged man in dingy overalls. He was waiting on the porch, carrying a battered suitcase. He had a grimy, good-natured face and sharp restless little eyes.

"Is this the Cain place?" he asked.

"Yes," Liz answered.

"Some hills you got here in San Francisco, lady." He set down his suitcase with a sigh of relief. "I'm Homer Hatch, from the shipyards. Would you mind showing me to my room?"

CHAPTER III

It was Liz's uncle, Brian Cain, who broke the amazed silence.

"I'm afraid I don't understand, my friend," he said. "Does this look like a rooming house?"

"The City Housing Bureau sent me," the man explained. "This address is listed there as being open for tenants."

"The Housing Bureau?"

"Look," the man said. "If anything's gone haywire, it ain't me. I've got credentials." He pulled a sheaf of papers and cards out of his pocket and began thumbing through them. "See—here's my union card—Homer Hatch. I've been a top-hand welder for years. I work at Marinship. Take a gander at my gate pass and my button. All right, so far?"

"All right." Uncle Brian nodded. "So you're Homer Hatch, a shipyard worker. But who sent you to this address?"

"I'm coming to that. Now have a squint at this letter from the Housing Bureau. It says: 'Report to home of Mrs. Michael Cain.'" He held up the letter for them to read. "You can see for yourselves."

Liz glanced at her mother. Her married name

was Mrs. Michael Cain. Liz saw memory dawning in her mother's eyes and with it a trace of guilt.

"Mother!" Liz cried.

Suddenly Mrs. Cain was all the gracious hostess. "I remember!" she cried. "You're the man I'm taking in for Mrs. Vansittart! Do come right on in!"

It was Homer Hatch's turn to look puzzled.

"Lady, I don't know no Mrs. Vansittart," he said. "But I want a room and a clean bed so bad that I ain't arguing. Not even if Mrs. Vansittart's in it." He saw the nuns and hastily added, "Meaning no offense, y'understand, Sisters."

"Now, let me see!" Mrs. Cain began to calculate aloud. "You're going to remain over until tomorrow, Brian, because this is a family gathering. You can use the small room downstairs near the kitchen just for tonight, and I'll put Mr. Hatch in Graffer's old room. There! That's settled."

"How about grandfather?" Mr. Hatch asked. "Maybe I ought to tell you—I snore some."

"Oh, so does Graffer. But I meant the room he just left, which is vacant. Now, Brian, will you show Mr. Hatch upstairs while Liz and I look after Sherry and Sister Veronica?"

"Ursula," the nun said quietly. Her face was calm, beautiful, serene.

Hatch reached down and picked up his suitcase. "Let's go. Lead the way, Mister." He walked into the house.

"My name is Cain," said Uncle Brian, closing the door after him. "Come on, Hatch. We'll see how you like the room."

"If it's got four walls and a bed, I'll like it," said Hatch.

Liz watched the two men ascend the big staircase and disappear at the top.

"Now, Mother," she said.

With Mrs. Cain leading, and Liz, Sister Ursula, and Sherry following, the four women started upstairs. The two nuns quietly but firmly had insisted on carrying their own bags. All the way up to the second floor, Mrs. Cain kept chattering away steadily.

"It was Mrs. Vansittart's idea," Mrs. Cain explained. "At the Tuesday Morning club she told me all about the housing shortage and I foolishly expressed sympathy for the poor shipyard workers. Then she told me everybody with spare rooms should register with the Housing Bureau and I let her call up and put in my name. That was a month ago. I never dreamed your grandfather would be so ill, and I thought you, Liz, would be off somewhere, ferrying airplanes."

They had reached the second floor now and were moving along the hall. Mrs. Cain was trotting ahead, brisk and chipper. From behind, Liz could hear the soft sound of Sherry's laughter. Sherry's laugh had always been low and musical, but now Liz thought she had never heard anything sound so soft and contented.

"You haven't changed a bit, Aunt Vicky," Sherry called out. "You don't know how nice it is to hear you all muddled, after the sensible women I have recently met." Liz glanced back over her shoulder and saw Sherry exchanging a smile with Sister Ursula.

"Sherry, here's a real muddle for you," said Liz. "First we'll show you to your rooms. Then, believe it or not, Mother and I are going to get dinner, and not out of cans either. Can you put up with what two amateurs can dredge out of the pantry, Sherry?" Liz had dropped back beside them.

"If a cook is all you need, may I offer to help?" suggested Sister Ursula.

"Can you cook?" Liz faltered, glancing at the long draped sleeves of the nun's habit. It was very strange. She had never thought of a nun standing before a stove.

Sister Ursula laughed. "Oh, these roll back easily. Housework is our specialty, you know. We are the Sisters of Martha of Bethany. And Martha, you remember, was the one who did all the housework."

"Then Sherry is going to do housework?" Liz stared at her cousin in surprise. "I didn't understand. I thought she would turn to other things."

"Spending a life of cloistered contemplation behind an iron grille?" Sister Ursula was smiling broadly. "I'm afraid we're not that kind of nuns. Not good enough, perhaps. I doubt if Sherry here could ever measure up to such a life. I'm sure I couldn't."

"But I thought nuns were devoted to prayer, and acts of charity and mercy."

"There are nuns and nuns," Sister Ursula said. "Brother Gregory used to say, 'There are three things known only to God in his infinite wisdom. One is how much a Dominican knows. Another is what a Jesuit is thinking about. And the third is how many Orders of Sisterhoods there are.' Ours—well, we're the etceteras who do the work. And now about dinner. How many do you expect?"

Later, as Liz set the table—making an awkward job of it with her one arm—she was more puzzled than ever. The other nun—was her name Ursula? She was a surprising person. She was so quiet you didn't know she was there, at first— just a funny habit with a round face looking out. Until she spoke. Then, in a few sentences, she had become a clear and definite person— efficient, administrative, capable, wise, and even humorous. If that was what the Sisters of Martha of Bethany did to you, maybe Sherry's choice made sense after all.

Liz was remembering. It had been ten or twelve years ago—the time she and Sherry had stayed overnight at Mina Drake's house. They had sat up until all hours, sleepless and babbling, plotting their futures and leaving brown smudges of chocolate on Mrs. Drake's sheets.

Mina was going to be an actress like Jean Harlow, who had just burst on an astonished public in *Hell's Angels*.

"And when he comes to see her on account of his friend, he starts to fall for her himself," Mina had said. "She wore a white evening dress and she looked *simply gorgeous*!"

Liz had liked *Hell's Angels*. In fact, she thought it was the most wonderful picture she had ever seen, but not because of Miss Harlow.

"I know," she had answered. "That's the one

where the Zeppelin comes out of the clouds over London and he crashes his ship into it. But, Mina, who wants to be like that kind of a woman? What's the fun of letting the man do all the flying?" Her own idol had been Amelia Earhart.

Sherry had been very quiet until they finally asked her, "And how about you?"

"Oh," Sherry said simply. "I'm going to be a nun."

They'd hooted at that, Mina and Liz. It was so silly. Why, Sherry hadn't even been disappointed in love yet.

Sherry hadn't mentioned her choice of vocation again for years. She'd led a normal life on campus, spent a couple of years employed as a secretary. Then she had disappeared.

Liz had heard it first from Ben. That was when Ben Latimer was Sherry's young man, and Liz had thought men were all very well as mechanics or co-pilots, but otherwise unnecessary.

There'd been a long postmortem after she'd heard Hinchcliff read his paper on his new direction finder, and she got home late. She had heard voices in the west room and had wandered in. Even before Sherry hastily excused herself and went upstairs, Liz realized she'd interrupted a scene. Liz hadn't known whether to go or remain, so she'd stood there, looking at Latimer.

Ben had taken a long time lighting his pipe.

"I want you to be the first to know, Liz," he said at last. "I've been jilted."

Liz gasped. "Why, Ben! We've all always believed it was completely settled."

Ben got up from the chair slowly, standing very tall and straight. He was still in uniform then.

"I've bumped into a powerful rival," he said. "A rival too strong to buck. The Church. Sherry's determined to become a nun. There's nothing I can do about it."

Afterwards, when Liz had gone upstairs to bed, Sherry had told her about it.

"I didn't want to do it blind, Liz," Sherry

had said. "I wanted to see enough of the world first so I'd be sure. And now I know. There's no mistake about it."

Now here it was, settled. All the hopes of that chocolate-smeared confab had been carried out. Wilhelmina—now Lorna—Drake was in Hollywood, and one of the most celebrated stars in the country, for reasons which had not been especially apparent twelve years ago. Liz was a grade A aviator—she hated the word "aviatrix"—and would be flying again as soon as this damned arm healed. And Sherry was a nun—or at least, well on the road to being one.

How about that? How close to being a nun was a novice? How irrevocable was it if you changed your mind? Liz wasn't sure. But she felt absurdly glad that Ben Latimer wouldn't be present for dinner tonight. Liz even hoped something might come up to keep him busy for the next few days.

CHAPTER IV

Dr. Frayne tasted the contents of the casserole and his white teeth glistened as he beamed with pleasure above his beard.

"Magnificent!" he proclaimed. "And you concocted this out of canned remnants, Vicky?"

Mrs. Cain shook her head. "She did it. Sister Helena."

"Ursula," the nun said quietly.

Dr. Frayne turned his smile down the table and eyed her with an approving gaze.

"As an atheist of long and solid standing, I have always admired monks, if only because they know how to make wine and liqueurs," Dr. Frayne announced. "But I had no notion that nuns had their fleshly virtues, too. If this is a sample, Sister, you must publish a Convent Cook Book."

"As a matter of fact, I didn't learn this in a convent," the nun confessed. "Oh, we cook, of course—and Sister Immaculata could shame many a *cordon bleu*—but this recipe I learned from the wife of a lieutenant on the Homicide Squad. She is the best cook I have ever known."

Liz felt a little shudder run up and down her

spine. A lieutenant on the Homicide Squad? She hadn't mentioned Ben Latimer since Sherry had arrived. Now she let her eyes meet those of her cousin, and wondered if her own were as unreadable as Sherry's. She caught sight of a dangerous smile on Roger Garvey's handsome features and saw his full lips part as if to speak.

Hastily she plunged in. "How on earth do you happen to know such strange people, Sister?"

She didn't hear what Garvey said, though she knew it was some question directed at Sherry and Ben. His speech and hers had overlapped and canceled each other. There was another awkward silence.

Then Liz's mother took a taste and stared at the untouched plate before Uncle Brian Cain.

"Brian, Dr. Frayne's right," Mrs. Cain said. "It really is wonderful. I'm almost tempted to enter a convent myself. How can you sit there, not touching a morsel of it. You look pale." Her face grew anxious. "Are you ill?"

"I'm all right, Vicky." Brian Cain forced a smile. "Something must have upset me at lunch. I feel a little squeamish."

"Overwork," Dr. Frayne diagnosed. "You won't be much use to the war effort if you wear yourself out, Brian."

Mrs. Cain spoke to everyone. "There's plenty of seconds for everybody." Her face brightened. "Ah—I know!"

"What, Mother?" Liz always feared the worst from her mother's sudden inspirations.

"That poor Mr. Thatch! He must be terribly hungry after welding things all day. I'm sure he'd be glad to eat up whatever is left over."

She bustled out of the room. Sister Ursula smiled approval, but Roger Garvey lifted his carefully brushed eyebrows.

"At least I hope she's able to persuade Hatch to wash his hands," Roger said. "Changing his clothes would be too much to hope for."

Nobody had a chance to answer him. From the second floor they heard Mrs. Cain's shrill, terrified scream.

It was an unearthly sound that came quavering through the old house. It caused them to hold their knives and forks suspended and sit for a brief space in stunned surprise.

Dr. Frayne recovered first. His professional duties had trained him to rise to emergencies. He jumped out of his chair and darted out of the room. Sister Ursula was not far behind him. Liz and Sherry momentarily got tangled up in the doorway, then went racing for the stairs, with Brian Cain close on their heels. Only Roger Garvey did not move. He shrugged wearily and went on eating.

When Liz reached the bend, Sister Ursula was already well up the steps. But Dr. Frayne had halted at the small table at the bottom of the flight and was looking about him in a perplexed manner.

"Where is it?" he was muttering. "I'm sure I left it here."

Then he looked under the table, saw his bag, snatched it up, and started to climb the steps, two at a time. Liz followed.

There had been only one scream. Now silence reigned on the upper floor. Automatically Liz headed for Graffer's room.

"The poor old man is dead and Mother must have found him," she was thinking. "Too bad! But perhaps it's for the best. He's been in pain so long."

Just as she remembered about Fists and those threatening notes, she saw Graffer's door open and Miss Kramer, starched and efficient, with her cap on, come out into the hall. As the nurse headed toward the east bedroom, Liz glanced into Graffer's room. The old man was sleeping peacefully, with his veined aged hands resting upon the folded sheet.

Liz turned and hastened toward the east bedroom, too. Down the hall she could see Sister Ursula about to enter that room. Liz ran forward past Miss Kramer and stopped in the doorway. Her mother was lying on the floor in a faint, but when Liz's glance went to the bed, she forgot about everything else.

The little shipyard worker, who had been so perkily alive an hour before, was lying upon the bed with his head on the pillow, face upward.

He was dead. But it was something more than mere death that halted Liz in the doorway of the room—something which jarred her nerves as they had never been jarred before. It was the expression upon the face of the corpse. The features were screwed up into a grin which was indescribably appalling.

Grins are supposed to depict mirth but this grimace was anything but humorous. It expressed pain—nothing else. Homer Hatch had died in agony and that last contortion of his features remained frozen there.

The effect was heightened by the stringy, greasy hair that hung down over his high forehead and the gleam of his yellow, bared teeth.

It was Dr. Frayne's dry voice, behind Liz, as he spoke to the nurse, which broke the spell of her horror.

"Miss Kramer, you stay here and assist me," said the doctor, as he pushed Liz to one side, and moved forward into the room. He glanced at Sister Ursula who had stopped at the foot of the bed. "Everybody else must clear out. Brian, carry Vicky to her room. Liz, you go with him, undress her and put her to bed. No—of course you can't do that with your lame arm. Sister, will you help?"

The nun nodded and Liz, recovering from her shock, turned. They were all there now, Uncle Brian, Sherry, Miss Kramer—everybody except Roger Garvey.

Brian Cain picked up Mrs. Cain and went out, followed by Liz, Sherry, and Sister Ursula. Miss Kramer remained with Dr. Frayne who stood at the door and closed it after them. They followed Brian as he carried his sister-in-law down the hallway.

Sherry had lingered in the doorway. Her face was as white as her wimple.

"Is—is Hatch dead?" she asked Liz.

"Yes."

"I never saw death like that before," Sherry said in shaky tones. "I know I'll have to. We do so much nursing work. But it's awful, just the same."

Her voice dropped. For the first time since her mother's scream Liz had the chance to ask herself how, what, why? Why had Hatch died almost on the instant he entered their home?

She had plenty of time to think, too, for when they arrived at Vicky's room and Uncle Brian had laid her down on a couch, Sister Ursula took charge and shooed them all out, just as Dr. Frayne had done.

Brian Cain went downstairs again, perhaps to finish his interrupted dinner. Liz and Sherry remained in the hallway, too excited to care about food. The two girls didn't say much to each other. They just stood there, thinking about what had happened.

After about fifteen minutes had passed, the doorway of the east bedroom opened and Miss Kramer came out. She motioned to them and they hurried forward.

"I'm going to see how Mrs. Cain is getting along," said the nurse. "Dr. Frayne told me to. You better go in and see if you can help him. He may need someone."

Then with a nod at Liz, she went up the hall to Mrs. Cain's room.

Liz could feel Sherry steeling herself, tightening her nerves against the death-chamber. She took the novice's hand in her good one and squeezed it reassuringly.

"Come on," she whispered.

The body had been clothed at Liz's first glimpse of it. Now the clothing lay on the floor, and when Dr. Frayne caught sight of the two girls, he hastily pulled a sheet over the corpse.

"Have to report this to the coroner's office right away," he told them. "Although I couldn't very well give a certificate, I was curious to see for myself."

"Why did he die?" Liz asked. She tried to forget about that grin.

The doctor frowned and tugged at his beard. "Damned if I know why, but I'm getting an idea of how. Thought at first it was tetanus. Typical enough spasm. But if that was it, we'd have noticed he was sick when he came."

"He looked fine then," Liz said. "Just a little tired."

"Sure. That's why I checked over the body. Tetanus could have resulted from an industrial accident but with modern precautions, it's unlikely. Also, there's no abrasion or wound on the body."

"Then what killed him?"

Dr. Frayne pulled down the sheet. The distorted grin seemed to have no effect upon his hardened nerves.

"Look at those eyebrows," the physician said. "Look at the mouth. Indisputable signs. Has to be either tetanus or strychnine. Since it wasn't tetanus, it must have been strychnine."

Liz shuddered. She heard a small groan from Sherry. "You mean he killed himself?"

"That's what the poor devil wanted the room for. Suicide in privacy. That's why he needed a room so badly. He did it quick, too."

"But if it's suicide, shouldn't there be a glass or something?" Liz asked.

"Why?" Dr. Frayne retorted. "Pills in your pocket—gulp 'em down." He was still oblivious of the girls' reaction to the casual vividness of his picture and the twisted features of the dead man.

There was a sound from the doorway and Liz glanced around to see Sister Ursula standing there. How long she had been in the doorway Liz didn't know.

"May I come in?" the nun asked "Mrs. Cain is in bed. She seems to have passed into a normal sleep. And this poor man, God rest his soul! I wonder where he got the strychnine."

Dr. Frayne raised his eyebrows. He could not conceal his astonishment. "You go in for diagnosis, too, Sister? Or did you hear what I said?"

"No, I didn't hear." The nun gestured at the contorted dead face. "It is easy to surmise the cause of death must have been strychnine."

The doctor grunted. "Also, it might have been tetanus. Trust an amateur to jump to the sensational."

"Remember, Doctor, I saw him only an hour ago. He was well then." She moved quietly to the bed. "He'd been drinking, hadn't he?"

Dr. Frayne nodded. "Common prelude. Nerve yourself up to it."

"But when he came here, I stood close to him and smelled no liquor. Have you sent for the police?"

"Police?" Sherry gasped.

"They check up on suicides," Dr. Frayne said. "Liz, will you please put in the call?"

CHAPTER V

Liz left the room. As she walked out she heard the nun's quiet voice.

"Dr. Frayne, why are you so sure it was suicide?"

Liz dialed OPERATOR and said, "I want a policeman." She gave the address and hung up. When she turned, Roger Garvey was standing behind her.

He glanced at her unsteady hand and wordlessly offered her a cigarette. After he had lighted it, he puffed on his own.

"I know to my sorrow, my dear Felicity, that you yearn for a specific policeman," he drawled. "But what drives you to this step? What has been happening?"

"You don't know?"

"When a woman screams, and a doctor, a nurse, and a nun are all available, it strikes me that I'd be more of a hindrance than a help. I decided to finish dinner. But what happened?"

"That little defense worker, Mr. Hatch, just killed himself in the room Mother let him have."

Garvey blew out a smoke ring. "And you still find death moving? Even in this year of death? But why the police?"

"Dr. Frayne says suicides must be reported."

"Of course. I should have remembered. But why just 'a policeman'? Why not give the family business to a family friend?"

"Please, Roger. Don't heckle me. I've got to get back."

Roger Garvey halted her by placing his hand on her shoulder.

"Felicity, you still misunderstand me. I don't mean to heckle. I only want you to see yourself clearly. Don't you know why you didn't call Ben?"

Liz's eyebrows went up.

"Why should I? It isn't his sort of job. He wouldn't want to be bothered."

"Of course, you can rationalize it." Roger sounded impatient. "But can't you see why you subconsciously shrank from calling Ben? Because you don't want him to come here, not while Sherry is in the house. It's because you still aren't sure of him."

"Let me go, Roger."

"Felicity." His voice was low and urgent. "You could be sure of me. You should know that."

"Let me go!"

She jerked away and ran upstairs. She could almost feel Garvey's eyes following her, although he had let her go.

At the head of the stairs she met Miss Kramer.

"Oh, Miss Cain," the nurse said, "would you please go in to your grandfather? He's awake now and he's demanding to see you and Miss—Sister—his other granddaughter," she concluded, uncertain of the correct designation for a novice.

"Right away." Liz again went into the room where Hatch had died. "I put in that call, Doctor," she told Frayne. "A prowl car should be here any minute."

"Thank you, Liz." The doctor turned to the nun. "And please, Sister Ursula! Leave it up to them when they arrive. After all, it's their business."

"I hope they know their business," the nun said.

Liz turned away and hurried up the hall to see her grandfather.

Graffer had always been old, as Liz remembered him. He had always had that white hair, that heavily lined face. But there had been strength and vigor under the semblance of age; now he was just an old man, weak and helpless and very much alone.

He sat propped up with pillows and a bedrest. He smiled as Liz came in. The smile lit up his gray, wrinkled face.

"Did you see your young man today?" he asked. His voice was gentle, but probing.

She understood what he meant. "He said he'd see to it, Graffer. He promised to have men posted around the house. You can rely on him. He'll take care of it."

"Good. I feel like an old fool, calling for help from the police." His withered face took on a cunning expression. "But Vitelli always meant what he said. Can't take chances with you and your mother here in the house. What's been happening?" he demanded with considerable abruptness.

Liz tried to stall off his question. "I haven't heard the news yet this evening," she said. "What makes you ask that?"

"People tramping up and down halls, in and out of rooms. What's been going on? Or has that fool of a doctor decided it's not good for my heart to let me know? Come on. Tell me."

Liz tried to smile. "You're imagining things, Graffer. Of course, it takes a lot of shuffling around, getting people settled in guest rooms, when we're having a family reunion."

He gave Liz a skeptical stare, then shrugged his shoulders.

She was glad that Sherry came in just then. Graffer took one look at this other granddaughter and shut his eyes in a wry grimace.

"Mary Sheridan Cain!" he barked. "What are you doing in that masquerade costume?"

Sherry stiffened. "It's my uniform," she said.

Graffer snorted. "Hmf! I warned your father what would come of your mother's religion. But I never expected to see a granddaughter of mine dressed that way."

"If we're going to start this again, I think I'd better go," Sherry answered quietly.

Graffer opened his eyes and laughed. "You're a good girl, Sherry," he said. "You know what you want and you've got the courage to stick to it. You're kind enough to come to see your old grandfather because the idiot doctors say he's dying. But you're strong enough to hold on to what you believe, and no pampering of an old man who might cut you out of his will. You're all right, Sherry. And I like your uniform."

Sherry stood still for an instant of amazement. Then she moved swiftly and gracefully to the side of the bed, leaned over, and kissed the old man.

"I'm glad," she said simply. "I've prayed that we could love and understand each other again."

They were silent for a moment. Liz smiled and felt good—the kind of feeling that leaves your eyes not quite dry.

"Intolerance is a bane of good times," Graffer said slowly. "I've been pig-headed in my day. I've been proud of it, and declaimed that tolerance is the limp virtue of the feebleminded. But I was a fool. Emotions run high. Hatred runs high. What might have been mere irritable prejudice ten years ago now can turn to vicious hate. We've got to watch ourselves. We've got to understand—and to love."

He paused and then barked out a loud laugh. "How the boys down at the Hall of Justice would enjoy this! Old Tim Cain turns soft! But Sherry understands."

"Yes, Graffer."

There were noises in the hall—the clumping of heavy feet.

"Sherry, now that we're friends again, maybe you'll tell me what the hell goes on out there?"

"What do you mean, Graffer?"

"Why are the bulls here?"

"Bulls?"

"Or do you forget such words in the convent? The harness bulls, the cops. After ten years in the district attorney's office and twenty on the bench, do you think I don't know a policeman's footsteps when I hear them?"

He was leaning forward from his pillows, his old blue eyes aglint.

"I'll go see, Graffer," Liz said. "You stay here, Sherry."

Miss Kramer was in the hall. "I thought he wanted to see you alone," the nurse said to Liz. "That's why I didn't interrupt you."

Liz nodded. "Thanks. But please go in now and see if you can calm him down. He knows something's going on and he wants to hear all about it."

The nurse went into Graffer's room, while Liz followed the sound of loud bass voices to the room that had been Homer Hatch's.

Dr. Frayne was there, and Sister Ursula, and two men in uniform. They paid no attention to Liz. The short and wiry policeman was talking to the doctor.

"And nobody around this place ever seen this Joe before today?" he asked.

"No one," Dr. Frayne said. "It was pure chance that the Housing Bureau should have sent him here."

The officer turned to the nun. "And you still insist this ain't no suicide?"

"I do," said Sister Ursula firmly.

"Look, Sister. Accordin' to you, inside an hour after he gets a room here, he makes a total stranger mad enough to kill him. The mysterious stranger has strychnine somewheres, and this dope obligingly ups and drinks it. Now I ask you does that make sense?"

"Patience is one of the seven cardinal virtues," Sister Ursula answered with a sigh. "In this instance, I fear time will show I am correct."

"Huh?"

"I was simply reminding myself. Let me tell you again, officer, when I saw the man this afternoon there was no liquor on his breath. When I saw him dead there was a pronounced smell of whisky. Dr. Frayne will corroborate me."

"So what? He took one to give himself some Dutch courage."

"And what did he drink it out of? There is no glass here."

"Look, Sister. Not everybody's so polite they got to drink out of a glass."

"Then where is the flask or bottle or whatever he had?"

"Maybe he got really good and mellow and heaved it out the window."

"Better search for it before you dismiss this as suicide. If you don't find it, admit that someone must have been drinking with him, and that someone carried away the flask or glasses. No one in this house confesses to having visited Hatch."

The policeman was heavily patient. "Sister,

you been reading stuff they hadn't ought to let get into convents. This poor sap comes here to bump himself off in peace and quiet. So let him. Leave him alone. Chuck, you go phone the coroner's office and let 'em cart him to the morgue."

The doorbell rang just as Sister Ursula started to speak. Liz thought hastily of where the others were, and concluded answering door-bells was her job. She turned toward the hall.

"I should warn you that, with the family's permission, I intend to report this death to the proper authorities," she heard Sister Ursula say as she left the room.

CHAPTER VI

Descending the stairs, Liz reached the front door and opened it. The man there promptly kissed her.

"Good evening, darling," said Detective-lieutenant Ben Latimer.

"Oh, Ben! My! I *am* glad to see you!"

Ben looked at her upturned face, smiled, and kissed her again. Then he released her reluctantly.

"Fun's fun, but what's been going on here?" he asked.

"I don't know. It's all so confused. But maybe you can help me. Mother went and told the Housing Bureau that we could rent a room to a defense worker. Then she forgot all about it and today, in the midst of everything, he showed up, and now he's dead and—my, it's even got me talking like Mother."

"Dead? Uh—naturally?"

"We don't know. Sister Ursula was talking about notifying Homicide, but now you're here, there's no necessity for that." She stopped short.

"What's the matter?"

"You're here."

"Yes?"

"But why? It's marvelous and just when we need you; but how could you know?"

Ben grinned. "Fine chance for an act, isn't it?

I could spin you a nice convincing story about a detective's intuition. But no mirrors are needed, darling. It's all perfectly straight-forward. My men, who were watching the house, saw the patrol car drive up and thought I ought to be told about it."

"Your men, of course! I almost forgot them. Did they see any strangers around?" Liz had a crawling premonition of what their presence might disclose. "But come on upstairs. Now that you're here I feel as if everything's going to turn out all right."

The two men in uniform were leaving Hatch's room. The short policeman recognized Latimer and stopped.

"Nothing for you, sir," he said. "Suicide, even if that good Sister in there does insist—"

Ben interrupted him. "Come on back inside with me while I take a look."

Liz tried to keep her eyes from the bed as she made introductions. "Sister Ursula, this is Lieutenant Latimer. Dr. Frayne, you know Ben?"

The doctor nodded. "Of course. Glad you came, my boy. We need the professional mind."

"Sister Ursula?" Ben repeated musingly. "Sister, do you know Terence Marshall, on the Los Angeles force?"

"Very well. In fact, I'm his daughter's god-mother."

Ben turned to the men in uniform. "I think you might pay some attention to what she says. I met Marshall while I was down south on the Rothmann matter. He told me that the two toughest cases in his entire career had been broken by his friend, Sister Ursula."

The short policeman's eyes boggled.

"Sister Ursula—Jeeze!" he said. "So it's *her*! Yeah, I know."

"Please, Lieutenant," said Sister Ursula. "I've simply taken an interest in Lieutenant Marshall's cases because my father, God rest his soul, was a chief of police back in Iowa. There was a time when I almost became a policewoman myself and naturally I was interested. It also made it impossible for me to remain silent when I knew there was something very wrong."

"Of course," Ben said. "Now will somebody give me a clear idea of just what happened?"

He listened to Dr. Frayne's terse, clear account, occasionally nodding or frowning. At the end he said:

"To sum up—pending the findings of an autopsy, we can assume that this man died of strychnine poisoning. Natural or accidental death is therefore out. Suicide and murder remain, but are equally unlikely. Until we investigate his past, we can't speak of motives, but renting a room through the Housing Bureau for the purpose of having a place to gulp down strychnine doesn't seem plausible. Yet as to murder—he's a stranger to everybody here, and his coming was purest chance, unless some enemy had trailed him to this house.

"But he's dead. So murder or suicide it must be. And the one piece of evidence pointing either way is the fact that he had a drink of whisky from a vanished container."

"That's what I told you, Lieutenant," the shorter man in uniform persisted. "There ain't a thing to show it was murder."

"But there isn't a thing to let you write it off so easily as suicide, either," Ben answered. "Further investigation is indicated. I want a look. Would you like to leave Sister, or Liz?"

Liz couldn't move. She stood rooted—fascinated—while Ben Latimer walked over to the bed. He pulled down the sheet, and her throat went dry as she saw Hatch's sardonic smile again, those stringy locks of hair, those yellow teeth. Ben stooped over the bed, then abruptly straightened up, with something in his hand.

"I don't think there's much doubt of murder, now," he said slowly. "This is a case for the Homicide Department, all right. Doctor, you examined the body?"

"Yes. When I thought it might be tetanus—looking for a wound—focus of infection."

"And did you notice this?" Ben held up what he had found so all could see it. It was a small rumpled oblong sheet of white paper.

"There was a scrap of paper like that on the bed, yes," Frayne said. "The body was partly rolled over on it. Didn't notice what it was. Thought it was a farewell note."

Ben turned the paper so Liz and Sister Ursula could observe it. It bore nothing but the outline of a clenched fist, with the index finger extended.

Liz looked up at Ben Latimer. For years he had been a friend, and for almost a year he had been the man she loved and was going to marry. Now he was a detective, working on a case. His lips, his eyes, the set of his jaw—everything about him was new and unfamiliar to her.

This strange Lieutenant Latimer turned to the short policeman. "You'll relieve him until I can get more men out here. You," he added to the other officer, "round up all the people in this house and take them to the drawing-room, downstairs."

"But Ben," Liz protested. "You can't go sending a man around into all these rooms. Graffer's sick, and the shock might be fatal. And I don't know if Mother's come to yet. She found the body."

"Very well. I'll give you that job, Liz. Round everybody up."

"Miss Kramer will have to stay with her patient, Judge Cain," Dr. Frayne broke in authoritatively. "I will not permit him to be left alone."

"All right." Ben gave his assent impatiently. "Officer, I'll leave you here with the body until the boys come. Dr. Frayne, Sister—you will please go down to the drawing-room and wait for me."

He left the room. Liz followed him. She felt helpless, caught up in something vast and stern and machinelike. An hour earlier domestic life had been chaotic, but at least it had been familiar. Now a stranger had died, and everything was changed. The police were in charge and they were giving orders, and she had her job to do. Round them up, he had said, as though her people were so many cattle.

But it would keep her occupied. It would be something which might efface the haunting memory of Hatch's bared teeth and grotesque smile.

Liz received two surprises during the

roundup. The first came when she found Uncle Brian visiting in Roger Garvey's room. This was totally unexpected and a complete reversal of Uncle Brian's ideas of social propriety. He had never bothered to conceal his dislike and distrust of Graffer's secretary. The antagonism between the two men was evident even now, when Liz opened the door to their call and delivered her message.

They had been talking—Liz could see that. Brian Cain had been chewing on a cigar and glowering, while Roger Garvey was looking pale and distraught. It was the first time Liz had ever seen the secretary when he didn't seem sure of himself.

"In the drawing-room?" Uncle Brian said, rising to his feet. "Sure. I'll come with you, right now."

"I'll be along in a minute or so," said Roger.

It was Uncle Brian who closed the door. As he walked down the hallway with Liz, he muttered aloud:

"I can't see how Father tolerates that young upstart. His ideas are all twisted."

"I don't think he talks much about them to Graffer."

"The nerve of him—asking me for a job! Why is he so anxious to get out of this house all of a sudden? I don't understand it."

The second surprise Liz was to remember came when she stopped to tell Miss Kramer to remain with Graffer until relieved. Sherry was also in the room, so Liz took her down the hall to sit for a while with Mrs. Cain.

"You'll watch after Mother, won't you, Sherry?" Liz said. "Later, when she wakes up, you can bring her downstairs to the drawing-room, if you feel she's up to it. Ben Latimer wants to question her."

Sherry nodded. Then she said slowly, "So Ben is here."

Liz said, "Yes."

"You said 'Ben Latimer wants' as though it were—oh, just anybody."

"That's the way he is now. He's different, all of a sudden."

"But he's there. Ah!"

Sherry turned away, crossed the room to the window, and stood looking out with her back to Liz.

CHAPTER VII

Slowly Liz walked downstairs to the drawing-room. There she found Dr. Frayne, Sister Ursula, Roger Garvey, and Uncle Brian gathered in a group, waiting for Ben Latimer. They did not talk much. They were silent and nervous. And all the time the golden hands of the marble clock, on the huge old-fashioned mantel, kept ticking noisily along, just as if nothing at all were happening.

"But why here?" Liz thought, and was amazed to discover she had spoken aloud.

Dr. Frayne jumped. "What do you mean, Liz?"

"I mean, whoever killed Hatch. Why should he follow Hatch here?"

"Nobody killed Hatch." It was Uncle Brian who spoke. He was still skeptical.

"But if someone did, why did he choose this house? It's strange, with Graffer so sick and Sherry arriving on a visit."

Sister Ursula said, "There was a reason." It was hard to tell whether it was a theoretical remark or deduction.

Ben came in then. Or rather Detective-lieutenant Latimer came in.

"I've talked to Sergeant Verdi," he said. "There isn't much else I can do until the squad gets here, except talk to you. Perhaps I may be able to turn up something that will give the squad a lead. That room used to be Judge Cain's, didn't it?"

"Until this morning," Liz said.

"So that anything we find there, from prints to the traditional gold cuff links, might reasonably belong there. They are either his or those of visitors who called on your grandfather?"

"Lieutenant!" said Brian Cain, suddenly.

"Yes, Mr. Cain?"

Uncle Brian had a sudden light in his eyes. "If that poor devil Hatch was in my father's room, perhaps somebody made a mistake—a perfectly natural one, under the circumstances. The Judge changed his room only today."

Liz uttered a gasp. "I see what you mean." She looked at Ben Latimer. "It was the Fist, Ben. Remember those threatening notes? It fits. They thought Hatch was Graffer."

"Ingenious," Ben said dryly. "And it might make good sense if Hatch had been, say, shot through the window. But a murderer who could get close enough to Homer Hatch to poison him and still be unable to distinguish him from your grandfather must be a curious individual. I'd like to meet him."

"How did the poison get into the room?" Uncle Brian asked.

His question aroused a doubt in Liz's mind also. It was odd about the poison. How *had* it gotten into the room? The more she thought of it, the more puzzled she became.

"That's right," she said. "It is mysterious. How was the poison put into Hatch's room? Was it by some strange method? You read about poison wallpaper, pillows, and things like that. Could it have been something similar?"

Dr. Frayne emitted a snort of disgust.

"No." Ben shook his head at Liz. "Strychnine gas doesn't explain it either. Hatch was poisoned in the normal manner. Somebody gave him poisoned whisky. Which means, in all likelihood, that he knew and trusted his murderer and would accept a drink from him. You still maintain that none of you knew him?"

The silence was sufficient answer.

"And no one recognized him after Mr. Cain showed him to his room?"

Again there was silence. Liz happened to be watching Roger Garvey. She wondered what that quick puzzled contraction of his features meant, and whether Ben also had noticed it.

Dr. Frayne said, "Then you're sure that it's murder?"

"Not sure, no. But sure that it deserves investigation. If my man can't find a whisky bottle within throwing range of that window, I'll be morally certain he didn't kill himself. Then again there's the Fist. That we should find that symbol of death and revenge beside a suicide is asking too much of coincidence."

"Are you suggesting there were two victims in the same house?" Liz exclaimed in shocked tones. "I mean two persons condemned to death by the Fist?"

Uncle Brian started. "What on earth are you driving at, Liz? Two? Has someone else here had trouble with the Fists?" He seemed to understand abruptly. "Oh!"

Ben nodded. "Today your father sent word to me by Liz that he'd been threatened. He asked me to put a guard on the house. And that brings me to the most important point in this case."

He paused. At that moment the door slid back and Sherry appeared, helping Mrs. Cain into the room.

They stood near the doorway for an instant. There was a lamp on a low table beside Sherry, throwing its light upward at an oblique angle, giving that oval face a quality at once both ethereal and human. Yes, Sherry was beautiful.

Ben turned and faced her. For a terrible moment Liz held her breath. They'd met again now, under strange and frightening circumstances. What would Ben do? What would he say?

Lieutenant Latimer spoke curtly. "Good. Now we're all here. Sit down, please."

Uncle Brian hardly waited for his sister-in-law to settle herself. "Well, Lieutenant? What is this important point you mentioned?"

"I complied with your father's request for protection," Ben said slowly. "I sent two good men out here. They're experts, both of them, and this house is simple to watch from a spotter's viewpoint. The two of them have had it constantly covered."

"Yes?"

"They got here shortly before Hatch arrived. Verdi saw him go up the steps and was preparing to intervene when Mrs. Cain apparently welcomed him. They've been on guard ever since. No one has entered or left this house."

The clock ticked very loudly while the group assimilated that explanation. It was Dr. Frayne who summed it up.

"That shows that the murderer got here before Hatch and was here waiting for him?"

"Yes," Ben said.

"And he's still here?"

"He's still here," Ben replied.

Uncle Brian was on his feet. "Then we've got to search this house from top to bottom. We've got him trapped. If he tries to sneak out, your men will get him. He hasn't got a chance."

"We'll postpone the searching party till my squad gets here," Ben said.

His voice, however, told how slight was his hope of their finding anything.

"I'll take the women first," Ben continued. "After that they can go to bed and get some rest. Mrs. Cain, will you come to the library with me? Sergeant Verdi can remain with the rest of you."

He paused in the doorway and added, "Maybe you'd better come with us, Liz."

Liz smiled to herself. She understood the suggestion; anyone interviewing her mother would need an interpreter.

But there was nothing to interpret. Out of all the blithe chaos of her mother's remarks, out of all the dissertations on domestic problems and all the questions from Mrs. Vansittart on the Housing Situation, there emerged not a single fact beyond what was already known. Mrs. Vansittart had been responsible for Hatch's arrival. Apparently it was purest chance that he, rather than any other stranger, should have been sent by the Housing Bureau.

"So you see, Ben, it was all just fate," Mrs. Cain concluded. "Why don't you go home, take a hot bath and get a good night's sleep? Because you can't arrest fate, can you?"

Ben nodded to himself as Mrs. Cain left. "The damnedest thing is that in a way she's right. Call it fate, call it circumstance, call it the pure cussedness of things, but too many times a detective discovers a criminal is almost guiltless of his own crime. Since you can't arrest the true causes, you nab some poor dope because there has to be an arrest. Now tell me what you know, Liz."

Liz found that she was hardly more helpful than her mother. A stranger had come to the house and died there. That was all she knew.

When she had finished her futile contribution, she studied the face of the detective-lieutenant.

"Ben," she said.

"Yes?"

"Will you tell me what you think about this?"

Ben hesitated. "If it wasn't for that Fist, I might ignore even Sister Ursula's point about the bottle," he admitted. "The whole situation is unique—such an unlikely set-up for murder. But I can't disregard the Fist. And I can't get what we know to make sense either. Poisoning Hatch by mistake for your grandfather is impossible, but the Fist angle positively connects Hatch's death with these threats. I've got to plow through this until I turn up the explanation."

There was a knock at the door, and Sergeant Verdi came in. He was tall for an Italian, and his body was built along generous lines. Now, obviously, he found it awkward to maintain a professional attitude in front of Liz whom he had met a dozen times before as the "Loot's" girl friend.

"The squad's here," he said. "You want to talk to 'em before they start in?"

Ben rose. "I guess that's all we're apt to get out of you, Liz. Go catch yourself some sleep while the search goes on."

"What about Graffer?" she said. "Hadn't I better look in his room myself? If the squad goes bursting in there, he might get excited."

"Right. I'll send a man with you to stay outside within easy earshot. And here. You might need this." He handed her his service automatic.

CHAPTER VIII

The men from Homicide were waiting in the front hall. Ben gave them their instructions briefly. They were to search every inch of hiding place in the house. But before they could set off,

Sister Ursula entered the hall from the drawing-room.

"Lieutenant!" she called out sharply.

Sergeant Verdi had followed her in. His sheepish face and his clumsily gesticulating hands seemed to say, "I know I should've stopped her, but you can't lay hands on a nun, can you?"

Ben grinned at him. "All right, Sergeant," he said. "What is it, Sister?"

"Are you sending your search party into old Mr. Cain's room?"

"No. Miss Cain thought of that; she's taking that room herself."

The nun sighed with relief. "Thank God! And thank you, Felicity."

"Hooker, you go with Miss Cain, and do whatever she says," Ben said. "And since you're here, Sister, I'll take you next."

The lanky, gangling Hooker talked cheerfully as he and Liz went upstairs.

"Want some gum, Miss? Always helps me concentrate when I'm working and I ain't supposed to smoke. Used to buy gum by the carton, I did, until we got into this here shortage. Got this pack from a soldier. Give him a lift across the bridge and he says to me, 'Guess a pack of gum is the least we can do to help the morale on the home front!'"

Liz hardly heard him. The automatic she was still holding seemed to weigh tons. It felt awkward and strange in her left hand. Because of her interest in aviation, she understood engines, and her hands had developed a knack with machines, but firearms were something else again. If she had to use this weapon, she wondered what she would do.

Also, her mind fretted over Sister Ursula's sudden appearance in the hall. Of course, it was important that Graffer shouldn't be disturbed or shocked. But the nun had seemed to lay more importance on it than simply that. There had been worried tension on her usually smooth face. The nun had thought of something. It was not obvious. It was some new and perilous reason why the police must not penetrate the bedchamber.

She reached Graffer's room. Here there was peace. Outside the door Hooker took his post, a living symbol of the new strangeness that had invaded the house. Across the hall was the room where Homer Hatch still lay grinning. But here there was only an old man calmly asleep and a nurse seated under a shaded reading lamp. Miss Kramer looked up and said, "Sh!" to Liz.

Yet this peaceful room was somehow the focus of all that new strangeness. For the threat of the Fists had been directed at this room, and the sign of the Fists had tied into Hatch's death. With her body Liz shielded the automatic from Miss Kramer's eyes, but she held a firm and ready grip on it.

Searching the room was simple. There were only a couple of places to look—the closet and the window recess. Both were empty. The nurse watched Liz curiously, but her sleeping patient kept her from asking questions.

The bed was a low one. There could be no hiding place underneath. This room was safe.

Liz returned to the hall, thanked Hooker, and went downstairs again. Catch some sleep, Ben had said. But who could sleep while murder stalked near at hand?

Liz saw Sister Ursula come out of the library, and hurried toward her. She had questions to ask.

"Sister, why were you so worried about having the squad search Graffer's room?"

"How are you fixed here for cocoa?" the nun replied.

"Why, I think we have some."

"One never knows, nowadays, if anyone has anything. Would you like to join me in the kitchen for a hot cup? We can talk better there," she added.

"Thanks. I think I'd better give this gun back to Ben first. See you in a minute." She knocked on the library door and went in.

She made a left-handed mock salute and said, "Special Agent Cain reporting, sir. No one in Graffer's bedroom. And here is the sidearm issued to me."

Ben took it and held it tentatively in his hands. "You wouldn't like to keep it?"

"Why?"

"You're the most sensible and capable person I know here."

Liz could not conceal her astonishment. "But why should I need it?"

"If the squad flushes this murderer, there could be trouble," Ben said. "He mightn't like being arrested. And if they don't flush him, you might feel better if you have it."

He hadn't said what he really meant. He didn't need to. "If they don't flush him, then you're living with a murderer," was his implication.

Liz shook her head. "Thanks. I'll make out."

"As you please." He looked down at three almost blank sheets of paper before him. "I'll take Sherry next, and doubtless will continue to learn precisely nothing. Will you please send her in?"

Out in the kitchen with Sister Ursula, the cocoa was hot and rich and soothing.

"You're wise, Sister," Liz said. "You know what people need."

"I'm afraid I know very little," said Sister Ursula. "But I must confess, to avoid the appearance of false modesty, that my guesses have a very high average of success."

"Sister," Liz began, then stopped in embarrassment.

"Yes?"

"What is a novice?"

The nun looked surprised. "I thought you were going to ask me about the murder."

"Later. But what is a novice?"

"Why, I suppose you might say a novice is an apprentice nun, an undergraduate of the Order."

"Just—just in training for it? Not really one yet?" Liz felt her face flush. Also, to her mortification, she had stumbled over the words.

"Not really, no." Sister Ursula's eyes had begun to twinkle. She was shrewd, clever. How much had she guessed? How much did she know? How well did she understand?

"And if she changes her mind?" Liz went on.

"Then she does as her changed mind indicates."

"But I thought novices had to go through with it."

Sister Ursula smiled. "I'm not surprised. You've heard stories of the unwilling novices and bitter frustrated lives, to say nothing of the juicier tales of immurings. But girls who become nuns against their will are forced into it by their parents or by circumstances, certainly not by the Order. It wouldn't make sense. The Army exempts conscientious objectors and neurotics and others, not so much out of kindness, but simply because they'd make very bad soldiers. We feel the same way. A woman who became a nun against her will would be useless to the Order."

"Then Sherry can still change her mind!" Liz took a deep breath and sipped more cocoa. "Now, please tell me about Graffer."

"There isn't anything to tell. I don't know anything. But I did think of a possible new motive for the death of poor Mr. Hatch."

"Why was he killed?"

"Suppose he was murdered by the Fists, as their trademark indicates. Why should they kill Hatch for revenge, and not your grandfather? Could killing him have been a device—a step in an elaborate plan? What was the result of Hatch's death?"

"I don't know. We don't know anything about Hatch."

The nun smiled. "I realize that. But what is the one result that we know? Something went wrong. The police found out about it too quick. His death brought the Homicide Squad into this house and gave them unlimited access to every room."

She paused. Liz slowly assimilated the nun's meaning, though her mind was still distracted by earlier thoughts. "But what was their plan, in the first place?"

"I know my theory leaves too much unexplained. It isn't even, I'm afraid, one of my better guesses. But outside enemies must be taken into consideration, and guarded against."

Liz nodded. But she kept thinking, "Ben and Sherry are alone together. And nothing is irrevocable."

Roger Garvey came in just then. The secretary had changed even in the brief time since Liz last had seen him. His fine regular features looked drawn and pale, and his fingers were twitching.

Liz looked up and said, "Hello."

"Sergeant Verdi said I might come out here." He seemed nervously anxious to justify himself. "Your uncle wants a drink and I was the only one who knew where to get the liquor." He crossed the room to the cellar door and hesitated. "Did they—have they made certain the cellar is all right?"

"I believe the usual routine is to start at the top of the house," said Sister Ursula. "I doubt if they've searched the cellar yet."

"Oh!" Roger's hand faltered on the knob. But at last he gathered courage and went clattering down the cellar steps.

"It isn't comfortable, living in a house with murder," Liz said. "I've never seen Roger so nervous."

Sister Ursula frowned. "That young man isn't nervous. He's mortally afraid."

Roger Garvey soon came back with a bottle of whisky. "Would either of you care for some?"

The women shook their heads, so he poured himself a good four ounces and gulped them with a haste that was an insult to the label on the bottle. He stood still a moment and let the shudder run through him. Then he straightened up.

"Sister Ursula," he said, "you know a great deal about murder, don't you?"

"I have had a little experience."

"Then tell me. Tonight, in this house, is there going to be another killing?"

The nun framed her words cautiously. "It is hard to say. The pattern is thus far so unclear that it's impossible to tell what the murderer's next step must be. It is conceivable, perhaps even possible. Why?"

"I've got to get out of here," he said, almost to himself. "Because there will be another. I didn't even need you to tell me. I knew it all the time. But I wanted to hear you say so."

"What do you mean?" Sister Ursula demanded. "You assert you know all this?"

"Of course. Because you see, I'm to be the victim." He poured another quick one, gulped it, and hurried from the room, paying no attention to the nun's attempt to detain him.

"I don't understand why he said that," Liz mused. "Earlier this evening, Uncle Brian was telling me how anxious Roger seemed to get out of this house. But why should he think he's in danger?"

The kitchen extension of the phone rang. At the second ring, Liz rose to her feet.

"With everybody tied up maybe I'd better answer it," she said. She crossed the room.

CHAPTER IX

Someone else on another extension in the house got on the phone just as Liz picked up the receiver. She was about to replace it, then curiosity prevented her, for she had heard an official-sounding voice say, "Latimer?"

"Speaking," Ben answered.

"We've collared Vitelli," the voice said. "Rather, the Feds grabbed him. Jumping parole and sending death-threats don't count for much, but he forgot to notify his draft board of his new address. So the Feds moved in and tracked him down, and he tried to shoot it out. That was a mistake."

She heard Ben say, "Dead?" There was disappointment in his voice.

"Dying, maybe. If you want his statement about those notes, you'd better hustle down to the hospital pronto."

The vocabulary of Ben's comments indicated that the novice Sherry was no longer in the room.

"All right," he concluded. "Be there in fifteen minutes."

Liz heard the wire click and hung up, too. She found Sister Ursula looking at her reproachfully.

"Murder has a shocking effect on the character, as De Quincey pointed out," the nun said. "And you're reduced to eavesdropping?"

"I'm glad I did. Now I know what to do next."

Sister Ursula paused a moment. "I shan't ask you," she said. "But from what I've seen and heard of you, Felicity, I know that inaction is the most unbearable of tortures for you. If you've found something to do—do it and God bless you."

"Thanks, Sister." Liz smiled, and felt a little more like herself.

The only way to do this was openly, so openly that nothing could be suspected.

Try to sneak out, and the guards wouldn't appreciate your motives. She calmly walked down the steps of the back porch and approached the uniformed policeman who was on guard.

"Lieutenant Latimer is taking me down to help identify a suspect and I'm to meet him out here. Where's his car?"

Her unofficial standing as the "Loot's" girl doubtless helped. The cop did not question her story, but pointed the car out to her.

After fifteen minutes and two cigarettes, she began to wonder if her plan had miscarried. Could Ben have gone some other way? But just as she stubbed out the second cigarette, he appeared and climbed in behind the wheel.

"Hello," she said.

He turned on her. "Felicity Cain—" he began with formal fury.

"Oh, but please, Ben! I'm going nuts cooped up in that house. Let me ride down with you and talk to you. I've got to do something."

He turned the ignition switch. "Who's arguing?" he snorted. "I've been spending the last fifteen minutes hunting for you. You're the closest of anybody to your grandfather and know most about these Fist notes. I want you with me when I quiz Vitelli. Where've you been hiding?"

"Here," said Liz meekly. "And it's a fine thing," she added ruefully, "when a girl can't think up a really smart lie without having it turn into the truth!"

Ben didn't answer. He swung the car out of the driveway and pressed down hard on the accelerator. They went humming along the paved road out in front, under the dark, leafy branches of trees.

"It seems so strange to be going at fifty," Liz observed.

"You cost me fifteen minutes," Ben grunted. "Then Ryan decided to tell me you were in this car. Vitelli may not wait for tire conservation."

Liz laughed. Already her spirits were beginning to improve.

"Fifty used to be nothing and already it feels like zooming with a Pratt-Whitney," she said. "Funny how quickly you get used to things. Like Jeff Carey who just came back from Iowa and said, 'And you know what? At night the streets there are *all lit up*!' He sounded awed. But I wonder if you can ever get used to it?"

"Used to what?" Ben prompted.

"Used to murder. If it was murder," she added hastily.

"It was murder, all right. No bottle was found within possible heaving distance of that window."

"Oh. You got that report already?"

"Yes."

"And the other report?"

"What other—oh, yes," Ben said slowly. "I got that, too."

"And nobody was found hiding anywhere in the house?" Liz began to grow frightened. Could someone in the family be a murderer?

Ben surmised what she was thinking and tried to reassure her. "Of course no search is absolutely conclusive."

Liz was distressed. "Don't, Ben. It's kind of you to try to soften the news, but I understand what it means. A killer among those you trust and love—that's horrible!"

Ben's voice was officially dry. "No one entered or left that house since Hatch arrived. There is no one in it now but the members of the household. And Hatch was murdered."

"In all the questioning did anything come up that might be useful in finding out who's guilty?"

"Not a thing."

"Not from Sherry, either?"

"Why Sherry?"

"I just wondered what you discussed."

"Interesting girl," Ben mused aloud.

"Damned interesting. She didn't have anything helpful on Hatch, but we talked quite a bit. Somehow she makes me see lots of subjects from a new point of view."

His voice trailed off. Liz was silent, too, as they drove on through the tree-lined streets. Finally a brightly lighted hospital loomed up before them.

They got out of the car and went in.

"There's nothing we can do to save him," the intern of the ward said. "Internal hemorrhage. He's going fast."

"Can he talk?" Ben demanded.

"I think he can. But he hasn't so far. Lafferty's in there with him."

Ben greeted the moon-faced FBI man in the ward as an old colleague.

"Hi! Fine service I get from the Government, shooting up the man I need for questioning. What do you think I pay taxes for?"

Lafferty shrugged. "Don't blame me, Latimer. It was his idea. And one of my men is down the hall, in just about as bad shape."

"Vitelli won't talk?"

"Try what you can get out of him. I've sent for Belcore to help out."

"Good."

Liz kept looking at the man in the bed. This whole terrible night had revolved around men in beds. That was the *leitmotiv*. And they had all smiled—Graffer with the peaceful smile of tired age, Hatch with that frightful contorted smile of strychnine and this man with a blend of cunning and triumph which was fully as horrible.

Ben said, "Vitelli!"

The man gave no sign of hearing. He just went on smiling.

"You're going to die, Vitelli. And you know why? Because you can't trust the Fists. Because they aren't yours any more. One of them turned you in to the Feds."

Vitelli lay impassive, content.

"Yes, one of them snitched," Ben went on. "Here's your chance to get even. Spill what you know, and they'll all land in prison. And you'll die in peace."

Vitelli shook his head with slow pleasure.

A dapper long-faced man with keen button eyes came into the room. He was dressed in a single-breasted, rather worn suit of dark clothes. His black eyes sparkled as he saw the man on the bed, and his black mustache twitched happily.

"Lieutenant Belcore, you know Lafferty, don't you?" Ben said. "And this is Liz Cain."

For the first time there was a response from the man on the bed. He lifted one feeble hand and made a scornful gesture with his thumb and fingers.

Lieutenant Belcore invoked the body of Bacchus and sketchily outlined the possible ancestry of any man who could make such a gesture to a lady. Vitelli replied briefly, using a few hoarse, labored words.

His tones were harsh and rasping. He had little breath to give it. But underneath the rasp could be detected a voice which had once been slow and oily and cold.

Liz knew a good deal of the man from her grandfather. She knew how he had perverted the original liberal, revolutionary tendencies of Italian secret societies into a personal racket for himself. It used to be said that Vitelli had tears in his eyes whenever he collected protection money. The payment had robbed him of the pleasure he could have derived in punishing non-payment.

Twenty years in prison had not changed Vitelli. His voice was the vocal horror that was to be expected from a man of his stamp.

"What did Vitelli say?" Ben asked Belcore.

Belcore looked at Liz. "It was not necessary to translate."

"Ask him what good he expects to get out of being stubborn?"

But Vitelli had propped himself up on one elbow and was speaking unprompted. His words were a deadly flow of some new acid that froze even as it burned. And the light in his little eyes was that of wicked exultation. The words went on monotonously until a sudden spasm of coughing interrupted them. The blood on his mouth was even redder than his lips.

"What did he say?" Ben asked.

"He said he is glad Miss Cain is here. He says

he wants her to know that her grandfather took twenty years out of his life but that payment has been arranged and will be made. He asserts the plans are all perfected and the collection may take place this very night. Now he does not care if he dies; it is all fixed."

Ben whirled to the bed. "What plans? Who's doing it? You can talk English if you want to. Spill it, Vitelli, or we'll round up every relative you've got in North Beach and give them the works."

Another fit of coughing shook Vitelli. Liz turned her eyes away as the blood gushed forth. There was a ghastly rattle in the wounded man's throat, but he managed to speak once more, and for the first time in English.

"Go to hell!" he said.

His defiance still sounded in the room when his breathing finally stopped.

Those were the last words of Angelo Vitelli.

CHAPTER X

It was not until the doctors and nurses had been called and certain formalities were finished that Ben Latimer gave full expression to his inward disgust.

He took a rapid turn up and down the room, his broad shoulders very straight and stiff, his eyes grim and hard, then stopped and spoke tersely to the waiting FBI agent.

"That fellow died like just what he was—a sewer rat," he said. "But at least, with rats you know exactly where you stand. They don't beat around the bush. They don't pretend."

"Knowing that doesn't help us," the FBI man complained. "It's too bad he didn't talk. I've an idea he might have been able to give us some very useful information. He probably could have told us where to pick up the rest of his mob. Now it'll take months and months of hard digging."

Lieutenant Belcore twisted his hat around in his hands. He looked a little tired and annoyed. His voice, too, carried a distinct note of weariness.

"Not much you can do with fellows like Vitelli. They usually resent other mobsters muscling in on their people."

"I just wonder what, if anything, Vitelli knew about the killing of a certain shipyard worker," Ben mused. "If the war were still going on you might be tempted to label it as sabotage."

Belcore frowned. "I wish we could truthfully say all these rats were fascist tools," he went on. "It is hard to realize that some men who helped fight for liberty are as bitterly against the law."

He paused briefly, then glanced sharply at Latimer.

"You mentioned a shipyard worker, Lieutenant. You remember that homicide case last week in my North Beach territory?"

"I left it up to Verdi," Ben admitted. "Nothing much you can do when an unidentified drifter gets his skull cracked. Routine takes its course."

"Well, he is no longer unidentified. You will get the full report tomorrow, but I thought you might like to know. And he was no drifter. He had a good paying job at Marinship."

"So?"

"A check-up on fingerprints at all the plants revealed a lot." Belcore nodded. "Your unidentified man is named Homer Hatch."

Ben's face went through contortions such as are seldom seen even in a hospital. "Homer Hatch!" he repeated. "And at Marinship. It couldn't be the same!"

He took from his pocket an identification card and handed it to the Italian, who whipped out a notebook and compared its number with what was written there.

"I don't know where you got this card," Belcore said. "But it's the same Homer Hatch."

Ben whistled. "This is one for the book, boys. I'm investigating two separate murders, and both corpses are the same man!"

Liz tried to talk on the way back, but she was rebuffed by a growl. Not until they were almost home did Ben break his silent pondering.

"I've been trying to find a pattern in this damn thing," he apologized gruffly. "Sorry if I barked at you."

"And have you found a pattern?"

"The hell of it is, I've found at least three. They go like this. The Cain Homer Hatch, our Hatch, the poisoned Hatch, is a phony. So what follows from that? Why should anybody be posing as a murdered shipyard worker? The answer is simple."

Ben cleared his throat. "Pattern A. Our Hatch was a labor saboteur. He killed the real Hatch to take over his job and raise hell at Marinship. Someone in the house is his confederate who arranged for him to make his headquarters there. He and the confederate quarreled and the confederate disposed of him. Objections?"

Liz hotly vented her scorn. "Plenty. Nobody in our house would be the confederate of such a man!"

"Leave personalities out, Liz. Under the proper circumstances, anyone can be and do anything. That's something you learn on the Force. Can you suggest other objections?"

"Yes. There wasn't time for them to have a quarrel. Hatch was killed almost as soon as he got there."

"I don't know about that," Ben said. "Ten minutes is enough to provide a motive for murder. Suppose he was backing out on the plan, threatening to give it away. That might be plenty to make somebody want to kill him. But let's go on to the next."

"All right," said Liz. "Let's hear it."

"Pattern B. First part same as before, but no confederate. Instead somebody in the house recognized Hatch for what he is and wipes him out. Objections?"

Liz shook her head. "That's even weaker. Why murder him? If someone recognized him as a phony and probably a saboteur, why not just turn him over to the authorities?"

"Suppose you didn't have enough evidence but wanted to keep him from doing damage?"

"His working in a defense plant under false identification would be enough to hold him, wouldn't it?"

"Yes, I guess so. Well, Pattern C. We still have the original Hatch killed by a subversive element

for their own dastardly purpose. And our Hatch is a private eye or an undercover Fed taking his place to try to track down his murderers. But they get him instead. Objections?"

"That would still mean that somebody in the house was a fifth columnist. And that isn't possible."

"Isn't possible? After you've heard Garvey shooting his mouth off about saving the world for the British Empire and the rest of his line?"

"Just because a man talks that way doesn't mean he's a traitor. Roger couldn't really *do* anything that would injure the war effort."

"Any other objections?"

"Yes. Two that apply to all these ideas. One, they all depend on the mere chance that the Housing Bureau sent Hatch to our house. Isn't that hanging a lot on coincidence?"

"Coincidences happen," Ben said. "I've got to work on what might have occurred, Liz, not on what we both would like to be true."

"All right." Liz's voice became crisp. "This is no sentimental objection. How did the murderer give Hatch—I suppose we've got to go on calling him that—how did he give him the strychnine? Under any of your patterns, Hatch would have good reasons for being wary. If Hatch was acquainted with the murderer, he'd know better than to take a drink from him. If the murderer spotted him without being recognized, Hatch would surely become suspicious if a total stranger wandered into his bedroom and said, 'Here, have a drink!'"

Ben thought a while. Then he said "Thanks."

"Did I help any?" Liz asked.

"Frankly, no. I'd been making all those objections to myself. But I wanted to see if they were obvious or if I was being professionally overcautious. They're obvious all right, and valid. Especially the last. Furthermore, until I can figure out how Hatch was persuaded to drink that strychnine, I haven't got a case."

The car chugged slowly up the cobbled hill. The night was moon-bright and peaceful—the sort of a still night when it is almost impossible to believe that not many months ago shells were falling on distant islands across the sea while the world was locked in a violent war.

Ben must have been thinking along those lines, too.

"War and hate—they seem impossible under such a moon," he said.

"I know. Peaceful nights like this are too good to last."

"No more peace in a minute. We'll be back at the house. There's nothing I can really accomplish until I check on Hatch's identity tomorrow. Yet I'd like to get the rest of these stories straightened out tonight if I can. I never saw a case with so few leads of any description."

The night's peace was indeed too good to last. It was shattered now by a half dozen shots.

The car leaped ahead with a jolt that almost threw Liz from her seat. Then as it swerved to the curb by the house, a black figure darted in front of its headlights. There was a squeal of brakes, another jolt and the car stopped. The person lying on the street in front of it was still, too.

Liz leaped out of the car almost as quickly as Ben did. She was beside him as he bent over the figure.

"Thank God for good brakes," Latimer muttered. "I barely nudged him. But he's bleeding badly—and not from what the car did to him either. It's a bullet hole."

Liz shrank back. "Who is it?"

Ben turned the figure face up. Roger Garvey's fine handsome features gleamed pallidly in the moonlight.

"Oh!" Liz gasped and shuddered. "It's the Fist again. He was right. He predicted this. So they got him, too!"

Ben looked up to see Sergeant Verdi approaching. He rose angrily to his feet.

"Well, what goes on here? The house full of police and the murderer still gets away with another try? This one'll live, I think, but that's no thanks to you."

"Aw, we're doin' our best."

"Nix on the alibis, Verdi. But I hope to God you've got the killer this time. If you haven't, it's

back to a beat for you. All right, Sergeant. Who shot this man?"

"I hate to tell you about it."

"Come on! Who shot him?"

Sergeant Verdi looked glum. He swallowed. "Er-ah, I'm sorta afraid it was me."

Ben stared at him. "You! *What's that?*"

Verdi gulped again. "He'd been hitting the bottle pretty hard and he kept carrying on about how he had to get the hell out of this house or they'd bump him next. So at last he tries to make a break for it. Ryan tackles him in the hall, but he wrenches himself loose. Then I yells for him to stop or I'll shoot."

"So?"

"So he didn't stop."

Ben leaned over and slipped his hands under Garvey's armpits.

"Take the feet, Verdi," he said. "And there's one consolation," he added. "At least I know who this is."

CHAPTER XI

Ryan was standing at the door, keeping the household inside. Dr. Frayne stepped forward as they brought the wounded man in.

"I think he'll be okay, Doctor," Ben said. "If you'd look him over and give me a report, I'd be obliged. We'll get the police surgeon out here but that bleeding ought to be stopped right away. Verdi, you and McGinnis carry him up to his room. You direct them, will you, Doctor? Thanks. McGinnis! You'll stay there with him."

Sherry came downstairs. As she passed the men carrying Garvey, she cringed away from them, but Dr. Frayne quietly reassured her. When she reached the hall, Sister Ursula asked a question.

"Your grandfather?"

"He slept through it, thank heaven."

Uncle Brian made a loud noise intended to indicate relief.

"Ben—Lieutenant—I want to talk to you," he said.

"Fine. With Garvey and the doctor out of the way for the moment, you're the only one left for me to interview. Shall we go into the library?"

"What I've got to say I'd just as soon the women heard." Brian Cain's voice was hearty and his manner easy, but he wasted no words. Just as Ben had become Lieutenant Latimer, after Hatch's death, so Liz now saw her Uncle Brian change into Mr. Cain, the executive.

"First to clear up a foolish minor point. We all told you no one saw this Hatch after his arrival. Well, I'm afraid I did. It's not important. After I'd showed him to his room, I remembered a Hatch who was shop foreman for me some ten years ago. First-rate man. Never knew what became of him, and I needed an experienced foreman in the plant. He resembled the Hatch I had known, so I went to see him. If he was related to the fellow I knew, I wanted to ask where to find him. I had no luck, however. He offered me a drink, but I wasn't feeling well and turned the offer down. That's all I know. Everything.

"But when our roomer was murdered and you began your inquisition, I got the jitters—which was idiotic, of course. Since nobody had seen me, I decided just to forget the episode. You can understand why. I was the last man to see him alive and all that. But tonight I thought it over and realized how foolishly I acted."

Ben's eyes met those of Sister Ursula. "He offered you a drink?" Ben asked.

The nun waited eagerly for the answer.

"Yes. Seemed a friendly sort of fellow."

"What sort of a drink?"

"I didn't even notice. Hard liquor of some sort. Bottle was a fifth, I think." Brian Cain waved his hand. "But enough of this, Ben. These irrelevant matters may be professional, but they aren't getting us any place. There's something else I wanted to discuss."

"Yes?" Ben showed curiosity.

"My father is a very sick man," went on Brian, unheeding. "Sudden shock could eas-

ily kill him. If he should learn that there was a murderer loose in this house tonight—well, he might die. If he does, I'll hold you responsible. Dr. Frayne gave him a sedative and I think he'll sleep through tonight. But tomorrow morning he'll be anxious to know what's been going on here. In time he's bound to learn. When that happens, I want him to learn that the case is solved, the murderer arrested, and all danger has departed."

Ben Latimer nodded. "I understand how you feel, sir. But it isn't possible to have everything break the way we wish. There's a lot of essential routine work which I can't handle until offices are open tomorrow."

"I'm not asking you what's possible," Cain shot back crisply. "The Government doesn't ask me what's possible when it wants planes. It tells me what must be done, and I see to it that it is done. Now I'm telling you that this case should be solved tonight. You're Liz's friend, Ben, and I respect your professional status. Nevertheless, you've only got tonight. In the morning I'll put the Golden West Agency on the job. They're used to my ways, and they never yet wasted time complaining about bad breaks."

Ben stared after Brian Cain as he stalked away. He had given Ben his ultimatum.

"The Golden West," Ben muttered. "If they could solve murders as well as they can break strikes, everything would be rosy."

"The trouble with being a giant is that you're forever disappointed with pigmies," Sister Ursula said. "Mr. Cain is really flattering you, Lieutenant. He expects you to find murderers the way he builds planes."

"You'd all better go to bed, ladies," Ben said. "I think you've told me all you can. And don't be worried. There'll be men in the halls all night."

Without saying anything more, he walked off, frowning.

"You two go," Sister Ursula said to Liz and Sherry. "I want a word with the lieutenant."

The two girls silently climbed the stairs. As they reached the top, Liz turned to her cousin.

She hardly knew what she was going to say—something to convey a little human understanding in this coldly official night. Whatever was on her lips died there when she saw that the novice was crying.

Liz took her hand. "I know, Sherry," she said.

Sherry's husky voice was shaky. "It's so different. I wanted to come home and make Graffer feel good so we'd all be happy for a little while. Now this had to happen."

"I know," Liz repeated.

Sherry snuffled and fumbled in her long sleeve for a handkerchief. "You can leave the world but the world doesn't leave you," she said. "Good night, Liz." She went into her room.

Liz walked down the hall, nodding abstractedly at the guard stationed outside Graffer's room. Further on she met Dr. Frayne as he came out of Roger Garvey's bedroom.

"Oh! Hello, Liz."

"Hello." Before he shut the door, she caught a glimpse of Roger in bed, pale and still. He was asleep. Men in beds—so many of them!

"Is he all right?" Liz asked.

"He'll be fine in the morning after a sleep. And once I thought I had retired! In all my hectic G. P. days up in the Sierras, I never really spent a night like this. Get some sleep, Liz. You look ragged."

"I'll try."

"Would you like a sedative?"

"No, thanks. Oh, Doctor?"

"Yes?"

"Has Ben talked to you yet?"

"Not yet. Why?"

"I was wondering. When we came out from dinner after Mother screamed, you couldn't find your bag for a minute. Remember?"

"I'm old, I guess. Always putting things down and never remembering where they are."

He lifted his head and glanced sharply at Liz. "Hum! Could be! But that's nonsense. Ridiculous. But I'll tell your Ben. You're a smart girl, Liz."

Smart girl? She smiled wryly as she closed herself in her own room. "I'm so smart I can't even get myself straightened out inside," she murmured. "I keep worrying about Ben and about Graffer, and I see that dreadful Vitelli lying there dying, and I hear Roger saying he'll be next. It's awful!"

I'd take a drink now, she thought. I'd even take a drink from that bottle Uncle Brian saw and that's vanished so completely. I wonder if their search was thorough. Of course, they were hunting for a man, not a bottle, and when I get to thinking this way it sets me worrying about Mother. Probably there's no need to worry about her because tomorrow she'll have decided this was all a special persecution devised just to worry her.

Her mind was still working busily an hour after she got into bed. Even her room, that bare narrow room which seemed more nun's cell than boudoir, seemed strange to her. She was lonely and lost and she longed to talk with somebody. She needed human companionship.

She also wanted to cry, she realized suddenly. Not because of any sorrow—she was too confused to feel sorrow—but the satisfactory release of crying, the easing of physical and mental tension. She needed a shoulder for tears.

But Ben had become Detective-lieutenant Latimer and Graffer, the best shoulder in the world, must not be disturbed. And Sherry was too closely involved in what troubled Liz. She naturally never thought of her mother, for Mrs. Cain's shoulders were not that kind. There was one person in this house who would do. Sister Ursula!

Liz slipped into her plain tailored robe and her mules. It was an absurd nocturnal expedition she had planned. But she had made up her mind and was determined to go through with it. She opened her door.

In the hall Graffer's guard stopped her. "Okay, lady," he said. "What goes?"

Her explanation sounded foolish. "I just wanted to go down and talk to Sister Ursula for a while."

"Uh-uh." The detective was polite enough, but plainly he disapproved. "We got orders nobody goes prowling around tonight, see?"

"But I won't do any harm."

"Yep, and I bet if we had run into the duck who was going into Hatch's room, he'd have said the same thing. Not that I mean you're up to anything like that, you understand, but orders is orders."

The old house was dark and still, and the officer kept his voice to a gruff whisper.

"I'm warning you, officer, I've got to have a shoulder to cry on and, if you keep me here, I'll damned well use yours," Liz told him.

The officer made a warding movement. "Keep back, lady. I'm married. I dunno what this means, but you better get right back to your room."

"Oh, officer!" Liz almost choked with suppressed mirth. Already she was feeling much better. This argument was so absurd the hysterical symptoms were departing.

At this moment Sergeant Verdi came around the corner from the direction of the stairs. When he caught sight of Liz he quickened his pace.

"Hello, Miss Cain," he said, stopping near her. "This is luck. I'm glad you are still up. I was just coming after you. Sister Ursula wants to see you."

Liz stared at him in surprise. "That's strange," she said. "By an odd coincidence, I was just starting out to see Sister Ursula on my own hook. I couldn't sleep. But this officer halted me."

Verdi nodded at the detective. "It's all right. She can go." He looked at Liz. "I'll just walk along with you to see that you get there safely. Sister Ursula is in the room near the kitchen."

"I know." Liz grinned at the guard. "Better luck next time."

CHAPTER XII

There was a light in the library, but Liz knew that Ben would not want to see her now.

When they reached the room which had once been occupied by the cook downstairs, Sergeant Verdi left Liz. She knocked, and Sister Ursula opened the door.

"Come in, my dear," said Sister Ursula. "It was nice of you to come."

"That's all right," Liz said. "I've been hoping to see you."

Suddenly words were pouring out in a confused torrent. Sister Ursula listened quietly, with a tender smile of understanding on her lips. Finally the words stopped and the tears came.

When it was over, Liz found cigarettes in the pocket of her robe and lighted one.

"I didn't know why I acted so silly. You've got a good shoulder, Sister."

"I need one. Often. But you're a child, Liz. In your own life, you're a woman—no, let us say an adult—with no sex distinction. But since you've been cut off from your chosen career by your arm, you're falling back on your emotions, and there you're a child. You speak of Ben as though he were nobody himself—just a stock figure for women to dispute about. He's not. Lieutenant Latimer is a man who has a very difficult job to do and is doing it well. He can't be your gallant lover every minute of the day."

Liz nodded. "But you can't expect me to be sensible tonight, can you? With all that has happened?"

"No." The nun's quiet voice was grave. "But someone has to be sensible. I've tried to be. That's why I sent for you."

"I don't think I understand."

"I have a certain theory I'd like to test. I believe you heard Lieutenant Latimer mention that this is not my first contact with murder?"

"Yes. And the way you pounced on the point about that bottle was astonishing. It had uncomfortable possibilities. I'm afraid I'm still not being sensible. Anyway, you mean you're still trying to solve the murder?"

"I have solved it. That's why I wanted to talk to you. I wanted to tell you about it and see how the solution sounds."

Solution to murder! The words rang in Liz's

ears. For the first time she perceived their full implication. It had been murder and the nun knew the answer. Suddenly Liz realized that this was it. A quiet scene here. Two women talking in a downstairs room of a silent old house. This was what the events had all been leading up to. This was the crucial moment.

It all seemed so peaceful, so undramatic. Sister Ursula began to speak.

"There are so many things we have to account for, so many little things," she said. "If we can find a pattern embracing all of them, we can be almost sure that that pattern is the truth. And we need the truth, and need it now. Your uncle is right. Your grandfather must know a safe truth tomorrow. We must spare your family the pain of a long investigation, and the worry of your uncle's private detectives."

"Also the danger of another murder," Liz said. "Roger was so afraid."

"Needlessly," said Sister Ursula. "Mr. Garvey's life is in no danger, unless my answer is shockingly wrong. Not at the moment, at least. But let me try to list what we have to explain:

"The murder of the real Hatch. The presence of the Fist under the body of the false Hatch. The disappearance of the bottle which your uncle saw. The shifting of Dr. Frayne's medicine case. Roger Garvey's fear of death in this house. Vitelli's conviction that his plans will be carried out. Your uncle's indisposition when we were all eating together."

Liz had been listening quietly and nodding as the nun ticked off each point, but now she broke in.

"Uncle Brian. You think that the food poisoning, or whatever happened to him, was maybe a rehearsal?"

"I think your uncle's poisoning is one of the most vital points in this whole case.

"Let us look at the murder of the real Hatch. It seems fruitless to search for motives in his personal history which we don't as yet know. If he were killed for personal reasons and his impersonator happened to be killed for others, that explains much. I think we must assume that

he was killed by the impersonator, and for the purposes of imposture. Now why should he be impersonated?"

"Because he worked at Marinship, I guess. That's all we know about him."

"No, Liz. We know one other thing about him. He worked at Marinship, and the Housing Bureau had assigned him a room here. Now as to the presence of the Fist; the symbol of the Fist has been found often before beside bodies, and always it was left there by the murderer. So we easily assumed that it had been left by the murderer in this case, too. But there is another possibility—it was left by the lodger before he became a corpse. It was in his possession before the murder, and fell out of his pocket in his spasms.

"Put those two ideas together. The real Hatch was killed because he had a room here, and the Fist symbol belonged to the false Hatch."

Liz gasped aloud. "Then—then the impostor was a Fist. They killed the real Hatch so they could smuggle a man in here for evil purposes! They guessed we'd have a police guard after the threats, but they knew we wouldn't turn away a defense worker from the Housing Bureau. And that's what Vitelli meant. He didn't know his man was dead."

"Let us try to reconstruct it from there," the nun said. "The false Hatch came to this house to kill your grandfather. But instead he was himself murdered. Why? It is next to impossible to assume that he knew anyone in this house. He would be running too great a risk of detection if he did. Or if the person was an ally who would not betray him, then that person could have undertaken the job himself without this elaborate masquerade. The false Hatch did not know anyone here. But he might have recognized someone, or have been recognized.

"Say that he knew something vital about the past of an individual here in this house. He may have attempted blackmail, or the individual may simply have feared that he might and forestalled him. The individual saw his chance in Dr. Frayne's case.

"As to Mr. Garvey's fright, ask yourself what

happened after he announced that he would be the next victim?" Sister Ursula's voice was insistent and loud. "What vital fact came to light in the evidence?"

"After Roger was shot, Uncle Brian told us about the bottle."

Sister Ursula smiled. It was a mechanical, unhappy smile.

"The bottle!" she said. "And there we are at the crux of the whole case. How was that strychnine administered? According to your uncle, Hatch was drinking from the bottle. There was no glass for the murderer to poison. He would have to poison the bottle itself. And yet Hatch would be on his guard. He was here on a dangerous mission. All men were his enemies. Would he accept a drink from a person whom he distrusted?"

"It doesn't seem likely."

"But there is a way. One way in which that poison could have been administered with complete confidence. If the murderer himself drank from the same bottle."

"But if you did that, you would poison yourself!" Liz protested.

There was the click of a light switch and the room was in darkness.

CHAPTER XIII

Out of the darkness a voice spoke. Its tones were hollow, almost inhuman.

"There was no policeman in the hall," it said. "Such negligence on the part of the authorities is a lucky break for me. I am here to kill you both. No, do not scream. That would force me to fire in the darkness and possibly only maim you. I am giving you this moment of darkness for your prayers."

The voice was ghastly, unrecognizable. It is what the voice of Death would sound like, Liz thought.

"It will all explain itself," the voice went on. "You sent for Liz, Sister. They know that. It will be clear that you wished to confront her

with evidence of her guilt. She killed you out of spite, herself from remorse. The picture will be plain."

There was no sound in the darkness but the tiny clicking of Sister Ursula's rosary beads.

"You are wise to attempt nothing," the voice went on. "Since you must die, die in peace."

The light came on. Liz's blinking eyes saw the figure in the doorway, and her brain whirled. Then she heard the shot.

But it did not come from the automatic pistol in the figure's hand. That automatic fell to the floor as blood spurted from the hand holding it and a look of terrified amazement spread over Uncle Brian's face.

For Liz, the darkness grew and enveloped her. . . .

Sister Ursula was sitting by the bed when Liz opened her eyes. She shuddered as memory came back. "Is it all over? Was it really Uncle Brian?"

Sister Ursula nodded.

"Where is he now? Was he killed?"

"He was only slightly wounded. He's down at Headquarters. Lieutenant Latimer phoned a few minutes ago. Brian Cain is making a complete confession."

"But how did you know?"

"Two things made me sure," the nun replied quietly. "One was the bottle and the other was the food poisoning. You remember I said there was one sure way of allaying Hatch's suspicion?"

"Yes, drinking it yourself. But how was it accomplished?"

"By drinking it himself—and then taking an emetic and an antidote before the poison could begin to work. There was some tincture of iodine missing from Dr. Frayne's bag, too. Diluted, that is a specific antidote for strychnine. The murderer drank with Hatch, then left him promptly and visited the bathroom. And of all the people in this house, only your uncle showed the effects of such treatment, though he attributed it to indisposition.

"Also on his word alone depended the evidence of the bottle. There was no bottle. The poisoned liquor was given in Mr. Cain's silver flask, relic of the twenties, which would never be noticed by police carefully hunting for a liquor bottle belonging to Hatch."

"But why should he have made up the bottle scene?"

"To distract us from the important fact that he had admitted being in Hatch's room. Why did he admit that? Because Roger Garvey saw him there. Garvey was afraid the murderer would kill him. Why? Because Garvey knew something dangerous. How did the murderer know he knew? Because Garvey had told the murderer, probably with a threat of blackmail. When the murderer refused to pay for silence, Garvey thought he was scheduled to die."

"Uncle Brian tried to kill us," Liz said. "Why didn't he kill Roger?"

"He was too wise," Sister Ursula said. "There was no need of it. Instead he drew the teeth of the blackmailer by admitting the visit himself, and adding a distracting touch with the bottle."

"Have you seen Roger?"

"Yes. He talked this morning. And his blackmail was not for money. You remember when he was pressing your uncle for a job? After he heard Mr. Cain deny returning to Hatch's room, he tried to use his knowledge as a lever to get that job. It never entered his head that Mr. Cain might refuse."

"But he has a good job here."

"His employer may die soon, ending the job. But that was not the main point. Employed by the Cain aeroplane plant, he might get draft deferment, which he could not hope for here. He risked his life, as he thought, with a murderer and got himself shot by the police, in order that he might not be shot by the enemy."

"But if you knew all this, why didn't you tell Ben and have him attend to Uncle Brian?"

"I did tell Lieutenant Latimer. That was why we arranged last night's scene. We did not have a case for a jury. We needed more evidence. You remember that your mother's shuffling of rooms ended up with your uncle and me in the servant's quarters? I arranged to explain my theory to you loudly enough so that he would hear it in the next room. I hoped that he would betray himself, and Lieutenant Latimer was ready in the closet when he did."

At this moment Dr. Frayne poked his bearded face in at the door. "Feeling chipper again, Liz?"

"I guess so. As chipper as I can under the circumstances. How's Graffer?"

"I haven't seen him yet. Overslept this morning myself after last night's strenuous duties." He withdrew his head.

"Sister Ursula," Liz said. "Why on earth did Uncle Brian kill that Fist impostor?"

"Because Hatch recognized him. At least that's what I surmise. Do you remember back during the Sinclair campaign when there was talk about the New Vigilantes? They were going to protect and save the State after it was plunged into Socialistic chaos.

"No one ever knew who the important men in the organization were. The group had fascist connections. The Fists were anti-fascist, and Hatch's assignment then was to study them in North Beach. As an apparent fascist, he got high enough in the New Vigilantes to meet the leaders. When he saw Mr. Cain again, he recognized him.

"Revelation of the Vigilante business would ruin the reputation of a hero of modern industry."

Ben came in, then, to interrupt them. He said nothing until he had kissed Liz.

Then as he started to speak, she said. "Don't ask me how I am and am I chipper. What do you expect?"

"Ostrich feathers," said Ben. "At least I can ask how you are, Sister?"

Sudden realization hit Liz. "And if I am all right, it isn't much thanks to you, Ben Latimer! You—you used me for bait!"

Before Ben could answer, the door opened. It was Dr. Frayne again.

"Don't worry about your grandfather's grieving over the news," the physician said. "He won't ever know—here." They looked at him, and he added, "Last night. In his sleep." Frayne shut the door.

"He was a good man," said Ben.

Liz's eyes were dry with that dryness that stings so much worse than tears.

"Now look, Liz," Ben went on. "Don't be sore at me. You say I used you. Okay. Maybe that's even true. I guess it is. But don't you see why I used you? Sister Ursula wanted to call Sherry, but I vetoed it."

Liz's temper flashed through her grief. "So you wouldn't risk her precious neck, but with me it was all right?"

"Uh-huh. Because I can use you, you see. Just like I can use my own hand. I wouldn't have the right to go risking a stranger. But you're part of me."

Liz smiled up at him. Out of the corner of her eye she saw Sister Ursula quietly leaving the room.

THE RIDDLE OF THE BLACK MUSEUM

Stuart Palmer

A DESCENDENT OF COLONISTS who settled in Salem, Massachusetts, in 1634, Charles Stuart Palmer (1905–1968) led a picaresque American life before becoming a successful writer, holding such jobs as iceman, sailor, publicity man, apple picker, newspaper reporter, taxi driver, poet, editor, and ghostwriter.

The Penguin Pool Murder (1931) introduced the popular spinster-sleuth Hildegarde Withers. Formerly a schoolteacher, the thin, angular, horse-faced snoop devotes her energy to aiding Inspector Oliver Piper of the New York City Police Department, driving him slightly crazy in the process. She is noted for her odd, even eccentric, choice of hats. Palmer stated that she was based on his high school English teacher, Miss Fern Hackett, and on his father.

There were thirteen more novels in the Miss Withers series, the last, *Hildegarde Withers Makes the Scene* (1969), being completed by Fletcher Flora after Palmer died. There also were four short story collections, with the first, *The Riddles of Hildegarde Withers* (1947), being selected as a *Queen's Quorum* title. It was followed by *The Monkey Murder and Other Hildegarde Withers Stories* (1950) and *People vs. Withers and Malone* (1963), in conjunction with Craig Rice, which also featured her series character, John J. Malone. The fourth, *Hildegarde Withers: Uncollected Riddles* (2002), was published posthumously.

The film version of *The Penguin Pool Murder* was released in 1932 and spurred five additional comic mystery films. The first three of the six featured Edna May Oliver in a perfect casting decision, followed by Helen Broderick, and then two with Zasu Pitts, including the last, *Forty Naughty Girls* (1937). Piper was played by James Gleason in all films.

The success of the series gained Palmer employment as a scriptwriter with thirty-seven mystery screenplays to his credit, mostly for such popular series as Bulldog Drummond, the Lone Wolf, and the Falcon.

"The Riddle of the Black Museum" was originally published in the March 1946 issue of *Ellery Queen's Mystery Magazine*; it was first collected in *The Riddles of Hildegarde Withers* (New York, Jonathan Press, 1947).

The Riddle of the Black Museum

STUART PALMER

MR. HUBERT HOLCOMB lay on his back in a cleared space at the far end of the long narrow cellar room, beyond the lines of shelves with their dusty, grim exhibits. The flashbulbs exploded almost in his face, but Holcomb did not mind. He did not even blink, for he had been dead since early that afternoon. Between two and three, the assistant medical examiner thought.

There were a number of plainclothesmen around the body. Inspector Oscar Piper, looking more than ever like a graying, housebroken leprechaun, surveyed the remains without visible enthusiasm. Then he looked carefully all around on the stone floor, not that he expected to find anything. But it was up to the skipper of the Homicide squad to act as if he knew what he was doing. Besides, it gave him time to think.

But there didn't seem to be any clues. Nothing, that is, except the long rope of cunningly-woven fine black silk which was still looped once around the dead man's neck, the ends extending for more than four feet in either direction, like an over-length skating scarf.

The Inspector relighted his dead cigar and said, "Identification done?"

Blunt-faced Sergeant Hardesty nodded. "Preliminary. From papers in his pocket. Social Security stuff, letters, all like that. He's Hubert Holcomb, age 58, lives 422 East 73rd Street, Manhattan."

"He used to be headwaiter or something like that at the old Hotel Grande," put in another detective. "What'd the Doc have to say?"

"He was strangled, Doc Fink says. A slow, nasty job. No fracture of the vertebrae or the hyoid bone."

The Inspector nodded sagely and looked at his watch. Then he turned toward the door, which stood at the other end of the narrow central corridor, and his normally crisp and rasping voice swelled to a roar. "Breck!"

The door opened and a sweating young patrolman, new to the Bureau, poked in his blank, reddish face.

"Yes, Inspector?"

"Any messages?"

"No, sir. Only word to call the Commissioner when it's convenient."

Piper winced. He had already talked to the Commissioner, or at least listened to him. "Was there nobody else? I was expecting another message."

"No, sir. There were some newspaper guys outside, but I gave 'em the bum's rush. Then there were the usual nuts who always try to get to the scene of a crime. Rubberneck stuff. One in particular—I thought I'd never brush her off, but I managed it."

"Good, good," commended the Inspector absently. Then he turned. "By any chance was this nut you brushed off a sort of angular, middle-aged dame?"

Breck smiled. "I guess you musta had trouble with her before, huh? Yeah, she was about that. Weight around 135, height five nine. . . ."

"Never mind that. Was she wearing a hat that looked like it had been made by somebody who had heard of hats but never actually seen one? Did she have a face like Whirlaway's mother?"

"Why—yeah, I mean yes, sir. But don't worry. I told her you were busy with a homicide, and couldn't be disturbed. So she's gave up by now."

Piper sighed. "That lady happens to be a special side-kick of mine. I've been trying to get hold of her all afternoon. She wouldn't give up, no matter what you said. So go find her, fast!"

It turned out that the unhappy officer had only to open the hall door, and Miss Hildegarde Withers sailed in, glaring one of her best glares at the Inspector. "Really! I hardly expected—" Then she saw where she was. "Oscar, this is the Black Museum!"

"So what? It's one hell of a place to have a murder committed, right here across the street from Headquarters. Fine publicity it will make!"

"Fine indeed," agreed the schoolteacher absently. She came slowly along the narrow passage between the crowded shelves, her eyes bulging at the accumulation of gruesome relics. She looked upon knives and swords and hatchets, curved scimitars and straight razors, saw-edged krisses and stilettos with long needle points. There were automatics and revolvers, great horse-pistols which a man could hardly lift with one hand, tiny derringers which could slip out of sight up a gambler's sleeve, antique blunderbusses and modern shotguns, rifles with barrels as long as a tall man and chased with silver.

There were ropes and infernal machines, hammers and blackjacks and sash-weights and hatpins, and a hundred other articles the exact use of which one might only imagine. But the general effect was all too clear. She stood among a thousand weapons, each of which was collected here in this room because it had done a man

to death. Here was Manhattan's version of the world-famous Black Museum at New Scotland Yard, with an American accent.

"Mercy me!" said the maiden schoolma'am. "Look at all the dust and spiderwebs, too. Makes one want to get busy with a broom!"

Piper lowered his voice, so that the detectives at the farther end of the room could not hear. "Makes me want to get out of here," he confided. "Just a minute, Hildegarde. The body is back there. But before you have a look, let me fill in the picture. At two o'clock this afternoon three men were admitted to this place. They were all strangers to each other, all very interested in having a look at the Black Museum. The attendant in charge was called away to the phone on some routine matter, and while he was gone it happened—apparently an impromptu job. As he came back he heard somebody yelling for help and pounding on the door, which he had locked from the outside. When he got in he found that Holcomb was strangled, and each of the survivors was pointing at the other and screaming 'He did it! I saw him!'"

Miss Withers sniffed. "That simplifies our problem. Only two suspects."

"Yeah, it simplifies things to the point where I'm about to get rousted out of the Force. Because the Commissioner hit the ceiling. He's given me until six P.M. tomorrow to solve this thing, or else accept indefinite suspension without pay. And it's a physical impossibility to solve it. The killer was smart enough to tell exactly the same story as the innocent bystander. And you can't break it from motive, because Holcomb was a little nonentity whom nobody could have had reason to bump."

"So far as we know," Miss Withers reminded him gently.

"Yeah. So I sent for you because—well, two or three times in the past you managed to stumble on the truth, with your blind luck, and—"

"Blind luck!" echoed the schoolteacher indignantly. "I stumbled, did I? Well—"

But whatever else she was about to say was lost as Miss Hildegarde Withers found herself staring down at the body of the rotund little old man with the polished bald head, the face still purplish and distorted, the silken rope around his neck. "Oh, dear!" gasped Miss Withers, and turned away.

"What we figure happened," Piper continued, "is that when the attendant went out of the room, the three visitors split up and went wandering around looking at what interested them. Holcomb came back here, and one of the others followed him, snatched up that noose, and had him strangled before the other man knew about it or could do anything."

"I see." Miss Withers was peering at a nearby exhibit, consisting of a champagne bottle, the base of which had been smashed into jagged shards, now tipped with brownish-black stains. The card propped before it read: *Bottle used by Stanik Bard in murder of Hyman Kinch, Hotel Grande Ballroom, October 1921*.

"Now if you want to see the attendant—" Piper was saying.

"I would rather see the card. All the exhibits have cards. If the murderer reached up and grabbed the most convenient weapon, namely the noose, then where is the card?"

The Inspector demanded of his detectives if any of them had seen a card on the floor. Nobody had. Everybody looked. But it was Miss Withers who first gave tongue above the quarry, perhaps because she started looking at the end of the room farthest from the corpse and nearest the door. The card, still in its place, read: *Assassin's noose, Moslem origin, used by Ab-el-Harun in murder of Mary Malone, Central Park, August 1917*.

"I remember that case," the Inspector was beginning. "I saw him burned, too—"

Miss Withers looked at him, and sniffed. "Oscar, I think I've seen enough of this place. It seems to have a definite *odor*."

"I know what you mean. Remember, I used to keep some of these exhibits up in my office—the ones I'd worked on, I mean. But I got the feeling they gave me the willies." He held the door open for her. "Now I suppose you want to see

the suspects? They're pretty big shots, both of 'em, and have to be handled with kid gloves. We're holding Charley Thayer, the wonder boy of politics, and Dexter Moore, the famous war correspondent."

"My, my," murmured Miss Withers. "Death loves a shining marksman, doesn't he? But Oscar, while we're here, I believe I would like a word with the attendant."

"That you'll have," said the Inspector, and led her into a little cubby of an office beneath the stair, where they faced a paunchy old man in police uniform but without the badge. He had a day's beard and a handsome, ruined face with eyes, the schoolteacher thought, like cold boiled onions. "This is Captain Halverstadt, retired," Piper introduced them. "Hal's in charge of the lower floors of the Criminal Courts Building here. Tell us about it again, oldtimer."

The voice was cracked and whining. "Well— you see, we got orders not to let just anybody into the Museum, on account we don't want any of the weapons filched and maybe used again. So we sorta give conducted tours, usually at ten in the morning and two in the afternoon. Comes two o'clock today and only Mr. Holcomb, that's the victim, showed up. But at the last minute the two others arrive—"

"Together?" demanded Miss Withers.

"No, ma'am. One of them as we was coming down the stairs, and the other just as I unlocked the Museum door. Mr. Thayer, it was, who came last. I got them inside and was just going into the little spiel I always give when I heard the phone ringing here in the office. So I had to excuse myself for just a minute. But to make sure that nobody got away with anything, I locked the door behind me when I went out."

"How long were you gone?" Piper asked.

"Maybe ten, fifteen minutes."

"And when you unlocked the door you didn't notice anything that would help us to figure out which man was telling the truth and which was lying?"

"No, Inspector. Both of them looked scared and excited. But neither man was rumpled up any. They were both talking all at once, so I couldn't make much sense of it. But I saw the corpse, so I held 'em both while the boys got here from across the street."

"I see," said Miss Withers in a faraway voice. "'I see, said the blindman. . . .' By the way, Captain, do visitors to the Museum have to give a reason for wanting to see the place?"

Captain Halverstadt hesitated. "Well, I got orders to make sure they're not *wrongos*, looking for a gun to snatch. Now this Mr. Holcomb, he had a good reason. He said he used to be maître d'hôtel at the Grande, and he wanted a look at the broken bottle that figured in a murder when he was working there. Mr. Thayer said he was interested in studying crime prevention because he was running for office on a reform ticket, and Mr. Moore said he was hipped on old guns and heard we had an 1854 derringer here. With people like that we don't ask much. . . ."

"Not even enough," Miss Withers observed softly. "Tell us, Captain. Do you have any ideas? What is your theory about the case?"

The old man blinked. "It's not really a theory, mind. It's just that the place gets you, when you have to be in there alone so much like I do. You get to thinking and—and hearing things. All those bloody knives and old guns and so forth, they were made for killing and they were used for killing, and sometimes you sort of hear them whispering in the back of your mind. They sort of say 'Go on, use me again, I want to do it again. . . .'" He shook his head. "Excuse me, I was just day-dreaming out loud."

He watched them through his rheumy eyes, still shaking his head, until they were up the stairs. "Batty as a bed-bug," the Inspector decided.

"There are more things in heaven and earth . . ." put in the schoolteacher.

"Well, now for the suspects. That is, if they're not being beaten into unconsciousness with a rubber hose in the back room somewhere."

The Inspector grinned. "I only wish we could settle it that easy, but the old days are gone. Besides, these suspects aren't people you can

work over with a rubber hose. Come on, we'll take the short cut."

He led the way up another flight of stairs, and then across the covered bridge to Headquarters. Then instead of turning down the hall to his own office he took her past a grilled, guarded door and finally down a hall to another door bearing the legend: *Detective Bureau, Preliminary Investigation—Private.* At that moment the door opened suddenly and there emerged a small untidy lawyer with a big cigar tilted skywards. "Oh, oh," said the Inspector. In tow of the little man was a handsome figure with a tanned face and wavy gray hair.

"Evening, Inspector," said the lawyer. "As you see, I got a writ. Book 'em or let 'em go, I always say." He touched his client's elbow. "Come on, Mr. Thayer."

But the man held back, drew himself up to his full height, and faced the Inspector. "Just a moment. I wish to make two things clear. As candidate for the Assembly I have the right to ask that you take special care in any releases you may make to the press. And I ask you to make clear the fact that I have not been under arrest, that I have made a detailed voluntary statement, that I will hold myself in readiness to cooperate with the police at any time of the day or night, and that I can prove that I have never met the victim of this infamous murder in all my life." He paused.

"Come on, Mr. Thayer," urged the lawyer, a little uneasily.

"Good evening, Inspector," said Charles Robin Thayer, and departed.

Miss Withers stared after him. "He might have said good evening to me, too. Women have the vote in New York State. At any rate, Oscar, he doesn't look like a murderer. So few of them do, though."

The Inspector led the way into the office, where a desk sergeant quickly stood up, shaking his head at the implied question in his superior's eye. "Nothing new in his statement, sir. Claims he didn't touch a single object in the room—was just looking, getting material for a talk on crime prevention, and all of a sudden he turned his head and saw Mr. Moore laying Mr. Holcomb's body down at the other end of the room."

"I know, I know. Look here, Hildegarde." The Inspector led the way across the office and slid back a wooden panel in the wall. Behind it was a sheet of cloudy glass, through which they could see a small room bright with one glaring lamp that shone into the eyes of a tanned, dapper man who sat on the edge of a hard chair, surrounded by three detectives. He looked far less worried than his inquisitors. "This thing," continued the Inspector, "is a mirror on the other side. They can't see or hear us."

"I gather," asked Miss Withers, "that this is Dexter Moore, the sole remaining suspect?"

He nodded. "Was overseas for Midwest Press for four years in the European theater. An expert on guns, to hear him tell it. He likes to collect them from dead Germans, Bulgarians, Rumanians, and anybody."

"Nice and ghoulish, isn't he?" Miss Withers squinted closer. "Not as handsome as the other suspect, but rugged and useful looking. He seems quite pleased with himself."

They watched the pantomime, as the detectives, obviously referring to a typed statement, hurled barrage after barrage of questions at the man in the chair. Now and again he shook his head, with amused patience.

"Moore will have to be turned loose in a minute," Piper decided. "His statement is exactly the same as Thayer's—but in reverse! Besides, we can't hold a man on suspicion when he's got three medals and is a front-page hero. But blast it, somebody committed that murder! Holcomb didn't murder himself!" The panel closed. "And if I don't get busy, I'm going to be hunting a job."

Silently the schoolteacher followed the Inspector back to his own office, where he sank unhappily into the chair behind his desk and picked up carbon copies of the twin statements signed *Dexter N. Moore* and *Charles Robin Thayer*. He read them through, then tossed them aside. "Moore's has more adjectives, but Thayer winds up with

a better climax. They both add up to the same thing."

The schoolteacher glanced at them, and nodded. "They read like truth. Which is natural, because whichever was the guilty one, he was smart enough to pull a complete switch of viewpoint."

"Yeah. If I had a motive, just a tiny little motive."

Miss Withers, who had been staring at a nearby brick wall through the open window, now turned quickly. "Oscar, an innocent man might lie—I mean a man innocent of murder. He might hate somebody so much that he would try to incriminate him. . . ."

"Look, Hildegarde. They don't even know each other. We've proved that, as clearly as anyone can. They never met. Thayer was secretary of an educational association upstate when Moore went overseas. Moore's only been back four days. I don't see—"

"Oscar, do you remember the impression the Black Museum made on us both? Isn't it within the realm of possibility that a mind might snap from the sheer weight of the exhibits, from the poisonous aura they give off?"

The Inspector was amused. "Look, Hildegarde. You saw Thayer and Moore. They're not the type to change into murderous maniacs instanter, just from being in a museum like that. They're hard-headed, ambitious citizens. Try again."

"Perhaps I will. By the way, Oscar, has it occurred to you that the murder would never have happened but for the accident of that telephone call. If there ever was a telephone call. . . ."

Just at that moment the telephone rang, with a loud angry clang. "Yes?" said the Inspector. "Oh, yes, Commissioner. Yes, I know—"

Miss Withers waved good-bye at her unhappy sparring-partner, and then went quietly out of the room.

Later that night, back in her own little apartment on West 73rd Street, the schoolteacher bent over her aquarium of fancy tropical fish and soberly addressed a fantastic and ornate *scalare*, who stared back at her and worked its shark-mouth foolishly. "The main problem," she was saying, "is the motive. Why should anybody want to kill a harmless little retired hotel employee?"

A black mollie, fat and sleek, swam past the angel-fish, who took out furiously after it, snapping at fin and tail. "Or," continued Miss Withers to her oblivious audience, "did somebody just have an overwhelming urge to kill, and take the nearest victim?" The schoolteacher sighed and snapped out the overhead light, reducing fairyland into a muddy puddle of water, sand, and weeds, peopled by nondescript gray minnows.

The lightless pool, she fancied, was like her own mind at the moment—a dark and clouded place. Well, she might as well sleep on it. "To sleep, perchance to dream, I hope," said she, and went off to bed.

Dream she did that night. As a matter of fact, the Inspector was of the opinion that she was still dreaming when she stalked into his office shortly after nine o'clock next morning, announcing that a substitute was taking over her little charges at Jefferson School, and that she intended to devote her time to saving his precious skin.

"Don't you worry," she told him. "My subconscious worked it all out for me in my sleep. I dreamed—"

"My old father, good man that he was, always said he would rather hear rain on a tin roof than hear a woman tell her dreams," interrupted the Inspector. "And for your information, if you're still worrying about that telephone call, it was on the level all right. Those calls all pass through the Headquarters switchboard, and Cap Halverstadt had a call just after two yesterday. It was from Western Union, a long complicated telegram about a three horse parlay at Rockingham, signed Sam."

"Oh," said the schoolteacher. "Well, about the dream. I dreamed I was playing cards with two suspects and there came time for a show-

down. But one of them refused to put down his cards—and that one was the murderer! Only I don't remember which of them it was."

"Marvelous, Hildegarde!"

"Well, the meaning is clear. Oscar, an innocent and a guilty man must react in different ways to the same stimuli. That's the principle of the lie detector."

"Sure, sure. And I get booted out of the Force if I don't wash up this case before the Commissioner has his second cocktail tonight. And all because of the killing of a useless little old guy who was good for nothing but the writing of some reminiscences of the Good Old Days, that nobody would want to read about. . . ."

"Oh, Oscar!" cried Miss Withers. "Sometimes you are brilliant!"

A pleased but vague smile crossed the Inspector's face, but it died away as he heard the door close behind his visitor. Nor did he hear any more from her until a short time after noon that day, when she called on the phone and requested that he show up at her apartment as soon as convenient. Curiosity, and the lack of any other hopeful portent, brought him there within fifteen minutes. He found the maiden schoolteacher leisurely removing signs of unwonted make-up from her face. She had combed her gray-brown hair back into a violent upsweep hair-do, and otherwise attired herself fearfully and quite wonderfully.

"For God's sake, Hildegarde, you look like Carrie Nation!"

"Well put, Oscar. Permit me to introduce myself. I am none other than Miss Miriam Whitehead Jones, world-famous impressionist poet. In impressionist circles only, of course. Having laid aside my fading laurels I have decided to set down on paper the memories of a busy life, filled with reminiscences of the great and the near-great who have been my friends and my—er, my intimates. I have been seeking a publisher for my memoirs. And since they will naturally be a bit on the racy side, I had to find one who was not too squeamish about the danger of libel suits."

"I still don't get it."

"You will. I happened at last to be success-ful, Oscar, although I was forced to spend the entire morning tramping up and down Madison Avenue. But I finally located a Mr. Hoppman, of Klaus Hoppman and Sons, who seems just the perfect publisher. You would not care for him, Oscar. He is a dusty little man, with a scrawny neck and a head as bare and reptilian as a turtle's. But he seems to specialize in the publication of memoirs such as mine will be, especially when the author contributes most of the expense. Indeed, I have learned that he has already set in type the first volume of 'Forty Years of Scandals at the Grande Hotel,' by Hubert Holcomb."

The Inspector took a deep breath, and nodded. "You figure you got a motive—that somebody might not want to be included in Hol-comb's memoirs. And that somebody—"

"Oscar, if we were at 221B Baker Street I should ask you to take down the commonplace books and the indexes, but lacking Sherlock Holmes's library, do you know any local news-paperman who could sneak me into the paper's morgue?"

Piper hesitated. "Well, I know Weatherby over at the Brooklyn Falcon. He's been there since the year One. But what you expect to find—"

"I haven't the slightest idea. But I'll find it all the same."

A short time later she found herself seated at a battered oak table in a small room crowded with musty, tattered volumes. Miss Hildegarde With-ers sneezed, sneezed again, and began to shuffle through interminable envelopes filled with dry and brittle press clippings. But her progress was very slow, and the hands of her watch moved swiftly.

The Inspector, a very worried man indeed, met her by appointment at her own apartment shortly before five. "Not that your wild ideas will do any good. The Commissioner means it this time, too. I had my boys pick up Cap Halver-stadt, just in case he might have gone nuts from being in that place too long, but they couldn't get anything on him. We've been watching Moore

and Thayer, too, but they're acting like com-pletely innocent bystanders."

"Did your men report that both Mr. Thayer and Mr. Moore received special delivery mes-sages this afternoon? Because they did, and the messages were from me. Asking them to drop in here. I think they'll come, too. Because I hinted to each of them that he would meet an eye-witness to the murder. Meaning the other, of course. You see, Oscar, in the newspaper files I found what I had hoped to find. *Voilà*, the motive."

The Inspector eagerly seized the yellow clipping which she produced from her capa-cious bag. "German-Americans Affirm Faith in Future Amity," he read. "At a gala dinner in the Hotel Grande last evening, prominent New Yorkers representing the German-American Bund, the Brooklyn Turn-Verein, and other organizations interested in German-American cordiality, met to toast the New Germany. . . ."

"You can skip down to the last paragraph," Miss Withers said. "See here? 'Among the speakers were Hans Von Drebber, of the Ger-man Embassy in Washington, Ludwig Kraus, the famous author, and Carl Thayer, well-known Albany educator.'"

"I begin to see," said the Inspector.

"Just suppose," Miss Withers continued tri-umphantly, "that in his memoirs Hubert Hol-comb happened to remember that early Nazi dinner at his hotel, and mentioned prominent guests? Suppose that Mr. Hoppman, the pub-lisher, realizing that disclosure of such leanings on the part of Thayer would at this time wreck his political career, attempted a quiet bit of blackmail before publication?"

Piper nodded. "But Hildegarde, now that you've got a motive for Thayer, why not call off the invitation to Moore?"

"It's only fair that since the man has been under suspicion, he is here to see himself cleared. Besides, there are a few points that aren't worked out quite right as yet. I'm counting on you for that. Remember, I'm only an amateur, a self-appointed gadfly to the police department, as you so often remind me. You'll have to take over at the proper time. By the way, did you bring what I asked for?" The Inspector felt in his pocket, and then produced the silken noose which was to be, he hoped, Exhibit A in the case of the State of New York versus the murderer of Hubert Holcomb. The schoolteacher took it gingerly and placed it on the table, directly under the rays of the lamp.

Then came a hammering of the door-knocker. A moment later Dexter Moore was facing them. He wore a debonair, quizzical smile, a little too much on the Richard Harding Davis type, Miss Withers thought. She preferred her foreign correspondents to be like Ernie Pyle.

"I thought this was to be a private interview," he said stiffly.

"Don't mind me, Mr. Moore," the Inspector told him easily. "I'm just the innocent bystander. But we want to finish this thing up, don't we?"

Moore took a few steps into the room, and then his eye fell upon the silken noose. "Are you infantile enough to suppose that you can disturb nerves as cool as mine by showing me the weapon in the case? After what I went through in the Black Museum yesterday—"

He was interrupted by a second hammering of the knocker. This time it was Mr. Thayer, who had changed into a dinner jacket. He surveyed them all with the perfect aplomb, the trained gestures, of the professional man of politics. "I don't understand your note, Miss Withers. And I don't think I like remaining here in the company of a man whom I know to be a murderer. . . ."

"Sit down, Thayer, and let the lady say her say," cut in Dexter Moore, smiling a brave, grim smile. "You know very well which of us is the murderer. Let's get on with it."

Miss Withers sniffed. "I intend to. You see, gentlemen, it is important that before we leave this room we establish for all time, to the satisfaction of the police and the public, just which one of you is guilty and which is innocent."

"Is this going to be a long lecture?" Thayer looked at his watch.

"Just long enough, I hope. Mr. Holcomb, for whose murder you are both under suspicion, was killed because in writing his reminiscences of a busy life as *maître d'hôtel* at a notorious gathering place of the city that was New York, he touched upon an old scandal in the past of one of you gentlemen. His publishers, either for their own protection or for purposes of polite blackmail, brought the matter to the attention of the murderer. No doubt they contacted dozens of people who were mentioned in the manuscript. But one person had too much to lose. He followed Holcomb, learned he was waiting to see the interior of the Black Museum, and slipped away to send a complicated telegram to the attendant, which would take at least ten or fifteen minutes to deliver by phone. It is possible to specify the exact time of delivery for a telegram, you see. That would, he expected, leave him alone with his unsuspecting victim. As fate would have it, he wasn't alone. But he went ahead with it, figuring that at worst it would be only one man's word against another's. But you see, it is not impossible to delve back into a man's forgotten past and to discover just what secret it was that would make him murder. . . ."

The Inspector, on his toes, was watching Thayer. That was why he very nearly swallowed his cigar when he saw Dexter Moore spring to his feet. "So what!" the man cried. "Suppose you did find out about what happened that night in the suite at the Grande! Suppose I did go out of the window in my underwear—I didn't know it was a water pistol the fellow threatened us with! Anyway, the hotel hushed up the whole thing, and I was just another newspaperman then. But if it came out *now*—"

He stopped, swallowed. "But I wouldn't kill to keep that secret. Besides, who knows but Mr. Thayer here has a similar old scandal in *his* past."

"As a matter of fact," the Inspector put in, "we know about Mr. Thayer's secret. It was a certain dinner, with some speakers since grown famous. Or infamous."

"Okay!" cut in Thayer. "And you're right back where you started. Either of us has a motive, of a sort. But I say that Dexter Moore killed Holcomb. He says that I killed him. It's up to the police department to prove which of us it was."

Miss Hildegarde Withers looked across the room toward the tank of tropical fish. The reflecting light was shining now, and the place was a fairyland again, a lambent tropical forest filled with glittering, phosphorescent beings, angel-fish, neons, golden tetras, mollies, and jewelled butterfly bettas moved magically and surely through the turquoise water. . . .

And then she knew.

She turned suddenly to face the two men. "Two negatives make a positive," said Hildegarde Withers. "Each of you blames the other. Captain Halverstadt says that neither of you showed signs of a struggle, that your clothes were not disheveled. The police have proved that neither of you knew Hubert Holcomb, and that you had never met one another—except perhaps between the pages of his manuscript. But it is plain as the nose on my face, gentlemen. Each of you came there to kill him. You read the intent in each other's eyes, and then and there was born the unholy inspiration to kill him *together*!"

Dexter Moore laughed harshly. "There is no proof in all that, no case the Inspector can ever hand over to a district attorney. It is still Thayer's word against mine, mine against his, yours against ours."

"I have another witness," promised Miss Hildegarde Withers. She held up the silken rope. "This is almost nine feet long, gentlemen. In the old days, when such things as these were used by the assassins, they made a noose and gave one swift jerk, snapping the victim's neck. According to my encyclopedia, the Hashhashim—or hashish-eaters—used to kill Christians with this, by the dozens. But according to the assistant medical examiner Holcomb was strangled to death *slowly*! That takes time."

"There could have been time enough," Thayer put in. "I was very interested in some exhibits at the other end of the room."

"There was time enough," Miss Withers raced desperately on, "for either of you separately to creep up on Holcomb and to strangle him. But that would have given Holcomb a chance to fight back, however feebly. He would have clawed at your face, your clothing. Were there any signs—any signs at all—of such a struggle? No! But if you were to hold—*each* of you—an end of this rope, if you were to loop it once around his neck and both stand well out of reach, *if you were to play tug-of-war* until he collapsed, wouldn't that do the job neatly? Don't answer. I can read it in your faces. You knew that the individual cases against you would cancel out—and you took a chance—"

"They still cancel out," Thayer said wearily. "Look at the Inspector. He knows the case would be laughed out of court."

Slowly the Inspector nodded. Miss Withers sneaked a glance at her watch, and a look of quiet triumph came over her face. "There's one thing that won't be laughed out of court," she said. "One little detail that you murderers didn't know and couldn't know. Exhibits in the Black Museum are stained with an invisible powder, known to chemists as oxy-methane blue. The idea was to prevent pilfering, since oxy-methane blue after some hours forms an indelible stain upon the human skin. And both of you claimed you didn't touch anything in the Black Museum—not even the murder rope!"

The two men looked incredulously at their right hands, and both kept staring, for a deep blue stain marked their palms. Then followed what Miss Withers would rather not have witnessed, for both broke down into sobbing, frenzied confessions, screaming, ranting, struggling against the detectives who poured in from the hall. But finally they were taken away.

The Inspector made his triumphant phone call to the Commissioner and then sank down wearily beside his old friend. "You sure had me going for a minute," he confessed. "Hildegarde, what's this about ox-something blue powder on the exhibits in the Black Museum? I never heard of it."

She smiled. "It wasn't in the museum. We used it in the school last fall, to catch a child who was pilfering in the cloak room. It doesn't work

in a few hours, it works in a few minutes. Look at your own palm, Oscar."

He looked, and gasped. "But, Hildegarde—"

"It was smeared on my doorknocker," confessed the schoolteacher.

MEREDITH'S MURDER

Charlotte Armstrong

IT IS NOT UNCOMMON for a mystery writer to find, or to focus on, a specialty of some kind—a theme or subject in which they flourish. For Charlotte Armstrong (1905–1969), the attraction was creating stories and novels of suspense and peril to the young and to the elderly.

In no work is this characterized more graphically than in *Mischief* (1950), in which a psychopathic hotel babysitter gradually becomes unglued as she contemplates killing her young charge. Filmed as *Don't Bother to Knock* (1952), it starred the young and beautiful Marilyn Monroe in a rare villainous role. Directed by Roy Baker, it also starred Richard Widmark, Anne Bancroft, and Elisha Cook, Jr.

Another of Armstrong's powerful suspense novels to be filmed was *The Unsuspected* (1946), a controversial novel that was both praised by critics for its writing skill and lambasted for disclosing the identity of the killer almost at the outset. A famous radio narrator steals money from his ward's inheritance, and, when his secretary discovers his thievery, he kills her. More deaths follow before he confesses—on air. It was filmed under the same title and released in 1947 to excellent reviews. Directed by Michael Curtiz, it starred Claude Rains, Joan Caulfield, and Audrey Totter.

During the filming of *The Unsuspected*, Armstrong and her family permanently moved from New York to California, where she continued to write stories and more than twenty novels, one of which, *A Dram of Poison* (1956), won the Edgar as the best novel of the year. She also wrote television scripts, including several that were produced by Alfred Hitchcock.

"Meredith's Murder" was originally published in the Fall 1953 issue of *Conflict—Stories of Suspense*; it was first collected in *The Albatross* by Charlotte Armstrong (New York, Coward-McCann, 1957) with the title "The Hedge Between," under which it often has been reprinted.

Meredith's Murder

CHARLOTTE ARMSTRONG

THE MAN NAMED RUSSELL, who happened to be a lawyer, sat full in the light of a solitary lamp. It shone upon the brown-covered composition book in his hands. A man named John Selby, a merchant in the small city, was seated in a low chair. He hung his head; his face was hidden; the light washed only his trembling head and the nervous struggle of his fingers. The Chief of Police, Barker, was seated in half shadow. And Doctor Coles loomed against the wall beside a white door that was ajar. It was one o'clock in the morning.

Doctor, Lawyer, Merchant, Chief . . .

"Well?" the Chief challenged. "Okay, Russell. You're smart, as Selby says you are. You come running when you're called, listen to five minutes' talk about this kid, and you predict there's got to be some such notebook around. Well? Now you've found it, why don't you see what it says?"

"I'm waiting for a direction," said the lawyer mildly. "It's not for me to turn this cover. Look at the big black letters. *Meredith Lee. Personal and Private.* It's not up to me to violate her privacy. But Selby's her kin. Coles is her doctor. And you are law and order in this town."

The doctor turned his head suddenly to the crack of the door.

"Any change?" the Chief asked eagerly.

"No. She's still unconscious. Go ahead, Russell. Don't be squeamish. She's a child, after all."

"See if there's anything helpful in there," the Chief of Police said, "See if that notebook can explain . . ."

"Explains," the lawyer mused, "how a fifteen-year-old girl solved a seven-year-old murder mystery in four days . . ."

"She didn't solve it all the way," said the Chief impatiently.

Russell ignored him. "What do you say, Selby? She's your niece. Shall we read her private notebook?"

Selby's hands came palms up, briefly. The policeman spoke again, "Read it. I intend to, if you don't. I've got to get the straight of it. My prisoner won't talk."

The doctor said pompously, "After all, it may be best for the girl."

Russell said dryly, "I'm just as curious as the rest of you."

He opened the book and began to read aloud.

Meredith Lee. New Notes and Jottings.
July 23rd.

Here I am at Uncle John's. The family has dumped me for two weeks while they go to New York. I don't complain. It is impossible for me to get bored, since I can always study human nature.

Uncle John looks much the same. Gray hairs show. He's thirty-seven. Why didn't he marry? Mama says he's practicing to stuff a shirt. He was very Uncle-ish and hearty when I got dumped last night, but he actually has no idea what to do with me, except tell the servants to keep me clean and fed. It's a good thing I've got resources.

Russell looked up. The Chief was chewing his lip. The doctor was frankly smiling. John Selby said, painfully, "She's right about that. Fool I was . . . I *didn't* know what to do with her." His head rolled in his hands.

"Go on," the Chief prodded.

Russell continued reading.

Went to the neighborhood drug store, first thing. Snooped down the street. I'd forgotten it, but my goodness, it's typical. Very settled. Not swank. Not poor, either. Very middle. No logic to that phrase. A thing can't be *very* middle, but it says what I feel. On the way home, a Discovery! There's a whopping big hedge between Uncle John's house and the house next door. The neighbor woman was out messing in her flower beds. Description: petite. Dark hair, with silver. Skillfully made up. Effect quite young. (N.B. What a bad paragraph! Choppy!)

So, filled with curiosity, I leaned over her gate and introduced myself. She's a Discovery! She's a Wicked Widow and she's *forbidden*! I didn't know that when I talked to her.

(N.B. Practice remembering dialogue accurately.)

Wicked Widow: Mr. Selby's niece, of course. I remember you, my dear. You were here as a little girl, weren't you? Wasn't the last time about seven years ago?

Meredith Lee: Yes, it was. But I don't remember you.

W.W.: Don't you? I am Josephine Corcoran. How old were you then, Meredith?

M.L.: Only eight.

W.W.: Only eight?

We came to a stop. *I* wasn't going to repeat. That's a horrible speech habit. You can waste hours trying to communicate. So I looked around and remembered something.

M.L.: I see my tree house has disintegrated.

W.W.: Your tree house? (N.B. She repeated everything I said, and with a question mark. Careless habit? Or just pace?) Oh, yes, of course. In that big maple, wasn't it?

M.L.: Mr. Jewell—you know, Uncle John's gardener?—he built it for me. I had a cot up there and a play ice-box and a million cushions. I wouldn't come down.

W.W.: Wouldn't come down? Yes, I remember. Eight years old and your Uncle used to let you spend the night— (N.B. She looked scared. Why? If I'd fallen out and killed myself seven years ago, I wouldn't be talking to her. Elders worry retroactively.)

M.L.: Oh, Uncle John had nothing to do with it. Mama's rational. She knew it was safe. Railings, and I always pulled up my rope ladder. Nobody could get up, or get me down without an awful lot of trouble. I was a tomboy in those days.

W.W.: Tomboy? Yes, seven years is a long time. (N.B. No snicker. She looked serious and thoughtful, just standing with the trowel in her hand, not even smiling. That's when I got the feeling I could really communicate and it's very unusual. She must be thirty. I get that feeling with really old people or people about eighteen, sometimes. But people in between, and especially thirty, usually act like Uncle John.)

Now I forget . . . her dialogue wasn't so sparkling, I guess, but she was understanding. Did I know any young people? I said No, and she politely hoped I wouldn't be lonely. I explained that I hoped to be a Writer, so I would probably always be lonely. And she said she supposed that was true. I liked that. It's not so often somebody listens. And while she may have looked surprised at a new thought, she didn't look *amused*. My object in life is not to *amuse*, and I get tired of those smiles. So I liked her.

But then, at dinner time, just as soon as I'd said I'd met her, she got forbidden.

Uncle John: (clearing his throat) Meredith, I don't think you had better . . . (He stuck. He sticks a lot.)

M.L.: Better what?

Uncle John: Er . . . (N.B. *English* spelling. Americans say uh. I am an American.) Uh . . . Mrs. Corcoran and I are not . . . uh . . . especially friendly and I'd rather you didn't . . . (Stuck again)

M.L.: Why not? Are you feuding?

Uncle John: No, no. I merely . . .

M.L.: Merely what? I think she's very nice.

Uncle John: Uh . . . (very stuffy) . . . You are hardly in a position to know anything about it. I'm afraid she is not the kind of woman your mother would . . .

M.L.: What kind is she? (You have to really pry at Uncle John.)

Uncle John: (finally) Not socially acceptable.

M.L.: What! Oh, for heaven's sakes, Uncle John! That's the stuffiest thing I *ever* heard! Why?

Uncle John: It's not stuffy, Meredith, and it's not easy to explain why. (Looks at me as if he wonders whether I understand English.) Maybe, if you knew that there was a strange business, years ago . . . Her husband was . . . uh . . . shot in rather mysterious circum . . .

M.L.: Shot! Do you mean killed? Do you mean *murdered*? Really? Oh, boy! How? When? Who did it? What happened?

Now, why did Uncle John act so surprised? Did he think I'd be scared? Don't people who are thirty ever remember how they didn't used to be *scared* by interesting things? But he *was* surprised and also very sticky and stuffy for a while. But I kept prying.

And I think it's just pitiful. I don't know why Uncle John can't see how pitiful it is. Poor Mrs. Corcoran. Her husband came home late one night and as he was standing at his own front door, somebody shot him from behind. They found the gun but nothing else. He wasn't robbed. It's just a mystery. So, just because it is a mystery and nobody knows, they've treated her as if she were a murderess! I can just see how it's been and I'm ashamed of Uncle John. He sure is practicing to stuff a shirt. He lets the hedge grow, and he goes along with the stupid town. It sounds as if nobody has accepted her socially ever since. Fine thing! She is supposed to be a wicked widow, just because her husband got murdered by person or persons unknown. Probably the town thinks such a thing couldn't happen to a respectable person. But it *could*. I'm very sorry for her.

The thing I'm saving for the bottom of this page is—it's my murder! I got that out of Uncle John. What do you know! What do you know! *I* was in my tree house that very night!

I'm just faintly remembering how I got whisked out of here so fast, that time. I never did know why. Holy cats! Eight years old. I'm asleep in a tree and a murder takes place right under me! And I never even knew it! They didn't tell me! They didn't even ask me a single question! A fine thing! A real murder in my own life, and I can't remember even one thing about it!

The lawyer paused. The doctor stirred, looked through the door. Three raised heads queried him. He said, "Nothing. It may be a good while yet before she is conscious. Don't . . . worry."

Selby turned to stare blindly at the lamp. "My sister should never—should never have left her with me. I had no business—no business to tell her a word about it."

"You thought she'd be scared away from the widow?"

"I suppose so."

The Chief said, "Now, wait a minute. The girl puts down in there that she *couldn't remember even one thing* about the killing? But that makes no sense at all."

"That's the July twenty-third entry," said Russell. "Here is July twenty-fifth. Let's see."

I couldn't stand it—I just can't think about anything else but my murder. I had to find out more. This afternoon I had tea with the widow. I don't think she's wicked at all. She's very sad, actually. She was in the garden again. I just know she was conscious of me, on Uncle John's side of the hedge, all day yesterday. Today, finally, she spoke to me. So I went around and leeched onto her.

(N.B. Practice getting the "saids" in)

Nervously, she said, "I hope your Uncle won't be angry."

I said, pretending to blurt, "Oh, Mrs. Corcoran, Uncle John told me about the awful thing that happened to your husband. And to think I was right up in my tree house. I can't stop thinking about it."

"Don't think about it," she said, looking pretty tense. "It was long ago, and there is no need. I'm sorry he spoke of it."

"Oh, I made him," said I. "And now when I think that for all I know, I might have seen and heard exactly what happened, and the only trouble is, I was so little, I can't *remember*—it just about makes me wild!"

She looked at me in a funny way. I thought she was going to blurt, "Oh, if only you could remember . . ." But actu-

ally, she said, "If you would like more cake please help yourself."

"It's too bad it's a mystery," I said (cried). "Why couldn't they solve it? Don't you wish they could solve it? Maybe it's not too late."

She looked startled. (N.B. What happens to eyes, anyhow, to make the whites show more? Observe.)

"I wish you would tell me the details," I said. "Couldn't they find out *anything*?"

"No, no. My dear, I don't think we had better talk about it at all. It's not the sort of thing a sweet child ought to be brooding about," she said.

I was desperate. "Mrs. Corcoran, the other day I thought better of you. Because you didn't laugh, for instance, when I mentioned that I used to be a tomboy, years ago. Most older people would have laughed. I'll never understand why. Obviously, I'm quite different and seven years has made a big change, and why it's so *funny* if I *know* that, I cannot see." She was leaning back and feeling surprised, I judged. "So don't disappoint me now and think of me as an eight-year-old child," I said, "when I may have the freshest eye and be the open-mindedest person around."

She nibbled her lips. She wasn't offended. I think she's very intelligent and responding.

"I'm *going* to brood and you can't stop that," I told her. "I just wish I could help. I've been thinking that maybe if I tried I *could* remember."

"Oh, no. No, my dear. Thank you," she said. "I know you would like to help. But you were only eight at that time. I don't suppose, then or now, anyone would believe you."

"And now I'm *only* fifteen," I said crossly, "and nobody will *tell* me."

She said sweetly. "You're rather an extraordinary fifteen, my dear. If I tell you about it, Meredith, and you see how hopeless it is, do you think perhaps then you can let it rest?"

I said I thought so. (What a lie!)

"Harry, my husband, was often late getting home, so that night," she said, "I wasn't at all worried. I simply went to bed, as usual, and to sleep. Something woke me. I don't know what. My window was open. It was very warm, full summer. I lay in my bed, listening. There used to be a big elm out there beside my walk. It got the disease all the elms are getting, and it had to be cut down and taken away. But that night I could see its leaf patterns on the wall, that the moon always used to make at night, and the leaves moving gently. There was a full moon, I remember. A lovely quiet summer night." (N.B. She's pretty good with a mood.)

"I had been awakened, yet I could hear nothing, until I heard the shot. It paralyzed me. I lay back stiff and scared. Harry didn't . . . cry out. I heard nothing more for a while. Then I thought I heard shrubs rustling. When I finally pulled myself to the window, your Uncle John was there." She stopped and I had to poke her up to go on.

"Your Uncle was forcing his way through the hedge, which was low, then. And I saw Harry lying on our little stoop. I ran to my bedroom door and my maid was standing in the hall, quite frightened, and we ran down. Your Uncle told me that Harry was . . . not alive. (N.B. Pretty delicate diction.) He was calling the doctor and the police from my phone. I sat down trembling on a chair in the hall. I remember, now, that as your Uncle started out of the house again, he seemed to recall where you were and went running to his garage for a ladder to get you down."

"Darn it," I said.

She knew what I meant, because she said right away, "You couldn't remember—

you must have been sleepy. Perhaps you didn't really wake up."

"I suppose so," said I disgustedly. "Go on."

"Well, the police came very quickly— Chief Barker himself. And of course, Doctor Coles. They did find the gun, caught in the hedge. They never traced it. There weren't any fingerprints anywhere. And no footprints in that dry weather. So they never found out . . ." She pulled herself together. "And that, my dear, is all." She started drinking her tea, looking very severe with herself.

I said, "There never was a trial?"

"There was never anyone to try."

"Not you, Mrs. Corcoran?"

"No one accused me," she said, smiling faintly. But her eyes were so sad.

"They did, though," I said, kind of mad. "They sentenced you, too."

"Dear girl," she said very seriously, "You mustn't make a heroine of me. Chief Barker and Doctor Coles . . . and your Uncle John, too, I'm sure . . . tried as helpfully as they could to clear it all up, but they never could find out who, or even why. You see? So . . ." She was getting pretty flustery.

"So the wind begins to blow against you," I said, mad as the dickens. "Or how come the hedge? Why does Uncle John tell me not to come here? What makes him think you're so wicked?"

"Does he?" she said, "I am not wicked, Meredith. Neither am I a saint. I'm human."

I always thought that was a corny saying. But it's effective. It makes you feel for whoever says it, as if they had admitted something just awful that you wouldn't admit, either—unless, of course, you were *trapped*.

"Harry and I were not always harmonious," she said. "Few couples are. He drank a good bit. Many men do. I suppose the neighbors noticed. Some of them, in fact, used to feel quite sorry for me. I . . ." Her face was real bitter, but she has a quick hunching way of pulling herself together. ". . . shouldn't be saying these things to you. Why do I forget you are so young? I shouldn't. Forgive me, and don't be upset."

"Not me," I told her. "I'm pretty detached. And don't forget my eye is fresh. I can see the trouble. There isn't anybody else to suspect. You need . . ."

"No, no. No more. I had no right to talk to you. And you'd better not come again. It is not I, my dear. I like you very much. I would love to see you often. But—"

I said, "I think Uncle John is a stuffy old stinker. To bend the way the wind blows. But *I* don't have to!"

"Yes, you do," she said, kind of fixing me with her eye. "It's not nice, Meredith, to be this side of the hedge. Now, please, never question your Uncle John's behavior." She was getting very upset. "You must . . . truly, you must . . . believe me . . . when I say . . . I think he meant . . . to be very kind . . . at that time." She spaced it like that, taking breaths in between.

"But that mean old hedge, for the whole town to see. It makes me mad!" I said.

She fixed me, again. She said very fast almost like whispering, "Perhaps it was I, Meredith, who let the hedge grow."

Naturally, my mouth opened, but before I got anything out she said, loudly, "It was best. There, now . . ."

(N.B. Yep. I was really disappointed. How I hate it when people say, "There, now." Implying that they know a million things more than me. And I better be comforted. I'm *not*. I'm irritated. It means they want to stop talking to me, and that's all.)

"It's all so old," she continued in that phony petting-the-kitty kind of way. "And

nothing will change it. Let it rest. Thank you for coming and thank you for being open-minded. But go away now, Meredith, and promise me not to think about it any more."

I fixed her with *my* eye. I said, "Thank you very much for the lovely cake."

But I'm not angry. I feel too sorry for her. Besides, she let out hints enough and I should have caught on. Well, I didn't, then. But after the session I had with Uncle John . . . *Are they ever dumb!*

We had finished dinner when I decided to see what more I could pry out of *him*. I said, "If Harry Corcoran was a drinking man he was probably drunk the night he got shot."

Uncle John nearly knocked his coffee over. "How do you know he was a drinking man?" roared he. "Have you been gossiping with Mrs. Jewell?" (Mrs. Jewell is the housekeeper. Vocabulary about one hundred words.)

"Oh, no, I haven't. Was he?"

"Who?"

"Harry Corcoran?"

"What?"

"Drunk?"

"So they say," bites Uncle John, cracking his teeth together, "Now, Meredith—"

"Where were you at the time of the murder?" chirped I.

(N.B. Nope. Got to learn to use the "saids." They're neutraller.)

"Meredith, I wish you—"

"I know what you wish, but I wish you'd tell me. Aw, come on, Uncle John. My own murder! Maybe if I had all the facts, I'd stop thinking so much about it. Don't you see that?"

(N.B. False. The more you know about anything the more interesting it gets. But he didn't notice.)

"I told you the facts," he said (muttered?), "and I wish I had kept my big mouth shut. Your mother will skin me alive. How the devil did I get into this?"

(N.B. I thought this was an improvement. He's usually so darned stuffy when he talks to me.)

"You didn't tell me any details. Please, Uncle John . . ." I really nagged him. I don't think he's had much practice defending himself, because finally, stuffy as anything, he talked.

"Very well. I'll tell you the details as far as I know them. Then I shall expect to hear no more about it."

"I know," said I. True. I knew what he *expected*. I didn't really promise anything. But he's not very analytical. "Okay. Pretend you're on the witness stand. Where were you at the time?"

"I was, as it happened . . . [N.B. Stuffy! Phrase adds nothing. Of course it happened.] . . . in the library that night working late on some accounts. It was nearly one in the morning, I believe . . . [N.B. Of course he believes, or he wouldn't say so] . . . when I heard Harry Corcoran whistling as he walked by in the street."

"What tune?"

"What?" (I started to repeat but he didn't need it. Lots of people make you repeat a question they heard quite well just so they can take a minute to figure out the answer.) "Oh, that Danny Boy song. Favorite of his. That's how I knew who it was. He was coming along from the end of town, past this house—"

"Was that usual?"

"It was neither usual nor unusual," said Uncle John crossly. "It's merely a detail."

"Okay. Go on."

"The next thing I noticed was the shot."

"You were paralyzed?"

"What?" He just about glared at me. "Yes, momentarily. Then I ran out my side door and pushed through the hedge and found him there on his own doorstep . . . uh . . ."

"Not living," I said delicately.

He gave me another nasty look. "Now, that's all there was to it."

"That's not all! What did you do then? Didn't you even look for the murderer?"

"I saw nobody around. I realized there might be somebody concealed, of course. So I picked up his key from where it had fallen on the stoop—"

"The Corcorans' door was locked?"

"It was locked and I unlocked it and went inside to the phone. As I was phoning, Mrs. Corcoran and her maid came downstairs. I called Chief Barker and Doctor Coles."

"Yes, I know. And then you ran to get the ladder and pulled me down out of my tree. Okay. But you're leaving things out, Uncle John. You are deliberately being barren. You don't give any atmosphere at all. What was Mrs. Corcoran's emotional state?"

"I haven't the slightest idea," said Uncle John with his nose in a sniffing position, "and if I had, it would not be a fact."

I pounced. "You think she did it?"

He pulled his chin practically to the back of his neck. "I wish you would not say that. I have little right to speculate and none to make a judgment. There was no evidence."

"But you did pass judgment. You told me she was a certain kind of—"

"Meredith, I know only one fact. Your mother would not like this at all. In any case, I will not discuss Mrs. Corcoran's character with you. I must insist you take my word for it. There is no way. . . ." He kind of held his forehead.

"Uncle John, who let the hedge grow?"

"What? The hedge belongs to me."

"That ain't the way I heared it," said stupid I.

So *he* pounced. "Where have you been hearing things? Who told you Harry Corcoran was a drinking man? Where have you been, Meredith?"

So I confessed. No use writing down the blasting I got. It was the usual. Bunch of stuff about my elders wanting no harm to come to me, things not understood in my philosophy, mysterious evils that I wot not of, and all that sort of stuff. Why doesn't he tell me plain out that it's none of my business?

Well, I don't think it's evil. I think it's foolishness. I think that Uncle John's too sticky and stuffy to tell me . . . (Probably thinks I never heard of s-blank-x) . . . is that he used to be romantic about the pretty lady next door. Probably Uncle John saw a lot of Harry's drunken comings-home and heard plenty of the disharmonizing. Probably he is one neighbor who felt sorry for her. Wonder if they were in love and said so. I doubt it. Probably they just cast glances at each other over the hedge and said nothing. That would be just like Uncle John.

Anyhow, when somebody shoots Harry Corcoran in the back, the widow gets it into her head that Uncle John did it. After all, she heard things—rustling bushes—looked out, and there he was. But gosh, even if she felt romantic about him too, she'd draw the line at murder! But of course, Uncle John didn't do it. He thinks *she* did. He knows she was unhappy with Harry. But he draws the line at murder, too. So these dopes, what do they do? They have no "right" to pass "judgment" or "accuse" anybody. They pull themselves in, with the hedge between. All these years, with their very own suspicions proving that neither one could have done it . . . Probably if they'd had sense enough to speak out and have a big argument, they could have got married and been happy long ago.

Oh, how ridiculous! How pitiful! And oh, that I was born to put it right! (N.B. Who said that?)

The lawyer put the book down. John Selby groaned. "I had no idea . . . no idea what she had in her head. I knew she was bright . . ."

"Bright, yes," said Doctor Coles, "but that kid's so insufferably condescending!"

"You wouldn't like it even if she guessed right," said Russell thoughtfully. "The girl's got a hard way to go. She'll be lonely."

"Thought she was smart, all right," growled Barker. "Wasn't as smart as she thought. She was wrong, I take it?"

Selby didn't answer. His gaze was fixed on the lawyer's face.

"You shouldn't blame her for being wrong," Russell murmured. "She's not yet equipped to understand a lot of things. But she is compelled to try. There's her intelligent curiosity fighting a way past some clichés, but the phrase 'feel romantic' is flat, for her, and without shading."

"I still can't see what happened," Barker broke in to complain. "Never mind the shading. Go ahead—if there's more of it."

"Yes, there's more. We come to July twenty-sixth—yesterday." Russell began to read once more.

I've figured. I know exactly how to do it. I'll say *I can remember*! I'll tell them that when I was up in my tree that night the shot or something woke me, and I saw a stranger running away . . .

"So she made it up! Told a story!" Chief Barker slapped his thigh. "But . . . now wait a minute . . . you believed her, Selby?"

"I believed her," her uncle sighed.

"Go on. Go on," the doctor said.

I know how to make them believe me, too. This will be neat! I'll tell Uncle John first, and I'll mix into the story I tell him all the little bits I got from her that he doesn't know I've been told. So, since *they'll* be true, he'll be fooled, and think I really remember. Then I'll go to her, but in the story I tell her, all I have to do is mix in the bits I got from Uncle John that she doesn't know I've been told. It'll work! Ha, they'll never catch on to the trick of it. They'll believe me! Then they can get together, if they still want to. I'm not worried about telling a kind of lie about it. If anybody official starts asking questions I can always shudder, and be too young and tender, and clam up.

Get it exactly right. Make lists.

Russell looked up. "Meredith's good at math, I suppose?"

"A plus," her uncle groaned. "She scares me." Russell nodded and began to read again.

List No. 1. For Uncle John. Things she told me.

1. Warm night. Full moon.
2. The elm tree that used to be there.
3. The gun was found *in the hedge.*
4. Harry didn't yell.

Now, put all these points in. Future dialogue. By Meredith Lee.

M.L.: Oh, Uncle John, I do remember now!

Uncle John: What?

(Whoops! Since this is in the future, I better not write *his* dialogue. It might confuse me.)

M.L.: I was up in my room, thinking, and I began to hum that tune. That Danny Boy. It made the whole thing come back to me like a dream. Now I remember waking up on my cot and hearing that whistling. I peeked out between my railings. The moon was very bright that night. It was warm, too, real summer. I could see the elm tree by the Corcorans' walk. (Pause. Bewildered.) Which elm tree, Uncle John?

There's none there now. *Was* there an elm tree, seven years ago?

(Ha, ha, that'll *do* it!)

I saw a man come up their walk. I must have heard the shot. I thought somebody had a firecracker left over from Fourth of July. I saw the man fall down but he didn't make any noise, so I didn't think he was hurt. I thought he fell asleep.

(What a touch! Whee!)

Then I saw there was another man, down there, and he threw something into the hedge. The hedge crackled where it landed. Then this man jumped through their gate and ran, and then you came out of this house . . .

(By this time the stuffing should be coming out of Uncle John.)

I'll say I don't know who the stranger was. "But it wasn't you, Uncle John," I'll say, "and the widow Corcoran's been thinking so for seven years and I'm going to tell her . . ."

Then I'll run out of the house as fast as I can.

He'll follow—he'll absolutely have to!

Russell looked up. "Was it anything like that?"

"It was almost exactly like that," said John Selby, lifting his tired, anxious face. "And I did follow. She was right about that. I absolutely had to."

"Smart," said Chief Barker, smacking his lips, "the way she worked that out."

"Too smart," the doctor said, and then, "Nurse? Yes?" He went quickly through the door.

"My sister will skin me alive," said John Selby, rousing himself. "Kid's had me jumping through hoops. Who am I to deal with the likes of her? Looks at me with those big brown eyes. Can't tell whether you're talking to a baby or a woman. Everything I did was a mistake. I never had the least idea what she was thinking. You're smart about people, Russell—that's why I need you. I feel as if I'd been through a wind-tunnel. Help me with Meredith. I feel terrible about the whole thing, and if she's seriously hurt and I'm responsible . . ."

"You say you don't understand young people," began Russell, "but even if you did, this young person . . ."

"You take it too hard, John," said Chief Barker impatiently. "Doc doesn't think she's hurt too seriously. And she got herself into it, after all. Listen, go on. What did she say to the widow? That's what I need to know. Is it in there?"

"It must be," said Russell. "She made another list."

List No. 2. For the widow. Things Uncle John told me.

1. Harry was whistling Danny Boy.
2. He came in the direction that passed this house.
3. He was drunk.
4. He dropped his key.

Not so good. Yes it is, too. What woke her? She doesn't know, but I do! Future dialogue:

M.L.: Oh, Mrs. Corcoran, I think I'm beginning to remember! I really think so! Listen, I think I heard a man whistling. And it was that song about Danny Boy. And he was walking from the east, past our house. Would it have been your husband?

(Ha! She's going to *have* to say Yes!)

And he . . . it seems to me that he didn't walk right. He wobbled. He wobbled up your walk and he dropped something. Maybe a key. It must have been a key because I saw him bending over to hunt for it but . . .

(Artistic pause here? I think so.)

Oh, now I remember! He straightened up. He couldn't have found it because he called out something. It was a name! It must have been . . . Oh, Mrs. Corcoran, could it have been your name, being called in the night, that woke you up?

(Betcha! Betcha!)

Well the rest of hers goes on the same. Stranger, throws gun, runs away, just as Uncle John comes out. "So it wasn't you," I'll say, "and I can prove it! But poor Uncle John has been afraid it *was*."

Then what? I guess maybe I'd better start to bawl.

Yep. I think that will do it. I think that's pretty good. They're bound to believe me. Of course, the two stories are not identical, but they can't be. *They'll* never notice the trick of it. They'll just have to be convinced that it wasn't either one of them who shot Harry Corcoran. I can't wait to see what will happen. What will they *do*? What will they *say*? Oh-ho-ho, is this ever research! I better cry soft enough so I can hear and memorize.

When shall I try it? I can't wait! Now is a good time. Uncle John is in the library and she's home. I can see a light upstairs in her house. Here goes, then.

(N.B. Would I rather be an actress? Consider this. M.L.)

The lawyer closed the book. "That's all." He put his hand to his eyes but his mouth was curving tenderly.

"Some scheme," said Barker in awe. "Went to a lot of trouble to work up all that plot . . ."

"She had a powerful motive," Russell murmured.

"My romance," said Selby bitterly.

"Oh, no. Research for her," the lawyer grinned.

"Whatever the motive, this remarkable kid went and faked those stories and she had it wrong," growled Barker. "But she must have got something right. Do you realize that?" He leaned into the light. "Selby, as far as you were concerned, you believed that rigmarole of hers. You thought she *did* remember the night of the killing and she *had* seen a stranger?"

"I did," John Selby said, sounding calmer. "I was considerably shaken. I had always suspected Josephine Corcoran, for reasons of my own."

"Lots of us suspected," the Chief said dryly, "for various reasons. But never could figure how she managed, with you rushing out to the scene so fast and the maid in the upstairs hall."

"What were your reasons, John?" Russell asked.

"In particular, there was a certain oblique conversation that took place in the course of a flirtation that appalls me, now. It seemed to me, one evening, that she was thinking that the death of her husband might be desirable—and might be arranged. I can't quote her exactly, you understand, but the hint was there. She thought him stupid and cruel and intolerable, and the hint was that if he were dead and gone she'd be *clean*. The shallow, callous, self-righteous . . . the *idea*! As if her life should rightfully be cleared of him with no more compunction than if he'd been . . . well, a wart on her hand." He held his head again. "Now, how is a man going to explain to his fifteen-year-old niece just what makes him think a woman is wicked? The feeling you get, that emanates from the brain and body?" He groaned. "That little talk pulled me out of my folly, believe me. That's when I shied off and began to let the hedge grow. When you realize that not long after that he *did* die, you'll see how I've lived with the memory of that conversation for seven years. Wondering. Was I right about what she had in mind and did I perhaps not recoil enough? Had I not sufficiently discouraged the . . . the idea? There was no evidence. There was nothing. But I've had a burden close to guilt and I've stayed on my side of the hedge, believe me, and begun to study to stuff a shirt." He groaned again and shifted in the chair. "When I thought the child had really seen a stranger with that gun, I was stunned. As soon as I realized where Meredith had gone . . ."

"You followed. You saw them through the widow's front door?" The Chief was reassembling this testimony.

"Yes. I could see them. At the top of the stairs. Mrs. Corcoran standing by the newel post and Meredith talking earnestly to her."

"You couldn't hear?"

"No, unfortunately. But if Meredith had rehearsed it, if she stuck to her script, then we must have it here."

"If it's there, I don't get it." Chief Barker passed his hand over his face. "Now, suddenly, you say—in the middle of the girl's story—the widow yelled something that you *could* hear?"

"She yelled, '*I told you to keep out of this, you nosy brat!*' And then she pushed Meredith violently enough to send her rolling down the stairs." Selby began to breathe heavily.

"And you got through the door . . ."

"By the time I got through the door, she was on the girl like a wildcat. She was frantic. She *meant* to hurt her." John Selby glared.

"So you plucked the widow off her prey and called us for help? Did Mrs. Corcoran try to explain at all?" Russell inquired.

"She put out hysterical cries. 'Poor dear! Poor darling!' But she meant to hurt Meredith. I heard. I saw. I know. And she knows that I know."

"Yes, the widow gave herself away," said Russell. "She was wicked, all right."

"So we've got her," the Chief growled, "for the assault on Meredith. Also, we know darned well she shot her husband seven years ago. But she won't talk. What I need," the Chief was anxious, "is to figure out what it was that set her off. What did the kid say that made her nerve crack? I can't see it. I just don't get it."

The doctor had been standing quietly in the door. Now he said, "Maybe Meredith can tell us. She's all right. Almost as good as new, I'd say."

John Selby was on his feet. So was Chief Barker. "Selby, you go first," the doctor advised. "No questions for the first minute or two."

The Chief turned and sighed. "Beats me."

Russell said, "One thing, Harry Corcoran never called out his wife's name in the night. Selby, who heard a whistle, would have heard such a cry."

"Do I see what you're getting at?" said Barker shrewdly. "It shows the kid didn't get *that far* in the story or the widow would have known she was story-telling."

"She certainly didn't get as far as any guilty stranger, or the widow would have been delighted. Let's see."

"There was something. . . ."

"Was it the tune? No, that's been known. Selby told that long ago. Was it Harry's drunkenness? No, because medical evidence exists. Couldn't be that."

"For the Lord's sakes, let's *ask* her," the Chief said.

They went through the door. The nurse had effaced herself watchfully. Four men stood around the bed. Doctor, Lawyer, Merchant, Chief . . .

Young Meredith Lee looked very small, lying against the pillow with her brown hair pressed back by the bandages, her freckles sharpened by the pallor of her face, her big brown eyes round and shocked.

"How do you feel, honey?" rumbled the Chief.

"She pushed me down." Meredith's voice was a childish whimper.

Her Uncle John patted the bed and said compulsively, "There, Meredith. There now . . ."

"Don't say that," the Chief put in with a chuckle. "It just annoys her."

The girl saw her notebook in Russell's hands. She winced and for a flash her eyes narrowed and something behind the child face was busy reassessing the situation.

"Miss Lee," said the lawyer pleasantly, "my name is Russell. I'm a friend of your Uncle John's. I'm the one who ferreted out your notes. I hope you'll forgive us for reading them. Thanks to you, now we know how wicked the widow was seven years ago."

"I only pretended," said Meredith in a thin treble. "I was only eight. I don't really remember anything at all." She shrank in the bed, very young and tender.

Her uncle said, "We know how you pretended. I . . . I had no idea you were so smart."

"That was some stunt," the doctor said.

"Very clever," the lawyer said, "the two stories as you worked them out."

"You're quite a story-teller, honey," chimed in Chief Barker.

On the little girl's face something struggled and lost. Meredith gave them one wild indignant look of pure outraged intelligence before her face crumpled. "I am not either!" she bawled. "I'm not any good! I got it all wrong! Didn't get the plot right. Didn't get the characters right. I guess I don't know *anything*! I guess I might as well give up . . ." She flung herself over and sobbed bitterly.

Chief Barker said, "She's okay, isn't she? She's not in pain?"

The nurse rustled, muttering "shock." The doctor said stiffly, "Come now, Meredith. This isn't a bit good for you."

But Selby said, to the rest of them, "See? That's the way it goes. She's eight and she's eighty. She can cook up a complex stunt like that and then bawl like a baby. I give up! I don't know what you should do with her. I've wired my sister. She'll skin us both, no doubt. Meredith, *please.* . . ."

Meredith continued to howl.

The lawyer said sharply. "That's right, Meredith. You may as well give up trying to be a writer if you are going to cry over your first mistakes instead of trying to learn from them. Will you be grown-up for a minute and listen? We seriously want your help to convict a murderess."

"You do not," wailed Meredith. "I'm too stupid!"

"Don't be a hypocrite," snapped the lawyer. "You are not stupid. As a matter of fact, you are extremely stuffy—as this book proves to us."

Meredith choked on a sob. Then slowly she opened one brown eye.

"The average young person," hammered the lawyer, "has little or no respect for an elder's experience and nothing can make him see its value until he gets some himself. But even a *beginning* writer should have a less conventional point of view."

"Now wait a minute," bristled John Selby. "Don't scold her. She's had an awful time. Listen, she meant well . . ."

Meredith sat up and mopped her cheek with the sheet. The brown eyes withered him. "Pul-lease, Uncle John," said Meredith Lee.

So John Selby raised his head and settled his shoulders. "Okay." He forced a grin. "Maybe I'm not too old to learn. You want me to lay it on the line? All right, you *didn't* mean well. You were perfectly vain and selfish. You were going to fix up my life and Josephine Corcoran's life as a little exercise for your superior wisdom." His stern voice faltered. "Is that better?"

Meredith said, tartly, "At least, it's ratio-nal." She looked around and her voice was not a baby's. "You are all positive the widow is a mur-deress," she said flatly.

Chief Barker said, "Well, honey, we always did kind of think so."

"Don't talk down to her," snapped John Selby, "or she'll talk down to you. I . . . I get that much."

"Who are you, anyhow?" asked Meredith of the Chief.

He told her. "And I am here to get to the bot-tom of a crime. Now, young lady," the Chief was no longer speaking with any jovial look at all, "you jumped to a wrong conclusion, you know. She *was* guilty."

"I don't see *why* you've always thought so," said Meredith rebelliously.

"I guess you don't," said Barker. "Because it's a matter of experience. Of a lot of things. In the first place, I know what my routine investiga-tion can or cannot turn up. When it turns up *no* sign of any stranger whatsoever, I tend to believe that there wasn't one."

The Chief's jaw was thrust forward. The lit-tle girl did not wince. She listened gravely.

"In the second place, as you noticed yourself, there's nobody else around here to suspect. In the third place, nine times out of ten, only a wife is close enough to a man to have a strong enough motive."

"Nine times out of ten," said Meredith scornfully.

"That's experience," said Barker, "and you scoff at the nine times because you think we for-get that there can be a tenth time. You are wrong, young lady. Now, somebody shot Harry Corco-ran . . ."

"Why don't you suspect Uncle John?" flashed Meredith.

"No motive," snapped Barker.

"Meredith," began her Uncle, "I'm afraid you . . ."

"Speak up," said Russell.

"Yes. Right." Selby straightened again. "Well, then, listen. I'd no more murder a man as a favor to a neighbor than I'd jump over the moon. Your whole idea—that Josephine Corcoran would *think* I had—is ridiculous. Whatever she is, she's too mature for that. Furthermore, I never did want to marry her. And your mother may skin me for this but so help me you'd better know, men sometimes don't and women know it." Meredith blinked. "Also, even if I had," roared her Uncle John, "Barker knows it might occur to me that there is such a thing as divorce. Just as good a way to get rid of a husband, and a lot safer than murder."

Meredith's tongue came out and licked her lip.

"Now, as to her motive, she hated Harry Corcoran bitterly . . . bitterly. She's . . . well, she's wicked. To know that is . . . is a matter of experience. You spot it. Some cold and selfish, yet hot and reckless thing. That's the best I can do."

"It's not bad," said Meredith humbly, "I mean, thank you, Uncle John. Where is she now?"

"In the hospital," said Chief Barker, "with my men keeping their eye on her."

"Was she hurt?"

The doctor cleared his throat. "She's being hysterical. That is, you see, she was startled into making a terrible mistake when she pushed you, my dear. Now, all she can think to do is fake a physical or psychic collapse. But it's strictly a phony. I can't tell you exactly how I know that . . ."

"I suppose it's experience," said Meredith solemnly. She seemed to retreat deeper into the pillow. "I was all wrong about her. The town was *right*!" She looked as if she might cry, having been forced to this concession.

Russell said briskly. "That's not enough. No good simply saying you were wrong. You need to understand what happened to you, just how you were led."

"Led?" said Meredith distastefully.

"The widow was guilty," Russell said. "Begin with that. Now look back at the time you first hung over her gate. You couldn't know she was guilty or even suspect it, because you hadn't so much as heard about the murder yet. How could you guess the fright she got, remembering that little girl in the tree? You thought it was retroactive worry—that you might have fallen. Because that is a kind of fear in your experience. Do you see, now, when you turned up, so full of vigor and intelligence, that she never felt less like smiling in her life. *Of course* she took you seriously. And you were charmed."

"Naturally," said Meredith bravely.

"I can see, and now you should be able to see, how she tried to use your impulsive sympathy. Maybe she hoped that when you tried—as you were bound to try—to remember the night, long ago, that your imagination would be biased in her favor."

"I guess it was," said Meredith bleakly.

"Probably, she tried to put suspicion of your Uncle John into your head, not from innocence, but to supply a missing suspect to the keen and much too brainy curiosity that had her terrified. Now, don't be downcast," the lawyer added, his warm smile breaking. "I'd have been fooled, too. After all, this is hindsight."

"Probably you wouldn't have been fooled," said Meredith stolidly. "Experience, huh?"

"I've met a few murderers before," said Russell gently.

"Well, I've met a murderess now," said Meredith gravely. "Boy, was I ever dumb!" She sighed.

The Chief said, "All clear? Okay. Now, what do you say we find out where you were *smart*? What *did* it? Can't we get to that?"

"Smart?" said Meredith.

"This is our question to you, young lady. What cracked Mrs. Corcoran's nerve? Where were you in the story when she flew at you and pushed you down the stairs?"

The girl was motionless.

"You see, dear," began the doctor.

"She sees," said her Uncle John ferociously.

Meredith gave him a grateful lick of the eye. "Well, I was just past the key . . ." she said. She frowned. "And *then* she yelled and pushed me." The brown eyes turned, bewildered.

"What were the exact words?" said Barker briskly, "Russell, read that part again."

But Russell repeated, lingeringly, "Just past the key . . . ?"

"I don't get it," Barker said. "Do you?"

"I just thought she'd be glad," said Meredith in a small groan. "But she pushed me and hurt me. I got it *wrong*." She seemed to cower. She was watching Russell.

"You got it right," said he. "Listen. And follow me. Harry Corcoran was shot in the back."

"That's right," the Chief said.

"The key was on the doorstep." The lawyer was talking to the girl.

"I picked it up," said Selby.

"All this time we've been assuming that he dropped the key *because he was shot*. But that isn't what you said, Meredith. *You* said that he dropped the key *because he was drunk*. Now, all this time we have assumed that he was shot from behind, from somewhere near the hedge. But if you got it right, when he bent over to pick up the key . . . and was shot in the back . . ." Russell waited. He didn't have to wait long.

"*She* shot him from above," said Meredith, quick as a rabbit. "*She* was upstairs."

"From *above*," said Barker, sagging. "And the widow's been waiting for seven years for some bright brain around here to think of that. Yep. Shot from a screenless window. Threw the gun out, closed the window, opened her door, faced her maid. Pretty cool. Pretty lucky. Pretty smart. And there is nothing you could call evidence, even yet." But the Chief was not discouraged or dismayed. He patted the bed covers. "Don't you worry, honey. You got her, all right. And I've made out with less. By golly, I got her method, now, and that's going to be leverage. And, by golly, one thing she's going to have to tell me, and that is *why* she pushed you down the stairs."

"She needn't have," said Meredith, in the same thin, woeful voice. "*I* didn't know . . . *I* didn't understand." Then her face changed and something was clicking in her little head. "But she still *thinks* I saw him drop the key. Couldn't I go where she is? Couldn't I . . . break her down? I could *act*." The voice trailed off. They weren't going to let her go, the four grown men.

"*I'm* going," said Selby grimly. "I'll break her down."

"Stay in bed," said the doctor, at the same time. "Nurse will be here. I may be needed with the widow."

"And I," said Russell. But still he didn't move. "Miss Lee," he said to the little girl, "may I make a prophecy? You'll go on studying the whole world, you'll get experience, and acquire insight, and you will not give up until you become a writer." He saw the brown eyes clear; the misting threat dried away. He laid the notebook on the covers. "You won't need to be there," he said gently, "because you can imagine." He held out a pencil. "Maybe you'd like to be working on an ending?" She was biting her left thumb but her right hand twitched as she took the pencil.

"Meredith," said her Uncle John, "here's one thing you can put in. You sure took the stuffing out of me. And I don't care what your mother's going to say . . ."

Meredith said, as if she were in a trance, "When is Mama coming?"

"In the morning. I wish I hadn't wired—I wish I hadn't alarmed her . . . We're going to be in for it."

"Oh, I don't know, Uncle John," said Meredith. The face was elfin now, for a mocking second of time. Then it was sober. She put the pencil into her mouth and stared at the wall. The nurse moved closer. The four men cleared their throats. Nothing happened. Meredith was gone, imagining. Soon the four grown men tiptoed away.

Meredith Lee. New notes and Jottings.

July 27th.

Early to bed. Supposed to be worn out. False, but convenient for all of us.

Everybody helped manage Mama. Doctor Coles put a small pink bandage on me. Chief Barker and Mr. Russell met her train and said gloating things about the widow confessing.

But, of course, Mama had to blast us some. She was just starting to rend Uncle John when I said, "Don't be so cross with him, Mama. He is the Hero. Saved my life." That took her aback. She was about to start on me, but Uncle John jumped in. "Meredith's the Heroine, sis. She broke the case."

Well, Mama got distracted. She forgot to be mad at us any more. "What's going on with you two?" she wanted to know. Well, I guess she could see that the stuffing was out of both of us.

(N.B. Men are interesting. M.L.)

FLOWERS FOR AN ANGEL

Nigel Morland

THE INDEFATIGABLE NIGEL MORLAND, who was born Carl Van Biene (1905–1986), wrote approximately three hundred books under his own name and a gallimaufry of pseudonyms that included John Donavan, Norman Forrest, Roger Garnett, and Neal Shepherd.

Self-educated, Morland worked in printing, bookbinding, and advertising, as a mortuary assistant, and in journalism, covering crime stories in China and working for several Far Eastern newspapers while studying forensic medicine as a sideline. He edited numerous magazines, several fiction but mainly medical, notably *The Criminologist*, which he edited from its inception in 1966 until his death.

His most controversial novel was *Death Takes an Editor* (1949), which dealt with masochistic sex—a subject never before portrayed candidly in a mystery novel—shocking to readers as it came from the pen of an author whose work generally was on the cozy side.

Morland's most successful mysteries featured Mrs. Palmyra Pym, deputy assistant commissioner of the Metropolitan Police, who appeared in more than twenty books, beginning with *The Phantom Gunman* (1935). Mrs. Pym—yes, she was married, but be prepared for her wrath if you mention it, as she regards it as the biggest (perhaps only) mistake she's ever made—is an indomitable detective who will go to any lengths to bring a criminal to justice and has no problem carrying an automatic pistol, though she doesn't really know how to use it, so sometimes winds up brawling with bad guys, the same as any other cop.

Morland wrote the original story and some of the dialogue for *Mrs. Pym of Scotland Yard* (1940), which starred Mary Clare as the titular character and Edward Lexy as Detective Inspector Shott.

"Flowers for an Angel" was originally published in the September 1951 issue of *Ellery Queen's Mystery Magazine*; it was first collected in *Mrs. Pym and Other Stories* (Henley-on-Thames, Aiden Ellis, 1976).

Flowers for an Angel

NIGEL MORLAND

SOME WOMEN HAVE SAID that Mrs. Pym was never young, that even in her initial stages she was probably an elderly baby. Obviously, such women should drink milk out of saucers; still, it is a fact that Mrs. Pym was somehow stolid, enormously capable, and frequently harsh, even in the early 1920's when she must have been around thirty.

She affected the same ugly tweeds, the same enchantingly insane hats, and the same air of magnificent omnipotence as she does today. But her hair was brown then, with only the faintest touch of her current greyness. Her speech was as biting, and her contempt for authority and inefficiency as ready as on that notable day when she crashed the shocked portals of New Scotland Yard, the first woman ever to hold rank in Central C.I.D., where, in these present jittery times of nuclear fission and H-bombs, she is Mrs. Assistant-Commissioner Pym.

In those extraordinary 1920's she had drifted away from the job of chief secretary to the Director of Remounts (War Office, Special Service) in China, where they were still talking about her merciless "I think we're supposed to mount the British Army on Mongolian ponies; God knows why, but we Islanders are notable at confounding the enemy—particularly with the war over and done with!" She arrived, of all places in this world, as a woman detective-sergeant in the sur-

prised ranks of the Shanghai Municipal Police Force.

I was still a cub reporter on the Shanghai *Evening Star.* "Still," because I had publicly stated that Benjamin Cudworth, that aristocratic darling of the Shanghai Club, was selling guns to Wu Pei-fu (which later turned out to be the truth). It made me less than the dust beneath worthy British shoes—me, the Chinese, the Griffins, and the miserable itinerants who were not even Shanghailanders. But it was enough for Mrs. Pym; if she'd been in India she would have turned up at a Hindu dinner-party with an Untouchable. That seemingly granite exterior regarded all stiles as something to help lame dogs over—even if she usually kicked them on their way.

I used to go round to her flat in Bubbling Well Road, where I could watch the races, or the golfers in the middle of the central racecourse. She always had a liking for reporters—wasn't she one herself for a year?—though what she told me about the local social set should not have been poured into my nineteen-year-old ears: I thought the Country Club people were next to holiness—*she* stripped off their outward façades with the zest of a kid tearing the wrapping off candy.

Her private life was a mystery to me. I knew Richard Pym had been a retired ironmaster, that he had died a few months after their marriage (the Country Club went to town on that!), and that because the Municipal Council was regretting her appointment she was given no more than routine assignments—mostly traffic violations and such things—which were not C.I.D. work at all.

But when Klara Dimmick came drifting down the Whangpoo one chill winter's night, it became Mrs. Pym's business. She and I were in a large sampan, illegally moored off the Customs' Wharf. She was bartering for some rather nice jade which the boatman said was his father's—he claimed to be a refugee from Nanking. I daresay the jade was loot, since Wu Pei-fu was on the rampage: when those old-time *tuchuns* broke out, it was every native for himself.

An uproar from the family end of the sampan brought Mrs. Pym from under the reed-matted mid-structure, and there was Klara, large, Nordic, and beautiful, sitting gracefully in the stern of a dinghy, drifting superbly on the muddy, littered current.

The dinghy was gaffed. Mrs. Pym craned over to have a look, with the help of my pocket torch.

"Klara Dimmick," I said, "wife of——"

"All right, son, I know Dimmick of China Oil. H'm . . . that looks like a dagger wound in her front."

"Murder?"

"Could be." She snapped at the chattering sampan family in Shanghai dialect which, naturally, none of them understood; but her tone promoted something like silence. "Showy piece, isn't she?" Mrs. Pym's sniff was loud. A violent woman herself, she dislikes physically ostentatious human beings. "Lug her to the bank and we'll have a look-see."

You can't keep anything quiet in China. Every idler on the Bund had gathered round when we checked over Klara on the edge of the Customs' Wharf. The Chinese spectators were I-told-you-so-ing for all they were worth because, they maintained, her red hair was the unluckiest thing that could happen to her. I suggested the dagger wound was more immediately so. Mrs. Pym grimaced.

"Don't be childish, boy." She picked out an intelligent looking coolie and told him to nip along the Dzing-boo-vaung for help—the very mention of the police station scared him off. Finally, a stout Chinese who looked like, and admitted he was, a compradore agreed to do the job if she paid for a rickshaw on a generous basis—a Scot has nothing on a Chinese when it comes to money.

Mrs. Pym, wearing a camel's hair overcoat which gave her an impressive heaviness, crouched on the edge of the Wharf, studying the corpse. I knelt beside her, focusing the torch.

"That's a good coat she's wearing, though it's the wrong shade of mauve for a redhead, and she's too big for the double-breasted style." Her blue-grey eyes glanced at me with faint malice. "One of her earrings has fallen off—see it, caught in the coat folds? Not there, you blind young ass—on the left side, where it's buttoned." I saw the gewgaw and nodded my comprehension. "I doubt if it means anything much. Oh, we-tsen, we-tsen!" The encroaching crown moved back at the order. "Haul that painter up and let's see." Mrs. Pym paused. I had grabbed the rope, pulling its sodden, clammy length. At the end, attached with a bit of baling wire, was a bunch of ordinary red poppies, though the river had washed many of the heads away.

Mrs. Pym's snort was terrific.

"Is that supposed to be significant? Our thoughtful murderer! A coffin would have been more useful—here; give me those flowers." She wrapped them in the man's handkerchief she always carried, for though she was not that major horror, a masculine woman, she loathed the frail, feminine fripperies women are said to prefer.

"Won't there be trouble if you take those flowers?"

"Son, I've had trouble all my life. This is my case and I'll damn' well handle it Pym fashion. I'm sick of chasing birds who sound their hooters after midnight—this time I'm having my own way." She turned at the tramp of feet on the road. Inspector Gaylor, that big, amiable police officer from Wicklow, was there with his squad. "Oh, it's you, Inspector, somebody stabbed a hole in Klara Dimmick, chucked her in this dinghy, and I'm handling the case—and no loopy S.M.C. councillor is going to stop me!"

Gaylor waved protestingly.

"Why, ma'am, would you have me comment?" His smile was infectious—at least, I smiled back. "I'm only a poor cop, doing his duty. Now why would I be wanting to take the case away from you?"

When the examination was over, Gaylor said: "Sort of thing a native would do."

"Native my foot!" Mrs. Pym gestured irately. "You never came across one of them with that kind of imagination—betcha million dollars you never did! No," she added, shaking the orthodox Gaylor to the roots, "we'll find the beginnings of this somewhere in our own sacred upper crust, and when I've finished, I'll teach that socially-elect jellyfish to swing something out of Nick Carter on me!"

Ernest Dimmick was roused from bed at two o'clock in the morning. He lived in a very respectable house opposite the French Club. It did not matter a row of native beans to Mrs. Pym that she was in the French Concession on her official occasions; she administered the law as it stood, and when it didn't, she made personal adjustments.

The Number One boy brought him down, and Dimmick received us in the florid sitting-room. He was a gentle little man, with brown hair and brown eyes behind thick-glassed spectacles. You could almost see Mrs. Pym wondering why meek, small men always marry massive women, seemingly chosen from the front row of the Valkyrie chorus.

"Good evening," said Dimmick, as politely as if he were receiving expected guests. The Shanghai papers had made a sensation out of Mrs. Pym's appointment to the S.M.P., so he knew his visitor. "Is there something I can do for you?"

"I came about Mrs. Dimmick."

"Klara? Oh, yes. Er—perhaps there's something I can do—you see, my wife is at the Light Horse Ball."

"I see. Alone?"

"Oh, no. Won't you sit down? Drinks, perhaps?" Dimmick glanced at me helplessly in face of uncompromising refusals. "Mrs. Dimmick went with Mr. Thrane and his party. I felt somewhat unwell, so I did not go with them."

"Anything serious?"

"Serious?" Dimmick's brown eyes were anxious. "Oh, I see what you mean. No, nothing. A touch of dysentery, I think. I foolishly ate some Chinese melon two days ago. It was that, I imagine."

"What time did Mrs. Dimmick leave?"

"At six, I'm told. They were dining at the Palace, and going on to the Astor House for the ball. Is there anything wrong?"

"I'm afraid there is." Bluntly, but not unkindly, she told him what had happened. Dimmick took it badly. He sank into an armchair and covered his eyes with one hand, a gesture that would have looked theatrical in a more positive man.

"Mrs. Pym, I don't know what to say. I can't—can't think who would have done such a dreadful thing. And I never even saw her!"

"What do you mean?"

"I did not get home from the office till seven. She had already left. I haven't seen her since yesterday morning, and to think I might have spent the day . . ." There was nothing more we could do. We left little Dimmick with his grief.

Mrs. Pym owned a noisy red Bugatti, fast predecessor of the mechanical bullets she was to favour in later life. On the way back to the Settlement she drove with her customary violence.

"Went to a ball in a dark blue dress and a double-breasted coat!" Her sniff was devastating. "Dimmick's being taken for a sucker, if you ask me, son"—she paused to bang the horn at a dawdling rickshaw coolie, cursing him liberally as she went by—"son, there's more in this than meets a blind cat's eye. Know anything about Klara?"

"Social, or otherwise?"

"Otherwise."

"Not much. She was a Klara Zimmermann before she married. Came from Tsingtao, where the Germans are. She's about thirty, I think. Got a good reputation. She's on the board of the Rickshawmen's Mission. I've never heard anything but good about her."

"Huh! That tells me what I want to know." The uncharitable remark was typical. "No children?" I shook my head. "My friend, if you ever want to be suspicious, then suspect a good German girl with a nice little husband when she has no children." She braked the Bugatti in front of central police headquarters. "Come on in. I'll see the dogs don't bite you."

Lights were burning and there was an air of excitement. A murdered European was something apart from routine—the police station felt like my office when an exclusive story comes in. The Shanghai Municipal Council, in the form of the chairman, a tubby little man named Belper—he made half a million when he started the omnibus service—was there, throwing his weight about.

"This has got to be cleared up, and cleared up quick," he was telling gentle old Superintendent Laystall as we entered the general office. "Who the devil said that woman was to be in charge?"

"I said so." Mrs. Pym tramped across the boards, her eyes bleak and her hands deep in her pockets. Though she is of middle height, she made Belper look small. "I found the body, and I'm in charge."

"Says who?" Belper wanted to know. "You haven't got your superior officer's permission, and the Council won't stand for it."

"The Council can lump it. Police procedure——"

"Police fiddlesticks!" Belper looked as if he would dance with rage. "This is a serious matter. I'm not going to——"

"No?" Her strong mouth became a thin line; I felt for Belper when her hands went on her hips. "Mr. Belper, I am a properly constituted law-enforcement officer. I was there when the body of Klara Dimmick was found, and as a ranking C.I.D. detective I'm taking charge." She moved forward, Belper skipped towards Laystall, who was trying not to smile. "I don't give a minor hoot in Hades for the S.M.C. I'm handling this case until I'm officially taken off it. You're chairman of the Council, but in this office at this time you're an ordinary citizen. Take it or leave it."

"I'll take it. I'll call a meeting tomorrow and have you thrown out." Belper was livid. "I opposed your appointment in the first place, and I'm not going to stand for this!" He stormed towards the door, ridiculously like a cockerel. But he came to a halt and we saw his ears become bright red as Mrs. Pym said mildly:

"If you want to borrow my car, you may. You'll never get a taxi to Nadja Sheridan's little flat in Jessfield Park at this time of morning."

Belper went out quietly. Even Laystall laughed, later in the day, when we heard Belper had gone up-country on urgent business for a week. But now the superintendent was not laughing.

"Mrs. Pym, you know that's no way to behave."

Her slight smile was frosty.

"No, sir. We girls get our tantrums." Her bleak eyes dared him to laugh at the feeble jest. "What about Klara?"

"Dr. Swann has seen the coroner and he'll be at work in the hour. We agreed on that, rather than wait till a more reasonable hour."

"What about identification, sir?"

"Her Number One boy is coming down. I spoke to Dimmick. He's upset—and you can't blame him. He thought the world of her. By the way, what were you doing in the French Concession?"

"Our friend here," Mrs. Pym waved to me without hesitation, "is a journalist and wanted to interview Dimmick. The least I could do was give him a lift." She nodded as if pleased. "I'm not officially on duty, y'know."

"Aren't you?" Laystall was surprised. "I thought . . ."

"According to Belper, we don't think, sir, we're S.M.C. puppets. However, that's not important. D'you know anything about Klara Dimmick? Had she any lovers, or that sort of thing?" Mrs. Pym looked down her nose: she is no puritan, but she is a fastidious woman.

"Klara Dimmick!" Laystall was shocked. "Good Lord, no! Don't you go asking things like that or there really will be trouble. Why, she gave a thousand dollars to the Police Charity last November."

"Our friend here," she waved to me again, "told me she's the goddess of the Rickshaw-men's Mission as well—a spreader of sweetness and light." Her eyes were sardonic. "Where does she get that much money—on Dimmick's pay?"

"He's Number Three man in China Oil," Laystall protested.

"He still wouldn't have that much to spare, not in Shanghai with a wife who wears imported Paris models."

"What about asking Stein? She banks with him," I suggested.

Mrs. Pym never wastes time asking how you know things. She got on the phone and routed Stein out of bed, which, as president of the New York–Oriental Banking Corporation, he resented.

"I'm sorry to spoil your beauty sleep." She briefly explained what had happened. "I'm asking you, unofficially, to tell me Klara Dimmick's position. Eh? A rich woman, is she?" Mrs. Pym listened and put down the receiver, turning to us. "Worth more than a hundred thousand, he says: usually banks about ten thousand a few times every year, in cash."

I whistled. "Smelly?"

Laystall was offended.

"I don't think you should talk like that about her. I've never heard a thing to her discredit."

Mrs. Pym shrugged.

"Superintendent, you've got a nice mind; I haven't. True virtue, as our native friends insist, shelters behind a polite palm; a parade of good works is intended to distract the eye from other, less virtuous, things."

There was nothing more to be done then. Mrs. Pym ran me home to my digs in Yangtze-poo, telling me I could tag along with her if I was at her flat not later than eight-thirty—that meant turning my story early. I didn't mind.

"It looks good," I said, climbing out of the Bugatti into the chill, faintly hot-oil-and-garlic atmosphere which is pure Shanghai background. "As a rule, you don't get out-and-out thrillers in China."

Mrs. Pym wrinkled her nose.

"Go to bed and dream, or do a little research, son. Shinaingan was writing first-class thrillers here—with fingerprints and all—when Edgar Allan Poe's ancestors were being seasick on the *Mayflower*. Night-night."

Mrs. Pym's office was a small room at the top of police headquarters from which, if she felt like looking, she had a nice view of the S.M.C. building. Enthroned behind her neat, ancient desk, she permitted me to stay on the condition I took notes and kept my mouth shut. Her net had been cast ruthlessly, and before me was a list:

Johnnie Thrane
Elise Sartoris
Benjamin Cudworth
Lily Rogers
Ernest Dimmick
Fu Chwang
Dr. Swann
Morris Stein

The system of interviewing them was equally ruthless. Johnnie Thrane was first, and when he sat down it was as if a breath of Bond Street had entered the drab office.

"Mr. Thrane, you will have seen the morning papers. I want you to tell me what happened last night."

Thrane bowed.

"There is so little to say, dear lady. Mrs. Dimmick, Mrs. Sartoris, Mrs. Rogers, Mr. Cudworth, and myself were a small dinner party. We dined at the Palace and reached the Astor House just before nine."

"You were in evening dress?"

"But naturally!" Thrane was shocked. "It was a most formal affair."

"I know my manners, too. Okay, carry on."

"We—ah—did the usual things." Thrane went on in a hurt voice. "At ten Mrs. Dimmick was called to the telephone, and excused herself rather hurriedly."

"Why?"

"One of her protégés was ill. The dear lady was a great one for good works. We simply could not induce her to stay, and off she went."

Elise Sartoris, blonde and languid, substantiated the story, and so did the impeccable Lily Rogers, the Settlement's social leader. Little Benjamin Cudworth, who was always broke but whose connections were blue-blooded, added that Mrs. Dimmick had mentioned she would have to "pop home and change."

Ernest Dimmick admitted he had gone over to the French Club to look at the snooker, and must have missed his wife when she came in.

"I'm not surprised to hear your story," he told Mrs. Pym during his second interview. "Klara had only two passions in life—her benevolent institutions and the works of Richard Wagner. I am not being disloyal but they were, perhaps, almost more important than our—ah—married life . . ."

Fu Chwang, his Number One houseboy, admitted that since his master was out, he was out too—an old China custom.

"Master and mississy no have got. My pay talkee my mama."

"What side mama b'long?" Mrs. Pym wanted to know.

"B'long amah, Tracey Terrace–side. My go maybe one hour."

"You saw your mississy?"

Fu Chwang shook his head. "My cousin b'long rickshaw-coolie. Talkee me mississy ride him rickshaw. Catchee house ten o'clock. Catchee diff'runt clothes, then she go."

"What side?"

"Zeh-lok-phoo, Zikawe Creek-side."

"The end of the French Bund at Siccawei Creek?" Mrs. Pym was surprised. "How fashion what thing?"

"No savvy." Fu Chwang shrugged. "Catchee tall blown house that side. My cousin he talkee me mississy pay him small money. He say, no good, fare one dollah Mex. Wanchee big money. Mississy say 'yeu-tse, yeu-tse!' Very unkind."

"She'd paid enough, had she?" Mrs. Pym turned to me. "Gave the poor devil dimes, obviously."[*] She dismissed Fu Chwang when she found that his cousin had not followed Klara Dimmick, after the usual fashion of a swindled coolie.

In the time-honoured way of all police surgeons, Swann bustled in as if devils were after him.

"Got an appointment," he announced, leaning heavily on his brown leather work-case placed on the edge of the desk. "The corpse was well nourished and all that. Died of a knife thrust. Dead very few hours when I saw her." He twinkled because he liked Mrs. Pym.

"No exciting news?"

"No. With exposure to cold, then being messed about and brought into hot places—well, how can I give any time?"

"No, I see that."

"Nice of you." Swann nodded cheerfully. "Well-built, full-blooded German wench with years of life in her—her mortal twain was neatly cut and now she's buried in a rut . . . or soon will be." Swann beamed. He was given to those appalling, homemade couplets. Mrs. Pym smiled in a sour manner and sat back to wait for Morris Stein.

He was the most unhelpful of the lot. Private bankers in the Far East, then, had never made up their minds if they equalled God, or a mere archangel. Stein belonged to the former school.

---

[*] In those days, ten dimes legally equalled a dollar Mex, but local exchange was such that for a silver dollar one could get anything from ten to fourteen dimes in an exchange bureau, or, in copper, up to nearly two hundred pennies.

He answered Mrs. Pym's questions guardedly. No, he did not know where she got those sums of regular cash she deposited. They were always in twenties, fifties, and hundreds.

Mrs. Pym glared at the stout and impatient banker.

"Look here, Stein, I don't give a copper cash if you're the biggest gun in the Settlement—and there isn't one of your lot who wouldn't steal the wool off the Lamb of God, if he got the chance. I want to know where Klara got that money!"

Stein purpled.

"Mrs. Pym, I'll have you——"

"Oh, bosh. Bankers know everything about their clients. Where did she get it?"

"If I knew, I couldn't reveal professional secrets."

"Professional twiddle! This is a police office and I want your help. Look, friend, shall I tell this lad here—he's a reporter—that you cleared a million running guns up to Mukden for Chang Tso-lin?"

The banker gestured hurriedly.

"Rank libel! I told you I don't know anything. Mrs. Dimmick married an important man. Maybe it wasn't the best of marriages; he's only a runt, after all, and she's a fine woman, or was. There's not a breath of scandal associated with her name."

She let Stein ramble on and dismissed him, ignoring his threats.

"We're nowhere, son," she told me. "Problem is, who killed that lily-white child? I don't believe in white-wash, and, if nothing else, swindling that coolie out of a few dimes convinces me. She's hiding something, and that something is big. Wait a tick." She grabbed the phone and talked to Lorrie Bala, head of China Oil.

Lorrie, who was an Armenian, believed in nothing that was not good legal currency.

"Yes, I know about Dimmick," he said. "Klara? A nice woman. Yes. Did lots of good, wasting money, too, on tramps. Happy? Well, you might say, but she played him around a bit. He is a frustrated little perisher, but Ernie adored her. I don't think she'd risk a lover, but it puzzles me. You know these—well . . . but I never heard anything wrong about her."

Slightly pink, Mrs. Pym told me the story, adding:

"I just don't get it."

"Maybe she *was* a good woman? Maybe it was robbers, or something?"

"Laid her out in a dinghy and hung flowers on it? Don't be so damn silly. It was a man, and a white man."

"It might've been a woman, surely?"

"It was a man and you're blind if you can't see that. The answer's—hell, I'm slipping! Get a wiggle on—we're going to be busy."

The Bugatti went hurtling through the crowded streets. Mrs. Pym always drives as if she's one minute ahead of death. This time she rounded the Bund corner on two wheels, dodging rickshaws, great barrows with their "hi-yah"-ing coolies, and cars, with inspired directness. We raced across the French Concession and reached Siccawei Creek in nine minutes flat from police headquarters, which was impossible.

She walked to a gaunt brown house in Seh-lok-phoo with a little painted sign of a bunch of red poppies over the door. I thought all sorts of things in puzzled wonder.

She spent, she told me, thirty minutes interviewing a stout and unpleasant man named Chow Ling, a typically squat Cantonese. He was not prepared to talk, and once, waiting outside, I heard a muted yell. It worried me. She is never gentle with people who keep their mouths shut when she wants information.

"He wouldn't talk," she explained, when we were haring back to the Settlement. Her eyes were hard. "So I made him."

"How?"

"Proposed to light a little fire on his chest. When that didn't work, he'd spiked my guns. So I found a kitchen knife and made big play that I'd cut off one of his arms." Her eyes were icy. "I'd have been in a hell of a mess if he kept holding out on me! But he talked—there never was a Chinese who'd stand up to the idea of going to his eventual grave with an incomplete body."

"Ah! Did you get anything?"

"What d'you think?"

Superintendent Laystall saw her in his office. He was nice enough to let me be present, on the condition that he saw my story when I'd written it.

Mrs. Pym was cock-a-hoop, even though her face was stony.

"Dirty, filthy case, every bit of it." She frowned at me as if she didn't like my being there. "You and your angelic Klara!" She seemed to be addressing the whole of Shanghai. "A cold and frigid woman to that poor little husband of hers, and as moral as an alley cat outside the house!"

Laystall was shocked.

"I beg your pardon?"

"Granted. Do you know what? Klara Dimmick owned Chow Ling's calling-house! Yes, my gullible and credulous friends—a brothel! That's where she got the cash."

I was shaken. I knew of Chow Ling's only by hearsay—a discreet, exclusive establishment where all the girls were white and desperately expensive. Its watchword was complete ano-nymity and, being in the Chinese City, it could not be touched by the law, for it obviously paid plenty of local *cumshaw*.

"She *owned* it?" Laystall was almost incoherent.

"And she was the highest-priced article there." Mrs. Pym glowered awfully. She is a nice-minded woman, and I could see that she hated telling this story. "It's all been kept very quiet." She told us something of the place.

When Laystall had recovered he asked another question.

"You've found out who killed her?"

"Easily. I told our friend here it was a man when I saw her coat buttoned up, man-fashion."

"And the man?"

"One of her intimate circle—one of those who, like this whole damned town, thought she was an angel."

"Yes?"

"What would you do," she asked Laystall in a different voice, "if you brought yourself to go to one of those places, telephoned, ordered the best in the house"—Mrs. Pym frowned heavily—"and then found yourself in the room *with your own wife*?"

THERE'S DEATH FOR REMEMBRANCE

Frances & Richard Lockridge

PERHAPS THE MOST FAMOUS and successful crime-fighting couple in all of detective fiction (skipping Nick and Nora Charles, who, after all, appeared in only a single book) is Mr. and Mrs. North, the creations of Frances Louise Davis Lockridge (1896–1963) and her husband, Richard Orson Lockridge (1898–1982).

Richard Lockridge was a reporter in Kansas and then drama critic for the *New York Sun*. In the 1930s, he was a frequent contributor to *The New Yorker*, his short stories and articles winning him praise as the archetypical writer for that magazine. His series of non-mystery stories about a publisher and his wife were collected in *Mr. and Mrs. North* (1936).

When Frances Lockridge decided to write a detective story, she became bogged down, and he suggested that she use his creations as the main characters. She devised the plot, he did the actual writing, and the result was *The Norths Meet Murder* (1940), the first of a series of twenty-seven detective novels that ended with *Murder by the Book* in 1963, when Frances died.

The series garnered a great deal of critical praise for its humor and the portrayal of the Greenwich Village neighborhood in which the authors and the Norths lived, but it fell into formulaic plots that disenchanted some critics. Pam's penchant for fearlessly wandering into the villain's path and needing to be rescued in the last chapter irked more than a few readers. Jerry spends most of his time reading manuscripts for his mystery magazine while Pam takes care of the cats and stumbles across bodies, then looks for murderers.

The Norths came to Broadway in *Mr. and Mrs. North* (1941), a comic play by Owen Davis, which served as the basis for a 1942 motion picture of the same title that starred Gracie Allen and William Post, Jr. In the same year, a charming radio series also titled *Mr. and Mrs. North* made its debut and became an instant and enduring success. Barbara Britton and Richard Denning starred in the television series that ran for fifty-seven half-hour episodes (1952–1954).

"There's Death for Remembrance" was originally published in the November 16, 1955, issue of *This Week*; it has been frequently reprinted as "Pattern for Murder" and "Murder for Remembrance."

There's Death for Remembrance

FRANCES & RICHARD LOCKRIDGE

FERN HARTLEY CAME TO NEW YORK to die, although that was far from her intention. She came from Centertown, in the Middle West, and died during a dinner party—given in her honor, at a reunion of schoolmates. She died at the bottom of a steep flight of stairs in a house on West Twelfth Street. She was a little woman and she wore a fluffy white dress. She stared at unexpected death through strangely bright blue eyes. . . .

There had been nothing to foreshadow so tragic an ending to the party—nothing, at any rate, on which Pamela North, who was one of the schoolmates, could precisely put a finger. It was true that Pam, as the party progressed, had increasingly felt tenseness in herself; it was also true that, toward the end, Fern Hartley had seemed to behave somewhat oddly. But the tenseness, Pam told herself, was entirely her own fault, and as for Fern's behavior—well, Fern *was* a little odd. Nice, of course, but—trying. Pam had been tried.

She had sat for what seemed like hours with a responsive smile stiffening her lips and with no comparable response stirring in her mind. It was from that, surely, that the tenseness—the uneasiness—arose. Not from anything on which a finger could be put. It's my own fault, Pam North thought. This is a reunion, and I don't reunite. Not with Fern, anyway.

It had been Fern on whom Pam had responsively smiled. Memories of old days, of schooldays, had fluttered from Fern's mind like pressed flowers from the yellowed pages of a treasured book. They had showered about Pam North, who had been Fern's classmate at Southwest High School in Centertown. They had showered also about Hortense Notson and about Phyllis Pitt. Classmates, too, they had been those years ago—they and, for example, a girl with red hair.

"—*red* hair," Fern Hartley had said, leaning forward, eyes bright with memory. "Across the aisle from you in Miss Burton's English class. Of *course* you remember, Pam. She went with the boy who stuttered."

I *am* Pamela North, who used to be Pamela Britton, Pam told herself, behind a fixed smile. I'm not an impostor; I did go to Southwest High. If only I could prove it by remembering something—anything. Any *little* thing.

"The teacher with green hair?" Pam North said, by way of experiment. "Streaks of, anyway? Because the dye—"

Consternation clouded Fern's bright eyes. *"Pam!"* she said. "That was another one entirely. Miss Burton was the one who—"

It had been like that from the start of the party—the party of three couples and Miss Fern Hartley, still of Centertown. They were gathered in the long living room of the Stanley Pitts' house—the gracious room which ran the depth of the small, perfect house—an old New York house, retaining the charm (if also something of the inconvenience) of the previous century.

As the party started that warm September evening, the charm was uppermost. From open casement windows at the end of the room there was a gentle breeze. In it, from the start, Fern's memories had fluttered.

And none of the memories had been Pam North's memories. Fern has total recall; I have total amnesia, Pam thought, while keeping the receptive smile in place, since one cannot let an old schoolmate down. Did the others try as hard? Pam wondered. Find themselves as inadequate to recapture the dear, dead days?

Both Hortense Notson and Phyllis Pitt had given every evidence of trying, Pam thought, letting her mind wander. Fern was now reliving a perfectly wonderful picnic, of their junior year. Pam was not.

Pam did not let the smile waver; from time to time she nodded her bright head and made appreciative sounds. Nobody had let Fern down; all had taken turns in listening—even the men. Jerry North was slacking now, but he had been valiant. His valor had been special, since he had never even been in Centertown. And Stanley Pitt had done his bit, too; of course, he was the host. Of course, Fern was the Pitts' house guest; what a lovely house to be a guest in, Pam thought, permitting her eyes briefly to accompany her mind in its wandering.

Stanley—what a distinguished-looking man he is, Pam thought—was with Jerry, near the portable bar. She watched Jerry raise his glass as he listened. Her own glass was empty, and nobody was doing anything about it. An empty glass to go with an empty mind, Pam thought, and watched Fern sip ginger ale. Fern never drank anything stronger. Not that she had anything against drinking. Of course not. But even one drink made her feel all funny.

"Well," Pam had said, when Fern had brought the subject up, earlier on. "Well, that's more or less the idea, I suppose. This side of hilarious, of course."

"You know," Fern said then, "you always did talk funny. Remember when we graduated and you—"

Pam didn't remember. Without looking away from Fern, or letting the smile diminish, Pam nevertheless continued to look around the room. How lovely Phyllis is, Pam thought—really is. Blonde Phyllis Pitt was talking to Clark Notson, blond also, and sturdy, and looking younger than he almost certainly was.

Clark had married Hortense in Centertown. He was older—Pam remembered that he had been in college when they were in high school. He had married her when she was a skinny, dark girl, who had had to be prouder than anyone else because her parents lived over a store and not, properly, in a house. And look at her now, Pam thought, doing so. Dark still—and slim and quickly confident, and most beautifully arrayed.

Well, Pam thought, we've all come a long way. (She nodded, very brightly, to another name from the past—a name signifying nothing.) Stanley Pitt and Jerry—neglecting his own wife, Jerry North was—had found something of fabulous interest to discuss, judging by their behavior. Stanley was making points, while Jerry listened and nodded. Stanley was making points one at a time, with the aid of the thumb and the fingers of his right hand. He touched thumbtip to successive fingertips, as if to crimp each point in place. And Jerry—how selfish could a man get—ran a hand through this hair, as he did when he was interested.

"Oh," Pam said. "Of course I remember *him*, Fern."

A little lying is a gracious thing.

What a witness Fern would make, Pam thought. Everything that had happened—beginning, apparently, at the age of two—was brightly clear in her mind, not muddy as in the minds of so many. The kind of witness Bill Weigand, member in good standing of the New York City Police Department, always hoped to find and almost never did—never had, that she could remember, in all the many investigations she and Jerry had shared since they first met Bill years ago.

Fern would be a witness who really remembered. If Fern, Pam thought, knew something about a murder, or where a body was buried, or any of the other important things which so often come up, she would remember it precisely and remember it whole. A good deal of sifting would have to be done, but Bill was good at that.

Idly, her mind still wandering, Pam hoped that Fern did not, in fact, know anything of buried bodies. It could, obviously, be dangerous to have so total a recall and to put no curb on it. She remembered, and this from association with Bill, how often somebody did make that one revealing remark too many. Pam sternly put a curb on her own mind and imagination. What could Fern—pleasant, bubbling Fern, who had not adventured out of Centertown, excepting for occasional trips like these—know of dangerous things?

Pam North, whose lips ached, in whose mind Fern's words rattled, looked hard at Jerry, down the room, at the bar. Get me out of this, Pam willed across the space between them. Get me out of this! It had been known to work or had sometimes seemed to work. It did not now. Jerry concentrated on what Stanley Pitt was saying. Jerry ran a hand through his hair.

"Oh, dear," Pam said, breaking into the flow of Fern's words, as gently as she could. "Jerry wants me for something. You know how husbands are."

She stopped abruptly, remembering that Fern didn't, never having had one. She got up—and was saved by Phyllis, who moved in. What a hostess, Pam thought, and moved toward Jerry and the bar. The idea of saying that to poor Fern, Pam thought. This is certainly one of my hopeless evenings. She went toward Jerry.

"I don't," she said when she reached him, "remember anything about anything. Except one teacher with green hair, and that was the wrong woman."

Jerry said it seemed very likely.

"There's something a little ghoulish about all this digging up of the past," Pam said. "Suppose some of it's still alive?" she added.

"Huh?" Jerry said.

He was told not to bother. And that Pam could do with a drink. Jerry poured, for them both, from a pitcher in which ice tinkled.

"Sometime," Pam said, "she's going to remember that one thing too many. That's what I mean. You see?"

"No," Jerry said, simply.

"Not everybody," Pam said, a little darkly, "wants everything remembered about everything. Because—"

Stanley Pitt, who had turned away, turned quickly back. He informed Pam that she had something there.

"I heard her telling Hortense—" Stanley Pitt said, and stopped abruptly, since Hortense, slim and graceful (and *so* beautifully arrayed) was coming toward them.

"How Fern doesn't change," Hortense said. "Pam, do you remember the boy next door?"

"I don't seem to remember anything," Pam said. "Not anything at all."

"You don't remember," Hortense said. "I don't remember. Phyllis doesn't. And with it all, she's so—sweet." She paused. "Or is she?" she said. "Some of the things she brings up—always doing ohs, the boy next door was. How does one do an oh?"

"Oh," Jerry said, politely demonstrating, and then, "Was he the one with green hair?" The others looked blank at that, and Pam said it was just one of the things she'd got mixed up, and now Jerry was mixing it worse. And, Pam said, did Hortense ever feel she hadn't really gone to Southwest High School at all and was merely pretending she had? Was an impostor?

"Far as I can tell," Hortense said, "I never lived in Centertown. Just in a small, one-room vacuum. Woman without a past." She paused. "Except," she said, in another tone, "Fern remembers me in great detail."

Stanley Pitt had been looking over their heads—looking at his wife, now the one listening to Fern. In a moment of silence, Fern's voice fluted. "Really, a dreadful thing to happen," Fern said. There was no context.

"Perhaps," Stanley said, turning back to them, "it's better to have no past than to live in one. Better all around. And safer."

He seemed about to continue, but then Clark Notson joined them. Clark did not, Pam thought, look like a man who was having a particularly good time. "Supposed to get Miss Hartley her ginger ale," he said. He spoke rather hurriedly.

Jerry, who was nearest the bar, said, "Here," and reached for the innocent bottle—a bottle, Pam thought, which looked a little smug and virtuous among the other bottles. Jerry used a silver opener, snapped off the bottle cap. The cap bounced off, tinkled against a bottle.

"Don't know your own strength," Clark said, and took the bottle and, with it, a glass into which Jerry dropped ice. "Never drinks anything stronger, the lady doesn't," Clark said, and bore away the bottle.

"And doesn't need to," Hortense Notson said, and drifted away. She could drift immaculately.

"She buys dresses," Pam said. "Wouldn't you know?"

"As distinct—?" Jerry said, and was told he knew perfectly well what Pam meant.

"Buys them for, not from," Pam said.

To this, Jerry simply said, "Oh."

It was then a little after eight, and there was a restless circulation in the long room. Pam was with Phyllis Pitt. Phyllis assured her that food would arrive soon. And hadn't old times come flooding back?

"Mm," Pam said. Pam was then with Clark Notson and, with him, talked unexpectedly of tooth paste. One never knows what will come up at a party. It appeared that Clark's firm made tooth paste. Stanley Pitt joined them. He said Clark had quite an operation there. Pam left them and drifted, dutifully, back to Fern, who sipped ginger ale. Fern's eyes were very bright. They seemed almost to glitter.

(But that's absurd, Pam thought. People's don't, only cats'.)

"It's so exciting," Fern said, and looked around the room, presumably at "it." "To meet you all again, and your nice husbands and—" She paused. "Only," she said, "I keep wondering . . ."

Pam waited. She said, "What, Fern?"

"Oh," Fern said. "Nothing dear. Nothing really. Do you remember—"

Pam did not. She listened for a time, and was relieved by Hortense, and drifted on again. For a minute or two, then, Pam North was alone and stood looking up and down the softly lighted room. Beyond the windows at the far end, lights glowed up from the garden below. The room was filled, but not harshly, with conversation—there seemed, somehow, to be more than the seven of them in it. Probably, Pam thought, memories crowded it—the red-haired girl, the stuttering boy.

Fern laughed. Her laughter was rather high in pitch. It had a little "hee" at the end. That little "hee," Pam thought idly, would identify Fern—be something to remember her by. As Jerry's habit of running his hand through his hair would identify him if, about all else, she suddenly lost her memory. (As I've evidently begun to do, Pam North thought.) Little tricks. And Fern puts her right index finger gently to the tip of her nose, presumably when she's thinking. Why, Pam thought, she did that as a girl, and was surprised to remember.

Her host stood in front of her, wondering what he could get her. She had, Pam told him, everything.

"Including your memories?" Stanley Pitt asked her. Pam noticed a small scar on his chin. But it wasn't, of course, the same thing as—as running a hand through your hair. But everybody has something, which is one way of telling them apart.

"I seem," Pam said, "a little short of memories."

"By comparison with Miss Hartley," Stanley said, "who isn't? A pipe line to the past. Can't I get you a drink?"

He could not. Pam had had enough. So, she thought, had all of them. Not that anybody was in the least tight. But still . . .

Over the other voices, that of Fern Hartley was raised. There was excitement in it. So it isn't alcohol, Pam thought, since Fern hadn't had any. It's just getting keyed up at a party. She looked toward Fern, who was talking, very rapidly, to Jerry. No doubt, Pam thought, about what I was like in high school. Not that there's anything he shouldn't know. But still . . .

Fern was now very animated. If, Pam thought, I asked whether anyone here was one cocktail up I'd—why, I'd say Fern. Fern, of all people. Or else, Pam thought, she has some exciting surprise.

It was now eight thirty. A maid appeared at the door, waited to be noticed, and nodded to Phyllis Pitt, who said, at once, "Dinner, everybody." The dining room was downstairs, on a level with the garden. "These old stairs," Phyllis said. "Everybody be careful."

The stairs were, indeed, very steep, and the treads very narrow. But there were handrails and a carpet. The stairway ended in the dining room, where candles glowed softly on the table, among flowers.

"If you'll sit—" Phyllis said, starting with Pam North. "And you and—" They moved to the places indicated. "And Fern—" Phyllis said, and stopped. "Why," she said, "where is—"

She did not finish, because Fern Hartley stood at the top of the steep staircase. She was a slight figure in a white dress. She seemed to be staring fixedly down at them, her eyes strangely bright. Her face was flushed and she made odd, uncertain movements with her little hands.

"I'm—" Fern said, and spoke harshly, loudly, and so that the word was almost a shapeless sound. "I'm—"

And then Fern Hartley, taking both hands from the rails, pitched headfirst down the staircase. In a great moment of silence, her body made a strange, soft thudding on the stairs. She did not cry out.

At the bottom of the red-carpeted stairs she lay quite still. Her head was at a hideous angle to her body—an impossible angle to her body. That was how she died.

Fern Hartley died of a broken neck. There was no doubt. Six people had seen her fall. Now she lay at the bottom of the stairs and no one would ever forget her soft quick falling down that steep flight. An ambulance surgeon confirmed the cause of her death and another doctor from up the street—called when it seemed the ambulance would never get there—confirmed it, too.

But after he had knelt for some time by the body the second doctor beckoned the ambulance surgeon and they went out into the hallway. Then the ambulance surgeon beckoned one of the policemen who had arrived with the ambulance, and the policeman went into the hall with them. After a few minutes, the policeman returned and asked, politely enough, that they all wait upstairs. There were, he said meaninglessly, a few formalities.

They waited upstairs, in the living room. They waited for more than two hours, puzzled and in growing uneasiness. Then a thinnish man of medium height, about whom there was nothing special in appearance, came into the room and looked around at them.

"Why, *Bill*!" Pam North said.

The thinnish man looked at her, and then at Jerry North, and said, "Oh." Then he said there were one or two points.

And then Pam said, "Oh," on a note strangely flat.

How one introduces a police officer, who happens to be an old and close friend, to other friends who happen to be murder suspects—else why was Bill Weigand there?—had long been a moot question with Pam and Jerry North. Pam said, "This is Bill Weigand, everybody. Captain Weigand. He's—he's a policeman. So there must be—" And stopped.

"All right, Pam," Bill Weigand said. Then, "You all saw her fall. Tell me about it." He looked around at them, back at Pam North. It was she who told him.

Her eyes had been "staring"? Her face flushed?

Her movements uncertain? Her voice hoarse? "Yes," Pam said, confirming each statement. Bill Weigand looked from one to another of the six in the room. He received nods of confirmation. One of the men—tall, dark-haired but with gray coming, a little older than the others—seemed about to speak. Bill waited. The man shook his head. Bill got them identified then. The tall man was Stanley Pitt. This was his house.

"But," Bill said, "she hadn't been drinking. The medical examiner is quite certain of that." He seemed to wait for comment.

"She said she never did," Pam told him.

"So—" Bill said.

Then Hortense Notson spoke, in a tense voice. "You act," she said, "as if you think one of us pushed her."

Weigand looked at her carefully. He said, "No. That didn't happen, Mrs. Notson. How could it have happened? You were all in the dining room, looking up at her. How could any of you have pushed her?"

"Then," Clark Notson said, and spoke quickly, with unexpected violence. "Then why all this? She . . . what? Had a heart attack?"

"Possibly," Bill said. "But the doctors—"

Again he was interrupted.

"I've heard of you," Notson said, and leaned forward in his chair. "Aren't you homicide?"

"Right," Bill said. He looked around again, slowly. "As Mr. Notson said, I'm homicide." And he waited.

Phyllis Pitt—the pretty, the very pretty, light-haired woman—had been crying. More than the rest, in expression, in movements, she showed the shock of what had happened. "Those dreadful stairs," she said, as if to herself. "Those dreadful stairs."

Her husband got up and went to her and leaned over her. He touched her bright hair and said, very softly, "All right, Phyl. All right."

"Bill," Pam said. "Fern fell downstairs and—and died. What more is there?"

"You all agree," Bill said, "that she was flushed and excited and uncertain—as if she had been drinking. But she hadn't been drinking. And . . ."

the pupils of her eyes were dilated. That was why she seemed to be staring. Because, you see, she couldn't see where she was going. So . . ." He paused. "She walked off into the air. I have to find out why. So what I want . . ."

It took him a long time to get what he wanted, which was all they could remember, one memory reinforcing another, of what had happened from the start of the dinner party until it ended with Fern Hartley, at the foot of the staircase, all her memories dead. Pam, listening, contributing what she could, could not see that a pattern formed—a pattern of murder.

Fern had seemed entirely normal—at least, until near the end. They agreed on that. She had always remembered much about the past and talked of it. Meeting old school friends, after long separation, she had seemed to remember everything—far more than any of the others.

"Most of it, to be honest, wasn't very interesting." That was Hortense Notson. Hortense looked at Pam, at Phyllis Pitt.

"She was so sweet," Phyllis said, in a broken voice.

"So—so interested herself." Pam said. "A good deal of it was pretty long ago, Bill."

Fern had shared her memories chiefly with the other women. But she had talked of the past, also, with the men.

"It didn't mean much to me," Stanley Pitt said. "It seemed to be all about Centertown, and I've never been in Centertown. Phyllis and I met in New York." He paused. "What's the point of this?" he said.

"I don't know," Bill Weigand told him. "Not yet. Everything she remembered seemed to be trivial? Nothing stands out? To any of you?"

"She remembered I had a black eye the first time she saw me," Clark Notson said. "Hortense and I—when we were going together—ran into her at a party. It was a long time ago. And I had a black eye, she said. I don't remember anything about it. I don't even remember the party, actually. Yes, I'd call it pretty trivial."

"My God," Stanley Pitt said. "*Is* there some point to this?"

"I don't know," Bill said again, and was patient. "Had you known Miss Hartley before, Mr. Pitt?"

"Met her for the first time yesterday," Stanley told him. "We had her to dinner and she stayed the night. Today I took her to lunch, because Phyl had things to do about the party. And—" He stopped. He shrugged and shook his head, seemingly at the futility of everything.

"I suppose," Jerry North said, "the point is— did she remember something that somebody— one of us—wanted forgotten?"

"Yes," Bill said. "It may be that."

Then it was in the open. And, with it in the open, the six looked at one another; and there was a kind of wariness in the manner of their looking. Although what on earth I've got to be wary about I don't know, Pam thought. Or Jerry, she added in her mind. She couldn't have told Jerry anything about me. Well, not anything important. At least not very . . .

"I don't understand," Phyllis said, and spoke dully. "I just don't understand at all. Fern just— just fell down those awful stairs."

It became like a game of tennis, with too many players, played in the dark. "Try to remember," Bill had told them; and it seemed they tried. But all they remembered was apparently trivial.

"There was something about a boy next door," Phyllis Pitt remembered. "A good deal older than she was—than we all were. Next door to Fern. A boy named—" She moved her hands helplessly. "I've forgotten. A name I'd never heard before. Something—she said something dreadful—happened to him. I suppose he died of something."

"No," Hortense Notson said. "She told me about him. He didn't die. He went to jail. He was always saying 'oh.'" She considered. "I think," she said, "he was named Russell something." She paused again. "Never in my life, did I hear so much about people I'd never heard of. Gossip about the past."

Stanley Pitt stood up. His impatience was evident.

"Look," he said. "This is my house, Captain. These people are my guests. Is any of this badgering getting you anywhere? And . . . where is there to get? Maybe she had a heart attack. Maybe she ate something that—" He stopped, rather abruptly; rather as if he had stumbled over something.

Weigand waited, but Pitt did not continue. Then Bill said they had thought of that. The symptoms—they had all noticed the symptoms— including the dilation of the pupils, might have been due to acute food poisoning. But she had eaten almost nothing during the cocktail period. The maid who had passed canapés was sure of that. Certainly she had eaten nothing the rest had not. And she had drunk only ginger ale, from a freshly opened bottle.

"Which," Bill said, "apparently you opened, Jerry."

Jerry North ran his right hand through his hair. He looked at Bill blankly.

"Of course you did," Pam said. "So vigorously the bottle cap flew off. Don't you—"

"Oh," Jerry said. Everybody looked at him. "Is that supposed—"

But he was interrupted by Pitt, still leaning forward in his chair. "Wait," Pitt said, and put right thumb and index finger together, firmly, as if to hold a thought pinched between them. They waited.

"This place I took her to lunch," Stanley said. "It's a little place—little downstairs place, but wonderful food. I've eaten there off and on for years. But . . . I don't suppose it's too damned sanitary. Not like your labs are, Clark. And the weather's been hot. And—" He seemed to remember something else and held this new memory between thumb and finger. "Miss Hartley ate most of a bowl of ripe olives. Said she never seemed to get enough of them. And . . . isn't there something that can get into ripe olives? That can poison people?" He put the heel of one hand to his forehead. "God," he said. "Do you suppose it was that?"

"You mean food poisoning?" Weigand said. "Yes—years ago people got it from ripe olives.

But not recently, that I've heard of. New methods and—"

"The olives are imported," Pitt said. "From Italy, I think. Yes. Dilated pupils—"

"Right," Bill said. "And the other symptoms match quite well. You may—"

But now he was interrupted by a uniformed policeman, who brought him a slip of paper. Bill Weigand looked at it and put it in his pocket and said, "Right," and the policeman went out again.

"Mr. Notson," Bill said, "you're production manager of the Winslow Pharmaceutical Company, aren't you?"

Notson looked blank. He said, "Sure."

"Which makes all kinds of drug products?"

Notson continued to look blank. He nodded his head.

"And Mr. Pitt," Bill Weigand said. "You're—"

He's gone off on a tangent, Pam North thought, half listening. What difference can it make that Mr. Notson makes drugs—or that Mr. Pitt tells people how to run offices and plants better—is an "efficiency engineer"? Because just a few minutes ago, somebody said something really important. Because it was wrong. Because— Oh! Pam thought. It's on the tip of my mind. If people would only be quiet, so I could think. If Bill only wouldn't go off on these—

"All kinds of drugs," Bill was saying, from his tangent, in the distance. "Including preparations containing atropine?"

She heard Clark Notson say, "Yes. Sure."

"Because," Bill said, and now Pam heard him clearly—very clearly—"Miss Hartley had been given atropine. It might have been enough to have killed her, if she had not had quick and proper treatment. She'd had enough to bring on dizziness and double vision. So that, on the verge of losing consciousness, she fell downstairs and broke her neck. Well?"

He looked around.

"The ginger ale," Jerry said. "The ginger ale I opened. That . . . opened so easily. Was that it?"

"Probably," Bill said. "The cap taken off carefully. Put back on carefully. After enough atropine

sulphate had been put in. Enough to stop her remembering." Again he looked around at them; and Pam looked, too, and could see nothing—except shock—in any face. There seemed to be fear in none.

"The doctors suspected atropine from the start," Bill said, speaking slowly. "But the symptoms of atropine poisoning are very similar to those of food poisoning—or ptomaine. If she had lived to be treated, almost any physician would have diagnosed food poisoning—particularly after Mr. Pitt remembered the olives—and treated for that. Not for atropine. Since the treatments are different, she probably would not have lived." He paused. "Well," he said, "what did she remember? So that there was death for remembrance?"

Phyllis Pitt covered her eyes with both hands and shook her head slowly, dully. Hortense Notson looked at Weigand with narrowed eyes and her husband with—Pam thought—something like defiance. Stanley Pitt looked at the floor and seemed deep in thought, to be planning each thought between thumb and finger, when Weigand turned from them and said, "Yes?" to a man in civilian clothes. He went to talk briefly with the man. He returned. He said the telephone was a useful thing; he said the Centertown police were efficient.

"The boy next door," Weigand said, "was named Russell Clarkson. He was some years—fifteen, about—older than Fern Hartley. Not a boy any more, when she was in high school, but still 'the boy next door.' He did go to jail, as you said, Mrs. Notson. He helped set up a robbery of the place he worked in. A payroll messenger was killed. Clarkson got twenty years to life. And—he escaped in two years, and was never caught. And—*he was a chemist*. Mr. Notson. As you are. Mr. *Clark* Notson."

Notson was on his feet. His face was very red and he no longer looked younger than he was. He said, "You're crazy! I can prove—" His voice rose until he was shouting across the few feet between himself and Weigand.

And then it came to Pam—came with a

kind of violent clarity. "Wait, Bill. *Wait!*" Pam shouted. "It wasn't 'ohs' at all. Not *saying* them. That's what was wrong."

They were listening. Bill was listening.

Then Pam pointed at Hortense. "You," she said, "the first time you said *doing* ohs. Not saying 'Oh.' You even asked how one *did* an oh. We thought it was the—the o-h kind of O. But—it was the *letter* O. And—*look at him now!* He's doing them now. *With his fingers.*"

And now she pointed at Stanley Pitt, who was forming the letter O with the thumb and index finger of his right hand; who now, violently, closed into fists his betraying hands. A shudder ran through his body. But he spoke quietly, without looking up from the floor.

"She hadn't quite remembered," he said, as if talking of something which had happened a long time ago. "Not quite." And he put the thumb and index finger tip to tip again, to measure the smallness of a margin. "But—she would have. She remembered everything. I've changed a lot and she was a little girl, but . . ."

He looked at his hands. "I've always done that, I guess," he said. He spread his fingers and looked at his hands. "Once it came up," he said, "there would be fingerprints. So—I had to try." He looked up, then, at his wife. "You see, Phyl, that I had to try?"

Phyllis covered her face with her hands.

After a moment Stanley Pitt looked again at his hands, spreading them in front of him. Slowly he began to bring together the fingertips and thumbtips of both hands; and he studied the movements of his fingers intently, as if they were new to him. He sat so, his hands moving in patterns they had never been able to forget, until Weigand told him it was time to go.

MOM SINGS AN ARIA

James Yaffe

MOST OF THE STORIES AND NOVELS of James Yaffe (1927–2017) have featured his most popular detective character, Mom, a Jewish widow who lives in the Bronx. A true armchair detective, Mom solves cases for her son, a detective, merely by listening to his accounts of the evidence during their traditional Friday-night dinners. These stories were frequent winners in the annual *Ellery Queen's Mystery Magazine* contests and spawned five novels, beginning with *A Nice Murder for Mom* (1988).

Born in Chicago, Yaffe moved to New York City at an early age and wrote his first story while still in high school. That effort, "Department of Impossible Crimes," was published in *Ellery Queen's Mystery Magazine*, launching a series of stories about Paul Dawn and the fictional division of the NYPD that he heads. The clever plotting garnered Yaffe a following deeply devoted to his exceptional narratives of fair-play detective fiction.

After Yaffe graduated from Yale, he served in the navy and spent a full year in Paris before launching his writing career. A book of non-mystery stories, *Poor Cousin Evelyn* (1951), received good reviews, followed by *Nothing but the Night* (1957), a fictionalized version of the famous Leopold-Loeb murder trial. He wrote several plays, the best known being *The Deadly Game* (1960), an adaptation of Friedrich Dürrenmatt's *Traps*; it was the basis for a 1982 television movie with George Segal, Trevor Howard, and Robert Morley. With Jerome Weidman, Yaffe wrote the drama *Ivory Tower* (1969), in which an American poet in 1943 calls for soldiers to lay down their arms in the face of the Nazi onslaught and is accused of treason. Yaffe wrote for numerous television series, including *Studio One*, *The U.S. Steel Hour*, *Suspicion*, and *The Alfred Hitchcock Hour*.

"Mom Sings an Aria" was originally published in the October 1966 issue of *Ellery Queen's Mystery Magazine*; it was first collected in *My Mother, the Detective* (Norfolk, Virginia, Crippen & Landru, 1997).

Mom Sings an Aria

JAMES YAFFE

IT WAS ONE OF THE GREATEST disappointments of my mother's life that I never turned out to be a musical genius. For a couple of years, when I was a kid, Mom made me take violin lessons. At the end of the first year I played a piece called "Rustling Leaves." At the end of the second year I was still playing "Rustling Leaves." Poor Mom had to admit I wasn't another Jascha Heifetz, and that was the end of my musical career.

Mom has always been crazy about music herself. She did a little singing when she was a girl, and might have done something with her voice—instead she got married, moved up to the Bronx, and devoted herself to raising a future Lieutenant in the New York City Homicide Squad. But she still listens regularly to the Saturday afternoon broadcasts of the Metropolitan Opera, and she can still hum along with all the familiar arias. That was why—when my wife Shirley and I went up to the Bronx the other night for our regular Friday dinner—I knew Mom would be interested in my latest case.

"You're a music lover, Mom," I said. "Maybe you can understand how a man could love music so much that he'd commit murder for it."

"This is hard to understand?" Mom said, looking up from her roast chicken. "Why else did I stop your violin lessons? Once, while you were playing one of your pieces, I happened to take a look at your teacher, Mrs. Steinberg—and on her face was murder, if I ever saw it!"

"You don't mean that literally, do you, Mother?" Shirley said. "A woman wouldn't *really* feel like murdering a little boy because he played the violin badly."

"People can have plenty feelings that were never in your psychology books at college," Mom said. "Believe me, in my own family—my Aunt Goldie who thought the pigeon outside her window was actually her late husband Jake—"

Mom went into detail, and her story was fascinating. Then she passed the chicken a second time, and I was able to get back to my murder.

"Have you ever seen the standing-room line at the Metropolitan Opera House?" I said. "Half an hour before every performance the box office sells standing-room tickets at two-fifty each, on a first-come first-served basis. The opera lovers start lining up outside the house hours ahead of time. They stand on their feet for three hours *before* the opera just so they can stand on their feet for three hours *during* the opera! Talk about crazy human motives!"

"People with no ears in their heads," Mom said, "shouldn't be so quick to call other people crazy." And she gave me one of those glares which has been making me feel like a naughty little five-year-old ever since I *was* a naughty little five-year-old.

I turned my eyes away and pushed on. "Well, there are certain people who show up on the opera standing-room line night after night, for practically every performance throughout the season. These 'regulars' are almost always at the head of the line—they come earlier than anyone else, wait longer, and take the best center places once they get inside the house. And since most of them have been doing this for years, they know each other by name, and they pass the time gossiping about the opera singers and discussing the performances. You could almost say they've got an exclusive little social club all their own—only their meeting place isn't a clubhouse, it's the sidewalk in front of the Met. Anyway, you couldn't imagine a more harmless collection of old fogeys—the last group on earth where you'd expect to find a murderer!"

"Even an opera lover has to have a private life," Mom said. "He enjoys himself with the beautiful music—but he's still got business troubles or love troubles or family troubles waiting for him at home."

"That's just it, Mom. If one of these standing-room regulars had gone home and killed his wife or his mother-in-law or his business partner, this would just be a routine case. But what happened was, he killed one of the other people in the standing-room line."

Mom was looking at me with her eyes narrowed—a sure sign that I had her interested. "The two oldest regulars in the standing-room line," I said, "the charter members of the club, are Sam Cohen and Giuseppe D'Angelo. Cohen used to be a pharmacist, with his own drugstore on West Eighty-third Street. He retired fifteen years ago, after his wife died, and turned the management of the store over to his nephew, though he went on living in the apartment above it. As soon as he retired, he started going to the opera almost every night of the season.

"D'Angelo was in the exterminating business out in Queens—insects, rodents, and so on—but *he* retired fifteen years ago too. His wife is alive, but she doesn't care for music, so he's been in the habit of going to the opera by himself—almost every night of the season, just like Cohen.

"The two old men met on the standing-room line fifteen years ago, and have seen each other three or four nights a week ever since—but only at the opera, never anywhere else. As far as we know, they've never met for a drink or a lunch, they've never been to each other's homes, and they've never seen each other at all in the summer, when the opera is closed.

"Opera is the biggest thing in both their lives. Cohen's mother was a vocal coach back in Germany, and he cut his teeth on operatic arias—D'Angelo was born and brought up in the city of Parma, which they tell me is the most operatic city in Italy—"

"I've read about Parma," Mom said. "If a tenor hits a bad note there, they run him out of town."

"How horrible!" Shirley said. "It's positively uncivilized!"

Mom shrugged. "A little less civilization here in New York, and maybe we wouldn't hear so many bad notes."

I could see the cloud of indignation forming on Shirley's face—she never *has* caught on to Mom's peculiar sense of humor. I hurried on, "Well, the two old men both loved opera, but their opinions about it have always been diametrically opposed. So for fifteen years they've been carrying on a running argument. If Cohen likes a certain soprano, D'Angelo can't stand her. If D'Angelo mentions having heard Caruso sing *Aida* in 1920, Cohen says that Caruso never sang *Aida* till 1923.

"And the old men haven't conducted these arguments in nice soft gentlemanly voices either. They yell at each other, wave their arms, call each other all sorts of names. 'Liar' and 'moron' are about the tamest I can think of. In spite of their bitterness, of course, these fights have never lasted long—before the night is over, or at least by the time of the next performance, the old men always make it up between them—"

"Until now?" Mom said.

"I'll get to that in a minute, Mom. Just a little

more background first. According to the other regulars on the standing-room line, the fights between Cohen and D'Angelo have become even more bitter than usual in recent years. They've been aggravated by a controversy which has been raging among opera lovers all over the world. Who's the greatest soprano alive today—Maria Callas or Renata Tebaldi?"

Mom dropped her fork and clasped her hands to her chest, and on her face came that ecstatic, almost girlish look which she reserves exclusively for musical matters. "Callas! Tebaldi! Voices like angels, both of them! That Callas—such fire, such passion! That Tebaldi—such beauty, such sadness! To choose which one is the greatest—it's as foolish as trying to choose between noodle soup and borscht!"

"Cohen and D'Angelo made their choices, though," I said. "D'Angelo announced one day that Tebaldi was glorious and Callas had a voice like a rooster—so right away Cohen told him that Callas was divine and Tebaldi sang like a cracked phonograph record. And the argument has been getting more and more furious through the years.

"A week ago a climax was reached. Callas was singing *Traviata*, and the standing-room line started to form even earlier than usual. Cohen and D'Angelo, of course, were right there among the first. Cohen had a bad cold—he was sneezing all the time he stood in line—but he said he wouldn't miss Callas's *Traviata* if he was down with double pneumonia. And D'Angelo said that personally he could live happily for the rest of his life without hearing Callas butcher *Traviata*—he was here tonight, he said, only because of the tenor, Richard Tucker."

"That Richard Tucker!" Mom gave her biggest, most motherly smile. "Such a wonderful boy—just as much at home in the *schul* as he is in the opera. What a proud mother he must have!" And Mom gave me a look which made it clear that she still hadn't quite forgiven me for "Rustling Leaves."

"With such a long wait on the standing-room line," I said, "Cohen and D'Angelo had time to whip up a first-class battle. According

to Frau Hochschwender—she's a German lady who used to be a concert pianist and now gives piano lessons, and she's also one of the standing-room regulars—Cohen and D'Angelo had never insulted each other so violently in all the years she'd known them. If the box office had opened an hour later, she says they would have come to blows.

"As it turned out, the performance itself didn't even put an end to their fight. Ordinarily, once the opera began, both men became too wrapped up in the music to remember they were mad at each other—but this time, when the first act ended, Cohen grabbed D'Angelo by the arm and accused him of deliberately groaning after Callas's big aria. 'You did it to ruin the evening for me!' Cohen said. He wouldn't pay attention to D'Angelo's denials. 'I'll get even with you,' he said. 'Wait till the next time Tebaldi is singing!'"

"And the next time Tebaldi was singing," Mom said, "was the night of the murder?"

"Exactly. Three nights ago Tebaldi sang *Tosca*—"

"*Tosca!*" Mom's face lighted up. "Such a beautiful opera! Such a sad story! She's in love with this handsome young artist, and this villain makes advances and tries to force her to give in to him, so she stabs him with a knife. Come to think of it, the villain in that opera is a police officer."

I looked hard, but I couldn't see any trace of sarcasm on Mom's face.

"Those opera plots are really ridiculous, aren't they?" Shirley said. "So exaggerated and unrealistic."

"Unrealistic!" Mom turned to her sharply. "You should know some of the things that go on—right here in this building. Didn't Polichek the janitor have his eye on his wife's baby sitter?"

Another fascinating story came out of Mom, and then I went on. "Anyway, for the whole weekend before *Tosca*, D'Angelo worried that Cohen would do something to spoil the performance for him. He worried so much that the night before, he called Cohen up and pleaded with him not to make trouble."

"And Cohen answered?"

"His nephew was in the room with him when the call came. He was going over some account books and didn't really pay attention to what his uncle was saying—but at one point he heard Cohen raise his voice angrily and shout out, 'You can't talk me out of it! When Tebaldi hits her high C in the big aria, I'm going to start booing!'"

Mom shook her head. "Terrible—a terrible threat for a civilized man to make! So does D'Angelo admit that Cohen made it?"

"Well, yes and no. In the early part of the phone conversation, D'Angelo says he and Cohen were yelling at each other so angrily that neither of them listened to what the other one was saying. But later on in the conversation—or so D'Angelo claims—Cohen calmed down and promised to let Tebaldi sing her aria in peace."

"Cohen's nephew says he didn't?"

"Not exactly. He left the room while Cohen was still on the phone—he had to check some receipts in the cash register—so he never heard the end of the conversation. For all he knows Cohen *might* have calmed down and made that promise."

"And what about D'Angelo's end of the phone conversation? Was anybody in the room with *him*?"

"His wife was. And she swears that he *did* get such a promise out of Cohen. But of course she's his wife, so she's anxious to protect him. And besides she's very deaf, and she won't wear a hearing aid—she's kind of a vain old lady. So what it boils down to, we've got nobody's word except D'Angelo's that Cohen didn't intend to carry out his threat."

"Which brings us," Mom said, "to the night Tebaldi sang *Tosca*?"

"Cohen and D'Angelo both showed up early on the standing-room line that night. Frau Hochschwender says they greeted each other politely, but all the time they were waiting they hardly exchanged a word. No arguments, no differences of opinion—nothing. And her testimony is confirmed by another one of the regulars who was there—Miss Phoebe Van Voorhees. She's in her seventies, always dresses in black.

"Miss Van Voorhees came from a wealthy New York family, and when she was a young woman she used to have a regular box at the opera—but the money ran out ten or twelve years ago, and now she lives alone in a cheap hotel in the East Twenties, and she waits on the standing-room line two nights a week. She's so frail-looking you wouldn't think she could stay on her feet for five minutes, much less five hours—but she loves opera, so she does it."

"For love," Mom said, "people can perform miracles."

"Well, Miss Van Voorhees and Frau Hochschwender both say that Cohen and D'Angelo were unusually restrained with each other. Which seems to prove that they were still mad at each other and hadn't made up the quarrel over the phone, as D'Angelo claims—"

"Or maybe it proves the opposite," Mom said. "They *did* make up the quarrel, and they were so scared of starting another quarrel that they shut up and wouldn't express any opinions."

"Whatever it proves, Mom, here's what happened. On cold nights it's the custom among the standing-room regulars for one of them to go to the cafeteria a block away and get hot coffee for the others—meanwhile they hold his place in the line. The night of Tebaldi's *Tosca* was very cold, and it was D'Angelo's turn to bring the coffee.

"He went for it about forty-five minutes before the box office opened, and got back with it in fifteen or twenty minutes. He was carrying four cardboard containers. Three of them contained coffee with cream and sugar—for Frau Hochschwender, Miss Van Voorhees, and D'Angelo himself. In the fourth container was black coffee without sugar—the way Cohen always took it.

"Well, they all gulped down their coffee, shielding it from the wind with their bodies—and about half an hour later the doors opened. They bought their tickets, went into the opera house, and stood together in their usual place in the back at the center.

"At eight sharp the opera began. Tebaldi was in great voice, and the audience was enthusiastic. At the end of the first act all of the standing-room regulars praised her—except Cohen. He just grunted and said nothing. Frau Hochschwender and Miss Van Voorhees both say that he looked pale and a little ill.

"'Wait till she sings her big aria in the second act,' D'Angelo said. 'I hope she sings it good,' Cohen said—and Frau Hochschwender says there was a definite threat in his voice. But Miss Van Voorhees says she didn't notice anything significant in his voice—to her it just sounded like an offhand remark. Then the second act began, and it was almost time for Tebaldi's big aria—"

"Such a beautiful aria!" Mom said. "*Vissy darty.* It's Italian. She's telling that police officer villain that all her life she's cared only for love and for art, and she never wanted to hurt a soul. She tells him this, and a little later she stabs him." And in a low voice, a little quavery but really kind of pretty, Mom began to half sing and half hum—"*Vissy darty, vissy damory*—" Then she broke off, and did something I had seldom seen her do. She blushed.

There was a moment of silence, while Shirley and I carefully refrained from looking at each other. Then I said, "So a few minutes before Tebaldi's big aria, Cohen suddenly gave a groan, then he grabbed hold of Frau Hochschwender's arm and said, 'I'm sick—' And then he started making strangling noises, and dropped like a lead weight to the floor.

"Somebody went for a doctor, and D'Angelo got down on his knees by Cohen and said, 'Cohen, Cohen, what's the matter?' And Cohen, with his eyes straight on D'Angelo's face, said, 'You no-good! You deserve to die for what you did!' Those were his exact words, Mom—half a dozen people heard them.

"Then a doctor came, with a couple of ushers, and they took Cohen out to the lobby—and D'Angelo, Frau Hochschwender, and Miss Van Voorhees followed. A little later an ambulance came, but Cohen was dead before he got to the hospital.

"At first the doctors thought it was a heart attack, but they did a routine autopsy—and found enough poison in his stomach to kill a man half his age and twice his strength. The dose he swallowed must've taken two to three hours to produce a reaction—which means he swallowed it while he was on the standing-room line. Well, nobody saw him swallow *anything* on the standing-room line except that container of hot black coffee."

"And when the doctors looked at the contents of his stomach?"

"They found the traces of his lunch, which *couldn't* have contained the poison or he would've died long before he got to the opera house—and they found that coffee—and that was all they found. So the coffee had to be what killed him."

"And since that old man D'Angelo was the one who gave him the coffee, you naturally think he's the murderer."

"What else can we think, Mom? For five minutes or so—from the time he picked up the coffee at the cafeteria to the time he gave it to Cohen at the opera house—D'Angelo was alone with it. Nobody was watching him—he could easily have slipped something into it. And nobody *else* had such an opportunity. Cohen took the coffee from D'Angelo, turned away to shield the container from the cold wind, and drank it all down then and there. Only D'Angelo *could* have put the poison into it."

"What about the man at the cafeteria who made the coffee?"

"That doesn't make sense, Mom. The man at the cafeteria would have no way of knowing who the coffee was meant for. He'd have to be a complete psycho who didn't care *who* he poisoned. Just the same, though, we checked him out. He poured the coffee into the container directly from a big urn—twenty other people had been drinking coffee from that same urn. Then in front of a dozen witnesses he handed the container to D'Angelo without putting a thing in it—not even sugar, because Cohen never took his coffee with sugar. So we're right back to D'Angelo—he *has* to be the murderer."

"And where did he get it, this deadly poison? Correct me if I'm wrong, but such an item isn't something you can pick up at your local supermarket."

"Sure, it's against the law to sell poison to the general public. But you'd be surprised how easy it is to get hold of the stuff anyway. The kind that killed Cohen is a common commercial compound—it's used to mix paints, for metallurgy, in certain medicines, in insecticides. Ordinary little pellets of rat poison are made of it sometimes, and you can buy them at your local hardware store—a couple of dozen kids swallow them by accident in this city every year. And don't forget, D'Angelo used to be in the exterminating business—he knows all the sources, it would be easier for him to get his hands on poison than for most other people."

"So you've arrested him for the murder?" Mom said.

I gave a sigh. "No, we haven't."

"How come? What's holding you up?"

"It's the motive, Mom. D'Angelo and Cohen had absolutely no connection with each other outside of the standing-room line. Cohen didn't leave D'Angelo any money, he wasn't having an affair with D'Angelo's wife, he didn't know a deep dark secret out of D'Angelo's past. There's only one reason why D'Angelo could have killed him—to stop him from booing at the end of Renata Tebaldi's big aria. That's why he committed the murder. I'm morally certain of it, and so is everyone else in the Department. And so is the D.A.'s office—but they won't let us make the arrest."

"And why not?"

"Because nobody believes for one moment that we can get a jury to believe such a motive. Juries are made up of ordinary everyday people. They don't go to the opera. They think it's all a lot of nonsense—fat women screaming at fat men, in a foreign language. I can sympathize with them—I think so myself. Can you imagine the D.A. standing up in front of a jury and saying, 'The defendant was so crazy about an opera singer's voice that he killed a man for disagreeing with him!' The jury would laugh in the D.A.'s face."

I sighed harder than before. "We've got an airtight case. The perfect opportunity. No other possible suspects. The dying man's accusation—'You no-good! You deserve to die for what you did!' But we don't dare bring the killer to trial."

Mom didn't say anything for a few seconds. Her eyes were almost shut, the corners of her mouth were turned down. I know this expression well—her "thinking" expression. Something always comes out of it.

Finally she looked up and gave a nod. "Thank God for juries!"

"What do you mean, Mom?"

"I mean, if it wasn't for ordinary everyday people with common sense, God knows *who* you experts would be sending to jail!"

"Mom, are you saying that D'Angelo *didn't*—"

"I'm saying nothing. Not yet. First I'm asking. Four questions."

No doubt about it, whenever Mom starts asking her questions, that means she's on the scent, she's getting ready to hand me a solution to another one of my cases.

My feelings, as always, were mixed. On the one hand, nobody admires Mom more than I do—her deep knowledge of human nature acquired among her friends and neighbors in the Bronx; her uncanny sharpness in applying that knowledge to the crimes I tell her about from time to time.

On the other hand—well, how ecstatic is a man supposed to get at the idea that his mother can do his own job better than *he* can? That's why I've never been able to talk about Mom's talent to anybody else in the Department—except, of course, to Inspector Milner, my immediate superior, and only because he's a widower, and

Shirley and I are trying to get something going between Mom and him.

So I guess my voice wasn't as enthusiastic as it should have been, when I said to Mom, "Okay, what are your four questions?"

"First I bring in the peach pie," Mom said.

We waited while the dishes were cleared, and new dishes were brought. Then the heavenly aroma of Mom's peach pie filled the room. One taste of it, and my enthusiasm began to revive. "What *are* your questions, Mom?"

She lifted her finger. "Number One: you mentioned that Cohen had a cold a week ago, the night Maria Callas was singing *Traviata*. Did he still have the same cold three nights ago, when Tebaldi was singing *Tosca*?"

By this time I ought to be used to Mom's questions. I ought to take it on faith that they're probably not as irrelevant as they sound. But I still can't quite keep the bewilderment out of my voice.

"As a matter of fact," I said, "Cohen *did* have a cold the night of the murder. Frau Hochschwender and Miss Van Voorhees both mentioned it—he was sneezing while he waited in line, and even a few times during the performance, though he tried hard to control himself."

Mom's face gave no indication whether this was or wasn't what she had wanted to hear. She lifted another finger. "Number Two: after the opera every night, was it the custom for those standing-room regulars to separate right away—or did they maybe stay together for a little while before they finally said good night?"

"They usually went to the cafeteria a block away—the same place where D'Angelo bought the coffee that Cohen drank—and sat at a table for an hour or so and discussed the performance they'd just heard. Over coffee and doughnuts—or Danish pastry."

Mom gave a nod, and lifted another finger. "Number Three: at the hospital you naturally examined what was in Cohen's pockets? Did you find something like an envelope—a small envelope with absolutely nothing in it?"

This question really made me jump. "We did find an envelope, Mom! Ordinary stationery size—it was unsealed, and there was no address or stamp on it. But how in the world did you—'"

Mom's fourth finger was in the air. "Number Four: how many more times this season is Renata Tebaldi supposed to sing *Tosca*?"

"It was Tebaldi's first, last, and only performance of *Tosca* this season," I said. "The posters in front of the opera house said so. But I don't see what that has to do with—"

"You don't see," Mom said. "Naturally. You're like all the younger generation these days. So scientific. Facts you see. D'Angelo was the only one who was ever alone with Cohen's coffee—so D'Angelo must have put the poison in. A fact, so you see it. But what about the *people* already? Who is D'Angelo—who was Cohen—what type human beings? This you wouldn't ask yourself. Probably you wouldn't even understand about my Uncle Julius and the World Series."

"I'm sorry, Mom. I never knew you *had* an Uncle Julius—"

"I don't have him no more. That's the point of the story. All his life he was a fan of the New York Yankees. He rooted for them, he bet money on them, and when they played the World Series he was always there to watch them. Until a couple of years ago when he had his heart attack, and he was in the hospital at World Series time.

"'I'll watch the New York Yankees on television,' he said. 'The excitement is too much for you,' the doctor said, 'it'll kill you.' But Uncle Julius had his way, and he watched the World Series. Every day he watched, and every night the doctor said, 'You'll be dead before morning.' And Uncle Julius said, 'I wouldn't die till I know how the World Series comes out!' So finally the New York Yankees won the World Series—and an hour later Uncle Julius went to sleep and died."

Mom stopped talking, and looked around at Shirley and me. Then she shook her head and said, "You don't follow yet? A man with a love for something that's outside himself, that isn't even his family—with a love for the New York Yankees or for Renata Tebaldi—in such a man this feeling is stronger than his personal worries or his personal ambitions. He wouldn't let anything interrupt his World Series in the middle, not even dying. He wouldn't let anything interrupt his opera in the middle—not even murdering."

I began to see a glimmer of Mom's meaning. "You're talking about D'Angelo, Mom?"

"Who else? Renata Tebaldi was singing her one and only *Tosca* for the year, and for D'Angelo, Renata Tebaldi is the greatest singer alive. Never—in a million years, never—would he do anything to spoil this performance for himself, to make him walk out of it before the end. Let's say he *did* want to murder Cohen. The last time in the world he'd pick for this murder would be in the middle of Tebaldi's *Tosca*—her one and only Tosca! Especially since he could wait just as easy till after the opera, when the standing-room regulars would be having cake and coffee at the cafeteria—he could just as easy poison Cohen *then*."

"But Mom, isn't that kind of far-fetched, psychologically? If the average man was worked up enough to commit a murder, he wouldn't care about hearing the end of an opera first!"

"Excuse me, Davie—the average man's psychology we're not talking about. The opera lover's psychology we are talking about. This is why you and the Homicide Squad and the District Attorney couldn't make heads and tails from this case. Because you don't understand from opera lovers. In this world they don't live—they've got a world of their own. Inside their heads things are going on which other people's heads never even dreamed about. To solve this case you have to think like an opera lover."

"To solve this case, Mom, you have to answer the basic question: if D'Angelo didn't poison that coffee, who *could* have?"

"Who says the coffee was poisoned?"

"But I told you about the autopsy. The poison took two to three hours to work, and the contents of Cohen's stomach—"

"The contents of his stomach! You should show a little more interest in the contents of Cohen's pockets!"

"There was nothing unusual in his pockets—"

"Why should a man carry in his pocket an empty unsealed envelope, without any writing on it, without even a stamp on it? Only because it wasn't empty when he put it there. Something was in it—something which he expected to need later on in the evening—something which he finally took out of the envelope—"

"What are you talking about, Mom?"

"I'm talking about Cohen's cold. An ordinary man, he don't think twice about going to the opera with a cold. What's the difference if he sneezes a little? It's only music. But to an opera lover, sneezing during a performance, disturbing people, competing with the singers—this is worse than a major crime. A real opera lover like Cohen, he'd do everything he could to keep his cold under control.

"Which explains what he put in that envelope before he left his home to go to the opera house. A pill, what else? One of these new prescription cold pills that dries up your nose and keeps you from sneezing for five-six hours. And why was the envelope empty when you found it in his pocket? Because half an hour before the box office opened, he slipped out his pill and swallowed it down with his hot black coffee."

"Nobody *saw* him taking that pill, Mom."

"Why should anybody see him? Like you explained yourself, to drink his coffee he had to turn his body away and shield the container from the wind."

I was beginning to be shaken, no doubt about it. But Shirley spoke up now, in her sweet voice, the voice she always uses when she thinks she's one up on Mom. "The facts don't seem to bear you out, Mother. All the witnesses say that Mr. Cohen went on sneezing *after* the opera had begun. Well, if he really did take a cold pill, as you believe, why didn't it have any effect on his symptoms?"

A gleam came to Mom's eyes, and I could see

she was about to pounce. The fact is that Shirley never learns.

So to spare my wife's feelings I broke in quickly, before Mom could open her mouth. "I'm afraid that confirms Mom's theory, honey. The reason why the cold pill didn't work was that it wasn't a cold pill. It looked like one on the outside maybe, but it actually contained poison."

"I always knew I didn't produce a dope!" Mom said, with a big satisfied smile. "So now the answer is simple, no? If Cohen was carrying around a poison pill in his pocket, where did he get it? Who gave it to him? Why should he think it was a cold pill? Because somebody told him it was. Somebody he thought he could trust—not only personally but professionally. Somebody he went to and said, 'Give me some of that new stuff, that new wonder drug, that'll keep me from sneezing during the opera—'"

"His nephew!" I interrupted. "My God, Mom, I think you're right. Cohen's nephew *is* a pharmacist—he manages the drug store that Cohen owned. He has access to all kinds of poison and he could make up a pill that would look like a real cold pill. And what's more, he's the only relative Cohen has in the world. He inherits Cohen's store and Cohen's savings."

Mom spread her hands. "So there you are. You couldn't ask for a more ordinary, old-fashioned motive for murder. Any jury will be able to understand it. It isn't one bit operatic."

"But Mom, you must've suspected Cohen's nephew from the start. Otherwise you wouldn't have asked your question about the empty envelope."

"Naturally I suspected him. It was the lie he told."

"What lie?"

"The night before the opera D'Angelo called up Cohen and tried to make up their quarrel. Now according to the nephew, Cohen made a threat to D'Angelo over the phone. 'When Tebaldi hits her high C in the big aria, I'm going to start booing!' A terrible threat—but Cohen never could have made it."

"I don't see why not—"

"Because Cohen was an opera lover, that's why. A high C—this is a tenor's note. It's the top of his range—when he hits one, everybody is thrilled and says how wonderful he is. But for a soprano a high C is nothing special. She can go a lot higher than that. A high E—sometimes even an E sharp—*this* is the big note for a soprano. In the *Vissy darty* from *Tosca*, any soprano who couldn't do better than a high C would be strictly an amateur. People who are ignoramuses about opera—people like Cohen's nephew—they never *heard* of anything except the high C. But an opera lover like Cohen—he positively couldn't make such a mistake. Now excuse me, I'll bring in the coffee."

Mom got to her feet, and then Shirley called out, "Wait a second, Mother. If his nephew committed the murder, why did Cohen accuse D'Angelo of doing it?"

"When did Cohen accuse D'Angelo?"

"His dying words. He looked into D'Angelo's face and said, 'You no-good! You deserve to die for what you did!'"

"He looked into D'Angelo's face—but how do you know it was D'Angelo he was seeing? He was in delirium from the weakness and the pain, and before his eyes he wasn't seeing any D'Angelo, he wasn't seeing this world that the rest of us are living in. He was seeing the world he'd been looking at before he got sick, the world that meant the most to him—he was seeing the world of the opera, what else? And what was happening up there on that stage just before the poison hit him? The no-good villain was making advances to the beautiful heroine, and she was struggling to defend herself, and pretty soon she was going to kill him—and Cohen, seeing that villain in front of his eyes, shouted out at him, 'You no-good! You deserve to die for what you did!'"

Mom was silent for a moment, and then she went on in a lower voice, "An opera lover will go on being an opera lover—right up to the end."

She went out to the kitchen for the coffee,

and I went to the phone in the hall to call the Homicide Squad.

When I got back to the table, Mom was seated and the coffee was served. She took a few sips, and then gave a little sigh. "Poor old Cohen—such a terrible way to go!"

"Death by poisoning *is* pretty painful," I said.

"Poisoning?" Mom blinked up at me. "Yes, this is terrible too. But the worst part of all—the poor man died fifteen minutes too soon. He never heard Tebaldi sing the *Vissy darty.*"

And Mom began to hum softly.

THE MODERN ERA

ALL THE LONELY PEOPLE

Marcia Muller

ALTHOUGH SELDOM ACKNOWLEDGED FOR ITS SIGNIFICANCE, the publication of Marcia Muller's (1944–   ) *Edwin of the Iron Shoes* in 1977 was a pivotal point in the history of American detective fiction. The novel introduced Sharon McCone, the first female private eye character written by a woman. McCone wasn't a sidekick, didn't inherit the agency, and didn't need to be rescued by a man when the going got tough. A few years later, Sue Grafton (who described Muller as "the founding mother of the contemporary female hard-boiled private eye") and Sara Paretsky followed in Muller's footsteps, becoming household names with their bestselling novels.

Muller was born in Detroit and earned a B.A. in English and an M.A. in journalism from the University of Michigan, but after her move to San Francisco, she set almost all her books in the Bay Area. The region is an integral part of her work, especially the McCone series, which numbers more than thirty novels and numerous short stories. Muller's other series characters include Elena Oliverez, a Mexican-American art expert; Joanna Stark, an art and alarm security consultant for museums; and Carpenter and Quincannon, detectives in nineteenth-century San Francisco; that series is cowritten with her husband, Bill Pronzini, a prolific mystery writer best known for his Nameless Detective series.

McCone worked her way through college doing security work for a department store, liked it, and decided to make it a career, joining All Souls, a San Francisco legal co-op, as an investigator, where she worked for many years, mainly on cases that involved social issues, before opening her own agency.

Muller was named a Grand Master by the Mystery Writers of America in 2005 and given "The Eye" by the Private Eye Writers of America in 1993, both for lifetime achievement.

"All the Lonely People" was originally published in *Sisters in Crime*, edited by Marilyn Wallace (New York, Berkley, 1989).

All the Lonely People

MARCIA MULLER

"NAME, SHARON McCONE. Occupation . . . I can't put private investigator. What should I be?" I glanced over my shoulder at Hank Zahn, my boss at All Souls Legal Cooperative. He stood behind me, his eyes bemused behind thick horn-rimmed glasses.

"I've heard you tell people you're a researcher when you don't want to be bothered with stupid questions like 'What's a nice girl like you . . .'"

"*Legal* researcher." I wrote it on the form. "Now—'About the person you are seeking.' Age—does not matter. Smoker—does not matter. Occupation—does not matter. I sound excessively eager for a date, don't I?"

Hank didn't answer. He was staring at the form. "The things they ask. Sexual preference." He pointed at the item. "Hetero, bi, lesbian, gay. There's no place for 'does not matter.'"

As he spoke, he grinned wickedly. I glared at him. "You're enjoying this!"

"Of course I am. I never thought I'd see the day you'd fill out an application for a dating service."

I sighed and drummed my fingertips on the desk. Hank is my best male friend, as well as my boss. I love him like a brother—sometimes. But he harbors an overactive interest in my love life and delights in teasing me about it. I would be hearing about the dating service for years to come. I asked, "What should I say I want the guy's cultural interests to be? I can't put 'does not matter' for everything."

"I don't think burglars *have* cultural interests."

"Come on, Hank. Help me with this!"

"Oh, put film. Everyone's gone to a movie."

"Film." I checked the box.

The form was quite simple, yet it provided a great deal of information about the applicant. The standard questions about address, income level, whether the individual shared a home or lived alone, and hours free for dating were enough in themselves to allow an astute burglar to weed out prospects—and pick times to break in when they were not likely to be on the premises.

And that apparently was what had happened at the big singles apartment complex down near the San Francisco–Daly City line, owned by Hank's client, Dick Morris. There had been three burglaries over the past three months, beginning not long after the place had been leafleted by All the Best People Introduction Service. Each of the people whose apartments had been hit were women who had filled out the application forms; they had had from two to ten dates with men with whom the service had put them in touch. The burglaries had taken place when one renter was at work, another away for the weekend, and the third out with a date whom she had also met through Best People.

Coincidence, the police had told the renters and Dick Morris. After all, none of the women had reported having dates with the same man. And there were many other common denominators among them besides their use of the service. They lived in the same complex. They all knew one another. Two belonged to the same health club. They shopped at the same supermarket, shared auto mechanics, hairstylists, dry cleaners, and two of them went to the same psychiatrist.

Coincidence, the police insisted. But two other San Francisco area members of Best People had also been burglarized—one of them male—and so they checked the service out carefully.

What they found was absolutely no evidence of collusion in the burglaries. It was no fly-by-night operation. It had been in business ten years—a long time for that type of outfit. Its board of directors included a doctor, a psychologist, a rabbi, a minister, and a well-known author of somewhat weird but popular novels. It was respectable—as such things go.

But Best People was still the strongest link among the burglary victims. And Dick Morris was a good landlord who genuinely cared about his tenants. So he put on a couple of security guards, and when the police couldn't run down the perpetrator(s) and backburnered the case, he came to All Souls for legal advice.

It might seem unusual for the owner of a glitzy singles complex to come to a legal services plan that charges its clients on a sliding-fee scale, but Dick Morris was cash-poor. Everything he'd saved during his long years as a journeyman plumber had gone into the complex, and it was barely turning a profit as yet. Wouldn't be turning any profit at all if the burglaries continued and some of his tenants got scared and moved out.

Hank could have given Dick the typical attorney's spiel about leaving things in the hands of the police and continuing to pay the guards out of his dwindling cash reserves, but Hank is far from typical. Instead he referred Dick to me. I'm All Souls' staff investigator, and assignments like this one—where there's a challenge—are what I live for.

They are, that is, unless I have to apply for membership in a dating service, plus set up my own home as a target for a burglar. Once I started "dating," I would remove anything of value to All Souls, plus Dick would station one of his security guards at my house during the hours I was away from there, but it was still a potentially risky and nervous-making proposition.

Now Hank loomed over me, still grinning. I could tell how much he was going to enjoy watching me suffer through an improbable, humiliating, *asinine* experience. I smiled back—sweetly.

"'Your sexual preference.' Hetero." I checked the box firmly. "Except for inflating my income figure, so I'll look like I have a lot of good stuff to steal, I'm filling this out truthfully," I said. "Who knows—I might meet someone wonderful."

When I looked back up at Hank, my evil smile matched his earlier one. He, on the other hand, looked as if he'd swallowed something the wrong way.

My first "date" was a chubby little man named Jerry Hale. Jerry was *very* into the singles scene. We met at a bar in San Francisco's affluent Marina district, and while we talked, he kept swiveling around in his chair and leering at every woman who walked by. Most of them ignored him, but a few glared; I wanted to hang a big sign around my neck saying, "I'm not really with him, it's only business." While I tried to find out about his experiences with All the Best People Introduction Service, plus impress him with all the easily fenceable items I had at home, he tried to educate me on the joys of being single.

"I used to be into the bar scene pretty heavily," he told me. "Did all right too. But then I started to worry about herpes and AIDS—I'll let you see the results of my most recent test if you want—and my drinking was getting out of hand. Besides, it was expensive. Then I went the other way—a health club. Did all right there too. But goddamn, it's *tiring*. So then I joined a bunch of church groups—you meet a lot of horny women there. But churches encourage matrimony, and I'm not into that."

"So you applied to All the Best People. How long have you—?"

"Not right away. First I thought about joining AA, even went to a meeting. Lots of good-looking women are recovering alcoholics, you know. But I like to drink too much to make the sacrifice. Dear Abby's always saying you should enroll in courses, so I signed up for a couple at U.C. Extension. Screenwriting and photography."

My mouth was stiff from smiling politely, and I had just about written Jerry off as a possible suspect—he was too busy to burglarize anyone. I took a sip of wine and looked at my watch.

Jerry didn't notice the gesture. "The screenwriting class was terrible—the instructor actually wanted you to write stuff. And photography—how can you see women in the darkroom, let alone make any moves when you smell like chemicals?"

I had no answer for that. Maybe my own efforts at photography accounted for my not having a lover at the moment. . . .

"Finally I found All the Best People," Jerry went on. "Now I really do all right. And it's opened up a whole new world of dating to me—eighties-style. I've answered ads in the paper, placed my own ad too. You've always got to ask that they send a photo, though, so you can screen out the dogs. There's Weekenders, they plan trips. When I don't want to go out of the house, I use the Intro Line—that's a phone club you can join, where you call in for three bucks and either talk to one person or on a party line. There's a video exchange where you can make tapes and trade them with people so you'll know you're compatible before you set up a meeting. I do all right."

He paused expectantly, as if he thought I was going to ask how I could get in on all these good eighties-style deals.

"Jerry," I said, "have you read any good books lately?"

"Have I . . . *what?*"

"What do you do when you're not dating?"

"I work. I told you, I'm in sales—"

"Do you ever spend time alone?"

"Doing what?"

"Oh, just being alone. Puttering around the house or working at hobbies. Just thinking."

"Are you crazy? What kind of a computer glitch are you, anyway?" He stood, all five-foot-three of him quivering indignantly. "Believe me, I'm going to complain to Best People about setting me up with you. They described you as 'vivacious,' but you've hardly said a word all evening!"

Morton Stone was a nice man, a sad man. He insisted on buying me dinner at his favorite Chinese restaurant. He spent the evening asking me questions about myself and my job as a legal researcher; while he listened, his fingers played nervously with the silverware. Later, over a brandy in a nearby bar, he told me how his wife had died the summer before, of cancer. He told me about his promise to her that he would get on with his life, find someone new, and be happy. This was the first date he'd arranged through All the Best People; he'd never done anything like that in his life. He'd only tried them because he wasn't good at meeting people. He had a good job, but it wasn't enough. He had money to travel, but it was no fun without someone to share the experience with. He would have liked to have children, but he and his wife had put it off until they'd be financially secure, and then they'd found out about the cancer. . . .

I felt guilty as hell about deceiving him, and for taking his time, money, and hope. But by the end of the evening I'd remembered a woman friend who was just getting over a disastrous love affair. A nice, sad woman who wasn't good at meeting people; who had a good job, loved to travel, and longed for children. . . .

Bob Gillespie was a sailing instructor on a voyage of self-discovery. He kept prefacing his remarks with statements such as, "You know, I had a great insight into myself last week." That was nice; I was happy for him. But I would rather have gotten to know his surface persona before probing into his psyche. Like the two previous men, Bob didn't fit any of the recognizable profiles of the professional burglar, nor had he had any great insight into how All the Best People worked.

Ted Horowitz was a recovering alcoholic, which was admirable. Unfortunately he was also the confessional type. He began every anecdote with the admission that it had happened "back when I was drinking." He even felt compelled to describe how he used to throw up on his ex-wife. His only complaint about Best People—this with a stern look at my wineglass—was that they kept referring him to women who drank.

Jim Rogers was an adman who wore safari clothes and was into guns. I refrained from telling him that I own two .38 Specials and am a highly qualified marksman, for fear it would incite him to passion. For a little while I considered him seriously for the role of burglar, but when I probed the subject by mentioning a friend having recently been ripped off, Jim became enraged and said the burglar ought to be hunted down and shot.

"I'm going about this all wrong," I said to Hank.

It was ten in the morning, and we were drinking coffee at the big round table in All Souls' kitchen. The night before I'd spent hours on the phone with an effervescent insurance underwriter who was going on a whale-watching trip with Weekenders, the group that god-awful Jerry Hale had mentioned. He'd concluded our conversation by saying he'd be sure to note in his pocket organizer to call me the day after he returned. Then I'd been unable to sleep and had sat up hours longer, drinking too much and

listening for burglars and brooding about loneliness.

I wasn't involved with anyone at the time—nor did I particularly want to be. I'd just emerged from a long-term relationship and was reordering my life and getting used to doing things alone again. I was fortunate in that my job and my little house—which I'm constantly remodeling—filled most of the empty hours. But I could still understand what Morton and Bob and Ted and Jim and even that dreadful Jerry were suffering from.

It was the little things that got to me. Like the times I went to the supermarket and everything I felt like having for dinner was packaged for two or more, and I couldn't think of anyone I wanted to have over to share it with. Or the times I'd be driving around a curve in the road and come upon a spectacular view, but have no one in the passenger seat to point it out to. And then there were the cold sheets on the other side of the wide bed on a foggy San Francisco night.

But I got through it, because I reminded myself that it wasn't going to be that way forever. And when I couldn't convince myself of that, I thought about how it was better to be totally alone than alone *with* someone. That's how *I* got through the cold, foggy nights. But I was discovering there was a whole segment of the population that availed itself of dating services and telephone conversation clubs and video exchanges. Since I'd started using Best People, I'd been inundated by mail solicitations and found that the array of services available to singles was astonishing.

Now I told Hank, "I simply can't stand another evening making polite chitchat in a bar. If I listen to another ex-wife story, I'll scream. I don't want to know what these guys' parents did to them at age ten that made the whole rest of their lives a mess. And besides, having that security guard on my house is costing Dick Morris a bundle that he can ill afford."

Helpfully Hank said, "So change your approach."

"Thanks for your great suggestion." I got

up and went out to the desk that belongs to Ted Smalley, our secretary, and dug out a phone directory. All the Best People wasn't listed. My file on the case was on the kitchen table. I went back there—Hank had retreated to his office—and checked the introductory letter they'd sent me; it showed nothing but a post-office box. The zip code told me it was the main post office at Seventh and Mission streets.

I went back and borrowed Ted's phone book again, then looked up the post office's number. I called it, got the mail-sorting supervisor, and identified myself as Sharon from Federal Express. "We've got a package here for All the Best People Introduction Service," I said, and read off the box number. "That's all I've got—no contact phone, no street address."

"Assholes," she said wearily. "Why do they send them to a P.O. box when they know you can't deliver to one? For that matter, why do you accept them when they're addressed like that?"

"Damned if I know. I only work here."

"I can't give out the street address, but I'll supply the contact phone." She went away, came back, and read it off to me.

"Thanks." I depressed the disconnect button and redialed.

A female voice answered with only the phone number. I went into my Federal Express routine. The woman gave me the address without hesitation, in the 200 block of Gough Street near the Civic Center. After I hung up I made one more call: to a friend on the *Chronicle*. J. D. Smith was in the city room and agreed to leave a few extra business cards with the security guard in the newspaper building's lobby.

All the Best People's offices took up the entire second floor of a renovated Victorian. I couldn't imagine why they needed so much space, but they seemed to be doing a landslide business, because phones in the offices on either side of the long corridor were ringing madly. I assumed it was because the summer vacation season was

approaching and San Francisco singles were getting anxious about finding someone to make travel plans with.

The receptionist was more or less what I expected to find in the office of that sort of business: petite, blond, sleekly groomed, and expensively dressed, with an elegant manner. She took J. D.'s card down the hallway to see if their director was available to talk with me about the article I was writing on the singles scene. I paced around the tiny waiting room, which didn't even have chairs. When the young woman came back, she said Dave Lester would be happy to see me and led me to an office at the rear.

The office was plush, considering the attention that had been given to decor in the rest of the suite. It had a leather couch and chairs, a wet bar, and an immense mahogany desk. There wasn't so much as a scrap of paper or a file folder to suggest anything resembling work was done there. I couldn't see Dave Lester, because he had swiveled his high-backed chair around toward the window and was apparently contemplating the wall of the building next door. The receptionist backed out the door and closed it. I cleared my throat, and the chair turned toward me.

The man in the chair was god-awful Jerry Hale.

Our faces must have been mirror images of shock. I said, "What are *you* doing here?"

He said, "You're not J. D. Smith. You're Sharon McCone!" Then he frowned down at the business card he held. "Or is Sharon McCone really J. D. Smith?"

I collected my scattered wits and said, "Which are you—Dave Lester or Jerry Hale?"

He merely stared at me, his expression wavering between annoyance and amusement.

I added, "I'm a reporter doing a feature article on the singles scene."

"So Marie said. How did you get this address? We don't publish it because we don't want all sorts of crazies wandering in. This is an exclusive service; we screen our applicants carefully."

They certainly hadn't screened me; otherwise they'd have uncovered numerous deceptions. I said, "Oh, we newspaper people have our sources."

"Well, you certainly misrepresented yourself to us."

"And you misrepresented yourself to *me!*"

He shrugged. "It's part of the screening process, for our clients' protection. We realize most applicants would shy away from a formal interview situation, so we have the first date take the place of that."

"You yourself go out with *all* the women who apply?"

"A fair amount, using a different name every time, of course, in case any of them know each other and compare notes." At my astonished look he added, "What can I say? I like women. But naturally I have help. And Marie"—he motioned at the closed door—"and one of the secretaries check out the guys."

No wonder Jerry had no time to read. "Then none of the things you told me were true? About being into the bar scene and the church groups and the health club?"

"Sure they were. My previous experiences were what led me to buy Best People from its former owners. They hadn't studied the market, didn't know how to make a go of it in the eighties."

"Well, you're certainly a good spokesman for your own product. But how come you kept referring me to other clients? We didn't exactly part on amiable terms."

"Oh, that was just a ruse to get out of there. I had another date. I'd seen enough to know you weren't my type. But I decided you were still acceptable; we get a lot of men looking for your kind."

The "acceptable" rankled. "What exactly *is* my kind?"

"Well, I'd call you . . . introspective. Bookish? No, not exactly. A little offbeat? Maybe intense? No. It's peculiar . . . you're peculiar—"

"Stop right there!"

Jerry—who would always be god-awful Jerry and never Dave Lester to me—stood up and came around the desk. I straightened my posture. From my five-foot-six vantage point I could see the beginnings of a bald spot under his artfully styled hair. When he realized where I was looking, his mouth tightened. I took a perverse delight in his discomfort.

"I'll have to ask you to leave now," he said stiffly.

"But don't you want Best People featured in a piece on singles?"

"I do not. I can't condone the tactics of a reporter who misrepresents herself."

"Are you sure that's the reason you don't want to talk with me?"

"Of course. What else—"

"Is there something about Best People that you'd rather not see publicized?"

Jerry flushed. When he spoke, it was in a flat, deceptively calm manner. "Get out of here," he said, "or I'll call your editor."

Since I didn't want to get J. D. in trouble with the *Chron*, I went.

Back at my office at All Souls, I curled up in my ratty armchair—my favorite place to think. I considered my visit to All the Best People; I considered what was wrong with the setup there. Then I got out my list of burglary victims and called each of them. All three gave me similar answers to my questions. Next I checked the phone directory and called my friend Tracy in the billing office at Pacific Bell.

"I need an address for a company that's only listed by number in the directory," I told her.

"Billing address, or location where the phone's installed?"

"Both, if they're different."

She tapped away on her computer keyboard. "Billing and location are the same: two-eleven Gough. Need anything else?"

"That's it. Thanks—I owe you a drink."

————

In spite of my earlier determination to depart the singles scene, I spent the next few nights on the phone, this time assuming the name of Patsy Newhouse, my younger sister. I talked to various singles about my new VCR; I described the sapphire pendant my former boyfriend had given me and how I planned to have it reset to erase old memories. I babbled excitedly about the trip to Las Vegas I was taking in a few days with Weekenders, and promised to make notes in my pocket organizer to call people as soon as I got back. I mentioned—in seductive tones—how I loved to walk barefoot over my genuine Persian rugs. I praised the merits of my new microwave oven. I described how I'd gotten into collecting costly jade carvings. By the time the Weekenders trip was due to depart for Vegas, I was constantly sucking on throat lozenges and wondering how long my voice would hold out.

Saturday night found me sitting in my kitchen sharing ham sandwiches and coffee by candlelight with Dick Morris's security guard, Bert Jankowski. The only reason we'd chanced the candles was that we'd taped the shades securely over the windows. There was something about eating in total darkness that put us both off.

Bert was a pleasant-looking man of about my age, with sandy hair and a bristly mustache and a friendly, open face. We'd spent a lot of time together—Friday night, all day today—and I'd pretty much heard his life story. We had a lot in common: He was from Oceanside, not far from where I'd grown up in San Diego; like me, he had a degree in the social sciences and hadn't been able to get a job in his field. Unlike me, he'd been working for the security service so long that he was making a decent wage, and he liked it. It gave him more time, he said, to read and to fish. I'd told him my life story, too: about my somewhat peculiar family, about my blighted romances, even about the man I'd once had to shoot. By Saturday night I sensed both of us were getting bored with examining our pasts, but the present situation was even more stultifying.

I said, "Something has *got* to happen soon."

Bert helped himself to another sandwich. "Not necessarily. Got any more of those pickles?"

"No, we're out."

"Shit. I don't suppose if this goes on that there's any possibility of cooking breakfast tomorrow? Sundays I always fix bacon."

In spite of having just wolfed down some ham, my mouth began to water. "No," I said wistfully. "Cooking smells, you know. This house is supposed to be vacant for the weekend."

"So far no one's come near it, and nobody seems to be casing it. Maybe you're wrong about the burglaries."

"Maybe . . . no, I don't think so. Listen: Andie Wyatt went to Hawaii; she came back to a cleaned-out apartment. Janie Roos was in Carmel with a lover; she lost everything fenceable. Kim New was in Vegas, where I'm supposed to be—"

"But maybe you're wrong about the way the burglar knows—"

There was a noise toward the rear of the house, past the current construction zone on the back porch. I held up my hand for Bert to stop talking and blew out the candles.

I sensed Bert tensing. He reached for his gun at the same time I did.

The noise came louder—the sound of an implement probing the back-porch lock. It was one of those useless toy locks that had been there when I'd bought the cottage; I'd left the dead bolt unlocked since Friday.

Rattling sounds. A snap. The squeak of the door as it moved inward.

I touched Bert's arm. He moved over into the recess by the pantry, next to the light switch. I slipped up next to the door to the porch. The outer door shut, and footsteps came toward the kitchen, then stopped.

A thin beam of light showed under the inner door between the kitchen and the porch—the burglar's flashlight. I smiled, imagining his surprise at the sawhorses and wood scraps and exposed wiring that make up my own personal urban-renewal project.

The footsteps moved toward the kitchen door again. I took the safety off the .38.

The door swung toward me. A half-circle of light from the flash illuminated the blue linoleum. It swept back and forth, then up and around the room. The figure holding the flash seemed satisfied that the room was empty; it stepped inside and walked toward the hall.

Bert snapped on the overhead light.

I stepped forward, gun extended, and said, "All right, Jerry. Hands above your head and turn around—slowly."

The flash clattered to the floor. The figure—dressed all in black—did as I said.

But it wasn't Jerry.

It was Morton Stone—the nice, sad man I'd had the dinner date with. He looked as astonished as I felt.

I thought of the evening I'd spent with him, and my anger rose. All that sincere talk about how lonely he was and how much he missed his dead wife. And now he turned out to be a common crook!

"You son of a bitch!" I said. "And I was going to fix you up with one of my friends!"

He didn't say anything. His eyes were fixed nervously on my gun.

Another noise on the back porch. Morton opened his mouth, but I silenced him by raising the .38.

Footsteps clattered across the porch, and a second figure in black came through the door. "Morton, what's wrong? Why'd you turn the lights on?" a woman's voice demanded.

It was Marie, the receptionist from All the Best People. Now I knew how she could afford her expensive clothes.

"So I was right about *how* they knew when to burglarize people, but wrong about *who* was doing it," I told Hank. We were sitting at the bar in the Remedy Lounge, his favorite Mission Street watering hole.

"I'm still confused. The Intro Line is part of All the Best People?"

"It's owned by Jerry Hale, and the phone equipment is located in the same offices. But as Jerry—Dave Lester, whichever incarnation you prefer—told me later, he doesn't want the connection publicized because the Intro Line is kind of sleazy, and Best People's supposed to be high-toned. Anyway, I figured it out because I noticed there were an awful lot of phones ringing at their offices, considering their number isn't published. Later I confirmed it with the phone company and started using the line myself to set the burglar up."

"So this Jerry wasn't involved at all?"

"No. He's the genuine article—a born-again single who decided to put his knowledge to turning a profit."

Hank shuddered and took a sip of Scotch.

"The burglary scheme," I went on, "was all Marie Stone's idea. She had access to the addresses of the people who joined the Intro Line club, and she listened in on the phone conversations and scouted out good prospects. Then, when she was sure their homes would be vacant for a period of time, her brother, Morton Stone, pulled the jobs while she kept watch outside."

"How come you had a date with Marie's brother? Was he looking you over as a burglary prospect?"

"No. They didn't use All the Best People for that. It's Jerry's pride and joy; he's too involved in the day-to-day workings and might have realized something was wrong. But the Intro Line is just a profit-making arm of the business to him—he probably uses it to subsidize his dating. He'd virtually turned the operation of it over to Marie. But he did allow Marie to send out mail solicitations for it to Best People clients, as well as mentioning it to the women he 'screened,' and that's how the burglary victims heard of it."

"But it still seems too great a coincidence that you ended up going out with this Morton."

I smiled. "It wasn't a coincidence at all. Morton also works for Best People, helping Jerry screen the female clients. When I had my date with Jerry, he found me . . . well, he said I was peculiar."

Hank grinned and started to say something, but I glared.

"Anyway, he sent Mort out with me to render a second opinion."

"Ye gods, you were almost rejected by a dating service."

"What really pisses me off is Morton's grieving-widower story. I really fell for the whole tasteless thing. Jerry told me Morton gets a lot of women with it—they just can't resist a man in pain."

"But not McCone." Hank drained his glass and gestured at mine. "You want another?"

I looked at my watch. "Actually, I've got to be going."

"How come? It's early yet."

"Well, uh . . . I have a date."

He raised his eyebrows. "I thought you were through with the singles scene. Which one is it tonight—the gun nut?"

I got off the bar stool and drew myself up in a dignified manner. "It's someone I met on my own. They always tell you that you meet the most compatible people when you're just doing what you like to do and not specifically looking."

"So where'd you meet this guy?"

"On a stakeout."

Hank waited. His eyes fairly bulged with curiosity.

I decided not to tantalize him any longer. I said, "It's Bert Jankowski, Dick Morris's security guard."

BLOOD TYPES

Julie Smith

AFTER A LONG AND SUCCESSFUL CAREER as a journalist, Julienne Drew Smith (1944–) turned to fiction writing. Having graduated from the University of Mississippi, she took a job as a reporter for the New Orleans *Times-Picayune*, followed by stints at the *San Francisco Chronicle* and the *Santa Barbara News-Press*. Other jobs included writing catalog copy for Banana Republic, serving as press officer for the San Francisco district attorney, and, with fellow mystery writer Marcia Muller and others, forming Invisible Ink, a consulting company that provided editing and writing services.

Death Turns a Trick (1982), Smith's first mystery, introduced Rebecca Schwartz, a San Francisco attorney who, against her father's wishes, followed in his career footsteps. She is smart, ambitious, independent, Jewish, and a feminist—as she is quick to tell anyone who will listen. She appeared in five novels before Smith began to focus on Skip Langdon, who made her debut in *New Orleans Mourning* (1990), which won the Edgar for best novel of the year. Langdon has been the protagonist in eight additional novels.

Langdon, a former debutante and Carnival queen, works as a policewoman in New Orleans—an unlikely choice for a woman who had been a petty thief and a drug user and had flunked out of Tulane. She may be the most recognizable cop in the NOPD being six feet tall, big-boned, with lots of long curly hair and bright green eyes.

"Blood Types" was originally published in *Sisters in Crime*, edited by Marilyn Wallace (New York, Berkley, 1989).

Blood Types

JULIE SMITH

"REFRESH MY RECOLLECTION, counselor. Are holographic wills legal in California?"

Though we'd hardly spoken in seven years or more, I recognized the voice on the phone as easily if I'd heard it yesterday. I'd lived with its owner once. "Gary Wilder. Aren't you feeling well?"

"I feel fine. Settle a bet, okay?"

"Unless you slept through more classes than I thought, you know perfectly well they're legal."

"They used to be. It's been a long time, you know? How are you, Rebecca?"

"Great. And you're a daddy, I hear. How's Stephanie?"

"Fine."

"And the wee one?"

"Little Laurie-bear. The best thing that ever happened to me."

"You sound happy."

"Laurie's my life."

I was sorry to hear it. That was a lot of responsibility for a ten-month-old.

"So about the will," Gary continued. "Have the rules changed since we were at Boalt?"

"A bit. Remember how it could be invalidated by anything preprinted on it? Like in that case where there was a date stamped on the paper the woman used, and the whole thing was thrown out?"

"Yeah. I remember someone asked whether you could use your own letterhead."

"That was you, Gary."

"Probably. And you couldn't, it seems to me."

"But you probably could now. Now only the 'materially relevant' part has to be handwritten. And you don't have to date it."

"No? That seems odd."

"Well, you would if there were a previous dated will. Otherwise just write it out, sign it, and it's legal."

Something about the call, maybe just the melancholy of hearing a voice from the past, put me in a gray and restless mood. It was mid-December and pouring outside—perfect weather for doleful ruminations on a man I hardly knew anymore. I couldn't help worrying that if Laurie was Gary's whole life, that didn't speak well for his marriage. Shouldn't Stephanie at least have gotten a small mention? But she hadn't, and the Gary I knew could easily have fallen out of love with her. He was one of life's stationary drifters—staying in the same place but drifting from one mild interest to another, none of them very consuming and none very durable. I hoped it would be different with Laurie; it wouldn't be easy to watch your dad wimp out on you.

But I sensed it was already happening. I suspected that phone call meant little Laurie, who was his life, was making him feel tied down and he was sending out feelers to former and future lady friends.

The weather made me think of a line from a poem Gary used to quote:

Il pleure dans mon coeur
Comme il pleut sur la ville.

He was the sort to quote Paul Verlaine. He read everything, retained everything, and didn't do much. He had never finished law school, had sold insurance for a while and was now dabbling in real estate, I'd heard, though I didn't know what that meant, exactly. Probably trying to figure out a way to speculate with Stephanie's money, which, out of affection for Gary, I thanked heaven she had. If you can't make up your mind what to do with your life, you should at least marry well and waffle in comfort.

Gary died that night. Reading about it in the morning *Chronicle*, I shivered, thinking the phone call was one of those grisly coincidences. But the will came the next day.

The *Chronicle* story said Gary and Stephanie were both killed instantly when their car went over a cliff on a twisty road in a blinding rainstorm. The rains were hellish that year. It was the third day of a five-day flood.

Madeline Bell, a witness to the accident, said Gary had swerved to avoid hitting her Mercedes as she came around a curve. The car had exploded and burned as Bell watched it roll off a hill near San Anselmo, where Stephanie and Gary lived.

Even in that moment of shock I think I felt more grief for Laurie than I did for Gary, who had half lived his life at best. Only a day before, when I'd talked to Gary, Laurie had had it made—her mama was rich and her daddy good-looking. Now she was an orphan.

I wondered where Gary and Stephanie were going in such an awful storm. To a party, probably, or home from one. It was the height of the holiday season.

I knew Gary's mother, of course. Would she already be at the Wilder house, for Hanukkah, perhaps? If not, she'd be coming soon; I'd call in a day or two.

In the meantime I called Rob Burns, who had long since replaced Gary in my affections, and asked to see him that night. I hadn't thought twice of Gary in the past five years, but something was gone from my life and I needed comfort. It would be good to sleep with Rob by my side and the sound of rain on the roof—life-affirming, as we say in California. I'd read somewhere that Mark Twain, when he built his mansion in Hartford, installed a section of tin roof so as to get the best rain sounds. I could understand the impulse.

It was still pouring by mid-morning the next day, and my throat was feeling slightly scratchy, the way it does when a cold's coming on. I was rummaging for vitamin C when Kruzick brought the mail in—Alan Kruzick, incredibly inept but inextricably installed secretary for the law firm of Nicholson and Schwartz, of which I was a protesting partner. The other partner, Chris Nicholson, liked his smart-ass style, my sister Mickey was his girlfriend, and my mother had simply laid down the law—hire him and keep him.

"Any checks?" I asked.

"Nope. Nothing interesting but a letter from a dead man."

"What?"

He held up an envelope with Gary Wilder's name and address in the upper left corner. "Maybe he wants you to channel him."

The tears that popped into my eyes quelled even Kruzick.

The will was in Gary's own handwriting, signed, written on plain paper, and dated December 17, the day of Gary's death. It said: "This is my last will and testament, superseding all others. I leave everything I own to my daughter, Laurie Wilder. If my wife and I die before her 21st birthday, I appoint my brother, Michael Wilder, as her legal guardian. I also appoint my brother as executor of this will."

My stomach clutched as I realized that Gary had known when we talked that he and Stephanie were in danger. He'd managed to seem his usual happy-go-lucky self, using the trick he had of hiding his feelings that had made him hard to live with.

But if he knew he was going to be killed, why hadn't he given the murderer's identity? Perhaps he had, I realized. I was a lawyer, so I'd gotten the will. Someone else might have gotten a letter about what was happening. I wondered if my old boyfriend had gotten involved with the dope trade. After all, he lived in Marin County, which had the highest population of coke dealers outside the greater Miami area.

I phoned Gary's brother at his home in Seattle but was told he'd gone to San Anselmo. I had a client coming in five minutes, but after that, nothing pressing. And so, by two o'clock I was on the Golden Gate Bridge, enjoying a rare moment of foggy overcast, the rain having relented for a while.

It was odd about Gary's choosing Michael for Laurie's guardian. When I'd known him well he'd had nothing but contempt for his brother. Michael was a stockbroker and a go-getter; Gary was a mooner-about, a romantic, and a rebel. He considered his brother boring, stuffy, a bit crass, and utterly worthless. On the other hand, he adored his sister, Jeri, a free-spirited dental hygienist married to a good-natured sometime carpenter.

Was Michael married? Yes, I thought. At least he had been. Maybe fatherhood had changed Gary's opinions on what was important—Michael's money and stability might have looked good to him when he thought of sending Laurie to college.

I pulled up in front of the Wilder-Cooper house, a modest redwood one that had probably cost nearly half a million. Such were real-estate values in Marin County—and such was Stephanie's bank account.

At home were Michael Wilder—wearing a suit—and Stephanie's parents, Mary and Jack Cooper. Mary was a big woman, comfortable and talkative; Jack was skinny and withdrawn. He stared into space, almost sad, but mostly just far-away, and I got the feeling watching TV was his great passion in life, though perhaps he drank as well. The idea, it appeared, was simply to leave the room without anyone noticing, the means of transportation being entirely insignificant.

It was a bit awkward, my being the ex-girlfriend and showing up unexpectedly. Michael didn't seem to know how to introduce me, and I could take a hint. It was no time to ask to see him privately.

"I'd hoped to see your mother," I said.

"She's at the hospital," said Mary. "We're taking turns now that—" She started to cry.

"The hospital!"

"You don't know about Laurie?"

"She was in the accident?"

"No. She's been very ill for the last two months."

"Near death," said Mary. "What that child has been through shouldn't happen to an animal. Tiny little face just contorts itself like a poor little monkey's. Screams and screams and screams; and *rivers* flow out of her little bottom. *Rivers*, Miss Schwartz!"

Her shoulders hunched and began to shake. Michael looked helpless. Mechanically Jack put an arm around her.

"What's wrong?" I asked Michael.

He shrugged. "They don't know. Can't diagnose it."

"Now, Mary," said Jack. "She's better. The doctor said so last night."

"What hospital is she in?"

"Marin General."

I said to Michael: "I think I'll pop by and see your mother—would you mind pointing me in the right direction? I've got a map in the car."

When we arrived at the curb, I said, "I can

find the hospital. I wanted to give you something."

I handed him the will. "This came in today's mail. It'll be up to you as executor to petition the court for probate." As he read, a look of utter incredulity came over his face. "But . . . I'm divorced. I can't take care of a baby."

"Gary didn't ask in advance if you'd be willing?"

"Yes, but . . . I didn't think he was going to die!" His voice got higher as reality caught up with him. "He called the day of the accident. But I thought he was just depressed. You know how people get around the holidays."

"What did he say exactly?"

"He said he had this weird feeling, that's all—like something bad might happen to him. And would I take care of Laurie if anything did."

"He didn't say he was scared? In any kind of trouble?"

"No—just feeling weird."

"Michael, he wasn't dealing, was he?"

"Are you kidding? I'd be the last to know." He looked at the ground a minute. "I guess he could have been."

Ellen Wilder was cooing to Laurie when I got to the hospital. "Ohhhh, she's much better now. She just needed her grandma's touch, that's all it was."

She spoke to the baby in the third person, unaware I was there until I announced myself, whereupon she almost dropped the precious angel-wangel and dislodged her IV. We had a tearful reunion, Gary's mother and I. We both missed Gary, and we both felt for poor Laurie.

Ellen adored the baby more than breath, to listen to her, and not only that, she possessed the healing power of a witch. She had spent the night Gary and Stephanie were killed with Laurie, and all day the next day, never even going home for a shower. And gradually the fever had broken, metaphorically speaking. With Grandma's loving attention, the baby's debilitating

diarrhea had begun to ease off, and little Laurie had seemed to come back to life.

"Look, Rebecca." She tiptoed to the sleeping baby. "See those cheeks? Roses in them. She's getting her pretty color back, widdle Waurie is, yes, her is." She seemed not to realize she'd lapsed into baby talk.

She came back and sat down beside me. "Stephanie stayed with her nearly around the clock, you know. She was the best mother anyone ever—" Ellen teared up for a second and glanced around the room, embarrassed.

"Look. She left her clothes here. I'll have to remember to take them home. The *best* mother . . . she and Gary were invited to a party that night. It was a horrible, rainy, rainy night, but poor Stephanie hadn't been anywhere but the hospital in weeks—"

"How long had you been here?"

"Oh, just a few days. I came for Hanukkah—and to help out if I could. I knew Stephanie had to get out, so I offered to stay with Laurie. I was just dying to have some time with the widdle fweet fing, anyhow—" This last was spoken more or less in Laurie's direction. Ellen seemed to have developed a habit of talking to the child while carrying on other conversations.

"What happened was Gary had quite a few drinks before he brought me over. Oh, God, I never should have let him drive! We nearly had a wreck on the way over—you know how stormy it was. I kept telling him he was too drunk to drive, and he said I wanted it that way, just like I always wanted him to have strep throat when he was a kid. He said he felt fine then and he felt fine now."

I was getting lost. "You *wanted* him to have strep throat?"

She shrugged. "I don't know what he meant. He was just drunk, that's all. Oh, God, my poor baby!" She sniffed, fumbled in her purse, and blew her nose into a tissue.

"Did he seem okay that day—except for being drunk?"

"Fine. Why?"

"He called me that afternoon—about his will. And he called Michael to say he—well, I guess to say he had a premonition about his death."

"His will? He called you about a will?"

"Yes."

"But he and Stephanie had already made their wills. Danny Goldstein drew them up." That made sense, as Gary had dated his holograph. Danny had been at Boalt with Gary and me. I wondered briefly if it hurt Ellen to be reminded that all Gary's classmates had gone on to become lawyers just like their parents would have wanted.

A fresh-faced nurse popped in and took a look at Laurie. "How's our girl?"

"Like a different baby."

The nurse smiled. "She sure is. We were really worried for a while there." But the smile faded almost instantly. "It's so sad. I never saw a more devoted mother. Laurie never needed us at all—Stephanie was her nurse. One of the best I ever saw."

"I didn't know Stephanie was a nurse." The last I'd heard she was working part-time for a caterer, trying to make up her mind whether to go to chef's school. Stephanie had a strong personality, but she wasn't much more career-minded than Gary was. Motherhood, everyone seemed to think, had been her true calling.

"She didn't have any training—she was just good with infants. You should have seen the way she'd sit and rock that child for hours, Laurie having diarrhea so bad she hardly had any skin on her little butt, crying her little heart out. She must have been in agony like you and I couldn't imagine. But finally Stephanie would get her to sleep. Nobody else could."

"Nobody else could breast-feed her," I said, thinking surely I'd hit on the source of Stephanie's amazing talent.

"Stephanie couldn't, either. Didn't have enough milk." The nurse shrugged. "Anyone can give a bottle. It wasn't that."

When she left, I said, "I'd better go. Can I do anything for you?"

Ellen thought a minute. "You know what you could do? Will you be going by Gary's again?"

"I'd be glad to."

"You could take some of Stephanie's clothes and things. They're going to let Laurie out in a day or two and there's so much stuff here." She looked exasperated.

Glad to help, I gathered up clothes and began to fold them. Ellen found a canvas carryall of Stephanie's to pack them in. Zipping it open, I saw a bit of white powder in the bottom, and my stomach flopped over. I couldn't get the notion of drugs out of my mind. Gary had had a "premonition" of death, the kind you might get if you burned someone and they threatened you—and now I was looking at white powder.

I found some plastic bags in a drawer that had probably once been used to transport diapers or formula, and lined the bottom of the carryall with them, to keep the powder from sticking to Stephanie's clothes.

But instead of going to Gary's, I dropped in at my parents' house in San Rafael. It was about four o'clock and I had some phoning to do before five.

"Darling!" said Mom. "Isn't it awful about poor Gary Wilder?"

Mom had always liked Gary. She had a soft spot for ne'er-do-wells, as I knew only too well. She was the main reason Kruzick was currently ruining my life. The person for whom she hadn't a minute was the one I preferred most—the blue-eyed and dashing Mr. Rob Burns, star reporter for the San Francisco *Chronicle*.

Using the phone in my dad's study, Rob was the very person I rang up. His business was asking questions that were none of his business, and I had a few for him to ask.

Quickly explaining the will, the odd phone call to Michael, and the white powder, I had him hooked. He smelled the same rat I smelled, and more important, he smelled a story.

While he made his calls I phoned Danny Goldstein. "Becky baby."

"Don't call me that."

"Terrible about Gary, isn't it? Makes you *think*, man."

"Terrible about Stephanie too."

"I don't know. She pussy-whipped him."

"She was better than Melissa."

Danny laughed unkindly, brayed you could even say. Everyone knew Gary had left me for Melissa, who was twenty-two and a cutesy-wootsy doll-baby who couldn't be trusted to go to the store for a six-pack. Naturally everyone thought *I* had Gary pussy-whipped when the truth was, he wouldn't brush his teeth without asking my advice about it. He was a man desperate for a woman to run his life, and I was relieved to be rid of the job.

But still, Melissa had hurt my pride. I thought Gary's choosing her meant he'd grown up and no longer needed me. It was a short-lived maturity, however—within two years Stephanie had appeared on the scene. I might not see it exactly the way Danny did, but I had to admit that if he'd had any balls, she was the one to bust them.

"I hear motherhood mellowed her," I said.

"Yeah, she was born for it. Always worrying was the kid too hot, too cold, too hungry—one of those poo-poo moms."

"Huh?"

"You know. Does the kid want to go poo-poo? Did the kid already go poo-poo? Does it go poo-poo enough? Does it go poo-poo too much? Is it going poo-poo *right now*? She could discuss color and consistency through a whole dinner party, salmon mousse to kiwi tart."

I laughed. Who didn't know the type? "Say, listen, Danny," I said. "Did you know Laurie's been in the hospital?"

"Yeah. Marina, my wife, went to see Stephanie—tried to get her to go out and get some air while she took care of the baby, but Stephanie wouldn't budge."

"I hear you drew up Gary's and Stephanie's wills."

"Yeah. God, I never thought—poor little Laurie. They asked Gary's sister to be her guardian—he hated his brother and Stephanie was an only child."

"Guess what? Gary made another will just before he died, naming the brother as Laurie's guardian."

"I don't believe it."

"Believe it. I'll send you a copy."

"There's going to be a hell of a court fight."

I wasn't so sure about that. The court, of course, wouldn't be bound by either parent's nomination. Since Stephanie's will nominated Jeri as guardian, she and Michael might choose to fight it out, but given Michael's apparent hesitation to take Laurie, I wasn't sure there'd be any argument at all.

"Danny," I said, "you were seeing a lot of him, right?"

"Yeah. We played racquetball."

"Was he dealing coke? Or something else?"

"Gary? No way. You can't be a dealer and be as broke as he was."

The phone rang almost the minute I hung up. Rob had finished a round of calls to what he called "his law-enforcement sources." He'd learned that Gary's brakes hadn't been tampered with, handily blowing my murder theory.

Or seemingly blowing it. Something was still very wrong, and I wasn't giving up till I knew what the powder was. Mom asked me to dinner, but I headed back to the city—Rob had said he could get someone to run an analysis that night.

It was raining again by the time I'd dropped the stuff off, refused Rob's dinner invitation (that was two) and gone home to solitude and split pea soup that I make up in advance and keep in the freezer for nights like this. It was the second night after Gary's death; the first night I'd needed to reassure myself I was still alive. Now I needed to mourn. I didn't plan anything fancy like sackcloth and ashes, just a quiet night home with a book, free to let my mind wander and my eyes fill up from time to time.

But first I had a message from Michael Wilder. He wanted to talk. He felt awful calling me like this, but there was no one in his family he felt he could talk to. Couldn't we meet for coffee or something?

Sure we could—at my house. Not even for Gary's brother was I going out in the rain again.

After the soup I showered and changed into jeans. Michael arrived in wool slacks and a sport coat—not even in repose, apparently, did he drop the stuffy act. Maybe life with Laurie would loosen him up. I asked if he'd thought any more about being her guardian.

It flustered him. "Not really," he said, and didn't meet my eyes.

"I found out the original wills named Jeri as guardian. If Stephanie didn't make a last-minute one, too, hers will still be in effect. Meaning Jeri could fight you if you decide you want Laurie."

"I can't even imagine being a father," he said. "But Gary must have had a good reason—" he broke off. "Poor little kid. A week ago everyone thought *she* was the one who was going to die."

"What's wrong with her—besides diarrhea?" I realized I hadn't had the nerve to ask either of the grandmothers because I knew exactly what would happen—I'd get details that would give *me* symptoms, and two hours later, maybe three or four, I'd be backing toward the door, nodding, with a glazed look on my face, watching matriarchal jaws continue to work.

But Michael only grimaced. "That's all I know about—just life-threatening diarrhea."

"Life-threatening?"

"Without an IV, a dehydrated baby can die in fifteen minutes. Just ask my mother." He shrugged. "Anyway, the doctors talked about electrolyte abnormalities, whatever they may be, and did every test in the book. But the only thing they found was what they called 'high serum sodium levels.'" He shrugged again, as if to shake something off. "Don't ask—especially don't ask my mom or Stephanie's."

We both laughed. I realized Michael had good reasons for finding sudden parenthood a bit on the daunting side.

I got us some wine and when I came back, he'd turned deadly serious. "Rebecca, something weird happened today. Look what I found." He held out a paper signed by Gary and headed "Beneficiary Designation."

"Know what that is?"

I shook my head.

"I used to be in insurance—as did my little brother. It's the form you use to change your life insurance beneficiary."

The form was dated December 16, the day before Gary's death. Michael had been named beneficiary and Laurie contingent beneficiary. Michael said, "Pretty weird, huh?"

I nodded.

"I also found both Gary's and Stephanie's policies—each for half a million dollars and each naming the other as beneficiary, with Laurie as contingent. For some reason, Gary went to see his insurance agent the day before he died and changed his. What do you make of it?"

I didn't at all like what I made of it. "It goes with the will," I said. "He named you as Laurie's guardian, so he must have wanted to make sure you could afford to take care of her."

"I could afford it. For Christ's sake!"

"He must have wanted to compensate you." I stopped for a minute. "It might be his way of saying thanks."

"You're avoiding the subject, aren't you?"

I was. "You mean it would have made more sense to leave the money to Laurie directly."

"Yes. Unless he'd provided for her some other way."

"Stephanie had money."

"I don't think Gary knew how much, though."

I took a sip of wine and thought about it, or rather thought about ways to talk about it, because it was beginning to look very ugly. "You're saying you think," I said carefully, "that he knew she was going to inherit the half million from Stephanie's policy. Because she was going to die and he was the beneficiary, and he was going to die and his new will left his own property to Laurie."

Michael was blunt: "It looks like murder-suicide, doesn't it?"

I said, "Yeah," unable to say any more.

Michael took me over ground I'd already mentally covered: "He decided to do it in a hurry, probably because it was raining so hard—an accident in the rain would be much more plausible. He made the arrangements.

Then he called me and muttered about a premonition, to give himself some sort of feeble motive for suddenly getting his affairs in order; he may have said the same thing to other people as well. Finally he pretended to be drunk, made a big show of almost having an accident on the way to the hospital, picked up Stephanie, and drove her over a cliff."

Still putting things together, I mumbled, "You couldn't really be sure you'd die going over just any cliff. You'd have to pick the right cliff, wouldn't you?" And then I said, "I wonder if the insurance company will figure it out."

"Oh, who cares! He probably expected they would but wanted to make the gesture. And he knew I didn't need the money. That's not the point. The point is why?" He stood up and ran his fingers through his hair, working off excess energy. "Why kill himself, Rebecca? And why take Stephanie with him?"

"I don't know," I said. But I hadn't a doubt that that was what he'd done. There was another why—why make Michael Laurie's guardian? Why not his sister as originally planned?

The next day was Saturday, and I would have dozed happily into mid-morning if Rob hadn't phoned at eight. "You know the sinister white powder?"

"Uh-huh."

"Baking soda."

"That's all?"

"That's it. No heroin, no cocaine, not even any baby talc. Baking soda. Period."

I thanked him and turned over, but the next couple of hours were full of vaguely disquieting dreams. I woke upset, feeling oddly tainted, as if I'd collaborated in Gary's crimes. It wasn't till I was in the shower—performing my purification ritual, if you believe in such things—that things came together in my conscious mind. The part of me that dreamed had probably known all along.

I called a doctor friend to find out if what I suspected made medical sense. It did. To a baby Laurie's age, baking soda would be a deadly poison. Simply add it to the formula and the excess sodium would cause her to develop severe, dehydrating diarrhea; it might ultimately lead to death. But she would be sick only as long as someone continued to doctor her formula. The poisoning was not cumulative; as soon as it stopped, she would begin to recover, and in only a few days she would be dramatically better.

In other words, he described Laurie's illness to a *T*. And Stephanie, the world's greatest mother, who was there around the clock, must have fed her—at any rate, would have had all the opportunity in the world to doctor her formula.

It didn't make sense. Well, part of it did. The part I could figure out was this: Gary saw Stephanie put baking soda in the formula, already knew about the high sodium reports, put two and two together, may or not have confronted her . . . no, definitely didn't confront her. Gary never confronted anyone.

He simply came to the conclusion that his wife was poisoning their child and decided to kill her, taking his own aimless life as well. That would account for the hurry—to stop the poisoning without having to confront Stephanie. If he accused her, he might be able to stop her, but things would instantly get far too messy for Gary-the-conflict-avoider. Worse, the thing could easily become a criminal case, and if Stephanie was convicted, Laurie would have to grow up knowing her mother had deliberately poisoned her. If she were acquitted, Laurie might always be in danger. I could follow his benighted reasoning perfectly.

But I couldn't, for all the garlic in Gilroy, imagine why Stephanie would want to kill Laurie. By all accounts, she was the most loving of mothers, would probably even have laid down her own life for her child's. I called a shrink friend, Elaine Alvarez.

"Of course she loved the child," Elaine explained. "Why shouldn't she? Laurie perfectly answered her needs." And then she told me some things that made me forget I'd been planning to consume a large breakfast in a few minutes. On the excuse of finally remembering to take Stephanie's clothes, I drove to Gary's house.

The family was planning a memorial service in a day or two for the dead couple; Jeri had just arrived at her dead brother's house; friends had dropped by to comfort the bereaved; yet there was almost a festive atmosphere in the house. Laurie had come home that morning.

Michael and I took a walk. "Bullshit!" he said. "Dog crap! No one could have taken better care of that baby than Stephanie. Christ, she martyred herself. She stayed up night after night—"

"Listen to yourself. Everything you're saying confirms what Elaine told me. The thing even has a name. It's called Munchausen Syndrome by Proxy. The original syndrome, plain old Munchausen, is when you hurt or mutilate yourself to get attention.

"'By proxy' means you do it to your nearest and dearest. People say, 'Oh, that poor woman. God, what she's been through. Look how brave she is! Why, no one in the world could be a better mother.' And Mom gets off on it. There are recorded cases of it, Michael, at least one involving a mother and baby."

He was pale. "I think I'm going to throw up."

"Let's sit down a minute."

In fact, stuffy, uptight Michael ended up lying down in the dirt on the side of the road, nice flannel slacks and all, taking breaths till his color returned. And then, slowly, we walked back to the house.

Jeri was holding Laurie, her mother standing over her, Mary Cooper sitting close on the couch. "Oh, look what a baby-waby. What a darling girly-wirl. Do you feel the least bit hot? Laurie-baurie, you're not running a fever, are you?"

The kid had just gotten the thumbs-up from a hospital, and she was wrapped in half a dozen blankets. I doubted she was running a fever.

Ellen leaned over to feel the baby's face. "Ohhh, I think she might be. Give her to Grandma. Grandma knows how to fix babies, doesn't she, Laurie girl? Come to Grandma

and Grandma will sponge you with alcohol, Grandma will."

She looked like a hawk coming in for a landing, ready to snare its prey and fly up again, but Mary was quicker still. Almost before you saw it happening, she had the baby away from Ellen and in her own lap. "What you need is some nice juice, don't you, Laurie-bear? And then Meemaw's going to rock you and rock you . . . oh, my goodness, you're burning up." Her voice was on the edge of panic. "Listen, Jeri, this baby's wheezing! We've got to get her breathing damp air. . . ."

She wasn't wheezing, she was gulping, probably in amazement. I felt my own jaw drop and, looking away, unwittingly caught the eye of Mary's husband, who hadn't wanted me to see the anguish there. Quickly he dropped a curtain of blandness. Beside me, I heard Michael whisper, "My God!"

I knew we were seeing something extreme. They were all excited to have Laurie home, and they were competing with each other, letting out what looked like their scariest sides if you knew what we did. But a Stephanie didn't come along every day. Laurie was in no further danger, I was sure of it. Still, I understood why Gary had had the sudden change of heart about her guardianship.

I turned to Michael. "Are you going to try to get her?"

He plucked at his sweater sleeve, staring at his wrist as if it had a treasure map on it. "I haven't decided."

An image from my fitful morning dreams came back to me: a giant in a forest, taller than all the trees and built like a mountain; a female giant with belly and breasts like boulders, dressed in white robes and carrying, draped across her outstretched arms, a dead man, head dangling on its flaccid neck.

In a few days Michael called. When he got home to Seattle, a letter had been waiting for him—a note, rather, from Gary, postmarked the day of his death. It didn't apologize, it didn't explain—it didn't even say, "Dear Michael." It was simply a quote from *Hamlet* typed on a piece of paper, not handwritten, Michael thought, because it could be construed as a confession and there was the insurance to think about.

This was the quote:

Diseases desperate grown
By desperate appliance are relieved,
Or not at all.

I didn't ask Michael again whether he intended to take Laurie. At the moment, I was too furious with one passive male to trust myself to speak civilly with another. Instead, I simmered inwardly, thinking how like Gary it was to confess to murder with a quote from Shakespeare. Thinking that, as he typed it, he probably imagined grandly that nothing in his life would become him like the leaving of it. The schmuck.

A POISON THAT LEAVES NO TRACE

Sue Grafton

AS THE DAUGHTER of mystery novelist C. W. Grafton, Sue Taylor Grafton (1940–2017) unsurprisingly became a detective novelist as well. She had two major inspirations: Ross Macdonald, the writer she admired more than any other, and her ex-husband, with whom she engaged in a bitter divorce and child custody battle that lasted six years. As the ugly war proceeded, she kept thinking of new ways to kill him and finally put them down on paper, unplanned research for future novels.

After graduating from the University of Louisville, the city in which she was born and raised, Grafton took jobs as a hospital admissions clerk, cashier, and medical secretary before turning to writing. After producing seven novels (only two of which were published) and screenplays for television, either on her own or with her future husband, Steven Humphrey, she began the work that made her an international bestseller: the "alphabet novels" featuring private investigator Kinsey Millhone, each book beginning with a letter of the alphabet in sequential order. The novels, beginning with *"A" Is for Alibi* (1982), were one of the major contributing elements of the boom of female writers producing tougher, more hard-boiled detective fiction that began in the 1980s.

Although Grafton has described her series character as "a younger, smarter, and thinner" version of herself, that is not entirely accurate. While Millhone is a loner who prefers not to have intense relationships, the relentlessly charming Grafton was married to Humphrey for nearly forty years. The series is set in Santa Teresa (a fictionalized Santa Barbara) as an homage to Macdonald, whose Lew Archer novels were also set there.

One of the most honored authors of her time, Grafton was given lifetime achievement awards by the Mystery Writers of America, the (British) Crime Writers' Association, the Private Eye Writers of America, and Malice Domestic.

"A Poison That Leaves No Trace" was originally published in *Sisters in Crime 2*, edited by Marilyn Wallace (New York, Berkley, 1990); it was first collected in *Kinsey and Me* (Santa Barbara, California, Bench Press, 1991).

A Poison That Leaves No Trace

SUE GRAFTON

THE WOMAN WAS WAITING outside my office when I arrived that morning. She was short and quite plump, wearing jeans in a size I've never seen on the rack. Her blouse was tunic-length, ostensibly to disguise her considerable rear end. Someone must have told her never to wear horizontal stripes, so the bold red-and-blue bands ran diagonally across her torso with a dizzying effect. Big red canvas tote, matching canvas wedgies. Her face was round, seamless, and smooth, her hair a uniformly dark shade that suggested a rinse. She might have been any age between forty and sixty. "You're not Kinsey Millhone," she said as I approached.

"Actually, I am. Would you like to come in?" I unlocked the door and stepped back so she could pass in front of me. She was giving me the once-over, as if my appearance was as remarkable to her as hers was to me.

She took a seat, keeping her tote squarely on her lap. I went around to my side of the desk, pausing to open the French doors before I sat down. "What can I help you with?"

She stared at me openly. "Well, I don't know. I thought you'd be a man. What kind of name is Kinsey? I never heard such a thing."

"My mother's maiden name. I take it you're in the market for a private investigator."

"I guess you could say that. I'm Shirese Dunaway, but everybody calls me Sis. Exactly how

long have you been doing this?" Her tone was a perfect mating of skepticism and distrust.

"Six years in May. I was with the police department for two years before that. If my being a woman bothers you, I can recommend another agency. It won't offend me in the least."

"Well, I might as well talk to you as long as I'm here. I drove all the way up from Orange County. You don't charge for a consultation, I hope."

"Not at all. My regular fee is thirty dollars an hour plus expenses, but only if I believe I can be of help. What sort of problem are you dealing with?"

"Thirty dollars an hour! My stars. I had no idea it would cost so *much*."

"Lawyers charge a hundred and twenty," I said with a shrug.

"I know, but that's in case of a lawsuit. Contingency, or whatever they call that. Thirty dollars an *hour* . . ."

I closed my mouth and let her work it out for herself. I didn't want to get into an argument with the woman in the first five minutes of our relationship. I tuned her out, watching her lips move while she decided what to do.

"The problem is my sister," she said at long last. "Here, look at this." She handed me a little clipping from the Santa Teresa newspaper. The death notice read: "Crispin, Margery, beloved mother of Justine, passed away on December 10. Private arrangements. Wynington–Blake Mortuary."

"Nearly two months ago," I remarked.

"Nobody even told me she was sick! That's the point," Sis Dunaway snapped. "I wouldn't know to this day if a former neighbor hadn't spotted this and cut it out." She tended to speak in an indignant tone regardless of the subject.

"You just received this?"

"Well, no. It come back in January, but of course I couldn't drop everything and rush right up. This is the first chance I've had. You can probably appreciate that, upset as I was."

"Absolutely," I said. "When did you last talk to Margery?"

"I don't remember the exact date. It had to be eight or ten years back. You can imagine my shock! To get something like this out of a clear blue sky."

I shook my head. "Terrible," I murmured. "Have you talked to your niece?"

She gestured dismissively. "That Justine's a mess. Marge had her hands full with that one," she said. "I stopped over to her place and you should have seen the look I got. I said, 'Justine, whatever in the world did Margery die of?' And you know what she said? Said, 'Aunt Sis, her heart give out.' Well, I knew that was bull the minute she said it. We have never had heart trouble in our family. . . ."

She went on for a while about what everybody'd died of; Mom, Dad, Uncle Buster, Rita Sue. We're talking cancer, lung disorders, an aneurysm or two. Sure enough, no heart trouble. I was making sympathetic noises, just to keep the tale afloat until she got to the point. I jotted down a few notes, though I never did quite understand how Rita Sue was related. Finally, I said, "Is it your feeling there was something unusual in your sister's death?"

She pursed her lips and lowered her gaze. "Let's put it this way. I can smell a rat. I'd be willing to *bet* Justine had a hand in it."

"Why would she do that?"

"Well, Marge had that big insurance policy. The one Harley took out in 1966. If that's not a motive for murder, I don't know what is." She sat back in her chair, content that she'd made her case.

"Harley?"

"Her husband . . . until he passed on, of course. They took out policies on each other and after he went, she kept up the premiums on hers. Justine was made the beneficiary. Marge never remarried and with Justine on the policy, I guess she'll get all the money and do I don't know what. It just doesn't seem right. She's been a sneak all her natural life. A regular con artist. She's been in jail four times! My sister talked till she was blue in the face, but she never could get Justine to straighten up her act."

"How much money are we talking about?"

"A hundred thousand dollars," she said. "Furthermore, them two never did get along. Fought like cats and dogs since the day Justine was born. Competitive? My God. Always trying to get the better of each other. Justine as good as told me they had a falling-out not two months before her mother died! The two had not exchanged a word since the day Marge got mad and stomped off."

"They lived together?"

"Well, yes, until this big fight. Next thing you know, Marge is dead. You tell me there's not something funny going on."

"Have you talked to the police?"

"How can I do that? I don't have any *proof*."

"What about the insurance company? Surely, if there were something irregular about Marge's death, the claims investigator would have picked up on it."

"Oh, honey, you'd think so, but you know how it is. Once a claim's been paid, the insurance company doesn't want to hear. Admit they made a mistake? Uh-uh, no thanks. Too much trouble going back through all the paperwork. Besides, Justine would probably turn around and sue 'em within an inch of their life. They'd rather turn a deaf ear and write the money off."

"When was the claim paid?"

"A week ago, they said."

I stared at her for a moment, considering. "I don't know what to tell you, Ms. Dunaway. . . ."

"Call me Sis. I don't go for that Ms. bull."

"All right, Sis. If you're really convinced Justine's implicated in her mother's death, of course I'll try to help. I just don't want to waste your time."

"I can appreciate that," she said.

I stirred in my seat. "Look, I'll tell you what let's do. Why don't you pay me for two hours of my time. If I don't come up with anything concrete in that period, we can have another conversation and you can decide then if you want me to proceed."

"Sixty dollars," she said.

"That's right. Two hours."

"Well, all right. I guess I can do that." She opened her tote and peeled six tens off a roll of bills she'd secured with a rubber band. I wrote out an abbreviated version of a standard contract. She said she'd be staying in town overnight and gave me the telephone number at the motel where she'd checked in. She handed me the death notice. I made sure I had her sister's full name and the exact date of her death and told her I'd be in touch.

My first stop was the Hall of Records at the Santa Teresa County Courthouse two and a half blocks away. I filled out a copy order, supplying the necessary information, and paid seven bucks in cash. An hour later, I returned to pick up the certified copy of Margery Crispin's death certificate. Cause of death was listed as a "myocardial infarction." The certificate was signed by Dr. Yee, one of the contract pathologists out at the county morgue. If Marge Crispin had been the victim of foul play, it was hard to believe Dr. Yee wouldn't have spotted it.

I swung back by the office and picked up my car, driving over to Wynington-Blake, the mortuary listed in the newspaper clipping. I asked for Mr. Sharonson, whom I'd met when I was working on another case. He was wearing a som-

ber charcoal-gray suit, his tone of voice carefully modulated to reflect the solemnity of his work. When I mentioned Marge Crispin, a shadow crossed his face.

"You remember the woman?"

"Oh, yes," he said. He closed his mouth then, but the look he gave me was eloquent.

I wondered if funeral home employees took a loyalty oath, vowing never to divulge a single fact about the dead. I thought I'd prime the pump a bit. Men are worse gossips than women once you get 'em going. "Mrs. Crispin's sister was in my office a little while ago and she seems to think there was something . . . uh, irregular about the woman's death."

I could see Mr. Sharonson formulate his response. "I wouldn't say there was anything *irregular* about the woman's death, but there was certainly something sordid about the circumstances."

"Oh?" said I.

He lowered his voice, glancing around to make certain we couldn't be overheard. "The two were estranged. Hadn't spoken for months as I understand it. The woman died alone in a seedy hotel on lower State Street. She drank."

"Nooo," I said, conveying disapproval and disbelief.

"Oh, yes," he said. "The police picked up the body, but she wasn't identified for weeks. If it hadn't been for the article in the paper, her daughter might not have ever known."

"What article?"

"Oh, you know the one. There's that columnist for the local paper who does all those articles about the homeless. He did a write-up about the poor woman. 'Alone in Death' I think it was called. He talked about how pathetic this woman was. Apparently, when Ms. Crispin read the article, she began to suspect it might be her mother. That's when she went out there to take a look."

"Must have been a shock," I said. "The woman did die of natural causes?"

"Oh, yes."

"No evidence of trauma, foul play, anything like that?"

"No, no, no. I tended her myself and I know they ran toxicology tests. I guess at first they thought it might be acute alcohol poisoning, but it turned out to be her heart."

I quizzed him on a number of possibilities, but I couldn't come up with anything out of the ordinary. I thanked him for his time, got back in my car, and drove over to the trailer park where Justine Crispin lived.

The trailer itself had seen better days. It was moored in a dirt patch with a wooden crate for an outside step. I knocked on the door, which opened about an inch to show a short strip of round face peering out at me. "Yes?"

"Are you Justine Crispin?"

"Yes."

"I hope I'm not bothering you. My name is Kinsey Millhone. I'm an old friend of your mother's and I just heard she passed away."

The silence was cautious. "Who'd you hear that from?"

I showed her the clipping. "Someone sent me this. I couldn't believe my eyes. I didn't even know she was sick."

Justine's eyes darkened with suspicion. "When did you see her last?"

I did my best to imitate Sis Dunaway's folksy tone. "Oh, gee. Must have been last summer. I moved away in June and it was probably some time around then because I remember giving her my address. It was awfully sudden, wasn't it?"

"Her heart give out."

"Well, the poor thing, and she was such a love." I wondered if I'd laid it on too thick. Justine was staring at me like I'd come to the wrong place. "Would you happen to know if she got my last note?" I asked.

"I wouldn't know anything about that."

"Because I wasn't sure what to do about the money."

"She owed you money?"

"No, no. I owed *her* . . . which is why I wrote."

Justine hesitated. "How much?"

"Well, it wasn't much," I said, with embarrassment. "Six hundred dollars, but she was such a doll to lend it to me and then I felt so bad when I couldn't pay her back right away. I asked her if I could wait and pay her this month, but then I never heard. Now I don't know what to do."

I could sense the shift in her attitude. Greed seems to do that in record time. "You could pay it to me and I could see it went into her estate," she said helpfully.

"Oh, I don't want to put you to any trouble."

"I don't mind," she said. "You want to come in?"

"I shouldn't. You're probably busy and you've already been so nice. . . ."

"I can take a few minutes."

"Well. If you're sure," I said.

Justine held the door open and I stepped into the trailer, where I got my first clear look at her. This girl was probably thirty pounds overweight with listless brown hair pulled into an oily ponytail. Like Sis, she was decked out in a pair of jeans, with an oversize T-shirt hanging almost to her knees. It was clear big butts ran in the family. She shoved some junk aside so I could sit down on the banquette, a fancy word for the ripped plastic seat that extended along one wall in the kitchenette.

"Did she suffer much?" I asked.

"Doctor said not. He said it was quick, as far as he could tell. Her heart probably seized up and she fell down dead before she could draw a breath."

"It must have been just terrible for you."

Her cheeks flushed with guilt. "You know, her and me had a falling-out."

"Really? Well, I'm sorry to hear that. Of course, she always said you two had your differences. I hope it wasn't anything serious."

"She drank. I begged her and begged her to give it up, but she wouldn't pay me no mind," Justine said.

"Did she 'go' here at home?"

She shook her head. "In a welfare hotel. Down on her luck. Drink had done her in. If only I'd known . . . if only she'd reached out."

I thought she was going to weep, but she couldn't quite manage it. I clutched her hand. "She was too proud," I said.

"I guess that's what it was. I've been thinking to make some kind of contribution to AA, or something like that. You know, in her name."

"A Marge Crispin Memorial Fund," I suggested.

"Like that, yes. I was thinking this money you're talking about might be a start."

"That's a beautiful thought. I'm going right out to the car for my checkbook so I can write you a check."

It was a relief to get out into the fresh air again. I'd never heard so much horsepuckey in all my life. Still, it hardly constituted proof she was a murderess.

I hopped in my car and headed for a pay phone, spotting one in a gas station half a block away. I pulled change out of the bottom of my handbag and dialed Sis Dunaway's motel room. She was not very happy to hear my report.

"You didn't find anything?" she said. "Are you positive?"

"Well, of course I'm not positive. All I'm saying is that so far, there's no evidence that anything's amiss. If Justine contributed to her mother's death, she was damned clever about it. I gather the autopsy didn't show a thing."

"Maybe it was some kind of poison that leaves no trace."

"Uh, Sis? I hate to tell you this, but there really isn't such a poison that I ever heard of. I know it's a common fantasy, but there's just no such thing."

Her tone turned stubborn. "But it's possible. You have to admit that. There could be such a thing. It might be from South America . . . darkest Africa, someplace like that."

Oh, boy. We were really tripping out on this one. I squinted at the receiver. "How would Justine acquire the stuff?"

"How do I know? I'm not going to set here and solve the whole case for you! You're the one gets paid thirty dollars an hour, not me."

"Do you want me to pursue it?"

"Not if you mean to charge me an arm and a leg!" she said. "Listen here, I'll pay sixty dollars more, but you better come up with something or I want my money back."

She hung up before I could protest. How could she get her money back when she hadn't paid this portion? I stood in the phone booth and thought about things. In spite of myself, I'll admit I was hooked. Sis Dunaway might harbor a lot of foolish ideas, but her conviction was unshakable. Add to that the fact that Justine was lying about *something* and you have the kind of situation I can't walk away from.

I drove back to the trailer park and eased my car into a shady spot just across the street. Within moments, Justine appeared in a banged-up white Pinto, trailing smoke out of the tail pipe. Following her wasn't hard. I just hung my nose out the window and kept an eye on the haze. She drove over to Milagro Street to the branch office of a savings and loan. I pulled into a parking spot a few doors down and followed her in, keeping well out of sight. She was dealing with the branch manager, who eventually walked her over to a teller and authorized the cashing of a quite large check, judging from the number of bills the teller counted out.

Justine departed moments later, clutching her handbag protectively. I would have been willing to bet she'd been cashing that insurance check. She drove back to the trailer where she made a brief stop, probably to drop the money off.

She got back in her car and drove out of the trailer park. I followed discreetly as she headed into town. She pulled into a public parking lot and I eased in after her, finding an empty slot far enough away to disguise my purposes. So far, she didn't seem to have any idea she was being tailed. I kept my distance as she cut through to State Street and walked up a block to Santa Teresa Travel. I pretended to peruse the posters in the window while I watched her chat with the travel agent sitting at a desk just inside the front door. The two transacted business, the agent handing over what apparently were pre-arranged tickets. Justine wrote out a check. I busied myself at a newspaper rack, extracting a paper as she came out again. She walked down State Street half a block to a hobby shop where she purchased one of life's ugliest plastic floral wreaths. Busy little lady, this one, I thought.

She emerged from the hobby shop and headed down a side street, moving into the front entrance of a beauty salon. A surreptitious glance through the window showed her, moments later, in a green plastic cape, having a long conversation with the stylist about a cut. I checked my watch. It was almost twelve-thirty. I scooted back to the travel agency and waited until I saw Justine's travel agent leave the premises for lunch. As soon as she was out of sight, I went in, glancing at the nameplate on the edge of her desk.

The blond agent across the aisle caught my eye and smiled.

"What happened to Kathleen?" I asked.

"She went out to lunch. You just missed her. Is there something I can help you with?"

"Gee, I hope so. I picked up some tickets a little while ago and now I can't find the itinerary she tucked in the envelope. Is there any way you could run me a copy real quick? I'm in a hurry and I really can't afford to wait until she gets back."

"Sure, no problem. What's the name?"

"Justine Crispin," I said.

I found the nearest public phone and dialed Sis's motel room again. "Catch this," I said. "At four o'clock, Justine takes off for Los Angeles. From there, she flies to Mexico City."

"Well, that little shit."

"It gets worse. It's one-way."

"I knew it! I just knew she was up to no good. Where is she now?"

"Getting her hair done. She went to the bank first and cashed a big check—"

"I bet it was the insurance."

"That'd be my guess."

"She's got all that money *on* her?"

"Well, no. She stopped by the trailer first and then went and picked up her plane ticket. I think

she intends to stop by the cemetery and put a wreath on Marge's grave. . . ."

"I can't stand this. I just can't stand it. She's going to take all that money and make a mockery of Marge's death."

"Hey, Sis, come on. If Justine's listed as the beneficiary, there's nothing you can do."

"That's what you think. I'll make her pay for this, I swear to God I will!" Sis slammed the phone down.

I could feel my heart sink. Uh-oh. I tried to think whether I'd mentioned the name of the beauty salon. I had visions of Sis descending on Justine with a tommy gun. I loitered uneasily outside the shop, watching traffic in both directions. There was no sign of Sis. Maybe she was going to wait until Justine went out to the gravesite before she mowed her down.

At two-fifteen, Justine came out of the beauty shop and passed me on the street. She was nearly unrecognizable. Her hair had been cut and permed and it fell in soft curls around her freshly made-up face. The beautician had found ways to bring out her eyes, subtly heightening her coloring with a touch of blusher on her cheeks. She looked like a million bucks—or a hundred thousand, at any rate. She was in a jaunty mood, paying more attention to her own reflection in the passing store windows than she was to me, hovering half a block behind.

She returned to the parking lot and retrieved her Pinto, easing into the flow of traffic as it moved up State. I tucked in a few cars back, all the while scanning for some sign of Sis. I couldn't imagine what she'd try to do, but as mad as she was, I had to guess she had some scheme in the works.

Fifteen minutes later, we were turning into the trailer park, Justine leading while I lollygagged along behind. I had already used up the money Sis had authorized, but by this time I had my own stake in the outcome. For all I knew, I was going to end up protecting Justine from an assassination attempt. She stopped by the trailer just long enough to load her bags in the car and then she drove out to the Santa Teresa Memorial Park, which was out by the airport.

The cemetery was deserted, a sunny field of gravestones among flowering shrubs. When the road forked, I watched Justine wind up the lane to the right while I headed left, keeping an eye on her car, which I could see across a wide patch of grass. She parked and got out, carrying the wreath to an oblong depression in the ground where a temporary marker had been set, awaiting the permanent monument. She rested the wreath against the marker and stood there looking down. She seemed awfully exposed and I couldn't help but wish she'd duck down some to grieve. Sis was probably crouched somewhere with a knife between her teeth, ready to leap out and stab Justine in the neck.

Respects paid, Justine got back into her car and drove to the airport where she checked in for her flight. By now, I was feeling baffled. She had less than an hour before her plane was scheduled to depart and there was still no sign of Sis. If there was going to be a showdown, it was bound to happen soon. I ambled into the gift shop and inserted myself between the wall and a book rack, watching Justine through windows nearly obscured by a display of Santa Teresa T-shirts. She sat on a bench and calmly read a paperback.

What was going on here?

Sis Dunaway had seemed hell-bent on avenging Marge's death, but where was she? Had she gone to the cops? I kept one eye on the clock and one eye on Justine. Whatever Sis was up to, she had better do it quick. Finally, mere minutes before the flight was due to be called, I left the newsstand, crossed the gate area, and took a seat beside Justine. "Hi," I said, "Nice permanent. Looks good."

She glanced at me and then did a classic double take. "What are you doing here?"

"Keeping an eye on you."

"What for?"

"I thought someone should see you off. I suspect your Aunt Sis is en route, so I decided to keep you company until she gets here."

"Aunt *Sis*?" she said, incredulously.

"I gotta warn you, she's not convinced your mother had a heart attack."

"What are you talking about? Aunt Sis is dead."

I could feel myself smirk. "Yeah, sure. Since when?"

"Five years ago."

"Bullshit."

"It's not bullshit. An aneurysm burst and she dropped in her tracks."

"Come on," I scoffed.

"It's the truth," she said emphatically. By that time, she'd recovered her composure and she went on the offensive. "Where's my money? You said you'd write a check for six hundred bucks."

"Completely dead?" I asked.

The loudspeaker came on. "May I have your attention, please. United Flight 3440 for Los Angeles is now ready for boarding at Gate Five. Please have your boarding pass available and prepare for security check."

Justine began to gather up her belongings. I'd been wondering how she was going to get all that cash through the security checkpoint, but one look at her lumpy waistline and it was obvious she'd strapped on a money belt. She picked up her carry-on, her shoulder bag, her jacket, and her paperback and clopped, in spike heels, over to the line of waiting passengers.

I followed, befuddled, reviewing the entire sequence of events. It had all happened today. Within hours. It wasn't like I was suffering brain damage or memory loss. And I hadn't seen a ghost. Sis had come to my office and laid out the whole tale about Marge and Justine. She'd told me all about their relationship, Justine's history as a con, the way the two women tried to outdo each other, the insurance, Marge's death. How could a murder have gotten past Dr. Yee? Unless the woman wasn't murdered, I thought suddenly. Oh.

Once I saw it in *that* light, it was obvious.

Justine got in line between a young man with

a duffel bag and a woman toting a cranky baby. There was some delay up ahead while the ticket agent got set. The line started to move and Justine advanced a step with me right beside her.

"I understand you and your mother had quite a competitive relationship."

"What's it to you," she said. She kept her eyes averted, facing dead ahead, willing the line to move so she could get away from me.

"I understand you were always trying to get the better of each other."

"What's your point?" she said, annoyed.

I shrugged. "I figure you read the article about the unidentified dead woman in the welfare hotel. You went out to the morgue and claimed the body as your mom's. The two of you agreed to split the insurance money, but your mother got worried about a double cross, which is exactly what this is."

"You don't know what you're talking about."

The line moved up again and I stayed right next to her. "She hired me to keep an eye on you, so when I realized you were leaving town, I called her and told her what was going on. She really hit the roof and I thought she'd charge right out, but so far there's been no sign of her. . . ."

Justine showed her ticket to the agent and he motioned her on. She moved through the metal detector without setting it off.

I gave the agent a smile. "Saying good-bye to a friend," I said, and passed through the wooden arch right after she did. She was picking up the pace, anxious to reach the plane.

I was still talking, nearly jogging to keep up with her. "I couldn't figure out why she wasn't trying to stop you and then I realized what she must have done—"

"Get away from me. I don't want to talk to you."

"She took the money, Justine. There's probably nothing in the belt but old papers. She had plenty of time to make the switch while you were getting your hair done."

"Ha, ha," she said sarcastically. "Tell me another one."

I stopped in my tracks. "All right. That's all I'm gonna say. I just didn't want you to reach Mexico City and find yourself flat broke."

"Blow it out your buns," she hissed. She showed her boarding pass to the woman at the gate and passed on through. I could hear her spike heels tip-tapping out of ear range.

I reversed myself, walked back through the gate area and out to the walled exterior courtyard, where I could see the planes through a windbreak of protective glass. Justine crossed the tarmac to the waiting plane, her shoulders set. I didn't think she'd heard me, but then I saw her hand stray to her waist. She walked a few more steps and then halted, dumping her belongings in a pile at her feet. She pulled her shirt up and checked the money belt. At that distance, I saw her mouth open, but it took a second for the shrieks of outrage to reach me.

Ah, well, I thought. Sometimes a mother's love is like a poison that leaves no trace. You bop along through life, thinking you've got it made, and next thing you know, you're dead.

DISCARDS

Faye Kellerman

AS A PRACTICING ORTHODOX JEW, Faye Marder Kellerman (1952–) has brought the doctrine and practice of her faith into many of her bestselling novels about Rina Lazarus, also an Orthodox Jew, and Los Angeles Police Department Sergeant Peter Decker, an ethnic Jew raised as a Southern Baptist by his adoptive parents who embraces Judaism when he falls in love with Rina, a widow with two children when they meet in their first adventure, *The Ritual Bath* (1986).

Kellerman suffers from dyslexia, so she disliked reading and English classes, receiving a B.A. in theoretical mathematics from UCLA, followed by a doctorate in dental surgery. Her plans to practice dentistry were derailed when she became pregnant with her first child, Jesse (who has gone on to be a bestselling writer like his mother and father, Jonathan Kellerman), and then had three more. Having a career that allowed her to stay home led her to write about her imaginary friends, as she has described it.

Of Kellerman's more than thirty novels, more than twenty are police procedurals featuring Decker and Lazarus, many of which deal with Jewish themes. The series was enhanced for readers by the love affair that quickly bloomed between the two characters, eventually resulting in their somehow inevitable marriage.

Among her non-series books are two cowritten with her husband, *Double Homicide* (2004) and *Capital Crimes* (2006), and *The Quality of Mercy* (1989), a historical novel that is remarkably similar to the movie *Shakespeare in Love* (1998), resulting in her filing a plagiarism suit in Federal Court in 1999.

"Discards" was originally published in *A Woman's Eye*, edited by Sara Paretsky (New York, Delacorte, 1991); it was first collected in *The Garden of Eden and Other Criminal Delights* by Faye Kellerman (New York, Warner, 2006).

Discards

FAYE KELLERMAN

BECAUSE HE'D HUNG AROUND long enough, Malibu Mike wasn't considered a bum but a fixture. All of us locals had known him, had accustomed ourselves to his stale smell, his impromptu orations and wild hand gesticulations. Malibu preaching from his spot—a bus bench next to a garbage bin, perfect for foraging. With a man that weatherbeaten, it had been hard to assign him an age, but the police had estimated he'd been between seventy and ninety when he died—a decent stay on the planet.

Originally they'd thought Malibu had died from exposure. The winter has been a chilly one, a new arctic front eating through the god-awful myth that Southern California is bathed in continual sunshine. Winds churned the tides gray-green, charcoal clouds blanketed the shoreline. The night before last had been cruel. But Malibu had been protected under layers and layers of clothing—a barrier that kept his body insulated from the low of forty degrees.

Malibu had always dressed in layers even when the mercury grazed the hundred-degree mark. That fact was driven home when the obituary in the Malibu *Crier* announced his weight as 126. I'd always thought of him as chunky, but now I realized it had been the clothes.

I put down the newspaper and turned up the knob on my kerosene heater. Rubbing my hands together, I looked out the window of my trailer. Although it was gray, rain wasn't part of the forecast and that was good. My roof was still pocked with leaks that I was planning to fix today. But then the phone rang. I didn't recognize the woman's voice on the other end, but she must have heard about me from someone I knew a long time ago. She asked for *Detective* Darling.

"Former detective," I corrected her. "This is Andrea Darling. Who am I talking to?"

A throat cleared. She sounded in the range of middle-aged to elderly. "Well, you don't know me personally. I am a friend of Greta Berstat."

A pause allowing me to acknowledge recognition. She was going to wait a long time.

"Greta Berstat," she repeated. "You were the detective on her burglary? You found the men who had taken her sterling flatware and the candlesticks and the tea set?"

The bell went off and I remembered Greta Berstat. When I'd been with LAPD, my primary detail was grand theft auto. Greta's case had come my way during a brief rotation through burglary.

"Greta gave you my phone number?" I inquired.

"Not exactly," the woman explained. "You see, I'm a local resident and I found your name in the Malibu Directory—the one put out by the

Chamber of Commerce? You were listed under Investigation right between Interior Design and Jewelers."

I laughed to myself. "What can I do for you, Ms. . . ."

"Mrs. Pollack," the woman answered. "Deirdre Pollack. Greta was over at my house when I was looking through the phone book. When she saw your name, her eyes grew wide and my-oh-my did she sing your praises, Detective Darling."

I didn't correct her this time. "Glad to have made a fan. How can I help you, Mrs. Pollack?"

"Deirdre, please."

"Deirdre it is. What's up?"

Deirdre hemmed and hawed. Finally, she said, "Well, I have a little bit of a problem."

I said, "Does this problem have a story behind it?"

"I'm afraid it does."

"Perhaps it would be best if we met in person?"

"Yes, perhaps it would be best."

"Give me your address," I said. "If you're local, I can probably make it down within the hour."

"An hour?" Deirdre said. "Well, that would be simply lovely!"

From Deirdre's living room I had a one-eighty-degree view of the coastline. The tides ripped relentlessly away at the rocks ninety feet below. You could hear the surf even this far up, the steady whoosh of water advancing and retreating. Deirdre's estate took up three landscaped acres, but the house, instead of being centered on the property, was perched on the edge of the bluff. She'd furnished the place warmly—plants and overstuffed chairs and lots of maritime knickknacks.

I settled into a chintz wing chair; Deirdre was positioned opposite me on a loveseat. She insisted on making me a cup of coffee, and while she did I took a moment to observe her.

She must have been in her late seventies, her face scored with hundreds of wrinkles. She was short with a loose turkey wattle under her chin, her cheeks were heavily rouged, her thin lips painted bright red. She had flaming red hair and false eyelashes that hooded blue eyes turned milky from cataracts. She had a tentative manner, yet her voice was firm and pleasant. Her smile seemed genuine even if her teeth weren't. She wore a pink suit, a white blouse, and orthopedic shoes.

"You're a lot younger than I expected," Deirdre said, handing me a china cup.

I smiled and sipped. I'm thirty-eight and have been told I look a lot younger. But to a woman Deirdre's age, thirty-eight still could be younger than expected.

"Are you married, Detective?" Deirdre asked.

"Not at the moment." I smiled.

"I was married for forty-seven years." Deirdre sighed. "Mr. Pollack passed away six years ago. I miss him."

"I'm sure you do." I put my cup down. "Children?"

"Two. A boy and a girl. Both are doing well. They visit quite often."

"That's nice," I said. "So . . . you live by yourself."

"Well, yes and no," she answered. "I sleep alone but I have daily help. One woman for weekdays, another for weekends."

I looked around the house. We seemed to be alone and it was ten o'clock Tuesday morning. "Your helper didn't show up today?"

"That's the little problem I wanted to tell you about."

I took out my notebook and pen. "We can start now if you're ready."

"Well, the story involves my helper," Deirdre said. "My housekeeper. Martina Cruz . . . that's her name."

I wrote down the name.

"Martina's worked for me for twelve years," Deirdre said. "I've become quite dependent on her. Not just to give me pills and clean up the house. But we've become good friends. Twelve years is a long time to work for someone."

I agreed, thinking: twelve years was a long time to do anything.

Deirdre went on. "Martina lives far away from Malibu, far away from me. But she has never missed a day in all those years without calling me first. Martina is very responsible. I respect her and trust her. That's why I'm puzzled even though Greta thinks I'm being naïve. Maybe I am being naïve, but I'd rather think better of people than to be so cynical."

"Do you think something happened to her?" I said.

"I'm not sure." Deirdre bit her lip. "I'll relate the story and maybe you can offer a suggestion."

I told her to take her time.

Deirdre said. "Well, like many old women, I've acquired things over the years. I tell my children to take whatever they want but there always seem to be leftover items. Discards. Old flower pots, used cookware, out-of-date clothing and shoes and hats. My children don't want those kinds of things. So if I find something I no longer need, I usually give it to Martina.

"Last week, I was cleaning out my closets. Martina was helping me." She sighed. "I gave her a pile of old clothes to take home. I remember it well because I asked her how in the world she'd be able to carry all those items on the bus. She just laughed. And oh, how she thanked me. Such a sweet girl . . . twelve years she worked for me."

I nodded, pen poised at my pad.

"I feel so silly about this," Deirdre said. "One of the robes I gave her . . . it was Mr. Pollack's old robe, actually. I threw out most of his things after he died. It was hard for me to look at them. I couldn't imagine why I had kept his shredded old robe."

She looked down at her lap.

"Not more than fifteen minutes after Martina left, I realized why I hadn't given the robe away. I kept my diamond ring in one of the pockets. I have three different diamond rings—two

of which I keep in a vault. But it's ridiculous to have rings and always keep them in a vault. So this one—the smallest of the three—I kept at home, wrapped in an old sock and placed in the left pocket of Mr. Pollack's robe. I hadn't worn any of my rings in ages, and being old, I guess it simply slipped my mind.

"I waited until Martina arrived home and phoned her just as she walked through her door. I told her what I had done and she looked in the pockets of the robe and announced she had the ring. I was *thrilled*—delighted that nothing had happened to it. But I was also extremely pleased by Martina's honesty. She said she would return the ring to me on Monday. I realize now that I should have called my son and asked him to pick it up right at that moment, but I didn't want to insult her."

"I understand."

"Do you?" Deirdre said, grabbing my hand. "Do you think I'm foolish for trusting someone who has worked for me for twelve years?"

Wonderfully foolish. "You didn't want to insult her," I said, using her words.

"Exactly," Deirdre answered. "By now you must have figured out the problem. It is now Tuesday. I still don't have my diamond and I can't get hold of Martina."

"Is her phone disconnected?" I asked.

"No. It just rings and rings and no one answers it."

"Why don't you just send your son down now?"

"Because . . ." She sighed. "Because I don't want him to think of his mother as an old fool. Can you go down for me? I'll pay you for your time. I can afford it."

I shrugged. "Sure."

"Wonderful!" Deirdre exclaimed. "Oh, thank you so much."

I gave her my rates and they were fine with her. She handed me a piece of paper inked with Martina's name, address, and phone number. I didn't know the exact location of the house, but I knew the area. I thanked her for the information, then said, "Deirdre, if it looks like Martina took off with the ring, would you like me to inform the police for you?"

"No!" she said adamantly.

"Why not?" I asked.

"Even if Martina took the ring, I wouldn't want to see her in jail. We have too many years together for me to do that."

"You can be my boss anytime," I said.

"Why?" Deirdre asked. "Do you do house-keeping too?"

I informed her that I was a terrible house-keeper. As I left, she looked both grateful and confused.

Martina Cruz lived on Highland Avenue south of Washington—a street lined by small houses tattooed with graffiti. The address on the paper was a wood-sided white bungalow with a tar paper roof. The front lawn—mowed but devoid of shrubs—was bisected by a cracked red plaster walkway. There was a two-step hop onto a porch whose decking was wet and rotted. The screen door was locked, but a head-size hole had been cut through the mesh. I knocked through the hole but no one answered. I turned the knob and, to my surprise, the door yielded, screen and all.

I called out a "hello," and when no one answered, I walked into the living room—an eight-by-ten rectangle filled with hand-me-down furnishings. The sofa fabric, once gold, had faded to dull mustard. Two mismatched chairs were positioned opposite it. There was a scarred dining table off the living room, its centerpiece a black-and-white TV with rabbit ears. Encircling the table were six folding chairs. The kitchen was tiny, but the counters were clean, the food in the refrigerator still fresh. The trash hadn't been taken out in a while. It was brimming over with Corona beer bottles.

I went into the sole bedroom. A full-size mattress lay on the floor. No closets. Clothing was neatly arranged in boxes—some filled with little-girl garments, others stuffed with adult apparel. I quickly sifted through the piles, trying to find Mr. Pollack's robe.

I didn't find it—no surprise. Picking up a corner of the mattress, I peered underneath but didn't see anything. I poked around a little longer, then checked out the backyard—a dirt lot holding a rusted swing set and some deflated rubber balls.

I went around to the front and decided to question the neighbors. The house on the immediate left was occupied by a diminutive, thickset Latina matron. She was dressed in a floral print muumuu and her hair was tied in a bun. I asked her if she'd seen Martina lately, and she pretended not to understand me. My Spanish, though far from perfect, was understandable, so it seemed as if we had a little communication gap. Nothing that couldn't be overcome by a ten-dollar bill.

After I gave her the money, the woman informed me her name was Alicia and she hadn't seen Martina, Martina's husband, or their two little girls for a few days. But the lights had been on last night, loud music booming out of the windows.

"Does Martina have any relatives?" I asked Alicia in Spanish.

"Ella tiene una hermana pero no sé a donde vive."

Martina had a sister but Alicia didn't know where she lived. Probing further, I found out the sister's name—Yolanda Flores. And I also learned that the little girls went to a small parochial school run by the *Iglesia Evangélica* near Western Avenue. I knew the church she was talking about.

Most people think of Hispanics as always being Catholic. But I knew from past work that Evangelical Christianity had taken a strong foothold in Central and South America. Maybe I could locate Martina or the sister, Yolanda, through the church directory. I thanked Alicia and went on my way.

The Pentecostal Church of Christ sat on a quiet avenue—an aqua-blue stucco building that looked more like an apartment complex than a house of worship. About twenty-five primary-grade children were playing in an outdoor parking lot, the perimeters defined by a cyclone fence. The kids wore green-and-red uniforms and looked like moving Christmas tree ornaments.

I went through the gate, dodging racing children, and walked into the main sanctuary. The chapel wasn't large—around twenty by thirty—but the high ceiling made it feel spacious. There were three distinct seating areas—the Pentecostal triad: married women on the right, married men on the left, and mixed young singles in the middle. The pews faced a stage that held a thronelike chair upholstered in red velvet. In front of the throne was a lectern sandwiched between two giant urns sprouting plastic flowers. Off to the side were several electric guitars and a drum set, the name *Revelación* taped on the bass drum. I heard footsteps from behind and turned around.

The man looked to be in his early thirties with thick dark straight hair and bright green eyes. His face held a hint of Aztec warrior—broad nose, strong cheekbones and chin. Dressed in casual clothing, he was tall and muscular, and I was acutely aware of his male presence. I asked him where I might find the pastor and was surprised when he announced that he was the very person.

I'd expected someone older.

I stated my business, his eyes never leaving mine as I spoke. When I finished, he stared at me for a long time before telling me his name—Pastor Alfredo Gomez. His English was unaccented.

"Martina's a good girl," Gomez said. "She would never take anything that didn't belong to her. Some problem probably came up. I'm sure everything will work out and your *patrona* will get her ring back."

"What kind of problem?"

The pastor shrugged.

"Immigration problems?" I probed.

Another shrug.

"You don't seem concerned by her disappearance."

He gave me a cryptic smile.

"Can you tell me one thing?" I asked. "Are her children safe?"

"I believe they're in school," Gomez said.

"Oh." I brightened. "Did Martina bring them in?"

"No." Gomez frowned. "No, she didn't. Her sister brought them in today. But that's not unusual."

"You haven't seen Martina today?"

Gomez shook his head. I thought he was telling me the truth, but maybe he wasn't. Maybe the woman was hiding from the INS. Still, after twelve years, you'd think she'd have applied for amnesty. And then there was the obvious alternative. Martina had taken the ring and was hiding out somewhere.

"Do you have Martina's husband's work number? I'd like to talk with him."

"José works construction," Gomez said. "I have no idea what crew he's on or where he is."

"What about Martina's sister, Yolanda Flores?" I said. "Do you have her phone number?"

The pastor paused.

"I'm not from the INS." I fished around inside my wallet and came up with my private investigator's license.

He glanced at it. "This doesn't mean anything."

"Yeah, that's true," I put my ID back in my purse. "Just trying to gain some trust. Look, Pastor, my client is really worried about Martina. She doesn't give a hoot about the ring. She specifically told me *not* to call the police even if Martina took the ring—"

Gomez stiffened and said, "Martina wouldn't do that."

"Okay. Then help us both out, Pastor. Martina might be in some real trouble. Maybe her sister knows something."

Silently, Gomez weighed the pros and cons of trusting me. I must have looked sincere because he told me to wait a moment, then came back with Yolanda's work number.

"You won't regret this," I assured him.

"I hope I don't," Gomez said.

I thanked him again, taking a final gander at those beautiful green eyes before I slipped out the door.

I found a pay booth around the corner, slipped a quarter in the slot, and waited. An accented voice whispered hello.

Using my workable Spanish, I asked for Yolanda Flores. Speaking English, the woman informed me that she was Yolanda. In the background I heard the wail of a baby.

"I'm sorry if this is a bad time," I apologized. "I'm looking for your sister."

There was a long pause at the other end of the line.

Quickly, I said, "I'm not from *inmigración*. I was hired by Mrs. Deirdre Pollack to find Martina and was given your work number by Pastor Gomez. Martina hasn't shown up for work in two days and Mrs. Pollack is worried about her."

More silence. If I hadn't heard the same baby crying, I would have thought she'd hung up the phone.

"You work for Missy Deirdre?" Yolanda asked.

"Yes," I said. "She's very worried about your sister. Martina hasn't shown up for work. Is your sister okay?"

Yolanda's voice cracked. "Es no good. Monday *en la tarde*, Martina husband call me. He tell me she don' work for Missy Deirdre and she have new job. He tell me to pick up her girls cause Martina work late. So I pick up the girls from the school and take them with me.

"Later, I try to call her, she's not *home*. I call and call but no one answers. I don' talk to José, I don' talk to no one. I take the girls to school this morning. Then José, he call me again."

"When?"

"About two hour. He ask me to take girls. I say jes, but where is Martina? He tell me she has to sleep in the house where she work. I don' believe him."

It was my turn not to answer right away. Yolanda must have been bouncing the baby or something because the squalling had stopped.

"You took the children yesterday?" I asked.

"I take her children, jes. I no mind takin' the kids but I want to talk to Martina. And José . . . he don' give me the new work number. I call Martina's house, no one answer. I goin' to call Missy Deirdre and ask if Martina don' work there no more. *Ahorita*, you tell me Missy Deirdre call *you*. I . . . scared."

"Yolanda, where can I find José?"

"He works *construcción*. I don' know where. Mebbe he goes home after work and don' answer the phone. You can go to Martina's house tonight?"

"Yes, I'll do that," I said. "I'll give you my phone number, you give me yours. If you find out anything, call me. If I find out something, I'll call you. Okay?"

"Okay."

We exchanged numbers, then said good-bye. My next call was to Deirdre Pollack. I told her about my conversation with Yolanda. Deirdre was sure that Martina hadn't taken a new job. First of all, Martina would never just leave her flat. Secondly, Martina would never leave her children to work as a sleep-in housekeeper.

I wasn't so sure. Maybe Martina had fled with the ring and was lying low in some private home. But I kept my thoughts private and told Deirdre my intention to check out Martina's house tonight. She told me to be careful. I thanked her and said I'd watch my step.

At night, Martina's neighborhood was the mean streets, the sidewalks supporting pimps and prostitutes, pushers and buyers. Every half hour or so, the homeboys cruised by in souped-up low riders, their ghetto blasters pumping out body-rattling bass vibrations. I was glad I had my Colt .38 with me, but at the same time I wished it were a Browning Pump.

I sat in my truck, waiting for some sign of life at Martina's place, and my patience was rewarded two hours later. A Ford pickup parked in front of the framed house, and out came four dark-complexioned males dressed nearly identically:

jeans, dark windbreakers zipped up to the neck, and hats. Three of them wore ratty baseball caps; the biggest and fattest wore a bright white painter's cap. Big-and-Fat was shouting and singing. I couldn't understand his Spanish—his speech was too rapid for my ear—but the words I could pick up seemed slurred. The other three men were holding six-packs of beer. From the way all of them acted, the six-packs were not their first of the evening.

They went inside. I slipped my gun into my purse and got out of my truck, walking up to the door. I knocked. My luck: Big-and-Fat answered. Up close he was nutmeg-brown with fleshy cheeks and thick lips. His teeth were rotten and he smelled of sweat and beer.

"I'm looking for Martina Cruz," I said in Spanish.

Big-and-Fat stared at me—at my *Anglo* face. He told me in English that she wasn't home.

"Can I speak to José?"

"He's no home, too."

"I saw him come in." It wasn't really a lie, more of an educated guess. Maybe one of the four men was José.

Big-and-Fat stared at me, then broke into a contemptuous grin. "I say he no home."

I heard Spanish in the background, a male voice calling out the name José. I peered around Big-and-Fat's shoulders, trying to peek inside, but he stepped forward, making me back up. His expression was becoming increasingly hostile, and I always make it a point not to provoke drunk men who outweigh me.

"I'm going," I announced with a smile.

"Pasqual," someone said. A thinner version of Big-and-Fat stepped onto the porch. "Pasqual, *qué pasó*?"

Opportunity knocked. I took advantage.

"I'm looking for José Cruz," I said as I kept walking backward. "I've been hired to look for Martin—"

The thinner man blanched.

"Go away!" Pasqual thundered out. "Go or I kill you!"

I didn't stick around to see if he'd make good on his threat.

The morning paper stated that Malibu Mike, having expired from natural causes, was still in deep freeze, waiting for a relative to claim his body. He'd died buried under tiers of clothing, his feet wrapped in three pairs of socks stuffed into size twelve mismatched shoes. Two pairs of gloves had covered his hands, and three scarves had been wrapped around his neck. A Dodgers' cap was perched atop a ski hat that cradled Malibu's head. In all those layers, there was not one single piece of ID to let us know who he really was. After all these years, I thought he deserved a decent burial, and I guess I wasn't the only one who felt that way. The locals were taking up a collection to have him cremated. Maybe a small service, too—a few words of remembrance, then his ashes would be mixed with the tides.

I thought Malibu might have liked that. I took a twenty from my wallet and began to search the trailer for a clean envelope and a stamp. I found what I was looking for and was addressing the envelope when Yolanda Flores called me.

"Dey find her," she said, choking back sobs. "She *dead*. The police find her in a trash can. She beat to death. Es *horrible*!"

"Yolanda, I'm so sorry." I really was. "I wish I could do something for you."

"You wan' do somethin' for me?" Yolanda said. "You find out what happen to my sister."

Generally I like to be paid for my services, but my mind flashed to little dresses in cardboard boxes. I knew what it was like to live without a mother. Besides, I was still fuming over last night's encounter with Pasqual.

"I'll look into it for you," I said.

There was a silence across the line.

"Yolanda?"

"I still here," she said. "I . . . surprise you help me."

"No problem."

"Thank you." She started to cry. "Thank you very much. I pay you—"

"Forget it."

"No, I work for you on weekends—"

"Yolanda, I live in a trailer and couldn't find anything if you cleaned up my place. Forget about paying me. Let's get back to your sister. Tell me about José. Martina and him get along?"

There was a very long pause. Yolanda finally said, "José no good. He and his brothers."

"Is Pasqual one of José's brothers?"

"How you know?"

I told her about my visit with Pasqual the night before, about Big-and-Fat's threat. "Has he ever killed anyone before?"

"I don' know. He drink and fight. I don' know if he kill anyone when he's drunk."

"Did you ever see Pasqual beating Martina?"

"No," Yolanda said. "I never see that."

"What about José?"

Another moment of silence.

Yolanda said, "He slap her mebbe one or two time. I tell her to leave him but she say no 'cause of the girls."

"Do you think José could kill Martina?"

Yolanda said, "He slap her when he drink. But I don' think he would kill her to kill her."

"He wouldn't do it on purpose."

"Essackly."

"Yolanda, would José kill Martina for money?"

"No," she said firmly. "He's *Evangélico.* A bad *Evangélico,* but not *el diablo.*"

"He wouldn't do it for *lots* of money?"

"No, he don' kill her for money."

I said, "What about Pasqual?"

"I don' think so."

"Martina have any *enemigos*?"

"*Nunca persona!*" Yolanda said. "No one want to hurt her. She like sugar. Es so *terrible*!"

She began to cry. I didn't want to question her over the phone. A face-to-face meeting would be better. I asked her when was the funeral service.

"Tonight. *En la iglesia a las ocho.* After the *culto funeral,* we go to *cementerio.* You wan' come?"

"Yes, I think that might be best." I told her I knew the address of the church and would meet her eight o'clock sharp.

I was unnerved by what I had to do next: break the bad news to Deirdre Pollack. The old woman took it relatively well, never even asked about the ring. When I told her I'd volunteered to look into Martina's death, she offered to pay me. I told her that wasn't necessary, but when she insisted, I didn't refuse.

I got to the church by eight, then realized I didn't know Yolanda from Adam. But she picked me out in a snap. Not a plethora of five-foot-eight, blond, blue-eyed Salvadoran women.

Yolanda was petite, barely five feet and maybe ninety pounds tops. She had yards of long brown hair—Evangelical women don't cut their tresses—and big brown eyes moistened with tears. She took my hand, squeezed it tightly, and thanked me for coming.

The church was filled to capacity, the masses adding warmth to the unheated chapel. In front of the stage was a table laden with broth, hot chocolate, and plates of bread. Yolanda asked me if I wanted anything to eat and I declined.

We sat in the first row of the married women's section. I glanced at the men's area and noticed Pasqual with his cronies. I asked Yolanda to point out José: the man who had come to the door with Pasqual. The other two men were also brothers. José's eyes were swollen and bright red. Crying or post-alcohol intoxication?

I studied him further. He'd been stuffed into an ill-fitting black suit, his dark hair slicked back with grease. All the brothers wore dark suits. José looked nervous, but the others seemed almost jocular.

Pasqual caught me staring, and his expression immediately darkened, his eyes bearing down on me. I felt needles down my spine as he began to rise, but luckily the service started and he sank back into his seat.

Pastor Gomez came to the dais and spoke

about what a wonderful wife and mother Martina had been. As he talked, the women around me began to let out soft, muted sobs. I did manage to sneak a couple of sidelong glances at the brothers. I met up with Pasqual's dark stare once again.

When the pastor had finished speaking, he gave the audience directions to the cemetery. Pasqual hadn't forgotten about my presence, but I was too quick for him, making a beeline for the pastor. I managed to snare Gomez before Pasqual could get to me. The fat slob backed off when the pastor pulled me into a corner.

"What happened?" I asked.

Gomez looked down. "I wish I knew."

"Do the police—"

"Police!" The pastor spat. "They don't care about a dead Hispanic girl. One less flea in their country. I was wearing my work clothes when I got the call this morning. I'd been doing some plumbing and I guess they thought I was a wetback who didn't understand English." His eyes held pain. "They joked about her. They said it was a shame to let such a wonderful body go to waste!"

"That stinks."

"Yes, it stinks." Gomez shook his head. "So you see I don't expect much from the police."

"I'm looking into her death."

Gomez stared at me. "Who's paying you to do it?"

"Not Yolanda," I said.

"Martina's *patrona*. She wants her ring."

"I think she wants justice for Martina."

The pastor blushed from embarrassment.

I said, "I would have done it gratis. I've got some suspicions." I filled him in on my encounter with Pasqual.

Gomez thought a moment. "Pasqual drinks even though the church forbids alcohol. Pasqual's not a bad person. Maybe you made him feel threatened."

"Maybe I did."

"I'll talk to him," Gomez said. "Calm him down. But I don't think you should come to the *cementerio* with us. Now's not the time for accusations."

I agreed. He excused himself as another parishioner approached and suddenly I was alone. Luckily, Pasqual had gone somewhere else. I met up with Yolanda, explaining my reason for not going to the cemetery. She understood.

We walked out to the school yard, into a cold misty night. José and his brothers had already taken off their ties and replaced their suit jackets with warmer windbreakers. Pasqual took a deep swig from a bottle inside a paper bag, then passed the bag to one of his brothers.

"Look at them!" Yolanda said with disgust. "They no even wait till after the funeral. They nothing but *cholos*. Es terrible!"

I glanced at José and his brothers. Something was bothering me and it took a minute or two before it came to me. Three of them—including José—were wearing old baseball caps. Pasqual was the only one wearing a painter's cap.

I don't know why, but I found that odd. Then something familiar began to come up from the subconscious, and I knew I'd better start phoning up bus drivers. From behind me came a gentle tap on my shoulder. I turned around.

Pastor Gomez said, "Thank you for coming, Ms. Darling."

I nodded. "I'm sorry I never met Martina. From what I've heard, she seemed to be a good person."

"She was." Gomez bowed his head. "I appreciate your help and I wish you peace."

Then he turned and walked away. I'd probably never see him again and I felt a little bad about that.

I tailed José the next morning. He and his brothers were part of a crew framing a house in the Hollywood Hills. I kept watch from a quarter block away, my truck partly hidden by the overhanging boughs of a eucalyptus. I was trying to figure out how to get José alone, and then I got a big break. The roach wagon pulled in and José was elected by his brothers to pick up lunch.

I got out of my truck, intercepted him as he carried an armful of burritos, and stuck my .38

in his side, telling him if he said a word, I'd pull the trigger. My Spanish must have been very clear, because he was as mute as Dopey.

After I got him into the cabin of my truck, I took the gun out of his ribs and held it in my lap.

I said, "What happened to Martina?"

"I don' know."

"You're lying," I said. "You killed her."

"I don' kill her!" José was shaking hard. "*Yo juro!* I don' kill her!"

"Who did?"

"I don' know!"

"You killed her for the ring, didn't you, José?" As I spoke, I saw him shrink. "Martina would never tell you she had the ring: she knew you would *take* it from her. But *you* must have found out. You asked her about the ring and she said she didn't have any ring, right?"

José didn't answer.

I repeated the accusation in *español*, but he still didn't respond. I went on.

"You didn't know what to do, did you, José? So you waited and waited and finally, Monday morning, you told your brothers about the ring. But by *that* time, Martina and the ring had already taken the bus to work."

"All we wan' do is talk to her!" José insisted. "Nothin' was esupposed to happen."

"What wasn't supposed to happen?" I asked.

José opened his mouth, then shut it again.

I continued. "Pasqual has a truck—a Ford pickup." I read him the license number. "You and your brothers decided to meet up with her. A truck can go a lot faster than a bus. When the bus made a stop, two of you got on it and made Martina get off."

José shook his head.

"I called the bus company," I said. "The driver remembered you and your brother—two men making this woman carrying a big bag get off at the stop behind the big garbage bin. The driver even asked if she was okay. But Martina didn't want to get you in trouble and said *todo está bien*—everything was fine. But everything wasn't fine, was it?"

Tears welled up in José's eyes.

"You tried to force her in the truck, but she fought, didn't she?"

José remained mute.

"But you did get her in Pasqual's truck," I said. "Only you forgot something. When she fought, she must have knocked off Pasqual's Dodgers' cap. He didn't know it was gone until later, did he?"

José jerked his head up. "How you know?"

"How do I know? I *have* that cap, José." Not exactly true, but close enough. "Now, why don't you tell me what happened?"

José thought a long time. Then he said, "It was assident. Pasqual no mean to hurt her bad. Just get her to talk. She no have ring when we take her off the bus."

"Not in her bag—*su bolsa?*"

"*Ella no tiena niuna bolsa.* She no have bags. She tell us she left ring at home. So we took her home, but she don' fin' the ring. That make me mad. I *saw* her with ring. No good for a wife to *lie* to husband." His eyes filled with rage, his nostrils flared. "No good! A wife must always tell husband the truth!"

"So you killed her," I said.

José said, "Pasqual . . . he did it. It was assident!"

I shook my head in disgust. I sat there in my truck, off guard and full of indignation. I didn't even hear him until it was too late. The driver's door jerked open and the gun flew out of my lap. I felt as if I'd been wrenched from my mother's bosom. Pasqual dragged me to the ground, his face looming over me, his complexion florid and furious. He drew back his fist and aimed it at my jaw.

I rolled my head to one side and his hand hit the ground. Pasqual yelled but not as loud as José did, shouting at his brother to *stop*. Then I heard the click of the hammer. Pasqual heard it too and released me immediately. By now, a crowd had gathered. Gun in hand, José looked at me, seemed to speak English for my benefit.

"You kill Martina!" José screamed out to Pasqual. "I'm going to kill you!"

Pasqual looked genuinely confused. He spoke

in Spanish. "*You* killed her, you little shit! You beat her to death when we couldn't find the ring!"

José looked at me, his expression saying: do you understand this? Something in my eye must have told him I did. I told him to put the gun down. Instead, he turned his back on me and focused his eyes on Pasqual. "You lie. You get drunk, you kill Martina!"

In Spanish, Pasqual said, "I tried to stop you, you *asshole*!"

"You lie!" José said. And then he pulled the trigger.

I charged him before he could squeeze another bullet out of the chamber, but the damage had been done. Pasqual was already dead when the sirens pulled up.

The two other brothers backed José's story. They'd come to confront Martina about the ring. She told them she had left it at home. But when they returned to the house and the ring wasn't around, Pasqual, in his drunken rage, beat Martina to death and dumped her body in the trash.

José will be charged with second degree murder for Pasqual, and maybe a good lawyer'll be able to bargain it down to manslaughter. But I remembered a murderous look in José's eyes after he'd stated that Martina had lied to him. If I were the prosecutor, I'd be going after José with charges of manslaughter on Martina, Murder One on Pasqual. But that's not how the system works. Anyway, my verdict—rightly or wrongly—wouldn't bring Martina back to life.

I called Mrs. Pollack after it was all over. Through her tears, she wished she'd never remembered the ring. It wasn't her fault but she still felt responsible. There was a small consolation. I was pretty sure I knew where the ring was.

I'm not too bad at guesses—like the one about Pasqual losing his hat in a struggle. That simple snapshot in my mind of the brothers at the church—three with beat-up Dodgers' caps, the fourth wearing a *new* painter's cap. Something off kilter.

So my hunch had been correct. Pasqual had once owned a Dodgers' cap. Where had it gone? Same place as Mr. Pollack's robe. Martina had packed the robe in her bag Monday morning. When she was forced off the bus by José and his brothers, I pictured her quickly dumping the bag in a garbage bin at the bus stop, hoping to retrieve it later. She never got that chance.

As for the ring, it was right where I thought it would be: among the discards that had shrouded Malibu Mike the night he died. The Dodgers' cap on Malibu's head got me thinking in the right direction. If Malibu *had* found Pasqual's cap, maybe he found the other bag left behind by Martina. After all, that bin had been his spot.

Good old Malibu. One of his layers had been a grimy old robe. Wedged into the corner of its pocket, a diamond ring. Had Malibu not died that Monday, José might have been a free man today.

Mrs. Pollack didn't feel right about keeping the ring, so she offered it to Yolanda Flores. Yolanda was appreciative of such generosity, but she refused the gift, saying the ring was cursed. Mrs. Pollack didn't take offense; Yolanda was a woman with pride. Finally, after a lot of consideration, Mrs. Pollack gave the ring to the burial committee for Malibu Mike. Malibu never lived wealthy, but he sure went out in high style.

SPOOKED

Carolyn G. Hart

THE AUTHOR OF APPROXIMATELY SIXTY BOOKS, Carolyn Gimpel Hart (1936–   ) had indifferent success during her first dozen years as an author, during which time she wrote six books, four published only in England. Everything changed when she created the charming Death on Demand series featuring Annie Laurance and her boyfriend (later husband), Max Darling.

The Death on Demand bookstore is located on an island off the coast of South Carolina that, for all its coziness, is a lightning rod for murder and violence, with Annie often the brains behind an investigation. The series of bibliomysteries (mystery and crime fiction with the world of books as its background) has drawn a wide audience as it features the one thing that mystery readers have in common: the love of mysteries. The setting enables the characters to discourse on mystery writers and books, past and present, in a totally natural way. The first book in the series (of twenty-seven) was titled, perhaps not unsurprisingly, *Death on Demand* (1987).

Beginning her writing career as a journalist, Hart graduated, a Phi Beta Kappa, with a journalism degree from the University of Oklahoma, where she went on to become an assistant professor in the School of Journalism and Mass Communication. She has been a full-time mystery writer since 1986, being nominated for and winning numerous mystery awards since then, most notably the Grand Master Award in 2014 for lifetime achievement, presented by the Mystery Writers of America.

"Spooked" was originally published in the March 1999 issue of *Ellery Queen's Mystery Magazine*; it was first published in book form in *Murder on Route 66*, edited by Carolyn Wheat (New York, Berkley, 1999).

Spooked

CAROLYN G. HART

THE DUST FROM THE CONVOY rose in plumes. Gretchen stood on tiptoe waving, waving.

A soldier leaned over the tailgate of the olive drab troop carrier. The blazing July sun touched his crew cut with gold. He grinned as he tossed her a bubble gum. "Chew it for me, kid."

Gretchen wished she could run alongside, give him some of Grandmother Lotte's biscuits and honey. But his truck was twenty feet away and another one rumbled in front of her. She ran a few steps, called out, "Good luck. Good luck!" The knobby piece of gum was a precious lump in her hand.

She stood on the edge of the highway until the last truck passed. Grandmother said Highway 66 went all the way to California and the soldiers were on their way to big ships to sail across the ocean to fight the Japs. Gretchen wished she could do something for the war. Her brother Jimmy was a Marine, somewhere in the South Pacific. He'd survived Iwo Jima. Every month they sent him cookies, peanut butter and oatmeal raisin and spice, packed in popcorn. When they had enough precious sugar, they made Aunt Bill's candy but Mom had to find the sugar in Tulsa. Mr. Hudson's general store here in town almost never had sacks of sugar. Every morning she and Grandmother sat in a front pew of the little frame church in the willows and prayed for Jimmy and for all the boys overseas and for Gretchen's mom

working so hard at the defense plant in Tulsa. Her mom only came home about one weekend a month. Grandmother tried to save a piece of meat when she could. Grandmother said her mom was thin as a rail and working too hard, but Gretchen knew it was important for her mom to work. They needed everybody to help and Mom was proud that she put radio parts in the big B-24 Liberators.

Gretchen took a deep breath of the hot heavy air, still laced with dust, and walked across the street to the café. Ever since the war started, they'd been busy from early morning until they ran out of food, sometimes around five o'clock, never later than seven. Of course, they had special ration books for the café, but Grandmother said they couldn't use those points to get sugar for Jimmy. That wouldn't be right.

Gretchen shaded her eyes and looked at the plate glass window. She still felt a kind of thrill when she saw the name painted in bright blue: Victory Café. A thrill but also a tightness in her chest, the kind of feeling she once had when she climbed the big sycamore to get the calico kitten and a branch snapped beneath her feet. For an instant that seemed to last forever, she was falling. She whopped against a thick limb and held on tight. She remembered the sense of strangeness as she fell. And disbelief, the thought that this couldn't be happening to her. There was a strangeness in the café's new name. It had been Pfizer's Café for almost twenty years, but now it didn't do to be proud of being German. Now Grandmother didn't say much in the café because her accent was thick. She was careful not to say *ja* and she let Gretchen do most of the talking. Grandmother prayed for Jimmy and for her sister's family in Hamburg.

Gretchen tucked the bubble gum in the pocket of her pedal pushers. Grandmother wouldn't let her wear shorts even though it was so hot the cotton stuck to her legs. She glanced at the big thermometer hanging by the door. Ninety-eight degrees and just past one o'clock. They'd sure hit over a hundred today, just like every day for the past few weeks. They kept the front door propped, hoping for a little breeze through the screen.

The café was almost as much her home as the boxy three-bedroom frame house a half mile away down a dirt road. Her earliest memories were playing with paper dolls in a corner of the kitchen as her mother and grandmother worked hard and fast, fixing country breakfasts for truck drivers in a hurry to get to Tulsa and on to Oklahoma City and Amarillo with their big rigs. Every morning grizzled old men from around the county gathered at Pfizer's for their newspapers and gossip as well as rashers of bacon, a short stack and scrambled eggs. But everything changed with the war. Camp Crowder just over the line in Missouri brought in thousands of soldiers. Of course, they were busy training, but khaki uniforms were no stranger to the Victory Café even though the menu wasn't what it had been before the war. Now they had meatless Tuesdays and Grandmother fixed huge batches of macaroni and cheese. Sometimes there wasn't any bacon but they had scrambled eggs and grits and fried potatoes. Instead of roast beef, they had hash, the potatoes and meat bubbly in a vinegary sauce. But Grandmother never fixed red cabbage or sauerkraut anymore.

It was up to Gretchen to help her grandmother when her mom moved to Tulsa. She might only be twelve, but she was wiry and strong and she promised herself she'd never complain, not once, not ever, not for the duration. That's what everybody talked about, the duration until someday the war was over. On summer evenings she was too tired to play kick the can and it seemed a long-ago memory when she used to climb up into the maple tree, carrying a stack of movie magazines, and nestle with her back to the trunk and legs dangling.

She gave a swift professional glance around the square room. The counter with red leatherette stools was to the left. The mirror behind the counter sparkled. She'd stood on a stool to polish it after lunch. Now it reflected her: black pig-tails, a skinny face with blue eyes that often looked tired and worried, and a pink Ship 'n Shore blouse and green pedal pushers. Her blouse had started the day crisp and starched, but now it was limp and spattered with bacon grease.

Four tables sat in the center. Three wooden booths ran along the back wall and two booths to the right. The jukebox was tucked between the back booths and the swinging door to the kitchen. It was almost always playing. She loved "Stardust" and "Chattanooga Choo Choo" but the most often played song was "Praise the Lord and Pass the Ammunition." A poster on the wall beside the jukebox pictured a sinking ship and a somber Uncle Sam with a finger to his lips and the slogan: LOOSE LIPS SINK SHIPS. Grandmother told her it meant no one should talk about the troop convoys that went through on Highway 66 or where they were going or talk about soldiers' letters that sometimes carried information that got past the censors. Grandmother said that's why they had to be so careful about the food to make sure there was enough for Jimmy and all the other boys. And that's why they couldn't drive to Tulsa to see Mom. There wasn't enough gas. Grandmother said even a cupful of gas might make a difference one day whether some boy—like Jimmy—lived or died.

Two of the front tables needed clearing. But she made a circuit of the occupied places first.

Deputy Sheriff Carter flicked his cigar and

ash dribbled onto his paunch which started just under his chin and pouched against the edge of the table. He frowned at black and white squares on the newspaper page. He looked at Mr. Hudson across the table. "You know a word for mountain ridge? Five letters." He chewed on his pencil. "Oh, yeah," he murmured. He marked the letters, closed the paper, leaned back in the booth. "Heard they been grading a road out near the McLemore place."

Mr. Hudson clanked his spoon against the thick white coffee mug. "Got some more java, Gretchen?"

She nodded.

Mr. Hudson pursed his thin mouth. "Bud McLemore's son-in-law's a county commissioner, Euel. What do you expect?"

Gretchen hurried to the hot plates behind the counter, brought the steaming coffee pot, refilled both men's mugs.

The deputy sheriff's face looked like an old ham, crusted and pink. "Never no flies on Bud. Maybe my youngest girl'll get herself a county commissioner. 'Course, she spends most of her time at the USO in Tulsa. But she's makin' good money at the Douglas plant. Forty dollars a week." Then he frowned. "But it's sure givin' her big ideas."

Gretchen moved on to the next booth, refilled the cups for some Army officers who had a map spread out on the table.

The younger officer looked just like Alan Ladd. "I've got it marked in a grid, Sir. Here's the last five places they spotted the Spooklight."

The bigger man fingered his little black mustache. "Lieutenant, I want men out in the field every night. We're damn all going to get to the bottom of this business."

Gretchen took her time moving away. The Spooklight. Everybody in town knew the army had set up a special camp about six miles out of town just to look for the Spooklight, those balls of orange or white that rose from nowhere and flowed up and down hills, hung like fiery globes in the scrawny bois d'arc trees, sometimes ran

right up on porches or over barns. Some people said the bouncing globes of light were a reflection from the headlights on Highway 66. Other folks scoffed because the lights had been talked about for a hundred years, long before cars moved on the twisting road.

Gretchen put the coffee on the hotplate, picked up a damp cloth and a tray. She set to work on the table closest to the Army officers.

". . . Sergeant Ferris swore this light was big as a locomotive and it came rolling and bouncing down the road, went right over the truck like seltzer water bouncing in a soda glass. Now, you can't tell me," the black mustache bristled, "that burning gas acts like that."

"No, Sir." The lieutenant sounded just like Cornel Wilde saluting a general in that movie about the fall of Corregidor.

The kitchen door squeaked open. Her grandmother's red face, naturally ruddy skin flushed with heat from the stove, brightened and she smiled. But she didn't say a word. When Gretchen was little, she would have caroled, "*Komm her, mein Schatz.*" Now she waved her floury hands.

Gretchen carried the dirty dishes into the kitchen. The last words she heard were like an Abbott and Costello radio show, a nonsensical mixture, ". . . soon as the war's over . . . set up search parties . . . I'm gonna see if I can patch those tires . . . good training for night . . ."

Four pies sat on the corner table, steam still rising from the latticed crust. The smell of apples and cinnamon and a hint of nutmeg overlay the onions and liver and fried okra cooked for lunch.

"Oh, Grandmother." Gretchen's eyes shone. Apple pie was her most favorite food in all the world. Then, without warning, she felt the hot prick of tears. Jimmy loved apple pie, too.

Grandmother's big blue eyes were suddenly soft. She was heavy and moved slowly, but her arms soon enveloped Gretchen. "No tears. Tomorrow ve send Jimmy a stollen rich with our own pecans. Now, let's take our pies to the counter. But first," she used a sharp knife, cut a generous wedge, scooped it out and placed it on a plate, "I haf saved one piece—*ein*—for you."

The pie plates were still warm. Gretchen held the door for her grandmother. It was almost like a festive procession as they carried the pies to the counter.

The officers watched. Mr. Hudson's nose wrinkled in pleasure. Deputy Carter pointed at the pie plate. "Hey, Lotte, I'll sure take one of those." There was a chorus of calls.

Grandmother dished up the pieces, handing the plates to Gretchen, then stood at the end of the counter, sprigs of silver-streaked blond hair loose from her coronet braids, her blue eyes happy, her plump hands folded on her floury apron. Gretchen refilled all the coffee cups.

Grandmother was behind the cash register when Mr. Hudson paid his check. "Lotte, the deputy may have to put you in jail you make any more pies like that."

Grandmother's face was suddenly still. She looked at him in bewilderment.

Mr. Hudson cackled. "You sure don't have enough sugar to make that many pies. You been dealing in the black market?"

Grandmother's hands shook as she held them up, as if to stop a careening horse. "Oh, *nein*, *ne*—no, no. Not black market. Never. I use honey, honey my cousin Ernst makes himself."

The officers were waiting with their checks. The younger blond man, the one who looked like Alan Ladd, smiled warmly. "*Sprechen Sie deutsch? Dies ist der beste Apfelkuchen den ich je gegessen habe.*"

The deputy tossed down a quarter, a dime, and a nickel for macaroni and cheese, cole slaw, pie, and coffee. He glowered at Grandmother. "No Heine talk needed around here. That right, Lotte?" He glared at the soldier. "How come you speak it so good?"

The blond officer was a much smaller man, but Gretchen loved the way he looked at the deputy like he was a piece of banana peel. "Too bad you don't have a German *Grossmutter* like

she and I do." He nodded toward Gretchen. "We're lucky, you know," and he gave Grandmother a gentle smile. "*Danke schön.*"

But Grandmother's shoulders were drawn tight. She made the change without another word, not looking at any of the men, and when they turned toward the front door, she scuttled to the kitchen.

Gretchen waited a moment, then darted after her.

Grandmother stood against the back wall, her apron to her face, her shoulders shaking.

"Don't cry, Grandmother." Now it was Gretchen who stood on tiptoe to hug the big woman.

Her grandmother wiped her face and said, her accent even more pronounced than usual, "Ve haf vork to do. Enough now."

As her grandmother stacked the dirty dishes in the sink, Gretchen took a clean recipe card. She searched through the file, then printed in large block letters:

LOTTE'S APPLE HONEY VICTORY PIE

6 tart apples
1 cup honey
2 T. flour
1 tsp. cinnamon
dash nutmeg
dash salt
pastry

She took the card and propped it by the cash register.

Back in the kitchen, Grandmother scrubbed the dishes in hot soapy water, then hefted a tea-kettle to pour boiling water over them as they drained. Gretchen mopped the floor. Every so often, the bell jangled from the front and Gretchen hurried out to take an order.

The pie and all the food were gone before five. Grandmother turned the sign in the front window to CLOSED. Then she walked wearily to the counter and picked up the recipe Gretchen had scrawled.

"Let's leave it there, Grandmother." Gretchen was surprised at how stern she sounded.

Her grandmother almost put it down, then shook her head. "Ve don't vant to make the deputy mad, Gretchen."

Gretchen hated hearing the fear in Grandmother's voice. She wanted to insist that the recipe remain. She wanted to say that they hadn't done anything wrong and they shouldn't have to be afraid. But she didn't say anything else as her grandmother held the card tight to her chest and turned away.

"You go on home, Grandmother. I'll close up." Gretchen held up her hands as her grandmother started to protest. "You know I like to close up." She'd made a game of it months ago because she knew Grandmother was so tired by closing time that she almost couldn't walk the half mile to the house and there was still the garbage to haul down to the incinerator and the menus to stack and silverware to roll up in the clean gingham napkins and potatoes to scrub for tomorrow and the jam and jelly jars to be wiped with a hot rag.

Gretchen made three trips to the incinerator, hauling the trash in a wheelbarrow. She liked the creak of the wheel and the caw of the crows and even though it was so hot she felt like an egg on a sizzling griddle, it was fun to use a big kitchen match and set the garbage on fire. She had to stay until she could stir the ashes, be sure the fire was out. She tipped the wheelbarrow over and stood on it to reach up and catch a limb and climb the big cottonwood. She climbed high enough to look out over the town, at the café and at McGrory's gas station and at the flag hanging limp on the pole outside the post office.

If it hadn't been for the ugly way the deputy had acted toward Grandmother, Gretchen probably would never have paid any attention to him. But he'd been mean and she glowered at him through the shifting leaves of the cottonwood.

He didn't see her, of course. He was walking along the highway. A big truck zoomed over the hill. When the driver spotted the deputy's high crowned black hat and khaki uniform, he abruptly slowed. But the deputy wasn't paying any attention, he was just strolling along, his hands in his pockets, almost underneath Gretchen's tree.

A hot day for a walk. Too hot a day for a walk. Gretchen wiped her sticky face against the collar of her blouse. She craned for a better look. Oh, the deputy was turning into the graveyard nestled on the side of the hill near the church. The graveyard was screened from most of the town by a stand of enormous evergreens so only Gretchen and the crows could see past the mossy stone pillars and the metal arch.

Gretchen frowned and remembered the time when Mrs. Whittle caught Sammy Cooper out in the hall without a pass. She'd never forgotten the chagrin on Sammy's face when Mrs. Whittle said, "Samuel, the next time you plan to cut class, don't walk like you have the Hope diamond in your pocket and there's a policeman on every corner." Gretchen wasn't sure what the Hope diamond was, but every time any of the kids saw Sammy for the next year, they'd whistle and shout, "Got the Hope diamond, Sammy?"

The deputy stopped in a huge swath of shade from an evergreen. He peered around the graveyard. What did he expect to see? Nobody there could look at him.

Gretchen forgot how hot she was. She even forgot to be mad. She leaned forward, and grabbed the closest limb, moved it so she could see better.

The deputy made a full circle of the graveyard which was maybe half as big as a football field, no more than forty or fifty headstones. He passed by the stone angel at Grandpa Pfizer's grave and her dad's stone that had a weeping willow on it. That was the old part of the cemetery. A mossy stone, half fallen on one side, marked the grave of a Confederate soldier. Mrs. Peters took Gretchen's social studies class there last year and showed them how to do a rubbing of a stone even though the inscription was scarcely legible. Gretchen shivered when she saw the wobbly indistinct gray letters: Hiram Kelly,

Age 19, wounded July 17, 1863, in the Battle of Honey Springs, died July 29, 1863. Beloved Son of Robert and Effie Kelly, Cherished Brother of Corinne Kelly. Some of the graves still had little American flags, placed there for the Fourth. A half dozen big sprays marked the most recent grave.

Back by the pillars, the deputy made one more careful study of the church and the graveyard, then he pulled a folded sheet of paper from his pocket and knelt by the west pillar. He tugged at a stone about three inches from the ground.

Gretchen couldn't believe her eyes. She leaned so far forward her branch creaked.

The kneeling man's head jerked up.

Gretchen froze quieter than a tick on a dog.

The sun glistened on his face, giving it an unhealthy coppery glow. The eyes that skittered over the headstones and probed the lengthening shadows were dark and dangerous.

A crow cawed. A heavy truck rumbled over the hill, down main street. The faraway wail of Cal Burke's saxophone sounded sad and lonely.

Gradually the tension eased out of the deputy's shoulders. He turned and jammed the paper into the small dark square and poked the stone over the opening, like capping a jar of preserves. He lunged to his feet and strode out of the cemetery, relaxing to a casual saunter once past the church.

Gretchen waited until he climbed into his old black Ford and drove down the dusty road.

She swung down from the tree, thumped onto the wheelbarrow, and jumped to the ground. The bells in the steeple rang six times. She had to hurry. Grandmother would have a light supper ready, pork and beans and a salad with her homemade Thousand Island dressing and a big slice of watermelon.

Gretchen tried not to look like she had the Hope diamond in her pocket. Instead, she whistled as though calling a dog and clapped her hands. A truck roared past on its way north to Joplin. Still whistling, she ran to the stone posts. Once hidden from the road, she worked fast. The oblong slab of stone came right off in her hand. She pulled out the sheet of paper, unfolded it.

She'd had geography last spring with Mrs. Jacobs. She'd made an A. She liked maps, liked the way you could take anything, a mountain, a road, an ocean, and make it come alive on a piece of paper.

She figured this one at a glance, the straight line—though really the road curved and climbed and fell—was Highway 66. The little squiggle slanting off to the northeast from McGrory's station was the dusty road that led to an abandoned zinc mine, the Sister Sue. The X was a little off the road, just short of the mine entrance. There was a round clock face at the top of the sheet. The hands were set at midnight.

She stuffed the folded sheet in its dark space, replaced the stone. X marks the spot. Not a treasure map. That was kid stuff in stories by Robert Louis Stevenson. But nobody hid a note in a stone post unless they were up to something bad, something they didn't want anybody to know about. Tonight. Something secret was going to happen tonight. . . .

Gretchen pulled the sheet up to her chin even though the night oozed heat like the stoves at the café. She was dressed, a tee shirt and shorts, and her sneakers were on the floor. She waited until eleven, watching the slow crawl of the hands on her alarm clock and listening to the summer dance of the June bugs against her window screen. She unhooked the screen, sat on the sill, and dropped to the ground. She wished she could ride her bike, but somebody might be out on the road and see her and they'd sure tell Grandmother. Instead, she figured out the shortest route, cutting across the McClelland farm, careful to avoid the pasture where Old Amos glared out at the world with reddish eyes, and slipping in the shadows down Purdy Road.

The full moon hung low in the sky, its milky radiance creating a black and cream world, making it easy to see. She stayed in the shadows. The buzz of the cicadas was so loud she couldn't hear the cars, so she kept a close eye out for head-lights coming over the hill or around the curve.

Once near the abandoned mine, she moved from shadow to shadow, smelling the sharp scent of the evergreens, feeling the slippy dried nee-dles underfoot. A tremulous, wavering, plaintive shriek hurt her ears. Slowly, it subsided into a moan. Gretchen's heart raced. A sudden flap and an owl launched into the air.

Gretchen looked uneasily around the clear-ing. The boarded-over mine shaft was a dark mound straight ahead. There was a cave-in years ago, and they weren't able to get to the miners in time. In the dark, the curved mound looked like a huge gravestone.

The road, rutted and overgrown, curved past the mine entrance and ended in front of a ram-shackle storage building, perhaps half as large as a barn. A huge padlock hung from a rusty chain wound around the big splintery board that barred the double doors.

Nothing moved though the night was alive with sound, frogs croaking, cicadas rasping.

Gretchen found a big sycamore on the hill-side. She climbed high enough to see over the cleared area. She sat on a fat limb, her back to the trunk, her knees to her chin.

The cicada chorus was so loud she didn't hear the car. It appeared without warning, headlights off, lurching in the deep ruts, crushing an over-growth of weeds as it stopped off the road to one side of the storage shed. The car door slammed. In the moonlight, the deputy's face was a pale mask. As she watched, that pale mask turned ever so slowly, all the way around the clearing.

Gretchen hunkered into a tight crouch. She felt prickles of cold though it was so hot sweat beaded her face, slipped down her arms and legs.

A cigarette lighter flared. The end of the deputy's cigar was a red spot. He leaned inside the car, dragging out something. Metal clanked as he placed the thing on the front car fender. Suddenly he turned toward the rutted lane.

Gretchen heard the dull rumble, too, loud enough to drown out the cicadas.

Dust swirled in a thick cloud as the wheels of the army truck churned the soft ruts.

The sheriff was already moving. He propped a big flashlight on the car fender. By the time the driver turned and backed the truck with its rear end facing the shed, the sheriff was snipping the chain.

The driver of the truck wore a uniform. He jumped down and ran to help and the two men lifted up the big splintery board, tossed it aside. Each man grabbed a door. They grunted and strained and pulled and finally both doors were wide open. The soldier hurried to the back of the truck, let down the metal back.

Gretchen strained to catch glimpses of the soldier as he moved back and forth past the flashlight. Tall and skinny, he had a bright bald spot on the top of his head, short dark hair on the sides. His face was bony with a beaked nose and a chin that sank into his neck. He had ser-geant stripes on his sleeves. He was a lot smaller and skinnier than the deputy but he was twice as fast. They both moved back and forth between the truck and the shed, carrying olive green gas-oline tins in each hand.

Once the sergeant barked, "Get a move on. I've got to get that truck back damn quick."

Even in the moonlight, the deputy's face looked dangerously red and he huffed for breath. He stopped occasionally to mop his face with an oversize handkerchief. The sergeant never paused, and he shot a sour look at the bigger man.

Gretchen tried to count the tins. She got confused, but was sure there were at least forty, maybe a few more.

When the last tin was inside the shed, the doors shoved shut, the chains wrapped around the board, the deputy rested against his car, his breathing as labored as a bulldogger struggling with a calf.

The sergeant planted himself square in front of the gasping deputy and held out his hand.

"Goddam, man"—the deputy's wind whis-tled in his throat—"you gotta wait 'til I sell the stuff. I worked out a deal with a guy in Tulsa.

Top price. A lot more than we could get around here. Besides, black market gas out here might get traced right back to us."

"I want my money." The sergeant's reedy voice sounded edgy and mean.

"Look, fella." The deputy pushed away from the car, glowered down at the smaller man. "You'll get your goddam money when I get mine."

The soldier didn't move an inch. "Okay. That's good. When do you get yours?"

The deputy didn't answer.

"When's the man coming? We'll meet him together." A hard laugh. "We can split the money right then and there."

The deputy wiped his face and neck with his handkerchief. "Sure. You can help us load. Thursday night. Same time."

"I'll be here." The sergeant moved fast to the truck, climbed into the front seat. After he revved the motor, he leaned out of the window. "I'll be here. And you damn sure better be."

Grandmother settled the big blue bowl in her lap, began to snap green beans.

Gretchen was so tired her eyes burned and her feet felt like lead. She swiped the paring knife around the potato. "Grandmother, what does it mean when people talk about selling gas on the black market?"

Grandmother's hand moved so fast, snap, snap, snap. "We don't have much of that around here. Everyone tries hard to do right. The gas has to be used by people like the farmers and Dr. Sherman so he can go to sick people and the Army. The black market is very wrong, Gretchen. Why, what if there wasn't enough gas for the jeeps and tanks where Jimmy is?"

There wasn't much sound then but the snap of beans and the soft squish as the potato peelings fell into the sink.

Gretchen tossed the last potato into the big pan of cold water. "Grandmother," she scooped up the potato peels, "who catches these people in the black market?"

Grandmother carried her bowl to the sink. "I don't know," she said uncertainly. "I guess in the cities the police. And here it would be the deputy. Or maybe the Army."

Gretchen put the dirty dishes on the tray, swiped the cloth across the table.

Deputy Carter grunted, "Bring me some more coffee," but he didn't look up from his copy of the newspaper. He frowned as he printed words in the crossword puzzle.

Across the room, the officer who looked like Alan Ladd was by himself. He smiled at Gretchen. "Tell your grandmother this is the best food I've had since I was home."

Gretchen smiled shyly at him, then she blurted, "Are you still looking for the Spooklight?"

His eyebrows scooted up like snapped window shades. "How'd you know that?"

She polished the table, slid him an uncertain look. "I heard you yesterday," she said softly.

"Oh, sure. Well," he leaned forward conspiratorially, "my colonel thinks it's a great training tool to have the troops search for mystery lights. The first platoon to find them's going to get a free weekend pass."

Gretchen wasn't sure what a training tool was or a free pass, but she focused on what mattered to her. "You mean the soldiers are still looking for the lights? They'll come where the lights are?"

"Fast as they can. Of course," he shrugged, "nobody knows when or where they're going to appear so it's mostly a lot of hiking around in the dark and nothing happens."

Gretchen looked toward the deputy. He was frowning as he scratched out a word, wrote another one. She turned until her back was toward the sheriff. "They say that in July the lights dance around the old Sister Sue mine. That's what I heard the other day." Behind her, she heard the creak as the sheriff slid out of the booth, clumped toward the cash register. "Excuse me," she said quickly and she turned away.

The sheriff paid forty-five cents total, thirty for the Meatless Tuesday vegetable plate, ten for raisin pie, a nickel for coffee.

When the front door closed behind him, Gretchen hurried to the table. As she cleared it, she carefully tucked the discarded newspaper under her arm.

"A cherry fausfade, please." She slid onto the hard metal stool. The soda fountain at Thompson's Drugs didn't offer comfortable stools like those at the Victory Café.

"Cherry phosphate," Millard Thompson corrected. He gave her his sweet smile that made his round face look like a cheerful pumpkin topped by tight coils of red hair. Millard was two years older than she and had lived across the alley all her life. He played the tuba in the junior high band, had collected more tin cans than anybody in town, and knew which shrubs the butterflies liked. Once he led her on a long walk, scrambling through the rugged bois d'arc to a little valley covered with thousands of Monarchs. And in the Thompson wash room, he had two shelves full of chemicals and sometimes he let her watch his experiments. He even had a Bunsen burner. And Millard's big brother Mike was in the 45th, now part of General Patton's Seventh Army. They hadn't heard from him since the landings in Sicily and there was a haunted look in Mrs. Thompson's eyes. Mr. Thompson had a big map at the back of the store and he moved red pins along the invasion route. Mike's unit was reported fighting for the Comiso airport.

Gretchen looked around the store, but it was quiet in midafternoon. Millard's mother was arranging perfumes and powders on a shelf behind the cash register. His dad was in the back of the store behind the pharmacy counter. "Millard," she kept her voice low, "do you know about the black market?"

He leaned his elbow on the counter. "See if I got enough cherry in. Yeah, sure, Gretchen. Dad says it's as bad as being a spy. He says

people who sell on the black market make blood money. He says they don't deserve to have guys like Mike ready to die for them."

Gretchen loved cherry fausfades, okay, she knew it was phosphate but it had always sounded like fausfade to her, but she just held tight to the tall beaded sundae glass. "Okay, then listen, Millard . . ."

Gretchen struggled to stay awake. She waited a half hour after Grandmother turned off her light, then slipped from her window. Millard was waiting by Big Angus's pasture.

As they hurried along Purdy Road, Millard asked, "You sure it was Deputy Carter? And he said it was for the black market?"

"Yes."

Millard didn't answer but she knew he was struggling with the truth that they couldn't go to the man who was supposed to catch bad guys. When they pulled the shed doors wide and he shone his flashlight over the dozens and dozens of five-gallon gasoline tins, he gave a low whistle. Being Millard, he picked up a tin, unscrewed the cap, smelled.

"Gas, all right." There was a definite change in Millard's voice when he spoke. He sounded more grownup and very serious. "We got to do something, Gretchen."

She knew that. That's why she'd come to him. "I know." She, too, sounded somber. "Listen, Millard, I got an idea . . ."

He listened intently while she spoke, then he looked around the clearing, his round face was intent, measuring. Then he grinned. "Sure. Sure we can. Dad's got a bunch of powdered magnesium out in the storeroom. They used to use it with the old-fashioned photography." He looked at her blank face. "For the flash, Gretchen. Here's what we'll do . . ."

Gretchen could scarcely bear the relief that flooded through her when the young lieutenant stopped in for coffee and pie Wednesday afternoon. When she refilled his cup, she said quickly, "Will you look for the Spooklight tonight?"

The lieutenant sighed. "Every night. Don't know why the darned thing's disappeared just when we started looking for it."

"A friend of mine saw it last night. Near the Sister Sue mine." She gripped her cleaning cloth tightly. "If you'll look there tonight, I'm sure you'll find it."

It was cloudy Wednesday night, the last night before the man from Tulsa would come to get that gas. Gretchen and Millard moved quickly around the clearing, Gretchen clambering up in the trees, Millard handing her the pie tins Gretchen brought from the café's kitchen. She scrambled to high branches, fastened the tins with duct tape.

"You think they'll come," Millard asked as they unwrapped the chain, lifted the board and tugged the doors to the storage shed wide open. Gretchen carefully tucked the newspaper discarded by the sheriff between two tins.

"Yes." There had been a sudden sharpness in the young officer's eyes. She'd had the feeling he really listened to her. Maybe she felt that way because she wanted it so badly, but there was a calmness in her heart. He would come. He would come.

Millard took his place high in the branches of an oak that grew close to the boarded-over mine shaft. Gretchen clutched the oversize flashlight and checked over in her mind which trees had the pie tins and how she could move in the shadows to reach them.

Suddenly Millard began to scramble down the tree. "Gretchen, Gretchen, where are you?"

"Over here, Millard." She moved out into the clearing. "What's wrong?"

He was panting. "It's the army, but they're going down the wrong road. They're on the road to Hell Hollow. They won't come close enough to see us."

Gretchen could hear the noise now from the road on the other side of the hill.

"I'll go through the woods. I've got my stuff." And Millard disappeared in the night.

Gretchen almost followed. But if Millard decoyed them this way, she had to be ready to do her part.

Suddenly a light burst in the sky and it would be easily seen from Hell Hollow road. Nobody who knew beans would have thought it was the Spooklight but, by golly, it was an odd, unexplained flash in the night sky. Then came another flash and another.

Shouts erupted. "Look, look, there it is."

"Quick. This way."

"Over the hill."

If Millard had been there, she would have hugged him. He'd taken lumps of the powdered magnesium, wrapped them in net (Gretchen had found an old dress of her mom's and cut off the net petticoat), and added a string wick they'd dipped in one of the gas tins. He lighted the wick and used his slingshot to toss the soon-to-explode packet high in the air.

Gretchen heard Millard crashing back through the woods. He just had enough time to climb the oak when the soldiers swarmed into the clearing. Gretchen slithered from shadow to shadow, briefly shining the flash high on the tins. The reflected light quivered oddly high in the branches. She made her circuit, then slipped beneath a thick pine and lay on her stomach to watch.

Two more flares shone in the sky and then three in succession blazed right in front of the open shed doors.

The local *Gazette* used headlines as big as the Invasion of Sicily in the Friday morning edition.

ARMY UNIT FINDS
BLACK MARKET GAS
AT SISTER SUE MINE

Army authorities revealed today that unexplained light flashing in the sky led a patrol to a cache of stolen gasoline . . .

It was the talk of the town. Five days later, when Deputy Sheriff Euel Carter was arrested, the local breakfast crowd was fascinated to hear from Mr. Hudson who heard it from someone who heard it on the post, "You know how Euel always did them damfool crossword puzzles. Well," Mr. Hudson leaned across the table, "seems he left a newspaper right there in the storage shed and the puzzle was all filled out in his handwriting. Joe Bob Terrell from the *Gazette* recognized his handwriting, said he'd seen it a million times in arrest records. The newspaper had Euel's fingerprints all over it and they found his prints on the gas tins. They traced the tins to Camp Crowder and they checked the prints of everybody in the motor pool and found some from this sergeant and his were on half the tins and on the boards that sealed up that shack by the Sister Sue. They got 'em dead to rights."

Gretchen poured more coffee and smiled. At lunch the nice officer—she'd known he would come that night—had left her a big tip. He'd looked at her, almost asked a question, then shook his head. She could go to Thompson's for a cherry fausfade in a little while and tell Millard everything she'd heard. It was too bad they couldn't tell everyone how clever Millard had been with the magnesium. But that was okay. What really mattered was the gas. Now maybe there'd be enough for Jimmy and Mike.

MAKING LEMONADE

Barbara Paul

SOME PEOPLE TURN TO WRITING because it's fun, or because they feel unsuited to any other type of employment, or because they are driven to it by a passionate desire to tell stories, unable to stop unleashing the creativity that is wildly screaming to be let loose. For Barbara Jeanne Paul (1931–   ), who was working as a teacher, the reason she turned to producing fiction, she claimed, is that she simply could not stand the notion of reading another undergraduate paper.

After an early career writing science fiction, beginning with *An Exercise for Madmen* (1978), followed by three more sci-fi books in the next three years, she switched to mystery novels and quickly became established in that genre.

Her first mystery novel, *The Fourth Wall* (1979), reflected her affection for the theater. Her second, *Liars and Tyrants and People Who Turn Blue* (1980), combined science fiction with mystery. As a test to determine how fast a full-length novel could be written, she wrote, in two weeks, *Your Eyelids Are Growing Heavy* (1981), about a woman who deduces that she has been hypnotized when a large piece of her life has vanished from her memory. Paul wrote three historical mysteries featuring the great opera singer Enrico Caruso: *A Cadenza for Caruso* (1984), *Prima Donna at Large* (1985), and *A Chorus of Detectives* (1987). Her series protagonist, Marian Larch of the New York Police Department, starred in seven novels, beginning with *The Renewable Virgin* (1984). Paul's 1985 novel *Kill Fee* was the inspiration for the 1990 made-for-television movie titled *Murder C.O.D.*, in which a Chicago cop is being blackmailed for having an extramarital affair. When he and his wife move to Portland, Oregon, the blackmailer follows. It starred Patrick Duffy and William Devane.

"Making Lemonade" was originally published in *Sisters in Crime 4*, edited by Marilyn Wallace (New York, Berkley, 1991).

Making Lemonade

BARBARA PAUL

THE DEAD MAN WAS JAPANESE, dressed in a Ralph Lauren suit that had amazingly little blood on it. Mid-forties, dapper even in death. His second-floor apartment reflected an almost stereotypical love of order, of serenity, of delicate objects, at the same time avoiding any chauvinism in its decoration: the clean-lined sofa was a German design, the lighting fixtures were from Sweden. But the ambience remained unquestionably Japanese—the expanse of open floor space, the lack of clutter, the exact positioning of one perfect bowl on the reflecting surface of a table. The normally bull-voiced uniformed cops who'd invaded the dead man's sanctuary spoke in muted tones, unconsciously adjusting to their environment; designed to soothe, the apartment could also intimidate. Detective Sergeant Marian Larch knelt on the floor and examined the three small bullet holes in the dead man's chest. *What a waste,* she thought.

His name was Tatsuya Nakamoto, and he was with Sony Corporation; that much she knew. A wedding ring said there was a Mrs. Nakamoto. The owner of the ground-floor apartment directly under Nakamoto's had called the police; he'd heard the shots and had even caught a glimpse of the killer from the back as he ran out of the building. Thin, Caucasian, brown hair, under six feet. Scruffy-looking. Only about a million people in New York who fit that description.

A pane in a glass door leading to the second-floor balcony had been broken from the outside. Next to the balcony grew an elm tree, graceful and decorative, and, apparently, climbable. The building itself was on Second Avenue in the East Village; fully renovated and almost lavishly decorated, it was a four-story home to four upscale families who were doing their part to help gentrify the part of Manhattan that fell within the city's Ninth Precinct. Three blocks away were slums; five blocks away were the project houses. Haves unwittingly daring the have-nots to prey upon them; the have-nots frequently taking the dare.

"A doper," said Foley. "Thinks the place is empty. Shinnies up that tree to grab what he can carry in one trip and out again. But Nakamoto surprises him. The doper pops him up close three times with his little twenty-two and hightails it outta here."

Marian nodded; her partner probably had it right. No billfold on the body . . . but an expensive watch and ring were left; the killer must be new at this. She went out onto the balcony. No leaves, no twigs or little pieces of bark. She reached up and touched the nearest branch of the elm; two leaves detached themselves and drifted to her feet. Marian went back in and gestured to one of the uniformed officers; she asked him to go down and see if he could find any signs that the tree had been climbed. Then if he couldn't, find out if the tree *could* be climbed.

"You want me to climb the tree."

"That's right."

"How far?"

"All the way, if you can."

The officer didn't quite roll his eyes as he went out. Marian followed him to the door and checked the lock. No sign of a forced entry. She went into the kitchen looking for a back door and found one; the lock had not been forced there either. Using a handkerchief she carried for the purpose, she grasped the base of the knob and opened the door; on the other side was a landing in the service stairway.

On the landing she spotted a white plastic card of the size meant to be carried in a billfold. Marian picked it up carefully by the edges. On one side was a calendar in print so tiny as to be virtually unreadable. On the other side were the name, address, and phone number of a local pharmacy. *24-Hr Delivery*, it said. Marian put the card in a plastic evidence bag.

"Shit!" came Foley's voice from the living room. The only environment that ever intimidated Foley was the precinct captain's office. Marian went back in and found him bending over the body. "He's still wearing his wristwatch. And a ring."

Glad you noticed, Marian thought.

"We got a amateur here," her partner complained. "This one's gonna be a bitch."

"Amateurs make mistakes." She held up the plastic bag.

Foley turned his head sideways to read the print. "Markham's Pharmacy? Where'd you find it?"

"Service stairway outside the back door. Technically off the premises? But close enough."

Foley snorted. "It fell out of a package being delivered. And the delivery coulda been for another floor."

"True. But how does a card 'fall out' of a package? We'll have to check if Markham's Pharmacy made any deliveries here today."

Foley grunted assent. "And we better find out the last time that stairway was cleaned."

"Good idea." Marian wandered through the rest of the apartment. The bedroom was spacious and masculine-looking, with separate dressing rooms and closets. With her handkerchief she opened one of the closets. About three-fourths of the space was taken up with men's suits and shirts; the rest was filled with kimonos. So Nakamoto dressed the part when he was out in the world, but at home he liked the old ways. Marian opened the other closet and found just the opposite proportion: Mrs. Nakamoto had a few suits and dresses, but kimonos made up the bulk of her wardrobe. You didn't have to be a genius to figure that one out.

Marian found no other beds in the apartment; evidently the Nakamotos never entertained overnight guests. She did find a separate dining room, a home office complete with computer and filing cabinets, a room filled with electronic equipment in which a large-screen Sony dominated, several sitting/thinking/whatever rooms; one looked like a small art gallery. And everywhere the decor was pronouncedly masculine. *Or maybe it only looks that way to me,* Marian thought. The difference could be one of culture, not of gender.

She went back into the living room where Foley stood with his hands in his pockets, scowling at the body on the floor. They were limited in what they could do until the Crime Scene Unit arrived; the CSU almost always beat the detectives to the scene, but not today. The officer Marian had sent down to check the elm tree came back and said, "Sergeant Larch? There was leaf litter all over the ground, but I couldn't see any marks on the bark or broken-off twigs or anything like that. Didn't look to me as if anybody'd been climbing that tree."

"Did you climb it yourself?"

"Tried to, but the damned thing started bending over before I got all the way up to the second-floor balcony. I thought it was going to break. The only one who could climb that tree is a monkey or maybe a small child."

Marian cast an appraising eye over the officer.

"Hundred seventy-six pounds," he said.

She gave him a smile and a thank-you and turned back to Foley. "The glass in the balcony door was broken to make it look as if that's the way the killer got in. But he came in through one of the doors."

Foley scowled. "Nakamoto let him in."

"Or he had a key."

"Either way, it's still no professional hit. The killer's a first-timer."

Marian thought so too. "The Crime Scene Unit's here," she said.

The team of Larch and Foley split up for the time being, a procedure they opted for as frequently as possible. Foley stayed to interview the neighbors and check with the medical examiner; Marian went to break the news to Mrs. Nakamoto. After dusting for prints and taking pictures, the Crime Scene Unit had found two things of interest. One was Nakamoto's billfold in a bureau drawer; it held over four hundred dollars. The other was an appointment calendar that said Mrs. Nakamoto would be at the American Red Cross headquarters on Amsterdam Avenue the entire day. "I'll stop off at Markham's Pharmacy on the way back," Marian said to her partner. "See if you can find out when the service stairs were last cleaned."

Foley grunted the grunt that Marian had learned meant *Okay*. She took the car and headed across town to the West Side Highway, which she followed uptown and then cut over to Amsterdam. She got lucky and found an illegal parking place.

Inside the Red Cross offices, a man named Greg Seaver told her Mrs. Nakamoto was in a fund-raising committee meeting. "May I help you? Or would you like to wait?"

Marian showed him her badge. "Sergeant Larch, NYPD. It can't wait, Mr. Seaver. I need to talk to her now."

Either her tone of voice or her badge convinced him. "I'll get her. Wait here, please."

"We'll need a private place to talk."

"You can use my office."

He returned immediately with a small Japanese woman wearing American clothing easily and even with flair. She had her hair cut short and was carefully made up—model-pretty, in fact. "Mieko, this is Sergeant Larch of the police." When he'd finished his half an introduction, Seaver withdrew from his office and left them alone.

"Yes?" Mieko Nakamoto said with that strong upward lilt that made the word sound like a challenge even though it was not intended as such.

Marian had her sit down, and as gently as possible she explained what the police had found in the Nakamoto apartment. She told the new widow that her husband had almost surely died immediately and did not suffer. Mrs. Nakamoto's eyes grew bigger as she listened while her mouth seemed to grow smaller. In her lap her small-boned hands clasped and unclasped themselves. Finally after an extended silence she stood up and excused herself. Through the glass wall of the office Marian watched her walking rigidly toward the ladies' room. She made no move to follow; the woman needed privacy.

Greg Seaver was hovering anxiously outside the office. With a sigh Marian motioned him in and told him that Tatsuya Nakamoto had been murdered.

"Oh my god," he gasped. "What a dreadful—oh, poor Mieko! Murdered? Who . . . ?"

"It's too early yet," Marian said. "Mr. Seaver, did you know Mr. Nakamoto?"

"I met him once. A very formal, traditional man. I don't think he entirely approved of Mieko's working here. Damn—what a godawful thing to happen!"

"He didn't approve?"

"Well, he asked me if I thought it was *gracious* to importune strangers for money," Seaver said with an annoyed laugh. "Gracious! But he'd disapprove of any place Mieko worked. I remember thinking at the time that he probably wanted her to stay at home and wear a kimono. I know he looked offended when I addressed her by her first name."

"Does Mrs. Nakamoto have a salaried position here?"

"Oh no, she does volunteer work. Mieko has a real talent for fund-raising—we're lucky to have her."

"I'd have thought the Red Cross used professional fund-raisers."

"National Headquarters does. We're just the local chapter here."

"Ah. Tell me, what time did Mrs. Nakamoto come in today?"

He gave her a strange look. "Is it true, you always suspect the spouse first? Mieko came in around ten this morning, and she's been here ever since." They both looked at their watches; it was 11:50 A.M. "Sergeant, if Mr. Nakamoto was killed any time after ten this morning, there's no way Mieko could have done it."

Marian didn't mention that the police had been called around nine-thirty. Mrs. Nakamoto came back, minus much of her make-up; she'd probably washed her face with cold water. Greg Seaver tried to tell her how sorry he was, but it was an awkward moment. He obviously wanted to put an arm around her and comfort her, but Mrs. Nakamoto's entire demeanor said Don't-Touch-Me. Finally at a look from Marian, Seaver edged out and left them alone again.

"Where is my husband?" Mrs. Nakamoto asked in a high voice.

Marian explained about the medical examiner and the law's requirement that autopsies be performed in all cases of violent death. In response to Marian's questions, Mrs. Nakamoto said her husband had been working at home today, in preparation for a meeting tomorrow morning. No, his working at home was not unusual; he had done it several times before. No, he was not expecting anyone, as far as she knew. The widow could have been an automaton, answering precisely and briefly, volunteering nothing. Marian said she'd like her to check the apartment to see if anything was stolen.

"Yes. I will do that now." Without another word, Mrs. Nakamoto rose and walked out. Marian watched her go, stiff-backed, taking small steps, head not moving. She marched past Greg Seaver without a glance.

Marian walked over to him and asked, "Is it the bad news, or is she always that withdrawn?"

He sighed. "Most of the time she's friendly in a shy sort of way, but sometimes she's exactly the way you saw her. With Mieko, it's hard to know what's going on."

It is indeed, Marian agreed.

It was close to four before Marian and Foley got together in the Precinct Detectives Unit room on the second floor of the Ninth Precinct stationhouse. Foley reported that the neighbors had nothing to tell him about the Nakamotos; the Japanese couple were quiet people who kept to themselves. They'd bought the apartment about two years ago and were on courteous speaking terms with the other three families in the building. And that was it.

"The outfit that does maintenance for the building was there yesterday," Foley said, "and they cleaned the service stairway as well as the main entry and the elevators. I asked 'em what they'd do if they found a cheap plastic billfold calendar, and they said they'd toss it."

"What time were they there?" Marian asked.

"Late afternoon. So that calendar was dropped either last night or earlier today. What about Markham's Pharmacy—did you talk to 'em? Any deliveries?"

"Not within the past two weeks. They do deliver regularly to the building, though, to the Nakamotos and to the family living on the fourth floor. Markham is the pharmacist and owner, and he told me they put some sort of promotional material in every package they deliver—this month it happens to be billfold calendars. But get this, Foley. Every package is sealed with tape before it leaves the pharmacy so nothing will get lost. There's no way the plastic calendar could have fallen out of a package, even if there had been a delivery this morning."

"Hah. So chances are good it did belong to the killer. Maybe he tried to use it to force the lock."

"It wouldn't have worked. Too much overlap by the door frame."

"I *know* it wouldn't have worked, Larch," Foley said irritably. "I said maybe he *tried* to use it. This is a fuckin' amateur we're dealing with, remember?"

"All right, all right. But I did get something from Markham. I asked him if his delivery boy was thin, brown-haired, scruffy-looking, and he said no, he was plump and had curly red hair. But then he said the description did fit his *former* delivery boy, whom he'd had to let go just a couple of weeks ago. Seems the kid was good on the job but he had a way of not showing up for work a lot, and Markham needed someone he could rely on."

Foley grinned. "Name and address?"

"Derek Brown. He lives in the projects. So what are we waiting for? Let's go."

"First thing tomorrow morning," Foley said, getting up and putting on his coat. "It's five after four—we're off duty."

Marian made a noise of exasperation. "Foley, sometimes I don't believe you! Here we have the name and address of a probable killer, and you want to let it ride because we're *off duty*?"

"Better say that a little louder, Larch," Foley scoffed. "I'm not sure the captain heard you." And with that he was gone.

Marian slapped at her desk in frustration. Then she too got up and put on her coat; she could no more let her curiosity about Derek Brown go until next morning than she could do without food for a month. She left her car in the lot across the street from the stationhouse on East Fifth and walked the two blocks to the Lillian Wald project houses between Columbia Street and FDR Drive.

Derek Brown lived on the third floor of his building; Marian took the stairs rather than risk the elevator. The smell of spicy cooking mingled with the odor of urine and stale marijuana; the din from televisions and boom boxes was formidable. A more different atmosphere from the one in the Nakamoto apartment Marian couldn't imagine. The dirty walls were covered with graffiti; gang signs adorned most of the doors. Two black boys of about eleven or twelve raced noisily down the hall, banging on doors as they passed. One of them tried to give Marian's backside a squeeze, but she stiff-armed the kid and sent him on his way.

She came to the door she was searching for and knocked. After a moment it opened the width of its restraining chain and the suspicious face of a little girl peered up at her. Someone was coughing in the room behind the child. "Hi, I'm here to see Derek," Marian said. "Is he home?"

The girl disappeared without a word and her place at the barely opened door was taken by a thin-faced young man with deep shadows under his eyes. "You want to see me?"

Marian held up her badge. "Derek Brown? I need to ask you some questions. May I come in?"

"Look, I'm not feeling so hot. Could you come back another time?"

"It won't take long. Let me in."

He did, reluctantly, turning his head aside to cough. Marian stepped into a dark room that held only a few pieces of shabby furniture; except for a pillow and a rumpled blanket on the sofa, the place was as neat as the people living in such a dump could make it. Marian turned and faced Derek Brown; he fit the neighbor's description of the killer exactly, even to the scruffy-looking part. Brown looked about thirty, maybe a little older. And it was clear he felt rotten.

He sank down on the sofa and pointed to an aluminum kitchen chair against the wall. Marian sat down and introduced herself; she asked the girl her name. The child didn't want to answer at first, but Brown murmured something and she said, defiantly, "My name is Alison—all right?" A big chip on that small shoulder.

"Your daughter?" Marian asked Brown.

He managed a laugh that turned into a cough. "Alison is ten. I'm nineteen. Even if it were possible, at nine I hated girls. No, Alison's my sister."

Nineteen. She'd thought he was thirty. Before Marian could start on her questions, a woman's voice called out from the apartment's only other room. "Derek? Who is it?"

"Police, Mom."

A woman in a wheelchair maneuvered her way through the doorway separating the two rooms. Late forties, heavy arms and shoulders, shriveled legs. Bifocals, fading brown hair. She looked straight at Marian and said, "If it's about that Hernandez boy, we didn't see anything."

"No, ma'am, I'm not here about that." Marian would have preferred to interrogate Brown alone; but the apartment was so small that even if she did ask the other two to go into the bedroom, they still would have heard every word that was said. "Where's Mr. Brown?" she asked the woman in the wheelchair.

"Gone." She added no explanation.

Marian turned back to the young man on the sofa. "You used to work at Markham's Pharmacy?"

He nodded. "Up until a couple of weeks ago."

"Until old man Markham fired him 'cause he got sick," Alison spoke up belligerently.

"Alison," Mrs. Brown said firmly. "Keep quiet."

"Did you ever make a delivery to the Nakamoto apartment on Second Avenue?"

"Yeah, and to the Wyatts too," Brown said. "Fourth floor, same building."

"When was the last time you made a delivery to the Nakamotos?"

"Oh, uh, about a month ago, I guess. Why?"

"Mr. Nakamoto was murdered earlier today."

All three of them reacted differently. Mrs. Brown looked shocked. Alison's eyes narrowed and she moved to put the sofa between herself and Marian. Brown closed his eyes and turned his head away. After a moment he looked back at her and said, "I'm sorry to hear that."

"How well did you know Mr. Nakamoto?"

"I never met him. Mrs. Nakamoto took all the deliveries. Nice lady."

"Were you in their building today?"

"Me? No!"

Mrs. Brown gripped the arms of her wheelchair. "Are you accusing my son of murder?"

"I'm not accusing anyone of anything. I just want to know if he had any reason to be in that building today."

"What reason could he have? He lost his job, you know that. Besides, he hasn't been anywhere. Look at him! Can't you tell he's sick?"

"Mom." Brown cleared his throat. "I've been here all day, Sergeant."

"Yeah, and we'll swear to that in court!" Alison piped up.

Funny thing for a ten-year-old to say. "The killer was seen leaving the building," Marian went on, "and you answer the description."

"It wasn't Derek!" Alison screeched. "He was here!"

"Would you be willing to participate in a line-up?" It was a test question; a line-up would be of no use since the neighbor never saw the killer's face.

Brown passed the test . . . almost. "Sure, why not? Only not right now. I really don't feel well, Sergeant."

"It's time for you to go," Mrs. Brown said abruptly. "Go on—leave him alone. Get out."

Alison left her safe place behind the sofa and ran to open the door. Marian stood up. "Have you seen a doctor?" she asked Brown. He nodded weakly.

"*Go away!*" Alison commanded.

Marian went away.

At eight o'clock the following morning Marian and Foley were sitting in Captain DiFalco's office, all three of them wanting another cup of coffee before getting on with the day's work. "Of course they'd alibi him," DiFalco growled in response to Marian's report. "His mother and his sister? You didn't believe 'em, did you?"

"No," Marian said. "But it's a tough situation, Captain. Derek Brown is the sole support of a crippled mother and a ten-year-old sister, and he's just lost his job. The Browns are a family that's obviously come down in the world. They're well-spoken people and still civilized, in spite of living in the projects for god knows how long. The girl's starting to turn, though.

They need money to get out of there, and Brown could be desperate enough to kill for it."

"Did Mrs. Nakamoto let us know if anything was stolen?"

"Not yet. I thought I'd go talk to her when we finished here."

"Why bother?" Foley asked. "She don't know anything."

"I want to ask her about Derek Brown, for one thing—if she's seen him in the last couple of days, like that. Besides, she wasn't very communicative yesterday, understandably. I just want to wrap it up."

"Okay," DiFalco said, "but one of you ought to go to Sony—they haven't been told yet, have they?"

Foley said, "Not unless Mrs. Nakamoto called them. I'll go. You don't need two of us to talk to the lady." So once again the team of Foley and Larch would be able to split up.

"Any reason to treat this as anything other than a straight shoot-and-grab?" the captain asked.

"No," said Foley.

"Maybe," said Marian. "What about the faked entry? An ordinary shoot-and-grab wouldn't try to make it look as if he'd entered one way when in fact he'd come in by another. Why bother? The killer must have had a key—Nakamoto wouldn't have let a stranger into his home."

"He was their drugstore's delivery boy, for Christ's sake!" Foley snorted. "Nakamoto would let *him* in."

"Derek Brown told me he'd made all the deliveries to the wife. The husband wouldn't have known who he was."

"*If* Brown was telling the truth."

Captain DiFalco was scowling. "Still, it's a loose end. Foley, nose around a bit while you're over at Sony. Find out if Nakamoto had any problems, see if he confided in anyone. You know what to look for."

Foley grunted. "Anything else?"

"Both of you call in when you're finished. The lab report should come through sometime this morning. And take tape recorders with you—see if you can get some statements."

Mieko Nakamoto opened the door to Marian's ring; she was dressed in an American blouse and skirt, and she admitted Marian courteously but with no show of either resentment or welcome. Marian asked if anything had been stolen.

"Oh yes," Mrs. Nakamoto said in her high voice. "Two things. A thirteen-inch television we kept in the kitchen, and a compact disc player."

"Where was the disc player?"

"It was in the room with the big television." Mrs. Nakamoto swallowed. "Do you think he takes only what he can carry under each arm?"

"Either that," Marian said, "or that's what we're supposed to think. Why didn't he take the computer? That's worth more than the TV. And the watch your husband was wearing was worth more than both of them together. There was cash in the apartment—four hundred dollars in your husband's billfold. But the killer didn't touch that." Marian looked around her. "As far as that goes, there are any number of things he could have taken from right here in the living room. But instead he goes into the kitchen for a small TV set and into a different room for a CD player. Why the kitchen at all? Doesn't make sense."

Mrs. Nakamoto started to say something, but then pressed her lips together and kept quiet.

Marian took a deep breath and said, "Mrs. Nakamoto, I want you to let me take a look at your husband's papers—bank statements, that sort of thing. I can get a warrant, but you'd save me time if you just give your permission."

The Japanese woman's face was blank. "But what do bank statements have to do with the burglar?"

"Maybe he wasn't an ordinary burglar. Please, Mrs. Nakamoto—it's better if you give permission."

She assented, although it was clear the request disturbed her. She led the way into her husband's home office, where Marian was surprised to find the bank statements already spread out on the desk. "I was trying to understand my financial situation," Mrs. Nakamoto explained.

Marian nodded and sat down at the desk, determined to make it fast; the woman obviously felt invaded. The bank records proved what Marian had suspected. The various accounts were all in Tatsuya Nakamoto's name. There were health, auto, and home protection insurance policies, but no life insurance. Nakamoto had accumulated extensive stock holdings, also in his name alone. Mieko didn't have a cent of her own.

Mrs. Nakamoto's face finally showed some expression when Marian left; it was relief. Down on the street, Marian found a phone and called in, as instructed. She told Captain DiFalco what she'd learned.

"Uh-huh. This one's sounding phonier by the minute," he said. "He passed up that roomful of electronic equipment except for one CD player, but he checked out the *kitchen* before he left? Something going on there, but for now just bring Derek Brown in—I've already asked for a warrant. I got the lab report, and his prints are on that plastic calendar you found, clear as daylight. He was there, all right."

"Hm. How'd we happen to have his prints?"

"He once tried to hold up a liquor store—get this—with a baseball bat. But the owner had a gun. Chased him off with no trouble at all. The charges were eventually dropped because the owner didn't want to close the store long enough to come in and testify."

"Good god."

"Yeah. Foley hasn't called in yet. Stay where you are, and I'll send you a couple of uniforms for back-up."

"Not necessary, Captain. Derek Brown is sick, and he's stick-thin anyway. I could pick him up and carry him in."

"And so he's not dangerous? For god's sake, Larch, the guy's a killer! You know better than that."

Marian sighed. "Yes, sir." She told him where she was and waited.

In less than five minutes a Radio Motor Patrol car pulled up to the curb. Marian climbed into the backseat and learned the two uniformed officers sent to back her up were called Washington and Esposito. She explained that she was to arrest a sick nineteen-year-old, and that their main function was to stand there and look authoritative. Washington and Esposito allowed as how they could handle that, and Esposito headed the RMP back toward the project houses.

Esposito found an unused fire hydrant to park by, and the three headed inside, automatically bypassing the elevator in favor of the stairs. Marian knocked politely on the Browns' door, and then less politely, and finally ended up pounding with both fists and yelling "Police!" At last the door opened a crack and Mrs. Brown looked up at her from her wheelchair.

"Mrs. Brown, I'm Sergeant Larch. I was here yesterday."

"I remember you." She didn't sound happy about it.

Marian didn't blame her. "I'm sorry to tell you this, but I'm here to arrest Derek. Please open the door."

"You can't arrest him! He hasn't done anything!"

"Open the door, Mrs. Brown. We have to come in."

"Derek isn't here!"

"Let us come in and see for ourselves."

"He isn't here! Go away!"

Marian turned to the two officers, none too fond of this part of her job. "Break it down," she said.

"No! Wait, wait!" Mrs. Brown closed the door long enough to slip off the chain and then let them in. Washington and Esposito immediately searched the two-room apartment, a task that took all of ten seconds. "Nobody here," Washington said.

"Where is he, Mrs. Brown?" Marian asked.

The woman in the wheelchair started crying, making Marian feel even worse than she already felt. The two uniformed officers shifted their weight uncomfortably and exchanged a look; suddenly they were the heavies.

"Mrs. Brown?" Marian nudged gently. "Where's Derek?"

The older woman took several deep gulps of

air and blurted, "He's in the hospital! *Now* will you leave him alone?"

Marian knelt down by the wheelchair so her face was level with the other woman's. "Mrs. Brown," she said softly, "your son has AIDS, hasn't he?"

All the fight seemed to go out of the crippled woman. She dropped her face into her hands and her whole body began to shake with great wracking sobs. She didn't make a sound, but the three cops in the room heard every cry.

They were able to track down the overworked doctor at Bellevue who'd seen Derek Brown when he was admitted. The doctor told them bluntly that Brown wouldn't be leaving the hospital, ever. It was a matter of days, perhaps hours. He should have been in the hospital long ago, the doctor complained; they could have at least made him more comfortable. No more than one visitor at a time, please. The doctor hurried away without a backward glance.

Marian turned to Washington and Esposito. "I guess I won't be needing you anymore. Thanks for your help." The two men mumbled something and left, eager to get away from the place.

The ward where Derek Brown was to spend his last hours was depressing and a little scary, with its run-down look and its battered metal carts of Dr. Frankenstein medical equipment and its rows of curtained-off beds—*dying places*, Marian thought. A nurse directed her to Derek Brown's bed; Marian opened the curtain and slipped inside.

In spite of thinking she was prepared, she was shocked by his appearance. He looked ten pounds lighter and twenty years older than yesterday; she wondered how he managed to keep breathing. After a moment he opened his eyes and saw her standing there. He twisted his thin lips into a wry smile. "I thought I'd be seeing you again," he rasped.

There was no chair and no bedside table. Marian gritted her teeth and took out the tape recorder; she identified herself, Derek Brown, the time, the place. Then she put the machine on his pillow and asked if he understood he was being recorded. He said he did.

She hated what she had to do. "You know why I'm here, don't you?" she said slowly. "You left your calling card for us to find. We know who killed Mr. Nakamoto, and we know why. We don't have the gun yet, but we do have your prints at the scene. And we know why you let yourself get sucked into such a scheme. But it was all for nothing. It's over, Derek."

A long silence followed. Then a raspy sigh floated up from the bed. "Yes, it's all over." He breathed noisily for a moment or two. "I'm not sure I ever believed it would work."

"It was part of the deal you made," Marian went on, "that you leave something behind to incriminate yourself. You knew you weren't going to live long enough to be prosecuted— you'd never go to prison. So you agreed to take the blame in exchange for . . . security for your family? How was that supposed to work, Derek?"

There were tears in his eyes. "A trust fund. For my mother and my sister."

"And you trust a murderer to keep her word?"

"It was already set up. All she had to do was sign one paper, as soon as Mr. Nakamoto was dead and the money was hers." A look of pain crossed his face. "That man never did anything to me. I'm sorry he's dead." He was quiet a moment. "It was the only chance I had of getting my family out of the projects. Do you know Alison carries a knife? A ten-year-old girl carrying a knife. And Sergeant, I couldn't tell her not to." A long spasm of coughing overtook him.

"Take your time," Marian said.

When he'd recovered a little strength, he actually mustered up a smile. "You know what they say you're supposed to do when life hands you a lemon . . . well, I tried. I did the best I could."

He probably had, at that. "Where's the gun?"

"Pushed down between the sofa back and the seat . . . you know, that sofa where I sleep. You'll find only my fingerprints on it." He coughed again. "I got that gun for her—not hard to do, where I live."

"Were you there when she shot him?"

"In the kitchen." He had to wait until he had the breath to go on. "I heard the three shots, and then she brought the gun to me. I dropped the little calendar with my fingerprints on it and stumbled down the back stairs making as much noise as I could."

"How did she get out of the building without being seen?"

"Out the front way, while the guy downstairs was busy gawking at me." Another pause. "Sergeant, what's going to happen to my mom and my sister?"

"They won't be abandoned," Marian promised. "I'll call Social Services today. They'll work out something—don't worry about your family. They'll be taken care of."

He closed his eyes. "It was Social Services that put them in the project house."

There was nothing she could say to that. The Social Services Department would do the best it could—but it was never enough. Never.

His breathing seemed shallower. "Sergeant," he whispered, "I did the best I could."

"I know," she said.

A few minutes of silence passed and Marian began to fear he was dead. But then she saw his chest rising slightly and falling again; only sleeping. Grateful that she wouldn't have to watch him die and ashamed for being grateful, she turned off the tape recorder and made her way out of the depressing ward.

She barely saw where she was going. The mother in a wheelchair, the son with AIDS, and the ten-year-old daughter carrying a knife to protect herself. *You know what they say you're supposed to do when life hands you a lemon.* And a small Japanese woman had provided him with the means for doing it.

Marian took a cab back to where she'd left her car parked near the Nakamoto apartment on

Second Avenue. She should phone for Washington and Esposito, but she wanted to handle this alone. She'd worry about Captain DiFalco later.

Mrs. Nakamoto answered the door with the same expressionless face she'd shown Marian earlier. "Sergeant Larch. This is the second time you have been here today."

"It will be the last. May I come in?"

The Japanese woman stepped back and allowed her to enter—an important legal nicety, since Marian didn't have a warrant. Standing just inside the door and without offering a word of explanation, she took out the tape recorder and started it playing.

As Mrs. Nakamoto came to understand what she was listening to, her shoulders began to slump and her head bowed. Already small, she seemed to shrink to child-size as Marian watched. The small-boned hands clasped each other so tightly the knuckles were white. When at last she lifted her head, it was to show Marian the face of despair. "It was my chance," she whispered. "It was my only chance."

Marian turned off the tape recorder. "No, it wasn't," she said, more harshly than she intended. "You didn't have to kill him. There were other ways."

The small woman flared, the first sign of passion she'd shown. "You know nothing of my life! You know nothing of our *ways*!"

"Perhaps not," Marian said, "but I do know the laws of this country. You didn't have to kill him, and you didn't have to bribe that poor sick boy to take the fall for you. You have the right to remain silent—"

"It was the best I could do!"

Marian continued reading her her rights, and then told her to get a coat. "You can call your lawyer from the station," she said, "as soon as we book you."

Mrs. Nakamoto asked permission to bring a purse; Marian told her all right, but it would be taken away from her once she was booked. The Japanese woman moved slowly, so slowly, trying to postpone the inevitable. At last she was ready, and Marian waited while she locked the front door. The cop handed the prisoner a set of handcuffs and told her to put them on.

In the car, the silence stretched out painfully. Then Mrs. Nakamoto said, in a voice even higher than usual, "I wish to honor my commitment to Mrs. Brown and the girl."

Marian took her eyes off the traffic for a moment to stare at her; could she truly be that naive? "The law says you can't profit from a felony. You're not going to get one cent of your husband's money."

"I understand that." Her hands were clasping and unclasping again. "But all that is required to make the trust fund legal at this point is my signature. I have not been, ah, booked yet, and the money is mine right now. *Right now*, at this moment, it is mine. I can sign it away to Mrs. Brown if I wish."

"That's crazy. Once you're booked, the trust will be invalidated."

"Perhaps . . . but perhaps not. How is the law to know of the arrangement? The bank officer will not wish to lose the administration of the trust. Neither Mrs. Brown nor I will speak of it. Only you, Sergeant Larch, stand in the way. But if you take me to the bank before you book me, then Derek's mother and sister will be taken care of."

"Crazier and crazier. Even if your bank officer were willing to turn a blind eye—and I think you're assuming a hell of a lot there—too many other people at the bank will know about the trust. You think they're all going to break the law just to help you ease your conscience?"

Mrs. Nakamoto's breathing was becoming shallower. "People . . . do not wish to trouble themselves, on the whole. I understand there are many ways the trust may fail. But if there is even one small chance it will succeed . . . then I must try, do you not see?"

Oh, Jesus! "Mieko, do you have any idea what you're asking me to do?" Marian said miserably.

"I understand. And I ask."

They rode in silence, for one city block, then another. At last Marian said tightly, "Which bank?"

The Japanese woman named an address.

Marian turned the car uptown. One man was dead, another was dying, and a woman was going to prison. But maybe Alison Brown wouldn't have to carry a knife anymore. "This isn't going to work," she muttered.

"Perhaps not." Mrs. Nakamoto stared straight ahead. "But I am doing the best I can."

"Yes," Marian said, and pressed down on the accelerator.

LOUISE

Max Allan Collins

MAX ALLAN COLLINS (1948–   ) has created several diverse series characters, including Quarry, a hit man; Nolan, a professional thief; Mallory, a midwestern mystery writer who solves crimes; Eliot Ness, the real-life FBI agent of the Prohibition era; Dick Tracy, the famous character created by Chester Gould (when Gould retired, Collins wrote the comic strips, a novelization of the *Dick Tracy* movie, and two additional novels); and his most successful character, Nate Heller, a Chicago private eye whose cases were mainly set in the 1930s and 1940s. Many of the novels involve famous people of the era, including Al Capone, Frank Nitta, and Eliot Ness in the first book, *True Detective* (1983), as well as featuring such notorious cases as the kidnapping of Charles and Ann Lindbergh's baby in *Stolen Away* (1991), the disappearance of Amelia Earhart in *Flying Blind* (1998), and the Black Dahlia murder in *Angel in Black* (2001).

Collins is also the author of the graphic novel *Road to Perdition* (1998), the basis for the 2002 Tom Hanks film, and several sequels, and has written numerous stand-alone novels and coauthored many books and stories with Mickey Spillane, completing works that were left unfinished when Spillane died.

Ms. Tree is the heroine of a popular comic book series featuring Michael Tree, a private detective who takes charge of the agency when her husband is murdered. She is tough and fearless, inspired, according to the author, by Velda, Mike Hammer's secretary and girlfriend.

"Louise" was originally published in the anthology *Deadly Allies*, edited by Robert J. Randisi and Marilyn Wallace (New York, Doubleday, 1992).

Louise

MAX ALLAN COLLINS

HER FACE WAS PRETTY AND HARD; her eyes were pretty and soft.

She was a waif in a yellow-and-white peasant dress, a Keane painting child grown up, oval freckled face framed by sweeping blond arcs. She wore quite a bit of make-up, but the effect was that of a school-girl who'd gotten into mommy's things. She stood with her purse held shyly before her, a guilty Eve with a brown patent-leather fig leaf.

"Miss Tree?" she asked tentatively, only half-stepping inside my private office, despite the fact my assistant had already bid her enter.

I stood, paying her back the respect she was showing, and tried to put her at ease with a smile. "I prefer 'Ms.,'" I told her, sitting back down, and gestured toward the chair opposite me.

She settled gradually into the chair and straightened her skirt primly, though her manner was at odds with the scoop neck that showed more bosom than modesty would allow. "I never been to a office on Michigan Avenue before," she said, her big blue eyes taking in the stark lines of my spacious but austere inner chamber. "You sure have a nice one."

"Thank you, Miss Evans."

Pretty as she was, she had the sort of countenance that wore more suffering than even heavy make-up could hide; so it was kind of a shock when her face brightened with a smile.

"Louise," she said, and she extended her tiny hand across the desk, with a deliberation that revealed the courage she'd had to summon to behave so boldly, "call me Louise. Please."

"My assistant tells me you were quite insistent about seeing me personally."

She nodded and lowered her head. "Yes. I'm sorry."

"Don't be sorry, Miss Evans."

"It's Mrs. Evans. Excepting, I'd like you to call me Louise. I need us to be friends."

"All right," I said. This wasn't going to be easy, was it? "You said this is about your daughter. That your daughter is in trouble."

I was too busy for this, with Gold Coast divorce cases, legal work, and corporate accounts, but it hadn't been the kind of plea you could turn down.

"Terrible trouble," she said, and her lower lip trembled; the blue eyes were filling up. "My husband . . . I'm afraid of what he might . . ."

Then she began to weep.

I got up, came around and knelt beside her as she dug embarrassedly for Kleenex in her purse. She was so much smaller than me, I felt like an adult comforting a child as I slipped an arm around her.

"You can tell me," I said. "It'll be all right."

"She's gone," she said. "He took her."

"Your husband took your daughter?"

"Months ago. Months ago. God knows what he done her, by this time."

"Tell me about it. Start at the beginning. Start anywhere."

But she didn't start. She grabbed my arm and her tiny fist gripped me hard. As hard as the life that had made the sweet features of her young face so old.

"I wish I was like you," she said. Her voice had an edge.

"Louise . . ."

"I've read about you, Ms. Tree. You're a strong woman. Nobody messes with you. Nobody pushes you around."

"Please . . ."

"You're big. You killed bad men before."

That was me—a cross between King Kong and the Lone Ranger, in a dress. Frankly, this petite if buxom woman did make me feel "big"; at five ten, one-hundred-forty pounds, I sure wasn't small. My tombstone would likely read: "Here Lies Michael Tree—She Never Did Lose That Ten Pounds."

And so I was to be Louise's savior; her avenger. I sighed, smiled and said, "You really should tell me about your daughter, Louise—and your husband."

"That's why I come here. I need somebody like you to go get Maggie back. He took her, and the law can't do nothing." I got a chair and sat next to her, where I could pat her reassuringly when necessary, and, finally, she told me her story.

Her husband Joe was "a good man, in lots of ways," a worker in a steel mill in Hammond. They met when she was working in a McDonald's in South Chicago, and they'd been married six years. That was how old Maggie, their only child, was.

"Joey's a good provider," she said, "but he . . . gets rough sometimes."

"He beat you?"

She looked away, nodded. Battered women feel ashamed, even guilty, oftentimes; it makes no logical sense, but then neither does a man beating on a woman.

"Has he beaten your daughter, too?"

She nodded. And she started to weep again.

She was out of Kleenex; I got up and got her some.

"But that . . . that's not the worst part," she said, sniffling. "Maggie is a pretty little girl. She got blond hair, just like mine. And Joey was looking at her . . . you know. *That* way. The way my daddy done me."

"Do you think your husband ever . . . ?"

"Not while I was around. But since he runned off with her, that's what I'm afraid of most."

I was a little confused; I had been assuming that this was a child custody situation. That the divorced husband had taken advantage of his visitation rights to disappear with his daughter.

"You haven't said anything about divorce," I said. "You and your husband *are* divorced?"

"No. We was talking about it. I think that's why he done it the way he done."

"What do you mean, Louise?"

"He knew that that if we was divorced, the courts'd give Maggie to me. And he didn't want me to have her. Ms. Tree, when I was Maggie's age, my daddy beat on me. And he done other things to me. You know what kind of things."

I nodded.

"Ms. Tree, will you take my case? All I got is two hundred dollars I saved. Is that going to be enough?"

"It's going to be like McDonald's, Louise," I said.

"Huh?"

"You're going to get back some change."

Louise had reported her husband's disappearance to the police, but in the five months since Joey Evans and his daughter vanished, there had been little done. My contact at the police department confirmed this.

"The Missing Persons Bureau did what they could," Rafe Valer said, sitting on the edge of his desk in his small cluttered office at Homicide.

"Which is what, exactly?"

Rafe shrugged. Darkly handsome describes him, but considering he's black, saying so may be in poor taste. Thirty, quietly ambitious and as dependable as a pizza at Gino's, Lt. Valer had been my late husband Mike's partner, before Mike went private.

"Which is," he said, "they asked around Hammond, and South Chicago, talking to his relatives and friends. They found that one day, five months ago, Joe Evans quit his job, sold his car for cash, packed his things and left."

"With his six-year-old daughter."

"With his six-year-old daughter. The assumption is, Evans has skipped the state."

I almost shouted. "Then this is an FBI matter!"

"Michael," Rafe said, calmly, smoothly, brushing the air with a gentle hand as if stroking an unruly pet, "it isn't kidnapping when a natural parent takes a child along when they take off."

"This is a case of child abuse, Rafe. Possibly sexual abuse!"

"I understand that," Rafe said, his voice tightly patient, "but Louise Evans never filed charges of any kind against her husband, before or after he ran off. Nor has she filed for divorce."

"Goddamnit. So what does that leave her with?"

"You," Rafe said.

As if I were dealing a hand of cards, I tossed a photo of rugged, weak-jawed Joe Evans onto the conference-room table; then a photo of blond little Maggie, her mother's cute clone; then another of the family together, in what seemed happier times, unless you looked close and saw the strain in the faces of both adults.

"Sweet looking child," Dan Green said, softly, prayerfully.

Dan, not yet thirty, was the younger of my two partners, a blond, mustached, good-looking kid whose regular features were slightly scarred from a fire an arsonist left him to die in. He'd lost an eye in that fire, too, and a hand; a glass eye and a hook took their place.

"Right now," I said, "she's very likely enduring hell on earth."

"Sexual abuse at any age is a tragedy," Roger Freemont said, taking Maggie's photo from Dan. His deep voice was hollow. "At this age, no word covers it."

Roger, balding, bespectacled, with a fullback's shoulders, was the rock of Tree Investigations, Inc. He'd been my husband's partner in the business; like Rafe Valer, Roger had worked with Mike in the Detective Bureau.

"I accepted a retainer of fifty dollars from Louise Evans," I said.

The two men gave me quick, searching looks, then shrugged and gave their attention back to the photos spread before them.

"Of course I did that for the sake of her self-respect," I said. "She works at a White Castle. She had two hundred bucks she'd saved and wanted to give it all to me."

"Fifty bucks will cover it," Roger said.

"Easily," Dan said. "So—where do we start?"

"They've been gone five months," Roger said, "and that's in our favor."

"Why?" Dan asked.

Roger shrugged. "He's settled in to his new life. Enough time has passed for him to think he's gotten away with something. So he gets careless. Enough time has passed for him to start seriously missing family and friends. So he makes phone calls. Writes letters."

Dan was drinking this in.

"Evans has a big family," I said, referring to my notes from several conversations with Louise. "They're a tight-knit working-class bunch. Two brothers and three sisters, all grown adults like Joey. One brother and two of the sisters live in the area—Hammond, Gary, South Chicago. Another brother lives in Dallas."

"*That* sounds like a good bet," Dan said. "I bet Joey's deep in the heart of you-know-where."

"Maybe. He also has a sister in Davenport, Iowa."

Roger perked up. "What is that? A three-hour drive?"

"Around," I said.

"Close to home," Roger said, eyes narrowing, "but far enough away."

"Where do we start?" Dan asked.

"You're going to go by the book, Dan. And Roger—you aren't."

Dan said, "Huh?" while Roger only nodded.

I assigned Dan to check up on Evans's last place of employment—the steel mill—to see if Evans used the place as a reference for a new job; ditto Evans's union—that union card would be necessary for Evans to get a similar job elsewhere.

"If Evans wanted to drop out," Dan said, "he wouldn't have used the mill as a reference, or maintained his union card . . ."

"Right," I said. "But we can't assume that. He may not be using an assumed name. Maybe he's still living as Joe Evans, just somewhere else. Also, Dan I want you to go over Louise Evans's phone bills for the six months prior to her husband leaving. Find out what, if any, out-of-town calls he was making."

Dan nodded.

"Any credit card trail?" Roger asked.

I shook my head no. "The only credit card the Evanses had was an oil company card, and Louise received no bills incurred by her husband after he took off."

"Any medical problems, for either the father or child?" Roger asked.

"No."

"Damn," Roger said.

"Why 'damn'?" Dan asked him.

"Prescription medicine would give us a trail," Roger said. "And we could check the hospitals and clinics in areas where we suspect they might be staying."

"They're both in fine health," I said. "Except, of course, for whatever physical and mental traumas the son of a bitch is inflicting on that child."

The two men shook their heads glumly.

"Roger," I said, "you talk to Evans's family members—his father's deceased, but mother's still alive. She may be the best bet. Anyway, after you've talked to them all, keep ma under surveillance. Go through all their trash, of course—phone bills, letters."

Roger nodded, smiled a little. This was old hat to him, but Dan was learning.

"Better cook up some jive cover story, for when you talk to the family," Dan advised him. "Don't tell them you're a detective."

Roger smirked at him. But he let him down easy: "Good idea, kid." There was no sarcasm in his voice; he liked Dan. "I'll tell 'em I'm trying to track Joey down for a credit union refund. They'll want to help him get his money."

Dan grinned. "I like that."

"Make it fifty-dollar refund check," I said.

"I like that figure, too," Roger said.

Dan made it unanimous.

Three days later, we had something.

It hadn't come from Dan, not much of it anyway. The by-the-book route had only confirmed what Missing Persons found: one day, Joe Evans quit and took off, abandoning if not quite burning all his bridges behind him. His boss at the steel mill had not been called upon for a reference, nor had his union card been kept active. And his friends at the mill claimed not to have heard from him.

"None of his pals saw it coming," Dan said. "Or so they say."

"What about the phone records Louise provided?"

Dan checked his notes. "Joey talked to both his brother in Dallas and his sister in Davenport, a number of times in the six months prior to his disappearance. They're a close family."

"Which sibling got the most attention? Texas or Iowa?"

"Iowa. That's where little sister is. Agnes, her name is. He must've called her twenty times in those six months."

Roger fleshed out the picture.

"They're a close family, all right," he said. "Even when a business-like stranger comes around with fifty bucks for their brother, they clam up. Nobody wanted the refund check except the gal in charge—Loretta Evans, the matriarch, a tough old cookie who could put the battle in battleaxe. Come to think of it, she could put the axe in, too."

"She took the check?"

"She did. And she mailed it out the same day. I saw her do it. Speaking of mail, I checked trashcans all over Indiana, feels like. I got to know the Evanses better than the Evanses know the Evanses. I could save 'em some money."

"How's that?"

"They should share a copy of the National Enquirer. Just pass one around, instead of all picking it up."

"Speaking of inquiring minds, what did yours find out?"

"Exactly what it wanted to know," Roger said. "The family seems close in general, but in particular, they seem to want to keep in touch with Agnes."

"Joe's sister."

"His baby sister. She's only twenty-two. Anyway, they been calling her a lot. All of 'em."

"Interesting."

"There's also a bar in Davenport, called Bill's Golden Nugget, where they call from time to time. Maybe she works there."

"It's a lead, anyway," I said. "Damn—I wish I knew where that letter Loretta Evans mailed went to."

"It went to Agnes," Roger said. He was smiling smugly.

"How do you know?"

"Because I waited around on the corner where she mailed it till a postman came around to empty the box and told him I slipped an important letter in that I thought I forgot to put a stamp on. I had a hysterical expression on my face and a stamp ready in my hand, and the bastard took pity on me and let me sort through looking for my letter."

"And you found one addressed to Agnes Evans."

"Sure."

"What did you do with it?"

"Left it right there," he said. "You don't think I'd tamper with the U.S. mail do you?"

A foul, pungent odor from Oscar Mayer permeated the working-class neighborhood the massive plant bordered; but nobody seemed to notice, on this sunny June afternoon, or anyway care. Ragamuffin kids played in the streets and on the sidewalks, wearing dirt-smudged cheeks that knew no era, and housewives hung wash on lines strung across porches, apparently enjoying a breeze that to me only emphasized the slaughterhouse stench.

The address I had for Agnes Evans was 714½ Wundrum; it turned out to be a paint-peeling clapboard duplex in the middle of a crowded block.

My Buick was dirty enough to be at home in the neighborhood, and in my plaid shirt, tied into a halter top, and snug blue jeans, I fit in, too. I felt pretty much at home, actually; with a cop for a father, I had grown up in neighborhoods only a small step up from this—minus the slaughterhouse scent, thankfully.

I knocked at 714½ and then knocked again. The door opened cautiously and a round-faced woman in her early twenties peeked out at me. She had permed dishwater-blond hair, suspicious eyes, and her brother's weak jaw.

"Yeah?"

Pleasant, not at all pushy, I said, "I'm looking for Doris Wannamaker."

"No Doris anybody here," Agnes Evans said. She eased the door open somewhat; not all the way, but I could get a better look at her. She wore tight jeans with fashion-statement holes in the knees and a blue tee-shirt with "QUAD CITIES USA" in flowing white letters. She was slim, attractive and wore no make-up.

I said, "Isn't this 714½?"

"Yeah." I could hear a TV inside; a cartoon show.

"Wundrum Street?"

"That's right."

I sighed. "She's gone, huh. I guess that's the way it goes these days. Wonder how much I missed her by."

"I lived here six months," she said. "I don't know who lived here before me."

I shrugged, smiled. "We was in beauty school together, Doris and me. I was just passing through town and wanted to surprise her. Sorry to bother."

Agnes Evans finally smiled. It was an attractive smile. "I went to beauty school. At Regent."

Of course, I'd known that.

I said, "I went to the University of Beauty Science in Cedar Falls."

"Supposed to be a good school," Agnes allowed. "I graduated, Regent. I didn't keep my certificate up, though."

"Me neither," I said.

The door was open wider. I could see the little girl, wearing a red tee-shirt and underpants, sitting like an Indian in front of the TV, watching Tom bash Jerry with a skillet.

"Sure sorry I bothered you," I said.

"No problem."

"Look, uh . . . is there any chance I could use your phone? I want to try to catch my boyfriend at the motel, before he goes out."

"Well . . ."

"I thought I was going to have the afternoon filled with seeing Doris and talking old times, but now . . . could I impose?"

She shrugged, smiled tightly, but opened the screen and said, "Come on in."

The house was neat as a pin; neater. The furniture was the kind you rented to own, but it was maintained as if owning it was the plan. The TV was a big portable on a stand, and there was a Holiday Inn–type landscape over the plastic-covered sofa. A window air-conditioner chugged and the place was almost chilly, and the smell of whatever-goes-into-weenies wasn't making it inside.

"Hi, honey," I said, stopping near the little girl.

She didn't look up at me; she was watching Jerry hit Tom with a toaster. "Hi," she said.

Maggie looked older than her picture, but not much. A little child with almost white blonde hair, and a lot of it, a frizzy frame around a cameo face that was blank with TV concentration.

I pretended to use the phone in the kitchen—which was tidy and smelled of macaroni and cheese—while Agnes stood with her arms folded

and studied me as she smoked a cigarette. She was still just a little suspicious.

"I'll see you later, then," I told the dial tone, and hung up and smiled at Agnes and shrugged. "Men," I said.

She smirked and blew smoke and nodded in mutual understanding.

As I walked out, she followed. I said, "So you're not in hair anymore?"

"No. My boyfriend Billy runs a bar. I work there most evenings."

"Really? Who looks after your little girl?"

"That's not my little girl. Cindy is, uh, a friend of mine's kid. I look after her, days."

"Sweet little girl," I said.

"She's a honey," Agnes said.

I left them there, in the neat house in the foul-smelling neighborhood. I wasn't worried about leaving Maggie in Agnes's care. It was someone else's care I was worried about.

The someone who was with Maggie, nights.

Bill's Golden Nugget was a country-western bar on Harrison, a one-way whose glory days—at least along this saloon-choked stretch—were long gone. I parked on a side street, in front of a natural-food co-op inhabited by hippies who hadn't noticed the sixties were over. The Nugget was between a pawn shop and a heavy-metal bar.

It was mid-afternoon and the long, narrow saloon was sparsely populated—a few out-of-work blue-collar urban cowboys were playing pool; a would-be biker played the Elvira pinball machine; a couple of guys in jeans and workshirts were at the bar, having an argument about baseball. Just enough patrons to keep the air smoky and stale. A Johnny Paycheck song worked at blowing out the jukebox speakers. The room's sole lighting seemed to be the neon and/or lit-up plastic signs which bore images of beer, Marlboro men, and *Sports Illustrated* swimsuit models, none of which had the slightest thing to do with the Nugget. Except for the beer.

A heavy-set, bearded, balding blond man in his late twenties was behind the bar. He wore a plaid shirt that clashed with mine and red suspenders that clashed with his. I heard somebody call him Bill.

He seemed pleasant enough, but he was watching me warily; I was new, and maybe I was a hooker.

I took a stool.

"What'll it be, sweet thing?" he said. There was nothing menacing about it. Not even anything condescending. But he was eyeing me carefully. Just a good on-top-of-it bar owner who was probably his own bouncer.

"What have you got on tap that I'd like, big guy?"

"Coors," he said, and it was sort of a question.

"You kidding, Bill? Drinking that stuff is like makin' love in a boat."

"Huh?"

"Fucking close to water," I said, and I grinned at him. He liked that.

"I also got Bud," he said.

"Bodacious," I said.

He went away smiling, convinced I was not a hooker, just available. Even a guy with a good-looking girl like Agnes at home has his weaknesses.

I milked the Bud for fifteen minutes, tapping my toes to the country music, some of which was pretty good. That Carlene Carter could sing. Nobody hit on me, not even Bill, and that was fine. I just wanted to fit in.

There was a room in back that was at least as big as the front, with tables and a dance floor and a stage for a band and a second bar; it wasn't in use right now, but some beer-ad lighting was on and somebody was back there working, loading in boxes of booze or whatever, through the alley door.

When the guy finished, he came up front; he was in a White Sox sweatshirt with cut-off sleeves and blue jeans. He was a brawny character, maybe twenty-five, good looking except for a weak chin.

He was Joey Evans.

I had a second Bud and eavesdropped as Evans—whose voice was high-pitched and husky, not suited to his rather brutish build—asked if he could take a break.

"Sure, Freddy," Bill said. "Take five, but then I need you with me behind the bar. It's damn near happy hour, kid."

Freddy/Joey went behind the bar and got himself a can of Diet Coke. He went to a table, away from any patrons, and sat quietly sipping.

I went over to him. "You look like you could use some company. Hard day?"

"Hard enough," he said. He took my figure in, trying to be subtle; it was about as successful as McGovern's run at the Presidency.

"Have a seat," he said, and stood, and pushed out a chair.

I sat. "Hope you don't mind my being so forward. I'm Becky Lewis." I stuck out my hand. We shook; his grip was gentle. Right.

"You're from Chicago, aren't you, Becky?" he said. He smiled boyishly; his eyes were light faded blue, like stonewashed denims.

I was supposed to be the detective. "How did you gather that?"

"The accent," he said. "I'd know that flat nasal tone anywhere."

He should: he had it himself.

"I figured you for Chicago, too. South side?"

"Close," he said. "How . . . ?"

"You're not wearing a Cubbies sweatshirt, now, are ya?"

He grinned. "Hell, no! Screw them and their Yuppie fans."

"You got that right. Let me buy you a beer . . . Freddy, is it?"

"Freddy," he said. "No thanks. I'm workin'. But I'll buy you one."

"I already got one. Let's just get to know each other a little."

There was not much to know, he said. He was fairly new to the area, working as a bartender for Bill, who was a friend of a friend.

"You got strong hands, Freddy," I said, stroking one. "Working hands. Steel mill hands."

His eyes flared. Maybe I'd gone too far.

"I . . . I got tired of factory life. Just too

damn hard. I need to be sharp, not wasted, when I spend time with my kid. I'm a single parent, you know. I'm trying for that quality time thing, you know."

I bet he was.

"How many kids you got, Freddy?"

"Just the one. Sweet little girl. Cindy. Starts first grade next year. You got any kids?"

"I'm divorced, but I never had any kids. Didn't think I was cut out for it."

"Oh, you should reconsider. There's nothing like it. Being a parent—it's the best thing that ever happened to me." Really.

"I don't know," I said, "I'm afraid I might lose my temper around 'em or something."

"That can be a problem," he admitted. "But I'd never lay a hand on Cindy. Never."

"Spare the rod and spoil the child, Clyde."

His brow knit. "I don't believe in that shit. Look—I used to have a bad temper. I'll be honest with you, Becky. I used to . . . well, I used to get a little rough with the ladies sometimes."

I stroked his hand, and almost purred: "I like it a little rough."

Gag me, as they say, with a spoon.

"I don't mean that. I don't mean horseplay or nothing. I mean, I hit women before. Okay? See this Diet Coke? It's not just 'cause I'm workin'. I don't drink anymore. I get nasty when I drink, so I don't drink."

"It's a little rough, being a recovering alcoholic, isn't it, working in a bar?"

"Being somebody who don't drink is a valuable commodity when you work in a bar-type situation. That's what Bill likes about me."

"You're not . . . tempted?"

"No. I haven't had a drink in five years."

"Five years?" Was he lying, or crazy? Or both? Was this a trick question? He swirled the Diet Coke in the can. "Five years sober. Five years dry. Besides, Becky—this job was all I could get."

"A strapping boy like you?"

His expression darkened. "I got my reasons. If you want to be my friend, you got to respect my privacy, okay?"

Funny, coming from a guy I just met who already had admitted he was a reformed drunk and supposedly reformed woman-beater. Was there something psychotic in those spooky faded blue eyes?

"Sure, honey," I said, "I'll respect your privacy. If you respect me in the morning."

He grinned again, shyly. "I got to get behind the bar, 'fore Bill tears me a new you-know-what."

"Can we get together after you get off work?"

"I got to spend the evening with my little girl."

"Right. Quality time."

"That's it. But I ought to have her in bed by nine o'clock."

I bet.

"You could stop over after that," he said. "I can give you the address. . . ."

Louise sat next to me in the front seat. She wore the same peasant dress she'd worn to my office; clutched the same patent-leather purse. Her heavy make-up, in the darkness as we sat in the car at the curb, gave her a Kabuki-like visage.

I had phoned her long distance, right after my encounter with Joey at the Nugget. She'd been standing by for my call, as I'd primed her that if I found Maggie, I'd need her to come immediately. I couldn't take Maggie without Louise present, and not just because the child would rightfully resist going with a stranger.

The fact was, with Louise along, taking Maggie would not be kidnapping. Without her, it would be.

"Are you all right, Louise?"

She nodded. We were in my Buick; we had left her Datsun in a motel parking lot near the Interstate. That's where we had met, after she made the three-hour drive in two and a half hours. It was now approaching nine-thirty and the sky was a brilliant dark blue with more stars than any child could ever hope to dream upon. Moving clouds seemed to rise cotton-candy-like, but it was only smoke from Oscar Mayer.

We were several blocks from Agnes Evans's

duplex, but the meat-packing smell still scorched the air. Joey Evans and his daughter lived in a single-family, single-story clapboard, smaller and newer than his sister's place. Built in the fifties sometime. I lived in a house like this when I was six.

"He's expecting me," I told her. I'd already told her this, but I'd been telling her a lot of things and I wasn't sure anything was sticking. She nodded.

"I'll go up, and knock, and after he lets me in, I'll excuse myself to go to the restroom, I'll find the back door, unlock it, and you come in and I'll keep him busy while you find your way to Maggie's room."

She nodded.

"Then you slip out the back door with her. When you're in the car with her, safe, honk twice. Short honks. Then I'll get out of there on some excuse, and we're outa here. You girls will be on your way home."

She smiled wanly. "Ms. Tree—thank you. Thank you so very much. I knew you could do it. I knew you could."

"I haven't done it yet. *We* haven't. Now, you need to have a clear head about you, Louise! I want to get you in and out, with Maggie, without him knowing till we're tail-lights. I don't want *any* violence going down—that husband of yours looks like he could bench-press a grand piano."

She nodded.

"Wait five minutes after I go to the door; then go around behind the house and find the back door. How long?"

"Five minutes."

"When you're safe in the car, how many times will you honk?"

She raised two fingers, as if making the peace sign. "Short honks."

"Good, Louise." I patted her shoulder. I felt confident about this. About as confident as you feel when you make your first dental visit in five years.

He answered my first knock. He was wearing a blue and white checked sportshirt and jeans; he looked nice. He asked me to come in, and I did. He smelled like Canoe cologne; I didn't even know they still made that stuff.

"It's not much, Becky," he said, gesturing about, "but it's enough for Cindy and me."

Whether he and his sister had similar decorating styles, or whether one of them had done the other's home, I couldn't say; but it was the same rent-to-buy decor, just a tad sparser than sis's place. The TV was a console, apparently an old used model, with a Nintendo unit on the floor in front representing the only visible extravagance. Over the couch was another discount-store oil painting, this one a sad-eyed Gacy-like clown handing a red balloon to a little girl who looked disturbingly like Maggie.

"You really keep the place neat," I said, sitting on the couch.

"Cindy helps me. She's really the strong one in the family."

"I'd love to meet her."

"Maybe next time. She's asleep. Besides, I don't like her to see me with other ladies."

"Other ladies?"

"Other than her mommy."

"But you're divorced."

"I know. But she's only six. She doesn't understand stuff like that. Of course, then, neither do I."

What sort of sick relationship did this son of a bitch have with little Maggie? Had he turned her into a "wife"? A six-year-old wife? This guy was lucky I wasn't armed.

"Look," I said, smiling, trying to maintain the pretense of warmth, "I need to use the little girl's room. Where . . . ?"

He pointed the way. It was through a neat compact kitchen, which connected to a hall off of which was Maggie's room. Or, Cindy's room. At least she didn't sleep with her daddy.

She sure looked angelic right now, blond hair haloing her sweet face on the overstuffed pillow. Her room was the only one that wasn't spare—even in the meager glow of the night light, I could see the zoo of stuffed animals, the clown and circus posters, the dolls and their little dresses. Daddy gave her everything.

The sick bastard.

When I returned, having flushed a toilet I really had had to use, I left the back door, off the kitchen, unlocked.

I sat down next to Joey—keeping in mind I needed to call him Freddy—and he said, "I can get you a beer, if you like."

The last thing in the world I wanted was for him to go traipsing through the kitchen while Louise was sneaking in.

"No thanks, I'm fine. I just got *rid* of a beer, honey."

He laughed embarrassedly. I nudged him with an elbow, gently. "What are you doing with beer in the house, anyway? You haven't had a drink in five years, right?"

A smile creased his pleasant face. "You're sure a suspicious girl. I keep a few brews in the fridge for company."

"You entertain a lot?"

"Not much. My sih . . ."

He started to say "sister," I think; then shifted gears.

"My friends Bill and Agnes both like their beer. In fact, Bill sometimes likes it too much." He shook his head. "A guy who runs a bar shouldn't drink up the profits."

"He's lucky to have you around."

"Actually, he is. I only hope he can stay in business. I sure need this job."

The child's scream shook the house.

Evans and I both bolted off the couch, and then, framed in the archway of the hall leading to the kitchen, there was Louise, pulling the unwilling little girl by the arm. The child, wearing an oversize, man's white tee-shirt with Bart Simpson on it, was screaming.

Louise, her eyes crazed, her Kabuki face frozen with rage, slapped the little girl savagely; it rang like a gunshot off the swirl-plaster walls.

That silenced the little girl's screams, but tears and whimpering took their place.

"Louise!" Evans said, face as white as a fish's underbelly. "What . . ."

Her purse had been tucked under one arm. Now, still clinging to the little girl with one hand, she dug her other hand into the brown patent-leather bag and came back with a snout-nosed black revolver.

"You bastard," she said, "you sick bastard . . ."

Those had been my thoughts, exactly, earlier, but now I was having new thoughts. . . .

"Louise," I said, stepping forward. "Put the gun down."

"You did it to her, didn't you?" she said to him. "You did it to her! You fucked her! You've been fucking her!"

The little girl was confused and crying.

Evans stepped forward, carefully; he was patting the air gently. "Louise—just because your father . . ."

"Shut-up!" she said, and she shot at him. He danced out of the way as the shot rang and echoed in the confined space; the couch took the slug.

I wasn't waiting to see who or what took the next one: I moved in and slapped the gun out of her hand; then I slapped her face, hard.

I had a feeling I wasn't the first one to do that to Louise. She crumpled to the floor and she wept quietly, huddling fetally; her little girl sat down close to her, stroking her mother's blond hair.

"Mommy," Maggie said. "Don't cry, mommy. Don't cry."

I picked up the gun.

Evans was standing looking down at his wife and child. He looked at me sharply, accusingly.

"I'm a private detective," I explained. "She hired me to get Maggie back."

"She told you I beat Maggie, right?" he snapped. "And worse?"

I nodded.

"Why the hell do you think I ran from her?" he said, plaintively; his face was haunted, his eyes welling. "*I* wasn't the one beating Maggie! But the courts would've given Maggie to her mommy. They would never have believed me over her. How *else* could I have stopped this?"

I didn't have an answer for him; he wasn't necessarily right—the courts might have realized Louise was the abusing parent. But they might not have. I sure hadn't.

He knelt beside his wife; the little girl was on

one side of her, and he was on the other. They were mostly in the kitchen. Louise didn't seem to notice them, but they tried to soothe her just the same.

"Her father did terrible things to her," he said softly. "She got me all confused with him. Looked at me and saw her daddy—thought I'd do the same things to Maggie he done to her."

"But the only one imitating her father," I said, "was Louise."

"Mommy doesn't mean to hurt me," the little girl said. "She loves me." It was almost a question.

Sirens were cutting the air; responding to the gun shot.

"I was wrong," he said, looking at me with eyes that wanted absolution. "I shouldn't have run. I should have stayed and tried to fix things."

Who could blame him, really?

Something in Louise had been broken so very long ago.

But as I watched them there, the little family huddling on the cold linoleum, I had to hope that something at long last could start being mended.

STRUNG OUT

Sara Paretsky

ONE OF THE MOST SIGNIFICANT figures in the ascent of female mystery writers in the last quarter of the twentieth century is Sara Paretsky (1947–   ). Not only has her tough private eye character, Victoria Iphigenia (generally and under-standably known as V.I., but called "Vic" by her friends) Warshawski, been one of the most famous and popular fictional detectives in America for more than three decades, but Paretsky was the guiding force in the creation of Sisters in Crime, the highly successful organization devoted to getting more attention for women crime writers.

Her education indicated a political or sociological career (she received a B.A. in political science from the University of Kansas, a Ph.D. in history from the University of Chicago, and an M.B.A., also from Chicago), and she worked in community service in Chicago before turning to writing mystery fiction. The first V. I. Warshawski novel, *Indemnity Only*, was published in 1982, and there have been more than twenty books since then, all but two featuring her hard-boiled P.I.

V.I. earned a law degree and worked for a short time as a public defender but soon went out on her own to become a private investigator specializing in white-collar crimes that frequently turn violent. She is physically fearless, with a background in karate and street fighting developed in her early years in a tough neighborhood on the South Side of Chicago—and she carries a Smith & Wes-son automatic.

Among Paretsky's numerous awards is a Grand Master for lifetime achieve-ment given by the Mystery Writers of America.

"Strung Out" was originally published in *Deadly Allies*, edited by Robert J. Randisi and Marilyn Wallace (New York, Doubleday, 1992).

Strung Out

SARA PARETSKY

I

PEOPLE BORN NEAR the corner of 90th and Commercial used to have fairly predictable futures. The boys grew up to work in the mills; the girls took jobs in the bakeries or coffee shops. They married each other and scrimped to make a down payment on a neighborhood bungalow and somehow fit their large families into its small rooms.

Now that the mills are history, the script has changed. Kids are still marrying, still having families, but without the certainty of the steel industry to buoy their futures. The one thing that seems to stay the same, though, is the number who stubbornly cling to the neighborhood even now that the jobs are gone. It's a clannish place, South Chicago, and people don't leave it easily.

When Monica Larush got pregnant our senior year in high school and married football hero Gary Oberst, we all just assumed they were on their way to becoming another large family in a small bungalow. She wasn't a friend of mine, so I didn't worry about the possible ruin of her life. Anyway, having recently lost my own mother to cancer, I wasn't too concerned about other girls' problems.

Monica's and my lives only intersected on the basketball court. Like me, she was an aggres-sive athlete, but she clearly had a high level of talent as well. In those days, though, a pregnant girl couldn't stay in school, so she missed our championship winter. The team brought her a game ball. We found her, fat and pasty, eating Fritos in angry frustration in front of the TV in her mother's kitchen. When we left, we made grotesque jokes about her swollen face and belly, our only way of expressing our embarrassment and worry.

Gary and Monica rewrote their script, though. Gary got a job on the night shift at Inland Steel and went to school during the day. After the baby—Gary Junior—was born, Monica picked up her GED. The two of them scrimped, not for a down payment, but to make it through the University of Illinois's Chicago campus. Gary took a job as an accountant with a big Loop firm, Monica taught high school French, and they left the neighborhood. Moved north was what I heard.

And that was pretty much all I knew—or cared—about them before Lily Oberst's name and face started popping up in the papers. She was apparently mopping up junior tennis competition. Tennis boosters and athletic-apparel makers were counting the minutes until she turned pro.

I actually first heard about her from my old basketball coach, Mary Ann McFarlane. Mary Ann's first love had always been tennis. When she retired from teaching at sixty, she continued to act as a tennis umpire at local high school and college tournaments. I saw her once a year when the Virginia Slims came to Chicago. She worked as a linesperson there for the pittance the tour paid—not for the bucks, but for the excitement. I always came during the last few days and had dinner with her in Greek Town at the end of the finals.

"I've been watching Lily Oberst play up at the Skokie Valley club," Mary Ann announced one year. "Kid's got terrific stuff. If they don't ruin her too young she could be—well, I won't say another Martina. Martinas come once a century. But a great one."

"Lily Oberst?" I shook my head, fishing for why the name sounded familiar.

"You don't remember Monica? Didn't you girls keep in touch after your big year? Lily is her and Gary's daughter. I used to coach Monica in tennis besides basketball, but I guess that wasn't one of your sports."

After that I read the stories in detail and got caught up on twenty years of missing history. Lily grew up in suburban Glenview, the second of two children. The *Herald-Star* explained that both her parents were athletic and encouraged her and her brother to go out for sports. When a camp coach brought back the word that Lily might have some tennis aptitude, her daddy began working with her every day. She had just turned six then.

Gary put up a net for her in the basement and would give her an ice cream bar every time she could hit the ball back twenty-five times without missing.

"He got mad when it got too easy for me," Lily said, giggling, to the reporter. "Then he'd raise the net whenever I got to twenty-four."

When it became clear that they had a major tennis talent on their hands, Monica and Gary put all their energy into developing it. Monica quit her job as a teacher so that she could travel to camps and tournaments with Lily. Gary, by then regional director for a pharmaceutical firm, persuaded his company to put in the seed money for Lily's career. He himself took a leave of absence to work as her personal trainer. Even now that she was a pro, Monica and Gary went with her everywhere. Of course Lily had a professional coach, but her day always started with a workout with Daddy.

Gary Junior didn't get much print attention. He apparently didn't share the family's sports mania. Five years older than Lily, he was in college studying for a degree in chemical engineering, and hoping to go off to Procter & Gamble in Cincinnati.

Lily turned pro the same year Jennifer Capriati did. Since Capriati was making history, joining the pros at thirteen, Lily, two years older, didn't get the national hoopla. But Chicago went wild. Her arrival in the Wimbledon quarterfinals that year was front-page news all over town. Her 6–2, 6–0 loss there to Monica Seles was shown live in every bar in the city. Fresh-faced and smiling under a spiky blond hairdo, she grinned through her braces and said it was just a thrill to be on the same court with players like Seles and Graf. The city fell in love.

So when it was announced that she was coming to Chicago to play in the Slims in February the tournament generated more publicity than it had ever known. After a year and a half on the pro circuit Lily was ranked eighth in the world, but the pictures of her arrival at the family home still showed an ingenuous grin. Her Great Dane, standing on his hind legs with his paws on her shoulders, was licking her face.

Mary Ann McFarlane called me a few days after the Obersts arrived back in town. "Want to come up to Glenview and watch the kid work out? You could catch up with Monica at the same time."

That sounded like a treat that would appeal to Monica about as much as it did to me. But I had never seen a tennis prodigy in the making. I agreed to drive out to Glenview on Friday morning. Mary Ann and I would have lunch with Monica after Lily's workout.

The Skokie Valley Tennis Club was just off the Edens Expressway at Dempster. Lily's workout started at eight but I hadn't felt the need to watch a sixteen-year-old, however prodigious, run laps. I arrived at the courts a little after ten.

When I asked a woman at the reception desk to direct me to Lily, she told me the star's workout was off-limits to the press today. I explained who I was. She consulted higher authority over the phone. Mary Ann had apparently greased the necessary skids: I was allowed past a bored guard lounging against a hall door. After showing him my driver's license, I was directed down the hall to the private court where Lily was practicing. A second guard there looked at my license again and then opened the door for me.

Lily had the use of three nets if she needed them. A small grandstand held only three people: Mary Ann and Monica and a young man in a workout suit with "Artemis" blazoned across the back. I recognized Monica from the newspaper photos, but they didn't do justice to her perfectly styled gold hair, the makeup enhancing her oval face, or the casual elegance of her clothes. I had a fleeting memory of her fat, pasty face as she sat eating Fritos twenty years ago. I would never have put those two images together. As the old bromide has it, living well is the best revenge.

Mary Ann squeezed my hand as I sat on her other side. "Good to see you, Vic," she whispered. "Monica—here's Vic."

We exchanged confused greetings across our old coach, me congratulating her on her daughter's success, she exclaiming at how I hadn't changed a bit. I didn't know if that was a compliment or not.

The man was introduced as Monte Allison, from Artemis Products' marketing department. Artemis supplied all of Lily's tennis clothes and shoes, as well as a seven-figure endorsement contract. Allison was just along to protect the investment, Mary Ann explained. The equipment maker heard her and ostentatiously turned his left shoulder to us.

On the court in front of us Lily was hitting tennis balls. A kid in white shorts was serving to her backhand. A dark man in shabby gray sweats stood behind her encouraging her and critiqu-

ing her stroke. And a third man in bright white clothes offered more forceful criticisms from the sidelines.

"Get into the shot, Lily. Come'n, honey, you're not concentrating."

"Gary," Mary Ann muttered at me. "That's Paco Callabrio behind her."

I don't know much about tennis, but even I'd heard of Callabrio. After dominating men's tennis in the sixties he had retired to his family home in Majorca. But five years ago he'd come out of seclusion to coach a few selected players. Lily had piqued his interest when he saw her at the French Open last year; Monica had leaped at the opportunity to have her daughter work with him. Apparently Gary was less impressed. As the morning wore on Gary's advice began clashing with Paco's more and more often.

In the midst of a heated exchange over Lily's upswing I sensed someone moving onto the bench behind me. I turned to see a young woman leaning at her ease against the bleacher behind her. She was dressed in loose-fitting trousers that accentuated the long, lean lines of her body.

Lily saw the newcomer at the same time I did. She turned very red, then very white. While Paco and Gary continued arguing, she signaled to the young man to start hitting balls to her again. She'd been too tired to move well a minute ago, but the woman's arrival infused her with new energy.

Mary Ann had also turned to stare. "Nicole Rubova," she muttered to me.

I raised my eyebrows. Another of the dazzling Czech players who'd come to the States in Martina's wake. She was part of the generation between Martina and Capriati, a year or so older than Graf but with time ahead of her still to fight for the top spots. Her dark, vivid beauty made her a mediagenic foil to Graf's and Lily's blondness, but her sardonic humor kept her from being really popular with the press.

"Gary's afraid she's going to rape his baby. He won't let Lily go out alone with any of the women on the circuit." Mary Ann continued to mutter at me.

I raised my brows again, this time amazed at Mary Ann's pithy remarks. She'd never talked so bluntly to me when she was my basketball coach.

By now Gary had also seen Rubova in the stands. Like Lily he changed color, then grew even more maniacal in his demands on his daughter. When Paco advised a rest around eleven-thirty, Gary shook his head emphatically.

"You can't spoil her, Paco. Believe me, I know this little girl. She's got great talent and a heart of gold, but she's lazy. You've got to drive her."

Lily was gray with exhaustion. While they argued over her she leaned over, her hands on her knees, and gasped for air.

"Mr. Oberst," Paco said, his chilly formality emphasizing his dislike, "you want Lily to be a great star. But a girl who plays when she is this fatigued will only injure herself, if she doesn't burn out completely first. I say the workout is over for the day."

"And I say she got to Wimbledon last year thanks to my methods," Gary yelled.

"And she almost had to forfeit her round of sixteen match because you were coaching her so blatantly from the seats," Paco shouted back. "Your methods stink, Oberst."

Gary stepped toward the Catalan, then abruptly turned his back on him and yelled at his daughter, "Lily, pick up your racket. Come on, girl. You know the rules."

"Really, Oberst," Monte Allison called tentatively down to the floor from the stands. "We can't injure Lily—that won't help any of us."

Monica nodded in emphatic agreement, but Gary paid no attention to either of them. Lily looked imploringly from Paco to Gary. When the coach said nothing else, she bent to pick up her racket and continued returning balls. She was missing more than she was hitting now and was moving leadenly around the court. Paco watched for about a minute, then turned on his heel and marched toward a door in the far wall. As he disappeared through it, Monica got up from Mary Ann's left and hurried after him.

I noticed a bright pink anorak with rabbit fur around the hood next to where she'd been sitting, and two furry leather mittens with rabbits embroidered on them.

"That's Lily's," Mary Ann said. "Monica must have forgotten she was holding them for her. I'll give them to the kid if she makes it through this session."

My old coach's face was set in angry lines. I felt angry, too, and kept half rising from my seat, wondering if I ought to intervene. Paco's departure had whipped Gary into a triumphant frenzy. He shooed the kid serving balls away and started hitting ground strokes to his daughter at a furious pace. She took it for about five minutes before collapsing on the floor in tears.

"I just can't do it anymore, Daddy. I just can't."

Gary put his own racket down and smiled in triumph.

A sharp clap came from behind me, making me jump. "Bravo, Gary!" Nicole cried. "What a man you are! Yes, indeed, you've proved you can frighten your little girl. Now the question is: Which matters more to you? That Lily become the great player her talent destines her to be? Or that you prove that you own her?"

She jumped up lightly from the bench and ran down to the court. She put an arm around Lily and said something inaudible to the girl. Lily looked from her to her father and shook her head, flushing with misery. Nicole shrugged. Before leaving the court she and Gary exchanged a long look. Only an optimist would have found the seeds of friendship in it.

II

The Slims started the next Monday. The events at the Skokie Valley Tennis Club made me follow the newspaper reports eagerly, but the tournament seemed to be progressing without any open fireworks. One or two of the higher seeds were knocked out early, but Martina, Rubova, Lily, and one of the Maleeva sisters were all winning on schedule, along with Zina Garrison. Indeed, Martina, coming off knee surgery, seemed to be playing with the energy of a woman half her age.

I called Mary Ann McFarlane Thursday night to make sure she had my pass to the quarterfinal matches on Friday. Lily was proving such a hit that tickets were hard to get.

"Oh, yes," she assured me. "We linespersons don't have much leverage, but I got Monica to leave a pass for you at the will-call window. Dinner Sunday night?"

I agreed readily. Driving down to the Pavilion on Friday, I was in good time for the noon match, which pitted Martina against Frederica Lujan.

Lujan was seeded twelfth to Martina's third in world rankings, but the gap between their games seemed much wider than those numbers. In fact, halfway through the first set Martina suddenly turned her game up a notch and turned an even match into a rout. She was all over the court, going down for shots that should have been unhittable.

An hour later we got the quarterfinal meeting the crowd had come to see: Lily against Nicole Rubova. When Lily danced onto the court, a vision in pink and white with a sweatband pulling her blond spikes back from her face, the stands roared with pleasure. Nicole got a polite round of applause, but she was only there to give their darling a chance to play.

A couple of minutes after they'd started their warm-up, Monica came in. She sat close to the court, about ten rows in front of me. The man she joined was Paco Callabrio. He had stood next to Lily on the court as she came out for her warm-ups, patted her encouragingly on the ass, and climbed into the stands. Monica must have persuaded him not to quit in fury last week.

At first I assumed Gary was boycotting the match, either out of dislike of Paco or for fear his overt coaching would cause Lily to forfeit. As play progressed, though, I noticed him on the far side of the court, behind the chair umpire, making wild gestures if Lily missed a close shot, or if he thought the linespersons were making bad calls.

When play began Rubova's catlike languor vanished. She obviously took her conditioning seriously, moving well around the court and playing the net with a brilliant ferocity. Mary Ann might be right—she might have designs on Lily's body—but it didn't make her play the youngster with any gentleness.

Lily, too, had a range of motion that was exciting to watch. She was big, already five ten, with long arms and a phenomenal reach. Whether due to Gary's drills or not, her backhand proved formidable; unlike most women on the circuit she could use it one handed.

Lily pushed her hard but Rubova won in three sets, earning the privilege of meeting Navratilova the next afternoon. It seemed to me that Lily suddenly began hitting the ball rather tentatively in the last few games of the final set. I wasn't knowledgeable enough to know if she had suddenly reached her physical limit, or if she was buckling under Rubova's attack.

The crowd, disappointed in their favorite's loss, gave the Czech only a lukewarm hand as she collected her rackets and exited. Paco, Monica, and Gary all disappeared from the stands as Lily left the court to a standing ovation.

Mary Ann had been a linesperson on the far sideline during the Rubova match. Neither of the players had given the umpire a hard time. Rubova at one point drew a line on the floor with her racket, a sarcastic indicator of where she thought Mary Ann was spotting Lily. Another time Lily cried out in frustration to the chair umpire; I saw Monica's shoulders tense and wondered if the prodigy was prone to tantrums. More likely she was worried by what Gary—turning puce on the far side—might do to embarrass her. Other than that the match had gone smoothly.

Doubles quarterfinals were on the agenda for late afternoon. I wasn't planning on watching those, so I wandered down to the court to have a word with Mary Ann before I left.

She tried to talk me into staying. "Garrison has teamed up with Rubova. They should be fun to watch—both are real active girls."

"Enough for me for one day. What'd you think of the kid in tournament play?"

Mary Ann spread her hands. "She's going to go a long way. Nicole outplayed her today, but she won't forever. Although—I don't know—it looked to me in the last couple of games as though she might have been favoring her right shoulder. I couldn't be sure. I just hope Gary hasn't got her to injure herself with his hit-till-you-drop coaching methods. I'm surprised Paco's hanging on through it."

I grinned suggestively at her. "Maybe Monica has wonderful powers of persuasion."

Mary Ann looked at me calmly. "You're trying to shock me, Vic, but believe me, I was never a maiden aunt. And anyway, nothing on this circuit would shock me. . . . They have free refreshments downstairs for players and crew. And press and hangers-on. Want to come have some coffee before you go? Some of the girls might even be there."

"And be a hanger-on? Sure, why not?" Who knows, maybe Martina would meet me and remember an urgent need for some detective work.

A freight elevator protected by guards carried the insiders to the lower depths. Mary Ann, in her linesperson's outfit, didn't need to show any identification. I came in for more scrutiny, but my player's-guest badge got me through.

The elevator decanted us onto a grubby corridor. Young people of both sexes hurried up and down its length, carrying clipboards at which they frowned importantly.

"PR staff," Mary Ann explained. "They feed all the statistics from the match to different wire services and try to drum up local interest in the tournament. Tie-ins with the auto show, that kind of thing."

Older, fatter people stood outside makeshift marquees with coffee and globular brownies. At the end of the hall I could see Paco and Monica huddled together. Gary wasn't in sight.

"Lily may have gone back in for a massage; I think she already did her press interview. Gary must be inside with her. He won't let her get a workover alone."

"Inside the locker room?" I echoed. "I know she's Daddy's darling, but don't the other women object to him being there while they're changing? And can she really stand having him watch her get massaged?"

"There's a lounge." Mary Ann shepherded me into the refreshment tent—really a niche roped off from the cement corridor with a rather pathetic plastic canopy overhead. "Friends and lovers of the stars can sit there while the girls dress inside. I don't expect he actually hangs around the massage table. Don't go picturing some fabulous hideaway, though. This is a gym at a relatively poor university. It's purely functional. But they do have a cement cubbyhole for the masseuse—that sets it apart from the normal school gym."

I suddenly realized I was hungry—it was long past lunchtime. The Slims catering was heavy on volume and carbohydrates. I rejected fried chicken wings and rice and filled a plastic bowl with some doubtful-looking chili. Mary Ann picked up a handful of cookies to eat with her coffee.

We settled at an empty table in the far corner and ate while Mary Ann pointed out the notables to me. Zina Garrison's husband was at the buffet next to Katarina Maleeva. The two were laughing together, trying to avoid a fat reporter who was unabashedly eavesdropping on them.

A well-groomed woman near the entrance to the marquee was Clare Rutland, the doyenne of the tour, Mary Ann explained. She had no formal title with the Slims, but seemed to be able to keep its temperamental stars happy, or at least functioning.

As I ate my chili, six or seven people stopped to talk to Rutland. They'd nod at her remarks and race off again. I imagined tennis stars' wishes, from lotus blossoms to Lotus racers, being satisfied at the wave of her hand.

Mary Ann, talking to acquaintances, began picking up some of the gossip buzzing the room: Lily might have strained her shoulder. Maybe torn her rotator cuff. In this kind of environment the worst scenarios are generated rapidly from the whiff of an idea. And Gary apparently had been thrown out of Lily's press conference and was now sulking in the women's lounge.

A collective cry from the group across the room made me jerk my head around. Nicole Rubova was sprinting down the hall, wet, a towel haphazardly draping her midriff.

"Clare," she gasped.

Clare Rutland was on her feet as soon as she heard the out-cry, almost before Rubova came into view. She took off her cardigan and draped it across the player's shoulders. Rubova was too far from us for me to be able to hear her, but the reporters in the room crowded around her, tournament etiquette forgotten.

It only took a minute for Mary Ann to get the main point of the story from one of them: Gary Oberst was on the couch in the players' lounge. Someone had wrapped a string from a tennis racket around his neck a few times.

It was only later that everyone realized Lily herself had disappeared.

III

Clare Rutland curled one foot toward her chin and massaged her stockinged toes. Her face, rubbed free of makeup, showed the strain of the day in its sharply dug lines.

"This could kill the Slims," she remarked to no one in particular.

It was past midnight. I was in the windowless press room with her, Mary Ann, and a bunch of men, including Jared Brookings, who owned the PR firm handling the Slims in Chicago. Brookings had come in in person around nine, to see what could be done to salvage the tournament. He'd sent his fresh-faced minions packing long ago. They'd phoned him in terror when the police arrested Nicole Rubova, and clearly were not up to functioning in the crisis.

Arnold Krieger was there, too, with a handful of other reporters whose names I never learned. Krieger was the fat man who'd been listening in on Zina Garrison's husband earlier in the dining

area. He covered tennis for one of the wire services and had made himself at home in the press room when the cops commandeered it for their headquarters.

"She'll be out on bond in the morning, right?" Krieger palmed a handful of nuts into his mouth as he started to talk, so his words came out clogged. "So she can play Martina at one, per the schedule."

Clare looked at him in dismay but didn't speak.

Brookings put his fingertips together. "It all depends, doesn't it? We can't be too careful. We've spent two decades building these girls up, but the whole fabric could collapse at any minute."

I could see Mary Ann's teacher instincts debating whether to correct his mixed metaphors and deciding against it. "The problem isn't just having one of the stars arrested for murder," she said bluntly. "Lily Oberst is a local heroine and now everyone is going to read that an evil lesbian who had designs on her killed her father because he stood between them. Chicago might rip Nicole apart. They certainly won't support the tournament."

"Besides," Clare Rutland added in a dull voice, "two of the top seeds withdrew when they heard about Rubova's arrest. They've gone off to locate a lawyer to handle the defense. The other Czechs may not play any more Slims this year if a cloud hangs over Rubova. Neither will Freddie Lujan. If they drop out, others may follow suit."

"If a cloud hangs over Rubova, it's over the whole tour," Monte Allison, the Artemis Products representative, spoke for the first time. "We may withdraw *our* sponsorship for the rest of the year—I can't speak for Philip Morris, of course. That's a corporate decision, naturally, not mine, but we'll be making it tomorrow or—no, tomorrow's Saturday. We'll make it Monday. Early."

I'd never yet known a corporation that could make an important decision early Monday just because one of its vice presidents said so in a forceful voice. But Allison was fretful because none of the tennis people was paying attention to him. Since Artemis also helped Philip Morris promote the tour, Allison was likely to urge that they withdraw their sponsorship just because he didn't like the way Clare Rutland kept snubbing him.

I muttered as much to Mary Ann.

"If they have to make a decision Monday, it gives you two days to solve the crime, Vic," she said loudly.

"You don't believe Rubova killed Oberst?" I asked her, still sotto voce.

"I believe the police wanted to arrest her because they didn't like her attitude," Mary Ann snapped.

The investigation had been handled by John McGonnigal, a violent crimes sergeant I know. He's a good cop, but a soignée, sardonic woman does not bring out the best in him. And by the time he'd arrived Nicole had dressed, in a crimson silk jumpsuit that emphasized the pliable length of her body, and withdrawn from shock into mockery.

When McGonnigal saw me slide into the interrogation room behind Rubova, he gave an exaggerated groan but didn't actively try to exclude me from his questioning sessions. Those gave me a sense of where everyone claimed to have been when Gary was killed, but no idea at all if McGonnigal was making a mistake in arresting Nicole Rubova.

Police repugnance at female-female sexuality might have helped him interpret evidence so that it pointed at her. I hadn't been able to get the forensic data, but the case against Rubova seemed to depend on two facts: she was the only person known to be alone with Gary in the locker room. And one of her rackets had a big section of string missing from it. This last seemed to be a rather slender thread to hang her on. It would have taken a good while to unthread enough string from a racket to have enough for a garrote. I didn't see where she'd had the time to do it.

McGonnigal insisted she'd spent Lily's press conference at it, dismissing claims from Frederica Lujan that she'd been talking to Nicole while it was going on. Some helpful person

had told him that Frederica and Nicole had had an affair last year, so McGonnigal decided the Spanish player would say anything to help a friend.

None of the Slims people questioned my sitting in on the inquiry—they were far too absorbed in their woes over the tournament. The men didn't pay any attention to Mary Ann's comment to me now, but Clare Rutland moved slightly on the couch so that she was facing my old coach directly. "Who is this, Mary Ann?"

"V. I. Warshawski. About the best private investigator in the city." Mary Ann continued to speak at top volume.

"Is that why you came to the matches today?" The large hazel eyes looked at me with intense interest. I felt the power she exerted over tennis divas directed at me.

"I came because I wanted to watch Lily Oberst. I grew up playing basketball with her mother. Mary Ann here was our coach. After watching Gary train Lily last week I would have thought the kid might have killed him herself—he seemed extraordinarily brutal."

Clare smiled, for the first time since Nicole Rubova had come running down the hall in her towel ten hours ago. "If every tennis kid killed her father because of his brutal coaching, we wouldn't have any parents left on the circuit. Which might only improve the game. But Oberst was one of the worst. Only—why did she have to do it *here*? She must have known—only I suppose when you're jealous you don't think of such things."

"So you think Rubova killed the guy?"

Clare spread her hands, appealing for support. "You don't?"

"You know her and I don't, so I assume you're a better judge of her character. But she seems too cool, too poised, to kill a guy for the reason everyone's imputing to her. Maybe she was interested in Lily. But I find it impossible to believe she'd kill the girl's father because he tried to short-circuit her. She's very sophisticated, very smart, and very cool. If she *really* wanted to have an affair with Lily, she'd have figured out a way. I'm not sure she wanted to—I think it amused her to see Lily blush and get flustered, and to watch Gary go berserk. But if she did want to kill Gary she'd have done so a lot more subtly, not in a fit of rage in the locker room. One other thing: If—*if*—she killed him like that, on the spot, it must have been for some other reason than Lily."

"Like what?" Arnold Krieger had lost interest in Monte Allison and was eavesdropping on me, still chewing cashews.

I hunched a shoulder. "You guys tell me. You're the ones who see these prima donnas week in and week out."

Clare nodded. "I see what you mean. But then, who did kill Oberst?"

"I don't know the players and I don't have access to the forensic evidence. But—well, Lily herself would be my first choice."

A furious uproar started from Allison and Brookings, with Clare chiming in briefly. Mary Ann silenced them all with a coach's whistle—she still could put her fingers in her mouth and produce a sound like a steam engine.

"She must have been awfully tired of Gary sitting in her head," I continued when Mary Ann had shut them up. "She could hardly go to the bathroom without his permission. I learned today that he chose her clothes, her friends, ran her practice sessions, drove away her favorite coaches. You name it."

The police had found Lily quickly enough—she'd apparently had a rare fight with Gary and stormed away to Northwestern Hospital without telling Monica. Without her entourage it had taken her a while to persuade the emergency room that her sore shoulder should leap ahead of other emergencies. Once they realized who she was, though, they summoned their sports medicine maven at once. He swept her off in a cloud of solicitude for X rays, then summoned a limo to take her home to Glenview. There still would have been plenty of time for her to kill Gary before she left the Pavilion.

"Then there's Monica," I went on. "She and Paco Callabrio have been pretty friendly—

several people hinted at it during their interviews this afternoon. She and Gary started dating when they were fifteen. That's twenty-four years with a bully. Maybe she figured she'd had enough.

"I don't like Paco for the spot very well. He's like Nicole—he's got a life, and an international reputation; he didn't need to ruin it by killing the father of one of his pupils. Although, apparently he came out of retirement because of financial desperation. So maybe he was worried about losing Lily as a client, and his affair with Monica deranged him enough that he killed Oberst."

"So you think it's one of those three?" Clare asked.

I shrugged. "Could be. Could be Allison here, worried about his endorsement contract. He watched Gary driving Lily to the breaking point. Artemis could lose seven, eight million dollars if Lily injured herself so badly she couldn't play anymore."

Allison broke off his conversation with Brookings when he heard his name. "What the hell are you saying? That's outrageous. We're behind Lily all the way. I could sue you—"

"Control yourself, Monte," Clare said coldly. "No one's accusing you of anything except high-level capitalism. The detective is just suggesting why someone besides Nicole might have killed Gary Oberst. Anything else?"

"The hottest outsider is Arnold Krieger here."

Two of the anonymous reporters snickered. Krieger muttered darkly but didn't say anything. The tale of Lily's interview with him had come out very early in McGonnigal's questioning.

Tennis etiquette dictates that the loser meet journalists first. The winner can then shower and dress at her leisure. After her match Lily had bounced out, surrounded by Paco, Gary, and Monica. She'd giggled with the press about her game, said she didn't mind losing to Nicole because Nicole was a great player, but she, Lily, had given the game her best, and anyway, she was glad to have a few extra days at home with Ninja, her Great Dane, before flying off to Palm Springs for an exhibition match. People asked about her shoulder. She'd said it was sore but nothing serious. She was going over to Northwestern for X rays just to be on the safe side.

Arnold Krieger then asked whether she felt she ever played her best against Rubova. "After all, most people know she's just waiting for the chance to get you alone. Doesn't that unnerve you?"

Lily started to giggle again, but Gary lost his temper and jumped Krieger on the spot. Security guards pried his hands from the journalist's throat; Gary was warned out of the press room. In fact, he was told that one more episode would get him barred from the tour altogether.

The cops loved that, but they couldn't find anyone who'd seen Krieger go into the locker room afterwards. In fact, most of us could remember his staying near the food, playing tag team with Garrison's husband.

"Don't forget, it was Rubova's racket the string was missing from," Krieger reminded me belligerently.

Clare eyed Krieger as though measuring him for an electric chair, then turned back to me. "What do you charge?"

"Fifty dollars an hour. Plus any unusual expenses—things above the cost of gas or local phone bills."

"I'm hiring you," Clare said briskly.

"To do what? Clear Nicole's name, or guarantee the tour can go on? I can only do the first—if she's not guilty. If it turns out to be Lily, or any of the other players, the Slims are going to be under just as much of a cloud as they are now."

Clare Rutland scowled, but she was used to being decisive. "Clear Nicole for me. I'll worry about the Slims after that. What do you need me to do to make it official?"

"I'll bring a contract by for you tomorrow, but right now what I really want is to take a look at the women's locker room."

"You can't do that," one of the anonymous reporters objected. "The police have sealed it."

"The police are through with it," I said.

"They've made their arrest. I just need someone with a key to let me in."

Clare pinched the bridge of her nose while she thought about it. Maybe it was the objections the men kept hurling at her that made her decide. She stood up briskly, slipped her feet into their expensive suede pumps, and told me to follow her. Mary Ann and I left the press room in her wake. Behind us I could hear Allison shouting, "You can't do this."

IV

I tore the police seal without compunction. If they'd been in the middle of an investigation I would have honored it, but they'd had their chance, made their arrest.

The locker room was a utilitarian set of cement cubes. The attempt to turn the outermost cube into a lounge merely made it look forlorn. It held a few pieces of secondhand furniture, a large bottle of spring water, and a telephone.

Gary had been sitting on a couch plunked into the middle of the floor. Whoever killed him had stood right behind him, wrapping the racket string around his throat before he had time to react—the police found no evidence that he had been able even to lift a hand to try to pull it loose. A smear of dried blood on the back cushion came from where the string had cut through the skin of his neck.

Whoever had pulled the garrote must have cut her—or his—hands as well. I bummed a pad of paper from Clare and made a note to ask McGonnigal whether Nicole had any cuts. And whether he'd noticed them on anyone else. It was quite possible he hadn't bothered to look.

The lounge led to the shower room. As Mary Ann had warned, the place was strictly functional—no curtains, no gleaming fittings. Just standard brown tile that made my toes curl inside my shoes as I felt mold growing beneath them, and a row of small, white-crusted shower heads.

Beyond the showers was a bare room with hooks for coats or equipment bags and a table for the masseuse. A door led to the outer hall.

"It's locked at all times, though," Clare said.

"*All* the time? I expect someone has a key."

She took the notepad from me and scribbled on it. "I'll track that down for you in the morning."

A barrel of used towels stood between the showers and the massage room. For want of anything better to do I poked through them, but nothing unusual came to light.

"Normally all the laundry is cleared out at the end of the day, along with the garbage, but the maintenance crews couldn't come in tonight, of course," Clare explained.

The garbage bins were built into the walls. It was easy to lift the swinging doors off and pull the big plastic liners out. I took them over to the masseuse's corner and started emptying them onto the table piece by piece. I did them in order of room, starting with the lounge. Police detritus—coffee cups, ashes, crumpled forms—made up the top layer. In the middle of the styrofoam and ash, I found two leather mittens with bunnies embroidered on them. The palms were cut to ribbons.

I went through the rest of the garbage quickly, so quickly I almost missed the length of nylon wrapped in paper towels. One end poked out as I perfunctorily shook the papers; I saw it just as I was about to sweep everything off the massage table back into the bag.

"It's racket string," Mary Ann said tersely.

"Yes," I agreed quietly.

It was a piece about five inches long. I unrolled all the paper toweling and newsprint a sheet at a time. By the time I finished I had three more little pieces. Since the garrote that killed Gary had been deeply embedded in his throat, these might have been cut from Nicole's racket to point suspicion at her.

"But the mittens . . ." My old coach couldn't bring herself to say more.

Clare Rutland was watching me, her face frozen. "The mittens are Lily's, aren't they?

Her brother got them for her for Christmas. She showed them off to everyone on the tour when we had our first post–Christmas matches. Why don't you give them to me, Vic? The string should be enough to save Nicole."

I shook my head unhappily. "Could be. We'd have to have the lab make sure these pieces came from her racket. Anyway, I can't do that, Clare. I'm not Gary Oberst's judge and jury. I can't ignore evidence that I've found myself."

"But, Vic," Mary Ann said hoarsely, "how can you do that to Lily? Turn on her? I always thought you tried to help other women. And you saw yourself what her life was like with Gary. How can you blame her?"

I felt the muscles of my face distort into a grimace. "I don't blame her. But how can you let her go through her life without confronting herself? It's a good road to madness, seeing yourself as above and beyond the law. The special treatment she gets as a star is bound to make her think that way to some degree already. If we let her kill her father and get away with it, we're doing her the worst possible damage."

Mary Ann's mouth twisted in misery. She stared at me a long minute. "Oh, *damn* you, Vic!" she cried, and pushed her way past me out of the locker room.

The last vestiges of Clare Rutland's energy had fallen from her face, making her cheeks look as though they had collapsed into it. "I agree with Mary Ann, Vic. We ought to be able to work something out. Something that would be good for Lily as well as Nicole."

"No," I cried.

She lunged toward me and grabbed the mittens. But I was not only younger and stronger, my Nikes gave me an advantage over her high heels. I caught up with her before she'd made it to the shower-room door and gently took the mittens from her.

"Will you let me do one thing? Will you let me see Lily before you talk to the police?"

"What about Nicole?" I demanded. "Doesn't she deserve to be released as soon as possible?"

"If the lawyer the other women have dug up for her doesn't get her out, you can call Sergeant McGonnigal first thing in the morning. Anyway, go ahead and give him the string now. Won't that get her released?"

"I can't do that. I can't come with two separate pieces of evidence found in the identical place but delivered to the law eight hours apart. And no, I damned well will not lie about it for you. I'll do this much for you: I'll let you talk to Lily. But I'll be with you."

Anyway, once the cops have made an arrest they don't like to go back on it. They were just as likely to say that Nicole had cut the string out herself as part of an elaborate bluff.

Clare smiled affably. "Okay. We'll go first thing in the morning."

"No, Ms. Rutland. You're a hell of a woman, but you're not going to run me around the way you do the rest of the tour. If I wait until morning, you'll have been on the phone with Lily and Monica and they'll be in Majorca. We go tonight. Or I stick to you like your underwear until morning."

Her mouth set in a stubborn line, but she didn't waste her time fighting lost battles. "We'll have to phone first. They're bound to be in bed, and they have an elaborate security system. I'll have to let them know we're coming."

I breathed down her neck while she made the call, but she simply told Monica it was important that they discuss matters tonight, before the story made national headlines.

"I'm sorry, honey, I know it's a hell of an hour. And you're under a hell of a lot of strain. But this is the first moment I've had since Nicole found Gary. And we just can't afford to let it go till morning."

Monica apparently found nothing strange in the idea of a two A.M. discussion of Lily's tennis future. Clare told her I was with her and would be driving, so she turned the phone over to me for instructions. Monica also didn't question what I was doing with Clare, for which I was grateful. My powers of invention weren't very great by this point.

V

A single spotlight lit the gate at Nine Nightingale Lane. When I leaned out the window and pressed the buzzer, Monica didn't bother to check that it was really us: she released the lock at once. The gate swung in on well-oiled hinges.

Inside the gate the house and drive were dark. I switched my headlights on high and drove forward cautiously, trying to make sure I stayed on the tarmac. My lights finally picked out the house. The drive made a loop past the front door. I pulled over to the edge and turned off the engine.

"Any idea why the place is totally dark?" I asked Clare.

"Maybe Lily's in bed and Monica doesn't want to wake her up."

"Lily can't sleep just knowing there's a light on somewhere in the house? Try a different theory."

"I don't have any theories," Clare said sharply. "I'm as baffled as you are, and probably twice as worried. Could someone have come out here and jumped her, be lying in ambush for us?"

My mouth felt dry. The thought had occurred to me as well. Anyone could have lifted Lily's mittens from the locker room while she was playing. Maybe Arnold Krieger had done so. Gotten someone to let him in through the permanently locked end of the women's locker room, lifted the mittens, garroted Gary, and slipped out the back way again while Rubova was still in the shower. When he realized we were searching the locker room, he came to Glenview ahead of us. He'd fought hard to keep me from going into the locker room, now that I thought about it.

My gun, of course, was locked away in the safe in my bedroom. No normal person carries a Smith & Wesson to a Virginia Slims match.

"Can you drive a stick shift?" I asked Clare. "I'm going inside, but I want to find a back entrance, avoid a trap if I can. If I'm not out in twenty minutes, drive off and get a neighbor to call the cops. And lock the car doors. Whoever's in the house knows we're here: they released the gate for us."

The mittens were zipped into the inside pocket of my parka. I decided to leave them there. Clare might still destroy them in a moment of chivalry if I put them in the trunk for safekeeping.

I took a pencil flash from the glove compartment. Using it sparingly, I picked my way around the side of the house. A dog bayed nearby. Ninja, the Great Dane. But he was in the house. If Arnold Krieger or someone else had come out to get a jump on us, they would have killed the dog, or the dog would have disabled them. I felt the hair stand up on the back of my neck.

A cinder-block cube had been attached to the back of the house. I shone the flash on it cautiously. It had no windows. It dawned on me that they had built a small indoor court for Lily, for those days when she couldn't get to the club. It had an outside door that led to the garden. When I turned the knob, the door moved inward.

"I'm in here, Vic." Monica's voice came to me in the darkness. "I figured you'd avoid the house and come around the back."

"Are you all right?" I whispered loudly. "Who's inside with Lily?"

Monica laughed. "Just her dog. You worried about Paco interrupting us? He's staying downtown in a hotel. Mary Ann called me. She told me you'd found Lily's mittens. She wanted me to take Lily and run, but I thought I'd better stay to meet you. I've got a shotgun, Vic. Gary was obsessive about Lily's safety, except, of course, on the court. Where he hoped she'd run herself into early retirement."

"You going to kill me to protect your daughter? That won't help much. I mean, I'll be dead, but then the police will come looking, and the whole ugly story will still come out."

"You always were kind of a smart mouth. I remember that from our high school days. And how much I hated you the day you came to see me with the rest of the team when I was pregnant with little Gary." Her voice had a conversa-tional quality. "No. I can persuade the cops that I thought my home was being invaded. Someone coming to hurt Lily on top of all she's already been through today. Mary Ann may figure it out, but she loves Lily too much to do anything to hurt her."

"Clare Rutland's out front with the car. She's going for help before too long. Her story would be pretty hard to discount."

"She's going to find the gate locked when she gets there. And even Clare, endlessly clever, will find it hard to scale a ten-foot electrified fence. No, it will be seen as a terrible tragedy. People will give us their sympathy. Lily's golden up here, after all."

I felt a jolt under my rib cage. "*You* killed Gary."

She burst out laughing. "Oh, my goodness, yes, Vic. Did you just figure that out, smart-ass that you are? I was sure you were coming up here to gun for me. Did you really think little Lily, who could hardly pee without her daddy, had some sudden awakening and strangled him?"

"Why, Monica? Because she may have hurt her shoulder? You couldn't just get him to lay off? I noticed you didn't even try at her practice session last week."

"I always hated that about you," she said, her tone still flat. "Your goddamned high-and-mightiness. You don't—didn't—ever stop Gary from doing some damned thing he was doing. How do you think I got pregnant with little Gary? Because his daddy said lie down and spread your legs for me, pretty please? Get out of your dream world. I got pregnant the old-fashioned way: he raped me. We married. We fought—each other and everything around us. But we made it out of that hellhole down there just like you did. Only not as easily."

"It wasn't easy for me," I started to say, but I sensed a sudden movement from her and flung myself onto the floor. A tennis ball bounced off the wall behind me and ricocheted from my leg.

Monica laughed again. "I have the shotgun. But I kind of like working with a racket. I was pretty good once. Never as good as Lily, though.

And when Lily was born—when we realized what her potential was—I saw I could move myself so far from South Chicago it would never be able to grab me again."

Another *thwock* came in the dark and another ball crashed past me.

"Then Gary started pushing her so hard, I was afraid she'd be like Andrea Jaeger. Injured and burned out before she ever reached her potential. I begged him, pleaded with him. We'd lose that Artemis contract and everything else. But Gary's the kind of guy who's always right."

This time I was ready for the swish of her racket in the dark. Under cover of the ball's noise, I rolled across the floor in her direction. I didn't speak, hoping the momentum of her anger would keep her going without prompting.

"When Lily came off the court today favoring her shoulder, I told him I'd had it, that I wanted him out of her career. That Paco knew a thousand times more how to coach a girl with Lily's talent than he did. But Mr. Ever-right just laughed and ranted. He finally said Lily could choose. Just like she'd chosen him over Nicole, she'd choose him over Paco."

I kept inching my way forward until I felt the net. One of the balls had stopped there; I picked it up.

Monica hadn't noticed my approach. "Lily came up just then and heard what he said. On top of the scene he'd made at her little press doohickey it was too much for her. She had a fit and left the room. I went down the hall to an alcove where Johnny Lombardy—the stringer—kept his spool. I just cut a length of racket string from his roll, went back to the lounge, and—God, it was easy."

"And Nicole's racket?" I asked hoarsely, hoping my voice would sound as though it was farther away.

"Just snipped a few pieces out while she was in the shower. She's another one like you—snotty know-it-all. It won't hurt her to spend some time in jail."

She fired another ball at the wall and then, unexpectedly, flooded the room with light. Nei-ther of us could see, but she at least was prepared for the shock. It gave her time to locate me as I scrambled to my feet. I found myself tangled in the net and struggled furiously while she stead-ied the gun on her shoulder.

I wasn't going to get my leg free in time. Just before she fired, I hurled the ball I'd picked up at her. It hit her in the face. The bullet tore a hole in the floor inches from my left foot. I finally yanked my leg from the net and launched myself at her.

VI

"I'm sorry, Vic. That you almost got killed, I mean. Not that I called Monica—she needed me. Not just then, but in general. She never had your, oh, centeredness. She needed a mother."

Mary Ann and I were eating in Greek Town. The Slims had limped out of Chicago a month ago, but I hadn't felt like talking to my old coach since my night with Monica. But Clare Rutland had come to town to meet with one of the tour sponsors, and to hand me a check in person. And she insisted that the three of us get together. After explaining how she'd talked the spon-sors and players into continuing, Clare wanted to know why Mary Ann had called Monica that night.

"Everyone needs a mother, Mary Ann. That's the weakest damned excuse I ever heard for try-ing to help someone get away with murdering her husband."

Mary Ann looked at me strangely. "Maybe Monica is right about you, Victoria: too high-and-mighty. But it was Lily I was trying to help. I wouldn't have done it if I'd known Monica was going to try to kill you. But you can take care of yourself. You survived the encounter. She didn't."

"What do you mean?" I demanded. "All I did was bruise her face getting her not to shoot me. And no one's going to give her the death penalty. I'd be surprised if she served more than four years."

"You don't understand, Vic. She didn't have anything besides the . . . the scrappiness that got her and Gary out of South Chicago. Oh, she learned how to dress, and put on makeup, and what kinds of things North Shore people eat for dinner. Now that the fight's gone out of her she doesn't have anything inside her to get her through the bad times. You do."

Clare Rutland interrupted hastily. "The good news is that Lily will recover. We have her working with a splendid woman, psychotherapist, I mean. She's playing tennis as much as she wants, which turns out to be a lot. And the other women on the circuit are rallying around in a wonderful way. Nicole is taking her to Maine to spend the summer at her place near Bar Harbor with her."

"Artemis dropped their endorsement contract," I said. "It was in the papers here."

"Yes, but she's already made herself enough to get through the next few years without winning another tournament. Let's be honest. She could live the rest of her life on what she's made in endorsements so far. Anyway, I hear Nike and Reebok are both sniffing around. No one's going to do anything until after Monica's trial—it wouldn't look right. But Lily will be fine."

We dropped it there. Except for the testimony I had to give at Monica's trial I didn't think about her or Lily too much as time went by. Sobered by my old coach's comments, I kept my time on the stand brief. Mary Ann, who came to the trial every day, seemed to be fighting tears when I left the courtroom, but I didn't stop to talk to her.

The following February, though, Mary Ann surprised me by phoning me.

"I'm not working on the lines this year," she said abruptly. "I've seen too much tennis close up. But Lily's making her first public appearance at the Slims, and she sent me tickets for all the matches. Would you like to go?"

I thought briefly of telling her to go to hell, of saying I'd had enough tennis—enough of the Obersts—to last me forever. But I found myself agreeing to meet her outside the box office on Harrison the next morning.

BENEATH THE LILACS

Nevada Barr

IT IS NOT UNCOMMON for fictional detectives to share the same career path as their creators; mystery novels and short stories abound with mystery-writing sleuths, lawyers, and journalists. It is a little more uncommon to share a calling as a park ranger, as Nevada Barr (1952–   ) does with her series protagonist, Anna Pigeon.

Soon after receiving a master's degree in drama, Barr worked as an actress in New York and Minneapolis, appearing in off-Broadway plays, movies, television, commercials, and radio voice-overs. When her first husband, a director, became interested in environmental issues, she began working as a park ranger during the summer, and then full-time, until she became a bestselling author and devoted all her time to writing books.

The tough-talking Pigeon is a hard-working law enforcement park ranger with the United States National Park Service in nineteen novels, beginning with *Track of the Cat* (1993), which won both the Agatha and Anthony Awards as the best first novel of the year. Barr got the idea for the plot while walking through the woods and thinking of the many ways a person could die—and the people she believed would be better off dead. Since then, she (and Pigeon) have been regulars on the bestseller list. Curiously, Pigeon's adventures have been set in a different national park in every book as she solves mysteries in the wilderness and historic locales, generally involving natural resources.

"Beneath the Lilacs" was originally published in *Women on the Case*, edited by Sara Paretsky (New York, Delacorte, 1996).

Beneath the Lilacs

NEVADA BARR

LILAC TREES, two in white, two in plum, and two in the palest lavender, had grown up as Gwen had grown. Now she was in her forties and the lilacs were higher than the eaves of the house. One of the plum-colored trees had died. Slash, piled shoulder-high, lay on the concrete between the garden and the alley. It had taken Gwen all morning to cut it down and haul the withered limbs out to where the garbage men might deign to take them.

Digging out the last of the grasping roots, Gwen uncovered the bone. A museum curator, she knew a finger bone when she saw one. Letting her rump fall back on the freshly dug earth, she contemplated her find.

The day was still and warm, a hint of the hard winter past making the fragile spring almost unbearably precious. Growing up in Minnesota, there'd been many days like this one. Payoff days, her mother called them. Days when you were paid in full for chilblains, dead batteries, frozen nose hairs.

Here in the arbor behind her mother's house in Minneapolis, two blocks from Lake Nokomis, Gwen had spent those days curled down in the fertile earth arranging tiny plastic soldiers on the rooted mounds beneath the lilacs and fighting glorious bloodless battles till the last Horatio fell heroically defending the last bridge.

When had a real corpse come to join those of her phantom armies?

An Indian, perhaps, buried before whites settled the area. A homesteader, laid to rest in a family plot long since forgotten, sold and resold till at length a city had crept over sod and sodbuster alike.

Gwen looked up from the earth between her feet. Beyond the shade-dappling the sun shone with an unwavering intensity that by July would seem harsh. So close in winter's shadow it was a promise of renewal and, so, eternal life. Every leaf, each blade of grass, was wreathed in light. Spring's coronation.

The glare was not so kind to man-made structures. Mullions in the many-paned bay window were peeling, white paint curling off in strips like sunburned flesh; a crack ran up the foundation where the water faucet poked through the cement; the little statue of the Virgin Mary listed drunkenly, attesting to a neglect Gwen's mother would once have been incapable of.

At some point during the twenty-six years Gwen had been gone, Madolyn Clear had gotten old. A pang of guilt and one sharper for opportunities lost cut through Gwen's chest. She pulled up her knees and hugged them close.

She had always thought of her mother as a rock, remaining unchanged as the oceans of life broke against her. For a little girl that brought with it a strong sense of security and not a little loneliness.

A memory from childhood, a snapshot without cause or effect, rose in Gwen's mind. She was very young, not more than two or three. It must have been around the time her father died, though there were no cerebral Polaroids of that. She was dressed in a T-shirt and underpants, her short hair molded into sleepy spikes. Mud mottled the carpet under her bare feet. One plump hand, fingers spread like a starfish, was pressed against her mother's bedroom door at the top of the stairs. Inside she knew her mother was crying.

Idly, Gwen wondered if she'd pushed open that door or stayed lonely and lost in the hallway. Probably the latter. There were no memories of seeing her mother cry. Not ever. Everybody cried. Madolyn must have felt safe only in private.

Privacy, her mother's one indulgence, was all but lost to her now. Since the stroke the sitting room had become her bedroom. The stairs effectively banning her from the rest of her house, she spent her days in the bay window, propped up in the hideous comfort of a hospital bed looking out on her garden.

Light glittered off the windowpanes. Gwen couldn't see inside, but she waved anyway.

Her mother was no longer a poor woman. Money could buy cooks and nurses and therapists. Gwen had been asked to tend the garden. So much needed to be done with love and not just with a spade. Turned firmly out-of-doors, she nurtured the flowers with the tenderness she was forbidden to lavish on her mother.

And a skeleton lay beneath the lilacs.

Gwen wondered if she should tell her. "No shocks," Dr. Korver had warned, but Gwen doubted a corpse would distress Madolyn. Pragmatism had soaked so deep into her mother's bones it was sometimes hard to reconcile the woman as she was with the photos of her as a young bride, dripping with white after the wed-

ding mass, decked in the ruffles and lace of her going-away suit.

And, too, there was nothing awful about a skeleton so long and so quietly dead. Her mother might even be intrigued, delighted. Who wouldn't be delighted to find a skeleton in the arbor? A story to dine out on for years to come. Still Gwen felt an odd reluctance to tell her. Perhaps it was simply a reluctance to move. The heady scent of the lilacs wrapped around her in a gauzy cloak. Like Dorothy in her poppy field, Gwen was paralyzed with the perfume.

Wriggling her feet deeper in the warm soil, she watched the dirt cascade over the rolled cuffs of her trousers. The house had its ghosts, its lonely hallways, as all houses did, but not the arbor. Bootsies and Tippies and Pinky-Winkies lay interred in various corners and there were remembrances of skinned knees and broken arms and once she'd dislocated Ricky Harper's little finger, but none of that marred the garden's perfect peace. Despite Minnesota's snows Gwen remembered it always sunny, always in bloom. As one remembers childhood.

A second snapshot materialized. This one was captioned, a single line of dialogue in a familiar yet unnameable voice. Gwen was at the piano pretending to play. Her feet didn't reach the floor; a dress in rustling pink frothed around her little bottom. On the high back of the old upright sat a yellow cat. His tail, fat as a striped sausage, switched down near the pages of music. The window to the garden was open and there was a faint pleasant sound of distant laughter.

The voice wasn't her mother's—a neighbor lady probably. "At least now you can keep the house full of flowers," she'd said. "Small blessings."

Gwen's house in Pasadena, California, was always filled with flowers. Her first husband had been allergic to them and to her cats. After the divorce her mother said it wasn't wise to completely trust a man who was allergic to cats. It meant they were part rat.

". . . now you can keep the house full of flowers. Small blessings." Who had been allergic? Not Gwen, not her mother. Not you, Gwen thought, looking at the spectral finger beckoning amid the roots. At least not for a long time.

Gwen seldom thought of the past. She and her mother didn't discuss it by mutual if unspoken agreement. Yet here under the lilacs the past seemed to rise up from the earth as insistent and cloying as the scent of the blooms overhead.

Coming home, Gwen thought, and her mother's stroke proving a mortality neither wished to admit. Gwen's age. She'd found herself getting in touch with old college friends, thinking fondly of reunions. The mad scrabble to grow up, to do and be and speak, was over and there was a desire to recapture the things undervalued in the rush to adulthood.

Surely it had been more than a decade since she'd thought of Ricky Harper, though they'd dated in high school and he'd gotten even with her for dislocating his little finger by breaking her heart. Disasters of about equal magnitude.

"Lit out," Ricky had said. Gwen remembered the words clearly. He'd said it of her father, hence the damaged pinky.

She turned her thoughts back to the bony pinky protruding from the rich black dirt.

The strange and dreaming lethargy lifted and she rubbed her face like a woman coming out of a long sleep. A curator's instincts reasserted themselves and she pulled off her mother's gardening gloves—heavy white cotton decorated with apple-green sprigs. The kind old ladies wear. The hands that were exposed were starting to wrinkle, age spots beginning to form from so many years working out-of-doors, and Gwen smiled at her snobbery.

Kneeling over the bone, she carefully swept away the earth. Without access to a lab, she couldn't tell how old the find was, but the knuckle was still intact. Bit by bit she removed the soil until wrist, thumb, and index finger were exposed. Probably it was nothing, still she felt excitement building. Anthropologists, even those who've long since left fieldwork, dream of finding a Lucy the way gamblers dream of the big jackpot.

Several more minutes work raised Gwen's hopes even further. On the third finger of the right hand—for it was a right hand—something glowed dull and coppery. Gwen allowed herself a snort of derision as images of Aztec gold and Ojibwa copper danced incongruously through her head.

With great care, not as if the finger could still feel, but as if prying eyes might see and suddenly cry "Thief!" Gwen worked the ring free and polished the face of it clean with the tail of her shirt.

1946. University of Minnesota.

Modern dead; not history but murder.

Panic clouded Gwen's mind. Nausea threatened to rob her of her senses, and though she was sitting, she felt as if she would fall and clung to the sturdy trunk of a lilac.

Numbers, clear and neat as arithmetic problems, clicked through her thoughts. In 1945 her parents were married and bought the house. One year later her father graduated from the University of Minnesota and went to work for the city.

Without looking at it again, Gwen slipped the ring in her pocket and gently pushed dirt back over the bones.

Cancer, her mother had said.

"Lit out."

Never once had Gwen visited her father's grave. Buried in Sioux Falls, her mother told her, in his hometown. Gwen had never been there. Madolyn was estranged from her husband's family. Religious differences was how she explained it and, assuming they were Protestant, Gwen hadn't asked again.

Cards addressed to Gwen came at Christmas and on birthdays till she was out of school. Grandparents she'd never seen and did not mourn died while she worked on her doctorate at Stanford.

Gwen eased up from the ground and started to brush the dirt from her trousers, but the effort proved too great. The forty feet to the back door stretched an impossible distance and she found herself shuffling along the walk, the noise of her dragging steps clogging her ears.

As she passed through the front hall her mother called to her, but she pretended not to hear. Mud from the newly opened grave tracked the sage-green carpet of the upstairs hall and the snapshot came again: the little bare feet, the starfish hand, the mud, the weeping behind the closed door. Someone had tracked freshly dug earth upstairs that day as well.

Gwen's head swam and she stumbled the last few steps to collapse on Madolyn's bed; hers now.

She closed her eyes and would have closed her mind had she been able. Images chased each other around inside her skull like maddened ferrets. She imagined she could feel the weight of the ring in her pocket pressing on her thigh. Soon she would take it out, examine it again, but there was no hurry. An old photograph of her father had served as the springboard for the ten thousand daydreams of a lonely child. The ring was his. She'd memorized it along with the grain, the light, and the shadows of the photo.

Anger plucked her from the bed like a giant hand, and in anger, she snatched up the phone. There was no statute of limitations on murder.

Before the second ring she laid the receiver back in its cradle and sat down on the edge of the bed. Her knees were shaking too badly to support her.

Lots of men must have graduated from the University of Minnesota in 1946. They would all wear the same ring. The corpse could have been a classmate of her father's, a family friend.

Buried in the backyard.

A lover then; her mother took a lover, her father killed him then "lit out." Or died of cancer as her mother said, taking his secret with him. Madolyn may not even have known of the murder. It could have taken place when she was out of town for some reason.

Gwen felt herself calming down, her breathing leaving off the ragged pattern of tears. Hysteria was being replaced by a lifetime's habit of rational thought. Explanations could be found. Truth was seldom more awful than one's febrile imaginings. She smiled, if weakly, at the lurid picture she'd conjured of her mother wild-eyed and blood-spattered wielding Norman Bates's knife.

For several minutes Gwen sat, her feet flat on the floor, her back bowed, staring at the carpet and thinking nothing at all. Too many electrical impulses at once had short-circuited her brain. From below the sweet strains of Doris Day's "Sentimental Journey" filtered up through the heater vents.

Of course Gwen would have to pursue it. Letting sleeping skeletons lie was out of the question. Her mother was too fragile to confront, the police too abrasive. Not that the Minneapolis police weren't as polite as midwestern myth would paint them, but there would be digging literally and figuratively. Strangers couldn't be expected to take the time and energy that delicacy required.

Again she picked up the phone. Grandmother and Granddad were dead, but Gwen assumed Sioux Falls still existed. Seven phone calls to the seven cemeteries and mausoleums didn't turn up any Gerald Clear interred in 1950.

Nausea returned. Gwen put her head between her knees. Her hands fell to the carpet like leaves and she found herself staring at the dirt-encrusted nails with morbid fascination as if they were the hands that buried the corpse, not the ones to unearth it after so many years.

Pushing herself to her feet, she made her way toward the bathroom to wash. On the wall above the light switch was a small wooden cross adorned with a long-suffering silver Jesus. Clawing it down, she hurled it against the far wall. From downstairs her mother called: "Honey, are you okay?"

"I'm okay, Ma," Gwen shouted.

"Come downstairs when you're done."

Gwen turned on both taps to drown out her mother's voice and watched the dirt from her hands sully the white porcelain of the old-fashioned sink.

There was an uncle in Des Moines, she remembered. Once or twice as a child she'd seen him, but relations between him and her mother were strained. Gwen didn't even know if he was still living. If so, he would be close to eighty.

Her old bedroom had been converted to a study some years after she left home. Oblivious to the mess she made, or on some level relishing the release of destruction, Gwen turned it upside down searching for his address. She was almost disappointed when she found it fairly quickly under *C* in her mother's well-ordered Rolodex.

Lest thought rob her of courage, Gwen punched in his number not knowing what she would say if he should answer. When an old voice creaked "Hello," she was momentarily stunned. At the third repetition, she found her tongue. "Uncle Daniel?"

"This is Daniel Clear," the man said with unconcealed annoyance.

Gwen introduced herself in greater detail and the annoyance evaporated. She told him her mother had had a stroke. Daniel took that as the reason for the call and Gwen didn't disabuse him of the notion. Had it not been for the skeleton, she wondered if she would have thought to inform him. Probably not.

"Tell me about Dad," she said when the preliminaries were behind them.

Uncle Daniel didn't find it an odd question and Gwen realized she'd been wanting to ask it for a long time. The romantic fog of perfect love her mother had generated around her father's memory had ceased to be enough after Gwen's own marriage failed in mutual acrimony.

The picture Daniel painted of his little brother had grit, sand, and spice, and Gwen knew when this was over she would seek the old man out.

Daniel remembered an altar boy, quick with his fists, hot-tempered, a favorite with the girls and the apple of his mother's eye.

His memories dwindled and he began wandering to second cousins and others Gwen neither knew nor cared about. She asked him why he—all of her father's family—had become estranged from her mother.

"It may seem like a little thing to a modern young lady like yourself," he said. "But to us it wasn't. It nearly killed your grandma. Your mother just went and buried him up in the cities. Never invited any of us to the funeral. Didn't even tell us till it was all over."

Gwen sat in the wreck of the study and grasped at straws of justification. Hot-tempered, quick with his fists, a favorite with the girls. People didn't kill without reason. Had her father cheated, been killed in a moment of passion? Had he beaten her mother? Was he killed to protect Gwen? Gwen had no memories of abuse, but people sometimes didn't.

The thought physically sickened her. A glimpse of herself, face half in shadow, hankie clutched to her eyes, on *Oprah*, leavened the horror with absurdity. Vaguely she remembered repressed memories, like chicken pox, were more or less age-specific. Mid-thirties rang a bell. She comforted herself with that.

And the lies of True Love and her sainted father? Fairy tales to delight a little girl? Or to rewrite history for a shattered and disappointed woman? The crosses, the statues, mass and communion and confession: the ultimate hypocrisy or lifelong penance?

The phone was still cradled on Gwen's knees. With one hand she flipped through the Rolodex, then punched in the number for Dr. Korver's office. In his seventies, he still ran a practice. Gwen pleaded emergency and because Annie, the receptionist, had known her since she was three years old, she was given an appointment.

Compelled by some outdated formality that overtook her when she returned to childhood haunts, Gwen divested herself of jeans and slipped on a fitted rayon dress and flats. The short, graying hair got a few licks with a brush but, as always, it did what it did. Without saying good-bye to her mother, she lifted the car keys from the hook under the kitchen cupboard and slunk out the back door.

Dr. Korver looked much as he had as long as Gwen could remember: bow tie, suspenders, a clean-shaven and age-defying baby face. His hair was white but was still so thick and lush, one could almost believe he had it bleached to reassure his older patients.

Perched fully dressed on the examination table, Gwen knew neither of them was completely at ease.

"Annie said an emergency," Dr. Korver said for starters.

"I need to talk to you." Dr. Korver didn't do anything so crass as to glance at his watch, but he fidgeted and Gwen could read the impatience just as clearly. From the look on his face, talk wouldn't take precedence over so much as an ingrown toenail. "I need to know how my father died," Gwen said abruptly.

"Cancer. Surely your mother told you?"

Gwen nodded. "Did you see him?" she pressed.

"If I remember rightly, he died in Sioux City or somewhere, visiting I think. You should be asking your mother these questions, Gwen."

"You never saw him dead?"

He shrugged his shoulders. This time he did look at his watch.

"So you don't know that he died?" Gwen sounded accusing and he reacted in kind, his avuncular manner disappearing behind a mask of injured pride.

"He had an inoperable brain tumor. Unless he got hit by a truck first, he died of it," he said bluntly, and stood to indicate the interview was over.

Gwen caught hold of his arm. "Please," she said. "Could I see my medical records and Mom's?"

Dr. Korver looked at her for a moment. His visage softened. He'd come to recognize pain in all its guises. "What's wrong, Gwen?"

She said nothing and the kindness was pushed aside by irritation. "You can see your medical records, though I don't know what good it'll do you. I can't let you see your mother's without her permission." He left and Gwen felt as cold and exposed as if she wore only a backless paper gown.

After pulling her file, Annie left Gwen alone in the records room. Quickly, she flipped through the pages. Though she was healthy, so many years

of care made it thick. Before 1952 there were seven entries: three general check-ups, an ear infection, fever, a scald on her left forearm, and a hairline fracture of her left foot.

Taking advantage of Annie's trusting nature, Gwen moved to the filing cabinet and walked her fingers through the *C*'s. Her father's file was gone, taken to storage years before no doubt, but her mother's was there. Still standing Gwen scanned the entries from 1945 to 1952: influenza, broken rib, tonsillitis, sprained wrist. The box marked INSURANCE/HEALTH/LIFE had the word "None" scribbled in it twice. No wonder there was such a paucity of doctor's visits during those years.

Footsteps sounded on the linoleum outside the door and Gwen hastily fumbled the file back into place. Her heart pounded as if peeking at her mother's medical history were a capital crime. No one entered the records room and Gwen took a moment to pull herself together before she ventured out and said her good-byes to Annie.

She couldn't bring herself to go back to her mother's, not yet. She chewed mechanically through a late lunch at Kapoochi's on Nicollet and Eighth. The food was more an excuse for the glass of Chardonnay than an end in itself.

When the dishes had been cleared and only another solitary glass or dessert could excuse lingering, Gwen returned to the festive crush on Nicollet.

Because the sun shone, Minnesotans made it a holiday. Flower vendors lined the street. People walked and waited for buses and shopped and chattered in groups. Gwen joined the loiterers gathering sun on the wide brick sills of the Conservatory.

Fortified with wine, she could again think of the skeleton, her mother, and murder. Broken rib, sprained wrist, scalded arm, fractured foot; a history of abuse or just the vagaries of living? Gwen had nothing to compare it to, no government statistics on how often the average mother and daughter damaged themselves in the pursuit of daily life.

Why kill a dying man? Surely it was easier and safer to let nature take its course. Self-defense? Possibly. A favorite with the girls: killed in a moment of jealous rage or because he was going to leave? Also possible.

Madolyn Clear never remarried and Gwen had believed it was because she never stopped loving her dead husband. Could it be that memories of a bad marriage made her shy of the institution? And the lilacs? "Now you can keep the house full of flowers. Small blessings." Revenge? Planting a man allergic to lilacs under six trees of blooms? Each thought was more wretched than the last, sick-making, and Gwen shook herself free of them as a dog rids its fur of raindrops.

Too many years had passed since the death of a father she had never known for the lash of his murder to cut too deep. Betrayal of truth was the injury; loss of the idea that love existed, that she was born from it and to it. Death of the possibility, of the dream.

Gwen relinquished her place in the sun to a polite young woman with tricolor hair and two nose rings. There was one more stop to be made and then she must go home.

St. Bartholomew's was in South Minneapolis in what was considered a bad section of town, though to Gwen's perception—altered by years in other cities—the homes still retained their dignity and the people on the streets didn't appear to have lost their hope. The church was staid and conservative, an edifice of brick and mortar that blended well with the apartment houses that had sprung up around it in the 1940s. The front lawn was badly in need of attention and the steps had deteriorated, not from the constant tread of feet but from disuse and neglect.

The front doors were locked. Gwen picked her way through the struggling rhododendrons to the rectory behind the church. Decay had taken the small brick dwelling as well. Windows were draped as if against terrible cold, and leaves from the previous autumn lay in dusty piles in the corners of the porch.

After two tries with the doorbell and a rapping that left her knuckles burning, Gwen was turning to go. Soft shuffling from within stopped her. Unconsciously donning a pious look, she waited in feigned patience.

A man so old he looked elemental—cracked stone and sere earth—opened the door and blinked up at her from eyes made milky with cataracts. Beyond the changed flesh Gwen could barely recognize Father Davis, the priest to whom she'd poured out childish confessions. Cataracts and time had clearly robbed him of all recollection of her.

"I'm Gwendolyn Clear," she told him. "My mother, Madolyn Clear, and I used to attend mass at St. Bartholomew's."

For long moments he stared at her. Minute workings of the muscles around his mouth attested to some kind of mental process. "Gwennie," he said at last, and she was impressed. "Do come in. You're just in time for something, I'm sure. Tea? Sherry? Coffee? It's always a good time for company."

Inside, the rectory was dark and stifling. Father Davis wore wool trousers and a pullover sweatshirt and tapped at the thermostat as he passed, his old bones needing heat from without.

Ensconced in a worn chair by a blessedly dead fire, Gwen accepted a glass of orange juice as the quickest way to absolve both of them of the niceties and waited while Father Davis settled himself. Scooping a tiger cat from the seat of the chair opposite her, he lowered himself carefully into its depths then arranged the cat across his knees like a rug.

"I no longer say mass," he said. "But I still occasionally hear confessions of the very wicked." He smiled to let her know he was teasing.

Because he was a priest and because he was Father Davis, Gwen told him everything. She finished and the silence between them was long and comfortable. The old man stroked the tiger cat, the muscles around his mouth twitching as he thought.

"As a priest I'm not allowed to speak of much the good Lord has seen fit to let me remember," he said at last. "But you mustn't let these shadows from the past blot out your faith in the things that are good: love and forgiveness, sacrifice, redemption. I have known you all of your life and known your mother most of hers. All I can tell you that might be of help is that to my knowledge your mother loved your father dearly. Indeed, loved him more than she feared God."

Blinking again in the clear sunlight, Gwen fished sunglasses from her bag as she skirted the shrubbery in favor of paving stones on the way back to where she'd parked the car.

Time had poured its obscuring dust over events but still she held some facts—or educated guesses that she would use in lieu of facts. Gerald Clear had a temper. Gerald Clear was beloved of the ladies. Gerald Clear had inoperable brain cancer. Her mother had killed him or knew the person who had, and hid the crime by burying him in the backyard. Madolyn loved him "more than she feared God." Medical records catalogued four possible abuse injuries in seven years.

Gwen drove back to Lake Nokomis so slowly that cars honked at her more than once, but she scarcely acknowledged them. At a stop sign less than a block from the house her car came to rest. Traffic was light and no other vehicle appeared to remind her of the business of driving. As the car idled in neutral, the doctor's reports filtered back through her mind.

No insurance. Not life. Not health.

In 1952 the Clears were poor—poor as church mice, her mother was fond of saying. There would be no money for the medical bills from an extended illness. Dad was going to kick the bucket anyway so what the hey?

Gwen shook her head as if disagreeing with some unseen adversary. Madolyn had loved her husband more than she feared God. And the pieces fell in place. Sudden tears choked Gwen and she sat at the intersection and cried till the pressure of a Volvo in the rearview mirror forced her to move.

Madolyn Clear was propped up in her hospital bed, sun from the bay window making a patchwork of light and shadow across her legs. While Gwen had been out she'd been given a shampoo and short snow-white hair fell in natural curls. A pair of reading glasses hung around her neck on a cord of psychedelic colors. One hand, slightly gnarled with arthritis, rested on the book she'd been reading.

When Gwen came in she smiled. The teeth were yellowed and crooked but they were all her own and Gwen thought her smile beautiful. It faded to a look of concern as Gwen crossed the hardwood floor close enough that her mother could read the strange lines her face had fallen into after the storm of tears.

Gwen sat in the window seat, the light at her back, and took the ring from the pocket of her dress. Laying it on the coverlet between her mother's hands, she said: "I know all about Daddy."

Madolyn stroked the dull gold with one finger as if it were a tiny living creature. "And do you hate me?" she asked without looking up. Beneath white lashes tears sparkled in the sun. Gwen pretended not to notice. Her mother had seen fit to hide them for over forty years. It would be ungracious to discover them now.

"No, Momma." Gwen wanted to take her hand but lacked the courage. Instead she laid hers on the coverlet touching her mother's as if by accident. "I admire you. I've always admired you."

They sat for a time without speaking. A house finch came and hopped along the windowsill beyond the glass and Madolyn's old Siamese cat crept close to fantasize.

"Why lilacs?" Gwen asked. "Dad was allergic, wasn't he?"

Madolyn looked startled, then laughed. "That's right, he was. It's been a very long time. Gerry said they were his favorite flower because they gave me so much joy. He knew he couldn't be buried in consecrated ground so he asked to have lilacs planted over his grave. So I'd visit often, he said."

"Was he afraid of the pain? Of losing his faculties?" Gwen asked.

"Your father wasn't afraid of anything," Madolyn said. Then: "Of course he was. Who wouldn't be? But he would have faced it as he faced everything. He knew he was dying and that the medical costs would eat up our savings, our car, even our home. You and I would be left alone with nothing. He loved us very much." Tears trickled from beneath the papery lids and found channels in the wrinkled cheeks. This time Gwen did take her mother's hand and Madolyn held tight, her grip warm and dry.

"But he didn't kill himself," Gwen said.

"It would have meant his soul," Madolyn said. "And there never was a finer."

MISS GIBSON

Linda Barnes

WHEN LINDA JOYCE APPELBLATT BARNES (1949–   ) became a full-time writer after working as a drama teacher and director, she created a series about Michael Spraggue, a wealthy actor and private eye, which lasted for four books, beginning with *Blood Will Have Blood* (1982). Carlotta Carlyle pops up now and then in a relatively minor role. The character proved to be so good that Barnes decided to create a series for her. She made her solo debut in *A Trouble of Fools* (1987) and starred in an additional eleven novels before Barnes wrote her first stand-alone mystery, *The Perfect Ghost* (2013).

Carlotta Carlyle began as a police officer but now is a pretty tough Boston taxi driver when she is not being a pretty tough Boston private investigator. She's an imposing figure at six feet, one inch tall, though she regularly weighs only about 155 pounds; when her weight drops below that number, she says "I get demoted from thin to skinny." Bright red hair tops off her appearance, making it difficult to fail to notice her.

The daughter of a deceased Scottish-Irish policeman and a Jewish mother, Carlotta is close only to her Jewish grandmother, for whom she tenderly cares. While a member of the Boston Police Department, she was close to Joe Mooney and has occasionally given him tips. Her part-time job as a cabdriver brought her in close proximity to Sam Gianelli, a law-abiding member of a Mafia family.

"Miss Gibson" was originally published in *Women on the Case*, edited by Sara Paretsky (New York, Delacorte, 1996).

Miss Gibson

LINDA BARNES

I HATE TO TRAVEL except by car or cab. Even then I like to call the shots, do the driving. If you see me on board an airplane, someone else is surely footing the bill. If you find me flying first class—United #707 to Denver, connecting first class to United #919 to Portland, Oregon—you can be absolutely certain that the lady paying the freight is Dee Willis.

You remember Dee, the pop/blues singer who snatched seven Grammys after twenty years of hard-luck bar gigs. The hot new songbird with—can it be? is it possible?—a shred of dignity, a smidgen of integrity. Stubborn as they come, Dee couldn't be bothered following trends. She just kept on doing what she always did. Never dumbed down her act for an audience. The fans had to catch up to her.

Hell, even I have to admit it: Dee's got more than a few remnants of tattered integrity. She supports good causes, sings her heart out at benefits for sick musicians and AIDS-infected kids. I tend to choke on her acts of kindness because I've been jealous of Dee as long as I can remember: first and always for her sweet soaring soprano; second, because some time ago she ran off with a Cajun bass player, my then husband, Cal Therieux.

No surprise that her hastily scrawled plea hadn't been enough to make me abandon my Cambridge, Mass., digs. Neither was her prom-ise of primo plane and concert tickets. Only a carefully negotiated fee had me peering nervously from the Boeing 737's pitiful excuse for a window.

Dee owns one item I'd rather have than anything you can name, and I certainly do not speak of my ex-husband, who's no longer a member of Dee's band and was never her "possession" to give or to take. Twenty-five years ago, Dee studied at the feet of the Reverend Gary Davis, the blind bluesman who wrote holy spirituals and, when the spirit moved him, played such hymns to human weakness as "Baby, Let Me Follow You Down." The Reverend was so taken with Dee that he willed her Miss Gibson, his favorite guitar. Dee hardly plays Miss Gibson anymore, what with her stock of custom-made electrics and glittering Stratocasters. I'd treat Miss Gibson right, give her a better home.

The vision of the Reverend Davis's Gibson keeping company with my old National Steel guitar had me up above the clouds, grasping the armrests, trying to fly the plane via mind control.

Ridiculous. I took six deep breaths, accepted the futility of telekinesis, and lapsed into fitful sleep.

I switched planes at Denver's International Airport, wandering into a nearby ladies' room, where I splashed my face with cold water, shook out my red hair, glared at the mirror, and hoped the lighting was bad. A mother of twins maintained serene calm while one offspring vomited and the other wailed.

While we were waiting to take off for Portland, a guy across the aisle asked the flight attendant for a Baileys-on-the-rocks. I hadn't indulged during the Boston-to-Denver leg in spite of the free flow of liquor, but Baileys sounded like such a good idea I decided to join the party.

Baileys was my dad's home tipple of choice. At bars, it was a shot and a beer, like the other Irish cops. Even after my folks split, Mom kept a bottle for him. She drank schnapps. Peppermint. Disgusting.

Many Baileys later, the jolt of the plane's wheels smacking the Portland landing strip made me grind my teeth. I didn't relax my jaw till the damn thing slowed. Out of control, that's how airplanes make me feel.

Dee Willis always had style, now she's got the cash to go with it: a guy in full livery waited at the gate with CARLYLE printed neatly on a signboard. Broad-shouldered and burly, he resisted conversational gambits and stood at attention until the luggage carousel disgorged my bag. Hefting it, he gawked at its pathetic lightness, staring me down with narrowed eyes, as if he wanted to ask why I couldn't have carried my stuff on board and saved us the twenty-minute wait.

I saw no reason to explain that I needed to check my luggage because it contained a Smith & Wesson 4053, two magazines, and sufficient ammunition to turn an aircraft fuselage into Swiss cheese. I'm no U.S. marshal, just a private investigator; I can't carry on planes. To carry at all, I'd have to check in with the Portland cops, explain my mission, and get a temporary license.

I'd told Dee to hire somebody local. Seems like I've been giving Dee good advice all my life and she never takes one word to heart.

"Stalker," she'd said in her increasingly urgent phone calls. At every concert in every city, always seated in the same section, wearing colorful western gear, almost like he wanted her to notice him,

wanted to stand out in the crowd. Always too damn close.

Ron, Dee's longtime lead guitar, and some of the other guys in the band had braced the man one night. He hadn't seemed fazed, hadn't backed off an inch. Showed up at the next performance bold as brass—and now he, or somebody, was sending wilted flowers, sending nasty letters. She'd FedExed a sample, of a semilyrical nature:

Our lives are linked with chains of steel,
Chains of steel, my Lady Blue.
Saw a chainsaw in a hardware store.
Thought of you, babe. Thought of you.

Block print in a Neanderthal hand. Cheap ballpoint ink. Unsigned. Hardly Dee's favorite fan mail. And no proof that the "stalker" had sent it.

Dee was set for three shows in Portland due to a venue screw-up. She'd been scheduled to play one date in a major arena; her manager had discovered the booking error after the tickets went SRO. Not wanting to disappoint the legions who'd finally made her a star, she'd rented a smaller hall. Intimate. Close to the audience. Close to the stalker. She was scared.

Bodyguard, I'd advised.

You, she'd insisted. We'd discussed terms, including Miss Gibson. Then the tickets came. For the planes and all three shows.

Great seats.

"I thought it didn't snow in Portland," I muttered as the chauffeur and I struggled through gusts of icy wind layered with flakes as soft and wet as soapsuds.

"First blizzard since '89," he grumbled. "Just for you."

"You drive in snow much?" I asked.

"Nope," he said, brushing ineffectually at the windshield with a gloved hand.

In the terminal I'd noticed folks standing around, eyes glued to picture windows, staring with wide-eyed wonder at a paltry six inches Bostonians would have shrugged off with a laugh. I felt a jolt of pity for these two-season folk—rainy and dry—wished I had a shovel to offer the driver instead of a handgun.

I blinked bleary eyes, figured that since the flight had landed after one in the morning, it was now past 4:00 A.M. Boston time. The little sleep I'd enjoyed on the Denver leg had been more than countered by the Baileys binge. I could barely stand upright in the slashing wind.

I was grateful when the chauffeur opened the passenger-side back door, understanding when he didn't wait politely to close the door behind me. I heard the lid of the trunk open, felt a brief stab of regret. Separated from my luggage again.

I drive a cab part-time when I can't make enough PI money to crack my monthly nut. My eye went automatically to the front visor. No photo, no license. Not to worry, I told myself. It's not a cab; it's a limo. No regulations, most cities.

I halted, one foot poised on the shag carpet. The front door locks were shaped like tiny letter *T*'s. The rear locks were straight, smooth, and short, like the filed-off jobs in the backseats of patrol cars.

I engineered a quick reverse, backing into a pile of slush that soaked through my thin boots. "Have a scraper in the trunk?" I asked as casually as I could manage, trying to come up beside the chauffeur.

He gave way. "Jeez, I dunno. You wanna look?"

The leather soles of my boots slipped on the slick stuff coating the pavement. I had to concentrate on my footing. No excuse, just the truth. When the "chauffeur" tackled me high, midback, he had no trouble flipping me head over heels. I barely had the presence of mind to tuck my head to my chin. If I hadn't, I might have snapped my neck as the huge trunk lid came slamming down.

Thank God and the Ford Motor Company for the depth of Lincoln Town Car trunks. Ditto for the plush carpeting. My head thunked against my soft-sided duffel.

Dammit. Yes, I was jetlagged, half drunk, in a strange city at a beastly hour, but Dee had described her "stalker": heavyset, big as a small refrigerator, built on the same square lines as my "chauffeur." I cursed and cursed again. Uniforms'll get you every time; you *trust* a guy in livery, a guy parading your name on a signboard.

The engine revved far too quickly for my assailant to have cleared the windows properly. As we fishtailed into motion I tested the limits of my confinement, reaching out with my right arm, then my left, pushing the trunk lid with both arms, then both feet, in case the latch had failed to catch. No such luck.

Seven plus two, I thought. Seven plus two.

I drive an old Toyota, but as a car freak in good standing, I pore over *Consumer Reports* New Car Yearbooks at newsstands or libraries, anyplace I don't have to fork over cash. Seven plus two is the way *CR* indicates a huge trunk, one with room for seven pullman cases and two weekenders. I spent a while pondering the word "pullman," which reeked of ancient railroad lore, and rubbing my head. Cubic feet, as in amount of available air, would have been a better measurement considering my predicament. Dual exhausts on a new Town Car. I hoped they were working well, discharging their fumes behind the car, not underneath it.

Lying on my back, I approximated the position of a helpless turtle. My duffel bag, probably less than "weekender" size, was next to my head. My knees grazed the top of the trunk. The darkness was total, absolute. We careened around a corner and I found myself unwillingly shifted to an even less comfortable angle.

Did the Lincoln Town Car possess a trunk pass-through to the backseat? I didn't think so. Most of those are found in cars with less trunk capacity. I tried a crab-crawl deeper into the trunk, felt around for some doodad that might lead to the passenger compartment. Lots of effort; no result. Except sweat.

It was going to have to be the duffel bag, maneuvering it, opening it, locating the 40 in its silica-lined case, finding a magazine, loading it. Not shooting off a round by mistake. I imagined one ricocheting through the trunk till it found a soft, cozy home in my body. Imagined igniting the gas tank. Even if the slug miraculously missed me and any flammable fluids, I'd wind up stone-deaf from the enclosed explosion.

We turned a corner too fast. I tried to anchor myself, but I slid to the right, away from my bag.

The "stalker" had an ally in Dee's camp. Deeply embedded there. Dee's no loudmouth, no idle gossiper. She doesn't share her plans with roadies or groupies. Would she have told anyone I was arriving? Left a note by the telephone? Had someone overheard her call a travel agent? Had she relegated the duty to some gofer who'd been suborned by the stalker?

Who'd want to stop Dee? Scare Dee off the circuit?

She'd never harbored a female backup vocalist, didn't tour with a regular opening act. Nobody in her entourage would cherish delusions of replacing Dee Willis.

Her recording company might hire a goon to get her offstage and into the studio. Dee doesn't cut many albums; she likes the rush of live performance. Says she's the leader of a road band and proud of it. Her last two CDs went platinum practically overnight. More studio recordings might make a mint for some MCA/America exec.

Would an entertainment giant hire a thug to frighten one of their stars? Not much I'd put past those L.A. suits.

I wriggled closer to my suitcase.

First step: simple. Unlock the duffel. Keys in my back pocket; I'm not a handbag toter. For the first time since high school I found myself wishing I were less than six feet one. I rolled onto my side, slid an arm behind me, and inched the key out. Might sound easy. Try it in the dark, in a trunk, in a lurching, skidding vehicle.

My fingers found the lock, unbuckled and unzipped the bag from memory and touch, located the gun case. I placed it between my shaky knees. Then it was a race against time, my fingers steadily more numb, more unwieldy as they grew icy. It was not a job for gloved hands.

I couldn't find a magazine. Something sharp

jabbed my hand. What? A nail scissor protruding from my plastic makeup sack? Blood welled from the cut and I made sure to smear some on the carpet. Evidence. Just in case. A snakelike garment grabbed my wrist. Panty hose. There. My hand closed on a rectangle of metal. The box of shells was at the bottom of the case.

Which way to face when he opened the trunk? Should I try for a full rotation, a rollover to get my elbows on the floor? The car stopped. Red light? Traffic jam? I heard a door open, slam. What if he was stopping for backup? What if he abandoned the car? "Woman frozen in freak Portland blizzard." Maybe he'd come back in a week, dump my body in a river.

I clicked the magazine home.

I forced myself to breathe. In and out. Slowly, regularly. I couldn't hear footsteps.

The trunk opened so fast I only caught a glimpse of a hand holding an upraised crowbar before the flashlight blinded me. The beam gave me a target to sight on. My neck ached from holding my head upright. I kept my teeth from chattering as I yelled, "Hold it there. Drop the iron."

Never pull your piece unless you intend to shoot. Never shoot unless you mean to kill. That's what they taught me at the police academy. I'd have shot the chauffeur without a qualm, just for being a lousy goddamn driver, but I wanted answers.

If he'd flicked off the light and made a sudden move, he might have gotten me. My finger tightened against the trigger. If the light died I'd fire.

It didn't. It wavered and I heard a soft thud, like a tire iron landing in snow.

"Hey," he said, his voice a good two notes higher than before. "Relax. Take it easy. I look mean, but I'm not."

"I don't look mean, but I am," I said menacingly, wondering how the hell I was going to get out of the trunk without at least wounding the jerk, giving him something to hold his attention while I clambered over the rear bumper.

"You got the safety catch on?" he asked nervously.

"Guess," I said. "Take five steps back and lie down in the snow."

"Lie down?"

"Faceup. Make me a snow angel, and I mean a good one."

"A snow angel?" he echoed.

"It's like doing jumping jacks lying down," I said. "What's your name?"

"Why?"

"Because I've got a gun and you don't, moron."

"Name's Clay," he muttered.

"Well, Clay. I want to hear you flap those arms and legs. I want to hear your hands clap over your head, okay? Real loud and regular. If I even suspect you're going for the tire iron, not to mention anything else, you're going to be missing a kneecap."

I didn't move till I heard a snort, followed by the scuffing of snow, and rhythmic clapping. Then I stretched my legs over the edge of the trunk, and lifted myself to a semi-sitting position using a combo of abdominals and my left arm.

"Okay, angel," I said once I'd struggled to my feet. My legs felt tingly and achy. My left arm burned. I wanted to sit in the snow and cry. Lie down. Make my own angel.

"What?" he said.

"Are we going to chat or shoot?"

"Can I get up?"

"Why? You want to die like a man?"

"It's colder than a witch's tit down here. If we're gonna talk this thing out, let's get in the car and turn on the heater."

"I have a better idea," I said, reaching behind me and lifting my bag out of the trunk.

"What?"

"Keep flapping those arms. I am now going to take ten steps away from the car. Don't worry. That won't put me out of firing range. Then you will stand *when I tell you to*, and you will march over to the car, and get in the trunk."

"In the trunk?"

"We're trading places."

"Then what?"

His voice hailed from somewhere south. No wonder he didn't know how to make a snow angel. His accent reminded me of someone else's; its cadence was familiar, but not the same. His voice was higher pitched.

"I didn't get a chance to ask 'then what?' when you shoved me in," I said reasonably. "Now, did I?"

He glared. No reply.

"I'm taking my ten steps," I said. "You can get up now."

He followed orders.

"Who hired you to freak Dee Willis?" I asked. No response.

"Come on," I urged. "You think I couldn't shoot you dead and walk, buddy? Think it over. I'm a legit private eye on a legit case. My gun's legal. There's evidence—my blood and sweat and hair—in the damn trunk. Your fingerprints on the tire iron. There's self-defense written all over this baby."

Nothing.

"So who hired you?"

I was freezing my ass for nothing. I don't know, in the movies, somebody's got a gun, they ask questions, and people tell them what they want to know. In real life, I get perps too stupid to plan beyond their next meal.

I blew out a steamy breath, said, "Okay. Let's do it the hard way. Empty your pockets. Drop everything straight down in the snow. I want to see the car keys drop. I want to see your wallet drop. I expect you have a knife, and I would like to see that hit the ground, too."

"Shit." His drawl split the word into two syllables. "I ain't got a knife."

I sighted to the left of his foot, pressed the trigger gently, hit closer than I'd intended. The ground jumped four inches from his toe.

"Knife," I said.

"Jesus, lady," he said. "It's in my boot."

"Well, sit your fat butt on the ground and take your boots off. Easy, now. Rest your weight on your right hand. Like that. Take your boots off with your left. One at a time. Slow and easy.

Lay the blade on the ground. Take your socks off, too, while you're at it."

"I could get frostbit."

"You could get dead," I said pleasantly. "Okay. Now stand up and walk to the car. Hands over your head, please. Take one step toward me, make a move for the knife or the tire iron, and you're meat, understand? My hands are getting too cold to go for anything but gut shots. And, trust me, I will empty the magazine. I've got seven left. And they're not twenty-twos."

I felt better as soon as I'd slammed the trunk. I grabbed the keys from the snow and locked the damn thing just to make sure.

I slung my bag into the backseat, then gathered up the "chauffeur's" belongings, boots, smelly socks, and all.

In the driver's seat, I turned on the engine and let blessed heat flow over my shaking hands and chilled feet. I set the safety on the 40 and stuck it in the glove compartment.

I searched for a map. Nothing in the dash. Nothing in any of the fancy seat pockets. As dawn brightened the sky, I settled down for a thorough exam of the man's wallet.

Cash: one hundred and eighty-seven bucks. A crumpled note giving my name—spelled wrong—airline—spelled right—and arrival time. I stuck it in my pocket, went on to examine a mine of contradictory ID. He had a California driver's license in the name of Claude Fillmer. A Discover card for one Clyde Fulton. Several business cards for Clyde, one introducing him as a claims rep for State Farm Insurance, another asserting his connection to California Security, Incorporated. He'd made himself vice-president. I wondered why he hadn't gone for the top job.

A motel key. Room 138.

A video-rental card for Claude.

A Burger King receipt. I was getting nowhere; I should have made him strip.

Mooney, my former boss at the Boston PD, once told me that ex-cons tend to keep more than knives in their boots. I could practically

hear his voice. I hoped I wasn't starting to hallucinate.

Inside the left boot, I felt the raised outline of a cardboard rectangle. I upended the sucker, shook it hard, but the card was stuck to the insole. It felt too thick and stiff for a manufacturer's label. I used Clay's (or Claude's or Clyde's) knife to pry it out, taking grim satisfaction in the gouges I hacked in the leather.

I found the kind of ID card that comes with cheap wallets. Clayton Fuller had filled out parts of it in a barely legible scrawl. If anything happened to Clayton, anything necessitating the removal and examination of his boots, he thought Mrs. Caroline Fuller of Hazlehurst, Mississippi, was most likely to care.

Hazlehurst, Mississippi. The name swam before my eyes.

Memphis means Elvis.

Detroit is Aretha.

Liverpool equals Lennon and McCartney.

Hazlehurst, Mississippi, is the birthplace of the legendary Robert Johnson, a man who recorded forty-one tunes in a tragically short twenty-nine-year life span and left his imprint on country blues forever. King of the Delta Blues, they called him. Any blues musician worth his salt would boast of sharing a hometown with Robert Johnson, even a player born years after Johnson's mysterious death in 1938.

One had.

I needed to rock the car to get us moving. I may have done it more vigorously than necessary out of consideration for my passenger in the trunk.

I had no idea where we were. I drove, searching for a convenience store, a phone booth, a police station. The Lincoln had half a tank of gas.

I pulled into the parking lot of a little mom-and-pop store near a crossroads, taking care to remove the keys and lock all the doors. Wouldn't do to have my possibly stolen car possibly stolen again. Mom-and-pop sported a Pacific Bell logo on their door. The clerk shook his head sadly as he informed me that I was in the town of Gresham, Oregon. Women drivers, his glance said, hardly ever knew where the hell they were. I was glad I'd left my gun in the glove compartment.

I requested a phone book and ten dollars' worth of change. I learned that all of Mississippi shares one area code: 601.

Clayton's mama was home, practically housebound, she said, what with the "artheritis" actin' up like it done, and just full of chitchat about her son and his best boyhood pals. What a memory.

I was exhausted by the time I talked her off the line. I used some of Clay's cash to buy a local *Oregonian*, a map, a cup of steaming coffee, and a huge Nestlé's Crunch bar.

Breakfast.

I knocked on the trunk in passing.

"I'm gonna faint in here," Clay yelled.

"Good," I hollered back.

God knows what the nosy clerk, peering through the blinds, thought. I gulped the coffee without tasting it, ate half the candy bar standing in the chill morning air. It felt fine to be outdoors in sunlight.

The air was different, canned and smoky, at Dee's first Portland gig. After managing a few hours' sleep, I entered the hall as soon as the doors opened, the first fan inside the tiny auditorium. The stalker was not in the house. The police had been glad to take him off my hands. We'd had a little private eye–to-felon chat before I turned him in. I'd mentioned the inadvisability of naming Dee Willis, unless he wanted his fifteen minutes of fame fast, followed by a lifetime of hate mail and hard prison time.

Dee's popular with inmates. She does jailhouse concerts.

I kept my lies simple. I'd landed late at the airport. No cabs. Guy had pretended to be a legit limo driver, offered me a ride into town for twenty bucks, tried to attack me. I showed my license, my Massachusetts permit to carry. Perp

had picked on the wrong victim. The cops were sympathetic. I presented them with Clayton's various IDs, suggested they check outstanding warrants and parole violations in all his assumed names as well as his own.

I didn't think they'd come up empty.

I watched the crowd filter in, young and old, dressed up, dressed down. Joking, laughing, getting ready for a great time.

No opening act. The curtain rose on the band, playing "For Tonight," the early rocker Dee had made her anthem. Her voice came from everywhere, amplified. The audience gawked, expecting her to enter from stage right, stage left, down one aisle, then another. She chose her moment brilliantly, theatrical as always, appearing suddenly behind an onstage scrim, rainbow lights glistening her white satin tux.

I settled into my crushed velveteen seat and fell for the magic. For glistening bodies shiny with sweat. For the beat and the lyrics and the glorious close harmonies. For the old songs, by John Lee Hooker and Robert Johnson and Son House and Mama Thornton, that Dee had taken, transformed, and made her own. I saw her through a looking-glass of memory at first, but she shattered the barrier with song after song, dragging me into the moment, her moment.

That's her gift. She makes you forget everything but the song. Makes you care about lyrics written seventy years ago by a Mississippi sharecropper, makes them more important than a crummy day at the office or a fight with the kids. Dee gets so deep into the music, it's a wonder she ever climbs out.

I didn't leave my seat at intermission. I didn't move until the last encore ended. Didn't stand till everyone else had gone. Then I parted a red velvet drape and mounted the steps leading backstage.

The dressing rooms were upstairs, eight of them, two per floor, four floors. The "chauffeur" had outlined the setup. I knew which room was Dee's. First floor back. I kept climbing, up to the second floor front. I knocked once, stepped inside. I kept my voice low; I didn't want Dee to hear.

The room was Spartan, linoleum floor, peeling paint on bare walls. Air freshener and body odor warred, neither victorious.

Dee and I have long shared a taste in men: tall, bone-thin, and musically inclined. Ron, in his early forties now, and Cal, my ex, shared enough superficial similarities to pass as a pair of matching bookends.

Ron was buttoning a purple silk shirt over his skinny torso, tucking the shirttail into tight jeans. The jeans disappeared into high snakeskin boots. His guitar lay across a countertop. I brushed a string to get his attention.

He glanced at my reflection in the mirror, sank into a hardbacked chair.

"Carlotta," he said, both grin and voice forced.

"Don't bother smiling for me, Ron."

"No bother," he lied. "Long time."

"I've had a talk with your boy, Clay."

He fumbled for an answer, an excuse. "Clay doesn't know shit," he said, after a long pause. "Clay's not my 'boy.'"

"He knows who hired him, Ron. He's real sure about that."

"You don't fuckin' understand," the lead guitar player said, slamming his fist down against the countertop.

"I understand that you love Dee, Ron. I understand that's hard."

He nodded, so slightly it was barely perceptible.

"I mean about Clay," he said. "There's no understanding Dee. I've given up on that. But with Clay, it got out of hand, Carlotta. I never meant it to get ugly."

"Ugly, Ron? You're talking about scaring somebody half to death. You're talking about a stalker. You're talking about a guy who tried to kill me last night."

"Shit." He split the word into two syllables, just like Clayton Fuller.

"Did you tell him I was coming?"

"Only reason I did was to scare him the hell off, Carlotta. Told him Dee'd hired a pro, somebody who'd nab his sorry ass. I figured he'd split. He's changed, you know? People fuckin' change on you. . . . He's somebody from the old days. Guy I played football with in high school. That's all."

"Hazlehurst," I said.

"Hazlehurst High, yeah. He was a tough guy then. Still is."

"You send for him?"

"He came to a concert. Out of the blue. We went out for a drink. He wanted me to introduce him to Dee. That's what every guy in the fuckin' country wants, an intro to Dee."

"So?"

"So I told him that Dee and I were . . . together, but we were having our troubles. You know, like we always had."

"Trouble staying faithful, you mean?"

"You know her."

I folded my arms under my breasts, gave him a look. "Whereas you were always a saint, Ron. I remember that."

"I only care for Dee. If she'd—"

"Did you ever ask her to marry you?"

"I always ask. Says she doesn't want kids, so what's the point?"

"And she likes men," I observed.

"Probably sucking some guy's dick right now," he said without skipping a beat. "Celebrating 'cause Clay didn't show." Ron's voice sounded dead as an urn full of ashes. "Wanna go check? It's not like I never walked in on her before."

"Let's not change the tune here, Ron. It's not illegal to sleep around. It is illegal to threaten somebody's life."

"Honest to God, I tried to stop him, Carlotta. Everybody in the band'll tell you that. He was like a hound on the scent, out to do me a favor whether I wanted one or not."

"You should have called the cops."

Ron swallowed. "I thought about it. I told him it'd gone too far. He kinda laughed, then he said he'd cut my hand, cut the tendons, so

I'd never play again. He swore if I turned him in he'd tell everybody it was my idea from the get-go."

"Wasn't it?"

"Carlotta, I *love* her. I might have said something to Clay, probably did after I'd downed a few shots. Like, you know, I wish to hell she'd stop screwing around. Clay took it real personal. Said he'd been through two divorces and every time it was his wife cheatin' on him, bangin' this guy or that guy while he's out earnin' bread for the table."

"And you believed him?"

Ron stared at his boots. I noticed a deep scratch across one toe. "I reckon if his wives ran off, they had good reason. I knew a girl he dated back in high school. She'd look at another guy, he'd smack her 'cross the mouth. She moved away, didn't tell anybody where she was headed. What I understand, one of his wives, at least, has got a restraining order out on Clay, maybe an arrest warrant. He told me he can't see his kids, called his wife a castrating bitch. Really got off on it, how wicked she was. Couldn't tell me enough about that evil woman."

Good, I thought, hoping for the arrest warrant. I wanted the bastard locked up, but not at the expense of involving Dee. She didn't need the tabloid coverage. She didn't need every jerk who could read the *Star* or the *Enquirer* getting the idea that stalking Dee Willis might be a fine way to pass the hours.

"Did she sound evil to you?" I asked Ron. "The wife?"

He shook his head. "Sounded like she didn't like gettin' the shit kicked out of her. Sounded like she'd had enough and wanted out."

I repeated, "You should have called the cops."

He faced me directly, stared at me with ice-blue eyes. His voice sounded low and raspy, exhausted. He shook his head, kept shaking it slowly, side to side, as he spoke. "I thought he'd stick around a few nights, maybe make her realize a true thing, Carlotta. Like it's not how it used to be out there. You know it isn't."

"How'd it used to be, Ron? I forget."

"You could get crabs, Carlotta. Maybe the clap. Shot of penicillin. Big fuckin' deal."

"You afraid she'll bring home AIDS? Stop sleeping with her. Use a condom."

"You think I'm just worrying about myself here? Goddammit, I love her."

"So you hire some jerk to scare her to death. What's he supposed to do for a finale? Kidnap her? Rape her?"

"I'd never—I only thought he'd keep her home nights. I thought she'd turn to me, for help, for protection. Instead, she called you."

The way he looked at me, I could tell Dee's cry for help, for *my* help, had been bitter medicine. Yet another injury to his pride.

"And just what was Clay going to do to me, Ron?"

"I dunno," he said, studying the linoleum like it was a work of art. "Man's a fool. I guess he figured he could scare you."

I thought about my time in the trunk. Especially the few moments when I hadn't known whether Clay would open it or walk away. . . .

He'd done his job.

Ron was speaking. "I think Clay's way past thinkin' about me, Carlotta. I'm afraid he really wants Dee. I'm scared he'll hurt her." He swallowed audibly. "I guess I'm ready to go to the cops."

I said, "No reason to, Ron. I've taken care of the cops. You're going to do something harder. Tell Dee. Every nasty detail."

"No."

"Then pack your bags and update your resumé, because she'll fire your ass. You know she will, if I tell her."

He didn't say anything, just stared into the mirror like he was saying good-bye to the best part of himself.

"Do it, Ron. Apologize. Stay with her."

"She's never loved anything but the music, Carlotta," he said, his Adam's apple working. "She doesn't love me."

"She comes back to you, Ron."

"She comes back."

"Maybe that's her kind of love. Maybe that's all the love she's got."

"I don't know if I can live with that," he said.

I wasn't sure if he was talking to me or to the pale skinny man in the mirror.

"Two days, Ron," I said. "You have two days to tell her, or else I will."

I flagged a cab and went straight to the airport. No trouble changing the tickets. Fly first class, they give you leeway.

Dee called late the next night, woke me from a sound sleep. I suppose Ron will always be her lead guitar.

Miss Gibson arrived via messenger. I've stroked her, held her, but I can't bring myself to play her. I try, but something keeps me mute. When I touch the strings, finger a chord, I'm overwhelmed by a sense of awe.

Maybe fear. With that precious battered guitar in hand, I guess I'm scared that I've come as close to the magic as I'll ever get.

HEADACHES AND BAD DREAMS

Lawrence Block

LAWRENCE BLOCK (1938–) has created numerous series characters, including the light humor of Bernie Rhodenbarr (star of the Burglar series); the shady lawyer, Ehrengraf, who has no problem subverting the law to free his clients; Keller, a hit man, who tries to kill only those who need killing; Chip Harrison (an homage to the Nero Wolfe character, written as Chip Harrison); Evan Tanner (a reluctant spy with a sleep disorder that keeps him constantly awake); and the dark Matthew Scudder series about an alcoholic former cop who functions as an unpaid private detective drawn into mysteries by a desire to help friends or just those who need help. It is generally acknowledged that the Scudder series is his greatest work, ranking among the best private eye fiction ever written. His body of work includes more than a hundred novels and short stories collections in every subgenre of the mystery field as well as more than a dozen soft-core porn novels produced in his earliest years as a professional writer.

Among the films inspired by Block's work are *Eight Million Ways to Die* (1986), a weak adaptation of the 1982 Matt Scudder novel, starring Jeff Bridges and Rosanna Arquette; *Burglar* (1987), a dreadful film based on the Rhodenbarr character that starred Whoopi Goldberg and Bobcat Goldthwait; and *A Walk Among the Tombstones* (2014), a very good rendering of the 1992 Scudder novel, starring Liam Neeson and Dan Stevens.

Block has won four Edgar Awards: three for best short story and one in 1992 for best novel with *A Dance at the Slaughterhouse* (1991). For lifetime achievement, the Mystery Writers of America honored him with the Grand Master Award in 1994.

"Headaches and Bad Dreams" was first published in the December 1997 issue of *Ellery Queen Mystery Magazine*; it was first collected in *The Collected Mystery Stories* (London, Orion, 1999).

Headaches and Bad Dreams

LAWRENCE BLOCK

THREE DAYS OF HEADACHES, three nights of bad dreams. On the third night she woke twice before dawn, her heart racing, the bedding sweat-soaked. The second time she forced herself up and out of bed and into the shower. Before she'd toweled dry the headache had begun, starting at the base of the skull and radiating to the temples.

She took aspirin. She didn't like to take drugs of any sort, and her medicine cabinet contained nothing but a few herbal preparations—echinacea and goldenseal for colds, gingko for memory, and a Chinese herbal tonic, its ingredients a mystery to her, which she ordered by mail from a firm in San Francisco. She took sage, too, because it seemed to her to help center her psychically and make her perceptions more acute, although she couldn't remember having read that it had that property. She grew sage in her garden, picked leaves periodically and dried them in the sun, and drank a cup of sage tea almost every evening.

There were herbs that were supposed to ease headaches, no end of different herbs for the many different kinds of headaches, but she'd never found one that worked. Aspirin, on the other hand, was reliable. It was a drug, and as such it probably had the effect of dulling her psychic abilities, but those abilities were of small value when your head was throbbing like Poe's telltale heart. And aspirin didn't slam shut the

doors of perception, as something strong might do. Truth to tell, it was the nearest thing to an herb itself, obtained originally from willow bark. She didn't know how they made it nowadays, surely there weren't willow trees enough on the planet to cure the world's headaches, but still . . .

She heated a cup of spring water, added the juice of half a lemon. That was her breakfast. She sipped it in the garden, listening to the birds.

She knew what she had to do but she was afraid.

It was a small house, just two bedrooms, everything on one floor, with no basement, and shallow crawl space for an attic. She slept in one bedroom and saw clients in the other. A beaded curtain hung in the doorway of the second bedroom, and within were all the pictures and talismans and power objects from which she drew strength. There were religious pictures and statues, a crucifix, a little bronze Buddha, African masks, quartz crystals. A pack of tarot cards shared a small table with a little malachite pyramid and a necklace of bear claws.

A worn oriental rug covered most of the floor, and was itself in part covered by a smaller rug on which she would lie when she went into trance. The rest of the time she would sit in the straight-backed armchair. There was a chaise as well, and that was where the client would sit.

She had only one appointment that day, but it was right smack in the middle of the day. The client, Claire Warburton, liked to come on her lunch hour. So Sylvia got through the morning by watching talk shows on television and paging through old magazines, taking more aspirin when the headache threatened to return. At 12:30 she opened the door for her client.

Claire Warburton was a regular, coming for a reading once every four or five weeks, upping the frequency of her visits in times of stress. She had a weight problem—that was one of the reasons she liked to come on her lunch hour, so as to spare herself a meal's worth of calories—and she was having a lingering affair with a married man. She had occasional problems at work as well, a conflict with a new supervisor, an awkward situation with a coworker who disapproved of her love affair. There were always topics on which Claire needed counsel, and, assisted by the cards, the crystals, and her own inner resources, Sylvia always found something to tell her.

"Oh, before I forget," Claire said, "you were absolutely right about wheat. I cut it out and I felt the difference almost immediately."

"I thought you would. That came through loud and clear last time."

"I told Dr. Greenleaf. 'I think I may be allergic to wheat,' I said. He rolled his eyes."

"I'll bet he did. I hope you didn't tell him where the thought came from."

"Oh, sure. 'Sylvia Belgrave scanned my reflex centers with a green pyramid and picked up a wheat allergy.' Believe me, I know better than that. I don't know why I bothered to say anything to him in the first place. I suppose I was looking for male approval, but that's nothing new, is it?" They discussed the point, and then she said, "But it's so hard, you know. Staying away from wheat, I mean. It's everywhere."

"Yes."

"Bread, pasta. I wish I could cut it out completely, but I've managed to cut way down, and it helps. Sylvia? Are you all right?"

"A headache. It keeps coming back."

"Really? Well, I hate to say it, but do you think maybe you ought to see a doctor?"

She shook her head. "No," she said. "I know the cause, and I even know the cure. There's something I have to do."

When Sylvia was nineteen years old, she fell in love with a young man named Gordon Sawyer. He had just started dental school, and they had an understanding; after he had qualified as a dentist, they would get married. They were not officially engaged, she did not have a ring, but they had already reached the stage of talking about names for their children.

He drowned on a family canoe trip. A couple of hours after it happened, but long before anybody could get word to her, Sylvia awoke from a nightmare bathed in perspiration. The details of the dream had fled, but she knew it had been awful, and that something terrible had happened to Gordon. She couldn't go back to sleep, and she had been up for hours with an unendurable headache when the doorbell rang and a cousin of Gordon's brought the bad news.

That was her first undeniable psychic experience. Before that she'd had feelings and hunches, twinges of perception that were easy to shrug off or blink away. Once a fortune-teller at a county fair had read her palm and told her she had psychic powers herself, powers she'd be well advised to develop. She and Gordon had laughed about it, and he'd offered to buy her a crystal ball for her birthday.

When Gordon died her life found a new direction. If Gordon had lived she'd have gone on working as a salesgirl until she became a full-time wife and mother. Instead she withdrew into herself and began following the promptings of an inner voice. She could walk into a bookstore and her feet would lead her to some arcane volume that would turn out to be just what she needed to study next. She would sit in her room in her parents' house, staring for hours at a candle flame, or at her own reflection in the mirror. Her parents were worried, but nobody did anything beyond urging her to get out more and meet people. She was upset over Gordon's death, they agreed, and that was understandable, and she would get over it.

"Twenty-five dollars," Claire Warburton said, handing over two tens and a five. "You know, I was reading about this woman in *People Magazine*, she reads the cards for either Oprah or Madonna, don't ask me which. And do you know how much she gets for a session?"

"Probably more than twenty-five dollars," Sylvia said.

"They didn't say, but they showed the car she drives around in. It's got an Italian name that sounds like testosterone, and it's fire-engine red, naturally. Of course, that's California. People in this town think you'd have to be crazy to pay twenty-five dollars. I don't see how you get by, Sylvia. I swear I don't."

"There was what my mother left," she said. "And the insurance."

"And a good thing, but it won't last forever. Can't you—"

"What?"

"Well, look into the crystal and try to see the stock market? Or ask your spirit guides for investment advice?"

"It doesn't work that way."

"That's what I knew you'd say," Claire said. "I guess that's what everybody says: You can't use it for your own benefit or it doesn't work."

"That's as it should be," she said. "It's a gift, and the Universe doesn't necessarily give you what you want. But you have to keep it. No exchanges, no refunds."

She parked across the street from the police station, turned off the engine and sat in the car for a few moments, gathering herself. Her car was not a red Testarossa but a six-year-old Ford Tempo. It ran well, got good mileage, and took her where she wanted to go. What more could you ask of a car?

Inside, she talked to two uniformed officers before she wound up on the other side of a desk from a balding man with gentle brown eyes that belied his jutting chin. He was a detective, and his name was Norman Jeffcote.

He looked at her card, then looked directly at her. Twenty years had passed since her psychic powers had awakened with her fiancé's death, and she knew that the years had not enhanced her outward appearance. Then she'd been a girl with regular features turned pretty by her vital energy, a petite and slender creature, and now she was a little brown-haired mouse, dumpy and dowdy.

"'Psychic counseling,'" he read aloud. "What's that exactly, Ms. Belgrave?"

"Sometimes I sense things," she said.

"And you think you can help us with the Sporran kid?"

"That poor little girl," she said.

Melissa Sporran, six years old, only child of divorced parents, had disappeared eight days previously on her way home from school.

"The mother broke down on camera," Detective Jeffcote said, "and I guess it got to people, so much so that it made some of the national newscasts. That kind of coverage pulls people out of the woodwork. I got a woman on the phone from Chicago, telling me she just knows little Melissa's in a cave at the foot of a waterfall. She's alive, but in great danger. You're a local woman, Ms. Belgrave. You know any waterfalls within a hundred miles of here?"

"No."

"Neither do I. This woman in Chicago, see, may have been a little fuzzy on the geography, but she was good at making sure I got her name spelled right. But I won't have a problem in your case, will I? Because your name's all written out on your card."

"You're not impressed with psychic phenomena," she said.

"I think you people got a pretty good racket going," he said, "and more power to you if you can find people who want to shell out for whatever it is you're selling. But I've got a murder investigation to run, and I don't appreciate a lot of people with four-leaf clovers and crystal balls."

"Maybe I shouldn't have come," she said.

"Well, that's not for me to say, Ms. Belgrave, but now that you bring it up—"

"No," she said. "I didn't have any choice. Detective, have you heard of Sir Isaac Newton?"

"Sure, but I probably don't know him as well as you do. Not if you're getting messages from him."

"He was the foremost scientific thinker of his time," she said, "and in his later years he became quite devoted to astrology, which you may take as evidence either of his openmindedness or of encroaching senility, as you prefer."

"I don't see what this has to—"

"A colleague chided him," she said, brooking no interruption, "and made light of his enthusiasm, and do you know what Newton said? 'Sir, I have investigated the subject. You have not. I do not propose to waste my time discussing it with you.'"

He looked at her and she returned his gaze. After a long moment he said, "All right, maybe you and Sir Isaac have a point. You got a hunch about the Sporran kid?"

"Not a hunch," she said, and explained the dreams, the headaches. "I believe I'm linked to her," she said, "however it works, and I don't begin to understand how it works. I think . . ."

"Yes?"

"I'm afraid I think she's dead."

"Yes," Jeffcote said heavily. "Well, I hate to say it, but you gain in credibility with that one, Ms. Belgrave. We think so, too."

"If I could put my hands on some object she owned, or a garment she wore . . ."

"You and the dogs." She looked at him. "There was a fellow with a pack of bloodhounds,

needed something of hers to get the scent. Her mother gave us this little sunsuit, hadn't been laundered since she wore it last. The dogs got the scent good, but they couldn't pick it up anywhere. I think we still have it. You wait here."

He came back with the garment in a plastic bag, drew it out and wrinkled his nose at it. "Smells of dog now," he said. "Does that ruin it for you?"

"The scent's immaterial," she said. "It shouldn't even matter if it's been laundered. May I?"

"You need anything special, Ms. Belgrave? The lights out, or candles lit, or—"

She shook her head, told him he could stay, motioned for him to sit down. She took the child's sunsuit in her hands and closed her eyes and began to breathe deeply, and almost at once her mind began to fill with images. She saw the girl, saw her face, and recognized it from dreams she thought she had forgotten.

She felt things, too. Fear, mostly, and pain, and more fear, and then, at the end, more pain.

"She's dead," she said softly, her eyes still closed. "He strangled her."

"He?"

"I can't see what he looks like. Just impressions." She waved a hand in the air, as if to dispel clouds, then extended her arm and pointed. "That direction," she said.

"You're pointing southeast."

"Out of town," she said. "There's a white church off by itself. Beyond that there's a farm." She could see it from on high, as if she were hovering overhead, like a bird making lazy circles in the sky. "I think it's abandoned. The barn's unpainted and deserted. The house has broken windows."

"There's the Baptist church on Reistertown Road. A plain white building with a little steeple. And out beyond it there's the Petty farm. She moved into town when the old man died."

"It's abandoned," she said, "but the fields don't seem to be overgrown. That's strange, isn't it?"

"Definitely the Petty farm," he said, his voice quickening. "She let the grazing when she moved."

"Is there a silo?"

"Seems to me they kept a dairy herd. There'd have be a silo."

"Look in the silo," she said.

She was studying Detective Jeffcote's palm when the call came. She had already told him he was worried about losing his hair, and that there was nothing he could do about it, that it was inevitable. The inevitability was written in his hand, although she'd sensed it the moment she saw him, just as she had at once sensed his concern. You didn't need to be psychic for that, though. It was immediately evident in the way he'd grown his remaining hair long and combed it to hide the bald spot.

"You should have it cut short," she said. "Very short. A crew cut, in fact."

"I do that," he said, "and everybody'll be able to see how thin it's getting."

"They won't notice," she told him. "The shorter it is, the less attention it draws. Short hair will empower you."

"Wasn't it the other way around with Samson?"

"It will strengthen you," she said. "Inside and out."

"And you can tell all that just looking at my hand?"

She could tell all that just looking at his head, but she only smiled and nodded. Then she noticed an interesting configuration in his palm and told him about it, making some dietary suggestions based on what she saw. She stopped talking when the phone rang, and he reached to answer it.

He listened for a long moment, then covered the mouthpiece with the very palm she'd been reading. "You were right," he said. "In the silo, covered up with old silage. They wouldn't have found her if they hadn't known to look for her.

And the smell of the fermented silage masked the smell of the, uh, decomposition."

He put the phone to his ear, listened some more, spoke briefly, covered the mouthpiece again. "Marks on her neck," he said. "Hard to tell if she was strangled, not until there's a full autopsy, but it looks like a strong possibility."

"Teeth," she said suddenly.

"Teeth?"

She frowned, upset with herself. "That's all I can get when I try to see *him*."

"The man who—"

"Took her there, strangled her, killed her. I can't say if he was tall or short, fat or thin, old or young."

"Just that he had teeth."

"I guess that must have been what she noticed. Melissa. She must have been frightened of him because of the teeth."

"Did he bite her? Because if he did—"

"No," she said sharply. "Or I don't know, perhaps he did, but it was the appearance of the teeth that frightened her. He had bad teeth."

"Bad teeth?"

"Crooked, discolored, broken. They must have made a considerable impression on her."

"Jesus," he said, and into the mouthpiece he said, "You still there? What was the name of that son of a bitch, did some handyman work for the kid's mother? Henrich, Heinrich, something like that? Looked like a dentist's worst nightmare? Yeah, well, pick him up again."

He hung up the phone. "We questioned him," he said, "and we let him go. Big gangly overgrown kid, God made him as ugly as he could and then hit him in the mouth with a shovel. This time I think I'll talk to him myself. Ms. Belgrave? You all right?"

"Just exhausted, all of a sudden," she said. "I haven't been sleeping well these past few nights. And what we just did, it takes a lot out of you."

"I can imagine."

"But I'll be all right," she assured him. And, getting to her feet, she realized she wouldn't be needing any more aspirin. The headache was gone.

The handyman, whose name turned out to be Walter Hendrick, broke down under questioning and admitted the abduction and murder of Melissa Sporran. Sylvia saw his picture on television but turned off the set, unable to look at him. His mouth was closed, you couldn't see his teeth, but even so she couldn't bear the sight of him.

The phone rang, and it was a client she hadn't seen in months, calling to book a session. She made a note in her appointment calendar and went into the kitchen to make a cup of tea. She was finishing the tea and trying to decide if she wanted another when the phone rang again.

It was a new client, a Mrs. Huggins, eager to schedule a reading as soon as possible. Sylvia asked the usual questions and made sure she got the woman's date of birth right. Astrology wasn't her main focus, but it never hurt to have that data in hand before a client's first visit. It made it easier, often, to get a grasp on the personality.

"And who told you about me?" she asked, almost as an afterthought. Business always came through referrals, a satisfied client told a friend or relative or coworker, and she liked to know who was saying good things about her.

"Now who was it?" the woman wondered. "I've been meaning to call for such a long time, and I can't think who it was that originally told me about you."

She let it go at that. But, hanging up, she realized the woman had just lied to her. That was not exactly unheard of, although it was annoying when they lied about their date of birth, shaving a few years off their age and unwittingly providing her with an erroneous astrological profile in the process. But this woman had found something wholly unique to lie about, and she wondered why.

Within the hour the phone rang again, another old client of whom she'd lost track. "I'll bet you're booked solid," the woman said. "I just hope you can fit me in."

"Are you being ironic?"

"I beg your pardon?"

"Because you know it's a rare day when I see more than two people, and there are days when I don't see anyone at all."

"I don't know how many people you see," the woman said. "I do know that it's always been easy to get an appointment with you at short notice, but I imagine that's all changed now, hasn't it?"

"Why would it . . ."

"Now that you're famous."

Famous.

Of course she wasn't, not really. Someone did call her from Florida, wanting an interview for a national tabloid, and there was a certain amount of attention in the local press, and on area radio stations. But she was a quiet, retiring woman, hardly striking in appearance and decidedly undramatic in her responses. Her personal history was not interesting in and of itself, nor was she inclined to go into it. Her lifestyle was hardly colorful.

Had it been otherwise, she might have caught a wave of publicity and been nationally famous for her statutory fifteen minutes, reading Joey Buttafuoco's palm on "Hard Copy," sharing herbal weight-loss secrets with Oprah.

Instead she had her picture in the local paper, seated in her garden. (She wouldn't allow them to photograph her in her studio, among the candles and crystals.) And that was enough to get her plenty of attention, not all of which she welcomed. No one actually crept across her lawn to stare in her window, but cars did slow or even stop in front of her house, and one man got out of his car and took pictures.

She got more attention than usual when she left the house, too. People who knew her congratulated her, hoping to hear a little more about the case and the manner in which she'd solved it. Strangers recognized her—on the street, in the supermarket. While their interest was not intrusive, she was uncomfortably aware of it.

But the biggest change, really, was in the number of people who suddenly found themselves in need of her services. She was bothered at first by the thought that they were coming to her for the wrong reason, and she wondered if she should refuse to accommodate such curiosity seekers. She meditated on the question, and the answer that came to her was that she was unequipped to judge the motivation of those who sought her out. How could she tell the real reason that brought some troubled soul to her door? And how could she determine, irrespective of motivation, what help she might be able to provide?

She decided that she ought to see everyone. If she found herself personally uncomfortable with a client's energy, then she wouldn't see that person anymore. That had been her policy all along. But she wouldn't prejudge any of them, wouldn't screen them in advance.

"But it's impossible to fit everyone in," she told Claire Warburton. "I'm just lucky I got a last-minute cancellation or I wouldn't have been able to schedule you until the end of next week."

"How does it feel to be an overnight success after all these years?"

"Is that what I am? A success? Sometimes I think I liked it better when I was a failure. No, I don't mean that, but no more do I like being booked as heavily as I am, I'll tell you that. The work is exhausting. I'm seeing four people a day, and yesterday I saw five, which I'll never do again. It drains you."

"I can imagine."

"But the gentleman was so persistent, and I thought, well, I do have the time. But by the time the day was over . . ."

"You were exhausted."

"I certainly was. And I hate to book appointments weeks in advance, or to refuse to book them at all. It bothers me to turn anyone away, because how do I know that I'm not turning away someone in genuine need? For years I had less business than I would have preferred, and

now I have too much, and I swear I don't know what to do about it." She frowned. "And when I meditate on it, I don't get anywhere at all."

"For heaven's sake," Claire said. "You don't need to look in a crystal for this one. Just look at a balance sheet."

"I beg your pardon?"

"Sylvia," Claire said, "raise your damn rates."

"My rates?"

"For years you've been seeing a handful of people a week and charging them twenty-five dollars each, and wondering why you're poor as a churchmouse. Raise your rates and you'll increase your income to a decent level—*and* you'll keep yourself from being overbooked. The people who really need you will pay the higher price, and the curiosity seekers will think twice."

"But the people who've been coming to me for years—"

"You can grandfather them in," Claire said. "Confine the rate increase to new customers. But I wouldn't."

"You wouldn't?"

"No, and I'm costing my own self money by saying this, but I'll say it anyhow. People appreciate less what costs them less. That woman in California, drives the red Tosteroni? You think she'd treasure that car if somebody sold it to her for five thousand dollars? You think *People Magazine* would print a picture of her standing next to it? Raise your rates and everybody'll think more of you, and pay more attention to the advice you give 'em."

"Well," she said, slowly, "I suppose I could go from twenty-five to thirty-five dollars . . ."

"Fifty," Claire said firmly. "Not a penny less."

In the end, she had to raise her fee three times. Doubling it initially had the paradoxical effect of increasing the volume of calls. A second increase, to seventy-five dollars, was a step in the right direction, slowing the flood of calls; she waited a few months, then took a deep breath and told a caller her price was one hundred dollars a session.

And there it stayed. She booked three appointments a day, five days a week, and pocketed fifteen hundred dollars a week for her efforts. She lost some old clients, including a few who had been coming to her out of habit, the way they went to get their hair done. But it seemed to her that the ones who stayed actually listened more intently to what she saw in the cards or crystal, or channeled while she lay in trance.

"Told you," Claire said. "You get what you pay for."

One afternoon there was a call from Detective Jeffcote. There was a case, she might have heard or read about it, and could she possibly help him with it? She had appointments scheduled, she said, but she could come to the police station as soon as her last client was finished, and—

"No, I'll come to you," he said. "Just tell me when's a good time."

He turned up on the dot. His hair was very short, she noticed, and he seemed more confident and self-possessed than when she'd seen him before. In the living room, he accepted a cup of tea and told her about the girl who'd gone missing, an eleventh-grader named Peggy Mae Turlock. "There hasn't been much publicity," he said, "because kids her age just go off sometimes, but she's an A student and sings in the church choir, and her parents are worried. And I just thought, well . . ."

She reminded him that she'd had three nights of nightmares and headaches when Melissa Sporran disappeared.

"As if the information was trying to get through," he said. "And you haven't had anything like that this time? Because I brought her sunglasses case, and a baseball jacket they tell me she wore all the time."

"We can try," she said.

She took him into her studio, lit two of the new scented candles, seated him on the chaise and took the chair for herself. She draped Peggy Mae's jacket over her lap and held the green vinyl eyeglass case in both hands. She closed her eyes, breathed slowly and deeply.

After a while she said, "Pieces."

"Pieces?"

"I'm getting these horrible images," she said, "of dismemberment, but I don't know that it has anything to do with the girl. I don't know where it's coming from."

"You picking up any sense of where she might be, or of who might have put her there?"

She slowed her breathing, let herself go deep, deep.

"Down down down," she said.

"How's that, Ms. Belgrave?"

"Something in a well," she said. "And old rusty chain going down into a well, and something down there."

A search of wells all over the country divulged no end of curious debris, including a skeleton that turned out to be that of a large dog. No human remains were found, however, and the search was halted when Peggy Mae came home from Indianapolis. She'd gone there for an abortion, expecting to be back in a day or so, but there had been medical complications. She'd been in the hospital there for a week, never stopping to think that her parents were afraid for her life, or that the police were probing abandoned wells for her dismembered corpse.

Sylvia got a call when the girl turned up. "The important thing is she's all right," he said, "although I wouldn't be surprised if right about now she wishes she was dead. Point is you didn't let us down. You were trying to home in on something that wasn't there in the first place, since she was alive and well all along."

"I'm glad she's alive," she said, "but disappointed in myself. All of that business about wells."

"Maybe you were picking up something from fifty years ago," he said. "Who knows how many wells there are, boarded up and forgotten years ago? And who knows what secrets one or two of them might hold?"

"Perhaps you're right."

Perhaps he was. But all the same the few days when the police were looking in old wells was a professional high water mark for her. After the search was called off, after Peggy Mae came home in disgrace, it wasn't quite so hard to get an appointment with Sylvia Belgrave.

Three nights of nightmares and fitful sleep, three days of headaches. And, awake or asleep, a constant parade of hideous images.

It was hard to keep herself from running straight to the police. But she forced herself to wait, to let time take its time. And then on the morning after the third unbearable night she showered away the stale night sweat and put on a skirt and a blouse and a flowered hat. She sat in the garden with a cup of hot water and lemon juice, then rinsed it in the kitchen sink and went to her car.

The car was a Taurus, larger and sleeker and, certainly, newer than her old Tempo, but it did no more and no less than the Tempo had done. It conveyed her from one place to another. This morning it brought her to the police station, and her feet brought her the rest of the way— into the building, and through the corridors to Detective Norman Jeffcote's office.

"Ms. Belgrave," he said. "Have a seat, won't you?"

His hair was longer than it had been when he'd come to her house. He hadn't regrown it entirely, hadn't once again taken to combing it over the bald spot, but neither was it as flatteringly short as she'd advised him to keep it.

And there was something unsettling about his energy. Maybe it had been a mistake to come.

She sat down and winced, and he asked her if she was all right. "My head," she said, and pressed her fingertips to her temples.

"You've got a headache?"

"Endless headaches. And bad dreams, and all the rest of it."

"I see."

"I didn't want to come," she said. "I told myself not to intrude, not to be a nuisance. But it's just like the first time, when that girl disappeared."

"Melissa Sporran."

"And now there's a little boy gone missing," she said.

"Eric Ackerman."

"Yes, and his address is no more than half a mile from my house. Maybe that's why all these impressions have been so intense."

"Do you know where he is now, Ms. Belgrave?"

"I don't," she said, "but I do feel connected to him, and I have the strong sense that I might be able to help."

He nodded. "And your hunches usually pay off."

"Not always," she said. "That was confusing the year before last, sending you to look in wells."

"Well, nobody's perfect."

"Surely not."

He leaned forward, clasped his hands. "The Ackerman boy, Ms. Belgrave. You think he's all right?"

"Oh, I wish I could say yes."

"But you can't."

"The nightmares," she said, "and the headaches. If he were all right, the way the Turlock girl was all right—"

"There'd be no dreams."

"That's my fear, yes."

"So you think the boy is . . ."

"Dead," she said.

He looked at her for a long moment before he nodded. "I suppose you'd like some article connected with the boy," he said. "A piece of clothing, say."

"If you had something."

"How's this?" he said, and opened a drawer and brought out a teddy bear, its plush fur badly worn, the stitches showing where it had been ripped and mended. Her heart broke at the sight of it and she put her hand to her chest.

"We ought to have a record of this," he said, propping a tape recorder on the desk top, pressing a button start it recording. "So that I don't miss any of the impressions you pick up. Because you can probably imagine how frantic the boy's parents are."

"Yes, of course."

"So do you want to state your name for the record?"

"My name?"

"Yes, for the record."

"My name is Sylvia Belgrave."

"And you're a psychic counselor?"

"Yes."

"And you're here voluntarily."

"Yes, of course."

"Why don't you take the teddy bear, then. And see what you can pick up from it."

She thought she'd braced herself, but she was unprepared for the flood of images that came when she took the little stuffed bear in her hands. They were more vivid than anything she'd experienced before. Perhaps she should have expected as much; the dreams, and the headaches, too, were worse than they'd been after Melissa Sporran's death, worse than years ago, when Gordon Sawyer drowned.

"Smothered," she managed to say. "A pillow or something like it over his face. He was struggling to breathe and . . . and he couldn't."

"And he's dead."

"Yes."

"And would you happen to know where, Ms. Belgrave?"

Her hands tightened on the teddy bear. The muscles in her arms and shoulders went rigid, bracing to keep the images at bay.

"A hole in the ground," she said.

"A hole in the ground?"

"A basement!" Her eyes were closed, her heart pounding. "A house, but they haven't finished building it yet. The outer walls are up but that's all."

"A building site."

"Yes."

"And the body's in the basement."

"Under a pile of rags," she said.

"Under a pile of rags. Any sense of where,

Ms. Belgrave? There are a lot of houses under construction. It would help if we knew what part of town to search."

She tried to get her bearings, then realized she didn't need them. Her hand, of its own accord, found the direction and pointed.

"North and west," he said. "Let's see, where's there a house under construction, ideally one they stopped work on? Seems to me there's one just off Radbourne Road about a quarter of a mile past Six Mile Road. You think that might be the house, Ms. Belgrave?"

She opened her eyes. He was reaching across to take the teddy bear from her. She had to will her fingers to open to release it.

"We've got some witnesses," he said, his voice surprisingly gentle. "A teenager mowing a lawn who saw Eric Ackerman getting into a blue Taurus just like the one you've got parked across the street. He even noticed the license plate, but then it's the kind you notice, isn't it? 2ND SITE. Second sight, eh? Perfect for your line of work."

God, her head was throbbing.

"A woman in a passing car saw you carrying the boy to the house. She didn't spot the vanity plate, but she furnished a good description of the car, and of you, Ms. Belgrave. She thought it was odd, you see. The way you were carrying him, as if he was unconscious, or even dead. Was he dead by then?"

"Yes."

"You killed him first thing? Smothered him?"

"With a pillow," she said. "I wanted to do it right away, before he became afraid. And I didn't want him to suffer."

"Real considerate."

"He struggled," she said, "and then he was still. But I didn't realize just how much he suffered. It was over so quickly, you see, that I told myself he didn't really suffer a great deal at all."

"And?"

"And I was wrong," she said. "I found that out in the dreams. And just now, holding the bear . . ."

He was saying something but she couldn't

hear it. She was trembling, and the headache was too much to be borne, and she couldn't follow his words. He brought her a glass of water and she drank it, and that helped a little.

"There were other witnesses, too," he said, "once we found the body, and knew about the car and the license plate. People who saw your car going to and from the construction site. The chief wanted to have you picked up right away, but I talked him into waiting. I figured you'd come in and tell us all about it yourself."

"And here I am," she heard herself say.

"And here you are. You want to tell me about it from the beginning?"

She told it all simply and directly, how she'd selected the boy, how she got him to come into the car with her, how she'd killed him and dumped the body in the spot she'd selected in advance. How she'd gone home, and washed her hands, and waited through three days and nights of headaches and bad dreams.

"Ever kill anybody before, Ms. Belgrave?"

"No," she said. "No, of course not."

"Ever have anything to do with Eric Ackerman or his parents?"

"No."

"Why, then?"

"Don't you know?"

"Tell me anyway."

"Second sight," she said.

"Second . . ."

"Second sight. Vanity plates. Vanity."

"Vanity?"

"All is vanity," she said, and closed her eyes for a moment. "I never made more than a hundred fifty dollars a week," she said, "and nobody knew me or paid me a moment's attention, but that was all right. And then Melissa Sporran was killed, and I was afraid to come in but I came in anyway. And everything changed."

"You got famous."

"For a little while," she said. "And my phone started ringing, and I raised my rates, and my phone rang even more. And I was able to help people, more people than I'd ever helped before, and they were making use of what I gave them, they were taking it seriously."

"And you bought a new car."

"I bought a new car," she said, "and I bought some other things, and I stopped being famous, and the ones who only came because they were curious stopped coming when they stopped being curious, and old customers came less often because they couldn't afford it, and . . ."

"And business dropped off."

"And I thought, I could help so many more people if, if it happened again."

"If a child died."

"Yes."

"And if you helped."

"Yes. And I waited, you know, for something to happen. And there were crimes, there are always crimes. There were even murders, but there was nothing that gave me the dreams and the headaches."

"So you decided to do it yourself."

"Yes."

"Because you'd be able to help so many more people."

"That's what I told myself," she said. "But I was just fooling myself. I did it because I'm having trouble making the payments on my new car, a car I didn't need in the first place. But I need the car now, and I need the phone ringing, and I need—" She frowned, put her head in her hands. "I need aspirin," she said. "That first time, when I told you about Melissa Sporran, the headache went away. But I've told you everything about Eric Ackerman, more than I ever planned to tell you, and the headache hasn't gone away. It's worse than ever."

He told her it would pass, but she shook her head. She knew it wouldn't, or the bad dreams, either. Some things you just knew.

AN AFFAIR OF INCONVENIENCE

Anne Perry

AN INTERNATIONALLY BESTSELLING AUTHOR of historical mystery fiction with nearly twenty-eight million copies sold, Anne Perry (1938–) has produced nearly eighty books, most of them classic Victorian-era detective novels about Thomas and Charlotte Pitt or about William Monk. Among much else, she has written a dozen highly successful Christmas-themed novellas in which Lady Vespasia Cumming-Gould is featured, plus works set during World War I.

Perry's first book, *The Cater Street Hangman* (1979), featured Thomas Pitt, a Victorian policeman, and his highborn wife, Charlotte, who helps her husband solve mysteries out of boredom. She is of enormous help to him as she is able to gain access to people of a high social rank, which would be extremely difficult for a common police officer to do. There are nearly thirty books in the series, set in the 1880s and 1890s. With *Twenty-One Days* (2017), the Pitts's son Daniel has been persuaded to take on his own case in what may be the start of a new series.

The Monk series, with more than twenty novels, beginning with *The Face of a Stranger* (1990), is set in the 1850s and 1860s. Monk, a private detective, is assisted on his cases by an excitable nurse, Hester Latterly.

After winning the Edgar in 2000 for her short story "Heroes," set during World War I, Perry began a series of novels featuring its protagonist, British Army chaplain Joseph Reavley, whose exploits and character were suggested by the author's grandfather; the first book was *No Graves as Yet* (2003).

Lady Vespasia Cumming-Gould has been a secondary character in the Pitt series but is the author's favorite. "She's always been one of my favorite characters," Perry has said, "and she's who I would like to be. She has courage for life, she has wit, and she has intelligence and grace and [beauty], but her beauty is more than just a matter of her features; it's something within her." She is noted for expressing her opinion of how women are treated in England at the time.

"An Affair of Inconvenience" was originally published in the Fall 1998 issue of *Mary Higgins Clark Mystery Magazine*.

An Affair of Inconvenience

ANNE PERRY

IT HAD BEEN QUITE DISTINCTLY the sound of breaking glass, once, sharply, and then silence. Lady Vespasia Cumming-Gould sat up in bed. It had come from the room next door, the only unoccupied guest room in the house.

On a long country weekend such as this, when the London season was over and the Queen and Prince Albert had retired to the late-summer pleasures of Osbourne, it was not unusual for there to be a number of romantic affairs conducted with discretion but distinct relish. An assignation in the middle of the night was not of itself remarkable. But it should not entail the smashing of glass. That sounded more like an accident, or even an intruder.

Vespasia fumbled in the dark for a moment, found the matches, and lit the lamp on the table beside her. She rose and pulled her ivory silk robe over her shoulders without bothering to straighten the cascades of lace or arrange her hair carefully. She picked up the lamp and walked softly across to the door and opened it.

The corridor outside was dimly lit from the gas bracket halfway along, turned down as low as possible until it burned yellow. There was no one there and total silence.

She tiptoed along to the next door and put her hand on the knob. She turned it slowly and pushed. It swung open.

Lady Oremia Blythe was standing in the cen-ter of the room, her abundant fair hair streaming around her shoulders, her yellow peignoir with its gleaming satin and extravagant ribbons hang-ing open over her nightgown. In her right hand was the brass base of an oil lamp. The splintered shards of its mantle lay on the floor around the recumbent body of Sir Ferdinand Wakeham. The crown of his bald head was bleeding a lit-tle. He was wearing a paisley robe and a striped cotton nightshirt. Oremia was ashen-faced, her eyes wide with horror.

Vespasia glanced automatically at the bed. The four-poster had been made carefully but not with the skill or the neatness with which a chambermaid would have done it. The corners were uneven. The coverlet was not smoothed under the pillows. Its recent use was apparent.

What was far less apparent was why Oremia should have struck Ferdie senseless, or in fact why she had been with him at all! Vespasia had been observing the gathered company all week-end. She had seen the covert glances and smiles, the twitching of skirts, the dropped handker-chiefs, the unnecessary errands, the laughter and lingering moments. She was well aware that Ferdie's interests lay elsewhere.

She gazed at Oremia with raised eyebrows.

"Oh . . . er . . . Vespasia . . ." Oremia began awkwardly, blinking at last. Her hand holding the remnants of the lamp was trembling very slightly. She licked dry lips. "I . . . er . . ." She swallowed. Her voice cracked. "Vespasia! What am I going to do? For God's sake . . . help me!"

Vespasia closed the door behind her softly and turned to face Oremia, whom she was not particularly fond of. But she would help for Oremia's husband's sake. Toby Blythe was not merely an old friend who deserved better than the scandal and the mockery this would cause, he was a man with a public reputation to preserve, upon which his position depended and his power to do a great deal of good—good about which Vespasia cared profoundly. He was a man ahead of his time in seeking to widen the franchise, an altruistic but unpopular cause among his peers. Ridicule would be the most potent of weapons against him.

"What happened?" she inquired, not entirely sympathetically. Certainly she was curious.

Oremia was torn between the desire to defend herself and a need to enlist Vespasia's help. Self-preservation won. "I . . ." She steeled herself, her expression reflecting her dilemma. "I had an . . . assignation here. My lover"— she said the word with a brightness in her eyes and the flicker of a smile on her lips—"my lover had not yet left when Ferdie came in. I had no choice!" She raised her shoulders in an elegant shrug. "I could not allow him to find us here! I did the only thing I could. I had the lamp in my hand . . . I used it."

"I see," Vespasia said dryly.

"For heaven's sake, what am I to do?" Oremia's voice was rising, and there was a note of panic in it. "Help me!"

Vespasia forced herself to think of Toby and stifle the response that came naturally to her tongue. Toby had been not unadmiring of Vespasia in the past. She had most agreeable memories of him. She could smile even now as she thought of them. Her mind raced. How many believable explanations were there for this rather ridiculous scene?

"It's not amusing!" Oremia snapped, her face pink. "Have you any idea—"

"A very vivid idea," Vespasia said coolly. "A great many ribald jokes, none of them flattering." She had no knowledge who the lover might have been and did not choose to ask. The solution was now fully formed in her mind. "Put that lamp down, or what remains of it . . . there!" She pointed to the floor about a yard from Ferdie's head. "And go back to your bed. Close your door. As far as the rest of the world is concerned, you slept through the night without waking. You heard and saw nothing at all."

Oremia stared at her as if she hardly dared believe her.

"Go on!" Vespasia ordered. "Before Ferdie comes to his senses and it's too late!"

"Oh! Yes. Yes, of course. Vespasia . . ." Still, she hesitated, breathing heavily.

"No, I won't tell Toby," Vespasia said, answering the unspoken question. "Now hurry, and do exactly as I told you."

"Yes. I will." And this time she swept past Vespasia, who caught her by the arm as she was about to fling the door open.

"Watch!" she hissed. "Make sure there is no one there! You can't afford to be seen!" She nearly added "you fool!" and bit her tongue only at the last moment. Vespasia was still the most beautiful woman in the house, perhaps even in England, but she was twenty years older than Oremia Blythe, and she had learned a little wisdom and perhaps a little regret.

Oremia caught her breath in a sob, keeping her back to Vespasia, her shoulders stiff. Possibly it was embarrassment, but more likely it was anger. She put her hand on the doorknob and turned it very slowly. The latch freed, and she pulled it open no more than three inches, then four, then a foot. "There's no one here," she said with satisfaction, as if she had known it all along.

"Then go quickly," Vespasia commanded. "And stay in your room unless something happens that would waken the dead."

Oremia swung around. "Such as what?"

"An explosion or a fire alarm!" Vespasia said tartly. "I don't know!"

Oremia disappeared along the corridor and around the corner. Vespasia turned back into the room. Mercifully, Ferdie Wakeham was still insensible. She wondered if she ought to hit him again, just to make sure he remained that way. She still had a considerable amount to do, for which she required his mental absence. But she did not wish to injure the poor man beyond what was absolutely necessary.

She paused only a moment. She would trust to luck. Besides, what she planned to do must be done immediately, and there was no other weapon readily to hand.

She went over to the window and opened it, gave him a last swift look to make sure he was still showing no signs of returning to consciousness, then slipped out the door herself and went along the corridor to the linen cupboard. She opened the door and whisked inside, pulling it almost closed, and waited, her eye to the crack.

She was just in time. She had barely arranged herself when a figure passed by—a lush, feminine figure, all gleaming skin and rustling silk, most inappropriate for a discreet assignation. It was the Honorable Mrs. Leonora Vickery—fourth bedroom on the left, east wing.

As soon as Leonora had passed on her way to the spare room—and passed Ferdie Wakeham, whom she would expect to be there awaiting her—Vespasia came out of the linen cupboard, picked up her skirts and ran down the corridor, across the landing and into the east wing. She passed the first door, second, third, and opened the fourth. She went in, swung around, closed the door silently and immediately turned up the gas, which was so low as to be barely burning at all.

She looked around the room. The bedcovers were thrown back where Leonora had climbed out. The brushes and combs were set out on the dressing table, the chair askew where she had sat arranging her hair before leaving. There was her jewel box. That was what Vespasia needed. In half a dozen strides she passed to the window and threw up the sash. The night air was warm and faintly scented with cut grass. One of the gardeners had trimmed the croquet lawn in the afternoon.

She went back to the dressing table and picked up the jewel box, making sure all the drawers were closed, then took it to the window and threw it out, sending it as far as she could. She closed the window, as quietly as possible. Even so, it made a slight click.

She turned down the gas again and opened the door a crack. Thank heaven there was no one else about. She could not afford to hesitate even an instant. Leonora would have found Ferdie by now and with any luck would have realized she could not afford to be discovered in the west wing at this hour of the night. Even if he had cried out, she could not possibly have heard him had she been in her own room, or anywhere else for which she could provide a reasonable explanation. And a glance would tell her Ferdie needed some medical attention.

The only disaster would be if Leonora panicked, or if Ferdie had not enough sense to realize he needed assistance, or conceivably if Leonora were so in love with him that she threw caution and both their reputations to the wind and summoned help on the spot. Mercifully, not likely!

Vespasia came out of the east wing onto the landing and passed the foot of the stairs leading up to the attic, where the servants had their rooms. This flight of stairs was for convenience, for valets and ladies' maids to come as soon as summoned. There was a large vase of flowers on a table. It was crooked, as if someone had knocked it in the extremely dim light.

She turned into the west wing and stopped abruptly, her heart beginning to beat violently. Someone was moving at the far end! Leonora! Vespasia had meant to be back in the linen cupboard by now. She had been too slow! If she were caught here, Leonora would be bound to leap to the conclusion that Vespasia was out of her bed for the same purpose she was herself!

Vespasia would greatly prefer not to give Leonora such a weapon in her hand. Should she turn the landing light down so far that she would not be seen?

Yes!

No! Then Leonora might fall over something in the dark and possibly raise the house. Vespasia could just imagine the scene if Leonora knocked over the vase of flowers at the bottom of the servants' stairs. Or the jardiniere by the banisters. How could she possibly explain that? Inebriated—at the very kindest! But on the landing in the middle of the night?

More likely, Leonora would turn up the gas again, and certainly see Vespasia, and wonder what in heaven's name she was doing. Then there would be only one conclusion—and not a charitable one.

She was coming. Vespasia could hear the rustle of silks. Stupid woman!

Vespasia flattened herself against the wall next to the potted palm and stood rigid, almost breathless.

Leonora came out of the corridor and passed within a yard of her. Her almond-flower perfume was sweet in the air. She was tiptoeing, watching where she was going. She was breathing heavily. Not surprising. She had just found Ferdie senseless on the floor and debated what to do. Vespasia had relied on the shock causing her to pause at least a few moments before leaving.

Now Leonora was going back to her own room. She passed by the newel post of the main stairway down, safely negotiated around the jardiniere and then the table at the bottom of the servants' stairs. A moment later she was into the east corridor and back in her own room.

The instant the crack of light disappeared from under Leonora's door, Vespasia swung around and ran along the west corridor past her own room and into the unoccupied room where Ferdie Wakeham still lay amid the shattered pieces of the lamp. He was just beginning to stir.

"Oh, Ferdie!" Vespasia exclaimed with horror. "How incredibly brave of you!"

"Wha . . . What?" He blinked, opened his eyes and winced sharply as the light caught them. "Ooh! Ooooh." He put out his hand and caught it on a piece of broken glass. He swore loudly and snatched his hand away, putting it to his lips to stop the blood. "What in hell happened?"

"You must have caught him," Vespasia said, as if it were the only possible answer.

"Caught him?" He remained motionless, acutely aware of the glass around him.

"The burglar! You heard him and came to tackle him. You caught him right here, only he seized"—she looked around, then down at the floor—"the lamp and struck you over the head." She let her expression convey her admiration for his courage and quick action. "No doubt he fled, leaving you here." She glanced meaningfully toward the window. "Please allow me to help. We owe you so much." She bent down and very carefully began picking up shards of glass and putting them in the wastebasket.

He sat blinking uncertainly.

She put the last of the pieces into the basket. "There. Now you may rise without further injury. You may be feeling a little dizzy." She looked at his head earnestly. "He appears to have struck you rather hard. I dare say he was a very large person, a complete ruffian."

"Yes . . ." Ferdie agreed. "Yes, he was rather large."

"Allow me." She offered him her hand, and he took it, climbing to his feet rather shakily. Poor Ferdie was looking very much the worse for wear. Yet had he regained his senses any sooner it would have been most unfortunate.

"Thank you." He accepted her help, swaying a little. "Yes . . . a real ruffian. I am most obliged to you. I assume you heard the . . . the lamp breaking?"

"Yes," she said quite truthfully. "I sat in bed some minutes, gathering my wits before I realized there must be something very wrong. I think I was deeply asleep."

"Yes," he nodded, and winced, standing suddenly very still. It had not been a good idea to move his head. He groaned involuntarily. "Yes, of course," he whispered.

"I think we had better raise the servants and see what damage he has done," she said. "And perhaps get some ministration for your head. That cut looks rather unpleasant. I don't doubt you will have a severe headache in the morning, if you have not one already."

"I have," he said ruefully. "I've never had a hangover like it." He smiled at her. "This is worse than rough cider . . . or at least as bad."

"Come." She offered her arm again and, when he took it, led him to the door and back along the corridor to the landing. She sat him in the only comfortable chair and turned up the gas in all the brackets. There was still no noise in the house. If anyone was awake, he or she was being remarkably discreet, assuming the movement was all illicit and better unobserved.

Vespasia went to the foot of the servants' stairs, ready to go up if necessary and waken one of the valets to minister to Ferdie. She noticed the crooked vase again. It was exactly where someone would have caught it on the way up if passing in a hurry, or in the dim light. Who would be going up there in the half dark and not want to straighten a vase he or she had knocked?

Oremia's lover! Because he did not want to be seen and feared he might be—after Ferdie had intruded into the bedroom he presumed not occupied, only to find a previous pair of lovers about to leave.

And the lover would go up there rather than to his own room, unless his own room were indeed up there. Oremia had been sleeping with one of the servants!

Vespasia knew which one it would be—the remarkably handsome young footman with the dark hair and the curving lips and fine legs. Really, how could Oremia be so—so incredibly, monumentally stupid? To betray Toby with one of his friends was bad enough, with a footman was appalling! If it became known, Toby would be mocked or pitied, or both. His effectiveness to do good, his life's goals, would be nullified. Who would take him seriously?

Vespasia was so furious she could hardly swallow. All for the sake of a few moments' utterly selfish gratification! Oremia had known the wretched man barely a week, and she had used him simply for her own enjoyment. He was hardly in a position to refuse her. She could ruin him with a word, and if rejected might well do so out of spite! Vespasia felt the anger settle inside her like a stone, but she was helpless to do anything about it. She must protect Oremia for Toby's sake, and because she had said she would.

She marched up the stairs, fists clenched, and knocked lightly and firmly on the butler's bedroom door, and then again, in case he should doubt what he had heard.

It was opened after several moments, and a very anxious face appeared in the crack, his nightcap askew. He blinked before he recognized Vespasia.

"Lady Cumming-Gould! Is something amiss, my lady?"

"Yes, I am afraid so, Harcourt. It seems Sir Ferdinand has disturbed an intruder and been attacked when he tried to apprehend him. He is not very seriously hurt, but he was knocked insensible for some few minutes and has a very nasty cut on his head. We are not aware of anything that has been taken."

"Oh, dear." Harcourt gathered his wits very quickly. "That is dreadful. Are you all right, my lady?"

"Yes, thank you, Harcourt, I am quite unhurt. Perhaps you might call whoever on the staff is best able to minister to injury and a severe headache, and then see if anything is missing or anyone else disturbed. Although I have heard no other sound."

"Certainly, my lady. That would be most wise. I shall come straight down," and he retreated behind the door. Vespasia assumed he was arranging his clothing with a suitable dignity. After all, he was the principal among the servants and must always appear to be in command.

She went downstairs again and found Ferdie still looking pained and very groggy, propped up by the chair rather than sitting in it. "I think you need a stiff brandy," she observed. "Or perhaps one of my maid's herbal preparations against headache and a brandy afterward."

"I think I'll take the brandy," he said with more decision than she had thought him capable of.

Vespasia smiled. "You don't surprise me," she murmured. "Although, Ferdie, I do think the herbs might have a more lasting result."

"I'll have the brandy," he repeated.

She smiled very slightly. "I think next time you hear burglars in the night, you would be wise not to involve Leonora," she said casually.

"Oh . . ." He looked nonplussed, then suddenly blushed deeply. "Oh, yes . . . of course. I . . ."

She turned away, so as not to witness his embarrassment. She had said enough. He knew she knew.

Harcourt came down the stairs looking purposeful, with two ladies' maids and a valet behind him. The brandy was sent for, and the herbs, plus a bowl of hot water, ointment, and plaster.

Within minutes doors were knocked on, and people began to appear in various stages of sleepiness and disarray. A full ten minutes passed before Leonora Vickery came stumbling out of her room, wailing loudly that her jewelry had been stolen—all of it, even including the case in which she kept it. It was monstrous! She had been robbed of everything!

"Not quite everything," Vespasia observed in an aside. "I rather fancy something of it you were willing to give." But fortunately, no one heard her, or if they did, they were too stunned and generally dazed to take it in or question her meaning. Not that people often questioned Vespasia, in any event.

By three o'clock in the morning Ferdie's wound had been seen to, and he had been returned to his bed. Leonora had been comforted and assured that every possible avenue would be pursued in order to recover her jewels. Finally,

everyone else in the household had gone back to their rooms.

At nine o'clock in brilliant sunlight Vespasia came along the corridor to the landing, ready to go downstairs for the day. By now, no doubt, the garden staff would have found Leonora's jewel box and everything would be returned to her. Ferdie would have a resounding headache, but it would eventually go, and he would be little the worse for the adventure. At least he could pose as the hero. He would certainly never deny that.

On the whole, Vespasia felt rather pleased with herself, and as always she looked magnificent.

Toby Blythe was going down the stairs. Vespasia watched his straight back and dark head, now definitely touched with gray here and there, and smiled with delightful memory.

Then Oremia swirled out of the east corridor, her skirts flying in an enormous bouffant of rose-pink and wine. Her face was sickeningly pale and her eyes like sockets in her head.

Vespasia was startled and her composure completely shaken. "What is it?" she gasped. "Oremia!"

"My diamonds, Vespasia!" Oremia said in a dry whisper, so quiet Vespasia barely heard her. "My diamonds have been stolen!"

Vespasia drew in her breath, her hands flew to her lips and she stifled a laugh. "Oh, my dear!" she said with only the merest shred of sympathy. "If you will sleep with the footman, you must expect a certain inconvenience!"

Oremia glared at her, then whirled around and sailed down the stairs after her husband.

Vespasia sighed, and smiled, then followed her down, her head high, her ivory skirts touching the banister rails on both sides.

BEAUBIEN

Deborah Morgan

RAISED ON A RANCH in Grove, Oklahoma, Deborah Morgan (1955–) went on to become a rodeo queen, so it is not surprising that she has great affection for writing westerns as well as mystery fiction; she is an award-winning writer in both genres.

Death Is a Cabaret (2001), the first novel in her antiques-lover's mystery series featuring former FBI agent Jeff Talbot, was nominated for the Barry Award, won the Reader's Choice Award at Chicago's Love is Murder conference, and was one of only two paperback original mysteries to be noted in *Publishers Weekly*'s "The Year in Books" (2001). All five novels in the series made the Independent Mystery Booksellers Association bestseller list, with the third (*The Marriage Casket*, 2003) taking the number one slot.

Before moving to Michigan in 1993 to "join typewriters" with Loren D. Estleman, Morgan was managing editor of a biweekly newspaper in southeast Kansas and earlier was managing editor of the nation's number one treasure-hunting magazine. She also served as editor of the Private Eye Writers of America newsletter for three years.

When asked to submit a private eye story featuring Mary Shelley, her private eye character, for the anthology *Mystery Street*, Morgan chose to set it on Motown's Beaubien Street, home to the Detroit Police Department for ninety years, drawing on her observations during her years as a dispatcher for her hometown police department and later for the Oklahoma Highway Patrol.

"Beaubien" was originally published in *The Private Eye Writers of America Presents: Mystery Street #2*, edited by Robert J. Randisi (New York, Signet, 2001); it was first collected in *Junction* (Hertford, North Carolina, Crossroad Press, 2015).

Beaubien

DEBORAH MORGAN

AS MANY TIMES as I've walked into Detroit Police Headquarters, it still makes me nervous.

I can't think why. I'm not a criminal. But my heart thuds like a Ford engine on a cold morning, then gains rpm's and pounds hell against my ribcage. My *nerve* begs for a shot of anything. My senses are never sharper.

You know the feeling. The nervousness causes one of three reactions at any given time: fear (always visible in one form or another), cockiness (on the defense and ready to take on anything and anybody), or innocence (coupled with a determination to prove it by keeping a low profile). Point of fact: any one of these emotions will put the cops on red alert.

We're screwed, no matter what.

Today, I opted for low profile. Lieutenant Harold Bittenbinder had asked me to come by for a piece of birthday cake that the department had ordered. Rumor had it Harry was turning 55 on Saturday. Since my father never reached that age and Harry doesn't have any daughters, I was honored to be included.

I made it through the metal detector without a peep from either of us. That always surprises me.

Down the hall, just outside the bank of elevators, was a display case containing memorabilia for sale. I wondered how many of the navy blue coffee mugs emblazoned with *Detroit P.D.* in gold were being unwrapped on the fourth floor by our birthday boy.

By the time I arrived the party was in full swing. Harry spotted me and made his way through the post-battle confusion of uniforms and smoke, a Polaroid shot in one hand and a mug from the case downstairs in the other. Instinctively, I looked at his desk. Triplets.

If a two-hundred-forty-pound German American can bubble, Harry was bubbling. "Look at this, Mary!" He shoved a photo of the cake up to my face. It had been designed in the image of a double-nickel speed limit sign. Catchy.

"Where's the real thing, Harry? I haven't eaten all day."

"You don't wanna see it. It looks like a train wreck."

I was starving, so I took my chances. After surviving two pieces of cake and countless curious stares directed my way, I went back in search of Harry. I hadn't planned ahead, but hoped he was free for dinner. When I found him, he was talking with a young uniformed officer who looked like she'd be more at home on the cover of *Vogue* than in a squad car.

"Lee Khrisopoulis," Harry said, "meet Mary Shelley, a good friend and a hell of a PI. Mary, Lee's one of the best cops we've got."

She awkwardly shifted a cigarette to her left hand and took my extended right. I noted that her grip was as firm as my own.

"Harry says you're the best PI since Philip Marlowe."

"That's saying a lot, coming from this old man." I squeezed his arm. "The cake was great, Harry, but I need to find something more substantial. Can you join me?"

Just then, Harry was hailed from across the room. "Can't. I'll call you later." He left, and I turned to Lee.

Her smile behind the olive skin was still intact, but her dark eyes told me something was up. "Meet me. Pegasus. Fifteen."

I nodded, understanding, and smiled. "A pleasure meeting you, too."

I walked out the front door and onto Beaubien, fed the meter on the way past my Chevy, then turned the corner and took in the aromas of skordalia, baklava, and ouzo. If I worked down here, I'd gain back every pound I'd lost since my divorce.

The only person I know who can bake better than the Greeks is my son, Vic. He learned in Michigan's culinary institute called the state prison system from a French-trained chef who had used his knife to fillet a restaurant owner for shorting his paycheck.

As I walked, I caught myself hoping that Officer Khrisopoulis was being melodramatic. Vic was joining me for the Fourth of July festivities, with a Tigers game and some cold ones thrown in, and I didn't want to spend my time playing gumshoe.

When I arrived at the Pegasus, instinct told me to search out a more secluded table. I ordered a beer and a sampler plate of appetizers that included spanakopita, dolmathes yalantzi, and saganaki. Apparently, I'd bastardized the pronunciations so much that the waitress repeated my order of spinach triangles, stuffed grape leaves, and cheese that's been set on fire in English so I'd know what I was in for.

When Lee arrived by way of the back door, she slid into the chair opposite me and ordered coffee. "I don't have much time, so I'll cut to it. The powers that be want to partner me up with a new cop on the force for a special detail. I'd like to know more about him beforehand."

My brows shot up. "You pulled cloak-and-dagger crap on me for this? Why didn't you have someone at headquarters get you the lowdown? Harry, for instance?"

"No. Even if I weren't a female cop—which I am—it'd be difficult to check out another officer."

"Yeah, for all of us. Do you have any reason not to trust this new cop?"

"Nothing like that. Just trying to watch my back is all." The waitress put our drinks in front of us. Officer Khrisopoulis gulped the steaming liquid and set the cup down with a thud. "No one can know about this. Not even Harry. Got it?"

"I can handle that."

"I'd like a daily report, too. Meet me here at the same time every day and I'll pay you for the extra trouble. Can you handle that, too?"

I said I could. "But I'll warn you, I may not have much to report by tomorrow. Could be a challenge to dig up much on a new cop, working from the outside in."

"Easier than from the inside out." She pulled a cigarette from her pocket and lit it and took a ragged drag. "The cop's name is Joey Partello. Just over six feet, dark, buff—some would say sexy, if you're into the Italian lover type."

"Anything distinguishing?"

"That's not distinguishing enough for you?"

"I like my men short and near-sighted. Less competition that way." I waited for a smile. She didn't oblige. "What does he drive?"

"When he's off duty, he drives a dark blue Jimmy, loaded."

"Off duty is when?"

"The harsh, bright light of day."

I nodded.

The waitress showed up with my appetizers, touched a match to the saganaki and yelled

Opaa! Khrisopoulis was gone before the flames died out.

It was getting close to five o'clock, so I made the appetizers serve as dinner, then searched out the pay phone and called my source at the Secretary of State's office. If you're not in Michigan, you probably know it as the DMV. There is the seldom, wonderful occasion when the computers aren't down, and this was one of them. I obtained Officer Partello's address, and decided to make a swing-by to check it out.

For the most part, the old Italian neighborhood hadn't changed since FDR was president and Ford was making bomber parts for the war effort. Joey Partello's house looked pretty much like the other clapboard homes that lined the street—for now, anyway. A sign out front boasted TRIPLE A CONSTRUCTION and on the driveway were stacks of smooth-planed lumber. Sacks of cement formed a barricade in front. Footings had been trenched along the east side of the original structure, about ten feet out; they cornered and continued out of sight around back.

Our Officer Partello was sinking a hefty chunk into a major addition.

I drove to the next block and pulled over to where a plump Italian woman was walking along the edge of the yard, picking tomatoes from vines that formed a frame around the property and hammocking them in a red-stained apron. Anywhere but here and I'd have thought it was blood. Hell, I'd have thought the same thing in an Italian restaurant. In the safety of the neighborhood, though, it was always tomato sauce.

"Nice house," I said by way of introduction.

She glanced up, then went back to picking tomatoes. When she spoke, her accent was as thick as marinara. "We've been here since '42."

I took that to mean she liked the place.

She stopped picking, then, and sized me up. "You looking for a house?"

I love it when they make the job this easy. "Yes, ma'am. I thought that was a for sale sign."

I pointed toward Partello's. "Turns out it's a construction outfit advertising what they haven't done yet."

"That's the way of things these days. Joey would like to sell out, but—" she paused to cross herself—"he knows his mother would haunt him from the grave, so he's changing everything he can about the look of the place." She pulled a guilty look, as if she'd spoken out of turn. Apparently in order to absolve herself, she added, "He's paying cash, though. That's a good sign he's sticking with the old ways."

"A tough order nowadays."

"For some, I suppose." She paused, then picked up a small basket of tomatoes and handed it to me. "Go home and make some spaghetti. You're rail thin."

I didn't have the heart to tell her I couldn't cook.

There wasn't much more I could do that night, so I went home and drew a hot bath in the old clawfoot tub I'd rescued from the junk pile that came with the place. After an admirable attempt at becoming a prune, I set my alarm for God-awful early and turned in.

At three minutes after seven the next morning, I was at the intersection of Clinton and Beaubien when Partello pulled the Jimmy out of police parking and headed over to Brush. Tailing the cop was as easy as following a train down a railroad track. He took a left on Madison and nosed the Jimmy in for valet parking at the Detroit Athletic Club. I breezed on by.

The DAC. I knew the place, only because I'd once had a client ask me to meet him there in the Grill Room. With the annual membership fee of thirty-five hundred dollars, I had to wonder if I should trade in my plastic badge for a cop's shield.

While Partello spent the next hour working up a sweat in the comfort of an air-conditioned weight room, I trolled for parking under anything that looked like it might offer some shade. Giving that up, I sat and perspired.

My Corsica's air conditioner blew as hot as Ross Perot and by the time my cop emerged at eight fifteen, I was mopping up rivulets of sweat that ran between my breasts and down my stomach with a Subway napkin I'd found under the front seat.

The Jimmy took off and I tailed it until it entered Partello's neighborhood. I figured him to be going home for some sleep. I made my way to the City-County Building, thinking that a peek at some of the cases featuring Partello would give me an idea about how this new little rich cop was getting along with the fine citizens of Detroit.

As I walked past the bronzed, muscular statue of a man known as the Spirit of Detroit, it only served to remind me how much time had passed since I'd been laid.

Public records are a private eye's best friend. According to them, Joey Partello had been on the Motor City's payroll longer than Chrysler had sucked hind tit to Chevrolet. I traced cases back five, ten, twelve, sixteen years—Partello's name was all over the place.

It didn't make any sense. I wasn't sure how long Lee Khrisopoulis had been with the force, but she'd have to have her head buried not to know that Partello was a fixture. I knew one thing: Our prearranged meeting wasn't soon enough.

I drove to headquarters.

The officer standing guard at the metal detector checked his roster and told me that Khrisopoulis was on days off.

I debated looking in on Harry, but what was I going to say? I was admittedly confused, even a little ticked off. But until I knew what this goose chase was about, Lee Khrisopoulis was my client and I had promised confidentiality. I'd give it, too, at least until the odds showed that I needed to do otherwise.

For the second time in recent history, I called the Secretary of State's office. My source asked if my calls were going to come in threes, like death.

"You never know until that third one hits, do you?"

He didn't have a comeback, so he gave me the information I needed and hung up.

The house looked like a Norman Rockwell painting in a Norman Rockwell neighborhood, light years from the barred windows and graffiti of downtown Detroit. I hurried up the concrete walk that led to the front door, noting that the flower gardens were in need of weeding. I had a sudden image of America's Painter turning in his grave.

I stood head-on in front of the fisheye, figuring that any smart cop would check the peephole before opening the door.

Lee Khrisopoulis didn't disappoint me. She flung the door open and yelled, "What in the hell do you think you're doing?"

"Turn that question around and walk it right back at yourself." I eyed her evenly. "Joey Partello has been on the force nearly as long as Coleman Young was in office. But you knew that already, didn't you?"

She grabbed my arm and pulled me inside. As thoughts of police brutality shot through my mind, she slammed the door, jerked the cigarette from her mouth, and jammed her eye to the peephole.

I'd never seen anyone look more disgusting with a smoke. But I hadn't been sent here from Lung Patrol. "You're paying me for this little game," I started, "so here's your money's worth. He's got some dough. I don't know how he's making it, but I can find that out, too, if it's important to you. Also got a major remodel going on, and he's apparently making enough money to join the crowd at the DAC."

She turned, surprised. "You got all that in twenty-four hours?"

"Hell, don't you know anything about gathering information? I had all that before your first cup of coffee this morning."

"Harry told me you were good," she said matter-of-factly.

"Did Harry put you up to this? Tell him April Fools was three months ago."

"No, Harry doesn't know about this." She took another drag, went for the peephole again, then backed up and fanned smoke like she was fighting off bees. "I meant it when I said no one else could know about this. I had to be sure you could do a job quickly and without anyone getting suspicious. Besides, I figured my odds were better with you since you're a woman. I thought you would understand."

"The first thing *you* need to understand is that acting like a damn woman will bring six courses of hell down on you. Start acting like a cop."

"You're right." She made a sound that could've passed for either a laugh or a cry. "Of course, if I weren't a woman, I wouldn't be in this damn mess."

"You're giving men way too much credit."

"Possibly, but I have reason to. Do you know what kind of danger you've put me in by coming here? Not to mention yourself."

"Since you seem to be playing some sort of game with me, how the hell am I *supposed* to know? It took me no time to get the scoop on Joey Partello. I sure as hell wasn't going to wait around for our meeting this afternoon. Now, are you going to tell me what this is about, or do I walk?"

"I'm paying you five hundred a day." She turned and glared at me. "That should be enough to make you stick to the game plan."

"I don't play games, Officer." I grabbed for the doorknob.

She stopped me. "You can't leave now."

"Watch me."

"I'm not the one watching." She let go of my arm and nodded toward the door.

It was my turn to check the spy hole. There was a blue sedan parked up the street, the same one I'd noticed earlier when I'd pulled up.

She started walking. "Come sit down. I'll tell you the whole sordid story."

The officer's home was immaculate, except for an ashtray full of butts on the coffee table. When she started to light up another smoke, I frowned.

She paused, then slid it back in the pack. "I didn't smoke before . . . well, before everything. Thought it would calm my nerves, but it probably just shows how much of a wreck I really am, doesn't it?"

"Pretty much."

She nodded. "Have you ever had your privacy violated, Mrs. Shelley?"

"Mary."

"Mary. Your home invaded? Things taken?"

We were seated on the couch, angled toward each other. I shook my head, waited for her to continue.

"It started three months ago. I work the Property Room at headquarters. Items began disappearing. When I reported what was going on, I started getting threats.

"Then someone gained entry to my house, my *home*. It wasn't a B and E, and it didn't look like anything was missing. But I knew someone had been in here." She shuddered slightly, then went on with her story.

"Do you know what it's like to realize that? To walk into a room and *know* that someone had been there? To wonder, Did he sit on that chair? Did he go through my clothing? Did he see his reflection in the bathroom mirror—the mirror I have to look in every day? And the kitchen. Did he put poison in my orange juice? Did he hide something in the cereal box?

"It almost drove me insane. I ended up throwing out everything in the house. But I couldn't figure out what he'd been doing here."

"How do you know it was a he?"

"He called, finally. Asked if I'd determined what was missing."

"So he *did* take something."

"Oh, yeah, he took something, all right."

I waited for her to tell me what it was. She didn't offer. "So?" I prodded.

"How in the hell do I say this?" She buried her face in her hands.

"Just say it, Lee. You're not going to shock me."

She looked at me. "Okay. Panties. He stole a pair of panties from the bathroom hamper."

"Panties? Why in the hell would he want—" I stopped. There could only be one explanation, unless he was a pervert. "DNA, right?"

"Yes. Damn it. Partello found out I was having an affair with a married man. Worse than that, actually—a fellow officer. The DNA from the panties can prove it.

"That's why I think he's the one. Partello. The one who was here, the one who's been calling, threatening me, threatening us. And if my friend's wife finds out, well . . . It will kill him if he loses his wife and kids.

"You see, my friend found out about a crooked cop ring. He doesn't have proof yet, but he's getting close—and it looks like Partello is the leader. So, my friend confronted him—I begged him not to, but he really thought he could use the cops' unwritten code of loyalty. Partello just told him that loyalty was a two-way street. Apparently, he started doing some investigating of his own. He threatened to expose us. Leverage, you know.

"Only now, my friend is wondering if he should bust the ring—for the greater cause. He feels that less people will be hurt in the long run, that it may be worth risking his marriage. It's eating him up."

I waited, taking it all in. When she didn't volunteer any more information I said, "What do you think?"

"At first, I thought all I wanted was to get the panties back. Remove the incriminating evidence from the equation. But now, laying it all out like this?" She shrugged. "Nothing makes me sicker than crooked cops. The police department is supposed to be made up of people who are willing to serve and protect. Sounds corny, sometimes, when you boil it down to that. But I don't want to see the department under siege from within."

"You're a twenty-first-century Beaubien."

"What?"

"Mademoiselle Beaubien?" I watched her face, but nothing registered. "Don't tell me they let you work at 1300 Beaubien without telling you where the name came from. Chief Pontiac united all the Indian tribes in the Northwest Territory to lay siege against Fort Detroit."

"When the hell did this happen?"

"Something like three hundred years ago. This young French woman named Beaubien—I don't know her first name—learned of it and warned the Fort's commander. Saved the day, as it were. More than that, really. She saved Detroit."

"You're our Beaubien," I continued, "only you're already on the inside. You need to dig the department out of this. We just have to figure out how."

"I don't know about that, but I do know one thing. I don't want this to hinge on an incriminating pair of panties." She lit a cigarette, then laughed bitterly. "Sounds like the damned White House, doesn't it?"

"Just like," I said.

"Well, I can't help that. But I can tell you that I haven't been with my friend since Partello was in my home."

"The property that's missing. What is it?"

For the first time, she looked truly frightened. "Drugs," she said. "Meth, crack, coke, heroin, GHB—a.k.a. the date-rape drug—tons of marijuana. Drugs. Lots and lots of drugs."

We talked over options, laid some new ground rules that we both could live with, and worked on our strategy.

I asked about the blue sedan.

"One of Partello's boys. Been watching the house, but I haven't caught anyone tailing me while I'm at work. My guess is there are enough cops involved to watch me while I'm on duty." A tremor shook her body. "It's scary, not knowing who to trust."

I told her where I'd parked and asked if my car was blocking hers in the garage.

"No. I'm on the other side."

"Good. I'll leave it here for now." I told her my plan while I made a call from my cellphone. I wasn't sure if I could trust her line not to be tapped.

In twenty minutes, Vic was following my

instructions to the letter, slowly pulling through the alley behind Lee's house. I darted across the lawn, keeping the house between me and the surveillance goon. On my cue, Vic made a rolling stop and I slipped into the back seat of his beige Plymouth.

The bland set of wheels was the last thing you'd expect someone who looked like Vic to drive. He's got a shaved head, more holes than Dillinger, and he's on the annual Christmas card lists of four tattoo emporiums.

He'd recently begun working for a lawn service so he was tanned, and his tall, slim physique was quickly showing some muscled definition. He'd be perfect for the job I had in mind.

I asked him to swing by MC Sports on the way home. He frowned, but obliged, and I made a quick run inside while he circled the parking lot so he could keep the air conditioner humming.

Plastic bag in hand, I crawled back into Vic's car and told him to swing by my office. Prometheus Investigations offers about as much leg room as a crop-duster, but its location just off Woodward is handy to my downtown haunts.

"You're always wanting to help out, right?" I asked Vic after we'd climbed the stairs to my office.

"Sure," he answered, giving the word an extra syllable with a wary lilt. He lit a Camel as if he knew he was going to need something to steady his nerves.

I handed him the shopping bag. "Here's your costume."

He leaned over a round coffee table the size of a Frisbee, ground out the cigarette in an ashtray with HOLIDAY INN printed in the bottom, and headed for the bathroom.

Plastic crackled on the other side of the bathroom door, then everything was quiet. When Vic spoke, I could barely hear his voice from the other side of the door. He'd uttered a confused-sounding *What the hell?* that was followed by more silence.

Then: "No way!"

That, I could've heard from Cleveland.

"Mom," he said then with that two-syllable singsong he'd used as a teenager when he was annoyed with me, "you gotta be shitting me."

"You can get in the men's locker room at the DAC a hell of a lot easier than I can. Besides, you pick locks better than I do."

He was still cursing as he walked out of the bathroom, wearing the tennis whites and carrying a racket and a navy duffel bag. "I look like a damn Harvard prep."

"Not yet you don't. Tuck in the shirttail and lose the nose ring. Where's the belt I bought?"

Getting the panties was as simple as throwing fifty bucks out the window. There's always someone around to pick it up.

Vic told me how he'd gone about it, how the kid gathering up towels in the locker room had told him he looked ridiculous in that get-up.

Vic paused and gave me a told-you-so smirk. When I didn't say anything, he got back down to business.

He'd agreed with the guy, then cut to the chase and told him it was a front. This excited the kid, so Vic pulled the fifty from his pocket and asked which of the vertical coffins belonged to Partello. The kid spit out the number, took the bill, and offered to stand watch while Vic picked the lock. The red lace panties were zipped up tight in a plastic evidence bag inside a sneaker.

Sometimes you had to wonder how a crooked cop ever hooked together enough brain cells to pull off a scam.

I arranged a meeting with Harry while Vic paid a few calls to his connections in Detroit's underworld. Don't ask; I don't and I never will. After getting Vic out from under his father's spell, I learned to thank God for every day I have with my son. I can't do much more than that. After all he's been through, my son is in many ways a lot older than I am.

We—Vic and I—reconnoitered at my office and, after an all-clear from Lee, swung by her place and picked up my Corsica. I checked the glove compartment first thing for my Smith & Wesson .22 snub-nose.

We subverted, snaking our way along backroads and through subdivisions in what we determined was a successful job of arriving at my house un-tailed. We had a pizza delivered and waited for nightfall.

Besides the oppressive humidity, another drawback of summer is the challenge of where to hide a gun on you without the benefit of jackets. At least my weapon's small, so I can usually come up with something.

Tonight I opted for a stylish rendition of a fishing vest I'd bought in khaki and dyed black for just such occasions. It's longer than a man's vest and the zip pockets are priceless for stakeouts, bugouts, and my all-too-infrequent campouts. It's made of lightweight cotton with an elastic insert at the middle of the back which provides just enough gathers to camouflage the .22 I had tucked in my waistband.

I was parked down Beaubien, as far away from police headquarters as I could get and still be able to see anything. I'd driven my pickup—a '56 GMC stepside, ginger metallic—in case Lee's goon was watching for my Chevy, and had let Vic out to walk from my office.

I watched for him now, using the binoculars he'd given me for Christmas. When I saw him climb the steps and go through the doors of 1300, something gripped my chest like a vise and I regretted having ever dragged him into this.

I thought about the conversation I'd had earlier with Harry. I'd persuaded him to trust me on this one, told him that Vic had a great *in*, that he was going to tell the guy in Property to use his cellphone and call the cop ring's street connection to verify that Vic had been sent there to pick up the goods.

"Vic's not in that racket anymore," Harry had said.

"I know that, and you know that. As it turns out, the other guy doesn't know that."

"Hell, Mary, how can you be sure?"

"I guess I can't be, but Vic told me not to ask questions. He just said that the thing he has on this drug dealer is a hell of a lot more dangerous to the guy than a few crooked cops." I closed my eyes, as if that would erase my fears. "Harry, if I knew the things Vic learned under the tutelage of his father and his years in Jackson prison . . . well, it would scare me a damn sight more than his trying to buy drugs from a cop while you're hiding in the wings."

Bittenbinder sighed heavily. "What if something goes wrong? If Vic gets hurt—"

"You think I haven't thought of that? If I didn't think Vic could handle it, I'd nix the whole thing right now. But remember, Harry, you have no choice. You can't use a cop on this one. We'll just have to make sure we cover every base. You can position yourself so that Vic's covered. Lee will be there, too.

"You know how good Vic is with electronics," I went on. "He's rigged up a recorder in this huge gothic cross he wears on a chain around his neck—"

"We'll modify it," Harry said, "make it a wire and put one of my men at the other end."

"Let's get on it, then." I'd said, glad to see that Harry was back in cop mode.

I knew I wouldn't make it past the metal detector, so I gave Harry a call like we'd planned earlier and he got me in by way of an old service entrance that most of the newcomers don't know about. He stashed me in a supply closet and told me to stay put until it was all over. I said okay. The lie came easily. But I wasn't about to hang back when my son might be in the cross fire.

I'd learned the layout of police headquarters earlier from Lee, so I knew I wasn't too far from the Property Room. I stepped into the hallway and moved close enough to hear what was going on inside.

"You Rutledge?" It was Vic's voice.

"Who's asking?" Cocky attitude.

I could envision Vic pointing to his tee shirt, which was being used as the code. It had a picture of Curious George lying unconscious on the ground beside an open bottle of ether. "George needs something to wake him up."

"Then I'll need to call the doctor for a prescription." More code.

I could hear the faint, high-pitched beeps as Rutledge punched buttons on a cellphone. "Yeah, Doc. I gotta sick monkey here." A pause, then: "Ether. Yep. That's the one." Another pause. "Okay. Got it." Another beep sounded as he ended the call. "Doc says you're cool. I'll go in back and get the stuff. Anybody comes down here, you play like you're lost, got it?"

"Got it," Vic said.

The time stretched on with the flesh-tingling tension of a Hitchcock film. I considered going in, but thought I heard some sort of movement so I stayed put. More time passed.

The next thing I heard was Vic ask, "What's goin' on?"

"Looks like the doctor is in." That was Rutledge's voice, sarcastic.

There was a shuffling noise. I moved closer to the door. I wanted to peek inside, see how many there were, but decided not to take the chance. Not yet.

"We've got a deal, Rutledge," Vic said. "I gave Doc, here, fifty large this afternoon. Now, tell your goon to get the gun off me." Goon. The guy from Lee's house, the blue sedan.

"Trouble down here?" It was Lee's voice. Her coming out of hiding meant only one thing: The deal had turned sour.

"Nothing that a little showdown won't fix." This was a new voice.

"Don't try it, Partello—" Lee's voice—"I've got you covered."

"The only thing you're covering is your boyfriend's ass."

"Wrong, Partello. That would be Bittenbinder covering my ass." I figured this had to be Lee's friend. "He's bearing down on you right now."

"You expect me to believe that?"

I'm not sure why, but I took that as my cue. Maybe, if I could get in there in time, Partello wouldn't check whether or not Harry was behind him. Maybe the wondering would slow him down. I pulled my gun and walked gingerly through the door.

The only thing that registered when I got in there was the gun pointed at Vic.

Words can't describe what I felt, seeing that gun zeroed in on my son. In that instant, I saw Vic—the infant I had bonded with as only a mother can; the toddler who had come to me when he fell down; the schoolboy who had come to me when he was knocked down; the teenager who had gotten snared into white-collar crime by his own father; the man who had overcome it. I saw all the incarnations that were my son, and I knew that I would kill the man who was holding a gun on him now. I knew I was going to kill Joey Partello.

I forced myself to concentrate. My heart pounded in my ears and I wasn't sure if anyone was talking, but then someone spoke and the pounding subsided. My focus had never been keener. My aim had never been sharper.

The Property Room was set up similar to an old bank, with teller windows framed in by glass partitions and a single door at one end providing access to the back where the loot was kept. Standing in that doorway was Joey Partello.

In front of Vic, on the other side of the opening, was a young male officer I took for Rutledge, and behind him was another officer—the goon—with a massive forearm across the neck of a very thin man in dark, baggy clothes. Doc. Behind Vic, and off to the right, was Lee Khrisopoulis. To her right was a uniformed officer—the boyfriend.

"Who's that?" Partello's tone told me he expected me to identify myself. He didn't move his aim away from Vic.

"You don't need to know that," Lee said.

"Shut up, bitch." Partello spoke through gritted teeth.

"Watch your mouth." This was Harry's voice.

Partello swung the gun away from Vic and toward the back, where Harry had been waiting silently.

Partello had made his mistake. As he swiveled, I put a bullet behind his right ear. He fired as he crumpled, squeezing off three rounds before he hit the ground. Everyone opened fire.

Vic lunged to the floor and slid on his stomach toward me like he was stealing home plate. Rutledge, who had fired at Vic and missed, readjusted and drew a bead on Lee and the uniformed cop opened a hole in Rutledge's chest, but not before he'd squeezed off a shot. Lee fell.

The goon, who was still holding Doc, swung around to fire on Harry and Lee's friend capped him before he got off a round. Doc pulled free of the falling man, then rolled himself up in a ball in the corner.

The gunfire stopped.

Vic and I each made sure the other hadn't been hit, then we both went to Lee. Her friend was already there, cradling her in his arms and stroking her face.

Blood was seeping from her chest, but not enough to cause the dark red puddle quickly growing under her.

I looked at the officer inquiringly.

"Ricochet got her in the back."

"Mary?" Raspy coughs came from Lee's throat.

"Yes, Lee. I'm right here." I grasped her hand.

"That French woman—Beaubien? Was she injured?"

"No, I don't think so."

"That's good." She coughed some more. "I'm a cop. I'm supposed to be ready to die."

"You're not going to die. Don't you know that?"

Lee looked at the man holding her. She tried to swallow, made a choking noise. When she spoke again, her voice was congested with liquid. "No, I can tell. But it was worth it."

"What was?" I asked.

"Saving the fort."

We left her alone with her friend.

I looked around the room. It had filled with officers. Many I recognized from Harry's birthday party, only now their faces were behind guns.

The paramedics arrived, counted fallen bodies, and called for some backup of their own.

Vic and I picked up Harry around eleven on Sunday and headed to Comerica Park. Crappy name for a baseball stadium, if you ask me. I don't care how many fountains and Ferris wheels they add, it'll never replace Tiger Stadium. Apparently, though, they've got all us die-hard fans by the balls, because we were out in full force, shoving through the wide concrete ramps toward the seats like so many cattle in the chutes.

After Harry and Vic and I had eaten our hot dogs and gotten a second round of brewskies from a vendor in an orange cap with peach fuzz on his face, Harry updated us on what he'd learned so far about the cop ring.

Five officers were involved. The two still alive after last night's shootout decided to stay that way by singing like Joe Valachi.

In spite of our efforts when Vic picked me up in Lee's alley, Goon had figured something out and tailed us. He had Polaroids of both of us on his person when he died.

Harry wrapped up by telling us that Lee Khrisopoulis's funeral would be Wednesday.

We were silent for a while and then Vic asked Harry if he knew the meaning of the word Beaubien.

"No. Do you?"

"Sure. It means 'beautiful and good.' You need to teach that to your cops."

Harry sat quietly and drank his beer.

DOUBLE-CROSSING DELANCEY

S. J. Rozan

IT WAS ALWAYS THE DREAM of Shira Judith Rozan (1950–   ) to become an architect, and when she succeeded, she decided she'd prefer to be a writer—and has succeeded at that, too. A native New Yorker (she was born in the Bronx), Rozan set her mystery novels and short stories mainly in various parts of the city.

Although Rozan has written a couple of stand-alone novels—*Absent Friends* (2004) and *In This Rain* (2006), and cowritten (with Carlos Dews) two paranormal novels under the Sam Cabot pseudonym, *Blood of the Lamb* (2013) and *Skin of the Wolf* (2014)—it is her series about Lydia Chin and Bill Smith for which she is best known. Each takes turns being the central figure in alternate novels.

Chin and Smith are partners in a private detective agency, and although they are quite different from each other, they do not make an outlandish "odd couple" pairing. Rozan has knowingly described them as based on herself. "Lydia is me as I was when I was her age," she has explained. "She's optimistic and full of energy. She believes that the world can be saved. . . . Bill, on the other hand, is me as I am now—on a bad day. He's been through enough bad stuff in his life that he knows what can't be done."

Many of their cases take them to New York's Chinatown, an area Lydia knows well, as she lives there with her mother. While she is a thoroughly modern young woman, she respects the traditions of her culture, which often conflict with her job and her life.

Most of the books in the series have been nominated for or have won most of the major mystery awards; notably, *Winter and Night* (2002) won the Edgar for best novel of the year.

"Double-Crossing Delancey" was originally published in *The Private Eye Writers of America Presents: Mystery Street #2*, edited by Robert J. Randisi (New York, Signet, 2001).

Double-Crossing Delancey

S. J. ROZAN

I NEVER TRUSTED JOE DELANCEY, and I never wanted to get involved with him, and I wouldn't have except, like most people where Joe's concerned, I was drawn into something irresistible.

It began on a bright June morning. I was ambling through Chinatown with Charlie Chung, an FOB—Fresh Off the Boat—immigrant from Hong Kong. We had just left the dojo after an early-morning workout. The air was clear, my blood was flowing and I was ready for action.

"Good work this morning," I told Charlie. I stopped to buy a couple of hot dough sticks from the lady on the corner, who was even fresher off the boat than Charlie. "You keep up that kind of thing, you'll be a rank higher by next year." I handed him a dough stick. "My treat."

Charlie bowed his head to acknowledge the compliment, and the gift; then he grinned.

"Got big plans, next year, gaje," he declared. "Going to college." In Cantonese, "gaje" means "big sister." I'm not related to Charlie; this was his Chinese way of acknowledging my role as his wise advisor, his guide on the path of life. I tried to straighten up and walk taller.

"Really?" I asked.

Charlie nodded. "By next year," he told me with complete confidence, "my English gets better, also my pockets fills up."

In the dojo, Charlie and I practice kicks and punches on each other. Outside, Charlie prac-

tices his English on me. Sometimes it feels the same.

Nevertheless, I said, "Your English is coming along, Charlie."

"Practice make perfect," he grinned, confiding, "English saying." His eyes took on a distant look. "Maybe, can put English saying in fortune cookie, sell to China. Make big money."

Fortune cookies are unknown in China; they were invented by a Japanese man in New Jersey. "Not likely, Charlie. Chinese people are too serious about food."

"You think this, gaje?" A bus full of tourists pulled around the corner. Heads hung out windows and cameras pressed against faces. Charlie smiled and waved. "Probably, right," Charlie went on. "I go look for one other way, make big money. Maybe, import lychee nuts."

I munched on my dough stick. "Lychee nuts?"

He nodded. "In USA, too much canned lychees. Too sweet, no taste, pah!"

"You can get fresh lychees here."

"Saying fresh, but all old, dry, sour. Best lychees, can't find. Import best fresh lychees, sell like crazy."

"You know, Charlie, that's not a bad idea."

"Most idea of Charlie not bad idea! Plan also, import water buffalo. Pet for American children, better than dog."

Sometimes Charlie worries me. I mean, if I'm going to be the guy's gaje, I have responsibilities. "The lychees may be a good idea, Charlie. The water buffalo is not."

Charlie, his mouth full of warm, sweet dough, mumbled, "Not?"

"Not."

Charlie hasn't learned to shrug yet. He did what Chinese people have always done: he jutted his chin forward. "If you say, gaje. Before invest big money, asking you."

"That's smart."

"Maybe," Charlie grinned wickedly, "brother-in-law also come asking you, now."

"Your sister's husband? He needs advice?"

"Too late, advice. Brother-in-law one stupid shit."

I winced. "Remember I told you there are some words you can learn but not say?"

Charlie's brow furrowed. "Stupid?"

I shook my head.

"Oh." He grinned again, and blushed. "Okay. Brother-in-law one stupid jackass."

I guessed that was better. "What did he do that was stupid?"

"Brother-in-law buying two big crates, cigarettes lighters from China. Red, picture both sides of Chairman Mao." Charlie stopped on the sidewalk to bow elaborately. I wondered what both sides of Chairman Mao looked like. "Light cigarette, play 'East is Red' same time."

"Sounds great."

"Cost brother-in-law twelve hundreds of dollars. Thinks, sell to tourists on street, make big bucks. When crates come, all lighters don't have fluid, don't have wick."

"Oh, no."

"Brother-in-law complain to guy sold him. Guy saying, 'Why you thinking so cheap? Come on, brother-in-law, I have fluid, I have wicks sell you.' Now brother-in-law sitting home filling lighters all night after job, sticking wicks in. Don't know how, so half doesn't work. Now, sell cheap, lose money. Sell expensive, tourist don't want. Also, brother-in-law lazy jackass. By tomor-row, next day, give up. Many lighters, no wick, no fluid, no bucks for brother-in-law."

My eyes narrowed as I heard this story. Leaving aside Charlie's clear sense that no bucks was about what his brother-in-law deserved, I asked, "Who was the guy your brother-in-law bought these things from, do you know? Was he Chinese?"

"Not Chinese. Some *lo faan*, meet on Delancey Street. Say, have lighters, need cash, sell cheap. I tell brother-in-law, you stupid sh—" Charlie swallowed the word "—stupid jackass, how you trust *lo faan* guy with ruby in tooth?"

"Lo faan" means, roughly, barbarian; more broadly, it means anyone not Chinese. For emphasis Charlie tapped a tooth at the center of his own grin.

"Charlie," I said, "I have to go. So do you, or you'll be late." Charlie works the eight-to-four shift in a Baxter Street noodle factory. "See you tomorrow morning."

"Sure, gaje. See you."

With another grin and a wave, Charlie was off to work. With shoulders set and purposeful stride, so was I.

These clear June mornings in New York wilt fast. It wasn't quite so bright or early, I had accomplished a number of things, and I was sweaty and flagging a little by the time I finally spotted Joe Delancey on Delancey Street.

Delancey Street is the delta of New York, the place where the flood of new immigrants from Asia meets the river of them from the Caribbean and the tide from Latin America, and they all flow into the ocean of old-time New Yorkers, whose parents and grandparents were the last generation's floods and rivers and tides. Joe Delancey could often be found cruising here, looking for money-making opportunities, and I had been cruising for awhile myself, looking for Joe.

I stepped out in front of him, blocking his path on the wide sidewalk. "Joe," I said. "We have to talk."

Joe rocked to a halt. His freckled face lit

up and his green eyes glowed with delight, as though finding me standing in his way was a pleasure, and being summoned to talk with me was a joy he'd long wished for but never dared hope to have.

"Lydia! Oh exquisite pearl of the Orient, where have you been these lonely months?"

"Joe—"

"No, wait! Do not speak." He held up a hand for silence and tilted his head to look at me. "You only grow more beautiful. If we could bottle the secret of you, what a fortune we could make." I laughed; with Joe, though I know him, I often find myself laughing.

"Do not vanish, I beg you," he said, as though I were already shimmering and fading. "Now that I have at long last found you again."

"I was looking for you, Joe."

He smiled gently. "Because Fate was impatient for us to be together, and I too much of a fool to understand." He slipped my arm through his and steered me along the sidewalk. "Come. We shall have tea, and sit awhile, and talk of many things." We reached a coffee shop. Joe gallantly pulled open the door. As I walked in past him he grinned, and when he did the ruby in his front tooth glittered in the sun.

I'd once asked him what the story was on the ruby in his tooth.

His answer started with a mundane cavity, like all of us get. Because it was in the front, Joe's dentist had suggested filling it and crowning it. "In those days, I was seeing an Indian girl," Joe had said, making it sound like sometime last century. "A Punjabi princess, a sultry beauty with a ruby in her forehead. She gave me one that matched it, as a love token. When the embers of our burning affair had faded and cooled—"

"You mean, when you'd scammed her out of all you could get?"

"—I had Dr. Painless insert my beloved's gift in my tooth, where it would ever, in my lonely moments, remind me of her."

I hadn't fully believed either the ruby or the story, and I thought Joe Delancey's idea of what to do with a love token was positively perverse. But though I'm a licensed private investigator I'm also a well-brought-up Chinese girl, and I hadn't known the Punjabi princess. I'd just looked at my watch and had some place to be.

Now, on this June morning, Joe waved a waiter over and ordered tea and Danishes. "Tea in a pot," he commanded, "for the Empress scorns your pinched and miserly cups." He turned to me with a thousand-watt smile. "Anything your heart desires, oh beauteous one, within the limited powers of this miserable establishment, I will provide. Your money is no good with Joe. A small price to pay for the pleasure of your company."

I wasn't surprised that Joe was buying. That was part of his system, he'd once confided cheerfully. Always pay for the small things. You get a great reputation as a generous guy, cheap.

In Joe's business that was a good investment.

"Joe," I began when the tea had come, along with six different Danishes, in case I had trouble deciding which kind I wanted, "Joe, I heard about the lighters."

"Ah," Joe said, nodding. "You must mean Mr. Yee. An unfortunate misunderstanding, but now made whole, I believe."

"You believe no such thing. The guy's stuck with a garage full of garbage and no way to make up his investment. You've got to lay off the new immigrants, Joe."

"Lydia. My sweet. Where you see new immigrants, I see walking goldmines. And remember, darling, never was an honest man unhorsed by me."

"Aha. So you're known around here as 'Double-crossing Delancey' for no reason."

"Sticks and stones," he sighed.

"Oh, Joe. These people are desperate. It's not fair for you to take advantage of them."

"Taking advantage of people is inherently unfair," he reflected, lifting a prune Danish from the pile. "And you can be sure each recently-come representative of the huddled masses with whom I have dealings believes himself, at first, to be taking advantage of me."

"Still," I tried again. "You took twelve hundred dollars from this guy Yee. It's a lot of money."

"Fifteen hundred, with the fluid and the wicks," Joe corrected me. "He stands to make quite a lot more than that, with the right marketing plan."

"Marketing plan? Joe, the guy's a waiter!"

"And looking to better himself. An ambition to be commended."

I sighed. "Come on, Joe. Why don't you pick on someone your own size?"

Joe bit into his pastry. "My ancestors would spin in their graves. Surely you, a daughter of a culture famous for venerating the honorable ancestors, can understand that. This street, you know, is named for my family." I suspected the reverse was closer to the truth, but held my tongue. "It is peopled, now as ever, with newly-minted Americans seeking opportunity. For a Delancey, they are gift-wrapped presents, Christmas trinkets needing only to be opened."

"You're a rat, Joe."

"Not so. In fact, I detect in you a deep appreciation of my subtle art."

"You're reading me wrong."

"If so, why are you smiling? My glossy-haired beauty, I make my living reading people. I'm rarely wrong. It's you who're in the wrong profession. You have a great future elsewhere."

"You mean, doing the kind of work you do?"

"I do. With me beside you singing in the wilderness."

I sliced off a forkful of cherry Danish. Joe, by contrast, had his entire pastry in his hand and was gouging half-moon bites from it. "Not my calling, Joe," I said.

"I disagree. You have all the instincts. You could have been one of the greats—and owed it all to me. I'd have been famous, mentor to the renown Lydia Chin." He sighed, then brightened. "The offer's still open."

"I don't like cheating people."

A gulp of tea, a shake of the head, and the retort: "Thinning the herd, darling. I only take from beggars: people who beg me to."

An old line of Joe's I'd heard before. "I know, Joe. 'You can't catch a pigeon unless he sits still.'"

"Damn correct."

"That doesn't mean he wants to be caught."

"Wrong, oh glorious one. None of the people from whom I earn my bread will ever be rich, the brains to keep away from the likes of me being the minimal criteria for financial success. I at least offer them, though for but a fleeting moment, the warm and fuzzy sense that they might someday reach that dream."

"And you're doing them a favor?"

"Oh, I am, I am. Deep down, they know that fleeting moment is all they'll ever have, and they beg me to give them that. At least that. At most that. Joe, they say in their hearts—"

"Oh, stop it, Joe," I said in my mouth. "I've heard it before. And what about your Punjabi princess? Wasn't she rich?"

"You shock me, my sweet. Surely you cannot favor the grasping retention of unearned, inherited, caste-based wealth?"

"When the other choice is having it conned out of people by someone like you, I might."

"You cut me to the quick, my gorgeous friend. It pains me to feel your lack of respect for my ecological niche. Therefore let's cease talking about me and discuss you. How goes it with you? The detecting business treating you well?"

Joe winked and attacked his Danish. I sipped my tea. Around us bustled people making a living and people taking time out from making a living. I watched them and I watched Joe and finally I spoke. "Well, I have to admit that whoever told me this was no way to get rich was right."

"Wasn't that me?"

"Among others, maybe."

"I know I did. I thought, and think, you had, and have, chosen the wrong path. But enough of that. If the detecting of crime doesn't pay, what ecological niche do you propose to fill?"

I cut more Danish. "Oh, I'm not giving up the investigating business. But I do have to supplement it from time to time."

"And with what?"

"This and that. Nothing fun. A friend of mine came up with an idea this morning that sounded good, but then I thought about it. I don't know."

"And that would be what?"

"Lychee nuts."

"Lychee nuts? You intend to build your fortune on, excuse me, lychee nuts?"

"Well, exactly. He thinks it's a great idea, but I'm not sure. On the one hand, the best fresh lychees are hard to find in the US, and very big among Chinese people. You can get them canned, but they don't taste anything like the real thing. The fresh ones they import are third-rate. Premium fresh lychees, the best China has to offer, are very scarce and valuable."

"Really?" Joe sounded thoughtful. "How valuable is valuable?"

"Oh, not worth your time, Joe, not in your league. People would pay a lot, but they're expensive to import. You couldn't sell them down here. Just uptown, in the really fancy food shops." The waiter, to my surprise, had not only actually brought us our tea in a pot, but now replaced it with a fresh one. It's sometimes amazing what Joe can convince people to do. I filled both our cups. "You know, all those uptown Chinese doctors and investment bankers, the ones who buy raspberries in January and asparagus in November. They'd pay a fortune, if the lychees were really good. But the import business, I don't think I'm cut out for it."

Lifting his freshly-filled cup, Joe asked, "Is there none of this fabulous commodity on offer as we speak in New York, food capital of the world?"

"There's only one shop, actually just down Delancey about a block, that sells the big, premium ones. Really fresh and sweet, perfumey-tasting. Go ahead, make a face. Chinese people think of this stuff like caviar."

"Do they really? Then why not go for it?"

"Oh, I don't know. If I could get my hands on lychees from India, it might be worth it."

"They are thought to be special, India lychees?"

"I've actually never had one. They don't export them at all."

"Why not?"

"Some government restrictions, I don't know. But if I could sell those . . . On the other hand, this whole import thing probably isn't right for me."

I finished off my Danish, drained my tea. "You sure you won't reconsider your marks, Joe?"

Flashing the ruby again, Joe said, "Perhaps if you, oh stunning one, reconsider my offer."

I smiled too. "Not in this lifetime. Well, I tried. Thanks for the snack, Joe. I have to go."

"There are Danishes yet untouched." Joe pointed to the pile of pastries still on the plate.

"I've had enough," I said. "More would be greedy. And I know what happens to greedy people when they get around you."

Joe bowed his head, as Charlie had, to acknowledge the compliment. He stood when I did, and remained standing as I worked my way to the door, but then he sat again. As I left he was ordering more tea and reaching for a blueberry Danish. From the distant, dreamy look in his eyes I could tell he was searching for an angle on the lychee nut situation. I wondered if he'd find it.

Four days later, on the phone, I heard from Joe again.

"I must see you," he said. "I yearn."

"Oh, please, Joe."

"No, in truth. Actually I can help you."

"Do I need help?"

"You do. Let me provide it."

"Why don't I trust you? Oh, I remember, you're a con man."

"Lydia! This is your Joe! My motives in this instance are nefarious, it's true, but not in the way you think. One: I can be with you, motive enough for any man. Two: We can both make money, motive enough for any man or woman. And three: You can see how smart your Joe is, and perhaps be moved to reconsider my previous offer. Motive enough, by itself, for Joe."

"That one's not likely."

"Let me buy you a refreshing beverage and we can discuss the issue."

It was a soggy afternoon, and I was, as we delicately say in the detecting business, between cases. My office air conditioner thinks if it makes enough noise I won't notice it actually does nothing useful, but I'd noticed. I'd finished paying my bills and had been reduced to filing.

I gave up, locked up, and went out to meet Joe.

Joe's meeting place of choice was a bench in Sara Roosevelt Park just north of Delancey Street. The refreshing beverage was a seltzer for me and an orange soda for him from the cart with the big beach umbrella. Joe's Cheshire Cat smile was not explained until we sat side by side and with a flourish he poured into my lap the contents of the paper bag he'd been carrying. The ruby flashed as I picked up one of a pair of the biggest, most flawless, most perfect fresh lychees I'd ever seen.

"Where did these come from?" I marveled.

"Are you pleased, oh spectacular one? Has not your Joe done grandly?"

"Where did you get them?" I asked again. They were the size of tennis balls, which for a lychee is enormous.

"Sample one, my queen," said Joe.

"May I really?"

"They are for you, to lay at your feet. In the spirit of full disclosure I admit there were originally three. I tried one myself, and am left to conclude only that Chinese taste buds and Irish taste buds must have been created with irreconcilable differences."

"You didn't like it?" I bit into the lychee. It was firm and juicy, sweet and spicy, good beyond my wildest lychee dreams. As I dabbed a trickle of juice from my chin I wondered if Charlie had ever had one like it.

"Your verdict, please," Joe demanded. "Is this the lychee that will make us rich?"

"This is a great lychee, Joe," I said warily. "Totally top-notch, super-duper, one of the best. Where are they from?"

Joe had been leaning forward watching me

as though I were a race in which he had bet the rent on a horse. Now he leaned back, laced his fingers behind his head and stretched his legs. He grinned through the leafy canopy at the blue June sky.

"The Raj," he said. "The star of the Empire, the jewel in the crown. These are lychees from India, oh joy of my heart."

I stared. "You're kidding."

He spoke modestly, as befitted a man who had performed a miracle. "Procuring them was not a simple matter, even for your Joe. As you yourself stated so accurately, India does not as a matter of course export its lychees. But having been nearly engaged to a Punjabi princess does have its uses."

"You're not telling me her family still even speaks to you? They're willing to do business with you?"

Joe shuddered. "Heavens, no. Her male relatives would long since have sliced my throat, or other even more valuable parts of my person, had not my princess retained a soft spot for old Joe in her heart of hearts. But not all Indians of my acquaintance bear my former beloved's family good will, and the enemy of my enemy is, after all, my friend."

This was baroque enough to be pure Joe. "So you talked some other, what, Indian of your acquaintance into smuggling these for you? As a way to get back at your princess's family for whatever they were mad at them for?"

"Something like that. More important than those inconsequential details is the fact that there are, apparently, many more lychees where these came from."

"Is that a fact?"

"It is. And the fate of those lychees was quite a topic of conversation between myself and my South Asian acquaintances. We have, I am pleased to say, come close to a meeting of the minds. Of course," Joe paused significantly, "we also discussed remuneration, some serious compensation for their trouble, which will apparently include a certain amount of baksheesh to establish a home for blind customs officials."

"Really?" I asked. "How much did you promise them?"

Joe sent me a sideways glance. "I haven't, yet. That's why I needed to speak to you."

"Me? Why?"

"Well, putting aside my need for your mere nearness—"

"Say that again."

"What? My need for your mere nearness?"

"A great phrase, Joe. I just wanted to hear it twice. Go on."

He gave me an indulgent smile. "In any case: it is you and you alone who can set a price on these beauties. One beauty knowing another. What will your uptown Chinese pay? What shall I say we, therefore, will pay?"

"We?"

"We, oh shining vision! You and I! Your dream of riches! We shall reach the golden shore together. Whatever you say they're worth, I shall put up half. No questions asked. If you tell me these things will make us wealthy, then wealthy they will make us." He lifted the remaining lychee from my lap, flipped it high in the air, leaned forward and caught it behind his back. Tossing it again he listed like a sailboat in the wind, then looked around wildly for the lychee as though he'd lost it. Just before it beaned him, he reached up, caught it and produced it with a flourish. I burst out laughing.

"Do I entertain you?" Joe's eyes shone like the eyes of a puppy thrilled that its new trick had gone over well.

"You do. But what really makes me laugh is the idea of going into business with you."

"But Lydia! This is nearly legit! There's the small matter of Indian export regulations, to be sure, but that aside, just look how far I've compromised my principles. I'm proposing to involve the Delancey name in a venture almost honest, for the sake of this dream, your dream. Oh, the ancestors! Surely you can bend your principles too?"

"Joe," I said sweetly, "read my lips. I will not do business with you. Legit or shady, risky or insured by Lloyd's of London. I'm more amazed than I can tell you that you found a source for Indian lychees, but I will not invest in any scheme that comes attached to you."

Joe looked at the lychee in his hand. He flipped it in the air, not nearly as high as before. "Time," he said to it. "She needs time to consider." He caught it, tossed it again. "The idea is new, that's all. Once she's sat with it for a day, the rightness of it will become clear to her. The inevitability. The kismet—"

He stopped short as I leaned over and snatched the lychee in mid-descent. "Thanks, Joe. I have a friend who'll enjoy this." I gave him my brightest smile, not quite a thousand watts but as many as I had. "Good luck with Indian customs." I stood and walked away, leaving Joe looking puzzled and forlorn on a bench in Sara Roosevelt Park.

I had told Joe I wouldn't do business with him. This did not mean, however, that nothing he did was of interest to me. In dark glasses and big floppy hat, I was up and out early the next morning, plying my own trade on Delancey Street.

One thing you could say for Joe: he did not, as did many people in his line of work, yield to the temptation to indulge in layabout ways. Joe's work was despicable, but he worked hard. I picked him up just after nine A.M. and tailed him for nearly three hours, waiting in doorways and down the block while he went in and out of stores, sat in coffee shops, met people on park benches. Finally, at a hole-in-the-wall called "Curry in a Hurry," he was joined at a sidewalk table by a turbaned, bearded fellow who drank a lassi while Joe wolfed down something over rice. They spoke. Joe shrugged. The other man asked a question. Joe shook his head. Watching them from across the street, I was reminded that I was hungry. Luckily, their meeting was brief. When the turbaned gentleman left while Joe was still wolfing, I abandoned my pursuit of Joe and followed.

After a bit of wandering and some miscellaneous shopping, the turbaned gentleman entered a four-story building on the corner of Hester and

Delancey. An aluminum facade had been applied to the building's brick front sometime in the sixties to spiff the place up. Maybe it had worked, but the sixties were a long time ago.

I gave the gentleman a decent interval, then crossed to the doorway and scanned the names on the buzzers. They were many and varied: Wong Enterprises; La Vida Comida; Yo Mama Lingerie. The one that caught my eye, though, was Ganges, Ltd.

That was it for a while. Now I had to wait until Charlie got off work at four. I hoped the staff of Ganges, Ltd. was as assiduous as most immigrants, putting in long hours in the hope of making their fortunes. Right now, having put in some fairly long hours myself, I headed off down Delancey Street in the hope of lunch.

At twenty past four, with Charlie at my side, I was back on the corner of Hester and Delancey, pressing the button for Ganges, Ltd. After the back-and-forth of who and what, the buzzer buzzed and we were in.

Ganges, Ltd. occupied a suite on the second floor in the front, from which the swirling currents of life in the delta could be followed. A sari-wrapped woman in the outer office rose from her desk and led us into the private lair of the turbaned gentleman I had had in my sights. The nameplate on his desk made him out to be one Mr. Rajesh Shah.

"Thank you for seeing us without an appointment, Mr. Shah," I said. I sat in one of the chairs on the customer's side of the desk and Charlie took the other. Rajesh Shah had stood to shake our hands when we came in; now he sat again, eyebrows raised expectantly. His white turban and short-sleeved white shirt gleamed against his dark skin. "I'm sure you're a very busy man and I don't mean to be impolite, popping in like this," I went on, "but we have some business to discuss with you. I'm Lydia Chin; perhaps you've heard of me."

Shah's bearded face formed into an expression of regret. "It is I who find, to my despair, that I am in a position to be impolite. Your name is not, alas, familiar. A fault of mine, I am quite sure. Please enlighten me."

Well, that would be like Joe: giving away as little as possible, even to his business partner. Controlling the information minimizes the chance of error, misstep, or deliberate double-cross. As, for example, what Charlie and I were up to right now.

On a similar principle, I introduced Charlie by his first name only. Then I launched right into the piece I had come to say. "I believe you're acquainted with Joe Delancey."

Shah smiled. "It is impossible to be doing business in this neighborhood and not make the acquaintance of Mr. Delancey."

"It's also impossible to actually do business with Mr. Delancey and come out ahead."

"This may be true," Shah acknowledged, non-committal.

"Believe me, it is." I reorganized myself in the chair. "Mr. Delancey recently offered me a business proposition which was attractive," I said. "Except that he's involved in it. I won't do business with him. But if you yourself are interested in discussing importing Indian lychee nuts, I'm prepared to listen."

Rajesh Shah's eyebrows went up once again. He looked from me to Charlie. "The Indian government is forbidding the export of lychee nuts to the USA. This is until certain import restrictions involving Indian goods have been re-evaluated by your government."

"I know the US doesn't get Indian lychees," I said. "Like most Chinese people, Indian lychees have only been a legend to me. But Joe gave me a couple yesterday. They were every bit as good as I'd heard." I glanced at Charlie, who smiled and nodded vigorously. "Joe also gave me to understand you had found a way around the trade restrictions."

"You are a very blunt speaker, Miss Chin."

"I'm a believer in free speech, Mr. Shah, and also in free trade. It's ridiculous to me that lychees as good as this should be kept from people who would enjoy them—and would be willing to pay for them—while two governments who claim to be friendly to each other carry on like children."

Shah smiled. "I myself have seven children, Miss Chin. I find there is a wisdom in children that is often lacking in governments. What do you propose?"

"I propose whatever Joe proposed, but without Joe."

"This will not please Mr. Delancey."

"Pleasing Mr. Delancey is low on my list of things to do. You have to decide for yourself, of course, whether the money we stand to make is worth getting on Joe's bad side for."

"As to that, Mr. Delancey may be ubiquitous in this neighborhood but he is in no way omnipotent."

Charlie had been following our English with a frown of intense concentration. Now his eyes flew wide. I smothered my smile so as not to embarrass him, and made a mental note to teach him those words later.

"Charlie here," I said to Shah, "has some money he's saved. Not a lot of money, I have to warn you, just a few thousand. Joe talked about putting up half: I think you'll have to assume more of the responsibility than that."

Shah gave a thoughtful nod, as though this were not outside the realm of possibility.

I went on, "What we can really bring to the deal is a distribution network. Well," I reflected, "that's probably a little fancy. What I mean is, I assume the cost of bringing these lychees in would be high, and so the sale price would have to be high for us to make a profit."

Rajesh Shah nodded, so I went on.

"You couldn't sell them on the street in Chinatown if they're expensive. People down here don't have that kind of money. But in the last few days—since Charlie first proposed this lychee idea, and before I knew about the Indian ones— I've done some looking around. There are a number of stores in fancy neighborhoods that are interested. Because I'm Chinese they'll assume the fruit we bring them is from China. I'm sure you and Joe had already figured out a way to fake the paperwork."

Shah had the grace to blush. Then he smiled. "Of course."

"Well, then," I said. "What do you think?"

"Let me be sure I am understanding you," Shah said. "What you are proposing is that your associate—" a nod in Charlie's direction "—invest his modest sum and receive a return commensurate with that investment. You yourself would act as, I believe the expression is, 'front woman?' "

"I guess it is."

"And you would be receiving, in effect, a salary for this service."

"Sounds right."

"And Mr. Delancey would have no part in any of this."

"That's not only right, it's a condition."

Rajesh Shah nodded a few times, his gaze on his desk blotter as though he was working something out. "I think," he said finally, "that this could be a successful proposition. Mr. Charlie," he asked, "how much of an investment are you prepared to make?"

Since the talk of money had begun, Charlie had looked increasingly fidgety and anxious. This could have been fatigue from the strain of focusing on all this English; it turned out, though, to be something else.

Something much worse.

"Money," he mumbled, in an almost-inaudible, un-Charlie-like way. "Really, don't have money."

Shah looked at me. I looked at Charlie. "The money you saved," I said. "You have money put away for college. We talked about using some of that."

Charlie's face was that of a puppy that hadn't meant to get into the garbage and was very very sorry. I wondered in passing why all the men I knew thought dog-like looks would melt my heart. His beseeching eyes on mine, Charlie said, "You remember jackass brother-in-law?"

I nodded.

"Brother-in-law takes money for next great idea."

"Charlie. You let your brother-in-law have your money?"

Charlie's chin jutted forward. "In family account."

This was a very Chinese method of keeping money: in a joint account that could be accessed by a number of different family members. I wasn't surprised to hear that Charlie's brother-in-law was able to help himself. But: "He had the nerve? To take the joint money? After the disaster with the lighters?"

Rajesh Shah looked confused. Joe must not have shared the story of his triumphant swindle of jackass brother-in-law. But that wasn't my problem at the moment.

Charlie was nodding. "Brother-in-law have big money-making idea. Need cash, give to cousin."

"And what did your cousin do with it?"

"Cousin not mine. Cousin his," Charlie rushed to assure me. This was a distinction Charlie had learned in America. In a Chinese family the difference is non-existent: relations are relations, at whatever distance.

"His cousin," I said, my tone reflecting growing impatience. "What did his cousin do with your money?"

"Comes from China," he said. "Comes from China, brings . . ."

Charlie petered out. I finally had to demand, "Brings what?" Brought what, Lydia, I silently corrected myself. Or, bringing what. Even in the face of stress and strain, standards must be maintained. "What, Charlie?"

In a voice as apologetic as his face, Charlie answered, "Bear gall."

I counted to ten. When I spoke, my tone was ice. "Your cousin—no, all right, his cousin— brought bear gall from China into the US?"

Charlie nodded miserably.

Rajesh Shah spoke. "Excuse me, I am sorry, please: what is bear gall?"

My eyes still on Charlie, I answered, "It's gooey brown stuff from the gall bladders of bears. Certain uneducated, foolish, ignorant Chi-

nese people think it has medicinal properties. It doesn't, and besides that it's very painful to the bears to have it collected, and besides that it's illegal to bring it into this country."

Charlie stared at the floor and said nothing.

"How much, Charlie?" I asked. "How much did he bring?"

Charlie mumbled something I couldn't hear. Rajesh Shah also leaned forward as I demanded again, "How much?"

Just barely louder, Charlie said, "Four pounds."

"Four pounds!" I exploded. "That could get him put away for twenty years! And your jackass brother-in-law. And you, Charlie!"

"Me?" Charlie looked up quickly. "I don't know they doing this! Just brother-in-law, his cousin!"

"Tell that to the judge," I said disgustedly.

"Judge?" Charlie's eyes were wide. I didn't bother to explain. "I say this," Charlie said, shaking his head slowly. "I say, stupid guys, now what you think? Selling bear gall on street? Sign, big characters, 'Bear gall here'? But brother-in-law say, so much bear gall, make twenty thousand of bucks, send Charlie to college. Someone in family get to be smart, then everyone listen smart guy."

"Sounds to me like in your family it's too late for that."

"Excuse me." This was Rajesh Shah again. I frowned and Charlie blushed but we both turned to him. It was, after all, his office. "I must admit surprise on hearing these numbers. Four pounds of this bear gall can bring twenty thousand dollars, actually?"

"Probably more," I grumbled. "If it's a well-known brand people will pay close to five hundred dollars an ounce in this country because it's so hard to get. Because it's illegal," I snarled in Charlie's direction. "Because you can get arrested and put in jail for selling it. Or deported. Does your brother-in-law know that?"

"Brother-in-law know very little, I think. But say, know guy, going buy. Then brother-in-law, cousin, don't have bear gall, don't get arrested. Jeff Yang, on Mott Street?"

"Jeff Yang?" The words came slowly from my mouth. "Your brother-in-law is dealing with Jeff Yang?"

"Not dealing yet. Doesn't really know guy," he admitted. "Just hear guy buys bear gall."

"Jeff Yang," I said, emphasizing each word, as though I'd just discovered Charlie was a slow learner, "is the scum of the earth. I went to grade school with him, Charlie, I've known him forever. He used to steal other kids' lunch money. He'd sell you his grandmother if he could get a good price. Charlie, listen to me. You will not do business with Jeff Yang. Your brother-in-law, your cousin, his cousin, your kitchen god, nobody will do business with Jeff Yang. You will go home and flush this disgusting stuff down the toilet immediately."

Charlie looked stricken. I stood. "Well, so much for our plan, Charlie," I said. "Come on. Mr. Shah, I'm sorry we wasted your time."

Shah stood also. Reluctantly, so did Charlie.

"It is unfortunate we cannot do business," Shah said. He smiled in a kindly way at Charlie, then returned his gaze to me. "I must tell you, though, Miss Chin, that my door will continue to be open, if other possibilities occur to you."

"I don't think so," I said. "No offense, Mr. Shah, but I should have known better than to get involved in anything Joe Delancey had any part of. It can only lead to things like this, and worse."

Without a look at Charlie, I swept to the door and yanked it open. I nodded to the woman in the sari, crossed her office and stomped down the stairs. Charlie, with the look of a beaten pup, followed after.

The dog thing got him nowhere.

I was in my office early the next morning, stuffing papers in files and thinking I should sell my air-conditioner to Joe Delancey because it was a con artist, too—or maybe I could palm it off on Charlie's brother-in-law—when the phone rang.

Picking it up, I snapped, "Lydia Chin Investigations," in two languages. Then, because whoever this was might not deserve to be snapped

at, I added more politely, "Lydia Chin speaking. Can I help you?"

"I think you can," said a male voice from the other end. "How're you doing, Lydia? This is Jeff Yang."

Maybe the snapping hadn't been such a bad idea.

"Jeff," I said. "Good-bye."

"No," came the instant response. "Not until you hear the proposition."

"I can imagine," I said, because I could. "No."

"You can make money, and keep your friends out of trouble," Jeff said. "Or you can not make money, and they can get in trouble. What'll it be?"

An echo in Jeff's voice told me I was on the speakerphone in his so-called office, really a tiny room behind a Mott Street restaurant, and not a very good restaurant at that. Well, two could play that game. I punched my own speakerphone button and dropped into my desk chair.

"Go to hell, Jeff."

"You know you don't mean that."

"I mean so much more than that."

"I'll buy it, Lydia. The whole four pounds."

"I have nothing to sell, especially to you."

"Well, you can stay out of it. Just tell me where to find this guy Charlie and his relations."

"Jeff," I said, "I wouldn't tell you where to find a bucket of water if you were on fire."

"I always liked you, too. Holding your teddy bear hostage until you kissed me was just my way of showing that. Let's do business, Lydia."

"Even if I were inclined to do business with you, Jeff, which would be about two weeks after hell froze over, I wouldn't risk my reputation for whatever piddly sum you're about to offer and then cheat me out of."

"It'll be a good price. In cash. You'll have it at the same time as you turn over the goods."

"No cash, no goods, no thanks. If Chinatown found out I was dealing with you I'd never have a legit client again."

"I'll send someone else. No one will know it's me."

"Who, Rajesh Shah? Is that who's in your

office right now, Jeff? Is that why you have me on the damn speakerphone?"

Jeff ignored my question, a sure way of answering it. "Lydia," he said, "if you do a deal with me we can keep it quiet. If you don't, I'll do two things. One: I'll spread the word in Chinatown that you did do a deal with me, and you can kiss your legit clients goodbye. But that'll be the least of your problems, because two, I'll drop a dime on you, and you'll have to give the Customs people your friend Charlie and his brother-in-law to keep your own ass out of jail."

I was speechless. Then: "What?" I heard my voice, low and shocked. "Jeff, you—"

"Don't tell me I wouldn't, because you know I would. Lychee nuts are about your speed, Lydia. Bear gall is out of your league. Five thousand dollars, by noon."

"Five thousand dollars? For four pounds?"

"You're not in a great negotiating position."

"Neither are you. I told Charlie yesterday to flush the stuff down the toilet."

"And you know," Jeff said, "you just know that he didn't. Five thousand, in the park, noon. Or your reputation is what goes down the toilet. And your friend Charlie goes to jail. Sent there by you."

Charlie in jail, sent there by me. That was an ugly picture and I wiped it from my mind, replacing it with a vision of Jeff Yang in his back-room office. With Rajesh Shah.

"Ten," I said.

"Five."

"It's Golden Venture brand."

"Wrapped and labeled?"

"One-ounce packages."

The briefest of pauses, then, "Seven-five."

"I hope," I said, "that every ounce you sell takes a year off your life."

"The same to you," Jeff said. "See you in the park at noon."

"You must have missed it: I won't be seen with you, Jeff. Charlie will be there."

"How will I know him?"

"He'll find you. By your smell," I added, and hung up.

I called Charlie at the noodle factory. "I need you to be in the park at noon. With your brother-in-law's package."

Of course Jeff had been right: the package had not gone down the toilet. "Only get half hour lunch," Charlie said apologetically.

"This shouldn't take long." I hung up.

At noon, of course, I was in Sara Roosevelt Park too. I sat far away from the bench I had stationed Charlie at, half-screened by a hot dog vendor's cart. I just wanted to make sure everything went all right: I felt responsible for this.

It went without incident. I had shown Charlie a picture of Jeff Yang and he spotted him, followed him until he sat, and then, in a burst of creativity, ignored him, walked to a soda stand, bought himself a Coke, and meandered back to Jeff's bench. He put down the brown paper bag he was carrying and popped the can open. Charlie and Jeff exchanged a few words of casual conversation, two strangers enjoying a sunny June day. Charlie asked to glance at Jeff's newspaper, and Jeff obliged. Charlie opened the pages of the front section, slipping the back section unopened beneath him on the bench. When he was hidden behind the paper Jeff rose, told Charlie in a friendly way to keep the paper, and then set off down the path, the bag Charlie had arrived with under his arm.

In the early evening of the next day the light was honey-colored, the sky was cobalt, and the trees were a glorious emerald green as I strolled through the same park, Charlie at my side.

"Rajesh Shah, that man, I see him yesterday night, on Delancey Street," Charlie said.

"Really?"

"Yes. He say, hear you have money now, Charlie. Asking if I want invest in lychees, still. From India."

"What did you do?" I asked, though I was pretty sure of the answer.

"I tell him, have to speak to gaje. Say Charlie not investing on own anymore."

"Very good, Charlie. Very, very good."

I had bought us pretzels from a cart and was explaining to Charlie the difference between

Kosher salt and the regular kind when a trio of men rose from a bench and stepped into our path.

"Lydia," said Joe, with his thousand-watt smile. Rajesh Shah, in turban and short-sleeved shirt, was on his left, and Jeff Yang, bulging shoulders straining his black muscle tee, was on his right. The grim and dark expressions on their faces wouldn't have powered a nightlight.

"Lydia," Joe said again, holding on his palm a paper-wrapped rectangle the size of a mahjongg tile. "Oh shining star of the east, what is this?"

I peered at the label around its middle. "You don't read Chinese, Joe? It says, 'Golden Venture Brand Bear Gall, Finest In All China.'"

"Yes, exquisite one," Joe agreed. "But what is it?"

"Prune paste, Joe. The stuff they put in Danishes." I gave him a big smile, too, and this time I was sure I hit a thousand watts.

Charlie, beside me, was also grinning. Shah and Yang frowned yet more deeply. Joe just looked sad.

"Did you try to sell it?" I asked sympathetically.

"Indeed I did. And for my trouble was chased from the back alleys of Chinatown by dangerous men with meat cleavers. The damage to my reputation for veracity in those precincts is incalculable."

"No kidding? Nice side benefit," I said.

"Lydia." Joe shook his head, as though the depth of his disappointment was bottomless. "You have cheated your Joe?"

"Well, I was hoping you were behind Jeff's offer," I admitted, "but I was prepared to cheat Mr. Shah if he was all I could get."

"All the packages are prune paste? There is no bear gall?"

"There isn't, and there never was."

"You set us up?"

"I did."

"Lydia," Joe repeated, in a voice of deep grief. "You set up your Joe?"

"My Joe, my foot. Show some respect. You were setting me up and I out-set you."

"I?" Bewildered innocence. "But—"

"Oh, Joe. Indian lychees. You know, you keep saying I have all the instincts. I don't, but I figured if I thought like you everything would work out."

"How so, my duplicitous darling?"

"When I turned down your offer, right on that bench over there—which you knew I would—I asked myself, what would Joe do if he were turning down an offer from a middleman he didn't trust?" Joe wrinkled his nose at "middleman" but didn't protest. "Joe would try to cut the middleman out," I said. "So let's see how easy Joe makes it for me to cut him out. You led me around for awhile the next morning, and finally you let me see you with Mr. Shah."

"I did notice you following me," Joe conceded.

"I should hope so. I couldn't have been more obvious except by waving to you. You really think that's the best I can do? Joe, you show very little appreciation for my ecological niche."

"Touché, fair one. And then?"

"Well, you clearly wanted me to go to Mr. Shah and do a deal, leaving you behind. Then you and he would split whatever cash Mr. Shah was able to con us out of, right? Of course there were never any Indian lychees any more than there was bear gall. But when Charlie and I figured that out, who were we going to complain to? I was the one who'd said importing them was illegal in the first place."

Joe sighed. "So, knowing the sting was on, you stung first?"

"Wouldn't you have?"

"I would indeed. And Mr. Yang, so reviled by you when suggested by Charlie as a purchaser for the non-existent bear gall, had in fact been suggested by you to Charlie as a name to bring up at the appropriate moment, in order to draw in Mr. Shah?"

Jeff Yang was glowering at Joe's side. I said, "Well, Jeff was perfect for the spot. In a million years Jeff would never risk a nickel of his own on a deal like this. If he did a deal, someone would have to be financing it. I hope," I said to Jeff, "you charged a commission. Something for your trouble."

Jeff Yang's frown became fiercer and his hands curled into fists. I could feel Charlie next to me watching him, tensing.

Joe sighed. "We're all so very, very disappointed."

"No, you're not, Joe. You're impressed."

"Well," Joe conceded, "perhaps I am. But now, my unequalled Asian mistress of mystery, the game is over. Yes, you have won, and I will proclaim that truth to all who ask. Now is the time to return your cleverly-gotten gains so that we can go our separate ways, with no hard feelings."

Charlie's face fell at this prospect.

"You have to be kidding, Joe," I said. "When was the last time you gave back money you'd conned somebody out of fair and square?"

"Ah," Joe said, "but I would not—especially in my amateur days, which status I fear you have not yet left behind—have worked a con on such a one as Mr. Yang." He indicated Jeff Yang, whose fists were clenched, angry frown fixed in place. To emphasize the danger, Joe stepped away a little, Rajesh Shah with him, leaving Charlie and me marooned with Jeff Yang in the center of the pathway. "I fear I will not be able to restrain the good Mr. Yang from putting into play his threatened destruction of your professional reputation, unless we are all satisfied. Not to mention what look like fairly dire designs on your person."

This was, finally, too much for Jeff Yang. The frown exploded into a great bellowing laugh.

Whatever else you want to say about Jeff Yang, his laugh has always been infectious. I cracked up too.

So did Charlie.

Jeff, wheezing from laughter, turned to Joe. "I do have designs on Lydia's person, but not that kind. I've spent my whole life trying to make up for the teddy bear kidnapping incident. I'll do anything she asks. I'm putty in her hands. I'll even pretend to be a big-time China-town gangster if Lydia wants me to." He pulled a fan of bills from his pocket and waved them in the air. "I charged ten per cent," he said to me. "If I buy you dinner, will you finally forgive me?"

"I'll never forgive you," I said. "But you might as well buy me dinner." I slipped my arm into his. Just before Jeff, Charlie, and I walked off in the golden evening I spoke once more to Joe, who stood open-mouthed on the path.

"Oh, and thanks for the lychees, Joe. They were China's finest. From that place on Delancey, right? And do keep in touch with your friend Mr. Shah. When they start growing lychees in India, if they ever do, I'm sure he'll let you know."

Mr. Shah blushed and frowned. But Joe, with a wide smile breaking over his face like sun through clouds, swept forward into a low, graceful bow. He came up with a flourish and a grin. I bowed my head to acknowledge the compliment. The ruby in Joe's tooth flashed in a final ray of light as, with Jeff and Charlie, I turned and walked away.

THE SHOESHINE MAN'S REGRETS

Laura Lippman

ALTHOUGH BORN IN ATLANTA, GEORGIA, Laura Lippman (1959–   ) is closely associated with Baltimore, Maryland, where she has lived most of her life. She was a longtime reporter for the *Baltimore Sun* before becoming a full-time fiction writer who has had numerous books on bestseller lists for the past decade.

In addition to nine stand-alone novels and a short story collection, Lippman has written a dozen detective novels in her Tess Monaghan series, including the Edgar-winning *Charm City* (1997), which won for best paperback original of the year; Lippman has been nominated for six other Edgars (twice each for paperback original, short story, and novel).

In a 2006 profile of Monaghan (full name: Theresa Esther Weinstein Monaghan), Lippman described her as "perhaps Baltimore's best-known private investigator," working as the sole employee of Keys Investigations, Inc., technically co-owned by Edward Keys, a retired Baltimore police detective. Monaghan has described herself as an "accidental detective" after trying to help a friend and botching it badly. She helped his lawyer, who then pressed her to work for him as an investigator, soon pushing her out to start her own agency. She is a workaholic with a longtime boyfriend and a good, slightly sarcastic sense of humor.

"The Shoeshine Man's Regrets" was originally published in *Murder . . . and All That Jazz*, edited by Robert J. Randisi (New York, Signet, 2004). It was selected by Joyce Carol Oates for inclusion in *The Best American Mystery Stories 2005*.

The Shoeshine Man's Regrets

LAURA LIPPMAN

"BRUNO MAGLI?"

"Uh-uh. Bally."

"How can you be so sure?"

"Some kids get flashcards of farm animals when they're little. I think my mom showed me pictures of footwear cut from magazines. After all, she couldn't have her only daughter bringing home someone who wore white patent loafers, even in the official season between Memorial Day and Labor Day. Speaking of which—there's a full Towson."

"Wow—white shoes *and* white belt and white tie, and ten miles south of his natural habitat, the Baltimore County courthouse. I thought the full Towson was on the endangered clothing list."

"Bad taste never dies. It just keeps evolving."

Tess Monaghan and Whitney Talbot were standing outside the Brass Elephant on a soft June evening, studying the people ahead of them in the valet parking line. A laundry truck had blocked the driveway to the restaurant's lot, disrupting the usually smooth operation, so the restaurant's patrons were milling about, many agitated. There was muttered talk of symphony tickets and the Orioles game and the Herzog retrospective at the Charles Theatre.

But Tess and Whitney, mellowed by martinis, eggplant appetizers, and the perfect weather, had no particular place to go and no great urgency about getting there. They had

started cataloging the clothes and accessories of those around them only because Tess had confided to Whitney that she was trying to sharpen her powers of observation. It was a reasonable exercise in self-improvement for a private detective—and a great sport for someone as congenitally catty as Whitney.

The two friends were inventorying another man's loafers—Florsheim, Tess thought, but Whitney said good old-fashioned Weejuns—when they noticed a glop of white on one toe. And then, as if by magic, a shoeshine man materialized at the elbow of the Weejun wearer's elbow.

"You got something there, mister. Want me to give you a quick shine?"

Tess, still caught up in her game of cataloging, saw that the shoeshine man was old, but then, all shoeshine men seemed old these days. She often wondered where the next generation of shoeshine men would came from, if they were also on the verge of extinction, like the Towson types who sported white belts with white shoes. This man was thin, with a slight stoop to his shoulders and a tremble in his limbs, his salt-and-pepper hair cropped close. He must be on his way home from the train station or the Belvedere Hotel, Tess concluded, heading toward a bus stop on one of the major east-west streets farther south, near the city's center.

"What the—?" Mr. Weejun was short and compact, with a yellow polo shirt tucked into lime green trousers. A golfer, Tess decided, noticing his florid face and sunburned bald spot. She was not happy to see him waiting for a car, given how many drinks he had tossed back in the Brass Elephant's Tusk Lounge. He was one of the people who kept braying about his Orioles tickets.

Now he extended his left foot, pointing his toe in a way that reminded Tess of the dancing hippos in *Fantasia*, and stared at the white smear on his shoe in anger and dismay.

"You *bastard*," he said to the shoeshine man. "How did you get that shit on my shoe?"

"I didn't do anything, sir. I was just passing by, and I saw that your shoe was dirty. Maybe you tracked in something in the restaurant."

"It's some sort of scam, isn't it?" The man appealed to the restless crowd, which was glad for any distraction at this point. "Anyone see how this guy got this crap on my shoe?"

"He didn't," Whitney said, her voice cutting the air with her usual conviction. "It was on your shoe when you came out of the restaurant."

It wasn't what Mr. Weejun wanted to hear, so he ignored her.

"Yeah, you can clean my shoe," he told the old man. "Just don't expect a tip."

The shoeshine man sat down his box and went to work quickly. "Mayonnaise," he said, sponging the mass from the shoe with a cloth. "Or salad dressing. Something like that."

"I guess you'd know," Weejun said. "Since you put it there."

"No, sir. I wouldn't do a thing like that."

The shoeshine man was putting the finishing touches on the man's second shoe when the valet pulled up in a Humvee. Taxicab yellow, Tess observed, still playing the game. Save the Bay license plates and a sticker that announced the man as a member of an exclusive downtown health club.

"Five dollars," the shoeshine man said, and Weejun pulled out a five with great ostentation— then handed it to the valet. "No rewards for scammers," he said with great satisfaction. But

when he glanced around, apparently expecting some sort of affirmation for his boorishness, all he saw were shocked and disapproving faces.

With the curious logic of the disgraced, Weejun upped the ante, kicking the man's shoeshine kit so its contents spilled across the sidewalk. He then hopped into his Humvee, gunning the motor, although the effect of a quick getaway was somewhat spoiled by the fact that his emergency brake was on. The Humvee bucked, then shot forward with a squeal.

As the shoeshine man's hands reached for the spilled contents of his box, Tess saw him pick up a discarded soda can and throw it at the fender of the Humvee. It bounced off with a hollow, harmless sound, but the car stopped with a great squealing of brakes and Weejun emerged, spoiling for a fight. He threw himself on the shoeshine man.

But the older man was no patsy. He grabbed his empty box, landing it in his attacker's stomach with a solid, satisfying smack. Tess waited for someone, anyone, to do something, but no one moved. Reluctantly she waded in, tossing her cell phone to Whitney. Longtime friends who had once synched their movements in a women's four on the rowing team at Washington College, the two could still think in synch when necessary. Whitney called 911 while Tess grabbed Weejun by the collar and uttered a piercing scream as close to his ear as possible. "Stop it, asshole. The cops are coming."

The man nodded, seemed to compose himself—then charged the shoeshine man again. Tess tried to hold him back by the belt, and he turned back, swinging out wildly, hitting her in the chin. Sad to say, this physical contact galvanized the crowd in a way that his attack on an elderly black man had not. By the time the blue-and-whites rolled up, the valet parkers were holding Weejun and Whitney was examining the fast-developing bruise on Tess's jaw with great satisfaction.

"You are so going to file charges against this asshole," she said.

"Well, I'm going to file charges against him,

then," Weejun brayed, unrepentant. "He started the whole thing."

The patrol cop was in his midthirties, a seasoned officer who had broken up his share of fights, although probably not in this neighborhood. "If anyone's adamant about filing a report, it can be done, but it will involve about four hours down at the district."

That dimmed everyone's enthusiasm, even Whitney's.

"Good," the cop said. "I'll just take the bare details and let everyone go."

The laundry truck moved, the valet parking attendants regained their usual efficiency, and the crowd moved on, more anxious about their destinations than this bit of street theater. The shoeshine man started to walk away, but the cop motioned for him to stay, taking names and calling them in, along with DOBs. "Just routine," he told Tess, but his expression soon changed in a way that indicated the matter was anything but routine. He walked away from them, out of earshot, clicking the two-way on his shoulder on and off.

"You can go," he said to Whitney and Tess upon returning. "But I gotta take him in. There's a warrant."

"Him?" Whitney asked hopefully, jerking her chin at Weejun.

"No, him." The cop looked genuinely regretful. "Could be a mix-up, could be someone else using his name and DOB, but I still have to take him downtown."

"What's the warrant for?" Tess asked.

"Murder, if you really want to know."

Weejun looked at once gleeful and frightened, as if he were wondering just whom he had taken on in this fight. It would make quite a brag around the country club, Tess thought. He'd probably be telling his buddies he had taken on a homicidal maniac and won.

Yet the shoeshine man was utterly composed. He did not protest his innocence or insist that it was all a mistake, things that even a guilty man might have said under the circumstances. He simply sighed, cast his eyes toward the sky, as if asking a quick favor from his deity of choice, then said: "I'd like to gather up my things, if I could."

"It's the damnedest thing, Tess. He couldn't confess fast enough. Didn't want a lawyer, didn't ask any questions, just sat down and began talking as fast as he could."

Homicide detective Martin Tull, Tess's only real friend in the Baltimore Police Department, had caught the shoeshine man's case simply by answering the phone when the patrol cop called him about the warrant. He should be thrilled—it was an easy stat, about as easy as they come. No matter how old the case, it counted toward the current year's total of solved homicides.

"It's a little too easy," Tull said, sitting with Tess on a bench near one of their favorite coffeehouses, watching the water taxis zip back and forth across the Inner Harbor.

"Everyone gets lucky, even you," Tess said. "It's all too incredible that the warrant was lost all these years. What I don't get is how it was found."

"Department got some grant for computer work. Isn't that great? There's not enough money to make sure DNA samples are stored safely, but some think tank gave us money so college students can spend all summer keystroking data. The guy moved about two weeks after the murder, before he was named in the warrant. Moved all of five miles, from West Baltimore to the county, but he wasn't the kind of guy who left a forwarding address. Or the cop on the case was a bonehead. At any rate, he's gone forty years wanted for murder, and if he hadn't been in that fight night before last, he might've gone another forty."

"Did he even know there was a warrant on him?"

"Oh, yeah. He knew exactly why he was there. Story came out of him as if he had been rehearsing it for years. Kept saying, 'Yep, I did it, no doubt about it. You do what you have to do, Officer.' So we charged him, the judge put a hundred-grand bail on him, a bail bondsman put up ten thousand, and he went home."

"I guess someone who's lived at the same address for thirty-nine years isn't considered a flight risk."

"Flight risk? I think if I had left this guy in the room with all our opened files, he would have confessed to every homicide in Baltimore. I have never seen someone so eager to confess to a crime. I almost think he wants to go to jail."

"Maybe he's convinced that a city jury won't lock him up, or that he can get a plea. How did the victim die?"

"Blunt-force trauma in a burglary. There's no physical evidence, and the warrant was sworn out on the basis of an eyewitness who's been dead for ten years."

"So you probably couldn't get a conviction at all if it went to trial."

"Nope. That's what makes it so odd. Even if she were alive, she'd be almost ninety by now, pretty easy to break down on the stand."

"What's the file say?"

"Neighbor lady said she saw William Harrison leave the premises, acting strangely. She knew the guy because he did odd jobs in the neighborhood, even worked for her on occasion, but there was no reason for him to be at the victim's house so late at night."

"Good luck recovering the evidence from Evidence Control."

"Would you believe they still had the weapon? The guy's head was bashed in with an iron. But that's all I got. If the guy hadn't confessed, if he had stonewalled me or gotten with a lawyer, I wouldn't have anything."

"So what do you want me to tell you? I never met this man before we became impromptu tag-team wrestlers. He seemed pretty meek to me, but who knows what he was like forty years ago? Maybe he's just a guy with a conscience, who's been waiting all these years to see if someone's going to catch up with him."

Tull shook his head. "One thing. He didn't know what the murder weapon was. Said he forgot."

"Well, forty years. It's possible."

"Maybe." Tull, who had already finished his coffee, reached for Tess's absent-mindedly, grimacing when he realized it was a latte. Caffeine was his fuel, his vice of choice, and he didn't like it diluted in any way.

"Take the easy stat, Martin. Guy's named in a warrant, and he said he did it. He does have a temper, I saw that much. Last night it was a soda can. Forty years ago, it very well could have been an iron."

"I've got a conscience, too, you know." Tull looked offended.

Tess realized that it wasn't something she knew that had prompted Tull to call her up, but something he wanted her to do. Yet Tull would not ask her directly, because then he would be in her debt. He was a man, after all. But if she volunteered to do what he seemed to want, he would honor *her* next favor, and Tess was frequently in need of favors.

"I'll talk to him. See if he'll open up to his tag-team partner."

Tull didn't even so much as nod to acknowledge the offer. It was as if Tess's acquiescence were a belch, or something else that wouldn't be commented on in polite company.

The shoeshine man—William Harrison, Tess reminded herself, she had a name for him now—lived in a neat bungalow just over the line in what was known as the Woodlawn section of Baltimore County. Forty years ago, Mr. Harrison would have been one of its first black residents, and he would have been denied entrance to the amusement park only a few blocks from his house. Now the neighborhood was more black than white, but still middle class.

A tiny woman answered the door to Mr. Harrison's bungalow, her eyes bright and curious.

"Mrs. Harrison?"

"*Miss.*" There was a note of reprimand for Tess's assumption.

"My name is Tess Monaghan. I met your brother two nights ago in the, um, fracas."

"Oh, he felt so bad about that. He said it was

shameful, how the only person who wanted to help him was a girl. He found it *appalling*."

She drew out the syllables of the last word, as if it gave her some special pleasure.

"It was so unfair what happened to him. And then this mix-up with the warrant . . ."

The bright catlike eyes narrowed a bit. "What do you mean by mix-up?"

"Mr. Harrison just doesn't seem to me to be the kind of man who could kill someone."

"Well, he says he was." Spoken matter-of-factly, as if the topic were the weather or something else of little consequence. "I knew nothing about it, of course. The warrant or the murder."

"Of course," Tess agreed. This woman did not look like someone who had been burdened with a loved one's secret for four decades. Where her brother was stooped and grave, she had the regal posture of a short woman intent on using every inch given her, but there was something blithe, almost gleeful, beneath her dignity. Did she not like her brother?

"It was silly of William"—she stretched the name out, giving it a grand, growling pronunciation, Will-yum—"to tell his story and sign the statement, without even talking to a lawyer. I told him to wait, to see what they said, but he wouldn't."

"But if you knew nothing about it . . ."

"Nothing about it until two nights ago," Miss Harrison clarified. That was the word that popped into Tess's head, clarified, and she wondered at it. Clarifications were what people made when things weren't quite right.

"And were you shocked?"

"Oh, he had a temper when he was young. Anything was possible."

"Is your brother at home?"

"He's at work. We still have to eat, you know." Now she sounded almost angry. "He didn't think of that, did he, when he decided to be so noble. I told him this house may be paid off, but we still have to eat and buy gas for my car. Did you know they cut your Social Security off when you go to prison?"

Tess did not. She had relatives who were far from pure, but they had managed to avoid doing time. So far.

"Well," Miss Harrison said, "they do. But Will-yum didn't think of that, did he? Men are funny that way. They're so determined to be *gallant*"—again, the word was spoken with great pleasure, with the tone of a child trying to be grand—"that they don't think things through. He may feel better, but what about me?"

"Do you have no income, then?"

"I worked as a laundress. You don't get a pension for being a laundress. My brother, however, was a custodian for Social Security, right here in Woodlawn."

"I thought he shined shoes."

"Yes, *now*." Miss Harrison was growing annoyed with Tess. "But not always: William was enterprising, even as a young man. He worked as a custodian at Social Security, which is why he has Social Security. But he took on odd jobs, shined shoes. He hates to be idle. He won't like prison, no matter what he thinks."

"He did odd jobs for the man he killed, right?"

"Some. Not many. Really, hardly any at all. They barely knew each other."

Miss Harrison seemed to think this mitigated the crime somehow, that the superficiality of the relationship excused her brother's deed.

"Police always thought it was a burglary?" Tess hoped her tone would invite a confidence, or at least another clarification.

"Yes," she said. "Yes. That, too. Things were taken. Everyone knew that."

"So you were familiar with the case, but not your brother's connection to it?"

"Well, I knew the man. Maurice Dickman. We lived in the neighborhood, after all. And people talked, of course. It was a big deal, murder, forty years ago. Not the *happenstance* that it's become. But he was a showy man. He thought awfully well of himself, because he had money and a business. Perhaps he shouldn't have made such a spectacle of himself, and then no one would have tried to steal from him. You know what the Bible says, about the rich man and the camel and the eye of the needle? It's true, you know. Not always, but often enough."

"Why did your brother burglarize his home? Was that something else he did to supplement his paycheck? Is that something he still does?"

"My brother," Miss Harrison said, drawing herself up so she gained yet another inch, "is not a thief."

"But—"

"I don't like talking to you," she said abruptly. "I thought you were on our side, but I see now I was foolish. I know what happened. You called the police. You talked about pressing charges. If it weren't for you, none of this would have happened. You're a terrible person. Forty years, and trouble never came for us, and then you undid everything. You have brought us nothing but grief, which we can ill afford."

She stamped her feet, an impressive gesture, small though they were. Stamped her feet and went back inside the house, taking a moment to latch the screen behind her, as if Tess's manners were so suspect that she might try to follow where she clearly wasn't wanted.

The shoeshine man did work at Penn Station, after all, stationed in front of the old-fashioned wooden seats that always made Tess cringe a bit. There was something about one man perched above another that didn't sit quite right with her, especially when the other man was bent over the enthroned one's shoes.

Then again, pedicures probably looked pretty demeaning, too, depending on one's perspective.

"I'm really sorry, Mr. Harrison, about the mess I've gotten you into." She had refused to sit in his chair, choosing to lean against the wall instead.

"Got myself into, truth be told. If I hadn't thrown that soda can, none of this would have happened. I could have gone another forty years without anyone bothering me."

"But you could go to prison."

"Looks that way." He was almost cheerful about it.

"You should get a lawyer, get that confession thrown out. Without it, they've got nothing."

"They've got a closed case, that's what they've got. A closed case. And maybe I'll get probation."

"It's not a bad bet, but the stakes are awfully high. Even with a five-year sentence, you might die in prison."

"Might not," he said.

"Still, your sister seems pretty upset."

"Oh, Mattie's always getting upset about something. Our mother thought she was doing right by her, teaching her those Queen of Sheba manners, but all she did was make her perpetually disappointed. Now, if Mattie had been born just a decade later, she might have had a different life. But she wasn't, and I wasn't, and that's that."

"She did seem . . . refined," Tess said, thinking of the woman's impeccable appearance and the way she loved to stress big words.

"She was raised to be a lady. Unfortunately, she didn't have a lady's job. No shame in washing clothes, but no honor in it either, not for someone like Mattie. She should have stayed in school, become a teacher. But Mattie thought it would be easy to marry a man on the rise. She just didn't figure that a man on the rise would want a woman on the rise, too, that the manners and the looks wouldn't be enough. A man on the rise doesn't want a woman to get out of his bed and then wash his sheets, not unless she's already his wife. Mattie should never have dropped out of school. It was a shame, what she gave up."

"Being a teacher, you mean."

"Yeah," he said, his tone vague and faraway. "Yeah. She could have gone back, even after she dropped out, but she just stomped her feet and threw back that pretty head of hers. Threw back her pretty head and cried."

"Threw back her pretty head and cried— why does that sound familiar?"

"I couldn't tell you."

"Threw back her pretty head . . . I know that, but I can't place it."

"Couldn't help you." He began whistling a tune, "Begin the Beguine."

"Mr. Harrison—you didn't kill that man, did you?"

"Well, now, I say I did, and why would anyone want to argue with me? And I was seen coming from his house that night, sure as anything. That neighbor, Edna Buford, she didn't miss a trick on that block."

"What did you hit him with?"

"An iron," he said triumphantly. "An iron!"

"You didn't know that two days ago."

"I was nervous."

"You were anything but, from what I hear."

"I'm an old man. I don't always remember what I should."

"So it was an iron?"

"Definitely, one of those old-fashioned ones, cast iron. The kind you had to heat."

"The kind," Tess said, "that a man's laundress might use."

"Mebbe. Does it really matter? Does any of this really matter? If it did, would they have taken forty years to find me? I'll tell you this much—if Maurice Dickman had been a white man, I bet I wouldn't have been walking around all this time. He wasn't a nice man, Mr. Dickman, but the police didn't know that. For all they knew, he was a good citizen. A man was killed, and nobody cared. Except Edna Buford, peeking through her curtains. They should have found me long ago. Know something else?"

"What?" Tess leaned forward, assuming a confession was about to be made.

"I *did* put the mayonnaise on that man's shoe. It had been a light day here, and I wanted to pick up a few extra dollars on my way home. I'm usually better about picking my marks, though. I won't make that mistake again."

A lawyer of Tess's acquaintance, Tyner Gray, asked that the court throw out the charges against William Harrison on the grounds that his confession was coerced. A plea bargain was offered instead—five years probation. "I told you so," Mr. Harrison chortled to Tess, gloating a little at his prescience.

"Lifted up her lovely head and cried," Tess said.

"What?"

"That's the line I thought you were quoting. You said 'threw,' but the line was lifted. I had to feed it through Google a few different ways to nail it, but I did. 'Miss Otis Regrets.' It's about a woman who kills her lover, and is then hanged on the gallows."

"Computers are interesting," Mr. Harrison said.

"What did you really want? Were you still trying to protect your sister, as you've protected her all these years? Or were you just trying to get away from her for a while?"

"I have no idea what you're talking about. Mattie did no wrong in our mother's eyes. My mother loved that girl, and I loved for my mother to be happy."

So Martin Tull got his stat and a more-or-less clean conscience. Miss Harrison got her protective older brother back, along with his Social Security checks.

And Tess got an offer of free shoeshines for life, whenever she was passing through Penn Station. She politely declined Mr. Harrison's gesture. After all, he had already spent forty years at the feet of a woman who didn't know how to show gratitude.

DUST UP

Wendy Hornsby

THE UNDERAPPRECIATED WENDY HORNSBY (1947–   ) is best known for her series of novels about documentary filmmaker Maggie MacGowen, who somehow becomes entangled in mysteries and murder as an amateur sleuth. That sounds like the makings of a nice cozy series, but no, it's not. The author's exploration of the dark side of ever-sunny Los Angeles has been compared to Raymond Chandler's by more than one critic.

Maggie first encounters violence in *Telling Lies* (1992) and now has ten books in the series, the most recent being *Disturbing the Dark* (2016).

It is in Hornsby's short fiction that the real darkness descends. "Nine Sons" is a disturbing, heartbreaking tale of a family that lives on the Northern Plains during the Great Depression. It won the Edgar for best short story of the year in 1992. It serves as the title story of a collection of her tales, *Nine Sons Collected Mysteries* (2002), a volume that also includes the masterpiece of noir "Ghost Caper." The story in this anthology, "Dust Up," has the kind of ending one might expect from Cormac McCarthy or Jim Thompson. The protagonist is named Pansy. Do not be fooled!

A lifelong Southern Californian, Hornsby graduated from UCLA with a degree in history and went on to become a tenured professor at Long Beach City College.

"Dust Up" was originally published in *Murder in Vegas*, edited by Michael Connelly (New York, Forge, 2005).

Dust Up

WENDY HORNSBY

PANSY REYNARD lay on her belly inside a camouflaged bird blind, high-power Zeiss binoculars to her eyes, a digital sound amplifier hooked over her right ear, charting every movement and sound made by her observation target, an Aplomado falcon hatchling. As Pansy watched, the hatchling stretched his wings to their full thirty-inch span and gave them a few tentative flaps as if gathering courage to make his first foray out of the nest. He would need some courage to venture out, she thought. The ragged, abandoned nest his mother had appropriated for her use sat on a narrow rock ledge 450 vertical feet above the desert floor.

"Go, baby," Pansy whispered when the chick craned back his neck and flapped his wings again. This was hour fourteen of her assigned nest watch. She felt stiff and cramped, and excited all at once. There had been no reported Aplomado falcon sightings in Nevada since 1910. For a mated Aplomado falcon pair to appear in the Red Rock Canyon area less than twenty miles west of the tawdry glitz and endless noise of Las Vegas, was singular, newsworthy even. But for the pair to claim a nest and successfully hatch an egg was an event so unexpected as to be considered a miracle by any committed raptor watcher, as Pansy Reynard considered herself to be.

The hatchling watch was uncomfortable, perhaps dangerous, because of the ruggedness of the desert canyons, the precariousness of Pansy's rocky perch in a narrow cliff-top saddle opposite the nest, and the wild extremes of the weather. But the watch was very likely essential to the survival of this wonder child. It had been an honor, Pansy felt, to be assigned a shift to watch the nest. And then to have the great good fortune to be on site when the hatchling first emerged over the top of the nest was, well, nearly overwhelming.

Pansy lowered her binocs to wipe moisture from her eyes, but quickly raised them again so as not to miss one single moment in the life of this sleek-winged avian infant. She had been wakened inside her camouflage shelter at dawn by the insistent chittering of the hatchling as he demanded to be fed. From seemingly nowhere, as Pansy watched, the mother had soared down to tend him, the forty-inch span of her black and white wings as artful and graceful as a beautiful Japanese silk-print kite. The sight of the mother made Pansy almost forgive Lyle for standing her up the night before.

Almost forgive Lyle: This was supposed to be a two-man shift. Lyle, a pathologist with the Department of Fish and Game, was a fine bird-watcher and seemed to be in darned good physical shape. But he was new to the Las Vegas office and unsure about his readiness to face the desert overnight. And he was busy. Or so he said.

Pansy had done her best to assure Lyle that he would be safe in her hands. As preparation, she had packed two entire survival kits, one for herself and one for him, and had tucked in a very good bottle of red wine to make the long chilly night pass more gently. But he hadn't come. Hadn't even called.

Pansy sighed, curious to know which he had shunned, an evening in her company or the potential perils of the place. She had to admit there were actual, natural challenges to be addressed. It was only mid-April, but already the desert temperatures reached the century mark before noon. When the sun was overhead, the sheer vertical faces of the red sandstone bluffs reflected and intensified the heat until everything glowed like—and felt like—the inside of an oven. There was no shade other than the feathery shadows of spindly yucca and folds in the rock formations.

To make conditions yet more uncomfortable, it was sandstorm season. Winds typically began to pick up around noon, and could drive an impenetrable cloud of sand at speeds surpassing eighty miles an hour until sunset. When the winds blew, there was nearly no way to escape both the heat and the pervasive, intrusive blast of sand. Even cars were useless as shelter. With windows rolled up and without the AC turned on you'd fry in a hurry. With the AC turned on, both you and the car's engine would be breathing grit. If you could somehow navigate blind and drive like hell, you might drive clear of the storm before sand fouled the engine. But only if you could navigate blind.

People like Pansy who knew the area well might find shelter in random hollows among the rocks, such as the niche where the hatchling sat in his nest. Or the well prepared, for instance Pansy, might hunker down inside a zip-up shelter made to military specs for desert troops, like the one that was tucked inside her survival pack. Or navigate using digital GPS via satellite— Global Positioning System.

Not an environment for neophytes, Pansy

conceded, but she'd had high hopes for Lyle, and had looked forward to an evening alone with him and the falcons under the vast blackness of the desert sky, getting acquainted.

Pansy knew she could be a bit off-putting at first meeting. But in that place, during that season, Pansy was in her métier and at her best. Her preparations for the nest watch, she believed, were elegant in their simplicity, completeness, and flexibility: a pair of lightweight one-man camouflage all-weather shelters, plenty of water, a basic all-purpose tool, meals-ready-to-eat, a bodacious slingshot in case snakes or vultures came to visit the nest, good binocs, a two-channel sound amplifier to eavesdrop on the nest, a handheld GPS locator, and a digital palm-sized video recorder. Except for the water, each kit weighed a meager twenty-seven pounds and fit into compact, waterproof, dust-proof saddlebags she carried on her all-terrain motorcycle. The bottle of wine and two nice glasses were tucked into a quick-release pocket attached to the cycle frame. She had everything: shelter, food, water, tools, the falcon, a little wine. But no Lyle.

Indeed, Lyle's entire kit was still attached to the motorcycle she had stashed in a niche in the abandoned sandstone quarry below her perch.

A disturbing possibility occurred to Pansy as she watched the hatchling: Maybe Lyle was a little bit afraid of her. A champion triathlete and two-time Ironman medalist, Lieutenant Pansy Reynard, desert survival instructor with the Army's SFOD-D, Special Forces Operational Detachment—Delta Force, out of the Barstow military training center, admitted that she could be just a little bit intimidating.

10:00 A.M., APRIL 20
Downtown Las Vegas

Mickey Togs felt like a million bucks because he knew he looked like a million bucks. New custom-made, silver-gray suit with enough silk in the fabric to give it a little sheen. Not flashy-shiny, but sharp—expensively sharp, Vegas player sharp. His shirt and tie were of the same silver-gray color, as were the butter-soft handmade shoes on his size eight, EEE feet. Checking his reflection in the shiny surface of the black Lincoln Navigator he had acquired for the day's job, Mickey shot his cuffs, adjusted the fat Windsor knot in his silver-gray necktie, dusted some sand kicked up from yesterday's storm off his shoes, and grinned.

Yep, he decided as he climbed up into the driver's seat of the massive SUV, he looked every penny like a million bucks, exactly the sort of guy who had the *cojones* to carry off a million-dollar job. Sure, he had to split the paycheck a few ways because he couldn't do this particular job alone, but the splits wouldn't be equal, meaning he would be well paid. One hundred K to Big Mango the trigger-man, one hundred to Otto the Bump for driving, another hundred to bribe a cooperative federal squint, and then various payments for various spotters and informants. Altogether, after the split, Mickey personally would take home six hundred large; damn good jack for a morning's work.

Mickey Togs felt deservedly cocky. Do a little morning job for the Big Guys, be back on the Vegas Strip before lunch, get a nice bite to eat, then hit the baccarat salon at the Mirage with a fat stake in his pocket. Mickey took out a silk handkerchief and dabbed some sweat from his forehead; Mickey had trained half his life for jobs like this one. Nothing to it, he said to himself, confident that all necessary preparations had been made and all contingencies covered. A simple, elegant plan.

Mickey pulled the big Navigator into the lot of the Flower of the Desert Wedding Chapel on South Las Vegas Boulevard, parked, and slid over into the front passenger seat, the shotgun position. The chapel was in a neighborhood of cheap old motels and auto shops, not the sort of place where Mickey and his hired help would be noticed. In a town where one can choose to be married by Captain Kirk, Elvis Presley, or Marilyn Monroe, where brides and grooms

might dress accordingly, wedding chapels are good places not to be noticed. Even Big Mango, an almost seven-foot-tall Samoan wearing a turquoise Hawaiian shirt and flip-flops, drew hardly a glance as he crossed the lot and climbed into the backseat of the Navigator.

Otto the Bump, a one-time welterweight boxer with cauliflower ears and a nose as gnarled as a bag full of marbles, ordinarily might draw a glance or two, except that he wore Vegas-style camouflage: black suit, starched white shirt, black tie, spit-shined black brogans, a clean shave and a stiff comb-over. He could be taken for a maitre d', a pit boss, a father of the bride, a conventioneer, or the invisible man just by choosing where and how he stood. As he hoisted himself up into the driver's seat of the Navigator, Otto looked every inch like a liveried chauffeur.

"What's the job?" Otto asked as he turned out of the lot and into traffic.

"The Feds flipped Harry Coelho," Mickey said. "He's gonna spill everything to the grand jury this morning, and then he's going into witness protection. We got one shot to stop him. Job is to grab him before he gets to the courthouse, then take him for a drive and lose him as deep as Jimmy Hoffa."

"A snitch is the worst kind of rat there is," Otto groused. "Sonovabitch deserves whatever he gets."

"Absolutely," Mickey agreed. Big Mango, as usual, said nothing, but Mickey could hear him assembling the tools for his part of the job.

"How's it going down?" Otto asked.

"Federal marshals are gonna drive Harry from the jail over to the courthouse in a plain Crown Victoria with one follow car."

"Feds." Otto shook his head. "I don't like dealing with the Feds."

"Don't worry, the fix is in," Mickey said, sounding smug. "I'll get a call when the cars leave the jail. The route is down Main to Bonneville, where the courthouse is. You get us to the intersection, park us on Bonneville at the corner. We'll get a call when the cars are approaching the intersection. When they make the turn, you get us between the two cars and that's when we grab Harry."

"Whatever you say." Otto checked the rear-view mirror. "But what's the fix?"

Mickey chuckled. "You know how federal squints are, doughnut-eating civil servants with an itch to use their guns; they get off playing cops and robbers. A simple, good follow plan just doesn't do it for them, so they gotta throw in some complication. This is it: Harry leaves the jail in the front car. Somewhere on the route, the cars are going to switch their order so when they get to the courthouse Harry will be in the second car."

"How do you know they'll make the switch?"

"I know my business," Mickey said, straightening his tie to show he had no worries. "I got spotters out there. If the switch doesn't happen or the Feds decide to take a different route or slip in a decoy, I'll know it." He snapped his manicured fingers. "Like that."

Otto's face was full of doubt. "How will you know?"

"The phone calls?" Mickey said. "They're coming from inside the perp car. I bought us a marshal."

"Yeah?" Otto grinned, obviously impressed. "You got it covered, inside and outside."

"Like I say, I know my business," Mickey said, shrugging. "Here's the plan: Otto, you get us into position on Bonneville, and we wait for the call saying they're approaching. When the first car makes the turn off Main, you pull in tight behind it and stop fast. From then till we leave, you need to cover the first car; don't let anyone get out. Mango, you take care of the marshals in the second car any way you want to, but if you gack the marshal riding shotgun, you can have the rest of the bribe payment I owe him."

"Appreciate it," Mango said. "You want me to take out Harry, too?"

"Not there. I'll go in myself and get him. Otto, you stay ready to beat us the hell out when I say. We're taking Harry for a little drive and getting him lost. Are we clear?"

"Candy from a little baby," Otto said. Mango,

in the backseat, grunted. Could be gas, could be agreement, Mickey thought. Didn't much matter. Mango got paid to do what he did and not for conversation. With a grace that belied his huge size, Mango rolled into the back deck of the vast SUV and began to set up his firing position at the back window. Quiet and efficient, Mickey thought, a true pro.

The first call came. Harry Coelho left the Clark County jail riding in the backseat of a midnight blue Crown Victoria. The follow car was the same make, model, color. After two blocks, as planned, the cars switched positions, so that the follow car became the lead, and Harry Coelho's ass was hanging out in the wind with no rear cover.

When the second call came, the Navigator was in position on Bonneville, a half-block from the courthouse, waiting.

The snatch went smooth, by the book exactly the way Mickey Togs wrote it, the three of them moving with synchronicity as honed as a line of chorus girls all high-kicking at the same time. The first Crown Vic made the turn. Otto slipped the massive Navigator in behind it and stopped so fast that the second Crown Vic rear-ended him; the Crown Vic's hood pleated up under the Navigator's rear bumper like so much paper, didn't leave a mark on the SUV. Before the Crown Vic came to a final stop, Mango, positioned in the back deck, flipped up the rear hatch window and popped the two marshals in the front seat—fwoof, fwoof, that breezy sound the silencer makes—just as Mickey snapped open the back door and yanked out Harry Coelho, grabbing him by the oh-so-convenient handcuffs. They were back in the Navigator and speeding away before the first carload of Feds figured out that they had a problem on their hands.

No question, Otto was the best driver money could buy. A smooth turn onto Martin Luther King, then a hop up onto the 95 freeway going west into the posh new suburbs where a behemoth of an SUV like the Navigator became as anonymous and invisible as a dark-haired nanny pushing a blond-haired baby in a stroller.

After some maneuvers to make sure there was no tail, Otto exited the Interstate and headed up into Red Rock Canyon.

10:50 A.M.
Red Rock Canyon

The hatchling was calling out for a feeding again when Pansy Reynard heard the rumble of a powerful engine approaching. Annoyed that the racket might frighten her falcons, she peered over the edge of her perch.

The sheer walls of the abandoned sandstone quarry below her were a natural amplifier that made the vehicle sound larger than it actually was, but it was still huge, the biggest, blackest pile of personal civilian transport ever manufactured. Lost, she thought when she saw the Navigator, and all of its computer-driven gadgets couldn't help it get back to the freeway where it belonged.

For a moment, Pansy considered climbing out of her camouflaged blind and offering some help. But she sensed there was something just a little hinky about the situation. Trained to listen to that quiet inner warning system, Pansy held back, focused her binoculars on the SUV, and waited.

The front, middle, and back hatch doors opened at once and four men spilled out: two soft old guys wearing suits and dress shoes, a Pacific Islander dressed for a beach party, and a skinny little man with a hood over his head and his hands cuffed behind his back. The hood muffled the little man's voice so that Pansy couldn't understand his words, but she certainly understood his body language. Nothing good was happening down there. She set the lens of her palm-sized digital video recorder to zoom, and started taping the scene as it unfolded below.

The hooded man was marched to the rim over a deep quarried pit. His handlers stood him facing forward, then stepped aside. With a cool and steady hand, Beach Boy let off two silenced shots. A sudden burst of red opened out of the center of the hood, but before the man had time to crumple to the sandstone under him, a second blast hit him squarely in the chest and lifted him enough to push him straight over the precipice and out of sight.

"Kek, kek, kek." The mother Aplomado falcon, alarmed perhaps by the eerie sound of the silencer or maybe by the burst of energy it released, screeched as she swooped down between the canyon walls as if to dive bomb the intruders and distract them away from her nest. The two suits, who peered down into the abyss whence their victim had fallen, snapped to attention. Beach Boy, in a clean, fluid motion, pivoted the extended gun arm, spotted the mother and—fwoof, fwoof—she plunged into a mortal dive.

The hatchling, as if he saw and understood what had happened, set up his chittering again. Pansy saw that gun arm pivot again, this time toward the nest.

"No!" Pansy screamed as she rose, revealing herself to draw fire away from the precious, now orphaned hatchling. Binoculars and camera held aloft where they could be seen she called down, "I have it all on tape, you assholes. Come and get it."

Pansy kept up her screaming rant as she climbed out of the blind and rappelled down the backside of the cliff, out of view of the miscreants, but certainly within earshot. She needed them to come after her, needed to draw them away from the nest.

When she reached the canyon floor, Pansy pulled her all-terrain motorcycle out of its shelter among the rocks, gunned its powerful motor and raced toward the access road where the men could see her. The survival kit she had packed for Lyle—damn him, anyway—was still attached to the cycle's frame.

Otto the Bump scrambled back into the Navigator while Mickey and Mango pushed and pulled each other in their haste to climb inside lest they get left behind.

"Feds," Otto growled between clenched teeth as he started the big V-8 engine. "I told you, I don't like messing with Feds."

"She ain't the freaking Feds," Mickey snapped. His face red with anger, he turned on Mango. "You want to shoot off that piece of yours, you freaking idiot, shoot that damn girl. Otto, go get her."

The old quarry made a box canyon. Its dead-end access road was too narrow for the Navigator to turn around, so it had to back out the way it came in. Pansy was impressed by the driver's skill as he made a fast exit, but she still beat the Navigator to the mouth of quarry. For a moment, she stopped her bike crosswise to the road, blocking them. There was no way, she knew, that she could hold them until the authorities might arrive. Her entire purpose in stopping was to announce herself and to lure them after her, away from the nest. She hoped that they would think that size and firepower were enough to take her out.

Pansy'd had enough time to get a good look at her opponents, to make some assessments. The two little guys were casino rats with a whole lot of starched cuff showing, fusspot city shoes, jackets buttoned up when it was a hundred freaking degrees out there. Beach Boy would be fine in a cabana, but dressed as he was and without provisions . . . Vegas rats, she thought; the desert would turn them into carrion.

Rule one when outmanned and outgunned is to let the enemy defeat himself. Pansy figured that there was enough macho inside the car that once a little-bitty girl on a little-bitty bike challenged them to a chase, they wouldn't have the courage to quit until she was down or they were dead. Pansy sniffed as she lowered her helmet's face guard; overconfidence and geographic naïvete had brought down empires. Ask Napoleon.

Pansy didn't hear the burst of gunfire, but twice she felt the air wiffle past her head in that particular way that makes the hair of an experienced soldier stand up on end. As she bobbed and wove, creating an erratic target, she also kept herself just outside the range of the big handgun she had seen. Still, she knew all about random luck, and reminded herself not be too cocky herself, or too reliant on the law of averages.

Because she was in the lead, Pansy set the course. Her program involved stages of commitment: draw them in, give them a little reward as encouragement, then draw them in further until their training and equipment were overmatched by the environment and her experience. Play them.

The contest began on the decently paved road that headed out of Lee Canyon. Before the road met the freeway, Pansy veered onto a gravel by-road that took them due north, bisecting the canyons. When the road became a dry creek bed, Pansy disregarded the dead-end marker and continued to speed along; the Navigator followed. The canyons had been cut by eons of desert water runoff. The bottoms, except during the rainy season, were as hard-packed as fired clay and generally as wide as a two-lane road, though there were irregular patches of bone-jarring imbedded rocks and small boulders and some narrows. The bike could go around obstacles; the four-wheel-drive Navigator barreled over them.

Pansy picked up a bit of pavement in a flood control culvert where the creek passed under the freeway, and slowed slightly to give the Navigator some hope of overtaking her. But before they could quite catch her, she turned sharply again, this time onto an abandoned service road, pulling the Navigator behind as she continued north.

At any time, Pansy knew she could dash up into any of the narrow canyons that opened on either side of the road, and that the big car couldn't follow her. She held on to that possibility as an emergency contingency as she did her best to keep her pursuers intrigued.

The canyons became smaller and broader, the terrain flatter and Pansy more exposed. Sun bore down on her back and she cursed the wusses behind her in their air-conditioned beast. At eleven o'clock, right on schedule, the winds began to pick up. Whorls of sand quickly escalated to flurries and then to blinding bursts. Pansy pulled down the sand screen that was attached to her face guard, but she still choked on grit, felt fine sand grind in her teeth. None of this, as miserable as it made her feel, was unfamiliar or anything she could not handle.

Always, Pansy was impressed by the skill of the driver following her, and by his determination. He pushed the big vehicle through places where she thought he ought to bog down. And then there were times that, if he had taken more risk, he could have overcome her. That he had refrained, clued Pansy to the strategy: The men in the car thought they were driving her to ground. They were waiting for her to fall or falter in some way. She used this assumption, feigning, teasing, pretending now and then to weaken, always picking up her speed or maneuvering out of range just before they could get her, to keep them engaged. Some birds used a similar ploy, pretending to be wounded or vulnerable as a feint to lure predators away from their nests.

The canyons ended abruptly and the terrain became flat, barren desert bottom. There was no shelter, no respite, only endless heat and great blasts of wind-whipped sand. Pansy could no longer see potholes or boulders, nor could any of them see roadside markers. Though Pansy could not see the road, and regularly hit bone jarring dips and bumps, she was not navigating blind. Three times a year she ran a survival course through the very same area. She had drawn her pursuers into the hollow between Little Skull and Skull Mountains, headed toward Jackass Flats, a no-man's-land square in the middle of the Nellis Air Force Base gunnery range.

"Get her," Mickey growled. The silk handkerchief he held against his nose muffled his words. "I have things to do in town. Take her out. Now."

Mango's only response was to reload.

Otto swore as he switched off the AC and shut down the vents. Sand so fine he could not see it ground under his eyelids, filled his nose and throat, choked him. Within minutes the air inside the car was so hot that sweat ran in his eyes, made his shirt stick to his chest and his

back, riffled down his shins. There was no water, of course, because this was supposed to be a quick job, out of Vegas and back in an hour. He had plenty besides heat and thirst to make him feel miserable. First, he thought he could hear the effects of grit on the car's engine, a heaviness in its response. Next, he had a pretty good idea what Mickey would do to him if he let the girl get away.

How could they have gotten so far into this particular hell? Otto wondered. In the beginning, it had seemed real simple. Follow the girl until they were out of the range of any potential witnesses, then run over the girl and her pissant bike like so much road kill. But every time he started to make his move, she'd pull some damn maneuver and get away: she'd sideslip him or head down a wash so narrow that he had to give the road—such as it was—his undivided attention. The SUV was powerful, but it had its limitations, the first of which was maneuverability: it had none.

And then there was Mickey and his constant nudging, like he could do any better. By the time they came out of the canyons and onto the flats, Otto was so sick and tired of listening to Mickey, contending with the heat, the sand, and the damn girl and her stunts that he didn't care much how things ended, only that they ended immediately. He knew desperation and danger could be found on the same page in the dictionary, but he was so desperate to be out of that place that he was ready to take some risks; take out the girl and get back up on the freeway and out of the sand, immediately.

Between gusts Otto caught glimpses of the girl, so he knew more or less where she was. Fed up, he put a heavy foot on the accelerator and waited for the crunch of girl and bike under his thirty-two-inch wheels.

Pansy heard the SUV's motor rev, heard also the big engine begin to miss as it became befouled by sand. With the Navigator accelerating toward her, Pansy snapped the bottle of wine out of its break-away pouch, grasped it by the neck, gave it a wind-up swing as she spun her bike in a tight one-eighty, and let the bottle fly in a trajectory calculated to collide dead center with the rapidly approaching windshield.

As she headed off across the desert at a right angle to the road, she heard the bottle hit target and pop, heard the windshield give way, heard the men swear, smelled the brakes. The massive SUV decelerated from about fifty MPH to a dead, mired stop in the space of a mere sixty feet. Its huge, heavy-tread tires sliced through the hard desert crust and found beneath it sand as fine as talcum powder and as deep as an ocean. Forget four-wheel drive; every spin of the wheels merely kicked up a shower of sand and dug them in deeper. The behemoth SUV was going nowhere without a tow.

When she heard the rear deck hatch pop open, Pansy careened to a stop and dove behind a waist-high boulder for cover. As Beach Boy, leaning out the back hatch, unloaded a clip in her general direction, Pansy, lying on her belly, pulled out her slingshot, strapped it to her wrist, reached into the pouch of three-eighths-inch steel balls hanging from her belt, and, aiming at the dull red flashes coming from the end of Beach Boy's automatic, fired back. She heard random pings as her shot hit the side of the Navigator.

"She's packing heat," Otto yelled. Pansy continued to ping the side of the car with shot; sounded enough like bullet strikes.

Mango finally spoke. More exactly, Mango let out an ugly liquid-filled scream when Pansy's steel balls pierced his throat and his cheek. Mortally hit, he grabbed his neck as he fell forward, tumbling out of the SUV. With the big back window hanging open, the SUV quickly filled with fire hot, swirling yellow sand.

"She got Mango!" Otto yelled in Mickey's direction. "We try to run for it, she'll get us, too."

Mickey Togs, feeling faint from the heat, barely able to breathe, pulled his beautiful silver-gray suit coat over his head, being careful not to wrinkle it or get sweat on it, and tried, in vain, to get a signal on his cell phone. He didn't know who to call for help in this particularly humiliating situation, or, if he should be able to get a call out—and he could not—just where he happened to be for purposes of directing some sort of rescue.

Otto the Bump heard Mickey swear at his dead phone, and nearly got hit with it when Mickey, in a rage, threw the thing toward the cracked and leaking windshield. Not knowing what else to do, Otto reached for the little piece strapped to his left ankle.

"I'm making a run for it," Otto said.

"Idiot, what are your chances?" Mickey asked. "You got thirty, forty miles of desert, no water, can't see through that damn sand, and a lunatic out there trying to kill you."

"If I stay in this damn car or I make a run for it, I figure it's eighty-twenty against me either way," Otto said. "I prefer to take it on the run than sitting here waiting."

"Ninety-five to five." Mickey straightened the knot in his tie. "You do what you think you gotta do. I'm staying put."

"Your choice, but you still owe me a hundred K," Otto said. He chambered a round as he opened the car door, brought his arm against his nose, and dropped three feet down to the desert floor.

Without pausing for so much as a perfunctory hello to the clerk on duty, Pansy Reynard strode past the reception desk of the regional office of the Department of Fish and Game and straight back to the pathology lab. Pansy had showered and changed from her dirty desert camouflage BDUs—battle-dress utilities—into sandals, a short khaki skirt, and a crisp, sleeveless linen blouse; adaptability, she knew well, is the key to survival.

She opened the lab door and walked in. When Lyle, the so recently absent Lyle, looked up, she placed a large bundle wrapped in a camouflage tarp onto his desk, right on top of the second half of a tuna sandwich he happened to be eating, and then she flipped her sleek fall of hair over her shoulder for effect.

Eyes wide, thoroughly nonplused, Lyle managed to swallow his mouthful of sandwich and to speak. "What's this?"

"I went back to the nest this afternoon after the sandstorm blew out." Pansy unfastened the bundle and two long, graceful wings opened out of the tarp chrysalis. "I found her in the canyon."

"Oh, damn." Lyle stood, ashen-faced now, tenderly lifted the mother Aplomado falcon and carried her to a lab bench. He examined her, discovered the deep crimson wound in her black chest. Through gritted teeth he said, "Poachers?"

"Looks like it," Pansy said.

"What about the hatchling?"

"He's okay but he has to be hungry." With reverent sadness, Pansy stroked the mother falcon's smooth head. "Another week or two and the baby will be ready to fend for himself. But in the meantime, someone needs to get food to him. Or he needs to be brought in to a shelter."

Lyle sighed heavily. He was obviously deeply moved by this tragedy, a quality that Pansy found to be highly attractive.

"What are you going to do, Lyle?"

"I'll ask for a wildlife team to come out," he said. "Someone will get up there tomorrow to rescue the hatchling. Too bad, though. We've lost a chance to reestablish a nesting pattern."

"Tomorrow?" There was a flash of indignation in her tone.

"He'll be okay overnight."

"What if the poachers come back tonight?"

Again he sighed, looked around at the cluttered lab and the stacks of unfinished paperwork. Then he turned and looked directly into Pansy's big brown eyes.

"Pansy, I need help," he said. "Will you watch the nest tonight?"

"Me?" She touched her breastbone demurely, her freshly scrubbed hand small and delicate looking. "Alone? Lyle, there are people with guns out there."

"You're right," he said, chagrined. "Sorry. Of course you shouldn't be alone. You shouldn't have been alone last night and this morning, either. It's just, I got jammed up here in the office with a possible plague case in a ground squirrel, Chamber of Commerce all in a lather that word would get out. I couldn't break away."

"Ground squirrels aren't in danger of extinction," she said.

"I am sorry, very sorry," Lyle said, truly sounding sorry. "Look, Pansy, I really need you. If I join you, will you be willing to go back to the nest tonight?"

She took a long breath before responding, not wanting to sound eager. After a full ten count, during which he watched her with apparent interest, she nodded.

"The two of us should be able to handle just about anything that comes up," she said. "I'll meet you out front in five minutes."

"In five," he said as he peeled off his lab coat. "In five."

THE CASE OF THE PARR CHILDREN

Antonia Fraser

HAVING ALREADY ESTABLISHED a reputation as a writer of popular history and biographies about Mary, Queen of Scots, Oliver Cromwell, various episodes in British history, and the kings and queens of England, Lady Antonia Margaret Caroline Fraser (1932–) turned to writing detective stories about Jemima Shore, a television investigative reporter, producing ten novels between 1977 and 1995.

The daughter of Lord Longford, himself a writer, Antonia earned a B.A. and an M.A. in history from Oxford. She married Hugh Fraser when she was twenty-four, divorcing him twenty-one years later in a highly publicized breakup when she began an affair with the married playwright Harold Pinter, marrying him three years later.

Jemima Shore was introduced in *Quiet as a Nun* (1977), and the character was featured in a British television series, *Jemima Shore Investigates*, which lasted for only twelve episodes in 1983. Shore is a modern woman and reflects society in the last quarter of the twentieth century. The author has stated that her primary influence as a mystery writer was Dorothy L. Sayers and her protagonist is an up-to-date version of Harriet Vane. Although Shore does not have a Lord Peter Wimsey in her life, she is not relegated to existence without a man. Or, more accurately, men. Bringing a new element to mystery fiction, Shore may be the first literary detective to sleep with people who may be involved in murder, as she does in *The Wild Island* (1978).

"The Case of the Parr Children" was originally published in *Ms. Murder*, edited by Marie Smith (London, Xanadu, 1989); it was first collected in *Jemima Shore's First Case* (New York, Norton, 1987).

The Case of the Parr Children

ANTONIA FRASER

"I'VE COME ABOUT THE CHILDREN."

The woman who stood outside the door of the flat, her finger poised to ring the bell again, looked desperate. She also looked quite unknown to the owner of the flat, Jemima Shore. It was ten o'clock on Sunday morning; an odd time for anyone to be paying a social call on the celebrated television reporter. Jemima Shore had no children. Outside her work she led a very free and very private existence. As she stood at the door, unusually dishevelled, pulling a dark-blue towelling robe round her, she had time to wonder rather dazedly: Whose children? Why here? Before she decided that the stranger had rung the wrong bell of the flat, and very likely in the wrong house in Holland Park. "I've come about the children."

The woman before her was panting slightly as she repeated the words. But then Jemima Shore's flat was the top floor. It was her appearance which on closer inspection was odd: she looked smudged and dirty in like a charcoal drawing which has been abandoned. Her beltless mackintosh had presumably once been white; as had perhaps her ancient tennis shoes with their gaping canvas, and her thick woollen socks. The thin dark dress she wore beneath her mackintosh, hem hanging down, gave the impression of being too old for her until Jemima realized that it was the dress itself which was decrepit. Only

her hair showed any sign of care: that had at least been brushed. Short and brown, it hung down straight on either side of her face: in this case the style was too young.

The woman before Jemima might have been a tramp. Then there was the clink of a bottle at her feet as she moved uneasily towards Jemima. In a brown paper bag were the remains of a picnic which had clearly been predominantly alcoholic. The image of the tramp was confirmed.

"Jemima Shore Investigator?" she gasped. "You've *got* to help me." And she repeated for the third time: "You see, I've come about the children."

Jemima recoiled slightly. It was true that she was billed by this title in her programmes of serious social reportage. It was also true that the general public had from time to time mistaken her for a real investigator as a result. Furthermore, lured by the magic spell of know-all television, people had on occasion brought her problems to solve; and she had on occasions solved them. Nevertheless early on a Sunday morning, well before the first cup of coffee, seemed an inauspicious moment for such an appeal. In any case by the sound of it, the woman needed a professional social worker rather than an amateur investigator.

Jemima decided that the lack of coffee could at least be remedied. Pulling her robe still further around her, and feeling more than slightly cross, she led the way into her elegant little kitchen. The effect of the delicate pink formica surfaces was to make the tramp-woman look grubbier than ever. At which point her visitor leant forward on her kitchen stool, covered in pretty rose-coloured denim, and started to sob loudly and incontrolledly into her hands. Tears trickled between her fingers. Jemima noticed with distaste that the finger-nails too were dirty. Coffee was by now not so much desirable as essential. Jemima proceeded first to make it, and then to administer it.

Ten minutes later she found herself listening to a very strange story indeed. The woman who was telling it described herself as Mrs. Catharine Parr.

"Yes, just like the wretched Queen who lost her head, and I'm just as wretched, I'm quite lost too." Jemima raised her eyebrows briefly at the historical inaccuracy—hadn't Catharine Parr, sixth wife of Henry VIII, died in her bed? But as Mrs. Parr rushed on with her dramatic tale, she reflected that here was a woman who probably embellished everything with unnecessary flourishes. Mrs. Parr was certainly wretched enough; that went without question. Scotland. She had come overnight from Scotland. Hence of course the mackintosh, even the picnic (although the empty wine bottles remained unexplained). Hence the early hour, for Mrs. Parr had come straight from Euston Station, off her sleeper. And now it was back to the children again.

At this point, Jemima Shore managed at last to get a word in edgeways: "Whose children? Your children?"

Mrs. Parr, tears checked, looked at Jemima as though she must already know the answer to that question: "Why, the *Parr* children of course. Don't you remember the case of the Parr children? There was a lot about it on television," she added reproachfully.

"The Parr children: yes, I think I do remember something—your children, I suppose."

To Jemima's surprise there was a pause. Then Mrs. Parr said with great solemnity:

"Miss Shore, that's just what I want you to

find out. I just don't *know* whether they're my children or not. I just don't *know*."

"I think," said Jemima Shore Investigator, resignedly drinking her third cup of coffee, "you had better tell me all about it from the beginning."

Oddly enough Jemima genuinely did remember something about the episode. Not from television, but from the newspapers where it had been much discussed, notably in the *Guardian*; and Jemima was a *Guardian* reader. It had been a peculiarly rancorous divorce case. The elderly judge had come down heavily on the side of the father. Not only had he taken the unusual step of awarding Mr. Parr care and custody of the two children of the marriage—mere babies—but he had also summed up the case in full for the benefit of the Press.

In particular he had dwelt venomously on the imperfections of Mrs. Parr and her "trendy amoral Bohemianism unsuitable for contact with any young creature." This was because Mrs. Parr had admitted having an affair with a gypsy or something equally exotic. She now proposed to take her children off with him for the glorious life of the open road; which, she suggested, would enable her children to grow up uninhibited, loving human beings. Mr. Parr responded with a solid bourgeois proposition, including a highly responsible Nanny, a general atmosphere of nursery tea now, private schools later. Columnists had had a field-day for a week or two, discussing the relative merits of bourgeois and Bohemian life-styles for children. On the whole Jemima herself had sympathized with the warm-blooded Mrs. Parr.

It transpired that Jemima's recollection of the case was substantially correct. Except that she had forgotten the crucial role played by the so-called Nanny; in fact no Nanny but a kind of poor relation, a trained nurse named Zillah. It was Zillah who had spoken with calm assurance of the father's love for his children, reluctantly of the selfish flightiness of the mother. She had known her cousin Catharine all her life, she said, although their material circumstances had been very different. She pronounced with regret that in her opinion Catharine Parr was simply not fitted to have sole responsibility for young children. It was one of the reasons which had prompted her to leave her nursing career in order to look after the Parr babies.

Since Zillah was clearly a detached witness who had the welfare of the children at heart, her evidence was regarded as crucial by the judge. He contrasted Catharine and Zillah: "two young women so outwardly alike, so inwardly different." He made this also a feature of his summing-up. "Miss Zillah Roberts, who has had none of the benefits of money and education of the mother in the case, has nevertheless demonstrated the kind of firm moral character most appropriate to the care of infants . . . etc. etc."

In vain Mrs. Parr had exploded in court: "Don't believe her! She's his mistress! They're sleeping together. She's been jealous of me all her life. She always wanted everything I had, my husband, now my children." Such wild unsubstantiated talk did Mrs. Parr no good at all, especially in view of her own admitted "uninhibited and loving" behaviour. If anything, the judge's summing-up gained in vinegar from the interruption.

Mrs. Parr skated over the next part of her story. Deprived of her children, she had set off for the south of Ireland with her lover. Jemima had the impression, listening to her, that drink had played a considerable part in the story— drink and perhaps despair too. Nor did Mrs. Parr enlarge on the death of her lover, except to say that he had died as he had lived: "violently." As a result Jemima had no idea whether Mrs. Parr regretted her bold leap out of the bourgeois nest. All she discovered was that Mrs. Parr had had no contact whatsoever with her children for seven years. Neither sought nor proffered. Not sought because Mr. Parr had confirmed Mrs. Parr's suspicions by marrying Zillah the moment his divorce became absolute: "and *she* would never have permitted it. Zillah." Not proffered, of course, because Mrs. Parr had left no address behind her.

"I had to make a new life. I wouldn't take any money from him. They'd taken my children away from me and I had to make a new life."

It was only after the death of Mrs. Parr's lover that, destitute and friendless, she had returned to England. Contacting perforce her ex-husband's lawyer for funds of some sort, she had discovered to her astonishment that Mr. Parr had died suddenly several months earlier. The lawyers had been trying in their dignified and leisurely fashion to contact his first wife, the mother of his children. In the meantime the second Mrs. Parr, Zillah, the children's ex-Nanny and step-mother had taken them from Sussex off to a remote corner of the Scottish Highlands. As she put it to the lawyer, she intended "to get them and me away from it all." The lawyer had demurred with the question of the children's future outstanding. But Zillah, with that same quiet air of authority which had swayed the divorce-court judge, convinced him. It might be months before the first Mrs. Parr was contacted, she pointed out. In the meantime they had her address. And the children's.

"And suddenly there I was!" exclaimed Mrs. Catharine Parr to Jemima Shore, the vehemence returning to her voice. "But it was too late."

"Too late?"

"Too late for Zillah. You see, Miss Shore, Zillah was dead. She was drowned in a boating accident in Scotland. It was too late for Zillah." Jemima, sensing the depth of Mrs. Parr's bitterness, realized that what she really meant was: Too late for vengeance.

Even then, Mrs. Parr's troubles were not over. The encounter with the children had been even more upsetting. Two children, Tamsin nearly nine and Tara nearly eight, who confronted her with scared and hostile eyes. They were being cared for at the lodge which Zillah had so precipitately rented. A local woman from the village, responsible for the caretaking of the lodge, had volunteered. Various suggestions had been made to transfer the children to somewhere less lonely, attended by less tragic memories. However, Tamsin and Tara had shown such extreme distress at the idea of moving away from their belongings and the home they knew that the plan had been abandoned. In the meantime their real mother had announced her arrival.

So Mrs. Parr took the sleeper to Inverness.

"But when I got to Scotland I didn't recognize them!" cried Mrs. Parr in a return to her dramatic style. "So I want you to come back to Scotland with me and *interview* them. Find out who they are. You're an *expert* interviewer: I've seen you on television. That programme about refugee children. You talk to them. I beg you, Miss Shore. You see before you a desperate woman and a fearful mother."

"But were you likely to recognize them?" enquired Jemima rather dryly. "I mean you hadn't seen either of them for seven years. How old was Tamsin then—eighteen months? Tara—what—six months?"

"It wasn't a question of *physical* recognition, I assure you. In a way, they *looked* more or less as I expected. Fair. Healthy. She'd looked after them all right, Zillah, whoever they are. She always looked after people, Zillah. That's how she got him of course."

"Then why—" began Jemima hastily.

Mrs. Parr leant forward and said in a conspiratorial tone: "It was spiritual recognition I meant. Nothing spoke to me and said: these are my children. In fact a voice deep in me cried out: Zillah! These are Zillah's children. This is Zillah's revenge. Even from the grave, she won't let me have my own children." She paused for effect.

"You see Zillah had this sister Kitty. We were cousins, I think I told you. Quite close cousins even though we had been brought up so differently. That's how Zillah came to look after the children in the first place: she wanted a proper home, she said, after the impersonality of nursing. But that didn't satisfy Zillah. She was always on at me to do something about this sister and her family—as though their awful lives were my fault!"

She went on: "Kitty had two little girls, almost exactly the same ages as my two. Quite fair then, though not as fair as Zillah and not as fair as my children. But there was a resemblance, everyone said so. People sometimes took them for my children. I suppose our relationship accounted for it. Kitty was a wretched creature but physically we were not unalike. Anyway, Zillah thought the world of these babies and was always having them round. Kitty was unhappily married: I believe the husband ran off before the last baby was born. Suddenly, looking at this pair, I thought: little cuckoos. Zillah has taken her own nieces, and put them into my nest—"

"—Which you had left of your own accord." But Jemima did not say the words aloud. Instead she asked with much greater strength:

"But *why?*"

"The money! That's why," exclaimed Mrs. Parr in triumph. "The Parr money in trust for them. Parr Biscuits. Doesn't that ring a bell? The money only went to the descendants of Ephraim Parr. *She* wouldn't have got a penny—except what *he* left her. Her nieces had no Parr blood either. But my children, because they were Parrs, would have been, *are* rich. Maybe my poor little children died, ran away, maybe she put them in an orphanage—*I* don't know. Or"—her voice suddenly changed totally, becoming dreamy, "Or perhaps these are my children after all. Perhaps I'm imagining it all, after all I've been through. Miss Shore, this is just what I've come all the way from Scotland to beg you to find out."

It was an extraordinary story. Jemima's original impulse had been to give Mrs. Catharine Parr a cup of coffee and send her gently on her way. Now the overriding curiosity which was definitely her strongest attribute would not let her be. The appeals of the public to Jemima Shore Investigator certainly fell on compassionate ears; but they also fell on very inquisitive ones. In this instance she felt she owed it to the forces of common sense to point out first to Mrs. Parr that lawyers could investigate such matters far more efficiently than she. To this Mrs. Parr answered quite reasonably that lawyers would take an age, as they always did:

"And in the meantime what would happen to

me and the children? We'd be getting to know each other, getting fond of each other. No, Miss Shore, *you* can settle it. I know you can. Then we can all get on with our lives for better or for worse."

Then Jemima caved in and acceded to Mrs. Parr's request.

It was in this way, for better or for worse as Mrs. Parr had put it, that Jemima Shore Investigator found herself the following night taking the sleeper to Inverness.

The sleeping-car attendant recognized Mrs. Parr quite merrily: "Why, it's you again Mrs. Parr. You'll keep British Rail in business with your travelling." Then of course he recognized Jemima Shore with even greater delight. Later, taking her ticket, he was with difficulty restrained from confiding to her his full and rich life story which he was convinced would make an excellent television documentary. Staved off, he contented himself with approving Jemima's modest order of late-night tea.

"You're not like your friend, then, Mrs. Parr . . ." he made a significant drinking gesture. "The trouble I had with her going north the first time. Crying and crying, and disturbing all the passengers. However, she was better the second time, and mebbe now you'll have a good influence on her now, Miss Shore. I'll be seeing her now and asking her if this time she'll have a late-night cup of tea." He bustled off, leaving Jemima faintly disquieted. She hoped that Mrs. Parr had no drink aboard. The north of Scotland with an alcoholic, probably a fantasist into the bargain . . .

Morning found her in a more robust mood. Which was fortunate since Jemima's first sight of Kildrum Lodge, standing on the edge of a dark, seemingly endless loch, shut in by the mountains, was once again disquieting. It was difficult for her to believe that Zillah could have brought the children to such a place out of sheer love for Scottish scenery and country pursuits such as fishing, swimming, and walking. The situation of the lodge itself even for Scotland was so extremely isolated. Nor was the glen which

led up to the lodge notably beautiful. A general lack of colour except blackness in the water reflected from the skies made it in fact peculiarly depressing. There was a lack of vegetation even on the lower slopes of the mountains, which slid down straight into the loch. The single-track road was bumpy and made of stones. It was difficult to imagine that much traffic passed that way. One could imagine a woman with something to hide—two children perhaps?—seeking out such a location, but not a warm comforting body hoping to cheer up her charges after the sudden death of their father.

The notion of Zillah's sinister purpose, far-fetched in London, suddenly seemed horribly plausible. And this was the loch, the very loch, in which Zillah herself had drowned. No, Kildrum to Jemima Shore did not have the air of a happy uncomplicated place. She looked across at Mrs. Parr, in the passenger seat of the hired car. Mrs. Parr looked pale. Whether she had passed the night consuming further bottles of wine or was merely dreading the next confrontation with the Parr children, the hands with which she was trying to light a cigarette were shaking. Jemima felt once more extremely sorry for her and glad that she had come to Kildrum.

They approached the lodge. It was surrounded by banks of dark-green rhododendrons, growing unrestrained, which did nothing to cheer the surroundings. There was no other garden, only rough grass going down to the loch. The large windows of the lodge looked blank and unwelcoming. As Jemima drove slowly up the stony road, the front door opened and something white was glimpsed within. It was eerily quiet once the car's engine stopped. Then the door opened further and the flash of white proved to be a girl wearing jeans and a blue jersey. She had extremely fair, almost lint-white hair, plaited. For a girl of eight she was quite well built—even stocky.

"Tamsin," said Mrs. Parr. She pronounced the name as though for Jemima's benefit; but it was once again disquieting that she made no move towards the child. The interior of the house, like the glen itself and the mountains, was dark. Most of the paintwork was brown and the chintz curtains were patterned in a depressing brown and green. Nevertheless, some energy had obviously been spent recently in making it cosy. There were cheerful traces of childish occupation, books, a bright red anorak, shiny blue gumboots. Pot plants and an arrangement of leaves bore witness to the presence of a domestic spirit in the house—once upon a time.

In the large kitchen at the back of the house where Jemima insisted on repairing for coffee there was also an unmistakeable trace of modern civilization in the shape of a television set. There was a telephone too—but that was black and ancient looking. Tamsin went with them, still silent. In the kitchen they were immediately joined by Tara, equally silent, equally blonde.

The two sisters stared warily at the women before them as if they were intruders. Which in a sense, thought Jemima, we are. Her eyes caught and held by the two striking flaxen heads, she recalled Mrs. Parr's words concerning Zillah's nephew and niece: "Quite fair too then, but not as fair as Zillah's and not as fair as my children . . ." Could children actually become fairer as the years went by? Impossible. No one became fairer with time except out of a bottle. Even these children's hair was darkening slightly at the roots. Jemima felt that she had a first very positive clue that the Parr children were exactly what they purported to be. She was so relieved that a feeling of bonhomie seized her. She smiled warmly at the children and extended her hand.

"I'm Jemima Shore—"

"Investigator!" completed Tamsin triumphantly. And from her back she produced a large placard on which the cheering words: "Welcome Jemima Shore Investogator" were carefully inscribed in a variety of lurid pentel colours.

"I did it," exclaimed Tara.

"I did the spelling," said Tamsin proudly.

Jemima decided it would be tactful to congratulate her on it. At least fame on the box granted you a kind of passport to instant friendship, whatever the circumstances. In the kitchen too was another figure prepared to be an instant friend: Mrs. Elspeth Maxwell, caretaker of the lodge and since the death of Zillah, *in loco parentis* to the Parr children. Elspeth Maxwell, as Jemima quickly appreciated, was a woman of uncertain age but certain garrulity. Instinctively she summed people up as to whether they would make good or bad subjects for an interview. Mrs. Parr, madness and melodrama and all, would not in the end make good television. She was perhaps too obsessional at centre. But Elspeth Maxwell, under her flow of anecdote, might give you just that line or vital piece of information you needed to illuminate a whole topic. Jemima decided to cultivate her; whatever the cost in listening to a load of irrelevant gossip.

As a matter of fact Elspeth Maxwell needed about as much cultivation as the rhododendrons growing wild outside the house. During the next few days, Jemima found that her great problem consisted in getting away from Elspeth Maxwell, who occupied the kitchen, and into the children's playroom. Mrs. Parr spent most of the time in her bedroom. Her public excuse was that she wanted to let Jemima get on with her task, which had been described to Tamsin and Tara as investigation for a programme about children living in the Highlands. Privately she told Jemima that she wanted to keep clear of emotional involvement with the children "until I'm *sure*. One way or the other." Jemima thought there might be a third reason: that Mrs. Parr wanted to consume at leisure her daily ration of cheap red wine. The pile of empty bottles on the rubbish dump behind the rhododendrons continued to grow and there was a smell of drink upstairs emanating from Mrs. Parr's bedroom. Whenever Mrs. Parr chose to empty an ash-tray it was overflowing.

On one occasion Jemima tried the door. It was locked. After a moment Mrs. Parr called out in a muffled voice: "Go away. I'm resting."

It was conclusive evidence of Mrs. Parr's addiction that no drink was visible in the rest of the house. Jemima was never offered anything alcoholic nor was any reference made to the subject. In her experience of alcoholics, that was far more damning than the sight of a rapidly diminishing sherry bottle in the sitting-room.

Elspeth on the subject of the children was interminable: "Ach, the poor wee things! Terrible for them, now, wasn't it? Their mother drowned before their very eyes. What a tragedy. Here in Kildrum."

"Step-mother," corrected Jemima. Elspeth swept on. But the tale was indeed a tragic one, whichever way you looked at it.

"A fearful accident indeed. Though there's other people been drowned in the loch, you know, it's the weeds, those weeds pull you down, right to the bottom. And it's one of the deepest lochs in the Highlands, deeper than Loch Ness, nearly as deep as Loch Morar, did you know that, Miss Shore? Then their father not so long dead, I believe, and this lady coming, their real mother, all on top of it. Then you, so famous, from television . . ."

The trouble was that for all her verbiage, Elspeth Maxwell could not really tell Jemima anything much about Zillah herself, still less about her relationship with Tamsin and Tara. It was Elspeth who had had the task of sorting out Zillah's effects and putting them into suitcases, still lying upstairs while some sort of decision was reached as to what to do with them. These Jemima made a mental note to examine as soon as possible. Otherwise Elspeth had seen absolutely nothing of Zillah during her sojourn at Kildrum Lodge.

"She wanted no help, she told the Estate Office. She could perfectly well take care of the lodge, she said, and the children. She was used to it. And the cooking. She wanted peace and quiet, she said, and to fish and walk and swim and go out in the boat—" Elspeth stopped, "Ah well, poor lady. But she certainly kept herself very close, herself and the children. No one knew her in Kildrum. Polite, mind you, a very polite lady, they said at the Estate Office, wrote very polite letters and notes. But very close."

And the children? The verdict was more or less the same. Yes, they had certainly seemed very fond of Zillah whenever glimpsed in Kildrum. But generally shy, reserved. And once again polite. Elspeth could only recall one conversation of any moment before Zillah's death, out of a series of little interchanges and that was when Tamsin, in Kildrum Post Office, referred to the impending arrival of Mrs. Parr. Elspeth, out of motherly sympathy for their apparent loneliness, had invited Tamsin and Tara to tea with her in the village. Tamsin had refused: "A lady's coming from London to see us. She says she's our Mummy. But Billy and me think Zillah is our Mummy."

It was, remarked Elspeth, an unusual burst of confidence from Tamsin. She had put it down to Tamsin's distaste at the thought of the arrival of "the lady from London"—while of course becoming madly curious about Tamsin's family history. As a result of a "wee discussion" of the subject in her own home, she had actually put two and two together and realized that these were the once famous Parr children. Elspeth, even in Kildrum, had naturally had strong views on *that* subject. How she would now have adored some contact with the household at Kildrum Lodge! But that was politely but steadfastly denied her. Until Zillah's death, ironically enough, brought to Elspeth exactly that involvement she had so long desired.

"I did think: mebbe she has something to hide, and my brother-in-law, Johnnie Maxwell, the ghillie, he thought mebbe the same. Keeping herself so much to herself. But all along, I dare say it was just the fear of the other mother, that one"—Elspeth rolled her eyes to the ceiling where Mrs. Parr might be supposed to lie "resting" in her bedroom—"fear of her finding the children. Ah well, it's difficult to judge her altogether wrong. If you know what I mean. The dreadful case. All that publicity."

But Elspeth looked as if she would readily rehash every detail of the case of the Parr children, despite the publicity, for Jemima's benefit.

None of this was particularly helpful. Nor did inspection of Zillah's personal belongings, neatly sorted by Elspeth, bring any reward. It was not that Jemima expected to find a signed confession: "Tamsin and Tara are imposters. They are the children of my sister . . ." Indeed, she was coming more and more to the conclusion that Mrs. Parr's mad suspicions were the product of a mind disordered by alcohol. But Jemima did hope to provide herself with some kind of additional picture of the dead woman, other than the malevolent reports of the first Mrs. Parr, and the second-hand gossip of Elspeth Maxwell. All she discovered was that Zillah, like Jemima herself, had an inordinate fondness for the colour beige, presumably for the same reason, to complement her fair colouring; and like a good many other Englishwomen bought her underclothes at Marks & Spencer. Jemima did not like to speculate where and when Mrs. Parr might have last bought her underclothes.

There were various photographs of Tamsin and Tara but none predating Scotland. There were also some photographs of Zillah's sister Kitty; she did look vaguely like Mrs. Parr, Jemima noticed, but no more than that; their features were different; it was a question of physical type rather than strict resemblance. There were no photographs of Kitty's children. Was that sinister? Conceivably. Or maybe she had merely lost touch with them. Was it also sinister that Zillah had not preserved photographs of Tamsin and Tara in Sussex? Once again: conceivably. On the other hand Zillah might have packed away all her Sussex mementoes (there were no photographs of Mr. Parr either). Perhaps she came into that category of grief-stricken person who prefers not to be reminded of the past.

From the Estate Office Jemima drew another blank. Major Maclachlan, who had had the unenviable task of identifying Zillah's body, was polite enough, particularly at the thought of a television programme popularizing his corner of the Highlands. But he added very little to the public portrait of a woman whose chief characteristic was her reserve and determination to guard her privacy—her own and that of the children. Her love of country sports, especially

fishing, had however impressed him: Major Maclachlan clearly found it unjust that someone with such admirable tastes should have perished as a result of them.

Only Johnnie Maxwell, Elspeth's brother-in-law who was in charge of fishing on the loch, contributed anything at all vivid to her enquiries. For it was Johnnie Maxwell who had been the principal witness at the inquest, having watched the whole drowning from the bank of the loch. To the newspaper account of the tragedy, which Jemima had read, he added some ghoulish details of the pathetic cries of the "wee girl," unable to save Zillah. The children had believed themselves alone on the loch. In vain Johnnie had called to them to throw in the oar. Tamsin had merely screamed and screamed, oar in hand, Tara had sat quite still and silent, as though dumbstruck in horror. In their distress they did not seem to understand, or perhaps they could not hear him.

Altogether it was a most unfortunate, if not unparalleled accident. One moment Zillah was casting confidently ("Aye, she was a grand fisherwoman, the poor lady, more's the pity"). The next moment she had overbalanced and fallen in the water. There was no one else in the boat except the two children, and no one else to be seen on the shores of the loch except Johnnie. By the time he got his own boat to the children, Zillah had completely vanished and Tamsin was in hysterics, Tara quite mute. Helpers came up from the Estate. They did not find the body till the next morning, when it surfaced in the thick reeds at the shore. There were some bruises on it, but nothing that could not be explained by a fall from the boat and prolonged immersion.

That left the children. Jemima felt she owed it to Mrs. Parr to cross-examine them a little on their background. Confident that she would turn up nothing to their disadvantage, she could at least reassure Mrs. Parr thoroughly as a result. After that she trusted that her eccentric new contact would settle into normal life or the nearest approximation to it she could manage. Yes, the gentle, efficient cross-examination of Tamsin and Tara would be her final task and then Jemima Shore Investigator would depart for London, having closed the case of the Parr children once and for all.

But it did not work out quite like that.

The children, in their different ways, were friendly enough. Tamsin was even quite talkative once her initial shyness wore off. She had a way of tossing her head so that the blonde pigtails shook, like a show pony shaking its mane. Tara was more silent and physically frailer. But she sprang into life whenever Tamsin felt the need to contradict her, as being her elder and better. Arguing with Tamsin made even Tara quite animated. You could imagine both settling down easily once the double shock of Zillah's death and their real mother's arrival had been assimilated.

Nevertheless something was odd. It was instinct, not reason, that guided her. Reason told her that Mrs. Parr's accusations were absurd. But then nagging instinct would not leave her in peace. She had interviewed too many subjects, she told herself, to be wrong . . . Then reason reasserted itself once more, with the aid of the children's perfectly straightforward account of their past. They referred quite naturally to their life in Sussex.

"We went to horrid school with nasty rough boys—" began Tara.

"It was a *lovely* school," interrupted Tamsin, "I played football with the boys in my break. Silly little girls like Tara couldn't do that." All of this accorded with the facts given by the lawyer: how the girls had attended the local primary school which was fine for the tomboy Tamsin, not so good for the shrinking Tara. They would have gone to the reputedly excellent school in Kildrum when the Scottish term started had it not been for the death of Zillah.

Nevertheless something was odd, strange, not quite right.

Was it perhaps the fact the girls never seemed to talk amongst themselves which disconcerted her? After considerable pondering on the subject, Jemima decided that the silence of Tamsin and Tara when alone—no happy or unhappy sounds coming out of their playroom or bedroom—was the most upsetting thing about them. Even the sporadic quarrelling brought on by Tamsin's bossiness ceased. Yet Jemima's experience of children was that sporadic quarrels in front of the grown-ups turned to outright war in private. But she was here as an investigator not as a child analyst (who might or might not have to follow later). Who was she to estimate the shock effect of Zillah's death, in front of their very eyes? Perhaps their confidence had been so rocked by the boating accident that they literally could not speak when alone. It was, when all was said and done, a minor matter compared to the evident correlation of the girls' stories with their proper background.

And yet . . . There was after all the whole question of Zillah's absent nieces. Now was that satisfactorily dealt with or not? Torn between reason and instinct Jemima found it impossible to make up her mind. She naturally raised the subject, in what she hoped to be a discreet manner. For once it was Tara who answered first:

"Oh, no, we never see them. You see they went to America for Christmas and they didn't come back." She sounded quite blithe.

"Canada, silly," said Tamsin.

"Same thing."

"It's not, silly."

"It is—"

"Christmas?" pressed Jemima.

"They went for a Christmas holiday to America. Aunt Kitty took them and they never came back."

"They went *forever*," interrupted Tamsin fiercely. "They went to Canada and they went *forever*. That's what Zillah said. Aunt Kitty doesn't even send us Christmas cards." Were the answers, as corrected by Tamsin, a little too pat?

A thought struck Jemima. Later that night she consulted Mrs. Parr. If Zillah's sister had been her next of kin, had not the lawyers tried to contact her on Zillah's death? Slightly reluctantly Mrs. Parr admitted that the lawyers had tried and so far failed to do so. "Oddly enough it seemed I was Zillah's next of kin after Kitty," she added. But Kitty had emigrated to Canada (yes, Canada, Tamsin as usual was right) several years earlier and was at present address unknown. And she was supposed to have taken her two daughters with her.

It was at this point Jemima decided to throw in her hand. In her opinion the investigation was over, the Parr children had emerged with flying colours, and as for their slight oddity, well, that was really only to be expected, wasn't it? Under the circumstances. It was time to get back to Megalith Television and the autumn series. She communicated her decision to Mrs. Parr, before nagging instinct could resurrect its tiresome head again.

"You don't feel it then, Jemima?" Mrs. Parr sounded for the first time neither vehement nor dreamy but dimly hopeful. "You don't sense something about them? That they're hiding something? Something strange, unnatural . . ."

"No, I do not," answered Jemima Shore firmly. "And if I were you, Catharine"—they had evolved a spurious but convenient intimacy during their days in the lonely lodge—"I would put all such thoughts behind you. See them as part of the ordeal you have suffered, a kind of long illness. Now you must convalesce and recover. And help your children, your own children, to recover too." It was Jemima Shore at her most bracing. She hoped passionately not so much that she was correct about the children—with every minute she was more convinced of the rightness of reason, the falseness of instinct—but that Mrs. Parr would now feel able to welcome them to her somewhat neurotic bosom. She might even give up drink.

Afterwards Jemima would always wonder whether these were the fatal words which turned the case of the Parr children from a mystery into a tragedy. Could she even then have realized or guessed the truth? The silence of the little girls together: did she gloss too easily over that? But by that time it was too late.

As it was, immediately Jemima had spoken, Mrs. Parr seemed to justify her decision in the most warming way. She positively glowed with delight. For a moment Jemima had a glimpse of the dashing young woman who had thrown up her comfortable home to go off with the raggle-taggle-gypsies seven years before. This ardent and presumably attractive creature had been singularly lacking in the Mrs. Parr she knew. She referred to herself now as "lucky Catharine Parr," no longer the wretched Queen who lost her head. Jemima was reminded for an instant of one of the few subjects who had bested her in argument on television, a mother opposing organized schooling, like Catharine Parr a Bohemian. There was the same air of elation. The quick change was rather worrying. Lucky Catharine Parr: Jemima only hoped that she would be third time lucky as the sleeping-car attendant had suggested. It rather depended on what stability she could show as a mother.

"I promise you," cried Mrs. Parr interrupting a new train of thought, "I give you my word. I'll never ever think about the past again. I'll look after them to my dying day. I'll give them all the love in the world, all the love they've missed all these years. Miss Shore, Jemima, I told you I trusted you. You've done all I asked you to do. Thank you, thank you."

The next morning dawned horribly wet. It was an added reason for Jemima to be glad to be leaving Kildrum Lodge. A damp Scottish August did not commend itself to her. With nothing further to do, the dripping rhododendrons surrounding the lodge were beginning to depress her spirits. Rain sheeted down on the loch, making even a brisk walk seem impractical. With the children still silent in their playroom and Mrs. Parr still lurking upstairs for the kind of late-morning rise she favoured, Jemima decided to make her farewell to Elspeth Maxwell in the kitchen.

She was quickly trapped in the flood of Elspeth's reflections, compared to which the rain outside seemed suddenly mild in contrast. Television intrigued Elspeth Maxwell in general, and Jemima, its incarnation, intrigued her in particular. She was avid for every detail of

Jemima's appearance on the box, how many new clothes she needed, television make-up and so forth. On the subject of hair, she first admired the colour of Jemima's corn-coloured locks, then asked how often she had to have a shampoo, and finally enquired with a touch of acerbity:

"You'll not be putting anything on, then? I'm meaning the colour, what a beautiful bright colour your hair is, Miss Shore. You'll not be using one of those little bottles?"

Jemima smilingly denied it. "I'm lucky." She wasn't sure whether Elspeth believed her. After a bit Elspeth continued: "Not like that poor lady." She seemed obsessed with the subject. Was she thinking of dyeing her own hair? "The late Mrs. Parr, I mean, when I cleared out her things, I found plenty of bottles, different colours, dark and fair, as though she'd been making a wee experiment. And she had lovely fair hair herself, or so they said, Johnnie and the men when they took her out of the water. Just like the children. Look—" Elspeth suddenly produced two bottles from the kitchen cupboard. One was called Goldilocks and the other Brown Leaf. Jemima thought her guess was right. Elspeth was contemplating her own wee experiment.

"I'm thinking you'll not be needing this on your *natural* fair hair." There was a faint ironic emphasis in Elspeth's tone. "And Tamsin and Tara, they'll have lovely hair too when they grow up. They won't need Goldilocks or such things. And who would want Brown Leaf anyway with lovely fair hair like theirs? And yours. Brown Leaf would only hide the colour." Elspeth put the bottles back in the cupboard as though that settled the matter.

Irritated by her malice—there was nothing wrong with dyeing one's hair but Jemima just did not happen to do it—Jemima abandoned Elspeth and the kitchen for the playroom. Nevertheless, Elspeth's words continued to ring in her head. That and another remark she could not forget. Tamsin and Tara were both reading quietly, lying on their tummies on the floor. Tamsin looked up and smiled.

"When will the programme be, Miss Shore?"

she asked brightly. "When will you come back and film us? Oh, I'm so sad you're going away."

Jemima was standing by the mantlepiece. It had a large mirror over it, which gave some light to the dark room. In the mirror she gazed back into the room, at the striking blonde heads of the two children lying on the floor. It was of course a mirror image, reversed. The sight was symbolical. It was as though for the first time she was seeing the case of the Parr children turned inside out, reversed, black white, dark fair . . . Lucky children with their mother restored to them. A mother who drank and smoked and was totally undomesticated. But was still their mother. Zillah had done none of these things—but she had done worse: she had tried to keep the children from the mother who bore them. Lucky. Third time lucky.

Jemima stood absolutely still. Behind her back Tamsin smiled again that happy innocent smile. Tara was smiling too.

"Oh yes, Miss Shore," she echoed, "I'm so sad you're going away." For once Tara was in total agreement with her sister. And in the mirror Jemima saw both girls dissolve into soundless giggles, hands over their mouths to stifle the noise. She continued to stare at the children's blonde heads.

With sudden horrible clarity, Jemima knew that she was wrong, had been wrong all along. She would have to tell the woman resting upstairs that the children were not after all her own. A remark that had long haunted her came to the front of her mind. Catharine Parr: "Just like the wretched Queen who lost her head, and I'm just as wretched." And now she knew why it had haunted her. Catharine Parr had not been executed by Henry VIII, but she had been childless by him. Now she would have to break it to Mrs. Parr that she too was childless. Would be childless in the future.

It had to be done. There was such a thing as truth. Truth—and justice. But first, however dreadfully, she had to confront the children with what they had done. She had to make them admit it.

Wheeling round, she said as calmly as possible to the little girls: "I'm just going to drive to the telephone box to arrange with my secretary about my return. This telephone is out of order with the storm last night." She thought she could trust Tamsin to accept the story. Then Jemima added:

"And when I come back, we'll all go out in the boat. Will you tell your—" she paused in spite of herself, "Will you tell your Mummy that?"

The children were not smiling now.

"The boat!" exclaimed Tamsin. "But our Mummy can't swim. She told us." She sounded tearful. "She told us not to go in the boat, and anyway we don't want to. She told us we'd never ever have to go in the boat again."

"Oh don't make us go in the horrid boat, Miss Shore," Tara's eyes were wide with apprehension. "Please don't. We can't swim. We never learnt yet."

"I can swim," replied Jemima. "I'm a strong swimmer. Will you give your Mummy my message?"

When Jemima got back, Mrs. Parr was standing with Tamsin and Tara by the door of the lodge, holding their hands (the first time Jemima had glimpsed any sign of physical affection in her). She was looking extremely distressed. She was wearing the filthy torn mackintosh in which she had first arrived at Jemima's flat. Her appearance, which had improved slightly over the last few days, was as unkempt and desperate as it had been on that weird occasion.

"Miss Shore, you mustn't do this," she cried, the moment Jemima was out of the car. "We can't go out in the boat. It's terrible for the children—after what happened. Besides, I can't swim—"

"I'm sorry, Catharine," was all Jemima said. She did not relish what she had to do.

Perhaps because she was childless herself, Jemima Shore believed passionately that young children were basically innocent whatever they did. After all, had the Parr children ever really had a chance in life since its disturbing beginnings? And now she, the alleged protector of the

weak, the compassionate social campaigner, was going to administer the *coup de grâce*. She wished profoundly that she had not answered the bell to Mrs. Parr that fatal Sunday morning.

The rain had stopped. The weather was clearing above the mountains in the west, although the sky over the loch remained sullen. In silence the little party entered the rowing boat and Jemima pushed off from the soft ground of the foreshore.

"Come on, Tamsin, sit by me. Row like you did that afternoon with Zillah."

Mrs. Parr gave one more cry: "Miss Shore! No." Then she relapsed with a sort of groan into the seat at the stern of the boat. Tara sat beside her, facing Jemima and Tamsin.

After a while Jemima rested on her oar. They were near the middle of the loch. The lodge looked small and far away, the mountains behind less menacing. Following the rain the temperature had risen. Presently the sun came out. It was quite humid. Flies buzzed round Jemima's head and the children. Soon the midges would come to torture them. The water had a forbidding look: she could see thick green weeds floating just beneath the surface. An occasional fish rose and broke the black surface. No one was visible amongst the reeds. They were, the silent boat load, alone on the loch.

Or perhaps they were not alone. Perhaps Johnnie Maxwell the ghillie was somewhere amid the sedge, at his work. If so he would have seen yet another macabre sight on Loch Drum. He would have seen Jemima Shore, her red-gold hair illuminated by the sunlight, lean forward and grab Tara from her seat. He would have seen her hurl the little girl quite far into the lake, like some human Excalibur. He would have heard the loud splash, seen the spreading circles on the black water. Then he would surely, even at the edge of the loch—for the air was very still after the rain—heard Tara's cries. But even if Johnnie Maxwell had been watching, he would have been once again helpless to have saved the drowning person.

Mrs. Parr gave a single loud scream and

stood up at the stern of the boat. Jemima Shore sat grimly still, like a figure of vengeance. Tamsin got to her feet, wielded her oar and tried in vain to reach out to the child, splashing hopelessly now on, now under the surface of the loch. Jemima Shore continued to sit still.

Then a child's voice was heard, half choking with water: "Zillah, save me! Zillah!"

It seemed as though the woman standing at the stern of the boat would never move. Suddenly, uncontrollably, she tore off her white mackintosh. And without further hesitation, she made a perfect racing dive on to the surface of the loch. Minutes later Tara, still sobbing and spluttering, but alive, was safely out of the water. Then for the first time since she had thrown Tara into the loch, Jemima Shore made a move—to pull the woman who had called herself Mrs. Catharine Parr back into the boat.

"The police are coming of course," said Jemima. They were back at the house. "You killed her, didn't you?"

Tamsin and Tara, in dry clothes, had been sent out to play among the rhododendrons which served for a garden. The sun was gaining in intensity. The loch had moved from black to grey to slate-blue. Tara was bewildered. Tamsin was angry. "Good-bye, *Mummy*," she said fiercely to Zillah.

"Don't make her pretend any longer," Jemima too appealed to Zillah. And to Tamsin: "I know, you see. I've known for some time."

Tamsin then turned to her sister: "Baby. You gave it away. You promised never to call her Zillah. Now they'll come and take Zillah away. I won't ever speak to you again." And Tamsin ran off into the dark shrubberies.

Zillah Parr, wearing some of her own clothes fished out of Elspeth's packages, was sitting with Jemima by the playroom fire. She looked neat and clean and reassuring, a child's dream mother, as she must always have looked during the last seven years. Until she deliberately assumed the messy run-down identity of Mrs.

Parr, that is. How this paragon must have hated to dirty her finger-nails! Jemima noticed that she had seized the opportunity to scrub them vigorously while she was upstairs in the bathroom changing.

Now the mirror reflected a perfectly composed woman, legs in nice shoes, neatly crossed, sipping the glass of whiskey which Jemima had given her.

"Why not?" said Zillah coolly. "I never drink you know, normally. Unlike *her*. Nor do I smoke. I find both things quite disgusting. As for pretending to be drunk! I used to pour all those bottles of wine down the sink. But I never found a good way of producing cigarette stubs without smoking. Ugh, the smell. I never got used to it. But I feel I may need the whiskey this afternoon."

Silence fell between them. Then Zillah said quite conversationally: "By the way, how did you know?"

"A historical inaccuracy was your first mistake," replied Jemima. They might have been analysing a game of bridge. "It always struck me as odd that a woman called Catharine Parr, an educated woman to boot, would not have known the simple facts of her namesake's life. It was Catharine Howard, by the way, who lost her head, not Catharine Parr."

"Oh, really." Zillah sounded quite uninterested. "Well, I never had any education. I saw no use for it in my work, either."

"But you made other mistakes. The sleeping-car attendant: that was a risk to take. He recognized you because of all the drinking. He spoke of you being third time lucky, and at first I thought he meant your quick journey up and down from London to Inverness and back. But then I realized that he meant that this was your third journey *northwards*. He spoke of you 'going north' the second time and how you weren't so drunk as the first time. She went up first, didn't she? You killed her. Then faked your own death, and somehow got down to London secretly, perhaps from another station. Then up and down again under the name of Catharine Parr."

"That was unlucky." Zillah agreed. "Of course I didn't know that he'd met the real Catharine Parr when I travelled up under her name the first time. I might have been more careful."

"In the end it was a remark of Elspeth Maxwell's which gave me the clue. That, and your expression."

"That woman! She talks far too much," said Zillah with a frown.

"The dyes: she showed me the various dyes you had used, I suppose to dye Mrs. Parr's hair blonde and darken your own."

"She dyed her own hair," Zillah sounded positively complacent. "I've always been good at getting people to do things. I baited her. Pointed out how well I'd taken care of myself, my hair still blonde and thick, and what a mess she looked. Why, I looked more like the children's mother than she did. I knew that would get her. We'd once been awfully alike, you see, at least to look at. You never guessed that, did you? Kitty never really looked much like her, different nose, different shaped face. But as girls, Catharine and I were often mistaken for each other. It even happened once or twice when I was working for her. And how patronizing she was about it. 'Oh, that was just Zillah' she used to say with that awful laugh of hers when she'd been drinking 'Local saint and poor relation.' I was like her but not like." Zillah hesitated and then went on more briskly.

"I showed her the bottle of Goldilocks, pretended I used it myself and she grabbed it. 'Now we'll see who the children's real mother is' she said, when she'd finished."

"The bottle did fool me at first," admitted Jemima. "I thought it must be connected somehow with the children's hair. Then Elspeth gave me the key when she wondered aloud who would ever use Brown Leaf if they had fair hair: 'It would only hide the colour.'" She paused. "So you killed her, blonde hair and all."

"Yes I killed her," Zillah was still absolutely composed. She seemed to have no shame or even fear. "I drowned her. She was going to take the children away. I found out that she couldn't swim, took her out in the boat in the morning when I knew Johnnie Maxwell wasn't around. Then I let her drown. I would have done anything to keep the children," she added.

"I told the children that she'd gone away," she went on. "That horrid drunken old tramp. Naturally I didn't tell them I'd killed her. I just said that we would play a game. A game in which I would pretend to fall into the lake and be drowned. Then I would dress up in her old clothes and pretend to *be* her. And they must treat me just as if I *was* her, all cold and distant. They must never hug me as if I was Zillah. And if they played it properly, if they never talked about it to anyone, not even to each other when they were alone, the horrid mother would never come back. And then I could be their proper mother. Just as they had always wanted. Zillah, they used to say with their arms round me, we love you so much, won't you be our Mummy forever?" Her voice became dreamy and for a moment Zillah was reminded of the person she had known as Catharine Parr. "I couldn't have any children of my own, you see; I had to have an operation when I was quite young. Wasn't it unfair? That she could have them, who was such a terrible mother, and I couldn't. All my life I've always loved other people's children. My sister's. Then his children."

"It was the children all along, wasn't it? Not the money. The Parr Trust: that was a red herring."

"The money!" exclaimed Zillah. Her voice was full of contempt. "The Parr Trust meant nothing to me. It was an encumbrance if anything. Little children don't need money: they need love and that's exactly what I gave to them. And she would have taken them away, the selfish good-for-nothing tramp that she was, that's what she threatened to do, take them away, and never let me see them again. She said in her drunken way, laughing and drinking together. 'This time my fine cousin Zillah, the law will be on my side.' So I killed her. And so I defeated her. Just as I defeated her the last time when she tried to take the children away from me in court."

"And from their father," interposed Jemima.

"The judge knew a real motherly woman when he saw one," Zillah went on as though she had not heard. "He said so in court for all the world to hear. And he was right, wasn't he? Seven years she left them. Not a card. Not a present. And then thinking she could come back, just like that, because their father was dead, and claim them. All for an accident of birth. She was nothing to them, *nothing*, and I was everything."

And Jemima herself? Her mission?

"Oh yes, I got you here deliberately. To test the children. I was quite confident, you see. I knew they would fool you. But I wanted them to know the sort of questions they would be asked—by lawyers, even perhaps the Press. I used to watch you on television," she added with a trace of contempt. "I fooled that judge. He never knew about their father and me. I enjoy fooling people when it's necessary. I knew I could fool you."

"But you didn't," said Jemima Shore coldly. She did not like the idea of being fooled. "There was one more clue. An expression. The expression of triumph on your face when I told you I was satisfied about the children and was going back to London. You dropped your guard for a moment. It reminded me of a woman who had once scored over me on television. I didn't forget that." She added, "Besides, you would never have got away with it."

But privately she thought that if Zillah Parr had not displayed her arrogance by sending for Jemima Shore Investigator as a guinea pig she might well have done so. After all, no one had seen Catharine Parr for seven years; bitterly she had cut herself off completely from all her old friends when she went to Ireland. Zillah had also led a deliberately isolated life after her husband's death; in her case she had hoped to elude the children's mother should she ever reappear. Zillah's sister had vanished to Canada. Elspeth Maxwell had been held at arm's length as had the inhabitants of Kildrum. Johnnie Maxwell

had met Zillah once but there was no need for him to meet the false Mrs. Parr, who so much disliked fishing.

The two women were much of an age and their physical resemblance in youth striking: that resemblance which Zillah suggested had first attracted Mr. Parr towards her. Only the hair had to be remedied, since Catharine's untended hair had darkened so much with the passing of the years. As for the corpse, the Parr family lawyer, whom Zillah had met face to face at the time of her husband's death, was, she knew, on holiday in Greece. It was not difficult to fake a resemblance sufficient to make Major Maclachlan at the Estate Office identify the body as that of Zillah Parr. The truth was so very bizarre: he was hardly likely to suspect it. He would be expecting to see the corpse of Zillah Parr, following Johnnie's account, and the corpse of Zillah Parr, bedraggled by the loch, he would duly see.

The unkempt air of a tramp was remarkably easy to assume: it was largely a matter of externals. After a while the new Mrs. Catharine Parr would have discreetly improved her appearance. She would have left Kildrum—and who would have blamed her?—and started a new life elsewhere. A new life with the children. Her own children: at last.

As all this was passing through Jemima's head, suddenly Zillah's control snapped. She started to cry: "My children, my children. Not hers, Mine—". And she was still crying when the police car came up the rough drive, and tall men with black and white check bands round their hats took her away. First they had read her the warrant: "Mrs. Zillah Parr, I charge you with the murder of Mrs. Catharine Parr, on or about the morning of August 6 . . . at Kildrum Lodge, Inverness-shire."

As the police car vanished from sight down the lonely valley, Tara came out of the rhododendrons and put her hand in Jemima's. There was no sign of Tamsin.

"She will come back, Miss Shore, won't

she?" she said anxiously. "Zillah, I mean, not that Mummy. I didn't like that Mummy. She drank bottles all the time and shouted at us. She said rude words, words we're not allowed to say. I cried when she came and Tamsin hid. That Mummy even tried to hit me. But Zillah told us she would make the horrid Mummy go away. And she did. When will Zillah come back, Miss Shore?"

Holding Tara's hand, Jemima reflected sadly that the case of the Parr children was probably only just beginning.

FAST

Jeffery Deaver

JEFFERY DEAVER (1950–   ) has written more than a dozen novels about Lincoln Rhyme, the brilliant quadriplegic detective who made his debut in *The Bone Collector* (1997), which was filmed and released by Universal in 1999 and starred Denzel Washington and Angelina Jolie. Other Rhyme novels are *The Coffin Dancer* (1998), *The Empty Chair* (2000), and, most recently, *The Cutting Edge* (2018).

He has also written more than twenty stand-alone and other series novels, most notably those featuring Kathryn Dance, who made her debut in *The Cold Moon* (2006), a Lincoln Rhyme novel in which she makes a brief appearance, followed by her first star turn in *The Sleeping Doll* (2007). Dance, an agent in the California Bureau of Investigation, is brilliant in the art of interrogation and is a highly accomplished reader of body language.

Deaver was born outside Chicago and received his journalism degree from the University of Missouri, becoming a newspaperman, after which he received his law degree from Fordham University, practicing for several years. A poet, he wrote his own songs and performed them across the country.

His works have been translated into twenty-five languages and are perennial bestsellers in America and elsewhere. Among his many honors are seven nominations for Edgar Awards (twice for best paperback original, five times for best short story), three Ellery Queen Readers Awards for best short story of the year, and the Ian Fleming Steel Dagger Award from the (British) Crime Writers' Association for *Garden of Beasts* (2004).

His non-series novel *A Maiden's Grave* (1995) was adapted for an HBO movie titled *Dead Silence* (1997) and starred James Garner and Marlee Matlin. His suspense novel *The Devil's Teardrop* (1999) was a 2010 made-for-television movie of the same name.

"Fast" was originally published in *Trouble in Mind* (New York, Grand Central, 2014).

Fast

JEFFERY DEAVER

THEY WERE JUST ABOUT TO SEE the octopus when she received a text alerting her that two hundred people were going to die in two hours.

Kathryn Dance rarely received texts marked with exclamation points—the law enforcement community tended not to punctuate with emotion—so she read it immediately. Then called her office, via speed dial three.

"Boss," the young man's voice spilled from her iPhone.

"Details, TJ?"

Over their heads:

"Will the ticket holders for the one-thirty exhibition make their way inside, please."

"Mom!" The little girl's voice was urgent. "That's us."

"Hold on a second, honey." Then into the phone: "Go on."

TJ Scanlon said, "Sorry, boss, this's bad. On the wire from up north."

"Mom . . ."

"Let me talk, Mags."

"Long story short, Alameda was monitoring this domestic separatist outfit, planning an attack up there."

"I know. Brothers of Liberty, based in Oakland, white supremacists, antigovernment. Osmond Carter, their leader, was arrested last week and they threatened retaliation if he's not released."

"You knew that?"

"You read the statewide dailies, TJ?"

"Mean to."

". . . the Monterey Bay Aquarium is pleased to host the largest specimen of Enteroctopus dofleini *on exhibit in the northern California area, weighing in at a hundred and twenty-one pounds! We know you're going to enjoy viewing our visiting guest in his specially created habitat."*

"Okay. What's the story?" Dance persisted into the phone as she and her children edged closer to the exhibit hall. They'd waited forty-five minutes. Who would have thought octopuses, *octopi*, would be such a big draw?

TJ said, "Everybody believed they were going to hit somewhere up there, Alameda, Contra Costa, San Fran, but maybe there was too much heat. Oakland PD had a CI inside the group and he said two of their people came down here, set up something. And—"

She interrupted. " 'Set up something.' What does that mean?"

"An attack of some kind. He doesn't know what exactly. Maybe an IED, maybe chemical. Probably not bio but could be. But the number of victims is for sure, what I texted you. Two hundred plus or minus. That's confirmed. And whatever it is, it's up and running; the perps set it and they were headed back. The CI said four P.M. is when the attack goes down."

Two and a half hours. A little less. Lord . . .

"No idea of the victims, location?"

TJ Scanlon offered, "None."

"But you said they 'were' headed back."

"Right, we caught a break. There's a chance we can nail 'em. The CI gave us the make of the car—a 2000 Taurus, light blue. CHP spotted one in Marina and went after it. The driver took off. Probably them. They lost the pursuit on surface roads. Everybody's searching the area. Bureau's coming in from the field office. Hold on, boss. I'm getting something."

Dance happened to glance up and see her reflection in the glass panel on the other side of which elegant and eerie sea horses floated with sublime, careless ease. Dance noted her own still gaze looking back at her, in a narrow, Cate Blanchett face, hair in a ponytail, held taut by a black-and-green scrunchy installed that morning by her ten-year-old daughter, currently champ-ing beside her. Her mop-headed son, Wes, twelve, was detached from mother and sister. He was less intrigued by cephalopods, however big, and more by an aloof fourteen-year-old in line, a girl who should have been a cheerleader if she wasn't.

Dance was wearing jeans, a blue silk blouse and a tan quilted vest, comfortably warm. Sunny at the moment, the Monterey Peninsula could be quite fickle when it came to weather. Fog mostly.

"*Mom*, they're calling us," Maggie said in her weegee voice, the high pitch that conveyed exas-peration really well.

"One minute, this's important."

"First, it was a second. Now it's a minute. Jeez. One one-thousand, two one-thousand . . ."

Wes was smiling toward, but not at, the cheerleader.

The line inched forward, drawing them seductively closer to the Cephalopod of the Century.

TJ came back on the line. "Boss, yep, it's them. The Taurus's registered to the Brothers of Liberty. CHP's in pursuit."

"Where?"

"Seaside."

Dance glanced around her at the dim con-crete and glass aquarium. It was holiday break—ten days before Christmas—and the place was packed. And there were dozens of tourist attrac-tions like this in the area, not to mention movie theaters, churches, and offices. Some schools were closed but others not. Was the plan to leave a bomb in, say, that trash can out front? She said into the phone, "I'll be right in." Turning to the children, she grimaced at their disappointed faces. She had a theory—possibly unfounded—that her two children were more sensitive to dis-appointment than other kids their age because they were fatherless . . . and because Bill had died suddenly. There in the morning, and then never again. It was so very hard for her to say what she now had to: "Sorry, guys. It's a big problem at work."

"Aw, Mom!" Maggie grumbled. "This is the last day! It's going to San Diego tomorrow." Wes, too, was disappointed, though part of this wasn't sea life but pretty cheerleaders.

"Sorry, guys. Can't be helped. I'll make it up to you." Dance held the phone back to her ear and she said firmly to TJ, "And tell everybody: No shooting unless it's absolutely necessary. I don't want either of them killed."

Which brought conversation around them in the octopus line to a complete stop. Everyone stared.

Speaking to the wide-eyed blonde, Wes said reassuringly, "It's okay. She says that a lot."

The venue for the party was good. The Mon-terey Bay Seaside Motel was near the water, north of the city. And what was especially nice about this place was that unlike a lot of banquet rooms this one had large windows opening onto a stretch of beach.

Right now, Carol Messner noted, the beach had that December afternoon look to it: bleached, dusty, though the haze was mostly mist with a bit of fog thrown in. Not so focused, but, hey, a beach view beat a Highway 1 view any day, provided the sun held.

"Hal," she said to her associate. "You think we need more tables over there? It looks empty."

Carol, president of the local branch of the California Central Coast Bankers' Association, was a woman in her sixties, a grandmother several times over. Although her employer was one of the larger chain banks that had misbehaved a bit a few years ago, she'd had no part of mortgage-backed securities; she firmly believed banks did good. She wouldn't have been in the business if she didn't think that. She was living proof of the beneficence of the world of finance. Carol and her husband had comfortable retirement funds thanks to banks, her daughter and son-in-law had expanded their graphic arts business and made it successful thanks to banks, her grandsons would be going to Stanford and UC-Davis next fall thanks to student loans.

The earth revolved around money, but that was a good thing—far better than guns and battleships—and she was happy and proud to be a part of the process. The diminutive, white-haired woman wouldn't have been in the business for forty-six years if she'd felt otherwise.

Hal Reskin, her second in command at the CCCBA, was a heavyset man with a still face, a lawyer specializing in commercial paper and banking law. He eyed the corner she pointed at and agreed. "Asymmetrical," he said. "Can't have that."

Carol tried not to smile. Hal took everything he did quite seriously and was a far better i-dotter than she. "Asymmetrical" would be a sin, possibly mortal.

She walked up to the two motel employees who were organizing the room for the Christmas party, which would last from three to five today, and asked that they move several of the round ten-tops to cover the bald spot on the banquet room floor. The men hefted the tables and rearranged them.

Hal nodded.

Carol said, "De-asymmetricalized."

Her vice president laughed. Taking his tasks seriously didn't mean he was missing a sense of humor.

Hal took the room in. "Looks good to me. Double-check the sound system. Then we'll get the decorations up."

"The PA?" she asked. "I tried it yesterday. It was fine." But being the i-dotting banker that she was, Carol walked to the stage and flicked on the PA system.

Nothing.

A few more flicks of the off-on toggle.

As if that would do any good.

"This could be a problem."

Carol followed the cord but it disappeared below the stage.

"Maybe those workers," Hal said, peering at the microphones.

"Who?"

"Those two guys who were here a half hour ago. Maybe before you got here?"

"No, I didn't see anybody. José and Miguel?" she asked, nodding at the men on the motel staff, now setting up chairs.

"No, other ones. They asked if this is where the banking meeting was going to be. I told them yes and they said they had to make some repairs under the stage. They were under there for a few minutes, then they left."

She asked the two motel workers in the corner, "Did you hear that there was a problem with the sound system?"

"No, ma'am. Maria, Guest Services, she handle everything with the microphones and all that. She said it was fine this morning. But she off now."

"Where are those other workers?" Carol asked. After receiving blank stares, she explained what Hal had told her.

"I don't know who they'd be, ma'am. We're the ones, José and me, who set up the rooms."

Walking toward the access door to the stage, Hal said, "I'll take a look."

"You know electronics?" she asked.

"Are you kidding? I set up my grandson's Kinect with his XBox. All by my little ole lonesome."

Carol had no idea what he was talking about but he said it with such pride she had to smile.

She held open the access door as he descended beneath the stage. "Good luck."

Three minutes later the PA system came on with a resonant click through the speakers.

Carol applauded.

Hal appeared and dusted off his hands. "Those guys earlier, they knocked the cord loose when they were under there. We'll have to keep an eye out, they don't do it again. I think they'll be back."

"Really?"

"Maybe. They left a toolbox and some big bottles down there. Cleaner, I guess."

"Okay. We'll keep an eye out." But the workmen were gone from Carol's mind. Decorations had to be set up, food had to be arranged. She wanted the room to be as nice as possible for the two hundred CCCBA members who'd been looking forward to the party for months.

A stroke of luck . . . and good policing.

The CHP had collared the Brothers of Liberty perps.

Kathryn Dance, who'd dropped the disgruntled children off with her parents in Carmel, was standing in the weedy parking lot of an outlet mall only six miles from the California Bureau of Investigation's Monterey Office, where she worked. Michael O'Neil now approached. He looked like a character from a John Steinbeck novel, maybe Doc in *Cannery Row*. Although the uniform of the MCSO was typical county sheriff's khaki, Chief Detective O'Neil usually dressed soft—today in sport coat and tan slacks and blue dress shirt, no tie. His hair was salt-and-pepper and his brown eyes, beneath lids that dipped low, moved slowly as he explained the pursuit and collar. His physique was solid and his arms very strong—though not from working out in a gym (that was amusing to him) but from muscling salmon and other delicacies into his boat in Monterey Bay every chance he got.

O'Neil was taciturn by design and his face registered little emotion, but with Dance he could usually be counted on to crack a wry joke or banter.

Not now. He was all business.

A fellow CBI agent, massive shaved-headed Albert Stemple, stalked up and O'Neil explained to him and Dance how the perps had been caught.

The fastest way out of the area was on busy Highway 1 north, to 156, then to 101, which would take the suspected terrorists directly back to their nest in Oakland. That route was where the bulk of the searchers had been concentrating—without any success.

But an inventive young Highway Patrol officer had asked himself how would *he* leave the area, if he knew his mission was compromised. He decided the smartest approach would be to take neighborhood and single-lane roads all the way to Highway 5, several hours away. And so he concentrated on small avenues like Jacks and Oil Well and—this was the luck part—he spotted the perps near this strip mall, which was close to Highway 68, the Monterey-Salinas Highway.

The trooper had called in backup, then lit 'em up.

After a twenty-minute high-speed pursuit, the perps skidded into the mall, sped around back and vanished, but the trooper decided they were trying a feint. He didn't head in the same direction they were; instead, he squealed to a stop and waited beside a Tires Plus operation.

After five excessively tense minutes, the Brothers of Liberty had apparently decided they'd misled the pursuit and sped out the way they'd come in, only to find the trooper had anticipated them. He floored the cruiser, equipped with ram bars, and totaled the Taurus. The perps bailed.

The trooper tackled and hog-tied one. The other galloped toward a warehouse area three or four hundred yards away, just as backup arrived. There was a brief exchange of gunfire and the second perp, wounded, was collared, too. Several CHP officers and a colleague of Dance's at the CBI, TJ Scanlon, were at that scene.

Now, at the outlet mall, the perp who'd been

tackled, one Wayne Keplar, regarded Dance, Stemple, and O'Neil and the growing entourage of law enforcers.

"Nice day for an event," Keplar said. He was a lean man, skinny, you could say. Parentheses of creases surrounded his mouth and his dark, narrow-set eyes hid beneath a severely straight fringe of black hair. A hook nose. Long arms, big hands, but he didn't appear particularly strong.

Albert Stemple, whose every muscle seemed to be massive, stood nearby and eyed the perp carefully, ready to step on the bug if need be. O'Neil took a radio call. He stepped away.

Keplar repeated, "Event. Event . . . Could describe a game, you know." He spoke in an oddly high voice, which Dance found irritating. Probably not the tone, more the smirk with which the words were delivered. "Or could be a tragedy. Like they'd call an earthquake or a nuclear meltdown an 'event.' The press, I mean. They love words like that."

O'Neil motioned Dance aside. "That was Oakland PD. The CI's reporting that Keplar's pretty senior in the Brothers of Liberty. The other guy—the wounded one . . ." He nodded toward the warehouses. "Gabe Paulson, he's technical. At least has some schooling in engineering. If it's a bomb, he's probably the one set it up."

"They think that's what it is?"

"No intelligence about the means," O'Neil explained. "On their website they've talked about doing anything and everything to make their point. Bio, chemical, snipers, even hooking up with some Islamic extremist group and doing a quote 'joint venture.'"

Dance's mouth tightened. "We supply the explosives, you supply the suicide bomber?"

"That pretty much describes it."

Her eyes took in Keplar, sitting on the curb, and she noted that he was relaxed, even jovial. Dance, whose position with the CBI trumped the other law enforcers, approached him and regarded the lean man calmly. "We understand you're planning an attack of some sort—"

"Event," he reminded her.

"Event, then, in two and a half hours. Is that true?"

"'Deed it is."

"Well, right now, the only crimes you'll be charged with are traffic. At the worst, we could get you for conspiracy and attempt, several different counts. If that event occurs and people lose their lives—"

"The charges'll be a *lot* more serious," he said jovially. "Let me ask you—what's your name?"

"Agent Dance. CBI." She proffered her ID.

He smacked his lips. As irritating as his weaselly voice. "Agent Dance, of the CBI, let me ask you, don't you think we have a few too many laws in this country? My goodness, Moses gave us *ten*. Things seemed to work pretty well back then and now we've got Washington and Sacramento telling us what to do, what not to do. Every little detail. Honestly! They don't have faith in our good, smart selves."

"Mr. Keplar—"

"Call me 'Wayne,' please." He looked her over appraisingly. Which cut of meat looks good today. "I'll call you Kathryn."

She noted that he'd memorized her name from the perusal of the ID. While Dance, as an attractive woman, was frequently undressed in the imaginations of the suspects she interviewed, Keplar's gaze suggested he was pitying her, as if she were afflicted with a disease. In her case, she guessed, the disease was the tumor of government and racial tolerance.

Dance noted the impervious smile on his face, his air of . . . what? Yes, almost triumph. He didn't appear at all concerned he'd been arrested.

Glancing at her watch: 1:37.

Dance stepped away to take a call from TJ Scanlon, updating her on the status of Gabe Paulson, the other perp. She was talking to him when O'Neil tapped her shoulder. She followed his gaze.

Three black SUVs, dusty and dinged but imposing, sped into the parking lot and squealed to a halt, red and blue lights flashing. A half-dozen men in suits climbed out, two others in tactical gear.

The largest of the men who were Brooks Brothers–clad—six two and two hundred pounds—brushed his thick graying hair back and strode forward.

"Michael, Kathryn."

"Hi, Steve."

Stephen Nichols was the head of the local field office of the FBI. He'd worked with Dance's husband, Bill Swenson, a bureau agent until his death. She'd met Nichols once or twice. He was a competent agent but ambitious in a locale where ambition didn't do you much good. He should have been in Houston or Atlanta, where he could free-style his way a bit further.

He said, "I never got the file on this one."

Don't you read the dailies?

Dance said, "We didn't either. Everybody assumed the BOL would strike up near San Francisco, *that* bay, not ours."

Nichols said, "Who's he?"

Keplar stared back with amused hostility toward Nichols, who would represent that most pernicious of enemies—the federal government.

Dance explained his role in the group and what it was believed they'd done here.

"Any idea exactly what they have in mind?" another agent with Nichols asked.

"Nothing. So far."

"There were two of them?" Nichols asked.

Dance added, "The other's Gabe Paulson." She nodded toward the warehouses some distance away. "He was wounded but I just talked to my associate. It's a minor injury. He can be interrogated."

Nichols hesitated, looking at the fog coming in fast. "You know, I have to take them, Kathryn." He sounded genuinely regretful at this rank pulling. His glance wafted toward O'Neil, too, though Monterey was pretty far down on the rung in the hierarchy of law enforcement here represented and nobody—even the sheriff himself—expected that the County would snag the bad boys.

"Sure." Dance glanced toward her watch.

"But we haven't got much time. How many interrogators do you have?"

The agent was hesitating. "Just me for now. We're bringing in somebody from San Francisco. He's good."

"Bo?"

"Right."

"He's good. But—" She tapped her watch. "Let's split them up, Steve. Give me one of them. At least for the time being."

Nichols shrugged. "I guess."

Dance said, "Keplar's going to be the trickiest. He's senior in the organization and he's not the least shaken by the collar." She nodded toward the perp, who was lecturing nearby officers relentlessly about the destruction of the Individual by Government—he was supplying the capitalization. "He's going to be trickier to break. Paulson's been wounded and that'll make him more vulnerable." She could see that Nichols was considering this. "I think, our different styles, background, yours and mine, it'd make sense for me to take Keplar, you take Paulson."

Nichols squinted against some momentary glare as a roll of fog vanished. "Who's Paulson exactly?"

O'Neil answered, "Seems to be the technician. He'd know about the device, if that's what they've planted. Even if he doesn't tell you directly, he could give something away that'd let us figure out what's going on." The Monterey detective wouldn't know exactly why Dance wanted Keplar and not Gabe but he'd picked up on her preference and he was playing along.

This wasn't completely lost on the FBI agent. Nichols would be considering a lot of things. Did Dance's idea to split up the interrogation make sense? Did she and he indeed have different interrogation styles and background? Also, he'd know that O'Neil and Dance were close and they might be double teaming him in some way, though he might not figure out to what end. He might have thought she was bluffing, hoping that he'd pick Wayne Keplar, because she herself wanted Gabe Paulson for some reason.

Or he might have decided that all was good and it made sense for him to take the wounded perp.

Whatever schematics were drawn in his mind, he debated a long moment and then agreed.

Dance nodded. "I'll call my associate, have Paulson brought over here."

She gestured to the two CHP officers towering over Wayne Keplar. He was hoisted to his feet and led to Dance, O'Neil, and Nichols. Albert Stemple—who weighed twice what the suspect did—took custody with a no-nonsense grip on the man's scrawny arm.

Keplar couldn't take his eyes off the FBI agents. "Do you know the five reasons the federal government is a travesty?"

Dance wanted him to shut up—she was afraid Nichols would change his mind and drag the perp off himself.

"First, economically. I—"

"Whatever," Nichols muttered and wandered off to await his own prisoner.

Dance nodded and Stemple escorted Keplar to a CBI unmarked Dodge and inserted him into the backseat.

Michael O'Neil would stay to supervise the crime scene here, canvassing for witnesses and searching for evidence—possibly items thrown from the car that might give them more information about the site of the attack.

As she got into her personal vehicle, a gray Nissan Pathfinder, Dance called to Nichols and O'Neil, "And remember: We have two and a half hours. We've got to move fast."

She pulled out her phone, briefed TJ Scanlon about Paulson and Nichols and turned on the flashing lights suctioned to her windshield.

1:52.

Dance left rubber on the concrete as she sped out of the parking lot.

Fast . . .

Albert Stemple was parked outside CBI, looking with some contempt at the press vans that were lolling near the front door. Dance parked behind him. She strode to the Dodge.

A reporter—a man with an aura of Jude Law, if not the exact looks—pushed to the barricade and thrust a microphone their way.

"Kathryn! Kathryn Dance! Dan Simmons, The True Story dot com."

She knew him. A sensationalist reporter who oozed toward the tawdrier aspects of a story like slugs to Dance's doomed vegetable garden.

Simmons's cameraman, a squat, froggy man with crinkly and unwashed hair, aimed a fancy Sony video cam their way as if about to launch a rocket-propelled grenade.

"No comment on anything, Dan." She and Stemple shoehorned Wayne Keplar out of the car.

The reporter ignored her. "Can you give us your name?" Aimed at the suspect.

Keplar was all too happy to talk. He shouted out, "The Brothers of Liberty," and began a lecturette about how the fourth estate was in the pocket of corporate money and the government.

"Not all reporters, Wayne," Simmons said. "Not us. We're with you, brother! Keep talking."

This impressed Keplar.

"Quiet," Dance muttered, leading him toward the front door.

"And we're about to strike a blow for freedom!"

"What are you going to do, Wayne?" Simmons shouted.

"We have no comment," Dance called.

"Well, *I* do. I've only been *arrested*," Wayne offered energetically, with a smile, ignoring Dance and mugging for the reporter, whose disheveled photographer was shooting away with his fancy digital video camera. "I'm not under a gag order. Freedom of speech! That's what the founders of this country believed in. Even if the people in charge now don't."

"Let him talk, Agent!" the reporter called.

"I have no comment at this time."

Simmons replied, "We don't want *your* comment, Kathryn. We want Wayne's." He then added, "Were you hurt, Wayne? You're limping."

"They hurt me in the arrest. That'll be part of the lawsuit."

He hadn't been limping earlier. Dance tried to keep the disgust off her face.

"We heard there were other suspects. One's wounded and in FBI custody. The other's at large."

Police scanners. Dance grimaced. It was illegal to hack cell phones, but anybody could buy a scanner and learn all they wanted to about police operations.

"Wayne, what do you expect to achieve by what you're doing?"

"Makin' the people aware of the overbearing government. The disrespect for the people of this great nation and—"

Dance actually pushed him through the door into the CBI Monterey headquarters, an unimpressive building that resembled one of the insurance agencies or law offices in this business park east of the airport on the way to Salinas, off Highway 68.

Simmons called, "Kathryn! Agent Dance—"

The CBI's front door was on a hydraulic closer but she would have slammed it if she could have.

Dance turned to him. "Wayne, I've read you your rights. You understand you have the right to an attorney. And that anything you say can and will be used against you in court."

"Yes, ma'am."

"Do you wish to waive your right to an attorney and to remain silent?"

"Yup."

"You understand you can break off our interview at any time."

"I do now. Thanks very much. Informative."

"Will you tell us where you're planning this attack? Do that and we'll work out a deal."

"Will you let our founder, Osmond Carter, go free? He's been illegally arrested, in contravention of his basic human rights."

"We can't do that."

"Then I think I'm not inclined to tell you what we've got in mind." A grin. "But I'm happy to talk. Always enjoy a good chin-wag with an attractive woman."

Dance nodded to Stemple, who guided Keplar through the maze of hallways to an interrogation room. She followed. She checked her weapon and took the file that a fellow agent had put together on the suspect. Three pages were in the manila sleeve. That's all? she wondered, flipping open the file and reading the sparse history of Wayne Keplar and the pathetic organization he was sacrificing his life for.

She paused only once. To glance at her watch and learn that she had only two hours and one minute to stop the attack.

Michael O'Neil was pursuing the case at the crime scene, as he always did: meticulously, patiently.

If an idea occurred to him, if a clue presented itself, he followed the lead until it paid off or it turned to dust.

He finished jotting down largely useless observations and impressions of witnesses in front of where the trooper rammed the suspects' car. ("Man, it was totally, like, loud.") The detective felt a coalescing of moisture on his face; that damn Monterey fog—as much a local institution as John Steinbeck, Cannery Row, and Langston Hughes. He wiped his face with broad palms. On the water, fishing from his boat, he didn't think anything of the damp air. Now, it was irritating.

He approached the head of his Forensic Services Unit, a dark-complexioned man, who was of Latino and Scandinavian heritage, Abbott Calderman. The CBI didn't have a crime scene operation and the FBI's closest one was in the San Jose–San Francisco area. The MCSO provided most of the forensics for crimes in this area. Calderman's team was clustered around the still-vaporing Taurus, practically dismantling it, to find clues that could tell them about the impending attack. Officers were also examining, then bagging and tagging, the pocket litter from the two suspects—the police term for wallets, money, receipts, twenty-dollar bills (serial numbers, thanks to ATMs, revealed more than you'd think), sunglasses, keys, and the like. These items would be logged and would ultimately end up at the jail where the men would be booked—Salinas—but for now the team would examine the items for information about the "event" Wayne Keplar had so proudly referred to.

Calderman was speaking to one of his officers, who was swathed in bright blue crime scene overalls, booties, and a surgeon's shower cap.

"Michael," the CS head said, joining the detective. "My folks're going through the car." A glance at the totaled vehicle, air bags deployed. "It's real clean—no motel keys, letters or schematics."

Rarely were perps discovered with maps in their possession with a red grease pencil X, the legend reading: "Attack here!"

"We'll know more when we analyze the trace from the tires and the floor of the passenger compartment and the trunk. But they did find something you ought to know about. A thermos of coffee."

"And it was still hot?"

"Right." Calderman nodded that O'Neil caught the significance of the discovery. "And no receipts from Starbucks or a place that sells brewed coffee."

"So they might've stayed the night here somewhere and brewed it this morning."

"Possibly." Oakland was a long drive. It could take three hours or more. Finding the thermos suggested, though hardly proved, that they'd come down a day or two early to prepare for the attack. This meant there'd probably be a motel nearby, with additional evidence. Though they'd been too smart to keep receipts or reservation records.

The Crime Scene head added, "But most important: We found three cups inside. Two in the cup holders in the front seat, one on the floor in the back, and the rear floor was wet with spilled coffee."

"So, there's a third perp?" O'Neil asked.

"Looks that way—though the trooper who nailed them didn't see anybody else. Could've been hiding in the back."

O'Neil considered this and called Oakland PD. He learned that the CI had only heard about Paulson and Keplar, but it was certainly possible he decided to ask someone else along. The snitch had severed all contact with the BOL, worried that by diming out the operation he'd be discovered and killed.

O'Neil texted Dance and let her know about the third perp, in case this would help in the interrogation. He informed the FBI's Steve Nichols, too.

He then disconnected and looked over the hundred or so people standing at the yellow police tape gawking at the activity.

The third perp . . . Maybe he'd gotten out of the car earlier, after setting up the attack but before the CHP trooper found the suspects.

Or maybe he'd bailed out here, when the Taurus was momentarily out of sight behind the outlet store.

O'Neil summoned several other Monterey County officers and a few CHP troopers. They headed behind the long building searching the loading docks—and even in the Dumpsters—for any trace of the third suspect.

O'Neil hoped they'd be successful. Maybe the perp had bailed because he had particularly sensitive or incriminating information on him. Or he was a local contact who did use credit cards and ATM machines—whose paper trail could steer the police toward the target.

Or maybe he was the sort who couldn't resist interrogation, perhaps the teenage child of one of the perps. Fanatics like those in the Brothers of Liberty had no compunction about enlisting—and endangering—their children.

But the search team found no hint that someone had gotten out of the car and fled. The rear of the mall faced a hill of sand, dotted with succulent plants. The area was crowned with a tall chain-link fence, topped with barbed wire. It would have been possible, though challenging, to escape that way, but no footprints in the sand led to the fence. All the loading dock doors were locked and alarmed; he couldn't have gotten into the stores that way.

O'Neil continued to the far side of the building. He walked there now and noted a Burger King about fifty or sixty feet away. He entered the restaurant, carefully scanning to see if anyone avoided eye contact or, more helpfully, took off quickly.

None did. But that didn't mean the third perp wasn't here. This happened relatively often. Not because of the adage (which was wrong) about returning to or remaining at the scene of the crime out of a subconscious desire to get caught. No, perps were often arrogant enough to stay around and scope out the nature of the investigation, as well as get the identities of the investigators who were pursuing them—even, in some cases, taking digital pictures to let their friends and fellow gangbangers know who was searching for them.

In English and Spanish he interviewed the diners, asking if they'd seen anyone get out of the perps' car behind the outlet store. Typical of witnesses, people had seen two cars, three cars, no cars, red Tauruses, blue Camrys, green Chryslers, gray Buicks. No one had seen any passengers exit any vehicles. Finally, though, he had some luck. One woman nodded in answer to his questions. She pulled gaudy eyeglasses out of her blond hair, where they rested like a tiara, and put them on, squinting as she looked over the scene thoughtfully. Pointing with her gigantic soda cup, she indicated a spot behind the stores where she'd noticed a man standing *next* to a car that could've been blue. She didn't know if he'd gotten out or not. She explained that somebody in the car handed him a blue backpack and he'd left. Her description of the men—one in combat fatigues and one in black cargo pants and a black leather jacket—left no doubt that they were Keplar and Paulson.

"Did you see where he went?"

"Toward the parking lot, I guess. I, like, didn't pay much attention." Looking around. Then she stiffened. "Oh . . ."

"What?" O'Neil asked.

"That's him!" she whispered, pointing to a sandy-haired man in jeans and work shirt, with a backpack over his shoulder. Even from this dis-tance, O'Neil could see he was nervous, rocking from foot to foot, as he studied the crime scene. He was short, about five three or so, explaining why the trooper might easily miss him in the back of the Taurus.

O'Neil used his radio to call an MCSO deputy and have her get the woman's particulars. She agreed to stay here until they collared the perp so she could make a formal ID. He then pulled his badge off his neck and slipped it into the pocket of his jacket, which he buttoned, to conceal the Glock.

He started out of the Burger King.

"Mister . . . Detective," the woman called. "One thing . . . that backpack? You oughta know, when the guy handed it to him, they treated it real careful. I thought maybe it had something breakable in it. But now maybe I'm thinking it could be, you know, dangerous."

"Thanks."

It was then that the sandy-haired man glanced toward O'Neil.

And he understood.

He eased back into the crowd. Hiking the backpack higher on his shoulder, he turned and began to run, speeding between the buildings to the back of the mall. There he hesitated for only a moment, charged up the sand hill and scaled the six-foot chain-link O'Neil had surveyed earlier, shredding part of his jacket as he deftly vaulted the barbed wire. He sprawled onto the unkempt land on the other side of the fence, also mostly sand. It was a deserted former military base, hundreds of acres.

O'Neil and two deputies approached the fence. The detective scaled it fast, tearing his shirt and losing some skin on the back of his hand as he crested the barbed wire. He leaped to the sand on the other side. He rolled once, righted himself and drew his gun, anticipating an attack.

But the perp had disappeared.

One of the deputies behind him got most of the way up the fence, but lost his grip and fell. He dropped straight down, off balance, and O'Neil heard the pop of his ankle as it broke.

"Oh," the young man muttered as he looked

down at the odd angle. He turned as pale as the fog and passed out.

The other deputy called for a medic then started up the fence.

"No!" O'Neil shouted. "Stay there."

"But—"

"I'll handle the pursuit. Call a chopper." And he turned, sprinting through the sand and succulents and scrub oak and pine, dodging around dunes and stands of dry trees—behind any one of which an armed suspect could be waiting.

He hardly wanted to handle the pursuit alone but he had no choice. Just after he'd landed, he'd seen a sign lying face up on the sand.

DANGER UXO
UNEXPLODED ORDNANCE

It featured a picture of an explosion coming up from the ground. Red years ago, the paint was now pink.

This area had been part of the military base's artillery range, and reportedly thousands of tons of shells and grenades were buried here, waiting to be cleared as soon as the Pentagon's budget allowed.

But O'Neil thought of the two hundred people who'd die in less than two hours and began to sprint along the trail that the suspect had been kind enough to leave in the sand.

The unreasonable idea occurred to him that if he took Kathryn Dance's advice—to move *fast*—he might be past the cannon shell when it detonated.

He didn't, however, think an explosion like that was something you could outrun.

Kinesic analysis works because of one simple concept, which Dance thought of as the Ten Commandments Principle.

Although she herself wasn't religious, she liked the metaphor. It boiled down to simply: Thou Shalt Not . . .

What came after that prohibition didn't matter. The gist was that people knew the difference between right and wrong and they felt uneasy doing something they shouldn't.

Some of this stemmed from the fear of getting caught, but still we're largely hardwired to do the right thing.

When people are deceptive (either actively misstating or failing to give the whole story) they experience stress and this stress reveals itself. Charles Darwin said, "Repressed emotion almost always comes to the surface in some form of body motion."

The problem for interrogators is that stress doesn't necessarily show up as nail biting, sweating and eye avoidance. It could take the form of a pleasant grin, a cheerful nod, a sympathetic wag of the head.

You don't say . . .

Well, that's terrible . . .

What a body language expert must do is compare subjects' behavior in nonstressful situations with their behavior when they might be lying. Differences between the two suggest—though they don't prove—deception. If there *is* some variation, a kinesic analyst then continues to probe the topic that's causing the stress until the subject confesses, or it's otherwise explained.

In interrogating Wayne Keplar, Dance would take her normal approach: asking a number of innocuous questions that she knew the answers to and that the suspect would have no reason to lie about. She'd also just shoot the breeze with him, no agenda other than to note how he behaved when feeling no stress. This would establish his kinesic "baseline"—a catalog of his body language, tone of voice, and choice of expressions when he was at ease and truthful.

Only then would she turn to questions about the impending attack and look for variations from the baseline when he answered.

But establishing the baseline usually requires many hours, if not days, of casual discussion.

Time that Kathryn Dance didn't have.

It was now 2:08.

Still, there was no option other than to do the best she could. She'd learned that there was another suspect, escaping through the old military ordnance storage and practice ground, with Michael O'Neil in pursuit (she knew the dangers of the base and didn't want to think of the risks to him). And the Monterey crime scene team was still going over the Taurus and the items that Paulson and Keplar had on them when arrested. But these aspects of the investigation had produced no leads.

Dance now read the sparse file once more quickly. Wayne Keplar was forty-four, high school educated only, but he'd done well at school and was now one of the "philosophers" at the Brothers of Liberty, writing many of the essays and diatribes on the group's blogs and website. He was single, never married. He'd been born in the Haight, lived in San Diego and Bakersfield. Now in Oakland. He didn't have a passport and had never been out of the country. His father was dead—killed in a Waco/Ruby Ridge–type stand-off with federal officers. His mother and sister, a few years older than he, were also involved in the BOL, which despite the name, boasted members of both sexes. Neither of these family members had a criminal record.

Keplar, on the other hand, did—but a minor one, and nothing violent. His only federal offense had been graffiti-ing an armed forces recruitment center.

He also had an older brother, who lived on the East Coast, but the man apparently hadn't had any contact with Keplar for years and had nothing to do with the BOL.

A deep data mine search had revealed nothing about Keplar's and Gabe Paulson's journey here. This was typical of militia types, worried about Big Brother. They'd pay cash for as much as they could.

Normally she'd want far more details than this, but there was no more time.

Fast . . .

Dance left the folder at the desk out front and entered the interrogation room. Keplar glanced up with a smile.

"Uncuff him," she said to Albert Stemple, who didn't hesitate even though he clearly wasn't crazy about the idea.

Dance would be alone in the room with an unshackled suspect, but she couldn't afford to have the man's arms limited by chains. Body language analysis is hard enough even with all the limbs unfettered.

Keplar slumped lazily in the gray padded office chair, as if settling in to watch a football game he had some, but not a lot of, interest in.

Dance nodded to Stemple, who left and closed the thick door behind him. Her eyes went to the large analog clock at the far end of the room.

2:16.

Keplar followed her gaze then looked back. "You're goin' to try to find out where the . . . *event*'s takin' place. Ask away. But I'll tell you right now, it's going to be a waste of time."

Dance moved her chair so that she sat across from him, with no furniture between them. Any barrier between interviewer and subject, even a small table, gives the perp a sense of protection and makes kinesic analysis that much harder. Dance was about three feet from him, in his personal proxemic zone—not so close as to make him stonewall, but near enough to keep him unsettled.

Except that he wasn't unsettled. At all. Wayne Keplar was as calm as could be.

He looked at her steadily, a gaze that was not haughty, not challenging, not sexy. It was almost as if he were sizing up a dog to buy for his child.

"Wayne, you don't have a driver's license."

"Another way for the government to keep tabs on you."

"Where do you live?"

"Oakland. Near the water. Been there for six years. Town has a bad rap but it's okay."

"Where were you before that?"

"San Diego."

She asked more about his personal life and travels, pretending not to know the answers. She'd left the file outside.

His responses were truthful. And as he spoke she noted his shoulders were forward, his right hand tended to come to rest on his thigh, he looked her straight in the eye when he spoke, his lips often curled into a half smile. He had a habit of poking his tongue into the interior of his cheek from time to time. It could have been a habit or could be from withdrawal—missing chewing tobacco, which Dance knew could be as addictive as smoking.

"Why'd you leave San Diego, Wayne? Weather's nicer than Oakland."

"Not really. I don't agree with that. But I just didn't like it. You know how you get a vibration and it's just not right."

"That's true," she said.

He beamed in an eerie way. "Do you? You know that? You're a firecracker, Kathryn. Yes, you are."

A chill coursed down her spine as the near-set eyes tapped across her face.

She ignored it as best she could and asked, "How senior are you in the Brothers of Liberty?"

"I'm pretty near the top. You know anything about it?"

"No."

"I'd love to tell you. You're smart, Ms. Firecracker. You'd probably think there're some pretty all right ideas we've got."

"I'm not sure I would."

A one-shoulder shrug—another of his baseline gestures. "But you never know."

Then came more questions about his life in Oakland, his prior convictions, his childhood. Dance knew the answers to some but the others were such that he'd have no reason to lie and she continued to rack up elements of baseline body language and verbal quality (the tone and speed of speech).

She snuck a glance at the clock.

"Time's got you rattled, does it?"

"You're planning to kill a lot of people. Yes, that bothers me. But not you, I see."

"Ha, now you're sounding just like a therapist. I was in counseling once. It didn't take."

"Let's talk about what you have planned, the two hundred people you're going to kill."

"Two hundred and *change*."

So, more victims. His behavior fit the baseline. This was true; he wasn't just boasting.

"How many more?"

"Two hundred twenty, I'd guess."

An idea occurred to Dance and she said, "I've told you we're not releasing Osmond Carter. That will never be on the table."

"Your loss . . . well, not yours. Two hundred and some odd people's loss."

"And killing them is only going to make your organization a pariah, a—"

"I know what 'pariah' means. Go on."

"Don't you think it would work to your advantage, from a publicity point of view, if you call off the attack, or tell me the location now?"

He hesitated. "Maybe. That could be, yeah." Then his eyes brightened. "Now, I'm not inclined to call anything off. That'd look bad. Or tell you direct where this thing's going to happen. But you being Ms. Firecracker and all, how 'bout I give you a chance to figure it out. We'll play a game."

"Game?"

"Twenty Questions. I'll answer honestly, I swear I will."

Sometimes that last sentence was a deception flag. Now, she didn't think so.

"And if you find out where those two hundred and twenty souls're going to meet Jesus . . . then good for you. I can honestly say I didn't tell you. But you only get twenty questions. You don't figure it out, get the morgue ready. You want to play, Kathryn? If not, I'll just decide I want my lawyer and hope I'm next to a TV in"—he looked at the clock—"one hour and forty-one minutes."

"All right, let's play," Dance said, and she subtly wiped the sweat that had dotted her palms. How on earth to frame twenty questions to narrow down where the attack would take place? She'd never been in an interrogation like this.

He sat forward. "This'll be fun!"

"Is the attack going to be an explosive device?"

"Question one—I'll keep count. No."

"What will it be?"

"That's question two but, sorry, you know Twenty Questions: has to be yes or no answers. But I'll give you a do-over."

"Will it be a chemical/bio weapon?"

"Sorta cheating there, a twofer. But I'll say yes."

"Is it going to be in a place open to the public?"

"Number three. Yes, sorta public. Let's say, there'll be public access."

He was telling the truth. All his behavior and the pitch and tempo of voice bore out his honesty. But what did he mean by public access but not quite public?

"Is it an entertainment venue?"

"Question four. Well, not really, but there will be entertainment there."

"Christmas related?"

He scoffed. "That's five. Are you asking questions wisely, Ms. Firecracker? You've used a quarter of them already. You could have combined Christmas and entertainment. Anyway, yes, Christmas is involved."

Dance thought this curious. The Brothers of Liberty apparently had a religious side, even if they weren't born-again fanatics. She would have thought the target might be Islamic or Jewish.

"Have the victims done anything to your organization personally?"

Thinking police or law enforcement or government.

"Six. No."

"You're targeting them on ideological grounds?"

"Seven. Yes."

She asked, "Will it be in Monterey County?"

"Number eight. Yes."

"In the city of . . ." No, if she followed those lines of questioning, she'd use up all the questions just asking about the many towns and unincorporated areas in Monterey County. "Will it be near the water?"

"Sloppy question. Expect better from you, Ms. Firecracker. Do-over. Near the *what*?"

Stupid of her, Dance realized, her heart pounding. There were a number of bodies of water and rivers in the area. And don't ask about the ocean. Technically, Monterey wasn't on the Pacific. "Will it be within a half mile of Monterey Bay?"

"Good!" he said, enjoying himself. "Yes. That was nine. Almost halfway there."

And she could see he was telling the truth completely. Every answer was delivered according to his kinesic baseline.

"Do you and Gabe Paulson have a partner helping you in the event?"

One eyebrow rose. "Yes. Number ten. You're halfway to saving all them poor folks, Kathryn."

"Is the third person a member of the Brothers of Liberty?"

"Yes. Eleven."

She was thinking hard, unsure how to finesse the partner's existence into helpful information. She changed tack. "Do the victims need tickets to get into the venue?"

"Twelve. I want to play fair. I honestly don't know. But they did have to sign up and pay. That's more than I should give you, but I'm enjoying this." And indeed it seemed that Keplar was.

She was beginning to form some ideas.

"Is the venue a tourist attraction?"

"Thirteen. Yes, I'd say so. At least near tourist attractions."

Now she felt safe using one of her geographical questions. "Is it in the city of Monterey?"

"No. Fourteen."

"Carmel?"

"No. Fifteen."

Dance kept her own face neutral. What else should she be asking? If she could narrow it down a bit more, and if Michael O'Neil and his Crime Scene team came up with other details, they might cobble together a clear picture of where the attack would take place then evacuate every building in the area.

"How you doing there, Kathryn? Feeling the excitement of a good game? I sure am." He looked at the clock. Dance did, too. Hell, time had sped by during this exchange. It was now 2:42.

She didn't respond to his question, but tried a different tack. "Do your close friends know what you're doing?"

He frowned. "You want to use question sixteen for that? Well, your choice. Yes."

"Do they approve?"

"Yes, all of them. Seventeen. Getting all you need here, Kathryn? Seems you're getting off track."

But she wasn't. Dance had another strategy. She was comfortable with the information she had—tourist area, near the water, a paid-for event, Christmas related, a few other facts—and with what O'Neil found, she hoped they could narrow down areas to evacuate. Now she was hoping to convince him to confess by playing up the idea raised earlier. That by averting the attack he'd still score some good publicity but wouldn't have to go to jail forever or die by lethal injection. Even if she lost the Twenty Questions game, which seemed likely, she was getting him to think about the people he was close to, friends and family he could still spend time with—if he stopped the attack.

"And family—do your siblings approve?"

"Question eighteen. Don't have any. I'm an only child. You only got two questions left, Kathryn. Spend 'em wisely."

Dance hardly heard the last sentences. She was stunned.

Oh, no . . .

His behavior when he'd made the comment about not having siblings—a bald lie—was identical to that of the baseline.

During the entire game he'd been lying.

Their eyes met. "Tripped up there, didn't I?" He laughed hard. "We're off the grid so much, didn't think you knew about my family. Shoulda been more careful."

"Everything you just told me was a lie."

"Thin air. Whole cloth. Pick your cliché, Ms. Firecracker. Had to run the clock. There's nothing on God's green earth going to save those people."

She understood now what a waste of time this had been. Wayne Keplar was probably incapable of being kinesically analyzed. The Ten Commandments Principle didn't apply in his case. Keplar felt no more stress lying than he did telling the truth. Like serial killers and schizophrenics, political extremists often feel they are doing what's right, even if those acts are criminal or reprehensible to others. They're convinced of their own moral rectitude.

"Look at it from my perspective. Sure, we would've gotten *some* press if I'd confessed. But you know reporters—they'd get tired of the story after a couple days. Two hundred dead folk? Hell, we'll be on CNN for weeks. You can't *buy* publicity like that."

Dance pushed back from the table and, without a word, stepped outside.

Michael O'Neil sprinted past ghosts.

The Monterey area is a place where apparitions from the past are ever present.

The Ohlone Native Americans, the Spanish, the railroad barons, the commercial fisherman . . . all gone.

And the soldiers, too, who'd inhabited Fort Ord and the other military facilities that once dotted the Monterey Peninsula and defined the economy and the culture.

Gasping and sweating despite the chill and mist, O'Neil jogged past the remnants of barracks and classrooms and training facilities, some intact, some sagging, some collapsed.

Past vehicle pool parking lots, supply huts, rifle ranges, parade grounds.

Past signs that featured faded skulls and crossed bones and pink explosions.

UXO . . .

The suspect wove through the area desperately and the chase was exhausting. The land had been bulldozed flat in the 1930s and '40s for the construction of the base but the dunes had reclaimed much of the landscape, rippled mounds of blond sand, some of them four stories high.

The perp made his way through these valleys in a panicked run, falling often, as did O'Neil because of the dicey traction—and the fast turns and stop-and-go sprinting when what looked like a potential explosives stash loomed.

O'Neil debated about parking a slug in the man's leg, though that's technically a no-no. Besides, O'Neil couldn't afford to miss and kill him.

The suspect chugged along, gasping, red-faced, the deadly backpack over his shoulder bouncing.

Finally, O'Neil heard the thud thud thud of rotors moving in.

He reflected that a chopper was the only smart way to pursue somebody through an area like this, even if it wasn't technically a minefield. The birds wouldn't trip the explosives, as long as they hovered.

And what were the odds that he himself would detonate some ordnance, mangling his legs?

What about the kids then?

What about his possible life with Kathryn Dance?

He decided that those questions were pointless. This was military ordnance. He'd end up not an amputee but a mass of red jelly.

The chopper moved closer. God, they were loud. He'd forgotten that.

The suspect stopped, glanced back and then turned right, disappearing fast behind a dune.

Was it a trap? O'Neil started forward slowly. But he couldn't see clearly. The chopper was raising a turbulent cloud of dust and sand. O'Neil waved it back. He pointed his weapon ahead of him and began to approach the valley down which the perp had disappeared.

The helicopter hovered closer yet. The pilot apparently hadn't seen O'Neil's hand gestures. The sandstorm grew fiercer. Some completely indiscernible words rattled from a loudspeaker.

"Back, back!" O'Neil called, uselessly.

Then, in front of him, he noticed what seemed to be a person's form, indistinct in the miasma of dust and sand. The figure was moving in.

Blinking, trying to clear his eyes, he aimed his pistol. "Freeze!"

Putting some pressure on the trigger. The gun was double-action now and it would take a bit of poundage to fire the first round.

Shoot, he told himself.

But there was too much dust to be sure this was in fact the perp. What if it was a hostage or a lost hiker?

He crouched and staggered forward.

Damn chopper! Grit clotted his mouth.

Which was when a second silhouette, smaller, detached from the first and seemed to fly through the gauzy air toward him.

What was—?

The blue backpack struck him in the face. He fell backward, tumbling to the ground, the bag resting beside his legs. Choking on the sand, Michael O'Neil thought how ironic it was that he'd survived a UXO field only to be blown to pieces by a bomb the perp had brought with him.

The Bankers' Association holiday party was under way. It had started, as they always did, a little early. Who wanted to deny loans or take care of the massive paperwork of approved ones when the joy of the season beckoned?

Carol and Hal were greeting the CCCBA members at the door, showing them where to hang coats, giving them gift bags and making sure the bar and snacks were in good supply.

The place did look magical. She'd opted to close the curtains—on a nice summer day the water view might be fine but the fog had descended and the scenery was gray and gloomy. Inside, though, with the holiday lights and dimmed overheads, the banquet room took on a warm, comfy tone.

Hal was walking around in his conservative suit, white shirt and oversized Santa hat. People sipped wine and punch, snapped digital pictures and clustered, talking about politics and sports and shopping and impending vacations.

Also, a lot of comments about interest rates, the Fed, and the euro.

With bankers you couldn't get away from shop talk. Ever.

"We heard there's a surprise, Carol," one of the members called.

"What?" came another voice.

"Be patient," she said, laughing. "If I told you it wouldn't be a surprise, now would it?"

When the party seemed to be spinning along on its own, she walked to the stage and tested the PA system once again. Yes, it was working fine.

Thank goodness.

The "surprise" depended on it. She'd arranged for the chorus from one of her grandson's high schools to go up onstage and present a holiday concert, traditional and modern Christmas and Hanukkah songs. She glanced at her watch. The kids would arrive at about 3:45. She'd heard the youngsters before and they were very good.

Carol laughed to herself, recalling the entertainment at last year's party. Herb Ross, a VP at First People's Trust, who'd injected close to a quart of the "special" punch, had climbed on the table to sing—and even worse (or better, for later water cooler stories) to act out—the entire "Twelve Days of Christmas" himself, the leaping lords being the high point.

Kathryn Dance spent a precious ten minutes texting and talking to a number of people in the field and here at headquarters.

It seemed that outside the surreality of the interrogation room, the investigation hadn't moved well at all. Monterey's Forensic Services Unit was still analyzing trace connected with the Taurus and the suspects' pocket litter and Abbott Calderman said they might not have any answers for another ten or fifteen minutes.

Lord, she thought.

Michael O'Neil, when last heard from, had been pursuing the third conspirator in the abandoned army base. A police chopper had lost him in a cloud of dust and sand. She'd had a brief conversation with FBI agent Steve Nichols in a nearby mobile command post, who'd said, "This Paulson isn't saying anything. Not

a word. Just stares at me. I'd like to waterboard him."

"We don't do that," Dance had reminded.

"I'm just daydreaming," Nichols had muttered and hung up.

Now, returning to the interrogation room with Wayne Keplar, Dance looked at the clock on the wall.

3:10.

"Hey," said Wayne Keplar, eyeing it briefly, then turning his gaze to Dance. "You're not mad at me, are you?"

Dance sat across the table from him. It was clear she wasn't going to power a confession out of him, so she didn't bother with the tradecraft of kinesic interviewing. She said, "I'm sure it's no surprise that, before, I tried to analyze your body language and was hoping to come up with a way to pressure you into telling me what you and Gabe and your other associate had planned."

"Didn't know that about the body language. But makes sense."

"Now I want to do something else, and I'm going to tell you exactly what that is. No tricks."

"Shoot. I'm game."

Dance had decided that traditional analysis and interrogation wouldn't work with someone like Wayne Keplar. His lack of affect, his fanatic's belief in the righteousness of his cause made kinesics useless. Content-based analysis wouldn't do much good either; this is body language's poor cousin, seeking to learn whether a suspect is telling the truth by considering if what he says makes sense. But Keplar was too much in control to let slip anything that she might parse for clues about deception and truth.

So she was doing something radical.

Dance now said, "I want to prove to you that your beliefs—what's motivating you and your group to perform this attack—they're wrong."

He lifted an eyebrow. Intrigued.

This was a ludicrous idea for an interrogator. One should never argue substance with a suspect. If a man is accused of killing his wife, your job is to determine the facts and, if it appears that he did indeed commit murder, get a confession or at least gather enough information to help investigators secure his conviction.

There's no point in discussing the right or wrong of what he did, much less the broader philosophical questions of taking lives in general or violence against women, say.

But that was exactly what she was going to do now.

Poking the inside of his cheek with his tongue once more, thoughtful, Keplar said, "Do you even know what our beliefs are?"

"I read the Brothers of Liberty website. I—"

"You like the graphics? Cost a pretty penny."

A glance at the wall. 3:14.

Dance continued. "You advocate smaller government, virtually no taxes, decentralized banking, no large corporations, reduced military, religion in public schools. And that you have the right to violent civil disobedience. Along with some racial and ethnic theories that went out of fashion in the 1860s."

"Well, 'bout that last one—truth is, we just throw that in to get checks from rednecks and border control nuts. Lot of us don't really feel that way. But, Ms. Firecracker, you done your homework, sounds like. We've got more positions than you can shake a stick at but those'll do for a start . . . So, argue away. This's gonna be as much fun as Twenty Questions. But just remember, maybe I'll talk *you* into my way of thinking, hanging up that tin star of yours and coming over to the good guys. What do you think about that?"

"I'll stay open-minded, if you will."

"Deal."

She thought back to what she'd read on the group's website. "You talk about the righteousness of the individual. Agree up to a point, but we can't survive as individuals alone. We need government. And the more people we have, with more economic and social activity, the more we need a strong central government to make sure we're safe to go about our lives."

"That's sad, Kathryn."

"Sad?"

"Sure. I have more faith in humankind than

you do, sounds like. We're pretty capable of taking care of ourselves. Let me ask you: You go to the doctor from time to time, right?"

"Yes."

"But not very often, right? Pretty rare, hmm? More often with the kids, I'll bet. Sure, you have kids. I can tell."

She let this go with no reaction.

3:17.

"But what does the doctor do? Short of broken bone to set, the doctor tells you pretty much to do what your instinct told you. Take some aspirin, go to bed, drink plenty of fluids, eat fiber, go to sleep. Let the body take care of itself. And ninety percent of the time, those ideas work." His eyes lit up. "That's what government should do: Leave us alone ninety-nine percent of the time."

"And what about the other one percent?" Dance asked.

"I'll give you that we need, let's see, highways, airports, national defense . . . Ah, but what's that last word? 'Defense.' You know, they used to call it the 'War Department.' Well, then some public relations fellas got involved and 'War' wouldn't do anymore, so they changed it. But that's a lie. See, it's not just defense. We go poking our noses into places that we have no business being."

"The government regulates corporations that would exploit people."

He scoffed. "The government helps 'em do it. How many congressmen go to Washington poor and come back rich? Most of them."

"But you're okay with some taxes?"

He shrugged. "To pay for roads, air traffic control, and defense."

3:20.

"The SEC for regulating stocks?"

"We don't need stocks. Ask your average Joe what the stock market is and they'll tell ya it's a way to make money or put something away for your retirement fund. They don't realize that that's *not* what it's for. The stock market's there to let people buy a company, like you'd go to a used car lot to buy a car. And why do you want to buy a company? Beats me. Maybe a few people'd buy stock because they like what the company does or they want to support a certain kind of business. That's not what people want them for. Do away with stocks altogether. Learn to live off the land."

"You're wrong, Wayne. Look at all the innovations corporations have created: the lifesaving drugs, the medical supplies, the computers . . . that's what companies have done."

"Sure, and iPhones and BlackBerrys and laptops have replaced parents, and kids learn their family values at porn sites."

"What about government providing education?"

"Ha! That's another racket. Professors making a few hundred thousand dollars a year for working eight months, and not working very hard at that. Teachers who can hardly put a sentence together themselves. Tell me, Kathryn, are you happy handing over your youngsters to somebody you see at one or two PTA meetings a year? Who knows what the hell they're poisoning their minds with."

She said nothing, but hoped her face wasn't revealing that from time to time she did indeed have those thoughts.

Keplar continued, "No, I got two words for you there. 'Home schooling.'"

"You don't like the police, you claim. But we're here to make sure you and your family're safe. We'll even make sure the Brothers of Liberty're free to go about their business and won't be discriminated against and won't be the victim of hate crimes."

"Police state . . . Think on this, Ms. Firecracker. I don't know what *you* do exactly here in this fancy building, but tell me true. You put your life on the line every day and for what? Oh, maybe you stop some crazy serial killer from time to time or save somebody in a kidnapping. But mostly cops just put on their fancy cop outfits and go bust some poor kids with drugs but never get to the *why* of it. What's the reason they were scoring pot or coke in the first place? Because the government and the institutions of this country failed them."

3:26.

"So you don't like the federal government. But it's all relative, isn't it? Go back to the eighteenth century. We weren't just a mass of individuals. There was state government and they were powerful. People had to pay taxes, they were subject to laws, they couldn't take their neighbors' property, they couldn't commit incest, they couldn't steal. Everybody accepted that. The federal government today is just a bigger version of the state governments in the 1700s."

"Ah, good, Kathryn. I'll give you that." He nodded agreeably. "But we think state and even *local* laws are too much."

"So you're in favor of no laws?"

"Let's just say a lot, lot less."

Dance leaned forward, with her hands together. "Then let's talk about your one belief that's the most critical now: violence to achieve your ends. I'll grant you that you have the right to hold whatever beliefs you want—and not get arrested for it. Which, by the way, isn't true in a lot of countries."

"We're the best," Keplar agreed. "But that's still not good enough for us."

"But violence is hypocritical."

He frowned at this. "How so?"

"Because you take away the most important right of an individual—his life—when you kill him in the name of your views. How can you be an advocate of individuals and yet be willing to destroy them at the same time?"

His head bobbed up and down. A tongue poke again. "That's good, Kathryn. Yes."

She lifted her eyebrows.

Keplar added, "And there's something to it . . . Except you're missing one thing. Those people we're targeting? They're not individuals. They're part of the system, just like you."

"So you're saying it's okay to kill them because they're, what? Not even human?"

"Couldn't have said it better myself, Ms. Firecracker." His eyes strayed to the wall. 3:34.

The helicopter set down in a parking lot of the outlet mall in Seaside and Michael O'Neil and a handcuffed suspect—no ID on him—climbed out.

O'Neil was bleeding from a minor cut on the head incurred when he scrabbled into a cluster of scrub oaks escaping the satchel bomb.

Which turned out to be merely a distraction.

No IEDs, no anthrax.

The satchel was filled with sand.

The perp had apparently disposed of whatever noxious substance it contained on one of his crosscut turns and weaves, and the evidence or bomb or other clue was lost in the sand.

The chopper's downdraft hadn't helped either.

What was most disappointing, though, was that the man had clammed up completely.

O'Neil was wondering if he was actually mute. He hadn't said a word during the chase or after the detective had tackled and cuffed him and dragged him to the helicopter. Nothing O'Neil could say—promises or threats—could get the man to talk.

The detective handed him over to fellow Monterey County Sheriff's Office deputies. A fast search revealed no ID. They took his prints, which came back negative from the field scanner, and the man was processed under a John Doe as "UNSUB A."

The blond woman with the big soda cup—now mostly empty—who'd spotted him in the crowd now identified him formally and she left.

The Crime Scene boss strode up to O'Neil. "Don't have much but I'll say that the Taurus had recently spent some time on or near the beach along a stretch five miles south of Moss Landing." Calderman explained that because of the unique nature of cooling water from the power plant at Moss Landing, and the prevailing currents and fertilizer from some of the local farms, he could pinpoint that part of the county.

If five miles could be called pinpointing.

"Anything else?"

"Nope. That's it. Might get more in the lab." Calderman nodded to his watch. "But there's no time left."

O'Neil called Kathryn, whose cell phone went right to voice mail. He texted her the information. He then looked over at the smashed Taurus, the emergency vehicles, the yellow tape stark in the gray foggy afternoon. He was thinking: It wasn't unheard of for crime scenes to raise more questions than answers.

But why the hell did it have to be this one, when so little time remained to save the two hundred victims?

Hands steady as a rock, Harriet Keplar was driving the car she'd stolen from the parking lot at the outlet mall.

But even as her grip was firm, her heart was in turmoil. Her beloved brother, Wayne, and her sometimes lover, Gabe Paulson, were in custody. After the bomb detonated shortly, she'd never see them again, except at trial—given Wayne's courage, she suspected he'd plead not guilty simply so he could get up on the stand and give the judge, jury and press an earful, rather than work a deal with the prosecutor.

She pulled her glasses out of her hair and regarded her watch. Not long now. It was ten minutes to the Dunes Inn, which had been their staging area. And would have been where they'd wait out the next few days, watching the news. But now, sadly, Plan B was in effect. She'd go back to collect all the documents, maps, extra equipment and remaining explosives and get the hell back to Oakland. She bet there was a goddamn snitch within the Brothers of Liberty up there—how else would the police have known as much as they did?—and Harriet was going to find him.

It was a good thing they'd decided to split up behind the outlet mall. As the Taurus had temporarily evaded the Highway Patrol trooper and skidded to a stop, Harriet in the backseat, Wayne decided they had to make sure somebody got back to the motel and ditched the evidence—which implicated some very senior people at the BOL.

She jumped out with the backpack containing extra detonators and wires and tools and phony IDs that let them get into the banquet hall where the CCCBA was having their party. Harriet had been going to hijack a car and head back to the Dunes Inn, but the asshole of a trooper had rammed Gabe and Wayne. And police had descended.

She'd slipped into a Burger King, to let the dust settle. She'd ditched the contents of the satchel, but, to her dismay, the police were spreading out and talking to everybody at the mall. Harriet decided she had to find a fall guy to take attention away from her. She'd spotted a solo shopper, a man about her height with light hair—in case the trooper had seen her in the backseat. She stuck her Glock in his ribs, pulling him behind the BK, then grabbed his wallet. She found a picture of three spectacularly plain children and made a fake call on her cell phone to an imaginary assistant, telling him to get to the poor guy's house and round up the kidlings.

If he didn't do exactly as she said, they'd be shot, oldest to youngest. His wife would be the last to go.

She got his car keys and told him to stand in the crowd. If any cops came to talk to him he was to run and if he was caught he should throw the pack at them and keep running. If he got stopped he should say nothing. She, of course, was going to dime him out—and when the police went after him she would have a chance to take his car and leave. It would have worked fine, except that goddamn detective—O'Neil was his name—had her stay put so she could formally ID the sandy-haired guy. Oh, how she wanted to get the hell out of there. But she couldn't arouse suspicion, so Harriet had cooled her heels, sucking down Diet Coke, and tried to wrestle with the anger and sorrow about her brother and Gabe.

Then O'Neil and the poor bastard had returned. She'd IDed him with a fierce glance of warning and given them some fake information on how to reach her.

And now she was in his car, heading back to the Dunes Inn.

Oh, Wayne, I'll miss you! Gabe, too.

The motel loomed. She sped into the parking lot and braked to a stop.

She was then aware of an odd vibration under her hands. The steering column. What was it?

An earthquake?

A problem with the car?

She shut the engine off but the vibration grew louder.

Leaves began to move and the dust swirled like a tornado in the parking lot.

And Harriet understood. "Oh, shit."

She pulled her Glock from her bag and sprinted toward the motel door, firing blindly at the helicopter as it landed in the parking lot. Several officers and, damn it, that detective, O'Neil, charged toward her. "Drop the weapon, drop the weapon!"

She hesitated and laid the gun and her keychain on the ground. Then she dropped facedown beside them.

Harriet was cuffed and pulled to her feet.

O'Neil was approaching, his weapon drawn and looking for accomplices. A cluster of cops dressed like soldiers was slowly moving toward the motel room.

"Anyone in there?" he asked.

"No."

"It was just the three of you?"

"Yes."

The detective called, "Treat it dynamic in any case."

"How'd you know?" she snapped.

He looked her over neutrally. "The cargo pants."

"What?"

"You described the man in the car and said one was wearing cargo pants. You couldn't see the pants of somebody inside a car from sixty feet away. The angle was wrong."

Hell, Harriet thought. Never even occurred to her.

O'Neil added that the man they'd believed was one of the conspirators was acting too nervous. "It occurred to me that he might've been set up. He told me what you'd done. We tracked his car here with his GPS." O'Neil was going through her purse. "You're his sister, Wayne's."

"I'm not saying anything else." Harriet was distracted, her eyes taking in the motel room.

O'Neil caught it and frowned. He glanced down at her keychain, which held both a fob for her car and the second one.

She caught his eye and smiled.

"IED in the room!" he called. "Everybody back! Now."

It wasn't an explosive device, just a gas bomb Gabe had rigged in the event something like this happened. It had been burning for three minutes or so—she'd pushed the remote control the second she'd seen the chopper—but the smoke and flames weren't yet visible.

Then a bubble of fire burst through two of the windows.

Armed with extinguishers, the tactical team hurried inside to salvage what they could, then retreated as the flames swelled. One officer called, "Michael! We spotted a box of plastic explosive detonators, some timers."

Another officer ran up to O'Neil and showed him what was left of a dozen scorched documents. They were the floor plan for the site of the attack at the CCCBA party. He studied it. "A room with a stage. Could be anywhere. A corporation, school, hotel, restaurant." He sighed.

Harriet panicked, then relaxed, as she snuck a glimpse and noted that the name of the motel was on a part of the sheet that had burned to ash.

"Where is this?" O'Neil asked her bluntly.

Harriet studied it for a moment and shook her head. "I've never seen that before. You planted it to incriminate me. The government does that all the time."

At the Bankers' party the high school students arrived, looking scrubbed and festive, all in uniforms, which Carol approved of. Tan slacks and blazers for the boys, plaid skirts and white blouses for the girls.

They were checking out the treats—and the boys were probably wondering if they could cop a spiked punch—but would refrain from anything until after the twenty-minute concert. The kids took their music seriously and sweets tended to clog the throat, her grandson had explained.

She hugged the blond, good-looking boy and shook the hand of the chorus director.

"Everyone, everyone!" she called. "Take your seats."

And the children climbed up onstage, taking their positions.

The clock in the interrogation room registered 3:51.

Dance broke off the debate for a moment and read and sent several text messages, as Wayne Keplar watched with interest.

3:52.

"Your expression tells me the news isn't good. Not making much headway elsewhere?"

Kathryn Dance didn't respond. She slipped her phone away. "I'm not finished with our discussion, Wayne. Now, I pointed out you were hypocritical to kill the very people you purport to represent."

"And I pointed out a hole a mile wide with that argument."

"Killing also goes against another tenet of yours."

Wayne Keplar said calmly, "How so?"

"You want religion taught in school. So you must be devout. Well, killing the innocent is a sin."

He snickered. "Oh, please, Ms. Firecracker. Read the Bible sometime: God smites people for next to nothing. Because somebody crosses Him or to get your attention. Or because it's Tuesday, I don't know. You think everybody drowned in Noah's flood was guilty of something?"

"So al-Qaeda's terrorist tactics are okay?"

"Well, al-Qaeda itself—'cause they want the strongest government of all. It's called a theocracy. No respect for individuals. But their tactics? Hell, yes. I admire the suicide bombers. If I was in charge, though, I'd reduce all Islamic countries to smoking nuclear craters."

Kathryn Dance looked desperately at the clock, which showed nearly 3:57.

She rubbed her face as her shoulders slumped. Her weary eyes pleaded. "Is there anything I can say to talk you into stopping this?"

3:58.

"No, you can't. Sometimes the truth is more important than the individuals. But," he added with a sincere look. "Kathryn, I want to say that I appreciate one thing."

No more Ms. Firecracker.

"What's that?" she said in a whisper, eyes on the clock.

"You took me seriously. That talk we just had. You disagree, but you treated me with respect."

4 P.M.

Both law officer and suspect remained motionless, staring at the clock.

A phone in the room rang. She leaned over and hit the speaker button fast. "Yes?"

The staticky voice, a man's. "Kathryn, it's Albert. I'm sorry to have to tell you . . ."

She sighed. "Go on."

"It was an IED, plastic of some sort . . . We don't have the count yet. Wasn't as bad as it could be. Seems the device was under a stage and that absorbed some of the blast. But we're still looking at fifteen or so dead, maybe fifty injured . . . Hold on. CHP's calling. I'll get back to you."

Dance disconnected, closed her eyes briefly then glared at Keplar. "How *could* you?"

Wayne frowned; he wasn't particularly triumphant. "I'm sorry, Kathryn. This is the way it had to be. It's a war out there. Besides, score one for your side—only fifteen dead. We screwed up."

Dance shivered in anger. But she calmly said, "Let's go."

She rose and knocked on the door. It opened immediately and two large CBI agents came in, also glaring. One reshackled Keplar's hands behind him, hoping, it seemed, for an excuse to Taser the prisoner. But the man was the epitome of decorum.

One agent muttered to Dance, "Just heard, the death count's up to—"

She waved him silent, as if denying Keplar the satisfaction of knowing the extent of his victory.

She led the prisoner out the back of CBI, toward a van that would ultimately transport him to the Salinas lockup.

"We'll have to move fast," she told the other agents. "There're going to be a lot of people who'd like to take things into their own hands."

The area was largely deserted. But just then Dan Simmons, the blogger who'd pestered Dance earlier, the Jude Law lookalike, peered around the edge of the building as if he'd been checking every few minutes to see if they'd make a run for it this way. Simmons hurried toward them, along with his unwashed cameraman.

Dance ignored him.

Simmons asked, "Agent Dance, could you comment on the failure of law enforcement to stop the bombing in time?"

She said nothing and kept ushering Keplar toward the van.

"Do you think this will be the end of your career?"

Silence.

"Wayne, do you have anything to say?" the blog reporter asked.

Eyes on the camera lens, Keplar called, "It's about time the government started listening to people like Osmond Carter. This never would have happened if he hadn't been illegally arrested!"

"Wayne, what do you have to say about killing innocent victims?"

"Sacrifices have to be made," he called.

Simmons called, "But why these particular victims? What's the message you're trying to send?"

"That maybe bankers shouldn't be throwing themselves fancy holiday parties with the money they've stolen from the working folk of this country. The financial industry's been raping citizens for years. They claim—"

"Okay, hold it," Dance snapped to the agents flanking Keplar, who literally jerked him to a stop.

Dance was pulling out a walkie-talkie. "Michael, it's Kathryn, you read me?"

"Four by four. We've got six choppers and the entire peninsula com network standing by. You're patched in to all emergency frequencies. What do you have?"

"The target's a party—Christmas, I'd guess—involving bankers, or savings and loan people, bank regulators, something like that. It *is* a bomb and it's under the stage in that room you texted me about."

Wayne Keplar stared at her, awash in confusion.

A half-dozen voices shot from her radio, variations of *"Roger . . . Copy that . . . Checking motels with banquet rooms in the target zone, south of Moss Landing . . . Contacting all banks in the target zone."*

"What is this?" Keplar raged.

Everyone ignored him.

A long several minutes passed, Dance standing motionless, head down, listening to the intersecting voices through the radio. And then: "This is Major Rodriguez, CHP. We've got it! Central Coast Bankers' Association, annual Christmas party, Monterey Bay Seaside Motel. They're evacuating now."

Wayne Keplar's eyes grew wide as he stared at Dance. "But the bomb . . ." He glanced at Dance's wrist and those of the other officers. They'd all removed their watches, so Keplar couldn't see the real time. He turned to an agent and snapped, "What the hell time is it?"

"About ten to four," replied Dan Simmons, the reporter.

He blurted to Dance, "The clock? In the interrogation room?"

"Oh," she said, guiding him to the prisoner transport van. "It was fast."

A half hour later Michael O'Neil arrived from the motel where the bankers' party had been interrupted.

He explained that everyone got out safely, but there'd been no time to try to render the device safe. The explosion was quite impressive. The material was probably Semtex, Abbott Calder-man had guessed, judging from the smell. The Forensic Services head explained to O'Neil that it was the only explosive ever to have its own FAQ on the Internet, which answered questions like: Was it named after an idyllic, pastoral village? (yes). Was it mass produced and shipped throughout the world, as the late President Václav Havel claimed? (no). And was Semtex the means by which its inventor committed suicide? (not exactly—yes, an employee at the plant did blow himself up intentionally, but he had not been one of the inventors).

Dance smiled as O'Neil recounted this trivia.

Steve Nichols of the FBI called and told her they were on the way to the CBI to deliver the other suspect, Gabe Paulson. He explained that since she'd broken the case, it made sense for her to process all the suspects. There would be federal charges—mostly related to the explosives—but those could be handled later.

As they waited in the parking lot for Nichols to arrive, O'Neil asked, "So, how'd you do it? All I know is you called me about three, I guess, and told me to get choppers and a communications team ready. You hoped to have some details about the location of the attack in about forty-five minutes. But you didn't tell me what was going on."

"I didn't have much time," Dance explained. "What happened was I found out, after wasting nearly an hour, that Keplar was kinesics proof. So I had to trick him. I took a break at three and talked to our technical department. Seems you can speed up analog clocks by changing the voltage and the frequency of the current in the wiring. They changed the current in that part of the building so the clock started running fast."

O'Neil smiled. "That was the byword for this case, remember. You said it yourself."

And remember: We have two and a half hours. We've got to move fast . . .

Dance continued, "I remembered when we got to CBI Keplar started lecturing Dan Simmons about his cause."

"Oh, that obnoxious reporter and blogger?"

"Right. I called him and said that if he asked

Keplar why he picked those particular victims, I'd give him an exclusive interview. And I called you to set up the search teams. Then I went back into the interrogation. I had to make sure Keplar didn't notice the clock was running fast so I started debating philosophy with him."

"Philosophy?"

"Well, Wikipedia philosophy. Not the real stuff."

"Probably real enough nowadays."

She continued, "You and the Crime Scene people found out that it was probably a bomb and that it was planted in a large room with a stage. When the clock hit four in the interrogation room, I had Albert call me and pretend a bomb had gone off and killed people but the stage had absorbed a lot of the blast. That was just enough information so that Keplar believed it had really happened. Then all I had to do was perp walk him past Simmons, who asked why those particular victims. Keplar couldn't keep himself from lecturing.

"Sure was close."

True. Ten minutes meant the difference between life and death for two hundred people, though fate sometimes allowed for even more narrow margins.

One of the FBI's black SUVs now eased to a stop beside Dance and O'Neil.

Steve Nichols and another agent climbed out and helped their shackled prisoner out. A large bandage covered much of his head and the side of his face. O'Neil stared at him silently.

The FBI agent said, "Kathryn, good luck with this fellow. Wish you the best but he's the toughest I've ever seen—and I've been up against al-Qaeda and some of the Mexican cartel drug lords. They're Chatty Cathy compared with him. Not a single word. Just sits and stares at you. He's all yours."

"I'll do what I can, Steve. But I think there's enough forensics to put everybody away for twenty years."

The law enforcers said good-bye and the feds climbed into the Suburban, then sped out of the CBI lot.

Dance began to laugh.

So did the prisoner.

O'Neil asked, "So what's going on?"

Dance stepped forward and undid the cuffs securing the wrists of her associate, TJ Scanlon. He removed the swaddling, revealing no injuries.

"Thanks, boss. And by the way, those're the first words I've said in three hours."

Dance explained to O'Neil, "Gabe Paulson's in a lot more serious condition than I let on. He was shot in the head during the takedown and'll probably be in a vegetative state for the rest of his life. Which might not be that long. I knew Nichols'd wanted to have a part of the case—and for all we knew at that point he had primary jurisdiction. I wanted to interrogate the only suspect we had—Keplar—so I needed to give Nichols someone. TJ volunteered to play Paulson."

"So you just deceived the FBI."

"Technically. I know Steve. He's a brilliant agent. I'd trust him with anything except an interrogation with a deadline like this."

"Three hours, boss," TJ said, rubbing his wrists. "Did I mention not speaking for three hours? That's very hard for me."

O'Neil asked, "Won't he find out, see the pictures of the real Paulson in the press?"

"He was pretty bandaged up. And like I said, it may come back to haunt me. I'll deal with it then."

"I thought I was going to be waterboarded."

"I told him not to do that."

"Well, he didn't share your directive with me. I think he would have liked to use cattle prods, too. Oh, and I would've given you up in five seconds, boss. Just for the record."

Dance laughed.

O'Neil left to return to his office in Salinas and Dance and TJ entered the CBI lobby, just as the head of the office, Charles Overby, joined them. "Here you are."

The agents greeted the paunchy man who was in his typical work-a-day outfit: slacks and white shirt with sleeves rolled up, revealing tennis- and golf-tanned arms.

"Thanks, Kathryn. Appreciate what you did."

"Sure."

"You were in the operation, too?" Overby asked TJ.

"That's right. FBI liaison."

Overby lowered his voice and said approvingly, "They don't seem to want a cut of the action. Good for us."

"I did what I could," TJ said. Then the young man returned to his office, leaving Dance and her boss alone.

Overby turned to Dance. "I'll need a briefing," he said, nodding toward the reporters out front. A grimace. "Something to feed to *them*."

Despite the apparent disdain, though, Overby was in fact looking forward to the press conference. He always did. He loved the limelight and would want to catch the 6 P.M. local news. He'd also hope to gin up interest in some national coverage.

Dance put her watch back on her wrist and looked at the time. "I can give you the bare bones, Charles, but I've got to see a subject in another matter. It's got to be tonight. He leaves town tomorrow."

There was a pause. "Well, if it's critical . . ."

"It is."

"All right. Get me a briefing sheet now and a full report in the morning."

"Sure, Charles."

He started back to his office and asked, "This guy you're meeting? You need any backup?"

"No thanks, Charles. It's all taken care of."

"Sure. 'Night."

"Good night."

Heading to her own office, Kathryn Dance reflected on her impending mission tonight. If Overby had wanted a report on the attempted bombing for CBI headquarters in Sacramento or follow-up interrogations, she would have gladly done that, but since he was interested only in press releases, she decided to stick to her plans.

Which involved a call to her father, a retired marine biologist who worked part-time at the aquarium. She was going to have him pull some strings to arrange special admission after hours for herself and the children tonight.

And the "subject" she'd told Overby she had to meet tonight before he left town? Not a drug lord or a terrorist or a confidential informant . . . but what was apparently the most imposing cephalopod ever to tour the Central Coast of California.

BAD GIRLS

THE WINGED ASSASSIN

L. T. Meade & Robert Eustace

ALTHOUGH ONLY SERIOUS AFICIONADOS of detective fiction remember her work today, Elizabeth Thomasina Meade Smith (1844–1914), whose nom de plume was L. T. Meade, wrote several volumes of detective fiction that are historically important.

Stories from the Diary of a Doctor (1894; second series 1896), written in collaboration with Dr. Edgar Beaumont (using the pseudonym Clifford Halifax), is the first series of medical mysteries published in England. Other memorable books by Meade include *A Master of Mysteries* (1898), *The Gold Star Line* (1899), and *The Sanctuary Club* (1900), which features an unusual health club in which a series of murders is committed by apparently supernatural means, all written in collaboration with Dr. Eustace Robert Barton (1868–1943), writing as Robert Eustace. *The Sorceress of the Strand* (1903) portrays Madame Sara, an utterly sinister villainess who specializes in murder.

The Brotherhood of the Seven Kings (1899), also a collaborative effort with Barton, is the first series of stories about a female crook. The thoroughly evil leader of an Italian criminal organization, the dazzlingly beautiful and brilliant Madame Koluchy, matches wits with Norman Head, a reclusive philosopher who had once joined her gang. The volume was selected by Ellery Queen for *Queen's Quorum* as one of the 106 most important collections of mystery short stories. Curiously, only Meade's name appears on the front cover and spine of the book, though Eustace is given credit as the cowriter on the title page.

Eustace is known mainly for his collaborations with other writers. In addition to working with Meade, he cowrote several stories with Edgar Jepson; a novel with the once-popular mystery writer Gertrude Warden, *The Stolen Pearl: A Romance of London* (1903); and, most famously, a novel with Dorothy L. Sayers, *The Documents in the Case* (1930).

"The Winged Assassin" was first published in the February 1898 issue of *The Strand Magazine*; it was first collected in *The Brotherhood of the Seven Kings* (London, Ward, Lock, 1899).

The Winged Assassin

L. T. MEADE & ROBERT EUSTACE

THAT A SECRET SOCIETY, *based upon the lines of similar institutions so notorious on the Continent during the last century, could ever have existed in the London of our day may seem impossible. Such a society, however, not only did exist, but through the instrumentality of a woman of unparalleled capacity and genius, obtained a firm footing. A century ago the Brotherhood of the Seven Kings was a name hardly whispered without horror and fear in Italy, and now, by the fascinations and influence of one woman, it began to accomplish fresh deeds of unparalleled daring and subtlety in London. By the wide extent of its scientific resources, and the impregnable secrecy of its organisations, it threatened to become a formidable menace to society, as well as a source of serious anxiety to the authorities of the law. It is to the courtesy of Mr. Norman Head that we are indebted for the subject-matter of the following hitherto unpublished revelations.*

My scientific pursuits no longer interested me. I returned to my house in Regent's Park, but only to ponder recent events. With the sanction of conscience I fully intended to be a traitor to the infamous Brotherhood which, in a moment of mad folly, I had joined. From henceforth my object would be to expose Mme. Koluchy. By so doing, my own life would be in danger; never-

theless, my firm determination was not to leave a stone unturned to place this woman and her confederates in the felon's dock of an English criminal court. To effect this end one thing was obvious: single-handed I could not work. I knew little of the law, and to expose a secret society like Mme. Koluchy's, I must invoke the aid of the keenest and most able legal advisers.

Colin Dufrayer, the man I had just met before my hurried visit to Naples, was assuredly the person of all others for my purpose. He was one of the smartest lawyers in London. I went therefore one day to his office. I was fortunate in finding him in, and he listened to the story, which I told him in confidence, with the keenest attention.

"If this is true, Head," he said, "you yourself are in considerable danger."

"Yes," I answered; "nevertheless, my mind is made up. I will enter the lists against Mme. Koluchy."

His face grew grave, furrows lined his high and bald forehead, and knitted themselves together over his watchful, grey eyes.

"If anyone but yourself had brought me such an incredible story, Head, I should have thought him mad," he said, at last. "Of course, one knows that from time to time a great master in crime arises and sets justice at defiance; but that this woman should be the leader of a deliberately organized crusade against the laws of England is almost past my belief. Granted it is so, however, what do you wish me to do?"

"Give me your help," I answered; "use your ingenuity, employ your keenest agents, the most trusted and experienced officers of the law, to watch this woman day and night, and bring her and her accomplices to justice. I am a rich man, and I am prepared to devote both my life and my money to this great cause. When we have obtained sufficient evidence," I continued, "let us lay our information before the authorities."

He looked at me thoughtfully; after a moment he spoke.

"What occurred in Naples has doubtless given the Brotherhood a considerable shock," he said, "and if Mme. Koluchy is as clever as you suppose her to be, she will remain quiet for the present. Your best plan, therefore, is to do nothing, and allow me to watch. She suspects you, she does not suspect me."

"That is certainly the case," I answered.

"Take a sea voyage, or do something to restore your equilibrium, Head; you look overexcited."

"So would you be if you knew the woman, and if you had just gone through my terrible experiences."

"Granted, but do not let this get on your nerves. Rest assured that I won't leave a stone unturned to convict the woman, and that when the right moment comes I will apply to you."

I had to be satisfied with this reply, and soon afterwards I left Dufrayer. I spent a winter of anxiety, during which time I heard nothing of Mme. Koluchy. Once again my suspicions were slumbering, and my attention was turned to that science which was at once the delight and solace of my life, when, in the May of the following year, I received a note from Dufrayer. It ran as follows:—

"MY DEAR HEAD,—I have received an invitation both for you and myself to dine and sleep next Friday at Sir John Winton's place at Epsom. You are, of course, aware that his horse, Ajax, is the favourite for the Derby. Don't on any account refuse this invitation—throw over all other engagements for the sake of it. There is more in this than meets the eye.

"Yours sincerely.
"COLIN DUFRAYER."

I wired back to Dufrayer to accept the invitation, and on the following Friday went down to Epsom in time for dinner. Dufrayer had arrived earlier in the day, and I had not yet had an opportunity of seeing him alone. When I entered the drawing-room before dinner I found myself one of a large party. My host came forward to receive me. I happened to have met Sir John several times at his club in town, and he now signified his pleasure at seeing me in his house. A moment afterwards he introduced me to a bright-eyed girl of about nineteen years of age. Her name was Alison Carr. She had very dark eyes and hair, a transparent complexion and a manner full of vivacity and intelligence. I noticed, however, an anxious expression about her lips, and also that now and then, when engaged in the most animated conversation, she lost herself in a reverie of a somewhat painful nature. She would wake from these fits of inattention with an obvious start and a heightened colour. I found she was to be my companion at dinner, and soon discovered that hers was an interesting, indeed, delightful, personality. She knew the world and could talk well. Our conversation presently drifted to the great subject of the hour, Sir John Winton's colt, Ajax.

"He is a beauty," cried the girl. "I love him for himself, as who would not who had ever seen him?—but if he wins the Derby, why, then, my gratitude—" She paused and clasped her hands, then drew herself up, colouring.

"Are you very much interested in the result of the race?" I could not help asking.

"All my future turns on it," she said, dropping her voice to a low whisper. "I think," she continued, "Mr. Dufrayer intends to confide in you. I know something about you, Mr. Head, for Mr. Dufrayer has told me. I am so glad to meet you. I cannot say any more now, but my position is one of great anxiety."

Her words somewhat surprised me, but I could not question her further at that moment. Later on, however, when we returned to the drawing-room, I approached her side. She looked up eagerly when she saw me.

"I have been all over Europe this summer," she said gaily; "don't you want to see some of my photographs?"

She motioned me to a seat near her side, and taking up a book opened it. We bent over the photographs; she turned the pages, talking eagerly. Suddenly, she put her hand to her brow, and her face turned deadly pale.

"What is the matter?" I asked.

She did not speak for a moment, but I noticed that the moisture stood on her forehead. Presently she gave a sigh of relief.

"It has passed," she said. "Yes, I suffer in my head an indescribable agony, but it does not last now more than a moment or two. At one time the pain used to stay for nearly an hour, and I was almost crazy at the end. I have had these sharp sort of neuralgic pains from a child, but since I have consulted Mme. Koluchy—"

I started. She looked up at me and nodded.

"Of course you have heard of her," she said; "who has not? She is quite the most wonderful, delightful woman in existence. She, indeed, is a doctor to have confidence in. I understand that the men of the profession are mad with jealousy, and small wonder, her cures are so marvellous. Yes, Mr. Head, I went to quite half a dozen of our greatest doctors, and they could do nothing for me; but since I have been to Mme. Koluchy the pain comes but seldom, and when it does arise from any cause it quickly subsides. I have much to thank her for. Have you ever seen her?"

"Yes," I replied.

"And don't you like her?" continued the girl eagerly. "Is she not beautiful, the most beautiful woman in the world? Perhaps you have con-sulted her for your health; she has a great many men patients."

I made no reply; Miss Carr continued to speak with great animation.

"It is not only her beauty which impresses one," she said, "it is also her power—she draws you out of yourself completely. When I am away from her I must confess I am restless—it is as though she hypnotized me, and yet she has never done so. I long to go back to her even when,—" She hesitated and trembled. Someone came up, and commonplace subjects of conversation resumed their sway.

That evening late I joined Dufrayer in the smoking-room. We found ourselves alone, and I began to speak at once.

"You asked me to come here for a purpose," I said. "Miss Carr, the girl whom I took in to dinner, further told me that you had something to communicate. What is the matter?"

"Sit down, Head; I have much to tell you."

"By the way," I continued, as I sank into the nearest chair, "do you know that Miss Carr is under the influence of Mme. Koluchy?"

"I know it, and before I go any further, tell me what you think of her."

"She is a handsome girl," I replied, "and I should say a good one, but she seems to have trouble. She hinted at such, and in any case I observed it in her face and manner."

"You are right, she is suffering from a very considerable anxiety. I will explain all that to you presently. Now, please, give your best attention to the following details. It is about a month ago that I first received a visit from Frank Calthorpe, Sir John Winton's nephew, and the junior partner of Bruce, Nicholson, & Calthorpe, the great stockjobbers in Garrick Gardens. I did some legal business for his firm some years ago, but the matter on which Calthorpe came to see me was not one connected with his business, but of a purely private character."

"Am I to hear what it is?"

"You are, and the first piece of information I mean to impart to you is the following. Frank Calthorpe is engaged to Miss Carr."

"Indeed!"

"The engagement is of three months' date."

"When are they to be married?"

"That altogether depends on whether Sir John Winton's favourite, Ajax, wins the Derby or not."

"What do you mean?"

"To explain, I must tell you something of Miss Carr's early history." I sat back in my chair and prepared to listen. Dufrayer spoke slowly.

"About a year ago," he began, "Alison Carr lost her father. She was then eighteen years of age, and still at school. Her mother died when she was five years old. The father was a West Indian merchant, and had made his money slowly and with care. When he died he left a hundred thousand pounds behind him and an extraordinary will. The girl whom you met tonight was his only child. Henry Carr, Alison's father, had a brother, Felix Carr, a clergyman. In his will Henry made his brother Alison's sole guardian, and also his own residuary legatee. The interest of the hundred thousand pounds was to be devoted altogether to the girl's benefit, but the capital was only to come into her possession on certain conditions. She was to live with her uncle, and receive the interest of the money as long as she remained single. After the death of the uncle she was still, provided she was unmarried, to receive the interest during her lifetime. At her death the property was to go to Felix Carr's eldest son, or, in case he was dead, to his children. Provided, however, Alison married according to the conditions of the will, the whole of the hundred thousand pounds was to be settled on her and her children. The conditions were as follows:

"The man who married Alison was to settle a similar sum of one hundred thousand upon her and her children, and he was also to add the name of Carr to his own. Failing the fulfilment of these two conditions, Alison, if she married, was to lose the interest and capital of her father's fortune, the whole going to Felix Carr for his life, and after him to his eldest son. On this point the girl's father seems to have had a crank—he was often heard to say that he did not intend to amass gold in order to provide luxuries for a stranger.

"'Let the man who marries Alison put pound to pound,' he would cry; 'that's fair enough, otherwise the money goes to my brother.'

"Since her father's death, Alison has had one or two proposals from elderly men of great wealth, but she naturally would not consider them. When she became engaged, however, to Calthorpe, he had every hope that he would be able to fulfil the strange conditions of the will and meet her fortune with an equal sum on his own account. The engagement is now of three months' date, and here comes the extraordinary part of the story. Calthorpe, like most of his kind, is a speculator, and has large dealings both in stocks and shares and on the turf. He is a keen sportsman.

"Now, pray, listen. Hitherto he has always been remarkable for his luck, which has been, of course, as much due to his own common sense as anything else; but since his engagement to Miss Carr his financial ventures have been so persistently disastrous, and his losses so heavy, that he is practically now on the verge of ruin. Several most remarkable and unaccountable things have happened recently, and it is now almost certain that some one with great resources has been using his influence against him. You will naturally say that the person whose object it would be to do so is Alison's uncle, but beyond the vaguest suspicion, there is not the slightest evidence against him. He has been interested in the engagement from the first, and preparations have even been made for the wedding. It is true that Alison does not like him, and resents very much the clause in the will which compels her to live with him; but as far as we can tell, he has always been systematically kind to her, and takes the deepest interest in Calthorpe's affairs. Day by day, however, these affairs grow worse and worse.

"About a fortnight ago, Calthorpe actually discovered that shares were being held against him on which he was paying enormous differences, and had finally to buy them back at tremendous loss. The business was done through a broker, but the identity of his client is a mystery.

We now come to his present position, which is a most crucial one. Next Wednesday is the Derby Day, and Calthorpe hopes to retrieve his losses by a big coup, as he has backed Ajax at an average price of five to two in order to win one hundred thousand on the horse alone. He has been quietly getting his money on during the last two months through a lot of different commission agents. If he secures this big haul he will be in a position to marry Alison, and his difficulties will be at an end. If, on the other hand, the horse is beaten, Calthorpe is ruined."

"What are the chances for the horse?" I asked.

"As far as I can tell, they are splendid. He is a magnificent creature, a bay colt with black points, and comes of a splendid stock. His grandsire was Colonel Gillingham's Trumpeter, who was the champion of his year, winning the Derby, the Two Thousand Guineas, and St. Leger. There is not a three-year-old with such a fashionable ancestry as Ajax, and Sir John Winton is confident that he will follow their glorious record."

"Have you any reason to suspect Mme. Koluchy in this matter?" I asked.

"None. Without doubt Calthorpe possesses an enemy, but who that enemy is remains to be discovered. His natural enemy would be Felix Carr, but to all appearance the man has not moved a finger against him. Felix is well off, too, on his own account, and it is scarcely fair to suspect him of the wish to deliberately ruin his niece's prospects and her happiness. On the other hand, such a series of disasters would not happen to Calthorpe without a cause, and we have got to face that fact. Mme. Koluchy would, of course, be capable of doing the business, but we cannot find that Felix Carr even knows her."

"His niece does," I cried. "She consults her—she is under her care."

"I know that, and have followed up the clue very carefully," said Dufrayer. "Of course, the fact that Alison visits her two or three times a week, and in all probability confides in her fully, makes it all-important to watch her carefully. That fact, with the history which you have unfolded of Mme. Koluchy, makes it essential that we should take her into our calculations, but up to the present there is not a breath of suspicion against her. All turns on the Derby. If Ajax wins, whoever the person is who is Calthorpe's secret enemy, will have his foul purpose defeated."

Early the following morning, Sir John Winton took Dufrayer and myself to the training stables. Miss Carr accompanied us. The colt was brought out for inspection, and I had seldom seen a more magnificent animal. He was, as Dufrayer had described him, a bright bay, with black points. His broad forehead, brilliant eyes, black muzzle, and expanded nostrils proclaimed the Arab in his blood, while the long, light body, with the elongated limbs, were essentially adapted for the maximum development of speed. As the spirited creature curveted and pranced before us, our admiration could scarcely be kept in bounds. Miss Carr in particular was almost feverishly excited. She went up to the horse and patted him on his forehead. I heard her murmur something low into his ear. The creature turned his large and beautiful eye upon her as if he understood; he further responded to the girl's caress by pushing his nose forward for her to stroke.

"I have no doubt whatever of the result," said Sir John Winton, as he walked round and round the animal, examining his points and emphasizing his perfections. "If Ajax does not win the Derby, I shall never believe in a horse again." He then spoke in a low tone to the trainer, who nodded; the horse was led back to his stables, and we returned to the house.

As we crossed the Downs I found myself by Miss Carr's side.

"Yes," she exclaimed, looking up at me, her eyes sparkling, "Ajax is safe to win. Has Mr. Dufrayer confided in you, Mr. Head?"

"He has," I answered.

"Do you understand my great anxiety?"

"I do, but I think you may rest assured. If I am any judge of a horse, the favourite is sure to win the race."

"I wish Frank could hear you," she cried; "he is terribly nervous. He has had such a queer succession of misfortunes. Of course, I would marry him gladly, and will, without any fortune, if the worst comes to the worst; but there will be no worst," she continued brightly, "for Ajax will save us both." Here she paused, and pulled out her watch.

"I did not know it was so late," she exclaimed. "I have an appointment with Mme. Koluchy this morning. I must ask Sir John to send me to the station at once."

She hurried forward to speak to the old gentleman, and Dufrayer and I fell behind.

Soon afterwards we all returned to London, and on the following Monday I received a telegram from Dufrayer.

"Come to dinner—seven o'clock, important," was his brief message.

I responded in the affirmative, and at the right hour drove off to Dufrayer's flat in Shaftesbury Avenue, arriving punctual to the moment.

"I have asked Calthorpe to meet you," exclaimed Dufrayer, coming forward when I appeared; "his ill-luck dogs him closely. If the horse loses he is absolutely ruined. His concealed enemy becomes more active as the crucial hour approaches. Ah, here he comes to speak for himself."

The door was thrown open, and Calthorpe was announced. Dufrayer introduced him to me, and the next moment we went into the dining-room. I watched him with interest. He was a fair man, somewhat slight in build, with a long, thin face and a heavy moustache. He wore a worried and anxious look painful to witness; his age must have been about twenty-eight years. During dinner he looked across at me several times with an expression of the most intense curiosity, and as soon as the meal had come to an end, turned the conversation to the topic that was uppermost in all our minds.

"Dufrayer has told me all about you, Mr. Head; you are in his confidence, and therefore in mine."

"Be assured of my keen interest," I answered.

"I know how much you have staked on the favourite. I saw the colt on Saturday. He is a magnificent creature, and I should say is safe to win, that is—" I paused, and looked full into the young man's face. "Would it not be possible for you to hedge on the most advantageous terms?" I suggested. "I see the price tonight is five to four."

"Yes, and I could win thirty thousand either way if I could negotiate the transaction, but that would not effect my purpose. You have heard, I know, from Dufrayer, all about my engagement and the strange conditions of old Carr's will. There is no doubt that I possess a concealed enemy, whose object is to ruin me; but if Ajax wins I could obtain sufficient credit to right myself, and also to fulfil the conditions of Carr's will. Yes, I will stand to it now, every penny. The horse can win, and by God he shall!"

As he spoke Calthorpe brought down his fist with a blow on the table that set the glasses dancing. A glance was sufficient to show that his nerves were strung up to the highest pitch, and that a little more excitement would make him scarcely answerable for his actions.

"I have already given you my advice on this matter," said Dufrayer, in a grave tone. He turned and faced the young man as he spoke. "I would say emphatically, choose the thirty thousand now, and get out of it. You have plunged far too heavily in this matter. As to your present run of ill-luck, it will turn, depend upon it, and is only a question of time. If you hedge now you will have to put off your marriage, that is all. In the long run you will be able to fulfil the strange conditions which Carr has enjoined on his daughter's future husband, and if I know Alison aright, she will be willing to wait for you. If, on the other hand, you lose, all is lost. It is the ancient adage, 'A bird in the hand.'"

"It would be a dead crow," he interrupted excitedly, "and I want a golden eagle." Two hectic spots burned his pale cheeks, and the glitter in his eye showed how keen was the excitement which consumed him.

"I saw my uncle this morning," he went on.

"Of course, Sir John knows my position well, and there is no expense spared to guard and watch the horse. He is never left day or night by old and trusted grooms in the training stables. Whoever my enemy may be, I defy him to tamper with the horse. By the way, you must come down to see the race, Dufrayer; I insist upon it, and you too, Mr. Head. Yes, I should like you both to be there in the hour of my great success. I saw Rushton, the trainer, today, and he says the race is all over, bar shouting."

This was Monday night, and the following Wednesday was Derby Day. On the next evening, impelled by an uncontrollable desire to see Calthorpe, I called a hansom and gave the driver the name of his club. I felt certain that I should find him there. When I arrived the porter told me that he was in the house, and sending up my card, I went across to the tape machine, which was ticking away under its glass case in the hall. Two or three men were standing beside it, chatting. The Derby prices had just come through, and a page-boy was tearing the tape into lengths and pinning them on a green baize board in the hall. I glanced hurriedly through them. Evens Ajax, four to one Bright Star, eleven to two Midge, eight to one Day Dawn. I felt a hand on my shoulder, and Calthorpe stood beside me. I was startled at his appearance. There was a haggard, wild look in his eyes.

"It seems to be all right," I said cheerfully. "I see Ajax has gone off a point since this morning, but I suppose that means nothing?"

"Oh, nothing," he replied; "there has been a pot of money going on Bright Star all day, but the favourite can hold the field from start to finish. I saw him this morning, and he is as fit as possible. Rushton, the trainer, says he absolutely can't lose."

A small, dark man in evening dress approached us and overheard Calthorpe's last remark.

"I'll have a level monkey about that, if you like, Mr. Calthorpe," he said, in a low, nasal voice.

"It's a wager," retorted Calthorpe, drawing out his pocket-book with silver-bound edges, and entering the bet. "I'll make it a thousand, if you like?" he added, looking up.

"With pleasure," cried the little man. "Does your friend fancy anything?"

"No, thank you," I replied.

The man turned away, and went back to his companions.

"Who is that fellow?" I asked of Calthorpe.

"Oh, a very decent little chap. He's on the Stock Exchange, and makes a pretty big book on his own account."

"So I should think," I replied. "Why do you suppose he wants to lay against Ajax?"

"Hedging, I should imagine," answered Calthorpe carelessly. "One thousand one way or the other cannot make any difference now."

He had scarcely said the words before Dufrayer entered the hall.

"I have been looking for you, Head," he said, just nodding to Calthorpe as he spoke, and coming up to my side. "I went to your house and heard you were here, and hoped I should run you to earth. I want to speak to you. Can you come with me?"

"Anything wrong?" asked Calthorpe uneasily.

"I hope not," replied Dufrayer, "but I want to have a word with Head. I will see you presently, Calthorpe."

He linked his hand through my arm, and we left the club.

"What is it?" I asked, the moment we got into the street.

"I want you to come to my flat. Miss Carr is there, and she wishes to see you."

"Miss Carr at your flat, and she wishes to see me?"

"She does. You will soon know all about it, Head. Here, let us get into this hansom."

He hailed one which was passing; we got into it and drove quickly to Shaftesbury Avenue. Dufrayer let himself in to his rooms with a latchkey, and the next moment I found myself in Alison's presence. She started up when she saw the lawyer and myself.

"Now, Miss Carr," said Dufrayer, shutting

the door hastily, "we have not a moment to lose, Will you kindly repeat the story to Head which you have just told me?"

"But is there anything to be really frightened about?" she asked.

"I do not know of any one who can judge of that better than Mr. Head. Tell him everything, please, and at once."

Thus adjured, the girl began to speak.

"I went as usual to Mme. Koluchy this afternoon," she began; "her treatment does me a great deal of good. She was even kinder than usual. I believe her to be possessed of a sort of second sight. When she assured me that Ajax would win the Derby, I felt so happy that I laughed in my glee. She knows, no one better, how much this means to me. I was just about to leave her when the door of the consulting-room was opened, and who should appear standing on the threshold but my uncle, the Rev. Felix Carr! There is no love lost between my uncle and myself, and I could not help uttering a cry, half of fear and half of astonishment. I could see that he was equally startled at seeing me.

"'What in the name of fortune has brought you to Mme. Koluchy?' he cried.

"Madame rose in her usual stately way and went forward to meet him.

"'Your niece, Alison, is quite an old patient of mine,' she said; 'but did you not receive my telegram?'

"'No; I left home before it arrived,' he answered. 'The pains grew worse, and I felt I must see you. I have taken a horrible cold on the journey.' As he spoke he took his handkerchief out of his pocket, and sneezed several times. He continued to stand on the threshold of the room.

"'Well, good-bye, Alison, keep up your courage,' cried Mme. Koluchy. She kissed me on my forehead and I left. Uncle Felix did not take any further notice of me. The moment I went out the door of the consulting-room was closed, and the first thing I saw in the corridor was a torn piece of letter. It lay on the floor, and must have dropped out of Uncle Felix's pocket. I recognized the handwriting to be that of Mme.

Koluchy, I picked it up, and these words met my eyes: 'Innocuous to man, but fatal to the horse.' I could not read any further, as the letter was torn across and the other half not in my possession, but the words frightened me, although I did not understand them. I became possessed with a dreadful sense of depression. I hurried out of the house. I was so much at home with Mme. Koluchy now that I could go in and out as much as I pleased. I drove straight to see you, Mr. Dufrayer. I hoped you would set my terrors at rest, for surely Ajax cannot be the horse alluded to. The words haunt me, but there is nothing in them, is there? Please tell me so, Mr. Head— please allay my fears."

"May I see the torn piece of paper?" I asked gravely.

The girl took it out of her pocket and handed it to me.

"You don't mind if I keep this?" I said.

"No, certainly; but is there any cause for alarm?"

"I hope none, but you did well to consult Dufrayer. Now, I have something to ask you."

"What is that?"

"Do not repeat what you were good enough to tell Dufrayer and me to Calthorpe."

"Why so?"

"Because it would give him needless anxiety. I am going to take the matter up, and I trust all will be well. Keep your own counsel; do not tell what you have just told us to another living soul; and now I must ask you to leave us."

Her face grew whiter than ever; her anxious eyes travelled from my face to Dufrayer's.

"I will see you to a hansom," I said. I took her downstairs, put her into one, and returned to the lawyer's presence.

"I am glad you sent for me, Dufrayer," I answered. "Don't you see how grave all this is? If Ajax wins the Derby, the Rev. Felix Carr—I know nothing about his character, remember— will lose the interest on one hundred thousand pounds and the further chance of the capital being secured to his son. You see that it would be very much to the interest of the Rev. Felix if

Ajax loses the Derby. Then why does he consult Mme. Koluchy? The question of health is surely a mere blind. I confess I do not like the aspect of affairs at all. That woman has science at her fingers' ends. I shall go down immediately to Epsom and insist on Sir John Winton allowing me to spend the night in the training stables."

"I believe you are doing the right thing," answered Dufrayer. "You, who know Mme. Koluchy well, are armed at a thousand points."

"I shall start at once," I said.

I bade Dufrayer good-bye, hailed a hansom, desired the man to drive me to Victoria Station, and took the next train to Epsom.

I arrived at Sir John Winton's house about ten o'clock. He was astonished to see me, and when I begged his permission to share the company of the groom in the training stables that night, he seemed inclined to resent my intrusion. I did not wish to betray Alison, but I repeated my request with great firmness.

"I have a grave reason for making it," I said, "but one which at the present moment it is best for me not to disclose. Much depends on this race. From the events which have recently transpired, there is little doubt that Calthorpe has a secret enemy. Forewarned is forearmed. Will you share my watch tonight in the training stables, Sir John?"

"Certainly," he answered. "I do not see that you have any cause for alarm, but under the circumstances, and in the face of the mad way that nephew of mine has plunged, I cannot but accede to your request. We will go together."

We started to walk across the Downs. As we did so, Sir John became somewhat garrulous.

"I thought Alison would have come by your train," he said, "but have just had a telegram asking me not to expect her. She is probably spending tonight with Mme. Koluchy. By the way, Head, what a charming woman that is."

"Do you know her?" I asked.

"She was down here on Sunday. Alison begged me to invite her. We all enjoyed her company immensely. She has a wonderful knowledge of horses; in fact, she seems to know all about everything."

"Has she seen Ajax?" I asked. My heart sank, I could not tell why.

"Yes, I took her to the stables. She was interested in all the horses, and above all in Ajax. She is certain he will win the Derby."

I said nothing further. We arrived at the stables. Sir John and I spent a wakeful night. Early in the morning I asked to be allowed to examine the colt. He appeared in excellent condition, and the groom stood by him, admiring him, praising his points, and speaking about the certain result of the day's race.

"Here's the Derby winner," he said, clapping Ajax on his glossy side. "He'll win the race by a good three lengths. By the way, I hope he won't be off his feed this morning."

"Off his feed," exclaimed Sir John. "What do you mean?"

"What I say, sir. We couldn't get the colt to touch his food last night, although we tempted him with all kinds of things. There ain't nothing in it, I know, and he seems all right now, don't he?"

"Try him with a carrot," said Sir John.

The man brought a carrot and offered it to the creature. He turned away from it, and fixed his large, bright eyes on Sir John's face. I fancied there was suffering in them. Sir John seemed to share my fears. He went up to the horse and examined it critically, feeling its nose and ears.

"Tell Saunders to step across," he said, turning to the groom. He mentioned a veterinary surgeon who lived close by. "And look you here, Dan, keep your own counsel. If so much as a word of this gets out, you may do untold mischief."

"No fear of me, sir," said the man. He rushed off to fetch Saunders, who soon appeared.

The veterinary surgeon was a thickly built man, with an intelligent face. He examined the horse carefully, taking his temperature, feeling him all over, and finally stepping back with a satisfied smile.

"There's nothing to be alarmed about, Sir John," he said. "The colt is in perfect health. Let him have a mash presently with some crushed corn in it. I'll look in in a couple of hours, but there's nothing wrong. He is as fit as possible."

As the man left the stables, Sir John uttered a profound yawn.

"I confess I had a moment's fright," he said; "but I believe it was more from your manner than anything else, Mr. Head. Well, I am sleepy. Won't you come back to the house and let me offer you a shake-down?"

"No," I replied, "I want to return to town. I can catch an early train if I start at once."

He shook hands with me, and I went to the railway station. The oppression and apprehension at my heart got worse moment by moment. For what object had Mme. Koluchy visited the stables? What was the meaning of that mysterious writing which I had in my pocket—"Innocuous to man, but fatal to the horse"? What did the woman, with her devilish ingenuity, mean to do? Something bad, I had not the slightest doubt.

I called at Dufrayer's flat and gave him an account of the night's proceedings.

"I don't like the aspect of affairs, but God grant my fears are groundless," I cried. "The horse is off his feed, but Sir John and the vet are both assured there is nothing whatever the matter with him. Mme. Koluchy was in the stables on Sunday; but, after all, what could she do? We must keep the thing dark from Calthorpe and trust for the best."

At a quarter to twelve that day I found myself at Victoria. When I arrived on the platform I saw Calthorpe and Miss Carr coming to meet me. Dufrayer also a moment afterwards made his appearance. Miss Carr's eyes were full of question, and I avoided her as much as possible. Calthorpe, on the contrary, seemed to have recovered a good bit of nerve, and to be in a sanguine mood. We took our seats, and the train started for Epsom. As we alighted at the Downs station, a man in livery hurried up to Calthorpe.

"Sir John Winton is in the paddock, sir," he said, touching his hat. "He sent me to you, and says he wishes to see you at once, sir, and also Mr. Head."

The man spoke breathlessly, and seemed very much excited.

"Very well; tell him we'll both come," replied Calthorpe. He turned to Dufrayer. "Will you take charge of Alison?" he said.

Calthorpe and I moved off at once.

"What can be the matter?" cried the young man. "Nothing wrong, I hope. What is that?" he cried the next instant.

The enormous crowd was increasing moment by moment, and the din that rose from Tattersall's ring seemed to me unusually loud so early in the day's proceedings. As Calthorpe uttered the last words he started and his face turned white.

"Good God! Did you hear that?" he cried, dashing forward. I followed him quickly; the ring was buzzing like an infuriated beehive, and the men in it were hurrying to and fro as if possessed by the very madness of excitement. It was an absolute pandemonium. The stentorian tones of a brass-voiced bookmaker close beside us fell on my ears:

"Here, I'll bet five to one Ajax—five to one Ajax!"

The voice was suddenly drowned in the deafening clamour of the crowd, the air seemed to swell with the uproar. Were my worst fears confirmed? I felt stunned and sick. I turned round; Calthorpe had vanished.

Several smart drags were drawn up beside the railings. I glanced up at the occupants of the one beside me. From the box-seat looking down at me with the amused smile of a spectator sat Mme. Koluchy. As I caught her eyes I thought I detected a flash of triumph, but the next moment she smiled and bowed gracefully.

"You are a true Englishman, Mr. Head," she said. "Even your infatuated devotion to your scientific pursuits cannot restrain you from attending your characteristic national fête. Can you tell me what has happened? Those men seem to have suddenly gone mad—is that a part of the programme?"

"'Innocuous to man, but fatal to the horse,'" was my strange reply. I looked her full in the face. The long lashes covered her brilliant eyes for one flashing moment, then she smiled at me more serenely than ever.

"I will guess your enigma when the Derby is won," she said.

I raised my hat and hurried away. I had seen enough: suspicion was changed into certainty. The next moment I reached the paddock. I saw Calthorpe engaged in earnest conversation with his uncle.

"It's all up, Head," he said, when he saw me.

"Don't be an idiot, Frank," cried Sir John Winton angrily. "I tell you the thing is impossible. I don't believe there is anything the matter with the horse. Let the ring play their own game, it is nothing to us. Damn the market! I tell you what it is, Frank. When you plunged as you did, you would deserve it if the horse fell dead on the course; but he won't—he'll win by three lengths. There's not another horse in the race."

Calthorpe muttered some inaudible reply and turned away. I accompanied him.

"What is the matter?" I asked, as we left the paddock.

"Saunders is not satisfied with the state of the horse. His temperature has gone up; but, there! my uncle will see nothing wrong. Well, it will be all over soon. For God's sake, don't let us say anything to Alison."

"Not a word," I replied.

We reached the grand stand. Alison's earnest and apprehensive eyes travelled from her lover's face to mine. Calthorpe went up to her and endeavoured to speak cheerfully.

"I believe it's all right," he said. "Sir John says so, and he ought to know. It will be all decided one way or another soon. Look, the first race is starting."

We watched it, and the one that followed, hardly caring to know the name of the winner. The Derby was timed for three o'clock—it only wanted three minutes to the hour. The ring below was seething with excitement, Calthorpe was silent, now gazing over the course with the vacant expression of a man in a day-dream.

Bright Star was a hot favourite at even money.

"Against Ajax, five to one," rang out with a monotonous insistence.

There was a sudden lull, the flag had fallen. The moments that followed seemed like years of pain—there was much senseless cheering and shouting, a flash of bright colours, and the race was over. Bright Star had won. Ajax had been pulled up at Tattenham Corner, and was being led by his jockey.

Twenty minutes later Dufrayer and I were in the horse's stable.

"Will you allow me to examine the horse for a moment?" I said to the veterinary surgeon.

"It will want some experience to make out what is the matter," replied Saunders; "it's beyond me."

I entered the box and examined the colt carefully. As I did so the meaning of Mme. Koluchy's words became plain. Too late now to do anything—the race was lost and the horse was doomed. I looked around me.

"Has any one been bitten in this stable?" I asked.

"Bitten!" cried one of the grooms. "Why, I said to Sam last night"—he apostrophized the stable-boy—"that there must be gnats about. See my arm, it's all inflamed."

"Hold!" I cried, "what is that on your sleeve?"

"A house-fly, I suppose, sir," he answered.

"Stand still," I cried. I put out my hand and captured the fly. "Give me a glass," I said. "I must examine this."

One was brought and the fly put under it. I looked at it carefully. It resembled the ordinary house-fly, except that the wings were longer. Its colour was like an ordinary humming-bee.

"I killed a fly like that this morning," said Sam, the stable-boy, pushing his head forward.

"When did you say you were first bitten?" I asked, turning to the groom.

"A day or two ago," he replied. "I was bitten by a gnat, I don't rightly know the time. Sam, you was bitten too. We couldn't catch it, and we wondered that gnats should be about so early in the year. It has nothing to do with the horse, has it, sir?"

I motioned to the veterinary surgeon to come forward, and once more we examined Ajax. He now showed serious and unmistakable signs of malaise.

"Can you make anything out?" asked Saunders.

"With this fly before me, there is little doubt," I replied; "the horse will be dead in ten days—nothing can save him. He has been bitten by the tse-tse fly of South Africa—I know it only too well."

My news fell on the bystanders like a thunderbolt.

"Innocuous to man, but fatal to the horse," I found myself repeating. The knowledge of this fact had been taken advantage of—the devilish ingenuity of the plot was revealed. In all probability Mme. Koluchy had herself let the winged assassin loose when she had entered the stables on Sunday. The plot was worthy of her brain, and hers alone.

"You had better look after the other horses," I said, turning to the grooms. "If they have not been bitten already they had better be removed from the stables immediately. As for Ajax, he is doomed."

Late that evening Dufrayer dined with me alone. Pity for Calthorpe was only exceeded by our indignation and almost fear of Mme. Koluchy.

"What is to happen?" asked Dufrayer.

"Calthorpe is a brave man and will recover," I said. "He will win Miss Carr yet. I am rich, and I mean to help him, if for no other reason than in order to defeat that woman."

"By the way," said Dufrayer, "that scrap of paper which you hold in your possession, coupled with the fact that Mr. Carr called upon Mme. Koluchy, might induce a magistrate to commit them both for conspiracy."

"I doubt it," I replied; "the risk is not worth running. If we failed, the woman would leave the country, to return again in more dangerous guise. No, Dufrayer, we must bide our time until we get such a case against her as will secure conviction without the least doubt."

"At least," cried Dufrayer, "what happened today has shown me the truth of your words—it has also brought me to a decision. For the future I shall work with you, not as your employed legal adviser, but hand in hand against the horrible power and machinations of that woman. We will meet wit with wit, until we bring her to the justice she deserves."

THE BLOOD-RED CROSS

L. T. Meade & Robert Eustace

BORN IN IRELAND, Elizabeth Thomasina Meade Smith (1844–1914) later moved to London, where she married, wrote prolifically under the pseudonym L. T. Meade, and became an active feminist and member of the Pioneer Club, a progressive women's club founded in 1892. In her spare time, she worked as the editor of *Atalanta*, a popular girls' magazine. It is difficult to know how much spare time she had, however, as she produced more than three hundred novels and short story collections in various genres.

Dr. Eustace Robert Barton (1868–1943) used the pseudonym Robert Eustace and collaborated with several authors, including Edgar Jepson, Gertrude Warden, and Dorothy L. Sayers, but most commonly with Meade. Although he worked with her on such significant books as *The Brotherhood of the Seven Kings* (1899) and *The Sanctuary Club* (1900), his name seldom appeared on book covers, only on the title pages, so one wonders if it was due to the author's diffidence or the publishers' lack of respect.

The early years of the mystery story featured quite a few female criminals, most of whom shared the traits of youth, beauty, charm, and a devoted male friend or gang. They tended also to be clever rogues who enjoyed the excitement and great good fun of stealing jewels, money, or a precious antique or painting.

Madame Sara is a different sort of woman, carrying about her an air of mystery. Although she appears to be a beautiful young woman of no more than twenty-five years, she reportedly attended a wedding thirty years prior to the story's setting and looked exactly the same. She is also a ruthless murderer, counting both male and female victims among her triumphs.

The diabolical "The Blood-Red Cross" was originally published in the November 1902 issue of *The Strand Magazine*; it was first collected in *The Sorceress of the Strand* (London, Ward, Lock, 1903).

The Blood-Red Cross

L. T. MEADE & ROBERT EUSTACE

IN THE MONTH OF NOVEMBER in the year 1899 I found myself a guest in the house of one of my oldest friends—George Rowland. His beautiful place in Yorkshire was an ideal holiday resort. It went by the name of Rowland's Folly, and had been built on the site of a former dwelling in the reign of the first George. The house was now replete with every modern luxury. It, however, very nearly cost its first owner, if not the whole of his fortune, yet the most precious heirloom of the family. This was a pearl necklace of almost fabulous value. It had been secured as booty by a certain Geoffrey Rowland at the time of the Battle of Agincourt, had originally been the property of one of the Dukes of Genoa, and had even for a short time been in the keeping of the Pope. From the moment that Geoffrey Rowland took possession of the necklace there had been several attempts made to deprive him of it. Sword, fire, water, poison had all been used, but ineffectually. The necklace with its eighty pearls, smooth, symmetrical, pear-shaped, of a translucent white colour and with a subdued iridescent sheen, was still in the possession of the family, and was likely to remain there, as George Rowland told me, until the end of time. Each bride wore the necklace on her wedding-day, after which it was put into the strong-room and, as a rule, never seen again until the next bridal occasion. The pearls were roughly estimated as worth from two to three thousand pounds each, but the historical value of the necklace put the price almost beyond the dreams of avarice.

It was reported that in the autumn of that same year an American millionaire had offered to buy it from the family at their own price, but as no terms would be listened to the negotiations fell through.

George Rowland belonged to the oldest and proudest family in the West Riding, and no man looked a better gentleman or more fit to uphold ancient dignities than he. He was proud to boast that from the earliest days no stain of dishonour had touched his house, that the women of the family were as good as the men, their blood pure, their morals irreproachable, their ideas lofty.

I went to Rowland's Folly in November, and found a pleasant, hospitable, and cheerful hostess in Lady Kennedy, Rowland's only sister. Antonia Ripley was, however, the centre of all interest. Rowland was engaged to Antonia, and the history was romantic. Lady Kennedy told me all about it.

"She is a penniless girl without family," remarked the good woman, somewhat snappishly. "I can't imagine what George was thinking of."

"How did your brother meet her?" I asked.

"We were both in Italy last autumn; we were staying in Naples, at the Vesuve. An English lady was staying there of the name of Studley.

She died while we were at the hotel. She had under her charge a young girl, the same Antonia who is now engaged to my brother. Before her death she begged of us to befriend her, saying that the child was without money and without friends. All Mrs. Studley's money died with her. We promised, not being able to do otherwise. George fell in love almost at first sight. Little Antonia was provided for by becoming engaged to my brother. I have nothing to say against the girl, but I dislike this sort of match very much. Besides, she is more foreign than English."

"Cannot Miss Ripley tell you anything about her history?"

"Nothing, except that Mrs. Studley adopted her when she was a tiny child. She says, also, that she has a dim recollection of a large building crowded with people, and a man who stretched out his arms to her and was taken forcibly away. That is all. She is quite a nice child, and amiable, with touching ways and a pathetic face; but no one knows what her ancestry was. Ah, there you are, Antonia! What is the matter now?"

The girl tripped across the room. She was like a young fawn; of a smooth, olive complexion—dark of eye and mysteriously beautiful, with the graceful step which is seldom granted to an English girl.

"My lace dress has come," she said. "Markham is unpacking it—but the bodice is made with a low neck."

Lady Kennedy frowned.

"You are too absurd, Antonia," she said. "Why won't you dress like other girls? I assure you that peculiarity of yours of always wearing your dress high in the evening annoys George."

"Does it?" she answered, and she stepped back and put her hand to her neck just below the throat—a constant habit of hers, as I afterwards had occasion to observe.

"It disturbs him very much," said Lady Kennedy. "He spoke to me about it only yesterday. Please understand, Antonia, that at the ball you cannot possibly wear a dress high to your throat. It cannot be permitted."

"I shall be properly dressed on the night of the ball," replied the girl.

Her face grew crimson, then deadly pale.

"It only wants a fortnight to that time, but I shall be ready."

There was a solemnity about her words. She turned and left the room.

"Antonia is a very trying character," said Lady Kennedy. "Why won't she act like other girls? She makes such a fuss about wearing a proper evening dress that she tries my patience—but she is all crotchets."

"A sweet little girl for all that," was my answer.

"Yes; men like her."

Soon afterwards, as I was strolling, on the terrace, I met Miss Ripley. She was sitting in a low chair. I noticed how small, and slim, and young she looked, and how pathetic was the expression of her little face. When she saw me she seemed to hesitate; then she came to my side.

"May I walk with you, Mr. Druce?" she asked.

"I am quite at your service," I answered. "Where shall we go?"

"It doesn't matter. I want to know if you will help me."

"Certainly, if I can, Miss Ripley."

"It is most important. I want to go to London."

"Surely that is not very difficult?"

"They won't allow me to go alone, and they are both very busy. I have just sent a telegram to a friend. I want to see her. I know she will receive me. I want to go tomorrow. May I venture to ask that you should be my escort?"

"My dear Miss Ripley, certainly," I said. "I will help you with pleasure."

"It must be done," she said, in a low voice. "I have put it off too long. When I marry him he shall not be disappointed."

"I do not understand you," I said, "but I will go with you with the greatest willingness."

She smiled; and the next day, much to my own amazement, I found myself travelling first-class up to London, with little Miss Ripley as my companion. Neither Rowland nor his sister had approved; but Antonia had her own way, and the fact that I would escort her cleared off some difficulties.

During our journey she bent towards me and said, in a low tone:—

"Have you ever heard of that most wonderful, that great woman, Madame Sara?"

I looked at her intently.

"I have certainly heard of Madame Sara," I said, with emphasis, "but I sincerely trust that you have nothing to do with her."

"I have known her almost all my life," said the girl. "Mrs. Studley knew her also. I love her very much. I trust her. I am going to see her now."

"What do you mean?"

"It was to her I wired yesterday. She will receive me; she will help me. I am returning to the Folly tonight. Will you add to your kindness by escorting me home?"

"Certainly."

At Euston I put my charge into a hansom, arranging to meet her on the departure platform at twenty minutes to six that evening, and then taking another hansom drove as fast as I could to Vandeleur's address. During the latter part of my journey to town a sudden, almost unaccountable, desire to consult Vandeleur had taken possession of me. I was lucky enough to find this busiest of men at home and at leisure. He gave an exclamation of delight when my name was announced, and then came towards me with outstretched hand.

"I was just about to wire to you, Druce," he said. "From where have you sprung?"

"From no less a place than Rowland's Folly," was my answer.

"More and more amazing. Then you have met Miss Ripley, George Rowland's *fiancée*?"

"You have heard of the engagement, Vandeleur?"

"Who has not? What sort is the young lady?"

"I can tell you all you want to know, for I have travelled up to town with her."

"Ah!"

He was silent for a minute, evidently thinking hard; then drawing a chair near mine he seated himself.

"How long have you been at Rowland's Folly?" he asked.

"Nearly a week. I am to remain until after the wedding. I consider Rowland a lucky man. He is marrying a sweet little girl."

"You think so? By the way, have you ever noticed any peculiarity about her?"

"Only that she is singularly amiable and attractive."

"But any habit—pray think carefully before you answer me."

"Really, Vandeleur, your questions surprise me. Little Miss Ripley is a person with ideas and is not ashamed to stick to her principles. You know, of course, that in a house like Rowland's Folly it is the custom for the ladies to come to dinner in full dress. Now, Miss Ripley won't accommodate herself to this fashion, but *will* wear her dress high to the throat, however gay and festive the occasion."

"Ah! there doesn't seem to be much in that, does there?"

"I don't quite agree with you. Pressure has been brought to bear on the girl to make her conform to the usual regulations, and Lady Kennedy, a woman old enough to be her mother, is quite disagreeable on the point."

"But the girl sticks to her determination?"

"Absolutely, although she promises to yield and to wear the conventional dress at the ball given in her honour a week before the wedding."

Vandeleur was silent for nearly a minute; then dropping his voice he said, slowly:—

"Did Miss Ripley ever mention in your presence the name of our mutual foe—Madame Sara?"

"How strange that you should ask! On our journey to town today she told me that she knew the woman—she has known her for the greater part of her life—poor child, she even loves her.

Vandeleur, that young girl is with Madame Sara now."

"Don't be alarmed, Druce; there is no immediate danger; but I may as well tell you that through my secret agents I have made discoveries which show that Madame has another iron in the fire, that once again she is preparing to convulse Society, and that little Miss Ripley is the victim."

"You must be mistaken."

"So sure am I, that I want your help. You are returning to Rowland's Folly?"

"Tonight."

"And Miss Ripley?"

"She goes with me. We meet at Euston for the six o'clock train."

"So far, good. By the way, has Rowland spoken to you lately about the pearl necklace?"

"No; why do you ask?"

"Because I understand that it was his intention to have the pearls slightly altered and reset in order to fit Miss Ripley's slender throat; also to have a diamond clasp affixed in place of the somewhat insecure one at present attached to the string of pearls. Messrs. Theodore and Mark, of Bond Street, were to undertake the commission. All was in preparation, and a messenger, accompanied by two detectives, was to go to Rowland's Folly to fetch the treasure, when the whole thing was countermanded, Rowland having changed his mind and having decided that the strong-room at the Folly was the best place in which to keep the necklace."

"He has not mentioned the subject to me," I said. "How do you know?"

"I have my emissaries. One thing is certain—little Miss Ripley is to wear the pearls on her wedding-day—and the Italian family, distant relatives of the present Duke of Genoa, to whom the pearls belonged, and from whom they were stolen shortly before the Battle of Agincourt, are again taking active steps to secure them. You have heard the story of the American millionaire? Well, that was a blind—the necklace was in reality to be delivered into the hands of the old family as soon as he had purchased it. Now,

Druce, this is the state of things: Madame Sara is an adventuress, and the cleverest woman in the world—Miss Ripley is very young and ignorant. Miss Ripley is to wear the pearls on her wedding-day—and Madame wants them. You can infer the rest."

"What do you want me to do?" I asked.

"Go back and watch. If you see anything to arouse suspicion, wire to me."

"What about telling Rowland?"

"I would rather not consult him. I want to protect Miss Ripley, and at the same time to get Madame into my power. She managed to elude us last time, but she shall not this. My idea is to inveigle her to her ruin. Why, Druce, the woman is being more trusted and run after and admired day by day. She appeals to the greatest foibles of the world. She knows some valuable secrets, and is an adept in the art of restoring beauty and to a certain extent conquering the ravages of time. She is at present aided by an Arab, one of the most dangerous men I have ever seen, with the subtlety of a serpent, and legerdemain in every one of his ten fingers. It is not an easy thing to entrap her."

"And yet you mean to do it?"

"Someday—someday. Perhaps now."

His eyes were bright. I had seldom seen him look more excited.

After a short time I left him. Miss Ripley met me at Euston. She was silent and unresponsive and looked depressed. Once I saw her put her hand to her neck.

"Are you in pain?" I asked.

"You might be a doctor, Mr. Druce, from your question."

"But answer me," I said.

She was silent for a minute; then she said, slowly:—

"You are good, and I think I ought to tell you. But will you regard it as a secret? You wonder, perhaps, how it is that I don't wear a low dress in the evening. I will tell you why. On my neck, just below the throat, there grew a wart or mole—large, brown, and ugly. The Italian doctors would not remove it on account of the position. It lies just over what they said was an *aberrant* artery, and the removal might cause very dangerous haemorrhage. One day Madame saw it; she said the doctors were wrong, and that she could easily take it away and leave no mark behind. I hesitated for a long time, but yesterday, when Lady Kennedy spoke to me as she did, I made up my mind. I wired to Madame and went to her today. She gave me chloroform and removed the mole. My neck is bandaged up and it smarts a little. I am not to remove the bandage until she sees me again. She is very pleased with the result, and says that my neck will now be beautiful like other women's, and that I can on the night of the ball wear the lovely Brussels lace dress that Lady Kennedy has given me. That is my secret. Will you respect it?"

I promised, and soon afterwards we reached the end of our journey.

A few days went by. One morning at breakfast I noticed that the little signora only played with her food. An open letter lay by her plate. Rowland, by whose side she always sat, turned to her.

"What is the matter, Antonia?" he said. "Have you had an unpleasant letter?"

"It is from—"

"From whom, dear?"

"Madame Sara."

"What did I hear you say?" cried Lady Kennedy.

"I have had a letter from Madame Sara, Lady Kennedy."

"That shocking woman in the Strand—that adventuress? My dear, is it possible that you know her? Her name is in the mouth of everyone. She is quite notorious."

Instantly the room became full of voices, some talking loudly, some gently, but all praising Madame Sara. Even the men took her part; as to the women, they were unanimous about her charms and her genius.

In the midst of the commotion little Antonia burst into a flood of tears and left the room. Rowland followed her. What next occurred I cannot tell, but in the course of the morning I met Lady Kennedy.

"Well," she said, "that child has won, as I knew she would. Madame Sara wishes to come here, and George says that Antonia's friend is to be invited. I shall be glad when the marriage is over and I can get out of this. It is really detestable that in the last days of my reign I should have to give that woman the *entrée* to the house."

She left me, and I wandered into the entrance hall. There I saw Rowland. He had a telegraph form in his hands, on which some words were written.

"Ah, Druce!" he said. "I am just sending a telegram to the station. What! do you want to send one too?"

For I had seated myself by the table which held the telegraph forms.

"If you don't think I am taking too great a liberty, Rowland," I said, suddenly, "I should like to ask a friend of mine here for a day or two."

"Twenty friends, if you like, my dear Druce. What a man you are to apologize about such a trifle! Who is the special friend?"

"No less a person than Eric Vandeleur, the police-surgeon for Westminster."

"What! Vandeleur—the gayest, jolliest man I have ever met! Would he care to come?"

Rowland's eyes were sparkling with excitement.

"I think so; more especially if you will give me leave to say that you would welcome him."

"Tell him he shall have a thousand welcomes, the best room in the house, the best horse. Get him to come by all means, Druce."

Our two telegrams were sent off. In the course of the morning replies in the affirmative came to each.

That evening Madame Sara arrived. She came by the last train. The brougham was sent to meet her. She entered the house shortly before midnight. I was standing in the hall when she arrived, and I felt a momentary sense of pleasure when I saw her start as her eyes met mine. But she was not a woman to be caught off her guard. She approached me at once with outstretched hand and an eager voice.

"This is charming, Mr. Druce," she said. "I

do not think anything pleases me more." Then she added, turning to Rowland, "Mr. Dixon Druce is a very old friend of mine."

Rowland gave me a bewildered glance. Madame turned and began to talk to her hostess. Antonia was standing near one of the open drawing-rooms. She had on a soft dress of pale green silk. I had seldom seen a more graceful little creature. But the expression of her face disturbed me. It wore now the fascinated look of a bird when a snake attracts it. Could Madame Sara be the snake? Was Antonia afraid of this woman?

The next day Lady Kennedy came to me with a confidence.

"I am glad your police friend is coming," she said. "It will be safer."

"Vandeleur arrives at twelve o'clock," was my answer.

"Well, I am pleased. I like that woman less and less. I was amazed when she dared to call you her friend."

"Oh, we have met before on business," I answered, guardedly.

"You won't tell me anything further, Mr. Druce?"

"You must excuse me, Lady Kennedy."

"Her assurance is unbounded," continued the good lady. "She has brought a maid or nurse with her—a most extraordinary-looking woman. That, perhaps, is allowable; but she has also brought her black servant, an Arabian, who goes by the name of Achmed. I must say he is a picturesque creature with his quaint Oriental dress. He was all in flaming yellow this morning, and the embroidery on his jacket was worth a small fortune. But it is the daring of the woman that annoys me. She goes on as though she were somebody."

"She is a very emphatic somebody," I could not help replying. "London Society is at her feet."

"I only hope that Antonia will take her remedies and let her go. The woman has no welcome from me," said the indignant mistress of Rowland's Folly.

I did not see anything of Antonia that morn-

ing, and at the appointed time I went down to the station to meet Vandeleur. He arrived in high spirits, did not ask a question with regard to Antonia, received the information that Madame Sara was in the house with stolid silence, and seemed intent on the pleasures of the moment.

"Rowland's Folly!" he said, looking round him as we approached one of the finest houses in the whole of Yorkshire. "A folly, truly, and yet a pleasant one, Druce, eh? I fancy," he added, with a slight smile, "that I am going to have a good time here."

"I hope you will disentangle a most tangled skein," was my reply.

He shrugged his shoulders. Suddenly his manner altered.

"Who is that woman?" he said, with a strain of anxiety quite apparent in his voice.

"Who?" I asked.

"That woman on the terrace in nurse's dress."

"I don't know. She has been brought here by Madame Sara—a sort of maid and nurse as well. I suppose poor little Antonia will be put under her charge."

"Don't let her see me, Druce, that's all. Ah, here is our host."

Vandeleur quickened his movements, and the next instant was shaking hands with Rowland.

The rest of the day passed without adventure. I did not see Antonia. She did not even appear at dinner. Rowland, however, assured me that she was taking necessary rest and would be all right on the morrow. He seemed inclined to be gracious to Madame Sara, and was annoyed at his sister's manner to their guest.

Soon after dinner, as I was standing in one of the smoking-rooms, I felt a light hand on my arm, and, turning, encountered the splendid pose and audacious, bright, defiant glance of Madame herself.

"Mr. Druce," she said, "just one moment. It is quite right that you and I should be plain with each other. I know the reason why you are here. You have come for the express purpose of spying upon me and spoiling what you consider my game. But understand, Mr. Druce, that there is danger to yourself when you interfere with the schemes of one like me. Forewarned is fore-armed."

Someone came into the room and Madame left it.

The ball was but a week off, and preparations for the great event were taking place. Attached to the house at the left was a great room built for this purpose.

Rowland and I were walking down this room on a special morning; he was commenting on its architectural merits and telling me what band he intended to have in the musicians' gallery, when Antonia glided into the room.

"How pale you are, little Tonia!" he said.

This was his favourite name for her. He put his hand under her chin, raised her sweet, blushing face, and looked into her eyes.

"Ah, you want my answer. What a persistent little puss it is! You shall have your way, Tonia—yes, certainly. For you I will grant what has never been granted before. All the same, what will my lady say?"

He shrugged his shoulders.

"But you will let me wear them whether she is angry or not?" persisted Antonia.

"Yes, child, I have said it."

She took his hand and raised it to her lips, then, with a curtsy, tripped out of the room.

"A rare, bright little bird," he said, turning to me. "Do you know, I feel that I have done an extraordinarily good thing for myself in secur-ing little Antonia. No troublesome mamma-in-law—no brothers and sisters, not my own and yet emphatically mine to consider—just the child herself. I am very happy and a very lucky fellow. I am glad my little girl has no past history. She is just her dear little, dainty self, no more and no less."

"What did she want with you now?" I asked.

"Little witch," he said, with a laugh. "The pearls—*the* pearls. She insists on wearing the great necklace on the night of the ball. Dear little girl. I can fancy how the baubles will gleam and shine on her fair throat."

I made no answer, but I was certain that little Antonia's request did not emanate from herself. I thought that I would search for Vandeleur and tell him of the circumstance, but the next remark of Rowland's nipped my project in the bud.

"By the way, your friend has promised to be back for dinner. He left here early this morn-ing."

"Vandeleur?" I cried.

"Yes, he has gone to town. What a first-rate fellow he is!"

"He tells a good story," I answered.

"Capital. Who would suspect him of being the greatest criminal expert of the day? But, thank goodness, we have no need of his services at Rowland's Folly."

Late in the evening Vandeleur returned. He entered the house just before dinner. I observed by the brightness of his eyes and the intense gravity of his manner that he was satisfied with himself. This in his case was always a good sign. At dinner he was his brightest self, courteous to everyone, and to Madame Sara in particular.

Late that night, as I was preparing to go to bed, he entered my room without knocking.

"Well, Druce," he said, "it is all right."

"All right!" I cried; "what do you mean?"

"You will soon know. The moment I saw that woman I had my suspicions. I was in town today making some very interesting inquiries. I am primed now on every point. Expect a *dénouement* of a startling character very soon, but be sure of one thing—however black appearances may be the little bride is safe, and so are the pearls."

He left me without waiting for my reply.

The next day passed, and the next. I seemed to live on tenter-hooks. Little Antonia was gay and bright like a bird. Madame's invitation had been extended by Lady Kennedy at Rowland's command to the day after the ball—little Anto-nia skipped when she heard it.

"I love her," said the girl.

More and more guests arrived—the days flew on wings—the evenings were lively. Madame was a power in herself. Vandeleur was another. These two, sworn foes at heart, aided and abetted each other to make things go brilliantly for the rest of the guests. Rowland was in the highest spirits.

At last the evening before the ball came and went. Vandeleur's *grand coup* had not come off. I retired to bed as usual. The night was a stormy one—rain rattled against the window-panes, the wind sighed and shuddered. I had just put out my candle and was about to seek forgetfulness in sleep when once again in his unceremonious fashion Vandeleur burst into my room.

"I want you at once, Druce, in the bed-room of Madame Sara's servant. Get into your clothes as fast as you possibly can and join me there."

He left the room as abruptly as he had entered it. I hastily dressed, and with stealthy steps, in the dead of night, to the accompaniment of the ever-increasing tempest, sought the room in question.

I found it brightly lighted; Vandeleur pacing the floor as though he himself were the very spirit of the storm; and, most astonishing sight of all, the nurse whom Madame Sara had brought to Rowland's Folly, and whose name I had never happened to hear, gagged and bound in a chair drawn into the centre of the room.

"So I think that is all, nurse," said Vandeleur, as I entered. "Pray take a chair, Druce. We quite understand each other, don't we, nurse, and the facts are wonderfully simple. Your name as entered in the archives of crime at Westminster is not as you have given out, Mary Jessop, but Rebecca Curt. You escaped from Portland prison on the night of November thirtieth, just a year ago. You could not have managed your escape but for the connivance of the lady in whose service you are now. Your crime was forgery, with a strong and very daring attempt at poisoning. Your victim was a harmless invalid lady. Your knowledge of crime, therefore, is what may be called extensive. There are yet eleven years of your sentence to run. You have doubtless served Madame Sara well—but perhaps you can serve me better. You know the consequence if you refuse, for I explained that to you frankly and clearly before this gentleman came into the room. Druce, will

you oblige me—will you lock the door while I remove the gag from the prisoner's mouth?"

I hurried to obey. The woman breathed more freely when the gag was removed. Her face was a swarthy red all over. Her crooked eyes favoured us with many shifty glances.

"Now, then, have the goodness to begin, Rebecca Curt," said Vandeleur. "Tell us everything you can."

She swallowed hard, and said:—

"You have forced me—"

"We won't mind that part," interrupted Vandeleur. "The story, please, Mrs. Curt."

If looks could kill, Rebecca Curt would have killed Vandeleur then. He gave her in return a gentle, bland glance, and she started on her narrative.

"Madame knows a secret about Antonia Ripley."

"Of what nature?"

"It concerns her parentage."

"And that is—?"

The woman hesitated and writhed.

"The names of her parents, please," said Vandeleur, in a voice cold as ice and hard as iron.

"Her father was Italian by birth."

"His name?"

"Count Gioletti. He was unhappily married, and stabbed his English wife in an excess of jealousy when Antonia was three years old. He was executed for the crime on the twentieth of June, 18—. The child was adopted and taken out of the country by an English lady who was present in court—her name was Mrs. Studley. Madame Sara was also present. She was much interested in the trial, and had an interview afterwards with Mrs. Studley. It was arranged that Antonia should be called by the surname of Ripley—the name of an old relative of Mrs. Studley's—and that her real name and history were never to be told to her."

"I understand," said Vandeleur, gently. "This is of deep interest, is it not, Druce?"

I nodded, too much absorbed in watching the face of the woman to have time for words.

"But now," continued Vandeleur, "there are

reasons why Madame should change her mind with regard to keeping the matter a close secret—is that not so, Mrs. Curt?"

"Yes," said Mrs. Curt.

"You will have the kindness to continue."

"Madame has an object—she blackmails the signora. She wants to get the signora completely into her power."

"Indeed! Is she succeeding?"

"Yes."

"How has she managed? Be very careful what you say, please."

"The mode is subtle—the young lady had a disfiguring mole or wart on her neck, just below the throat. Madame removed the mole."

"Quite a simple process, I doubt not," said Vandeleur, in a careless tone.

"Yes, it was done easily—I was present. The young lady was conducted into a chamber with a red light."

Vandeleur's extraordinary eyes suddenly leapt into fire. He took a chair and drew it so close to Mrs. Curt's that his face was within a foot or two of hers.

"Now, you will be very careful what you say," he remarked. "You know the consequence to yourself unless this narrative is absolutely reliable."

She began to tremble, but continued:—

"I was present at the operation. Not a single ray of ordinary light was allowed to penetrate. The patient was put under chloroform. The mole was removed. Afterwards Madame wrote something on her neck. The words were very small and neatly done—they formed a cross on the young lady's neck. Afterwards I heard what they were."

"Repeat them."

"I can't. You will know in the moment of victory."

"I choose to know now. A detective from my division at Westminster comes here early tomorrow morning—he brings hand-cuffs—and—"

"I will tell you," interrupted the woman. "The words were these:—

"'I AM THE DAUGHTER OF PAOLO GIOLETTI, WHO WAS EXECUTED FOR THE MURDER OF MY MOTHER, JUNE 20TH, 18—.'"

"How were the words written?"

"With nitrate of silver."

"Fiend!" muttered Vandeleur.

He jumped up and began to pace the room. I had never seen his face so black with ungovernable rage.

"You know what this means?" he said at last to me. "Nitrate of silver eats into the flesh and is permanent. Once exposed to the light the case is hopeless, and the helpless child becomes her own executioner."

The nurse looked up restlessly.

"The operation was performed in a room with a red light," she said, "and up to the present the words have not been seen. Unless the young lady exposes her neck to the blue rays of ordinary light they never will be. In order to give her a chance to keep her deadly secret Madame has had a large carbuncle of the deepest red cut and prepared. It is in the shape of a cross, and is suspended to a fine gold, almost invisible, thread. This the signora is to wear when in full evening dress. It will keep in its place, for the back of the cross will be dusted with gum."

"But it cannot be Madame's aim to hide the fateful words," said Vandeleur. "You are concealing something, nurse."

Her face grew an ugly red. After a pause the following words came out with great reluctance:—

"The young lady wears the carbuncle as a reward."

"Ah," said Vandeleur, "now we are beginning to see daylight. As a reward for what?"

"Madame wants something which the signora can give her. It is a case of exchange; the carbuncle which hides the fatal secret is given in exchange for that which the signora can transfer to Madame."

"I understand at last," said Vandeleur. "Really, Druce, I feel myself privileged to say that of all the malevolent—" he broke off abruptly. "Never mind," he said, "we are keeping nurse. Nurse, you have answered all my questions with praise-worthy exactitude, but before you return to your well-earned slumbers I have one more piece of information to seek from you. Was it entirely by Miss Ripley's desire, or was it in any respect owing to Madame Sara's instigations, that the young lady is permitted to wear the pearl neck-lace on the night of the dance? You have, of course, nurse, heard of the pearl necklace?"

Rebecca Curt's face showed that she un-doubtedly had.

"I see you are acquainted with that most interesting story. Now, answer my question. The request to wear the necklace tomorrow night was suggested by Madame, was it not?"

"Ah, yes—yes!" cried the woman, carried out of herself by sudden excitement. "It was to that point all else tended—all, all!"

"Thank you, that will do. You understand that from this day you are absolutely in my ser-vice. As long as you serve me faithfully you are safe."

"I will do my best, sir," she replied, in a mod-est tone, her eyes seeking the ground.

The moment we were alone Vandeleur turned to me.

"Things are simplifying themselves," he said.

"I fail to understand," was my answer. "I should say that complications, and alarming ones, abound."

"Nevertheless, I see my way clear. Druce, it is not good for you to be so long out of bed, but in order that you may repose soundly when you return to your room I will tell you frankly what my mode of operations will be tomorrow. The simplest plan would be to tell Rowland everything, but for various reasons that does not suit me. I take an interest in the little girl, and if she chooses to conceal her secret (at present, remember, she does not know it, but the poor child will certainly be told everything tomorrow) I don't intend to interfere. In the second place, I am anxious to lay a trap for Madame. Now, two things are evident. Madame Sara's object in coming here is to steal the pearls. Her plan is to terrify the little signora into giving them to her in order that the fiendish words written on the child's neck may not be seen. As the signora must wear a dress with a low neck tomorrow night, she can only hide the words by means of the red carbuncle. Madame will only give her the carbuncle if she, in exchange, gives Madame the pearls. You see?"

"I do," I answered, slowly.

He drew himself up to his slender height, and his eyes became full of suppressed laughter.

"The child's neck has been injured with nitrate of silver. Nevertheless, until it is exposed to the blue rays of light the ominous, fiendish words will not appear on her white throat. Once they do appear they will be indelible. Now, lis-ten! Madame, with all her cunning, forgot some-thing. To the action of nitrate of silver there is an antidote. This is nothing more or less than our old friend cyanide of potassium. Tomorrow nurse, under my instructions, will take the little patient into a room carefully prepared with the hateful red light, and will bathe the neck just where the baleful words are written with a solu-tion of cyanide of potassium. The nitrate of sil-ver will then become neutralized and the letters will never come out."

"But the child will not know that. The terror of Madame's cruel story will be upon her, and she will exchange the pearls for the cross."

"I think not, for I shall be there to prevent it. Now, Druce, I have told you all that is necessary. Go to bed and sleep comfortably."

The next morning dawned dull and sullen, but the fierce storm of the night before was over. The ravages which had taken place, however, in the stately old park were very manifest, for trees had been torn up by their roots and some of the stateliest and largest of the oaks had been deprived of their best branches.

Little Miss Ripley did not appear at all that day. I was not surprised at her absence. The time had come when doubtless Madame found it necessary to divulge her awful scheme to the unhappy child. In the midst of that gay house-ful of people no one specially missed her; even

Rowland was engaged with many necessary matters, and had little time to devote to his future wife. The ball-room, decorated with real flowers, was a beautiful sight.

Vandeleur, our host, and I paced up and down the long room. Rowland was in great excitement, making many suggestions, altering this decoration and the other. The flowers were too profuse in one place, too scanty in another. The lights, too, were not bright enough.

"By all means have the ball-room well lighted," said Vandeleur. "In a room like this, so large, and with so many doors leading into passages and sitting-out rooms, it is well to have the light as brilliant as possible. You will forgive my suggestion, Mr. Rowland, when I say I speak entirely from the point of view of a man who has some acquaintance with the treacherous dealings of crime."

Rowland started.

"Are you afraid that an attempt will be made here tonight to steal the necklace?" he asked, suddenly.

"We won't talk of it," replied Vandeleur. "Act on my suggestion and you have nothing to fear."

Rowland shrugged his shoulders, and crossing the room gave some directions to several men who were putting in the final touches.

Nearly a hundred guests were expected to arrive from the surrounding country, and the house was as full as it could possibly hold. Rowland was to open the ball with little Antonia.

There was no late dinner that day, and as evening approached Vandeleur sought me.

"I say, Druce, dress as early as you can, and come down and meet me in our host's study."

I looked at him in astonishment, but did not question him. I saw that he was intensely excited. His face was cold and stern; it invariably wore that expression when he was most moved.

I hurried into my evening clothes and came down again. Vandeleur was standing in the study talking to Rowland. The guests were beginning to arrive. The musicians were tuning up in the adjacent ball-room, and signs of hurry and festival pervaded the entire place. Rowland

was in high spirits and looked very handsome. He and Vandeleur talked together, and I stood a little apart. Vandeleur was just about to make a light reply to one of our host's questions when we heard the swish of drapery in the passage outside, and little Antonia, dressed for her first ball, entered. She was in soft white lace, and her neck and arms were bare. The effect of her entrance was somewhat startling and would have arrested attention even were we not all specially interested in her. Her face, neck, and arms were nearly as white as her dress, her dark eyes were much dilated, and her soft black hair surrounded her small face like a shadow. In the midst of the whiteness a large red cross sparkled on her throat like living fire. Rowland uttered an exclamation and then stood still; as for Vandeleur and myself, we held our breath in suspense. What might not the next few minutes reveal?

It was the look on Antonia's face that aroused our fears. What ailed her? She came forward like one blind, or as one who walks in her sleep. One hand was held out slightly in advance, as though she meant to guide herself by the sense of touch. She certainly saw neither Vandeleur nor me, but when she got close to Rowland the blind expression left her eyes. She gave a sudden and exceedingly bitter cry, and ran forward, flinging herself into his arms.

"Kiss me once before we part forever. Kiss me just once before we part," she said.

"My dear little one," I heard him answer, "what is the meaning of this? You are not well. There, Antonia, cease trembling. Before we part, my dear? But there is no thought of parting. Let me look at you, darling. Ah!"

He held her at arm's length and gazed at her critically.

"No girl could look sweeter, Antonia," he said, "and you have come now for the finishing touch—the beautiful pearls. But what is this, my dear? Why should you spoil your white neck with anything so incongruous? Let me remove it."

She put up her hand to her neck, thus covering the crimson cross. Then her wild eyes met

Vandeleur's. She seemed to recognise his presence for the first time.

"You can safely remove it," he said to her, speaking in a semi-whisper.

Rowland gave him an astonished glance. His look seemed to say, "Leave us," but Vandeleur did not move.

"We must see this thing out," he said to me.

Meanwhile Rowland's arm encircled Antonia's neck, and his hand sought for the clasp of the narrow gold thread that held the cross in place.

"One moment," said Antonia.

She stepped back a pace; the trembling in her voice left it, it gathered strength, her fear gave way to dignity. This was the hour of her deepest humiliation, and yet she looked noble.

"My dearest," she said, "my kindest and best of friends. I had yielded to temptation, terror made me weak, the dread of losing you unnerved me, but I won't come to you charged with a sin on my conscience; I won't conceal anything from you. I know you won't wish me *now* to become your wife; nevertheless, you shall know the truth."

"What do you mean, Antonia? What do your strange words signify? Are you mad?" said George Rowland.

"No, I wish I were; but I am no mate for you; I cannot bring dishonour to your honour. Madame said it could be hidden, that this"— she touched the cross—"would hide it. For this I was to pay—yes, to pay a shameful price. I consented, for the terror was so cruel. But I—I came here and looked into your face and I could not do it. Madame shall have her blood-red cross back and you shall know all. You shall see."

With a fierce gesture she tore the cross from her neck and flung it on the floor.

"The pearls for this," she cried; "the pearls were the price; but I would rather you knew. Take me up to the brightest light and you will see for yourself."

Rowland's face wore an expression impossible to fathom. The red cross lay on the floor; Antonia's eyes were fixed on his. She was no child to

be humoured; she was a woman and despair was driving her wild. When she said, "Take me up to the brightest light," he took her hand without a word and led her to where the full rays of a powerful electric light turned the place into day.

"Look!" cried Antonia, "look! Madame wrote it here—here."

She pointed to her throat.

"The words are hidden, but this light will soon cause them to appear. You will see for yourself, you will know the truth. At last you will understand who I really am."

There was silence for a few minutes. Antonia kept pointing to her neck. Rowland's eyes were fixed upon it. After a breathless period of agony Vandeleur stepped forward.

"Miss Antonia," he cried, "you have suffered enough. I am in a position to relieve your terrors. You little guessed, Rowland, that for the last few days I have taken an extreme liberty with regard to you. I have been in your house simply and solely in the exercise of my professional qualities. In the exercise of my manifest duties I came across a ghastly secret. Miss Antonia was to be subjected to a cruel ordeal. Madame Sara, for reasons of her own, had invented one of the most fiendish plots it has ever been my unhappy lot to come across. But I have been in time. Miss Antonia, you need fear nothing. Your neck contains no ghastly secret. Listen! I have saved you. The nurse whom Madame believed to be devoted to her service considered it best for prudential reasons to transfer herself to me. Under my directions she bathed your neck today with a preparation of cyanide of potassium. You do not know what that is, but it is a chemical preparation which neutralizes the effect of what that horrible woman has done. You have nothing to fear—your secret lies buried beneath your white skin."

"But what is the mystery?" said Rowland. "Your actions, Antonia, and your words, Vandeleur, are enough to drive a man mad. What is it all about? I will know."

"Miss Ripley can tell you or not, as she pleases," replied Vandeleur. "The unhappy child was to be blackmailed, Madame Sara's object being to secure the pearl necklace worth a King's ransom. The cross was to be given in exchange for the necklace. That was her aim, but she is defeated. Ask me no questions, sir. If this young lady chooses to tell you, well and good, but if not the secret is her own."

Vandeleur bowed and backed towards me.

"The secret is mine," cried Antonia, "but it also shall be yours, George. I will not be your wife with this ghastly thing between us. You may never speak to me again, but you shall know all the truth."

"Upon my word, a brave girl, and I respect her," whispered Vandeleur. "Come, Druce, our work so far as Miss Antonia is concerned is finished."

We left the room.

"Now to see Madame Sara," continued my friend. "We will go to her rooms. Walls have ears in her case; she doubtless knows the whole *dénouement* already; but we will find her at once, she can scarcely have escaped yet."

He flew upstairs. I followed him. We went from one corridor to another. At last we found Madame's apartments. Her bedroom door stood wide open. Rebecca Curt was standing in the middle of the room. Madame herself was nowhere to be seen, but there was every sign of hurried departure.

"Where is Madame Sara?" inquired Vandeleur, in a peremptory voice.

Rebecca Curt shrugged her shoulders.

"Has she gone down? Is she in the ball-room? Speak!" said Vandeleur.

The nurse gave another shrug.

"I only know that Achmed the Arabian rushed in here a few minutes ago," was her answer. "He was excited. He said something to Madame. I think he had been listening—eavesdropping, you call it. Madame was convulsed with rage. She thrust a few things together and she's gone. Perhaps you can catch her."

Vandeleur's face turned white.

"I'll have a try," he said. "Don't keep me, Druce."

He rushed away. I don't know what immediate steps he took, but he did not return to Rowland's Folly. Neither was Madame Sara captured.

But notwithstanding her escape and her meditated crime, notwithstanding little Antonia's hour of terror, the ball went on merrily, and the bride-elect opened it with her future husband. On her fair neck gleamed the pearls, lovely in their soft lustre. What she told Rowland was never known; how he took the news is a secret between Antonia and himself. But one thing is certain: no one was more gallant in his conduct, more ardent in his glances of love, than was the master of Rowland's Folly that night. They were married on the day fixed, and Madame Sara was defeated.

THE ADVENTURE OF THE CARNEGIE LIBRARY

John Kendrick Bangs

ONE OF THE MOST POPULAR American humorists of the late nineteenth and early twentieth centuries, John Kendrick Bangs (1862–1922) satirized virtually every living writer (and some not so living), but always in a good-natured way, eschewing the nastiness brought to that particular literary form by many other satirists, whether because of jealousy, sheer meanness, or because it's easier to laugh at an artist than to laugh with him.

Bangs skillfully and prolifically mined the extraordinary popularity of Sherlock Holmes with stories in numerous newspapers and magazines, collecting his burlesques in such books as *The Pursuit of the House-Boat* (1897), in which Holmes finds himself in Hades with other notables of the time; *The Dreamers: A Club* (1899); *The Enchanted Type-Writer* (1899); *Potted Fiction* (1908); and *Shylock Homes: His Posthumous Memoirs*, stories that had been syndicated in American newspapers in 1903 under the title *Adventures of Shylock Homes* but not collected until a limited edition was published in 1973. In addition to his success with the world's greatest detective, Bangs also brought the world's greatest jewel thief to his typewriter to produce *R. Holmes & Co.* (1906), introducing the son of Sherlock Holmes, who also happens to be the grandson of A. J. Raffles—if we are to believe all the character says.

"The Adventure of the Carnegie Library" was originally published in *Mrs. Raffles* (New York, Harper & Brothers, 1905).

The Adventure of the Carnegie Library

JOHN KENDRICK BANGS

"MERCIFUL MIDAS, BUNNY," said Henriette one morning as I was removing the breakfast-tray from her apartment. "Did you see the extent of Mr. Carnegie's benefactions in the published list this morning?"

"I have not received my paper yet," said I. "Moreover, I doubt if it will contain any reference to such matters when it does come. You know I read only the London *Times*, Mrs. Van Raffles. I haven't been able to go the American newspapers."

"More fool you, then, Bunny," laughed my mistress. "Any man who wants to pursue crime as a polite diversion and does not read the American newspapers fails to avail himself of one of the most potent instruments for the attainment of the highest artistic results. You cannot pick up a newspaper in any part of the land without discovering somewhere in its columns some reference to a new variety of house-breaking, some new and highly artistic method of writing another man's autograph so that when appended to a check and presented at his bank it will bear the closest scrutiny to which the paying-teller will subject it, some truly Napoleonic method of entirely novel design for the sudden parting of the rich from their possessions. Any university which attempted to add a School of Peculation to its curriculum and ignored the daily papers as a positive source of inspiration to the highest artistry in the profession would fail as ignobly as though it should forget to teach the fundamental principles of high finance."

"I was not aware of their proficiency in that direction," said I.

"You never will get on, Bunny," sighed Henriette, "because you are not quick to seize opportunities that lie directly under your nose. How do you suppose I first learned of all this graft at Newport? Why, by reading the newspaper accounts of their jewels in the Sunday and daily newspapers. How do I know that if I want to sand-bag Mr. Rockerbilt and rifle his pockets all I have to do is to station myself outside the Crackerbaker Club any dark opera night after twelve and catch him on his way home with his fortune sticking out all over him? Because the newspapers tell me that he is a regular habitué of the Crackerbaker and plays bridge there every night after the opera. How do I know just how to walk from my hall bedroom in my little East Side tenement up Fifth Avenue into Mrs. Gaster's dining-room, where she has a million in plate on her buffet, with my eyes shut, without fear of stumbling over a step or a chair or even a footstool? Because the newspapers have so repeatedly printed diagrams of the interior of the lady's residence that its halls, passages, doorways, exits, twists, turns, and culs-de-sac are indelibly engraved upon my mind. How did I acquire my wonderful knowledge of the exact number of pearls, rubies, diamonds, opals, tiaras, bracelets, necklaces, stomachers, and other gorgeous jewéls now in the possession of the smart set? Only by an assiduous devotion to the contents of the daily newspapers in their reports of the doings of the socially elect. I have a scrap-book, Bunny, that has been two years in the making, and there hasn't been a novel burglary reported in all that time that is not recorded in my book, not a gem that has appeared at the opera, the theatre, the Charity Ball, the Horse Show, or a monkey dinner that has not been duly noted in this vademecum of mine, fully described and in a sense located. If it wasn't for that knowledge I could not hope for success any more than you could if you went hunting mountain-lions in the Desert of Sahara, or tried to lure speckled-trout from the depths of an empty goldfish globe."

"I see," said I, meekly. "I have missed a great opportunity. I will subscribe to the *Tribune* and *Evening Post* right away."

I have never understood why Henriette greeted this observation with a peal of silvery laughter that fairly made the welkin ring. All I know is that it so irritated me that I left the room to keep from making a retort that might seriously have disturbed our friendship. Later in the day, Mrs. Van Raffles rang for me and I attended upon her orders.

"Bunny," said she, "I've made up my mind to it—I must have a Carnegie library, that is all there is about it, and you must help. The ironmaster has already spent thirty-nine million dollars on that sort of thing, and I don't see why if other people can get 'em we can't."

"Possibly because we are not a city, town, or hamlet," I suggested, for I had been looking over the daily papers since my morning's talk with the lady, and had observed just who had been the beneficiaries of Mr. Carnegie's benefactions. "He don't give 'em to individuals, but to communities."

"Of course not," she responded, quickly. "But what is to prevent our becoming a municipality?"

My answer was an amazed silence, for frankly I could not for the life of me guess how we were to do any such thing.

"It's the easiest thing in the world," she continued. "All you have to do is to buy an abandoned farm on Long Island with a bleak sea-front, divide it up into corner lots, advertise the lots for sale on the instalment plan, elect your mayor, and Raffleshurst-by-the-Sea, swept by ocean breezes, fifteen cents from the Battery, is a living, breathing reality."

"By the jumping Disraeli, Henriette, but you are a marvel!" I cried, with enthusiasm. "But," I added, my ardor cooling a little, "won't it cost money?"

"About fifteen hundred dollars," said Henriette. "I can win that at bridge in an hour."

"Well," said I, "you know you can command my services, Henriette. What shall I do?"

"Organize the city," she replied. "Here is fifty dollars. That will do for a starter. Go down to Long Island, buy the farm, put up a few signs calling on people to own their own homes; advertise the place in big capital letters in the Sunday papers as likely to be the port of the future, consider yourself duly elected mayor, stop in at some photograph shop in New York on your way back and get a few dozen pictures of street scenes in Binghamton, Oberlin, Kalamazoo, and other well-populated cities, and then come back here for further instructions. Meanwhile I will work out the other details of the scheme."

According to my habit I followed Henriette's instructions to the letter. A farm of five hundred acres was secured within a week, the bleakest, coldest spot ever swept by ocean breezes anywhere. It cost six hundred dollars in cash, with immediate possession. Three days later, with the use of a ruler, I had mapped out about twelve thousand corner lots on the thing, and, thanks to my knack at draughtsmanship, had all ready for anybody's inspection as fine a ground-plan of Raffleshurst-by-the-Sea as ever was got up by a land-booming company in this or any other country. I then secured the photographs desired by my mistress, advertised Raffleshurst in three Sunday newspapers to the tune of a half-page each, and returned to Newport. I flattered myself that the thing was well done, for on reading the advertisement nothing would do but that Henriette should visit the place in person. The ads were so phrased, she said, as to be irresistible.

"It's fine, Bunny," she cried, with an enthusiastic laugh as she gazed out over the broad acres of Raffleshurst and noted how well I had fulfilled her orders. "Under proper direction you are a most able workman. Nothing could be better. Nothing—absolutely nothing. And now for Mr. Carnegie."

I still did not see how the thing was coming out, but such was my confidence in my leader that I had no misgivings.

"Here is a letter from Mrs. Gaster introducing the Hon. Henry Higginbotham, mayor of Raffleshurst, to Mr. Carnegie," said Henriette. "You will call at once on the iron-master. Present this letter, keeping in mind of course that you are yourself the Hon. Henry Higginbotham. Show him these photographs of the City Hall at Binghamton, of the public park at Oberlin, the high school at Oswego, the battery walk at Charleston and other public improvements of various other cities, when he asks you what sort of a place Raffleshurst is; then frankly and fearlessly put in your application for a one-hundred-and-fifty-thousand-dollar library. One picture—this beautiful photograph of the music-hall at the St. Louis Exhibition—you must seem to overlook always, only contrive matters so that he will inquire what it is. You must then modestly remark that it is nothing but a little two-hundred-thousand-dollar art gallery you have yourself presented to the town. See?"

"H'm—yes, I see," said I. "But it is pretty risky business, Henriette. Suppose Mrs. Gaster asks for further information about Mayor Higginbotham? I think it was unwise of you to connect her with the enterprise."

"Don't bother about that, Bunny. *I* wrote that letter of introduction—I haven't studied penmanship for nothing, you know. Mrs. Gaster will never know. So just put on your boldest front, remember your name, and don't forget to be modest about your own two-hundred-thousand-dollar art gallery. That will inspire him, I think."

It took me a week to get at the iron-master; but finally, thanks to Mrs. Gaster's letter of introduction, I succeeded. Mr. Carnegie was, as always, in a most amiable frame of mind, and received me cordially, even when he discovered my real business with him.

"I hadn't intended to give any more libraries this year," he said, as he glanced over the pictures. "I am giving away lakes now," he added. "If you wanted a lake, Mr. Higginbotham, I—"

"We have such a large water-front already, Mr. Carnegie," said I, "and most of our residents are young married couples with children not over three and five. I am afraid they would regard a lake as a source of danger."

"That's a pretty playground," he suggested, glancing at the Oberlin Park. "Somehow or other, it reminds me of something."

I thought it quite likely, but, of course, I didn't say so. I may be a fool but I have some tact.

"It's at the far corner of the park that we propose to put the library if you are good enough to let us have it," was all I ventured.

"H'm!" he mused. "Well, do you know, I like to help people who help themselves—that's my system."

I assured him that we of Raffleshurst were accustomed to helping ourselves to everything we could lay our hands on, a jest which even though it was only too true seemed to strike him pleasantly.

"What is that handsome structure you always pass over?" he asked, as I contrived to push the music-hall photograph aside for the fifth time.

I laughed deprecatingly. "Oh, that," I said, modestly—"that's only a little two-hundred-thousand-dollar music-hall and art gallery I have built for the town myself."

Oh, that wonderful Henriette! How did she know that generosity even among the overgenerous was infectious?

"Indeed!" said Mr. Carnegie, his face lighting up with real pleasure. "Well, Mr. Higginbotham, I guess—I guess I'll do it. I can't be outdone in generosity by you, sir, and—er—I guess you can count on the library. Do you think one hundred and fifty thousand dollars will be enough?"

"Well, of course—" I began.

"Why not make my contribution equal to yours and call it an even two hundred thousand dollars?" he interrupted.

"You overwhelm me," said I. "Of course, if you wish to—"

"And the Raffleshurst common council will appropriate five per cent. of that amount annually for its maintenance?" he inquired.

"Such a resolution has already been passed," said I, taking a paper from my pocket. "Here is the ordinance, duly signed by myself as mayor and by the secretary of the council."

Again that extraordinary woman, to provide me with so necessary a document!

The millionaire rose with alacrity and with his own hand drew me the required check.

"Mr. Mayor," said he, "I like the quick, business-like way in which you do things. Pray present my compliments to the citizens of Raffleshurst-by-the-Sea, and tell them I am only too glad to help them. If you ever want a lake, sir, don't fail to call upon me." With which gracious words the millionaire bowed me out.

"*Two* hundred thousand dollars, Bunny?" cried Henriette when I handed her the check.

"Yep," said I.

"Well, that *is* a good day's sport!" she said, gazing at the slip. "Twice as much as I expected."

"Yes," said I. "But see here, Henriette, suppose Mr. Carnegie should go down to Raffleshurst to see the new building and find out what a bunco game we have played on him?"

"He's not likely to do that for two reasons, Bunny," she replied. "In the first place he suffers acutely from lumbago in winter and can't travel, and in the second place he'd have to find Raffleshurst-by-the-Sea before he could make the discovery that somebody'd put up a game on him. I think by the time he is ready to start we can arrange matters to have Raffleshurst taken off the map."

"Well, I think this is the cleverest trick you've turned yet, Henriette," said I.

"Nonsense, Bunny, nonsense," she replied. "Any idiot can get a Carnegie library these days. That's why I put *you* on the job, dear," she added, affectionately.

THE WOMAN FROM THE EAST

Edgar Wallace

AS THE MOST POPULAR WRITER in the world in the 1920s and 1930s, Richard Horatio Edgar Wallace (1875–1932) earned a fortune—reportedly more than a quarter of a million dollars a year during the last decade of his life—but his extravagant lifestyle left his estate deeply in debt when he died. The enormous success that he enjoyed in the 1920s and 1930s was unprecedented, with reports (perhaps exaggerated by his publishers) that one in every four books sold in Great Britain during those years had been from his pen.

The prolific Wallace reputedly wrote more than 170 novels, 18 stage plays, 957 short stories, and elements of numerous screenplays and scenarios, including the first British sound version of *The Hound of the Baskervilles* (1931); 160 films, both silent and sound, have been based on his books and stories, most famously *King Kong* (1933), for which he wrote the original story and film treatment.

The Ranee of Butilata is typical of the many rogues created by Wallace. As a populist writer, Wallace found that common people related to his rogues— criminals who were not violent or physically dangerous but whose talents and inclinations led them to the other side of the law. Others include Anthony Smith (*The Mixer*, 1927), (Elegant) Edward Farthindale (*Elegant Edward*, 1928), and Four Square Jane (*Four Square Jane*, 1929). Readers rooted for these and other of Wallace's numerous literary criminals, who always stole from the wealthy and powerful.

When we meet the future Ranee of Butilata, she is a frightened, innocent woman not yet eighteen. Circumstances change her.

"The Woman from the East" was originally published in *The Woman from the East and Other Stories* (London, Hutchinson, 1934).

The Woman from the East

EDGAR WALLACE

PROLOGUE
The Match-Maker

"OVERTURE AND BEGINNERS, PLEASE!"

The shrill voice of the call-boy wailed through the bare corridors of the Frivolity Theatre, and No. 7 dressing-room emptied with a rush. The stone stairs leading down to the stage level were immediately crowded with chattering chorus girls, arrayed in the fantastic costumes of the opening number.

Belle Straker lagged a little behind the crowd, for she had neither the heart nor the inclination to discuss the interminable nothings which were so fascinating to her sister artistes.

At the foot of the stairs a tired looking man in evening dress was waiting. Presently he saw the girl and raised his finger. She quickened her pace, for the stage-manager was an irascible man and somewhat impatient.

"Miss Straker," he said, "you are excused tonight."

"Excused?" she replied in surprise. "I thought . . ."

The stage manager nodded.

"I didn't get your note saying you wanted to stay off," he said. "Now hurry up and change, my dear. You'll be in plenty of time."

In truth he had received a note asking permission to miss a performance, but he had not known then that the dinner engagement, which Belle Straker was desirous of keeping, was with the eminent Mr. Covent. And Mr. Covent was not only a name in the City, but he was also a director of the company owning the Frivolity Theatre.

The girl hesitated, one foot on the lower stair, and the stage manager eyed her curiously. He knew Mr. Covent slightly, and had been a little more than surprised that Mr. Covent was "that kind of man." One would hardly associate that white-haired and benevolent gentleman with dinner parties in which chorus girls figured.

As for the girl, some premonition of danger made her hesitate.

"I don't know whether I want to go," she said.

"Don't be silly," said the stage-manager, with a little smile. "Never miss a good dinner, Belle—how are those dancing lessons getting on?"

She knew what he meant, but it pleased her to pretend ignorance.

"Dancing lessons?" she said.

"Those you are giving to the Rajah of Butilata," said the stage-manager. "What sort of a pupil does he make? It must be rather funny teaching a man to dance who cannot speak English."

She shrugged her shoulders in assumed indifference.

"He's not bad," she said, and turned quickly to run up the stairs.

The stage-manager looked after her, and his smile broadened. Then, of a sudden, he became grave. It was no business of his, and he was hardened to queerer kinds of friendship than that which might exist between a chorus girl and an Eastern potentate, even though rumour had it that His Highness of Butilata was almost white.

Even friendships between young and pretty members of the chorus and staid and respectable City merchants were not outside the range of his experience. He, too, shrugged and went back to the stage, for the strains of the overture were coming faintly through the swinging doors.

Belle Straker changed swiftly, wiped the make-up from her face, and got into her neat street clothes. She stopped on her way out of the theatre to enquire at the stage door-keeper's office whether there had been any letters.

"No, miss," said the man. "But those two men came back again this evening to ask if you were playing. I told them that you were off."

She nodded gratefully. Those two men were, as she knew, solicitors' clerks who had writs to serve upon her. She had large and artistic tastes which outstripped her slender income. She was in debt everywhere, and nobody knew better than she how serious was her position.

The theatres were filling up, so that there were plenty of empty taxicabs, and with a glance at the jewelled watch upon her wrist and a little exclamation of dismay, she gave directions and jumped into the first cab she could attract.

Five minutes later she was greeting an elderly man, who rose from a corner table in Penniali's Restaurant.

"I am so sorry, Mr. Covent. That stupid stage-manager did not get my note asking to stay off, and I went to the theatre thinking my request had been refused. I hope I haven't kept you waiting?"

Mr. Covent beamed through his gold-rimmed spectacles.

"My dear child," he said pleasantly, "I have reached the age in life when a man is quite content to wait so long as he has an evening paper, and when time indeed runs too quickly."

He was a fine, handsome man of sixty-five, clean-shaven and rubicund. His white hair was brushed back from his forehead and fell in waves over his collar, and despite his years his frank blue eyes were as clear as a boy's.

"Sit down, sit down," he said. "I have ordered dinner, and I'm extremely grateful that I have not to eat it alone."

She found him, as she had found him before, a very pleasant companion, courteous, considerate and anecdotal. She knew very little about him, except that he had been introduced about two months before, and all that she knew was to his credit. He had invariably treated her with the deepest respect. He was by all accounts a very wealthy man—a millionaire, some said—and she knew, at any rate, that he was the senior partner of Covent Brothers, a firm of Indian bankers and merchants with extensive connections in the East.

They came at last to the stage when conversation was easier. And then it was that Mr. Covent opened up the subject which was nearer to his heart, perhaps, than to the girl's.

"Have you thought over my suggestion?" he asked.

The girl made a little grimace.

"Oh yes, I've thought it over," she said. "I don't think I can do it, I really don't, Mr. Covent."

Mr. Covent smiled indulgently. In all the forty-five years in which he had been in business he had never approached so delicate or so vital a problem as this; but he was a man used to dealing with vital problems, and he was in no way dismayed by the first rebuff.

"I hope you will think this matter over well before you reject it," he said. "And I am afraid you will have to do your thinking tonight, because the Rajah is leaving for India next week."

"Next week!" she said in surprise, and with that sense of discomfort which comes to the opportunist who finds her chance slipping away before her eyes. "I thought he was staying for months yet."

John Covent shook his head.

"No, he's going back to his country almost immediately," he said. "Now, Miss Straker, I will speak plainly to you. I happen to know, through certain agencies with which I am associated, that you are heavily in debt, and that you have tastes which are—just a little beyond your means, shall I say? You love the good things of life—luxury, comfort and all that sort of thing; you hate sordid surroundings—er—landladies, shall I say?"

Belle shivered at the thought of an interview she had had that morning with "Ma" Hetheridge, who had demanded with violence the payment of two months' arrears.

"Here is a man," John Covent went on, ticking off the points on his fingers, "who is madly in love with you. It is true that he is an Indian, though he would pass for a European and is admitted to the very best of English society. But against his colour and his race there is the fact that he is enormously wealthy, that he can give you not a house but a palace, a retinue of servants, and the most luxurious surroundings that it is humanly possible to imagine. He can give you a position beyond your wildest dreams and make you famous."

The girl shook her head, half in doubt, but did not reply.

"I know the kingdom of Butilata very well," mused Mr. Covent reminiscently. "A gorgeous country, with the most lovely gardens. I particularly remember the Ranee's garden—that would be you, of course, and the garden would be your own property. A place of marble terraces, of fragrant heliotrope, of luxurious growths of the most exotic plants. And then the Ranee's Court! That, of course, would be yours, Miss Straker—a columned apartment, every pillar worth a fortune. A wonderful bathing-pool in the centre, lined with blue tiles. And then, of course, you would have riding, and a car of your own—the Prince has half a dozen cars in his garage, and has just bought another half a dozen—and all the best people in India would call upon you. You would be received by the Viceroy . . . and all that sort of thing."

The girl fixed her troubled eyes upon the man who sketched this alluring picture.

"But isn't it true," she said, "that rajahs have more than one wife? What would be my position supposing he got tired of me and——"

"Oh, tut, tut! Nonsense!" said Mr. Covent, smiling benignly. "Don't forget that you are an English girl, and you would have special claims! No, no, the Government of India would not allow that sort of thing to happen, believe me."

She twisted the serviette with her nervous fingers.

"When would he want——"

"The marriage ceremony should be performed tonight," said Mr. Covent. "It is a very simple ceremony, but, of course, quite binding."

"Tonight?" she said, looking at him in consternation, and Mr. Covent nodded.

"But couldn't I go out to India and marry there?"

"No, no," said John Covent. "That is impossible. Here is your opportunity to marry a man who is worth millions, occupying one of the most wonderful positions in India, tremendously popular with all classes—a man who loves you—don't forget that, my child, he loves you."

The girl laughed—a short, bitter laugh.

"I'm not worrying about that," she said. "The only thing that concerns me—is me."

John Covent inclined his head graciously.

"That I can well understand," said that grave man. "It is, of course, a very serious step in a girl's life, but few, I think, have been faced at such a crisis of their career with so pleasant a prospect."

He took from his pocket a notecase and opened it.

"It is a very curious position," he said. "Here am I, a very respectable old gentleman who should be in bed, engaged in a West End restaurant negotiating the marriage of an Indian Rajah."

He laughed pleasantly as he took from the case a wad of folded notes. The girl looked at the money with hungry eyes, and saw they were notes of high denomination.

"There is two thousand pounds here," he said slowly, "much more really than I can afford, although the Rajah is a great client of mine."

"What is it?" she asked.

"This was the wedding present that I was giving you," he said. "I thought of many presents which might be acceptable, but decided that after all perhaps you would prefer the money. Two thousand pounds!"

The girl drew a deep breath. Two thousand pounds! . . . And Butilata was not more unpleasant than the average young man. He had already treated her decently, and . . .

"All right," she said recklessly, and jerked on the squirrel cape which lay over the back of her chair. "Produce your Rajah!"

They left the restaurant together and drove in Mr. Covent's handsome little electric brougham to a big house off Eaton Square, and were instantly admitted by an Indian servant. She had been there before, but never so late. She expected to find the big saloon blazing with light, for here the Rajah loved to sit. She was surprised, however, to find only a small reading-lamp placed by the side of the big blue divan on which he lolled.

He rose unsteadily to his feet and came towards her, both hands outstretched.

"So you have come," he said. He spoke perfect English, but there was a thickness in his speech and a glaze to his eye which suggested that he too had dined well.

He took her by both hands and led her to the divan, then turned to the waiting Englishman. The girl looked across almost appealingly to John Covent. Strange it was that in that dim light the mask of benevolence should slip from his face, and there should be something menacing, sinister, in his mien. It was a trick of the light, perhaps, for his voice was as soft and as kindly as ever.

"I think you're doing very wisely, Miss Straker," he said; "very wisely indeed."

Yet she seemed to detect a hint of nervousness in the voice, and for a second became panic-stricken.

"I don't think I'll go on with this, Mr. Covent," she said unsteadily. "I don't think I want to—go on with this."

"My dear child"—his voice had a soothing quality, "don't be foolish."

The Rajah was looking down at them, for John Covent had seated himself on the divan by the girl's side, and on the Rajah's brown face was a little smile. Presently he clapped his hands.

"There shall be a ceremony," he said. "It shall be a small ceremony, my beautiful child."

A man appeared at the far end of the room in answer to his summons, and he fired a volley of sharp, guttural words at the attendant.

Half an hour later John Covent was rolling smoothly westward, leaning back in his car alone. A long cigar was between his white teeth and there was a smile in his eyes.

"Very satisfactory, very satisfactory," said John Covent.

Thus, on the 14th day of May, 1909, was Isabelle Straker, who, had she been married in a prosaic registry office, would have described herself as "Spinster, aged seventeen-and-a-half," married to His Highness Dal Likar Bahadur, Rajah of Butilata, by the custom of his land. She was his eighth wife—but this she did not know.

I

The Partners

In the year of grace 1919 there were two partners to the firm of Covent Brothers. John Covent had died suddenly in India, and the business had passed into the hands of his son and his nephew, the latter of whom had inherited his mother's share in a business which had been in the same family for two hundred years.

Martin Covent was a tall, well-dressed man of twenty-seven. He had none of his late father's genial demeanour. The lips were harder, the brow straighter and the face longer than the expansive representative of the firm who had preceded him.

He sat at his great table, his elbows on the blotting-pad, and looked across toward his junior partner. And a greater contrast between himself and his cousin could not be imagined.

Tom Camberley was two years his junior and looked younger. He had the complexion of a man who lived an open-door life, the eyes of one who found laughter easy. He was not laughing now. His forehead was creased into a little frown, and he was leaning back in his chair regarding Martin Covent through narrowed eyelids.

"I hate to say so, Martin," he said quietly, "but I must tell you that, in my judgment, your scheme is not quite straight."

Martin Covent laughed.

"My dear boy," he said, with a hint of patronage in his tone, "I am afraid the mysteries of the banking profession are still—mysteries to you."

"That may be so," returned Tom Camberley coolly. "But there are certain basic principles on which I can make no mistake. For example, I am never mystified in distinguishing between right and wrong."

Martin Covent rose.

"I have often thought," he said, with a hint of irritation in his voice, "that you're wasted on the Indian banking business, my dear Tom. You ought to be running the literary end of a Bible Mission. There's plenty of scope in India for you if your conscience will not permit you to soil your hands with sordid business affairs."

The other laughed quietly.

"You're always suggesting I should clear out of the firm, and I should love to oblige you. But, bad business man as I am, I know the advantage of holding a position which brings me in the greater part of ten thousand a year. Anyway, there's no sense in getting angry about it, Martin. I merely offer you an opinion that to employ clients' money for speculative purposes without having secured the permission of those clients is dishonest. And really, I don't know why you should do it. The firm is on a very sound basis. We are making big profits, and the prospect is in every way healthy."

The other did not immediately reply. He paced the big private office with his hands in his pockets, whistling softly. Suddenly he stopped in his stride and turned.

"Let me tell you something, Tom Camber-ley," he said, "and stick this in your mind. You think you're on a good thing in holding shares in Covent Brothers. So you are. But ten years ago this firm was on the verge of bankruptcy, and your shares would have been worth about two-pence net."

Tom raised his eyebrows.

"You're joking," he said.

"I'm serious," said the other grimly. "We're talking as man to man and partner to partner, and I tell you that ten years ago we were as near bankruptcy as that." He snapped his fingers. "Fortunately, the governor got hold of that fool Butilata. Butilata was rich; we were nearly broke. The governor took his finances in hand and rebuilt the firm."

"This is news to me," said Tom. "I was at school at the time."

"So was I, but the governor told me," said Martin. "It was touch and go whether Butilata put his affairs in the hands of Covent Brothers or not. Happily the governor was able to render him a service. Butilata was staying in this country, and when he wasn't drinking like a fish he was mad keen on dancing, and fell in love with a girl—an actress at one of the theatres here, who taught him a few steps. He married her——"

"Married?" said Tom incredulously. "Is the Ranee of Butilata an English girl?"

Martin nodded.

"It was the governor who brought it about. Clever old devil, God rest him! was the governor. Of course, he had his qualms about it. He often told me that he thought it wasn't playing the game. He knew the kind of life that she was going to; but after all she was only a chorus girl, and probably she had a much better time than you or I."

Tom Camberley made a little grimace.

"That sounds rather horrible," he said. "What happened to the girl?"

Martin shrugged his shoulders.

"She endured it," he replied. "They were married and went out the next week to India. The governor never saw her again, though he frequently went to Butilata. When the Rajah died she came to England. She doesn't suspect that we played the part we did, or we shouldn't have her account."

Tom shivered.

"It is not a nice story," he said. "I could wish that we had made our money in some other way."

"What do you mean?" asked Martin gruffly. "We didn't make it out of the girl. It is true that the governor put himself right with the Rajah over that business."

Tom laughed again, but this time there was a little note of hardness in his merriment.

"Butilata died a comparatively poor man, though his wife seems to have plenty of money— probably she bagged the Butilata pearls—good luck to her, poor girl!" he said dryly. "But if the Rajah of Butilata became poor, the firm of Covent Brothers became correspondingly rich. Did your father oblige the Rajah in any other way?"

The other shot a suspicious glance at him.

"If you're being sarcastic you're wasting your breath. I merely want to point out to you that this business, which you regard as the safest investment you could find, was re-established by a fluke. Now be sensible, Tom." He came round the desk and sat on a corner, looking down at the other. "Here we have a prospect of making a million by the use of a little common sense. I tell you, Rumania is a country of the future, and these oil properties which have been offered to us will be worth a hundred per cent more than we can get them for today—and that in a year's time."

Still Tom Camberley shook his head.

"If you want to invest money, why not approach your clients?" he said. "We have no right whatever to touch their reserves or engage in any speculation which is not to the advantage of those who trust us with their balances. I notice, too, from the memo you sent me that you have earmarked the balance of this very woman—the Ranee. Surely you have done the woman sufficient injury?"

Martin Covent slipped down from the table with a snort.

"Anyone would think, to hear you speak," he said sarcastically, "that we were the Bank of England or one of the big joint stock concerns. Can't you get it in your head that we are bankers and merchants, and being bankers and merchants, we are necessarily speculators?"

"Speculate with your own money," said the other doggedly, and Martin Covent slammed out of the office.

His cousin sat deep in thought for five minutes, then he pushed a bell. A little while later the door opened and a girl came in. He noticed with surprise that she was wearing a coat and hat, and looked up at the clock.

"Gracious heavens!" he said in comical despair. "I hadn't the slightest idea it was so late, Miss Mead."

The girl laughed. Tom noticed that she had a pretty laugh, that her teeth were very white and very regular, and that when she laughed there were pleasant little wrinkles on each side of the big grey eyes. He had duly noted long before that her complexion was faultless, that her figure was slim, and that her carriage and walk were delightfully graceful. Now he noticed them all over again, and with a start realized that he had got into this habit of critical and appreciative examination.

The girl noticed too, if the faint flush which came to her cheeks meant anything, and Tom Camberley rose awkwardly.

"I'm awfully sorry, Miss Mead," he said. "I won't keep you now that it is late."

"Is there anything I can do?" said the girl. "I have no particular engagement. Did you want me to type a letter?"

"Yes—no," said Tom, and cursed himself for his embarrassment. "The fact was, I wanted to see the Ranee of Butilata's account."

The girl smiled and shook her head.

"Miss Drew has the accounts, you know, Mr. Camberley. I only deal with the correspondence."

Tom Camberley did know. When he had pressed the bell he had had no plan in his mind, and was as far from any definite scheme now.

"Where does the Ranee live?" he asked.

"I can get that for you," said the girl, and disappeared, to return in a few minutes with a slip of paper.

"The Ranee of Butilata, Churley Grange, Newbury," she read.

"Do you know her?"

The girl shook her head.

"All her business is done by Miss Drew, who goes down to see her," she said. "Miss Drew told me that she is always veiled—she thinks that there is some facial disfigurement. Isn't it rather dreadful an English girl marrying an Indian? Would you like to see Miss Drew in the morning?"

"No, no," he said hastily. He had no desire to discuss the matter with Miss Drew. Miss Drew had complete control of the accounts, and he suspected her of enjoying more of his partner's confidence than he did. To him she was a statuesque, cold-blooded plodder with a mathematical mind, who was never known to smile, and he was a little in awe of the admirable Miss Drew.

"Sit down," he said, and after a second's hesitation the girl obeyed.

Tom walked to the door and shut it—a proceeding which, if it aroused any apprehension in the girl's mind, did not provoke any objection.

"Miss Mead," he said, "I am going to take you into my confidence. In fact, I am going to ask you to do something just outside your duty, and I am relying upon you to keep the matter entirely to yourself."

She nodded, wondering what was coming next.

"The Ranee is not one of our richest clients," he said. "But she has a large deposit account with us, and she has frequently invested money on our advice in certain speculative propositions which have been put before her. My partner and I have a scheme for buying up a block of oil properties in Rumania, and he—Mr. Covent—has told me that her highness is willing to invest to any extent."

He was doing something which he knew was unpardonable. Not only was he suspecting his partner of a lie, but he was conveying his suspicion to an employee in the firm. In his doubt and uncertainty he had blundered into an act which had the appearance of being dishonourable; for he was now within an ace of revealing the secrets of partnership, which should not go outside.

He looked round apprehensively towards the door through which his partner had disappeared. He knew, however, that Martin was a creature of habit, and by now would be driving away in his car, and that there was no fear of interruption. The girl was waiting patiently. To say that she was not curious would be to misstate her attitude. She had need of patience, for it was some time before he spoke; but when he did speak, his mind was made up.

"I want you to do me a favour," he said, "and undertake an unusual mission. Will you go down to Churley Grange tonight and see the Ranee?"

"Tonight?" said the girl in surprise.

He nodded.

"I have told you that this business is confidential, and I don't think it is necessary to emphasize that fact. I want you to see her as from me, and ask her the amount she wishes to invest in Rumanian Oils. You can say we have mislaid her letters, and that I have sent you down before the office opens in the morning so that no mistake shall be made. If she expresses surprise, and cannot recollect having authorized us to invest money in Rumanian Oils, I want you to pretend that there is some mistake and that you were not quite certain whether she was the client concerned, and use your native wit to get out of the situation as well as you can. You quite understand?"

She nodded slowly.

"I understand a little," she smiled. "But wouldn't it be better to see Miss Drew in the morning? She deals with the Ranee."

Tom shook his head.

"No, no," he said. "I want you to get down, and I don't want Miss Drew to know anything about it, nor my partner."

He looked at his watch.

"The trains to Newbury are fairly frequent, I think," he said, "and at any rate we will look up the time-table."

There was a train down in an hour; the last train back reached Paddington at half past eleven.

"I will be waiting for you at the station with a car," he said. "Here is five pounds for expenses. Now will you do this for me?"

"Certainly, Mr. Camberley," said the girl, and then, with a smile in her eyes, "It sounds horribly mysterious, but I just love mystery."

"And I just hate it," said Tom Camberley.

II
The Ranee

Churley Grange was five miles from Newbury Station—a piece of information which Dora Mead received with mixed feelings. Fortunately there were taxis at the station, and Tom Camberley had given her sufficient money to meet any contingency.

It was dark when she turned from the main London road into a side road which bore round in the direction of Reading. Churley Grange was a Georgian mansion which stood on the main London road. It was a big house with very little land attached, and that enclosed by a high brick wall which hid the house from the road. A pair of big green gates, flanked by a smaller wicket gate, gave admission to the grounds, and these were closed when the cab drew up. Dora Mead looked for a bell, and for some time failed to find one. Then she discovered a small knob by the side of the wicket gate, and painted the same colour so as to be almost indistinguishable, and pressed it. She had to wait a few minutes before the gate was opened by a dark-looking man, evidently an Indian.

He wore a blue uniform coat with small metal buttons bearing some sort of crest. This she noticed in the brief time he stood surveying her.

"Is this the Ranee of Butilata's house?" she asked.

The man nodded.

"I have some important business with her," said Dora.

"Have you an appointment?" demanded the gatekeeper. He pronounced his words so carefully that she knew for certain that he was not English, even if his swarthy countenance had not already betrayed the fact.

The girl hesitated.

"Yes," she said boldly.

"Where are you from?" asked the man.

She was about to say London, but changed her mind.

"Newbury," she replied.

"Come in," said the man curtly, and locked the door behind her.

She found herself in a beautiful garden and was conducted across a well-kept lawn to a flight of steps leading to the main door of the building. Here she was handed over to another servant, also a man, and, like the first, an Indian. The gateman said something to the other in a low voice, and the second servant led her through a wide hall into the drawing-room.

It might have been the drawing-room of a palace. It was certainly the home of one to whom money was no object. The room was illuminated by lights concealed in the cornices, the ceiling was beautifully carved in plaster in the Moorish style, and long blue silk curtains covered its three windows. The floor was of polished parquet, on which a number of costly rugs were spread, and one gorgeous screen of exquisite workmanship, which she judged to be Eastern, was so arranged that it hid a second door in one corner of the room.

She was admiring the taste and beauty of the furnishings when she heard a rustle of garments behind her and half turned. Instantly there was a cry, a click, and the room was in darkness.

The girl stepped back in alarm.

"Please don't be afraid," said a muffled voice. "The fuses have broken."

"I could believe that if I hadn't seen your hand turn the light out," said Dora, making an heroic attempt to keep her voice steady. "Are you the Ranee of—of Butilata?"

"That is my name," said the voice; "wait, I will get candles."

The door opened and closed, and she heard voices in the hall. Then the mysterious hostess returned.

"Why have you come here and what do you want?" she asked.

"I will discuss my business in the light," said Dora. She was shaking from head to foot, for there was something about this house and its gloomy servants which had struck a chill of terror to her soul—something now in the strange conduct of the mistress of the house which filled her with blind panic. She heard the creak of the door opening, but this time she did not see the dim light in the hall, and she knew that it had been purposely extinguished.

The hair at the nape of her neck began to rise, her scalp tingled with terror. Springing forward, she pushed the woman aside and groped for the switch. Her fingers were on the lever, when a cloth was thrown over her head and she was jerked violently to the floor. She opened her mouth to scream, but a big hand covered it, and then she fainted.

Tom Camberley paced the arrival platform at Paddington in an uncomfortable frame of mind. He had cursed himself for sending the girl on such an errand, and had consigned his partner, who had aroused these suspicions and doubts in his mind, to the devil and his habitation.

When the train drew in, a little of this discomfort vanished.

The girl was in a carriage at the rear of the train, and when he saw her at a distance he quickened his step. It was not until he was half a dozen paces from her that he saw her face in the light of an overhead electric lamp.

"My God!" he said. "What has happened?"

She was as white as death, and swayed when he took her arm so that she nearly fell.

"Take me home," she whispered.

His car was waiting in the station yard, and it was not until the girl was approaching her Bloomsbury lodgings that she could find her voice to tell him of the events of the evening.

"When I recovered consciousness," she said, "I was in the cab. The driver told me that the gateman had brought me out and said that I had fainted, and that the lady thought I had better sit in the open air for a little while until I recovered."

"You don't remember what happened after you fainted?"

She shook her head.

"Oh, it was dreadful, dreadful! I never felt so afraid in my life," she whispered.

"Did you see the Ranee?"

"No, I did not see her. Please God I will never see her. She is a dreadful woman."

"But why, why?" asked the perplexed young man. "Why did she do this?" Then, remembering the girl's distress: "You don't know how sorry I am, Miss Mead, that I have exposed you to this outrage. I will see the Ranee myself and demand some explanation. I will . . ."

He remembered that he was not in a position to demand any explanation, and that it was more likely, if this matter was exposed, that he would be called upon to furnish some account of Dora Mead's mission to the Anglo-Indian Princess.

"Please don't speak about it," said the girl, laying her hand on his arm. "I want to forget it. I was terrified to death, of course, but now it is all over I am inclined to see the humorous side of it."

Her obvious distress belied this cheerful view, but Tom Camberley was silent.

"I don't understand it," said the girl, returning to the subject herself. "It was so amazingly unreal that I feel as if I have had a very bad dream. Here we are," she said suddenly, pointing to a house, and Tom leaned forward and tapped the window, bringing the car to a standstill.

The sidewalks of the street were deserted,

and the girl shivered a little as she descended from the car.

"Do you mind waiting a little while," she begged, "while I open the door? My nerves have been upset by this business."

"Isn't your landlady up?" he asked, and she shook her head.

"This is a block of tiny flats," she said. "Mine is on the second floor."

Her hand was shaking so that he had to take the key and open the door for her.

"I insist upon coming up to your room, at any rate," he said, "to see that you are all right. You can't imagine how sorry I am that you have had this unhappy experience."

She demurred at first to his suggestion that he should go upstairs with her, but presently agreed, and he followed her up two flights, until they came to the door of the little flat. Again he had to use the key for her.

"I'll wait here while you put your lights on," he said. "Lights are great comforters."

She went inside, and suddenly he heard an exclamation of surprise. Without waiting for an invitation he followed her in. She was in a small sitting-room and was staring helplessly from side to side, as well she might, because the room had evidently been ransacked. The floor was covered with a litter of papers which had evidently been thrown from a small pigeon-hole desk against the wall. The drawers were open and articles of attire were scattered about; pictures were hanging awry as though somebody had been searching behind them.

They looked at each other in silence.

"Somebody's been here," said Tom unnecessarily, then stooped to pick something from the floor. It was a small brass button, bearing on its face an engraved design.

Tom Camberley turned it over and over in his hand.

"This crest seems familiar," he said, and the girl took the button from his hand.

She looked from the button to her employer.

"It is the crest of the Ranee of Butilata," she said.

III
To Dissolve a Partnership

Dora was early at the office the next morning, but there was one before her, a slim, pretty girl of twenty-six, who looked up under her level black eyebrows as Tom Camberley's secretary came into the office. She noted the girl's tired eyes and white face, but made no comment until she had hung up her coat and hat, then, waiting until Dora was seated at her desk, she lit a cigarette and swung round in her swivel chair.

If Dora saw the movement she took no notice. Martin Covent's confidential stenographer could not by any stretch of imagination be described as her friend. At the same time, she always felt that Grace Drew was not ill-disposed towards her, and had she been in a less perturbed frame of mind, she would have responded more quickly to this unaccustomed action on the part of her fellow worker.

"You went to the Ranee of Butilata's last night," said Grace quietly, and Dora looked round startled.

"Yes," she confessed, "I did. How do you know?"

Miss Drew laughed, a quiet little laugh that might have meant anything or nothing.

"She's been through on the 'phone this morning apologizing for her rudeness to you. Was she very rude, by the way?"

Briefly the girl related what had happened to her on the previous night, and Grace Drew listened with interest.

"She's a queer woman," she said, when the other had finished. "A little mad, I think."

"Have you ever seen her?" asked Dora with interest.

Miss Drew shook her head.

"She is usually veiled or else speaks to me through a curtain," she said. "Mr. Martin thinks that there is some deformity of face."

Dora nodded.

"It was dreadful, wasn't it?" she said.

"What was dreadful?" asked Miss Drew, puffing out a cloud of smoke and watching its flight ceilingward.

"She was an English girl," said Dora, "and was trapped into a marriage with an Indian."

"Who told you that?" asked Miss Drew quickly, and Dora laughed.

"I don't know it for certain," she said. "I do know she married the Indian, and somehow I have a feeling that she was trapped."

"I don't know that I should be sorry for her," said Miss Drew, after a pause; "she has plenty of money."

"Money is not the only thing," said Dora quietly. "I think you've got rather a wrong view of things, Grace."

"Maybe I have," said the other, turning to her work. "Anyway, you'll have to explain to Mr. Covent why you went to Newbury last night. I shall have to tell him because it was a message to him."

Dora shrugged her shoulders.

"I don't know that I shall tell him anything," she said. "I simply went . . ." she hesitated, "on instructions."

"On instructions from Mr. Camberley, I presume?" said Grace, without raising her eyes.

The girl made no reply.

Miss Drew opened a little ledger on her desk and ran through the pages with deft touch. It impressed Dora that she was doing this more or less mechanically and that her object was to gain time.

"The Ranee is coming up today," she said.

"To the office?"

Miss Drew nodded.

"She generally comes up once a month," she said. "Oh no, she never comes actually into the office, but poor I have to go out and interview her in her car. Would you like to meet her?"

Dora shuddered.

"No, thank you," she said promptly, and Grace Drew laughed.

Tom Camberley and his partner arrived at the office almost simultaneously, and Tom went straight to his room with no more than a brief nod to his secretary. Through the glass partition she saw him come out again after a few minutes and go into his partner's room. Grace Drew was also watching, it seemed, for a little smile was playing about the corner of her mouth.

"I don't think there will be any need for me to make my report," she said, without stopping her work, and her surmise was justified.

Tom Camberley walked into Martin's room and closed the door behind him.

"Hello," said Covent, "what's the trouble?"

Tom drew up a chair to the big desk and sat down.

"Martin," he said, "I'm going to be perfectly frank with you."

"That's a failing of yours," replied the other, with a suggestion of sarcasm.

"Last night," Tom went on, ignoring the interruption, "I was worried about this Rumanian oil deal of yours and particularly in reference to your scheme for applying clients' money."

"Are we going to have that all over again?" demanded Martin Covent wearily.

"Wait," said the other, "I haven't finished. I wasn't quite satisfied that you were playing the game with the Ranee of Butilata and I sent Miss Mead to Newbury——"

"The devil you did!" said Martin, flushing angrily. "That's a pretty low game to play, Camberley!"

"If you come to a question of ethics," said Tom, "I think the balance of righteousness is on my side. I tell you I sent Miss Mead to Newbury to interview the Ranee, and she was most disgracefully treated."

Martin was on his feet, red and lowering.

"I don't care a damn what happened to Miss Mead," he said. "What I want to know is what do you mean by sending a servant of the firm to spy on me and give me away? You must have taken the girl Mead into your confidence, or she would not have known what enquiries to make. The most disgraceful thing I've ever heard!"

"I dare say you'll hear worse," replied Tom coolly. "But that also is beside the question. I want to see the Ranee's account."

Neither man heard the gentle tap at the door, nor saw it open to admit Grace Drew.

"You want to see the Ranee's account, do you?" snarled Martin. "Well, it's open to you any time you want. And I guess you'd better see all the accounts, Camberley, because I'm not going to carry on this business on the present basis much longer."

"In other words, you would like to dissolve the partnership?" said Tom quietly.

"I should," was the emphatic reply, and Tom nodded.

"Very well then," he said. "We can't do much better than call in a chartered accountant to straighten things out and see where we stand. I am not going to be a party to these queer business methods of yours."

"What do you mean by queer business methods?"

"You told me yesterday," said Tom, "that the firm was built up on the suffering you brought to an innocent girl. You boasted of the fact that the firm of Covent Brothers took up slavery as a side-line."

"Innocent!" laughed the other harshly. "A chorus girl!"

"So far as you and I know, that girl was as straight and as pure as any," said Tom sternly, "but if she were the worst woman in the world I should still regard the transaction as beastly."

"Remember that you are talking about my father," stormed Martin.

"I am talking about the firm of Covent Brothers," said Tom Camberley, "and I repeat that you have done enough harm to this unfortunate woman without risking her money in your wildcat schemes."

Martin Covent was pacing the room in a fury, and now he turned suddenly and for the first time saw Miss Drew standing by the door. There were few secrets which he did not share with this girl, and possibly her presence was an incentive to his fury.

"I tell you, Camberley," he said, "that you have gone far enough. This woman—this Ranee—was business. I don't care a curse whether she was

happy or unhappy, she saved the firm from going to pot. And I tell you too that if the same opportunity occurred to me as occurred to my father, and I could save the firm by sacrificing a thousand chorus girls, I should do so."

Tom Camberley shrugged his shoulders, and amusement and disgust were blended in his face.

"That is your code, Covent," he said, "but it is not mine, and the sooner you bring in your chartered accountants the better."

Turning, he left the room. There was a silence which the girl broke.

"I don't think so," she said.

"Don't think what?" asked Covent, in a surprisingly mild tone.

"I don't think we'll call in the chartered accountants," said the girl coolly, and helped herself to a cigarette from the open silver box.

He stared gloomily through the window and followed the girl's example, lighting his cigarette from the glowing end of hers.

"If this had only happened in three months' time," he said, "when Rumanian Oils——"

She laughed.

"Rumanian Oils will be bound to get you out of your trouble, Martin," she said.

He sat at his desk, looking up at her from under his lowered brows.

"You know a great deal about the business of this firm," he said.

"I know enough to make it extremely unpleasant for you if you do not keep your promise to me," said the girl. "I know that you have been raiding your clients' accounts, and that the last person in the world you want to see in this office is a representative from a firm of chartered accountants."

"The firm is solvent," he growled.

She nodded.

"It may be solvent, and yet it would be very awkward if the accounts were examined."

She puffed a ring of smoke into the air, a trick of hers, and then asked:

"Why not offer Mr. Camberley a lump sum to get out?"

"What good would that do?" he asked.

"It would save an examination of the accounts," she repeated patiently, "and I rather fancy Mr. Camberley would accept if the sum were big enough. At any rate, you cannot push him off until the half-yearly audit."

"That's an idea," he said thoughtfully. "If the worst came to the worst, I know a pretty little villa in an Argentine town and a pretty little girl——" He reached out his hand for hers and caught it, but she made no response.

"I think there's an idea in what you say," he went on. "At any rate, I'll see Camberley and try to get him out for a fixed sum—I can raise the money."

"I wonder," said the girl.

"You wonder what?" he asked quickly.

"Oh, I wasn't thinking about the money, but I was wondering whether you meant what you said, that you would sacrifice any woman for the firm's interest?"

"Any woman but you, darling," he said and, rising, kissed her. "Now be a good girl and help me all you can. Someday you shall be Mrs. Covent, and who knows, Lady Covent?"

"Someday," she repeated.

IV
The Hand at the Window

Tom Camberley went back to his office and rang for Dora Mead.

"I'm leaving the firm," he said.

"Have you quarrelled?" she asked anxiously.

"Yes, we've quarrelled all right," said Tom grimly.

"Did he say anything about——?"

He shook his head.

"No, I didn't go very deeply into the question of your unfortunate adventure at Newbury," he said, "and I am as much in the dark today as I was last night. Why on earth did the Ranee treat you so badly?"

He followed the new train of thought musingly.

"I've been wondering too," said the girl. "I was telling Grace Drew and she said that the Ranee was a little mad."

Tom nodded.

"There's something in that, but it isn't a nice thought that the firm has a lunatic for a client."

He laughed.

"However, I shan't be a member of the firm much longer," he said.

He dictated some letters, but he was not in a good mood for business, and the rest of the morning was idled away in speculation. Once he walked to the window and, looking down into the busy street, saw a car drawn up before the main door. It was a beautiful car, and from the angle at which he surveyed it, he saw that the windows were heavily curtained. He was wondering who the owner was when Dora came quickly into the office.

"The Ranee is here," she said. "I wonder if she has come to complain——"

"The Ranee," he repeated quickly, "I should like to see that lady."

He put on his hat, walked out of his office and down the broad stairs to the main entrance. As he reached the pavement the car was moving away. Miss Drew, bare-headed, was nodding her farewell to the occupant. Tom had a glimpse of a slight figure in black behind the curtain, and then a hand came out to pull up the window. It was a curious hand, and Tom looking at it, gasped.

He turned to Miss Drew.

"That was the Ranee, Mr. Camberley. Have you ever seen her?" said the girl pleasantly.

"The Ranee, eh?" said Tom. "No, I have never seen her. I thought she was a young woman?"

"I think she is," said Miss Drew. "She is rather a trying woman. But what makes you think she is not young?"

"I saw her hand," said Tom, "and if that was the hand of a young Englishwoman then I am a Dutchman."

The girl raised her eyebrows.

"I've never noticed her hands," she said. "What was curious about it?"

Tom did not reply immediately.

"Have you ever seen a native's fingernails?" he asked.

"I don't remember," said the girl.

"Well, have a good look at the next native's you see. You will find a blue half-moon on each nail, and there was a blue half-moon on the nails of that hand that came to the window. I know that the girl who married the Rajah of Butilata has lived in India for some years, but I'll swear that she has not lived there long enough to display that characteristic of the native."

He left the girl standing in the street looking after the disappearing car.

Many things happened in the next six hours to make the day an eventful one for Tom Camberley. He received from his partner a formal offer of a very handsome sum on condition that the partnership was terminated then and there. At first he was for refusing this, and then, acting on impulse, he took a sheet of paper, wrote an acceptance and sent it by hand to Martin Covent's office. He was impatient to be done with the business. There was something unwholesome in it all. A formal audit of the books would take weeks, and those would be weeks charged with impatience and annoyance. And the sum was a large one, larger, in fact, than he expected to get as his share. He walked into Dora's office and found her alone.

"Miss Mead," he said, "I'm going to make a suggestion to you and I wonder if you'll be offended."

She laughed up at him.

"I shall be very much offended if you ask me to go to Newbury again," she said.

"Nothing so interesting as that," said he. "I was going to suggest that you come and dine with me tonight," and then at her quick glance of distrust (or was it merely embarrassment?) he added quickly, "I should hate you to bring a chaperone, but if you like you can. I want to tell you something of what has happened today. I am leaving the firm."

"Leaving the firm?" she said in such frank dismay that a pleasant little glow went through him. "Oh no, Mr. Camberley, you don't mean that!"

"I'll tell you all about it. Will you dine with me?"

She nodded.

They dined modestly and well at the Trocadero, and Tom told all that had happened that day.

"Curiously enough," he said, "the dissolution of our partnership is less interesting to me than my discovery this morning."

"Your discovery?"

He nodded.

"You remember I went down to the street intending to have a word with the Ranee of Butilata. The car was just moving off as I arrived, and I could only catch a glimpse of the lady inside. But just as the window came abreast of me I saw a hand come out to grip the strap which raised the window. And it was not the hand of a refined Englishwoman or even of a woman who was not refined."

"What do you mean?" asked the girl.

"It was the hand of a native," said Tom emphatically, "and I should say a native of between forty and fifty. The hands were gnarled and veined, and very distinctly I saw upon the fingernails the little blue half-moon which betrays the Easterner."

"But I thought the Ranee was——"

"An English girl?" nodded Tom. "Yes. I thought so too. Now I've got an idea that there's some queer work going on and that the so-called Ranee of Butilata is not the Ranee at all."

"What is your theory?" she asked curiously.

"My theory," said Tom, "is that the Ranee of Butilata is not in England. She is probably dead. Somebody is impersonating her for his or her own purpose. This afternoon I got her account and it is a curious one. She arrived in England two years ago and opened an account with us for six thousand pounds. I have very carefully checked the in-coming and out-going money, and it is clear to me that that six thousand pounds was expended on the house at Newbury and its furnishing. In fact, the lady only had a balance of a few pounds when, after the account had been opened some six months, the second payment was made to her credit. Since then, however, she has been receiving money from India pretty regularly, and has now a very respectable balance."

"But it's impossible that she can be anything but English," said Dora, shaking her head. "Miss Drew has often told me she has spoken to her and that her English is perfect."

"But she has never seen her face?"

"No," said the girl, after a moment's thought. "I believe the Ranee is always veiled."

"You are sure she always spoke good English," insisted Tom with a puzzled frown. "I wish I could speak to Miss Drew."

"Why not call on her?" asked the girl. "She has a little flat in Southampton Street."

Tom looked at his watch.

"Nine o'clock," he said. "I doubt whether she would be home."

"She always spends her evenings at home," said Dora. "She has often told me how dull she found time in London. I think she is studying accountancy in her spare time."

Tom hesitated.

"Do you know the address?"

"Yes," said the girl. "Kings Croft Mansions, number one hundred and twenty-three."

"We'll go," said Tom, and called the waiter.

They took a taxi to Kings Croft Mansions and found that they were a big block of very small flats obviously occupied by professional people. No. 123 was on the fifth floor, but happily there was a lift. There were, in fact, two lifts, as the lift-man explained when they asked if Miss Drew was in.

"I don't know, sir," he replied. "Sometimes she comes up this way and sometimes through the other entrance, and it's very difficult to know whether she is in or out. She hasn't been up this way for a long time."

They rang the bell at 123 and there was no response. Tom knocked, but there was no reply. Accidently he pushed the flap of the letter-box and uttered an exclamation.

"Why, the box is full of letters!" he said. "She has either a big correspondence or else she hasn't been here for days."

The mat beneath his feet felt uneven and he pulled it up. There were several newspapers all the same, but of different dates, and he took them out.

"Five days' newspapers," he said thoughtfully; "that's queer."

He went along the passage to the other lift.

"No, sir," said the liftman, "I haven't seen Miss Drew for several days. She hasn't been home, and sometimes she's away for weeks at a time. In fact, sir," he said, "Miss Drew very seldom stays here."

Then, realizing that he was betraying the confidence of one of the tenants of the house, he added hastily: "She's got a little cottage down in Kent, sir, and I suppose she spends her time there in the pleasant weather."

Tom parted from the girl and went home that night more puzzled than ever.

The night for him was a sleepless one. He was up at five in the morning working in his study, and at seven o'clock was in the street. The mystery of Miss Drew was almost as great as the mystery of the Ranee of Butilata. The solution baffled him, and he had thought of a dozen without finding one which was convincing. His feet strayed in the direction of Southampton Street, and he was within sight of the building when a mud-stained motor-car passed him like a flash and pulled up before the flats. The door opened and a girl jumped out. There was no need to ask who she was. It was Grace Drew. She wore a long black travelling cloak and her face was veiled, but he knew her.

She turned to the driver of the car and said something. Without another word the car moved on.

"Excuse me."

Grace Drew was in the hall when Camberley's hand fell on her arm. She turned with a little cry.

"Mr. Camberley," she stammered.

"I'm sorry to bother you at this hour of the morning," said Tom good-humouredly, "but I called to see you last night."

"I wasn't in, of course," she said hurriedly.

"I've got a little cottage down in Kent. One of my friends there was sending this car up to town and suggested that I should use it."

"You're a lucky girl to have such friends," said Tom.

He could see through the veil that the girl's face was white.

"Perhaps I'd better postpone my enquiries," he said, "until later in the day."

"Thank you," she replied.

He was turning away, lifting his hat, when she came after him.

"Mr. Camberley," she said, "I've no doubt you think it is very extraordinary that I should drive to this place in a motor-car."

She spoke quickly, and he could sense her agitation.

"I suppose you think also that this dress"—she threw aside the beautiful cloak she was wearing and revealed a costume which even to his inexperienced eyes must have cost more than a month's salary—"and all that sort of thing. But perhaps you know . . . I wanted to keep it a secret . . . Mr. Covent and I are going to be married."

"I'm awfully glad," said Tom awkwardly, and felt a fool. Though he had stumbled upon an *affaire* of his partner and the mystery, so far as Miss Drew was concerned, was a mystery no more.

"You won't say a word, will you—not for a day or two," she said.

"I will not say a word even in a year or two," smiled Tom and held out his hand. "I congratulate you, or shall I say I congratulate Covent."

He heard her laugh—a queer little laugh, he thought.

"Wait and see," she said mockingly, and ran up the stairs toward the lift.

V

Martin Goes Away

He had promised secrecy, but there was one person that he had to tell, and that for an excellent reason. If he had felt embarrassed at the interview in the morning, he felt more embarrassed that afternoon as he strolled with Dora Mead through Green Park. It was a glorious sunny Saturday and the park was filled with people, but for all he knew or saw there was only one other but himself, and that was the flushed girl who walked by his side.

"You see," he was saying, "we have an excellent precedent. I am going to start another business. Covent has been very prompt and sent me his cheque today and I have finished with the firm—and I want somebody with me, to work with me, somebody who will put my interests first."

He felt he was growing incoherent, and the girl, who was surprisingly cool for all the fluttering at her heart, nodded gravely.

"So you see, dear," said Tom more awkwardly than ever, "the least you can do is to marry me right away."

"Isn't this," she faltered, "a little quick?"

"Sudden is the word you wanted," he murmured, and they both laughed.

If the next few days were dream days for the two people who had lately been members of the firm of Covent Brothers, they were hectic days for Martin Covent. Something had happened to the market. A rumour of trouble in Persia had changed the government in Rumania, shares had wobbled and collapsed, and even gilded securities had lost some of their auriferous splendour.

One morning Martin Covent went the round of his banks and methodically and carefully collected large sums of money, and these had been changed in an American bank in Lombard Street into even more realizable security. In the afternoon he called Miss Drew into his private office and locked the door.

"Grace, my dear," he said flippantly, though his voice shook, "you may pack your bag and get ready for a quick move to Italy."

"What has happened?" she asked.

"I am catching the Italian mail from Genoa to Valparaiso. All the passports are in order——"

"So it has come to that, has it?" she asked, biting her lips thoughtfully.

"It has come to that," he repeated.

"And we are to be married—when?" she asked.

He shrugged his shoulders.

"My dear girl, we shall have to postpone the marriage for a little while, there is no time now."

"You expect me to go with you—unmarried?" she asked.

He took her by the shoulders and smiled down into her face.

"Can't you trust me?" he asked.

"Oh yes, I can trust you," she replied, and there was no tremor in her voice. "What train do we catch?"

"The train leaving Waterloo and connecting with the Havre boat," said he. "Will you meet me on the platform at nine?"

She nodded.

"What of your clients?" she said.

He laughed.

"I'm afraid we'll have to take liberties with their accounts. The unfortunate Ranee of Butilata is going to suffer another injustice at the hands of the firm," he chuckled.

"But suppose it is found out that you have bolted?" said the girl.

"How can it be? It is Friday today. I am never at the office on Saturday. By Sunday I shall be on the boat, and it will be difficult for even the most skilful firm of accountants to discover that the firm has gone bust, for a week. No, my dear, I've thought it out very carefully. You will meet me tonight at nine o'clock?"

She nodded and went back to her work, as though the firm of Covent Brothers still stood high in the stable traditions of the City.

It was all so very simple. The plans went so smoothly that it was a very high-spirited Martin Covent who stepped into the boat-train as it was moving and sat down by the girl's side. They were the only occupants of the compartment.

"Well, darling," he said exuberantly, "we're off at last. You're looking pale."

"Am I?" she said indifferently. "If I am, is it extraordinary?"

He laughed and took out of his inside pocket a bulky black leather portfolio.

"Feel the weight of that," he said, putting it into her hand. "There's happiness and comfort for all the days of our lives, Grace."

She took the portfolio and put it down between them.

"And a great deal of unhappiness for other people," she said. "What about the Ranee of Butilata. She will be ruined."

"That doesn't worry me a great deal," smiled the man. "People of that kind can always get money."

She took a little silver cigarette-case from her bag, opened it, and chose a cigarette.

"Give me one," he asked, and she obeyed. She struck a match and held it for him, then lit her own, and slipping away from the arm which sought to hold her, she took a place facing him on the opposite seat.

"Now you're to be good for a little while," she said. "You've got to keep your head clear."

He puffed away at the cigarette and she watched him.

"After all," he said, "the firm is fairly solvent. We have a lot of outstanding debts, and I suppose they'll call in Tom Camberley to straighten out the mess. I'm only taking my own money."

"That's a comforting way of looking at it," said the girl. "It seems to me that you've taken some of your customers' money too."

"And that doesn't worry me, either. Now, my dear, the object of life is to find as much happiness as one can and——"

He took the cigarette out of his mouth and looked at it.

"What weird stuff you smoke, Grace," he said.

"Get up!" Her voice was sharp and peremptory, and in his surprise he attempted to obey her, but his legs would not support him and it seemed that no muscle of his body was under control.

"What the devil is this?" he asked stupidly.

"Dracena," she said coolly. "You have never heard of Dracena. That is because you have never been to India."

"Dracena?" he repeated.

"It is a very simple drug. It paralyses the muscles and renders its victim helpless. In a quarter of an hour you will sink into a condition of insensibility." She spoke in such a matter-of-fact tone that he could hardly grasp the import of her words.

"This train will stop at a little wayside station," she went on. "You would not think it was possible to stop a boat express, but I have fixed it. One of my servants, the one who used to masquerade as the Ranee of Butilata, has arranged to board the train at that station and I have arranged to get out. My car will be waiting, and I hope to be back at Newbury in the early hours of the morning."

"At Newbury?" he gasped. "Then you— you——"

"I am the Ranee of Butilata," said the girl. "I am the woman your father sold into captivity, into a life which by every standard and by every test was hell! I was sold to a drunkard and a brute, and an Indian at that, to save the firm of Covent Brothers, and when my husband died I had to steal the money to bring me to England.

"I did not waste my time as the wife of Butilata," she went on quietly, but with a hardness in her voice which brought a twinge of terror to the paralysed man. "I learnt book-keeping because I thought one day I would come back to the firm of Covent Brothers and worm my way into its confidences. Butilata made no secret of the part your people played."

"You are the Ranee of Butilata! You lived a double life!" he said slowly, as though in order that he should hear and understand.

"I lived a double life," she said. "By day I was your clerk. In the evening I was the Ranee of Butilata, who gave parties to the countryside. My car was always waiting round the corner for me and brought me back the next morning. Once I was nearly betrayed. Dora Mead came to Newbury unexpectedly and would have recognized me, but I switched out the lights and had her removed from the house.

"By day I slaved for you for three pounds a week, using my position to rob your firm systematically and consistently. Yes, I robbed you," she went on. "All the thousands standing to the credit of my account were transferred from the profits of the firm. I came into your business to ruin you," she said, "and to ruin Tom Camberley too, but he was a decent man. And because he expressed his pity for the poor girl who had been sent out to Butilata, I persuaded you to buy him out and save his money from the wreck."

"You—you——!" hissed Covent. He made an attempt to lurch forward, but fell backward, and the girl, rising to her feet, lowered him to the seat. She covered him with a travelling rug, and presently the train began to slow down.

It was a dark and rainy night, and when the train came to a stop at the little platform she slipped out, closing the door behind her and disappeared into the gloom.

They found Martin Covent at Southampton and brought him back to town to face his outraged clients and the inexorable vengeance of the law. But the stout black wallet that carried the proceeds of his robbery was never recovered, and the Ranee of Butilata vanished as though the earth had opened and swallowed her.

SHE KNEW WHAT TO DO

Joseph Shearing

MOST OF THE BOOKS WRITTEN under Gabrielle Margaret Vere Long's (1885–1952) Joseph Shearing pseudonym are historical novels, usually based on real-life criminal cases. While, the other nom de plumes of the prolific author have faded into obscurity, the Marjorie Bowen and Shearing names endure.

Among Long's best-known Shearing crime novels are *Moss Rose* (1934), the basis for the 1947 film of the same name; *Blanche Fury*, released in 1948; and the psychological thriller *So Evil My Love* (1947), the basis for the 1948 film of the same name starring Ann Todd, Ray Milland, and Geraldine Fitzgerald.

"She Knew What to Do" was originally published in *Orange Blossoms* (London, Heinemann, 1938).

She Knew What to Do

JOSEPH SHEARING

MISS MILLY folded up the letter with a happy smile on her broad, red face that was slightly comic even when she was serious. Harry was getting married at last, and to the right girl; since he had been in petticoats, Miss Milly had been working for that match, Lily Drew had everything, besides, in the old phrase, "the estates marched"; Mereholme, that Miss Milly had ruled and cherished since Harry, a squealing orphan baby, was put into her charge, would be joined to Cluttersmere, and her beloved nephew would own what he might term "half the county."

The stout woman looked at the two ugly, stiff photographs that hung above her desk, an elder Harry, her brother, and Mary, his wife, he killed in the hunting-field, she dead of shock a few days later: "My dears," said Miss Milly, her round, hard eyes moist for once. "I've done it— it's not been so easy, but I've done it—he's safe."

She put the letter in her key basket; he was coming home tonight or tomorrow after what he termed "a champagne party" at Sir Edward Dreen's town house, where the engagement had been announced; yes, the wilful, weak young man, who was so charming and so unstable, was safe now, Lily, silver fair and tiny, had the makings of a possessive shrew as Miss Milly, who could read her own sex perfectly, had marked with deep satisfaction.

Perhaps Harry had noticed it, too, and that was why he had avoided all the efforts of Miss Milly and the Drews to entice him into this suitable match, fooling about with this girl and that, getting into scrapes from which his aunt had to extricate him with tact and good round sums of money.

"Still, I did it." She looked at herself in the old mirror that had reflected so many of her ancestors, the Pentelows of Mereholme, and smiled grimly at her weather-beaten face with the snub nose, cheeks flecked with red veins and taut lips faintly tinged with a smooth purple glaze; she wore a grey poplin bodice, fastened tightly with round buttons over her massive bosom, a crimped white frill close under her flat jowl; she picked up a black straw hat with an artificial parrot pinned on a bunch of dry grass; her hats were her one vanity.

She lived by routine and she would not allow this good news to excite her; she was due to visit Mrs. Webster, who lived beyond the woods, the waterfall, a pleasant autumn drive; Miss Milly went to see this pampered invalid once a fortnight with dainties and to read the Bible; one of her special prides was that never, since she had taken on the responsibility of the large estate, had she failed in the smallest duty; the universal admiration and respect that surrounded her always, found expression in a crisis in the murmured—"Miss Milly will know what to do."

She was getting old, sixty years made her a little slower and a little stiffer, but she was still more vigorous than most women and almost indecently healthy; it often made Harry, whose constitution had hardly been able to stand the strain he had put upon it, in what Miss Milly called "the pursuit of pleasure," peevish to see the steady strength, the cool nerves his aunt showed on every kind of occasion.

She touched the bell and drew on her big leather gloves, she drove the gig herself and got the most out of the spanking grey cob; with perfect smoothness the routine was followed, one of the parlour-maids, Jenkins, of the sandy hair and steel-rimmed glasses, brought in the basket of jams, jellies and soups; Miss Milly placed the Bible in the corner, covered it with a napkin, inspected the fare, and said it might be taken to the gig; she supposed the reason for her high good humour, Harry's engagement, must be announced formally to the whole gathered household; she was ready to start, when Jenkins said, hesitant, as one who breaks a rule:

"A young woman wants to see you, madam. I tried to send her away, but she was very insistent—it is Dora Greene, who works at the Rectory."

"She is spoilt. Her mother was a fool to let her go to that place in London. . . ."

"I think she is a good girl, madam." But the women exchanged a glance of eternal feminine suspicion.

"I really haven't time to see her now. . . ." Miss Milly checked herself; the door had been timidly pushed open and Dora Greene nervously edged herself into the stately, stuffy room. "You should have waited," said the great lady sternly. "I'm afraid you've lost all your manners, Dora."

"I *had* to see you, madam," said the girl, flushing furiously; with a side look at the bleak disapproval of Jenkins, she added feebly: "It is about a new place for my brother, madam." This was so obvious a lie that Miss Milly sent away the parlour-maid, sat down beside her desk with the basket and questioned the girl, who stood drooping, a charming figure in a small black and white check shawl and a bonnet trimmed with grey ribbons; Dora had bright golden eyes, a pure white skin and hair flushed through with brightness; she had been prettier, but she looked heavy, flushed, and her almost perfect mouth was ragged.

"It's about Harry, madam."

Miss Milly stiffened, she turned an ugly colour, but not with dismay; she had handled these situations before; while the girl stammered out an agonised tale, dull to others—to her a tragedy, Miss Milly was making plans. Money, Dora sent away, Harry not even to be bothered, the Drews, who were straightlaced, never to know; before the girl had finished she asked sharply with contempt:

"Why did you come to me? No one is responsible, you know, for your disgraceful behaviour."

"Everyone says—Miss Milly knows what to do—I think . . . I was in such trouble. . . ."

"You don't deserve any pity. But I'll give you another chance. I'll send you to a home I know of and—when it is all over, I'll find you another place. . . ."

She half rose, thinking the matter settled, but Dora was suddenly quite changed; she lost her timid, half-imbecile manner and said clearly:

"But Mr. Harry promised to marry me. I've got the letters. I'm not going into the workhouse— I'm to have *this*. That's why I came to you. You'd understand—justice, madam. I remembered all you taught us in the Sunday School."

Miss Milly felt old and beaten; rage and terror drained her forces, she sank into the chair again and the parrot fluttered as if about to fly away from her shaking head: "Letters," she repeated, "letters."

"Yes, madam, all his promises, calling me his wife again and again. I could bring a case for breach, but I don't want to—it's ugly and I can't believe he's really left me, but I've not heard for a month, he won't answer letters and they are saying in the village that he'll marry Miss Drew—so I came to you."

Dora sat down at the end of this hurried speech, and this liberty sent the outraged blood pounding in Miss Milly's cheeks; she kept her control, and glancing at the two staring photographs, she said:

"Not such a fool, eh, Dora?"

"I don't know, Miss Milly, I'm sure. But you see that Mr. Harry couldn't marry anyone but me, don't you?" She spoke with a mingled innocence and cunning absolutely maddening to Miss Milly, who forced a frightful smile and asked:

"Does anyone know of this?"

Dora swore that she had been faithful to the beautiful secret; she wouldn't even have told Miss Milly now—but for his silence and the trouble. Miss Milly sighed:

"I'm very sorry, Dora." She spoke softly, soothingly. "Of course you are right. Harry must marry you—we learnt all about right and wrong in the Bible classes, didn't we? Of course he loves you. I dare say he can explain why he is silent. Now will you let me manage this for you?"

Dora sparkled into happiness; she felt as much at ease as if an angel from heaven had taken charge of her affairs.

"Of course, Miss Milly! Oh, I thought you'd do so, anyway! But true love counts, don't it?" the girl cried with relief into the corner of her shawl.

"Have you got the letters, dear?"

"Here—I brought them to prove to you . . ." A thin packet was handed over—as easily as that! The creature was, after all, half-imbecile.

"I will keep them," said Miss Milly, "they are safer with me." As faint terror and distrust glittered in the golden eyes, she added in a tone of immense authority: "I have a Bible here, Dora, I will swear on it to respect your confidence"—she put her hand on the book among the jam-pots—"to help you all I can. You were right to trust me, I do know what to do. Mr. Harry is coming home tonight or tomorrow. I expect he will want to see you—where do you generally meet?"

"By the waterfall, beyond Merton Wood—but I'd like to come *here* openly," again the flash of obstinate courage showed in the simple face.

"Of course, so you shall. But if he asks you to go there once more, go. He will want to explain so much quietly. *I* shall have had a talk with him. He can bring you here afterwards and I will return your letters; now—go."

Mechanically responsive to authority, the girl left the room, murmuring gratitude; Jenkins came fidgeting in, angry about this unprecedented interruption in routine—was the gig still to wait?

"No, it is too late. Mr. Harry may be home tonight. I'll go tomorrow. Dora Greene *did* come about her brother, Jenkins, he is clever with horses and she wants to get him into Lord King's stables."

Miss Milly read the letters that were dull, foolish and utterly damaging to the honour of the writer—it was simple to burn them, and she knew that some women would have left it at that, brazening out her word against that of a village servant; but she was afraid of Harry's weakness, he might so easily break down, of the girl's flashes of strength, of the dreadful scandal, the story even without the letters would be . . . She stopped her thoughts and made her preparations.

Harry came home and Miss Milly spent a happy evening talking over the arrangements for the wedding; neither mentioned Dora Greene. The next day was busy, and no one would have guessed from Miss Milly's energy that she had not slept at all the night before; at five o'clock Jenkins brought up the basket for Mrs. Webster, and the Bible was again placed in the clean napkin; the old woman had her own Holy Book, but the print was too small. The gig was ready, Mottle was in good fettle and Miss Milly, a good woman on a good errand, bowled along the lonely lane round the golden wood; a small bridge spanned the curdling stream into which finally fell the water from Merton falls, and there Miss Milly descended from the gig and tied the reins to a larch-tree and proceeded to climb up through the yellow woods, over the newly fallen leaves; she wore a plaid jacket, a black skirt and the hat with the parrot; the wood was dark, dank and quiet, toadstools green on rotting, fallen branches, brambles, with fox red stems and purple fruit trailed above the beech mast.

"Supposing," thought Miss Milly, "it goes wrong?"

She climbed up until she reached the summit of the wooded hill and then walked through the trees until the rocky ground broke away and the water poured into the gorge below. Dora Greene was standing there in spangled light and shade; Miss Milly drew a deep breath—it had not gone wrong—"But I shall need a good rest."

The girl drew back, puzzled, startled—

"You, madam!"

"You didn't expect me?"

"Oh no, Mr. Harry wrote—asking me to come, I had the letter by the post this morning late." Dora peered, uneasily, and showed a piece of cheap paper on which a few lines were written in an awkward hand. "He says not to mind the pencil scrawl, he's hurt his finger."

"I came instead." Miss Milly sat on a stone and took off her gloves. "We must have a talk, this is a good place. Does anyone know you're here?"

"No."

"No one knows I'm here, either, so it will be just you and me."

"What do you mean, madam? You look so funny. I trusted you."

"Quite rightly. I do know what to do. Aren't you ever frightened meeting Mr. Harry here, above the falls? It is a dizzy height, a nasty drop. . . ."

"I never thought of it," the gleam of obstinate strength showed in the pretty, fevered face. "You're not making game of me, are you, Miss Milly?"

"Oh dear no! What a queer note for Harry to have written! And he could not have come, for he's gone to the station to meet the Drews." The old woman tore the note, screwed the bits together and threw them down the waterfall; Dora instinctively peered after it, and Miss Milly snatched her check shawl off her shoulders.

"What did you do that for, madam?"

Miss Milly had rested now; she exerted her full strength, she put her firm red hands on Dora's neck and bore her backwards over the rocky edge, instantly balancing herself by the larch-tree that overhung the first water-break; the girl's cry was lost in the roar of the falling stream that foamed, curled, and splashed from rock to rock; she fell, but not to the bottom pool; she struck a ledge and clung there pleading desperately for mercy; her bonnet had come off, her skirt was torn, blood, like a lock of red hair, lay on her forehead, her white stocks and high tight black boots showed like the legs of a doll as she struggled frantically for a foothold.

The water poured down with boom and splash, the sun struck level through the trees, birds hopped from bough to bough; Miss Milly went on her knees, carefully, and stared down the abyss.

"Fool, imbecile, insolent hussy! Do you remember the Sunday school and what you learnt of right and wrong? You're paying now for doing wrong."

She found a large smooth stone and aimed it carefully; it struck the girl's hands; she shrieked and the words "I trusted you" were born above the clatter of the water.

"Precisely," grinned Miss Milly, and cast another stone.

Dora's strength was exhausted; she was slipping fast, cold, deafened, dizzy with fright; her legs twisted grotesquely in an effort to gain a foothold, her round mouth seemed to fill all her face. Her fingers unclutched—she was gone, down to the curdling foam of the seething pool; the waters seethed and sucked round her and flowed on towards the stream.

Miss Milly rose to her feet, panting, it was a good deal of exertion for a woman of her age; the most tiresome thing she had ever done, even for Harry, but she could not rest, she must not miss that visit to Mrs. Webster, no one must know she had been near the waterfall. The spot was lonely, no one would ever connect her with the suicide of a village hussy who had got into trouble.

She returned to the gig, skirting the pool; she could see Dora, eddied into a clump of weeds and elder at the side, her silly feet in the cheap, black boots sticking up, her head down, the rushing water missing her but covering her with bubbles of foam.

With luck it would be days before she was discovered—how relieved Harry would be! He must have been secretly worried.

The sun sank, a cold wind blew suddenly out of the wood and a dark cloud shaped like a wing spread across the fading sky; Miss Milly took off her shaken hat and straightened the stuffed parrot.

THE FORGERS

Arthur B. Reeve

WHEN THE ADVENTURES of Sherlock Holmes became a monumental success, authors and publishers alike strove to find their ways into what was evidently about to become a huge market. In the United States, Arthur Benjamin Reeve (1880–1936) became the bestselling mystery writer in the country when he created Craig Kennedy, identified as "the scientific detective." The success of the stories and novels was enhanced by a series of silent film serials about a young heroine named Elaine who constantly finds herself in the clutches of villains, only to be rescued at the last moment by Kennedy.

Reeve is not much read today because the pseudoscientific methods and devices that were of great interest then are utterly outmoded today and most never had a solid technical basis in the first place. Still, he did apply Freudian technology to detection two decades before psychoanalysis gained substantial public acceptance. During World War I he was asked to help establish a spy and crime detection laboratory in Washington, DC.

Only four of Reeve's books did not involve Kennedy, one of which was *Constance Dunlap, Woman Detective* (1916), a collection of stories in which the highly intelligent and gritty protagonist becomes involved in a wide range of adventures. In "The Forgers," the first story in the book, she and her husband engage in a complex criminal plan that has unintended consequences.

"The Forgers" was first published in *Constance Dunlap, Woman Detective* (New York, Hearst's International Library Co., 1916).

The Forgers

ARTHUR B. REEVE

THERE WAS SOMETHING of the look of the hunted animal brought to bay at last in Carlton Dunlap's face as he let himself into his apartment late one night toward the close of the year.

On his breath was the lingering odor of whisky, yet in his eye and hand none of the effects. He entered quietly, although there was no apparent reason for such excessive caution. Then he locked the door with the utmost care, although there was no apparent reason for caution about that, either.

Even when he had thus barricaded himself, he paused to listen with all the elemental fear of the cave man who dreaded the footsteps of his pursuers. In the dim light of the studio apartment he looked anxiously for the figure of his wife. Constance was not there, as she had been on other nights, uneasily awaiting his return. What was the matter? His hand shook a trifle now as he turned the knob of the bedroom door and pushed it softly open.

She was asleep. He leaned over, not realizing that her every faculty was keenly alive to his presence, that she was acting a part.

"Throw something around yourself, Constance," he whispered hoarsely into her ear, as she moved with a little well-feigned start at being suddenly wakened, "and come into the studio. There is something I must tell you tonight, my dear."

"My dear!" she exclaimed bitterly, now seeming to rouse herself with an effort and pretending to put back a stray wisp of her dark hair in order to hide from him the tears that still lingered on her flushed cheeks. "You can say that, Carlton, when it has been every night the same old threadbare excuse of working at the office until midnight?"

She set her face in hard lines, but could not catch his eye.

"Carlton Dunlap," she added in a tone that rasped his very soul, "I am nobody's fool. I may not know much about bookkeeping and accounting, but I can add—and two and two, when the same man but different women compose each two, do not make four, according to my arithmetic, but three, from which,"—she finished almost hysterically the little speech she had prepared, but it seemed to fall flat before the man's curiously altered manner—"from which *I* shall subtract one."

She burst into tears.

"Listen," he urged, taking her arm gently to lead her to an easy-chair.

"No, no, no!" she cried, now thoroughly aroused, with eyes that again snapped accusation and defiance at him, "don't touch me. Talk to me, if you want to, but don't, don't come near me." She was now facing him, standing in the high-ceilinged "studio," as they called the room where she had kept up in a desultory manner for her own amusement the art studies which had interested her before her marriage. "What is it that you want to say? The other nights you said nothing at all. Have you at last thought up an excuse? I hope it is at least a clever one."

"Constance," he remonstrated, looking fearfully about. Instinctively she felt that her accusation was unjust. Not even that had dulled the hunted look in his face. "Perhaps—perhaps if it were that of which you suspect me, we could patch it up. I don't know. But, Constance, I—I must leave for the west on the first train in the morning." He did not pause to notice her startled look, but raced on. "I have worked every night this week trying to straighten out those accounts of mine by the first of the year and—and I can't do it. An expert begins on them in a couple of days. You must call up the office tomorrow and tell them that I am ill, tell them anything. I must get at least a day or two start before they—"

"Carlton," she interrupted, "what is the matter? What have you—"

She checked herself in surprise. He had been fumbling in his pocket and now laid down a pile of green and yellow banknotes on the table.

"I have scraped together every last cent I can spare," he continued, talking jerkily to suppress his emotion. "They cannot take those away from you, Constance. And—when I am settled—in a new life," he swallowed hard and averted his eyes further from her startled gaze, "under a new name, somewhere, if you have just a little spot in your heart that still responds to me, I—I—no, it is too much even to hope. Constance, the accounts will not come out right because I am—I am an embezzler."

He bit off the word viciously and then sank his head into his hands and bowed it to a depth that alone could express his shame.

Why did she not say something, do something? Some women would have fainted. Some would have denounced him. But she stood there and he dared not look up to read what was written in her face. He felt alone, all alone, with every man's hand against him, he who had never

in all his life felt so or had done anything to make him feel so before. He groaned as the sweat of his mental and physical agony poured coldly out on his forehead. All that he knew was that she was standing there, silent, looking him through and through, as cold as a statue. Was she the personification of justice? Was this but a foretaste of the ostracism of the world?

"When we were first married, Constance," he began sadly, "I was only a clerk for Green & Co., at two thousand a year. We talked it over. I stayed and in time became cashier at five thousand. But you know as well as I that five thousand does not meet the social obligations laid on us by our position in the circle in which we are forced to move."

His voice had become cold and hard, but he did not allow himself to be betrayed into adding, as he might well have done in justice to himself, that to her even a thousand dollars a month would have been only a beginning. It was not that she had become accustomed to so much in the station of life from which he had taken her. The plain fact was that New York had had an over-tonic effect on her.

"You were not a nagging woman, Constance," he went on in a somewhat softened tone. "In fact you have been a good wife; you have never thrown it up to me that I was unable to make good to the degree of many of our friends in purely commercial lines. All you have ever said is the truth. A banking house pays low for its brains. My God!" he cried, stiffening out in the chair and clenching his fists, "it pays low for its temptations, too."

There had been nothing in the world Carlton would not have given to make happy the woman who stood now, leaning on the table in cold silence, with averted head, regarding neither him nor the pile of greenbacks.

"Hundreds of thousands of dollars passed through my hands every week," he resumed. "That business owed me for my care of it. It was taking the best in me and in return was not paying what other businesses paid for the best in other men. When a man gets thinking that way, with a woman whom he loves as I love you—something happens."

He paused in the bitterness of his thoughts. She moved as if to speak. "No, no," he interrupted. "Hear me out first. All I asked was a chance to employ a little of the money that I saw about me—not to take it, but to employ it for a little while, a few days, perhaps only a few hours. Money breeds money. Why should I not use some of this idle money to pay me what I ought to have?

"When Mr. Green was away last summer I heard some inside news about a certain stock. So it happened that I began to juggle the accounts. It is too long a story to tell how I did it. Anybody in my position could have done it—for a time. It would not interest you anyhow. But I did it. The first venture was successful. Also the spending of the money was very successful, in its way. That was the money that took us to the fashionable hotel in Atlantic City where we met so many people. Instead of helping me, it got me in deeper.

"When the profit from this first deal was spent there was nothing to do but to repeat what I had done successfully before. I could not quit now. I tried again, a little hypothecation of some bonds. Stocks went down. I had made a bad bet and five thousand dollars was wiped out, a whole year's salary. I tried again, and wiped out five thousand more. I was at my wits' end. I have borrowed under fictitious names, used names of obscure persons as borrowers, have put up dummy security. It was possible because I controlled the audits. But it has done no good. The losses have far outbalanced the winnings and today I am in for twenty-five thousand dollars."

She was watching him now with dilating eyes as the horror of the situation was burned into her soul. He raced on, afraid to pause lest she should interrupt him.

"Mr. Green has been talked into introducing scientific management and a new system into the business by a certified public accountant, an expert in installing systems and discovering irregularities. Here I am, faced by certain exposure," he went on, pacing the floor and looking everywhere but at her face. "What should I do? Borrow? It is useless. I have no security that anyone would accept.

"There is just one thing left." He lowered his voice until it almost sank into a hoarse whisper. "I must cut loose. I have scraped together what I can and I have borrowed on my life insurance. Here on the table is all that I can spare.

"Tonight, the last night, I have worked frantically in a vain hope that something, some way would at last turn up. It has not. There is no other way out. In despair I have put this off until the last moment. But I have thought of nothing else for a week. Good God, Constance, I have reached the mental state where even intoxicants fail to intoxicate."

He dropped back again into the deep chair and sank his head again on his hands. He groaned as he thought of the agony of packing a bag and slinking for the Western express through the crowds at the railroad terminal.

Still Constance was silent. Through her mind was running the single thought that she had misjudged him. There had been no other woman in the case. As he spoke, there came flooding into her heart the sudden realization of the truth. He had done it for her.

It was a rude and bitter awakening after the past months when the increased income, with no questions asked, had made her feel that they were advancing. She passed her hands over her eyes, but there it was still, not a dream but a harsh reality. If she could only have gone back and undone it! But what was done, was done. She was amazed at herself. It was not horror of the deed that sent an icy shudder over her. It was horror of exposure.

He had done it for her. Over and over again that thought raced through her mind. She steeled herself at last to speak. She hardly knew what was in her own mind, what the conflicting, surging emotions of her own heart meant.

"And so, you are leaving me what is left, leaving me in disgrace, and you are going to do the best you can to get away safely. You want me to tell one last lie for you."

There was an unnatural hollowness in her voice which he did not understand, but which cut him to the quick. He had killed love. He was alone. He knew it. With a final effort he tried to moisten his parched lips to answer. At last, in a husky voice, he managed to say, "Yes."

But with all his power of will he could not look at her.

"Carlton Dunlap," she cried, leaning both hands for support on the table, bending over and at last forcing him to look her in the eyes, "do you know what I think of you? I think you are a damned coward. There!"

Instead of tears and recriminations, instead of the conventional "How could you do it?" instead of burning denunciation of him for ruining her life, he read something else in her face. What was it?

"Coward?" he repeated slowly. "What would you have me do—take you with me?"

She tossed her head contemptuously.

"Stay and face it?" he hazarded again.

"Is there no other way?" she asked, still leaning forward with her eyes fixed on his. "Think! Is there no way that you could avoid discovery just for a time? Carlton, you—we are cornered. Is there no desperate chance?"

He shook his head sadly.

Her eyes wandered momentarily about the studio, until they rested on an easel. On it stood a water color on which she had been working, trying to put into it some of the feeling which she would never have put into words for him. On the walls of the apartment were pen and ink sketches, scores of little things which she had done for her own amusement. She bit her lip as an idea flashed through her mind.

He shook his head again mournfully.

"Somewhere," she said slowly, "I have read that clever forgers use water colors and pen and ink like regular artists. Think—think! Is there no way that we—that I could forge a check that would give us breathing space, perhaps rescue us?"

Carlton leaned over the table toward her, fascinated. He placed both his hands on hers. They were icy, but she did not withdraw them.

For an instant they looked into each other's eyes, an instant, and then they understood. They were partners in crime, amateurs perhaps, but partners as they had been in honesty.

It was a new idea that she had suggested to him. Why should he not act on it? Why hesitate? Why stop at it? He was already an embezzler. Why not add a new crime to the list? As he looked into her eyes he felt a new strength. Together they could do it. Hers was the brain that had conceived the way out. She had the will, the compelling power to carry the thing through. He would throw himself on her intuition, her brain, her skill, her daring.

On his desk in the corner, where often until far into the night he had worked on the huge ruled sheets of paper covered with figures of the firm's accounts, he saw two goose-necked vials, one of lemon-colored liquid, the other of raspberry color. One was of tartaric acid, the other of chloride of lime. It was an ordinary ink eradicator. Near the bottles lay a rod of glass with a curious tip, an ink eraser made of finely spun glass threads which scraped away the surface of the paper more delicately than any other tool that had been devised. There were the materials for his, their rehabilitation if they were placed in his wife's deft artist fingers. Here was all the chemistry and artistry of forgery at hand.

"Yes," he answered eagerly, "there is a way, Constance. Together we can do it."

There was no time for tenderness between them now. It was cold, hard fact and they understood each other too well to stop for endearments.

Far into the night they sat up and discussed the way in which they would go about the crime. They practised with erasers and with brush and water color on the protective coloring tint on some canceled checks of his own. Carlton must get a check of a firm in town, a check that bore a genuine signature. In it they would make such trifling changes in the body as would attract no attention in passing, yet would yield a substantial sum toward wiping out Carlton's unfortunate deficit.

Late as he had worked the night before, nervous and shaky as he felt after the sleepless hours of planning their new life, Carlton was the first at the office in the morning. His hand trembled as he ran through the huge batch of mail already left at the first delivery. He paused as he came to one letter with the name "W. J. REYNOLDS CO." on it.

Here was a check in payment of a small bill, he knew. It was from a firm which habitually kept hundreds of thousands on deposit at the Gorham Bank. It fitted the case admirably. He slit open the letter. There, neatly folded, was the check:

No. 15711. Dec. 27, 191—.

THE GORHAM NATIONAL BANK

Pay to the order of. . . . . . . Green & Co. . . . . . .

Twenty-five 00/100. . . . . Dollars

$25.00/100

W. J. REYNOLDS CO.,

per CHAS. M. BROWN, Treas.

It flashed over him in a moment what to do. Twenty-five thousand would just about cover his shortage. The Reynolds firm was a big one, doing big transactions. He slipped the check into his pocket. The check might have been stolen in the mail. Why not?

The journey uptown was most excruciatingly long, in spite of the fact that he had met no one he knew either at the office or outside. At last he arrived home, to find Constance waiting anxiously.

"Did you get a check?" she asked, hardly waiting for his reply. "Let me see it. Give it to me."

The coolness with which she went about it amazed him. "It has the amount punched on it with a check punch," she observed as she ran her quick eye over it while he explained his plan. "We'll have to fill up some of those holes made by the punch."

"I know the kind they used," he answered. "I'll get one and a desk check from the Gorham. You do the artistic work, my dear. My knowledge of check punches, watermarks, and paper will furnish the rest. I'll be back directly. Don't forget to call up the office a little before the time I usually arrive there and tell them I am ill."

With her light-fingered touch she worked feverishly, partly with the liquid ink eradicator, but mostly with the spun-glass eraser. First she rubbed out the cents after the written figure "Twenty-five." Carefully with a blunt instrument she smoothed down the roughened surface of the paper so that the ink would not run in the fibers and blot. Over and over she practised writing the "Thousand" in a hand like that on the check. She already had the capital "T" in "Twenty" as a guide. During the night in practising she had found that in raising checks only seven capital letters were used—O in one, T in two, three, ten, and thousand, F in four and five, S in six and seven, E in eight, N in nine, and H in hundred.

At last even her practise satisfied her. Then with a coolness born only of desperation she wrote in the words, "Thousand 00/100." When she had done it she stopped to wonder at herself. She was amazed and perhaps a little frightened at how readily she adapted herself to the crime of forgery. She did not know that it was one of the few crimes in which women had proved themselves most proficient, though she felt her own proficiency and native ability for copying.

Again the eraser came into play to remove the cents after the figure "25." A comma and three zeros following it were inserted, followed by a new "00/100." The signature was left untouched.

Erasing the name of "Green & Co.," presented greater difficulties, but it was accomplished with as little loss of the protective coloring on the surface of the check as possible.

Then after the "Pay to the order of" she wrote in, as her husband had directed, "The Carlton Realty Co."

Next came the water color to restore the protective tint where the glass eraser and the acids had removed it. There was much delicate matching of tints and careful painting in with a fine camel's hair brush, until at last the color of those parts where there had been an erasure was apparently as good as any other part.

Of course, under the microscope there could have been seen the angry crisscrossing of the fibers of the paper due to the harsh action of the acids and the glass eraser. Still, painting the whole thing over with a little resinous liquid somewhat restored the glaze to the paper, at least sufficiently to satisfy a cursory glance of the naked eye.

There remained the difficulty of the protective punch marks. There they were, a star cut out of the check itself, a dollar sign and 25 followed by another star.

She was still admiring her handiwork, giving it here and there a light little fillip with the brush and comparing this check with some of those which had been practised on last night, to see whether she had made any improvement in her technique of forgery, when Carlton returned with the punch and the blank checks on the Gorham Bank.

From one of the blank checks he punched out a number of little stars until there was one which in watermark and scroll work corresponded precisely with that punched out in the original check.

Constance, whose fingers had long been accustomed to fine work, fitted in the little star after the *$25*, then took it out, moistened the edges ever so lightly with glue on the end of a toothpick, and pasted it back again. A hot iron completed the work of making the edges smooth and unless a rather powerful glass had been used no one could have seen the pasted-in insertion after the *$25.

Careful not to deviate the fraction of a hair's breadth from the alignment, Carlton took the punch, added three o's, and a star after the 25, making it *$25,000*. Finally the whole thing was again ironed to give it the smoothness of an original. Here at last was the completed work, the first product of their combined skill in crime:

No. 15711. Dec. 27,191—.

THE GORHAM NATIONAL BANK
Pay to the order of . . . The Carlton Realty Co.
Twenty-five Thousand 00/100. . . . . Dollars
$25,000.00/100
W. J. REYNOLDS CO.,

per CHAS. M. BROWN, Treas.

How completely people may change, even within a few hours, was well illustrated as they stood side by side and regarded their work with as much pride as if it had been the result of their honest efforts of years. They were now pen and brush crooks of the first caliber, had reduced forgery to a fine art and demonstrated what an amateur might do. For, although they did not know it, nearly half the fifteen millions or so lost by forgeries every year was the work of amateurs such as they.

The next problem was presenting the check for collection. Of course Carlton could not put it through his own bank, unless he wanted to leave a blazed trail straight to himself. Only a colossal bluff would do, and in a city where only colossal bluffs succeed it was not so impossible as might have been first imagined.

Luncheon over, they sauntered casually into a high-class office building on Broadway where there were offices to rent. The agent was duly impressed by the couple who talked of their large real estate dealings. Where he might have been thoroughly suspicious of a man and might have asked many embarrassing but perfectly proper questions, he accepted the woman without a murmur. At her suggestion he even consented to take his new tenants around to the Uptown Bank and introduce them. They made an excellent impression by a first cash deposit of the money Carlton had thrown down on the table the night before. A check for the first month's rent more than mollified the agent and talk of a big deal that was just being signed up today duly impressed the bank.

The next problem was to get the forged check certified. That, also, proved a very simple matter. Anyone can walk into a bank and get a check for $25,000 certified, while if he appears, a stranger, before the window of the paying teller to cash a check for twenty-five dollars he would almost be thrown out of the bank. Banks will certify at a glance practically any check that looks right, but they pass on the responsibility of cashing them. Thus before the close of banking hours Dunlap was able to deposit in his new bank the check certified by the Gorham.

Twenty-four hours must elapse before he could draw against the check which he had deposited. He did not propose to waste that time, so that the next day found him at Green & Co.'s, feeling much better. Really he had come prepared now to straighten out the books, knowing that in a few hours he could make good.

The first hesitation due to the newness of the game had worn off by this time. Nothing at all of an alarming nature had happened. The new month had already begun and as most firms have their accounts balanced only once a month, he had, he reasoned, nearly the entire four weeks in which to operate.

Conscience was dulled in Constance, also, and she was now busy with ink eraser, the water colors, and other paraphernalia in a wholesale raising of checks, mostly for amounts smaller than that in the first attempt.

"We are taking big chances, anyway," she urged him. "Why quit yet? A few days more and we may land something worth while."

The next day he excused himself from the office for a while and presented himself at his new bank with a sheaf of new checks which she had raised, all certified, and totaling some thousands more.

His own check for twenty-five thousand was now honored. The relief which he felt was tremendous after the weeks of grueling anxiety. At once he hurried to a broker's and placed an order for the stocks he had used on which to borrow. He could now replace everything in the safe, straighten out the books, could make everything look right to the systematizer, could blame any apparent irregularity on his old system. Even ignorance was better than dishonesty.

Constance, meanwhile, had installed herself in the little office they had hired, as stenographer and secretary. Once having embarked on the hazardous enterprise she showed no disposition to give it up yet. An office boy was hired and introduced at the bank.

The mythical realty company prospered, at least if prosperity is measured merely by the bank book. In less than a week the skilful pen and brush of Constance had secured them a balance, after straightening out Carlton's debts, that came well up to a hundred thousand dollars, mostly in small checks, some with genuine signatures and amounts altered, others complete forgeries.

As they went deeper and deeper, Constance began to feel the truth of their situation. It was she who was really at the helm in this enterprise. It had been her idea; the execution of it had been mainly her work; Carlton had furnished merely the business knowledge that she did not possess. The more she thought of it during the hours in the little office while he was at work downtown, the more uneasy did she become.

What if he should betray himself in some way? She was sure of herself. But she was almost afraid to let him go out of her sight. She felt a sinking sensation every time he mentioned any of the happenings in the banking house. Could he be trusted alone not to betray himself when the first hint of discovery of something wrong came?

It was now near the middle of the month. It would not pay to wait until the end. Some one of the many firms whose checks they had forged might have its book balanced at any time now.

From day to day small amounts in cash had already been withdrawn until they were twenty thousand dollars to the good. They planned to draw out thirty thousand now at one time. That would give them fifty thousand, roughly half of their forgeries.

The check was written and the office boy was started to the bank with it. Carlton followed him at a distance, as he had on other occasions, ready to note the first sign of trouble as the boy waited at the teller's window. At last the boy was at the head of the line. He had passed the check in and his satchel was lying open, with voracious maw, on the ledge below the wicket for the greedy feeding of stacks of bills. Why did the teller not raise the wicket and shove out the money in a coveted pile? Carlton seemed to feel that something was wrong. The line lengthened and those at the end of the queue began to grow restive at the delay. One of the bank's officers walked down and spoke to the boy.

Carlton waited no longer. The game was up. He rushed from his coign of observation, out of the bank building, and dashed into a telephone booth.

"Quick, Constance," he shouted over the wire, "leave everything. They are holding up our check. They have discovered something. Take a cab and drive slowly around the square. You will find me waiting for you at the north end."

That night the newspapers were full of the story. There was the whole thing, exaggerated, distorted, multiplied, until they had become swindlers of millions instead of thousands. But nevertheless it was their story. There was only one grain of consolation. It was in the last paragraph of the news item, and read: "There seems to be no trace of the man and woman who worked this clever swindle. As if by a telepathic message they have vanished at just the time when their whole house of cards collapsed."

They removed every vestige of their work from the apartment. Everything was destroyed. Constance even began a new water color so that that might suggest that she had not laid aside her painting.

They had played for a big stake and lost. But the twenty thousand dollars was something. Now the great problem was to conceal it and themselves. They had lost, yet if ever before they loved, it was as nothing to what it was now that they had tasted together the bitter and the sweet of their mutual crime.

Carlton went down to the office the next day, just as before. The anxious hours that his wife had previously spent thinking whether he might betray himself by some slip were comparative safety as contrasted with the uncertainty of the hours now. But the first day after the alarm of the discovery passed off all right. Carlton even discussed the case, his case, with those in the office, commented on it, condemned the swindlers, and carried it off, he felt proud to say, as well as Constance herself might have done had she been in his place.

Another day passed. His account of the first day, reassuring as it had been to her, did not lessen the anxiety. Yet never before had they seemed to be bound together by such ties as knitted their very souls in this crisis. She tried with a devotion that was touching to impart to him some of her own strength to ward off detection.

It was the afternoon of the second day that a man who gave the name of Drummond called and presented a card of the Reynolds Company.

"Have you ever been paid a little bill of twenty-five dollars by our company?" he asked.

Down in his heart Carlton knew that this man was a detective. "I can't say without looking it up," he replied.

Carlton touched a button and an assistant appeared. Something outside himself seemed to nerve him up, as he asked: "Look up our account with Reynolds, and see if we have been paid—what is it?—a bill for twenty-five dollars. Do you recall it?"

"Yes, I recall it," replied the assistant. "No, Mr. Dunlap, I don't think it has been paid. It is a small matter, but we sent them a duplicate bill yesterday. I thought the original must have gone astray."

Carlton cursed him inwardly for sending the bill. But then, he reasoned, it was only a question of time, after all, when the forgery would be discovered.

Drummond dropped into a half-confidential, half-quizzing tone. "I thought not. Somewhere along the line that check has been stolen and raised to twenty-five thousand dollars," he remarked.

"Is that so?" gasped Carlton, trying hard to show just the right amount of surprise and not too much. "Is that so?"

"No doubt you have read in the papers of this clever realty company swindle? Well, it seems to have been part of that."

"I am sure that we shall be glad to do all in our power to cooperate with Reynolds," put in Dunlap.

"I thought you would," commented Drummond dryly. "I may as well tell you that I fear some one has been tampering with your mail."

"Tampering with *our* mail?" repeated Dunlap, aghast. "Impossible."

"Nothing is impossible until it is proved so," answered Drummond, looking him straight in the eyes. Carlton did not flinch. He felt a new power within himself, gained during the past few days of new association with Constance. For her he could face anything.

But when Drummond was gone he felt as he had on the night when he had finally realized that he could never cover up the deficit in his books. With an almost superhuman effort he gripped himself. Interminably the hours of the rest of the day dragged on.

That night he sank limp into a chair on his return home. "A man named Drummond was in the office today, my dear," he said. "Some one in the office sent Reynolds a duplicate bill, and they know about the check."

"Well?"

"I wonder if they suspect me?"

"If you act like that, they won't suspect. They'll arrest," she commented sarcastically.

He had braced up again into his new self at her words. But there was again that sinking sensation in her heart, as she realized that it was, after all, herself on whom he depended, that it was she who had been the will, even though he had been the intellect of their enterprise. She could not overcome the feeling that, if only their positions could be reversed, the thing might even yet be carried through.

Drummond appeared again at the office the next day. There was no concealment about him now. He said frankly that he was from the Burr Detective Agency, whose business it was to guard the banks against forgeries.

"The pen work, or, as we detectives call it, the penning," he remarked, "in the case of that check is especially good. It shows rare skill. But the pitfalls in this forgery game are so many that, in avoiding one, a forger, ever so clever, falls into another."

Carlton felt the polite third degree, as he proceeded: "Nowadays the forger has science to contend with, too. The microscope and camera may come in a little too late to be of practical use in preventing the forger from getting his money at first, but they come in very neatly later in catching him. What the naked eye cannot see in this check they reveal. Besides, a little iodine vapor brings out the original 'Green & Co.' on it.

"We have found out also that the protective coloring was restored by water color. That was easy. Where the paper was scratched and the sizing taken off, it has been painted with a resinous substance to restore the glaze, to the eye. Well, a little alcohol takes that off, too. Oh, the amateur forger may be the most dangerous kind, because the professional regularly follows the same line, leaves tracks, has associates, but," he concluded impressively, "all are caught sooner or later—sooner or later."

Dunlap managed to maintain his outward composure admirably. Still the little lifting of the curtain on the hidden mysteries of the new detective art produced its effect. They were getting closer, and Dunlap knew it, as Drummond intended he should. And, as in every crisis, he turned naturally to Constance. Never had she meant so much to him as now.

That night as he entered the apartment he happened to glance behind him. In the shadow down the street a man dodged quickly behind a tree. The thing gave him a start. He was being watched.

"There is just one thing left," he cried excitedly as he hurried upstairs with the news. "We must both disappear this time."

Constance took it very calmly. "But we must not go together," she added quickly, her fertile mind, as ever, hitting directly on a plan of action. "If we separate, they will be less likely to trace us, for they will never think we would do that."

It was evident that the words were being forced out by the conflict of common sense and deep emotion. "Perhaps it will be best for you to stick to your original idea of going west. I shall go to one of the winter resorts. We shall communicate only through the personal column of the *Star.* Sign yourself Weston. I shall sign Easton."

The words fell on Carlton with his new and deeper love for her like a death sentence. It had never entered his mind that they were to be separated now. Dissolve their partnership in crime? To him it seemed as if they had just begun to live since that night when they had at last understood each other. And it had come to this—separation.

"A man can always shift for himself better if he has no impediments," she said, speaking rapidly as if to bolster up her own resolution. "A woman is always an impediment in a crisis like this."

In her face he saw what he had never seen before. There was love in it that would sacrifice everything. She was sending him away from her, not to save herself but to save him. Vainly he attempted to protest. She placed her finger on his lips. Never before had he felt such overpowering love for her. And yet she held him in check in spite of himself.

"Take enough to last a few months," she added hastily. "Give me the rest. I can hide it and take care of myself. Even if they trace me I can get off. A woman can always do that more easily than a man. Don't worry about me. Go somewhere, start a new life. If it takes years, I will wait. Let me know where you are. We can find some way in which I can come back into your life. No, no,"—Carlton had caught her passionately in his arms—"even that cannot weaken me. The die is cast. We must go."

She tore herself away from him and fled into her room, where, with set face and ashen lips, she stuffed article after article into her grip. With a heavy heart Carlton did the same. The bottom had dropped out of everything, yet try as he would to reason it out, he could find no other solution but hers. To stay was out of the question, if indeed it was not already too late to run. To go together was equally out of the question. Constance had shown that. "Seek the woman," was the first rule of the police.

As they left the apartment they could see a man across the street following them closely. They were shadowed. In despair Carlton turned toward his wife. A sudden idea had flashed over her. There were two taxicabs at the station on the corner.

"I will take the first," she whispered. "Take the second and follow me. Then he cannot trace us."

They were off, leaving the baffled shadow only time to take the numbers of the cab. Constance had thought of that. She stopped and Carlton joined her. After a short walk they took another cab.

He looked at her inquiringly, but she said nothing. In her eyes he saw the same fire that blazed when she had asked him if there was no way to avoid discovery and had suggested it herself in the forgery. He reached over and caressed her hand. She did not withdraw it, but her averted eyes told that she could not trust even herself too far.

As they stood before the gateway to the steps

that led down into the long under-river tunnel which was to swallow them so soon and project them, each into a new life, hundreds, perhaps thousands of miles apart, Carlton realized as never before what it all had meant. He had loved her through all the years, but never with the wild love of the past two weeks. Now there was nothing but blackness and blankness. He felt as though the hand of fate was tearing out his wildly beating heart.

She tried to smile at him bravely. She understood. For a moment she looked at him in the old way and all the pent-up love that would have, that had done and dared everything for him struggled in her rapidly rising and falling breast.

It was now or never. She knew it, the supreme effort. One word or look too many from her and all would be lost. She flung her arms about him and kissed him. "Remember—one week from today—a personal—in the *Star*," she panted.

She literally tore herself from his arms, gathered up her grip, and was gone.

A week passed. The quiet little woman at the Oceanview House was still as much a mystery to the other guests as when she arrived, travel-stained and worn with the repressed emotion of her sacrifice. She had appeared to show no interest in anything, to take her meals mechanically, to stay most of the time in her room, never to enter into any of the recreations of the famous winter resort.

Only once a day did she betray the slightest concern about anything around her. That was when the New York papers arrived. Then she was always first at the news-stand, and the boy handed out to her, as a matter of habit, the *Star*. Yet no one ever saw her read it. Directly afterward she would retire to her room. There she would pore over the first page, reading and rereading every personal in it. Sometimes she would try reading them backward and transposing the words, as if the message they contained might be in the form of a cryptograph.

The strain and the suspense began to show

on her. Day after day passed, until it was nearly two weeks since the parting in New York. Day after day she grew more worn by worry and fear. What had happened?

In desperation she herself wired a personal to the paper: "Weston. Write me at the Oceanview. Easton."

For three days she waited for an answer. Then she wired the personal again. Still there was no reply and no hint of reply. Had they captured him? Or was he so closely pursued that he did not dare to reply even in the cryptic manner on which they had agreed?

She took the file of papers which she kept and again ran through the personals, even going back to the very day after they had separated. Perhaps she had missed one, though she knew that she could not have done so, for she had looked at them a hundred times. Where was he? Why did he not answer her message in some way? No one had followed her. Were they centering their efforts on capturing him?

She haunted the news-stand in the lobby of the beautifully appointed hotel. Her desire to read newspapers grew. She read everything.

It was just two weeks since they had left New York on their separate journeys when, on the evening of another newsless day, she was passing the news-stand. From force of habit she glanced at an early edition of an evening paper.

The big black type of the heading caught her eye:

NOTED FORGER A SUICIDE

With a little shriek, half-suppressed, she seized the paper. It was Carlton. There was his name. He had shot himself in a room in a hotel in St. Louis. She ran her eye down the column, hardly able to read. In heavier type than the rest was the letter they had found on him:

My Dearest Constance,
When you read this I, who have wronged and deceived you beyond words, will be where I can no longer hurt you. Forgive

me, for by this act I am a confessed embezzler and forger. I could not face you and
tell you of the double life I was leading. So
I have sent you away and have gone away
myself—and may the Lord have mercy on
the soul of

Your devoted husband,
Carlton Dunlap

Over and over again she read the words, as
she clutched at the edge of the news-stand to
keep from fainting—"wronged and deceived
you," "the double life I was leading." What
did he mean? Had he, after all, been concealing
something else from her? Had there really been
another woman?

Suddenly the truth flashed over her. Tracked
and almost overtaken, lacking her hand which
had guided him, he had seen no other way out.
And in his last act he had shouldered it all on
himself, had shielded her nobly from the penalty,
had opened wide for her the only door of escape.

THE MEANEST MAN IN EUROPE

David Durham

FEW CRIMINALS ARE AS CHARMING as Fidelity Dove, the angelic-looking girl whose ethereal beauty has made emotional slaves of many men. She is a fearless and inventive crook whose "gang" consists of a lawyer, a businessman, a scientist, and other devoted servants. She always wears gray, partly because the color matches well with her violet eyes but also because it reflects her strict, puritanical life. She is committed to righting wrongs, to helping those who cannot help themselves, while also being certain that the endeavor is profitable to herself.

She is the creation of William Edward Vickers (1889–1965) under the nom de plume David Durham, and appears in a single collection of short stories, *The Exploits of Fidelity Dove* (1924), one of the rarest volumes of crime fiction of the twentieth century; it was reissued eleven years later as by Roy Vickers.

Her frustrated adversary is Detective-Inspector Rason, who, against his will, is fond of Fidelity, respects her exceptional intelligence, and seems bemused by her criminal endeavors. He finds greater success when he joins the Department of Dead Ends, Vickers's other memorable series. This obscure branch of Scotland Yard has the unenviable task of trying to solve crimes that have been abandoned as hopeless. The stories in this series are "inverted" detective tales in which the reader witnesses the crime being committed, is aware when the incriminating clue is discovered, and follows the police methods that lead to the arrest. The department's unusual cases are recorded in several short story collections, beginning with the *Queen's Quorum* title *The Department of Dead Ends* (1947); the British edition of 1949 contains mostly different stories.

"The Meanest Man in Europe" was originally published in *The Exploits of Fidelity Dove* (London, Hodder & Stoughton, 1924).

The Meanest Man in Europe

DAVID DURHAM

I

THE CASE OF MR. JABEZ CREWDE gives us another reason to believe that Fidelity Dove was at this time developing a conscience. She did not make very much money out of Jabez Crewde. True, she cleared her expenses, which were, as usual, on the grand scale, and she paid herself and her staff well for their time. It was the Grey Friars Hospital which benefited chiefly by this exploit. You, if you are of those who refuse to believe that she had a spark of goodness in her, you may say that she simply indulged her sense of humour in making the meanest man in Europe subscribe twenty thousand pounds to a hospital.

Jabez Crewde deserved his title. He was worth close upon two hundred thousand pounds, which he had made as a financier—for which you can read moneylender, though he never took ordinary moneylenders' risks. Moneylender's interest—banker's risk—that was the formula on which he had grown rich. He lived in a small, drab house in a drab quarter of Islington.

Fidelity would never have heard of him if he had not had a very mild attack of appendicitis. Feeling unwell one day, he had gone in his shabbiest clothes to the surgery of a struggling slum doctor. The doctor diagnosed appendicitis, and recommended an operation. Jabez was no physical coward, but he expressed the utmost horror.

An operation would ruin him. So the doctor, having been persuaded to accept half a crown instead of his usual fee of five shillings, recommended the meanest man in Europe for free treatment at the Grey Friars Hospital.

It was a simple operation—the convalescence was short. It was during the latter period that Gorse, more or less by chance, got to know about it and related it to Fidelity. Fidelity crossed her hands across the bosom of her dream-grey gown and sadly shook her head.

"Avarice is the very leprosy of the soul," she said. "I am revolted, Cuthbert."

"For once I feel myself able to echo your sentiments," said Gorse. "He's worth about a couple of hundred thousand."

"Those poor, underpaid doctors!" said Fidelity. "And the overworked nurses! And the needy cases crying for admission—or is it perhaps a wealthy hospital?"

"There's a notice up saying if they don't get twenty thousand in three months they will have to close a wing," said Gorse.

"They have given their skill unstintingly to a suffering fellow creature. They have but cast their bread upon the waters——"

"Fidelity!" groaned Gorse. He would have died for Fidelity, as would any other member of her gang, but he alone believed her to be an utter humbug.

"My friend, you are always cruel to me, though you love me," sighed Fidelity. "And because I love you, I must please you. Listen, and tell me if this pleases you."

"I'm listening," grunted Gorse, and waited.

Fidelity's voice, when she spoke again, held the low call of birds at dusk.

"Tell Varley, our jeweller, to buy fifty thousand pounds' worth of pearls from the best firms he can," she said.

Gorse brightened.

"I thought you'd get down to brass tacks sooner or later, Fidelity!" he said, and left the room to carry out her order.

II

Jabez Crewde had the usual handful of spare-time agents, and it took no more than a few days for Fidelity to contrive that one of them should approach her. Within a week of her conversation with Gorse, she was sitting timidly in a dingy room in the drab house in Islington, which served Mr. Crewde for an office as well as a living-room.

"I—I have heard that you were ill and I hope you are better," said Fidelity in the tone of one who desires to placate a moneylender.

"I *have* to be better, Miss Dove," answered Crewde. "In these hard times I cannot afford a long illness. What do you want me to do for you?"

"I—I understood you were a financier," began Fidelity, "and I am in a difficulty which you will understand even better than I. A friend of mine, who knows all about stocks and shares, has told me that if I could invest five thousand pounds now it would be worth *thirty*-five thousand in a few days."

Jabez Crewde had no difficulty in suppressing a smile. It was a part of his profession to listen to fantastic tales.

"Go on, Miss Dove," said Crewde. "As long as you're not going to suggest that I should lend you the five thousand."

"Oh, but I was going to suggest just that," said Fidelity. "You see, I have not the five thousand pounds, and it seems such an awful pity to miss this chance. I don't know anything about money, but with thirty-five thousand pounds I need never think about it again. That is why I am so anxious to avail myself of this opportunity."

Mr. Crewde's eyes strayed to Fidelity's bag. It was of grey brocade—a dainty, home-like affair that suggested knitting and mothers' meetings and little rewards for good children.

"Are you offering any security?" he asked.

"You mean stocks and shares," divined Fidelity. "I'm afraid I haven't any. The only thing I have of any value is the jewellery my great-uncle left me. I must not sell it, and—in my sect we do not wear jewellery—so I thought that if I were to leave the jewellery with you and pay you back when I have the thirty-five thousand pounds——?"

"Have you any idea what the jewellery is worth?" asked Crewde, while Fidelity produced and opened a number of leather cases.

"It was valued at the time of my uncle's death," said Fidelity. "The assessor said that it was worth a little over fifty thousand pounds. It seemed to me terrible that so much money should be spent upon adornments."

Mr. Crewde began an expert scrutiny of the pearls. He was inclined to agree with the assessor as to their worth. He was inclined to think, now that he had taken stock of Fidelity's perfect grey tailor-made and her little white hat, that she was an extravagant and helpless fool.

"They are good pearls, though they're not worth anything like that at the present time," he said presently. "And I don't as a rule lend money upon jewellery. Have you no other securities?"

"None whatever, I fear," said Fidelity in dejection.

That was what Mr. Crewde wanted to know. It is of little use to a moneylender to have a very valuable pledge on a small loan if the client has other securities, because the pledge can always be redeemed. But when the very valuable pledge represents the only security, it is reasonably certain to pass into the hands of the moneylender—especially when the loan is made for the purposes of a get-rich-quick scheme.

"Oh, well, I don't know I'm sure!" Mr. Crewde was muttering with professional reluctance. "Everybody seems to be borrowing money just now. How soon do you expect your—er—your profits to come in, Miss Dove?"

"My friend said in six weeks' time," answered Fidelity.

"Six weeks! H'm! I might just be able to manage it."

Fidelity began to thank him.

"You're quite sure you *can* pay it back in the six weeks, mind?" challenged Mr. Crewde.

"Oh, perfectly sure," exclaimed Fidelity. "My friend was most positive."

"Very well, then," said Mr. Crewde. "I'll put that into writing and I shall ask you to sign it. If you will come here tomorrow at this time, I'll have the agreement ready for you, together with the money."

Fidelity barely glanced at the document on the following day. Its numerous clauses and penalties had no direct interest for her. She signed the document, gave a receipt for the cheque, took a receipt for her pearls, and left the dingy house in Islington.

She had borrowed five thousand pounds at sixty per cent. interest on a security of pearls worth fifty thousand pounds.

III

The meanest man in Europe was very pleased at his latest deal. Twenty years' experience had taught him that Miss Fidelity Dove would return in six weeks with a tale of misfortune and beg a renewal of the loan. In a year, with careful manipulation, he would be able to sell the pledge for his own profit without advancing any more money. He was elaborating a scheme by which he could save excise stamps on the numerous documents that would be used in the transaction, when his clerk brought him a card.

"Mr. Abraham Behrein." The address was in Hatton Garden.

He nodded, and the caller was shown in. Behrein was a well-dressed man of Hebraic appearance, not a bit like Gorse to look at. He greeted Jabez with rather elaborate courtesy.

"I have come to ask a favour, Mr. Crewde," he began. "I have reason to believe that you had a business transaction yesterday with a lady—a Miss Dove."

"Well, what of it?" demanded Crewde. "She's turned twenty-one."

"Quite so!" said Behrein. "I simply wished to ask if you would allow me to look at the pearls she deposited with you. I am aware that the request is most irregular, but—I have reasons."

"What reasons?"

"I do not care to name them."

"Well, that's an end of it. Certainly not!" snapped Jabez Crewde.

"You refuse?" asked Behrein with an air.

"Of course I do. Grant, this gentleman can't find the door!"

Jabez Crewde was more than a little disturbed by the incident. Not so Behrein. Behrein got into the taxi that was waiting for him and drove to Scotland Yard.

Here he again presented his card, explained that he was a dealer in precious stones, and stated that he had been robbed. He wished to speak to a responsible official who would take up the case. There was a short delay, at the end of which he was shown into Detective-Inspector Rason's rooms.

"A short time ago," explained Behrein to the detective, "I bought a parcel of pearls of an approximate value of fifty thousand pounds. It is a big parcel, Mr. Rason, in these days, and my purchase attracted a certain amount of attention. I had many opportunities of unloading, but I was not in a hurry. A lady, not in the trade, was introduced to me in the belief that she might purchase the entire parcel for her personal use.

"The lady encouraged the belief. She came twice to my office to inspect the pearls and to discuss methods of purchase. Her last visit was on Monday of this week. She was a very pleasant, very well-bred lady, and when I was wanted on the telephone I had no hesitation in leaving her for a moment in possession of the pearls."

Detective-Inspector Rason grunted. He knew well enough what was coming. An oft-told tale!

"My client," continued Behrein, "renewed her expressions of approval, said that she had some final financial arrangements to make, and would call upon me in the following week. This morning I wished to show the pearls to another customer—I had not handled them since the visit of the lady—and I find—a parcel of pretty good imitations, worth possibly one hundred and fifty pounds. I cannot, of course, prove anything, but I am certain that the lady in the case made the substitution while I was answering the telephone."

"Did she give you a name?" asked Rason.

"She gave me the name of Fidelity Dove," said Behrein, "with an address in Bayswater, which I have no doubt is a false one."

"The address is right enough," Rason rapped out. "She's probably waiting for us to call. She's the coolest crook in London and then some. She never bothers to run away. I've been on her track a dozen times and she always manages so that you can't prove anything. In a way, she's a great woman."

"That is not very consoling to one who looks like losing fifty thousand pounds as the result of her ingenuity," said Behrein bitterly.

"We shall take the matter up, of course," said Rason.

"Then perhaps I could help you," said Behrein. "Chiefly by chance, I happen to know that this lady—if it be not absurd so to call her—borrowed money upon the security of pearls from a Mr. Jabez Crewde. I'm quite sure of my facts. Mr. Crewde underpays his staff, and—er——"

"Quite so," said Rason.

"I was at his house in Islington half an hour ago," continued Behrein. "I asked, with all civility I hope, to be allowed to look at the pearls.

He received my request very ill-temperedly and refused it."

Detective-Inspector Rason made a note.

"Did you tell him your suspicion?"

"I would have explained had he given me time," said Behrein. "As it was, I was being shown out of the place before I could explain anything.

"I have here," continued Behrein, "photographs of the pearls, together with an expert description. If you have means of forcing Mr. Crewde, these papers will dispose of any doubt."

"Of course, we could get a search-warrant if necessary," said Rason. "But we always avoid unpleasantness of that kind if we possibly can. I think it very likely that I could persuade Mr. Crewde to show me the pearls of his own accord."

"Would it be possible for me to accompany you?" asked Behrein. "I could tell at a glance."

The detective agreed to this readily enough, and in half an hour Behrein was again at the house in Islington, this time accompanied by Rason.

IV

When Jabez Crewde found himself confronted with a police officer, he "saw the red light" and made no further bones about producing the pearls.

He laid them out on the table, but before he had finished, Behrein intervened.

"These are my pearls, Mr. Crewde," he said. "I could produce a round dozen experts at an hour's notice to identify them. If you care to peruse these documents, you will be satisfied yourself. I—I am very sorry for you."

"*Your* pearls! What the dickens do you mean?"

Behrein, in his slow, heavy accents, re-told the story of the substitution of the pearls. The end of the story left Crewde babbling incoherently.

"Given that Mr. Behrein can substantiate his

account," said Rason, "he will be able to obtain the pearls from you by an order of the Court, as they are stolen goods. Do you wish to take the matter up on your own account, Mr. Crewde?"

"Yes, of course I'll take it up!" snapped Crewde. "No, I can't afford to pay a lot of thieving lawyers. It's a matter for the Public Prosecutor. I'll give evidence if you'll pay me for my time."

"I take it, Mr. Behrein, that you will prosecute," suggested Rason.

"I have no alternative," replied Behrein. "If you will tell me how to proceed——"

Rason was about to speak, and checked himself.

"If I were you," he said instead, "I'd proceed very carefully, Mr. Behrein. It looks a clear-cut case. But there have been one or two cases before against this particular lady that have looked just as clear-cut. If you like to charge her, of course I must take the charge, but I suggest that you wait till I've seen her."

Mr. Behrein bowed.

"As you please," he said. "You understand these things and I don't. I would like to have a private word with Mr. Crewde if he will allow me."

"Right!" said Rason. "I'll get along to Miss Dove."

"It looks," said Mr. Behrein when the detective had left, "as though you and I, Mr. Crewde, are going to be let in for a great deal of expense and a great deal of wasted time. Are you at all willing to discuss an arrangement?"

"What arrangement can we make?" demanded Crewde. "You are on velvet. I've lent five thousand pounds on those pearls. You can get them from me for nothing by an order of the Court."

"Well, Mr. Crewde," said Behrein indulgently, "I feel that men of our stamp must hang together when we're up against this kind of thing. I have no desire to stand on my rights at your expense. I'll be frank with you. I have a prospective purchaser for those pearls and time is of the utmost importance. If they are going to

be held up three months as exhibits in a trial—to say nothing of a civil action between you and me, which I would profoundly regret—I shall lose my customer. I think—well, now, I won't beat about the bush—I am content to carry the five thousand loss. If you like to hand those pearls to me, I'll give you a proper receipt and five thousand pounds and take my risk of getting my money back."

Jabez Crewde could scarcely believe his ears.

"Eh? What's that? Haven't quite got you," he muttered, and Behrein repeated his offer.

"Of course," said Behrein laboriously, "you will lose your profit on the transaction—but you will have lost that in any case—together with your principal of five thousand pounds. As you admit, I can get the pearls returned to me by an order of the Court. I had hoped that you would accept my offer——"

"I do accept it," said Crewde in haste.

Behrein took out his wallet.

"One has to carry large sums about one in my trade," he explained, and counted out five thousand pounds in notes.

He added a formal receipt for the pearls and left the meanest man in Europe trembling with relief at being spared the loss of five thousand pounds and the necessity of appearing in Court.

V

It was nearly lunch-time when Detective-Inspector Rason arrived at Fidelity's house in Bayswater. Fidelity, exquisite in grey taffetas, asked him to stay to lunch. Politely, he declined.

"You constantly refuse my invitations, Mr. Rason," she told him, her violet eyes clear and shining as a child's. "And you cannot have come on duty this time."

Rason made a grimace.

"I have come on a clear-cut case against you for jewel-robbery, Miss Dove," he said. "But I'm old enough now not to attach too much importance to that fact."

Fidelity's smile was seraphic.

"All the same," continued Rason, "I'm taking a pretty keen professional interest in this particular case. I've been trying to guess how you're going to keep out of prison this time, and I'll admit I've clean failed."

"There is an elusive suggestion of flattery in your words, Mr. Rason," reproved Fidelity. "And flattery falls strangely on my ears. Let me confess I cannot in the least understand what you are saying."

"Yesterday morning," said Rason, with a sigh, "you pledged with Mr. Jabez Crewde pearls which on Monday you are alleged to have stolen by means of substituting false ones from a Mr. Abraham Behrein. Mr. Behrein has photographs of the pearls and expert descriptions. They have been identified as the pearls you pledged with Mr. Crewde."

"Mr.—what is the name of the other gentleman—Berlein?"

"Behrein," said Rason. "Are you going to deny knowledge of him, Miss Dove?"

"Yes," said Fidelity. The word had all the sanctity of a vow.

For a moment there was silence. A look almost of fear flashed into Rason's eyes.

"May I use your telephone?" he asked.

Fidelity's little bow gave consent. Rason fluttered the leaves of the telephone book, looked for Behrein, and could not find him. He rang up the Holborn police.

He gave particulars of himself, and then:

"Abraham Behrein," he said, and gave the address in Hatton Garden. "Send a man at once to verify name and address. 'Phone me here." There followed Fidelity's number.

In a quarter of an hour, in which Fidelity spoke gracefully and well of pearls as mentioned in the scriptures, there came the return message. Abraham Behrein was unknown in Hatton Garden.

"And now, Mr. Rason," asked Fidelity, "are you going to apologize for doubting my word?"

"No," said Rason. The emphasis of his refusal left Fidelity's gravity undisturbed until he had left her drawing-room; but as he crossed the magnificent hall silvery laughter followed him and rang in his ears long after he had left the house.

VI

On the next day Mr. Jabez Crewde was severely startled at being told that Fidelity Dove was on the doorstep and wished to see him.

"Show her in, and run for the police," he whispered to the clerk.

Fidelity came in, gracefully as ever. She inclined her head in the *soupçon* of a bow.

"Oh, Mr. Crewde!" she said in clear tones. "I do not know how to thank you! The money that you lent me must veritably have been bewitched. The scheme was successful beyond my friend's wildest dreams. So much money has been made that—is it the firm or his stockbroker?—has advanced on account of my profits all the money I borrowed from you, and I have come to repay you five thousand five hundred pounds."

"Let's have a look at it," said Crewde coarsely.

"But of course I wish you not merely to look at it but to take it,"—and Fidelity laid the notes on the table.

Mr. Crewde counted the notes.

"You can leave those there," he said, and glanced towards the door. Then, for safety, he picked them up and put them in his pocket. Fidelity looked offended.

"Will you give me a receipt and return my pearls?" she asked.

"We'll see about that in a minute," snapped Crewde.

"Against my inclination, I am driven to believe that your manner is intentionally offensive," said Fidelity. "I will wait no longer. The receipt is of no importance, for my bankers have the numbers of the notes. You will please return the pearls to my private address."

"Your private address! Yes, I know it— Aylesbury prison it'll be in a week or two," jeered Crewde. "As for the pearls, they are back with Mr. Abraham Behrein, whom you stole them from."

"Oh! How can you——" Fidelity produced a handkerchief.

"Tell it all to the policeman," invited Mr. Crewde as the clerk returned with a constable.

"What's all this?" asked the constable.

"That's the woman you want. Fidelity Dove, she calls herself," shouted Crewde. "Scotland Yard knows all about her."

The policeman looked embarrassed.

"Do you give the lady in charge, sir?" he asked.

"No, I don't give her in charge," said Crewde. "I'm not going to be mixed up with it. It's a matter for the Public Prosecutor. Scotland Yard!"

"We've no orders to arrest anyone of that name as far as I know," said the constable. "I can't take the lady unless you charge her, sir."

"There is my card, constable," said Fidelity. "My car is outside if you care to take the number."

In the car Fidelity drove home.

As soon as she had left, Jabez Crewde telephoned to Scotland Yard. He was put through to Rason, who informed him that all efforts to trace Abraham Behrein had failed.

"It was a hoax of some kind, I'm afraid," said Rason. "But you're all right, Mr. Crewde. You have the pearls, I take it? It was apparently a swindle that didn't come off."

"But she's paid me back the money I lent her, and wants the pearls back," protested Crewde.

"Well, I can't advise you," said Rason. "But I should have thought the best thing to do would be to give them to her."

"But I haven't got them!" yelled Crewde. "I handed them to Behrein—they were his—and he gave me the five thousand I'd lent her."

"O-o-oh!" said Rason. It was a long-drawn sound that held a world of meaning.

"What's the good of saying 'oh,'" raged Crewde. "You're a pack of fools, that's what you are," he added, after he had replaced the receiver.

On the next morning Jabez Crewde received a letter from Fidelity Dove's solicitor, Sir Frank Wrawton, demanding the immediate return of the pearls or their value in cash, which had been estimated by competent and unassailable experts at fifty thousand pounds.

By eleven o'clock Jabez Crewde had learned that Sir Frank Wrawton was empowered merely to give him a receipt for the pearls or the cash equivalent.

By twelve o'clock he was at Fidelity's house in Bayswater.

He was received by Fidelity in the morning-room.

"I've been thinking about this," he shouted at Fidelity, "and I can see what's happened. That Behrein, as he calls himself, is a confederate of yours. You two are in it together. I'll show you the whole bag o' tricks. You bought those pearls—they were genuine. Then you borrowed five thousand from me, and paid back five thousand five hundred. You dropped that five hundred. Then your confederate dropped another five thousand in getting the pearls from me. That's five thousand five hundred you've dropped—and for that outlay you've landed me with a liability for fifty thousand pounds. Why, you probably had those pearls hidden away an hour after Behrein left me, and you'll sell them again quietly later on——"

"Have you also been thinking, Mr. Crewde, how you are going to establish this terribly slanderous theory in a court of law?" asked Fidelity, nun-like and serene.

"Bah! The lawyers are robbers, like the police——"

"And the hospitals?" asked Fidelity.

Crewde looked very nearly startled.

"They call you the meanest man in Europe, Mr. Crewde," said Fidelity. "I alone have maintained that that is a slander. I want you to prove my words. You owe me fifty thousand pounds. To dispute my claim would merely mean the loss of another thousand pounds or so in lawyers' expenses. It is a pleasure to wring money from a mean man, but it is no pleasure if the man be not mean. The Grey Friars Hospital requires twenty thousand pounds, I understand."

"Eh?" grunted Crewde. "I don't get you. D'you want me to give them twenty thousand? What if I do?"

"If you will write a cheque for twenty thousand pounds to the Grey Friars Hospital," said Fidelity, "I will withdraw one-fifth of my claim against you. Twenty thousand to the Grey Friars Hospital, twenty thousand to myself—and I will give you a receipt for fifty thousand pounds."

"That's close on fifteen thousand pounds clear profit to yourself," said Crewde, a ghastly pallor spreading over his face.

"You may phrase it so," said Fidelity. "Or you may say that I am offering you ten thousand pounds to remove from London the reproach of harbouring the meanest man in Europe. . . . Ah, I see you have no fountain-pen. I beg you to use mine."

FOUR SQUARE JANE UNMASKED

Edgar Wallace

RICHARD HORATIO EDGAR WALLACE (1875–1932) created any number of series characters, the longest-running being Commissioner Sanders, representative of the Foreign Office of Great Britain, whose job was to keep the king's peace in Africa's River territories; he appeared in about a dozen books, beginning with *Sanders of the River* (1911). Wallace's most popular series featured the coterie who first appeared in *The Four Just Men* (1905); there were actually three, as one died before the story begins. They were wealthy dilettantes who set out to administer justice when the law is unable or unwilling to do the job; there were five sequels. Most of his other series characters appeared in short stories published in various newspapers and magazines and then were collected in book form.

One of these was the titular figure in *Four Square Jane* (1929), the only book devoted to the young rogue's exploits. In the editor's note in the book edition, the "heroine" is described as an "extremely ladylike crook, an uncannily clever criminal who exercises all her female cunning on her nefarious work" and "makes the mere male detectives and policemen who endeavor to be on her tracks look foolish."

Jane is pretty, young, slim, and chaste, and she leaves her calling card at the scene of her robberies: a printed label with four squares and the letter "J" in the middle. She makes sure to do this so that none of the servants will be accused of the theft. She has a troupe of loyal associates on whom she calls as they are needed.

"Four Square Jane Unmasked" is a made-up title; none of the stories in the book publication has a title. It was originally serialized in *The Weekly News* from January 10 to February 7, 1920; it was first collected in *Four Square Jane* (London, Readers Library, 1929).

Four Square Jane Unmasked

EDGAR WALLACE

PETER DAWES, of Scotland Yard, and a very gloomy Lord Claythorpe sat in conference in the latter gentleman's City office. For Lord Claythorpe was a director of many companies and had interests of a wide and varied character.

The detective sat at a table, with a little block of paper before him, jotting down notes from time to time, and there was a frown upon his face which suggested that his investigations were not going exactly as he could have wished them.

"There is the case," said Lord Claythorpe. "The whole thing was a malicious act on the part of this wretched woman, directed against me, my son, and my niece."

"Is Miss Joyce Wilberforce your niece?" asked the detective, and Lord Claythorpe hesitated.

"Well, she is not my niece," he said at last. "Rather she was the niece of one of my dearest friends. He was an immensely wealthy man, and when he died he left the bulk of his property to his niece."

The detective nodded.

"Where does your interest come in, Lord Claythorpe?" he asked.

"I am her legal guardian," said his lordship, "although of course, she has a mother. That is to say, I am the trustee and sole executor of her estate, and there were one or two provisions especially made by my dear friend which gave me authority usually denied to trustees——"

"Such as the right of choosing her husband," said the detective quietly, and it was Lord Claythorpe's turn to frown.

"So you know something about this, do you?" he asked. "Yes, I have that right. It so happened that I chose my own son Francis as the best man for that position, and the lady was quite agreeable."

"Indeed!" said the polite Peter. He consulted his notes. "As far as I understand, this mysterious person, whom Mrs. Wilberforce believes to be a discharged employee named Jane Briglow, after making several raids upon your property, reached the culmination of her audacity by robbing your son of his wedding-ring and then burgling the house of the parson who was to marry them and stealing the license, which had been granted by the Bishop of London."

"That's it exactly," said Lord Claythorpe.

"And what of the wedding?" asked Peter. "There will be no difficulty of getting another license."

Lord Claythorpe sniffed.

"The only difficulty is," he said, "that the young lady is naturally prostrated by the humiliation which this villainous woman has thrust upon her. She was in such a state of collapse the following morning that her mother was compelled to take her—or rather, to send her—to a friend in the country. The wedding is postponed for, let us say, a month."

"One other question," asked the detective. "You say you suspect, in addition to Jane Briglow, a young man named Jamieson Steele, who was in a way engaged to Miss Joyce Wilberforce?"

"A fugitive from justice," said his lordship emphatically. "And why you police fellows cannot catch him is beyond my understanding. The man forged my name——"

"I know all about that," said the detective. "I had the records of the case looked out, and the particulars of the case were 'phoned to me here whilst you had gone upstairs to collect data concerning the previous robbery. As a matter of fact, although he is, as you may say, a fugitive from justice, having very foolishly run away, there is no evidence which would secure a conviction before a judge and jury. I suppose your lordship knows that?"

His lordship did not know that, and he expressed his annoyance in the usual manner—which was to abuse the police.

Peter Dawes went back to Scotland Yard, and consulted the officer who had been in charge of the forgery case.

"No, sir," said that individual, "we have not a picture of Mr. Steele. But he was a quiet enough young fellow—a civil engineer, so far as my memory serves me, in the employment of one of Lord Claythorpe's companies."

Peter Dawson looked at the other thoughtfully. His informant was Chief Inspector Passmore, who was a living encyclopædia, not only upon the aristocratic underworld, but upon crooks who moved in the odour of respectability.

"Inspector," said Peter, "what position does Lord Claythorpe occupy in the world of the idle rich?"

The inspector stroked his stubbly chin.

"He is neither idle nor rich," he said. "Claythorpe is, in point of fact, a comparatively poor man, most of whose income is derived from directors' fees. He has been a heavy gambler in the past, and only as recently as the last oil slump he lost a goodish bit of money."

"Married?" asked Peter, and the other nodded.

"To a perfectly colourless woman whom nobody seems to have met, though I believe she is seen out at some of the parties Lewinstein gives," he said.

"Do you know anything about the fortune of Miss Joyce Wilberforce?"

"Two hundred and fifty thousand pounds," said the other promptly. "Held absolutely by his lordship as sole trustee. The girl's uncle thought an awful lot of him, and my own opinion is that, in entrusting the girl's fortune to Claythorpe, he was a trifle mad."

The men's eyes met.

"Is Claythorpe crooked?" asked Dawes bluntly, and the detective shrugged his shoulders.

"Heaven knows," he said. "The only thing I am satisfied about is his association with Four Square Jane."

Peter looked at him with a startled gaze.

"What on earth do you mean?" he asked.

"Well," said the inspector, "don't you see how all these crimes which are committed by Four Square Jane have as their object the impoverishment of Claythorpe?"

"I have formed my own theory on that," said Peter slowly. "I thought Four Square Jane was a society crook doing a Claude Duval stunt, robbing the rich to keep the poor."

The inspector smiled.

"You got that idea from the fact that she gives the proceeds of her jewel robberies to the hospitals. And why shouldn't she? They're difficult to dispose of, and as a rule they're easily retrievable if old man Claythorpe will pay the price. But you never heard, when she took solid money, that that went to hospitals, did you?"

"There have been instances," said Peter.

"When it wasn't Claythorpe's money," said the other quickly. "When it was only the money belonging to some pal of Claythorpe's as shady as himself. The impression I get of Four Square Jane is that she's searching for something all the time. Maybe it's money—at any rate, when she gets money she sticks to it; and maybe its something else."

"What is your theory?" asked Dawes.

"My theory," said the inspector slowly, "is that Four Square Jane and Claythorpe were working in a crooked game together, and that he double-crossed her and that she is getting her revenge."

Lord Claythorpe had his office in the City, but most of his business was conducted in a much smaller office situated in St. James's Street. The sole staff of this bureau was his confidential clerk, Donald Remington, a sour-faced man of fifty, reticent and taciturn, who knew a great deal more about his lordship's business than possibly even Lord Claythorpe gave him credit for.

After his interview with the detective, Lord Claythorpe drove away from the city to the West End, and went up the one flight of stairs which led to the little suite—it was more like a flat than an office and occupied the first floor of a shop building, being approached by the side door—in an absent and abstracted frame of mind.

The silent Remington rose as his master entered, and Lord Claythorpe took the seat which his subordinate had occupied. For fully three minutes neither man spoke, and then Remington asked:

"What did the detective want your lordship for?"

"To ask about that infernal woman," replied the other shortly.

"Four Square Jane, eh? But did he ask you anything else?" His tone was one of respectful familiarity, if the paradox may be allowed.

Claythorpe nodded.

"He wanted to know about Miss Wilberforce's fortune," he said.

Another silence, and then Remington asked:

"I suppose you'll be glad when that wedding is through, now?"

There was a significant note in his voice, and Claythorpe looked up.

"Of course, I shall," he said sharply. "By the way, have you made arrangements about——"

Remington nodded.

"Do you think you're wise?" he asked. "The securities had better stay in the vaults at the bank don't you think, especially in view of this girl's activities?"

"Nothing of the sort," replied Claythorpe violently. "Carry out my instructions, Remington, to the letter. What the devil do you mean by questioning any act of mine?"

Remington raised his eyebrows the fraction of an inch.

"Far be it from me to question your lordship's actions; I am merely suggesting that——"

"Well, suggest nothing," said Lord Claythorpe. "You have given notice to the bank that I intend putting the bonds in a place of security?"

"I have," replied the other, "the manager has arranged for the box to be delivered here this afternoon. The assistant manager and the accountant are bringing it."

"Good!" said Claythorpe. "Tomorrow I will take it down to my country place."

Remington was silent.

"You don't think it wise, eh?" The small eyes of Lord Claythorpe twinkled with malicious humour. "I see you're scared of Four Square Jane, too."

"Not I," said Remington quickly. "When is this marriage to occur?"

"In a month," said his lordship airily. "I suppose you're thinking about your bonus."

Remington licked his dry lips.

"I am thinking about the sum of four thousand pounds which your lordship owes me, and which I have been waiting for very patiently for the last two years," he said. "I am tired of this kind of work, and I am anxious to have a little rest and recreation. I'm getting on in years, and it's very nearly time I had a change."

Lord Claythorpe was scribbling idly on his blotting-pad.

"How much do you think I will owe you, altogether, with the bonus I promised you for your assistance?"

"Nearer ten thousand pounds than four," replied the man.

"Oh!" said his lordship carelessly. "That is a large sum, but you may depend upon receiving it the moment my boy is married. I have been spending a lot of money lately, Remington. It cost a lot to get back that pearl necklace."

"You mean the Venetian Armlet?" said the other quickly. "I didn't know that you had the pearl necklace back?"

"Anyway, I advertised for it," said his lordship evasively.

"Fixing no definite reward," said Remington, "and for a very good reason."

"What do you mean?" asked Lord Claythorpe quickly.

"The pearls were faked," said the calm Remington. "Your fifty thousand pound necklace was worth little more than fifty pounds!"

"Hush! for heavens' sake," said Claythorpe. "Don't talk so loud." He mopped his brow. "You seem to know a devil of a lot," he said suspiciously. "In fact, there are moments, Remington, when I think you know a damn sight too much for my comfort."

Remington smiled for the first time—a thin hard smile that gave his face a sinister appearance.

"All the more reason why your lordship should get rid of me as soon as possible," he said. "I have no ambition except to own a little cottage in Cornwall, where I can fish, ride a horse, and idle away my time."

His lordship rose hurriedly and took off his coat, preparatory to washing his hands in a small wash-place leading from the office.

"It's getting late," he said. "I had forgotten I have to lunch with somebody. Your ambition shall be gratified—be sure of that, Remington," he said, passing into the smaller room.

"I hope so," said Remington. His eyes were fixed on the floor. In throwing down his coat a letter had dropped from Claythorpe's pocket, and Remington stooped to pick it up. He saw the postmark and the handwriting, and recognized it as that of Mrs. Wilberforce. He heard the splash of the water in the bowl and Lord Claythorpe's voice humming a little tune. Without a moment's hesitation he took it out and read it. The letter was short.

"My dear Lord Claythorpe," it ran. "Joyce is adamant on the point of the marriage, and says she will not go through with it for another twelve months."

He replaced the letter in the envelope, and put it back in the inside pocket of the coat.

Twelve months! Claythorpe had lied when he said a month, and was obviously lying with a purpose.

When his lordship emerged, wiping his hands on a towel, and still humming a little tune, Remington was gazing out of the window upon the chimney tops of Jermyn Street.

"I shall be back at half-past two," said Lord Claythorpe, perfunctorily examining a small heap of letters which lay on his desk. "The bank people will be here by then?"

Remington nodded.

"I am worried about this transfer of Miss Joyce's securities," he said. "They are safe enough in the bank. I do not think they will be safe with you."

"Rubbish," said his lordship. "I think I know how to deal with Four Square Jane. And besides, I am going to ensure the safety of the securities. Four Square Jane isn't the kind of person who would steal paper security. It wouldn't be any good to her, anyway."

"But suppose these documents disappear?" persisted Remington. "Though it might not assist Four Square Jane, it would considerably embarrass you and Miss Joyce. It would not be a gain, perhaps, to the burglar, but it would be a distinct loss to the young lady."

"Don't worry," said Claythorpe, "neither Four Square Jane nor her confederate, Mr. Jamieson Steele——"

"Jamieson Steele?" repeated Remington. "What has he to do with it?"

Lord Claythorpe chuckled.

"It is my theory—and it is a theory, I think, which is also held by the police—that Jamieson Steele is the gentleman who assists Miss Four Square Jane in her robberies."

"I'll never believe it," said Remington.

Lord Claythorpe had his hand on the door, preparatory to departing, and he turned at these words.

"Perhaps you do not believe that he forged my name to a cheque in this very office?" he said.

"I certainly do not believe that," said Remington. "In fact I know that that story is a lie."

Claythorpe's face went red.

"That is an ugly word to use to me, Remington," he said, "I think the sooner you go the better."

"I quite agree with your lordship," said Remington, and smiled as the door slammed behind his irate master.

When Claythorpe returned he was in a more amicable frame of mind, and greeted the two bank officials with geniality. On the big table was a black japanned box, heavily sealed. The business of transferring the sealed packages which constituted the contents of the box was not a long process. Lord Claythorpe checked them with a list he took from his case, and signed a receipt.

"I suppose your lordship would not like to break the seals of these envelopes?" said the assistant bank manager. "Of course, we are not responsible for their contents, but it would be more satisfactory to us, as I am sure it would be to your lordship, if you were able to verify the contents."

"It is not necessary," said Claythorpe, with a wave of his hand. "I'll just reseal the box and put it in my safe."

This he did in the presence of the manager, locking away the box in an old-fashioned steel safe—a proceeding which the bankers witnessed without enthusiasm.

"That doesn't seem very secure," said one, "I wish your lordship——"

"I wish you would mind your own business," said Lord Claythorpe, and the bankers left, "blessing" the truculent man under their breath.

At six o'clock that afternoon Claythorpe finished the work on which he had been engaged, closed and locked his desk, tried the safe, and put on his hat. He glanced through the front window and saw that his car was waiting, and that it was pelting with rain.

"Which way are you going, Remington?" he asked. "I can give you a lift as far as Park Lane."

"No, thank you, my lord," said Remington, struggling into his mackintosh. "I am going by tube, and I have not far to walk."

They went out of the office together, double-locking the stout door. Before leaving, Remington attached a burglar alarm which communicated with a large bell outside the building, and he repeated this process before the door was actually closed and double-locked.

"I want you to be here at nine o'clock tomorrow morning," said Claythorpe to his subordinate. "Good-night."

The inclemency of the weather increased as the evening advanced. A howling southwest gale swept over London, clearing the streets of idlers and limiting to some extent the activities of the police patrols. The police officer who was on duty within a few yards of the building, and who was relieved at eleven o'clock that night, stated that he saw or heard nothing of a suspicious character. In the course of his tour of duty, he tried the door which led to Lord Claythorpe's office but found it fastened. His relief, a man named Tomms, made an examination of the door at a quarter past eleven—it was his business to examine every door in the street to see that they were securely fastened—and, in addition, acting upon instructions received from Scotland Yard, "pegged" the door. That is to say, he inserted two small wedges of the size of match sticks, one in each door-post, and tied a piece of black cotton from one to the other.

At one o'clock he tried the door again, and flashed his lamp upon the black thread, and found that it had been broken. This could only mean that someone had passed into the office between eleven and one. He summoned assistance, and roused the caretaker, who lived in adjoining premises, and together they went into the darkened building, and mounted the stairs.

Lord Claythorpe's office door was apparently closed. It led, as the caretaker explained, directly into the main office. There was no sign of jemmy work, and the officers might have given up their investigations and found a simple explanation for the broken thread in the wildness of the night, when, flashing his lamp on the floor, one of the policemen saw a thin trickle of red coming from beneath. It was blood!

The police did not hesitate, but smashed open the door, and entered with some difficulty, for immediately behind the door was lying the body of a man. Tomms switched on the light and knelt down by the side of the body.

"He's dead," he said. "Do you know this man?"

"Yes, sir," said the white-faced caretaker, "that's Mr. Remington."

The police made a perfunctory examination.

"You'd better get the divisional surgeon, Jim," he said to his comrade. "But I'm afraid its no use. This poor fellow has been shot through the heart."

He looked round the apartment. The safe door was wide open and empty.

Half-an-hour later Peter Dawes arrived on the scene of the murder and made a brief examination. He looked at the body.

"Was he like this?" he asked, "when you found him?"

"Yes, sir," replied the officer.

"He has a knife in his hand."

Peter bent down and looked at the thin-bladed weapon, tightly clenched in the dead man's hand.

"What's that, sir?" said Tomms, pointing to the other hand. "It looks like a paper there."

The card in Remington's half-clenched fist was loosely held, and the detective gently withdrew it. It was a visiting-card, and the name inscribed thereon was, "Mr. Jamieson Steele, Civil Engineer." Peter Dawes whistled, and then walked across to the safe.

"That's queer," he said, and swung the door

of the safe closed in the hope of finding something behind it.

He found something, but not what he had expected. In the centre of the green steel door was a small label. It was a label bearing the mark of Four Square Jane.

Four Square Jane had committed a murder! It was incredible. All Peter Dawes's fine theories went by the board in that discovery. This was not the work of a society crook; it was not the work of a criminal philanthropist; there was evidence here of the most cold-blooded murder that it had been his business to investigate.

Summoned from his bed at three o'clock in the morning, Lord Claythorpe came to his office a greatly distressed man. He was shivering from sheer terror when he told the story of the securities which had been in the safe when he had left the office.

"And I was warned. I was warned!" he cried. "Poor Remington himself begged me not to do it. What a fool I am!"

"What was Remington doing here?" asked Peter.

The body of the murdered man had long since been removed to the mortuary, and only the dark stain on the floor spoke eloquently of tragedy.

"I haven't any idea," said his lordship. "I simply dare not let myself think. Poor fellow! It is a tragedy, an appalling tragedy!"

"I know all about that," said Peter drily. "Murders usually are. But what was Remington doing in this office between eleven at night and one o'clock in the morning?"

Lord Claythorpe shook his head.

"I can only offer you my theory," he said, "for what it is worth. Poor Remington was greatly worried about the securities being in this office at all, and he begged me to get a caretaker, a commissionaire or somebody, to sit in the office during the night. Very foolishly I rejected this excellent suggestion. I can only surmise that, worried by the knowledge that so many valuable securities were in this inadequate safe, Remington came in the middle of the night, intending to remain on guard himself."

Peter nodded. It was a theory which had the appearance of being a feasible one.

"Then you think that he was surprised by the burglar?"

"Or burglars," said Lord Claythorpe. "Yes, I do."

Peter sat at his lordship's desk, tapping at the blotting-pad with his fingers.

"There is a lot to support your theory," he said. "From the appearance of the body and the weapon in his hand, it is a likely suggestion that he was defending himself. On the other hand, look at this."

He took a crumpled envelope from his pocket and laid it on the table. It was stained with blood and the flap was heavily sealed.

"We found this under his body," said the detective. "You will note that the envelope has been slit open by some sharp instrument—in fact, such an instrument as was found in Remington's hand when the body was discovered."

His lordship pondered this.

"Possibly he surprised them in the act of opening the envelope, and snatched it away," he said, and again the detective nodded.

"I agree with you that that is also a plausible theory," he said. "Had he a key of the safe?"

Lord Claythorpe hesitated.

"Not that I know," he said. "Why, yes, of course, he had! I did not realize it. Yes, Remington had a key."

"And is this the key?" Peter Dawes handed his lordship a long steel key which he had taken from his pocket, and Lord Claythorpe examined it intently.

"Yes," he said, "that is undoubtedly one of the keys of the safe. Where did you find it?"

"Under the table," said the detective.

"Are there any other clues?" asked his lordship after a pause, and this time Peter did not immediately answer.

"Yes, there is one," he said. "We found in the dead man's hand a small visiting-card."

"What was the name?" asked the other quickly.

"The name was Mr. Jamieson Steele, who, I believe, was a former employee of yours."

"Steele! By heaven! That fits in with what I have been saying all along!" cried Claythorpe. "So Steele was in it!"

"It doesn't follow because this card was found in Remington's hand that the card belonged to the burglar," said Peter quietly. "It is not customary in criminal circles for murderers to leave their cards upon their victims, as I daresay your lordship knows."

Claythorpe looked at him sharply.

"This does not seem to me to be a moment when you can exercise your sarcasm at my expense," he growled. "I tell you Steele is a blackguard, and is the kind of man who would assist this notorious woman in her undertakings. Of course, if you're going to shield him——"

"I shield nobody," said Peter coldly. "I would not even shield your lordship if I had the slightest evidence against you. Of that you may be sure."

Lord Claythorpe winced.

"This is a heavy loss for you," said Peter, who was ignorant of the contents of the safe. Then, noticing the other's silence, he asked quickly: "You will, of course, give me the fullest information as to what the safe contained. And you can't do better than tell me now. Was it ready money?"

Lord Claythorpe shook his head.

"Nothing but securities," he said, "and those not of a negotiable character."

"Your securities?" asked Peter. "What was their value?"

"About a quarter of a million," said his lordship, and Peter gasped.

"Your money?" he asked again.

"No," hesitated Lord Claythorpe. "Not my money, but a trust fund——"

Peter sprang up from the table.

"You don't mean to say that this was the fortune of Miss Joyce Wilberforce about which we were talking this morning?"

His lordship nodded.

"It is," he said briefly. "It is a great tragedy,

and I don't know how I shall excuse myself to the poor girl."

"You, of course, know what the securities were?" said Peter in a dry, matter-of-fact voice, as he sat down once more at the table.

In that moment he betrayed no more emotion than if he had been investigating the most commonplace of shop robberies.

"I have a list," said Claythorpe, and for nearly an hour he was detailing particulars of the bonds which had been stolen.

Peter finished his inquiry at four in the morning, and went to his office to send out an all-Britain message.

It was not like Jane, this latest crime. It was certainly not like Jane or her assistant—if she had an assistant—to leave an incriminating visiting-card in poor Remington's hand.

Peter Dawes was wise in the ways of criminals, both habitual and involuntary. He had seen a great deal of the grim side of his profession, and had made a careful study of anatomy, particularly in relation to murdered people. He was satisfied in his own mind that the card that was held in the lightly clenched fist of the dead man had been placed there after he had been shot.

He expressed himself frankly to his chief.

"The card is evidently a plant to lead us off the track; and if it was put there by Four Square Jane it was designed with the object of switching suspicion from her on to the unfortunate Steele."

"Do you think you'll catch Steele?" asked the chief.

Peter nodded.

"Yes, sir, I can catch him just when I want him, I think," he said. "It was only because we didn't want to take this man that we have let him go loose so long. He was a fool to run away, because the evidence against him was pretty paltry."

Dawes had a large number of calls to make the following morning, and the first of these was on a firm of safemakers in Queen Victoria Avenue. He had the good fortune to find that the sales manager had been in control of the store for the past twenty years, and that he remembered distinctly selling the safe to Lord Claythorpe.

"That's a relief," smiled the detective. "I was afraid I should have to go all over London to find the seller. How many keys did you supply?"

"Two," said the man. "One for his lordship, and one for Mr. Remington."

"Was there any difference in the two keys?"

"None except the marking. Have you one of the keys here?"

The detective produced it from his pocket, but when the salesman put out his hand for it he shook his head, with a smile.

"No, I'll keep it in my own hand, if you don't mind. I have a special reason," he said. "Perhaps you will describe the marking."

"It's inside the loop of the handle," explained the salesman. "You will find a small number engraved there—No. 1 or No. 2. No. 1 was intended for his lordship, No. 2 for Mr. Remington. The numbers were put there at Lord Claythorpe's suggestion in order to avoid confusion. It sometimes happens that both keys are in use together, and it is obviously desirable that they should not be mixed."

Peter looked at the inside of the loop and saw the number, then placed the key in his pocket with a little smile.

"Thank you; I think you have told me all that I want to know," he said. "You are sure that there are not three keys?"

"Perfectly certain," said the man emphatically. "And what is more, it would have been impossible to have got these keys cut, except by our firm."

Peter went back to Scotland Yard to find a telegram waiting for him. It was handed in at Falmouth by the chief of the local constabulary, and read:—

"Jamieson Steele is here. Shall I arrest? We have undoubted evidence that he spent last night in Falmouth with his wife."

"His wife?" said the puzzled detective. "I didn't know Steele was married. Well, that lets him out as far as the murder's concerned. The question is shall we pinch him for the forgery?"

He consulted his friend the Inspector, and the advice he received with regard to the arrest on the lesser charge was emphatic.

"Leave him alone," said the wise man. "It does us no good to arrest a man unless we are certain of conviction, and the only real offence that Jamieson Steele has committed was the fool offence of running away when he ought to have stood his ground. I interviewed the bank manager immediately after that crime, and the bank manager swore that the signature was not a forgery, but was Lord Claythorpe's own; and with that evidence before the jury you're not going to get a conviction, young fellow!"

Peter debated this point, and at last decided to wire to Steele asking him to come up and meet him.

The papers were filled with the stories of Four Square Jane's latest exploit. This, indeed, was the culmination of a succession of sensational crimes. Her character, her eccentricities, the record of her several offences, appeared in every newspaper. There were witnesses who had seen a mysterious woman hurrying up St. James's Street a quarter of an hour after the crime must have been committed; there were others who were certain they saw a veiled woman getting into a car at the bottom of St. James's Street; in fact, the usual crop of rumours and evidence was forthcoming, none of which was of the slightest value to the police.

That afternoon the detective visited Lord Claythorpe. He found that gentleman in very close consultation with a grave Mr. Lewinstein. To the credit of that genial Hebrew financier it must be said that, however optimistic might be the prospectuses he framed from time to time, he was undoubtedly straight. And Mr. Lewinstein's gravity of demeanour was due to a doubt which had arisen in his mind for the first time as to the trustworthy character of his lordly business associate. They greeted the detective— his lordship suspiciously and a little nervously, Lewinstein with evident relief.

"Well," asked Claythorpe, "have you made any discovery?"

"Several," said Peter. "We have been able to reconstruct the crime up to a point, and we have also proved that Mr. Steele was in Falmouth when the murder was committed."

A little shade passed over the sallow face of Lord Claythorpe.

"How could you prove that when you don't know where he is?" he asked.

"We found where he was, all right," said Peter with satisfaction.

"And you have arrested him, of course?" demanded his lordship. "I mean for the forgery."

The other smiled.

"Honestly, Lord Claythorpe, do you seriously wish us to arrest Jamieson Steele, in view of the overwhelming evidence in support of his contention that the cheque was given to him by you, and signed by you?"

"It's a lie!" roared Lord Claythorpe, bringing his fist down on the table.

"It may be a lie," said Peter Dawes quietly, "but it is a lie the jury will believe, and I can't believe that the outcome of such a prosecution will be very profitable to your lordship."

Claythorpe was silent. Presently he looked up and caught Lewinstein's eye, and Lewinstein nodded.

"I quite agree," said that gentleman seriously. "I never thought there was much of a case against young Steele. He was a good boy. Why he got rattled and ran away heaven only knows."

Claythorpe changed the subject, which was wholly disagreeable to him.

"Have you found anything else?"

"Nothing except this," said Peter, taking a key from his pocket and laying it on the table before Lord Claythorpe. "Will you be kind enough to show me your key?"

Claythorpe looked at the other for fully a minute.

"Certainly," he said. He disappeared from the room and returned with a bunch of keys, on the end of which lay the facsimile of that which lay on the table.

Peter took the key and examined it. He

looked at the inside of the loop, and as he did so an involuntary cry broke from Claythorpe's lips.

"A jumping tooth," he mumbled in apology. "Well, what have you found?"

"I've found that your keys have got slightly mixed," said Peter. "You have Remington's, and the key found in the office after the murder is yours!"

"Impossible!" said Lord Claythorpe.

"It is one of the impossible things that has happened," said Peter.

"Well, there's an explanation for that," Claythorpe began, but Peter stopped him.

"Of course there is," he said. "There are a hundred explanations, all of which are quite satisfactory. I suppose you had the keys out together on the table, and they got mixed at some time or other, and you did not notice. I'm not suggesting that you can't explain. I merely point out this fact, which at present has no bearing, or very little, or any aspect of the case."

Lewinstein and the detective went from the house together. His lordship, left alone, paced the study restlessly. Then he sat down at his desk and began to write. He produced two large canvas envelopes from the drawer of his desk, and into one of these he inserted a square certificate. He examined it casually before he put it into the cover. It was a debenture certificate issued by the North American Smelter Corporation for five hundred thousand dollars, and there was a particular reason why he should not have this valuable and important document in his house. He addressed the envelope containing the cover to himself in London. This he crossed with blue pencil, and from a drawer took out a small box containing a number of unused stamps. They were not British stamps, but Colonial, including Australian, African, Indian, and British Chinese. He fixed two Australian stamps, and placed the envelope within another, a little bigger. This he addressed to the manager of a Tasmanian bank, with whom he had done some business. To this gentleman he wrote a letter, saying that he expected to be in Australia by the time this letter reached its destination.

"But," the letter went on, "if by any chance I am not able to get to Australia, and I do not call for this packet within a week after its arrival, or notify you by cable, asking you to keep it for me, will you please send it back to me by registered post."

That was a job well done, he thought, as he sealed the envelope. This incriminating document would at any rate be out of the country for three months. Should he register it? He scratched his chin dubiously. Registration literally meant registration. If people inquired as to whether he had made any important transfer by mail, there would be no difficulty in discovering, not only the fact that he had posted such a letter, but the address to which it had been posted. No, on the whole he thought it would be better if he sent the letter by ordinary post. He put on his hat and coat, and took the letter himself to the nearest post office. On his return his butler announced a visitor.

"Miss Wilberforce!" said his lordship in surprise, "I thought she was in the country."

"She arrived a few minutes after you left, m'lord."

"Excellent!" said Claythorpe. It was the last person he had expected to see, and he fetched a sigh of relief. It might have been awkward if she had arrived earlier—at any rate, it was a remarkable coincidence that she had come at all that evening.

He found her standing by his table, and went towards her with outstretched hands.

"My dear Joyce," he said, "whatever brings you here?"

"I had a telegram about the robbery," she said; and then for the first time he realized that he had not troubled to notify the only person who was really affected by the burglary.

"Who wired you?"

"The police."

Still he was puzzled.

"But you couldn't have had the wire till eleven," he said, "how on earth did you get here?"

She smiled rather quietly.

"I did rather an adventurous thing," she

replied. "There is an aeroplane service between Falmouth and London."

He could only stare at her.

"That was very enterprising of you, Joyce."

"Tell me," she said, "did you also wire about this robbery?"

"I've been waiting till I got the fullest details before I notified you," said Lord Claythorpe easily. "You see, my dear girl, I have no wish to worry or frighten you, and possibly there was some chance that this wretched woman would return the securities, or at any rate give me a chance of redeeming them."

She nodded.

"I see," she said. "Then I can do nothing?"

He shook his head.

"Absolutely nothing."

She pursed her lips irresolutely.

"Can I write a letter?" she asked.

"Sit down, sit down, my dear child," he fussed. "You'll find paper and envelopes in this case."

At eleven o'clock that night, South Western District Post Office No. 2 was a scene of animation. Postal vans, horse vans, and motors were pulled up level with the big platform which led from the sorting room, and a dozen porters were engaged in handling mail bags for various destinations. The vans conveying local London mails had been despatched to the various district offices, the last to leave being a small one-horse van carrying the foreign mails to the G.P.O. It was driven by a middle-aged attendant named Carter, and pulled out of the yard at a quarter to twelve.

The weather was a repetition of that which had been experienced on the previous night. The south-wester was still blowing, the rain was coming down in gusty squalls, and the driver, muffled up to the chin, whipped up his horse to face the blast. His way led through the most deserted part of London's West End—more deserted than usual on this stormy night. One of the main streets through which he had to pass was "up," being in the hands of the road repair-

ers, and he turned into a side street to make a detour which would bring him clear of the obstruction. He observed, as he again turned his horse into the narrow thoroughfare running parallel with the main road, that the street lamps were extinguished, and put this down to the storm. He was in the blackest patch of the road, when a red lamp flashed right ahead of him, and he pulled his horse back on its haunches.

"What's the trouble?" he said leaning down and addressing the figure that held the lamp.

For answer, a blinding ray of light, directed by a powerful pocket lamp, struck him full in the face, and before he realised what had happened, someone had leapt on to the wheel and was by his side, clutching at the rails on top of the van. Something cold and hard was pressed against his neck.

"Utter a sound and you're a dead man," said a man's voice.

A quarter of an hour later, all that stood for authority in London was searching for a dark low motor car, and Peter Dawes, sitting on the edge of his bed in his pyjamas, was eagerly questioning one of his junior officers over the 'phone.

"Robbed the mail? Impossible! How did it happen? Were they arrested? I'll be with you in ten minutes."

He slipped into a suit, buttoned his mackintosh, and stepped out into the wild night. His flat was opposite a cab rank, and in less than ten minutes he was at Scotland Yard.

". . . the man said the thing was over so quickly he hadn't a chance of shouting, besides which, the fellow who stood by his side threatened to shoot him."

"What have they taken?"

"Only one bag, so far as can be ascertained. They knew just what they were after, and when they had got it they disappeared. The constable at the other end of the street heard the man shout, and came running down just in time to see a motor car turn the corner."

Later, Peter interviewed the driver, a badly scared man, in the stable-yard of the contractor who supplied the horses for the post office vans.

The driver was a man who had been in the Government service for ten years, and had covered the route he was following that night—except that he had never previously taken the side street rendered necessary by the condition of the road—for the greater part of that time.

"Did you see anybody else except the man who sat by your side and threatened you?" asked Peter.

"Yes, sir," replied the man. "I saw what I thought was a girl in a black oilskin; she passed round to the back of the van."

"Where is the van? Is it here?" asked the detective, and they showed him a small, four-wheeled vehicle, covered in at the top and with two doors which were fastened behind by a steel bar and padlocked. The padlock had been wrenched open, and the doors now stood ajar.

"They had taken out the mail bags, sir, in order to sort them out to see what was gone."

Peter flashed his lamp in the interior, examining the floor and sides carefully. There was no clue of any kind until he began his inspection of the inside of the doors, and there, on the very centre, was the familiar label.

"Four Square Jane, eh?" said Peter, and whistled.

"I deeply regret that I found it necessary to interfere with His Majesty's mails. In a certain bag was a letter which was very compromising to me, and it was necessary that I should recover it. I beg to enclose the remainder of the letters which are, as you will see, intact and untampered with!"

This document, bearing the seal manual of Four Square Jane, was delivered to the Central Post Office accompanied by a large mail bag. The person who delivered it was a small boy of the District Messenger Service, who brought the package in a taxi-cab. He could give no information as to the person who had sent him except to say that it was a lady wearing a heavy veil, who had summoned him to a popular hotel and

had met him in the vestibule. They had taken a cab together, and at the corner of Clarges Street the cab had pulled up on the instructions of the lady; a man had appeared bearing a bundle that he had put into a cab which then drove on. A little later the lady had stopped the cab, given the boy a pound note, and herself descended. The boy could only say that in his opinion she was young, and undoubtedly in mourning.

Here was new fuel to the flames of excitement which the murder of Remington had aroused. A murder one day, accompanied by a robbery which, if rumour had any foundation, involved nearly a quarter of a million pounds, and this tragedy followed on the next day by the robbery of the King's mail; and all at the hands of a mysterious woman whose name was already a household word—these happenings apart from the earlier crimes were sufficient to furnish not only London but the whole of Britain with a subject for discussion.

Lord Claythorpe heard the news of the robbery with some uneasiness. Inquiries made at the local district office, however, relieved him of his anxiety. The mail bag which had been taken, he was informed, was part of the Indian mail. The Australian mail had been delivered at the General Post Office earlier in the evening by the service which left the district office at nine o'clock. It was as well for his peace of mind that he did not know how erroneous was the information he had been given. He had asked Joyce to breakfast with him, and had kept her waiting whilst he pursued these inquiries; for he had read of the robbery in bed, and had hurried round to the district office without delay.

"This is the most amazing exploit of all," he said to the girl, as he handed her the paper. "Take this," he said. "I have read it."

"Poor Jane Briglow!"

"Why Jane Briglow?"

The girl smiled.

"Mother insists that it is she who has committed all these acts. As a matter of fact, I happen to know that Jane is in good service in the North of England."

Claythorpe looked at her in surprise.

"Is that so?" he said incredulously. "Do you know, I'd begun to form a theory about that girl."

"Well, don't," said Joyce, helping herself to jam.

"I wonder whether they'll get the bag back," speculated his lordship. "There's nothing about it in the papers."

"It is very unlikely, I should think," said Joyce. She rolled up her table-napkin. "You wanted to see me about something this morning," she said.

He nodded.

"Yes, Joyce," he said. "I've been thinking matters over. I'm afraid I was rather prejudiced against young Steele." The girl made no reply. "I'm not even certain that he was guilty of the offence with which I charged him," Claythorpe went on. "You see, I was very worried at the time, and it is possible that I may have signed a cheque and overlooked the fact. You were very fond of Steele?"

She nodded.

"Well," said Lord Claythorpe heartily, "I will no longer stand in your way."

She looked at him steadily.

"You mean you will consent to my marriage?"

He nodded.

"Why not?" he asked.

"Why not, indeed?" she said, a little bitterly. "I understand that my fortune no longer depends upon whether I marry according to your wishes or not—since I have no fortune."

"It is very deplorable," said his lordship gravely. "Really, I feel morally responsible. It is a most stupendous tragedy, but I will do whatever I can to make it up to you, Joyce. I am not a rich man by any means, but I have decided, if you still feel you cannot marry my son, and would prefer to marry Mr. Steele, to give you a wedding gift of twenty thousand pounds."

"That is very good of you," said the girl politely, "but, of course, I cannot take your verbal permission. You will not mind putting that into writing?"

"With all the pleasure in life," said Lord Claythorpe, getting up and walking to a writing-table, "really Joyce, you're becoming quite shrewd in your old age," he chuckled.

He drew a sheet of paper from a writing-case and poised a pen.

"What is the date?" he asked.

"It is the nineteenth," said the girl. "But date it as from the first of the month."

"Why?" he asked in surprise.

"Well, there are many reasons," said the girl slowly. "I shouldn't like people to think, for example, that your liking for Mr. Steele dated from the loss of my property."

He looked at her sharply, but not a muscle of her face moved.

"That is very considerate of you," he said with a shrug, "and it doesn't really matter whether I make it the first or the twenty-first, does it?"

He wrote quickly, blotted the sheet, handed it to the girl, and she read it and folded the paper away in her handbag.

"Was that really the reason you asked me to date the permission back?" he asked curiously.

She shook her head.

"No," she said coolly. "I was married to Jamieson last week."

"Married!" he gasped. "Without my permission!"

"With your permission," she said, tapping her little bag.

For a second he frowned, and then he burst into a roar of laughter.

"Well, well," he said. "That's rather rich. You're a very naughty girl, Joyce. Does your mother know?"

"Mother knows nothing about it," said the girl. "There is one more thing I want to speak to you about, Lord Claythorpe, and that is in connection with the robbery of the mail last night."

It was at that moment that Peter Dawes was announced.

"It's the detective," said Lord Claythorpe with a little frown. "You don't want to see him?"

"On the contrary, let him come in, because what I am going to say will interest him," she said.

Claythorpe nodded to the butler, and a few seconds later Peter Dawes came into the room. He bowed to the girl and shook hands with Lord Claythorpe.

"This is my niece—well, not exactly my niece," smiled Claythorpe, "but the niece of a very dear friend of mine, and, in fact, the lady who is the principal loser in that terrible tragedy of St. James's Street."

"Indeed?" said Peter with a smile. "I think I know the young lady by sight."

"And she was going to make an interesting communication to me just as you came in," said Claythorpe. "Perhaps, Joyce, dear, you will tell Mr. Dawes?"

"I was only going to say that this morning I received this." She did not go to her bag, but produced a folded paper from the inside of her blouse. This she opened and spread on the table and Claythorpe's face went white, for it was the five hundred thousand dollar bond which he had despatched the day before to Australia. "I seem to remember," said the girl, "that this was part of my inheritance—you remember I was given a list of the securities you held for me?"

Lord Claythorpe licked his dry lips.

"Yes," he said huskily. "That is part of your inheritance."

"How did it come to you?" asked Peter Dawes.

"It was found in my letter-box this morning," said the girl.

"Accompanied by a letter?"

"No, nothing," said Joyce. "For some reason I connected it with the mail robbery, and thought that perhaps you had entrusted this certificate to the post—and that in your letter you mentioned the fact that it was mine."

"That also is impossible," said Peter Dawes quietly, "because, if your statement is correct, this document would have been amongst those which were stolen on the night that Remington was murdered. Isn't that so, Lord Claythorpe?"

Claythorpe nodded.

"It is very providential for you, Joyce," he said huskily. "I haven't the slightest idea how it

came to you. Probably the thief who murdered Remington knew it was yours and restored it."

The girl nodded.

"The thief being Four Square Jane, eh?" said Peter Dawes, eyeing his lordship narrowly.

"Naturally, who else?" said Claythorpe, meeting the other's eyes steadily. "It was undoubtedly her work, her label was on the inside of the safe."

"That is true," agreed Peter. "But there was one remarkable fact about that label which seems to have been overlooked."

"What was that?"

"It had been used before," said Peter slowly. "It was an old label which had previously been attached to something or somewhere, for the marks of the old adhesion were still on it when I took it off. In fact, there were only a few places where the gum on the label remained useful."

Neither the eyes of the girl or Lord Claythorpe left the other's face.

"That is curious," said Lord Claythorpe slowly. "What do you deduce from that?"

Dawes shrugged.

"Nothing, except that it is possible someone is using Four Square Jane's name in vain," he said, "someone who was in a position to get one of the old labels she had used on her previous felonies. May I sit down?" he asked, for he had not been invited to take a seat.

Claythorpe nodded curtly, and Dawes pulled a chair from the table and seated himself.

"I have been reconstructing that crime," he said, "and there are one or two things that puzzle me. In the first place, I am perfectly certain that no woman was in your office on the night the murder was committed."

Lord Claythorpe raised his eyebrows.

"Indeed!" he said. "And yet the constable who was first in the room told me that he distinctly smelt a very powerful scent—the sort a woman would use. I also noticed it when I went into the room."

"So did I," said Peter, "and that quite decided me that Four Square Jane had nothing to do with the business. A cool, calculating woman like Four Square Jane is certain to be a lady of more than ordinary intelligence and regular habits. She is not the kind who would suddenly take up a powerful scent, because it is possible to trace a woman criminal by this means, and it is certain that in no other case which is associated with her name was there the slightest trace or hint of perfume. That makes me more certain that the crime was committed by a man and that he sprinkled the scent on the floor in order to leave the impression that Four Square Jane had been the operator."

"What do you think happened?" asked Lord Claythorpe after a pause.

"I think that Remington went to the office with the intention of examining the contents of the safe," said Peter deliberately. "I believe he had the whole of the envelopes on the table, and had opened several, when he was surprised by somebody who came into the office. There was an argument, in the course of which he was shot dead."

"You suggest that the intruder was a burglar?" said Lord Claythorpe with a set face, but Peter shook his head.

"No," he said. "This man admitted himself to the office by means of a key. The door was not forced, and there was no sign of a skeleton key having been used. Moreover, the newcomer must have been well acquainted with the office, because, after the murder was committed he switched out the light and pulled up the blinds which Remington had lowered, so that the light should not attract attention from the street. We know they were lowered, because the constable on beat duty on the other side of the street saw no sign of a light. The blinds were heavy and practically light-proof. Now, the man who committed the murder knew his way about the office well enough to turn out the light, move in the dark, and manipulate the three blinds which covered the windows. I've been experimenting with those blinds, and I've found that they're fairly complicated in their mechanism."

Again there was a pause.

"A very fantastic theory, if you will allow me to say so," said Lord Claythorpe, "and not at all like the sensible, commonsense point of view that I should have expected from Scotland Yard."

"That may be so," said Peter quietly. "But we get romantic theories even at Scotland Yard."

He looked down at the bond, still spread out on the table.

"I suppose your lordship will put this in the bank after your unhappy experience?" he said.

"Yes, yes," said Lord Claythorpe briefly, and Peter turned to the girl.

"I congratulate you upon recovering a part of your property," he said. "I understand this is held in trust for you until you're married."

Lord Claythorpe started violently.

"Until you're married!" he said. "Why, why!" He caught the girl's smiling eyes. "That means now, doesn't it?" he said.

"Until your marriage is approved by me," said Lord Claythorpe.

"I think it is approved by you," said Joyce, and dived her hand into her bag.

"It will be delivered to you formally tomorrow," said his lordship stiffly.

Peter Dawes and the girl went out of the house together and walked in silence a little way.

"I'd give a lot to know what you're thinking," said the girl.

"And I'd give a lot to know what you know," smiled Peter, and at that cryptic exchange they parted.

That night Mr. Lewinstein was giving a big dinner party at the Ritz Carlton. Joyce had been invited months before, but had no thought of accepting the invitation until she returned to the hotel where she was staying.

A good-looking man rose as she entered the vestibule, and came towards her with a smile. He took her arm, and slowly they paced the long corridor leading to the elevator.

"So that's Mr. Jamieson Steele, eh?" said Peter Dawes, who had followed her to the hotel, and he looked very thoughtfully in the direction the two had taken.

He went from the hotel and called on Mr. Lewinstein by appointment, and that great financier welcomed him with a large cigar.

"I heard you were engaged upon the Four Square Jane case, Mr. Dawes," he said, "and I thought it wouldn't be a bad idea if I invited you to dinner tonight."

"Is this a professional or a friendly engagement?" smiled Peter.

"It's both," said Mr. Lewinstein frankly. "The fact is, Mr. Dawes, and I'm not going to make any bones about the truth, it is necessary in my business that I should keep in touch with the best people in London. From time to time I give a dinner-party, and I bring together all that is bright and beautiful and brainy. Usually these dinners are given in my own house, but I've had a rather painful experience," he said grimly, and Peter, who knew the history of Four Square Jane's robbery, nodded in sympathy.

"Now, I want to say a few words about Miss Four Square Jane," said Lewinstein. "Do you mind seeing if the door is closed?"

Peter looked outside, and closed the door carefully.

"I'd hate what I'm saying to be repeated in certain quarters," Lewinstein went on. "But in that robbery there were several remarkable coincidences. Do you know that Four Square Jane stole nothing, in most cases, except the presents that had been given by Claythorpe? Claythorpe is rather a gay old bird and has gone the pace. He has been spending money like water for years. Of course, he may have a big income, or he may not. I know just what he gets out of the City. On the night of the burglary at my house this girl went through every room and took articles which in many cases had been given to the various people by Claythorpe. For example, something he had presented to my wife disappeared; some shirt-studs, which he gave to me, were also gone. That's rather funny, don't you think?"

"It fits in with my theory," said Peter nodding, "that Four Square Jane has only one enemy in the world, and that is Lord Claythorpe."

"That's my opinion, too," said Lewinstein. "Now tonight I am giving a big dinner-party, as I told you, and there will be a lot of women there,

and the women are scared of my parties since the last one. There will be jewels to burn, but what makes me specially nervous is that Claythorpe has insisted on Lola Lane being invited."

"The dancer?" asked Peter in surprise, and the other nodded.

"She's a great friend of Claythorpe's—I suppose you know that? He put up the money for her last production, and, not to put too fine a point upon it, the old man is infatuated by the girl."

Mr. Lewinstein sucked contemplatively at one of his large cigars.

"I am not a prude, you understand, Mr. Dawes," he said, "and the way men amuse themselves does not concern me. Claythorpe is much too big a man for me to refuse any request he makes. In the present state of society, people like Lola are accepted, and it is not for me to reform the Smart Set. The only thing I'm scared about is that she will be covered from head to foot in jewels."

He pulled again at his cigar, and looked at it before he went on:

"Which Lord Claythorpe has given her."

"This is news to me," said Peter.

"It would be news to a lot of people," said Lewinstein, "for Claythorpe is supposed to be one of the big moral forces in the City." He chuckled, as though at a good joke. "Now, there's another point I want to make to you. This girl Lola has been telling her friends—at least, she told a friend of mine—that she was going to the Argentine to live in about six months' time. My friend asked her if Lord Claythorpe agreed to that arrangement. You know, these theatrical people are very frank, and she said 'Yes.' He looked at the detective.

"Which means that Claythorpe is going, too," said Peter, and Lewinstein nodded.

"That is also news," said Peter Dawes. "Thank you, I will accept your invitation to dinner tonight."

"Good!" said Lewinstein, brightening. "You don't mind, but I may have to put you next to Lola."

That evening when Peter strolled into the big reception hall which Mr. Lewinstein had engaged with his private dining-room, his eyes wandered in search of the lady. He knew her by sight—had seen her picture in the illustrated newspapers. He had no difficulty in distinguishing her rather bold features; and, even if he had not, he would have known, from the daring dress she wore, that this was the redoubtable lady whose name had been hinted in connection with one or two unpleasant scandals.

But chiefly his eyes were for the great collar of emeralds about her shapely throat. They were big green stones which scintillated in the shaded lights, and were by far the most remarkable jewels in the room. Evidently Lewinstein had explained to Lord Claythorpe the reason of the invitation, because his lordship received him quite graciously and made no demur at a common detective occupying the place by the side of the lady who had so completely enthralled him.

It was after the introduction that Peter had a surprise, for he saw Joyce Wilberforce.

"I didn't expect to see you again today, Miss Wilberforce," he said.

"I did not expect to come myself," replied the girl, "but my husband—you knew I was married?"

Mr. Dawes nodded.

"That is one of the things I did know," he laughed.

"My husband had an engagement, and he suggested that I should amuse myself by coming here. What do you think of the emeralds?" she asked mischievously. "I suppose you're here to keep a friendly eye on them?"

Peter smiled.

"They are rather gorgeous, aren't they? Though I cannot say I admire their wearer."

Peter was discreetly silent. He took the dancer in to dinner, and found her a singularly dull person, except on the question of dress and the weakness of her sister artistes. The dinner was in full swing when Joyce Wilberforce, who was sitting almost opposite the detective, screamed and hunched herself up in the chair.

"Look, look!" she cried, pointing to the floor. "A rat!"

Peter, leaning over the table, saw a small brown shape run along the wainscot. The woman at his side shrieked and drew her feet up to the rail of her chair. This was the last thing he saw, for at that second all the lights in the room went out. He heard a scream from the dancer.

"My necklace, my necklace!"

There was a babble of voices, a discordant shouting of instructions and advice. Then Peter struck a match. The only thing he saw in the flickering light was the figure of Lola, with her hands clasped round her neck.

The collar of emeralds had disappeared!

It was five minutes before somebody fixed the fuse and brought the lights on again.

"Let nobody leave the room!" shouted Peter authoritatively. "Everybody here must be searched. And——"

Then his eyes fell upon a little card which had been placed on the table before him, and which had not been there when the lights went out. There was no need to turn it. He knew what to expect on the other side. The four squares and the little J looked up at him mockingly.

Peter Dawes, of Scotland Yard, had to do some mighty quick thinking and, by an effort of will, concentrate his mind upon all the events which had immediately preceded the robbery of the dancer's necklace. First there was Joyce Wilberforce, who had undoubtedly seen a rat running along by the wainscot, and had drawn up her feet in a characteristically feminine fashion. Then he had seen the dancer draw up her feet, and put down her hands to pull her skirts tight—also a characteristically feminine action.

What else had he seen? He had seen a hand, the hand of a waiter, between himself and the woman on his left. He remembered now that there was something peculiar about that hand which had attracted his attention, and that he had been on the point of turning his head in order to see it better when Joyce's scream had distracted his attention.

What was there about that hand? He concentrated all his mind upon this trivial matter, realising instinctively that behind that momentary omen was a possible solution of the mystery. He remembered that it was a well-manicured hand. That in itself was remarkable in a waiter. There had been no jewels or rings upon it, which was not remarkable. This he had observed idly. Then, in a flash, the detail which had interested him came back to his mind. The little finger was remarkably short. He puzzled his head to connect this malformation with something he had heard before. Leaving the room in the charge of the police who had been summoned, he took a taxi and drove straight to the hotel where Joyce Steele was staying with her husband.

"Mrs. Steele is out, but Mr. Steele has just come in," said the hotel clerk. "Shall I send your name up?"

"It is unnecessary," said the detective, showing his card. "I will go up to his room. What is the number?"

He was told, and a page piloted him to the door. Without troubling to knock, he turned the handle and walked in. Jamieson Steele was sitting before a little fire, smoking a cigarette, and looked up at the intruder.

"Hullo, Mr. Dawes," he said calmly.

"You know me, eh?" said Peter. "May I have a few words with you?"

"You can have as many as you like," said Steele. "Take a chair, won't you? This is not a bad little sitting-room, but it is rather draughty. To what am I indebted for this visit? Is our wicked uncle pressing his charge of forgery?"

Peter Dawes smiled.

"I don't think that is likely," he said. "I have made a call upon you for the purpose of seeing your hands."

"My hands?" said the other in a tone of surprise. "Are you going in for a manicure?"

"Hardly," said Peter drily, as the other spread out his hands before him. "What is the matter with your little finger?" he asked, after a scrutiny.

Jamieson Steele examined the finger and laughed.

"He is not very big, is he?" he laughed. "Arrested development, I suppose. It is the one blemish on an otherwise perfect body."

"Where have you been tonight?" asked Peter quietly.

"I have been to various places, including Scotland Yard" was the staggering reply.

"To Scotland Yard?" asked Peter incredulously, and Jamieson Steele nodded.

"The fact is, I wanted to see you about the curious charge which Lord Claythorpe brings forward from time to time; and also I felt that some explanation was due to you as you are in charge of a case which nearly affects my wife, as to the reason I did a bolt when Claythorpe brought this charge of forgery against me."

"What time did you leave the Yard?"

"About half an hour ago," said Steele.

Peter looked at him closely. He was wearing an ordinary lounge suit, and a soft shirt. The hand which had come upon the table had undoubtedly been encased in a stiff cuff and a black sleeve.

"Why, what is the matter?" asked Steele.

"There has been a robbery at the Ritz Carlton tonight," Peter explained. "A man dressed as a waiter has stolen an emerald necklace."

"And naturally you suspect me," he said ironically. "Well, you're at liberty to search this apartment."

"May I see your dress clothes?" said Peter.

For answer, the other led him to his bedroom, and his dress suit was discovered at the bottom of a trunk, carefully folded and brushed.

"Now," said Peter, "if you don't mind, I'll conduct the search you suggest. You understand that I have no authority to do so, and I can only make the search with your permission."

"You have my permission," said the other. "I realise that I am a suspected person, so go ahead, and don't mind hurting my feelings."

Peter's search was thorough, but revealed nothing of importance.

"This is my wife's room," said Steele. "Perhaps you would like to search that?"

"I should," said Peter Dawes, without hesitation, but again his investigations drew blank.

He opened all the windows of the room, feeling along the window-sills for a tape, cord or thread, from which an emerald necklace might be suspended. It was an old trick to fasten a stolen article to a black thread, and the black thread to some stout gummed paper fastened to the window-sill; but here again he discovered nothing.

"Now," said the cheerful young man, "you had better search me."

"I might as well do the job thoroughly," agreed Peter, and ran his hands scientifically over the other's body.

"Not guilty, eh?" said Steele, when he had finished. "Now perhaps you'll sit down, and I'll tell you something about Lord Claythorpe that will interest you. You know, of course, that Claythorpe has been living on the verge of bankruptcy. Won't you sit down?" he said again, and Peter obeyed. "Here is a cigar which will steady your nerves."

"I can't stay very long," said Peter, "but I should like your end of the serial very much indeed."

He took the proffered cigar, and bit off the end.

"As I was saying," Steele went on, "Claythorpe has been living for years on the verge of bankruptcy. He is a man who, from his youth up, has been dependent on his wits. His early life was passed in what the good books called dissolute living. I believe there was a time when he was so broke he slept on the Embankment."

Peter nodded. He also had heard something to this effect.

"This, of course, was before he came into the title. He is a clever and unscrupulous man with a good address. And knowing that he was up against it, he set himself to gain powerful friends.

One of these friends was my wife's uncle—a good-natured innocent kind of man, who had amassed a considerable fortune in South Africa. I believe Claythorpe bled him pretty considerably, and might have bled him to death, only the old fellow died naturally, leaving a handsome legacy to his friends and the residue of his property to my wife. Claythorpe was made the executor, and given pretty wide powers. Amongst the property which my wife inherited—or rather, would inherit on her wedding day, was a small coal-mine in the North of England, which at the time of the old man's death was being managed by a very brilliant young engineer, whose name modesty alone prevents my revealing."

"Go on," said Peter, with a smile.

"Claythorpe, finding himself in control of such unlimited wealth, set himself out to improve the property. And the first thing he did was to project the flotation of my coal mine—I call it mine, and I always regarded it as such in a spiritual sense—for about six times its value."

Peter nodded.

"In order to bring in the public, it was necessary that a statement should be made with regard to the quantity of coal in the mine, the extent of the seams, etc., and it was my duty to prepare a most glowing statement, which would loosen the purse-strings of the investing public. Claythorpe put the scheme up to me, and I said, 'No.' I also told him," the young man went on, choosing his words carefully, "that, if he floated this company, I should have something to say in the columns of the financial Press. So the thing was dropped, but Claythorpe never forgave me. There was a certain work which I had done for him outside my ordinary duties and, summoning me to his St. James's Street office, he gave me a cheque. I noticed at the time that the cheque was for a much larger amount than I had expected, and thought his lordship was trying to get into my good books. I also noticed that the amount inscribed on the cheque had the appearance of being altered, and that even his lordship's signature looked rather unusual. I took the cheque and presented it to my bank a few days later, and was summoned to the office, where I was denounced as a forger," said the young man, puffing a ring of smoke into the air reflectively, "but it gives you a very funny feeling in the pit of the stomach. The heroic and proper and sensible thing to do was to stand on my ground, go up to the Old Bailey, make a great speech which would call forth the applause and approbation of judge and jury, and stalk out of the court in triumph. Under these circumstances, however, one seldom does the proper thing. Remington it was—the man who is now dead—who suggested that I should bolt; and, like a fool, I bolted. The only person who knew where I was was Joyce. I won't tell you anything about my wife, because you probably know everything that is worth knowing. I'll only say that I've loved her for years, and that my affection has been returned. It was she who urged me to come back to London and stand my trial, but I put this down to her child-like innocence—a man is always inclined to think that he's the cleverer of the two when he's exchanging advice with women. That's the whole of the story."

Peter waited.

"Now, Mr. Steele," he said, "perhaps you will explain why you were at the Ritz-Carlton Hotel tonight disguised as a waiter."

Steele looked at him with a quizzical smile.

"I think I could explain it if I'd been there," he said. "Do you want me to invent an explanation as well as to invent my presence?"

"I am as confident that you were there," said Peter, "as I am that you are sitting here. I am also certain that it will be next to impossible to prove that you were in the room." He rose from his seat. "I am going back to the hotel," he said, "though I do not expect that any of our bloodhounds have discovered the necklace."

"Have another cigar," said Steele, offering the open box.

Peter shook his head.

"No thank you," he said.

"They won't hurt you, take a handful."

Peter laughingly refused.

"I think I am nearly through with this Four Square Jane business," he said, "and I am pretty certain that it is not going to bring kudos or promotion to me."

"I have a feeling that it will not, either," said Steele. "It's a rum case."

Peter shook his head.

"Rum, because I've solved the mystery of Four Square Jane. I know who she is, and why she has robbed Claythorpe and his friends."

"You know her, do you?" said Steele thoughtfully, and the other nodded.

Jamieson Steele waited till the door closed upon the detective, and then waited another five minutes before he rose and shot the bolt. He then locked the two doors leading from the sitting-room, took up the box of cigars and placed it on the table. He dipped into the box, and pulled out handful after handful of cigars, and then he took out something which glittered and scintillated in the light—a great collar of big emeralds—and laid it on the table. He looked at it thoughtfully, then wrapped it in a silk handkerchief and thrust it into his pocket, replacing the cigars in the box. He passed into his bedroom, and came out wearing a soft felt hat, and a long dark-blue trench coat.

He hesitated before he unbolted the door, unbottoned the coat, and took out the handkerchief containing the emerald collar, and put it into his overcoat pocket. If he had turned his head at that moment, and looked at the half-opened door of his bedroom, he might have caught a glimpse of a figure that was watching his every movement. Peter Dawes had not come alone, and there were three entrances to the private suite which Mr. and Mrs. Steele occupied.

Then Jamieson Steele stepped out so quickly that by the time the watcher was in the corridor, he had disappeared down the lift, which happened to be going down at that moment. The man raced down the stairs three at a time. The last landing was a broad marble balcony which overlooked the hall, and, glancing down, he saw

Peter waiting. He waved his hand significantly, and at that moment the elevator reached the ground floor, and Jamieson Steele stepped out of it.

He was half way across the vestibule when Peter confronted him.

"Wait a moment, Mr. Steele. I want you," said Peter.

It was at that second that the swing doors turned and Joyce Steele came in.

"Want me?" said Steele. "Why?"

"I am going to take you into custody on the charge of being concerned in the robbery tonight," said the detective.

"You're mad," said Steele, with an immovable face.

"Arrest him? Oh no, no!" It was the gasping voice of the girl. In a second she had flung herself upon the man, her two arms about him. "It isn't true, it isn't true!" she sobbed.

Very gently Steele pushed her back.

"Go away, my dear. This is no place for you," he said. "Mr. Dawes has made a great mistake, as he will discover."

The watcher had joined the group now.

"He's got the goods, sir," he said triumphantly. "I watched him. The necklace was in a cigar box. He has got it in his pocket."

"Hold out your hands," said Peter, and in a second Jamieson Steele was handcuffed.

"May I come?" said the girl.

"It is better you did not," said Peter. "Perhaps your husband will be able to prove his innocence. Anyway, you can do nothing."

They left her, a disconsolate figure, standing in the hall, and carried their prisoner to Cannon Row.

"Now we'll search you, if you don't mind?" asked Peter.

"Not at all," said the other coolly.

"Where did you say he put it?"

"In his pocket, sir," said the spy.

Peter searched the overcoat pockets.

"There's nothing here," he said.

"Nothing there?" gasped the man in astonishment. "But I saw him put it there. He took it out of his hip pocket and——"

"Well, let's try his hip pocket. Take off your coat, Steele."

The young man obeyed, and again Peter's deft fingers went over him, but with no better result. The two detectives looked at one another in consternation.

"A slight mistake on your part, my friend," said Peter, "I'm sorry we've given you all this trouble."

"Look in the bottom of the cab," the second detective pleaded, and Peter laughed.

"I don't see what he could do. He had the bracelets on his hands, and I never took my eyes off them once. You can search the cab if you like—it's waiting at the door."

But the search of the cab produced no better result.

And then an inspiration dawned upon Peter, and he laughed, softly and long.

"I'm going to give up this business," he said. "I really am, Steele. I'm too childishly trustful."

Their eyes met, and both eyes were creased with laughter.

"All right," said Peter. "Let him go."

"Let him go?" said the other detective in dismay.

"Yes. We've no evidence against this gentleman, and we're very unlikely to secure it."

For in that short space of time, Peter had realized exactly the kind he was up against; saw as clearly as daylight what had happened to the emeralds, and knew that any attempt to find them now would merely lead to another disappointment.

"If you don't mind, Steele, I think I'll go back with you to your hotel. I hope you're not bearing malice."

"Not at all," replied Steele. "It's your job to catch me, and my job to——" he paused.

"Yes?" said Peter curiously.

"My job to get caught, obviously," said Steele with a laugh.

They did not speak again until they were in the cab on the way back to the hotel.

"I'm afraid my poor wife is very much upset."

"I'm not worrying about that," said Peter drily. "Steele, I think you are a wise man; and, being wise, you will not be averse to receiving advice from one who knows this game from A to Z."

Steele did not reply.

"My advice to you is, get out of the country just as soon as you can, and take your wife with you," said Peter. "There is an old adage that the pitcher goes often to the well—I need not remind you of that."

"Suppose I tell you I do not understand you," said Steele.

"You will do nothing so banal," replied Peter. "I tell you I know your game, and the thing that is going to stand against you is the robbery of the mail. That is your only bad offence in my eyes, and it is the one for which I would work night and day to bring you to justice."

Again a silence.

"Nothing was stolen from the mail, that I know," said Peter. "It was all returned. Your principal offence is that you scared a respectable servant of his Majesty into fits. Anyway, it is a felony of a most serious kind, and would get you twenty years if we could secure evidence against you. You held up his Majesty's mail with a loaded revolver——"

"Even that you couldn't prove," laughed Steele. "It might not have been any more than a piece of gaspipe. After all, a hardened criminal, such as you believe I am, possessed of a brain which you must know by this time I have, would have sufficient knowledge of the law to prevent his carrying lethal weapons."

"We are talking here without witnesses," said Peter.

"I'm not so sure," said Steele quickly. "I thought I was talking to you in my little sitting-room without witnesses."

"Anyway, you can be sure there are no witnesses here," smiled Peter, as the cab turned into the street where the hotel was situated. "And I am asking you confidentially, and man to man, if you can give me any information at all regarding the murder in St. James's Street."

Steele thought awhile.

"I can't," he said. "As a matter of fact, I was in Falmouth at the time, as you know. Obviously, it was not the work of the lady who calls herself Four Square Jane, because my impression of that charming creature is that she would be scared to death at the sight of a revolver. The card which was found in the dead man's hand——"

"How did you know that?" asked Peter quickly.

"These things get about," replied the other unabashed. "Has it occurred to you that it was a moist night, that the murderer may have been hot, and that on the card may be his fingerprints?"

"That did occur to me," said Peter. "In fact, it was the first thing I thought about. And, if it is any interest to you, I will tell you that there was a finger print upon that card, which I have been trying for the past few days to——" He stopped. "Here we are at your hotel," he said. "There's a good detective lost in you, Steele."

"Not lost, but gone before," said the other flippantly. "Good-night. You won't come up and have a cigar?"

"No thanks," said a grim Peter.

He went back to Scotland Yard. It was curious, amazingly curious, that Steele should have mentioned the card that night. It was not into an empty office that he went, despite the lateness of the hour. There was an important police conference, and all the heads of departments were crowded into the room, the air of which was blue with tobacco smoke. A stout, genial man nodded to Peter as he came in.

"We've had a devil of a job getting it, Peter, but we've succeeded."

Before him was a small visiting-card, bearing the name of Jamieson Steele. In the very centre was a violet finger print. The finger print had not been visible to the naked eye until it had been treated with chemicals, and its present appearance was the result of the patient work of three of Scotland Yard's greatest scientists.

"Did you get the other?" said Peter.

"There it is," said the stout man, and pointed to a strip of cardboard bearing two black finger prints.

Peter compared the two impressions.

"Well," he said, "at any rate, one of the mysteries is cleared up. How did you get this?" he asked pointing to the strip of cardboard bearing the two prints.

"I called on him, and shook hands with him," said the stout man with a smile. "He was horribly surprised and offended that I should take such a liberty. Then I handed him the strip of card. It was a little while later, when he put his hand on the blotting pad, that he discovered that his palm and finger-tips were black, and I think that he was the most astonished man I ever saw."

Peter smiled.

"He didn't guess that your hand would be carefully covered with lamp-black, I gather?"

"Hardly," said the fat man.

Again Peter compared the two impressions.

"There is no doubt at all about it," he said. He looked at his watch. "Half-past twelve. Not a bad time, either. I'll take Wilkins and Browne," he said, "and get the thing over. It's going to be a lot of trouble. Have you got the warrant?"

The stout man opened the drawer of his desk and passed a sheet of paper across. Peter examined it.

"Thank you," he said simply.

Lord Claythorpe was in his study taking a stiff whisky and soda when the detective was announced.

"Well?" he said. "Have you found the person who stole the emerald necklace?"

"No, my lord," said Peter. "But I have found the man who shot Remington."

Lord Claythorpe's face went ashen.

"What do you mean?" he said hoarsely. "What do you mean?"

"I mean," said Peter, "that I am going to take you into custody on a charge of wilful murder, and I caution you that what you now say will be used in evidence against you."

———

At three o'clock in the morning, Lord Claythorpe, an inmate of a cell at Cannon Row, sent for Peter Dawes. Peter was ushered into the cell, and found that Claythorpe had recovered from the crushed and hopeless man he had left: he was now calm and normal.

"I want to see you, Dawes," he said, "to clear up a few matters which are on my conscience."

"Of course, you know," said Peter, "that any statement you make———"

"I know, I know," said the other impatiently. "But I have this to say." He paced the short cell, his hands gripped behind him. Presently he sat down at Peter's side. "In the first place," he said, "let me tell you that I killed Donald Remington. There's a long story leading up to that killing, but I swear I had no intention of hurting him."

Peter had taken a notebook from one pocket and a pencil from another, and was jotting down in his queer shorthand the story the other told. Usually such a proceeding had the effect of silencing the man whose words were being inscribed, but Claythorpe did not seem to notice.

"When Joyce Wilberforce's uncle left me executor of his estate, I had every intention of going straight," he went on. "But I made bad losses in the Kaffir market, and gradually I began to nibble at her fortune. The securities, which were kept in sealed envelopes at the bank, were taken out one by one, and disposed of; blank sheets of paper were placed in the envelopes, which were resealed. And when the burglary occurred, there was only one hundred-thousand-pound bond left. That bond you will find in a secret drawer of my desk. I think Remington, who was in my confidence except for this matter, suspected it all along. When I took the securities from the bank, it was with the intention of raiding my own office that night and leaving the sign of Four Square Jane to throw suspicion elsewhere. I came back to the office at eleven o'clock that night, but found Remington was before me. He had opened the safe with his key, and was satisfying his curiosity as to the contents of the envelopes. He threatened to expose me, for he had already discovered that the envelopes contained nothing of importance.

"I was a desperate man. I had taken a revolver with me in case I was detected, intending to end my life then and there. Remington made certain demands on me, to which I refused to agree. He rose and walked to the door, telling me he intended to call the police; it was then that I shot him."

Peter Dawes looked up from his notes.

"What about Steele's card?" he said.

Lord Claythorpe nodded.

"I had taken that with me to throw suspicion upon Steele, because I believed, and still believe, that he is associated with Four Square Jane."

"Tell me one thing," said Peter. "Do you know or suspect Four Square Jane?"

Lord Claythorpe shook his head.

"I've always suspected that she was Joyce Wilberforce herself," he said, "but I've never been able to confirm that suspicion. In the old days, when the Wilberforces were living in Manchester Square, I used to see the girl, and suspected she was carrying notes to young Steele, who had a top-floor office at the corner of Cavendish Square."

"Where were you living at the time?" asked Peter quickly.

"I had a flat in Grosvenor Square," said Lord Claythorpe.

Peter jumped up.

"Was the girl's uncle alive at this time?"

Lord Claythorpe nodded.

"He was still alive," he said.

"Where was he living?"

"In Berkeley——"

"I've got it!" said Peter excitedly. "This was when all the trouble was occurring, when you were planning to rob the girl, and using your influence against her. Don't you see? 'Four Square Jane.' She has named the four squares where the four characters in your story lived."

Lord Claythorpe frowned.

"That solution never occurred to me," he said.

He did not seem greatly interested in a matter which excited Peter Dawes to an unusual extent. He had little else to say, and when Peter Dawes left him, he lay wearily down on the plank bed.

Peter was talking for some time with the inspector in charge of the station, when the gaoler called him.

"I don't know what was the matter with that prisoner, sir," he said, "but, looking through the peephole about two minutes ago, I saw him pulling the buttons off his coat."

Peter frowned.

"You'd better change that coat of his," he said, "and place him under observation."

They all went back to the cell together. Lord Claythorpe was lying in the attitude in which Peter had left him, and they entered the cell together. Peter bent down and touched the face, then, with a cry, turned the figure over on its back.

"He's dead!" he cried.

He looked at the coat. One of the buttons had been wrenched off. Then he bent down and smelt the dead man's lips, and began a search of the floor. Presently he found what he was looking for—a section of a button. He picked it up, smelt it, and handed it to the inspector.

"So that's how he did it," he said gravely. "Claythorpe was prepared for this."

"What is it?" asked the inspector.

"The second button of his coat has evidently been made specially for him. It is a compressed tablet of cyanide of potassium, coloured to match the other buttons, and he had only to tear it off to end his life."

So passed Lord Claythorpe, a great scoundrel, leaving his title to a weakling of a son, and very few happy memories to that obscure and hysterical woman who bore his name. Peter's work was done, save for the mystery of Four Square Jane, and even that mystery was exposed. The task he had set himself now was a difficult one, and one in which he had very little heart. He obtained a fresh set of warrants, and accompanied by a small army of detectives who watched every exit, made his call at the hotel at which Steele and his wife were staying.

He went straight up to the room, and found Joyce and her husband at breakfast. They were both dressed; the fact that several trunks were packed suggested that they were contemplating an early move.

Peter closed the door behind him and came slowly to the breakfast table, and the girl greeted him with a smile.

"You're just in time for breakfast," she said. "Won't you have some coffee?"

Peter shook his head. Steele was eyeing him narrowly, and presently the young man laughed.

"Joyce," he said, "I do believe that friend Dawes has come to arrest us all."

"You might guess again, and guess wrong," said Peter, sitting himself down and leaning one elbow on the table. "Mr. Steele, the game is up. I want you!"

"And me, too?" asked the girl, raising her eyebrows.

She looked immensely pretty, he thought, and he had a sore heart for her.

"Yes, you, too, Mrs. Steele," he said quietly.

"What have I done?" she asked.

"There are several things you've done, the latest being to embrace your husband in the vestibule of the hotel when we had arrested him for being in possession of an emerald necklace, and in your emotion relieving him of the incriminating evidence."

She laughed, throwing back her head.

"It was prettily done, don't you think?" she asked.

"Very prettily," said Peter.

"Have you any other charge?"

"None, except that you are Four Square Jane," said Peter Dawes.

"So you've found that out, too, have you?" asked the girl. She raised her cup to her lips without a tremor, and her eyes were dancing with mischief.

Peter Dawes felt that had this woman been engaged on a criminal character instead of devoting her life to relieving the man who had robbed her of his easy gains, she would have lived in history as the greatest of all those perverted creatures who set the law at defiance.

Steele took a cigarette from his pocket, and offered his case to the detective.

"As you say, the jig is up," said he, "and since we desire most earnestly that there should be no unpleasant scene, and this is a more comfortable place to make a confession than a cold, cold prison cell, I will tell you that the whole scheme of Four Square Jane was mine."

"That's not true," said the girl quietly. "You mustn't take either the responsibility or the credit, dear."

Steele laughed as he held a light to the detective's cigarette.

"Anyway, I planned some of our cleverest exploits," he said, and she nodded.

"As you rightly say, Dawes, my wife is Four Square Jane. Perhaps you would like to know why she took that name?"

"I know—or, rather, I guess," said Peter. "It has to do with four squares in London."

Steele looked surprised.

"You're cleverer than I thought," he said. "But that is the truth. Joyce and I had been engaged in robbing Claythorpe for a number of years. When we got some actual, good money from him, we held tight to it. Jewels we used either to send in to the hospitals——"

"That I know, too," said Peter, and suddenly flung away his cigarette. He looked at the two suspiciously, but neither pair of eyes fell. "Now then," said Peter thickly. "Come along. I've waited too long."

He rose to his feet and staggered, then took a halting step across the room to reach the door, but Steele was behind him, and had pinioned him before he went two paces. Peter Dawes felt curiously weak and helpless. Moreover, he could not raise his voice very much above a whisper.

"That—cigarette—was—drugged," he said drowsily.

"Quite right," said Steele. "It was one of my Never Fails."

Peter's head dropped on his breast, and Steele lowered him to the ground.

The girl looked down pityingly.

"I'm awfully sorry we had to do this, dear," she said.

"It won't harm him," said Steele cheerfully.

"I think we had better keep some of our sorrow for ourselves, because this hotel is certain to be surrounded. The big danger is that he's got one of his gentleman friends in the corridor outside."

He opened the door quietly and looked out. The corridor was empty. He beckoned the girl.

"Bring only the jewel-case," he said. "I have the money and the necklace in my pocket."

After closing and locking the door behind them, they passed down the corridor, not in the direction of the lift or the stairs, but towards a smaller pair of stairs, which was used as an emergency exit, in case of fire. They did not attempt to descend, but went up three flights, till they emerged on a flat roof, which commanded an excellent view of the West End of London.

Steele led the way. He had evidently reconnoitred the way, and did not once hesitate. The low roof ended abruptly in a wall on to which he climbed, assisting the girl after him. They had to cross a little neck of sloping ledge, before they came to a much more difficult foothold, a slate roof, protected only by a low parapet. They stepped gingerly along this, until they came to a skylight, which Steele lifted.

"Down you go," he said, and helped the girl to drop into the room below them.

He waited only long enough to secure the skylight, and then he followed the girl through the unfurnished room into which they had dropped, on to a landing.

In the meantime, Peter's assistant had grown nervous, and had come up to the room, and knocked. Getting no answer, he had broken in the door, to find his chief lying still conscious but helpless where he had been left. The rough-and-ready method of resuscitation to which the detective resorted, shook the drugged man from his sleep, and a doctor, hastily summoned, brought him back to normality.

He was still shaky, however, when he recounted the happenings.

"They haven't passed out of the hotel, that I'll swear," said the detective. "We're watching every entrance, including the staff entrance. How did it occur?"

Peter shook his head.

"I went like a lamb to the slaughter," he said, smiling grimly. "It was the promise of a confession, and my infernal curiosity which made me stay—to smoke a doped cigarette, too!" He thought a moment. "I don't suppose they depended entirely on the cigarette, though," he said. "And maybe it would have been a little more unpleasant for me, if I hadn't smoked."

An hour after he was well enough to conduct personally a search of the hotel premises. From cellar to roof he went, followed by two assistants, and it was not until he was actually on the roof that he discovered any clue. It was a small piece of beadwork against the wall which the girl had climbed, and which had been torn off in her exertions. They passed along the neck, and along the sloping roof till they came to the skylight, and this Peter forced.

He found, upon descending, that he was in the premises of Messrs. Backham and Boyd, ladies' outfitters. The floor below was a large sewing-room, filled with girls who were working at their machines, until the unexpected apparition of a pale and grimy man brought an end to their labours. Neither the foreman nor the forewoman had seen anybody come in, and as it was necessary to pass through the room to reach a floor lower down, this seemed to prove conclusively to Dawes that the fugitives had not made use of this method to escape.

"The only people who have been in the upstairs room," exclaimed the foreman, "are two of the warehousemen, who went up about two minutes ago, to bring down some bales."

"Two men?" said Peter quickly. "Who were they?"

But, though he pushed his inquiries to the lower and more influential regions of the shop, he could not discover the two porters. A lot of new men had been recently engaged, said the manager, and it was impossible to say who had been upstairs and who had not.

The door porter at the wholesale entrance, however, had seen the two porters come out, carrying their somewhat awkwardly-shaped bundles on their shoulders.

"Were they heavy?" asked Peter.

"Very," said the door-keeper. "They put them on a cart, and didn't come back."

Now if there was one thing more certain than another in Peter's mind, it was that Four Square Jane did not depend entirely upon the assistance she received from her husband. Peter recalled the fact that there had once been two spurious detectives who had called on Lord Claythorpe having the girl in custody. They were probably two old hands at the criminal game, enlisted by the ingenious Mr. Steele. This proved to be the case, as Peter was to find later. And either Four Square Jane or he might have planted these two men in an adjoining warehouse with the object of rendering just that kind of assistance, which, in fact, they did render.

Peter reached the streets again, baffled and angry. Then he remembered that in Lord Claythorpe's desk was a certain bond to bearer for five hundred thousand dollars. Four Square Jane would not leave England until she had secured this; and, as the thought occurred to him, he hailed a taxi, and drove at top speed to the dead man's house.

Already the news of the tragedy which had overcome the Claythorpe's household had reached the domestics: and the gloomy butler who admitted him greeted him with a scowl as though he were responsible for the death of his master.

"You can't go into the study, sir," he said, with a certain satisfaction, "it has been locked and sealed."

"By whom?" asked Peter.

"By an official of the Court, sir," said the man.

Peter went to the study door, and examined the two big red seals.

There is something about the seal of the Royal Courts of Justice which impresses even an experienced officer of the law. To break that seal without authority involves the most uncomfortable consequences, and Peter hesitated.

"Has anybody else been here?" he asked.

"Only Miss Wilberforce, sir," said the man.

"Miss Wilberforce?" almost yelled Peter. "When did she come?"

"About the same time as the officer who sealed the door," said the butler. "In fact, she was in the study when he arrived. He ordered her out pretty roughly, too, sir," said the butler with relish, as though finding in Miss Wilberforce's discomfiture some compensation for the tragedy which had overtaken his employer. "She sent me upstairs to get an umbrella she had left when she was here last, and when I came down she was gone. The officer grumbled something terribly."

Peter went to the telephone and rang up Scotland Yard, but they had heard nothing of the sealing of the house and suggested that he should seek out the Chancery officials to discover who had made the order and under what circumstances. Only those who have attempted to disturb the routine of the Court of Chancery will appreciate the unhappy hours which Peter spent that day, wandering from master to master, in a vain attempt to secure news or information.

He went back to the house at half-past four that evening, determined to brave whatever terror the Court of Chancery might impose, and again he was met by the butler on the doorstep, but this time a butler bursting with news.

"I'm very glad you've come, sir. I've got such a lot to tell you. About half-an-hour after you'd gone, sir, I heard a ripping and tearing in the study, and I went to the door and listened. I couldn't understand what was going on, so I shouted out: 'Who's there?' And who do you think replied?"

Peter's heart had sunk at the butler's words.

"I know," he said. "It was Four Square—it was Miss Joyce Wilberforce."

"So it was, sir," said the butler in surprise. "How did you know?"

"I guessed," said Peter shortly.

"It appeared she'd been locked in quite by accident by the officer of the Court," the butler went on, "and she was having a look through his lordship's desk to find some letters she'd left behind."

"Of course, sir, everybody knows that Lord Claythorpe's desk is one of the most wonderful in the world. It's full of secret drawers, and I remember Miss Joyce saying once that if his lordship wanted to hide anything it would take a month to find it."

Peter groaned.

"They wanted time—of course, they wanted time!"

What a fool he had been all through! There was no need for the butler to tell him the rest of the story, because he guessed it. But the man went on.

"After a bit," he said, "I heard the key turn in the lock, and out came Miss Joyce, looking as pleased as Punch. But you should have seen the state of that desk!"

"So she broke the seals, did she?" said Peter, with gentle irony.

"Oh, yes, she broke the seals, and she broke the desk, too," said the butler impressively. "And when she came out, she was carrying a big square sheet of paper in her hand—a printed-on paper, like a bank note, sir."

"I know," said Peter. "It was a bond."

"Ah. I think it might have been," said the butler hazily. "At any rate, that's what she had. 'Well,' she said, 'it took a lot of finding.' 'Miss,' said I, 'you oughtn't to take anything from his lordship's study until the law——' 'Blow the law,' said she. Them was her very words—blow the law, sir."

"She's blown it, all right," said Peter, and left the house. His last hope was to block all the ports, and in this way prevent their leaving the country. However, he had no great hopes of succeeding in his attempts to hold the volatile lady whose escapades had given him so many sleepless nights.

Two months later, Peter Dawes received a letter bearing a South American postmark. It was from Joyce Steele.

"You don't know how sorry I am that we had to give you so much trouble," it ran; "and really, the whole thing was ridiculous, because all the time I was breaking the law to secure that which was my own. It is true that I am Four Square Jane. It is equally true that I am Four Square Jane no longer, and that henceforth my life will be blameless! And really, dear Mr. Dawes, you did much better than any of the other detectives who were put on my track. I am here with my husband, and the two friends who very kindly assisted us with our many exploits are also in South America, but at a long distance from us. They are very nice people, but I am afraid they have criminal minds, and nothing appals me more than the criminal mind. No doubt there is much that has happened that has puzzled you, and made you wonder why this, or that, or the other happened. Why, for example, did I consent to go to church with that impossible person, Francis Claythorpe? Partly, dear friend, because I was already married, and it did not worry me a bit to add bigamy to my other crimes. And partly because I made ample preparations for such a contingency, and knew that marriage was impossible. I had hoped, too, that Lord Claythorpe would give me a wedding present of some value, which hope was doomed to disappointment. But I did get a lot of quite valuable presents from his many friends, and these both Jamieson and I most deeply appreciate. Jamieson was the doctor who saw me at Lewinstein's by the way. He has been my right-hand man, and my dearest confederate. Perhaps, Mr. Dawes, you will meet us again in London, when we are tired of South America. And perhaps when you meet us you will not arrest us, because you will have taken a more charitable view of our behaviour, and perhaps you will have induced those in authority to share your view. I am tremendously happy—would you be kind enough to tell my mother that? I do not think it will cheer her up, because she is not that kind.

"I first got my idea of playing Four Square Jane from hearing a servant we once employed—a Jane Briglow—discussing the heroic adventures of some fictional personage in whom she was interested. But it was a mistake to call me 'Jane.' The 'J' stands for Joyce. When you have time for a holiday, won't you come over and see us? We should love to entertain you."

There was a P.S. to the letter which brought a wry smile to the detective's face.

"P.S. Perhaps you had better bring your own cigarettes."

THE ADVENTURE OF THE HEADLESS STATUE

Eugene Thomas

WHEN EUGENE THOMAS (1894–?) began to write a series of real-life adventures about Vivian Legrand, the woman dubbed "The Lady from Hell," for *Detective Fiction Weekly*, one of the most successful of the mystery pulps, it became one of the most successful series that the magazine published. When her exploits continued to appear with relentless regularity, doubt was cast upon their veracity—with good reason. Without apology, *DFW* continued to run stories about Legrand, then acknowledging that the tales were fictional. Were any of the stories true? Was there really a woman named Vivian Legrand? There is little evidence either way, but only the most gullible would accept the notion that all the stories published as true had any genesis in reality.

The female spy was not exactly a heroic figure, earning her sobriquet over and over again. Beautiful, intelligent, and resourceful, she was also a liar, blackmailer, and thief who was responsible for her own father's death.

Thomas, the author of five novels, created another series character, Chu-Seng, typical of many other fictional Yellow Peril villains. A Chinese deaf-mute with paranormal abilities, he works with the Japanese in their espionage activities against the United States in *Death Rides the Dragon* (1932), *The Dancing Dead* (1933), and *Yellow Magic* (1934). He is thwarted by Bob Nicholson, an American agent; Lai Chung, a Mongol prince; and a team of lamas who counteract Chu-Seng's powers with their white magic.

"The Adventure of the Headless Statue" first appeared in the January 25, 1936, issue of *Detective Fiction Weekly*.

The Adventure of the Headless Statue

EUGENE THOMAS

CHAPTER I
Dictator's Loot

THE LADY FROM HELL turned the corner of the Calle el Sol and stepped into another world—a world of dirt and filth and crime, crime in its nakedness as only the Latins know how to strip it of its glamour. Halting a moment, she glanced back over her shoulder at the street she had just left. It was almost deserted in the noonday heat that slashed across Havana like a naked sword. Not even a beggar, Havana's chief crop, drowsed in the sharp pools of purple shadow.

She lifted one shoulder in a slight shrug. There was no reason for her to think that she might have been followed, but the note from Antonio Gonzales had been explicit as to secrecy—had, indeed, intimated that if her errand was known she might never reach the destination for which she was bound.

Satisfied, she turned back. Here, there was relief from the sun. The overhanging galleries cast a grateful shadow, making sharp contrast between the space where she walked and the intolerable light reflected from the center of the street. In the distance the twin towers of the ancient cathedral rose above the surrounding houses.

Back in Europe, Vivian Legrand, the Lady from Hell, had known the ruthless reputation of the man she was on her way to meet. She knew the rumors which linked him with murders from Manoas to Belize and suspected, if she did not know, that he had a finger in many of the revolutions that periodically flared up in Latin America.

But the reputation of a man, no matter how evil, did not prevent the Lady from Hell from utilizing him if the need arose. And back there in Paris he had had a part in several shady schemes she had engineered. When they were finished, Gonzales had taken his cut and disappeared, but Vivian had heard through underworld channels that he had been trapped in a robbery in Southern France, had shot a man, and, unable to claim a penny of the money which lay to his credit in Paris banks, had been compelled to flee for his life.

She had not known that Gonzales was in Havana. The note delivered to her hotel that morning, asking her to call at an address in the Calle el Sol, had come as a complete surprise. But she knew that underworld news travels fast, and realized that the news she had arrived from London with Adrian Wylie, her chief of staff, must have reached the ears of Gonzales within a few hours.

A poorly dressed white man, a Cuban by his garb, passed her with a quick glance and turned in at a fruit shop a few doors further on. As Vivian passed he was busily arguing with the proprietor and did not even glance in her direction.

She found the place she sought quite easily. First, because of its fairly neat appearance in a street of dirt and filth, and, second, because of the door described by Gonzales in his note—a thick, iron-bound slab of teakwood inset in the black masonry front of the house. It was the only door of its kind on the street.

The Lady from Hell could see no evidence that she was being followed, but there was a queer intuitive feeling deep within her that eyes were watching her as she lifted the great iron knocker and let it drop three times against the knocking plate.

An old Spaniard opened the door, only an inch or so, and peered out. Vivian could see that the door was on a short chain.

"I want to see Antonio Gonzales. My name is Mrs. Legrand," she said.

There was a surprising ease and richness about that voice. It rose resonant and bell-like, as if it came effortlessly.

The door was opened wider as an invitation for her to enter. She ran her eye expertly over the man's figure for a sign of concealed weapons, but she could detect no suspicious bulge.

The shadowed hall into which she stepped was a typical entrance to a Havana home of the old days. Running the full length of the building, it opened in the rear into the patio, now overgrown with weeds. At one side a staircase with a wrought iron balustrade ran to an upper floor.

"*Señor* Gonzales is upstairs," the ancient Spaniard said, in his native tongue, "and is expecting you. The open door at the head of the stairs is his."

Vivian went on up the stairs and stepped through the doorway he had indicated.

Gonzales lay in a bed drawn up close to the narrow slit of a window. He passed as a white man, yet his nose was a trifle too flat, his lips a bit thickish, his skin a shade too dark. But in countries where people do not attach too much importance to these things, and to the telltale

half moon at the base of the nails, he was classed as a white Spaniard.

He peered at Vivian through eyes that were still keen and crafty, despite the glaze of fever which covered them.

"I'm glad you're here. I thought you weren't coming," he said. "You're late."

"I had other things to do," she answered curtly. Then she plunged directly to the point. "What do you want to see me about?"

He did not answer directly. Instead he studied her a moment.

"I asked you to come here," he said slowly, "because you've got the reputation of never double-crossing anybody that plays square with you."

"So what?" she asked calmly, but the light that gleamed for a moment in her narrowed eyes belied the calmness of her words.

"I've got something on tap," he went on slowly, "but I'm sick . . . fever . . . I can't shake it off, and unless I hurry I'll lose my chance."

"So you want me to pull your chestnuts out of the fire for you," she shot at him. "I'm not interested."

He raised a protesting hand.

"Wait a minute," he said. "I want to offer you a partnership in it, because you're the only person I know who's got guts enough to pull it off and not double-cross me while I'm lying here unable to do anything myself."

"Well?" she said. Just the single clipped word. The Lady from Hell was playing poker and her face had slipped into an expressionless mask.

"It's big," Gonzales went on. He passed a hand across his hot brow. "Would you mind handing me a drink of water from the jug there? Thanks." He took a deep drink of the water and then lay back. "It's the biggest thing I ever tackled . . . got a million in it . . . two million, maybe . . . and I'm holed up here, unable to do a damn thing." He swore deeply.

"Come to the point," Vivian said crisply.

"Ever hear of Juan Cordoza?"

She pondered a moment, then shook her head.

"He was Ciprano Castro's minister of finance," Gonzales said slowly. "Does that mean anything to you?"

Enlightment flooded Vivian. She remembered now. Cordoza, chief confidante of the dictator of Venezuela, had seen the downfall of his master coming long before the Iron Man himself had read the portents aright. He had skipped out of the country, reaching the Dutch island of Curaçao before Castro was aware of the fact that he had gone, taking a large part of the contents of the treasury with him. After leaving Curaçao his trail had vanished, and before Castro could turn his army of spies and secret agents loose on the trail of his missing treasurer the dictator himself had been compelled to follow in his treasurer's footsteps and take refuge himself in Curaçao.

"Cordoza is in Paris, isn't he?" she asked, remembering rumors now and then that, even though it had happened years before, still floated through the underworld of Europe's capitals.

Gonzales shook his head. "He never reached Paris. He chartered a boat to take him to Havana from Curaçao. He got here all right, landed secretly without anyone learning of his presence. But he never left Cuba—and neither did the stuff he looted from the treasury of Venezuela."

Vivian leaned forward. There was excitement in those green eyes of hers now.

"You know where the stuff is?" she queried.

"I know," he said with triumph. "If I could get out of here long enough to strike a bargain with Chang Kai I could have my hands on it in two hours. But this cursed fever won't let me. I couldn't walk a dozen feet without collapsing. And I'm not fool enough to think that if I struck a bargain with Chang Kai and wasn't there to watch after my interests that he'd play square. Oh, no. I'd whistle for my share, after he got his hands on it. One of his hatchetmen would kill me."

"Who is Chang Kai and what has he got to do with it?" the Lady from Hell asked.

Gonzales feebly raised himself on one elbow.

"Chang Kai's the head Chino in Havana. Runs a curio store in the Chinese quarter as a blind for his real activities—slipping through aliens across to the Florida Keys at a thousand a head—dope smuggling—anything that's crooked and that's got money in it. He's known about the Cordoza loot for a long time—knows it's hidden in a house here in Havana—could put his hands right on it—*if he knew the house.* But that's where he's stymied. It might be any house in the city, so far as he knows. And I know where the house is, but not where it is hidden in that house."

"I don't see why you need to bother with Chang Kai if you have the address," Vivian said doubtfully. "Surely a million in loot cannot be hidden away like a pin, and even if it were I could find a pin, knowing it was hidden in a certain house and worth a million."

"But this is different," Gonzales told her. "I cannot gain access to the house. It is impossible. I know. I will explain it all to you later."

"Then you're stymied yourself, to a certain extent," Vivian said.

"Right," Gonzales answered. Then he looked at her keenly with his fever-bright eyes. "Do you want a cut of the stuff—if you can find it?"

There was no hesitation in Vivian's eyes as she faced the man in the bed.

"Done," she said.

"Your word," he insisted. "No double-crossing."

"My word," she told him, and the man sank back satisfied. He knew that the Lady from Hell was as ruthless as a striking snake; that she would no more hesitate to take human life than she would to step upon an insect, if that life stood in the path of one of her schemes—but he also knew that she would not double-cross a confederate who had played squarely with her.

"Here's the address," Gonzales said, reaching under his pillow and handing her a folded slip of paper. "Use your own judgment about how you go about it. Strike a bargain with Chang Kai if there's no other way, or tear the house to pieces until you find it. That's up to you."

Then he stiffened suddenly. "What's that?" he whispered.

The sound that had disturbed him could only have been heard by a man whose senses were almost abnormally developed by years of dependence upon them. It was not so much, perhaps a matter of hearing as an ability to select what was of importance in the symphony of sound that Havana is always playing. Vivian had caught the sound also a moment after he had called it to her attention. It might have been a stealthy footstep in the hall outside . . . it was so elusive that it defied identification.

She listened intently, wondering if her ears had not tricked her.

But all that she could hear was the strident cry of a mango seller and the faint squawk of a parrot somewhere in the distance.

"Could that man of yours be listening?" she asked, struck by a sudden thought.

"No," Gonzales said positively. "And if he were, it wouldn't do him any good. He understands no English."

"It sounded like a footstep," Vivian said, "the footstep of someone trying to walk without noise."

She got to her feet and, crossing the room, flung the door open. The corridor was deserted.

"I'm going to look on the stairs," she said.

"Want a gun?" Gonzales asked, and his hand went under the pillow.

Vivian shook her head in a negative gesture. There was a gun in the little hand bag she carried. A gun that she was seldom without—small but deadly. She went out into the corridor and descended the stairs cautiously. A faint sound of a song came from the rear of the house. She made her way in that direction. A partly opened door gave her a view of the kitchen, where the man who had admitted her stood before a table peeling potatoes. The sound she had heard had not come from him.

She made her way quickly back up the stairs toward the room on the second floor. Her suspicions had not been dispelled, but there seemed to be no one in the place save the three of them.

She reached the threshold of Gonzales's room and stopped short in amazement.

Gonzales was lying partially off the bed, face up, one arm dangling toward the floor, and a great pool of blood staining the bed covering from the gaping knife wound in his throat.

In the brief instant that Vivian had been absent from the room an assassin had struck, hoping, evidently, to silence Gonzales before he betrayed to her the hiding place of the dictator's treasure.

She smiled grimly at the thought. The assassin had been too late. In her hand bag was the slip of paper that Gonzales had given her, the slip that would lead her to a million or more in loot.

She opened it and consternation flooded her green eyes.

The slip of paper was blank.

CHAPTER II
Book and Dagger

Vivian's face was thoughtful as she reached her hotel. She tapped on the door of Wylie's bedroom. There was no answer. He evidently had not returned from the steamship office, where he had gone to secure passage to Haiti, and she turned back toward her own bedroom. And then stopped short, her green eyes narrowed.

Brilliant sunlight poured through the high arched window and splashed in a great pool on the polished table in the center of the room. And in that pool of light a book lay open, a silver pen-knife fashioned in the shape of a Malay creese lying across the open page—a beautifully engraved five-inch snaky blade.

That open book with the paper knife across it was a signal from Wylie—evidence that something had happened during her absence that menaced their safety. It was a prearranged signal, something that could be done with the utmost casualness without exciting suspicion.

Hurriedly she searched the room, ran through both bedrooms, but nothing had been disarranged.

She was stumped. Wylie was not there—

danger threatening from an unknown quarter—and now, when she thought she had her hands on the secret of what was likely to be their greatest haul, she drew a blank. That Gonzales had been sincere enough, she had no doubt. The man undoubtedly thought that he was delivering to her the hiding place of Cordoza's loot. The only explanation was that someone had reached him first, substituting the blank piece of paper for the one with the address. But who?

The Spaniard who had admitted her to the house? She gave the thought serious consideration and then dismissed it. If the man had attempted to double-cross Gonzales, he would not have remained at the house, when, at any moment, his duplicity might be discovered. And, equally, he could not have murdered Gonzales. He had been in the kitchen, and it would have been an impossibility for him to have killed his master, and then reached the kitchen ahead of her.

Chang Kai, the Chinese Gonzales had mentioned? Her mind toyed with the thought. But if Chang Kai had stolen the slip of paper before her arrival, and substituted a blank, why return to kill Gonzales? Unless, of course, there had been delay in reaching the hiding place of the paper, and Chang Kai or his emissary had seen her entering the house and had returned and killed Gonzales to prevent his revealing the secret to her.

She took out the slip of paper and studied it carefully again, as she had done a dozen times before. There it was, mocking her impotence with its blankness.

She looked up sharply at the sound of a light tap upon the door of the sitting room. She laid the slip on the table and opened the door.

The man who stood upon the threshold was tall and dark and slim—a Cuban undoubtedly, for he had the aquiline nose of the pure bred Spaniard and the feline grace that characterizes certain Latin types. But his face was unhealthily pale.

"May I come in, Mrs. Legrand?" he asked. "I have a message for you."

Vivian opened the door wider and indicated a chair for her guest. She crossed to the table and stood there, the brilliant sunlight streaming in from outside catching her hair and turning it into a halo of flame above her exquisitely lovely profile.

Her eyes were hard as the glitter of emeralds as she studied the man before her. Something was wrong here. In her profession no one was above suspicion; no incident, however trivial, below notice. Her life had more than once depended upon being prepared for any eventuality that might arise, and her movement had brought her hand in close proximity to the little revolver that lay on the table, screened by a book.

"What do you want?" she asked after a moment.

"May I introduce myself?" inquired the man ingratiatingly. "I am Leon Ortega."

He crossed his legs comfortably and lighted a cigarette.

"What do you want?" Vivian shot at him again, her drooping lashes screening the cold calculation of her eyes.

"It's purely a matter of business, Mrs. Legrand," he said. "But before we start let me advise you that if you do anything rash you will most certainly regret it."

"What do you want?" Vivian asked.

The man leaned forward.

"Just a matter of striking a bargain with you."

"A bargain?"

The man nodded. "We've got something that you want. You've got something that we want. But we're not hoggish. We're willing to give up what we've got for half of what you've got."

Vivian's greenish eyes were narrowed and the tiny flame in them might have warned the man, had he been observant, that danger was gathering about him like a thunderstorm.

"What have you got that I want?" she queried softly.

"A certain Mr. Adrian Wylie," the man said comfortably.

———

"Ah!" Vivian said. She knew then that this was what the sign of the open book and paper knife meant. "So Mr. Wylie is, shall we say, your guest?"

"That will do as well as any other," the man admitted. "We—er—persuaded him that it would be advisable to accompany us until such time as we could have a talk with you."

"And what have I got that you want?" Vivian queried.

"Half of the stuff that Cordoza left when he died," the man came back at her swiftly. Then, as Vivian started to speak, he went on: "I might say that it will be useless to attempt to persuade us that you do not know where it is. We know that you do. We know that you got the directions for finding it from Gonzales less than an hour ago. We saw you leave. So we immediately took what precautions we considered necessary to protect our interests."

"And why not obtain the same information from Gonzales that I obtained?" she asked. There was in her voice no intimation of her anxiety—of how much hung on the answer to that question of hers.

The man regarded her with a smile.

"My dear Mrs. Legrand, you really do not do us justice. It was only this morning that we learned of Gonzales's whereabouts. We hurried there. We saw you leave. And when we entered the house we found him murdered. The answer is obvious."

Vivian's eyes, hard as bits of emeralds, betrayed nothing of the consternation his words aroused in her. These men, then, had not killed Gonzales, and did not know that a third party had beaten them—did not know that the slip of paper Gonzales had given her was a blank piece of paper.

"Your offer then," she said slowly, "is to trade Adrian Wylie for half of the Cordoza loot?"

"Exactly," the man said. "And I might call to your attention, Mrs. Legrand, that his life depends on your agreeing. He obviously knows nothing that will be of value to us. He is worthless to us except as a hostage. So, whether he

lives or dies depends entirely upon your acceptance or refusal."

For a moment hell fires flared in Vivian's eyes. She had a strong desire to snatch the little gun from her hand bag on the table. But reason came to her rescue. She would gain nothing by violence. If this man did not return, undoubtedly Wylie would die. Strategy was called for.

"I shall have to think it over," she said slowly. "I am not alone in this, of course, and there are others that I must consult."

"Who?" he asked.

There was suspicion in his voice, but the next instant he was aware of the anxiety that lingered in the husky tones of her voice and flickered in the green depths of her eyes. The ability to dispel suspicion in a man by turning on the full force of her personality as one turns water on in a tap was always one of the greatest assets of the Lady from Hell.

"You could not expect me to tell you the names of those working with me," she said gently. "Sufficient to say that I came here for the purpose of seeing Gonzales, of obtaining information from him that I did obtain, and that I cannot make any such agreement without first consulting the people who are in on this with me. But in view of the situation I think they will agree."

The man stood up.

"Six o'clock is the deadline," he said curtly. "Let me warn you—don't try any tricks. An attempt at treachery would be fatal to the negotiations—and Mr. Wylie."

He turned with a sardonic smile and left the woman standing there beside the table in the center of the room, apparently defeated.

He did not see, as the door closed behind him, that bowed figure straighten up like a steel spring uncoiling and dash swiftly into the next room. Neither did he see, as he stepped into the car in which he had arrived, her slender figure slip through the hotel entrance.

But she did not make the mistake of letting the man she was following see her emerge. She remained just inside the arched colonnade for a moment, adjusting her hat, until his car swung into the traffic on the Prado.

"Follow that car," she said swiftly to the driver of a taxi at the curb. "Ten dollars if you do not lose him."

CHAPTER III
The Headless Statue

The great arched hall of the ruined monastery of San Fernando on the road to Gibara was a purple pool of shadow, although the afternoon sunlight still struck sharply across the landscape seen through the arched opening where the great iron barred doors had been flung open. A great flame tree that stood in the doorway was dropping its blossoms in the slight breeze like a blood-red rain. In the distance El Principe Castle, once one of Havana's guardians and now a prison, stood on the top of the cliff overlooking the sea.

Just inside the doorway lounged the figure of an armed man, obviously a guard.

The great hall had, probably, at one time served as a place of worship for the monks. The ruined pile of rotted wood and carved stonework at one end might conceivably have been the altar. From narrow slitted windows, high up, three slanting beams of light fell sharply athwart the gloom, bringing into sharp relief the carved, life-sized figures that stood in niches all around the walls. Some of the figures were in an almost perfect state of preservation. Others were headless, battered, parts of their stone garments broken off. They were raised some ten feet above the floor, recessed into the enormously thick walls and each reached by three little flights of steps that led up to the pedestal upon which they stood.

Seated on a low stool almost directly beneath one of these statues, Leon Ortega faced the man he had kidnaped.

"I have just left Mrs. Legrand," Ortega said. "She is a very sensible woman. Tonight at eight o'clock she delivers to me the secret of the hiding place of the gold that I seek. When I have verified her information you are free to go."

"You have her word?" Wylie questioned.

Knowing the Lady from Hell as he did, he knew that if she did indeed have the key to the hiding place to a cache of gold she had no intention of yielding it tamely to Ortega. As a last resort, he knew that her loyalty to him would force her to yield to save his life. But he knew that she would make some effort to turn the game her way before she gave in. His mind would have been less easy, however, had he known that Vivian had nothing to barter for his safety and that the situation was causing the usually adroit Lady from Hell considerable concern.

The two had first met in Manila, where Wylie was assistant to the ancient and incredibly evil Mandarin Hoang Ti Fu, and almost immediately their partnership had come into being. It had lasted for several years now, and he had sense enough to realize that he could not have continued to be a successful crook had it not been for his association with the Lady from Hell. Among other things he lacked the rare initiative and cold ruthlessness which distinguished her and had won for her the nickname of which she was known in the underworld of three continents. But, on the other hand, Wylie alone knew how heavily Vivian Legrand leaned upon him in certain phases of their work; how utterly she trusted him when she would not have dared trust another.

"I have her word," Ortega responded satisfied. "Tonight she yields it." He looked at Wylie. "Meanwhile, you would prefer to remain here? It is cooler than in the room in there." He nodded toward the narrow, iron-bound door at the rear of the great hall that opened into the cell-like room where Wylie had been confined until his return.

"I would prefer it," Wylie said, and his eyes flickered toward the open gateway.

Ortega caught the glance and smiled sardonically.

"There is only one guard at the gate," he told Wylie, "but there are others on watch above the gateway. Through windows like those," and he indicated the embrasures above their heads, "they command a view of the road and the approaches. You might overpower the guard, although I do not think it likely, but you would be shot down before you had gone ten feet."

Normally, Ortega would have kept his captive securely penned up until his objective had been reached. But, cleverer than most of his ilk, he was looking into the future. There was a chance, a bare chance, that the woman might be willing to sacrifice the life of her companion. In that case, there was a slim chance that the man himself had some clue to its whereabouts. If that were so, and Ortega had been able to gain his confidence by treating him more as a guest than a captive, he might secure that knowledge by a bargain. Providing, of course, that Wylie knew that the woman had been willing to sacrifice him.

With this in mind he was perfectly content to let Wylie roam about the place, secure in the knowledge that he could not escape.

Meanwhile, back in her sitting room in the hotel, Vivian was walking up and down, that keen brain of hers seeking a solution to the problem. She had found where Wylie was being kept prisoner—that great pile of ruined masonry on a hilltop outside Havana was an ideal place. It looked strong enough to withstand the battering of artillery. But now that she had trailed Ortega to his lair, what had she gained? She had no secret to barter to Ortega in return for Wylie's safety, and Ortega would never believe her when she told him that the paper she had received from Gonzales had been blank. He would deem it but a trick on her part—and she had no doubt that Wylie's life would answer for her failure to deliver the secret.

She stopped in her stride and reached out to pick up the slip of paper again from the place where it had been on the table since Ortega's visit, an hour or more before, and gasped in astonishment.

Thin, fine lines of writing were apparent upon it now—thin lines in brown.

And then she realized what had happened. Gonzales's secret had been hidden in writing done with invisible ink. And it would have stayed truly invisible, forever lost to her, had it not been for her casual gesture in dropping it on the table. To lie in the full glare of the tropical sun! That intense heat had developed the writing upon it.

Swiftly she snatched it up, eagerly reading the two brief lines which were perceptible.

Monastery of San Fernando

That was clear enough. But then, the second line, rather blurred . . . some sort of odd signature, perhaps?

the Headless Saint

Yes, that final word was "Saint." A code term? Saints truly were to be associated with a monastery. The monastery of San Fernando? But, of course, here in Havana! Another gasp escaped her as the implication of what she had learned burst upon her shrewd mind.

For a moment she stood in deep thought, and then, her green eyes glowing with exultation, ran for her bedroom. Here was a situation that could not have fitted her purpose more perfectly if she had planned it.

Dusk was in the offing as a tall, black-haired woman picked her way through the Chinese quarter of Havana. She was no longer young, this woman. There were lines about her mouth, lines on her forehead, and the black hair was streaked with gray here and there.

She seemed frightened as she picked her way through a maze of dim, tunneled lanes and alleys of gloom where lived the Mother of Smells. Curious eyes followed her as she moved up to the door of a store and entered, for a white woman was a rarity in that section of Havana.

Once inside the store she waved aside the clerk who came forward and asked in Spanish to see Chang Kai, the proprietor, at once. He came forward from behind the desk at the rear, his round, moonlike face wearing a look of polite inquiry.

"I wish to talk to you—to see you alone," she said with a furtive look around. "I have just come from Paris—and in Paris I was told that if I should need help that was—difficult to obtain—to come to you."

There was a look of speculation in the eyes of Chang Kai as he opened a door into his private apartment and motioned her to enter. It was not often that a white woman came to him seeking aid. Usually it was an alien who wished to be smuggled into the United States, a drug runner from Europe with a supply of cocaine or heroin to dispose of.

Once inside the room the woman glanced about her nervously.

"Can we be overheard?" she asked, in Spanish.

"We are quite alone," Chang Kai assured her. He pulled out a curved teakwood chair and she sank into it with a sigh, her fragile, worn hands clasped tightly in her lap.

"I am Dolores Cordoza," she said abruptly.

Chang Kai's eyes flickered slightly at the sound of the name, but otherwise he remained impassive, and she went on:

"At one time my father was Minister of Finance of Venezuela. He foresaw that the revolution was coming, and when it came he fled with a large amount of gold and jewels."

"That is history, *señorita*," Chang Kai informed her with a look of polite indifference. But a faint smile played around the corners of his mouth, making the lips the only living part of his features. It was almost as if he found the irony of the situation deeply amusing.

"He reached Havana," the woman told him, "and died here. But before he died he hid in a safe place the money he had brought away with him."

"And," finished Chang Kai, "the money was never found. That I know, *señorita*. The hiding place of the treasure has never been found."

"But I have found it," she declared earnestly, leaning forward. "That is why I have come to you. Looking through my father's papers a short time ago I came across something that had been hidden before—a slip of paper that told where the treasure was hidden here in Havana. I hastened here. But when I arrived I found the house where the treasure was hidden occupied by a gang of cutthroats. I can do nothing alone. That is why I seek your aid."

"Where is the treasure hidden, *señorita*?" Chang demanded. Strong as the control over his emotion was, he could not quench the blaze that came into his beady black eyes. What a fool this woman was, those eyes seemed to say; a deer walking into the jaws of the tiger.

The woman made a negative motion of her head.

"That I will not tell you," she said stubbornly, "unless you are willing to aid me. And if you are to aid me, it must be done tonight. There are others on the trail of my father's money—a woman, a Mrs. Legrand, who has obtained the secret."

"Have heard of this woman," Chang Kai admitted. "But how did she hear of the hiding place of your father's money? She arrived in Havana only this morning."

"A man named Gonzales, who had stolen the knowledge from me in Paris, sent for her. When she learned that he knew the secret she slew him."

Chang Kai's eyes flickered. Beneath the ice of his eyes fires were alive again, glowing as he stared unblinkingly at the woman.

"So Mrs. Legrand has the secret," he said, and if there was a curious note in his voice the woman did not seem to notice it.

"Yes," came the answer, "and tomorrow morning she strikes a bargain with the man who occupies the house where the treasure is hidden—and tomorrow it will be in their hands—lost to me."

"I will aid you—for a price," Chang told her.

"I will pay, of course," the woman declared feverishly. "Twenty-five per cent of the treasure will be yours."

"I must have half," Chang Kai declared

firmly, and if the gleam in his eyes meant that he had no intention of giving this woman half of the treasure, once it was in his hands, she did not see it.

"I cannot give you half," the woman said firmly. "I must make a bargain with the leader of these men who occupy this house—one Ortega, a Cuban—for twenty-five per cent of the gold. Otherwise we could not obtain it. The house is strong, almost a fortress, and his men are armed. But I dare not go there alone and reveal to him the hiding place of the treasure—I am not a fool. I know that I would not live five minutes after this scoundrel got his hands on the secret of the hiding place. That is why I wish you to go with me tonight at eight thirty, with your men, to protect me."

The smile that flitted across the face of the Chinese was so nebulous that it might have been merely a shifting of the light and shadow effect upon his face. His voice was polite as he queried:

"Where is the treasure, *señorita*?"

"In the ruined Monastery of San Fernando, on the road to Gibara," the woman told him. "My father had purchased it, with the intention of restoring it and making it into a residence. He hid the treasure there. And then he died. The sale was never recorded, and I do not know who owns it now."

Chang Kai rose to his feet, an alert look upon his face.

"I shall make the necessary arrangements at once," he declared with satisfaction.

"But there is likely to be trouble! This man Ortega, whose headquarters it is, may not be satisfied with twenty-five per cent. He may try to seize it all," she said anxiously.

"There may be trouble," Chang Kai admitted, "but I shall be prepared for it. You need have no further cause for worry. Leave this matter to me and by tomorrow morning your share of your father's vanished treasure shall be in your hands."

He did not see the deep light, like the blaze in the heart of a fire opal, that leaped into the narrowed, greenish eyes of the woman facing him. Vivian Legrand, the Lady from Hell, had a great deal of doubt that the matter was going to turn out precisely as Chang Kai anticipated.

CHAPTER IV
Secret Orders

For more than an hour Wylie had been sitting on the low stool, one of the few articles of furniture in the vast room, or wandering around the place on a tour of inspection. The guard at the door apparently paid no attention to him, but Wylie knew that he was under close scrutiny.

A shout in Spanish drew his attention to the guard now—a shout that was taken up somewhere else in the great building and passed along. A moment later Ortega came into the place, buckling on a gun belt.

The guard said, in rapid Spanish, that a Chinese was approaching up the road, and Wylie's eyes flickered from the guard to Ortega. It was evident, from the thoughtful expression on the latter's face, that the visitor, whoever he was, was unexpected. Ortega turned speculative eyes upon Wylie.

"I hope," he said softly, "that you are not raising false hopes about this being your opportunity to, shall I say, desert our hospitality? I should not, if I were you, make the attempt. You may remain here, and if I find that this visitor requires to talk with me privately I shall ask you to go inside for a little time."

Wylie had not, as a matter of fact, given much thought to the possibility of escape provided by the visitor. Ortega's warning about the guards stationed above the doorway had not left his mind.

Their visitor proved to be a young Chinese, his smooth yellow face wreathed in a bland smile beneath the wide, shadowing coolie hat of split bamboo. He might have passed for any one of the dozen market gardeners who trudge the road between their little vegetable *fincas* and the

Havana markets every day in the week. Loose cotton trousers flapped above dirty feet in rope-soled sandals. The dingy cotton shirt was several sizes too large for him.

The bland smile still wreathed his face, but the eyes beneath the shadowing hat were intent as he crossed the space between doorway and Ortega.

"I bring you a message," he announced abruptly in Spanish, stepping in front of Ortega.

"From whom?" the Cuban asked.

"From Chang Kai, chief of my tong," came the answer. "Here is a paper that tells you that I speak truth when I say that I am his messenger," and he extended a slip of rice paper on which was written a sentence in Spanish, the fine spider-like letters giving evidence that the man who had written them was an artist with ink and brush.

Ortega read the sentence swiftly. Wylie's eyes were fixed intently upon the young Chinese. He was tense, waiting for any emergency that might arise, his legs pressing the stone flooring like coiled steel springs ready to hurl him to his feet at an instant's notice.

"What is the message?" the Cuban asked.

"You seek the hiding place of the gold of Cordoza," came the sing-song answer. "So does the worthy Chang Kai."

"*Madre de Dios!*" ejaculated Ortega, sitting up in amazement. "Does all of Havana seek this gold?"

"Of that I know nothing," the Chinese said calmly. His eyes roved about the hall, seeming to be seeking, noting, verifying, flitting from one to another of the statues in their niches on the wall. "My message is this: Today you killed a man to obtain the secret of the hiding place of the gold. If by now you have read the paper on which the secret is written you know that you have but half of the secret. The other half is in the hands of the Worthy Chang Kai. Without his half you cannot find the gold. Without your half my master is helpless. I am instructed to say to you if you are willing to join forces my master is willing to share the treasure, half and half."

For an instant silence hung over the little group. Watching Ortega, Wylie could almost read the conflicting emotions that raced through his brain. He knew that Ortega did not have the secret of the treasure and he could see that the Cuban was torn between the desire to admit the fact and a desire to bluff it out until he had obtained the secret from Vivian at eight o'clock that night.

The eyes of the Chinese youth had flitted back to the statues again. They seemed to fascinate him. His head was slightly tilted as he moved a step or two toward one of them to examine it more closely.

And so intent was Ortega upon the problem confronting him that he did not notice the interest of the young Chinese, did not see the stealthy sidewise movement that brought him in front of Wylie. Nor did he catch the movement that sent a revolver slipping from its hiding place up the loose sleeve of the Chinese and the hand that extended it to Wylie.

Ortega got to his feet and paced up and down. And, as his back was turned, the revolver disappeared into Wylie's pocket, along with the folded paper that accompanied it.

It was the piece of paper the Lady from Hell had received from Gonzales, on which she had added a few terse instructions. Instructions so brief that to most men they would have seemed fantastic, but to Wylie, who knew from long experience the shrewd crystal-like clearness of Vivian's brain, they were simple enough.

We're on top of treasure now. Be ready to help. Sunlight developed secret ink. Let Ortega find loot hidden in headless statue. Chink will take it from him and then *be ready.*

And, in the voice of the Lady from Hell, there came to Wylie's ears a few whispered sentences:

"Don't try getaway. Read note. I'll return

tonight. Just before Chang Kai arrives tell Ortega that the loot is in the statue of Sebastian!"

Her low-voiced instructions left him with gleaming eyes. He had recognized Vivian immediately upon her arrival. That disguise and make-up of a Chinese youth was one that he himself had taught her.

He found himself perplexed as to the exact meaning of her orders. There had been so little time while Ortega's back was turned. Yet he knew the Lady from Hell well enough; hers were never idle instructions. Whatever plans she was now revolving, things she expected him to do were an integral part of them.

Besides, there was the note safe in his pocket. Her whispered, urgent words must have been rather an afterthought. Otherwise she would have written them out for him in advance, adding them to the folded paper and the welcome revolver. Obviously she was concerned about something which she could not have understood clearly before entering this very room.

Vivian's face had settled again into its smooth yellow mask and her hands were folded as Ortega turned back to her suddenly.

"You may tell Chang Kai," he said, "that I agree."

"All right," she answered. "Then I am to tell you that Chang Kai will arrive here tonight at eight thirty. He will join his knowledge with yours and together you will secure the treasure."

"Agreed," Ortega said, and with a bow the young Chinese turned away.

CHAPTER V
The She-Devil's Gems

That night the Lady from Hell slowed the car she had hired two-thirds of the way up the hill on which the ruined monastery stood and ran it behind a clump of young mango trees. A few branches snapped off and tucked here and there about the body of the car broke its outlines, gave effective camouflage. She would have need of

that car in a short time, and need it badly, if her plans went according to schedule.

The pile of ruined masonry loomed on the crest of the hill above her in charred tracery against the golden globe of the rising moon, looking like some fantastic monster crouched there ready to spring. A light gleamed through one of the narrow slitted windows as she made her way up the hill, keeping carefully in the shadow of the underbrush that lined the roadway. Only the faintest of rustlings betrayed her presence. But even that, to her strained ears in the quiet of the night, was magnified to enormous proportions.

Thirty feet from her stood the black wall of the ruined monastery, and halfway between where she stood and the door a man stood sentinel by the tall undergrowth at the edge of the road. To attempt to approach the door by the road would be madness, serve only to invite a bullet from the man on guard. To even attempt a dash up the road in the moonlight, now stronger, would betray her presence. And along the side of the road it was equally dangerous.

Her only chance was to slip through the undergrowth, and she knew that her chance of getting past the man unobserved was slight. To jump him, and then make for the door, gave her only the scantiest of chances, for there was the possibility that there were others on guard that she could not see. But it was a chance that must be taken.

She might have stolen by at that, reach the door in safety, if she had not stepped on a dried twig. It snapped with an explosion of a rifle there in the stillness.

Silence . . . strung . . . pulsating . . . a gruelling hiatus. Minutes were eons . . . From the crest of a nearby palm came a querulous rasp of a parakeet, the only sound in a vast and dark silence.

Then cautious footsteps.

Vivian tensed. She was armed, but she dare not shoot, except as a last desperate expedient. The sound would bring the pack to her heels in half a minute.

And then near disaster swept upon her with sinister swiftness.

An intuition, a sudden leaping of her nerves from no visible warning, saved Vivian. She leaped sidewise under this intuitive impulse as a man behind her aimed a blow at her head with a revolver.

And then he broke into a high-pitched, choking noise as he stumbled back, clawing frantically at his eyes, writhing like a man suddenly bereft of all reason.

"*Madre de Dios!*" he cried in terror. "My eyes—they are burned out! I am blind—"

Concentrated ammonia does that to a man. It burns his eyes. Renders him immediately helpless.

Vivian's weapon had been a small rubber syringe filled with the stuff, and she had squirted a fine spray of it into the man's face. Then the butt of her gun fell on the head of the moaning man again and again with all the power of her strong arm—and the thing was done. The man slipped to the ground unconscious.

Without stopping to see how badly hurt the man was, Vivian slipped on quietly toward the great door of the building.

Her chief fear was that it might be locked. But it was not.

A touch, and it moved slightly on well-oiled hinges. Another touch and Vivian could peer through into the long, spacious room.

Hurricane lanterns, placed on the rude table in the center of the room, cast an irregular circle of light that barely washed the walls with a dim glow and bathed the statues in their niches in faint luminescence. Another lantern, placed on the floor, but tilted back so that its tin reflector directed a concentrated beam of light, illuminated one of the statues . . . a headless, battered piece of polychrome.

She caught her breath in astonishment. Here was something that she had not planned, something that startled her, made her think for a moment that her carefully-laid plans had gone wrong. Then a partial solution dawned upon her, and her tense lips parted in a slight smile as she saw how she could turn it to her own advantage.

Ortega, standing on one of the steps a little below the headless statue, swung a heavy hammer against it with shattering force—another and another blow. An oval portion in the statue's midsection cracked loose and fell to the floor. Behind it was a sparkle, a glitter.

Ortega shouted his triumph, and the Lady from Hell caught her breath in excitement. This was the hiding place of Cordoza's loot—a battered statue, hollow inside, standing in the ruined hall of a ruined monastery.

Ortega rained blow after blow. The statue cracked into fragments and the upper part crashed to the floor. And, like grains of corn from a ripped sack, the hoarded treasure spilled to the floor—pearls, rubies, amethysts, opals, emeralds in a glittering cascade in which the red-gold of minted coins formed dancing highlights of flame.

Dropping his hammer, Ortega leaped to the floor and scooped up a handful of the glittering gems, let them trickle through his fingers in a shining stream.

It was his last act of life. A shriek of terror burst from his lips as he glanced up from the floor just in time to see Chang Kai, standing ten feet away, raising a gun. It spat flame. A red splash appeared on his forehead. He fell over on his side, twitched once or twice, and then lay still.

"Do not stir," the Chinese snapped sharply at Ortega's astounded followers, huddled in a little knot a dozen or so feet away. The Lady from Hell could see that Chang Kai's Chinese had them covered. The Cubans saw it also. They did not move. They dared not.

Every eye in the room was fixed on Chang Kai. Softly Vivian pushed the door open a little more, slipped into the room, and closed the door behind her. None of those inside heard a sound, caught her furtive movement.

"This man," Chang Kai said with a contemptuous smile, indicating the huddled form on the floor, "was foolish enough to think that

I would share Cordoza's treasure with him. He knows better now. It belongs to me."

"I'm afraid you're mistaken," Vivian said quietly from her position beside the doorway. "It belongs to me."

Chang Kai whirled, amazement upon his face, his gun held high. Then he smiled slowly as he saw that the intruder was only a woman, even though she was armed. His eyes swept her from flaming red hair beneath the trim white Panama, raked down the white silk suit and ended at the white buck-skin shoes.

"What makes you believe that it belongs to you?" he said silkily. But there was deadly menace beneath the silk.

"Because I planned that it should," the Lady from Hell told him coolly. "I knew that the treasure was here, but Ortega's presence prevented my searching for it. I knew that you knew the hiding place, but did not know the house in which it was hid. So I told you the address, and arranged for you to come here."

"You!" There was amazement in Chang Kai's eyes. "But—"

"Yes," Vivian cut him short. "I was *Señorita* Dolores Cordoza. You did exactly as I planned for you to do. You found the jewels. You removed Ortega. And now I have come for the treasure."

Chang Kai laughed. A lone woman, even though armed with a gun, to wrest a fortune from the hands of two dozen armed and desperate men. Ortega's men, he realized, had nothing to lose and everything to gain by fighting on his side, should a fight be necessary.

There was a stillness in the poise of the man opposite Vivian Legrand that told her his purpose as clearly as though the words had been spoken. Her nerves coiled like springs.

"Do not make the mistake of thinking me alone," she warned. "I would not be that foolish. You are covered by a dozen men—good shots all of them."

Chang Kai's eyes flashed about the room. It was empty save for Vivian, his own and Ortega's men. He laughed and gave a swift order in Chinese to his men.

"I warn you," Vivian said urgently, switching into staccato Cantonese, so that his men might not mistake her meaning. "Attack me and the souls of your men will leap the Dragon Gate this night, to join their ancestors!"

Chang Kai peered at her appraisingly, striving to pierce the veil of shadows that filled the room, and read the expression on her face. It seemed incredible this woman should have come here single-handed in an attempt to wrest the treasure from them.

And yet there was no evidence that she was not alone.

He flung an order at his men:

"Disarm her."

As if to put a period to his words a shot rang out from somewhere behind him. Cursing shrilly, Chang Kai dropped his revolver and spun about as a bullet shattered his arm above the elbow.

"I warned you," Vivian said, her voice cutting through the sudden hub-bub of chattering that had arisen from the Chinese. "Look!"

Every eye in the room followed her pointing hand.

From behind one of the statues, where he had been hidden, Wylie stepped forth, automatic in hand. And for the first time the two opposing parties, Chang Kai's Chinese and the dead Ortega's Cubans, noticed that from behind each of the statues lining the wall behind them a slender black muzzle peered menacingly down at them.

"My men are armed with automatic rifles," Vivian said. "One movement and they can rake this place with a cross fire that will leave not one of you alive."

After a second's pause she went on, and, had Chang Kai not been too busily occupied with the pain of his wound, he might have caught the palpable note of relief in her voice. "Drop your weapons on the floor and kick them toward me—all of you."

She raised her revolver menacingly, and again her eyes flickered toward the line of statues.

"Quick, or I fire! And the first shot will be the signal for my men to shoot."

A revolver dropped onto the stone flagging and skidded across the pavement toward her under the impetus of a hasty kick. Another—another—until the floor between Vivian and her opponents was littered with revolvers and knives.

Wylie stepped down from the niche in which he stood.

"Back, all of you," he said sternly. "Go through that doorway in the rear." He indicated the door to the room in which he had been placed.

Fear in their eyes, treading on one another's toes in their eagerness to get out of range of those deadly rifles peering menacingly down upon them, the two groups went backward and through the doorway Wylie had indicated. With a quick movement he slammed the door.

"There is no other exit?" Vivian queried.

"None," Wylie said.

"Good," Vivian said. "Now we've got work to do. I've a car hidden below and we can place this stuff in it," and she indicated the glittering heap of jewels and gold coins on the floor. Then she halted.

"But how in the world did you manage that?" and she indicated the slender, deadly muzzles that leered down at them in the half gloom.

"Oh, that!" Wylie said with a smile. "That was an inspiration. There was a pile of short lengths of pipe in my room. I thought I might as well make use of them."

THE MADAME GOES DRAMATIC

Perry Paul

RELENTLESS SEARCHING for information about Perry Paul, which may be a pseudonym, has been fruitless. He was identified in passing as a former crime reporter, but there the trail of facts ends.

What is known is that he wrote for the lowest level of pulps, cracking one of the better magazines, *Detective Fiction Weekly*, just once in his career. It was tough enough to earn a living at the rates the best magazines paid: two cents a word, or maybe three if one was a big enough name. But to make it at a half cent a word was impossible, no matter how fertile the imagination or how fast one could type.

That was Perry Paul's world. He wrote for *Airplane Stories*, *Ghost Stories*, *Complete Sky Novel*, and *Gun Molls* (which lasted for only nineteen issues between October 1930 and April 1932), producing twelve stories about the Madame. All of his work appeared in the brief period from 1930 to 1932, after which he undoubtedly gave up—or starved to death (pure speculation on the latter).

While no one will confuse Paul's work with Hammett's or Chandler's, his stories gallop along briskly, and the Madame was a good enough creation to develop a bit of a following. Like many female characters in fiction, especially pulp fiction, she is jaw-droppingly gorgeous. Although she is a fairly hardened criminal, she also helps others whenever she can. To publishers and readers, Robin Hood–type crooks were acceptable as heroes and heroines. The Madame is well regarded, even by her adversaries, described as "a straight shooter in a town where even the calendar was suspected of being fixed."

"The Madame Goes Dramatic" was originally published in the April 1931 issue of *Gun Molls*.

The Madame Goes Dramatic

PERRY PAUL

"I'LL FIX YOU SO YOU'LL NEVER TELL!"

A dull black automatic menaced a sinister, leering face.

The hand that held the gun shook.

The audience sat forward in its seats, tense.

Dorothy Devine, glorious Dorothy, had the center of the stage. The moment was hers.

For two acts and part of the third she had caused her audience alternately to roll in the aisles and flood their handkerchiefs. The play was a clever combination of pathos, melodrama, and comedy, with the latter element prevailing. It was the first time the sensational dramatic actress had attempted an essentially comic role, but in it she wowed her public limp.

In the first act she had portrayed a schoolgirl, in the second a glamorous woman of the world, but now she was a little frail old lady. At the moment she had put off her pose of a grande dame and in tattered garments had gained access to the office of a night club, whose proprietor was in possession of a secret that could compromise her granddaughter.

The set was the office of the night club. The proprietor and the little old lady faced each other across a table. The man's face was dark, sneering.

It was a moment of pure melodrama. Would the little old lady be able to conquer the fear of the thing in her hand and exact justice?

Dorothy Devine was superb.

The Saturday night audience froze in breathless expectancy.

In the third row on the center aisle, the Madame, that dynamic figure who was as much an enigma to the police as to the underworld where she was looked upon as nothing short of a criminal genius, sat forward in her seat. The slim, well-kept fingers that were equally at home with a tea cup, a jimmy, or a Tommy-gun, or could, when clenched, put a good lightweight to sleep, were twined in her lap.

The Madame seldom attended the theatre. The reason was simple. Inside her smartly cropped red-blonde head functioned the brain that had evolved all the super criminal coups that had mystified the New York police for the past thirteen months. With such a mind it was impossible not to solve instantly the course of even the most complicated dramatic plot, and the play ceased to interest her.

So when that enigmatic figure who was known to both the police and the underworld only as the Madame did select a show, it was always a light farce whose lines sparkled with wit and humor.

Tonight she had chosen "Love Runs Hot," the screaming comedy hit featuring Dorothy

Devine, sensation of the current dramatic season. Miss Devine's talented interpretation of her first comic role had twice during the first two acts caused the Madame to smile. And that in itself was an accomplishment, for no one had ever seen her laugh.

Tonight was something of a celebration—it marked the end of the Madame's meteoric gangland career. On the following Monday she would dismantle Le Parfum Shoppe, in whose back office had been cased the famous Granite Bank heist, Faire Long's fantastic shake-down, the Hotel Kid's gem haul at the Normandy, all of which had been but a prelude to the unaccountable suicide of the Big Shot, boss double-crosser of the underworld, which the Madame *alone knew* was not really a suicide at all. She knew because it was a perfectly planned and executed revenge—a revenge that had drawn her from nobody knew where to become the master of every criminal art from the technique of the dip, the cloaker, the cold-card artist, the stick-up guy to the pinnacle of gangland aristocracy—the peterman. And her revenge accomplished, she would leave as she had come—a mystery.

She could do this because the Madame had been smart. She had never participated in any of the jobs she planned, nor had she ever accepted a share of the loot. Her play was the head work and a build up of confidence that would enable her eventually to rub out the Big Shot. This had been done, and in so doing the Madame had allied herself to no faction, although her restless mind was equally facile at solving problems of the police or the underworld. And she had done both without losing caste or double-crossing either.

Both sides respected, feared, and trusted her implicitly, and agreed that the Madame was a wow.

"Love Runs Hot" amused her tremendously. She admired the polished technique of Dorothy Devine, for among her other accomplishments the Madame could be a consummate actress if the occasion demanded.

Dorothy Devine, as popular with society as she was with the members of her own profession, rose to the heights in her final scene. She *was* the little old lady with the blunt automatic in her fear-stricken hand. She feared the gun as she feared the rat she faced.

Would she use it?

The audience shivered with apprehension.

And in the end she did not. She bluffed the menacing underworld figure with a bit of shrewd bravado that would have done credit to the great Madame herself, saved her granddaughter, and was back in her comic character again as the curtain went down to a rolling roar of laughter and applause.

Again Dorothy Devine had triumphed. Society and Broadway rose to acclaim her.

But as the Madame left her seat with the lithe grace and sureness of action that characterized her every movement, the actress was playing out a real-life drama in her dressing-room.

Backed against her make-up shelf, Dorothy Devine stood at bay, her bosom rising and falling, her lips compressed into a thin crimson line. In the hand that had held the stage gun with such evident reluctance a business-like automatic nestled. The hand grasped the rod as though it were accustomed to it, and the hand did not tremble.

It pointed at two men who had forced their way, a moment before, into the star's dressing quarters.

"Get out!" the actress snarled.

The men looked at each other knowingly and laughed.

They were faultlessly dressed, but about them both was a furtive look. The taller had a scar across his cheek that might have been made by a burst of shrapnel except that it was a furrow dug by the pointed fingernail of an enraged woman. The other was smaller, with eyes that never remained fixed on one thing for more than a split second.

"Get out, I tell you!"

Dorothy Devine's voice was rising shrilly.

"Take it easy." The man with the scar waved

a well-manicured hand languidly. "Take it easy, kid."

"Leave me alone!" Dorothy almost screamed. "Why can't you leave me——"

As the man with the scar dropped his hand she sprang for the door, thrusting herself madly between them. But as her hand grasped the knob they closed in from either side, seized her wrists, and tore her away. In another instant she had been thrust into a chair.

The man with the scar bent over her, wrenched the gun away and tossed it on a chaise-longue across the room.

"Now, listen to what we have to say, kid." His tone was menacing. "And you better make up your mind right now that you're going to do what we want."

There was something at once pleading and yet hopeless in the look the actress shot up at him, and past him to the man with the shifty eyes who had slouched to the door and stood leaning against it, gnawing at his lip.

"Oh, can't you leave me alone?" she begged. "I've paid your dirty blackmail until you've practically bled me dry. Now, won't you leave me alone?"

But even as she spoke she realized that with these two pleading would do no good. They were out for the last penny.

The man with the scar allayed her fears with words for an instant, however.

"It's not money we want this time," he said easily, glancing down at his polished nails. "And I resent your use of that word blackmail. It has an ugly sound."

"But that's exactly what it is," she protested vehemently. "You—you——"

The man with the scar held up his hand.

"Please, please!" He bowed mockingly. "Do not over-excite yourself, Miss Devine—Molly Delaney Mulford Dorothy Devine."

The actress shrank away at the string of names as though she had been smacked in the mouth.

The man drew a perfumed handkerchief from his sleeve and flicked it across his nails to renew the lustre.

"Let us realize that this is a purely business transaction," he resumed. "We perform a service for you for which you have thus far paid us. You infer that your supply of ready funds is low." He shrugged. "We do not wish to press you. Hence we will continue to perform the same service for you, but in return you must perform one for us."

Dorothy Devine's hands clenched in her lap.

"You blood-suckers—you parasites!" she cried. "Just because you know something about me——"

"Exactly!" The man with the scar cut her short. "Just because we happen to know that when you were appearing in a tent show on some dizzy merry-go-round circuit in the Middle West you spent six months in one of the local jugs—for—well, we are able to perform a very valuable service for you. We prevent that information from reaching the ears of your swell and very elegant society friends, and we naturally expect a small payment for the service. If we allowed it to be known that the gorgeous Dorothy Devine was really Molly Delaney Mulford——"

He spread his hands.

The actress half rose from her chair.

"You beasts! You know perfectly well that I was framed. That my husband and I had not been paid in weeks—nor had any of the other members of the troupe. You know that the manager of the show had been trying to get his hands on me and was furious because I laughed at him. And you know that when Jack Mulford needed an emergency operation I took from the manager's box only what was rightly ours. But in spite of it my husband died."

Her face sank into her hands.

"That is what *you* say, kid."

The actress sprang to her feet and faced him.

"Yes, that's what *I* say—and it's *true*. And it's true that the manager testified that we had been paid and that I'd stolen the money from his box—and the rest of the troupe backed him up because they were afraid if they didn't they'd never see their own pay—and it's true that I spent six months in jail for it." She shook her fist under his nose. "And how do you happen to know all this? Because you were in the same jail because you're the cheapest and poorest pair of jewel thieves at present living off the lowest form of crookedness there is—blackmail!"

The man with the scar smiled, a thin-lipped cruel smile.

"That is what *you* say," he murmured, "but would your Park Avenue friends who so eagerly seek you as a dinner guest, or would the Lacey-Smythes whose car is waiting outside the stage door to carry you out to their Long Island estate for the week-end—would they believe it?" He shook his head. "I think not. Hence we will continue to perform our little service and you will continue to pay our modest fee."

Dorothy Devine dropped back into her chair with a beaten look.

"But I tell you I have no money. You know that as well as I do."

"My dear Miss Devine"—the man's tone was sardonic—"who said anything about money? All we ask is that you perform a small service for us in return."

The man at the door nodded in agreement.

"Well?" the girl asked helplessly.

The man with the scar leaned closer.

"Merely this. Listen carefully. You are to be the week-end guest of the Lacey-Smythes. Mrs. Lacey-Smythe's pearls are famous. We have read about them in the papers often." He tapped a folded paper that protruded from his pocket. "In fact, an article on the party she is giving tonight and at which you are to be a guest, contains another description of her five-hundred-grand necklace."

He tapped the tips of his fingers together and glanced down at the actress speculatively.

"We have had our eyes on those pearls for a long time," he continued. "To tell you the truth, we have cased the job thoroughly and we expect within twenty-four hours to be in possession of them."

The actress was on her feet again.

"No, no—not Mrs. Lacey-Smythe! You're not going to rob her!"

"But that's exactly what we *are* going to do—and you're going to help us."

He waved aside her stammered protests, and his voice grew hard.

"If you wish to keep them as your friends—if you wish them not to know that they are entertaining a jailbird—you will do as we say. After all it is really nothing. As I said before, we have cased the job thoroughly *except* that we have been unable to locate the wall safe where Mrs. Lacey-Smythe places her jewels when she retires."

Dorothy Devine waited, knowing that she was trapped, yet searching her brain for a way out.

"Now all that you have to do," the man with the scar continued, "is to ask your hostess's permission to put some of your own jewels in her safe. On some pretext or other see her when she puts them in. After you have gone to your room to retire for the night a servant will rap at your door to inquire if you wish anything." He bowed. "I will be the servant and you will tell me the location of the safe. Then you may sleep peacefully knowing that neither of us will trouble you again."

He grinned with his lips alone.

"It will be worth it to be rid of us that easily, won't it? For you may rest assured that with the proceeds of this job we will be on the downy for the rest of our lives. Remember——"

"No, no!" The actress covered her ears with her hands and tried to brush past him. "I will not do it."

The man with the scar seized her arm.

"Let me go!" she pleaded. "Let me go! I am late as it is."

"In just a moment, kid. I merely wish to remind you what will happen to society's darling if it becomes known that she was once a jailbird—but I see that you know."

He released her arm.

"When I rap at your door I shall expect you to give me the information we desire."

With a mock show of politeness he escorted her into the corridor.

"Good-evening, Miss Devine, and have a nice time at the party."

He turned to his companion when the stage door had banged behind the departing actress.

"She's made up her mind to give us the air," he said. "But she'll change it. I know her better than she knows herself."

And he was right.

On Monday morning the Madame sat at the fragile Louis Quatorze desk in the little office behind Le Parfume Shoppe. Her close-fitting grey frock, carefully calculated to blend harmoniously with the softly shaded hangings and old French furniture of the room, served to enhance her young blonde beauty. She looked exactly what she pretended to be—a smart perfumer offering a stock of imported wares for those to whom price was the only criterion of quality.

Her head was bent forward and supported by her hands. Her blue-grey eyes, luminous and a bit misty at the thought that today Le Parfume Shoppe would be closed for good, were desultorily scanning the headlines of the first edition of the *Evening Gazette*, one of the more lurid afternoon tabloids spread out on the desk before her.

Suddenly the eyes grew hard and metallic as they caught a headline sprawled across the third page:

GEM THIEVES CRACK SOCIETY SAFE

Lacey-Smythes' Country House Looted of Famous Pearls

By Jane Bradley

Some time before dawn Sunday a thief, or thieves, slipped through the cordon of guards in and around the palatial Long Island country house of the wealthy and socially prominent Charles H. D. Lacey-Smythe, gagged the popular hostess and trussed her securely in her bed, broke into the concealed wall safe in her boudoir, and made away with her internationally-known necklace of matched pearls valued at half a million dollars.

The Lacey-Smythes' week-end guests, who included the Reginalt Van Astorbilt, Jrs., the incomparable Dorothy Devine, and "Pony" Dibble, the high-goal polo star, were thrown into a fever of excitement when Mrs. Lacey-Smythe's maid came screaming into the library as they were assembling for a late breakfast. She said that she had gone to her mistress's room with her morning chocolate and found her tied to the bed with her jaws firmly bound with adhesive tape.

Guards supplied by a private detective agency to protect the jewels worn by the guests at a large party held in the house the night before were immediately summoned and the maid's story proved to be true.

The only information Mrs. Lacey-Smythe could supply the police was that when she awakened she found herself unable to move. She exhibited all the symptoms of a person recovering from the effects of chloroform, however, and as the odor of that drug was still discernable in the bedroom the police believe that Mrs. Lacey-Smythe was chloroformed into unconsciousness, bound and gagged, and then the robbery effected.

The antiquated wall safe had been cracked in fairly expert fashion, and the police believe it must have been the work of semi-professionals at least. They are carefully checking the movements of all known gem thieves.

Mrs. Lacey-Smythe is at a loss as to how whoever did the job learned the location of the safe, as it was concealed behind a secret panel whose whereabouts was known only to her husband and herself.

The pearls were the only articles of value the safe contained except for trinkets of sentimental value belonging to one of the guests, which had been entrusted to the hostess for safekeeping.

The guards supplied by the private agency are unable to explain how the thief, or thieves, were able to pass through their cordon and gain access to the bedroom. The window was opened, however, and it is supposed that a ladder was used, although no marks of any kind were discovered in the flower-beds beneath.

The only possible clue was a blood-stain on the end of one of the splinters protruding from the broken panel. Under microscopic examination this splinter revealed particles of rubber and it is thought that one of the robbers probably ran the splinter into his rubber-gloved thumb in the course of his operations.

"Find the man with a splinter hole in his thumb and the robbery is solved," the inspector in charge of detectives said in a special interview granted newspapermen late last night.

The Madame thrust the paper aside impatiently.

"'The guards supplied by the detective agency,' indeed!" she snorted. "'At a loss to explain how the thieves were able to pass through their cordon and gain access to the bedroom!'"

She twisted the paper and flung it into the waste-basket.

"It should be obvious to even the most ignorant policeman that the—ah—petermen—never even passed through the cordon. It was an inside job. While they're waiting for someone to tell them to check up on the servants, and especially the extra ones hired for the party, the—ah—gentlemen who cleaned the pete—are getting farther and farther away, and so are the pearls, unless they've already gone through the—ah—fence."

She shrugged her slender shoulders.

"But what is the matter with me? Force of habit, probably. Here I am through with any and every—ah—racket and I must start uncasing jobs I read about in the papers."

She shook her head disapprovingly.

"Come, come, Madame! Enough of this! You must get about the permanent closing of the shoppe and then, as your acquaintances in the underworld so aptly put it—take it on the hot. Now the first thing to do, obviously, is to call——"

She reached for the gilded telephone on her desk.

But her hand was destined not to touch it at that moment, for from the shoppe came the low whine of a buzzer.

Like a striking snake the Madame whipped around in her chair as a heavily-veiled figure slunk furtively through the door that led in from the street.

As the figure moved uncertainly past the glass cases with their load of exotic bottles that lined the walls, casting quick, hunted glances over its shoulder, the Madame's agile mind classified its impression of the visitor—woman, young, body trained in dancing or some other kindred profession. The latter gave her the clue she wanted and nodding her head imperceptibly she made a shrewd guess as to the woman's identity.

The woman came hesitatingly toward the door of the inner office, her feet making no sound on the thick carpet of the floor.

Suddenly the woman stiffened, and stifled a shriek with her black-gloved hand.

From the street came a loud report.

The Madame's nonchalant pose did not change. She had seen the heavy truck sweep past the door and had recognized the sound for what it was—a backfire. And to her already complete classification of her visitor the Madame added—in mortal terror of someone. But she was too shrewd to confuse her mind with suppositions as to the cause for the fear. That was the secret of the Madame's success, she reasoned only from facts.

The woman came through the inner door and paused, undecided, beside the desk.

The Madame waited.

The visitor's first words would answer one question, that of her identity, the Madame was sure. The heavy black veil hid her features completely and it was necessary that she speak to give the Madame her cue.

And it was as the Madame expected.

"You are the—the person known as the Madame?" the woman asked haltingly.

The Madame's guess as to the woman's identity proved correct as her answer showed.

"Yes, Miss Devine," she said with a gracious inclination of the head. "Won't you sit down?"

The visitor took a quick step backward, surprise and fear in the movement.

"But—but how did you know it was I?"

"It is my business to know such things, Miss Devine. But do sit down." She indicated the slim-legged chair beside her desk. "I enjoyed your performance so much on Saturday night."

The Madame's visitor took the chair and thrust up her veil.

It *was* Dorothy Devine.

"Thank you," she said from polite force of habit. "I am glad that you enjoyed my efforts. But it is a wonder that I was able to play any show at all. You see, I had—I had unwelcome callers and they frightened me nearly crazy."

The actress hesitated.

"And you are still terrified of them," the Madame supplied in a low, soothing tone. "Your entrance a moment ago showed that only too plainly. And if I may hazard a guess, it is of these same unwelcome callers that you have come to see me."

Dorothy Devine nodded.

The Madame's eyelids drew together, half filming the grey-blue eyes and turning the blue to a glinting, metallic grey; her lips compressed; her nostrils distended like a keen-nosed hunting dog that gets the first breath of scent. It was always that way with the Madame when she scented a problem against which she could pit her matchless mind. This savored of action, intrigue, complications. The ethics of the problem did not interest the Madame—whether it was a question of the weak menaced by the strong, or the lesser dog seeking to wrest its due from the greater—it was only the problem that counted.

She leaned forward.

"I am interested, Miss Devine." The words dropped from her lips like tense, brittle bits of steel. "Please be perfectly frank and perhaps I may be able to help you."

The actress moved uneasily in her chair, hesitated, and appeared finally to make up her mind.

"I have been told—er—Madame, that you have never violated a confidence."

The Madame acknowledged the compliment perfunctorily, eager for the actress to speak.

"Please tell me what is troubling you, Miss Devine."

Dorothy Devine rested an arm on the edge of the desk and looked the Madame in the eyes, every trace of the stage business gone.

"Blackmail!" she whispered.

"Ah!"

"And if it will not bore you, Madame, I will begin at the beginning and tell you everything."

She did.

The Madame listened intently to the harrowing recital which began with the actress's debut in the tent show, continued through her marriage, the death of her husband, the frame-up that sent her to jail and began the blackmail, and led finally to her interview with the man with the scar and his companion in the dressing-room.

"I swore to myself I would not do it, Madame!" Dorothy cried in a shaken voice. "But when the time came I did." She looked up pleadingly. "Oh, if you could only understand how I have struggled for recognition—the recognition of the people that counted—not only the people of the theatre, but of society. And when I once got it I could not let it go—I could not!"

Her head dropped tiredly on her arm.

The Madame reached out a hand and stroked the shaking shoulders.

"I understand," she said gently.

The actress raised her head.

"They promised that if I would do this one thing they would leave me alone for good. I should have known better. They are nothing but cheap crooks—scavengers. They wait for things to fall into their hands, that is why they are not well known to the police. They will only go after sure things. They read about my success in the papers and left a petty racket to come to New York and make me pay. They read about the Lacey-Smythe pearls in the paper, cased the job, and found it was simply too easy, the owners depending chiefly for protection on the fact that the safe was concealed. Once they learned its location there was nothing to it. The private guards did not count."

She paused for breath.

"But what have they done now?" the Madame asked.

"They came to me this morning, directly I had returned from Long Island. They said that they would not be able to make satisfactory arrangements with the fence for a few days and demanded money to tide them over. They showed me Mrs. Lacey-Smythe's pearls, and laughed in my face. But what could I do?"

Dorothy Devine spread her hands helplessly.

"They have bled me dry, Madame. My work is suffering, and so——"

"And so," the Madame cut in, with a trace of amused irony, "you decided to set a thief to catch a thief."

She waved the actress's protest aside.

"And not such a bad idea at that, Miss Devine."

The Madame sat back, smoothed her tawny hair reflectively, and gazed into space.

After what seemed an interminable period to the actress, the silence was broken.

"You wish to be permanently rid of these two men." The Madame was thinking aloud. "And in so doing you must not, to their knowledge, appear, otherwise your secret would become known. That is to be avoided at all costs. Violence I will not tolerate, so"—she lapsed for a moment into the vernacular of the underworld at which she was adept—"burning them down is out."

She swung around quickly on the waiting woman.

"You say these men first put the finger on you when they were with you in the same can?"

"Yes."

"Have they ever, to your knowledge, done time since?"

"Yes. Both of them. Three times, once for working a cheap con game on a farmer, once for a stick-up, and once for concealed weapons. Oh, I know their histories well."

"Fine!" the Madame interrupted. "All felonies. Have you an understudy who could take your part—say for a week, if necessary?"

The actress showed her surprise.

"Y-es," she answered.

"Good. How long have the men given you to produce the money?"

"Until tomorrow morning."

The Madame drummed for a moment upon the polished top of the desk.

"Tell me, Miss Devine, is there a service entrance in the rear of your apartment building—I mean, one which you could slip out of without being seen?"

The rapid-fire of questions had completely tied the actress's mental faculties in a knot.

"Why—why, I believe so," she stammered.

"Good. Now, Miss Devine, go back to your apartment and answer neither doorbell or telephone until I call. You will know my call because the phone will ring three times and stop. Approximately three minutes later it will ring again three times and again stop. You will answer it when it rings once more after a three-minute interval. It will be I and I will tell you what to do next."

Before the actress could express her thanks she found herself being ushered gently but firmly toward the outer door.

"Follow my instructions implicitly—and, by the way, stop at the theatre on your way home and pick up your make-up box. And now, please excuse me, for I shall be very busy."

A moment later the door closed behind her and the actress found herself alone in the street.

The Madame returned to her desk, sat down and thumbed rapidly through the telephone book. Finding the number she sought, she reached for the telephone and gave it to the operator.

In a moment she was connected with her party.

"A-1 Realty Corporation?" she asked. "I am interested in renting a furnished apartment—somewhere in the West 90's, near the Drive. . . . Yes. . . . Just a moment, while I note the address"—she scribbled rapidly on a pad—"I will call to inspect it this afternoon, and if it suits I wish to occupy it immediately. Good-bye."

She hung up and once more consulted the pages of the telephone directory, found her number and gave it to the operator.

"*Evening Gazette?* I wish to speak to Jane Bradley, please . . . thank you . . . Miss Bradley? . . . I have never had the pleasure of your acquaintance, but I want to tell you how much I enjoyed your story of the Lacey-Smythe robbery"—she laughed softly, although the expression of her face did not change—"you are speaking to the person known as the Madame, possibly . . . oh, you *have* heard of me . . . I wondered, Miss Bradley, if you would care to be instrumental in the capture of the two persons responsible for the Lacey-Smythe robbery? . . . Splendid . . . could you call at Le Parfume Shoppe immediately?" She gave the address. "And it is understood that until you have seen me you are to say nothing about this call . . . good . . . I will be waiting for you . . . Good-bye."

The Madame replaced the receiver on its hook.

Inside of half an hour Jane Bradley, police reporter for the *Gazette*, burst into the inner office of Le Parfume Shoppe. She was young, competent, and inclined toward beauty. But efficiently-cynical newspaper woman that she was, she was obviously awed at first in the presence of the famous Madame.

She was soon at her ease, however, and listened with increasing wonder as the Madame talked. In five minutes she was convinced.

"I'll do it!" she exclaimed excitedly. "We can just make the next edition of this afternoon's paper. And I'll get 'Big Dan' Murray for the other part. He's a young dick trying to get along. You'll like him."

"Good, Miss Bradley. Now listen——"

For five minutes more the Madame spoke, rapidly but without using a superfluous word, while the reporter took notes. When she finished, the girl sprang to her feet.

"I'll rush right over and shove it in as is, Madame!" she cried, on her way to the door. "The rest of your directions will be carried out to the letter. I'll wait in the city room for a call from you. And thanks awfully, Madame, you don't know what this beat will mean to me. Cheerio."

Less than an hour later the Madame was inspecting a furnished apartment at 493 West 97th Street. It was in a brownstone house, the first two floors, to be exact, and had been occupied for years by a somewhat eccentric widow. The furnishings were old and a bit antiquated, but it seemed to suit the Madame and she leased it on the spot, stipulating, however, that she be allowed to occupy it immediately. The permission was readily granted by the agent, who did not recognize the identity of his prospective tenant.

"And now I wish to telephone," she remarked as she folded the receipt and slipped it into her bag.

"You may do so from this apartment, if you wish," the agent suggested. "The telephone has been kept in service. It is in the library, and there is also an extension in the master bedroom on the second floor. Nothing has been touched here since the death of the owner."

"Thank you."

The agent complimented himself on a smooth piece of work and left.

The Madame hurried to the phone, took a watch from her bag and placed it beside the instrument, raised the receiver and gave the number. It was repeated by the operator, then came the faint purr that indicated that the bell at the other end of the wire was ringing. There was a pause, another purr, a pause, and a third purr. Halfway through it she hung up, glancing at the dial of the watch as she did so. Three minutes later she called again and the process was repeated.

At the end of another three-minute interval she again called the same number. Dorothy Devine's voice answered almost immediately.

The Madame's directions were brief and to the point. At their conclusion the actress repeated what was expected of her so there could be no slip.

"Good," the Madame replied, "and don't forget the address."

The Madame had yet one more call to make, and this time when the receiver had clicked back upon its hook she rubbed her hands.

"If I do say it, Madame," she remarked affably, "this is as fine a job of casing as you have ever done. The trap is set, now all we have to do is wait for the prey to smell the bait. It will be one grand job—*if it works.*"

It was ten o'clock that evening. Behind the drawn curtains of the library at 493 West 97th Street a fire glowed comfortably in the open grate. In its flickering light, for there was no other source of illumination, the ancient furniture cast grotesque moving shadows upon the dingy walls.

In a wing-chair, beside the fire sat a little frail old lady, looking, in her stiff silk dress with lace at the neck and wrists, as though she had stepped direct from a century-old painting. The lace cap on her head was scarcely whiter than the hair beneath and served to throw the transparent, wrinkled face under it into shadow.

From time to time the little old lady turned half around in her chair and glanced apprehensively to where the seeking fingers of ruddy light from the fireplace fell upon a squat, bulky object against the opposite wall that reflected the soft rays in sharp, alien glimmerings.

It was a small safe, obviously new.

And as the little old lady in the chair sat watching it a door at the far end of the room opened and a maid as old and bent and fragile as herself entered bearing a tray. Her uniform would have brought a snicker to the modern variety of servant, but it blended in perfectly with its present surroundings.

The maid came forward with the tiny, fumbling steps of the very aged, and placed the tray on a low table beside her mistress.

"Your tea and toast, Ma'am, and a newspaper with an article about the diamonds," she quavered.

Handing a folded copy of the last edition of the *Gazette* to her mistress, she pointed to the headlines:

LACEY-SMYTHE GEM ROBBERY BAFFLES POLICE

All Clues Fail

By Jane Bradley

For an instant their eyes met with a twinkle, as though they shared an amusing secret.

"The first part of the article is about that horrible business on Long Island. It's the last few paragraphs"—the maid indicated them with a pointing finger—"that's about the diamonds, Ma'am."

While the ancient maid poured the tea from an old-fashioned pot the little old lady read:

The ease with which the Lacey-Smythe pearls were stolen reveals a shocking condition which is prevalent throughout greater New York, where many thousands of dollars' worth of gems are nightly placed behind even less trustworthy safeguards.

Many instances of such carelessness could be cited, but probably the most flagrant of these is the case of the famous Musgrave diamonds.

The Musgrave diamonds, a necklace of twenty flawless stones totaling several hundreds of carats in weight, have long been kept by their owner, Mrs. Elvira P. Musgrave, in a secret compartment of a secretary in the library of her residence at 493 West 97th Street.

This necklace, while not as well known as some of the more historic collections resting in the guarded vaults of the larger jewelers' shops, is nevertheless of tremendous real and sentimental value to Mrs. Musgrave, as the stones were collected in all parts of the world by her late husband.

It is hoped that the many thousand owners of valuable jewelry will be warned by the Lacey-Smythe robbery and see that their gems are consigned to any one of the conventional places of safety, the best, of course, being a safe deposit box, in a bank.

"That article should be a warning to you, Ma'am," the maid remarked. "At any rate, I took the liberty of renting that safe for the diamonds. It can be returned when it has served its purpose and the fee is very reasonable. Your tea, Ma'am."

She handed the steaming beverage to her mistress.

"And a cup for yourself."

"Thanks, Ma'am."

They drank, nibbling at their toast, and talked in subdued tones.

The great clock in the hall struck eleven.

"It is time for bed, Ma'am," the maid suggested.

But her mistress demurred.

"Just a few minutes more."

The clock struck the half-hour, and as it did so, from somewhere in the rear of the house came the muffled clangor of the doorbell.

The two women looked at each other knowingly.

The maid arose and left the room. The sound of her tottering footsteps receded down the hall and gave place to a murmur of voices. Then the fumbling footsteps returned, followed by the tramp of heavier feet, and the maid ushered two men into the library.

They wore derby hats pushed on the backs of their heads, in their teeth were clenched fat black cigars. The taller had his right thumb stuck in the armhole of his vest, disclosing a shiny badge. When he dropped it to his pocket there was a glimpse of grimy adhesive tape.

"Police officers to see you, Ma'am," the maid announced, her voice quivering.

The taller of the two stepped forward into the light. Across his cheek stretched a livid scar. Behind him, his companion stood shifting his feet uneasily, his eyes traveling furtively about the room, never remaining fixed on one place for more than a split second.

"You are Mrs. Elvira P. Musgrave?" the man with the scar demanded.

The little old lady nodded.

"Well, we're detectives from the station house around the corner," he announced, displaying the shield on his vest by a backward flip of his coat.

Behind him his companion duplicated the action.

"The sergeant sent us around about this," the man with the scar went on, drawing a copy of the *Gazette* from his pocket and pointing to the paragraph that mentioned the Musgrave diamonds. "Have you seen it?"

Again the little old lady in the chair nodded.

"Well, the sergeant thought those were too valuable jewels to be kept simply in an old desk without any kind of protection—too many burglars about, you know. So he sent us over to keep an eye out for your diamonds until morning, when he suggests you hire a safety deposit box in a bank and put them in it. We're to wait until they're safe."

"That is very kind indeed of you, gentlemen," the little old lady answered. "Won't you sit down?"

She indicated the stiff horsehair sofa on the opposite side of the fire, and as the two men sank down upon its creaky springs her maid assisted her to move her own chair so that her face was in shadow. Then the ancient maid crossed to the sofa where the men sat blinking in the direction of the flames.

Without a change of expression she plucked the fat cigars from their mouths and tossed them into the fire. Then she removed an iron hat from each head and slammed it down on its owner's knees.

"Priscilla!" the horrified mistress exclaimed. "These gentlemen have come to protect the Musgrave diamonds until we can place them in the bank in the morning. You are forgetting yourself. Bring fresh tea and toast."

The maid shuffled over to the table and began placing the cups back on the tray.

The man with the scar leaned forward.

"Tell me, Mrs. Musgrave, is that story in the paper about your diamonds true? So often they are exaggerated, you know."

"Oh, yes, indeed, sir," the little old lady twittered.

The man with the scar turned and surveyed the room until his eyes came to a tall old-fashioned desk in the corner.

"And is that the secretary in which the jewels are kept?" he asked.

"*Were* kept," she corrected him. "As soon as my maid read that article in the paper she telephoned a concern that rents safes and had one delivered immediately. There it is"—she pointed—"and the diamonds are in it. But I shall certainly take your advice and have them placed in the bank in the morning."

Both men followed the direction of her pointing finger and their mouths dropped open. The shifty-eyed one blinked rapidly and the man with the scar looked as though he might have swallowed his teeth.

But the little old lady appeared not to notice.

"Would you like to hear about the Mus-grave diamonds?" she asked, folding her hands serenely in her lap.

The men nodded dumbly.

The maid picked up her tray and left the room.

When she returned her mistress was still rambling on. The men sat uneasily on the edge of the sofa. She served tea and toast to them while her mistress continued her chatty monologue.

Outside in the hall the clock struck midnight.

Still the little old lady rambled on.

When the clock finally chimed one, the maid approached her mistress.

"You must go to bed now," she insisted sternly. "It's long past your bedtime as it is."

An expression of relief crossed the faces of the men.

The little old lady arose with reluctance.

"But these gentlemen——" she protested.

"Don't mind about us, Mrs. Musgrave," the man with the scar hastened to assure her. "We'll make ourselves comfortable here until morning—sergeant's orders."

The little old lady turned to her maid.

"Perhaps the gentlemen would like something to drink, Priscilla."

The maid disappeared and returned shortly with a tray containing whisky, soda, and glasses. As she handed it to the man with the scar she noticed a patch of adhesive tape on the ball of his right thumb, and stifled a chuckle.

The little old lady bid her callers good-night, and, assisted by her maid, slowly climbed the stairs to the second floor.

Just as dawn was breaking the man with the scar straightened from a cramped kneeling position before the safe in the library of 493 West 97th Street.

"Damned lucky we thought to bring our tools and a slug of soup," he muttered to the man with the shifty eyes. "Now throw that wet rug over this here box while I give it a shot."

He wrapped a pair of wires, leading from a

cup-like contrivance attached to the iron door, around the handle of the safe and carried the two loose ends to a distance while his companion covered the box with a heavy wet rug.

"Quick now—everything set?" he snapped, drawing a flashlight battery from his pocket. "I hear a truck."

The man with the shifty eyes glanced around the closed doors.

"Okay."

The truck, a heavy one, apparently filled with milk cans, rumbled past.

The man with the scar scratched the ends of the wire on the exposed poles of the battery.

There was a dull thud, lost in the rumble of the truck, and the door of the safe swung open.

At the same moment the door from the hall burst inward and two men, followed by an eager-eyed girl, pushed in to the library.

"There they are, Dan!" the girl cried shrilly. "Get 'em, big boy!"

It was obvious that these men *were* dicks. There was no mistaking it by the way they went for their guns.

"Big Dan" Murray was in the lead.

For a moment the man with the scar and his companion stood paralyzed.

"Put 'em up!" Murray bellowed.

As he spoke the door leading from the rear of the house opened and the maid, followed by her mistress, and both with negligée hastily thrown over their old-fashioned night attire, stepped into the library.

The man with the scar saw his chance.

With a sardonic laugh he leaped for the rear door, the man with the shifty eyes half a jump behind.

The two detectives withheld their fire, fearful that a stray shot might take effect on the women.

The little old lady cowered against the wall as the robbers rushed toward them.

But the maid stood her ground. In fact, she took a half step forward and waited flat-footed.

A collision seemed inevitable. The dicks were in pursuit, fearful of finding the maid a complete wreck when they should reach her.

But instead of going down in front of the charge, the unexpected happened.

Shifting with unlooked-for agility the maid's right fist lashed out, landing smack against the oncoming jaw. The blow seemed to travel only a matter of inches, but the man with the scar went down as though he had suddenly encountered a Mack truck head-on.

The fall of his companion slowed up the man with the shifty eyes for an instant, and in that instant a knife gleamed in his hand. It glimmered upward in a flashing arc directly above the maid's head.

The dicks were thundering up, but obvious that they would be too late. The maid was doomed.

But she waited unperturbed for the descent of the blade.

It started.

The maid's right hand flicked out, snaked under the man's upper arm and her fingers twined about his wrist. Her left hand covered her right, an old jiu-jitsu trick. She pressed forward.

The man's feet rose in the air and he did a backward spin. There was a sharp snap. He screamed in agony and fell in a limp huddle at the detectives' feet.

"Pushed too hard," the maid remarked laconically, dusting off her hands. "Broke his arm I'm afraid."

Before the astonished detectives could speak she put an arm about her half-fainting mistress's waist and supported her from the room.

"Well, I'll be—I certainly will be——" Big Dan Murray stammered as he snapped the cuffs on the two prostrate robbers and jerked them to their feet.

He turned to the girl who had followed them upon their unceremonious entrance.

"Your tip sure was the goods, *Gazette*," he chuckled.

"But are these babies the ones?" she asked anxiously. It was Jane Bradley.

Murray pointed to the piece of adhesive tape

that decorated the thumb of the man with the scar.

"We'll probably find a hole made by a certain splinter under that tape," he remarked. "And by the way," he turned to the other dick, "just have a look and see what they've got on 'em."

The man stepped forward and went through their pockets.

With a grunt of satisfaction he stepped back, holding something out in his hand.

"The Lacey-Smythe pearls!" Murray exclaimed. "Well, I'll be damned!"

He turned swiftly on the girl reporter.

"I beg your pardon, *Gazette*, but tell me—how did you know this was coming off? I sure appreciate the tip-off, but I feel dumb having to be taught my business by a girl reporter."

Jane Bradley smiled wisely.

"We—I had a hunch that if I planted that phoney about the Musgrave diamonds in the paper it would draw something. This apartment was all a set-up."

"But the two old dames, *Gazette*, who are they?"

The girl laughed outright.

"Just a pair of—of actresses we hired for the evening. But what I want to know is this—how long will these babies go up for? I understand they have three previous convictions to their credit—three felonies."

Dan Murray grinned.

"Well, I should say that by the time we get through pinning safe cracking, carrying concealed weapons, attempted assault with a deadly weapon, and several other things on them neither one will come out of the big house until they carry them out feet first. Does that satisfy you?"

"Perfectly. And now I think I'll go upstairs and pay off the—actresses."

Murray detained her a moment more.

"I suppose you want us to suppress the report of this arrest for—how long?"

The girl looked at her watch.

"It's seven now. Could you hold it till nine? My story's written and set ready to go. All I can expect is a first edition scoop anyway."

"Gladly, *Gazette*, we certainly owe that much to you."

"You're an old dear."

The girl turned and dashed from the room.

Upstairs she encountered the two "old ladies" removing wigs and make-up.

"I want to congratulate you on the finest performance of your career, Miss Devine," the maid was saying.

Dorothy Devine scrubbed at her face with a sheet of tissue.

"If you should consider turning to the theatre, Madame," she laughed, "I can assure you of the lead in any one of three plays that I know of. You were marvelous."

"And I can assure you both," the girl reporter cut in, "that your two boy friends downstairs can't possibly get off without life and about a hundred extra years tacked on for good measure."

"Splendid," the Madame remarked, "but if the police expect witnesses of this little business I'm afraid you will *really* have to hire a pair of actresses for Miss Devine and I are going to scram, and that quickly. And you must forget that we have been here at all."

EXTENUATING CIRCUMSTANCES

Joyce Carol Oates

THE CASE HAS BEEN made that Joyce Carol Oates (1938–   ), with a career known for its excellence, popularity, and prolificacy, is the greatest living writer in the world to have not yet been awarded the Nobel Prize in Literature (she has been regarded as a favorite by readers, critics, and bookies for about twenty-five years).

Born in Lockport, New York, in the northwestern part of the state, she began to write as a young child, attended Syracuse University on scholarship, and won a *Mademoiselle* magazine short story award at nineteen. Her first novel, *With Shuddering Fall* (1964), has been followed by more than a hundred books, including more than fifty novels, forty short story collections, several books for children and young adult novels, ten volumes of poetry, fourteen collections of essays and criticism, and eight volumes of plays; eleven of her novels of suspense were released under the pseudonyms Rosamond Smith and Lauren Kelly. An overwhelming number of her novels and short stories feature such subjects as violence, sexual abuse, murder, racial tensions, and class conflicts. Many of her fictional works have been based on real-life incidents, including violent crimes.

As voluminous as her writing career has been, so, too, has been the extraordinary number of major literary prizes and honors awarded to her, including a National Book Award for *them* (1969), as well as five other nominations; five Pulitzer Prize nominations; two O. Henry Awards for short stories; and Bram Stoker Awards for the novel *Zombie* (1995) and the short story "The Crawl Space" (2016). Among her bestselling books have been *We Were the Mulvaneys* (1996), which was an Oprah Book Club selection and a film released in 2002 with Beau Bridges and Blythe Danner, and *Blonde* (2000; 2001 film with Poppy Montgomery), a novel based on the life of Marilyn Monroe. The 1996 film *Foxfire* (starring Cathy Moriarty, Hedy Burress, and Angelina Jolie) was an adaptation of Oates's 1993 novel *Foxfire: Confessions of a Girl Gang.*

"Extenuating Circumstances" was originally published in *Sisters in Crime 5*, edited by Marilyn Wallace (New York, Berkley, 1992).

Extenuating Circumstances

JOYCE CAROL OATES

BECAUSE IT WAS A MERCY. Because God even in His cruelty will sometimes grant mercy.

Because Venus was in the sign of Sagittarius.

Because you laughed at me, my faith in the stars. My hope.

Because he cried, you do not know how he cried.

Because at such times his little face was so twisted and hot, his nose running with mucus, his eyes so hurt.

Because in such he was his mother, and not you. Because I wanted to spare him such shame.

Because he remembered you, he knew the word *Daddy*.

Because watching TV he would point to a man and say *Daddy—?*

Because this summer has gone on so long, and no rain. The heat lightning flashing at night, without thunder.

Because in the silence, at night, the summer insects scream.

Because by day there are earth-moving machines and grinders operating hour upon hour razing the woods next to the playground. Because the red dust got into our eyes, our mouths.

Because he would whimper *Mommy?*—in that way that tore my heart.

Because last Monday the washing machine broke down, I heard a loud thumping that scared me, the dirty soapy water would not drain out.

Because in the light of the bulb overhead he saw me holding the wet sheets in my hand crying *What can I do? What can I do?*

Because the sleeping pills they give me now are made of flour and chalk, I am certain.

Because I loved you more than you loved me even from the first when your eyes moved on me like candle flame.

Because I did not know this yet, yes I knew it but cast it from my mind.

Because there was shame in it. Loving you knowing you would not love me enough.

Because my job applications are laughed at for misspellings and torn to pieces as soon as I leave.

Because they will not believe me when listing my skills. Because since he was born my body is misshapen, the pain is always there.

Because I see that it was not his fault and even in that I could not spare him.

Because even at the time when he was conceived (in those early days we were so happy! so happy I am certain! lying together on top of the bed the corduroy bedspread in that narrow jiggly bed hearing the rain on the roof that slanted down so you had to stoop being so tall and from outside on the street the roof with its dark shingles looking always wet was like a lowered brow over the windows on the third floor and the windows like squinting eyes and we would come home together from the University meeting at the Hardee's corner you from the geology lab or the library and me from Accounting where my eyes ached because of the lights with their dim flicker no one else could see and I was so happy your arm around my waist and mine around yours like any couple, like any college girl with her boyfriend, and walking *home*, yes it was *home*, I thought always it was *home*, we would look up at the windows of the apartment laughing saying who do you think lives there? what are their names? who are they? that cozy secret-looking room under the eaves where the roof came down, came down dripping black runny water I hear now drumming on this roof but only if I fall asleep during the day with my clothes on so tired so exhausted and when I wake up there is no rain, only the earth-moving machines and grinders in the woods so I must acknowledge *It is another time, it is time*) yes I knew.

Because you did not want him to be born.

Because he cried so I could hear him through the shut door, through all the doors.

Because I did not want him to be *Mommy*, I wanted him to be *Daddy* in his strength.

Because this washcloth in my hand was in my hand when I saw how it must be.

Because the checks come to me from the lawyer's office not from you. Because in tearing open the envelopes my fingers shaking and my eyes showing such hope I revealed myself naked to myself so many times.

Because to this shame he was a witness, he saw.

Because he was too young at two years to know. Because even so he knew.

Because his birthday was a sign, falling in the midst of Pisces.

Because in certain things he *was* his father, that knowledge in eyes that went beyond me in mockery of me.

Because one day he would laugh too as you have done.

Because there is no listing for your telephone and the operators will not tell me. Because in any of the places I know to find you, you cannot be found.

Because your sister has lied to my face, to mislead me. Because she who was once my friend, I believed, was never my friend.

Because I feared loving him too much, and in that weakness failing to protect him from hurt.

Because his crying tore my heart but angered me too so I feared laying hands upon him wild and unplanned.

Because he flinched seeing me. That nerve jumping in his eye.

Because he was always hurting himself, he was so clumsy falling off the swing hitting his head against the metal post so one of the other mothers saw and cried out *Oh! Oh look your son is bleeding!* and that time in the kitchen whining and pulling at me in a bad temper reaching up to grab the pot handle and almost overturning the boiling water in his face so I lost control slapping him shaking him by the arm *Bad! Bad! Bad! Bad!* my voice rising in fury not caring who heard.

Because that day in the courtroom you refused to look at me your face shut like a fist against me and your lawyer too, like I was dirt beneath your shoes. Like maybe he was not even your son but you would sign the papers as if he was, you are so superior.

Because the courtroom was not like any courtroom I had a right to expect, not a big dignified courtroom like on TV just a room with a judge's desk and three rows of six seats each and not a single window and even here that flickering light that yellowish-sickish fluorescent tubing making my eyes ache so I wore my dark glasses giving the judge a false impression of me, and I was sniffing, wiping my nose, every question they asked me I'd hear myself giggle so nervous and ashamed even stammering over my age and my name so you looked with scorn at me, all of you.

Because they were on your side, I could not prevent it.

Because in granting me child support payments, you had a right to move away. Because I could not follow.

Because he wet his pants, where he should not have, for his age.

Because it would be blamed on me. It *was* blamed on me.

Because my own mother screamed at me over the phone. She could not help me with my life she said, no one can help you with your life, we were screaming such things to each other as left us breathless and crying and I slammed down the receiver knowing that I had no mother and after the first grief I knew *It is better, so.*

Because he would learn that someday, and the knowledge of it would hurt him.

Because he had my hair coloring, and my eyes. That left eye, the weakness in it.

Because that time it almost happened, the boiling water overturned onto him, I saw how easy it would be. How, if he could be prevented from screaming, the neighbors would not know.

Because yes they would know, but only when I wanted them to know.

Because you would know then. Only when I wanted you to know.

Because then I could speak to you in this way, maybe in a letter which your lawyer would forward to you, or your sister, maybe over the telephone or even face to face. Because then you could not escape.

Because though you did not love him you could not escape him.

Because I have begun to bleed for six days quite heavily, and will then spot for another three or four. Because soaking the blood in wads of toilet paper sitting on the toilet my hands shaking I think of you who never bleed.

Because I am a proud woman, I scorn your charity.

Because I am not a worthy mother. Because I am so tired.

Because the machines digging in the earth and grinding trees are a torment by day, and the screaming insects by night.

Because there is no sleep.

Because he would only sleep, these past few months, if he could be with me in my bed.

Because he whimpered *Mommy!—Mommy don't!*

Because he flinched from me when there was no cause.

Because the pharmacist took the prescription and was gone such a long time, I knew he was telephoning someone.

Because at the drugstore where I have shopped for a year and a half they pretended not to know my name.

Because in the grocery store the cashiers stared smiling at me and at him pulling at my arm spilling tears down his face.

Because they whispered and laughed behind me, I have too much pride to respond.

Because he was with me at such times, he was a witness to such.

Because he had no one but his Mommy and his Mommy had no one but him. Which is so lonely.

Because I had gained seven pounds from last Sunday to this, the waist of my slacks is so tight. Because I hate the fat of my body.

Because looking at me naked now you would show disgust.

Because I *was* beautiful for you, why wasn't that enough?

Because that day the sky was dense with clouds the color of raw liver but yet there was no rain. Heat lightning flashing with no sound making me so nervous but no rain.

Because his left eye was weak, it would always be so unless he had an operation to strengthen the muscle.

Because I did not want to cause him pain and terror in his sleep.

Because you would pay for it, the check from the lawyer with no note.

Because you hated him, your son.

Because he was *our* son, you hated him.

Because you moved away. To the far side of the country I have reason to believe.

Because in my arms after crying he would lie so still, only one heart beating between us.

Because I knew I could not spare him from hurt.

Because the playground hurt our ears, raised red dust to get into our eyes and mouths.

Because I was so tired of scrubbing him clean, between his toes and beneath his nails, the insides of his ears, his neck, the many secret places of filth.

Because I felt the ache of cramps again in my belly, I was in a panic my period had begun so soon.

Because I could not spare him the older children laughing.

Because after the first terrible pain he would be beyond pain.

Because in this there is mercy.

Because God's mercy is for him, and not for me.

Because there was no one here to stop me.

Because my neighbors' TV was on so loud, I knew they could not hear even if he screamed through the washcloth.

Because you were not here to stop me, were you.

Because finally there is no one to stop us.

Because finally there is no one to save us.

Because my own mother betrayed me.

Because the rent would be due again on Tuesday which is the first of September. And by then I will be gone.

Because his body was not heavy to carry and to wrap in the down comforter, you remember that comforter, I know.

Because the washcloth soaked in his saliva will dry on the line and show no sign.

Because to heal there must be forgetfulness and oblivion.

Because he cried when he should not have cried but did not cry when he should.

Because the water came slowly to boil in the big pan, vibrating and humming on the front burner.

Because the kitchen was damp with steam from the windows shut so tight, the temperature must have been 100°F.

Because he did not struggle. And when he did, it was too late.

Because I wore rubber gloves to spare myself being scalded.

Because I knew I must not panic, and did not.

Because I loved him. Because love hurts so bad.

Because I wanted to tell you these things. Just like this.

PERMISSIONS ACKNOWLEDGMENTS

Charlotte Armstrong. "Meredith's Murder" by Charlotte Armstrong, copyright © 1953 by Charlotte Armstrong. Copyright renewed 1981 by The Jack and Charlotte Lewi Family Trust. Originally published in *The Albatross* (Coward-McCann, 1957). Reprinted by permission of Brandt & Hochman Literary Agents, Inc. All rights reserved.

Linda Barnes. "Miss Gibson" by Linda Barnes, copyright © 1996 by Linda Barnes. Originally published in *Women on the Case*, edited by Sara Paretsky (Delacorte, 1996). Reprinted by permission of Gina Maccoby Literary Agency.

Nevada Barr. "Beneath the Lilacs" by Nevada Barr, copyright © 1996 by Nevada Barr. Originally published in *Women on the Case*, edited by Sara Paretsky (Delacorte, 1996). Reprinted by permission of Gina Maccoby Literary Agency.

Phyllis Bentley. "The Missing Character" by Phyllis Bentley, copyright © 1937 by the Estate of Phyllis Bentley, renewed. Originally published in *Woman's Home Companion* (July 1937). Reprinted by permission of Peters Fraser & Dunlop (www.petersfraserdunlop.com) on behalf of the Estate of Phyllis Bentley.

Lawrence Block. "Headaches and Bad Dreams" by Lawrence Block, copyright © 1999 by Lawrence Block. Originally published in *Ellery Queen Mystery Magazine* (December 1997). Reprinted by permission of the author.

Anthony Boucher. "Vacancy with Corpse" by H. H. Holmes, copyright © 1955 by Anthony Boucher, renewed. Originally published in *Mystery Book Magazine* (February 1946). Reprinted by permission of Curtis Brown, Ltd.

Whitman Chambers. "The Old Maids Die" by Whitman Chambers, copyright © 2017 by Steeger Properties, LLC. All rights reserved. Originally published in *Detective Fiction Weekly* (December 26, 1936). Reprinted by permission of Steeger Properties, LLC.

Max Allan Collins. "Louise" by Max Allan Collins, copyright © 1992 by Max Allan Collins. Originally published in *Deadly Allies*, edited by Robert J. Randisi and Marilyn Wallace (Doubleday, 1992). Reprinted by permission of the author.

Jeffery Deaver. "Fast" by Jeffery Deaver, copyright © 2014 Gunner Publications, LLC. Originally published in *Trouble in Mind* (Grand Central, 2014). Reprinted by permission of the author.

Mignon G. Eberhart. "Introducing Susan Dare" by Mignon G. Eberhart, copyright © 1934, 1962 by Mignon G. Eberhart. Originally published in *Delineator* (April 1934). Reprinted by permission of Brandt & Hochman Literary Agents, Inc. All rights reserved.

T. T. Flynn. "The Letters and the Law" by T. T. Flynn, copyright © 2017 by Steeger Properties, LLC. All rights reserved. Originally published in *Detective Fiction Weekly* (June 27, 1936). Reprinted by permission of Steeger Properties, LLC.

Hulbert Footner. "The Almost Perfect Murder" by Hulbert Footner, copyright © 1933 by Hulbert Footner, renewed. Originally published in *The Almost Perfect Murder* (Collins, 1933). Reprinted by permission of Geoffrey Footner.

Gilbert Frankau. "Misogyny at Mougins" by Gilbert Frankau, copyright © 1931 by Gilbert Frankau, renewed. Originally published in *Concerning Peter Jackson and Others* (Hutchinson, 1931). Reprinted by permission of United Agents LLP on behalf of Timothy d'Arch Smith.

Antonia Fraser. "The Case of the Parr Children" by Antonia Fraser, copyright © 1989 by Antonia Fraser. Originally published in *Ms. Murder*, edited by Marie Smith (Xanadu, 1989). Reprinted by permission of Curtis Brown Group Ltd, London, on behalf of Antonia Fraser.

Sue Grafton. "A Poison That Leaves No Trace" by Sue Grafton, copyright © 1990 by Sue Grafton. Originally published in *Sisters in Crime 2*, edited by Marilyn Wallace (Berkley, 1990). Reprinted by permission of the author.

Carolyn G. Hart. "Spooked" by Carolyn G. Hart, copyright © 1999 by Carolyn G. Hart. Originally published in *Ellery Queen's Mystery Magazine* (March 1999). Reprinted by permission of the author.

Wendy Hornsby. "Dust Up" by Wendy Hornsby, copyright © 2005 by Wendy Hornsby. Originally published in *Murder in Vegas*, edited by Michael Connelly (Forge, 2005). Reprinted by permission of the author.

Faye Kellerman. "Discards" by Faye Kellerman, copyright © 1991 by Faye Kellerman. Originally published in *A Woman's Eye*, edited by Sara Paretsky (Delacorte, 1991). Reprinted by permission of the author.

Laura Lippman. "The Shoeshine Man's Regrets" by Laura Lippman, copyright © 2004 by Laura Lippman. Originally published in *Murder . . . and All That Jazz*, edited by Robert J. Randisi (Signet, 2004). Reprinted by permission of the author.

Frances & Richard Lockridge. "There's Death for Remembrance" by Frances and Richard Lockridge, copyright © 1957 by Frances & Richard Lockridge, renewed. Originally published in *This Week* (November 16, 1955). Reprinted by permission of Curtis Brown, Ltd.

D. B. McCandless. "Too Many Clients" by D. B. McCandless, copyright © 2017 by Steeger Properties, LLC. All rights reserved. Originally published in *Detective Fiction Weekly* (March 27, 1937). Reprinted by permission of Steeger Properties, LLC.

Gladys Mitchell. "The Case of the Hundred Cats" by Gladys Mitchell, copyright © 1938 by Gladys Mitchell, renewed. Originally published in *Fifty Famous Detectives of Fiction* (Odhams Press, 1938). Reprinted by permission of the Estate of Gladys Mitchell.

Deborah Morgan. "Beaubien" by Deborah Morgan, copyright © 2001 by Deborah A. Estleman. Originally published in *The Private Eye Writers of America: Mystery Street #2*, edited by Robert J. Randisi (Signet, 2001). Reprinted by permission of the author.

Marcia Muller. "All the Lonely People" by Marcia Muller, copyright © 1989 by the Pronzini-Muller Family Trust. Originally published in *Sisters in Crime*, edited by Marilyn Wallace (Berkley, 1989). Reprinted by permission of the author.

Frederick Nebel. "Red Hot" by Frederick Nebel, copyright © 2017 by Steeger Properties, LLC. All rights reserved. Originally published in *Dime Detective* (July 1, 1934). Reprinted by permission of Steeger Properties, LLC.

Joyce Carol Oates. "Extenuating Circumstances" by Joyce Carol Oates, copyright © 1992 by Joyce Carol Oates. Originally published in *Sisters in Crime 5*, edited by Marilyn Wallace (Berkley, 1992). Reprinted by permission of the author.

Stuart Palmer. "The Riddle of the Black Museum" by Stuart Palmer, copyright © 1946 by Stuart Palmer. Originally published in *Ellery Queen's Mystery Magazine* (March 1946). Reprinted by permission of the author's estate and JABberwocky Literary Agency, Inc.

Sara Paretsky. "Strung Out" by Sara Paretsky, copyright © 1992 by Sara Paretsky. Originally published in *Deadly Allies*, edited by Robert J. Randisi and Marilyn Wallace (Doubleday, 1992). Reprinted by permission of the author.

Q. Patrick. "Murder with Flowers" by Q. Patrick, copyright © 1941 by Q. Patrick, renewed. Originally published in *The American Magazine* (December 1941). Reprinted by permission of Curtis Brown, Ltd.

Barbara Paul. "Making Lemonade" by Barbara Paul, copyright © 1991 by Barbara Paul. Originally published in *Sisters in Crime 4*, edited by Marilyn Wallace (Berkley, 1991). Reprinted by permission of the author.

Perry Paul. "The Madame Goes Dramatic" by Perry Paul, copyright © 2017 by Steeger Properties, LLC. All rights reserved. Originally published in *Gun Molls* (April 1931). Reprinted by permission of Steeger Properties, LLC.

Anne Perry. "An Affair of Inconvenience" by Anne Perry, copyright © 1998 by Anne Perry. Originally published in *Mary Higgins Clark Mystery Magazine* (Fall 1998). Reprinted by permission of the author.

Mary Roberts Rinehart. "Locked Doors" by Mary Roberts Rinehart, copyright © 1925 by Mary Roberts; renewed by Rinehart Literary Trust. Originally published in *Mary Roberts Rinehart Crime Book* (Farrar & Rinehart, 1925). Reprinted by permission of MysteriousPress.com.

S. J. Rozan. "Double-Crossing Delancey" by S. J. Rozan, copyright © 2001 by S. J. Rozan. Originally published in *The Private Eye Writers of America Presents: Mystery Street #2*, edited by Robert J. Randisi (Signet, 2001). Reprinted by permission of the author.

Richard Sale. "Chiller-Diller" by Richard Sale, copyright © 2017 by Steeger Properties, LLC. All rights reserved. Originally published in *Detective Fiction Weekly* (June 24, 1939). Reprinted by permission of Steeger Properties, LLC.

Julie Smith. "Blood Types" by Julie Smith, copyright © 1989 by Julie Smith. Originally published in *Sisters in Crime*, edited by Marilyn Wallace (Berkley, 1989). Reprinted by permission of the author.

Eugene Thomas. "The Adventure of the Headless Statue" by Eugene Thomas, copyright © 2017 by Steeger Properties, LLC. All rights reserved. Originally published in *Detective Fiction Weekly* (January 25, 1936). Reprinted by permission of Steeger Properties, LLC.

Roger Torrey. "Rat Runaround" by Roger Torrey, copyright © 2017 by Steeger Properties, LLC. All rights reserved. Originally published in *Black Mask* (May 1937). Reprinted by permission of Steeger Properties, LLC.

Valentine. "The Wizard's Safe" by Valentine, copyright © 2017 by Steeger Properties, LLC. All rights reserved. Originally published in *Detective Fiction Weekly* (June 16, 1928). Reprinted by permission of Steeger Properties, LLC.

Ethel Lina White. "The Gilded Pupil" by Ethel Lina White, copyright © 1940 by Ethel Lina White, renewed. Originally published in *Detective Stories of To-day*, edited by Raymond Postgate (Faber & Faber, 1940). Reprinted by permission of Peters Fraser & Dunlop (www.petersfraserdunlop.com) on behalf of the Estate of Ethel Lina White.

James Yaffe. "Mom Sings an Aria" by James Yaffe, copyright © 1966 by James Yaffe. Originally published in *Ellery Queen's Mystery Magazine* (October 1966). Reprinted by permission of Curtis Brown, Ltd.

Arthur Leo Zagat. "The Passing of Anne Marsh" by Arthur Leo Zagat, copyright © 2017 by Steeger Properties, LLC. All rights reserved. Originally published in *Detective Tales* (April 1937). Reprinted by permission of Steeger Properties, LLC.